Deputy Keeper of Public Records in Ireland

Deputy Keeper of Public Records in Ireland : appendix VI to twenty-first report

Deputy Keeper of Public Records in Ireland

Deputy Keeper of Public Records in Ireland : appendix VI to twenty-first report

ISBN/EAN: 9783742810595

Manufactured in Europe, USA, Canada, Australia, Japa

Cover: Foto ©Andreas Hilbeck / pixelio.de

Manufactured and distributed by brebook publishing software
(www.brebook.com)

Deputy Keeper of Public Records in Ireland

Deputy Keeper of Public Records in Ireland : appendix VI to twenty-first report

CONTENTS

APPENDIX VI.

Index to Calendar of Fiants of Elizabeth—D to Z, . *pages* 285 to 862

(This index is continued from 21st Report, App. III. The Calendar to which it is an Index has been printed as Appendices to 11th, 12th, 13th, 15th, 16th, 17th, and 18th Reports.)

INDEX TO FIANTS—ELIZABETH.

Daly, Fedr., pardon, [illegible], [illegible].
„ Henry, pardon, [illegible].
„ Teig, pardon, [illegible].
„ Walter, pardon, [illegible].
„ Wm. [illegible], pardon, [illegible].
„ (L. or Y.). *See* O'Daly.
Dalye, James, pardon, [illegible].
Dalystown, co. Westm. *See* Dallstown.
Dam[illegible], John, [illegible], [illegible].
Damaghe. *See* Damenaghe.
Damaglass (Damages Upper and Lower, co. Kilk. ?), [illegible].
Damanestone (Dimanistown, co. Meath), [illegible].
Damanestown (Dumanistown), co. Meath, [illegible].
Damas, the, co. Dub., [illegible].
Damenaghe—Damaghe (Damma), co. Kilk., [illegible], 1871, 1316, [illegible]. *See* also Damaghes.
Damport—Damporte—Damporte, Robert, com., [illegible]; pardon, [illegible], [illegible]; [illegible], [illegible].
Damport (or Forsyth), Wm., customs controller of Dublin, [illegible], [illegible].
Damsalstown, co. Meath. *See* Danielstown.
Danbogan, co. Westm., [illegible].
Danbie, Tho., commission, [illegible].
Dandonan, co. Wex., [illegible].
Dandyston alias Danleston, co. Meath, [illegible].
Danell, John, [illegible], [illegible].
Danestown, co. Meath, [illegible], [illegible], [illegible]; rectory, [illegible], [illegible].
Danett. *See* Dannet.
Dangan, co. Clare. *See* Dongan, Dnyagle in Ybrycke.
Dangan, co. Meath. *See* Dongan.
Dangan, Sir John, [illegible].
Danganbeg, co. Kilk. *See* Dongin.
Danganberg, King's co. *See* Dengainbegge.
Danganbeg, co. Lim. *See* Dingenbegge.
Danganbrack, co. Clare. *See* Dangenbreake.
Dangandargan, co. Tip. *See* Dudinbargain.
Dangano (co. Clare ?), [illegible].
Dangan Eighter, co. Gal. *See* Dangin[illegible].
Dangansmore, co. Kilk. *See* Dungrimore.
Dangans, Queen's co. *See* Dinghenbegge, Dinghainmore.
Dangen (co. Kerry ?), [illegible].
Dangen—Dangin—Dangen—Dengin—Dungine, co. Rosc., [illegible], [illegible], [illegible], [illegible], [illegible], [illegible].
Dangenbreake—Daingenbrake—Dangenbreake—Dingenbrack (Dangenbrack), co. Clare, [illegible], [illegible], [illegible]; manor, [illegible].
Dangendricke, [illegible].
Dangenerick—Dangen Erick, co. Gal., [illegible], [illegible], [illegible].
Dangen y bygain, co. Clare, [illegible].
Danginmore, co. Kilk., [illegible].
Dangin, co. Clare, [illegible].
Dangin. *See* Dangen, co. Rosc.
Danginbegge—Danginbeg, co. Kilk., [illegible], [illegible].
Danginmore—Danginmore, co. Kilk., [illegible], [illegible], [illegible], [illegible].
Dangynacrydoge (co. Kilk. ?), [illegible].
Daniell—Danyell:
„ Alexander, pardon, [illegible].
„ Arte, pardon, [illegible].
„ Conoghor Sir John, pardon, [illegible].
„ Constance, pardon, [illegible].
„ Constance or Con, pardon, [illegible].
„ Denis, pardon, [illegible].
„ Edm. Sir Rich., pardon, [illegible].
„ John (of Castle Dermot), com., [illegible]; pardon, [illegible].
„ John, the earl of Ormond's man, [illegible].
John, pardon, [illegible], [illegible], [illegible], [illegible], [illegible], [illegible], [illegible].
„ alias Nyenry, Morris, pardon, [illegible].
„ Rowan, pardon, [illegible].
Terence, dean of Armagh, commissions, [illegible], [illegible], [illegible].
Tho., vicar of Fortaga, [illegible].
„ Tho., pardon, [illegible], [illegible].
„ Walter, pardon, [illegible].
„ Wm., Sch., T.C.D., [illegible]; preacher of Galway, [illegible]; ecclesiastical commission, [illegible], [illegible].
„ Wm., pardon, [illegible].
Danieldesten (Dimanistown), co. Meath, [illegible].
Danielston (Damnelstown), co. Meath, [illegible].
Danleston, alias Dandyston, co. Meath, [illegible].
Dannalkirran (Danakirran), co. Mon., [illegible].
Dannet—Danell—Dannett, John, second remembrancer of the Exchequer, [illegible], [illegible]; constable of Limerick castle, [illegible]; license of absence, [illegible]; death, [illegible].
Dansie. *See* Danseye.
Dansk, trade with, [illegible].
Danseye—Dansie, Richard, authority to impress hay, [illegible]; grant of a wardship, [illegible].
Dantanestowne (co. Kilk. ?), [illegible].
Danyell. *See* Daniell.
Danystone, co. Dub., [illegible].
Danyaghbrake. *See* Dangenbreake.
Daragill—Daragill (Darrigill, co. Wat.), [illegible], [illegible].
Daraken, co. Wat., [illegible].
Daramine, co. Kerry, [illegible], [illegible].
Daranishe (co. Car. or Wex. ?), [illegible].
Darbelstown, co. Wat., [illegible].
Darbie, William, maker of Dungleale fort, [illegible].
Darcey—Darcere—Darcie. *See* Darcy.
Darcelston, [illegible]

INDEX TO FIANTS—ELIZABETH.

Darcy—Darcie—Darcey—Darcye—Darcye—Darsey—Darcy:
" Arthur (of Little Grange), pardon, [illegible]; commissions, [illegible], 4[illegible].
" Arthur, pardon, [illegible], [illegible], [illegible].
" (or Fagan), Cecily, murder of, [illegible].
" Christopher (of Platten), wardship, 367, 454; livery, [illegible]; lease, 1547; commissions, [illegible], [illegible], [illegible], [illegible], [illegible]; license to remain in England, [illegible]; his heirs, [illegible], [illegible], [illegible], [illegible].
" Christopher, son of George (of Platten), wardship, [illegible].
" Edmund (of Jordanstown), grant of land, 1577; commissions, 1647, [illegible], [illegible]; leases, [illegible], [illegible], [illegible], [illegible], [illegible], [illegible], [illegible], [illegible], [illegible]; license to alien, [illegible], [illegible]; surrender, [illegible]; pardon, [illegible].
" Edmund (of Rathwyre), livery, [illegible].
" Edm. (of Dorpatrick), 3462.
" Edm. (of Redmondstown), commissions, 4141, 4[illegible].
" Edm., pardon, [illegible], [illegible].
" Edward, lease, 2647.
" Edward, pardon, [illegible], [illegible].
" Garrold, commission, [illegible].
" Genet, [illegible].
" George, brother of Chr., [illegible], 454, [illegible].
" George, son of Christopher (of Platten), wardship, [illegible], [illegible]; murder of his wife, [illegible]; wardship of his heir, [illegible].
" George, pardon, [illegible].
" Gerald, commission, [illegible].
" Giles, pardon, [illegible].
" James, pardon, [illegible], [illegible], [illegible].
" James, alderman of Galway, [illegible].
" John (of Rathwyre), livery to son, [illegible].
" John, chaplain, lease, [illegible].
" John, pardon, [illegible], [illegible], [illegible].
" John, grant recited, [illegible].
" Katherine, [illegible]; dower, [illegible].
" Katherine, pardon, [illegible].
" Margery, pardon, [illegible].
" Nicholas, pardon, [illegible].
" Richard (of Rathwyre), livery to son, [illegible].
" Rich., pardon, [illegible], [illegible].
" Rob., pardon, [illegible].
" Saely, pardon, [illegible].
" Thomas (of Balrath), freedom from subsidy, [illegible].
" Thomas (of Platten), commission, [illegible].
" Thomas (of Loghor), commission, [illegible].

Darcy—Thos. (of Donnow), pardon, [illegible]; commissions, [illegible], [illegible], 4[illegible].
" Thos., pardon, [illegible].
" Walter, commissions, 4141, 4[illegible], [illegible].
" William (of Platten), wardship of heir, 367, 454.
" Wm. (of Platten), pardon, [illegible], [illegible].
" Wm., pardon, 1178, [illegible], [illegible], [illegible], [illegible].
Dardes, Gerald, pardon, 94.
" Peter, pardon, 4577.
" Wm., pardon, [illegible].
Dardem, Wm., pardon, [illegible].
Dardeam, Godfrey, pardon, [illegible].
Dardeston (Dardistown), co. Meath, [illegible], [illegible], [illegible], 1174, [illegible], [illegible], [illegible], 4441, [illegible].
Dardeston—Dardiston (Dardistown), co. Westm., 4151, [illegible], [illegible], [illegible].
Dardestown—Dardiston (Dardistown), co. Dub., [illegible], [illegible].
Dardioye, James, pardon, 1575.
Dardiston. See Dardestown.
Dardis, Walter, pardon, [illegible].
Dardistown, co. Dub. See Dardestown.
" co. Meath. See Dardeston.
" co. Westm. See Dardeston, Dardiston.
Dardys, Thos., pardon, [illegible].
Daregill. See Daragill.
Darelare, co. Tip., [illegible].
Dareloskane (see Derryloskane), [illegible].
Dargan, Oisheen, pardon, [illegible].
Dargill, co. Wex., [illegible].
Darleskan (or Derryloskan), [illegible].
Darinlare, co. Wat., [illegible].
Darmaghe (co. Cork?), [illegible]; rectory, [illegible].
Darnstown, co. Long., [illegible].
Darndale, co. Dub. See Dornald.
Darragh, co. Lim. See Dirragh.
Darraghlan, co. Mon. See Dyrraghlan.
Darragh[illegible], alias Darmaghe (co. Cork?), rectory, [illegible].
Darrachebane, co. Kerry, [illegible].
Darragan, Dermod, pardon, [illegible].
" John, pardon, [illegible].
Darroloskan (or Derryloskane), [illegible].
Darrigall, co. Wat. See Daragill.
Darrigen (co. Cork?), [illegible].
Darroloskan—Darroloskane, Queen's co., [illegible], [illegible].
Darrotaghe, in Connaught, [illegible].
Darry, Edm. boy m'Donell, pardon, [illegible].
" Morrogh some m'Donell, pardon, [illegible].
Darrys, Dermod ne, pardon, [illegible].
Darryknockane: Derryknockane, co. Lim. (?), [illegible].

INDEX TO FIANTS—ELIZABETH.

Darrylare, co. Wat., [illegible].
Darrylish, co. Cav., [illegible].
Darsey, James, alderman, corp., [illegible].
Darsey. *See* Darcy.
Darston (Dardistown, co. Westm. ?), [illegible].
Darty. *See* Darcy.
Darius, James, coroner of Dublin, [illegible].
Dartarall, in Munster, [illegible].
Darwio—Dartry (Dartree barony), co. Mon., [illegible]; manors and lands in, surrendered, [illegible]; grant of lands in, [illegible], [illegible], [illegible].
Dartry, territory in bar. Rosseclogher, co. Leit., [illegible], [illegible], [illegible].
Darus, co. Gal., [illegible].
Darver, co. Louth. *See* Darver.
Darvino (co. Donegal), [illegible].
Dashowen, Donogho m'Shane y, pardon, [illegible].
Daton, Edm., pardon, [illegible], [illegible], [illegible], [illegible], [illegible].
„ Giles, pardon, [illegible].
„ Ellinor, pardon, [illegible].
„ Gerald, pardon, [illegible], [illegible], [illegible].
„ James, pardon, [illegible], [illegible], [illegible], [illegible], [illegible], [illegible], [illegible], [illegible].
„ John, pardon, [illegible], [illegible], [illegible], [illegible].
„ Katherine, pardon, [illegible].
„ Maurice, pardon, [illegible], [illegible], [illegible], [illegible], [illegible].
„ Morish, pardon, [illegible], [illegible].
„ Nich., pardon, [illegible], [illegible], [illegible].
„ Patr., pardon, [illegible], [illegible].
„ Peter, pardon, 1041, [illegible], [illegible], [illegible], [illegible].
„ Peirse, pardon, [illegible], [illegible].
„ Redmond, pardon, [illegible].
„ Rich., pardon, [illegible], [illegible], [illegible], [illegible], [illegible].
„ Theobald, pardon, [illegible], [illegible].
„ Walter, pardon, [illegible], [illegible], [illegible], [illegible].
„ William, pardon, [illegible], [illegible], [illegible], [illegible], [illegible], [illegible].
Dation, Patr. fitz Nich., pardon, [illegible].
„ William, pardon, [illegible], [illegible].
Davagh, co. Mon. *See* Ballydavagh.
Davallintama, co. Mon., two ballybetaghs of, [illegible].
Davan, John, house in Trim, [illegible].
„ John, killed, [illegible].
Davelstowne, co. Wexford, [illegible].
Davells—Davell—Davellse—Davels:
„ Henry, collector of wine duties in Youghal and Dungarvan, [illegible]; captain of the Cavanaghs, [illegible]; sheriff of Carlow, [illegible], [illegible]; captain of Dungarvan, [illegible], [illegible]; sheriff of co. Wat., [illegible]; ransomed by Hugh m'Shane, [illegible]; commissions, [illegible], [illegible], [illegible], [illegible],
Davells:
[illegible], [illegible], [illegible], [illegible], [illegible], [illegible], [illegible], [illegible], [illegible], [illegible], [illegible], [illegible], [illegible], [illegible]; grant of land, [illegible]; leases, [illegible], [illegible], [illegible], [illegible], [illegible]; grants of wardship, [illegible], [illegible]; surrender, [illegible]; pardon, [illegible], [illegible], [illegible]; pardon at his request, [illegible]; recommends an appointment, [illegible]; wardship of his heir, [illegible]; his fees, [illegible], [illegible], [illegible].
„ Henry, son of Henry, wardship, [illegible]; leases, [illegible], [illegible], [illegible], [illegible], [illegible]; sheriff of Carlow, com., [illegible]; pardon, [illegible].
„ John, pardon, [illegible].
„ Wm., pardon, [illegible].
Davers, Christopher, water bailiff of Shannon, [illegible], [illegible]; lease, [illegible], [illegible].
„ Griffin, soldier, slain, [illegible].
Daves, Tho., pardon, [illegible].
„ William, death of, [illegible].
Davestande alias Dawestande, co. Meath, [illegible].
Davestons, lands of (co. Meath), [illegible].
Davestown (co. Wex. ?), [illegible].
David, Honnery, pardon, [illegible].
Davidson, Honora, pardon, [illegible].
Davidstown, co. Tip., [illegible].
Davidstown—Davidston, co. Kilk., [illegible], [illegible].
Davies—Davis—Davyes—Davys:
„ Henry, [illegible].
„ James, grant of a wardship, [illegible].
„ John, sheriff of Kildare, commission, [illegible], [illegible], [illegible]; pardon, [illegible].
„ Nich., [illegible].
„ Rob., pardon, [illegible], [illegible].
„ Tho., pardon, [illegible].
„ Wm., pardon, [illegible], [illegible], [illegible].
Daviston, co. Dub., [illegible].
Daviston (Ballydavis, Queen's co.), [illegible].
Davis. *See* Davies.
Daviston (co. Kild. ?), [illegible].
Davoke, Tho., pardon, [illegible].
Davy, John, grant of lands, [illegible].
„ Henry, [illegible].
Davy, Wm., pardon, [illegible].
Davys, Morierty duff m'Wm., pardon, [illegible].
Davyes, James. *See* Davies.
Davys, John. *See* Davies.
Dawestown, co. Louth, [illegible].
Dawkins, Theobald, pardon, [illegible].
„ Walter, pardon, [illegible].
Dawndon, John, pardon, [illegible].
Dawry—Dawrin, co. Tip., [illegible].
Dawson, John, [illegible].
„ Laurence, pardon, [illegible].
Dawtes, Rich., pardon, [illegible].
Dawtoney, John, [illegible].

INDEX TO FIANTS—ELIZABETH.

Dawtrie — Dawtrey, Nich., seneschal of Clandeboy, 2877, [illegible], [illegible].
Daye, the, co. Gal., [illegible].
Dayagh in Thycke (Daingan, in bar. Bunratty), co. Clare, manor, 1[illegible].
Dayayay alias M'David, David m'Shane, pardon, 4414.
Deagle, Shane, pardon, [illegible].
Dealeerviscoghlan — Dealner'coghlan—Dealnerveoghlan. See Delvyn M'Coghlan.
Deamor. See Desmore.
Dean, the son of, a kern, [illegible].
Deane, Henry, lease, [illegible].
„ Tho., pardon, [illegible].
Deanerathe, co. Louth, [illegible].
de Angulo, Patrick (see Nangle), livery, [illegible].
de Angulo, Thomas, knt., livery to his heir, [illegible].
Deanies, John, pardon, 4114.
Deanrathe, co. Dub., 4[illegible].
Deanstown, co. Lim. See Ballindrynaghe, Ballydrynan.
de Astro B. Flidur abbey, co. Cork (see Gilley), [illegible].
Deardir, James, pardon, [illegible].
Deareroure (co. Cork ?), [illegible].
Dearne Loyne or Fanctorney, co. Antrim, [illegible].
Dearge, or Red river (Derg river, co. Donegal and Tyrone), [illegible], [illegible].
Deargh, Donell, pardon, [illegible].
Dearmod, Edm., pardon, [illegible].
Dearver. See Derver.
Deasaghe, John crone, pardon, [illegible].
Deare, Emarreel, pardon, [illegible].
Debnilldenegh (co. Ferm. ?), [illegible].
de Brunase, Hugh m'William, pardon (O'Byrne), 1[illegible].
Debts due by crown, released for a lease of lands, [illegible], [illegible].
„ to crown, commission to collect, [illegible].
de Burg ( ), pardon, [illegible].
de Burgo, Hugo alias Ulick. See Clanrikard, earl of.
de Burgo, Onoria, [illegible].
de Burgo, Sabina, pardon, [illegible].
de Burgo. See Bourke.
de Burgos, Rich. and Ulick. See Clanricard, earl of.
de Bustan, Adrian, English liberty, [illegible].
Dece, Rich., commissions, [illegible], [illegible].
Decem — Desies — Desees — Decyes, the (baronies of Decies), co. Wat., 1[illegible], [illegible], [illegible], [illegible].
Decies—Decy—Desies
„ Gerald, viscount of, commission, [illegible].
Decies — Maurice FitzGerald, created viscount of, [illegible]; commission, [illegible], [illegible]; livery to his heir, [illegible].
Dee, John, second chamberlain, Exchequer, [illegible], [illegible], [illegible]; lease, 1[illegible].
Decy, Gerald, viscount of. See Decies.
Deegrity, co. Lim. See Degreity.
Deelish, co. Lim. See Delis, Dilis, Dillis, Dowelyshe.
Deenes, co. Meath. See Downys.
Deerfell, used by glovers, [illegible].
„ illegal export of, [illegible].
Deering, Anthony (capt.), [illegible]; land grant, [illegible].
Defence of co. Meath, instruction for, [illegible].
de Fonte Vivo, abbey, co. Cork (see Mawer), [illegible].
Degew (co. Lett. ?), [illegible].
Degreity (Dengerty), co. Lim., [illegible].
De Gruchir, Robert, a Frenchman, pardon, [illegible].
Degeragh, Donell, pardon, [illegible].
de Hespinosa, Jaques, doctor, English liberty, [illegible].
De Horsey, James, pardon, [illegible].
Deice, James, pardon, [illegible].
Deidro( )town, co. Westm., [illegible].
Deinge, co. Wex., [illegible].
Deingleentore (co. Kilk. ?), [illegible].
Deingleituir (Dengan Eighter, co. Gal.), [illegible].
Deingle hussey—Deingyen ne quiss. See Dingle.
Deirmodie, More ny, pardon, [illegible].
Deirmody, Margaret ny, pardon, [illegible].
Deirwey, co. Meath, [illegible].
Deise, Garret, pardon, [illegible].
Deisert, Queen's co., [illegible].
Dekeyser, Tho., pardon, [illegible].
Dekefeld, Tho., pardon, [illegible].
Delahide—Dalahyde—Delahid—Dellahyde —Delahid—Delahuide—Dalahoyde—Delahyde:
„ Amable (or Browne), pardon, [illegible].
„ Anthony, wardship, [illegible].
„ Christopher, pardon, [illegible].
„ Edward, pardon, [illegible].
„ Egerton, [illegible].
„ Francis, lease, [illegible].
„ George, livery to his son, 1[illegible].
„ George, pardon, [illegible].
„ James, son of, [illegible].
„ James, pardon, [illegible].
„ Joan (or Hussey), grant of land, [illegible]; pardon, [illegible], [illegible].

INDEX TO FIANTS.—ELIZABETH.

Delahide—John (of Dunshaughlin), grant recited, [illegible]; wardship of heir, 3780; his grandson attainted, [illegible].
" John, son of Walter, attainted, [illegible].
" John (of Killagh, co. Kerry), pardon, [illegible].
" John, pardon, [illegible].
" Laurence (of Moyglare), grant of land, [illegible], [illegible]; com., [illegible], [illegible]; pardon, [illegible], [illegible], [illegible]; grant and pardon of alienation to his widow, [illegible], [illegible].
" Luke, wardship, [illegible].
" Michael, commissions, [illegible], [illegible], [illegible], [illegible], [illegible].
" Richard, chancellor of Exchequer, [illegible].
" Richard (of Moyglare), grant of land, [illegible]; wardship of heir, [illegible].
" Richard (of Loghshenny), livery, [illegible]; wardship of heir, [illegible].
" Rowland, constable of Enniscorthy, [illegible]; pardon, [illegible].
" Thomas, pardon, [illegible], [illegible].
" Thomas (alderman), collector of wine duty in Drogheda, [illegible].
" Walter (knt.), attainted, his possessions leased, 317, 1846, 1347, [illegible]; granted, 1347, [illegible]; his son and grandson, [illegible].
" Walter (of Amy), com., [illegible].
" Walter, freedom from subsidy, [illegible].
" Walter (of Dunshaughlin), wardship, [illegible]; his son, [illegible].
" Walter (of Moyglare), pardon, [illegible].
Delamare—de la Mare — Dellamar — Dellamare—Delamar — Delamare—Dellamar—Dellamare—Dellamart—Dellamare:
" Alson, lease, [illegible].
" Andrew, pardon, [illegible].
" Edmund, under-serjeant of Delamare's country, [illegible].
" Edmund, pardon, [illegible], [illegible], [illegible].
" Edward, pardon, [illegible], [illegible], [illegible], [illegible].
" Ebert, pardon, [illegible].
" Ferdorche, pardon, [illegible].
" Geoffrey, pardon, [illegible].
" Gerald, pardon, [illegible], [illegible], [illegible], [illegible].
" James, pardon, [illegible], [illegible].
" John, pardon, [illegible].
Delamare—Meiler or Myler, chief-serjeant of Delamare's country, [illegible]; chief of his name, commissions, [illegible], [illegible].
" Morice, pardon, [illegible].
" Myler, pardon, [illegible].
" Piers, pardon, [illegible].
" Rich., pardon, [illegible].
" Theobald, alienation to, [illegible]; pardon, [illegible], [illegible], [illegible], [illegible].
" Thomas, pardon, [illegible], [illegible], [illegible], [illegible].
" Walter, lands of, [illegible].
" Walter, pardon, [illegible]; commissions, [illegible], [illegible].
" Walter, freedom, [illegible], [illegible].
" Walter, com., [illegible].
" Walter (of Rosmagh), com., [illegible].
Delamare—Delamare's country in co. Westm., divided into ploughlands, [illegible]; chief serjeant appointed, [illegible].
Delawaye, John, soldier, pardon, [illegible].
Delegranbegg. See Delligrilrogo.
Delganye (co. Wicklow), rector of, [illegible].
Delgo, in Upper Ossory, [illegible].
Delgrilbego — Delegranbegg (Dellige, co. Cork), [illegible], [illegible].
Delligrie (Dellige, co. Cork), [illegible].
Delln (Dunlish), co. Lim., [illegible].
Dellamar—Dellamare. See Delamare.
Dellebe, in Isle of Man, rectory, [illegible], [illegible].
Dellige, co. Cork. See Delligrilrogo, Delligrie, Delligrycarraghe, Delligrilbegge.
Delligramore—Delligmore, co. Cork, [illegible], [illegible], [illegible].
Delligrycarraghe (Dellige, co. Cork), [illegible].
Delven, baron of. See Delvin.
Delvan M'Coghlan — Delvin M'Coghlane — Delvinmacoughlan — Delvinmacoghlan — Delvinnecoghlan — Delvyn M'Coghlan (Delvin Macoghlin) (the barony of Garrycastle, King's co.), country of, [illegible], [illegible], [illegible]; martial law in, [illegible]; made shire land, [illegible].
" seneschal of, [illegible].
Delves, George, grant of land, [illegible]; com., [illegible].
Delvin. See Castletown.
Delvin—Delvan—Delvyn:
" Richard Nugent, baron of, his widow, license to marry, [illegible]; his heir, [illegible].
" Christopher, baron of, grant of land, [illegible]; livery, [illegible]; his uncle, [illegible]; commissions, [illegible], 1108, 1771, [illegible], [illegible], [illegible], [illegible], [illegible], [illegible], [illegible], [illegible], [illegible], [illegible]; lands forfeited by

INDEX TO FIANTS—ELIZABETH.

Delvin:
rebellion of, [illegible]; commissions, [illegible]; letters, [illegible]; wardship grant, [illegible]; bounds of his lands, [illegible].
Delvyn M'Caythin. See Delvin M'Cahan.
Demalerres, Peter, trade licence, [illegible].
Demanys, John m'Wm., pardon, [illegible].
Demetrick, 6112.
Demore — Demore (Dunmore), co. Meath, [illegible]; manor, [illegible]; rectory, [illegible].
" vicar of, [illegible].
Dempsie — Dempsey — Dempsie — Dempsey — Dempsie — Demse — Dumse — Dempsy:
" Agnes, widow of Simon Bee, [illegible].
" Arthur, pardon, [illegible].
" Barnaby, pardon, [illegible].
" Brian m'Owen, pardon, [illegible].
" Cahir, pardon, [illegible].
" Caro or Kare, pardon, [illegible]; wife of, [illegible].
" Cormock oge, pardon, [illegible].
" Darby, pardon, [illegible].
" Darye, pardon, [illegible].
" Dermot oge, livery to son, [illegible].
" Dermot, pardon, [illegible].
" Dowe, pardon, [illegible].
" Edmund A., pardon to son, [illegible].
" Edm., pardon, [illegible].
" Elena, pardon, [illegible].
" Elinor, pardon, [illegible].
" Fally m'Garrald, pardon, [illegible].
" Feagh m'Owen, pardon, [illegible].
" Giles, widow, grant of land, [illegible]; abatement to, [illegible]; pardon, [illegible].
" Glasny m'Teige, pardon, [illegible].
" Dayo alias Fardorogh, pardon, [illegible].
" Joan, pardon, [illegible].
" John, pardon, [illegible].
" Knoor, pardon, [illegible].
" Laghlin, pardon, [illegible].
" Lisagh, pardon, [illegible].
" Margaret nyne Hugh, pardon, [illegible].
" Molaghlin, pardon, [illegible].
" Morrogh m'Lisagh, pardon, [illegible].
" Mortagh, pardon, [illegible].
" Owen M'Hugh. See O'Dempsey.
" Owen, pardon, [illegible].
" Pate, pardon, [illegible].
" Phelim, pardon, [illegible].
" Richard A., pardon, [illegible].
" Shane m'Dermot, pardon, [illegible].
" (or O'Dempsey) Teige or Thady, pardon, [illegible].

Dempsie—Terence. See O'Dempsie.
" Thomas, pardon, [illegible].
" Tybot m'Edm., pardon, [illegible].
" Tyrlagh m'Garrald, pardon, [illegible].
" Tirrelagh, pardon, [illegible].
" William, pardon, [illegible].
Dempsey's, possessions of the, [illegible].
Demserret, Morrice, pardon, 6172.
Den—Dene—Denne:
" Fowlke, pardon, [illegible].
" Oliver, pardon, [illegible].
" Pudge, pardon, [illegible].
" Patrick, pardon, [illegible].
" Phelan, pardon, [illegible].
" Rowland fitz Tho., pardon, [illegible].
" Thomas (of Grenan), com., [illegible]; pardon, [illegible].
" Thomas, pardon, [illegible].
" Walter, pardon, [illegible].
Denalle, John, pardon, [illegible].
Denamaton (Denhamstown), co. Meath, [illegible].
Deaane, Rich., pardon, [illegible].
Denchworth, Berkshire, [illegible].
Denalon, John, pardon, [illegible].
Dene, Richard, pardon, [illegible].
Denevel, John, [illegible].
Dengan — Dengin — Dengine — Denyn — Dingaine — Dingen — Dengyn (Dangan), co. Meath, [illegible].
Dengan—Dengen, co. Mon., [illegible].
Dengan (Dangan castle, in parish of Kilchrist, co. Clare), [illegible].
Dengen, in bar. Tulla, co. Clare, [illegible].
Dengen, town of (Dangan, in par. Quin), co. Clare, [illegible].
Dengen, co. Gal., [illegible].
Dengen (Dingle), co. Kerry ?), [illegible].
Dengen—Dengian, co. Kild., [illegible].
Dengen. See Dengan, co. Mon.
Dengen. See Dengen, co. Rosc.
Dengen, in the Moroes, co. Wex., [illegible].
Dengen Invrighell, co. Clare, [illegible].
Dengen Ibalke, co. Clare, [illegible].
Dengentyvire, co. Rosc., [illegible].
Denghain, fort of (Philipstown, King's co.), under of, [illegible].
Dengin (Dangan beg), co. Kilk., [illegible].
Dengin. See Dengan, co. Meath.
Dengin. See Dengen, co. Rosc.
Dengin, co. Wex., [illegible].
Dengine. See Dengan, co. Meath.
Dengine. See Dengen, co. Kild.
Dengine. See Dingen, co. Rosc.
Dengnetrick—Dengen Bricke. See Dangenbrick.
Dengtarick (co. Rosc. ?), 6112.

INDEX TO FIANTS—ELIZABETH.

Dengle (see Dingle), co. Kerry, [illegible].
Dengyn. See Dengan, co. Meath.
Dengynyvyrgan — Dyngynyvyrgan (the barony of Dunkelly), co. Clare, [illegible].
Denham, Wm., constable of Dublin Castle, [illegible].
Denhamstown, co. Meath. See Dennanston.
Denis, alias Power, Donald, pardon, [illegible].
Denn—Denne. See Den.
Dennery. See Denny.
Dennis (Dinish), co. Kerry, [illegible].
Denny—Denney, Edward, grant of land, [illegible]; lease, [illegible].
Densyn (Densen), co. Meath, [illegible].
Densyvale—Densyvalle, co. Kerry, seignory or lordship of, [illegible].
Denson, John, vicar of Outerarde, co. Kild., [illegible].
" William, wardship grant, [illegible].
Depys, archdeacon of Killenora, [illegible].
Deraloge, co. Lim., [illegible].
Deputy (lord), use of certain friaries, &c., reserved to, [illegible], [illegible], [illegible], [illegible];
" use of castle of Carlow reserved to, [illegible].
" place of residence for, erected in Dublin castle, [illegible].
" receives (?) of cows for nomination to captaincy of Irish country, [illegible], [illegible], [illegible], [illegible].
" household of, victual to be impressed for, [illegible]; purveyor for, [illegible].
" secretary of, [illegible].
" See under names of respective viceroys, and p. 20 of XXI. Report.
Dera (co. Westm. ?), [illegible].
de Rabeo, monastery, [illegible].
Deragho (Deragh, co. Long.), [illegible], 1401, [illegible].
Deraghe (co. Westm. ?), [illegible].
Derre, co. Rosc., [illegible].
Derby, John, pardon, [illegible].
Derbestown (co. Wat. ?), [illegible].
Derbiestowne, co. Wat., [illegible].
Derrerawn, co. Westm., [illegible].
Dere, Queen's co., [illegible], [illegible]; castle, [illegible].
Dere, Maurice, pardon, [illegible].
Dereclone (Derryclooney, co. Tip. ?), [illegible], [illegible].
Deredaragh, co. Gal., [illegible].
Deredleghe, co. Kilk., [illegible].
Derehyne (Derryhene ?), co. Cav., [illegible].
Derekny, King's co., [illegible].
Derelaskan. See Derrylosken.
Derem'cloghae — Derem'laghan — Derem'laghny (see Derrymaclaghny), [illegible], [illegible], [illegible].
Deremlaghilin, co. Gal., [illegible].
Deremlaghilin (see Derrymaclaghny), [illegible].
Deremagh, Shane m'Wm., pardon, [illegible].
Deremlay (Derrymaclaughlin ? co. Gal.), [illegible].
Derrerslaige (Derrymaslaige), co. Mon., [illegible].
Deremeshough (Queen's co. ?), [illegible].
Deremlebanesty, Queen's co., [illegible].
Deremaghlagh, King's co. (Derryoughter, now co. Kild.), [illegible], [illegible].
Dereroe (Derryroe, Queen's co. ?), [illegible].
Dereviglaghan (see Derrymaclaghny), [illegible].
Derevoy (Derryvough ?), co. Mon., [illegible].
Derfadd (Derradd), co. Westm., [illegible], [illegible]; wood called, [illegible].
Derg (lough), co. Donegal. See Red lough, [illegible], [illegible].
Derg (river). See Dearge or Red river, [illegible], [illegible].
Dergullen—Dergyllen, King's co., [illegible], [illegible].
Derhinkterb. See Derrynahensy.
Derian, King's co. See Derrivan.
Derick, John, collector of customs, Drogheda, [illegible].
Derick—Dercke (see Derrick), co. Meath, [illegible].
Dericke, Tho., pardon, [illegible].
Dericks. See Derrick, co. Meath.
Derien (Derryen ?), co. Kerry, [illegible], [illegible].
Derildaragh, co. Gal., [illegible].
Derigane, co. Long., [illegible].
Derige, Teige m'Shane, pardon, [illegible].
Derigetee (co. Cav. ?), [illegible].
Derigenell, co. Gal., [illegible].
Derigvane, co. Cork, [illegible].
Derilleerogh wagher, co. Kerry, [illegible].
Deringe, Anthony, pardon, [illegible].
Derialoghan (Derryloughan), co. Gal., [illegible].
Derivagh, Donell, pardon, [illegible].
Derymacloghney. See Derrymaclaghny, co. Gal.
Dermacoffin, co. Kild., [illegible].
Dermed, Margaret ny, pardon, [illegible].
Dermoddy, Sylly ny, pardon, [illegible].
Dermodie—Dermody, Ellen ny, pardon, [illegible], [illegible].
" Katherine ny, pardon, [illegible].
" More ny, pardon, [illegible].
" Shele ny, pardon, [illegible].
Dermody. See Dermodie.
Dermondstown, co. Dub., [illegible].
Dermor, or Dramor, co. Meath, manor, [illegible].
Dermot, Laurence, grant, [illegible].
" Owen ny ne, pardon, [illegible].
" Tho., [illegible].
" —Dermote — Dermott, William, chancellor of Christ Church, Dublin, English liberty, [illegible]; commissions, [illegible], [illegible], [illegible].
Dermott, William. See Dermot.
" Thomas, [illegible].
Dermothe, James, [illegible].

INDEX TO FIANTS—ELIZABETH.

Dergan roe, Kallerrynsy, pardon, [illegible].
" " Lisarna ny, pardon, [illegible].
Dermott, Reamonyne ny, pardon, [illegible].
" Kilee, pardon, [illegible].
" Ione uyne, pardon, [illegible].
" Moire nyn, pardon, [illegible].
" Owney nyne, pardon, [illegible], [illegible].
" William. See Dermot.
Dernadarrill, co. Mon. See Dirradarry.
Dernakirnah, co. Mon. See Dyrrenaghkirnahin.
Dernalowna, co. Mon. See Dirrelowad.
Dernamoyle, co. Mon. See Bellydyrrenamoyle.
Dernamoyly, co. Mon., [illegible].
Dernamuck, co. Mon. See Durnamurrack.
Dernavol, co. Mon. See Dyrrenarvel.
Derndall—Dernadall (Darndale), co. Dub., 1408, [illegible].
Dernenalinkney, or Derrynalinghney, co. Gal., [illegible].
Dernia, co. Clare, [illegible].
Dernisura (co. Cork?), [illegible].
Dernodall (see Derndall), 1440.
Dernymarhaghe (co. Westm.), [illegible].
Derongh, King's co., [illegible].
Derpatrick—Dirpatrick—Dirpatricke—Dyrpatrick—Dyrpatryck (Derrypatrick), co. Meath, 1463, [illegible]; rectory, [illegible], [illegible], [illegible].
Derpatrick, [illegible].
Derr—Derre, co. Kild., [illegible], [illegible], [illegible].
Derra (co. Westm.), [illegible].
Derradd, co. Westm. See Derfadd.
Derragh, co. Long. See Deraghe.
Derre (co. Cork?), [illegible].
Derre (co. Gal.?), [illegible].
Derre. See Derr, co. Kild.
Derre, co. Wex., [illegible].
Derrecrur( ), in Upper Ossory, [illegible].
Derrera, co. Kerry. See Dyrrinia.
Derrecnalleghian, co. Clare. See Derrynaleghan.
Derreleagh—Dirreleghe (Derryleigh), co. Tip., [illegible], [illegible].
Derreine, co. Lim., [illegible].
Derreleshan (see Derrylesshan), [illegible].
Derrenlaghe, (see Derrynaclaghny), [illegible].
Derreo (Derrie?), Queen's co., [illegible].
Derreneagha, Queen's co., [illegible].
Derrenagarranaghe, co. Westm., [illegible].
Derrenarmanagh (co. Kilk.?), 1976, [illegible].
Derreneshyre (Derrynaseera?), Queen's co., [illegible].
Derrenaknockane (Derryknockane, co. Lim.?), [illegible].
Derrenaullagh (Derrinaullagh) Queen's co., [illegible].
Derrelyn. See Derreyle.
Derreros (co. Cork?), [illegible].
Derreyle—Derrelyn (Derryrod, co. Donegal), [illegible].
Derrevolane, King's co., [illegible].
Derroverbele (co. Tip.?), [illegible].
Derriadde, co. Gal., [illegible].
Derrick (Great)—Derick—Derrike—Much Derieke—Derricke—Dirrike—Derryck, (Derrockstown), co. Meath, [illegible], [illegible], [illegible], [illegible], [illegible], [illegible], [illegible], [illegible], [illegible], [illegible], [illegible], [illegible].
Derrick (Little)—Derick—Derricke—Derryck—Derrike, co. Meath, [illegible], [illegible], [illegible], [illegible], [illegible], [illegible], [illegible], [illegible], [illegible], [illegible], [illegible].
Derricloan. See Derrycloney.
Derricrossan—Dyrrycrossane, co. Clare, [illegible], [illegible].
Derricrowen, [illegible].
Derrie (co. Lim.?), [illegible].
Derrie, the (co. Westm.?), [illegible].
Derriemockulle (co. Mayo?), [illegible].
Derrig (Abboydery), co. Long., [illegible].
Derrike, Great and Little. See Derrick.
Derrilegh—Dirclegh (co. Kilk.?), [illegible], [illegible].
Derris, Queen's co. See Derren, Derrya.
Derrinaullagh, Queen's co. See Derrenaullagh.
Derrinloney, co. Mon. See Dyrranlowna.
Derrirone (Derryrone), co. Cork, [illegible].
Derrockstown, co. Meath. See Derrick.
Derronston, co. Lim., castle and land. [illegible].
Derront, Gibbon, attainted, [illegible].
Derrowel, co. Mayo. See Drowle.
Derrowkey (co. Ros.?), [illegible].
Derry, the (co. Cav.?), [illegible].
Derry (co. Cork?), [illegible].
Derry, dean of, pardon, [illegible].
Derry, co. Down. See Dyrry.
Derry, co. Mon. See Dyrrye.
Derry alias Rannapak, Queen's co., [illegible].
Derry, Hugh m'Shane, pardon, [illegible].
Derrygart, co. Kild. See Dyrregart.
Derrybrook, Queen's co. See Derybroke, Dirrebrooke.
Derryck, Little and Much, co. Meath. See Derrick.
Derrycloney—Derricloan—Dirrecloney—Derrycloane (Derrycloney, co. Tip.), [illegible], [illegible], [illegible], [illegible]; grant, [illegible]. See also Derecloghe.
Derryeo, co. Kerry. See Derien.
Derryconnell, co. Cork. See Dirriconnell.
Derrydonnell—Derrydonell, co. Gal., [illegible], [illegible].
Derrye, co. Leit., [illegible].
Derrye, Queen's co., [illegible].
Derryowen, co. Gal., [illegible].
Derrygarran, King's co. See Diregarran.
Derrygarran, Queen's co. See Dirriegarran, Dirrygarran.

INDEX TO FIANTS—ELIZABETH.

Derrygart—Dirregart—Dirrigart, co. Kild., [illegible], 1347, [illegible].
Derrygaman, co. Mon. *See* Dyrromahell.
Derrygarroghan, co. Cav. *See* Dyrrykyrvihan.
Derrygile, Queen's co. *See* Derrykill.
Derrygolan, co. Westm. *See* Dirrigoolay.
Derrygunnigan, King's co. *See* Dirrykrony-kyne, Dirrynegonhan.
Derryhall, co. Westm. *See* Doryhalle, Dirrehall.
Derryhallogh, co. Mon. *See* Dyrrehalloghe.
Derryhane, co. Cav. *See* Derohyne.
Derryhellan, co. Mon. *See* Dirrehelan.
Derryhine (co. Mon.?), [illegible].
Derrykearn, Queen's co. *See* Dirrekerryne.
Derrykeagh, co. Mon., [illegible].
Derrykinard, co. Mon. *See* Dyrragkenard, Dyrrecrrynard.
Derryknockane, co. Lim. *See* Derryknockan, Derrenknockane, Dirrocknokan, Dirroknokan.
Derrylahan, Queen's co. *See* Dyrrylane.
Derryleaigh, co. Gal., [illegible].
Derrylemaylara, co. Cork, [illegible].
Derryleheo, co. Sligo. *See* Derrolyhyn.
Derryleigh, co. Tip. *See* Derreliagh.
Derrylevick, co. Mon. *See* Dyrrelamyvike.
Derryloskan—Daraloskane—Darlloskane—Derreloskan—Deroleskan—Derreloskan—Deryloskan—Diraloskane—Deroleskan—Derreloskan—Dyrreloskan (Derryluskan), co. Tip., [illegible], [illegible], 3[illegible], [illegible], [illegible], [illegible], [illegible], [illegible], [illegible].
Derryloughan, co. Gal. *See* Derrylaghan.
Derrymaclaghny—Derry m'Laghney—Derrym'laughlen—Dero m'loghne—Dere m'laghne—Dere m'laghny—Deremicklaghlin—Derevighlaghne—Dermaclaghney—Derem'laght—Derym'laghne—Derym'Laughane—Dirremacklaghny—Dirremacloghney—Dirricklaghny—Drymylaghny—Derrymaclaghlen—Dyrryvicklaghny (Derrymacloughna), co. Gal., 1[illegible], 13[illegible], 14[illegible], 1[illegible], 1[illegible], [illegible], [illegible], [illegible], [illegible], [illegible], [illegible], [illegible], [illegible], [illegible], [illegible], [illegible].
Derrymolica—Dirremolen, King's co., [illegible], [illegible], [illegible].
Derrymore, co. Kerry, [illegible].
Derrymore, co. Westm. *See* Dermore.
Derrymoyle, Queen's co. *See* Dermoyle.
Derryn (Derrin or Derreen) Queen's co., [illegible].
Derrynacaheragh, co. Cork. *See* Derrynicharraghe.
Derrynagalliagh, co. Long. *See* Dirrenegaleaghe, Dirrenegealleaghe.
Derrynanarragh, co. Westm. *See* Dirrenegarragh.
Derrynahinch, co. Kilk. *See* Derrynehinchy.
Derrynargel, co. Mon. *See* Dyrrenargard.
Derrynaseera, Queen's co. *See* Derrenesheyre, Dyrrenashyre.
Derrynashallog, co. Mon. *See* Derenashalge.
Derryne, co. Clare, [illegible].
Derrynehinchy—Derhinhinch (Derrynahinch), co. Kilk., [illegible], [illegible].
Derrynullagh (Queen's co.?), [illegible].
Derryonaghter, co. Kild. *See* Derenghlagh.
Derrypatrick, co. Meath. *See* Derpatrick.
Derryphalice, co. Ros. *See* Dyrrypalen.
Derryreel, co. Don. *See* Derreriye, Derreryle.
Derryree, Queen's co. *See* Derrere.
Derryunaloght—Dirryunaloghe—Dyrryunaloght (Dromalaght), co. Kerry, [illegible], [illegible], [illegible].
Derryvillane, co. Cork. *See* Dirryvallie.
Derryvough, co. Mon. *See* Derevoy.
Derryvehil, co. Cav. *See* Dyrrevehill.
Derrywode, co. Gal. *See* Dirrevode.
de Barpe, David (see Fermoy), [illegible].
de Barpe (see Roche, John boy, pardon), [illegible].
de Barpe (see Holy Abbey, co. Tip.), [illegible].
Derve, co. Cork, [illegible].
Dervackney, co. Cav., [illegible].
Derve, co. Louth, [illegible].
Dervor (Darver), co. Louth, 1[illegible], 1[illegible], [illegible], [illegible]; rector of, pardon, [illegible].
Dervor by the Bregy—Dearvor, co. Meath, 1104, [illegible].
Dervoy (co. Cav.?), [illegible].
Dery, co. Gal., [illegible].
Derybroke—Berybroke (Derrybrock), Queen's co., [illegible], [illegible].
Derydonell, Derydonill. *See* Derrydonnell.
Deryhalle (Derryhall, co. Westm.), [illegible].
Deryhowen, co. Gal., [illegible].
Derykill (Derrygile, Queen's co.), [illegible].
Deryloskan. *See* Derryloskan.
Derym'laghne—Derym'Laughane. *See* Derrymaclaghny.
Deryman, co. Kerry or Cork, [illegible].
Derynodoyhan (Dyrrewalloghan?), co. Clare, [illegible].
Derynikarraghe (Derrynacaheragh), co. Cork, [illegible].
Derynemoylie, co. Mon., [illegible].
Derysere (co. Long.?), [illegible].
de Saint John, Rob., [illegible].
De S. Laurence, Christopher (see Howth, lord), [illegible].
Desedery, James, pardon, [illegible].
Desert (see Dysert), [illegible].
Desert—Desertt, co. Clare, [illegible], [illegible].
Desert, co. Lim., [illegible].

INDEX TO FIANTS—ELIZABETH.

Desert, co. Mon. *See* Disert.
Desert, Queen's co., 2315.
Desert—Deserte, co. Westm., 4462, [illegible].
Deserte, co. Cork, 4467.
Deserte (Dysert), co. Kerry, 2818.
Deserte. *See* Dysert, Queen's co.
Deserte. *See* Desert, co. Westm.
Desertolaghe. *See* Dysertlarb.
Desertleran, co. Gal., [illegible].
Desertt (or Desert), [illegible].
Desies, the. *See* Decies.
Desmond, co. Cork, 3072.
Desmond—Desmonde—Desmounde, country, com. of peace, [illegible], [illegible]; grant of land in, [illegible], [illegible]; martial law, [illegible], [illegible]; to be made shire ground, 1948, 2798.
" county, 4613-9, 4322, 4364, 4478, 4477, 4479, 3178, [illegible], [illegible], [illegible], [illegible]-2, [illegible], [illegible], [illegible]; grants of land in, [illegible], [illegible], [illegible], [illegible], 6717.
" sheriff of, [illegible].
" lordship, [illegible].
" James Fitzgerald, earl of, late lord treasurer, 163.
" Gerald or Garrett, earl of, commissions, 253, [illegible]-7, [illegible], [illegible]; dispute with earl of Ormond, [illegible]-3, 1409; disputes with nobles and people, [illegible]; protection, [illegible]; pardon, [illegible]; lease, [illegible]; "arch traitor," 4474; his rebellion, [illegible], [illegible], 3741, [illegible], [illegible], [illegible], [illegible], [illegible]; soldier rewarded for slaying, [illegible]; attainder, [illegible]; custodiam of his lands, [illegible]-8; enquiry as to lands forfeited, 4811; com. to hear claims, [illegible]; rights of, [illegible]; rents payable to, [illegible], [illegible], [illegible], [illegible], [illegible]; land in Youghal, [illegible]; church patronage, [illegible]; his lands granted, [illegible], [illegible], [illegible], [illegible], [illegible], [illegible], [illegible], [illegible], [illegible], [illegible], [illegible]-3, [illegible], [illegible], [illegible], [illegible], [illegible]; leased, [illegible]; land held of, [illegible], [illegible]; his widow pardoned, [illegible].
" Elinor, countess of, pardon, 4478, [illegible]; pardon, [illegible].
" James m'Moris m'Shane (or Fitzgerald, James fitz Maurice), pardon, 667.
" Sir James of (brother of earl of Desmond), pardon, 3347; in rebellion, [illegible], [illegible]; lands forfeited by, 4814.
" James fitz John of, pardon, 3467.
Desmond—James fitz Thomas of, pardon to him and his men, 4478.
" Sir John FitzGerald of (of Desmond), commissions, [illegible], 3738, [illegible]; pardon, [illegible], 3778; pardon to his men, [illegible]-[illegible], [illegible]-1; pardon at suit of, [illegible]-1, [illegible]-1; rebellion, [illegible], [illegible], [illegible]; joins rebellion of Baltinglas, [illegible]; enquiry as to lands forfeited by, 4814; rent payable to, [illegible]; attainted, his lands leased, [illegible].
" John fitz John of, pardon, 3467.
" Katherine, countess of, [illegible].
" Sir Thomas of, pardon, 1578, 2374, 4478.
" Thomas fitz John of, pardon, 3467.
Desmondes country, co. Kerry, [illegible], [illegible].
Desses. *See* Decies.
Dessford, John, pardon, [illegible].
Deswellston. *See* Diswelston.
Desyes. *See* Decies.
de Valo alias Johnson, John, grant, 1778.
Devenisshe, Edm., merchant, [illegible].
Deventry, town of, delivered to king of Spain, [illegible].
Devereux—Deverax—Deverox—Deverouse—Deverouxe—Deveroux—Deverouxe—Devorax—Dewerax—Dewrax—Dewroux:
" Derby gowle, pardon, [illegible].
" Dermot, pardon, 1744.
" James, alienation to, [illegible]; pardon, [illegible]; livery to his heir, [illegible].
" John, dean of Ferns, 418.
" John, pardon, 4618, [illegible], [illegible], [illegible].
" Lawrence, pardon, [illegible].
" Mahowe, pardon, [illegible].
" Nicholas (knt., of Balmagyr), sheriff of co. Wex., [illegible], [illegible]; commissions, 64, 87, [illegible], [illegible], [illegible], 2117, 2345, 3444; his heir, [illegible].
" Nicholas, sheriff of Wexford, [illegible].
" Nicholas (of Adamstown), commission, [illegible]; pardon, [illegible].
" Nich., son of Nich. (of Balmagyr), pardon, 2841; livery, [illegible].
" Nich., commission, [illegible].
" Nich., pardon, [illegible], [illegible].
" Philip, alienation to, [illegible]; lease, 1829; livery, [illegible].
" Richard, archdeacon of Ferns, commissions, 3411, [illegible].
" Richard, pardon, [illegible], [illegible], [illegible].
" Stephen, 1637; pardon, [illegible], [illegible].
" Thomas, pardon, [illegible], [illegible], [illegible].
" Walter, pardon, [illegible], [illegible], 6727.

INDEX TO FIANTS—ELIZABETH.

Devereux—William, treasurer of Ferns, [illegible].
" William, rector of Taghmon, [illegible].
" William, pardon, [illegible], [illegible].
Devesion, co. Kilk., [illegible].
Devic, Tho., pardon, [illegible].
Devil's Hooke, alias Rich. m'Ricard Burke, pardon, [illegible].
Devinish, Rich., pardon, [illegible].
Devon county, undertakers from, for Munster lands, [illegible].
Devoreux—Deverox. See Devereux.
Devorewyn, Gerat, pardon, [illegible].
Devowroe or Devowrn, Nicholas, pardon, [illegible].
de Wale, Ullick, attainted (see Wale), [illegible].
de Wall, Shane, pardon, [illegible].
Dewaleke. See Duleeke.
Dewemac (co. Cork ?), [illegible].
Deworox. See Devereux.
Dewhessen, James, pardon, [illegible].
Dewleek—Dowlecke—Dewlek—Dewleke. See Duleeke.
Dewrox, Nicholas, pardon, [illegible].
Dewroux, Nicholas. See Devereux.
Dewyn, Donell, pardon, [illegible].
Dexster, Tho., pardon, [illegible].
Dexter, Robert, [illegible].
Deyne, co. Down, [illegible].
Deyrloghan, co. Down, [illegible].
Deyrmot, Geany oyne, pardon, [illegible].
Dexter, Richard, grant of a wardship, [illegible].
Diamor, co. Meath. See Demore.
Diane, George, license, [illegible].
Dice (Decies), barony, co. Meath, [illegible].
Dickens, George, commission, [illegible], [illegible].
Dicwood, co. Down, [illegible].
Diermot, Geney oge, pardon, [illegible].
Diffren—Diffrene. See Dufferin.
Digganbegg (Danganbeg ?), co. Lim., [illegible].
Digganmore, co. Lim., [illegible].
Digin, John, [illegible].
Digin, co. Lim., [illegible].
Digonan, Patr., pardon, [illegible].
Digname, Richard, pardon, [illegible].
Dilis (Denish, co. Lim., or Denis, co. Kerry), [illegible].
Dillan, John, pardon, [illegible].
Dillin, Donell m'Diermott oge oy, pardon, [illegible].
Dillonyfoggie (Dollian), co. Cork, [illegible].
Dillis (Denish), co. Lim., [illegible].
Dillon—Dyllon—Dyllone:
" Bartholomew, lands of, [illegible].
" Bartholomew (of Kappoke), wardship, [illegible]; livery, [illegible].
" Christopher, pardon, [illegible].
" Dermod, pardon, [illegible].
" Edmund, pardon, [illegible], [illegible].
" Edm. m'Iames (of Walterston), pardon, [illegible].
Dillon—Edm. (of Walterston), attainted, [illegible].
" Edm. m'Thomas, pardon, [illegible].
" Gerald, or Garret, knight, appointed captain of Dillon's country, [illegible]; commissions, [illegible], [illegible], [illegible], [illegible].
" Gerald (of Riverston), grant, [illegible].
" Gerald, clerk of the crown, Queen's Bench, [illegible]; made third justice, Queen's Bench, [illegible].
" Gerald (of Dryman), clerk of peace, Kildare, &c., [illegible]; conveyance to his use, [illegible].
" Garret (of S. Mallee), commission, [illegible].
" Gerald (of Ardbraccan), grant of land, [illegible].
" Gerald m'Gerald (of Ballimorley), attainted, [illegible].
" Gerald, or Garrett, pardon, [illegible], [illegible], [illegible], [illegible], [illegible].
" Henry, pardon, [illegible], [illegible], [illegible], [illegible].
" Hubert (of Belanaghgharew), commission, [illegible], [illegible].
" Hubert, pardon, [illegible], [illegible], [illegible].
" James (of Dundrill), commission, [illegible].
" James og (of Kilkenny, co. Westm.), commissions, [illegible], [illegible].
" James (of Moymet, son of Sir Lucas), lease, [illegible]; livery, [illegible]; commissions, [illegible], [illegible], [illegible].
" James, lease, [illegible].
" James, burgess of Athlone, [illegible].
" James, pardon, [illegible], [illegible], [illegible], [illegible], [illegible], [illegible], [illegible].
" John (of Dublin), [illegible], [illegible].
" John, in Lismore, [illegible].
" John, burgess of Athlone, [illegible].
" John, pardon, [illegible], [illegible], [illegible].
" Lucas (afterwards knight), chief solicitor, [illegible], [illegible]; attorney general, [illegible]; chief baron, [illegible], [illegible]; custodiam of manor of Newcastle, &c., [illegible], [illegible]; custodiam of bar. of Kilkenny West, [illegible], [illegible], [illegible]; commissions, [illegible]; report or note on pardons, [illegible], [illegible], [illegible], [illegible]; party to indenture with Ulster chief, [illegible]; license of absence, [illegible]; pardon, [illegible]; pardons at

Dillon:
his suit, [illegible], [illegible], [illegible], 4014; freedom from subsidy, 742; livery to, as son and heir of sir Rob. Dillon, [illegible]; pardon of alienation, [illegible]; leases, [illegible], 1[illegible], 1714, [illegible], 4[illegible], [illegible], [illegible]; grant of land, 1[illegible]; trustee for Cormac M'Carthy of Blarny, [illegible]; his son and heir, [illegible]; his man, [illegible]; livery to his heir, [illegible].
„ Margery, pardon, [illegible].
„ Matthew, pardon, [illegible].
„ Maurice, pardon, [illegible].
„ Moriah, pardon, [illegible].
„ Nathaniel, chief or general clerk of the council, [illegible], 4196, [illegible]; conveyance to him, [illegible]; license of absence, [illegible]; his man, [illegible].
„ Nicholas (of Keppoke), wardship and livery of his heir, 2080, [illegible]; his widow, [illegible].
„ Patrick, pardon, [illegible].
„ Peirs, pardon, [illegible], [illegible].
„ Peter, suit by, [illegible].
„ Peter (of Skryne), wardship and livery of his heir, [illegible], [illegible].
„ Peter, pardon, [illegible].
„ Redmund, pardon, 3[illegible], [illegible], [illegible].
„ Richard (of Proudston), second justice Queen's Bench, 373, 719; com., [illegible]; freedom from subsidy, [illegible]; pardon, [illegible].
„ Richard (of Drumrany), com., [illegible].
„ Rich., sheriff of Westmeath, pardon, [illegible]; com., [illegible].
„ Rich. (of Skreen), wardship, [illegible]; livery, [illegible].
„ Rich., [illegible]; pardon, 719, [illegible], [illegible].
„ Robert (of Newtown of Trim, afterwards knight), second justice Queen's Bench, 27; chief justice Common Pleas, 146; oath of supremacy, [illegible]; commissions, 146, 218, [illegible], [illegible], [illegible], [illegible], [illegible], 1417, 1424, 14[illegible], [illegible], [illegible], [illegible], [illegible], [illegible], [illegible], [illegible], [illegible], [illegible]; surrenders seneschalship of Kilkenny West, [illegible]; leases, [illegible], [illegible]; grant of land, [illegible]; alienation to, [illegible]; livery to his heir, [illegible]; pardon at his suit, [illegible].
„ Robert (of Dalnath and Riverstown, afterwards knight), second justice of Connaught, 1434; chancellor of the green-wax of the Exchequer, [illegible], [illegible]; second justice Common Pleas, [illegible], [illegible]; chief justice Common Pleas, [illegible]; surrender, [illegible]; re-appointed, [illegible], [illegible];

Dillon:
commissions, 1417–8, 1[illegible], [illegible]; licence of absence, [illegible]; alienation to, [illegible].
„ Robert, second baron of the Exchequer, [illegible].
„ Robert, pardon, [illegible], [illegible], [illegible].
„ Robert, burgess of Athlone, [illegible].
„ Roger, commissions, [illegible], [illegible].
„ Rose, [illegible].
„ Theobald or Tybbot (afterwards knight), chief serjeant of Connaught, [illegible]; commissions, [illegible], [illegible], [illegible], [illegible], [illegible], [illegible]; pardon, [illegible], [illegible], [illegible], [illegible].
„ Thomas, justice of the liberty of Wexford, [illegible], [illegible]; chief justice of Connaught, [illegible], [illegible]; third justice Common Pleas, [illegible]; commissions, [illegible].
„ Thomas (of Courtstown), chief chamberlain of the Exchequer, [illegible], [illegible], [illegible]; clerk of the Crown of Meath, &c., [illegible], [illegible], [illegible]; pardon, [illegible].
„ Thomas (of Ardnacrany), com., [illegible], [illegible].
„ Thomas (of Canonstown), com., [illegible], [illegible]; pardon, [illegible].
„ Thomas (of Newtown of Trim) grant of a wardship, [illegible]; lease, [illegible].
„ Thomas, his lands in Trim, [illegible], [illegible].
„ Thomas, pardon, [illegible], [illegible], [illegible], [illegible], [illegible].
„ Tibbot, pardon, [illegible], [illegible].
„ Walter, pardon, [illegible].
Dillon's country, or Maghercuirk (the barony of Kilkenny West), co. Westmeath, [illegible], [illegible], [illegible]; to be set out in plough lands, [illegible], [illegible], [illegible].
„ captain of, appointed, [illegible], [illegible].
Dimanstown, co. Meath. See Damanston, Damoageston, Danielleston.
Dun, Anthony, pardon, [illegible].
„ Rowland, pardon, [illegible].
„ William, pardon, [illegible].
Dingaine. See Dongan, co. Meath.
Dingan. See Dingle.
Dingan—Dynghain, King's co., [illegible], [illegible].
Dinganbeare (Danganbeg, King's co.), [illegible].

Dingen. *See* Dungan, co. Meath.
Dingenbrack. *See* Dangenbrack.
Dingenenrnich. *See* Dingle.
Dinghainbegge—Dynginbegge (Dangane), Queen's co., 468, 1718.
Dinghainmore—Dyngin Onore (Dangane), Queen's co., 436, 1718.
Dinghan, co. Meath, [illegible].
Dingill—Dingillychuse—Dingine ne quose—Dingine ne quine. *See* Dingle.
Dinginmore (Dangenmore, co. Kilk. ?), 6704.
Dingle—Dinglecushe—Dingillychuse—Daingiokeyowy—Dinglecoune—Dinglequiske—Dinglequisse—Dingle Ilussy—Dinglecuyshe—Dinglequin—Dingle ne guye—Dinglequisko—Dinglequisse—Dinglecushe—Dingill—Dangle—Diagan—Dingennotich—Dingine ne quose—Dingine ne quise—Doingyne ne quise—Dyngle—Dyngle na Cuyse, co. Kerry, 2849, 4758, 4936, 5461, 4183, 6024, 6665, 6308, 6873.
„ charter to provost &c., 4814.
„ burgesses, pardon, 4871.
„ merchants, 1771, 4854, 6404, 6373.
„ premises in, leased, 5173, 6347; granted, 6308.
„ rectory, 6173.
„ collector of wine duty, 1578, 4418, [illegible], [illegible], [illegible], 4621, 6941.
„ controller, [illegible], [illegible], 4617.
„ supervisor of port, [illegible].
Dingle Inrt (in Philipstown, King's co.), 1528.
Dinish, co. Kerry. *See* Dennis.
Dinshin, Edm., pardon, 4778.
Dion Canltruane (co. Sligo ?), 4738.
Dyppes—Dyppis—Dipsis (Deeps), co. Wex., 3414, 3838, [illegible], 4382; manor, 3418.
Dira (co. Westm.), [illegible].
Dirae, the (co. Gal. ?), 6488.
Diragh (co. Cork or Lim.), 4184.
Diram, co. Ross, 4468.
Dirchrocke (Derrybrock ?), Queen's co., 1264.
Dirovaill. *See* Dirriemmoll.
Dirogarran (Derrygarran), King's co., 5341.
Dirologh. *See* Derrilogh, co. Kilk.
Dirolosikane. *See* Derryloskan.
Dirore—Direroe. *See* Dirraroe.
Dirgawne (co. Long. ?), 5451.
Dirgowne (co. Long. ?), [illegible].
Dirhy, Edm. oge m'Edmond, pardon, 4944.
Dirhy, Ricard m'Edmond, pardon, 4944.
Dirincrowane. *See* Dirrycrowan.
Dirig, Ellis fitz John, pardon, 4656.
Dirighivine (co. Lim. ?), 4611.
Diriefulle, Queen's co., 6458.
Dirimoan (co. Cork ?), 6512.
Dirinloake (co. Tip. ?), 6708.
Dirlis (co. Kild.), 4258.
Dirmore (Derrymore), co. Westm., 4207.
Dirnehe (co. Long. ?), [illegible].
Dirpatrick—Dirpatrick. *See* Derpatrick.
Dirr, co. Kilk., 5207.
Dirra (co. Westm. ?), 1158.
Dirraghatricke, co. Tip., 6617.
Dirraghe (Darragh ?), co. Lim., 2878, 6617.
Dirre, the (co. Leit. ?), 5141.
Dirremagnelaghe (Derrymagallagh, co. Long.), 1178.
Dirremured (co. Leit. ?), 5441.
Dirreaknokan (Derryknockane), co. Lim., 6614.
Dirrealouey—Dirrealouye. *See* Derrylowny.
Dirrecarragh, co. Cork, 4465.
Dirredarry (Dromdarrick ?), co. Mon., 1572.
Dirredawe, co. Cav., 4881.
Dirregart. *See* Derrygart.
Dirregawny (co. Gal. ?), 5452.
Dirregrasore (co. Leit. ?), 5441.
Dirreh (co. Cork ?), 4878.
Dirrehill, co. Westm., 1652.
Dirreheinn (Derryhellan), co. Mon., 6873.
Dirrehoy[ ], in Upper Ossory, [illegible].
Dirrekowle, co. Mayo, 1604.
Dirrekurye (Derrykeare ?), Queen's co., 5860.
Dirreklagh, co. Mon., 5577.
Dirreknokan (Derryknockane), co. Lim., 6624.
Dirreloghe. *See* Derrolash.
Dirreloigh (co. Tip. ?), [illegible].
Dirrelle, co. Kild., 404.
Dirrelomed—Dirrelome (Derralomed), co. Mon., 5642, 6678.
Dirremacklaghny—Dirremacloghny. *See* Derrymacloghny.
Dirremalen. *See* Derrymallen.
Dirremore, co. Sligo, 5434, 4848.
Dirren, Rob., pardon, [illegible].
Dirres, Queen's co., 1567.
Dirremagarragh (Derrymagarragh ?), co. Westm., 6574.
Dirremagarragh, 5748.
Dirremagarran, Queen's co., 488.
Dirremagallaghe (Derrymagallagh, co. Long.), [illegible].
Dirremakeny, co. Cav., 4897.
Dirremaleght, co. Tip., 6734.
Dirremanulle, King's co., 5763.
Dirreny, co. Long., 1178.
Dirreroe—Direro—Dirroroe (co. Cork ?), 1788, 6784.
Dirrery, co. Mon., 5673.

INDEX TO FIANTS—ELIZABETH.

Dirrallmeady (co. Tip. or Kilk. ?), [illegible].
Dirrovale—Dyrevald (Derrywoola), co. Gal., [illegible], [illegible].
Dirrowmilly (co. Leit. ?), [illegible].
Dirrighe (Daikes, King's co.), 1491.
Durtconnell — Dirconnill — Dyrconnill — Dyrryconnell (Derryconnell), co. Cork, [illegible], 4039, [illegible], [illegible].
Dirrigarile (co. Cork ?), [illegible].
Dirrigart. See Derrygart.
Dirrick, mock and little. See Derrick.
Dirrikrossykyne. See Durrykrossykyne.
Dirrindon (co. Cork ?), 4571.
Dirrinlawy, in Upper Ossory, 4117.
Dirrindive, co. Kerry, 6117.
Dirrinegarran (Derrygarran), Queen's co., 1799.
Dirringoloky (Derrygolan), co. Westm., [illegible].
Dirrinhon, co. Leit., [illegible].
Dirrinkowne, co. Leit., [illegible].
Dirrirain, co. Kerry, [illegible].
Dirrirough, co. Cork, [illegible].
Dirrirowragh, co. Cork, [illegible].
Dirriyowragh (co. Cork ?), [illegible].
Dirrivagh (co. Cork ?), [illegible].
Dirrivickloghny. See Derrymacloghny.
Dirriwilliam, co. Cork, [illegible].
Dirriwilliam (co. Cork ?), [illegible].
Dirrisloane, co. Tip., [illegible].
Dirrane, Gybbon, [illegible], [illegible].
Dirrineghieky, co. Ross., [illegible].
Dirry (King's or Queen's co. ?), [illegible].
Dirry, co. Kild., [illegible].
Dirry, co. Gal., [illegible].
Dirrycrossan—Dirieroman, co. Clare, [illegible], [illegible], [illegible].
Dirrykrossykyne — Dirrikrossykyne, (perhaps Derrygunnigan), King's co., [illegible].
Dirryloughaghiry, co. Down, [illegible].
Dirrys, Walter, pardon, [illegible].
Dirrynagarran (Derrygarran), Queen's co., [illegible].
Dirryneguinan (Derrygunnigan), King's co., [illegible].
Dirrynagalloughe, 1178.
Dirryrow—Dirry Roe—Dirryrowe, co. Cork, [illegible], [illegible], [illegible].
Dirrymulaght. See Derrymulaght.
Dirsert Kellye. See Disert Kellye.
Dirryroe, co. Cork, [illegible].
Dirryvallie (Derryvillane), co. Cork, rectory, [illegible].
Disart, Queen's co., [illegible].
Disarte. See Dysarte, co. Kilk.
Disdulle, [illegible].
Dise, Theobald, pardon, [illegible].
Diss, barony (Deece, co. Meath), martial law in, [illegible].
Disert, co. Clare, [illegible], [illegible], [illegible], [illegible], [illegible].
Disert—Diserte, co. Cork, [illegible], [illegible], [illegible], [illegible].
Disert (Dysert), co. Kerry, rectory, [illegible].
Disert (co. Kilk. ?), [illegible].
Disert (co. Lim. ?), [illegible].
Disert, rectory (Dysart, co. Louth), 1198.
Disert (Dysert), co. Mon., 4677.
Disert. See Disertoncon, Queen's co.
Disert (Dysart, co. Westm.), [illegible].
Disert—Diserte—Disert, co. Westm., [illegible], [illegible], [illegible], [illegible], [illegible], [illegible].
Disertan—Disertanan, co. Kild., 1131, [illegible].
Disertaneveen. See Disertaneveen.
Disertbeagh (Dysart), co. Kilk., [illegible].
Disert Gorman, co. Gal., [illegible].
Diserte. See Disert, co. Cork.
Diserte (Dysart, co. Lim.), 6171.
Diserte. See Dysert, Queen's co.
Diserte, co. Ross, [illegible].
Diserte (see Disert, co. Westm.), [illegible].
Disertolyan. See Dysertlinch.
Disertinkyrand. See Castlekyrand.
Disert-encos—Disertinnecwon—Disert (Dysartenos), Queen's co., rectory, 1518.
„ prebendary of, [illegible].
Disertgallyn—Disertgallen—Disert Gallen. See Dysertgallyne.
Disertlinbegh, [illegible]; rectory, [illegible].
Disertkonrane, co. Meath, [illegible].
Disert Kellye—Dirsert Kellye (co. Gal. ?), [illegible].
Disertkilleghe, co. Westm., lease, [illegible].
Disharde, co. Westm., [illegible].
Disherencan. See Disertanan.
Diskarte—Diskirtis, co. Cork (co. Wat. ?), 1897, 3161.
Dispensations, commission for granting, [illegible].
Dissart, co. Cork, 6431.
Dissertenan — Disertenan (Dysartenos), county Kilk., rectory, [illegible], [illegible].
Dissert (Dysart), Queen's co., [illegible].
Disvert. See Disert.
Diswolston — Dorwolliston — Dorwellston (Diswellstown), co. Dub., [illegible], [illegible], [illegible].
Diwyragh, Wm., pardon, [illegible].
Dixon, Patrick, merchant, [illegible].
„ Wm., pardon, 4117.
Dixonic, Wm., pardon, [illegible].
Dizarte. See Dysart, Queen's co.
D'Loughlinan, co. Wat. See Drogheloe.
Doalcion (co. Long. ?), [illegible].
Doanaltown (Bushmilltown), co. Lim., [illegible].
Doally (co. Tip. ?), [illegible].
Doan, Mawiros A., pardon, [illegible].
Doawne, Durgan, pardon, [illegible].
Dobbin—Dobbine—Dobbyn—Dobbyne—Dobin—Dobin—Dobyn.
„ Adam, pardon, [illegible].

INDEX TO FIANTS—ELIZABETH.

Dobbyn—David, pardon, 1437, 2154.
" Edmund, pardon, 1493.
" James, pardon, 1437.
" Jonkin, pardon, 3637.
" John, pardon, [illegible].
" Laurence, pardon, 3451.
" Patrick (of Lismore), pardon, 28. 83.
" Patrick, alderman of Waterford, pardon, 3794; cont., 6087.
" Patrick, 6954.
" Peter, commission, 663.
" Peter, pardon, 1437, 4987, 6322.
" Piers, 3431.
" Rob., pardon, [illegible].
" Simon, pardon, 1846.
" Thomas, pardon, 86, 1841, 2254, 6380.
" Walter, pardon, [illegible], 6368.
" William, pardon, 26, 1140, 2462, 6388.
Dobbyne's Water, on the Nore, 1317.
Dobon—Dobin. See Dobbyn.
Doboragh (co. Meath ?), 4187, 6371.
Dobyn. See Dobbyn.
Docarran (co. Cork ?), [illegible].
Doctor Noyland, lands of, 4761.
Docwra — Dockwra — Dockwray — Dockwray, Henry (capt., afterwards knight), constable of Dungarvan castle, [illegible], [illegible]-78, 6312, 6317; chief commissioner and leader of the army in Connaught, [illegible]-7; commander of the forces at Loughfoyle, 6370-1, 6378.
Dod, Tho., commission, [illegible], 1864.
Dodd, Brian, pardon, 6428.
" George, pardon, 6494.
" Wm., lease, 3472.
Doddo, Peter, vicar of Kilcoan, 6166.
Dodder river, co. Dub., 4177-8.
Dole, Margaret alias Mogy Gall, pardon, 6654.
" Pierce, pardon, 6654.
Dodin, Owen m'Donogh, pardon, 2462.
Doelo, Edm. oge m'Edm., pardon, 2078.
Doell, Queen's co., 6626.
Doelinta, Piers, pardon, 5165.
Dorglain, Charles son of Fitzmaurice I., pardon, 4666.
Doeraba—Dawran alias Durlane (Derrane, co. Rosc.), priory leased, 1314, 2143, 2783.
Doerisallin, co. Cork, 5065.
Doeyry wales (co. Ferm. ?), 6082.
Doffe, Morogh, pardon, 2831.
Dofforig, Morogh bane, pardon, 6377.
Doffish—Duffiskin, beside Galway, 4018, 5628.
Dogan, Dorby, pardon, 4394.
Dogane, Donell m'Connoher I., pardon, 4672.
Doggeston (Dogstown, co. Meath), 65.
Doggel, John, alienation to, 342.
Dogharties, Ross of the, pardon to persons of the race of, 6464. See O'Doherty.
Dogherarrick (co. Lim. ?), 6443.
Doghell, Queen's co., 1622, 6626.
Dogher, co. Mayo, 4676.
Dogherdie, Nich., pardon, 4821.
Dogherdie, Wm. (clerk), pardon, 4681.
Dogheradan, co. Cork, 6793.
Dogstown, co. Meath. See Doggeston.
Dohalagh, co. Cork, 4731.
Doher, Dogald, 1878.
Doheil (Dunkip, co. Lim.), 3171.
Doherty, Edm. m'Brien m'Ma I. pardon, 6646.
Dohain, Ions (e), pardon, 6115.
Doillis, co. Cork, 4614.
Doin, Dionysius, pardon, 6466.
" Omey, pardon, 4451.
" alias m'Donnell, James, pardon, 4091.
" Katherine, pardon, 6393.
" Martin, pardon, 4631.
" Wm., pardon, 6352.
Doine, John, pardon, 6628.
" Morris A., pardon, 6363.
Doinge, Garrott, pardon, 5188.
" James, pardon, 5188.
Doire Aghan, co. Cav., 5466.
Doiran (co. Don.), 6563.
Doiran Korine, Donell O'Sullivan alias, 4544.
Doiry, co. Gal., 6564.
Dolangh (Donagh), co. Dub., 1462.
Doldam, Kallaghe oge ny, pardon, 6612.
Dolan, Simon, pardon, 4611.
Dolard, Wm., pardon, 2798.
Dolfin, Moyler m'Moyler m'Teir., pardon, 6673.
" Teir., pardon, 6598.
" Redmond, pardon, 6662.
" —Dolphine, Walter, pardon, 6468, 6598.
Dolfine, Moyler m'[ ] more, pardon, 4678.
" Wm. oge D. m'Walter Leo, 4678.
Dolfyn, Henry, pardon, 5634.
Dolling, Donell m'Gillpatrick, pardon, 4877.
" Morrogh m'Gillpatrick, pardon, 6877.
Dolinge, John, pardon, 6284.
Dollanstown, co. Meath, 4887.
Dollard, Rich., pardon, 2877.
Dollandstown. See Dollanstown.
Dollas, co. Lim. See Dolough.
Dollaughe. See Dollough.
Dollin (co. Lim. ?), 4411.
Dollis (co. Lim. ?), 2170.
Dollogh—Dolloughe—Dolloughe—Dollough—Dulloughe (co. Dub.), 797, 1739, 2694, 2675, 4672.
Dollogh—Dolloigh—Dulloigh, co. Lim., 1494, 5166, 6451.
Dolloughe. See Dollough.
Dollulgh. See Dollogh.
Dollurdbeaome, co. Kild., 6623.

INDEX TO FIANTS.—ELIZABETH.

Dollough. *See* Dollogh.
Dalloughe, the, co. Car. (containing the parish of Cloydagh), [illegible].
Dallymor, co. Lim., [illegible].
Dologh—Dolough, co. Leix, 4762, 6442.
Dologho (Dollas, co. Lim.), 6172.
Dolokye, Edm and m' Tirlagh roe, parden, 1557.
Dolondre, Edm., pardon, 6[illegible]1.
Dolough (see Dologh), [illegible].
Dolphins. *See* Dollin.
Domakomagh, co. Kilk., [illegible].
Domanq, King's co., [illegible].
Dombraddis, co. Leix, [illegible].
Domeghhill, co. Tip., [illegible].
Domen, co. Ros., [illegible].
Domonoghe, co. Gal., rectory, [illegible].
Domoristown — Domorston — Domeriston—Domeristowne, co. Kilk. [illegible], [illegible], [illegible], [illegible], [illegible], [illegible].
Dominploca (co. Gal. ?), [illegible].
Dominicans, Preachers, or Black Friars. *See* Adare, Athenry, Athy, Ballinclowra, co. Sligo, Cashel, Cork, Dublin, Elphin, Galway, Glasmor, Kilkenny, Kilmallock, Limerick, Lurgho, Mullingar, Rathbrenan, Rathmullen, Roscrea, Trim, Waterford, Youghal.
Domnomeyugre (co. Down or Antrim), [illegible].
Domnorvion, co. Tip., 6[illegible].
Domnyoyage (perhaps Tamaynane, co. Antrim), [illegible].
Domrowin, co. Cork, [illegible].
Don, Wm., Irish interpreter, [illegible].
Donaanyt (co. Cav. ?), [illegible].
Donabate, co. Dub. *See* Donabate.
Donabrooke, co. Dublin, [illegible].
Donacmlaga, co. Westm. or Long., 6974.
Donacarny — Donakarney — Donakarny—Donakarne — Donnakirne (Donacarny, co. Meath), 7[illegible], 14[illegible], [illegible], [illegible], [illegible], [illegible], [illegible].
Donade—Donadale, co. Kild., [illegible], [illegible], [illegible]; rectory, 1[illegible].
Donagan, co. Clare, [illegible], [illegible].
Donagh (Boyvagh, co. Meath—see Inqu., 37 Jac. I.), [illegible].
Donagh, co. Mon. *See* Donnagh.
Donagh, Iohannes tyne, pardon, [illegible].
Donagha Gallochriste ny, [illegible].
Donaghe, Ricard, pardon, [illegible].
Donaghamore. *See* Donaghmore.
Donagh enlorane (M'Carty?), lands of, [illegible].
Donaghintraine, co. Sligo. *See* Dowrachontrahan.
Donaghmayne (Dunmain), co. Wex., [illegible].
Donaghmore—Donaghmore — Donamore —Dowaghmore (co. Cork), [illegible], [illegible], [illegible], [illegible], [illegible], [illegible], [illegible], [illegible].
Donaghmore — Donaghmore — Donamore —Donaghmor—Dowaghmore, co. Kilk., [illegible], [illegible], [illegible]; rectory, 1174, [illegible], [illegible].
Donaghmore, co. Meath. *See* Donamore.
Donaghmore — Dowaghmore, Queen's co., [illegible], [illegible].
Donaghmore, co. Tip. *See* Donaghmore.
Donaghmore, co. Wick. *See* Donamore.
Donaghmore, [illegible].
Donagh moyle (al Dromlare, co. Lim.), attainted, [illegible], [illegible].
Donaghmoyne, co. Mon. *See* Donaghmayne, Donaghmoney, Dowaghmayne.
Donaghe, John m'Donnell y, pardon, [illegible].
Donaghmayne, co. Mon., rectory, [illegible].
Donagcrost, co. Clare, [illegible].
Donaghuile, co. Kilk. *See* Donaghill.
Donakorney—Donakarny. *See* Donacarny.
Donally, co. Tip., [illegible].
Donalstown, co. Dub., [illegible].
Donamagra, co. Kilk., [illegible].
Donamor, co. Cork, [illegible].
Donamore, [illegible].
Donamore. *See* Donaghmore, co. Kilk.
Donamore, co. Meath, [illegible].
Donamore (Donaghmore, bar. Ratoath), co. Meath, manor, [illegible], [illegible]; rectory, [illegible], [illegible], [illegible], [illegible].
Donamore near Navan, co. Meath, [illegible].
Donamore alias Donaghmore, co. Meath, [illegible].
Donamore—Donamore, co. Westm., [illegible], [illegible], [illegible].
Donamore Ameyle — Donamore (Donaghmore, co. Wick.), [illegible]; prebendary of, [illegible].
Donamahir, co. Clare, [illegible].
Donane, Redmund, pardon, [illegible].
Donankory, co. Cav., [illegible], [illegible].
Donany, co. Louth, [illegible], [illegible], 4[illegible]; rectory, 1[illegible].
Donanyne, co. Cork, 1[illegible].
Donanye (co. Cav. ?), [illegible].
Donarayle. *See* Downeraill.
Donard—Donarde (Donard, co. Wick.), [illegible], [illegible], [illegible], [illegible]; rectory, [illegible], [illegible].
Donarde (co. Meath ?), [illegible].
Donarde, co. Ross, [illegible], [illegible].
Donassy castle (Donass), co. Clare, [illegible].
Donasagh (Donagh), co. Mon., [illegible].
Donawnia, co. Kild., [illegible].
Donaloo (Dunbuy, co. Cork ?), [illegible].
Donboise. *See* Dunboyne.
Donboirge, co. Cork, [illegible].
Donbullogo (Dunbullogue), co. Cork, rectory, [illegible].
Donbo Roag (co. Cork), [illegible].
Donbollock (co. Cork), [illegible].
Donbologa, co. Cork, [illegible].

INDEX TO FIANTS—ELIZABETH.

Donboy. See Dunboy.
Donboyn—Donboyne. See Dunboyne.
Donbrenan (Dunbrin), Queen's co., [illegible].
Donbrewayne—Donbrewlan (co. Wat. ?), [illegible], [illegible].
Donbro. See Dunbro.
Donbrodie—Donbrody. See Dunbrody.
Donbryne (co. Car. ?), [illegible].
Donbury. See Dunboy.
Donbye (co. Gal. ?), [illegible].
Doncannon—Don Cannon. See Duncannon.
Doncormok, co. Wex., [illegible].
Doncoro, co. Sligo, [illegible].
Doncoro, Queen's co., [illegible].
Doncormock—Doncormoke. See Duncormock.
Dondalk—Dondalke. See Dundalk.
Dondanire (Dowdanaid near Innishannon, co. Cork), [illegible].
Dondarragh (co. Car. ?), [illegible].
Dondedy (Dundeady?), co. Cork, [illegible].
Dondermot (Dundermot), co. Rosc., [illegible].
Dondoly (co. Cork ?), [illegible].
Dondolf or Dungall, co. Wex., [illegible].
Dondon, Andrew, pardon, [illegible].
„ John, pardon, [illegible].
„ Peter, pardon, [illegible].
„ Rich., pardon, [illegible], [illegible].
„ Walter, pardon, [illegible].
Dondonnell (Dundonnell), co. Westm., [illegible].
Dondrum — Donirum (Dundrum), co. Down, [illegible], [illegible], [illegible].
„ collector of customs, [illegible].
Dondrom (Dundrum, co. Dub. ?), [illegible].
Dondrom (see Dundrum, co. Tip.), [illegible].
Dondrum. See Dondrom, co. Down.
Dondrume (co. Wick. ?), [illegible].
Dondremy. See Dondrum.
Done, Derby, pardon, [illegible].
Done, Wm., pardon, [illegible].
Donebate—Donabate (Donabate), co. Dub., [illegible]; vicarage, [illegible].
Donebrowne (co. Kilk. or Tip.), [illegible].
Donede, co. Kild., [illegible], [illegible].
Donedowne alias Owndufe (Owendaff), co. Wex., [illegible].
Donedrum. See Dundrum.
Donegal—Donnygall, commission to form county, [illegible].
„ sheriff, [illegible].
Donegall, commander of the forces at, [illegible].
Donegall, co. Cork. See Downegall.
Donegalell, [illegible].
Donegrol, co. Tip., [illegible].
Donehony (King's co.), [illegible].
Donehoyne, King's co., [illegible].
Donehye, co. Down, [illegible].
Donekerney, [illegible].
Donekylly, Queen's co., [illegible].
Donellane, Margaret alias, pardon, [illegible].
„ Rose ny, pardon, [illegible].
Donell, Andrew ny, pardon, [illegible], [illegible].
„ Brian fitz Alexander, pardon, [illegible].
„ Dae oge vic Dae vic, pardon, [illegible].
„ David, pardon, [illegible].
„ Ellen ny, pardon, [illegible], [illegible].
„ Fynnola or Fynoll ny, pardon, [illegible], [illegible].
„ Honor ny, pardon, [illegible], [illegible].
„ Jone—Johanna—Jonane—Jowan or Jenane ny, pardon, [illegible], [illegible], [illegible], [illegible], [illegible], [illegible].
„ John, pardon, [illegible].
„ Mary ny, pardon, [illegible], [illegible].
„ Meive ny, pardon, [illegible].
„ More alias, pardon, [illegible].
„ Owny ny, pardon, [illegible].
„ Rose ny Coll ny, pardon, [illegible].
„ Sawe ny, pardon, [illegible].
„ Shily ny, pardon, [illegible].
„ William, pardon, [illegible].
„ O or M. See O'Donell.
Donell oge, Ellen ny, pardon, [illegible].
Donell Roe brege, attainted, [illegible].
Donell mcbury, Katherine ny, pardon, [illegible].
Donell ydolough, Jone ny, pardon, [illegible].
Donemaynewy (Dunmanway), co. Cork, [illegible]; castle and lands, [illegible].
Donemone—Donemon—Donamony (Dunnamona ?), co. Westm., [illegible], [illegible], [illegible]; grant, [illegible].
Donemony, co. Mayo, [illegible].
Donemony. See Donemone.
Donemore (Dunmore, co. Donegal), [illegible].
Donemyinchall, co. Clare, castle and lands, [illegible].
Donenore—Donerale (co. Westmeath ?), [illegible], [illegible].
Donengore (co. Kilk. ?), [illegible].
Donemy (co. Dub. ?), [illegible].
Donemy, co. Kilk., [illegible].
Donevilla, co. Cork. See Downevell.
Donevyn, co. Westm., [illegible].
Donery, co. Cav., [illegible].
Doneskeagh, co. Tip., [illegible].
Donevan, Conoghor m'Dermody, pardon, [illegible].
„ Donald, called O'Donevan, pardon, [illegible].
„ Ellen ny, pardon, [illegible].
„ Jone ny, pardon, [illegible].
„ Shilie ny, pardon, [illegible].
Donevane, More ny, pardon, [illegible].
Donevayn, Katherine, pardon, [illegible].
Donevian, co. Kerry, [illegible].
Donfeighe—Dunfeighe, King's co., [illegible], [illegible], [illegible].

Donfert—Donferte—Donfort. *See* Dunfert.
Donfeighe. *See* Donfeighe.
Dongan, Agnes, [illegible].
„ Genet, widow, [illegible].
„ (or Dungan), John, second engrosser of Exchequer, 1612, [illegible]; second remembrancer, [illegible], 4144, [illegible]; keeper of records in Dublin castle, 6414; cess., [illegible]; pardon, 1[illegible], [illegible]; plaintiff in a matrimonial suit, [illegible]; leases, [illegible]74, [illegible], 4014, [illegible]; surrender, [illegible]; a trustee, [illegible]; security, [illegible]; widow and heir, [illegible].
„ Margaret, grant of a wardship, [illegible].
„ Tho., pardon, [illegible].
„ Walter, son of John, wardship, [illegible].
„ Wm., clerk of first fruits, 6415, pardon, [illegible], [illegible].
„ Wm. *See* Parr., pardon, [illegible].
Dongane, Sir John, vicar of Castleknock, [illegible].
Dongane (co. Tip. ?), [illegible].
Dongannon, Hugh, baron of. *See* O'Neill, Hugh, and Tyrone, earl of.
Dongannon — Dongannstowne (Dongannstown), co. Car., [illegible], [illegible], [illegible].
Dongannston, co. Meath, 1[illegible], [illegible].
Dongannstowne. *See* Dongannston.
Dongara (co. Ros. ?), [illegible].
Dongarbrie, co. Mon., [illegible].
Dongarvan—Dongarvaine. *See* Dungarvan.
Dongavon, co. Cavan, [illegible].
Donginloge, co. Cork, [illegible].
Dongell (co. Kerry ?), [illegible].
Dongan, co. Ros., [illegible].
Dongennyn, baron of. *See* O'Neill, Hugh.
Donglas (Douglas, co. Cork), [illegible].
Dongolman—Dongolmane (Dungolman, co. Westm.), [illegible], [illegible].
Dongorin, co. Cav., [illegible].
Dongorny — Dongornie — Donnegowrne (Dungourney, co. Cork), [illegible], [illegible], [illegible]74, [illegible].
Dongory, co. Clare, 1[illegible].
Dongovin, co. Mon., [illegible].
Dongowin, co. Kilk., [illegible].
Dongowre, co. Tip., 1[illegible]; rectory, [illegible].
Dongyn. *See* Dongen, co. Meath.
Donhanyvee river, co. Down, [illegible].
Donhogan, co. Clare, [illegible].
Donhilorton, co. Louth, 1[illegible].
Donill. *See* Dunhill.
Donill, Arable nine, pardon, 6[illegible].
„ Brain, pardon, [illegible].
„ (alias M'Donill), Edmund, pardon, [illegible].
„ Edm., pardon, [illegible].
„ Maurice, pardon, 1[illegible].
Donill, Omer, pardon, [illegible].
„ Rosa, pardon, 6[illegible].
„ Sorogho, pardon, [illegible].
„ Nich., pardon, [illegible].
„ (T). *See* O'Donell.
Donimg, Pair., pardon, [illegible].
Donina, co. Long., [illegible].
Doninahead, co. Cork, [illegible].
Doniston (co. Wat.?), [illegible].
Donivane, Dermot m'Ricard I., pardon, [illegible].
Donkenstrand (co. Sligo ?), [illegible].
Donkellie. *See* Dunkellie.
Donkellyn. *See* Dunkellin.
Donkerly, John. *See* Dunkerly.
Donkeron—Donkieran—Donkierain. *See* Dunkeran.
Donkipp. *See* Dunkypp.
Donkormik. *See* Dunkormuck.
Donlavan. *See* Dunlavan.
Donlogh, Tieg m'Donell, pardon, [illegible].
Donleky, co. Clare, [illegible].
Donler—Donlere. *See* Dunleru.
Donlevan. *See* Dunlevan.
Donlinyckney (Dunleckny), co. Car., rectory, 1[illegible].
Donlogh (co. Kerry ?), [illegible]74.
Donlogh (co. Kerry ?), [illegible].
Donlovan—Donlowan. *See* Dunlewan.
Donluce. *See* Dunluce.
Donlyer. *See* Dunlavore.
Donlyvore — Downelivore (Dunleever, co. Meath), [illegible], [illegible].
Donmaghan. *See* Dunmaghan.
Donmacknein, co. Mayo, [illegible].
Donmaghie. *See* Dunmaghan.
Donmahasnock — Donmahanacke — Donmahonacke—Donmahanocke—Donmahonacke (Dunmanoge or Mounmohonnock, co. Kild.), 1[illegible]; rectory, [illegible], 11[illegible], 1[illegible], [illegible], [illegible].
Donmanagh, co. Dub., [illegible].
Donmayn—Donmaynn (Dunmain, co. Wex., 1[illegible]; rectory, 1[illegible].
Donmayne Uriell, co. Mon., 1[illegible].
Donmellan (co. Car. ?), [illegible].
Donmillen—Donmillen—Don Millin—Don Millen. *See* Dunmaylan.
Donmocoughe, Queen's co., [illegible].
Donmolchane, co. Louth, [illegible].
Donmone—Donmoone (co. Wat.), 1[illegible], [illegible].
Donmanway — Downemanowye — Downmanvey—Downemanvey — Downmanwy (Dunmanway, co. Cork), [illegible], [illegible], [illegible], [illegible], [illegible].
Donmones (*see* Donmone), 1[illegible].
Donmore. *See* Dunmore, co. Gal.
Donmore (Dunmore, co. Wat. ?), [illegible].
Donmore. *See* Dunmore, co. Kilk.

INDEX TO FIANTS.—ELIZABETH.

Dunmore (co. Meath ?), [illegible].
Dunmore M'Orysh... See Dunmore, co. [illegible].
Dunmore, co. [illegible], [illegible].
Dunmow—Dunmowe, co. Meath, [illegible], [illegible], [illegible].
Dunmowe, co. Westm. (Dunmowe in [illegible]), [illegible], [illegible].
Donnoylin—Donnaulin. See [illegible].
Donnuhul. See Donnhulo.
Donnaghmore in Infany (Donaghmore, co. Meath), rectory, [illegible].
Donnaghmore. See Donaghmore, co. Kilk.
Donnaghmore. See Donaghmore, co. Cork.
Donnaghmore (see Dunmore), co. Meath, [illegible].
Donnaghmore (Donaghmore, co. Tip.), [illegible].
Donnaghstown, co. Meath, [illegible].
Donnalmanagh — Donnalmanagh. See Donnalmanagh.
Donnakirne—Donnakirne. See Donnakirne.
Dunnamon (Dunamon), co. [illegible], [illegible].
Donnamore. See Donaghmore.
Dunnamore, co. Tip., [illegible].
Donnamore. See Donamore, co. Westm.
Donnamoon (co. Cork ?), [illegible].
Donnanaghdadle. See Donnanaghdadle.
Donnanghmore (Dunmore), co. Wex., [illegible].
Donnaughdadle — Donnaughdadle, co. Kild., [illegible], [illegible].
Donnanny, co. Meath, [illegible].
Donnavan, Teige m'Dermod, pardon, [illegible].
Donne, Arte oge fitz Arte, pardon, [illegible].
Donnell fitz William, pardon, [illegible].
James, pardon, [illegible].
Johanna ny, pardon, [illegible].
John, pardon, [illegible].
Morrogh, pardon, [illegible].
Morrough m'William, pardon, [illegible].
Wm., master doctor, [illegible]; [illegible] interpreter, [illegible].
Wm. m'Moriertagh oge, pardon, [illegible].
Donnamore, in Clanrickard, [illegible].
Donnegarvan. See Dungarvan.
Donnelane, John, pardon, [illegible].
Donnell, Ellen ny, pardon, [illegible].
" Katherine fitzey, pardon, [illegible].
" James, pardon, [illegible], [illegible].
Mary ny, pardon, [illegible].
Owen m'Owen I., pardon, [illegible].
Shilly ny Phelemie V., pardon, [illegible].
Donnell, co. Sligo, [illegible].
Donnemore, co. Mayo, [illegible].
Donnemy (co. Cav. ?), [illegible].
Donnehanagh, co. Tip., [illegible].
Donnelleston, [illegible].
Donnerallinge, co. Cork, [illegible].
Donngarvan. See Dungarvan.
Donnghill. See Dunhill.
Donnhill, Mary, pardon, [illegible].
Donnillen, co. Meath, [illegible].
Donnimoule (co. Kerry ?), [illegible].
Donnough, Conor ny, pardon, [illegible].
Donnough oge, attainted, [illegible].
Donnoghe, Thos., [illegible].
Donnoghue, [illegible].
Donnoghowe, Awliffe m'Shane I., pardon, [illegible].
Donnoghowe, Fynin m'Donell I., pardon, [illegible].
Donnor, Darby, pardon, [illegible].
Donnora, co. Louth, [illegible].
Donnore. See Donowre, co. Meath.
Donnore, co. Wex., [illegible].
Donnough, Fynyely ny, pardon, [illegible].
Donnore, co. Meath, [illegible].
Donnowre—Donnowre. See Donnowre.
Donnugmore, co. Cork, [illegible].
Donnygall co. See Donegal.
Donnymale, co. Mayo, [illegible].
Donnym (co. Meath ?), [illegible].
Donoghue, Margaret ny, pardon, [illegible].
Donogh, Alison, pardon, [illegible].
" Donell m'Donnogh ny, pardon, [illegible].
" Donell m'Fynyn, pardon, [illegible].
" Dorren ny, pardon, [illegible].
" Ellen ny, pardon, [illegible], [illegible].
" Giles ny, pardon, [illegible].
" Honora ny, pardon, [illegible], [illegible].
" Joanna, pardon, [illegible].
" Katherine ny, pardon, [illegible].
" Margaret ny, pardon, [illegible], [illegible], [illegible].
" Rich., pardon, [illegible].
" Onora ny, pardon, [illegible].
" Rosse ny, pardon, [illegible], [illegible].
" Sawe ny, pardon, [illegible].
Donoghowe, Choghour m'Rory I., pardon, [illegible].
Donoghowe alias O'Donoghowe, Phelim m'Felim, pardon, [illegible].
Donoghe, Mary ny Vicar ny, pardon, [illegible].
Donoghe moyle, attainted, [illegible].
Donoghe, John m'Shane I., pardon, [illegible].
Donoghmore (co. Cork ?), [illegible].
Donoghill, co. Tip., [illegible].
Donogh Lynaghe, Thos., pardon, [illegible].
Donoghhyll—Donoghill, co. Tip., [illegible], [illegible].
Donoghmore, co. Cork, [illegible], [illegible].
Donoghmore (co. Leit. ?), [illegible], [illegible].
Donoghue, Ellen ny, pardon, [illegible].
" Onory ny, pardon, [illegible].
" Honor ny, pardon, [illegible].
Katherine ny, pardon, [illegible].
Margaret ny, pardon, [illegible].
Onora ny Shane I., pardon, [illegible].

Donaghu, Shily nyne Donill I., pardon, 6156.
Wm., pardon, 6469.
" (I. or Y.). See O'Donoghue.
Donaghue, Anstace nyne, pardon, 6482.
Donagh pen, Ellin ny, pardon, 6484.
Donagh oge, Katherine nyn, pardon, 6561.
Donaghow (T.). See O'Donoghue.
Donaghowe, Onory ny, pardon, 4896.
Donaghowe, Shillie ne Fynine I., pardon, 4884.
Donagh riaughe, indenture, 4996.
Donaghu, Rorie m'Conogher I., pardon, 4466.
Donagowne, co. Meath, 3404.
Donaskill, co. Tip., rectory, 305, 3372, 4166.
" See also Downeghalle.
Donchowe, Awlife m'Conogher I., pardon, 6768.
Donoman (Dunmanon), co. Gal., 4521.
Donore, co. Westm. See Donowre, Downore.
Donardaryne (co. Wat.?), 458.
Donortie, Philip m'Donell I., pardon, 4664.
Donavan (I.). See O'Donovan.
Donowre, co. Meath, 4146.
Donower — Donowen. See Donowre, co. Westm.
Donowre—Donnowre, co. Kild., 3804, 4917, 5967.
Donowre, Oldtown of (co. Kild.?), 4211.
Donowre—Dunnowe—Dunnowre, co. Meath, 598, 598, 4144, 4461, 5186, 5489.
Donowre — Donnowre — Donowre — Donower — Donower — Dunore — Dunowre (Donore), co. Westm., 1412, 1485, 1672, 1686, 2117, 2271, 2842, 3040, 3386, 3186, 3389, 3890, 4151, 4288, 4279, 4462, 5701, 5267, 5810, 6071, 6778.
Donrybrand (co. Ferm.?), 6602.
Donsaghlin—Donsaghlyn. See Dunshaughlin.
Donsallagh (Donsallagh), co. Clare?), 5681.
Donsandle—Donsandard, co. Gal., 3464, 2185.
Donsany—Donsayne. See Dunsany.
Donserle, co. Kild., 3484.
Donshaghlan — Donshaglan — Donshaghlin — Donshalen — Donshalane — Donsaghlin. See Dunshaughlin.
Donsoghly — Donsoghlaye — Donsoughley, See Dunsoghly.
Donsaak. See Dunsinke.
Dontaike, co. Wat., 3122.
Donugill ba Menagh (Donoughile, co. Kilk.), 3798.
Dunvellyn, co. Lim., 2787.
Donvoule, co. Sligo, 4866.
Donygan (co. Westm.?), 5663.
Dooyll, James fitzWm., pardon, 5899.
Odo, son of John Y., English liberty, 177.
Mary ny, pardon, 5361.
" Walter fitzWm., pardon, 4896.
Doonyne (co. Rosc.?), 5464.
Dorayne (co. Wat.?), 5165.
Doo (perhaps Dowth), co. Meath, 865.
Doowry, Queen's co. See Dowrery, Dowrey.
Dopuarrig, co. Kerry. See Downearrigg, Downe Carrig, Dullcarrig.
Dorsnakeen, co. Lim. See Doukeilen.
Doudo, Honora roogh ny, pardon, 5618.
Dooky Khudy. See Tuohy bhudy.
Doohyle, co. Lim. See Dolroll.
Doolagh, co. Dub. See Dolaugh.
Doolydown, co. Meath. See Dowlydowne.
Doon, co. Lim. See Dunlehy.
Doon, King's co. See Dowyne.
Doonally, co. Sligo. See Downally.
Doonfullen, co. Sligo. See Downefullan.
Doonamona, co. Westm. See Downamona.
Doonamoyntane, co. Kerry. See Downemoyntane.
Doonass, co. Clare. See Annaghaneen, Donassy, Downass.
Doonbeg, co. Clare. See Downbegg.
Doonbolgee, co. Lim. See Dunboleen.
Dooncahic, co. Lim. See Down Kahicy.
Dooncon, co. Lim. See Downin, Downyn.
Doonell, co. Sligo, 5963.
Dooneakey (co. Clare?), 6542.
Doondeasy, co. Mayo. See Downeasey.
Doonfin, co. Sligo. See Downefin, Downfin.
Doonkinroain (co. Sligo?), 5963.
Doonkapha (co. Kerry?), 2963.
Doonfionnain (co. Sligo?), 5663.
Doonbonn (co. Sligo?), 6654.
Doonalynn (co. Sligo), 5682.
Doonmacfelim, co. Clare. See Downemacfelym.
Doonmo'keeadoo (co. Sligo?), 5604.
Doonamonie (Doonamona?), co. Westm., 6591.
Doonnagore, co. Clare. See Dunnaugeare, Downnagarr.
Doonogan, co. Clare. See Downogan.
Doonsallagh, co. Clare. See Donsallagh.
Doony, co. Cork. See Downyn, Downyn.
Doone yeboly (co. Sligo), 5663.
Dooreyny, co. Sligo. See Dowrosheyne.
Doopark, Mellifont, co. Louth, 530, 3671.
Doores, King's co., 2178.
Doorue (co. Lim.?), 5481.
Dooway, co. Gal. See Clottow Durable.
Doorus, co. Gal. See Dowrys.
Dorl. Inginn, co. Lim., 4078.
Doran, Donell m'Neile, pardon, 3064.
" John, pardon, 4117.
Dorane, Mulmo m'Owen I., pardon, 2612.
Dorehy, co. Kerry, 6325.
Doreyne, co. Westm., 1706.
Dorby, Royne ny, pardon, 5618.
Dorelown, co. Meath, 5683.
Dorellam (co. Sligo?), 6963.
Dorlognan. See Dorrylorkan.
Durulyn (Dorrylehan), co. Sligo, 6663.

INDEX TO FIANTS—ELIZABETH.

Doran [illegible], pardon, [illegible].
Dorernas moor, Queen's co., [illegible].
Doremlorogh, King's co., [illegible].
Dorfingill church (now Kilpatrick, co. Westm.), 6797.
Dorgh, Donell, pardon, [illegible].
Dorho (King's co.), [illegible].
Dorhous, co. Meath, [illegible].
Dorio, More ny, pardon, [illegible].
Dorive alias O'Ryordane, Dermod, pardon, [illegible].
Dormer—Dormor, George, justice of liberty of Wexford, [illegible], [illegible]; commissions, [illegible], [illegible], [illegible].
„ Peter, clerk of crown and peace, co. Kilkenny, &c., [illegible], [illegible], co. Cork &c., [illegible], [illegible], Queen's co., [illegible]; pardon, [illegible].
„ Peter, clerk, pardon, [illegible], [illegible], [illegible], [illegible].
„ Walter, pardon, [illegible].
„ William, [illegible].
Dormiskell (co. Westm. ?), rectory, [illegible].
Dormoghe, Queen's co., [illegible].
Dormollen, co. Kild., [illegible].
Dormor. See Dormer.
Dormore, co. Westm., [illegible].
Dormoyle (Derrymoyle ?), Queen's co., [illegible].
Dornyngn, John and Catherine, [illegible].
Doro. See Durrow.
Dorologhe (Dorradagh, co. Lim.), [illegible], [illegible].
Dorarow, Thos., pardon, [illegible].
Dorogham, Wm. FitzGerald, pardon, [illegible].
Doroghe, Henry, pardon, [illegible], [illegible].
Doroghnaghmore, [illegible].
Doroghe alias M'Owen, Donell, pardon, [illegible].
Doromoone (co. Cork ?), [illegible].
Doromoyra. See Durrow, King's co.
Doroughow, Donell, pardon, [illegible].
Dorow—Dorowe. See Durrow, King's co.
Dorran, the, (co. Car. or Wex.), [illegible].
Dorran, John, authority to impress hay, [illegible].
Dorre, Wm., alias Baker, [illegible].
Dorre (co. Leit. ?), [illegible].
Dorre, co. Tip., [illegible].
Dorreghie, Ellyn ny, pardon, [illegible].
Dorrehede (co. Kilk. ?), [illegible].
Dorrelenkan. See Derrylenkan.
Dorrhe, co. Tip. See Dorroghe.
Dorrie, Margaret, pardon, [illegible].
Dorrie, Thos. oge, pardon, [illegible].
Dorrogh, Edm., pardon, [illegible].
Dorroghane, alias M'Inerick, Teige, pardon, [illegible].
Dorroghe—Dorroghen—Durhen (Dorrha), co. Tip., [illegible]; vicarage [illegible], [illegible].
Dorroly, co. Long., [illegible].
Dorrow—Dorrowe. See Durrow.
Dorry, co. Kild., [illegible].
Dorryah (Durrah ?), co. Lim., [illegible].
Dorrymakyllie, [illegible].
Dorsees, island of (Dursey island, co. Cork), [illegible].
Dorsetshire, undertakers from, for Munster lands, [illegible], persons from, [illegible].
Dorsye, James, pardon, [illegible].
Dortkierrye, co. Kerry, [illegible].
Dorycloma. See Derryclowny.
Dorygawne, co. Long., [illegible].
Dorynn, John m'Donogh Y, pardon, [illegible].
Dorwelomon. See Diswelston.
Dossle, Evelin ne, pardon, [illegible].
Doubal—Doudall. See Dowdall.
Douf, James, pardon, [illegible].
Dougaston (Dungarstown, co. Carlow), [illegible].
Dough castle, co. Clare. See Doweghyconnoghor.
Doughell, John fitz Wm., pardon, [illegible].
Doughyconoghor—Dough (Dough), co. Clare, [illegible]; manor, [illegible].
„ barony (Corcomroe), [illegible]; constable of, [illegible].
Douglas. See Dowglas.
Douglas, Morice m'Owen Y, pardon, [illegible].
Douhall (Duhallow ?), co. Cork, [illegible].
Doules (co. Kerry ?), [illegible].
Doulenton, co. Meath, [illegible].
Doumlaclan, co. Cav., [illegible].
Doun (co. Lim. ?), [illegible].
Doundalke. See Dundalk.
Dounden, Peter, pardon, [illegible].
Doundowne, Richard, [illegible].
Dounegarvan—Doungarvane. See Dungarvan.
Dounglee (co. Donegal), [illegible].
Dounkeran. See Dunkeran.
Dounkerley, John. See Dunkerly.
Dounkyne. See Dunkyne.
Dounkyne (Dunquin ?), co. Kerry, [illegible].
Dounnogurr (Doonnagore), co. Clare, [illegible].
Dounmoilin, co. Lim., [illegible].
Dounsaney. See Dunsany.
Dounshaghlin. See Dunshaghlin.
Dounye, Donne m'Wm. m'Dermod, pardon, [illegible].
Dourley, Donell m'Shane Y, (O'Dunlevy), pardon, [illegible].
Douske—Douske—Dusk (Graiguenamanagh), co. Kilk., [illegible], [illegible].
„ abbey, leased, [illegible]; granted, [illegible]; possessions granted, [illegible].
Douth. See Dowth.
Dovea—Dove, co. Tip., [illegible], [illegible], [illegible].

INDEX TO FIANTS—ELIZABETH.

Dovepark, in Mellifont, co. Louth, [illegible].
Dowin, alias Morinaagh, Donla ny, [illegible].
Down (Dungell), co. Kerry, [illegible], [illegible], [illegible], [illegible]; rectory, [illegible].
Downganilla, co. Wat., [illegible].
Downge, Morris, pardon, [illegible].
Downgh island (co. Donegal), [illegible].
Downgh ne lely, co. Lim. or Cork, [illegible].
Downglaconnoghor (Dongis castle—the barony of Corcomroe), co. Clare, [illegible].
Dowaile (co. Mon. ?), [illegible].
Dowall, Shane m'Mylish, pardon, [illegible].
Dowelle—Dowallie. See Dowally.
Dowallie, co. Lim., [illegible].
Dowally—Dowalle—Dowallie (Dunkilowry), co. Cork, [illegible], [illegible], [illegible]; lord and captain of, [illegible].
Dowan, Mahown and Wm. m'Tho. I., pardon, [illegible].
Dowane, Wm. A., pardon, [illegible].
Dowanston—Dowanstowne, co. Meath, [illegible], [illegible].
Dowanston (Downestown), co. Meath, [illegible].
Dowanston, co. Meath, [illegible].
Dowarry (Doairy ?), Queen's co., [illegible], [illegible].
Dowayne, Joanna or Jane, [illegible].
Dowdde (or Dowdal) boy, pardon, [illegible].
Dowarey (co. Donegal), [illegible].
Downrolighan, co. Mayo, [illegible].
Dowdale, Patr. fitz Walter, pardon, [illegible].
Dowdall, Christopher, pardon, [illegible], [illegible].
Anne, pardon, [illegible].
Christopher, constitution, [illegible], [illegible]; wardship of his heir, [illegible].
Henry, land in Kilmainham, [illegible].
George, wardship of his heir, [illegible].
Henry, pardon, [illegible], [illegible].
—Dowdal—Dowdall—Dowdalle—Dodall, James, afterwards knight, queen's or principal solicitor, [illegible], [illegible]; second justice, Queen's Bench, [illegible], [illegible], [illegible]; chief justice, [illegible], [illegible]; chief commissioner of Munster, [illegible], [illegible]; oath of supremacy, [illegible]; commissions, [illegible]; services in court of Castle Chamber, [illegible]; leases, [illegible], [illegible]; pension, [illegible]; alienations, [illegible].
John, pardon, [illegible].
sir John, commission, [illegible].
Katherine, pardon, [illegible].
Patrick, citizen of Dublin, [illegible].
Patrick, pardon, [illegible].
Patrick, engrosser, Exchequer, [illegible].
Dowdall—Patrick (of Termonfeckin), wardship, [illegible]; commissions, [illegible], [illegible].
" Patr., alderman; Dublin, [illegible].
" Rich., pardon, [illegible].
" Rob., chief justice, Common Pleas, temp. Henry VI., [illegible].
" Rob., pardon, [illegible].
" Rob., [illegible], justice, his house, [illegible].
" Stephen, [illegible].
" Stephen, pardon, [illegible], [illegible].
" Thomas, pardon, [illegible].
" Walter, wardship, [illegible].
Dowde, Mary ny, pardon, [illegible].
Dowdestown (Dowdestown ?), co. Meath, [illegible].
Dowdeston—Dowdestowne—Dowdlaton (Dowdstown), co. Louth, [illegible], [illegible], [illegible], [illegible].
Dowdey, John m'Conoghor I., pardon, [illegible].
Dowding, Rich., pardon, [illegible].
Dowdinge, James, pardon, [illegible].
Dowdingeston—Dowdingestowne, co. Kild., [illegible]; rectory, [illegible].
Dowdingston. See Dowdinston.
Dowdingston, co. Kild., [illegible].
Dowdinston—Dowdingeston (Dowdingstown, co. Kild.), [illegible], [illegible].
Dowdiston (see Dowdeston), [illegible].
Dowdstown, co. Louth. See **Dowdeston**, Dowdleston.
Dowdstown, co. Meath. See **Dowanston.**
Dowdrall, Owen, [illegible].
Dowdy, Patr., pardon, [illegible].
Dowgonarig, co. Cork (Doonarrig, co. Kerry ?), [illegible].
Dowdall. See Dowdall, James.
Dowerynshan, Furlone, pardon, [illegible].
Dowgh, co. Kild., [illegible].
Dowell, co. Tip., [illegible].
Dowell, John, pardon, [illegible].
" John m'Connoghor Y., pardon, [illegible].
" Morinagh m'Teige I., pardon, [illegible].
Dowellesion (Dowdstown, co. Louth, see [illegible]), [illegible].
Dowelongan (in Leix ?), [illegible].
Dowelphin (Dowlin ?), co. Lim., [illegible].
Dowen, co. Mon., [illegible].
Dowen, Conoghor, alias Conoghor oge, pardon, [illegible].
Dowes, co. Ross. or Gal., [illegible].
Doweston, church of (Dowdstown, co. Meath ?), [illegible].
Dowesth, co. Meath, [illegible].
Dowghil, co. Cork, [illegible].
Dowgan, Cornell, pardon, [illegible].
" Henry, pardon, [illegible].
Honor ny, pardon, [illegible].
John, pardon, [illegible].
Morough, [illegible].
Tho., pardon, [illegible].
William, pardon, [illegible].

Dowgane, Donell m'Donogho I, pardon, [illegible]
" John, pardon, 6515.
" Shylie, pardon, 6516
Dowgannion, co. Car., 1[illegible]
Dowganstoe (Duncannstown, co. Car.), [illegible]
Dowgara (co. Ross.?), [illegible]
Dowgeston, co. Meath, [illegible]
Dowgenstown, co. Meath, [illegible]
Dowgh. See Donaghyouneagher.
Dowgh, co. Clare, [illegible]
Dowghcyno, co. Sligo, 6490.
Dowghill, co. Lim. or Cork, [illegible]
Dowghyouneagher. See Doughyouneagher.
Dowglas—Douglas (Douglass), co. Cork, [illegible], 6515.
Dowglas, river (Douglass), Queen's co., [illegible]
Dowglas mill, Cork, [illegible]
Dowglas yornagha, near Cork city, [illegible]
Dowglasse, John, pardon, 1671.
Dowgrell, co. Tip. or Lim., [illegible]
Dowgulloe (co. Lim.?), [illegible]
Dowgwilliam, [illegible]
Dowgyn, Wm., pardon, [illegible]
Dowhanry (co. Tip.?), 4122.
Dowhaile (co. Mon.?), [illegible]
Dowharthe, Rich., pardon, [illegible]
Dowie, Katherine alis Wm. I, pardon, [illegible]
Dowille, co. Cork, [illegible]
Dowklonan, co. Long., [illegible]
Dowlagh, Brian, pardon, [illegible]
" John, pardon, 5616.
" Tirrelagh m'Brien, pardon, [illegible]
Dowlagho, Owen, pardon, [illegible]
" Teige, pardon, [illegible]
Dowlan, Rob., [illegible]
" Shane A., pardon, [illegible]
Dowle, Phelim oge, pardon, [illegible]
Dowlen (co. Lim.?), [illegible]
Dowles, Dermod m'Morris Y, and others of name, pardon, 6763.
Dowles, Rich., pardon, 3177.
Dowlerevagh (co. Gal.?), 4874.
Dowleston (Dowlystown, co. Meath), [illegible]
Dowley—Dowly:
" Dermicius, [illegible]
" John, pardon, 1617, [illegible], [illegible]
" Hugh, pardon, 611, 1316, 1617.
" Phillip, pardon, [illegible]
" Richard, pardon, [illegible], [illegible], [illegible]
" Thos., pardon, [illegible], [illegible]
" William, pardon, 1617.
Dowlfyn (co. Gal.?), [illegible]
Dowlie, Donell m'Shane m'Donell I, pardon, [illegible]
Dowlie, Shane reagh m'Dermod, pardon, [illegible]
Dowlian, Owen m'Teig m'Donell, pardon, [illegible]
Dowlin, co. Kild., [illegible]
Dowlin, Maurice, pardon, [illegible]
Dowline, Geoffrey, pardon, [illegible]
Dowling, Thady, vice-custos of spiritualities of Leighlin diocese, [illegible]
Dowlinge, Donald, clerk, Rosses, [illegible]
" John, pardon, [illegible]
" Rich., pardon, [illegible]
" Shane, pardon, [illegible]
Dowlly, Elinor fits Morris, pardon, [illegible]
Dowly, John, pardon. See Dowley.
Dowlyng, Hugh, homicide of, [illegible]
Dowmanis (co. Cork?) [illegible]
Down—Downe (Downpatrick), co. Down, [illegible]
" rectory, [illegible], [illegible], [illegible]
" monastery of S. Patrick, possessions leased, [illegible]
" house of nuns, possessions leased, [illegible]
" and Connor, bishop, Eugene Magennis, pardon, 71, 182.
" " " Hugh (Allen), com., [illegible]
" " " John, presentations to benefices, [illegible], [illegible]
" " " Hugh Hampton, appointed, [illegible]
Down county, commission to survey and set out the county, 1425, 1730; com. to inquire of lands of earl of Kildare in, [illegible]; martial law, [illegible], 1159, 1728, [illegible], [illegible], [illegible], [illegible], [illegible], [illegible], [illegible]; pardons in, [illegible], 6711, [illegible]
" " sheriff, 1728, [illegible], [illegible], [illegible], [illegible], [illegible]
" " clerk of the crown, &c., [illegible], [illegible], [illegible], [illegible]
Down, King's co. See Dowan, Doyne.
Down—Downe (co. Tip. or Lim.), [illegible], [illegible], [illegible], [illegible], [illegible]
Down—Downe, Little (co. Westm.?), [illegible], [illegible]
Down, Conner, pardon, [illegible]
" Dermod, pardon, [illegible]
Downaghmore. See Donaghmore.
Downarthmore (co. Tip.?), [illegible]
Downaske (co. Lim. or Clare), [illegible]
Downally — Downally (Donally?), co. Sligo, [illegible], [illegible]
Downally, co. Tip., [illegible]
Downamona (Dunamona co. Lim.), [illegible]
Downamona (co. Mayo?), [illegible]
Downan (co. Car.?), 148
Downany, [illegible]
Downpatrick (Downpatrick in par. Kilbride?), co. Mayo, [illegible], [illegible]
Downarum (co. Sligo?), [illegible]

INDEX TO FIANTS—ELIZABETH.

Downanac — Downanea — Downeaye — Downeaseo (Doonass, co. Clare), [illegible], 6781; castle, [illegible], 6781.
Downawna, co. Wex., [illegible].
Downbaheneo (Dunlahane? co. Cork), [illegible].
Downbally—Downbaillye, co. Gal., [illegible], [illegible].
Downbeneos. See Dunboman.
Downboge — Downboge (Doonbeg?), co. Clare, 6781; castle, 6781.
Downbill, (Dunbell), co. Kilk., 494; rectory, [illegible].
Downbollig—Downcolbollig—Downcboilloy—Downbowlogy (Dunbolloge, co. Cork), [illegible], [illegible], 6781; rectory, [illegible].
Downbrin, [illegible].
Downbrowen (co. Kerry?), [illegible], [illegible].
Downcleuninrahne (Doongidsirainu), co. Sligo, [illegible].
Downcomarche (co. Sligo?), [illegible].
Downdamagh (Dundamagh?), co. Mon., ironmaster, granted, [illegible].
Downdaniel, co. Cork. See Dundaniel.
Downdarykeo—Downdaroyrick—Downderkeo (Dundarirke), co. Cork, [illegible], [illegible], [illegible].
Downdorewe (Dundorrow), co. Cork, [illegible].
Downe, [illegible].
Downe, Donagh, pardon, [illegible].
Downe, John, pardon, [illegible].
Downe, co. Cav., [illegible].
Downe (co. Clare?), [illegible].
Downe (co. Cork?), [illegible], [illegible].
Downe, co. Cork, churchyard, [illegible], [illegible].
Downe. See Down, co. Down.
Downe, co. Gal., [illegible], [illegible], [illegible], [illegible], [illegible].
Downe (Down), King's co., [illegible], [illegible].
Downe, Queen's co., [illegible], [illegible].
Downe. See Down, co. Tip.
Downe abbey, co. Wex., leased, [illegible], [illegible], [illegible], [illegible], [illegible].
Downe (co. Wick.), [illegible].
Downe, Little (see Down), co. Westm., [illegible].
Downeally (see Downelly), [illegible].
Downeame, [illegible].
Downeame castle (see Downame), [illegible].
Downeballagh, co. Gal., [illegible].
Downebally, co. Ros., [illegible].
Downebracon—Downebeokola—Downebraney—Downebekhane. See Dunlanna.
Downeboge (co. Cork?), [illegible].
Downebollig — Downebolloy — Downebowlogy. See Downbollig.
Downeboy, co. Cork, [illegible].
Downe Carrig (Doncarrig, co. Kerry?), [illegible].
Downeboys—Downeonky (Doonyary), co. Sligo, [illegible], [illegible].
Downe Cormocke. See Dunmarmock.
Downedaeure — Downedaniar — Downedanyre (co. Cork?), [illegible], [illegible].
Downedarane (Dunlavane), co. Cav., [illegible].
Downederoyrick. See Downdarykeo.
Downedondy (Dundondy?), co. Cork, [illegible].
Downedorisko. See Downdarykeo.
Downedowrick, co. Cork, [illegible].
Downedlin—Downedlyn (Dounllin, co. Sligo), [illegible], [illegible].
Downegall—Downegale—Downegynale—Downegall (Dunegall, co. Cork), [illegible], [illegible], [illegible], [illegible].
Downegoryle, [illegible].
Downeghinane, co. Cork, [illegible].
Downeghamore (co. Lim.?), [illegible].
Downegonewylly (Dungonavillo), co. Lim., [illegible].
Downegore (co. Clare?), [illegible].
Downegorton, co. Cork, [illegible].
Downegrillin—Downegrillyne, co. Lim., 1531, [illegible].
Downehill. See Dunhill.
Downe Inchville (co. Clare?), [illegible].
Downe Irncy, [illegible].
Downe Kierane, co. Cork (Kerry?), [illegible].
Downekillen, baron of, pardon (see Clanricard, earl), [illegible].
Downe Kylly, co. Cork (Kerry?), [illegible].
Downeleyrane, co. Sligo, [illegible].
Downelokio (co. Clare?), [illegible].
Downelyvore. See Dunlyvore.
Downeloghie (co. Cork?), [illegible].
Downelowe (Dunlo, co. Gal.), [illegible].
Downeluage (co. Cork?), [illegible].
Downemamarraine (co. Gal.?), [illegible].
Downe m'More, co. Cork, [illegible].
Downe m'Namaras, co. Clare, [illegible].
Downem'oyne, co. Mayo, [illegible].
Downe M'Patrick (Downemipatrick), co. Cork, [illegible].
Downemaghan—Downemaghon—Downemaghin—Downemaniline. See Dunmaghon.
Downemaliane (Dunmaine?), co. Gal., [illegible], [illegible].
Downemanoo (co. Lim.?), [illegible].
Downemanoi (co. Lim.?), [illegible].
Downemanovyn. See Dunmanovy.
Downemanoh (Dunmanus? co. Cork), [illegible], [illegible].
Downemalane (Dunmanmane), co. Kerry, [illegible].
Downemanvoy (see Dunmanvoy), [illegible].
Downemayn (co. Lei.?), [illegible].
Downemayne (Dunnghmayne), co. Mon., [illegible].
Downemean (co. Tip.?), [illegible].
Downemeane (Dunmeane), co. Lim., [illegible].
Downemerhane, co. Cork, [illegible].
Downemokyne, co. Sligo, [illegible].
Downemoylya, co. Lim., [illegible].

INDEX TO FIANTS—ELIZABETH.

Dowamogan — Dowamogna (Dunamaggan ?), co. Kilk., 1987, 2208, 6728.
Dowanmolvihill (co. Cork ?), 6791.
Dowanpatte, co. Lim., 2873, 5121.
Dowanmanvoy. See Donmanvoy.
Dowanmore (see Dowanmore), 6617.
Dowanmorwan, co. Lim., 6417.
Dowanmoylin. See Dunmoylan.
Dowaoe. See Dowane.
Dowane, co. Kerry, 6158.
Dowane, co. Westm., 6767.
Dowanmaghe (Downing), co. Cork, 6467.
Dowane — Dowan (Dunany), co. Kild., rectory, 1667, 6790.
Dowanamale. See Downgall.
Dowanmagwreg, co. Clare, 6665.
Dowanmoheman, King's co., 884, 1854.
Downamie, co. Kild., 6146.
Dowanowrer in Kynaleheha, 726.
Dowanaymale. See Dowangall.
Downanwallo Iobarrin, co. Clare, 2665, 4574.
Dowanygnale (co. Cork ?), 6778.
Dowane Growmach (co. Tip. ?), 4828.
Dowane O'Mamon — Downe onamane — Dowmeana (Dunamon), co. Gal., 2334, 4119; manor, 3290.
Downequilian — Downequillan, co. Cork, 6287, 6423.
Downerail — Donerayle — Downerail — Downerabill — Downenayle — Downerayle — Downerail — Downerail (Doneraile), co. Cork, 526, 2944, 3040, 4111, 4166-7; rectory, 2940, 4282.
Downaryder, co. Cork, 6281.
Downeria, co. Gal., 6461.
Downerall. See Downerall.
Downeryine, co. Cork, 6792.
Downeandell. See Dunamdell.
Downeshallo — Downeshallye (co. Clare ?), 4478.
Downeslard. See Dunlalred.
Downestown, co. Meath. See Downestown.
Downealme (Doonalton), co. Sligo, 6484.
Downemllage (co. Cork ?), 6761.
Downey, Richard, English Sheriff, 681.
Downeyle, co. Sligo, 4485.
Downeynay (co. Mayo ?), 5788.
Downfin (Dunfin ?), co. Sligo, 5434.
Dowufearo — Dowulwarn, co. Sligo, 5441.
Dowgarr — Dowgarre (co. Mon. ?), 4728, 6428, 5447.
Dowgarvan. See Dungarvan, co. Kilk.
Dowgoghoe (Dungroha), co. Lim., 6782.
Dowgamyne (co. Westm. ?), 5481.
Dowgawcey (co. Gal. ?), 5228.
Dowgwary (co. Gal. ?), 4787.
Dowhill. See Dunhill.
Dowhisle, co. Sligo, 5434.
Dowigall. See Downegall.
Dowighmoe, co. Cork, 4741.
Dowilline (Dunmoylan ?), co. Lim., 3474.
Dowin (Doonoon), co. Lim., 4614.
Dowine (co. Cork ?), 6808.
Dowing, co. Cork. See Dowanmaghe.
Dowingto (co. Cork ?), 6463.
Dowinge (co. Kilk. ?), 1178.
Dowlinge (co. Cork ?), 4814.
Dowingen — Dowinan — Downyngen, co. Kild., 2884, 4464, 5434, 6349.
" rectory, 6721.
" vicar of, 6473.
Dowe Kelaine (Dunmaline), co. Lim., 3474.
Dowe Kelloe. See Dunkellin.
Dowekerran. See Dunkeran.
Dowekeiell — Dowelkeidill. See Dunkeelin.
Dowekypp, co. Lim., 6467.
Dowaley, Maurice, pardon, 6510.
Dowlogh (co. Kerry ?), 6576.
Dowlewan. See Dunlewan.
Dowalyn, co. Sligo, 5438.
Dowmarfallym — Dowmmacfallym — Dowmichfallam (Dunmacfelim), co. Clare, 3377, 4482, 4574.
Dowmakyrne (co. Mayo ?), 5462.
Dowmanamey (co. Clare ?), 4818.
Dowmanagnwick, co. Cork. See Downe M'Patrick, 5458.
Dowmanam (Dunamanan, co. Cork ?), 6701.
Dowmanowy. See Dunmoowey.
Dowmickfellum. See Dowmicafallym.
Dowmolte, co. Lim., 6167.
Dowmollin. See Dunmoylan.
Dowmangna. See Dowamogan.
Dowmaor. See Downmore, co. Clare.
Dowmmore, co. Cav., 6703.
Dowmore — Dowmor — Dowmore, co. Clare, 3477, 4417, 5784.
Dowmore. See Dunmore, co. Gal.
Dowmore. See Dunmore, co. Kilk.
Dowmore, co. Westm., 6767.
Dowmoylin — Dowmoylyn. See Dunmoylan.
Dowmarbe, co. Cork, 6488.
Dowmanartkle, co. Cork, 4494.
Downard, co. Wex., 2280.
Downageare (Doonagore), co. Clare, 4574.
Downanore (co. Clare or Gal. ?), 4548.
Downanvihill (co. Clare ?), 6624.
Downaor (Dunore, co. Westm. ?), 6213.
Downogan castle (Doonogan), co. Clare, 4762.
Downeghailo (Downhill, co. Tip. ?), 4468.
Downelee, co. Westm., 6288.
Downaman. See Downe O'Mamon.
Downamogna, co. Kilk., 428.
Downamoae (co. Mayo ?), 5434.
Downeyo (co. Westm. ?), 6888.
Downewrigg, co. Cork, 2348.

INDEX TO FIANTS—ELIZABETH.

Downpatrick, co. Down. See Down.
Downpatrick, co. Mayo. See Downpatrick.
Downralle—Downrall. See Downerall.
Downrien (co. Gal.), [illegible].
Downrydar, co. Cork. [illegible].
Downsaghlon. See Dunshaghlin.
Downskyagh (co. Tip. ?), [illegible].
Downvickburn, co. Gal. [illegible].
Downy, Ellinor ny, pardon, [illegible].
„ Teig m'Donell Y, pardon, [illegible].
„ Thady, pardon, [illegible].
Downye (Downy), co. Cork. [illegible].
Downyll. See Dunhill.
Downygrahmiddle, co. Clare, [illegible].
Downys—Downyne, co. Cork, [illegible], [illegible], [illegible], [illegible], [illegible], [illegible], [illegible], [illegible]; manor, [illegible], [illegible], [illegible].
Downys, co. Lim., [illegible].
Downys (Doonass), co. Lim., [illegible], [illegible].
Downys—Downyne, co. Ross., [illegible], [illegible].
Downyne. See Downys, co. Cork.
Downyne. See Downys, co. Ross.
Downyney (Doonfeeny, co. Mayo ?), [illegible].
Downynges. See Downings.
Downekeston—Dowekestown, co. Meath, [illegible], [illegible].
Downle or Dowble boy, [illegible].
Dowry (Downy), Queen's co., 1167, [illegible], [illegible].
Dowrath, co. Gal. or Mayo, [illegible].
Dowrcahible, co. Sligo, [illegible].
Dowres (Dourus), co. Gal., [illegible].
Dowrewarerwinshe, co. Gal., [illegible].
Dowrey, Donogh m., pardon, [illegible].
Dowrie, Dermott, master of hospital at Leighlin, [illegible].
Dowrishe, Walter, commission, [illegible].
Dowro (Durrow, King's co.), [illegible].
Dowrown, co. Wat., [illegible].
Dowry (co. Kild. ?), [illegible].
Dowrye or Dowryne, sir Edm., master of hospital at Leighlin, [illegible].
Dowsko (or Dowsk), [illegible].
Dowson, Arthur, [illegible].
Dowth—Douth—Dowthe, co. Meath, [illegible], [illegible], [illegible], [illegible], [illegible], [illegible]; rectory, [illegible], [illegible]. See also Due.
Dowymullin (co. Ferm. ?), [illegible].
Dowyn, King's co. or Meath, [illegible], [illegible].
Dowyne (or Dowrye), sir Edm., [illegible].
Doy, Thady, pardon, [illegible].
Doyare, co. Long., [illegible].
Doyle, Connor, pardon, [illegible].
„ Dennis, pardon, [illegible].
„ Laghlen, pardon, [illegible].
„ Tho., pardon, [illegible].
Doyle, co. Cork, [illegible].
Doyll, Tho., pardon, [illegible].
Doylle mullyn, Edmund, pardon, [illegible].
Doymaccono (co. Mayo ?), 4844.
Doymor (co. Mayo ?), 4844.
Doyn, James, [illegible].
„ John, pardon, [illegible].
„ John, [illegible].
„ Mahmury m'Brien, pardon, [illegible].
„ Patrick, clerk, Eng. liberty, [illegible].
„ Rich., pardon, [illegible].
„ Wm., pardon at suit of, [illegible]; Irish interpreter to the lord deputy, [illegible].
Doyne, Anstace ny, pardon, [illegible].
„ Brian, pardon, [illegible].
„ Daniel, pardon, [illegible].
„ Giles, pardon, [illegible].
„ James, pardon, [illegible], [illegible].
„ John, pardon, 1169, [illegible].
„ Mary, [illegible].
„ Walter, pardon, 1169, [illegible].
„ Wm., pardon, [illegible], [illegible].
Doyne (Down), King's co., 3167, [illegible].
Doyre, Graney ny, pardon, [illegible].
„ Morrys ny, pardon, [illegible].
„ Phillip, pardon, [illegible].
Doyvrye, Morgho, pardon, [illegible].
Dracoll. See Draycoll.
Draddie, James, pardon, [illegible].
„ Patr., pardon, [illegible].
Draelle, Morrice, priest, pardon, [illegible].
„ Patr., pardon, [illegible].
Draflorensho (Trusterragh ?), co. Gal., [illegible].
Dragane, co. Tip., [illegible].
Draicott—Draicoll. See Draycoll.
Drake, Alexander, pardon, [illegible].
„ Christopher, pardon, [illegible].
„ George, comm., [illegible]; pardon, [illegible], [illegible].
„ Garrett, pardon, [illegible].
„ Henry, pardon, [illegible].
„ John, pardon, [illegible], [illegible].
„ Oliver, pardon, [illegible].
„ Patr., pardon, [illegible].
„ Rich., pardon, 441.
„ Rob., pardon, [illegible], [illegible].
„ Walter, pardon, [illegible].
„ Wm., pardon, [illegible].
Drakerath, co. Meath, [illegible].
Drakeston—Drakestowne, co. Meath, [illegible], [illegible], [illegible], [illegible].
Drakevoye. See Dromaroy.
Dramalarwagh (co. Leit.), [illegible].
Dramkayo, co. Dub., rector of, [illegible].
Dramnabyer (co. Leit.), [illegible].
Drangan—Drangane—Drongan—Drongane, co. Tip., 847, [illegible], [illegible], [illegible], [illegible], [illegible], [illegible], [illegible], [illegible], [illegible], [illegible]; grant, [illegible], [illegible]; rectory, [illegible], [illegible].
Draper—Drapper, Rob., parson of Trim, pardon, [illegible], [illegible]; pardon at his suit, [illegible].
Draudrinagh (co. Gal. ?), [illegible].
Dravile, co. Cav., [illegible].

INDEX TO FIANTS—ELIZABETH.

Drawater, Conilaous, [illegible].
Drawght, co. Gal., [illegible].
Draycott — Draycot — Dracott — Draicot — Draicott, Henry, chief remembrancer, 23, 468, [illegible]; chancellor of the green wax of the Exchequer, 874, 1792, 2119; third baron of Exchequer, 472; master of the rolls, 804, [illegible], 1752; third baron of the Exchequer, 1446, [illegible]; treasurer of co. Wexford, [illegible]; commissions, [illegible], 468, 617, 672, 703–4, 762, [illegible], [illegible], 1437–8, 1634, [illegible]; licence of alienation, [illegible]; freedom from subsidy, 178; grant of lands, 163; surrender, 1149; lease [illegible]; licence to alien, 348; grant of a wardship, 484; licence to export wheat, 1737; pardon, 1752; wardship and livery to his heir, 5106, [illegible].
" John (afterwards sir John), son of Henry, wardship, [illegible]; livery, [illegible]; grant of a wardship, 5774; comm., [illegible].
Dreanagh, co. Kerry. See Drinagho.
Dreglin, James, pardon, [illegible].
Drehoiteniarny, co. Tip., [illegible].
Drelingo, Katherine, pardon, [illegible].
Drenanbraggie, co. Cork, [illegible].
Drennanstown (co. Kild. ?), [illegible].
Drenanagh. See Drennagh.
Dreomconnoghaue, co. Tip., [illegible].
Dreenagho (Drinagh), co. Cork, [illegible].
Dressan (co. Ross ?), 2454.
Drenkan, co. Tip., [illegible].
Dressilly, Fynass, pardon, [illegible].
Dress, English, to be worn, 474, [illegible].
Dressmine, co. Cork, rectory, [illegible].
Drett, Donogh ya, pardon, [illegible].
Drewys, Margaret, pardon, [illegible].
Drey'hode (co. Wex. ?), [illegible].
Dreymanston, co. Kild., [illegible].
Droyconagho (Drinanagh), co. Dub., [illegible].
Drialloneyn, co. Clare, [illegible].
Drilin—Drilon:
" James, pardon, [illegible].
" John, pardon, [illegible].
" Petre, pardon, [illegible].
" Wm., pardon, [illegible].
Drilling—Drillone—Dryling:
" James, pardon, [illegible].
" Peter or Piers, pardon, [illegible], [illegible], [illegible], [illegible].
Drimnaston, co. Kild., [illegible].
Drimo M'Voyran, co. Kilk., rectory, [illegible].
Drimnagh, co. Dub. See Dromnagh.
Drinagh, co. Cork. See Dreenagho.
Drinagho (Dreanagh), co. Kerry, [illegible].
Drinan (co. Cav. ?), [illegible].
Dringane, co. Tip., [illegible].
Drinishdayve (co. Ross ?), [illegible].
Drinmore, co. Westm. See Droynmore.
Drinnanstown, co. Kild. See Ballinbrinan.
Drinnie, Hotary ay, pardon, [illegible].
Driscoll, Tade m'Dermod Y. pardon, [illegible].
Drishagan, co. Gal., [illegible].
Drishaghan, co. Ross. See Drishighan.
Drishan. See Drishane.
Drishanbegg, near Youghal, [illegible].
Drishane—Drishan—Drishaler—Drisane—Drishann, co. Cork, [illegible], [illegible], [illegible], [illegible], [illegible], [illegible], [illegible], [illegible], [illegible].
Drishighan — Drysighan (Drishaghan, co. Ross), [illegible], [illegible].
Drisholle, Fynineu m'Donell, pardon, [illegible].
Driskell, Tade m'Conoghor, pardon, [illegible].
Drislortan, co. Cav., [illegible].
Drisnyn, co. Cork, [illegible].
Drissaghan, co. Gal., [illegible].
Drisshane. See Drishane.
Drissill, co. Cork, [illegible].
Drissne-Drishane. See Drishane.
Drisholke—Dryshoke—Dryssholke, co. Dub., [illegible], [illegible], [illegible].
Drissone (co. Cork ?), [illegible].
Drislan (co. Gal.), [illegible].
Drisleman (co. Louth ?), [illegible].
Drivagh, co. Cork, [illegible].
Dronney (co. Wat. ?), [illegible].
Droucht, co. Gal., [illegible].
Droughan, co. Tip., [illegible].
Drough, Donald, pardon, [illegible].
Drogheadd Ballanno, co. Gal., [illegible].
Droghailine (co. Cork ?), [illegible].
Drogheda — Droghedda — Drongheda — Drohada — Drohedagh — Drohydath — Tredagh, 77, 131, 218, [illegible], [illegible], [illegible], [illegible], [illegible], 1178, 2117, [illegible], [illegible]; fatal landing accident at, [illegible]; fair dated at, [illegible], [illegible]; similar privileges granted to other towns, [illegible], [illegible], [illegible]; Ulster chiefs treated with at, [illegible], [illegible], [illegible]; corn measure of, [illegible].
" mayor, commissions, [illegible], [illegible], [illegible], [illegible], [illegible], [illegible].
" mayor and commons, rent from, [illegible].
" mayor and sheriffs, comm., [illegible]; powers similar to, granted to other towns, [illegible], [illegible].
" sheriffs, pardon, [illegible].
" recorder, [illegible], [illegible], [illegible], [illegible], [illegible].

INDEX TO FIANTS—ELIZABETH.

Drogheda—town clerk, [illegible].
" coroner, [illegible], [illegible].
" alderman, [illegible], [illegible].
" merchants of, [illegible], [illegible], [illegible], [illegible], [illegible], [illegible].
" premises in, 247; leased, [illegible], [illegible], [illegible], [illegible], [illegible], [illegible]; granted, [illegible], [illegible], [illegible].
" hospital of S. John, [illegible].
" priory of the B. V. M. de Urso [illegible].
" parish of the B. V. M., [illegible], [illegible].
" parish of S. Peter, [illegible], [illegible].
" rectory of S. Mary, [illegible], [illegible].
" rectory of S. Peter, [illegible], [illegible].
" Bridge-street, [illegible], [illegible].
" Dyer gate, [illegible], [illegible].
" Fleash house, [illegible].
" our Lady Church, [illegible].
" Quay, [illegible], [illegible].
" S. Laurence gate, [illegible], [illegible], [illegible].
" S. Nicholas' church, [illegible], [illegible], [illegible].
" S. Saviour's church, [illegible], [illegible], [illegible].
" S. Saviour's quay, [illegible], [illegible], [illegible].
" Tolsell, [illegible], [illegible].
" West street, [illegible], [illegible], [illegible].
" port or haven, [illegible], [illegible], [illegible], [illegible]; export of wheat, [illegible], [illegible], [illegible], [illegible], [illegible]; monopoly of export of wool, &c., [illegible]; illegal exports, [illegible].
" customs leased, [illegible], [illegible], [illegible]; salary of Master of Rolls charged on, [illegible].
" wines discharged without paying duty, [illegible].
" wine impost leased, [illegible].
" customer and collector of customs, [illegible], [illegible].
" controller, [illegible], [illegible], [illegible], [illegible], [illegible], [illegible], [illegible], [illegible], [illegible], [illegible], [illegible], [illegible].
" supervisor, [illegible].
" searcher and gauger, [illegible], [illegible], [illegible], [illegible], [illegible], [illegible].
" collector of wine duty, [illegible], [illegible], [illegible], [illegible], [illegible], [illegible], [illegible], [illegible].
" controller of wine duty, [illegible], [illegible], [illegible], [illegible], [illegible], [illegible], [illegible].
" county of town, included in government of Ulster, [illegible].
" county of town, commission of peace, [illegible], [illegible], [illegible], [illegible], [illegible], [illegible], [illegible].
" county of town, clerk of the crown, [illegible], [illegible], [illegible], [illegible].
Drogheddia, [illegible].
Drogheddaniarny—Drohedaniarne—Drohidinefarny—Drohidinolarnyn, co. Tip., [illegible], [illegible], [illegible], [illegible], [illegible].
Droghid, Donell m'Teige in, pardon, [illegible].
Droghstroll, co. Louth, [illegible].
Drought—Droghie—Droghim. See Droughe, co. Gal.
Droghton (D'Loughtane), co. Wat., [illegible], [illegible].
Droghty, co. Gal., [illegible].
Drohanvagha (co. Rosc. ?), [illegible].
Drohada—Drohedagh. See Drogheda.
Drohedaniarne. See Droghedaniarny.
Drohidlynnaght, co. Cork, [illegible].
Drohidinolarny — Drohidinofearnye. See Droghedaniarny, co. Tipperary.
Drohydath. See Drogheda.
Droigher, Donogh m, pardon, [illegible].
Droimmonarke — Droimmarecke (Drumawark, co. Donegal), [illegible], [illegible].
Droimchallyn (co. Cav. ?), [illegible].
Droimchrein (Drumcrin, co. Cav. ?), [illegible].
Droimod (co. Leit. ?), [illegible].
Droin (King's co. ?), [illegible], [illegible].
Droimmarcke. See Droimmonarke.
Droin Dana (co. Donegal or Tyrone), [illegible].
Droimseran, co. Gal., [illegible].
Droinnagh (co. Westm. ?), [illegible].
Droica (co. Lim. ?), [illegible].
Drom, co. Long., [illegible].
Drom, co. Tip., [illegible], [illegible].
Drom, Wm., [illegible].
Drom, Wm. m'Shane, pardon, [illegible].
Dromacke (Drummuck), co. Mon., [illegible].
Dromadde — Dromaddye, co. Cork (see Dromaddie), [illegible], [illegible].
Dromadda, co. Cav., [illegible].
Dromaddagan (Dunmaddigan ?), co. Mon., [illegible].
Dromaddie—Dromadie—Dromady (Dromadda, co. Cork ?), [illegible], [illegible], [illegible], [illegible], [illegible], [illegible], [illegible].
Dromaddy (Drumavaddy ?), co. Mon., [illegible].
Dromaddye. See Dromadde, co. Cork.
Dromadie—Dromady. See Dromaddie.
Dromagh, co. Cork, [illegible], [illegible], [illegible], [illegible].
Dromaghgalvan (Drumagalvin), co. Mon., [illegible].
Dromahair — Dromaheir — Dromahar — Dromahier — Dromahir — Dromahire (Dromahairy), co. Leit., [illegible], [illegible], [illegible], [illegible], [illegible], [illegible]; manor, [illegible].
Dromaichoge — Dromaynhoge (Dromana), co. Wat., [illegible], [illegible].
Dromalain (co. Wat. ?), [illegible].
Dromaleanbane, co. Kerry, [illegible].
Dromalgagh in Ormany, [illegible].
Dromalgar (co. Rosc. or Sligo ?), [illegible].

INDEX TO FIANTS—ELIZABETH.

Dromalkan, co. Clare, 6617.
Dromallan (*see* Dromolan, co. Clare), 6716.
Dromalane, co. Mon., 4663.
Dromaltie (Dromalie, co. Lim.), 6474.
Dromana, co. Wat. *See* Dromany, Dromainbrye.
Dromane—Dromanie. *See* Dromany.
Dromanagh, co. Cork. *See* Dromyoyne.
Dromanaugh, 1312.
Dromannie (co. Ross.), 4692.
Dromanny (Drummany), co. Mon., 4648.
Dromany, 1254.
Dromany—Dromane—Dromanagh—Dromayne—Dromayny—Dromanie—Dromaany—Drommany (Dromana, co. Wat.), 77, 656-7, 634-5, 644, 1948, 2271-3, 2328-9, 3426, 3784, 3132, 4462, 4488, 4526, 4571, 5477, 6571, 6668, 6762.
baron of, Maurice Fitzgerald, created, 1946; created Viscount Decies, 1251. *See* Decies.
Dromaragh (Drumarah), co. Down, 6662.
Dromarekyn (Dromarparkie, co. Tip. ?), 6179.
Dromard—Dromarde—Dromarde—Dromarde (co. Leit. ?), 4785, 4794, 5428, 6441, 6746.
Dromard—Drummarde, co. Lim., 2376, 6171. 6183, 6178, 6487; castle and lands, 6172.
Dromard (co. Ross or Leit.), 6535.
Drom Arde magrall (co. Leit. ?), 4794.
Dromarde. *See* Dromard.
Dromardie (co. Leit. ?), 6746.
Dromargalias (Drummagavilla ?), co. Mon., 4691.
Dromarisse (co. Leit. ?), 6469.
Dromatroe (co. Gal. or Mayo ?), 6476.
Dromaraine—Dromarlin. *See* Drumaravlin.
Dromaryo in O'Kedrie, 6132.
Dromavaddy, co. Mon., 4618.
Dromavane, co. Mon., 4658.
Dromavile (Drumavoale), co. Mon., 4647.
Dromaynbrye (Dromana), co. Wat., 148.
Dromayne—Dromayny. *See* Dromany.
Drombanna (co. Lim. ?), 6170.
Dromban, co. Tip., 6344.
Drombanachar—Drumbanachar—Dromabanachar (Drumbanagher), co. Mon., 4603, 4688, 4678.
Drombane, co. Long., 4664.
Drombanny, co. Lim., 4623.
Drombany, co. Lim., 4582.
Drombaynne, co. Lim., 1541.
Drombayne (co. Tip. ?), 4667.
Drombanacher. *See* Drombanachar.
Drombeg (co. Cork ?), 2761.
Drombeg—Drombeagh—Drumoberry, co. Lim., 4568, 6444, 6478, 4603.
Drombeagh, co. Meath, 4688.
Drombior (Drumbore), co. Mon., 4667.
Drombo, co. Cav., 4687.
Dromboe (Drumboe), co. Mon., 4648.
Drombarisko (Drumbarish), co. Mon., 4624.
Drombrallen, co. Tip., 4688.
Drombrealle (Drumbreanlis ?), co. Leit., 4667.
Drombrislio (Drumbrislan), co. Mon., 4686.
Dromboughlake in Ulster, 1462.
Dromlbyne (co. Cav. ?), 4687.
Dromlbyrne (Drumbirn), co. Mon., 4673.
Drombyane, co. Mon., 4638.
Dromcahell—Dromcahill (Drumcall), co. Mon., 4623, 4648.
Dromcalpe—Dromcolalpe—Dromcoralpe (co. Leit. ?), 6468, 6762.
Dromcannan—Dromkannanc (Drumcannon), co. Wat., 1804; rectory, 4158.
Dromcassangho, co. Lim., 4647.
Dromcany (Westm. or King's co.), 6768.
Dromcar, co. Meath, rectory, 6718.
Dromcarfie, co. Cav., 4681.
Dromcarowne, co. Kerry, 4612, 6633.
Dromcarro, co. Cav., 4682.
Dromcaschell—Dromcashell. *See* Drumcashell.
Dromcatlan. *See* Dromcaw.
Dromcalpp. *See* Dromcalpe.
Dromchany, co. Mon., 4603.
Dromchanley (co. Cav. ?), 4678.
Dromchyne (co. Leit. ?), 4768.
Dromcleive—Dromo Cleve (Dromcliff), co. Clare, 4761, 4461.
Dromcliffe, co. Sligo, 4762.
Dromclogh (co. Cork ?), 6611, 6638. *See also* Dromo on Clabig.
Dromcolley—Drom Colly—Dromcowley (Drumcowly), King's co., 474, 1847, 6674.
Dromcora, co. Sligo, 5286, 6663.
Dromconlan, co. Cav., 6762.
Dromcorragh—Dromcorraigh—Dromcorraghe. *See* Dromcorraghe, co. Dub.
Dromcorraght (Drumcoralra), co. Mon., 4673.
Dromcorrane—Dromcorowe. *See* Dromcorraghe.
Dromcorraghe (co. Meath or Cav.), 4638.
Dromcowley. *See* Dromcolley.
Dromcroe—Dromcrore (Dromcrone), co. Westm., 648, 3844, 3886, 4161, 4316, 6661; rectory, 6616, 4868.
Dromcroy—Dromcroye (co. Leit. ?), 6463.
Dromcrumner, co. Cork. *See* Dromcrumyn.
Dromcurraghe. *See* Dromcorraghe.
Dromcurre, co. Wat., 4131, 4481.
Dromcurrel, co. Mon., 4673.
Dromd (*see* Dromud), 4441.
Dromdagowre, co. Kerry, 4132.
Dromdagrwand, co. Kerry, 4638.
Dromdaliege—Dromdaliege, co. Cork, [illegible], 4616.

INDEX TO FIANTS—ELIZABETH.

Drumdatophe (Drumdaff, co. Ross.), 1814, 6783.
Drumdaniel, co. Cork. *See* Drumadonell.
Drumdarragh, co. Leit., 4442.
Drumderrdrehs (co. Cork ?), 6764.
Drumderrick (co. Cork ?), 6764.
Drumdile—Drumdicle (Drumdool, co. Tip.), 4451, 6748.
Drumdona (co. Donegal ?), 5947.
Drumdowny (Drumdoney), co. Sligo, 4492.
Drumdowny, co. Cork, 3346, 3388, 5874.
Drumdownh, co. Cork. *See* Drumdaughbeggs, Drumdagher.
Drumdrasill, co. Cork. *See* Drowndrasell.
Drumdaughbegge (Drumdough), co. Cork, 5529.
Dromdyle (co. Tip. ?), 6764.
Drumdylly (co. Tip. ?), 6766.
Drume (co. Kilk. ?), 6794.
Drume, co. Tip., 4457, 6883, 6788.
Drumeran (co. Ferm. ?), 4818.
Drumcarmuse (co. Cork ?), 5666.
Dromeaniason (co. Leit. ?), 6446.
Dromeard, co. Cav., 4982.
Dromeardo. *See* Dromard.
Dromchany (co. Lim. ?), 6494.
Dromohany (Dromboy), co. Lim., [illegible].
Dromcrolpa. *See* Drumcolpe.
Dromacrowe, co. Cav., 4634.
Drome Clere. *See* Dromcleive.
Dromecrosygeanyne (Drumcaunig), co. Kerry, 6788.
Dromecrorwyre (Dromecunnear), co. Cork, [illegible].
Dromed, co. Cav., 4434.
Dromed—Dromd (co. Leit.), 4448, 4441-6.
Dromedaligo. *See* Dromdaliegs.
Dromedarvigo (co. Ferm. ?), 4818.
Dromede (Dromed), co. Kerry, rectory, 3946, 6172.
Dromede (co. Long. ?), 4902.
Dromedicle. *See* Dromdile.
Dromedogher (Dromdough ?), co. Cork, 4236.
Dromedonell (Dromdaniel), co. Cork, 6438.
Dromefeogh (Dromfeogh, co. Cork), 4384.
Dromegarif (Dromgarriff, co. Cork), 2384.
Dromegen, co. Cav., 4634.
Dromegrenn (Drumgrone ?), co. Mon., 6426.
Dromegryne (Dromgreany), co. Mon., 6494.
Dromekinnare, co. Leit., 6438.
Dromekire (co. Lim. ?), 6178.
Dromekinaghly, co. Long., 4982.
Drome Irish, co. Leit., 6438.
Dromekitern (Dromkeiran), co. Kerry, 6622.
Dromekayne (co. Lim. ?), 4384.
Dromekire (co. Lim. ?), 6438.
Dromekilrook, co. Kild., 1612, 6488.
Dromekyne, co. Kerry, 4278.
Dromekyne (co. Lim. ?), 6498.
Dromelahane (Dromelane, co. Armagh ?), 4608.
Dromelake. *See* Drumlaske.
Dromelakane (or Dromlochan) 4605.
Dromellagh (King's co. ?), 6101.
Dromeloghan. *See* Dromloughan.
Dromemarryne, co. Kerry, 4182.
Dromen (co. Wick.) 1045, 6268.
Dromen Orian (co. Lim. ?), 6494.
Dromene, co. Cav., 4682.
Dromene, co. Clare, 6616.
Dromeneerne, co. Clare, 6612.
Dromeneely—Dromeneolle (co. Cork ?), 6616.
Dromenafingles (co. Clare ?), 6612.
Dromenole (Drummoll), co. Mon., 4828.
Dromenmoleane, co. Kilk., 4288.
Dromenmagh, co. Mayo, rectory, 1404.
Dromentallo, co. Meath, 686.
Dromenmeolstie (co. Ross. ?), 4428.
Dromen ny feanan (co. Cork ?), 6616.
Drome on Clohig (perhaps Dromeclogh) co. Cork, 4438.
Dromerum (co. Leit. ?), 6438.
Dromeroll (Drumerroll), co. Mon., 4888.
Dromeranan (co. Leit. ?), 6438.
Drome Rastell. *See* Dromrastle.
Dromereoivre (Dromecroeve), co. Mon., 6644.
Dromereagh. *See* Dromreagh.
Dromereorrie (co. Leit. ?), 6448.
Dromerkeall (co. Lim. ?), 6172.
Dromerroley (co. Leit. ?), 4788.
Dromerrall (co. Leit. ?), 6438.
Dromerron, co. Kilk., 1134.
Dromeshetreane, co. Cav., 4682.
Dromesighane, co. Cork, 4761.
Dromesly (co. Cork ?), 6648.
Dromevaldre, co. Cav., 4634.
Dromeyabeoye (co. Leit. ?), 6448.
Dromfeogh, co. Cork. *See* Dromefyogh.
Dromfeogh—Dromfeogh—Dromfyogh, co. Cork, 6548, 6868, 6871.
Dromfingles, co. Clare, castle, 6611.
Dromfoe (Dromponah), co. Cork, 6683.
Dromfroine, co. Mon., 4467.
Dromfyegh (see Dromfeogh), 6548.
Dromgachon, co. Cav., 4457.
Dromgallon (Dromgallane), co. Wat., 964.
Dromgallon, co. Kerry, 6182.
Dromgathe, co. Ross., 4872.
Dromgarre (Dromgarre ?), co. Mon., 6682.
Dromgarriff, co. Cork. *See* Dromegarif.
Dromgawly (co. Mon. ?), 6698.
Dromgeronfe (co. Cork ?), 6616.
Dromgirle (co. Cav. ?), 6762.
Dromgo (co. Leit. ?), 4488.
Dromgoall (co. Leit. ?), 6448.
Dromgoill, co. Kilk., 6178.
Dromgologht (Dromgolal), co. Mon., 6876.

INDEX TO FIANTS—ELIZABETH.

Dromgole, Andrew, pardon, 4017.
" Nicholas, pardon, [illegible]
" Nicholas, 4[illegible]
" Patrick, pardon, [illegible]
Dromgolnalagan, co. Louth, [illegible]
Dromgonner, co. Mon., [illegible]
Dromgonny, co. Mon., [illegible]
Dromgoun (co. Cork ?), [illegible]
Dromgowan (co. Cav. ?), [illegible]
Dromgowla (Dromgole), co. Mon., [illegible]
Dromgowle, co. Wex., [illegible]
Dromgowly, co. Mon., [illegible]
Dromgrainle, co. Sligo, [illegible]
Dromgriffan—Dromgriffe—Dromgriffyn—Dromgryffan (Dromgriffin), co. Gal., [illegible], [illegible], [illegible].
Dromgrillan, co. Leit., [illegible]
Dromgryffan. See Dromgriffan.
Dromgryffe (co. Leit. ?), [illegible]
Dromhall ( ), co. Cav., [illegible]
Dromhallagh, co. Cav., [illegible]
Dromhane (Drommahane), co. Cork, [illegible]
Dromharvey (co. Leit. ?), [illegible]
Dromharle, co. Long., [illegible]
Dromharlagh—Dromhorlagh, co. Ros., [illegible], [illegible]
Dromhilleagh (Drumhilleagh), co. Mon., [illegible]
Dromhire (co. Leit. ?), [illegible]
Dromhirke (co. Leit. ?), [illegible]
Dromhirre (co. Leit.), [illegible]
Dromhorme, co. Cav., [illegible]
Dromhucke (Drumhirk ?), co. Mon., [illegible]
Dromhurke (Drumhirk), co. Mon., [illegible]
Dromilally (co. Kerry or Lim. ?), [illegible]
Dromillo (co. Leit. ?), [illegible]
Dromillon (co. Long. ?), [illegible]
Dromin, co. Lim. See Dromen.
Dromine, co. Cork. See Dromyne.
Dromine, co. Wat. See Drominacho.
Drominagh (co. Cork ?), [illegible]
Drominagho—Dromynaghe (Dromine), co. Wat., [illegible], [illegible]
Drominahen, co. Leit., [illegible]
Drominary (co. Clare ?), [illegible]
Dromino, King's co., [illegible]
Drominnada, co. Cav., [illegible]
Drominmore, co. Tip. See Dromynmore.
Drominochlie, co. Long., [illegible]
Drominine (Dromanoon), co. Cork, [illegible]
Dromin Mackurlagh, co. Lim. See Dromine M'Terrelaghe.
Drominyrusmalane (Dromagunnie), co. Kerry, [illegible]
Dromirrell (co. Leit. ?), [illegible]
Dromirvin, [illegible]
Dromiskillie, rectory of, [illegible]
Dromiskyn—Drommyskan—Dromyskan—Dromyskryne—Dromyskyn (Dromiskin), co. Louth, [illegible], [illegible], [illegible], [illegible], [illegible]
Dromkeathnane. See Dromeanan.
Dromkearne (co. Cork ?), [illegible]
Dromkeam, co. Kerry. See Dromokeame.
Dromkeen, co. Kerry. See Dromkyne.
Dromkenie (co. Kerry ?), [illegible]
Dromkeyne (co. Lim. ?), [illegible]
Dromkholin—Dromkholyn (Drumgooland, co. Down), rectory, [illegible], [illegible]
Dromkiddi, co. Cork, [illegible]
Dromkine (co. Lim. ?), [illegible]
Dromkirvin (co. Leit. ?), [illegible]
Dromklive, co. Sligo, [illegible]
Dromkrael, co. Leit. or Ros., [illegible]
Dromkyne (Dromkeen), co. Kerry, [illegible]
Dromkyne (co. Lim. ?), [illegible]
Dromlagh (co. Leit. ?), [illegible]
Dromlagh, rectory, [illegible]
Dromlahan. See Dromlahan.
Dromlaion. See Dromlayon.
Dromlane (co. Mon. ?), [illegible]
Dromlare, co. Lim. See Dromlarie.
Dromlargan (Dromlargan), co. Meath, [illegible], [illegible]
Dromlarie—Dromlarye (Dromlara), co. Lim., [illegible], [illegible]
Dromlayon—Dromlaion, rectory, co. Long. (Dromlumman, co. Cav. ?), [illegible], [illegible]
Dromleagh (co. Lim. ?), [illegible]
Dromlean. See Dromlahan.
Dromleeke—Dromeleke, co. Louth, [illegible], [illegible]
Dromlenna, co. Cork. See Dromlyne.
Dromlenagh, co. Kerry. See Dromlengaghe.
Dromlengaghe—Dromlyngaghe (co. Cork ?), [illegible], [illegible]
Dromleighe (Dromlough ?), co. Tip., [illegible]
Dromleyne, co. Cav., [illegible]
Dromleyne, co. Clare, [illegible]
Dromleyne, co. Mon., [illegible]
Dromlin, Queen's co., [illegible]
Dromlin, co. Clare, [illegible]
Dromlishamore—Dromlishamore (Dromlish), co. Ros., [illegible], [illegible]
Dromlive, co. Cav., [illegible]
Dromloghan, co. Lim., [illegible]
Dromloghane (Dromlohan), co. Lim., [illegible]
Dromloghane (Dromlohan), co. Wat., [illegible]
Dromloghen (Dromloughlin ?), co. Mon., [illegible]
Dromlomad (co. Tip. ?), [illegible]
Dromlomane (Dromlummin), co. Tip., [illegible], [illegible]
Dromloman—Dromloman (Dromlumman, co. Cav.), rectory, [illegible], [illegible]
Dromlone, Queen's co., [illegible]
Dromloughan — Dromologhan, co. Lim., [illegible], [illegible], [illegible]
Dromlonny, co. Cav., [illegible]
Dromlumy (Dromlomy), co. Mon., [illegible]

INDEX TO FIANTS—ELIZABETH.

Dromlyne (co. Clare ?), 4878, 6798.
Dromlynie (Dromlevane), co. Cork, [illegible].
Dromlyre (co. Meath ?), [illegible].
Dromlyrry (Dromlerry), co. Meath, [illegible].
Dromlyse (co. Long. ?), [illegible].
Drommacloonagh (co. Mon. or Cav.), [illegible].
Drommagh, co. Cork, [illegible].
Drommahane, co. Cork. See Dromahane.
Drommaslie—Drommany. See Drommany.
Drommartin—Drommartan—Dromartin, co. Kerry, [illegible], 6487, [illegible].
Drommeagh, co. Cav., [illegible].
Drommonmarkie. See Dromonarky.
Drommore. See Dromore, co. Cork.
Drommore. See Dromore, co. Clare.
Drommore. See Dromore, co. Cork.
Drommore, co. Mayo, 6777.
Drommore. See Dromore, co. Westm.
Drommoyre, co. Cav., [illegible].
Drommyne, co. Cork, [illegible], [illegible].
Drommyrhen. See Dromiskyn.
Drommnedrinhin, co. Cork. See Drommnickine.
Dromnagh—Dromnaghe—Dromnaghe—Dromnagh—Dronynagh (Drimnagh), co. Dub.), [illegible], 770, [illegible], 3111, 3404, [illegible], [illegible], 4169, [illegible]; manor, [illegible].
Dromnagh (co. Rosc. ?), [illegible].
Dromnaskea (co. Lim. ?), 6487.
Dromnasilly (co. Cork ?), [illegible].
Dromnane (co. Kerry ?), [illegible].
Dromnaughan (co. Cork ?), [illegible].
Dromneanrule, co. Cork, [illegible].
Dromnagralnabegh—Dromnagraney (Dromnagraghy, co. Sligo), [illegible], [illegible].
Dromnamonkill, co. Rosc., [illegible].
Dromnamore (co. Cork ?), [illegible].
Dromnavane (co. Kerry ?), [illegible].
Dromneave, co. Lim., [illegible].
Dromnelalde (co. Tip. ?), [illegible].
Dromnoghe. See Drumnagh.
Dromnoler (co. Lim. or Tip.), [illegible].
Dromnogarkie. See Dromonarky.
Dromnychroby, co. Clare, [illegible].
Dromnygaly, co. Meath, [illegible].
Dromnygrane (Dromagrane ?), co. Mon., [illegible].
Dromnyfertagh (Drummallaney ? co. Dun.), surrender, [illegible].
Dromnyle (co. Cork ?), [illegible].
Dromnyn, co. Lim., [illegible].
Dromnyne, co. Cork, [illegible], [illegible], [illegible].
Dromnyninkyrre, co. Westm., [illegible].
Dromod, co. Kerry. See Dromode.
Dromod, co. Leit., [illegible].
Dromod (co. Tip. ?), [illegible].
Dromodd, co. Long., [illegible].
Dromole, co. Gal., [illegible].
Dromodiam, co. Clare, [illegible].
Dromodymane (perhaps Dromnadearvane), co. Clare, [illegible].
Dromoharowe, co. Cork, rectory, [illegible].
Dromohair (co. Lim. ?), [illegible].
Dromohir, co. Clare, [illegible].
Dromoile (King's co. ?), 6191.
Dromoleyllane, co. Clare, [illegible], 4071.
Dromole (Dromeralle), co. Mon., [illegible].
Dromoleighe, co. Cav., [illegible].
Dromolen—Dromollen—Dromolane (Dromoland), co. Clare, [illegible], [illegible]; castle, [illegible].
Dromollan, co. Clare, [illegible].
Dromolyne (Dromoland ? co. Clare), manor, [illegible].
Dromolyne, co. Clare, 6617.
Dromolyne (Dromoland or Drumline), co. Clare, [illegible].
Dromonarky—Dromnomarkie—Dromnomarkie (Dromomarkie), co. Tip., 6193, [illegible]. See also Dromnarkye.
Dromone (co. Cav. ?), [illegible].
Dromona (Dromin), co. Lim., [illegible].
Dromone, co. Kild., [illegible].
Dromone (co. Cork ?), 6487.
Dromoneshrin (co. Cork ?), 6211.
Dromoor (see Dromore), co. Cork, 2257.
Dromoralleagh, co. Clare, [illegible].
Dromore—Dromnemore, co. Clare, [illegible], [illegible], [illegible], [illegible].
Dromore — Drommor — Drommore—Drumore, (in parish of Kilshannig, co. Cork), [illegible]-6, 2257, [illegible], [illegible]; castle and lands, [illegible], [illegible].
" baron of, Dermot O'Callaghan, [illegible].
Dromore—Drumore, co. Cork, [illegible], [illegible], [illegible], [illegible].
Dromore, co. Down, [illegible].
Dromore (co. Ferm. ?), [illegible].
Dromore (co. Gal. ?), [illegible].
Dromore, co. Kerry, [illegible], [illegible], [illegible].
Dromore, co. Mon., [illegible], [illegible], [illegible], [illegible], [illegible].
Dromore, co. Wat., [illegible].
" See also Cromore.
Dromore—Drommore, co. Westm., [illegible], [illegible], [illegible].
Dromore (co. Wick.), [illegible].
Dromorgall, co. Kerry, [illegible].
Dromorore, alias Dromore (co. Cav.), [illegible].
Dromoyle, [illegible].
Dromoylane, co. Clare, [illegible].
Drompeah, co. Cork. See Dromdea.
Dromrade, co. Cav., [illegible].
Dromrane, co. Leit., [illegible].
Dromrahye, co. Cork, [illegible].
Dromrehine, co. Sligo, [illegible].
Dromreaughe (Dromrahane), co. Lim., [illegible].
Dromreany (Dromraney), co. Westm., [illegible], [illegible], [illegible].
Dromreaslie—Drome Rastell (Dromrastill), co. Cork, [illegible], [illegible].
Dromreath, co. Westm., [illegible], [illegible].

INDEX TO FIANTS—ELIZABETH.

Drumrath (Drumcanery), co. Westm. rectory, [illegible].
Drumraghe — Drumrourah (Drumrough), co. Mayo, [illegible].
Drumregros (co. Cav. ?), [illegible].
Drumrey (Drumrough), co. Down, [illegible].
Drumro, co. Car., 1948.
Drumroish (co. Leit. ?), [illegible].
Drum Roraghe, co. Cav., [illegible].
Drumroske, co. Wat., 977.
Drumrotlagh (Drumrutagh), co. Mon., [illegible].
Drumroughill (Drumroughill), co. Mon., [illegible].
Drumry, co. Meath, [illegible].
Drumseackane (co. Cork ?), [illegible].
Drumsallagh, co. Lim., [illegible]; grant, [illegible].
Drumsnale, co. Mon., [illegible].
Drumsawry, co. Westm., [illegible], [illegible].
Drumselling (co. Gal.), [illegible].
Drumsnake (Drumsnak), co. Down, [illegible], [illegible].
Drumsherrale, co. Cork, [illegible].
Drumshenaty (Drumshinny), co. Mon., [illegible].
Drumsholtonis, co. Cav., [illegible].
Drumshrowallagh (co. Cav. ?), [illegible].
Drumsillagh (co. Leit. ?), [illegible].
Drumslowe (Drumslow), co. Mon., [illegible].
Drumsnale (Drumsnat), co. Mon., lessee, [illegible].
Drumsrwill (co. Ferm. ?), [illegible].
Drumswichin (perhaps Drumsnaschable), co. Cork, [illegible].
Drumtample. See Drumtample.
Drumtarriv (co. Cork ?), [illegible].
Drumtarriffe (Drumtarriff, co. Cork), [illegible].
Drumtrasna, co. Lim. See Drumtrasnaghe.
Drumtork, co. Lim., [illegible].
Drumtyclohy, co. Cork, [illegible].
Drumucke (Drumusak), co. Mon., [illegible].
Drumullion, co. Mon., [illegible].
Drumullothe (Drumully, co. Mon.), [illegible].
Drumullye rectory (Drumully, co. Mon.), [illegible].
Drumurtlelaghe (co. Cork ?), [illegible].
Drumy, alias Glastrym, co. Mon., [illegible].
Drumyache, co. Mon., [illegible].
Drumycullygramyhe — Drumycumygraye (Drumgraunig), co. Kerry, [illegible], [illegible].
Drumyaule (co. Cork ?), [illegible].
Drumyn, co. Cav., [illegible].
Drumyn, co. Cork, [illegible].
Drumyn, co. Gal., [illegible].
Drumyn, co. Louth, [illegible].
Drumyn (Drumman), co. Meath, [illegible].
Drumyn, co. Meath, [illegible], [illegible].
Drumyn, Queen's co., [illegible].
Drumyne (Dromine), co. Cork, [illegible].
Drumynacroyne, co. Long., [illegible].
Drumynagh (Drimnagh, co. Dub. ?), [illegible].
Dromynaghe. See Drumdunaghe.
Drumynaly (co. Mon. ?), [illegible].
Drumynan, co. Car., [illegible].
Drumyne, co. Cork, [illegible], [illegible].
Drumyne, co. Meath, [illegible], [illegible].
Drumyne, co. Ros., rectory, [illegible]; vicarage, [illegible]
Drumyneene. See Drumyrayne.
Drumynesuble, co. Dub., [illegible].
Drumynerowe, co. Long., [illegible].
Drumyneer (Dromineer, co. Tip. ?), [illegible].
Drumynagh, co. Cork, [illegible]
Drumynhassery, co. Cork, [illegible].
Drumyn Des (co. Lim. ?), [illegible].
Drumynlyn. See Drumynayne.
Drumynmoghlane, co. Clare, [illegible].
Drumynnis (Drumlonan), co. Mon., [illegible].
Drumynayne — Drumlinge — Drumynesne — Drumynvine (Drumanean), co. Cork, [illegible], [illegible], [illegible], [illegible], [illegible]; castle and land, [illegible], [illegible].
Drumyrane, co. Westm., [illegible].
Drumyskan — Drumyskcyne — Drumyskyn. See Drumiskyn, co. Louth.
Drumystchell (co. Meath ?), [illegible].
Drumytrasnaghe (Drumtrasna), co. Lim., [illegible].
Drungan—Drungane. See Drangan.
Drunlare, co. Lim., [illegible].
Drunkey, King's co., [illegible], [illegible], [illegible], [illegible].
Drunowise (co. Leit. ?), [illegible].
Drunrystbrony, [illegible].
Drunure M'Terlaghe (Drumte Mactarlogh), co. Lim., [illegible].
Droghede—Drumchela. See Drogheda.
Drought — Drogh: — Droghile—Droghlin — Droughtin, co. Gal., [illegible], [illegible], [illegible], [illegible], [illegible], [illegible], [illegible].
Drought, Donogh m'Morterto, pardon, [illegible].
Droughlin. See Drought.
Drummagimor, co. Cav., [illegible].
Drummahoo (co. Mon. ?), [illegible].
Drummaghanisho (Drumbrenagh, co. Leit. ?), [illegible].
Drumnabrenlishe (Drumbrenalis, co. Leit.), [illegible].
Drumndone, co. Cav., [illegible].
Drumngoilla (co. Leit. ?), [illegible].
Drumn hillough (co. Leit. ?), [illegible].
Drumnlain (see Drumlahan), [illegible].
Drumnalton, co. Cav., [illegible].
Drumnaloge, co. Cav., [illegible].
Drumnallough (Drumnallagh ?), co. Cav., [illegible].
Drowngarraff (Drumgarriff, co. Cork ?), [illegible].
Drowle (Darrowel, co. Mayo ?), [illegible].
Drowndrynsell (Drumdrasill), co. Cork, [illegible].

INDEX TO FIANTS—ELIZABETH.

Drowmon, (co. Wick.), [illegible].
Drowmenaye (Drumraisy, co. Ferm. ?) [illegible].
Drowmkannelly, co. Cav., [illegible].
Drowmlahir (co. Clare ?), [illegible].
Drowmlyn, co. Clare, [illegible].
Drowmorgan (co. Kilk. ?), burgess of, [illegible].
Drowmonell (co. Cork ?), [illegible].
Droymallennis (co. Leit. ?), [illegible].
Droymhoghley, co. Long., [illegible].
Droymlove, co. Long., [illegible].
Droymorris (co. Leit. ?), [illegible].
Droya, King's co., [illegible].
Droyalagre, co. Westm., [illegible].
Droymelale, co. Meath, [illegible].
Droyncrickey (co. Cav. ?), [illegible].
Droynmore (Drinmore), co. Westm., [illegible].
Dru[illegible]ke, co. Long., [illegible].
Drue, man called, 4117.
Druerye. See Drury.
Druggre (al Kilmainham), co. Dub., [illegible], [illegible], [illegible].
Druinon (co. Meath ?), [illegible].
Drum, co. Mon. See Drugan.
Drum, co. Ross., [illegible].
rum (alias Simson), George, pardon, [illegible].
rumacreeve, co. Mon. See Dromacreeve.
rumada, co. Long., [illegible].
rumadoney, co. Down. See Ballygromadoney.
rumagalvin, co. Mon. See Dromaghgalvin.
rumahaire, co. Leit. See Dromahair.
rumaknockan, co. Down (see Ballydromaknockan), [illegible].
rumalane, co. Arm. See Dromalane.
rumalis, co. Antrim. See Cloghdrumalis, Drumalis.
rumalught, co. Kerry. See Derrymalught.
rumanillra, co. Ross. See Ynchedromanillra.
rumanny, co. Mon. See Dromanny.
rumard, See Drumard, co. Lim.
rumarrell, co. Mon. See Dromarell.
rumatample, co. Ross. See Drumtample.
rumavaddy, co. Mon. See Dromaddy, Dromavaddy.
rumavain, co. Mon. See Dromavile.
rumawerk, co. Donegal. See Drummawerk.
rumbanagher, co. Mon. See Drumbanagher.
rumbane, co. Mon. See Drumbon.
rumbirne, co. Mon. See Drumbyrne.
rumboriek, co. Mon. See Drumboriske.
rumbreanlis, co. Leit. See Drumbreanlis and Drommbreanliske.
rumbrickan, co. Mon. See Drumbrickie.
rumbrughas, co. Cav., [illegible].
rumburre, co. Mon. See Drumbur.
.rumcall, co. Mon. See Drummall.
Drumcannon, co. Wat. See Dromcanan.
Drumcashell—Dromcashell (Drumcashel), co. Louth, [illegible], [illegible], [illegible].
(Drumcaw)—Drumcathe—Drumhath, co. Down, rectory, [illegible], [illegible].
Drumcharin, co. Donegal. See Drumcharye.
Drumcliff, co. Clare. See Dromcleive.
Drumcondra, co. Mon. See Dromconraghl.
Drumconraghe—Dromconragh—Dromconraigh—Dromconrath—Dromconrowe—Drumcurrathe (Drumcondra, co. Dub.), [illegible].
Drumcooly, King's co. See Dromcolley.
Drumcormick, co. Sligo. See Carrow Dromcarwycke.
Drumcree, co. Westm. See Dromcree.
Drumcrin, co. Cav. See Dromchrin.
Drumcunnig, co. Kerry. See Drommeunnygeenyne, Dromuinycomigonie and Drumycunnygeenyne.
Drumdall, co. Ross. See Drumdamphe.
Drumdiel, co. Tip. See Drumdile.
Drumdoney, co. Sligo. See Dromdoney.
Drumeighan. See Drumlahan.
Drumely (co. Cork ?), [illegible].
Drumeynagh, co. Cork, [illegible].
Drumfynin (co. Cork ?), [illegible].
Drumgallane, co. Wat. See Dromgallan.
Drumgarriff, co. Cork. See Drowgarriff.
Drumgarve, co. Mon. See Drumgarve.
Drumghes (co. Cav.), [illegible].
Drumgolan, co. Mon. See Dromgolaght.
Drumgole, co. Mon. See Dromgowle and Ballydromgowle.
Drumgooland, co. Down. See Dromaholin.
Drumgor, co. Mon. See Ballydromgor.
Drumgroony, co. Mon. See Dromogryne.
Drumgriffin, co. Gal. See Dromgriffen.
Drumgrone, co. Mon. See Dromogrome and Dromnygran.
Drumgull (Drumgrill), co. Mon., [illegible].
Drumgullane, co. Wat. See Dromgallan.
Drumhillagh, co. Mon. See Dromhillough.
Drumhirk, co. Mon. See Dromhurke, Ballydromhurke, Dromhacke.
Drumicahie (co. Long. ?), [illegible].
Druminchahie (co. Long. ?), [illegible].
Druminnis, co. Mon. See Dromynnis.
Druminath. See Drumenaw, co. Down.
Drumkerry (co. Leit. ?), [illegible].
Drumkyne, co. Lim., [illegible].
Drumkyren (co. Leit. or Ross.), [illegible].
Drumlahan—Drumlaghan—Dromlahan—Drumlean—Dromlahan—Dromlean—Dromlein (Drumlane, co. Cav.), [illegible], [illegible], [illegible].

INDEX TO FIANTS—ELIZABETH.

Drumlahan—monastery of the B. V. M., [illegible], [illegible], [illegible], [illegible].
Drumlahan, co. Down, [illegible].
Drumlion. See Drumlahan, co. Cav.
Drumline, co. Cav. See Drumlahan.
Drumloyan, co. Meath. See [illegible].
Drumlerin, co. Lim., [illegible].
Drumleagh, co. Tip. See [illegible].
Drumlone. See Drumlahan, co. Cav.
Drumlonnagher (Drumlonagh ?), co. Kerry, [illegible].
Drumlorry, co. Meath. See Drumlyrry.
Drumluckra—[illegible], co. Down (Lisdrumlukra, co. Armagh ?), [illegible], [illegible].
Drumlester, co. Mon., [illegible].
Drumlish, co. Kerr. See [illegible].
Drumlohan. See [illegible].
Drumlone, co. Mon. See [illegible].
Drumlough, co. Down or [illegible], [illegible].
Drumloughlin, co. Mon. See [illegible].
Drumlummin, co. Tip. See Drumlumman.
Drumlummon, co. Cav. See Drumlahan, Drumlayon.
Drumlunny, co. Mon. See Drumlunny.
Drumman'[illegible], co. Tip., rectory, [illegible].
Drumman, co. Meath. See [illegible].
Drummer, A, [illegible].
Drummogie, [illegible].
Drummuck, co. Mon. See Drumucke, Drumucke.
Drummucken, co. Gal., [illegible].
Drummuck, co. Mon. See Drumnole.
Drumnally, co. Mon. See Drumnolder, Drumnallye.
Drumnamuile, co. Kerry, [illegible].
Drumnamuleevan, co. Ulster. See Drumnaly-more.
Drumnamagh, co. Cork, [illegible].
Drumnavavilla, co. Mon. See Drumnavavilla.
Drumnagrasky, co. Sligo. See Drumnagralsbagh.
Drumnalleery, co. Donegal. See Drumnay-[illegible].
Drumneill, co. Mon. See [illegible].
Drumnoghe. See Drumnagh.
Drumore or Drumnarvo (co. Cav.), [illegible].
Drumore. See Dromore, co. Cork.
Drumorallie (co. Kerry ?), [illegible].
Drumraney, co. Ferm. See [illegible].
Drumraney, co. Westm. See Drumraney, Drumrath.
Drumraney, [illegible].
Drumreal, co. Sligo. See Drumrall.
Drumreagh, co. Down. See Dromory.
Drumreagh, co. Mayo. See Drumreragha.
Drumrorghill, co. Mon. See Drumraghill.
Drumrutagh, co. Mon. See Drumroilagh.
Drumsheake, co. Cav., [illegible].
Drumsnak, co. Down. See Drumsnake.
Drumshenny, co. Mon. See Drumshenny.
Drumsillagh, co. Cav. See Drumsillagh.
Drumsnow, co. Mon. See Drumsnowe.
Drumsnal, co. Mon. See Drumsnail.
Drumtample—Drumtample (Drumnaktemple, co. Ross.), [illegible]; rectory, [illegible].
Drumtrock, co. Ross., [illegible].
Drumtamporie (Drumtramory), co. Mon., [illegible].
Drumundro (co. Wexf.), [illegible].
Drunyne, co. Cork, [illegible].
Drumutaly, co. Leit., [illegible].
Drumryne, co. Cork, [illegible].
Drumruall (Drumraws), co. Sligo; vicarage, [illegible].
Drury—Drurie—Drewrye—Drurie:
„ Anne, daughter of Sir Wm., wardship, [illegible].
„ Elizabeth, daughter of Sir Wm., wardship, [illegible].
„ Francis, pardon, [illegible].
„ Jane, wardship, [illegible].
„ Sir William, lord president of Munster, [illegible], [illegible]; lord justice of Ireland, [illegible], [illegible]; commissions, [illegible], [illegible], [illegible], [illegible], [illegible]; pardon, [illegible]; pardon at his suit, [illegible], [illegible], [illegible], [illegible], [illegible], [illegible], [illegible]; grant of wardships, [illegible], [illegible]; leases, [illegible], [illegible], [illegible], [illegible]; wardship of his daughters, [illegible].
Drushane—Drushane (co. Cork ?), [illegible], [illegible].
Drayne (co. Donegal), [illegible].
Drayne [illegible]—Drayne[illegible] (Drumchria, co. Donegal), [illegible], [illegible].
Drogane (Drom), co. Mon., [illegible].
Draymullyn, co. Clare, [illegible].
Drewrye (Dunn ?, King's co.), [illegible].
Dryland, Peter, pardon (see Drilling), [illegible].
Dryland, Nicholas, pardon, [illegible].
Drylan, James, pardon, [illegible].
„ Peter, [illegible].
Drylin, Wm., pardon, [illegible].
Dryling, Peter, [illegible]. See Drilling.
Drymaneagh (co. Cav. ?), [illegible].
Drymanre (co. Kerry ?), [illegible].
Drymaylaghy. See Derrymaclaghny, co. Gal.
Drynagh (co. Cork ?), [illegible].
Drynagh (co. Leit. ?), [illegible].
Drynagh, co. Wexf., [illegible].
Drynam—Drynam, co. Dub., [illegible], [illegible], [illegible], [illegible], [illegible], [illegible], [illegible].
Drynan, co. Lim., [illegible] of, [illegible].
Drynan, Morris, pardon, [illegible].
„ Peter, [illegible], [illegible].
Drynanstown (King's co. ?), [illegible].
Drynany (co. Kilk. ?), [illegible].
Drynan, King's co., [illegible].
Dryne, co. Kerr., [illegible].

INDEX TO FIANTS—ELIZABETH.

Dryngans, [illegible].

Dryal, Donald I., pardon, [illegible].

Drynin, King's co., [illegible].

Drynim, co. Dub., [illegible].

Dryny alias M'Carry, Donogh ne Tuig, pardon, [illegible].

Drynmill, co. Clare, [illegible].

Dryshoke. See Drishoke.

Drywighan. See Drishighan.

Drywan, co. Clare, [illegible].

Drynshoke. See Drinshoke.

Drynemane (King's co.), [illegible].

Dunevan—Duncan Kinyldseraghe (Kilmacdaugh), co. Gal., [illegible].

Dunagh, co. Kerry. See Down, Dwagh.

Dunaghcallyne, co. Lim., [illegible].

Duaghes (co. Cork or Lim.), [illegible].

Dunevan. See Dunevan.

Dubinion, co. Kild., [illegible].

Dublin—Dublyn (mentioned), [illegible]; fiants, commissions, and patents, dated at, [illegible]; measure of corn of, [illegible]; trade with, [illegible]; illegal exports from, [illegible]; robberies at, [illegible]; city court, [illegible]; commission court, [illegible]; statute of, [illegible]; great house of earl of Kildare, [illegible]; house granted to Callough O'More, [illegible]; submission of earl of Thomond at, [illegible]; earl of Desmond to come to, [illegible]; McWilliam, [illegible]; tennis court and bowling alley for recreation of nobility and gentlemen, [illegible]; gunpowder accident, [illegible]; lands near, [illegible]; enquiry as to earl of Kildare's lands in, [illegible]; leases of premises in, [illegible]; grants, [illegible]; charter of incorporation of the guild of S. Mary Magdalene of Barbers and Surgeons, [illegible].

Dublin:

- mayor, sheriffs, commonalty and citizens, grant of premises in city, [illegible].
- mayor, and sheriffs, com. of muster, [illegible]; mandate to, [illegible].
- mayor, [illegible]; warrant to, [illegible], commissions, [illegible].
- sheriffs, [illegible].
- constables, [illegible].
- recorder, commissions, [illegible]; court, [illegible]; aldermen, [illegible]; merchants of, [illegible].
- Archbishop, Hugh Curwen, keeper of great seal, 1; lord chancellor, [illegible]; pardon, [illegible]; takes oath of supremacy, [illegible]; commissions, [illegible].
- - Adam. See Loftus.
- - lands of, in Kilmainham, [illegible].
- - vicar-general and official principal of, [illegible]; appeals from, [illegible].
- - surrogate of, as Master of Prerogative, [illegible].
- - liberties of, [illegible].
- - diocese, court of, faculties in, issued, [illegible]; rector in, [illegible], presentation to, [illegible].

INDEX TO FIANTS—ELIZABETH.

Dublin:
,, archbishop, first fruits of his province to be collected for S. Patrick's, [illegible], [illegible].
archdeacon, Robert Sutton, [illegible].
,, ,, Robert Wesley, takes oath of supremacy, [illegible]; commissions, [illegible], [illegible], [illegible], [illegible], [illegible], [illegible], [illegible], [illegible], [illegible], [illegible].
,, ,, See Usher, Henry.
,, cathedral of Holy Trinity or Christ Church, [illegible].
,, ,, prior, [illegible].
,, ,, dean and chapter, licence to alien, [illegible]; chief rent to, [illegible]; pension from, [illegible], lands of, [illegible].
,, ,, dean, alienation of lands, [illegible], [illegible].
,, ,, ,, Thomas Lockwood, takes oath of supremacy, [illegible]; commissions, [illegible], [illegible], [illegible].
,, ,, ,, John Garvey. See Garvey.
,, ,, ,, James Wheeler, [illegible], [illegible], licence of absence, [illegible].
,, ,, precentor, Christopher Maltho, refused oath of supremacy, [illegible].
,, ,, ,, Richard Tompson, licence of absence, [illegible].
,, ,, ,, Robert Richardson, [illegible], [illegible].
,, ,, ,, Robert Graves, [illegible].
,, ,, ,, Thomas Ham, [illegible].
,, ,, chancellor, John Herman, refused oath of supremacy, [illegible].
,, ,, ,, William Dermot, grant of English liberty, [illegible]; commissions, [illegible], [illegible], [illegible].
,, ,, treasurer, John Cardiff refused oath of supremacy, [illegible].

Dublin:
,, cathedral of Holy Trinity:
,, ,, treasurer, Thomas Mann, licence of absence, [illegible], [illegible].
,, ,, ,, Bartholomew Mann, [illegible].
,, ,, ,, Henry Usher. See Usher.
,, ,, ,, John Middleton, [illegible].
,, ,, ,, John Carpenter, [illegible].
,, ,, ,, Wm. Hickes, [illegible].
,, ,, ,, Chr. Hewetson, [illegible].
,, ,, prebendaries, vicars, &c., oath of supremacy tendered to, [illegible].
,, cathedral of S. Patrick, dean and chapter to collect first fruits of the province of Dublin for repair of the cathedral, [illegible], [illegible].
,, ,, dean, Adam Loftus. See Loftus.
,, ,, ,, Thomas Jones. See Jones.
,, ,, ,, Richard Meredith, [illegible]; made bishop of Leighlin, [illegible]; grant to a discharge from deanery in discharge of a fine in the Star Chamber, [illegible], [illegible]. See Meredith.
,, ,, ,, John Bidgs, licence of absence, [illegible]; commission, [illegible].
,, ,, precentor or chantor. See Graid, Thomas. Land of, near Athy, [illegible].
,, ,, chancellor, Robert Nangill, takes oath of supremacy, [illegible].
,, ,, ,, Nicholas Walshe. See Walshe.
,, ,, ,, Tho. Jones. See Jones.
,, ,, treasurer, Edmund Sarsewell, [illegible], [illegible].
,, ,, ,, John Kerry, commissions, [illegible], [illegible], [illegible], [illegible], [illegible].

INDEX TO FIANTS—ELIZABETH.

Dublin:
„ cathedral, treasurer, Richard Thompson or Thomson, commissions, [illegible], 4176, [illegible], [illegible], [illegible], [illegible].
archdeacon. See Usher.
prebendaries 7, [illegible], [illegible], [illegible], [illegible], [illegible], [illegible], [illegible].
vicars, lands of, [illegible].
vicars choral or petty canons, lands of, [illegible], [illegible].
Trinity College, foundation charter, [illegible]; first provost, fellows, and scholars, [illegible]; grant of lands to, [illegible]; fine for pardon to be paid to, [illegible]; annuity granted to, [illegible]; crown wards to be educated in, [illegible], [illegible], &c. See Trinity College.
„ provost of, [illegible], [illegible].
abbey of the B.V.M., or Mary's abbey; church, cemetery, dormitory, &c., granted, [illegible]; abbot's lodging, Ankerer's park, &c., leased, [illegible]; messuage and garden at outer gate leased, [illegible]; same with abbey green, granted, [illegible]; infirmary, &c., leased, [illegible], [illegible]; demesne, [illegible].
possessions of, leased, [illegible]; granted, [illegible], [illegible], [illegible], [illegible], [illegible], [illegible], [illegible], [illegible], [illegible], [illegible], [illegible], [illegible], [illegible]; lands of, [illegible], [illegible].
abbot, lease by, [illegible], [illegible].
procurations from rectories, [illegible].
abbey of S. Thomas the Martyr, called Thomas court, abbot of, leases from recited, [illegible], [illegible], [illegible], [illegible], [illegible], [illegible], [illegible], [illegible], [illegible].
possessions leased, [illegible],

Dublin:
[illegible], [illegible], [illegible], [illegible], [illegible], [illegible], [illegible], [illegible], [illegible], 4411, [illegible], [illegible], [illegible], [illegible], [illegible], [illegible], [illegible], [illegible], [illegible], [illegible], [illegible], [illegible], [illegible], [illegible]; granted, [illegible], [illegible], [illegible], [illegible], [illegible], [illegible], [illegible], [illegible], [illegible], [illegible], [illegible], [illegible].
„ „ procurations from rectories of, [illegible].
„ hospital of S. John without Newgate, site alleged, [illegible].
„ „ prior, [illegible]; lease recited, [illegible], [illegible]; possessions leased, [illegible]; granted, [illegible], [illegible], [illegible], [illegible], [illegible].
„ house of nuns of the Hogges, tenement of, [illegible]; possessions leased, [illegible], [illegible], [illegible], [illegible], [illegible]; granted, [illegible].
„ house of friars preachers, leased, [illegible], [illegible]; granted, [illegible]; possessions granted, [illegible], [illegible].
„ friars minor, land of, [illegible].
„ Abbey green, [illegible].
„ Abbot's chambers and lodgings, [illegible].
„ All hallows, [illegible].
„ Ankyrner's park, [illegible].
„ Aqueduct, or high pipe, [illegible], [illegible].
„ Ayspark, [illegible].
„ Back lane, [illegible].
„ Beggars' Bush, [illegible].
„ Bridge, chapel of our Lady at the, [illegible], [illegible], [illegible].
„ Bridge of the castle, [illegible].
„ Bullring — Bolbrige — Boldrynge, [illegible], [illegible], [illegible].
„ Burnell's lane, [illegible], [illegible].
„ Castle, escape of prisoners from, [illegible], [illegible]; prisoners in, [illegible], [illegible], [illegible], [illegible]; persons indicted of treason to surrender at, [illegible]; hostages of O'Donell, to be delivered at, [illegible]; privileges of, granted to Carrickfergus castle, [illegible]; fiants dated at, [illegible], [illegible]; chancery records kept in, [illegible]; records in Bermingham's tower, [illegible]; commission to enquire of houses and lands belonging to, [illegible]; ground adjoin-

INDEX TO FIANTS—ELIZABETH.

Dublin Castle :
ing leased, [illegible], 2231, [illegible], 2878, [illegible], [illegible], [illegible]; [illegible]ed, [illegible].
" " constable of, [illegible], [illegible], 3014, [illegible], 4314, [illegible], [illegible], [illegible], [illegible] n; pardon for escape of prisoners, [illegible]; payment to, for diet of prisoners, [illegible].
" " vice-constable of, 1784, [illegible].
" " surveyor of ordnance and works in, [illegible].
" " keeper of the new buildings and clock, [illegible], [illegible], [illegible].
" " keeper of the council chamber, [illegible], [illegible], [illegible].
" " keeper of the records in Bermingham's tower, 3214, [illegible], [illegible].
" " janitor or porter, [illegible], [illegible], [illegible], [illegible], [illegible], [illegible].
" " gunner of, [illegible], [illegible], [illegible].
" " soldiers in, [illegible], [illegible], [illegible].
" " bridge of, [illegible].
" " court of Castle Chamber held in. See Castle Chamber.
" " ditch leased, [illegible], [illegible], [illegible], [illegible], [illegible], [illegible], [illegible].
" Castle street, [illegible], [illegible], [illegible], [illegible], [illegible].
" Chapel of our Lady at north end of bridge, [illegible], [illegible], [illegible].
" Collett's Inns, [illegible], [illegible].
" Cokbyll, [illegible].
" Cook—Coke—Cock street, [illegible], [illegible], [illegible], [illegible].
" Corpus Christi, land of fraternity of, [illegible].
" Crockers lane, [illegible].
" Crokers barres — Crokersbarres — Crockers Bars, [illegible], [illegible], [illegible].
" Dames gate, [illegible], [illegible], [illegible], [illegible].
" Dames mill, [illegible].
" Fern street, [illegible].
" Fishamble Fyshe—Fysher, street, [illegible], [illegible], [illegible], [illegible].
" Gaol, keeper of, [illegible].
" Gibbet meadow or Hoggen Hog's mead, [illegible], [illegible], [illegible].
" Grangegorman by, [illegible].
" High cross, [illegible].
" High street, [illegible], [illegible], [illegible], [illegible], [illegible], [illegible], [illegible], [illegible], [illegible], [illegible], [illegible], [illegible], [illegible].
" Hoggen—Hoggen's green, [illegible], [illegible].
" Kings mill, [illegible], [illegible].
" Mary lane, [illegible].
" Merchant quay, [illegible], [illegible].

Dublin :
" Newgate, [illegible], [illegible], [illegible], [illegible]; prisoners in, [illegible].
" Newstreet, [illegible], [illegible], [illegible], [illegible], [illegible].
" Old exchequer, [illegible], [illegible].
" Oxmantown, [illegible], [illegible], [illegible], [illegible].
" Powers Inns, [illegible], [illegible], [illegible], [illegible].
" Powll—Powell mill, [illegible], [illegible].
" preceptory, al. Kilmainham, [illegible].
" quay—key, [illegible], [illegible], [illegible].
" Rochell lane, or Back lane, [illegible].
" Rocket lane, [illegible].
" S. Andrew, parish of, [illegible], [illegible], [illegible], [illegible].
" S. Andrew's lands, [illegible].
" S. Audoen—Andwyn—Andoenus—Owen, church, [illegible], [illegible]; parish, [illegible], [illegible], [illegible], [illegible], [illegible].
" S. Bride's street, [illegible].
" S. Francis street, [illegible], [illegible], [illegible], [illegible], [illegible], [illegible], [illegible], [illegible], [illegible].
" S. George, church of, [illegible], [illegible].
" S. James church, [illegible].
" " gate, [illegible], [illegible], [illegible].
" " parish, [illegible], [illegible], [illegible], [illegible], [illegible], [illegible], [illegible], [illegible].
" S. John the evangelist, church proctors of S. Mary in, [illegible].
" " rector, [illegible].
" " parish, [illegible], [illegible], [illegible], [illegible], [illegible].
" S. Katherine, parish, [illegible], [illegible], [illegible], [illegible], [illegible].
" S. Mary of the Dame or Dames, parish, [illegible], [illegible], [illegible].
" S. Michael, church, parsonage of, [illegible]; tenement of S. Mary in, [illegible]; churchyard, [illegible]; land of [illegible], [illegible].
" " parish, [illegible], [illegible], [illegible].
" S. Michan, cemetery of church, manslaughter in, [illegible], sanctuary by, [illegible].
" " parish, [illegible], [illegible], [illegible], [illegible], [illegible].
" S. Nicholas, lands, [illegible].
" " parish, [illegible], [illegible], [illegible], [illegible].
" " parish of S. N. in church of S. Patrick, [illegible], [illegible].
" " within, street of, [illegible].
" S. Olave or S. Tullock, church, [illegible], [illegible], [illegible], [illegible], [illegible]; proctors of, [illegible]; wardens of, [illegible].
" " rectory, [illegible], [illegible], [illegible], [illegible].

Dublin:
- „ S. Clare, parish, 1483, 1792, 2161, 2562, 2763, 3228, 3352, 1714, 4124.
- „ S. Patrick's church, garden behind, 1892, 4573; mortgage payable at font in, 6044. See above, cathedral of S. Patrick.
- „ S. Patrick's street, [illegible], [illegible], 2654, [illegible], [illegible].
- „ S. Thomas street, 1173, [illegible], 4514, [illegible], [illegible].
- „ S. Thomas street. See Thomas street.
- „ S. Tullock. See S. Clare.
- „ S. Warburg, parish, 1511, [illegible], 4314, [illegible].
- „ „ street, 1348.
- „ Scarlet lane, 2364, [illegible].
- „ Schoolhouse lane, [illegible].
- „ Skinners street, 1348.
- „ Staine, the, [illegible].
- „ Suburbs, 1142, 1314, 1424, 1739, 1878, 1884, 1493, [illegible], 3424, [illegible].
- „ Sythar lane, [illegible].
- „ Tailors Hall, 2371, 3567, [illegible].
- „ Tholsel, [illegible].
- „ Thomas court, 1762, [illegible].
- „ „ See Abbey of S. Thomas.
- „ Thomas street, 1144, 1163, 1167, 1637, 1783, [illegible], [illegible], 4714, [illegible], 5776–80, 5786, [illegible].
- „ Wall of city, 2377.
- „ Winetavern street, 1811, [illegible], [illegible], 3876, 4311.
- „ Wood quay, 1722, 2308, 2334, 2614, [illegible], 4314, 4426, [illegible].
- „ port or haven, 60–1, 63, [illegible].
- „ „ export of wheat, 1718, 1727, 1745, 1753, [illegible].
- „ „ „ of wool, &c., monopoly, [illegible].
- „ „ supervisor, [illegible].
- „ „ customs, bond, [illegible], 3413.
- „ „ customs, salary of Master of Rolls charged on, [illegible].
- „ „ customer and collector of customs, [illegible], [illegible].
- „ „ controller of customs, 3779, 4763, 5184, [illegible], [illegible], [illegible], 6701.
- „ „ searcher and gauger, [illegible], [illegible], 5184, [illegible], [illegible], [illegible], [illegible].
- „ „ collector of wine duty, [illegible], [illegible], 2764, [illegible], [illegible], [illegible], [illegible], [illegible].
- „ „ controller of wine duty, [illegible], 3168, [illegible], [illegible], [illegible], 4133, [illegible].
- „ county of the city, [illegible], [illegible], 5133, [illegible].
- „ „ „ commissions of peace, [illegible], [illegible], [illegible], [illegible], [illegible], [illegible].

Dublin:
- „ county of the city, messuages and land in, 317, 1360.
- „ county, sheriff, 86, 308, 367, 648, 836, [illegible], [illegible], [illegible], [illegible], [illegible], 3161, 3428, [illegible], 4285, 6041, [illegible].
- „ „ general cessor and collector of cess, [illegible], 4067.
- „ „ commission of peace, 378–81, [illegible], 643, 2448, 3183, [illegible], [illegible], [illegible], [illegible], [illegible], [illegible], [illegible], [illegible], [illegible], [illegible], [illegible], [illegible], [illegible], [illegible], [illegible], [illegible], 6438, [illegible].
- „ „ commissions of muster and array, [illegible], 1117, [illegible], 3444, 3118, 4148, 4462, [illegible].
- „ „ general of the forces in, [illegible], [illegible], 4116, [illegible].
- „ „ martial law, [illegible], [illegible], [illegible], [illegible], 1198, 1178, 1437, [illegible], [illegible], [illegible], [illegible], [illegible], [illegible], [illegible], [illegible], [illegible], [illegible], [illegible], 4047, [illegible], [illegible], [illegible], 4444, [illegible].
- „ „ wages of soldiers against O'Mores cessed on, 1971.
- „ „ ploughlands in, [illegible].
- „ „ com. to enquire of lands of Earl of Kildare, [illegible], 763.
- „ „ com. as to lands of Viscount Baltinglass, [illegible].
- „ „ inquiry as to property of parish churches, [illegible].
- „ „ escheator of issues in, [illegible].
- „ „ authority to impress hay, [illegible], 4081, 4173, 4488, [illegible], [illegible], 6412.
- „ „ marches of, [illegible]; martial law in, 182, 304, [illegible]; particularized and seneschal appointed, [illegible].

Ducnallo, co. Gal., [illegible].

Donate, mortgage of lands in Galway stated in, [illegible].

Duneyrahinge, co. Cav., [illegible].

Duchemin, Nicholas (a Frenchman), English liberty, 3842.

Duchman, Nicholas, a foreigner, instituted to a vicarage, [illegible].

Dunboiske, co. Clare, [illegible].

Duckett, James, pardon, [illegible].

Duckett, James, pardon, [illegible].

Dudall, James. See Dowdall.

Dudee, Dermod m'Shane, pardon, [illegible].

Dudeke. See Duleeke.

Duell, Donoghowe m'Donogh, pardon, [illegible].

INDEX TO FIANTS—ELIZABETH.

Duf, Cahell, pardon, 97.
" Edm., [illegible].
" Ennos, pardon, 97.
" Henry, pardon, 97.
" Hugh, pardon, [illegible].
" Melaughlen, pardon, 97.
" Teig, pardon, 148.
" Thadee, [illegible].
" Thomas, pardon, 97.
Dufe, John, English liberty, 428.
" Thady, pardon, 1178.
Duff, Arte, pardon, [illegible].
" Catherine, pardon, 316.
" Connor or Conoghor, pardon, [illegible], 6974.
" David, pardon, [illegible].
" Donald, [illegible].
" Edm., pardon, [illegible].
" Farry grani, pardon, [illegible].
" Gerald, pardon, [illegible].
" Gillpatrick oge, pardon, [illegible].
" Henry, abbot of Thomascourt, [illegible].
" Honora ny Dermodle, pardon, [illegible].
" John, livery to daughter of, [illegible].
" Loghlyn, pardon, 7729, [illegible].
" Maurice, pardon, [illegible].
" Murtagh, pardon, [illegible].
" Noyne bane, pardon, [illegible].
" Philip, pardon, [illegible].
" Rich., pardon, [illegible].
" Shane m'Thomas, pardon, [illegible].
" Susanna ny De, pardon, [illegible].
" Thady, license to, 81.
" Thomas, pardon, [illegible].
" Tho., lease of wines impost, [illegible].
" Wm., merchant, [illegible].
" Wm., pardon, [illegible], [illegible], [illegible], [illegible].
" alias Harve, Wm., pardon, [illegible].
Duffcarrig co. Cork (Dunrarrig, co. Kerry?), [illegible]-74.
Duffelonry (co. Long.?), [illegible].
Duffe, Ardell, pardon, [illegible].
" Unlo fitz Edmond, pardon, [illegible].
" Conbonachie Fitzdavid, pardon, [illegible].
" Dermod, pardon, 1417.
" Donnoghe, pardon, [illegible].
" Edm., pardon, [illegible], [illegible].
" Fallo, pardon, [illegible].
" Falye, pardon, [illegible].
" Farrye, pardon, [illegible].
" Fayle, pardon, [illegible].
" Gerald, pardon, [illegible], [illegible].
" Henry, pardon, [illegible], [illegible].
" Hugh m'Owen, pardon, [illegible].
" Honora, pardon, [illegible].
" Inshe m'Edmond, pardon, [illegible].
" James, pardon, [illegible].
" James, pardon, [illegible], [illegible].
" John, pardon, [illegible].
Duffe, Laghlen, [illegible].
" Laughlen, murder of, [illegible].
" Laurencius or Laughlen, pardon, [illegible].
" Maurice, pardon, [illegible].
" Michael, 1827.
" Morietagh, pardon, [illegible].
" Mortagh, pardon, [illegible].
" Patrick, pardon, [illegible], [illegible], [illegible], [illegible].
" Philip, pardon, 1571.
" Rich., [illegible].
" Shall m'Edmond, pardon, [illegible].
" Shane, pardon, [illegible].
" Shane m'Thomas and his followers, pardon, [illegible].
" Sheriam, pardon, [illegible].
" Stephen, pardon, [illegible].
" Tuhlowe or Teige, pardon, [illegible].
" Thomas, pardon, [illegible], 1114, [illegible], [illegible].
" Thomas, widow of, [illegible].
" Tirlagh, pardon, [illegible], [illegible].
" William, pardon, 8, 816, [illegible], [illegible], [illegible].
Duffer, co. Ross, [illegible].
" See Duffery, co. Wex.
Dufferin—Diffren—Diffrene—Dufferane—Dufferne—Duffery—Duffrain—Duffryn—Duffrom—Duffrin, co. Down, [illegible], [illegible], [illegible].
" to be made shire ground, [illegible], [illegible].
" comm. to punish rebels, [illegible].
" martial law, [illegible], [illegible], [illegible], [illegible], [illegible], [illegible], [illegible].
" seneschal of, [illegible], [illegible], [illegible].
" governor of, [illegible], [illegible].
Duffery—Duffer—Duffre—Duffree—Duffrie—Duffrin—Duffry, co. Wex., country of, [illegible], [illegible], [illegible], [illegible], [illegible], [illegible], [illegible], [illegible], [illegible], [illegible], [illegible].
" custom of land, [illegible] granted to earl of Ormond, [illegible].
" martial law in, [illegible].
" chief surgeon of, [illegible].
Duffolem, co. Meath, rectory, [illegible].
Duffoy (co. Tip.?), [illegible].
Duff, Owen, pardon, [illegible].
Duffrain—Duffraine. See Dufferin.
Duffre—Duffree. See Duffery.
Duffrene—Duffrone. See Dufferin.
Duffrie. See Duffery.
Duffrien. See Dufferin.
Duffrin. See Duffery.
Duffry—Duffryn. See Duffery.
Dugan, James, pardon, [illegible].
Duggaine, Diermott m Monlaghlen I, pardon, [illegible].
Dughill, in O'Moloye's country, [illegible]-84.
Dughmore (co. Kilk.?), [illegible].
Dugin, Peter, pardon, [illegible].
Duhallow. See Dowally, Douhall.

INDEX TO FIANTS.—ELIZABETH.

Dulane (co. Cork ?), 6871.
Duhar, co. Cav., 6467.
Duigin, Rory, pardon, 6614.
Duigenan, Patk., pardon, 5169.
Duine, Charles or Cahir, master in Chancery, 6878.
Dukerghan, co. Mayo, 4817.
Duke, Anne, wife of Edw. Loftus, [illegible].
" Edward, 848.
" Eliz., lease, [illegible], 848.
" Henry (afterwards knight), commissions, [illegible], 4684, 4149, 4461, [illegible], [illegible]; sheriff of Cavan, [illegible], [illegible]; sheriff of King's co., [illegible]; grants of land, 476, 848, 4578; leases, 1778, 6043, 6167, [illegible]; surrender, [illegible]; pardon, [illegible]; heirs of, [illegible].
" James, pardon, 6410.
" Mary, wife of Rich. Gyfford, [illegible].
" Rich., pardon, [illegible].
Dukerghan, co. Mayo, 4817.
Dulane, Phelim, pardon, 4169.
Dulany, Wm. m'Mahowy, pardon, 6763.
Dulastowne, co. Meath, 1574.
Dulehontie, More ny, pardon, 5684.
Dulenzie, Murtagh m'Dermodie I., pardon, 6444.
Duleeke—Dewleke—Dewlek—Dowlek—Dowleke—Duelake—Duleke—Dulleke—Dulyeke—Dulyke—(Duleek), co. Meath, 58, 715, [illegible], 1189, 1459; lands in, 153, 4612, 4718.
" monastery of the B. V. M. granted, 140; procurations, 6787.
" priory or cell, leased, 873, 1456–9, [illegible], [illegible], 6425; procurations, 6787.
" manor, 1456–60, 3842, 5864.
" rectory, 1460, 5864.
" college yard, 6482.
" carpenter's tenement, 6423.
" Church, 872, 6423.
" Frank house, 6412.
" Maudlyn meadow, 6423.
" Smyth's meadow, 6423.
Dulen, John a. pardon, 6117.
Dulieghe, Donell m'Owen m'Teig m'Donell, pardon, 6868.
Dullcke. See Duleeke.
Dulig, Owen m'Teig m'Donell, pardon, 6468.
Dulegh, Edm. m'Morish, pardon, 4111.
Dulish, John m'Conoghor, pardon, 6844.
Dulung, William, pardon, 2811.
Dullagh, Florence, [illegible].
Dullaghe, co. Meath, 4683.
Dullane, Andrew, pardon, 2821.
" John, pardon, 3434.
" Richard, felony by, 777.
Dullanie, Wm. oge, pardon, 6784.
Dullany, Dermot m'Wm. pardon, 6763.
" James (alias Brit), pardon, 4032.
" Rich., pardon, 3434.
" Thos., pardon, 3434.
Dullard, James, pardon, 4568, 6706.
" Walter, 1428.
" Wm., pardon, 4351.
Dullarde, Nicholas, pardon, 1318.
Dullardston—Dullardeston—Dullardiston—Dullardstone—Dollardstowne (Dollardstown), co. Kild., 1578, [illegible], 4836, 6234, 6776; rectory, 5361.
Dullardston—Dullardeston—Dullarston (Dollardstown), co. Meath, 803, 453, 1104, 1458, 1513, 4144, 4174, 4786, 4209, 6423, 6425, 6864; manor, 1494.
Dullhame, James, pardon, [illegible].
Dulloghe. See Dullogh.
Dultracke (co. Long. ?), 6838.
Dulyke—Dulyeke. See Duleeke.
Dumalee church (Drumaliss), co. Antrim, 5788.
Dunakyn (co. Mayo), 6017.
Dumalinghe, Uah reoghe ny, pardon, 4687.
Dumaldrum, co. Mon. See Drumaldrum.
Dumamon, co. Gal. See Downe O'Mannan, Downman, Downamaine.
Dumamore, co. Rosc. See Downamane.
Dumanon, co. Wex., 6767.
Dumbalcane (co. Gal. ?), 4872.
Dunbale, co. Gal. or Mayo, 5708.
Dunbaboye (co. Cork ?), 6781.
Dunbecon—Dowbeacon—Downebacane—Downebeacane—Downebeacon—Downebekane (Dunbeacon, co. Cork), 5865, 6288, 3436, 6814–6, 6868.
Dunbell, co. Kilk. See Dowbell.
Dunbeerne (Dunbeirne, co. Lim.), 6171.
Dunbeig, co. Cork, 6871.
Dunbeigh, co. Cork, 6834.
Dunbellan. See Dunboyne.
Dunboige, co. Cork, 6408.
Dunboy—Donboy—Donbwy—Dunbuy, co. Cork, 5662, 6194, 6811, 6878.
Dunboy. See Donbee.
Dunboy (co. Kerry ?), 6676.
Dunboyne—Donboyne—Donboyn—Donboyne—Dunboine—Dunboyn, co. Meath, 1284, 1777, 3439, 3850, 3851, 3843, 4171, 6416, 6478, 6216, 6467, 6777; rectory, 818, 878, 3183, 1169, 1174, 3578, 3441, 6456, 6878.
" baron of, Edmond Butler, commissions, 142, 646–7, 848; injuries to him and his men, 436; pardon, 467; conveyance by, 6445; livery to his heir, 1768.

INDEX TO FIANTS—ELIZABETH.

Dunboyne—baron, James, livery, 1760; commissions, 1846, 2140, 2761; pardon, 2368, [illegible]; pardon at his suit, 2477; lease, 2368; release of recognizances, 6108.
Dunbrin, Queen's co. *See* Dunbrenne.
Dunbro—Donbro—Dunbrowe, co. Dub., [illegible], 1287, 2117, 2864.
Dunbrockily, co. Wat., 6344.
Dunbrody — Donbrodie — Donbrody, co. Wex., 744, 1222, 2422, 6644, 6438.
„ abbey, leased, 1657; possessions of, 2768; granted, 2778, 4047; suit as to, 6684.
„ grange, 1622, 6472.
„ barony, suit as to, 6626.
Dunbrowe. *See* Dunbro.
Dunbullogy, co. Cork. *See* Duntoilligo and Downbolling.
Dunbury (*see* Dunboy), 6511.
Dunbwoge (co. Cork ?), 6628.
Duncannon — Doncannon (Duncannon), co. Wex., 1637; house or fort of, [illegible], 6432.
Duncardie (co. Ross ?), 6728.
Duncastlane, co. Wexm., 6624.
Duncromore—Duncromayne, co. Tip., 6831.
Dunconterohain, co. Sligo, 4666.
Duncormock—Duncormock — Doncormock —Doncormoke—Donkormik—Downe Cormocke (Duncormick), co. Wex., 366, 2688, 3342, 4894, 5840, 6747; rectory, 4666, 6428.
Duncref—Dunmreef alias Dunkeyt—Dunrial—Dunmroffle, co. Kild., 873, 2214, 4884, 6728.
Duncrowe (Duncrum), co. Antrim, 6436.
Duncrowe (little), co. Antrim, 6632.
Dundas, Gerrott, pardon, 6472.
„ John, „ 6604.
Dundalk—Dondalk—Dondalke—Donndalke—Dundalke, co. Louth, 323, 1576, 1788; same rights granted to other towns, 1480, 1600; road to, 5946; rent payable at, 2168, 4561; treaty with Tyrone at, 6051, 5773, 6084, 6137; garrison, 6284.
„ bailiffs, commissions, 881, 2117, 5442.
„ merchants, 4017, 6497.
„ inhabitants pardoned, 4017.
„ rectory, 3412.
„ hospital of S. Leonard, 162.
„ port or haven, 56-1, 58, 63, 6433.
„ „ exportation, 4689.
„ „ illegal exports, 3080.
„ customs leased, 2073.
„ „ on wine leased, 4314.
„ collector of wine duty, 1466, 3613, 4228, 6861, 6041.
„ controller of wine duty, 3144, 3628, 4253, 5617.
Dundareirke, co. Cork. *See* Downdearyke.
Dundavan, co. Cav. *See* Downedavane.
Dundeady, co. Cork. *See* Dondady and Downedeady.
Dundermot, co. Ross. *See* Dondermot.
Dunderrow, co. Cork. *See* Downderowe.
Dundirig—Downdirich, co. Cork, 6427, 6469, 6671.
Dundishort, co. Kerry, 6466.
Dundonagh, co. Mon. *See* Downdonaght.
Dundonnell, co. Westm. *See* Dondonnell.
Dundrames, co. Mon. *See* Downdram.
Dundrum, co. Down. *See* Dondrom.
Dundrum, co. Dub. *See* Dondrom.
Dundrum—Dondrom—Dondrome — Dunedrome, co. Tip., 3384, 4371, 6442, 4894, 6792.
Dune (co. Lim. ?), 6511.
Dune, Barnaby, pardon, 6744.
„ Wm., pardon, 6168.
Duneany, co. Kild. *See* Downeny.
Dunekanny (Dungany), co. Meath, 1490.
Dunemewe (co. Gal. ?), 4707.
Dunen, King's co., 4447.
Duneshead—Duneshade, co. Cork, [illegible], 6644.
Duneychoyn, co. Sligo, 4676.
Dunfert—Donfort—Donferte — Donferte—Dunferte, co. Kild., 1617, 2867, 3117, 3144, 3444, [illegible], 4169, [illegible], 4296, 5402, 5745, 6772.
Dunforde. *See* Dunsford.
Dunfore, co. Sligo, [illegible].
Dungall, co. Wex., 3146, 3169.
Dungan, John. *See* Dongan.
Dunganiston (co. Wex. ?), 6644.
Dungannon, co. Tyrone. *See* Donganon.
Dungany, co. Meath. *See* Dunekanny.
Dunganstown, co. Car. *See* Donganston, Dongarstown, Dowganston.
Dunganville, co. Lim. *See* Downeganerwylly.
Dungarron, co. Cork, 6618.
Dungarvan — Dongarvan — Dungarron — Dongarvane — Dowgarvan, co. Kilk., 1626, 1974, 4013, 4287, 4796, 5494, 5796; rectory, 2846.
Dungarvan — Dongarvan — Dongarvaine — Doungarvan, co. Wat., 944, 3747, 3917, 4314, 4189, 4460, 4786, 6477; cottages and gardens in, leased, 664.
„ provost and inhabitants of town and liberties, pardoned, 4318.
„ member of Parliament, 132.
„ captain of, 2317.
„ rectory, 944, 2123.
„ vicar of S. Mary, 792.
„ manor, 4127, 4318.
„ castle, constable of, 60, 61, 184, 714, 789, 658, 664-7, 4128, 4327, 3949, 6059-70, 6314, 6317;

INDEX TO FIANTS—ELIZABETH.

Dungarvan :
constable and warders discharged, 6519 ; vice-constable, 6779.
" house of Augustin friars leased, 526, 2183.
" port, 523.
" " supervisor, 6[illegible].
" " searcher, 6[illegible], 6[illegible].
" collector of wine duty, 1607, 2214, 2446, 4[illegible], 6[illegible], 6[illegible].
" controller of wine duty, [illegible], 4[illegible], 6[illegible].
Dungeeha, co. Lim. See Downgehoe.
Dungervan, co. Cork, 4216.
Dungevin (Dungiven, co. Lderry.), lands, &c., about, 6[illegible].
Dungillen (co. Cork ?), 4709.
Dungolman, co. Westm. See Dongolman.
Dungonyn, co. Cav., 4[illegible].
Dungonle, co. Kilk., 6[illegible].
Dungorvery, co. Cork. See Dongorwey.
Dungrott (co. Tip.?), 5[illegible].
Dungrarie, co. Gal., 4[illegible].
Dungwell (co. Kerry ?), 6[illegible].
Dunhill — Donill — Domill — Dowahill — Downehill—Dowyll, co. Wat., 160, 443, 1[illegible] ; rectory, 2[illegible], 1[illegible].
Dunisheal—Downeshed (Dun na Sead or Baltimore), co. Cork, 4[illegible], 4[illegible].
Dunkerne (co. Kerry ?), 6[illegible].
Dunkellin—Dunkillina—Dunkellyn—Down Kellen, co. Gal, 1413, 4[illegible], 4[illegible] ; manor, [illegible] ; barony, [illegible].
Dunkeran — Donkeron—Dunkieran — Dunkierrain—Doonkeran—Downkerran (Dunkerron, co. Kerry), 2[illegible], 2[illegible], 7[illegible], 6[illegible].
Dunkerran, co. Tip. (Dunkerrin, King's co.), rectory, [illegible].
Dunkerly — Donkerly—Dunkerley, John, sovereign of Naasgarden, 5 ; takes oath of supremacy, [illegible] ; grant of land, [illegible] ; pardon, 1[illegible].
Dunkeroun, co. Kerry. See Dunkeran.
Dunkettle—Dunkiddill— Donkadle — Downkettell—Dowskiddill, co. Cork, 4[illegible], 6[illegible], 6[illegible], 6[illegible], 6[illegible].
Dunkillino. See Dunkellin.
Dunkip, co. Lim. See Dunkypp.
Dunkirl, co. Kilk., 7[illegible], [illegible].
Dunkeyt alias Dunscrull, co. Kildare, 6[illegible].
Dunkyllin, baron of. See Clanrickard, earl of, 6[illegible].
Dunkyne (co. Kerry ?), 6[illegible].
Dunkypp—Donkipp—Doonkippe (Dunkip), co. Lim., 1[illegible], 5[illegible], 6[illegible].
Dunlavan — Donlavan — Dunlevan — Dunlovan — Dunlowan — Downlowane (Dunlavan, co. Wick.), 1414, 5[illegible], 6[illegible].
Dunlavan :
" prebendary of, 1[illegible], [illegible], [illegible], [illegible], [illegible], [illegible], [illegible].
Dunlechny, co. Car. See Donloyckney.
Dunleere — Dunleire — Donler — Donlere — Donlyer (Dunleer), co. Louth, 14[illegible], 17[illegible], [illegible], [illegible].
Dunleever, co. Meath. See Donlyvers.
Dunletey (Doon, co. Lim.), prebend, 84.
Dunlere. See Dunleere.
Dunlo, co. Gal. See Downelowe.
Dunlon, co. Sligo, 5[illegible].
Dunluce—Donluce (co. Antrim), castle, surrender, 6[illegible].
" constable, 4[illegible] ; slain, [illegible].
" Scots in, [illegible].
Dunmaddigan, co. Meat. See Drumaddegan.
Dunmaghen—Donmaghin—Donmaghan—Downmaghan—Downemaghan—Downemaghine (Dunmahon), co. Cork, 294, 2[illegible], 7[illegible], 2[illegible], 5[illegible], 6[illegible] ; rectory, 1[illegible], 5[illegible].
Dunmain, co. Wex. See Donmayn, Donaghmayne, and Donnaghmaine.
Dunmanoge, co. Kild. See Donmahannock.
Dunmanwis, co. Cork. See Downmanus, Downmanwish.
Dunmanway, co. Cork. See Donmaynewny, Donmanvey, Dwonmanewey, Dwnemanewaie.
Dunmeellan. See Dunmoylen.
Dunmore, co. Donegal. See Donmore.
Dunmore—Donmore—Donmore M'Crysho—Downmore, co. Gal., 1[illegible], 147[illegible]-4, 1[illegible], [illegible].
" house of Augustin friars leased, [illegible].
" barony, [illegible]. See also Bermingham (lord), country of.
Dunmore—Donmore—Downmore, co. Kilk., 1[illegible], 1[illegible], [illegible]-4 ; rectory, 1[illegible], [illegible].
Dunmore, co. Wat. See Donmore.
Dunmoylen — Donmoyllen — Domyllen — Don Millino—Dunmoylin—Donmollin—Dunmoillen—Dunmoylin — Doanmoylyn—Dunmoylyne — Downmoylin — Downmoillin — Downmoylin — Downmoylyn (Dunmoylen), co. Lim., [illegible], [illegible], [illegible], [illegible], [illegible], [illegible], [illegible], [illegible], [illegible], [illegible].
" manor, [illegible], [illegible].
" rectory, 5[illegible].
" tughe, [illegible].
Dunmore, vicarage, 64
Dunn, Ellis, pardon, [illegible].
" Wm., pardon, 6777.

INDEX TO FIANTS—ELIZABETH.

[illegible] ([illegible]), co. Kilk., [illegible]. See also [illegible].
[illegible], co. Lim. See [illegible].
[illegible], co. Wexf. See [illegible].
Dun [illegible] Head, co. Cork. See [illegible].
[illegible], co. Sligo, [illegible].
[illegible], [illegible].
[illegible], co. Mayo, [illegible].
[illegible] (co. [illegible] ?), [illegible].
[illegible]. See [illegible], co. Wexf.
[illegible] (co. Cork), [illegible].
[illegible]. See [illegible], co. Wexf.
[illegible], co. Kerry. See [illegible].
[illegible], co. Cork, [illegible].
[illegible]. See [illegible].
[illegible]—[illegible] ([illegible]), co. Gal., [illegible], [illegible].
[illegible], co. Gal., [illegible].
[illegible] — [illegible] — [illegible] — [illegible] — [illegible] — [illegible]:
" lord of, Christopher [illegible], commissioner, [illegible], [illegible], [illegible]; wardship of heir, [illegible].
" lord of, Patrick, wardship, [illegible]; commissioner, [illegible], [illegible], [illegible], [illegible], [illegible]; grant of a wardship, [illegible]; pardon at his suit, [illegible].
" lands of, [illegible].
[illegible], co. Antrim, lands of, [illegible].
[illegible] — [illegible] ([illegible]), co. Down, rectory, [illegible], [illegible].
[illegible] — [illegible] — [illegible] — [illegible] — [illegible] — [illegible] — [illegible] — [illegible] — [illegible] — [illegible] — [illegible] ([illegible]), co. Meath, [illegible], [illegible], [illegible], [illegible], [illegible].
" [illegible] farm, &c. [illegible].
" manor, [illegible].
" rectory, [illegible], [illegible], [illegible], [illegible], [illegible], [illegible], [illegible], [illegible], [illegible], [illegible], [illegible], [illegible], [illegible].
[illegible]—[illegible] ([illegible]), co. Dub., [illegible], [illegible].
[illegible]—[illegible]—[illegible]—[illegible]—[illegible], co. Dub., [illegible], [illegible], [illegible], [illegible], [illegible], [illegible], [illegible], [illegible], [illegible].
[illegible], co. Down. See [illegible].
[illegible], co. Cork. See [illegible].
[illegible], co. Sligo, [illegible].
[illegible] (co. Kerry ?), [illegible].
[illegible], co. Kilk., [illegible].
[illegible], co. Cork, [illegible].
[illegible] alias O'[illegible], Donogh, pardon, [illegible].
[illegible] (co. Wick. ?), [illegible].
[illegible], co. Mon., [illegible].
[illegible] (co. Gal. or Mayo), [illegible].
[illegible], [illegible].
[illegible], Richard, [illegible].
[illegible] (co. Kerry or Cork), [illegible].
[illegible]. See [illegible].
[illegible], [illegible].
[illegible] ([illegible]), co. Tip., vicarage, [illegible].
[illegible], co. Wexf., [illegible].
[illegible] — [illegible] ([illegible], co. Tip. ?), [illegible], [illegible].
[illegible]—[illegible]—[illegible], John, baron of the Exchequer, [illegible], [illegible], [illegible], [illegible], [illegible]; third baron of the Exchequer, [illegible].
[illegible], co. Lim. See [illegible].
[illegible], co. Tip., [illegible].
[illegible], co. Lim. See [illegible].
[illegible]. See Durrow, King's co.
[illegible] ([illegible]), co. Mon., [illegible].
[illegible] (co. Tip. ?), [illegible].
[illegible], co. Long., [illegible].
(Durrow)— [illegible] — [illegible] — [illegible] — Durrow — [illegible] — [illegible], King's co., [illegible], [illegible], [illegible].
" priory, leased, [illegible]; granted, [illegible].
" " prior pardoned, [illegible].
" rectory, [illegible].
[illegible]—Durrow, in Upper Ossory, Queen's co., [illegible], [illegible], [illegible].
[illegible]. See Durrow, King's co.
[illegible] (Durrus), co. Cork, vicarage, [illegible].
[illegible] island, co. Cork. See [illegible].
[illegible], rectory, [illegible].
[illegible], co. Long., [illegible].
[illegible]. See [illegible].
[illegible] (co. Kerry ?), [illegible].
[illegible]. See [illegible].
[illegible], co. Cav., [illegible].
[illegible], John, commissioner, [illegible].
" Mr., bearer of message from lord deputy, [illegible].
" Rich., usher of the Exchequer, [illegible]; lease, [illegible]; grant of a wardship, [illegible].
[illegible], Neill and [illegible], pardon, [illegible].
[illegible], Tho., pardon, [illegible].
[illegible], [illegible], pardon, [illegible].
[illegible] alias [illegible], [illegible], pardon, [illegible].
[illegible], John, pardon, [illegible].
[illegible] ([illegible], co. Kerry), [illegible], [illegible].
[illegible], [illegible] m'[illegible] I, pardon, [illegible].
[illegible], Owen, pardon, [illegible].
[illegible], co. Cork (perhaps [illegible]), [illegible].
[illegible], co. Lim., [illegible].
[illegible], co. [illegible] or Gal., [illegible].
[illegible], Margaret ny, pardon, [illegible].
[illegible], Dermod m'Donogh I, pardon, [illegible].

INDEX TO FIANTS—ELIZABETH.

Dwir, Gwilansil m'Teige y, pardon, 4[illegible]7.
Dwlagh, Edm. fitz Gerrott, pardon, [illegible].
Dwlagh, Gerrott oge, pardon, [illegible].
Dwlagh, James m'Gerrott, pardon, [illegible].
Dwle, Donell m'Donogh y, pardon, [illegible].
Dwlig, Shane m'Teige m'Donell, pardon, [illegible].
Dwne (co. Gal. ?), [illegible].
Dwnaghey, David m'Tho. y, pardon, [illegible].
Dwnamanwele (Dunmanway), co. Cork, [illegible].
Dwnla, Dermod m'Donell I, pardon, [illegible].
Dwnlnshew, co. Kild., [illegible].
Dwn[illegible]rran, co. Gal., [illegible].
Dwolie, Morish, pardon, [illegible].
Dwrry[illegible], co. Cork, [illegible].
Dwsker, Walter, pardon to widow of, [illegible].
Dwyer, Philip fitz Edm. of Clonculine, and others of the same, pardoned, [illegible].
Dwygan, Peter, pardon, [illegible].
Dwygin, Denis, pardon, [illegible].
Dwyle, Una nye, pardon, [illegible].
Dwyn, John, pardon, [illegible].
Dwynagho (co. Kerry ?), [illegible].
Dwynlowe, co. Wex., [illegible].
Dwyne, [ ] oge, pardon, [illegible].
Dwynyne, co. Cork, [illegible].
Dyconged, co. Down, [illegible].
Dyganer, co. Meath, [illegible].
Dyerland at Trim, co. Meath, [illegible].
Dygon, co. Lim., [illegible].
Dylie, John ny, pardon, [illegible].
Dylion. *See* Dillon.
Dymallagh, Donogho, pardon, [illegible].
Dymerisson, co. Kilk., [illegible].
Dymynay (co. Kilk. ?), [illegible].
Dyn, Dermot, premises of, [illegible].
Dyngam Oure. *See* Dinghain more.
Dynghain, King's co. (*see* Dingan), [illegible].
Dyngin begge. *See* Dinghain begge.
Dyngle—Dyngle ne Coyne. *See* Dingle.
Dyngynyvryvne. *See* Dengynyvryvne.
Dynky, Wm. m'Thomas, pardon, 4[illegible].
Dynowle, Donell, pardon, [illegible].
Dyreconell. *See* Derriconnell.
Dyreconnagh, Queen's co., [illegible].
Dyrenewrybye, King's co., [illegible].
Dyrenmooly, King's co., [illegible].
Dyrentonie (Derrintonny), co. Mon., [illegible].
Dyrevold. *See* Dirrevoda.
Dyriam, Gerald, pardon, [illegible].
Dyrealle (co. Long. ?), [illegible].
Dyrpatrick—Dyrpatryck. *See* Derpatrick.
Dyrraghanick, co. Tip., [illegible].
Dyrraghenard (Derrykinard), co. Mon., [illegible].
Dyrrandarragh (co. Cork ?), [illegible].
Dyrre (co. Cav.), [illegible].
Dyrre, Queen's co., [illegible].
Dyrreaghlin (Darraghlan), co. Mon., [illegible].
Dyrrearowne, Queen's co., [illegible].
Dyrreclone, co. Mon., [illegible].
Dyrrecrynard (Derrykinard ?), co. Mon. [illegible].
Dyrregart (Derrygart ?), co. Kild., [illegible].
Dyrregashell (Derrygonnelly), co. Mon., [illegible].
Dyrrehallaghe (Derryhallagh), co. Mon., [illegible].
Dyrrekowle, co. Mayo, [illegible].
Dyrrelaryne, Queen's co., [illegible].
Dyrrelawycke (Derrylevick), co. Mon., [illegible].
Dyrrelanna. *See* Derryleckan.
Dyrremohill (Derryvohil, co. Cav.), [illegible].
Dyrren (Derrin or Derren, Queen's co.), [illegible].
Dyrrenaere—Dyrremakre, Queen's co., [illegible], [illegible].
Dyrremeelaragh (King's co.), [illegible].
Dyrrenoyard (Derrynargel), co. Mon., [illegible].
Dyrrenegarragh, co. Westm., [illegible].
Dyrrenehinshe (Derrenhinsh), co. Mon., [illegible].
Dyrrenehollagh, co. Monaghan, [illegible].
Dyrrenekra. *See* Dyrremacra.
Dyrreneshyre (Derrymacrora ?), Queen's co., [illegible].
Dyrrevevel (Derravel), co. Mon., [illegible].
Dyrreryane, co. Mon., [illegible].
Dyrrewara, co. Mon., [illegible].
Dyrrewylliam, co. Cork, [illegible].
Dyrri, co. Gal., [illegible].
Dyrrie (co. Cork ?), [illegible], [illegible].
Dyrrine, co. Kerry, [illegible].
Dyrrinie (Derreen ?), co. Kerry, [illegible].
Dyrrmore, co. Kild., [illegible].
Dyrrwarge, co. Kild., [illegible].
Dyrry, co. Cork, [illegible], [illegible].
Dyrry (Derry), co. Down, [illegible], [illegible].
Dyrry, co. Lim., [illegible].
Dyrry (co. Long. ?), [illegible].
Dyrrychrosane, co. Ros., [illegible].
Dyrryconnell (Derryconnell), co. Cork, [illegible].
Dyrrycrossan. *See* Derricrossan.
Dyrrye (Derry), co. Mon., [illegible].
Dyrrygarrife (co. Cork ?), [illegible].
Dyrrykyrekhan (Derrygarraghan, co. Cav. ?), [illegible].
Dyrrylane (Derrylahan), Queen's co., [illegible].
Dyrryphaten (Derryphatten, co. Rosc.), [illegible].
Dyrryumloghe (*see* Derryumloght), [illegible].
Dyrryvicklaghny (*see* Derrymacloghny), [illegible].
Dyrryville, King's co., [illegible].
Dyrrymor, co. Kerry, [illegible].
Dysart, co. Kilk. *See* Disert begg.
Dysart, co. Louth. *See* Disert.
Dysart, Queen's co. *See* Dissert, Dysert.
Dysart, co. Westm. *See* Disert.
Dysartbeagh, Queen's co. *See* Dysertbeg.
Dysarte—Disarte (Dysart), co. Kilk., [illegible]; rectory, [illegible], [illegible].
Dysartenos, Queen's co. *See* Disertenos.

INDEX TO FIANTS.—ELIZABETH.

Dyrrigallan, Queen's co. See Dyrrigallyne.
Dyrrarmore, co. Kilk. See Disartmoran.
Dysert—Dysert, co. Clare, 1541, 4761.
Dysert, co. Gal., [illegible].
Dysert, co. Kerry. See Desertes, Disirt.
Dysert, co. Lim. See Diserte.
Dysert — Deserte — Diserte — Dysarte— Dysert — Dizarte (Dysart in par., Dysart-enos), Queen's co., 196, 1685, [illegible], [illegible], [illegible].
Dysert—Dysarte, co. Westm., [illegible], 917.
Dysarthish — Desertshelp — Disertshelane (Dysartbeagh), Queen's co., 1414, [illegible], xxxi.
Dysarte. See Dysert, Queen's co.
Dysarte (Dysart), co. Rosc., rectory, [illegible].
Dysarte. See Dysert, co. Westm.
Dysert gallyne—Disert gallyn—Disertgallen —Disert Galline (Dysartgallen), Queen's co., [illegible], [illegible]; rectory, 576, 1118. See also Galleyn, Galyn.
Dysarthoran (co. Meath ?), rectory, [illegible].
Dysert. See Dysert, co. Clare.
Dysert. See Dysert, Queen's co.
Dyrregalaraghe (co. Leit. ?), 4788.
Dyxson, William, assignee of, 1663.

Ea, Ever m'Donell I., pardon, [illegible].
„ Wm. m'Dermod I., pardon, 2941.
„ See O'Hea.
Eaber Ros—Eabber Ros, brush (co. Donegal), [illegible], [illegible].
Eadden (co. Sligo ?), 6818.
Eadestown, co. Kild. See Edeston.
Eadintyroclare (Edenticlare), co. Cav., [illegible].
Eagar, co. Mayo, 1581.
Eaghe, lough (Lough Neagh), 1620.
Eaghan, Dermot and John m'Teig, and Donald m'Mortertagh Y, pardon, [illegible].
Ealleston, co. Meath, 14[illegible].
Eallie, James m'Shane, pardon, [illegible].
Eallie, Milles fitz John, pardon, [illegible].
Eally. See Ely.
Ealy, Morish m'Shane, pardon, [illegible].
Eaman, Helena, Anor, and Shily nyn, pardon, 4111.
Eanagh, co. Sligo, [illegible].
Eanagher, co. Cork, [illegible].
Eancalis, Donell m'Teig oge, pardon, [illegible].
Earenagh, Randall, pardon, [illegible].
Earlis (co. Lim. ?), [illegible].
Earles meadow, Ross, co. Wex., 1172, [illegible].
Earlestowne—Erlestowne—Erleston — Edgton (Earlstown, co. Kilk.), [illegible], [illegible]; rectory, [illegible], [illegible].
Earlsgrove, co. Kilk. See Erles Grove.
Earl's meadow (co. Ant.), [illegible].
Earne, lough, (Erne), [illegible], [illegible].
Earne river (Erne), fishing of, [illegible].
Earrell, Shane m'Fergananim, pardon, [illegible].
Earston alias Ballyraw (co. Kilk. ?), [illegible].
Easke (co. Sligo ?), [illegible].
Eastoyn, co. Gal., [illegible].
Easterrow, co. Rosc. See Isserowe.
Eastkerany—East Kenrane—Eastcherane —Ester Kerane (Carnes, East ?), co. Meath, [illegible], [illegible], [illegible], [illegible].
Eastmeath co. See Meath.
Easton, John, pardon, [illegible].
Eaton, George, pardon, [illegible].
Eaye or Saye, Rich., pardon, [illegible].
E'buarke, Hubert boy, pardon, [illegible].
o Boye, Margaret wyne, pardon, [illegible].
Ebroghan, Terence, pardon, [illegible].
E Callough, Wm. m'Teige, pardon, [illegible].
Ecarnghan, Emon Condon, pardon, [illegible].
Ecarryn, Dermot, pardon, [illegible].
Ecabe, Edm., pardon, [illegible].
Ecclesia Magna (Kilmore, co. Cav.), [illegible].
Ecclesiastical Causes, high commissioners for, [illegible], [illegible], [illegible], [illegible], [illegible], [illegible], [illegible].
„ commission for province of Armagh, [illegible].
„ commission for Munster and part of Leinster, [illegible].
„ commission for Munster, [illegible], [illegible], [illegible], [illegible], [illegible], [illegible].
„ commission for Connaught and Thomond, [illegible], [illegible].
„ commission for co. Westmeath, [illegible].
„ powers of commissioners, [illegible], [illegible].
„ high commission, principal register, [illegible], [illegible], [illegible], [illegible], [illegible].
„ high commission, pursuivant, [illegible].
„ high commission, collector of fines, [illegible], [illegible].
„ high commission, marshal or gaoler, [illegible], [illegible], [illegible].
„ courts, appeals from, [illegible].
„ courts, local, dominated by un...ful tenure, [illegible].
„ obedience of people of Carrickfergus, [illegible].
Eccleston, Tristram, constable Dublin castle, [illegible].
Echoggie, Maller m'Edward, pardon, [illegible].
„ Teige m'Brien, pardon, [illegible].
Echons, Arte, pensioner, [illegible].
Echamper—Eschamper, Gerald, pardon, [illegible], [illegible].
Echoyn, Shane m'Teig, pardon, [illegible].
Ecoggie, John or Shane m'Edm., attainted, [illegible], [illegible].
„ Rich. m'Edm., attainted, [illegible], [illegible], [illegible].

INDEX TO FIANTS—ELIZABETH.

Ecortan, Morish m'Shane, pardon, [illegible].
" Boris m'Owen, pardon, [illegible].
Ecorwayne, Shane m'Teig, pardon, [illegible].
Ecoyne, James m'Teig, pardon, [illegible].
Edalagh, Shane beg, pardon, [illegible].
Edallagh, John fitz Donogh, pardon, [illegible].
Eddendery—Eddenderrie. See Edenderry.
Eddergowle, co. Gal., [illegible].
Eden, co. Antrim. See Edengreene.
Edenakeran, co. Cav. See Edenaferan.
Edengowanell, co. Down (see Ballyedenaghconle), [illegible].
Edenburte (Edenburgh), co. Cav., [illegible].
Edenderry — Edenderie — Eddenderrie — Eddendery—Edindery, King's co., [illegible], [illegible], [illegible], [illegible]; grants, [illegible], [illegible].
Edenferan (Edenaferan, co. Mon.), [illegible].
Edengreene (Eden), co. Ant., [illegible].
Edenmore—Edyne more, co. Leit., [illegible], [illegible].
Edennis, Owen m'Donlaer, pardon, [illegible].
Edenport (co. Cav. ?), [illegible].
Edenickey (co. Cav. ?), [illegible].
Edenticlare, co. Cav. See Eadintyclare.
Edenirilleck, co. Down (see Ballyedentrilleke), [illegible].
Edergole, co. Mon., [illegible], [illegible].
Edeston—Edyston (Eadestown), co. Kild., [illegible], [illegible].
Edgerton. See Egerton.
Edgworth, Edward, preacher, [illegible].
Edinderry. See Edenderry.
Edirtea Amnaic—Edirtealmmaa, co. Gal., [illegible], [illegible].
Edmonds, Pierce, grant, [illegible].
Edmondston (Edmondstown), co. Dub., [illegible].
Edmonston (Edmondstown, co. Westm.), [illegible].
Edmund burye, slain in rebellion (co. Mayo), [illegible].
" Duffe's country, co. Wex., [illegible], [illegible], [illegible].
" macteagh, attainted (co. Kerry), [illegible].
" oge of Brettfieldstown, co. Cork, [illegible].
" oge of Killyshowragh, co. Lim., [illegible].
" reagh of Kinnalegh, [illegible], [illegible].
" Honora ny, pardon, [illegible].
" Joan ny, pardon, [illegible].
" Katherine nyne, pardon, [illegible].
" Margaret ny, pardon, [illegible].
" Morreen ny, pardon, [illegible].
" Onora ny Dowinke, pardon, [illegible].
" Sawe ny, pardon, [illegible].
" Shane oge m'Shane, pardon, [illegible].
" oge, Ellen ny, pardon, [illegible].
Education, cognizance of, by ecclesiastical commission, [illegible].
Edwif, country (see Idough), [illegible], [illegible].
Edenmore (Edenmore, co. Leit. ?), [illegible].
Edwards, Rich., clerk of the pleas of the Exchequer, [illegible], [illegible], [illegible], [illegible], [illegible]; third baron, [illegible].
Edwards, Dionysius, [illegible].
" Tho., [illegible], [illegible].
" Wm., sheriff of Waterford, [illegible]; pardon, [illegible].
Edynemore. See Edenmore.
Edyston. See Edeston.
Eels, customary payment in, [illegible], [illegible].
Effingham, lord Howard of, [illegible].
Egallevan, Donell m'Connor, pardon, [illegible].
Egane, Rob., pardon, [illegible].
Egarran, Wm., pardon, [illegible].
Egerton—Edgerton—Egirton:
" Arthur, pardon, [illegible], [illegible].
" Charles, constable of Carrickfergus castle, [illegible], [illegible]; pardon, [illegible]; comm., [illegible], [illegible].
" John, pardon, [illegible].
" Rich., surgeon, [illegible].
" Silvester, registrar of faculties, [illegible].
" Symon, pardon, [illegible].
Egerstown, co. Meath, [illegible].
Egillin O'Roseie. See Eglian O'Roseie.
Eglishe, co. Wat., chapel, [illegible], [illegible].
Eglishecomane, co. Wat., [illegible], [illegible].
Eglishe ne gayly — Eglishe ne gallie—Eglishe ne gally, (Aglish), co. Wat., [illegible], [illegible].
Eglys O'Rosyre. See Eglise O'Roseie.
Eghome, co. Kilk., [illegible].
Eghtureghowe, John m'Connor, pardon, [illegible].
Eglingham, Charles, lease, [illegible], [illegible].
Egirton. See Egerton.
Eglan, Edm. m'Tho., pardon, [illegible], [illegible].
Eglanny, Cahir, [illegible].
Eglanne, Arthur m'Donagh, pardon, [illegible].
" John, pardon, [illegible].
" Teige m'Donagh, pardon, [illegible].
Egleaney, Donald O'Boyn, pardon, [illegible].
Eglesh. See Eglishe.
Eglenehan, Shane m'Donagh, pardon, [illegible].
Egline, Donogh m'Donell, pardon, [illegible].
Eglis, co. Kerry, [illegible].
Eglis (co. Ross. ?), [illegible].
Eglise O'Roseie—Eglys O'Rosyre (perhaps Iverus), co. Lim., [illegible]; rectory, [illegible], [illegible].
Eglish, co. Lim., [illegible].
Eglishe, co. Gal., [illegible].
Eglishe—Eglesh (Eglish, Queen's co.), [illegible], [illegible].
Egno, Fair., pardon, [illegible].
Egowle, Donogh m'Cahir, pardon, [illegible].
" Thady m'Cahir, pardon, [illegible].
Ehalueen, Tho. m'Wm., pardon, [illegible].
Eharkine (co. Cork or Lim.), [illegible].

INDEX TO FIANTS—ELIZABETH.

Ehigan, John, pardon, 4626.
Ehowlaghan, Connor m'Teige, pardon, [illegible].
Ehyreconnaght. See Iohar Connaght.
Eire, Rob. See Eyre.
Eighgian, Donogh, pardon, 5844.
Eight acre field, Fothard, 4894.
Eiltirconnaghty. See Iohar Connaght.
Eikiffe, Richard m'Donogh, pardon, 4449.
Eiran, Tho., brigantine, 6790.
Eirke—Eyrke (Erke, co. Kilk.), rectory, 6493.
" vicar of, 1771.
Ekenlan, Terrilagh, pardon, [illegible].
Elalogo, Dormod m'Teig, pardon, 5274.
Elagh, co. Donegal. See Iligh.
Elan, Tho. m'Wm., pardon, 1284.
Elankarwell—Elankarvell, co. Clare, [illegible], 4874.
Elanhakyon, co. Clare, [illegible], 4871.
Elanbrasey, co. Wat., 5864.
Elanykono (co. Wat.?), 1[illegible].
Elarike, Wm. m'Edm. m'Owen, pardon, 1871.
Elasche, James, pardon, [illegible].
" See also Desmond.
Ele. See Ely.
Eleanaghanagho or Insula Canonicorum, (see Canon Island), 3434.
Eleighane, Donald m'David, pardon, 5783.
Elenbeyre, Sawe ayre, pardon, 4674.
Elenegor, [illegible]. See Glenogor.
Elerdeny—Elerdyne (King's or Queen's co.), [illegible], 1064.
Elestone. See Elleyston.
Eleteran (co. Clare?), 6514.
Elfordstown, co. Cork. See Ellfordston.
Elfyn—Elfinn. See Elphin.
Ele O'Carroll. See Ely.
Elgin, Garald m'Wm., pardon, 4644.
Eli Karroll. See Ely.
Elingirile (Elinguirty), co. Tip., manor of, 2160.
Eliot. See Elliot.
Eliscranaghe (co. Gal. or Mayo), 4451.
Eliston. See Elleyston.
Elkyn, Reginald, searcher of Wexford, 5064.
Ellagh (Elly), co. Mayo, [illegible].
Ellanbrwy, co. Lim., 4175.
Ellane (co. Kerry?), 2461.
Ellanramore, co. Tip., 6708.
Ellard (co. Kilk.?), 2[illegible].
Elleighton. See Ellisdon.
Ellerstary (co. Gal.?), 4071.
Ellenevarde, co. Lim., [illegible].
Elles. See Ellis.
Elletonreade. See Ellistown Rede.
Elleyston—Eleston—Eliston—Elyston, co. Kild., 491, 3901, 6681.
Ellfordston (Elfordstown, co. Cork), 6477.
Ellice, Roger, pardon, [illegible].
Ellinaghbroche, co. Ross., [illegible].
Elliot—Elliott—Eliot—Elyot—Ellyott:
" Humphrey, pardon, 4691.
" John, baron of the Exchequer, 4384, 5045; comns., 4482, 5713, 6267; grant, 5742.
" Owen, lease, 5976.
" Rob., grant, 5404.
" Thomas, leases, 611, 1348, 1434, 5944, 6[illegible]; surrender, 1[illegible]; comns., [illegible]; pardon, [illegible]; master gunner, 6[illegible].
" William, searcher, [illegible].
Ellis—Elles, John, pardon, 5[illegible].
" Nich., 5015.
" Patrick, pardon, [illegible], [illegible].
" William, 1104, [illegible].
Elliston (Ellistown), co. Dub., 1[illegible].
Elliston Rede—Ellestonreade, co. Meath, [illegible], 4153, 4168, 4[illegible].
Elphin. See Elphin.
Ellton—Elltown. See Ellton.
Elltonstown—Ellwardston. See Elverston.
Elly, co. Mayo. See Ellagh.
Elly I Karroll. See Ely.
Ellyne, Sawe ayre, pardon, [illegible].
Ellyott. See Elliot.
Elmer, Nich., 6[illegible]. See Aylmer.
Eloghe, Teig m'Owen, pardon, [illegible].
Elonkyne (co. Mayo?), 4[illegible].
Eloyne, Donell, pardon, [illegible].
Elphin—Elphinn—Elfyn—Elfinn—Elfyn—Olfine—Olfinne—Olfynne, co. Ross., 3[illegible], [illegible], [illegible].
" abbey, possessions granted, [illegible].
" monastery of S. Dominic, leased, 5161, [illegible].
" house of friars, leased, 3484, 5108.
" diocese of, 2[illegible].
" possessions of bishop, [illegible], [illegible].
" bishop John Lynche, 6131; commissions, 4170, 6722, 6715, 6132, [illegible], [illegible].
Elton—Eltown—Ellton—Elltown (Elton), co. Lim., 4[illegible], [illegible], 6[illegible], [illegible].
Elonvarrye (Queen's co.?), 6[illegible].
Elvanmoney, co. Clare, 4[illegible].
Elverston — Elverstone — Elwardston — Elvalstone—Elwardstone—Elwardistowne—Elwardiston—Elwertstone (Elverstown, co. Kild.), 1[illegible], [illegible], [illegible], 4[illegible], [illegible], [illegible], 6[illegible].
Elvoy, co. Meat. See Nairn, [illegible].
Elvonke, co. Tip., [illegible].
Elwardston—Elwardistowne—Elwertston. See Elverston.

INDEX TO FIANTS.—ELIZABETH.

Ely—Ely O'Carroll—Ely I Kearowll—Eally—Eli Karroll—Elle O'Carroll—Elle—Elly I Karroll (the country of O'Carroll in King's co.), [illegible], 1280, 2778, [illegible], [illegible], 6782, 4474, [illegible], [illegible], [illegible], 4141, [illegible], [illegible]; captain of, [illegible], 374; to be made shire ground, 3783; surrendered by O'Carroll, [illegible]; granted to him, [illegible]; martial law, 4119, 6782.
Ely, James fitz Morogh I, pardon, [illegible].
Elyot. See Elliot.
Elyston. See Ellerystone.
Emagher, Hugh and Teig m'Donell m'Teig, pardon, [illegible].
Emalaghe. See Emelagh.
Emalaghmore (co. Rosc. ?), church, [illegible].
Emale (see Imayle), [illegible].
Embearkan, co. Cork, [illegible].
Emelagh — Emalaghe (Queen's co.), [illegible], [illegible]; grant, [illegible], [illegible].
Emelaghyshill. See Emlaghyshell.
Emelly—Emellie. See Emly.
Emelye (Emlaghmore), co. Gal., 6138-1.
Emlagh, co. Clare, [illegible].
Emlagh, co. Rosc. See Imlaghe.
Emlagh Beg, co. Rosc. See Ymolaghbegg.
Emlaghfad, co. Sligo. See Ymlaghfaddie and Ewlaghfadde.
Emlaghmore, co. Gal. See Emelye.
Emlaghmagree, co. Rosc. See Ymolaghmygry.
Emlaghyshell — Emelaghyshill — Imlaghyshell, co. Sligo, [illegible], [illegible], [illegible].
Emlevegger — Imlevegger (Emlybeg ?), co. Mayo, [illegible].
Emly — Emelly — Emellie, co. Tip., to be made shire ground, 2734.
 " diocese, [illegible], 1643, [illegible], 6412.
 " dean of, [illegible].
 " archdeacon of, [illegible], [illegible].
 " See Imily, Imemely.
Emlybeg, co. Mayo. See Emlevegger.
Emmel, King's co. See Lnell.
Emo, Queen's co. See Imo.
Emolan, Dermot m'Knowgher, pardon, [illegible].
Emoloughane, Teig, pardon, [illegible].
Emon, Ellen nyne, pardon, [illegible].
Emongan, Donogh m'Donogh, pardon, 4174.
Emoroughowe, Connor and Murtagh, pardon, [illegible].
Emosie, Dermod m'Finin, pardon, [illegible].
Emper—Imper—Yemper (co. Westm.), [illegible], 1349, [illegible], [illegible], [illegible], [illegible]; rectory, [illegible].
Emperor, denization of subjects of, [illegible].
Empson, John, pardon, [illegible].
Emy, co. Mon. See Nemore.
Ene, Richard, son of M'Redmond, [illegible].
Enace—Enas—Enes—Eneas:
 " Donell m'Tho., pardon, [illegible].
 " James m'Shane, pardon, [illegible].
Enace—John or Shane m'Tirlagh owre, pardon, [illegible], 6377.
 " Owen m'Teig, pardon, [illegible].
 " Rob., pardon, [illegible].
 " Teige m'Shane, pardon, 6377.
 " Tirlagh m'Shane, pardon, 6377.
 " Wm. m'Tho., pardon, [illegible].
 " See Enasey, Enass, Ennes.
Enacy, Walter fitz Thomas, pardon, [illegible].
Enagh, co. Clare, [illegible], [illegible], 6912.
Enagh, co. Gal., 4914, [illegible].
Enagh (co. Lim. ?), 4479.
Enagh, co. Mon. See Namagh.
Enaghan, King's co. See Eneghan.
Enaghe (co. Mayo ?), [illegible].
Enaghe in Ormond (Nenagh ?), co. Tip., rectory, [illegible].
Enagher (co. Cav. ?), [illegible].
Enaghmore, co. Lim., [illegible].
Enaheren, David roe m'Wm., pardon, [illegible].
Enas—Enase. See Enace.
Enassa, Brian m'Connor m'Shane, attainted, [illegible].
Enasl, Teige m'Shane, pardon, [illegible].
Enasy, Edm. duff m'Donell, pardon, [illegible].
 " See also Enace.
Enbuha, Dermod m'Teig, pardon, [illegible].
Encassance, Donaghie m'Ranie, pardon, [illegible].
Ench, co. Kilk., 1334.
Enchecrwester, co. Kild., [illegible].
Enche in Inistioge, co. Kilk., 1917.
Encorig — Encherigo — Enhorigire, David, pardon, 2444; attainted and his lands granted, [illegible], [illegible], [illegible].
Encrewile, John, pardon, [illegible].
Encrumpain, Tirrelagh, pardon, [illegible].
Enculling, Donald, pardon, [illegible].
Endacloghanolie—Endaghcleogh (King's co. or Kild.), [illegible], 1634.
Endirren, Edw. m'Rory, pardon, [illegible].
Endown, Tho. m'Roric, pardon, [illegible].
Endowne, Meyler, pardon, [illegible].
Endrum, King's co. See Idrowyne.
Ene—Eneraghe. See Inne.
Eneas, Wm., pardon, [illegible].
Eneghan (Enaghan), King's co., [illegible], [illegible].
Eneshowney, co. Lim., [illegible].
Enelan—Eneleyne—Enylian, Amane, pardon, [illegible], [illegible], [illegible], 6317.
Enellane, Teig, [illegible].
Eneryne, Tho. reagh m'Teige, pardon, [illegible].
Enesshoy (recte Enschoy ?—Ennisaoffey), church, [illegible].
Enescoffie (Ennisaoffey, co. Westm.), [illegible].
Enescole—Enesaoe—Enesooe — Enschoe — Enschoy — Enesshoye (Ennisaoffey, co. Westm. ?), 2134, [illegible]; rectory, [illegible], [illegible], 1717, [illegible], [illegible].

INDEX TO FIANTS.—ELIZABETH.

Ennemorthy — Enemorthe — Ennemorley — Ennemorphie. *See* Enniscorthy.
Ennisdale, Tho., pardon, 612.
Ennismorich—Ennyshorick, co. Gal., [illegible], [illegible].
Ennske, Shane m'Teig, pardon, 4918.
Enniskillen. *See* Enniskillen.
Ennskine (Monkstown), co. Cork, [illegible], [illegible].
Enoskey—Enoskoe. *See* Enoscola.
Ennslawnagh. *See* Inaslawnaght.
Enoxe, Rich., pardon, [illegible].
Ennemaglangha, Queen's co., 1817.
Ennstiman. *See* Ennistimon.
Ennsticke—Ennistocka. *See* Inistioke.
Ensalle, Elice oy, pardon, [illegible].
Enesy, David m'Donoghe Y, pardon, [illegible].
Enfohnamaghe (Feohanagh), co. Lim., [illegible].
Engalle, co. Mon., [illegible].
Engaan—Engawnae, Brian m'Donogh, pardon, [illegible], [illegible].
Engineer, pension granted to, [illegible].
England, exports to, [illegible], [illegible], 1719, 1737, [illegible], [illegible].
" her trade with Spain, [illegible].
" crimes committed in, excepted from pardon, [illegible].
" license for absence in, 7, 16, [illegible], [illegible], [illegible], [illegible], 445–6, [illegible], [illegible], [illegible], [illegible], [illegible], [illegible], [illegible], [illegible], [illegible], [illegible], [illegible], 1107, 1271, [illegible], [illegible], [illegible], [illegible], [illegible], [illegible], [illegible], [illegible], [illegible], [illegible], [illegible], 3107, 3175, [illegible], [illegible], 3476, [illegible], [illegible], [illegible], [illegible], [illegible], [illegible], 4011, [illegible].
" monasteries in. *See* Cartmell, Exeter, Furness, Lanthony.
" lord chancellor of, [illegible].
" lord treasurer of, [illegible].
" high admiral of, [illegible], [illegible].
" principal secretary of, [illegible], [illegible].
" lieutenant of the ordnance in, [illegible], [illegible].
" master of the rolls, Irish master to hold office as fully as, [illegible].
" attorney general. *See* Attorney.
" privy council in, its authority in Irish affairs, [illegible], [illegible], [illegible], [illegible], [illegible], [illegible]; grant under letters of, [illegible], [illegible], [illegible], [illegible], [illegible], [illegible], [illegible], [illegible].
" Chancery in, appeals to, [illegible], [illegible].
England, great seal of, grants under, [illegible], [illegible], [illegible].
England — Englant — Englond — Englont — Englond:
" Dermod, pardon, [illegible].
" Garrett, pardon, [illegible].
" James, pardon, [illegible], [illegible].
" John, pardon, [illegible].
" Oliver, pardon, [illegible].
" Patrick, pardon, [illegible].
" Philip, pardon, [illegible].
" Thomas, pardon, [illegible], [illegible], [illegible], [illegible], [illegible], [illegible].
" Wm., pardon, [illegible], [illegible]; license for tan house, [illegible].
" ( ), pardon, [illegible].
Englandstown—Englandston — Englandstowne — Enclustown (Ballyengland), co. Lim., [illegible], [illegible], [illegible], [illegible], [illegible], [illegible], [illegible]; grant, [illegible].
England—Englond—Englont. *See* England (surname).
Englontstown. *See* Englandstown.
Englishe — Englos — Englis. *See* English (surname).
Englotan, Morris m'Tho., pardon, [illegible].
English, apparel, Idle man must be accompanied by honest man in, [illegible].
" archers to be maintained by lessees, [illegible], [illegible], &c.
" horsemen to be maintained by grantees of lands, [illegible], [illegible], [illegible], [illegible], [illegible], [illegible], [illegible], [illegible], &c.
" inhabitants aiding rebels to be imprisoned, [illegible].
" language and dress to be used in King's and Queen's cos., [illegible]; in Kildare, [illegible].
" law, right of English subjects in Irish country to, [illegible].
" liberty, grants of, [illegible]; grant to be expedited as the person is necessary to be employed, 1404.
" order, habit, and language, statute for, to be enforced by ecclesiastical commission, [illegible].
" Pale, martial law in borders of, [illegible]; privilege of surrender of, [illegible].
" patents, [illegible], [illegible]. *See also* England, great seal.

English, privy council. *See* England, privy council of.
" race, assignments of crown lands to be made only to persons of, [illegible], [illegible], [illegible], [illegible], [illegible], [illegible], [illegible], [illegible], [illegible], [illegible], &c.
" race, soldiers to be of, [illegible].
" race, rights of subjects of, reserved, [illegible].
" subjects to be planted in Ocior, [illegible].
" undertakers, grant to, [illegible]. *See* also Undertakers.
English — Englyshe — Englise — Englishe — English — Inglishe:
" Edm., pardon, [illegible], [illegible], [illegible], [illegible], [illegible], [illegible], [illegible].
" Edm. fitz Eustace, pardon, [illegible], [illegible], [illegible].
" Edm. fitz John, pardon, [illegible], [illegible].
" Eustace — Ualtoe, pardon, [illegible], [illegible], [illegible].
" Garret, pardon, [illegible].
" James, pardon, [illegible], [illegible], [illegible].
" James fitz Edm., pardon, [illegible], [illegible].
" James fitz Walter, pardon, [illegible], [illegible].
" James reogh, pardon, [illegible], [illegible].
" John, pardon, [illegible], [illegible], [illegible], [illegible], [illegible], [illegible], [illegible], [illegible].
" Jonick, pardon, [illegible].
" Morrery, pardon, [illegible].
" Morish, pardon, [illegible], [illegible].
" Patrick, pardon, [illegible], [illegible], [illegible], [illegible], [illegible].
" Peter, pardon, [illegible].
" Philip, pardon, [illegible], [illegible], [illegible], [illegible], [illegible].
" Piers fitz Edm., pardon, [illegible], [illegible], [illegible].
" Raimund, pardon, [illegible], [illegible], [illegible], [illegible], [illegible].
" Richard, pardon, [illegible], [illegible], [illegible].
" Rich. fitz Walter, pardon, [illegible], [illegible].
" Richard, pardon, [illegible].
" Richard fitz Walter, pardon, [illegible], [illegible].
" Shane, pardon, [illegible], [illegible].
" Walter, pardon, [illegible].
" Walter boy, pardon, [illegible], [illegible].
" Walter fitz John, pardon, [illegible], [illegible], [illegible].
" William, pardon, [illegible], [illegible], [illegible], [illegible], [illegible], [illegible], [illegible], [illegible].
" Wm. fitz Eustace, pardon, [illegible], [illegible].
" Wm. fitz Jonick, pardon, [illegible], [illegible].
" Wm. leagh, pardon, [illegible], [illegible].
Englishe (co. Kerry ?), [illegible].
Englishetown — Englyshtowne — Englishtown (Ballyenglish), co. Lim., [illegible], [illegible], [illegible]. *See* Englandstown.
Englond, John (*see* England), [illegible].
Engowis, Wm. m'Donogh, pardon, [illegible].
EnGwoly, Henry, pardon, [illegible].
Enhill, co. Kild., [illegible].
Enias, Tho. fitz David, pardon, [illegible].
Eniscorthy — Eniscorthie. *See* Enniscorthy.
Enish—Enishe, [illegible].
Enishcaslor (co. Tip. ?), [illegible].
Enishmore in Loghgaune (Inchmore, co. Long.), [illegible]. *See* Inchemore.
Enishonoghane (co. Kilk. ?), [illegible].
Enisky, John m'Donogh Y., pardon, [illegible].
Eniskine—Enyskyne (Enniskeen, co. Cav.), [illegible].
Enismore (co. Kerry ?), [illegible].
Enistnage—Inistnage—Ynestnag (Enistiogg), co. Kilk., [illegible], [illegible], [illegible].
Enistrick (Inishtorkl), co. Gal. or Mayo, [illegible].
Enkorighe, David. *See* Encorig.
Enmyn, Derby m'Mclaghlin I., pardon, [illegible].
Ennaly (Annaly), [illegible].
Ennereily, co. Wick. *See* Enereilly.
Ennes, Wm. and Donell m'Tho. (*see* Ennes), [illegible].
Enneshoye. *See* Enescoie.
Enneskea. *See* Enniskimon.
Ennestioke—Ennestyock. *See* Inistioke.
(Ennis) — Inche — Inche of Clonraneta — Inish — Innysh — Enyshe — Ennys, co. Clare:
" messuages, &c., in, [illegible], [illegible].
" manor, [illegible].
" house of grey friars, [illegible], [illegible], [illegible], [illegible]; granted, [illegible].
" assizes at, [illegible].
" constable of gaol, [illegible], [illegible].
" county, commissioners in, [illegible].
Ennisboyne, co. Wick. *See* Inchoboyne, Enobothine.
Enniscorthy, co. Westm. *See* Enescodie and Enscoie.
(Enniscorthy)—Enniscorthie — Enescorthy — Enescortie — Enescorphie—Enescortey — Eniscorthie — Eniscorthye — Inescorthye — Inescortie, co. Wex., [illegible], [illegible], [illegible], [illegible], [illegible], [illegible], [illegible], [illegible]; grant, [illegible], [illegible].
" castle and manor, [illegible]; leased, [illegible], [illegible], [illegible], [illegible], [illegible], [illegible]; granted, [illegible], [illegible].
" fair and customs, [illegible], [illegible].

INDEX TO FIANTS—ELIZABETH.

(Enniscorthy)—house of friars, leased, [illegible], 1125-6, [illegible]; granted, [illegible], 6218.
Enniscoush, co. Lim. See [illegible].
Ennisharn, co. Cav. See [illegible].
Enniskean, co. Cork. See Iniskean and [illegible].
(Enniskillen)—Enniskellen—Inisskellin—Inishkellyn—Iniskillin—Innskillen—Iniskellin—Iniskillen—Inniskellen—Innyskillen—Innyskillen—Inyskillyn, co. Fermanagh, [illegible].
" county of (the co. of Fermanagh), 4910, [illegible].
Ennislawnagh. See Innislawnagh.
Ennismag, co. Kilk. See [illegible].
(Ennistimon)—Ennistimon—Ennestimon—Inistymayne—Inistdymane—Inistymayn—Inishtimon—Innistymoyne—Innistimon—Innystidyman, co. Clare, [illegible], 1034, 1077, [illegible], 4274-5, 4782, [illegible], [illegible].
Ennistioke. See Inistioke.
Ennistown, co. Meath. See [illegible].
Enos, Edw., pardon, [illegible]. See also Ennos and Enos.
Ennoscklowne—Ennoscklowne (Enniskeen, Queen's co. ?), [illegible], 1651.
Enoy in Ballibewer, co. Cav., [illegible].
Ennys. See Ennis.
Ennys, Donyl, pardon, [illegible].
Ennyskorick. See [illegible].
Enniskill (co. Ross. ?), [illegible].
Enoghmore—Enoghmore (King's co. ?), [illegible], 1654.
Enshanmacbrook, co. Kerry, [illegible].
Enswan, Philip, pardon, [illegible].
" Shane, pardon, [illegible].
Enereilly (Ennereilly), co. Wick., rectory, [illegible], 4480.
Enraghmore. See Enraghmore.
Enrie, Conor and Wm., pardon, [illegible].
Enos—Enos—Enowes:
" Anthony, controller of customs, [illegible]; [illegible] constable Dublin castle, [illegible]; lease, [illegible].
" David, pardon, [illegible].
" Donogh, pardon, [illegible].
" Magnus, pardon, [illegible].
" Murrogh, pardon, [illegible].
" Patrick, pardon, [illegible], [illegible], [illegible].
" Teig, pardon, [illegible].
" Walter (Enowes), pardon, [illegible].
" Wm., pardon, [illegible].
" See Eynos.
Enstown (Ennistown), co. Meath, [illegible].
Enowes. See Enos.
Enyrisowne, Donogh O'Callaghan, [illegible].
Enrathmore—Enraghmore (Rathmore ?), King's co., [illegible], 1654.
Enverr (co. Gal. ?), [illegible].
Enrowane, Fergananym m'Murrogh, pardon, [illegible].
Ensnighe (co. Cork ?), [illegible].
Enevmagran, [illegible].
Ervinalangert—Enshanloweghert, King's co., [illegible], 1654.
Enshyquin (Inchiquin ?), co. Cork, [illegible].
Ensign in army, [illegible], [illegible].
Ensylmoke (Inchinabacky, co. Cork), rectory, [illegible].
Entaghmorenagh, King's co., [illegible], 1654.
Entardierin, King's co., [illegible], 1654.
Enterymann, Conoghor m'Donogh, pardon, [illegible].
Entoskyne—Inishone, Mahon m'Donogh, pardon, [illegible].
" Donell m'Donogh, pardon, [illegible].
Enulawry, Conoghor, pardon, [illegible].
Enulevoshew, Donogh, pardon, [illegible].
Enulaghty, Donell, pardon, [illegible].
Ennet, Edward, pardon, [illegible].
Ennen, Art, pardon, [illegible].
" Donogh, pardon, [illegible].
" Nicholas, pardon, [illegible].
Enryne—Ewryne (Ballinvrony), co. Tip., [illegible], [illegible], [illegible], 4161.
Eny (Inny river), co. Westm. See Inny.
Enyghan (co. Westm. ?), [illegible].
Enylian, Shane (see Enelian), [illegible].
Enynise. See Ennis.
Enyshmore. See Inishmore, co. Long.
Enyskerry (Inishcarra ?), co. Cork, [illegible].
Enyskyne. See Enniskean.
Enysnean, co. Gal., 4818.
Enystymane. See Inistioke.
Enyforen, Gerald m'Wm. Y, pardon, [illegible].
Enoghilling, co. Gal., [illegible].
Enystry, David Fitz Maurice, pardon, [illegible].
Enyner, John Fitz Peers, pardon, [illegible].
Esbury, Stephen, clerk of ordnance, [illegible].
Erbyrgh (co. Ross. ?), [illegible].
Eree, Hugh m'Tho., pardon, [illegible].
Eregan. Eregan, country of. See Iregan.
Ereghloen (Fernanil), co. Mon., [illegible].
Erely, Nich., pardon, [illegible].
Erenagh (Ervina), co. Clare, [illegible].
Erenagh lands (see [illegible]), [illegible].
Ercman, Stephen, pardon, [illegible].
Erishe M'Ulaig, co. Gal., [illegible].
Eris, [illegible].
Erles, co. Kilk. See Erles.
Erlesgrange, co. Kilk., 1810.
Erles Grove (Earlsgrove, co. Kilk. ?), [illegible].
Erlesmedowe, co. Car., [illegible].
Erlestone. See Earlestown.

INDEX TO FIANTS—ELIZABETH.

Ericswood, co. Cork, [illegible].
Eriston. See Earlestown.
Erily, Donald m'Te., pardon, [illegible].
" Teig m'Kilsarky, pardon, [illegible].
Erne, lake and river. See Earne.
Erohill—Erochill (Ironhills), co. Kild., [illegible], [illegible], [illegible]; castle, 4121.
Erosk (co. Wex. ?), [illegible].
Erorremo, co. Leit., [illegible].
Errevoney, co. Donegal. See Errervoy.
Errr, co. Westm., 1178.
Erroe (Queen's co. or Kild. ?), [illegible]. See Erry, Queen's co.
Errogan. See Irrgan.
Errell (Errill), Queen's co., [illegible].
Errervoy (Errarooney, co. Donegal), [illegible].
Errervoy more (Errarooney More, co. Donegal), [illegible].
Errick (Errill ?), co. Mayo, [illegible], [illegible].
Errigal, co. Mon. See Ereghies.
Errill, Queen's co. See Errell.
Errim, co. Clare. See Drvragh.
Erris, co. Mayo. See Iarla, Orrus.
Erry—Errye—Erroe (Queen's co. ?), [illegible]; vicarage, [illegible], [illegible].
Erry—Irry—Irre, co. Tip., 1797, [illegible], [illegible], [illegible]; grange of, [illegible], [illegible].
Erward, Pat., pardon, [illegible].
Eryaagh (co. Mon. ?), [illegible].
Eryone, Joan, pardon, [illegible].
Eryve (co. Ross. ?), [illegible].
Escheator general and feodary, [illegible], [illegible], [illegible], [illegible].
" deputy. See Boyle, Rich., [illegible].
" of co. Cork and Limerick, [illegible].
Esgir—Esgyr. See Esker.
Esker, co. Dub., [illegible], [illegible].
" manor, [illegible], [illegible], [illegible], [illegible], [illegible], [illegible].
" mill, [illegible].
" parish, [illegible], [illegible].
" vicar of, English liberty, [illegible].
Esker—Esgir—Esgyr, King's co., [illegible], [illegible].
Esker, co. Mon. See Nosker, [illegible].
Esker—Isker, Queen's co., 1714, 1876, [illegible].
Esker Bog, King's co. See Iskerbog.
Eskerbegge—Eskerbegg, Queen's co., [illegible], [illegible].
Eskerghann, co. Gal., [illegible].
Eskeragh (co. Leit. ?), [illegible].
Eskernecoile, co. Gal., [illegible].
Eskeroan—Eskyrovan—Skyrowan (Iskeroon), co. Meath, [illegible], [illegible], [illegible].
Eskerrowe—Iskerroe (Eskerroe), co. Gal., [illegible], [illegible].
Esker Parke, Queen's co., 1216.
Eskeltine (co. Gal. ?), [illegible].
Eskirrowyshelane (King's co.), [illegible].
Eskirraysholane. See also Yskerrowshell.
Eskyrovan. See Eskeroan.
Eskeston (Earlstown), co. Kilk., rectory, [illegible].
Esmond—Esmonde, John, pardon, [illegible], [illegible].
" Lawrence (Capt.), pardon, [illegible]; grant, [illegible]; pardon at his suit, [illegible].
" Nich., pardon, [illegible].
" Peirse, pardon, [illegible].
" Peter, pardon, [illegible].
" Robert, grant, [illegible].
Essleston, co. Meath, [illegible].
Essex, Walter [Devereux], earl of, com. to raise and rule the people of Clandeboy, &c., [illegible]; captain general of Ulster, [illegible], [illegible], [illegible]; treats with Desmond, [illegible]; com., [illegible]; pardon at instance of, [illegible], [illegible], [illegible], [illegible]; victualling of his soldiers, [illegible], [illegible], [illegible], [illegible], [illegible]; captain of Iveagh nominated by, [illegible]; composition with Tirlogh Lenagh, [illegible]; grant of land recited, [illegible], [illegible]; earl marshal, [illegible]; license to leave and return to Ireland at will, [illegible].
" Robert, earl of, [illegible]; arrival as lord lieutenant, [illegible]; his lieutenant general, [illegible], [illegible]; com. of peace during his absence from Dublin, [illegible], [illegible]; submissions to him, [illegible], [illegible]; com. for the government on his recall, [illegible], [illegible].
Estaboithine, co. Dub. (Ennisboyne, co. Wick.), [illegible], [illegible].
Estorkeran. See Esatherne.
Estownow, co. Ross. See Issynowe.
Estine, Edm. Donogh I., pardon, [illegible].
Etagho, co. Tip. (Ettagh, King's co.), rectory, [illegible].
Etaller, Donnell, pardon, [illegible].
Etermyn—ctarmen, John or Shane, attainted, [illegible], [illegible], [illegible].
Etermyne, Shane, pardon, [illegible].
Etirrap, Brian, pardon, [illegible].
Etinhake (Inchinaracky), co. Cork, rectory, [illegible], [illegible].
Etoskon, Edm. m'Shane, pardon, [illegible].
Ethonye—Ethuye. See Inan.
Etherington, Jenkin (see Hetherington), [illegible].
Etinevy, Wm. m'Tho., pardon, [illegible].
Etinaghty, Wm. Shane, pardon, [illegible].
Etogher, Tyrlagh, pardon, [illegible].
Ettagh, King's co. See Etagho.
Etinevin, Teig m'Rory boy, pardon, [illegible].
Etwarboy (Tarboy), co. Long., [illegible].
Eughter carrowe—Eitrecarrowe (Ightercarrowragh, co. Cork), [illegible], [illegible].

INDEX TO FIANTS.—ELIZABETH.

Bury (co. Tip.?), [illegible].
Bury, Wm., pardon, [illegible].
Eustace — Ewstace — Ewstas — Ewstas — Ustace:
„ Alexander, [illegible]; pardon, [illegible], [illegible], [illegible].
„ Alson, pardon, [illegible].
„ Anne, pardon, [illegible], [illegible], [illegible].
„ Christopher, attainted, his possessions, [illegible], 190, [illegible], [illegible], [illegible], [illegible], 1152, [illegible], [illegible], [illegible], [illegible], [illegible], [illegible], [illegible], [illegible], 4737, [illegible], [illegible]; lands granted to his daughter, 4737, [illegible].
„ Christopher, [illegible]; pardon, [illegible], [illegible], [illegible], [illegible], [illegible], [illegible], [illegible], [illegible].
„ David, pardon, [illegible], [illegible], [illegible], [illegible], [illegible], [illegible].
„ Edmund (brother of lord Baltinglas), attainted, his possessions leased, 4162, [illegible], [illegible], [illegible]; granted, [illegible], [illegible], [illegible].
„ Edmund, [illegible], pardon, [illegible], [illegible], [illegible], [illegible], [illegible], [illegible], [illegible], [illegible], [illegible], [illegible], [illegible], [illegible], [illegible].
„ Edward, pardon, [illegible], [illegible], [illegible], [illegible].
„ Eleanor, pardon, [illegible], [illegible], [illegible].
„ Elizabeth, [illegible]; pardon, [illegible].
„ Geo fitz Edm., pardon, [illegible].
„ Gerrot, pardon, [illegible].
„ Ismay, pardon, [illegible], [illegible].
„ James, livery to his heir, [illegible].
„ James, commissions, [illegible], [illegible], [illegible].
„ James, son of viscount Baltinglas, pardon, [illegible], [illegible]; his rebellion, [illegible], [illegible]. See Baltinglas, James, viscount.
„ James, [illegible]; pardon, [illegible], [illegible], [illegible], [illegible], [illegible], [illegible], [illegible], [illegible], [illegible], [illegible], [illegible], [illegible], [illegible].
„ Jennet, pardon, [illegible].
„ Joan, pardon, [illegible], [illegible].
„ Joan, heiress of Chr., grant, [illegible], [illegible], [illegible].
„ John, pardon, [illegible], [illegible], [illegible], [illegible], [illegible]; lease, [illegible], [illegible], [illegible]; keeper of Naas gaol, [illegible].
„ John (of Castlemartin), sheriff of Kildare, 1140, 1318, [illegible]; justice of peace, [illegible]; commissions, [illegible], [illegible], [illegible], [illegible], [illegible], [illegible], [illegible], [illegible], [illegible], [illegible], [illegible], [illegible], [illegible], [illegible]; pardon, [illegible], [illegible], [illegible], [illegible]; licence, [illegible], [illegible]; his heir, [illegible].
Eustace — John (of Confey), livery to his heir, [illegible].
„ John (of Confey), livery, [illegible].
„ John (of Lemartin?), livery, [illegible].
„ John (of Newland), commissions, [illegible], [illegible].
„ John fitz Edm., pardon, [illegible]; commissions, [illegible], [illegible].
„ Margaret, pardon, [illegible], [illegible], [illegible]; will of, [illegible].
„ Mary, called viscountess Baltinglas, [illegible].
„ Maurice, [illegible], pardon, [illegible], [illegible], [illegible], [illegible], [illegible], [illegible].
„ Maurice, executed for high treason, [illegible]; attainted, his lands granted, [illegible], [illegible].
„ Maurice (of Clongowes-wood), com., [illegible], [illegible].
„ Nicholas, pardons, [illegible], [illegible], [illegible], [illegible], [illegible], [illegible], [illegible].
„ Nicholas (of Confey), livery, [illegible]; freedom from subsidy, [illegible]; com., [illegible]; livery to his heir, [illegible].
„ Nich. fitz Rich., pardon, [illegible], [illegible].
„ Oliver, [illegible], [illegible], [illegible]; pardons, [illegible], [illegible], [illegible], [illegible], [illegible], [illegible], [illegible], [illegible], [illegible].
„ Oliver, learned in the law, commissions, [illegible], [illegible], [illegible], [illegible], [illegible].
„ Peter, pardon, [illegible], [illegible].
„ Richard, [illegible]; pardon, [illegible], [illegible], [illegible], [illegible], [illegible], [illegible], [illegible], [illegible]; commissions, [illegible], [illegible].
„ Robert, [illegible].
„ Roland. See Baltinglas, Roland, viscount of.
„ Roland (of Bagotstown?), pardon, [illegible], [illegible], [illegible].
„ Roland, pardon, [illegible].
„ Rose, pardon, [illegible], [illegible].
„ Thomas, lord of Kilcullen, [illegible].
„ Thomas, pardon, [illegible], [illegible], [illegible], [illegible], [illegible].
„ Thomas (of Cardiffstown), attainted, his lands leased, [illegible], [illegible], [illegible], [illegible], [illegible], [illegible], [illegible], [illegible], [illegible], [illegible], [illegible], [illegible], [illegible]; his lands granted, [illegible], [illegible], [illegible], [illegible].
„ Thomas (of Mullacash?), [illegible], [illegible].
„ Walter, [illegible], [illegible].
„ Walter, brother of viscount Baltinglas, a traitor, [illegible].
„ William, pardon, [illegible], [illegible], [illegible], [illegible].

Eustace — William (of Castlemartin), 6745; grant, 2791, 3946; commission, 3136; pardon, 1874.
Wm. son Walter, pardon, 6063, 6271, 6800.
Eustace's—Ewstace's land, in Kilnalchain, 1548.
Evagha. See Evagh.
Evaghery, Teig m'Eiles, pardon, 5458.
" Tho., pardon, 4265.
Evallagh, Donell, pardon, 6067.
Evallie, Dermot, pardon, 5134.
Evally, Hames, pardon, 4283, 4808.
Evan. See Erin.
Evragh. See Evagh, co. Down.
Evenke, Brian, pardon, 5468.
Dermod, pardon, 5431.
Evally, Mariertagh m'Shane, pardon, 5603.
Evegillahoo, co. Lim. See Ogallahorn.
Evealy, Brian, pardon, 2460.
Even. See Erin.
Evenagha, co. Sligo; vicarage, 4036.
Evenline, Walter, pardon, 5584.
Everard — Everade — Everet — Evrard — Everitt:
James, com., 260; pardon, 4455, 694.
John, justice of liberty of Tipperary, 5487; justice of Chief Place, [illegible]; comm. in Munster, 4798, 4773.
Matthew, pardon, 2533.
Peers, licence, 3158.
Redmond, 4926; commissions, 2738, 3450; pardon, 6163.
Rich., pardon, 2796, 3420.
Evers, Fermo, pardon, 6317.
Evers, Charles, pardon, 4201.
" Walter, pardon, 4043.
Evereon, Edw., pardon, 5418.
Everson—Everston, Rob., pardon, 3046, 6473.
Everston, John, pardon, 4472.
Everye, Patrick, pardon, 2944.
Evin—Evan—Even—Eyen—Eryn (Monasterevin), co. Kild., 23, 233, 434, 6417.
manor, 1131, 1362, 3164.
" See also Monasterevin.
Evelyne, Edm., pardon, 1804.
Evan. See Erin.
Evony, Edm. O'Dowyre, 5056.
Evry, Isabella, pardon, 5550.
Evrard, Peers (see Everard), 3158.
Evrett, Rich. (see Everard), 3420.
Evryn, Rawney, pardon, 4265, 4558.
Evyn. See Erin.
Ewacious, Rich. fitz Piers, pardon, [illegible].
Ewan, Donell m'Don., pardon, 4697.
Ewe, James, pardon, 46.
Ewe, earl of. See Essex, Walter, earl of.
Ewar, Anne, pardon, 4400.
" Ralph, grant, 4012; claim in Aucher's pardon, 4215.
Ewery, John, 5445.
Ewleyn, co. Long., 2851.
Ewyhanell, Shane m'Dermot, pardon, 4016.
Ewnyfinlydon (Ennisfad?), co. Sligo, 3818.
Ewstace—Ewstas. See Eustace.
Ewyn, Aey m'yne, pardon, 4876.
Exeter. See Exeter.
Exchequer, com. to collect outstanding debts to the crown, 5067.
" court of, 406, 4788, 4906, 5108, 5821.
" officers and officers, account to, 1287, 3176, 4878, 4238, 4344, 5416, 3716, 5020, 6186.
" lease to be enrolled in, 1084, 1898. See Auditor-General.
" questions under seal of, 5035.
" proceedings of, placed under superintendence of Chief Justice Gardiner, 6805.
" officers of, to take oath of supremacy, 4631.
" chancellor of; or chancellor of the green wax, 224, 356, 2113, 3560, 4631, 5664-5, 6476, 6430.
" chief baron, 136, 429, 1287, 5024, 5677.
" second baron, 17, 128, 283, 1494, 5480, 3804, 4384.
" third baron, 472, 804, 1546, 2741, 5180, 3905, 5836.
" chamberlain, chief, 256, 2371, 3645, 7153, 5814, 6061.
" " second, 336, 871, 3240, 3427, 5061, 6302.
" engrosser, chief, or clerk of pipe, 176, 563, 2828, 3245, 4245, 4136, 6684.
" " second, 1546, 2182, 3676, 6364.
" marshal, 285, 837, 1590, 2237, 3646.
" pleas, clerk of, 2, 144, 249, 278, 5177, 5052, 6044.
" receiver general, 2542, 6673.
" remembrancer, chief, 23, 872, 1249, 2184, 2738, 2723, 3442, 4123.
" " chief, deputy of, 3570.
" " second, 2, 156, 271, 563, 446, 878, 1580, 2782, 2743, 4186, 5757, 6184.

INDEX TO FIANTS.—ELIZABETH.

Exchequer, chief remembrancer, 141, 273, 2934, 4390, 6378.
" transcriptor, 143, 154, 270, 378, 4201.
" usher, 147, 273, 272, 4150, 5703.
Exeter—Exceter—Exton, in England, priory of S. Nicholas, possessions leased, [illegible]: granted, [illegible], 3789.
Exports, prohibited, [illegible], [illegible], [illegible].
Exter, Tho., lease, 2081.
Exton. See Exeter.
E Xalleyle, Teig, attainted, [illegible].
Eyamowe. See Eymowe.
Eyan. See Eyn.
Eyaby, Teig m'Mortriagh I., pardon, 6475.
Eykildreagh (co. Mayo ?), [illegible].
Eylled rogha, More ny, pardon, 6641.
Eylleroogh, More ny, pardon, [illegible].
Eylmer, Nich., [illegible]. See Aylmer.
Eylwardstoune. See Aylwardstown.
Eylyward, John fitz Ulyx, pardon, [illegible].
Eymowe—Eyomowe, alias Homowe, co. Westm., [illegible], [illegible].
Eyn—Eyan (Eyne), Queen's co., [illegible], 1863, [illegible]. See Eynekellim.
Eyne—Eyn, Dowaltus, son of Owney, English liberty, 177.
" Donell m'Donogh, pardon, 1811.
" Evably ny, pardon, [illegible].
" John m'Owen, pardon, 1341.
Eyne water (Inny river). See Inne.
Eynegh, the, 6477.
Eynekellim—Eynekillimm—Eynekylmeme (Eyne ?), Queen's co., 1847, [illegible].
Eyran, Rory, pardon, [illegible].
Eyrim (co. Kerry ?), [illegible].
Eyre—Eier—Ayre—Aire:
" Elizabeth, [illegible].
" Robert, [illegible]; grant, 1834, livery to his son, [illegible].
" William, [illegible]; livery [illegible]; wardship of his heir, [illegible].
" William, wardship, [illegible].
Eyre, alias Tyre, Queen's co., 1642.
Eyrenaght, co. Mon., [illegible].
Eyrke (Erke), see Rirke, 1371.
Eyrrygh, co. Clare, [illegible].

Facholog (co. Gal. ?), 4478.
Faculties, commissioners under Act of Hen. VIII., [illegible].
" substitute or surrogate for, appeals from, 2431, 4428, 4483.
" registrar of, [illegible], 4158, [illegible].
" judges of Court of, 6177, 6154, [illegible], [illegible].
Fadd, Maloghlin, pardon, [illegible].
Faddan, co. Gal., [illegible].
Faddan Morwand Beg, King's co. See Faddans.
Fadera, co. Cork, [illegible].
Faenoyrorteg (Fanore Beg ?), co. Clare, [illegible], 4374.
Fach, the, country called (in barony Athlone), co. Rosc., [illegible].
Fagan, Cahell duffe, pardon, [illegible].
" Conly, murder of, [illegible].
" Christopher, pardon, [illegible].
" Christopher, licence to alien, [illegible]; wardship of granddaughter, [illegible].
" Cormock, pardon, [illegible].
" Edm. ban, pardon, [illegible].
" Elinore, wardship, [illegible].
" Ferrall, pardon, [illegible].
" George, house in Dublin, 1811; pardon, [illegible].
" Gillpatrick m'Conor, pardon, [illegible].
" James fitz Wm., pardon, [illegible].
" John, pardon, [illegible].
" Manus oge, pardon, [illegible].
" Nicholas, vicar of Old Ross, [illegible].
" Nich., pardon, [illegible].
" Teig m'Cahell, pardon, [illegible].
" Thomas, wardship of daughter, [illegible].
" Tho. m'Melaghlin, pardon, [illegible].
" Terrelagh, pardon, [illegible].
" Wm., pardon, [illegible], [illegible], [illegible].
Fagane, Christopher. See Fagan.
" James pardon, [illegible].
Faganstone (Fagansdown), co. Meath, 1494.
Fagans, James, pardon, [illegible].
" Wm., licence to sell aqua vitae, [illegible].
Facholton (co. Westm. ?), [illegible].
Fagbert, co. Louth, 1312.
Fagirio (see Fahlo), [illegible].
Faghinevarne Rogey (co. Lim. ?), [illegible].
Faghley—Faghly. See Faughley.
Faghy, Donogh, pardon, [illegible].
Fagneirt, Morogh, pardon, 4711.
Fagon, Morogh, pardon, [illegible].
Fahan, co. Cork, 2741.
Fahe (co. Gal. ?), [illegible].
Fahe, co. Lim. See Fahle, Fay.
Fahagh (co. Kerry ?), [illegible].
Fahagh (co. Wat. ?), [illegible].
Fahan, co. Donegal. See Faine.
Faho, in Connaught, [illegible].
Faho, John A., pardon, [illegible].
Fahlo—Faghrio (Fahe ?), co. Lim., [illegible], [illegible], [illegible].
Fahlo (Fahe), co. Lim., [illegible].
Fahin, alias Tobin, Tho. oe, pardon, [illegible].
Fahy in Ossebel, [illegible].
Fahy (co. Clare ?), [illegible].
Fahy, Donoghy m'Wame I., pardon, [illegible].
Fahy—Fahye, co. Gal., 1776, [illegible].
Fahynovar brogie, [illegible].
Faie, co. Gal., [illegible].

INDEX TO FIANTS—ELIZABETH.

Fain. *See* Fay.
Faidley, Donell m'Teige Y, pardon, [illegible].
Faigh—Faighe, the, in Mullingar, [illegible], [illegible].
Faigh, co. Wex., [illegible].
Faighe. *See* Faigh.
Failberg (co. Kilk. ?), [illegible].
Faine (Fahan, co. Donegal), [illegible], [illegible].
Fainestown, co. Wex., [illegible].
Fair, barons of, hold court to settle disputes, [illegible].
Fairo (King's co. ?), [illegible].
Fairweather, James, soymaster, [illegible].
Fairs at Athenry, grant of, [illegible].
" at Mullingar, grant of, [illegible].
Faithley—Faithlick—Faithlik—Faithlike—Faithlyk, co. Wat., [illegible], [illegible], 677, [illegible], [illegible], [illegible].
Falcons, rent of, [illegible].
Fale, the (co. Cork ?), [illegible].
Falisch (co. Wat. ?), [illegible].
Fallaghmore, Queen's co. *See* Farraghmore.
Falls at Belfast, [illegible].
Fallo, Philip, pardon, [illegible].
Falley, Teige m'Curtis Y, pardon, [illegible].
Fallie, Thady m'Corke, pardon, [illegible].
Falloglass, Queen's co., [illegible], [illegible].
Fallon, Daniel, burgess, Athlone, [illegible].
" Edm., burgess, Athlone, [illegible].
" Nich., burgess, Athlone, [illegible].
" Wm., burgess, Athlone, [illegible].
Fallon, grange of, in O'Fallon's country, [illegible].
Fallowes, Isabell, kern, [illegible].
" Robert, widow of, [illegible].
Fallowfeild, Henry, grant of a wardship, [illegible].
Fally, Donnell Ballif m'Awliffe Y, pardon, [illegible].
Falragh, co. Rosc., [illegible].
Faltagh, Ullick de Wale, [illegible], [illegible].
Faltagh, co. Mon., [illegible].
Faminge, Edmund, pardon, [illegible].
" Robert, pardon, [illegible].
" Thomas, pardon, [illegible].
Fanamerings (co. Wick.), [illegible].
Fanet, M'Swyne, grant of his country (Fanad, co. Donegal), [illegible].
Faning—Faninge. *See* Fanning.
Faning rowe, Oliver and Shane fitz Rob., pardon, [illegible].
Faningston — Fanyngestowne (Faningstown), co. Lim., [illegible], [illegible], [illegible].
Faningstown—Fanyngston, co. Cork, [illegible], [illegible].
Faninge woods—Faninisweild—Fanyngeswood, [illegible], [illegible], [illegible].
Faninisweild (*see* Faningewoods), [illegible].
Fanmore, co. Gal., [illegible].
Fann (co. Kerry ?), [illegible].
Fannaramaka—Fannarvaska (Fannarogaha), co. Clare, [illegible], [illegible].
Fannie, Rich., pardon, [illegible].
Fanning—Faning — Faninge — Fanninge — Fannyng—Fannynge— Fanyng —Fanynge.
" David, pardon, [illegible], [illegible], [illegible], [illegible], [illegible], [illegible].
" Edmund, pardon, [illegible], [illegible], [illegible].
" Geoffrey or Jeffrey, pardon, [illegible], [illegible], [illegible], [illegible].
" George, [illegible]; indenture, [illegible].
" Honor, pardon, [illegible].
" Jacob, pardon, [illegible].
" James, pardon, [illegible], [illegible], [illegible], [illegible], [illegible], [illegible], [illegible], [illegible].
" John, pardon, [illegible], [illegible], [illegible], [illegible], [illegible], [illegible], [illegible], [illegible], [illegible], [illegible].
" Manus, pardon, [illegible].
" Margaret, pardon, [illegible].
" Nicholas, pardon, [illegible], [illegible], [illegible], [illegible], [illegible], [illegible].
" Oliver, pardon, [illegible], [illegible], [illegible], [illegible], [illegible], [illegible], [illegible], [illegible], [illegible], [illegible], [illegible], [illegible], [illegible], [illegible].
" Patrick, pardon, [illegible].
" Ricard, pardon, [illegible].
" Richard, pardon, [illegible], [illegible], [illegible], [illegible], [illegible], [illegible], [illegible], [illegible], [illegible].
" Robert, pardon, [illegible], [illegible], [illegible], [illegible], [illegible], [illegible], [illegible].
" Shane, pardon, [illegible], [illegible], [illegible], [illegible], [illegible].
" Thomas, pardon, [illegible], [illegible], [illegible], [illegible], [illegible], [illegible].
" Thomas, treasurer of Limerick cathedral, [illegible].
" William, pardon, [illegible], [illegible], [illegible], [illegible], [illegible].
" William (of Farrancroy), pardon, [illegible], [illegible].
Fanningstown, co. Lim. *See* Ballyfanninge, Faningston.
Fannit, Oyvon, mayor of Galway, [illegible].
Fannunge, Rob., pardon, [illegible].
Fannygan, Eo and Moriagh m'Donell Y, pardon, [illegible].
Fannyn, Edm. fitz James, pardon, [illegible].
" Tho. m'Edm., pardon, [illegible].
Fannyng—Fannynge. *See* Fanning.
Fannyngestowne. *See* Faningston, co. Lim.
Fannyngeswood. *See* Faningewoods.
Fanore Beg, co. Clare. *See* Fernoyerbeg.
Fant, James, attainted, [illegible].
" Robert, attainted, [illegible].
Fanta, co. Clare, [illegible].
Fanleston, co. Cork, [illegible].
Fantra (co. Kerry ?), [illegible].
Fantstown, co. Lim., [illegible].
Fanygallovane, co. Clare, [illegible].
Fanying, Robert, pardon, [illegible].

INDEX TO FIANTS—ELIZABETH.

Panyn, James, pardon, [illegible].
„ Oliver, pardon, [illegible].
„ Wm., pardon, [illegible].
Fanyne, Geoffrey, pardon, [illegible].
„ James, pardon, [illegible].
„ John, pardon, [illegible].
„ Robert, pardon, [illegible].
„ Wm., pardon, [illegible].
Fanyng—Fanynge. See Fanning.
Fanyngston (see Faningestown), 6618.
Fanystown, co. Wex., 414.
Farald, Conhor A., pardon, [illegible].
Farall, Donell, pardon, [illegible].
„ John, pardon, [illegible].
„ Mary, pardon, [illegible].
„ Morish m'Shane dirry E., pardon, [illegible].
Farammurchan, King's co., [illegible].
Faramanachlyn, co. Lim., [illegible].
Faravaune (Farranawana), co. Kerry, [illegible].
Farbille—Farbyll—Forbill—Ferbilly—Forbyll (barony of Farbill), co. Westm., [illegible]; martial law in, [illegible].
Farcki (co. Cork ?), [illegible].
Farcollen. See Ferwallen.
Fardingreston (Farthingstown), co. Westm., [illegible].
Fardoragh, alias Rory m'Wm. M'Bryen, pardon, 1068.
Fardoragh, Hugh Dempsy, [illegible].
Fardoroghe m'Edmond, alias John Farrell, pardon, 1194.
Fardrome alias Kyllcmeloen, [illegible].
Fare or Fayre, co. Wex., chapel, [illegible].
Farehy—Farichie—Farihy—Farrahie—Farrohie—Faryhy—Faryhye (Farahy), co. Cork, [illegible]; castle, [illegible].
Farenchanagh, 6142.
Farenecorrenie. See Farrenecroyne.
Farenemorghan, King's co., [illegible].
Farerory. See Farrenrory.
Farender Buddory, co. Lim., [illegible].
Fargamoryn alias Broyn M'Shehy, pardon, [illegible].
Fargamqayrry alias Awlive M'Donall, pardon, [illegible].
Farichie—Farihy. See Farehy.
Farinegrallah, co. Kerry, [illegible].
Farinala, co. Kerry, [illegible].
Farinvosher, co. Kerry, [illegible].
Farmanagh—Farmanuagh. See Fermanagh.
Farmer, John, vicar of Kylaholine, [illegible].
Farmers, freeholders, and husbandmen, Queen's co., [illegible].
Farmers under Munster undertakers, [illegible].
Farmer, Wm., commission, [illegible].
Farnaghe (Farnagh), co. Westm.), [illegible].
Farnan—Farnane, Queen's co., [illegible].
Farnan (Farnane), Queen's co., [illegible].
Farnanston (Farrenandon ? co. Kild.), [illegible].
Farney, co. Mon. See Ferney.
Farnigh (co. Leit. ?), [illegible].
Farny priorye. See Farrinopriory.
Farraghlane, Queen's co., [illegible].
Farraghmore (Fallaghmore), Queen's co., [illegible].
Farrahie. See Farehy.
Farrall—Farrell, Barnaby, pardon, [illegible].
„ Daniel, pardon, [illegible].
„ Donell, pardon, [illegible].
„ Edm., pardon, [illegible].
„ Fergus, pardon, [illegible].
„ Gerald, pardon, [illegible].
„ James, [illegible].
„ James, pardon, [illegible].
„ Margaret, pardon, [illegible].
„ Mary, pardon, [illegible].
„ Owen, pardon, [illegible].
„ Ross, pardon, [illegible].
„ Shane, pardon, [illegible].
„ Unea (or Inveninella), pardon, [illegible].
Farranadoen, co. Kild. See Farnanston.
Farranagalliagh, co. Ross. See Ferannen Calliaghe.
Farranawana, co Kerry. See Faravaune.
Farranclanloremohe—Farrintlandcrumd (King's co. ?), [illegible].
Farraneleigh, in manor of Carlow, [illegible].
Farranechere, co. Cork, [illegible].
Farrancnamanaghe, co. Wat., [illegible].
Farranlabeabery, co. Cork. See Ferrolebenarne.
Farrannabine—Farrinlmabin—Farrymmabin, Queen's co., [illegible].
Farrannamoallere, co. Mayo. See Carrowfarrennalnfloge.
Farrenrorie. See Farrenrory.
Farrentirie (co. Car. ?), [illegible].
Farrenagh, co. Rosc., [illegible].
Farraye Donoghlyn, Queen's co., [illegible].
Farrelarlane, co. Cork, [illegible].
Farrohie. See Farehy.
Farrebountie, co. Tip., [illegible].
Farrell. See Farrall.
Farrenmore, co. Rosc., [illegible].
Farrenbrilldon, co. Gal., [illegible].
Farrencarraghe, co. Kilk., [illegible].
Farrenecroyne—Fareanocroggie—Farrencrois—Ferencroyne, alias the Cross lands, co. Westm., [illegible].
Farrendawkinne—Ferrendawkinne, King's co., [illegible].
Farrendonoghe Ferne, Queen's co., 1714.

INDEX TO FIANTS.—ELIZABETH.

Farrendaffe, co. Cork, 5464.
Farrenmurragh, co. Lim., 4463.
Farren Edylline, co. Kerry, 4379.
Farrenkallagh, co. Westm., 1471.
Farrenarumaghe, near Limerick, 6786.
Farrenmollaghe—Ferrenalagh, co. Wat., 4439, 6722.
Farrenetemagwele, co. Cork, 5151.
Farren Gillfferranrie, co. Cork, 5465.
Farrenhamon — Ferrenhamon, co. Wex., customs due from, 4342.
" chief serjeant of, 1868, 2344.
Farren Ilyen, co. Gal., 1519.
Farren in Ferchinlige, co. Lim., 4374.
Farrenknraghe ne Sondrye, co. Cork, 5718.
Farrenmarren (co. Lim. ?), 4372.
Farrenmarryne, co. Cork, 4468.
Farren ne brahar, alias Ramullen, co. Donegal, 6645.
Farren nagane, co. Kerry, 6632.
Ferren ny gallagh, co. Cork, 5645.
Farren O'Neill, co. Car. See Ferren O'Neyle, Ferren Enserie.
Farren Rory — Farrenrorye — Fararory — Farrarorie — Farriurorie — Farryno Rory — Farryrory — Ferrenrory (Farrenrory), co. Tip., 260, 676, 1461, 2011, 5767, 4573, 6452, 6525.
Farrenede Ruddorye of the Glin, co. Lim., 6138.
Farrensporine, co. Cork, 5761.
Farrentegin, co. Lim., 6171.
Farrentmraihe, co. Meath, 6383.
Farrenvickiane (Farrenmacshane, King's co.), 1661.
Farren Walter ffynne, co. Cork, 5535.
Farrenwater, co. Cork, 5658.
Farrenyvollaghe, near Limerick, 5972.
Farrice Thomas. See Farriathomas.
Farrie, Inyen duffe ny, pardon, 6193.
Farrill, Bicard, pardon, 6438.
Farriehlough, co. Lim., 6153.
Farrinbrock, co. Kilk., 5684.
Farrinelandermod. See Farranelandermothe.
Farrindal, Queen's co., 3358.
Farrinedmond, co. Kerry, 6123.
Farrinmrelagh, co. Lim., 6121.
Farrine neale (co. Car. ?), 6600.
Farrine priory — Farnyprynrye — Fernyprioria, alias Tymerhoo (Timahoe), Queen's co., manor, 1316; advowson, 476, 1622.
Farrinathenbarie (co. Cork ?), 6452.
Farrinamble. See Farranamlane.
Farrin m'eineh, in Crabough, co. Kerry, 6117.
Farrin m'Henrie Roe, co. Lim., 6121.
Farrinmadin, co. Kerry, 6117.
Farrin m'of Imr, co. Cork, 4468.
Farrinmaclone, co. Lim., 6152.
Farrin O'llyne, co. Kilk., 5684.
Farrinrorie. See Farren Rory.
Farrinstocke, co. Kerry, 6122.
Farrinthomas — Farrice Thomas (co. Cork ?), 6414, 6538.
Farrintemicke in Mynogahan, co. Kerry, 6117.
Farrinvollaghe, co. Lim., 5647.
Farrinwilliam, co. Kerry, 6117.
Farrowe (co. Mayo ?), 6768.
Farrowe (co. Westm. ?), 6772.
Farrrellagh. See Fartellagh.
Farrylli (co. Cork ?), 6294.
Farryle, Una ny, pardon (see Farrell), 6494.
Farryll, John, pardon, 3474.
Farryne Moricrie duff, co. Kild., 1947.
Farryne Rory. See Farrenrory.
Farrynamble. See Farranamlane.
Farrynemoeykean, co. Kerry, 6122.
Farryrrey (co. Tip. ?), 6764.
Farryarory. See Farrenrory.
Farrynyrede, co. Cork, 6163.
Farryre (co. Tip. ?), 1184.
Farshinge, Conner, pardon, 6478.
" Edm. O'Fowlwe, pardon, 6462.
Farsing, Donald, pardon, 3374.
Fartacherigh, co. Kilk., 4346.
Fartagh, co. Cav., 4434.
Fartagiar, co. Gal., 5717.
Fartenegeraghe, co. Kilk., 627.
Farthingstown, co. Westm. See Fardingeston.
Fartie. See Fartry.
Fartierne, David m'Edm., pardon, 4388.
" Edm. m'Shane, pardon, 4387.
" James m'Edm., pardon, 4388.
Fartimore, co. Gal., 4234.
Fartry—Fartie—Fartrye—Fertar—Fertrie—Fortar (a district in modern barony of Ballinacor N., co. Wick.; the name is preserved in Vartry river), 818, 1463, 6191, 6460; martial law in, 848, 988, 1126, 1230, 1812, 2163, 2393.
" seneschal of, 6246, 6416.
Fartullagh — Farriullagh — Fortollaghe — Fertulla — Fortullagh — Fortullogh — Fartullaghe (a country and barony in) co. Westm., 398, 877, 1136, 1868, 2617, 3363, 3644, 3301, 5548, 6185, 6786; martial law in, 60, 6368; divided into ploughlands, 1463.
" captain of, 564, 671.
Faryhy—Faryhye. See Farchy.
Faryne (co. Kilk. ?), 5915.
Farynomo ghays, King's co., 1398.
Fasbentry. See Fasaghbentry.

INDEX TO FIANTS.—ELIZABETH.

Faugh, co. Meath, [illegible].
Faughbontre—Faughbentry. See Faughbentry.
Faugh Roleas—Faughrolane. See Faughrolna.
Faughrowe. See Faughbrow.
Faurbancy alias the Downes Layes, co. Antrim, [illegible].
Faudinin barony, co. Kilk. See Idough.
Faughbentry—Faghbentry—Faughbentre—Faughbentry—Faughbentre—Faughbentres—Faughbentrie—Faughbentrie (Bantry barony), co. Wex., [illegible], 1173, [illegible], [illegible], [illegible], [illegible], [illegible]; martial law, 44, 87.
Faugh Coylly (co. Sligo ?), [illegible].
Faughrolane—Faughorolane—Faugh Rolane, co. Kild., [illegible].
" rectory, [illegible].
Faughbrow—Faughbrow—Faughbrowe (Fassaroe, co. Wick.), 1778, [illegible], [illegible].
Faughbentrie. See Faughbentry.
Faun (co. Gal. ?), [illegible].
Faihbeg or Faithbeg, co. Wat., [illegible].
Faiky (co. Tip. or Lim.), [illegible].
Fanganeaym, [illegible].
Fanghan, co. Londonderry. See Foghan.
Fanglar, co. Donegal. See Faghard.
Faughloy—Faghloy—Faghloy (Faughalstown), co. Westm., rectory, [illegible], [illegible], [illegible].
Fantarmoaks, co. Clare. See Fantarmoaks.
Fanuell, used by glovers, 2311.
Faunt—Fannte, James, pardon, [illegible].
" John, pardon, [illegible], [illegible], [illegible].
" Rich., pardon, [illegible].
Fawcett, Rich., porter, Maryborough fortress, [illegible].
Fawney, co. Kerry, [illegible].
Fawning, Oliver, pardon, [illegible].
Fay—Faye—Fain.
" Anne, pardon, [illegible].
" Edm., pardon, [illegible].
" Edw., pardon, [illegible], [illegible], [illegible], [illegible], [illegible].
" Ellenor, [illegible].
" Francis, pardon, [illegible], [illegible].
" Garod, pardon, [illegible].
" Geoffrey (of Trumroe), his heir, [illegible], [illegible].
" George, pardon, [illegible], [illegible].
" Gerald or Garrett (of Derrymagarragh), sheriff of Westmeath, pardon, [illegible]; commission, [illegible]; his heir, [illegible].
" Gerald (of Derrymagarragh), livery, [illegible].
" Gerald, pardon, [illegible].
" Garrett, pardon, [illegible], [illegible].
" Hubert, pardon, [illegible].
" James, pardon, [illegible], [illegible], [illegible].
" Jeffrey, pardon, [illegible].
Fay—Joan, pardon, [illegible].
" John, pardon, [illegible].
" Margaret, pardon, [illegible].
" Maurice, pardon, [illegible].
" Meiler (of Trumroe), wardship and livery, [illegible], [illegible].
" Meiler, Moyler, or Mylor, pardon, [illegible], [illegible], [illegible], [illegible].
" Nicholas, pardon, [illegible], [illegible].
" Patrick, pardon, [illegible], [illegible], [illegible].
" Peirce, pardon, [illegible].
" Peter, pardon, [illegible].
" Redmond, pardon, [illegible], [illegible], [illegible].
" Richard, pardon, [illegible].
" Richard, son of Geoffrey of Trumroe, [illegible], [illegible].
" Robert, pardon, [illegible], [illegible].
" Thomas, pardon, [illegible], [illegible].
" Thomas, escape from gaol, [illegible].
" Walter, pardon, [illegible], [illegible], [illegible].
" William, pardon, [illegible], [illegible].
Fay—Faye, co. Gal., [illegible], [illegible].
Fay—Faye (co. Gal. or Rosc.), [illegible], [illegible].
Fay (Fahe ?) co. Lim., [illegible].
Fay Inollowacklaugh (co. Leit. ?), [illegible].
Faymore, co. Donegal. See Fighmore.
Faynevlankalig, co. Kerry, [illegible].
Faywyn, Tho. fitz Wm., pardon, [illegible].
Fayre alias Faro, co. Wex., chapel, [illegible].
Fayre furlongs at Carrickfergus, [illegible].
Fayron—Fayrtown—Fiernan (Foyran), co. Westm., [illegible], [illegible], [illegible]; rectory, [illegible], [illegible].
Feadan, co. Gal., [illegible].
Feadam, co. Arm. or Down, [illegible].
Feadanmore, co. Lim., rectory, [illegible].
Feadymore (Fedamore), barony, co. Lim., [illegible].
" See also Kylfeadymore, [illegible].
Feach, Margery ving, pardon, [illegible].
Feagh, co. Gal. See Fow.
Feaghe (King's co. ?), [illegible].
Feaghe (co. Meath ?), [illegible].
Feaghelughiry (Lohiry ?), co. Cork, [illegible].
Feaghin, Teig m'Wm. I, pardon, [illegible].
Feakens, Rob., pardon, [illegible].
Feakins, Peter, pardon, [illegible].
Feale, Hubert m'Shane mc, pardon, [illegible].
Feale (co. Cork ?), [illegible], [illegible].
Feale, Tho., pardon, [illegible].
Fealy, John m'Edm. oy, pardon, [illegible].
Fealyn, Wm. fitz David fitz Nich., pardon, [illegible].
Fean in Oruhenagh, co. Kerry, [illegible].
Feanstown—Feanstone (Flemstown ?), co. Meath, [illegible], [illegible], [illegible].
Fearnaviegan, co. Kerry, [illegible].
Fearanmaldfihill, co. Kerry, [illegible].
Fearanmarrine (co. Lim. ?), [illegible].
Fearin m'Kenedowy (co. Cork ?), [illegible].

INDEX TO FIANTS—ELIZABETH.

Fearman, Tho., tailor, fort of Philipstown, King's co., 4[illegible], [illegible].
Fearmanagh — Fearmanagh. See Fermanagh.
Fearann (co. Wat. ?), [illegible].
Fearnes. See Ferns.
Fearny. See Fernsey.
Fearran amany (co. Ferm. ?), [illegible].
Fearran y harpo, co. Sligo, [illegible].
Fearrye Edmond roe, co. Cork, [illegible].
Feart, co. Kilk., [illegible].
Feart, the, co. Tip., [illegible].
Feartagh, co. Lim., [illegible].
Feartan, co. Clare, [illegible].
Feartmore, co. Gal., [illegible].
Featherbed stolen, value of, [illegible].
Feibo (or Furboe), in Dunboyne, 11[illegible], [illegible].
Feibie, Wm., pardon, [illegible].
Feck, co. Lim., [illegible].
Fecullye—Fecullye (Feighcullen), co. Kild., 1916, [illegible].
Fedamore, co. Lim., rectory, [illegible], [illegible].
" See Feadymore, Kylfeadymore.
Fedan. See Feddan, co. Gal.
Fedan. See Feddan, King's co.
Fedane. See Feddan, co. Gal.
Feddan, co. Down, [illegible].
Feddan—Fedan—Fedane—Feddane (Viddane ?), co. Gal., [illegible], [illegible], [illegible], [illegible], [illegible]; castle, [illegible].
Feddan—Fedan—Fedane—Feddane (Faddan), King's co., 1461, [illegible], [illegible], [illegible].
Feddan (Feddane), co. Mon., [illegible].
Feddan (co. Rosc. ?), [illegible].
Feddanes (co. Wat. ?), [illegible].
Feddane (co. Clare ?), [illegible].
Feddane. See Feddan.
Feddane (co. Westm. ?), [illegible].
Feddane (Fiddane, co. Cork), [illegible].
Feddane (two) (Faddan More and Beg, King's co.), 1801.
Feddart—Feddert, grange by, co. Tip., [illegible], [illegible].
Feddigan, Wm., pardon, [illegible].
Feddreth, co. Wex., [illegible].
Federt (co. Kild. ?), [illegible].
Fedmay (co. Lim. ?), [illegible].
Fedorgh, country of (co. Wex. ?), [illegible].
Fedowe (Fedoo), co. Mon., [illegible].
Fedowne (co. Kilk. ?), [illegible].
Fee Glassey, co. Tip., 777.
Feelde, Wm., rector of Holy Trinity, Cork, [illegible].
Feenagh, co. Clare. See Finaghe.
Fees on fiant, &c., 46; on pardon, remitted, [illegible].
Fegan, Richard, licence to, 31.
Feghard (Figart or Faugher, co. Donegal), [illegible].
Feghin's church (B. Feighins), co. Westm., [illegible].
Feghkins, Rob., pardon, [illegible].
Feghnam, co. Tip., [illegible].
Feighcullen, co. Kild. See Fecullye.
Feili—Feilde, Andrew, pardon, [illegible].
" David, pardon, 3164.
" Dermod, pardon, [illegible], [illegible], [illegible], [illegible].
" James, pardon, [illegible].
" John, pardon, [illegible].
" Manus, pardon, [illegible], [illegible].
" Margaret, pardon, [illegible].
" Matthew, wardship, 4116.
" Mornes, pardon, [illegible].
" Morice or Morris, pardon, [illegible], [illegible], [illegible].
" Owen, pardon, [illegible].
" Owen, surgeon, pardon, [illegible].
" Richard, 4116.
" Rob. (of Culdaff), wardship of his heir, 4116.
" Tho., 4116.
" Wm., surgeon, [illegible]; medicus, [illegible].
" Wm. oge, pardon, [illegible].
Feilly, John oy, pardon, [illegible].
Feiame, Connor m'Mclaghlen, pardon, [illegible].
Feian, Edm. fitz John, pardon, [illegible].
" Grany ool, pardon, [illegible].
Feiame, David, pardon, [illegible], [illegible].
" Dermot, pardon, [illegible].
" Donagh fitz Nicholas, pardon, [illegible], [illegible].
" Donald fitz Nicholas pardon, [illegible], [illegible].
" Edmond, pardon, [illegible], [illegible].
" Joan oy, pardon, [illegible].
" John, pardon, [illegible].
" Maurice fitz William, pardon, [illegible].
" Nicholas, pardon, [illegible], [illegible].
" Richard fitz Nicholas, pardon, [illegible], [illegible].
" Rossy, pardon, [illegible], [illegible].
" Thomas, pardon, [illegible], [illegible].
" William m'Richard, pardon, [illegible].
Feignston, co. Meath, [illegible].
Feicneston, mikle (Great Flemingstown, co. Meath), [illegible].
Feiwston (co. Westm. ?), [illegible].
Feieston (Feltstown ? co. Meath), 1174.
Feistcrache (of Ballyrobuck) pardon (see Ferrelow), [illegible].
Feltemston, co. Meath, 344.
Felemston, littell (Little Flemingstown, co. Meath), [illegible].
Feller, Maryol, 17[illegible].
Fellister, Nicholas, pardon, [illegible].
Feltrym (co. Dub.), [illegible].
Feltter, James, pardon, [illegible].

INDEX TO FIANTS—ELIZABETH.

Fox, Margaret, pardon, 3418.
" Nich., general escheator, [illegible]; [illegible], 3480; pardon, [illegible].
Foxaghes — Fennaughes (Fenaghs), co. Kild., [illegible], 3703.
Fe[illegible], alias Foyras, co. Westm., 1240.
Fosanghs (co. Leit. ?), 4128. See also Fynnagh.
Fenning, fatal accident at Drogheda, [illegible].
Fenry (King's co. ?), [illegible].
Fenell, David, pardon, [illegible].
" Edm. fitz David, pardon, [illegible].
" Garrett, pardon, [illegible].
Fenelle, James, pardon, [illegible].
Fenigan, Petr., pardon, [illegible].
Fenit, co. Kerry. See Feyeard, Fyoalit.
Fenlagh, co. Sligo, [illegible].
Fennagh (co. Tip. ?), [illegible].
Fennaghes in Iverculck, co. Kilk., [illegible].
Fennaght, [illegible].
Fennaghes. See Fenaghes.
Fenne, King's co., 172.
Fennell, James, pardon, 4634.
" James, physician, pardon, [illegible].
Fennersconte. See Fennors Corte.
Fennor, co. Cork, [illegible]. See also Fynnor.
Fennor (co. Kilk. ?), 1213, [illegible].
Fennor, co. Meath. See Fynnor.
Fennor by Fevagh, co. Meath, [illegible].
Fennor—Finnor (co. Tip. ?), [illegible], [illegible].
Fennor, co. Wat. See Fignore.
Fennor, co. Westm. See Forgara.
Fennora, co. Meath, rectory, [illegible].
Fennorstown (co. Kilk. ?), 1311.
Fennors, Connor, pardon, [illegible].
Fennors Corte—Fennorsconte, co. Kilk., [illegible], [illegible].
Fenoghe, co. Cav., [illegible].
Fenoghe (co. Kilk. ?), 6102.
Fenoystowne (co. Tip. ?), [illegible].
Fenor (Finnor), co. Lim., [illegible].
Fenore, Connor, pardon, [illegible].
Fent (co. Tip. ?), [illegible].
Fentire. See Fintier.
Fenton, Geoffrey (afterwards knight), secretary of state, [illegible], [illegible]; principal secretary of the council, [illegible], [illegible]; general cessor and collector of cess, [illegible], [illegible]; surveyor gen., [illegible], [illegible]; clerk gen. of works, [illegible], [illegible]; commissioner, [illegible]; indenture with Irish chief, [illegible]; grant of land, [illegible]; grant of possessions of vacant bishopric, [illegible]; grant of a wardship, [illegible]; lease, [illegible].
Fenloyge, co. Gal., [illegible].
Fenbary (or [illegible]), [illegible].
Feohanagh, co. Lim. (or [illegible]), [illegible].
Feole, Ricard m'Shane [illegible], [illegible].
Feolan, Florence macDavid, pardon, [illegible].
Feolane, Morrish, pardon, [illegible].
Feorna, co. Wex., [illegible].
Ferallo, Murtagh m'Conoghor I., pardon, [illegible].
Ferall Bane. See O'Ferrall.
Ferall, Donnvana, pardon, 6108.
" Uin., pardon, [illegible].
Ferancaharrowe, co. Lim., [illegible].
Feran O'Neile. See Feren O'Neyle.
Feranes. See Ferrans.
Ferantlorde, co. Gal., [illegible].
Ferbill—Ferbilly—Ferbyll. See Ferbille.
Fercall — Fercalle — Fercalle — Ferkall — Forgall — Ferkall — Ferkall — Ferkeall — Ferkill — Ferkyall — Fyrcall — Fherkeall (O'Molloys country, the baronies of Eglish, Ballyboy and Ballycowan), King's co., [illegible], [illegible], [illegible], [illegible], [illegible], [illegible], [illegible]; [illegible] of, pardoned, [illegible], [illegible], [illegible]; martial law in, [illegible], [illegible]; made shire land, 1554; surrender and regrant to chief, [illegible].
" captain of, [illegible], [illegible], [illegible], [illegible], [illegible].
" seneschal of, [illegible].
Fercullen — Farcollan — Farcullen — Fercollin — Fercollen — Ferculyn — Fercullen — Forcullyn, country (a district at this time nearly conterminous with the present parish of Powerscourt, co. Wick.), [illegible], [illegible], [illegible], [illegible], [illegible]; martial law in, [illegible], [illegible], [illegible], [illegible], [illegible], [illegible], [illegible].
" seneschal of, [illegible], [illegible].
Ferculleen, co. Wex., [illegible].
Fercullyn. See Fercullen, co. Wick.
Ferdorgh, James Sharkall, pardon, [illegible].
Ferdorogh or Ola-[illegible], [illegible].
Ferdorough, alias John Fercall, pardon, [illegible], [illegible], [illegible], [illegible].
Ferekall. See Fercall.
Fereman, Tho., sailor, Philipston fort, [illegible].
Feremantolshe, co. Kerry, [illegible].
Ferenokelly, Queen's co., [illegible].
Ferequille, co. Wat., [illegible].
Ferelor. See Ferreter.
Fergall. See Fercall.
Fergus river, co. Clare, weirs on, [illegible], [illegible], [illegible].
Ferinlosmill, co. Cav., [illegible].
Ferinkonie, co. Gal., [illegible].
Ferioughe, co. Kild., [illegible].
Ferkall — Ferkall — Ferkeall — Ferkill. See Fercall.

Fericmge, Walter, pardon, 6877.

Fermanagh—Farmanagh — Farmanagh—Fearmanagh—Fearmanagh—Fermanagh, [illegible], [illegible]; captain of, [illegible]; country surrendered, [illegible]; granted to Maguire, [illegible], 6169; made shire ground, [illegible]; men of pardoned, [illegible]; general of the forces in, [illegible], [illegible], [illegible]; commission to prosecute rebels, [illegible]-1.

Fermoia. See Fermoy.

Fermorie, 4169.

Fermoy—Ardmoye — Armoye — Fermoie—Fermoye — Firmoy —Larmoy—Lermoy, co. Cork, [illegible], [illegible], 3116, [illegible].

,, demesne lands, [illegible].

,, rectory, [illegible].

,, monastery leased, [illegible], 3182, [illegible]; granted, [illegible], [illegible]; possessions leased, [illegible], [illegible].

,, viscount of, Maurice Roche, livery to his heir, 3156.

,, viscount, David Roche, commission, 1[illegible], 1544; pardon, [illegible], 3191; livery, [illegible]; lands of, [illegible]; leader of people of his country, [illegible]; his sons, [illegible], [illegible], [illegible]; his wife, [illegible]; livery to his heir, [illegible]. See Roche.

,, viscount Maurice Roche, pardon, [illegible]; livery, [illegible]; commission, [illegible]; lease, [illegible]; grant of land, [illegible]; land of, [illegible], [illegible]; submission to earl of Essex, and pardon, [illegible]. See Roche.

Fermoyle. See Formoyle and Foremle.

Fermoyle—Formoyle, co. Sligo, [illegible], [illegible].

Fernagh (co. Cork ?), [illegible].

Fernaght, co. Long., [illegible], [illegible].

Fernan, Conoghor oge Mc Rory, pardon, [illegible].

,, Salomon, clerk, pardon, [illegible].

Fernas (co. Ross ?), [illegible].

Fernane (co. Cork ?), 6744.

Fernane Callaghe (Fernanegallagh), co. Ross., [illegible].

Fernay. See Ferney.

Ferne prior in Clanrycard, 1[illegible].

Ferneighe (co. Gal.), [illegible].

Ferers. See Ferns.

Ferney—Fearney—Ferny—Fernie — Fermy —[illegible]—Inferny (barony of Farney, co. Mon.), [illegible], 1[illegible], 1[illegible], [illegible], [illegible], [illegible], [illegible]; granted to Earl of Essex, [illegible]; commission to survey, [illegible]; general pardon to inhabitants, [illegible], [illegible].

,, captain of, [illegible], 1[illegible], [illegible], [illegible].

,, seneschal of, [illegible].

Fernie. See Ferney.

Ferns. See Ferns.

Fernock (co. Kilk. ?), [illegible].

Fernoknight, co. Meath, 1[illegible].

Fernoruthe, co. Louth, 341.

Fernought (co. Long. ?), [illegible].

Ferns—Fearnes—Fernes—Fernes, co. Wex., [illegible], 1[illegible], [illegible], [illegible], [illegible], [illegible], [illegible], [illegible], [illegible], [illegible], [illegible], [illegible], [illegible], [illegible].

,, castle and manor, [illegible]; leased, [illegible], [illegible].

,, constable of castle, [illegible], [illegible], [illegible], [illegible]; service due to, [illegible].

,, abbey leased, [illegible], 1[illegible], 1[illegible], 1[illegible], [illegible], [illegible].

,, bishop Alexander (Devereux), commission, [illegible].

,, ,, John (Devereux), commission, [illegible], [illegible].

,, ,, Hugh (Allen), commission, [illegible], [illegible].

,, ,, Robert Grave, appointed, [illegible]-10.

,, ,, Nicholas Stafford, appointed, [illegible]-[illegible]; commission, [illegible].

,, dean, [illegible], [illegible].

,, archdeacon, [illegible], [illegible].

,, treasurer of cathedral, [illegible], [illegible].

,, benefices in diocese, [illegible], [illegible]-[illegible], [illegible], [illegible], [illegible], [illegible].

,, county, [illegible], [illegible], [illegible]; martial law in, [illegible]; commission of peace, [illegible].

,, county, clerk of crown, &c., [illegible].

Ferrere (Fearne ?), co. Westm., 1[illegible].

Feray. See Ferney.

Feray-priorie. See Farrinopriory.

Ferons. See Fernes.

Ferragh (co. Donegal), [illegible].

Ferrall, Honor, pardon, [illegible].

Farrall, Brodagh, pardon, [illegible].

,, Caselyn, pardon, widow, [illegible].

,, Catherine ny, [illegible].

,, Donald, pardon, [illegible].

,, Edm., pardon, [illegible].

,, Fergus, pardon, [illegible].

,, Henry, pardon, [illegible].

,, James, pardon, [illegible].

,, Jane (or ny (Isabel)), pardon, [illegible].

,, John, pardon, [illegible].

,, Katherine, [illegible].

,, Mary ny, pardon, [illegible].

,, Wm., pardon, [illegible], [illegible].

Ferran an mullyn (co. Ferm. ?), [illegible].

Ferrainaroughie (co. Ferm. ?), [illegible].

Ferrens—Ferans — Ferens, co. Meath, [illegible], [illegible], [illegible].

INDEX TO FIANTS—ELIZABETH.

Farranshambouraghe, co. Lim., [illegible] of, [illegible].
Farne of Chastley, lord [illegible], earl of, [illegible].
Farrelchemorne [illegible] (co. Cork, [illegible].
Farrell, Dermot, English liberty, [illegible].
Ferrennaugh. See Fermanagh.
Ferrennannagh (co. Wat. ?), [illegible].
Farrennolagh. See Farrennemollaghe.
Farrenerois. See Farrenroyes.
Farrendawkinne. See Farrendawkinne.
Farrenroyes. See Farrenroyes.
Farrencknagh, co. Long., [illegible].
Farrennemannaghe. See Farrenhonnanaghe.
Farron Emery, co. Westm., [illegible].
Farren Hamrle (Farren O'Neill, co. Car. ?), [illegible].
Farrenleamon. See Farrenleamon.
Farrennemanaghe—Farrennenanaghe near Limerick, [illegible], [illegible].
Farren O'Neyle—Feran O'Neile, co. Carlow, country of, [illegible], [illegible].
Farrenrory. See Farrenrory.
Farron ros, pardon, [illegible].
Farrelor—Ferrier—Ferrier—Fistier—Firyter, Edm. (of Bally-[illegible]), pardon, [illegible], [illegible].
" John, pardon, [illegible].
" Nich., pardon, [illegible].
" See Foletorn[illegible].
Ferries of Waxford and Ross, granted, [illegible].
Ferrignacorry, co. Lim., [illegible].
Ferrinagiragh, co. Long., [illegible].
Ferris, Anthony, pardon, [illegible].
Ferris, co. Kerry, [illegible].
Ferriters cove, co. Kerry. See Foriors.
Ferrell, Brian [illegible], pardon, [illegible].
" Rossy [illegible], pardon, [illegible].
Ferrys, King's co., [illegible].
Ferryeokilie alias Tymoke, Queen's co., [illegible].
Fertagh, co. Kilk. See Fertengoragher.
Fertangor (co. Gal. or Mayo), [illegible].
Fertan, King's co., [illegible].
Fertay, co. Clare, [illegible].
Fertes. See Fartry.
Ferters crook (Ferriters cove, in par. of Dunurlin), co. Kerry, [illegible].
Fertengeraghe (Fertagh), co. Kilk., monastery leased, [illegible]; granted, [illegible].
" rectory, [illegible].
Fertallaghe. See Fartullagh.
Fertreany, co. Lim., [illegible].
Fertrie. See Fartry.
Fertullagh—Fertolla. See Fartullagh.
Fertullagh, rectory, [illegible].
Fertullaghe in the Annaly, [illegible].
Fertullagh. See Fartullagh.
Fertur. See Fartry.
Feryher, King's co., [illegible].
Feryarell. See Ferrall.
Ferys, King's co., [illegible].
Ferrypoonill, co. Car., [illegible].
Feryter. See Ferretor.
Fessel, Thomas, pension, [illegible].
Fethard—Fetherd—Fethards—Fethird—Fidderd—Feldrath—Fidert—Fitherd—Fyrherd—Fythert, co. Tip., [illegible], [illegible], [illegible], [illegible], [illegible], [illegible], [illegible], [illegible], [illegible]; sale of aqua vitae in, [illegible]; premises in, granted, [illegible].
" sovereign of, commissions, [illegible], [illegible], [illegible].
" " and commonalty pardoned, [illegible].
" abbey, [illegible], [illegible].
" Drake [illegible], [illegible].
" our Lady's street, [illegible].
" old gate, [illegible].
" priory, lands of, granted, [illegible].
" rectory, [illegible], [illegible].
" See Feldart.
Fethard—Fytherd, co. Wex., [illegible]; creek, [illegible].
Fethards. See Fethard.
Fetherdes bridge, in Clonmel, co. Tip., [illegible].
Fethird. See Fethard.
Fethmayne (Kilfithmone, co. Tip. ?), [illegible].
Fetigan, Wm., pardon, [illegible].
Fettiplace, George (chief justice of Munster), [illegible].
Few (Fough ?), co. Gal., [illegible].
Fewmagh (co. Rosc. ?), [illegible].
Fews, co. Armagh. See Fues.
Fews, co. Wat. See Tamplerary.
Feyonyd, island, [illegible] (Fenis), co. Kerry, [illegible].
Feyrm alias Feasshe, co. Westm., [illegible].
Feynore, co. Tip., rectory, [illegible].
Feynogues, in Munster, [illegible].
Fiale, co. Cork, [illegible], [illegible].
Fiall—Fyall, co. Cork, [illegible], [illegible].
Fian, George, [illegible].
" Rich., alderman, [illegible]; commission, [illegible].
" Robert, lease, [illegible].
" Tayler, Dermod O Canenan, pardon, [illegible].
" Tho., merchant, [illegible].
Fiane, William, pardon, [illegible].
Fianston — Fianstone — Fianstown. See Fyanston.
Fiant, Matthew, pardon, [illegible].
Fiant not sealed before deputy's departure, confirmed by successor, [illegible].
Fiarlighaline, co. Lim., [illegible].
Fiarlighane, [illegible].
Fiddan, in Connaught, [illegible].
Fiddane, co. Kerry, [illegible].

INDEX TO FIANTS—ELIZABETH.

Fiddan (co. Kilk. ?), 6704.
Fiddan—Fydan, co. Wat., 2626, 4714, 6476.
Fiddane, co. Cork. See Foidane—Nufeddane, [illegible].
Fiddane—Fyddane, co. Wat., 1616, 6176.
Fiddart. See Fethard.
Fiddaun, co. Gal. See Feddan.
Fiddert, co. Wex., [illegible].
Fiddown, co. Kilk. See Fidowne—Fidone.
Fiddrath—Fidert. See Fethard, co. Tip.
Fidone (Fiddown, co. Kilk. ?), 6541.
Fidorgh—Fidorghkearde (Fidorfe), co. Meath, 6[illegible].
Fidorthe—Fydorthe, co. Meath, [illegible], 1174.
Fidowne—Fydowne (Fiddown), co. Kilk., 1404, 6784; rectory, [illegible].
Field, John fitz Philip, pardon, 4616.
„ Wm., pardon, [illegible].
Fielr, Donogh m'Teig ny, 6464.
Fierne (co. Kerry ?), [illegible].
Fernaghtonna (Frevaunmish?), co. Westm., [illegible].
Fierles, co. Kerry. See Nedloyra.
Fiermore, co. Westm., 1702.
Fighmore (Faymore ?), co. Don., 6[illegible].
Filgyly, David, pardon, 2357.
Fild or O'Filly, Dermod, pardon, 4421.
„ Owen, pardon, 4421.
Filde or O'Filly, Owen, pardon, 1[illegible].
Filletten (co. Lim. ?), 6437.
Fillawston, co. Meath, [illegible]. See also Fyllerston.
Finaghe—Fynagh (Fenagh ?), co. Clare, [illegible], 6718.
Fynallymore, co. Kerry, [illegible].
„ See Fynallymore.
Finance: arrears of pay compounded for, [illegible].
Fine, Daniel, soldier, petition for livery of lands, [illegible]. See Flinn.
Fine for pardon of Magnire, &c., not known, [illegible]. See under Galway, Mullingar.
Fineclas, co. Galway, [illegible], 4[illegible].
Fineglas, co. Kerry, [illegible].
Finglas (co. Lim. ?), [illegible]. See also Fynoglas.
Finglas—Finglass—Fingiass—Fynglas—Fynglass:
„ Jennett, [illegible].
„ John (of Tipperswick), pardon, 7[illegible]; commissions, 4148, [illegible].
„ John (of Porterstown), wardship of heir, [illegible].
„ John, 1714, 2721.
„ John, sheriff of co. Dublin, [illegible], [illegible].
„ Patrick (of Westpalstown), [illegible], 2721.
„ Patrick, lease to, 1[illegible], 6[illegible], [illegible]; his land, [illegible], 1720, [illegible], [illegible], [illegible]; grant of a wardship, [illegible].
„ Richard (of Westpalstown), serjeant at law, 179, [illegible], [illegible]; takes oath of supremacy, [illegible], [illegible]; solicitor-gen., [illegible]; commissions, [illegible], [illegible], [illegible], [illegible], [illegible], [illegible], 1417-8, 1434, 2117, [illegible], 3444; freedom from subsidy, 179; lease, [illegible], 1[illegible], [illegible], [illegible].
„ Roger (of Porterstown), pardon, 1[illegible]; com., 300.
„ Roger, lease, 1[illegible]; com., [illegible].
„ Roger (of Porterstown), wardship, [illegible].
„ Thomas, 5144.
Finglass, co. Dub., [illegible].
Finylass. See Finglas.
Finlawton, co. Meath, 1944.
Finis, co. Clare, [illegible].
Finlecke, co. Ross. See Fynleckmore.
Finloge (co. Tip. ?), 6784.
Finlirie, King's co., [illegible].
Finlomston, co. Meath, 1614.
Finley (co. Clare ?), [illegible].
Finn, Donell, pardon, 6400.
„ Tirreagh, pardon, 4914.
Finnaghton lands, co. Dub., [illegible]. See Fynnaghton.
Finne, Robert, livery, [illegible].
„ —Fynne, Wm., grant of land, 1[illegible]; livery to son, [illegible].
„ See Finn.
Finniterstown, co. Lim. See Ballinfinter, Ballyfinter, Ballyfyntter.
Finnoe, co. Lim. See Fonoe, Fynowe.
Finnor (see Fonnor), [illegible].
Finnoure (co. Cork ?), [illegible]. See Fynnor.
Finnure, co. Gal. See Ballyfinnor.
Finowick—Fynowick (Fintoge ?), co. Kerry, [illegible], [illegible], [illegible].
Finowre (Fonnor, co. Wat. ?), 1048. See also Fynnor.
Finshean, Dermod, pardon, 6401.
Finter—Fontire—Fintire—Fintrie, King's co., 1394, 7071, 4384, [illegible]; rectory, 1[illegible], [illegible], [illegible].
Fintire in Geeshill (Finter, King's co.), [illegible].
Fintire. See Finter.
Finoge, co. Kerry. See Finowick.
Fircal, King's co. See Fercall.
Firemore, King's co., 478, [illegible], 6171.
Firtior. See Forrertor.
Firtshaw (co. Long. ?), [illegible].
Firron, [illegible]. See Feyron.
Firres of S. Mary abbey, Dublin, 4[illegible].
Firrys fitz, pardon, [illegible].
First Fruits, clerk of, appointed, [illegible], [illegible], 24[illegible].
„ clerk or remembrancer, 4[illegible], 5410, [illegible].
„ com. to inquire of, 4[illegible], [illegible].
„ com. to value bishoprics and benefices for, 4406, 4917.

INDEX TO FIANTS—ELIZABETH.

First Fruits of province of Dublin collected for repair of S. Patrick's, 481, [illegible]
Firrylor. *See* Ferrotor.
Fish, John. *See* Fishe.
Fish (salt), impressed for army, 454, [illegible], 1[illegible]
Fish, tithes of, 17[illegible].
Fishe—Fish, John, pardon, [illegible], [illegible].
Fisher, Henry, clerk of the ordnance, [illegible].
" Tho., pardon, 3482.
Fisherie, alias O'Ferrall, Connor roe, pardon, [illegible].
Fishers' stonie, near Limerick city, [illegible].
Fishery, duty on foreign fishing vessels, [illegible], [illegible]; great fleet of fishermen frequent Waterford, [illegible].
Fishing of Bann river, leased. *See* Bann.
Fishing of Carlingford, tithes of, leased, [illegible]; exemption from tithes, [illegible].
Fishing, Ros, at Carrickfergus free of customs, 1[illegible].
Fishing of Galway river, [illegible].
Fishe, George, pardon, [illegible].
Fissher, Peter, grant of a wardship, [illegible].
" Tho., commission, [illegible].
Fisherfield, co. Clare, [illegible].
Fitche, vicar of [illegible], [illegible].
Fithard. *See* Fethard, co. Tip.
Fithmone—Fythmone (Kilfithmone?), co. Tip., 12[illegible], [illegible].
Fiton—Fyton—Fytone—Fyttin—Fytton:
" Alexander, commission, [illegible]; pardon, [illegible].
" Anthony, searcher and gauger of Galway, [illegible], [illegible]; collector of wine duty at Galway, [illegible], [illegible], [illegible]; lease of customs of Galway, [illegible], [illegible].
" Edward, knight (alias Fyton), president of Connaught, [illegible], [illegible], [illegible]; chief commissioner of Connaught, [illegible]; vice treasurer, [illegible], [illegible]; commissions, 13[illegible], [illegible], [illegible], [illegible], [illegible], [illegible], [illegible], [illegible], [illegible], [illegible], [illegible], [illegible], [illegible], [illegible], [illegible], [illegible], [illegible], [illegible], [illegible], [illegible]; constable of castle of Athlone, [illegible]; pardon, [illegible]; licence of absence, [illegible].
" Edward, receiver general of the Exchequer, [illegible]; Sir Edward, a Munster undertaker, [illegible]; grant of land, [illegible]; lease recited, [illegible].
" George, commission, [illegible].
" *See* Fytton.
Fitz Alexander, Dermot, pardon, 1[illegible].
" Galloghe m'Tirrelagh (M'Donell?), pardon, [illegible].
" Edmund, sheriff of M'William's country, [illegible]; sheriff of Connaught, [illegible]; leases, [illegible], [illegible], [illegible], [illegible], [illegible], [illegible], [illegible], [illegible], [illegible]; pardon, [illegible]; executor of, [illegible].
" Gerald, pardon, [illegible].
" Tirrelagh, pardon, [illegible].
Fitz Andrewe, Donell, pardon, [illegible].
Fitz Benet, Edm., pardon, [illegible].
Fitz Christopher, Gerald, pardon, [illegible].
" Rich., pardon, [illegible].
" Rob., pardon, [illegible].
Fitz Cormack, Cormock fitz John, pardon, [illegible].
" Donogh, pardon, [illegible].
Fitz Conell, Dermod, pardon, [illegible].
Fitz Cowrogry, Moloughlin, pardon, [illegible].
Fitz Daniel, David, pardon, [illegible].
" John, pardon, [illegible].
" Margaret, pardon, [illegible].
" vel Morie, pardon, [illegible].
Fitz Darby, Daniel, pardon, [illegible].
" John, pardon, [illegible].
Fitz Davi. *See* Fitz Davy.
Fitz David, David, pardon, [illegible].
" Donogh, pardon, [illegible].
" Edmund (or Fitz Davy) (of Ballygallaghan, co. Lim.), pardon, 1[illegible], [illegible], [illegible].
" Edm., pardon, [illegible], [illegible].
" Ellen or Ellinor, pardon, [illegible], [illegible].
" Gerrot, [illegible].
" James, pardon, [illegible].
" John, pardon, [illegible], [illegible].
" Morris, pardon, [illegible].
" Patrick, pardon, [illegible], [illegible].
" Redmund, pardon, [illegible].
" Richard, pardon, [illegible], [illegible], [illegible].
" Theobald, pardon, [illegible].
" Thomas, pardon, [illegible].
" Wm., pardon, [illegible], [illegible].
Fitz Davy—Davie—Davi—Davye:
" Edmund, pardon, [illegible], [illegible], [illegible].
" Edm. *See* Fitz David.
" Gerald, pardon, [illegible].
" Jeffery or Seffrain, pardon, [illegible].
" John, pardon, [illegible], [illegible].
" Redmund, pardon, [illegible].
" Rich., pardon, [illegible], [illegible].
" Wm., pardon, [illegible].
Fitz Denis, Wm., pardon, [illegible].
Fitz Derby, Donogh, pardon, [illegible].
" John, pardon, [illegible].
" Tho., pardon, [illegible].
Fitz Dermod, Morie, pardon, [illegible].
" Teig, pardon, [illegible].
Fitz Dermot, Dermot, pardon, [illegible].
Fitz Desmond, John, knight, attainted, [illegible].

INDEX TO FIANTS—ELIZABETH.

Fitz Desmonde, Ellenor, widow of White Knight, [illegible], [illegible], [illegible], [illegible].
Fitz Dominick, Bartholomew, pardon, [illegible].
Fitz Donell, Johanna, pardon, 414.
Fitz Donell roe, Wm., pardon, [illegible].
Fitz Donill fitz Wm., Donogh, pardon, 1044.
" Edm., pardon, [illegible].
" William, pardon, 1044.
Fitz Donnell, Katherine, pardon, [illegible].
Fitz Donogh, Margaret, pardon, [illegible].
" Thady, pardon, [illegible].
Fitz Donoghe, Wm., pardon, [illegible].
Fitz Eddy, Ellis, pardon, [illegible].
Fitz Edmond — Edmonde — Edmound — Edmund:
" David or Davie, pardon, [illegible], [illegible], [illegible].
" Donill, pardon, [illegible].
" Edm., pardon, [illegible].
" Edm. oge, pardon, [illegible].
" Edm. oge, M'Ydeganie, pardon, 4413.
" Ellen, [illegible].
" Garrot, pardon, [illegible].
" Gerald, pardon, [illegible], [illegible].
" Gerald fitz John, pardon, [illegible].
" Gerald or Gerrott, pardon, [illegible], [illegible], [illegible].
" Gillduf, pardon, [illegible].
" Henry, pardon, [illegible], [illegible].
" James, pardon, [illegible], [illegible], [illegible], [illegible].
" John. See Fitz Gerald.
" John, pardon, 1043, 1342, [illegible], [illegible], [illegible], [illegible], [illegible], [illegible], [illegible], [illegible], [illegible].
" Jowan, pardon, [illegible].
" Katherine fitz John—Katherine ny tane, pardon, [illegible], [illegible].
" Katherine, pardon, [illegible].
" Margaret, pardon, [illegible], [illegible], [illegible].
" Maurice or Morris, pardon, [illegible], [illegible], [illegible], [illegible], [illegible], [illegible].
" Maurice (of the Geraldines), pardon, [illegible]; attainted, [illegible].
" Muris, pardon, [illegible].
" Nich., pardon, [illegible].
" Rich., pardon, [illegible], [illegible], [illegible], [illegible], [illegible], [illegible], [illegible].
" Richard, pardon, [illegible].
" Rob., pardon, [illegible], [illegible].
" Rory, pardon, [illegible].
" Teig, pardon, [illegible].
" Thomas (of co. Kildare), commission, [illegible].
" Thomas, pardon, [illegible], [illegible], [illegible], 4167, 4111, [illegible], [illegible], [illegible].
" Walter, pardon, [illegible], [illegible], [illegible], [illegible].
Fitz Edmond—William, pardon, [illegible], 1154, [illegible], [illegible], [illegible].
" William (of Ardry, co. Kild.), pardon, 1874, [illegible], [illegible].
Fitz Edmunde, John. See Fitz Gerald.
Fitz Edward, Chr., pardon, [illegible].
" Oliver, pardon, [illegible].
" Thomas, pardon, [illegible], [illegible].
Fitz Hugh, Rich., pardon, [illegible].
Fitz Elyah, John, pardon, [illegible].
Fitz Eustace—Ewstace:
" Edmund Ennyah, pardon, [illegible].
" Wm., pardon, [illegible].
Fitz Garald — Garrald — Garrall. See Fitz Gerald.
Fitz Garrett—Garret — Garrot — Garrot—Garrott:
" David, pardon, [illegible].
" David (or Barron), [illegible].
" Edw. (of Narney), pardon, [illegible].
" Ellen ny tane, pardon, [illegible].
" Garrot (or Desmond, earl of), [illegible].
" Garrott (in King's co.), commission, [illegible].
" Gerald (of Kildangan, co. Kild.), pardon, 1675.
" George, commissions, [illegible], [illegible].
" Henry (of Moyrett), pardon, [illegible].
" Hubert, pardon, [illegible].
" James, pardon, [illegible], [illegible], [illegible].
" John, pardon, [illegible], [illegible], [illegible], [illegible], [illegible], [illegible], [illegible], [illegible], [illegible].
" John, his land, co. Cork, [illegible].
" Morris, pardon, [illegible].
" Nicholas, pension, [illegible].
" Philip, pardon, [illegible].
" Piers, sheriff of Kildare, [illegible].
" Rich. (of Moyrot, Queen's co.), pardon, [illegible]; wardship of heir, [illegible].
" Rich., grant land, Queen's co., [illegible].
" Rich., pardon, [illegible].
" Rob., pardon, [illegible].
" Shane, pardon, [illegible].
" Thomas (of Moyrett), wardship, [illegible].
" Thomas (of Dowore, co. Kild.), pardon, [illegible].
" Thomas, pardon, [illegible], [illegible].
" Thomas (or Barron), pardon, [illegible].
" (of Baynnaragh, co. Wexm.), commission, [illegible].
Fitz Garrold—Garrolde. See Fitz Gerald.

INDEX TO FIANTS.—ELIZABETH.

Fitz Garret—Garrett. *See* Fitz Garrett.
Fitz Geffrey—Geoffrie:
Donell, pardon, [illegible].
" Patrick, pardon, [illegible].
" Walter, pardon, [illegible].
Fitz George, Morris, pardon, [illegible].
Fitz Gerald—Gerald—Geraild—Gerrald—Gerrold—Garrolde—Geralde—Geralt—Gerolde—Gerralde—Gerrolde—Gerralt—Gerrold:
" [ ], attainted (in co. Wexford), [illegible].
" Alson, pardon, [illegible].
" Anstace, pardon, [illegible].
" Anne, pardon, [illegible].
" Brian, pardon, [illegible].
" Catherine, [illegible].
" Christopher, son of Oliver, pardon, [illegible].
" Christopher, pardon, [illegible].
" David Duff, commission, [illegible]; attainted, [illegible].
" David, pardon, [illegible].
" Edmund, pardon, [illegible].
Edm. oge m'Edm. m'James (of Cloyne, co. Cork), pardon, [illegible].
Edm. fitz John (son of John fitz Edm. of Cloyne), pension, [illegible].
Edm. fitz John (son of seneschal of Imokilly), wardship, [illegible].
Edm. fitz Thomas (heir of Knight of the Valley), grant of lands, [illegible]; excepted from pardon, [illegible].
Edw., commission, [illegible].
Edw. (of Tecroghan, afterwards Knt.), wardship and livery, [illegible]; grants to, [illegible].
Edw. fitz James (of Blackhall), commissions, [illegible].
Edw. (son of Sir Maurice of Lackagh), grant of land, [illegible].
Edw., lease, [illegible].
Edw., pardon, [illegible].
Ellen, pardon, [illegible].
Ellice, pardon, [illegible].
Ellinor, pardon, [illegible].
Fitz Gerald—Ellis, pardon, [illegible].
Garret (of Ballyroche), commission, [illegible].
Garret, pardon, [illegible].
George, commissions, [illegible]; leases to his widow, [illegible]; his heir, [illegible].
Gerald. *See* Kildare, earl of.
Gerald. *See* Desmond, earl of.
Gerald, son of earl of Kildare, sent to the queen, [illegible].
Gerald (of Villaneuve, co. Westm.), lease, [illegible]; commissions, [illegible]; pardon, [illegible].
Gerald (co. Wexford), commissions, [illegible].
Gerald (of Annagh, co. Meath), assignment to, [illegible].
Gerald, grant of a wardship, [illegible].
Gerald (of Shian, co. Wat.), his [illegible], [illegible].
Gerald (co. Wat.), kinsmen pardoned, [illegible].
Gerald fitz John, knt., father of viscount Decies, [illegible].
Gerald m' Gerald m'Shane (of Larragh, co. Westm.), commissions, [illegible].
Gerald, son of James (of Desmond), wardship and livery, [illegible].
Gerald fitz Morice (of Allen), commissions, [illegible].
Gerald fitz Philip. *See* Fitz Philip.
Gerald fitz Maurice (of Dunbarry), pardon, [illegible]; rebellion of, [illegible].
Gerald m'Morish (of Thomastown), sheriff of Limerick, [illegible].
Gerald fitz Rich., brother of M'Thomas, grant, [illegible].
Gerald M'Rodery, pardon, [illegible].
Gerald oge, commissions, [illegible].
Gerald, pardon, [illegible].
Gerald or Garrett, pardon, [illegible].

INDEX TO FIANTS—ELIZABETH.

Fitz Gerald—Gibbon, pardon, [illegible].
„ Gruffy, pardon, [illegible].
„ Helen, pardon, 6744.
„ Henry, pardon, [illegible], 2271, [illegible], 3716, [illegible].
„ Hubert fitz James, pardon, [illegible].
„ James, attainted, his possessions granted or leased, [illegible], 1343, [illegible], [illegible], [illegible], [illegible], [illegible], [illegible], [illegible], [illegible], 6792.
„ sir James (of Dromana), pardon, [illegible], [illegible], [illegible]; pardon to his [illegible], [illegible], [illegible]; livery, [illegible]; his heir, [illegible], [illegible].
„ James, knt. (James of Desmond), traitor, [illegible].
„ James (of Dunoyre), commission, [illegible].
„ James (of Urangowellon), commission, [illegible]; pardon, [illegible].
„ James (of Ballymonan), commission, [illegible].
„ James (of Lackagh), pardon, [illegible], [illegible].
„ James, sheriff of Kildare, [illegible].
„ James, grant of land, [illegible], [illegible].
„ James (of Donecla), pardon, [illegible].
„ James, land of, [illegible].
„ James (of Walterstown), testamentary suit, [illegible].
„ James (see Barron), [illegible].
„ James fitz John (of Carrigkitiel), pardon, [illegible].
„ James fitz John (of Knockmoan). See Fitz John.
„ James fitz John (of Tinnecarty), pardon, [illegible].
„ James fitz John (of Stroncally), pardon, [illegible], [illegible]; attainted, [illegible].
„ James fitz Maurice (of Shian), pardon, [illegible], [illegible].
„ James fitz Morish of Desmond, a rebel, [illegible], [illegible], [illegible]; pardon, [illegible], [illegible]; archrebel, [illegible].
„ James fitz Piers (of Ballymonan), pardon, [illegible].
„ James, pardon, [illegible], [illegible], [illegible], [illegible], [illegible], [illegible], [illegible], [illegible], [illegible], [illegible], [illegible], [illegible], [illegible], [illegible], [illegible], [illegible].
„ Johan, pardon, 6744.
„ sir John (of Lisfinin). See Desmond, sir John of.
„ John fitz Edm. (of Cloyne, afterwards knt.), sheriff of Cork, 1518, [illegible]; commissions, 1518, [illegible], [illegible], [illegible], [illegible]; pardon, [illegible], [illegible], [illegible], [illegible]; pardon at his suit, [illegible]–[illegible]; grant of annuity, [illegible]; leases, [illegible], [illegible], [illegible], [illegible].
„ John fitz Edm. (of Clohermoney, co. Cork), grant of land, [illegible]; (of Cahirmoney), pardon, [illegible].
„ John fitz Edm. (of Ballymartyr), seneschal of Imokilly, pardon, [illegible], [illegible], [illegible], [illegible]; wardship of his heir, [illegible].
„ John, lands of (co. Cork), [illegible], [illegible].
„ John, attainted (co. Cork), [illegible].
„ John (Oldwood, co. Wat.), pardon, [illegible].
„ John fitz James, attainted, [illegible].
„ John (of Knockmoan). See Fitz Morish.
„ John fitz William, Knight of Kerry, com., [illegible].
„ John, pardon, [illegible], [illegible], [illegible], [illegible], [illegible], [illegible], [illegible], [illegible], [illegible], [illegible], [illegible], [illegible], [illegible], [illegible], [illegible].
„ Katherine, pardon, [illegible], [illegible], [illegible], [illegible], [illegible], [illegible].
„ Laurence, pardon, [illegible].
„ dame Margaret, wife of sir Maurice, [illegible].
„ Margaret, pardon, [illegible], [illegible].
„ Mary, wife of Oliver Grace, [illegible].
„ Mary, wife of Terence Dempsy, [illegible].
„ Mary, pardon, [illegible], [illegible], [illegible], [illegible].
„ Maurice (of Dromana, knt.), sheriff of co. Cork, 77; commissions, [illegible], [illegible], [illegible]–7, [illegible]; pardon, [illegible]; created baron of Dromana, 1949; created viscount Decies, 1951. See Decies, viscount.
„ Maurice fitz Thomas (of Lackagh, knt.), commissions, [illegible], [illegible], [illegible], [illegible], [illegible], [illegible], [illegible], [illegible], [illegible]; grant of land, [illegible]; lease, [illegible]; pardon to him and his servants, [illegible]; his land, [illegible]; grant to his son, [illegible].
„ Maurice (of Shian, co. Wat.), pardon, [illegible], [illegible], [illegible], [illegible]; attainted, [illegible].

INDEX TO FIANTS—ELIZABETH.

Fitz Gerald—Maurice fitz James (of Osberstown, co. Kild.), com., [illegible]; attainted, [illegible]; pardoned, [illegible], [illegible].
" Maurice fitz James (of Macollop, co. Wat.), pardon, [illegible], [illegible].
" Maurice fitz John (of Knockmoan, co. Wat.), pardon, [illegible], [illegible], [illegible].
" Maurice fitz Tho. (of Bealaborrow, co. Wexf.), pardon, [illegible], [illegible].
" Maurice fitz Philip. See Fitz Philip.
" Maurice fitz Redmond of Brohill. See Gerald.
" Maurice fitz Walter, pardon, [illegible], [illegible].
" Maurice fitz Walter (of Glascely, co. Kild.), pardon, [illegible], [illegible].
" Maurice or Morish, pardon, [illegible].
" Myles (see Barron), [illegible], [illegible].
" Nicholas, pardon, [illegible], [illegible].
" Oliver, attainted, his lands in co. Wexm. leased and granted, [illegible], [illegible], [illegible], [illegible], [illegible], [illegible], [illegible], [illegible], [illegible].
" Oliver, sons of, pardoned, [illegible].
" Oliver fitz Piers, pardon, [illegible], [illegible], [illegible], [illegible], [illegible].
" Oliver, pardon, [illegible], [illegible], [illegible], [illegible], [illegible], [illegible].
" Owny alias Oliver, pardon, [illegible], [illegible].
" Patrick, pardon, [illegible].
" Patrick, com., [illegible]; third justice of Common Bench, [illegible]; second justice, [illegible].
" Peter, pardon, [illegible], [illegible].
" Piers or Peter fitz James (of Ballysonan, afterwards knight), sheriff of Kildare, [illegible], [illegible], [illegible], [illegible]; sheriff of Carlow, [illegible]; commissions, [illegible], [illegible], [illegible], [illegible], [illegible], [illegible], [illegible], [illegible]; pardon, [illegible], [illegible], [illegible], [illegible]; pardon to his men, [illegible]; lease, [illegible].
" Piers or Peter fitz James (of Grangemellyn), sheriff of Kildare, [illegible], [illegible]; commissions, [illegible], [illegible], [illegible]; pardon, [illegible], [illegible].
Fitz Gerald—Pierse, pardon, [illegible], [illegible].
" Redmond (of Brohill), pardon, [illegible], [illegible].
" Redmond (son of Tho. of Cloonbeigh), wardship, [illegible], [illegible].
" Redmond oge (of Ballingan), sheriff of Kildare, pardon, [illegible]; freedom from subsidy, [illegible]; pardon of alienation, [illegible]; commissions, [illegible], [illegible], [illegible], [illegible]; lease, [illegible].
" Redmond, pardon, [illegible], [illegible], [illegible].
" Richard or Riccard (of Moyrough), pardon, [illegible].
" Richard Baron (of Burnchurch), sheriff of Kilkenny; com., [illegible]; pardon, [illegible], [illegible], [illegible] (see Barron).
" Richard, his cross, [illegible].
" Rich. See M'Thomas.
" Richard, pardon, [illegible], [illegible], [illegible], [illegible], [illegible], [illegible], [illegible], [illegible], [illegible], [illegible], [illegible], [illegible], [illegible], [illegible], [illegible], [illegible].
" Robert fitz Morice (of Osbertstown), pardon, [illegible]; rebellion, [illegible].
" Robert, pardon, [illegible], [illegible].
" Royer, pardon, [illegible].
" Shane, pardon, [illegible], [illegible].
" Shely, pardon, [illegible].
" Tebbott, pardon, [illegible].
" Sir Thomas (Silken Thomas), horse from, [illegible], [illegible].
" Thomas (son of Oliver), pardon, [illegible].
" Thomas (of Rath by Grenoks), surrender, [illegible].
" Thomas Adayre, pardon, [illegible].
" Thomas ne Cnutine, pardon, [illegible].
" Thomas of Desmond, knt., pardon, [illegible].
" Thomas fitz James (of Dromana), pardon, [illegible], [illegible], [illegible].
" Thomas fitz James (of Templemyrhell), pardon, [illegible].
" Thomas, Knight of the Valley or of Glin, attainted, lands of, [illegible], [illegible], [illegible], [illegible], [illegible].
" Thomas, son of preceding, attainted, [illegible].
" Thomas (of Tallow, co. Lim.), called M'Thomas, pardon, [illegible]; mortgage by, [illegible]. See M'Thomas.

INDEX TO FIANTS—ELIZABETH.

Fitz Gerald—Thomas (of Little Narragh), pardon, [illegible].
„ Thomas, sheriff of Kildare, [illegible].
„ Thomas, son of Sir Maurice of Lackagh, [illegible]; commissions, 4110, [illegible].
„ Thomas (of Clonbolgan), pardon, [illegible]; cons., 4110; his heir, [illegible], [illegible].
„ Thomas fitz William (of Newton, co. Dub.), pardon, [illegible].
„ Thomas, pardon, [illegible], [illegible], [illegible], [illegible], [illegible], [illegible], [illegible], [illegible], [illegible], [illegible], 6177, [illegible].
„ Walter, attainted, lands in co. Kild., [illegible], 1267, 1161, [illegible].
„ Walter reagh fitz Morice (of Glassely), pardon, 6111.
„ Walter, pardon, [illegible], [illegible], [illegible], [illegible], [illegible], [illegible], [illegible], [illegible], [illegible], [illegible], [illegible], [illegible].
„ William, vicar of Kilfinney, [illegible].
„ William Roe, pardon, [illegible], [illegible].
„ Wm. (of Rathcoman), pardon, [illegible].
„ Wm. fitz Knight (of Ballynaight), pardon, 6156.
„ William, pardon, [illegible], [illegible], [illegible], [illegible], [illegible], [illegible], [illegible], [illegible], [illegible], [illegible], [illegible], [illegible], [illegible].
„ See also Fitz Garrett, Fitz Garret, Gerald, Geraldine.
Fitz Gerat—Gerate—Gerod—Gerode. See Fitz Gerrot.
Fitz Geralde. See Fitz Gerald.
Fitz Gerot—Geroth—Gerott. See Fitz Gerrot.
Fitz Gerrald—Gerralde—Gerrale. See Fitz Gerald.
Fitz Gerralde og, Moriah gankagh, pardon, [illegible].
Fitz Gerrard, Gerrard fitz Rich. (of Ballyowan), pardon, [illegible].
Fitz Gerrat—Gerritt—Gerrod. See Fitz Gerrot.
Fitz Gerrald. See Fitz Gerald.
Fitz Gerrot—Gerrott—Gerat—Gerald—Gerod—Gerode—Gerot—Geroth—Gerott—Gerrat—Gerritt—Gerrod:
„ David, pardon, [illegible], [illegible], [illegible].
„ Donagh, pardon, [illegible].
„ Edmund, pardon, [illegible], [illegible], [illegible], [illegible].
„ Gerald, pardon, [illegible], [illegible], [illegible], [illegible], [illegible], [illegible].
„ Henry, pardon, [illegible], [illegible].
„ James (of Rathkiegh, co. Wexford), cons., [illegible].
Fitz Gerrot—James m'Shan, cons., [illegible].
„ James, pardon, [illegible], [illegible], [illegible], [illegible], [illegible], 6677.
„ John, murder of, [illegible].
„ John (of Drumkane, esq.), pardon, [illegible].
„ John, pardon, [illegible], [illegible], [illegible], [illegible], [illegible], [illegible], [illegible], [illegible].
„ Margaret, pardon, [illegible].
„ Maurice, rector of Kilcoursan, pardon, [illegible].
„ Maurice, pardon, [illegible], [illegible], [illegible], [illegible].
„ Oliver, pardon, [illegible].
„ Rieard, pardon, 4170.
„ Richard, pardon, 1760.
„ Robert (in co. Kerry), attainted, [illegible], [illegible].
„ Shane, pardon, [illegible].
„ Thomas fitz James (of Mocollop), pardon, [illegible].
„ Thomas, pardon, [illegible], [illegible], [illegible], [illegible].
„ Walter roogh, evil disposed person, [illegible].
„ William, pardon, [illegible], [illegible].
Fitz Gerrot brack, Gerald, pardon, [illegible].
Fitz Gibbon—Gibon—Gibbone—Gybon:
„ Edmund (son of John, the White Knight), pardon, [illegible], [illegible]; lease, [illegible], [illegible], [illegible]; surrender, [illegible], [illegible]; called White Knight, [illegible]; grant of lands, [illegible], [illegible]; pardon, [illegible], [illegible].
„ Edm., pardon, [illegible].
„ Ellen, pardon, [illegible].
„ Garrett m'Moriah, pardon, [illegible].
„ Gerald, pardon, [illegible], [illegible], [illegible].
„ Gibbon, pardon, [illegible].
„ James, pardon, [illegible].
„ John oge, the White Knight, pardon, [illegible], [illegible]; attainted, [illegible], [illegible], [illegible], [illegible], [illegible], [illegible]; his sons, [illegible]; widow, [illegible], [illegible], [illegible], [illegible].
„ John, pardon, [illegible].
„ Maurice or Moris, pardon, [illegible], [illegible], [illegible], [illegible].
„ Philip, pardon, [illegible].
„ Rich. (of Knocklong), his sons, [illegible].
„ William m'Moriah, pardon, [illegible].
„ William, pardon, [illegible].
Fitz Gillypoill, Owny, pardon, [illegible].
Fitz Gubbowne, John, pardon, [illegible].
Fitz Gwybon, Gerald, pardon, [illegible].
Fitz Gybon. See Fitz Gibbon

INDEX TO FIANTS—ELIZABETH.

Fitz Hamyn, Rich., pardon, 6341.
Fitz Harries—Harreis—Harres—Harris—Harry—Harrys:
,, Arthur, pardon, 1442.
,, Lawrence, pardon, 3112.
,, Marcus, pardon, [illegible].
,, Matthew (of Brashillane, seneschal of Wexford, pardon, 1442, 1749; commissions, 3177, [illegible], 3141, [illegible].
,, Robert, pardon, 6449, 6744.
,, Teig, pardon, 6447.
,, (or Fitz Henrie), William, pardon, [illegible].
Fitz Henry—Henrie:
,, Arthur, pardon, [illegible], 4[illegible].
,, Edm., pardon, 6432.
,, Edward, pardon, [illegible]; house in Maryborough, 1494, [illegible].
,, Edward (of Skerries, co. Dub.), pardon, [illegible]; com., 4[illegible].
,, James, pardon, 6153.
,, John, serjeant-at-arms, 5768.
,, Lawrence, pardon, 3[illegible], 6432, 6742.
,, Matthew, pardon, [illegible].
,, Nicholas, pardon, 72, [illegible], 1442, [illegible], [illegible], 6432, 6741.
,, Oliver, pardon, 6432.
,, Peter, pardon, [illegible], [illegible].
,, Teig, pardon, [illegible].
,, Thomas, 72.
,, Walter, pardon, 6[illegible], 6432.
,, William, pardon, [illegible].
Fitz Herries—Herrys, Nicholas, pardon, 72, [illegible].
Fitz Hubert, Margaret, pardon, 5796.
Fitzimons. See Fitz Symon.
Fitz James, David, pardon, 6442, [illegible].
,, Dermot, pardon, [illegible].
,, Edmund, pardon, 1046, [illegible], 4[illegible], 6511, [illegible], 6[illegible].
,, Edmund, attainted, 6117, [illegible].
,, Edward, com., [illegible].
,, Henry, pardon, [illegible].
,, Gerald, or Garret, pardon, [illegible], [illegible], 6312, [illegible], 6473, 6[illegible], [illegible].
,, Garret (in co. Kerry), attainted, 6472.
,, Henry, land of, granted, 5[illegible].
,, Hubert, pardon, [illegible].
,, James, pardon, 6701.
,, Johanna, or Jowan (Bourke), pardon, 4[illegible], [illegible].
,, John, [illegible]; pardon, 1257, 1514, [illegible], [illegible], 37[illegible], [illegible], [illegible], 4307, [illegible], [illegible], [illegible], 6478, 6477, 6485, [illegible], [illegible].
,, Margaret, pardon, 3414.
Fitz James, Maurice, pardon, 2274, [illegible], [illegible].
,, Oliver, pardon, [illegible], [illegible], 6477, 6[illegible].
,, Onora, pardon, 4[illegible].
,, Owny, pardon, 1514.
,, Peter, pardon, 1571.
,, Peirce, pardon, [illegible], 6479.
,, Redmond, pardon, 6511, [illegible].
,, Richard, pardon, 1044, [illegible], [illegible], [illegible], 6314, [illegible].
,, Robert, pardon, [illegible], 6601.
,, Theobald, pardon, [illegible], 6[illegible].
,, Thomas, pardon, [illegible], [illegible], [illegible].
,, William, pardon, 1[illegible], [illegible], 2274, [illegible], [illegible].
Fitz Jofferie, Thomas, pardon, [illegible].
Fitz Jeffrey, James, pardon 5[illegible].
,, William, pardon, [illegible].
Fitz Jerrowl, Rich., pardon, [illegible].
Fitz John, Brian, pardon, [illegible].
,, David, pardon, [illegible], 4[illegible], 4[illegible], 6176, 6450, [illegible].
,, Edm., pardon, [illegible], [illegible], 6173, [illegible], 6444, 6762.
,, Edward, pardon, [illegible].
,, Ellen, pardon, 4477.
,, Ellis, pardon, [illegible].
,, Gerald or Garrett, pardon, [illegible], 6[illegible], [illegible].
,, Granny, pardon, [illegible].
,, Harrys, pardon, [illegible].
,, James (of Knockmoan, Fitzgerald), grant of land, [illegible].
,, James, pardon, [illegible], 4[illegible], [illegible], [illegible], 6478, 6[illegible].
,, Joan, pardon, [illegible].
,, John, pardon, [illegible], 6[illegible], [illegible].
,, John fitz Teig, pardon, [illegible].
,, John oge, pardon, [illegible], 6173, 6[illegible], [illegible].
,, Malcom, pardon, [illegible].
,, Maurice. See Fitz Gerald.
,, Nicholas, pardon, 4118, [illegible].
,, Onora, pardon, [illegible].
,, Patrick, pardon, [illegible].
,, Peter, pardon, [illegible].
,, Philip, pardon, [illegible], [illegible].
,, Redmond, pardon, 4[illegible], [illegible].
,, Richard, pardon, 114, [illegible], [illegible], [illegible]:
,, Robert, pardon, [illegible].
,, Sandall, pardon, 5718.
,, Shane, pardon, 4[illegible].
,, Teig, pardon, [illegible].
,, Thomas (of Flaxdown, co. Meath), commissions, 4[illegible], [illegible]; his son, 5714.
,, Thomas, pardon, 1[illegible], [illegible], [illegible], [illegible], 6477, [illegible].
,, Tirlagh, pardon, [illegible].

INDEX TO FIANTS—ELIZABETH.

Fitz John, Walter, pardon, 1313, 4180.
,, William fitz Edm., pardon, [illegible].
,, William, pardon, 1702, 2881, 4116, 4172, 4172, 4457, 5[illegible], 6[illegible], 6617.
Fitz Johnes—Jones:
,, Christopher, son of Tho. (of Flemstown), pardon, 6713.
,, James, pardon, 3374.
,, John (of Flemstown), commission, [illegible].
,, Rich., pardon, 6[illegible].
Fitz Johnnin, Edm., pardon, 6[illegible].
Fitz Jones. See Fitz Johnes.
Fitz Jones, James, pardon, 4367.
Fitz Knight, Morris, pardon, [illegible].
,, Wm., pardon, 4[illegible].
Fitz Laurens, Matthias, pardon, 781.
Fitz Leons. See Fitz Lions.
Fitz Lewis, Barnaby. See Brian.
,, Cahir and Gerald, pardon, 1[illegible].
Fitz Lions—Leons, James, his lands in co. Dub., 1228, 4[illegible].
Fitz Lonergan, Ellen, pardon, 6[illegible].
Fitz Mahowne, Owen, pardon, 4[illegible].
Fitz Master, Gerald, pardon, 6[illegible].
Fitz Maurice, James, pardon, 1237.
,, Richard, pardon, 1237, 4[illegible].
,, See Fitz Morish.
Fitz Mary, John and Ulig, pardon, 6179.
Fitz Morler, Ulick, pardon, [illegible].
Fitz Morce. See Fitz Morish.
Fitz Morgan, Wm., pardon, 6[illegible].
Fitz Morion. See Fitz Morish.
Fitz Moriso[illegible], Tho. (of Champiers), pardon, 6[illegible].
Fitz Morighe, Patr., pardon, [illegible].
Fitz Morish — Morice — Morris — Moroe — Moris — Morishe — Morrish — Morrish — Morrishe — Morryshe:
,, David, pardon, 2310, [illegible], 4821, 4874, 6[illegible], 6[illegible], 6[illegible].
,, Dominick, pardon, [illegible].
,, Donough, pardon, 6[illegible].
,, Edmund, son of Tho., lord Lixnaw, pardon, 4[illegible], 6[illegible].
,, Edmund, attainted, 6[illegible].
,, Edmund, pardon, 1604, 3476, 4[illegible], 6[illegible], 6[illegible].
,, Edw., pardon, [illegible].
,, Ellen, pardon, 6[illegible].
,, Ellinor, pardon, 2[illegible], 4[illegible], 6[illegible].
,, Ellis, pardon, [illegible].
,, Gerald (of Mornas, co. Lim.), attainted, 4777, 6[illegible].
,, Gerald or Gerrot, pardon, [illegible], [illegible], [illegible], [illegible], [illegible], [illegible], [illegible], [illegible], [illegible], [illegible], [illegible], [illegible].
Fitz Morish — Gilleen, pardon, 4[illegible].
,, James. See Fitz Gerald.
,, James, pardon, [illegible], [illegible], [illegible], [illegible], [illegible], [illegible].
,, Jane, pardon, 4[illegible], [illegible].
,, John (Fitzgerald, of Knockmoan, co. Wat.), pardon, [illegible], [illegible], [illegible]; widow of, [illegible].
,, John, lands of, [illegible].
,, John (in co. Kerry), attainted, 6[illegible], [illegible].
,, John, glebe land set to, 6[illegible].
,, John, pardon, [illegible], [illegible], [illegible], [illegible], [illegible], [illegible], [illegible].
,, Joan, pardon, 6[illegible].
,, Margaret, pardon, 6[illegible].
,, Morish, pardon, [illegible], [illegible], [illegible], [illegible], [illegible].
,, Nich., pardon, 6[illegible].
,, Oliver, pardon, [illegible].
,, Patrick, pardon, 4[illegible]; late lord Fitz Morris, [illegible].
,, Redmond, pardon, [illegible].
,, Richard, pardon, [illegible].
,, Richard, attainted, [illegible].
,, Richard, pardon, [illegible], [illegible], [illegible], [illegible].
,, Robert, attainted, [illegible], [illegible].
,, Robert, pardon, [illegible], [illegible], [illegible], [illegible].
,, Thomas, lord Fitz Morish, commissions, 1018, [illegible]; pardon, 4[illegible].
,, Thomas (of Adamstown), livery, 1614.
,, Thomas, attainted, 6117.
,, Thomas, pardon, 1044, 4118, 4[illegible], [illegible], [illegible], [illegible].
,, Walter, pardon, 4[illegible].
,, William, pardon, [illegible], [illegible].
,, See M'Morrish, &c.
Fitz Morish dowlagh, John and Theobald, pardon, [illegible].
Fitz Moyler, Moyler and Walter, pardon, [illegible].
Fitz Muriagh, Patrick, pardon, [illegible].
Fitz Nicholas, Edmund, pardon, [illegible], [illegible], [illegible], [illegible].
,, Garrett, pardon, [illegible].
,, Gerrott, pardon, [illegible], [illegible].
,, Grany, pardon, [illegible].
,, James, pardon, [illegible], [illegible].
,, John, pardon, [illegible], [illegible], [illegible].
,, Maurice or Morris, pardon, [illegible], [illegible], [illegible], [illegible].
,, Philip, pardon, [illegible].
,, Richard, pardon, [illegible].
,, Rich., pardon, [illegible], [illegible], [illegible].
,, Theobald, pardon, [illegible].

INDEX TO FIANTS.—ELIZABETH.

Fitz Nicholas, Thomas, pardon, 2863, 4878.
" William, pardon, [illegible], 6481, 6494, 6504, 6871–4.
Fitz Nicholas duffe, Morris and Wm., pardon, [illegible].
Fitz Nichols, Wm., pardon, 6874.
Fitz Nicoles, Tho., pardon, 4293.
Fitz Oliver, James, pardon, 2048.
" Rich., pardon, [illegible].
" Tho., pardon, [illegible].
" Wm., pardon, [illegible].
Fitz Patrick—Patricke—Patryck—Patryk—Pattrick:
" Ardaco, pardon, 6447.
" Barnaby, first baron of Upper Ossory. *See* Upper Ossory.
" Barnaby or Brian, knt., captain of Upper Ossory, 1437; commissions, [illegible], 1830, [illegible], [illegible], [illegible], 2345; pardon, [illegible], 1768; pardon at his suit, 1822; grant of land, 1647; lease, 3370; succeeds as baron of Upper Ossory. *See* Upper Ossory.
" Barnaby or Brian (of Castletown, son of Florence), pardon, [illegible], [illegible], [illegible], [illegible].
" Brian, pardon, [illegible], [illegible].
" Dermod, pardon, 6110, 6451.
" Donell (of Gortenacloghe), pardon, [illegible].
" Donell m'Geffroy (of Ballyawly), pardon, 6116, 6441, 6732.
" Donell, pardon, 3431, [illegible], [illegible].
" Donogh, pardon, 6110, 6441, 6732.
" Donogho, pardon, [illegible].
" Dorhogh, pardon, 3431.
" Edmund, pardon, 4788, 6116, [illegible].
" Florence, pardon, [illegible]; succeeded as baron of Upper Ossory. *See* Upper Ossory.
" Florence (of [illegible]), pardon, 3431.
" Florence, pardon, 6794.
" Fynan, pardon, 6110, 6441, 6732.
" Geoffrey (of Ballyawly), pardon, 4117.
" Geoffrey (of Ballaghrahin), pardon, 6451.
" Geoffrey, pardon, [illegible], [illegible].
" Grany, pardon, [illegible].
" Harris, pardon, [illegible].
" Jonnes, pardon, 4417.
" John (of Ballygihen), pardon, [illegible]; sums of pardoned, [illegible].
" John (son of Florence, lord Upper Ossory), pardon, [illegible], [illegible].
Fitz Patrick—John, pardon, [illegible], 6461, 6794, [illegible], [illegible].
" Katherine, pardon, [illegible].
" McDarb, pardon, [illegible], [illegible].
" Margaret, pardon, 6116, 6794, [illegible].
" Matthew, pardon, [illegible].
" Patrick, pardon, [illegible].
" Shane m'Teig (of [illegible]), pardon, [illegible], [illegible].
" Shane, pardon, 6116, [illegible], [illegible], [illegible].
" Shane, pardon, [illegible].
" Thady, pardon, [illegible].
" Teig, pardon, [illegible].
" Teig or Thaddeus (of [illegible], son of Florence lord Upper Ossory), pardon, [illegible], [illegible], [illegible].
" Torlagh, pardon, 3421.
" Torrelagh, pardon, [illegible].
" Theobald, pardon, [illegible].
" Thomas, pardon, [illegible].
" Tirlagh or Therlagh, pardon, [illegible], 6116, [illegible].
" Walter, pardon, [illegible].
" William, pardon, [illegible], 6116, 6117, [illegible].
Fitz Patrick roe, James, grant, [illegible].
Fitz Pedree—Peirs. *See* Fitz Piers.
Fitz Perres, Tibbot, pardon, [illegible].
Fitz Pers. *See* Fitz Piers.
Fitz Phillibane, Edm., pardon, [illegible].
Fitz Philip—Phillipp—Phillip—Philipe—Phillipp:
" David, pardon, [illegible].
" David backagh, attainted, [illegible].
" Donell backagh, attainted, [illegible].
" Edmund, pardon, [illegible], [illegible].
" Gerald (Fitz Gerald?), co. Kild., com., [illegible], [illegible].
" Gerald (Fitz Gerald of Kilmaoge, co. Kild.), com., [illegible].
" Gerald (of Allon, co. Kild.), sheriff of Kildare, pardon, [illegible], [illegible].
" John, pardon, 3421, [illegible], [illegible].
" Maurice (Fitz Gerald of Allen), pardon, [illegible].
" Maurice, pardon, [illegible].
" Thomas, [illegible], [illegible].
" Thomas, pardon, [illegible].
" William (of co. Lim.), attainted, [illegible].
Fitz Philips, Gerald. *See* Fitz Philip.
Fitz Piers—Peirce—Peirs—Pers—Pierce:
" Edmund, pardon, [illegible], [illegible].
" Gerald or Gerrald, pardon, [illegible], [illegible], [illegible], [illegible].

INDEX TO FIANTS.—ELIZABETH.

Fitz Piers—Henry, pardon, 2778.
" John, pardon, 1461, [illegible].
" Martin, pardon, 2763.
" Oliver. See Fitz Gerald.
" Philip, pardon, 4417.
" Pierce, pardon, 5143.
" Robert, pardon, [illegible], [illegible].
" Tho., pardon, 2708.
Fitz Redmond—Redmund:
" John, pardon, [illegible], 4440, [illegible].
" Morris. See Gerald, [illegible].
" Nicholas, pardon, [illegible].
" Rich., pardon, 1910, [illegible].
" Thomas, com., [illegible].
Fitz Redmond og, Ricard, pardon, [illegible].
Fitz Henrick, Redmund, pardon, [illegible].
" Ricard, pardon, [illegible].
Fitz Richard, Tobbot, pardon, [illegible].
Fitz Richard—Richards:
" David, pardon, 2744, [illegible], [illegible], [illegible].
" Edm., pardon, [illegible].
" Edm. (of Curranevragh, co. Cork), attainted, 6178.
" Gerald or Gerott, pardon, [illegible], [illegible], [illegible], [illegible], [illegible], [illegible].
" James, pardon, 2740, [illegible], [illegible], [illegible], 4118, 2744, [illegible].
" Jeffery, pardon, [illegible].
" John, com., 1844.
" John, pardon, 1371, [illegible], [illegible], 6477, [illegible], [illegible], [illegible].
" Maurice or Morris, pardon, [illegible], [illegible], 6477, [illegible], [illegible].
" Peirs, pardon, [illegible].
" Philip, pardon, [illegible], [illegible].
" Redmund, pardon, 437.
" Richard, pardon, [illegible], [illegible], [illegible].
" Rob., pardon, [illegible], [illegible].
" Simon, pardon, 6541.
" Theobald, pardon, [illegible].
" Tho., pardon, [illegible], [illegible], [illegible].
" Wm., pardon, [illegible], [illegible], [illegible], [illegible].
Fitz Richard gankagh, Gerott, attainted, [illegible].
Fitz Richard oge, James, pardon, [illegible].
Fitz Richards, Peirce, pardon, [illegible].
Fitz Robert, Edm., pardon, [illegible].
" John, pardon, [illegible], [illegible], [illegible].
" Maurice, pardon, [illegible].
" Peter, pardon, 738.
" Philip, pardon, [illegible].
" Rich., pardon, 10[illegible], 4744, [illegible], [illegible].
" Thomas, pardon, [illegible], [illegible], [illegible].
" William, pardon, [illegible], [illegible].
Fitz Robert batiro, Edm., pardon, [illegible].
Fitz Rory, John, pardon, [illegible].
" Tiedy, pardon, [illegible].
Fitz Rowland, Alexander, pardon, [illegible].
" Walter, pardon, [illegible], [illegible].
Fitz Symon—Symons—Simon—Simond—Simondes—Simonson—Simons—Symond—Symondes—Symonds—Symone—Fitzsimons—Fytzsymondes:
" Alison, pardon, 6017.
" Beale, pardon, 4817.
" Christopher, pardon, [illegible], [illegible].
" Edm., pardon, 6711.
" Edward, justice of liberty of Wexford, [illegible], [illegible], [illegible], [illegible]; attorney general, [illegible], [illegible]; serjeant-at-laws, [illegible], [illegible], [illegible]; master of the rolls ad interim, [illegible], [illegible]; commissions, [illegible]; notes by, as fiants, [illegible], [illegible]; leases, [illegible], [illegible], 1812, [illegible], [illegible]; grant of a wardship, [illegible]; pardon, [illegible], [illegible], [illegible]; pardon at his suit, 4070.
" Edward, clerk of the crown in chancery, [illegible], [illegible].
" Edward, suit as to will of, [illegible].
" Edward (of Clontark, co. Westm.), pardon, [illegible], [illegible].
" Gerot, pardon, 6712.
" George, pardon, 5144.
" Gerald (of Tullynally, co. Westm.), pardon, [illegible]; commissions, [illegible], [illegible].
" Gerald, pardon, 3401, [illegible], [illegible], [illegible].
" Gulfdaff, pardon, [illegible].
" Henry, pardon, 6711.
" James, pardon, [illegible], [illegible], 6711.
" Jenkin, pardon, [illegible].
" John, house in Dublin, 1811, [illegible], 4714.
" John, lease, [illegible].
" John, pardon, [illegible], [illegible], [illegible], 6711.
" Lawrence, pardon, [illegible].
" Luke, export license, [illegible].
" Margaret, widow of Nich. Tirrell, [illegible], [illegible].
" Margaret, pardon, 4817.
" Michael, sheriff of Dublin city, [illegible]; house in Dublin, 1811.

INDEX TO FIANTS.—ELIZABETH.

FitzSymon—Michael, commissions, [illegible], 6087, [illegible].
" Michael, party to matrimonial suit, 5847.
" Michael, pardon, [illegible].
" Morris, pardon, 6711.
" Nicholas, sheriff of Dublin city, 48; alderman of Dublin, commissions, [illegible], 4748; comptroller of customs of Galway, [illegible]; party in suit, [illegible]; house of, [illegible].
" Nicholas, lease, 1646.
" Nicholas, pardon, [illegible].
" Oliver, pardon, 6711.
" Oliver, pardon, [illegible].
" Patrick, pardon, [illegible], [illegible], 6711.
" Redmond, pardon, [illegible], [illegible], 4762.
" Richard (of Balmadrogh?), his heir, [illegible], [illegible].
" Richard (of Ballyfad?, co. Wex.), livery, [illegible].
" Richard, pardon, [illegible], [illegible], [illegible], 6711.
" Robert, pardon, 1673, [illegible], [illegible], [illegible].
" Sampson, pardon, 6711.
" Thomas, house in Dublin, [illegible].
" Thomas, alderman, grant of land, [illegible]; lease, [illegible].
" Tho., pardon, [illegible], [illegible].
" Turlagh, pardon, [illegible].
" Walter (of Balmadrogh), wardship and livery, [illegible], [illegible].
" Walter, party to suit, [illegible].
" Walter, pardon, 6711.
" William, pardon, [illegible], [illegible], [illegible], 6711.
Fitz symon, land of (of Carrick?), [illegible].
" " in Kilmainham, [illegible].
Fitz Terrelagh, Donogh, pardon, [illegible].
Fitz Teige, John, pardon, [illegible].
" Donald, pardon, [illegible].
Fitz Terrelagh, Alexander, pardon, [illegible].
Fitz Theobald, Redmond, pardon, [illegible].
" Rich. pardon, [illegible], [illegible].
Fitz Theobald boy, Edm. (Burke?) pardon, [illegible].
Fitz Thomas, Andrew, pardon, [illegible].
" David, pardon, [illegible].
" Donogh, pardon, [illegible].
" Edmund, pardon, [illegible], [illegible].
" Ellice, pardon, [illegible].
" Gerald (or Garret) (of Pallas?, co. Lim.), pardon, [illegible], [illegible].
" Gerald or Garrett, lands late of, (in co. Lim.), granted, [illegible], [illegible]. See M'Thomas.
Fitz Thomas, Gerald, Garret or Gerrot, pardon, 1574, 2173, [illegible], [illegible], [illegible], [illegible], [illegible], [illegible], [illegible].
" Hellen, pardon, [illegible].
" James, pardon, [illegible], [illegible], [illegible].
" Johanna, pardon, [illegible].
" John, pardon, [illegible], [illegible], [illegible], [illegible], [illegible], [illegible], [illegible], [illegible], [illegible].
" Katherine, pardon, [illegible].
" Maurice (of Adamstown), livery to heir, [illegible].
" Maurice, pardon, [illegible].
" Melaghlin, pardon, [illegible].
" Meredith, pardon, [illegible].
" Morris or Morish, pardon, [illegible], [illegible], [illegible], [illegible], [illegible], [illegible], [illegible].
" Nich., pardon, [illegible].
" Owen, pardon, [illegible].
" Peter, pardon, [illegible], [illegible].
" Philip, pardon, [illegible], [illegible].
" Richard, pardon, [illegible], [illegible], [illegible].
" Richard, or M'Thomas, attainted, [illegible].
" Robert, pardon, [illegible], [illegible].
" Thady, pardon, [illegible].
" Walter, pardon, [illegible].
" William, lands of, [illegible], [illegible].
" Werrick, pardon, [illegible].
Fitz Thomas gancagh, John, pardon, [illegible].
Fitz Thomas reagh, Rich., pardon, [illegible].
Fitz Thomyne, Edm., pardon, [illegible].
Fitz Tibbot—Tibbott:
" David, pardon, [illegible].
" Geoffrey, attainted, [illegible].
" Jeffery, pardon, [illegible], [illegible].
" John, pardon, [illegible].
" Richard, pardon, [illegible].
" Thomas, pardon, [illegible].
" Walter, pardon, [illegible].
" William, pardon, [illegible].
Fitz Tirlogh, Brian and John, pardon, [illegible].
Fitz Tirrelagh, Murtagh, pardon, [illegible].
Fitz Ulick—Uly—Ullick:
" Gilbert, pardon, [illegible].
" John, pardon, [illegible].
" John fitz Edm., attainted, [illegible], [illegible].
" Redmond, pardon, [illegible].
" Ulick, pardon, [illegible].
" Wm., pardon, [illegible].
Fitz Ursley—Urseley—Ursyley, Rowe and Hugh. See M'Mahon.
Fitz Walter, David, pardon, [illegible].
" Edm., pardon, [illegible], [illegible], [illegible], [illegible].
" Gerald, pardon, [illegible].

INDEX TO FIANTS—ELIZABETH.

Fitz Walter, Gibbot, pardon, [illegible].
 " James, pardon, [illegible], [illegible].
 " John, pardon, [illegible], [illegible].
 " Maurice, pardon, [illegible].
 " Nich. fitz Rich., pardon, [illegible].
 " Piers, pardon, [illegible].
 " Rob. (of the Frohane), pardon, [illegible], [illegible].
 " Rob., pardon, [illegible].
 " Thady, attainted, 6404.
 " Thomas, pardon, [illegible].
Fitz Water, Maurice, pardon, [illegible].
Fitz William—Williams — William — Williame—Wylliam—Wyllyamer
 " Austace, pardon, [illegible].
 " Brian (signs Bryan Fytz-wyllyam), surrender of lease, [illegible]; pension, [illegible], [illegible]; grants of land, [illegible], [illegible], [illegible], [illegible], [illegible], [illegible], [illegible], [illegible]; leases, [illegible], [illegible], [illegible]; death, [illegible].
 " Conogher, pardon, [illegible].
 " David, pardon, [illegible], [illegible], [illegible].
 " Derby, pardon, [illegible].
 " Donogh, pardon, [illegible].
 " Gerald, pardon, [illegible].
 " Garrett, pardon, [illegible], [illegible], [illegible].
 " Hellen, pardon, 4744.
 " James, pardon, [illegible], [illegible], [illegible].
 " Joakin, pardon, [illegible].
 " Jeroite, pardon, [illegible].
 " John, grant of a wardship, [illegible]; custodiam grant, [illegible].
 " John, pardon, [illegible], [illegible], [illegible], [illegible], [illegible], [illegible], [illegible], [illegible], [illegible].
 " Jonan, pardon, [illegible].
 " Katherine, pardon, [illegible].
 " Kenedy, pardon, [illegible].
 " Maurice, pardon, [illegible].
 " Melaghlen, pardon, [illegible].
 " Michael, surveyor general, licence of absence, [illegible], [illegible]; prothonotary of Common Bench, [illegible], [illegible]; commissions, [illegible], [illegible]; leases, [illegible], [illegible], [illegible], [illegible], [illegible].
 " Morris, pardon, [illegible], [illegible], [illegible].
 " Murrough, pardon, [illegible].
 " Nicholas (of Dromard, co. Lim.), pardon, [illegible], [illegible], [illegible]; attainted, [illegible], [illegible].
 " Nich., pardon, [illegible].
 " Redmund, pardon, [illegible], [illegible].
 " Ricard, pardon, [illegible].
 " Richard (son of Tho. of Merrion), constable of Wicklow castle, [illegible], [illegible]; pardon, [illegible].
Fitz William—
 " Rich. (of Littleton, co. Kild.), pardon, [illegible], [illegible].
 " Rich. (in co. Lim.), attainted, [illegible].
 " Rich., pardon, [illegible].
 " Robert, pardon, [illegible], [illegible].
 " Stephen, commission, [illegible].
 " Teig, pardon, [illegible].
 " Thomas (of Merrion, knt.), seneschal of the marches of Dublin, [illegible]; sheriff of co. Dublin, [illegible]; constable of Wicklow castle, [illegible], [illegible], [illegible]; prothonotary of the Common Bench, [illegible], [illegible]; commissions, [illegible], [illegible], [illegible], [illegible], [illegible], [illegible], [illegible], [illegible], [illegible], [illegible], [illegible], [illegible], [illegible], [illegible], [illegible]; leases, [illegible], [illegible], [illegible]; pardon, [illegible], [illegible], [illegible], [illegible], [illegible], [illegible], [illegible]; pardon at his suit, [illegible], [illegible].
 " Thomas, pardon, [illegible], [illegible], [illegible], [illegible].
 " Walter, pardon, [illegible].
 " William (signs W. Fytz Wylliam), vice-treasurer and treasurer at war, [illegible], [illegible]; constable of castle of Athlone, [illegible]; lord justice of Ireland, [illegible], [illegible]; lord deputy, [illegible], [illegible], [illegible], [illegible]; commissions, [illegible], [illegible], [illegible], [illegible], [illegible], [illegible], [illegible]; leases, [illegible], [illegible], [illegible], [illegible]; pardon, [illegible].
 " William, lease, [illegible].
 " William (of Johnston), commission, [illegible].
 " William, collector of wine duty in port of Dublin, [illegible]; principal registrar, ecclesiastical commission, [illegible], [illegible], [illegible], [illegible].
 " William, pardon, [illegible], [illegible], [illegible].
Fitz William cam, John, pardon, [illegible].
Fitz William oge, Edm. (of Garran James), pardon, [illegible], [illegible], [illegible], [illegible].
 " Phillip, pardon, [illegible].
Fivagh, co. Antrim, [illegible].
Flabagh, David, pardon, [illegible].
Flaoritie. See Flahertie.
Flagheran. See Flahovan.
Flaghie, Wm., pardon, [illegible].
Flaghivagan. See Flahovan.
Flahertie—Flaortie—Flaherty:
 " John, pardon, [illegible].

INDEX TO FIANTS.—ELIZABETH.

Flaherrie—Onora ny, pardon, [illegible].
,, Petrus, pardon, [illegible].
,, Roger, pardon at his suit, [illegible].
,, Sarogho ny, pardon, [illegible].
Flaherty—Flaghevan—Flaghivane—Flahivane—Flahyvan:
,, David, pardon, [illegible].
,, John, pardon, 2373, [illegible].
,, Maurice, pardon, [illegible].
,, Rich., pardon, [illegible].
,, Rob., pardon, [illegible].
,, Shane, pardon, 2373.
,, Tho., pardon, [illegible].
Flanagan, John, pardon, [illegible].
Flanagtane, Brian, pardon, [illegible].
Flanders, trade with, 38, [illegible]; denization of native, [illegible]; manner of cultivating woad, &c., introduced into Ireland, [illegible]. See Flemings.
Flanegane, Donald, chaplain, English liberty, [illegible].
,, Redmond, chief of his name, pardon, [illegible].
Flanegane country. See O'Flanagan.
Flanell, James, pardon, [illegible].
Flanrie, Conoghor m'Dermod Y, pardon, [illegible].
Flanuan, Edm., sub-sheriff of King's co., [illegible].
,, John, pardon, [illegible].
,, Tho., pardon, [illegible].
,, Wm., pardon, [illegible].
Flasille, Sarogh ny, pardon, [illegible].
Flanegan—Flannegan—Flanigan:
,, Ellinor ny, pardon, [illegible].
,, Fynnoula ny, pardon, [illegible].
,, John, pardon, [illegible].
,, Nich., pardon, [illegible].
,, Sorogh ny, pardon, [illegible].
Flanelle, Wm., pardon, [illegible].
Flatisbury—Flatesberie—Flatisberie—Flatisbury—Flattesbury—Flattisbury—Flatysbury—Flatisbury:
,, Christopher (of Johnstown), commissions, [illegible]; a trustee, [illegible]; allotment to, [illegible].
,, Edm., pardon, [illegible].
,, James (of Johnstown), commissions, [illegible]; a trustee, [illegible]; exemption from subsidy, [illegible].
Flaughe, Thady, pardon, [illegible].
Fleaghmoney, co. Lim., [illegible].
Flemings. See Flanders.
Flevell, James, pardon, [illegible].
Fleywan, Wm., pardon, [illegible].
Flemings, Patrick, pardon, [illegible].
Flemyngo, John, pardon, [illegible].
,, Tho., pardon, [illegible].
Flean, co. Lim., [illegible]. See also Phillinge.
Fleaming, Alexander, and others of same (see Fleming), 1373.
Fleminstown. See Polumstown, Follomston, Fomastown.
Fleetewood, John, grant to his son, [illegible].
,, Thomas, grant of land, [illegible].
Fleghlow, John, English liberty, [illegible].
Flemingstown (co. Kilk.), [illegible].
Fleming—Flemynge—Flemyng—Flemynge—Flemminge—Flemmyng—Flemmynge—Flemyinge—Flemmyng:
,, Alexander, pardon, 1373, [illegible].
,, Ann, pardon, [illegible].
,, Andrew, porter of castle of Carrickfergus, [illegible].
,, Barnie, pardon, [illegible].
,, Caliherine, robbery from, [illegible]
,, Christopher, baron of Slane, descent from, [illegible].
Christopher, attorney general, [illegible]; commissions, [illegible]; grant of a wardship, [illegible].
,, Chr., commissioner, [illegible].
,, Chr., grant of land, [illegible].
,, Chr., pardon, [illegible].
,, Chr., pardon to son, [illegible].
,, David, pardon, [illegible].
,, Edmund, treasurer of Waterford cathedral, [illegible]; commissioner, [illegible]; pardon, [illegible].
,, Edm., pardon, [illegible].
,, Edm. (of Cashel), livery, [illegible]; pardon, [illegible].
,, George, [illegible]; pardon, [illegible].
,, Gerald (son of Patr. of Kells), wardship, [illegible].
,, Gerald (son of Patr. of Crevanstown), livery, [illegible].
,, Gerald, baron, [illegible].
,, Gerald, baron, [illegible]; commissions, [illegible].
,, Gerald (of Crevagh), pardon, [illegible].
,, Gerald, pardon, [illegible].
,, James. See Slane, baron of.
,, James, father of Tho., baron of Slane, [illegible].
,, James, pardon, [illegible].
,, John, pardon, [illegible].
,, John, vicar [illegible], [illegible].
,, Katherine, [illegible]; pardon, [illegible].
,, Margaret, [illegible].
,, Nicholas, pardon, [illegible].
,, Patrick (of Kells), his heir, [illegible].

INDEX TO FIANTS—ELIZABETH.

Fleming—Patrick (of Cormarkin), his heir, [illegible].
„ Patrick, burgess of Cashel, [illegible].
„ Patrick (of Garrandalon), pardon, 3437, 6726, 6788.
„ Patrick, pardon, [illegible], 3427, [illegible].
„ Richard, pardon, 1273, 1617, [illegible], 3434, 3437, [illegible].
„ Robert, pardon to wit, 712.
„ Robert, pardon, 151, 1272, 1170, [illegible], [illegible], 4848, [illegible].
„ Thomas (of Slevroston), commissions, 280, 2346; claim to lands [illegible]. See Slane, baron of.
„ Thomas (of Siddan), commissions, [illegible], 1097, 1238, 1412, 2344, [illegible], 4161, 4763; pardon, 171, 788, 1848, 3730, 3437, 3844, 3787, [illegible].
„ Tho. (son of preceding), pardon, 3437.
„ Tho., vicar of Rathmolane, [illegible].
„ Thomas, pardon, 1373, [illegible], 4723, 6173, 6184, [illegible], 6788.
„ Walter (of Cashel), livery to [illegible], [illegible].
„ Walter, pardon, [illegible], 6763.
„ William (of Stevenston), pardon, [illegible]; commissions, [illegible], 4461, 5182.
„ Wm. (of Laughor), grant, 3761.
„ Wm., collector of wine duty in Drogheda, 3761.
„ Wm., pardon, 743, 1048, 1373, 1738, 1788, 3478, 3824, 5155, 6438.
Flemings (people of Flanders), trade with, 1519, 1711; ships of, to be seized, [illegible]; destinations, [illegible], [illegible], [illegible].
Flemington — Flemingtowne — Flemingstowne—Flemyngton—Flemyngtowne, co. Kild., [illegible], 1473, [illegible], [illegible], [illegible], [illegible], 6701.
Flemington—Flemyngstone, co. Meath, 738, [illegible].
Fletcher, 45; office of, [illegible], 3574.
Fletcher, Edward, pursuivant, [illegible].
„ Robert, lease, 1789; pardon, [illegible].
„ Thomas the, 3574.
Flinn, David, pardon, [illegible].
Flocks, export of, [illegible], [illegible]: illegal export, [illegible].
Flody. See Fluddy.
Floine, John, pardon, [illegible].
Flood, Margaret, pardon, [illegible].
„ Oliver, a ward, 6746.
Florance, Thomas, [illegible].
Flory, M'John, pardon, [illegible].
Florence, Wm., constable of castle of Naas, pardon, [illegible]; lease, 1424.
Flowre, George, pardon, [illegible].
Flud, John, pardon, [illegible].
Fludd, Dionysius, or Donogh O'Mulkilly, pardon, [illegible].
„ Hugh or Ea, pardon, 4633, 6701.
Fluddy—Fludy:
„ David, grant of land, [illegible]; grant of a wardship, [illegible]; murdered, [illegible].
„ Hugh, murdered, [illegible].
„ Walter, pardon, 242.
Flynne, ( ), pardon, [illegible].
Flyn—Flynn—Flynne:
„ Cormyll, pardon, [illegible].
„ Darby, „ [illegible].
„ Donill, „ 6494.
„ Edmund, „ 3661, [illegible].
„ Gilles ny, „ [illegible].
„ John, „ [illegible].
„ Morish, „ [illegible].
„ Owen, 1610; „ 1863, 1868.
„ Shane, „ [illegible].
„ Thomas, „ 843.
Fogh (co. Wat.?), [illegible].
Foard, Rob., pardon, [illegible].
Fockeston, co. Meath, [illegible], [illegible].
Fockeston, [illegible].
Fochegge, co. Gal., [illegible].
Foelan, Walter, pardon, 6417.
Foeleston (Folistown), co. Meath, [illegible].
Foe, co. Westm., [illegible].
Forth lordship (barony of Forth), co. Car., 894. See Forth.
Fogertie, Philip, pardon, [illegible].
Foghan river, (Faughan, co. Londonderry), fishing, [illegible].
Fohor (King's co.), 1871.
Folertie, Teige ny, pardon, [illegible].
Foine, co. Lim., [illegible].
Folain—Folaine—Folane.
„ Boylius, pardon, 4039, [illegible], 4797, [illegible].
„ Donagh, pardon, 897.
„ Farrand, pardon, 6448.
„ Macktragh, pardon, 6448.
„ Nicholas, pardon, [illegible], 4272, 6448.
„ Shrewlagh, pardon, 6448.
„ Teig, pardon, 677.
Folawe, Donoghow m'Shane Y, pardon, [illegible].
Folestone, Little (Little Foolestown?), co. Meath, 347, [illegible].
Folestone, Mirbo (Great Foolestown?), co. Meath, 347, [illegible].
Folie, Syvenagh, pardon, [illegible].
Foliograith (co. Car.?), [illegible].
Folistown, co. Meath. See Fockeston, Folestone.
Foliane, Tho., robbery of, 841.
Folleston, co. Meath, 2818.
Follow, John, [illegible]; pardon, [illegible].
Followe, co. Wat., 72.
Folane, Nicholas, pardon, [illegible].
Fomberie, John, pardon, [illegible].
Fomer, co. Clare, [illegible].

INDEX TO FIANTS.—ELIZABETH.

Fomorlie—Fomorily, co. Clare, 4549, [illegible].
Fomorrdo (co. Ros. ?), [illegible].
Fonlaffe, co. Cork, [illegible].
Fonte, James, 1541.
Fonte Vivo, de, abbey. *See* Maure, [illegible], [illegible].
Fontevamle, co. Kild., [illegible].
Fontcolands, co. Lim., [illegible].
Fontlestown—Fontlestown, co. Kild., vicar of, 40.
" rectory, 1427, [illegible].
Fontis Vivi, Laurhoo in Ormonde, 2273.
Foorth, Ambrose. *See* Forth.
Fooshe, co. Kerry, [illegible].
Fooslo (co. Cork ?), [illegible].
Footmen, pay of, [illegible], [illegible].
Footstown, co. Meath. *See* Folestown.
Foramoyll (co. Kerry ?), [illegible].
Foran, William, pardon, 916.
Foran, Peter m'Teig, pardon, [illegible].
Forestall, Rich., pardon, [illegible].
Forbarne, Reyne, pardon, [illegible].
Forbatestown, co. Westm., [illegible].
Forcenage (co. Sligo ?), [illegible].
Ford, Tho., pardon, [illegible].
Forde, Ambrose. *See* Forth.
" Peter, clerk of works, [illegible].
" Walter, pardon, [illegible].
Fore — Fower — Fowre — Fouer — Fouro (Fore), co. Westm., [illegible], 1469, [illegible], [illegible], [illegible], 3178, [illegible], [illegible], [illegible].
" provost of, [illegible].
" rectory, 3478, [illegible].
" priory, leased, 1089, 3478, [illegible]; proxies, [illegible].
" Archadiorum in, 3478.
" S. Fechin, 3478.
" domus canonicorum, [illegible].
" barony, co. Westm., [illegible].
" " co. Meath, 41, [illegible].
Foreign fishing vessels, tax on, [illegible], [illegible].
" merchants not to sell by retail, [illegible]; permitted to import wine, &c., [illegible], [illegible].
Forest, Henry, clerk of first fruits, [illegible].
" Piers, pardon, [illegible].
Forest's lands, Youghal, [illegible].
Forestall, Redmond, pardon, [illegible].
Fore-stallers and regrators to be punished, [illegible].
Forfeited lands of Desmond and others, [illegible], [illegible].
Forganey (Forgney, co. Longf.), [illegible].
Forgus, co. Cork, [illegible].
Forgus, im provost, [illegible].
Forgy, Edm., pardon, [illegible].
Forhane, Dermot and Wm. m'Donell, pardon, [illegible].
Forkelstown (co. Wick. ?), [illegible].
Forkill, co. Long., [illegible].
Forlough (co. Wat. ?), [illegible].
Forlonge—Furlonge. *See* Furlong.
Formolle (co. Kerry ?), [illegible].
Formoyle (Fermoyle, co. Kerry ?), [illegible].
Formoyle. *See* Fermoyle, co. Sligo.
Formule (Formoyle ?), co. Cork, [illegible].
Formvill (co. Cork ?), [illegible].
Formwill (co. Cork ?), [illegible].
Fornan (co. Wat. ?), [illegible].
Fornan, Edm. m'Donill, pardon, [illegible].
Fornoy, co. Westm., [illegible], [illegible].
Fornoght, Little (co. Kild. ?), [illegible].
Foroghmore, co. Cork, [illegible].
Forooghmore, co. Kilk., [illegible].
Forrestall, Rob., pardon, [illegible].
Forrestalstown, co. Wex. *See* Forstalstown.
Forristall, James and Patr., pardon, [illegible].
Forroughmore, co. Kilk., [illegible].
Forryman, John m'Donell I., pardon, [illegible].
Forryne, Donell m'Brien oe, pardon, [illegible].
Forstal—Forstale. *See* Forstall.
Forstalstown (Forrestalstown), co. Wex., [illegible].
Forstall—Forstal—Forstale:
" Edm., pardon, [illegible].
" Edmund, pardon, 784, [illegible], [illegible], [illegible], [illegible], [illegible], [illegible], [illegible], [illegible], [illegible], [illegible], [illegible]; wife of, [illegible].
" Ellen, pardon, [illegible].
" Ellinor, pardon, [illegible].
" Garret, pardon, [illegible].
" Geoffrey, pardon, [illegible], [illegible].
" George, pardon, [illegible].
" Gibbon, pardon, [illegible], [illegible], [illegible].
" James, pardon, [illegible], [illegible], [illegible], [illegible], [illegible], [illegible], [illegible], [illegible], [illegible].
" John, pardon, [illegible], [illegible].
" Moriah, pardon, [illegible].
" Patrick, pardon, [illegible], 1087, [illegible], [illegible], [illegible], [illegible], [illegible], [illegible].
" Piers, pardon, [illegible], [illegible].
" Peter, pardon, [illegible], [illegible].
" Redmond, pardon, [illegible], [illegible], [illegible].
" Reymond, pardon, [illegible].
" Richard, pardon, 784, [illegible], [illegible], [illegible], [illegible], [illegible], [illegible], [illegible], [illegible], [illegible].
" Robert, [illegible]; pardon, [illegible], [illegible], [illegible], [illegible], [illegible], [illegible], [illegible], [illegible].
" Thomas, pardon, [illegible], [illegible].
" Walter, pardon, [illegible], [illegible], [illegible], [illegible], [illegible], [illegible], [illegible], [illegible], [illegible], [illegible], [illegible], [illegible].
" William, pardon, [illegible], [illegible], [illegible], [illegible].
Forstalstown—Forstallstowne—Forstalstowne, co. Kilk., [illegible], [illegible], [illegible], [illegible], [illegible], [illegible].
Forstallstowne, [illegible].
Forster, John, his house, [illegible]; alderman, [illegible]; mayor of Dublin, [illegible].

Forster, Walter, surrender, [illegible]-1.
" William, protection, [illegible].
Forte — Fort — Fowertymolane (Forth barony), co. Car., 471, [illegible]; lordship, [illegible]. See also Tortanoles, [illegible].
Forte alias Furlonge, John, pardon, [illegible].
Forth — Forthe — Fourth — Forde — Fourth,
Ambrose, master in chancery, [illegible], 6157, 6443; vicar general of Dublin, [illegible]; surrender for faculties and prerogative, [illegible], [illegible], [illegible]; judge of court of faculties and prerogative, [illegible], [illegible], [illegible], [illegible], [illegible], [illegible], [illegible]; judge of admiralty, [illegible], [illegible]; commissioner, [illegible]; licence of absence, [illegible], [illegible], [illegible], [illegible], [illegible], [illegible], [illegible]; leases, [illegible], [illegible], [illegible].
" Humfrey, surrender, [illegible]; lease, [illegible].
Fortifications to be erected, [illegible], [illegible]; chief to supply labour for, [illegible]; fortified house to be built by grantee, [illegible].
Fortill (King's co.?), [illegible].
Fortune/hi (co. Wat.?), [illegible].
Fosbyrr, Jacques, pardon, [illegible].
Fosare, co. Gal., [illegible].
Fosahen, co. Clare, [illegible].
Fossamore, co. Clare, [illegible].
Fosward, Patrick, pardon, 1417, [illegible].
Fosse (Fossy), Queen's co., [illegible], [illegible], [illegible].
FossmCoddle, co. Kilk., [illegible].
Foster, Edw., pardon, [illegible].
" Garrott, pardon, [illegible].
" James, pardon, 1547.
" John, pardon, [illegible].
" Margaret, grant of wardship, [illegible].
" Patrick, [illegible].
" Rich., pardon, [illegible].
" Tho., pardon, [illegible].
" William, porter of Dublin castle, [illegible], [illegible].
Fotterell. See Fottrell.
Fottleston alias Whitleston, co. Kild., [illegible].
Fottrell—Fotterell, Nich., [illegible], [illegible].
Foty (co. Cork?), [illegible].
Fouer. See Fore.
Foughe—Nough, the, co. Gal., [illegible], [illegible]. See also Fowragh.
Foulkescourt — Fowlkescourt — Fowrecourt — Phoulkecorte — Phowlkescourt (co. Kilk.), [illegible], [illegible], [illegible], [illegible], [illegible].
Foulkrath—Fowkerathe—Fowkrath—Fowlkesrath—Fowlkrath, co. Kilk., [illegible], [illegible], [illegible], [illegible], [illegible].
Foulle, Hugh glass m'Teig oe, pardon, [illegible].
Foulluc, Glass m'Conoher I, pardon, [illegible].
Founle, land in the tenure of, [illegible].
" Shane roe, pardon, [illegible].
Founteslande, co. Lim., [illegible].
Fountaston. See Fonthaston.
Four Courts, marshal of, [illegible], [illegible], [illegible], [illegible], [illegible], [illegible], [illegible].
Foure. See Fore.
Fourth, Ambrose. See Forth.
Fowragh (Fough), co. Gal., castle and land, [illegible]-1.
Fowere. See Fore.
Fowertymolane. See Forte.
Fowerye, John oe, pardon, [illegible].
Fowkerathe. See Foulkrath.
Fowkeston (co. Tip.?), [illegible].
Fowkrath. See Foulkrath.
Fowlaine, Wm., [illegible].
Fowle, Ralf, provost marshal of Connaught, [illegible], [illegible], [illegible]; commission, [illegible], [illegible], [illegible], [illegible], [illegible], [illegible], [illegible]; pardon, [illegible].
Fowle, Simon, pardon, [illegible].
" William, [illegible].
Fowler, John, pardon, [illegible].
Fowlers haggard, co. Wex., [illegible].
Fowlerston, co. Meath, [illegible].
Fowlkescort. See Foulkescourt.
Fowlkesrath—Fowlkrath. See Foulkrath.
Fowloe, Jenkin alias John, pardon, [illegible].
Fowloe, Thomas fitz Davy (?) priest, pardon, [illegible].
Fowlow, Maurice m'Dermot I, pardon, [illegible].
Fowlowe, Donogh m'Tho. E, pardon, [illegible].
" Tho., pardon, [illegible].
Fowlygrath (co. Tip.?), [illegible].
Fowran, co. Kerry, [illegible], [illegible], [illegible].
Fowre. See Fore.
Fowrebennare (Fonshin More), co. Gal., [illegible].
Fowrecourt. See Foulkescourt.
Fox—Foxe:
" Arte, son of, [illegible].
" Brasill (of Lehinch), chief of his name, pardon, [illegible], [illegible]; English liberty, [illegible].
" Brasill m'Brien, pardon, [illegible], [illegible].
" Brasell, son of Art, [illegible].
" Brasell, son of Neill (of Kilcoursey), [illegible].
" Brasell, pardon, [illegible], [illegible], [illegible], [illegible].
" Brian m'Cahir, pardon, [illegible].
" Cahir, pardon, [illegible].
" Cauberry, [illegible], [illegible], [illegible].
" Cohigorie, pardon, [illegible].
" Cowcogry m'Brien, pardon, [illegible].
" Dermot, pardon, [illegible].
" Donogh, pardon, [illegible].

INDEX TO FIANTS—ELIZABETH.

Fox—Edm., pardon, [illegible], [illegible], [illegible], [illegible], [illegible].
" Ellen fitz Gerrald, pardon, [illegible].
" Gibbon (of Down), pardon, [illegible].
" Hubert (of Lobinch), seneschal of Fox's country, [illegible]; surrender and regrant of possessions, [illegible], [illegible]; pension, [illegible].
" Hugh, pardon, [illegible].
" James (of co. Lim.), pardon, [illegible], [illegible], [illegible].
" James, son of Patr. (of Limerick), wardship, [illegible].
" John, rector of Old Ross, [illegible].
" Katherine, pardon, [illegible].
" Kedagh, pardon, [illegible].
" Laghlin, grant of land, [illegible].
" Lisagh, pardon, [illegible].
" alias Cavanagh, Margaret, pardon, [illegible].
" Neil, son of, grant, [illegible].
" Onie, pardon, [illegible].
" Owen (of Lisnaskey), grant, [illegible]; pardon, [illegible].
" Owen, pardon, [illegible], [illegible], [illegible], [illegible].
" Patr., pardon, [illegible], [illegible], [illegible], [illegible], [illegible].
" Patr. (of Limerick), heir of, [illegible].
" Patr., merchant of Youghal, [illegible].
" Phelim (of Clonbrin in the Brenaght), grant, [illegible]; pardon, [illegible].
" Phelim, pardon, [illegible].
" Philip, pardon, [illegible].
" Rich., land held by, [illegible], [illegible].
" Rich., pardon, [illegible], [illegible].
" Rorie, pardon, [illegible].
" Teig, pardon, [illegible].
" Theobald—Tibbot, pardon, [illegible], [illegible], [illegible].
" Tibbite, pardon, [illegible].
" Tirlagh, pardon, [illegible].
" See Sinnaghe.
Fox, the, lands surrendered by, [illegible].
Fox's country (barony of Kilcoursey, King's co.), [illegible], [illegible]; surrender and regrant, [illegible], [illegible].
" seneschal of, [illegible].
Foxes parks in Dublin, [illegible], [illegible], [illegible], [illegible].
Foxes lands, [illegible].
Foxley, George, lease, [illegible]; re-grant, [illegible], [illegible].
Foxx, Edm., pardon, [illegible].
Foye, illegal custom, [illegible].
Foylanstown, co. Westm., [illegible].
Foyle, John mc, pardon, [illegible].
Foyn, co. Lim., [illegible].
Foynes—Foyne—Foyen, co. Lim., [illegible], [illegible], [illegible].
Foyoke (co. Rosc.?), [illegible].
Foyran, co. Westm., [illegible]. See Fayron.
Foyre (co. Kerry?), [illegible].
Fragh (co. Tip.?), [illegible].

Fraane, John, pardon, [illegible].
Fraane—Frain—Fraine—Fraine—Frayne, co. Meath, [illegible], [illegible], [illegible], [illegible], [illegible], [illegible], [illegible], [illegible], [illegible], [illegible].
Fraine—Frayne, Garrett, pardon, [illegible].
" Gerald, pardon, [illegible].
" Gerrott, pardon, [illegible].
" James, pardon, [illegible], [illegible], [illegible], [illegible].
" John, pardon, [illegible].
" Oliver, pardon, [illegible].
" Peter, pardon, [illegible].
" Redmond, pardon, [illegible], [illegible].
" Rich., pardon, [illegible].
" Rob., pardon, [illegible].
" Walter, pardon, [illegible].
" Wm., pardon, [illegible], [illegible], [illegible].
Fraineston. See Frayneston.
France, war with, [illegible]; trade with, [illegible], [illegible], [illegible], [illegible], [illegible], [illegible], [illegible]; merchant of, protected, [illegible]; subjects of king pardoned, [illegible].
Franciscan or Grey Friars, or Friars minor, houses of. See Adare, Armagh, co. Mayo, Bonamargy, Carrickfergus, Clonmel, Clonkenkerill, Ennis, Galway, Kilcrea, Kildare, Killaly, Killeigh, Kinalehin, Lislaghtin, Moyne, co. Mayo, Quin, Rosserilly, Tomogan, Trim, Wexford, Wicklow, and Youghal.
Francomes land, co. Dub., [illegible].
Frank house in Cork, [illegible], [illegible].
" Drogheda, [illegible].
" Dublin, [illegible].
" Kilkenny, [illegible].
" Mullingar, [illegible], [illegible], [illegible].
" Naas, [illegible], [illegible].
" Navan, [illegible].
" Trym, [illegible], [illegible].
" Wicklow, [illegible], [illegible].
Franzesye, Anthonio, pardon, [illegible].
Frasnon—Frasstowne (co. Mon.?), [illegible].
Frawill, Fynolly or, pardon, [illegible].
Fraye—Frayne. See Fraine.
Frayne, Redmond, &c. See Fraine.
Frayne-ton—Fraineston—Frayneston—Frayneston (Frayne's ton), co. Wick., [illegible], [illegible], [illegible], [illegible], [illegible], [illegible], [illegible], [illegible].
Freatuane. See Freshane.
Freaghe, co. Cork, [illegible].
Freamoune, co. Westm., [illegible].
Freban—Frebane or Feba, in Dunboyne, [illegible], [illegible].
Freehane—Freshane—Freshan. See Freshane.
Freeholders of county Wexford to freedom from subsidy, [illegible].
" to hold by knights service, [illegible], [illegible], [illegible].
" under Dermod Cavenagh of Knockamorrow to be confirmed in their rights, [illegible].

INDEX TO FIANTS. ELIZABETH.

Freeholders exempted from martial law, 615, 643, 1196.
„ join in surrender, [illegible].
„ pardoned, [illegible], 6457, 6459, [illegible], 6517, [illegible], [illegible], [illegible], 6541, [illegible], 6561, [illegible], 6732.
„ services in Munster to be fixed, 6771.
„ under earl of Desmond, [illegible].
„ under Munster undertakers, [illegible], [illegible].
Freeston (Friarstown), co. Kild., 6811.
Freerton—Freertowne. See Frierston.
Frefayre alias Frevian, co. Meath, [illegible].
Fregkane (co. Cork ?), 6514.
Fregkane—Frehanes. See Frehane.
Frehane (co. Cork ?), 3353.
Frehane—Freaghane—Frechanes—Freehan—Freghans—Frehanes—Freighan, co. Tip., [illegible], 1578, [illegible], [illegible], [illegible], [illegible], [illegible], [illegible].
Frein, David, pardon, [illegible].
Freinle, James, pardon, [illegible].
Freine, Peirs, pardon, [illegible].
Frekelleston, co. Meath, 782.
Freman, Nich., pardon, [illegible], [illegible].
French trade, 60-1, 1516, 1711.
„ King's subjects, protection for, [illegible]; duty placed on goods imported by, [illegible].
„ ship despoiled at Limerick, 1812.
„ men, pardon, [illegible], denization of, [illegible], [illegible].
„ courts, Irish merchants fail to obtain redress in, [illegible].
„ See France.
French—Frenche:
„ Edm., lease, [illegible].
„ Edm., pardon, [illegible].
„ Josias, pardon, [illegible].
„ Oliver, [illegible].
„ Peter, pardon, [illegible], [illegible].
„ Robert, pardon, [illegible].
„ Tho., pardon, [illegible].
Frene, Edde, pardon, [illegible].
„ Leonard, pardon, [illegible].
„ Walter, pardon, [illegible], [illegible].
Frenyston (co. Kilk. ?), [illegible].
Freny—Fernecy—Frenye:
„ David, pardon, [illegible].
„ Edward, pardon, [illegible].
„ Eny, pardon, [illegible].
„ James, pardon, [illegible], [illegible], [illegible].
„ Jenny, pardon, [illegible].
„ Leonard, pardon, [illegible], [illegible], [illegible].
„ Oliver, pardon, [illegible], [illegible], [illegible], [illegible].
„ Peter, pardon, [illegible].
Freny—Frenoy—Frenye:—
„ Redmund, pardon, 677, [illegible], [illegible].
„ Robert, pardon, [illegible], [illegible].
„ Thomas, pardon, [illegible], [illegible], [illegible].
„ Walter, pardon, [illegible], [illegible], [illegible], [illegible].
Frenyston (co. Kilk. ?), [illegible].
Frereton (Friarstown), co. Kild., [illegible], [illegible].
Frereton (Friarstown), co. Lim., [illegible].
Frevian alias Frefayre, co. Meath, [illegible].
Frevan, co. Westm., [illegible].
Frevanagh, co. Westm. See Fleanghboune.
Frevanagh, co. Cav., [illegible].
Frevannaghe—Frevenaghe, co. Westm., [illegible], [illegible].
Frevar, co. Cav., [illegible].
Frevell. See Frevill.
Frevenagh. See Frevannaghe.
Frevill—Frevell, (license, grant of advowsons, [illegible], 512, [illegible].
Freyland, co. Lim., [illegible].
Freyne—Freyn, John, pardon, 1674.
„ Redmund reagh, pardon, [illegible], [illegible].
„ Richard, pardon, 1675.
„ Robert, pardon, [illegible].
„ Walter, pardon, 1674.
Freyneston, co. Wick. See Frayneston.
Freynshe, Nicholas, livery to son, [illegible].
„ Robert, livery, [illegible].
Freyny, Fowlk, pardon, [illegible].
„ Rowland, pardon, [illegible].
Freynelleston, co. Meath, 148.
Friers mill, Galway, [illegible].
Friars. See Carmelite, Dominican, Franciscan, Trinity. Also see Monastery.
Friarstown, co. Car. See Frierstone.
Friarstown, co. Kild. See Frereton, Freeston.
Friarstown, co. Lim. See Ballynebrahir, or Frereton.
Friekanston (co. Westm. ?), [illegible].
Friers island, Monaghan, [illegible].
Friarspark, Trim, [illegible].
Frierston—Freerton—Frierstone—Frirton (Friarstown), co. Car., [illegible], [illegible], [illegible], [illegible], [illegible].
Friers mill, co. Cork, [illegible].
Frirton. See Frierston.
Frompelstowne, co. Kild., 1654.
Frompstowne—Frompstone, co. Dub., [illegible], [illegible].
Frostinge, Rich., pardon, [illegible].
Fuchenbog (Fuchin Bog), co. Gal., [illegible].
Fuero, Edm., pardon, [illegible].
Fues (Fews, co. Armagh), [illegible]; commission to subdue, [illegible]; pardon to chief and people of, [illegible].

INDEX TO FIANTS.—ELIZABETH.

Fuce, Wm., pardon, [illegible].
Fulford, Henry, pardon, [illegible].
Fulke, Henry, vicar of Kilpatrick, [illegible].
Fulkescourt, co. Kilk., [illegible].
Fullam, Wm., pardon, [illegible].
Fullan, Simon, pardon, [illegible].
Fuller, pardons of a, 177, [illegible].
Fullerton, James, security for men of Hos-commons co., [illegible].
Fullwalk, [illegible].
Fullum, Simon, pardon, [illegible].
Fuame, Tho., pardon, [illegible].
Funchanagh (co. Kerr. ?), [illegible].
Funshin Beg, co. Gal. See Fachenbeg.
Funshin More, co. Gal. See Fuwalinmore.
Funsheg, co. Louth. See Upsbeker.
Funton ny Carty, Donel O'Swilivan, pardon, [illegible]. See also Fwoiles.
Fuoeyd, co. Kilkenny, [illegible].
Furayne, Shane m'Teig I., pardon, [illegible].
Furendall, John, pardon, [illegible].
Furlonge—Furlong—Furlong:
- Anastasia, pardon, [illegible].
- David, pardon, [illegible].
- Edmund, pardon, [illegible].
- Fowke, pardon, [illegible].
- Gerald, pardon, [illegible].
- Henry, pardon, [illegible].
- James (of Horeton), wardship and livery, [illegible]; his lands, [illegible].
- James, pardon, [illegible].
- John (of Horeton), sheriff of co. Wexford, [illegible]; commission, [illegible]; pardon, [illegible]; land of, [illegible]; his heir, [illegible].
- John, pardon, [illegible].
- Laurence, pardon, [illegible].
- Matthew, pardon, 748, [illegible].
- Matthew, rebellion of, [illegible].
- Matthias, pardon, [illegible].
- Nicholas, pardon, [illegible].
- Patrick, pardon, [illegible].
- Philip, pardon, [illegible]; son of, [illegible].
- Redmond, pardon, [illegible].
- Richard, pardon, [illegible].
- Robert, pardon, [illegible].
- Simon, pardon, [illegible].
- Thomas, pardon, [illegible].
- Walter, pardon, [illegible].
- William, heir of, [illegible].

Furlonge, William, pardon, [illegible].
Furlongstown, co. Wex., [illegible].
Furmoilke (co. Kilk. ?), [illegible].
Furness, England, monastery of, [illegible].
Furres, John, wardship, [illegible].
Furres—Fyrres, William, capt., com. for martial law, [illegible]; pardon, [illegible].
Furres—Furres, William (of Kilkenny), grant of land, [illegible]; son and heir of, [illegible].
- See Fyrres.
Furrisah, [illegible].
Furrs of St. Marie Abbie, Dublin, [illegible].
Furryhill, co. Kild. See Fyrhill.
Furtho, Mr., [illegible]. See Forth, Ambrose.
Furtollaghe. See Furtollagh.
Fury (King's co.), [illegible].
Fusey, tithes of, [illegible]; on fixed, [illegible].
Futley, Geoffrey, pardon, 147.
Fuyrabo lo, co. Kild., [illegible].
Fwoyle (King's co.), [illegible].
Fwoleo no twoly or boulo, Wm. M'Kellgoll, [illegible].
Fwrres, William. See Furres.
Fwyre—Fyrryo—Fywyre (Whitery), King's co., rectory, [illegible].
Fyaln, James, pardon, [illegible].
Fyall. See Fiall.
Fyan, Richard. See Fian.
Fyanston—Fyanceston—Fianstown—Fianstown (Fyanstown), co. Meath, [illegible].
Fydan. See Fiddan.
Fyddam. See Fiddam.
Fyddorth, co. Wat., [illegible].
Fyddown. See Fiddowne.
Fydortho. See Fidortho.
Fydy, co. Cork, [illegible].
Fyens (co. Wexford ?), [illegible].
Fyenot. See Fyenitt.
Fyenaugh (man's name), [illegible].
Fyenny, Cahill m'Teig I., pardon, [illegible].
- Donell and Rory m'Shane I., pardon, [illegible].
Fyenitt—Fyenot, co. Kerry, [illegible].
Fyeriagh, co. Tip., [illegible].
Fyherd, co. Tip., [illegible].
Fyine (co. Lim. ?), [illegible].
Fykinsion, co. Meath, [illegible].
Fyllandon, co. Meath, [illegible].
Fyllerton, co. Meath, [illegible].
Fymoan, co. Tip., rectory, [illegible].
Fymore, co. Tip., [illegible].
Fyn, Donogh m'Donell Y., pardon, [illegible].
- Rich., pardon, [illegible].
- Tirlagh, pardon, [illegible].
- Wm. fitz Thomas, pardon, [illegible].

INDEX TO FIANTS—ELIZABETH.

Fyna (co. Kild. ?), 3662.
Fynagh. See Finaghe.
Fynagh—Fynagh (co. Cork ?), 6511, 6764.
Fynagh, co. Gal., [illegible].
Fynallane, co. Kerry, 6417.
Fynallymore, co. Kerry, 5013, 6028.
„ See Finallimor.
Fynangh (co. Leit. ?), 6766.
Fynbeare. See Fynllane.
Fynchangrane (co. Long. ?), 6552.
Fyndemore (co. Long. ?), 6552.
Fyne, Richard, pardon, 776.
„ Thomas, 1011.
„ Tirlagh, pardon, 6564.
Fynel, co. Kerry, 4620.
Fynegina, co. Lim., 3781.
Fynaghede (co. Kerry ?), 4467.
Fynelay (co. Tip. ?), 6323.
Fynen, David m'Donogh, pardon, 6477.
„ Margaret ny, pardon, 6518.
„ Shily ny, pardon, 6518.
Fyner, 1368.
Fynet, Edm., pardon, 6172.
Fynglas—Fynglass, &c. See Finglas.
Fynkeslone, co. Meath, 325.
Fynbour—Fynbourne (Kilfenora, co. Clare), religious house, possessions leased, 1453, 6924.
Fynine, Donogh, pardon, 6333.
„ Onory ny, pardon, 6703.
„ Margaret ny, pardon, 6461.
„ Tirlagh, pardon, 6367.
Fynkilline—Fynicklyne—Fraynklyne (Finkeline ?), co. Ross., 1455, 2360, 4467.
Fynlie, co. Kerry, 4448.
Fynlestown (co. Lim. ?), 6477.
Fynn, Derby, pardon, 6741.
„ Hugh, m'Teige, pardon, 6268.
„ Margaret, pardon, 6478.
„ Nich., pardon, 6477.
„ Tirlagh, pardon, 6784.
Fynnaghes, co. Kild., 1369.
Fynnaghe's lands, co. Dub., 1233.
Fynnan, bog, King's co., 6786.
Fynne, William. See Finne.
Fynnevarre (co. Clare ?), 6818.
Fynnolan, Harrie, Morchoe and Shane m'Edm., pardon, 6517.
Fynnor, co. Cork, 3455.
Fynnor, (Fennor in par. Ardcath), co. Meath, 1463.
Fynnor, co. Meath, 1465.
Fynnor (Fennor, par. Oldcastle), co. Meath, 1466.
Fynnor, church of, co. Meath, 6797.
Fynnor, co. Wat., 326, 1068.
Fynnoy, Tho., pardon, 6452.
Fynowick. See Finowick.
Fynowr (Finnoe), co. Lim., 4123.
Fynter (co. Kild. ?), 6049.
Fynury, co. Rosc., 1469.
Fynwey, co. Cav., 6634.
Fyny, co. Clare, 2977.
Fynyd (co. Sligo ?), [illegible].
Fynye, Margaret ny, pardon, 6461.
Fynyskilyne. See Fynkilline.
Fyond, Cornell, 6498.
Fyrall. See Farrell.
Fyrhill (Ferryhill), co. Kild., 3140.
Fyric (King's co.), 6961.
Fyrres, William, grant of wardship, 688.
„ See Furres.
Fyrre alias Fywyre. See Fwyre.
Fytherd. See Fethard.
Fytherd. See Fethard, co. Wex.
Fythert. See Fetherd.
Fytkmoyn. See Fithmone.
Fyton—Fytonn—Fytten—Fytton. See Fitton.
Fytzgarrold. See Fitz Garrett.
Fytzgerald—Fytzgeralde. See Fitz Gerald.
Fyta Harries. See Fitz Harries.
Fyts Patrick—Fytzpatrick. See Fitz Patrick.
Fytzsymondes. See Fitz Symons.
Fyts Teige. See Fitz Teige.
Fyts William—Fytzwilliams—Fytzwylliam—Fyts Wylliams—Fytzwylliam. See Fitz William.

Gabbal Baghwall (co. Wick.) See Cowlmell, also Kilranelagh, 1538; Rosnlaghan, 6291.
Gaerye, co. Cork, 3140.
Gaffery — Gaffeney, Christopher, prebendary of Tipper, license of absence, 604; pardon, 681. See Ossory, bishop of.
Gafary — Gaffeny, co. Meath, 1468.
Gagell, co. Mayo, 1404.
Gagill, co. Rosc., 6462.
Gaiden, Nich., lease 4380.
„ Simon, lease, 4298.
Gaines lands by Callon, co. Wex., 4081.
Gainsborough. See Burgh, lord, 6123.
Gainston, co. Wex., 6668.
Galdeall (Chabol), Queen's co., 2286.
Galbellie (Gallbally, co. Wex. ?), 6454.
Gallbally, 6178.
Galbally, co. Lim., 3807, 4924, 5006; grant, 6178.
Galbon, John, 4168.
Galbardiston. See Galbertstown.
Galbegendon, in manor of Leixlip, 1568, 6668.
Galbertston—Galbardiston, co. Tip., 3023, 3448, 5523, 5850; castle, &c., 5945.

INDEX TO FIANTS—ELIZABETH.

Galbooly, co. Tip. *See* Gulrolly.
Galbraly (Gallbeley, co. Gal.), [illegible].
Galcown, Donell m'Donogh I., pardon, 6761.
„ Dwaltagh m'Tumalyn I., pardon, 6761.
„ Farrell m'Tomalyn I., pardon, 6761.
„ Owe m'Owen m'Adegane I., pardon, 6761.
Gald alias Hawe, Wm., pardon, 6764.
Galdey alias Butler, James, pardon, 6762.
Galdie, David m'Edmund, pardon, [illegible], [illegible].
„ Edmund. *See* Galdy.
Galdref, Theobald Fitz-Theobald, pardon, [illegible].
Galdy — Gaddie, alias Archdeacon, Edm., pardon, [illegible], [illegible].
Gale, Farrell m'Howge m'Dermot, pardon, [illegible].
Gale, James, pardon, [illegible], [illegible].
„ Richard, pardon, 1617.
„ Shane, m'Howge m'Dermot, pardon, [illegible]. *See* M'Dermot gale.
Galenaheras, co. Gal., [illegible].
Galeberg — Galloberg (Galeyberg), co. Ros., [illegible], [illegible].
Galemorryghily (co. Westm. ?), [illegible].
Galeras (*see* Galloroes), [illegible].
Galeston—Galestown. *See* Galleston, co. Meath.
Galey, co. Kerry. *See* Galle, Gallie.
Galeyberg, co. Ros. *See* Galeberg, Gayleberg.
Galgane—Galgrane, Darby, pardon, [illegible], [illegible].
Galgane, David, pardon, [illegible].
Galie (Galey), co. Kerry, [illegible], [illegible], [illegible], [illegible]; advowson, [illegible].
Galin, King's co., 1648.
Gall, David, pardon, 141, 437, [illegible], [illegible], [illegible], [illegible], [illegible], [illegible].
„ Edmund, pardon, 141, [illegible], [illegible], [illegible], [illegible], [illegible], [illegible], [illegible], [illegible], [illegible].
„ James, pardon, [illegible], [illegible], [illegible], [illegible], [illegible], [illegible].
„ John, pardon, [illegible], [illegible].
„ Mary alias Margaret Doile, pardon, [illegible].
„ Miles, pardon, [illegible].
„ Peter, pardon, 1974, [illegible].
„ Redmund, pardon, [illegible].
„ Richard, pardon, 141, 437, [illegible], [illegible], [illegible], [illegible], [illegible], [illegible], [illegible], [illegible], [illegible].
„ Robert, pardon, 912, [illegible].
„ Walter (of Gall-town), sheriff of Kilkenny, [illegible], [illegible], [illegible], [illegible]; commissions, [illegible], [illegible], [illegible], [illegible], [illegible]; pardon, 141, [illegible], [illegible].
„ Walter (of Garranconnan), com., [illegible]; pardon, 437, [illegible], [illegible], [illegible].
„ Walter, pardon, [illegible], [illegible].
Galla, Donell alias Donell m'Connor, pardon, [illegible].
Galla, Shane, pardon, [illegible].
Galla (co. Ros. ?), [illegible].
Gallagh — Gallaghe, co. Gal., [illegible], [illegible], [illegible], [illegible], [illegible], [illegible], [illegible], [illegible].
Gallagh, co. Ros., [illegible].
Gallane, co. Cork, [illegible].
Gallanaghry (King's or Queen's co.), [illegible], [illegible].
Gallavan, Conoghor m'Donoghe I., pardon, [illegible].
Galloway (co. Gal. ?), [illegible].
Galloway (Galway), [illegible]. *See* Galway.
Gallchery, Eugene (son of) Cormac I., pardon, [illegible].
Galle, Edm. roe, pardon, [illegible].
Galleberg. *See* Galeberg.
Gallen, King's co., [illegible].
„ monastery of canons, leased, [illegible], [illegible].
Gallerous—Galerus, co. Kerry, [illegible], [illegible].
Galleston. *See* Gauldstown, co. Kilk.
Galleston—Galeston—Galestown—(Gale's-town), co. Meath, [illegible], [illegible], 1460, [illegible], [illegible].
Gallestown. *See* Gauldtown, co. Kilk.
Gallevan, Donell m'Conoghor R., pardon, [illegible].
Galleys (Dymrighailes), Queen's co., [illegible].
Galleys to be maintained on Shannon, [illegible], [illegible], [illegible].
Gallgaher, Wm., pardon, [illegible].
Gallie (Galey), co. Kerry, [illegible]; grant, [illegible].
„ rectory, [illegible], [illegible], [illegible].
Gallie, Rich., pardon, [illegible].
Gallinshe (co. Ros. ?), [illegible].
Gallighe country (co. Armagh ?), [illegible].
Gallin, [illegible].
Gallirston. *See* Gauldstown, co. Kilk.
Gallmoyleon (co. Meath ?), [illegible].
Gallmorestown. *See* Galmorestown, co. Kild.
Gallmorestown, co. Meath, [illegible].
Gallmoriston. *See* Galmorestown.
Gallmoye. *See* Galmoy.
Gallo. *See* Gallowe.
Galloglass to be maintained by chief, [illegible], [illegible]; to be maintained by granters of lands, [illegible], [illegible], [illegible].
„ the queen's, bonaght of, [illegible]; agreement with chiefs of, [illegible].
Galloglasses, pardon of, [illegible], [illegible], [illegible].
Gallon of land, co. Cav., [illegible].
Gallons, Mary, custodiam ruled, [illegible].
Galloway, [illegible].
Gallowe—Gallo (Gallow), co. Meath, church, [illegible], 1948, [illegible].
Gallowlawe, Morrish Cosrian I., pardon, [illegible].
Gallowry (co. Clare ?) [illegible].
Gallstown. *See* Gaulstown, co. Kilk.
Gallmurry, Thos., pardon, [illegible].

INDEX TO FIANTS.—ELIZABETH.

Galluoly, co. Ross. or Gal., 4884
Gallvaine, Dermot, pardon, 6416.
,, John m'Teig Y., pardon, 4671.
Gallvally, co. Wex., 5737.
Gallvane, John, pardon, 5754.
Gallwaie. See Galway.
Gallwaie, 6124.
Gallwan, James, pardon, 1655.
Gallway. See Galway.
Gallway. See Galwey.
Gallways. See Galway.
Gallwelley in Lower Connaght, 6862.
Gallwey. See Galway.
Gallwey. See Galwey.
Gallwiston, co. Cork, 1687.
Galmarston, co. Kild., 1583.
Galmoie. See Galmoy.
Galmorestown—Galmerston—Gallmorestone—Gallmerstone, co. Kild., 994, 2366, 3423, 4665, 5393; castle and lands, 6576.
Galmoy—Gallmoye—Galmoie, co. Kilk., rectory, 2284, 2616, 4288, 5594.
Galrowston, co. Dub., 2673, 3047, 5236.
Galrotheston (Galrotestown), co. Louth, 6316, 6687.
Galveris, Tho., pardon, 6213.
Galtagh, Philip, pardon, 5463.
Galte alias FitzHarrice, William, pardon, 5933.
Galtire (Gualtier), co. Wat., 753.
Galtrim—Galtrym—Galtrym, co. Meath, 1653, 2166, 4149, 6387.
,, rectory, 443, 864–6, 898, 1560, 1662, 2614, 2968, 3424, 3426, 4514, 4250, 5678, 6343, 6787.
,, baron of. See Hussey.
Galtrym, Richard, sheriff and coroner, Dublin, 287.
,, Rose, pardon, 4917.
Galtrymo, baron of. See Hussey, Patrick.
Galty, John, pardon, 5044.
Galvally—Galvalley, co. Galway, 4874; castle, 5964.
Galvan, James fitz Edm., pardon, 4804.
Galvan's lands, in Youghal, 6658.
Galvani, Gabriel, license to, 86.
Galvei—Galvey. See Galway.
Galveye, Andrew. See Galwey.
Galvie. See Galway.
Galvelle, church of (Galbooly, co. Tip.), 687.
Galvey—Galvaye—Galwaie. See Galway.
Galwaie, Edmund. See Galwey.
Galwan, John, pardon, 6416.
Galway—Gallway—Gallwey—Galwaie—Galwey—Gallaway—Galvey—Galvie—Galvey, 1694, 3874, 3403, 3943, 4283, 4343, 4478, 4884, 4884, 4922, 4883, 5452, 5522, 5783, 5843, 6138; sums of civility in Connaught, 3731; foreign trade, 1711, 3736; fiants dated at, 3087, 3619-16, 3619-20, 4069; fine to be paid at, 1138, 3873-3; chief may be summoned to, 3791, 4628.
,, mayor, bailiffs, and commonalty, license, 1188, 3462-4; office of searcher granted to, 3734.
,, mayor, 968, 2964, 3367, 4234, 4436, 4631, 6188, 6083, 6727, 6062, 6606, 6328-4, 6640.
,, aldermen, 4876, 6069, 6640.
,, recorder, 6633.
,, merchants, 2478, 3071, 3583, 3718, 3777, 3941, 4238, 4464, 4783, 5470, 5737, 5882, 6862.
,, preacher of, 6384.
,, church of S. Nicholas, 2430.
,, ,, our Lady, 5737.
,, college, wardens and vicars, 6464.
,, Duffish, 4918, 6429.
,, Friar's mill, 5787.
,, gaol, keeper of, 4673.
,, Martin's mill, 3494, 5737, 6188.
,, mills on river, 1488, 6767.
,, monastery of S. Augustin, leased, 1409, 3424.
,, ,, S. Dominic, leased, 1418, 3428.
,, ,, S. Francis, leased, 1409, 6446.
,, premises in, 1488.
,, rectory, 343, 3429, 3442.
,, river fishery, 1559, 3494, 6188; tithes of fish, 3452.
,, river (or bay), 1774.
,, port, 888.
,, ,, supervisor, 6866.
,, customs leased, 2438, 2647, 2834, 3488.
,, ,, controller, 2762.
,, searcher and gauger, 2846, 2734, 6867.
,, wine impost, leased, 4132.
,, ,, collector, 1434, 2618, 2744, 3494, 5314, 5838, 6209, 6481, 6842.
,, ,, controller, 1674, 2138, 2763, 3494, 5158, 5578, 5868, 6482, 6817.
,, county, 1712, comn. to form, 1834.
,, ,, sheriff, 3887, 4048, 4264, 4886, 5741.
,, ,, comn. for government, 2703.
,, ,, comn. for martial law, 3887, 4848.
,, ,, persons of, pardoned, 3963, 3947, 4471, 4473-83, 4148, 5523, 6312, 4642, &c.

INDEX TO FIANTS—ELIZABETH.

Galway county, crimes outside excepted from pardons, [illegible], [illegible], [illegible].

Galwayes lands, Youghal, [illegible].

Galwale—Galwey. *See* Galwey.

Galwey—Gallwale—Galway—Gallwey—Galveye—Galwale—Galway—Galwaye—Galweye—Galwy.

" Anastasia, wardship, [illegible].

" Andrew, pardon, [illegible], [illegible], [illegible].

" Christopher, alienation in, [illegible]; wardship of heir, [illegible].

" David, pardon, [illegible].

" Edm., livery, [illegible].

" Ellen, pardon, [illegible].

" Geoffrey, pardon, [illegible], [illegible].

" James, [illegible]; leases, [illegible], [illegible], [illegible]; grant of a wardship, [illegible].

" John, alderman of Cork, pardon, [illegible].

" John, lease, [illegible]; searcher of Limerick, [illegible]; collector of Dingle, [illegible].

" John (of Limerick), [illegible].

" John (son of Walter of Cork), wardship and livery, [illegible], [illegible].

" Patrick, [illegible], [illegible]; comm., [illegible].

" Richard, [illegible].

" Stephen, pardon, [illegible].

" Walter (of Cork), pardon, [illegible]; his heir, [illegible], [illegible].

" William, searcher of Limerick, [illegible], [illegible].

" William (of Cork), pardon, [illegible]; his heir, [illegible].

Galwyle—Galweyle, co. Gal., [illegible], [illegible].

Galyn (Dysartgallen ?), Queen's co., [illegible], [illegible].

Gambon, Morice, pardon, [illegible].

Games played, [illegible], [illegible]; sledge throwing, [illegible]; bowls and bowling, [illegible], [illegible].

Gane, Margaret ny, pardon, [illegible].

Ganagh (co. Cork ?), [illegible].

Gancagh, Edmund, lands of, in co. Lim., granted, [illegible].

Ganderstown, co. Louth. *See* Ballymander, [illegible].

Gange (Granard O'Fullan), co. Ross., [illegible].

Gan [illegible], Tely O'Connellor, pardon, [illegible].

Gangion, Dermot [illegible] m'Tyrlagh m'Dermot [illegible], pardon, [illegible].

Gaol, built on private speculation, [illegible].

Gaol delivery, comm. for, by martial law, [illegible], [illegible].

Gaol at Naas, [illegible], [illegible].

" at Mullingar, erection of, [illegible].

Gaols. *See* prisoners, [illegible].

Gara, Katherine ny, pardon, [illegible].

Garagh, Turlogh m'Donogh Y, pardon, [illegible].

Garaghill (co. Car. ?), [illegible].

Garaldine, Shane m'Maurice, pardon, [illegible].

Garaldines, Sept of the, [illegible].

Garan grange, co. Kilk., [illegible].

Garan, co. Kilk., [illegible].

Garan (co. Lim. ?), [illegible].

Garandgorill, [illegible].

Garanegolane. *See* Garrangillane.

Garanevillen. *See* Garranvillan.

Garan James. *See* Garran James.

Garanreoghe in Munster, [illegible].

Garanraith (co. Clare ?), [illegible].

Garanyckle, co. Wex., [illegible].

Garbal [illegible], co. Meath. *See* Garblanghe, [illegible].

Garbally—Garbelly—Garvally—Garvelle, co. Gal., [illegible], [illegible], [illegible], [illegible]. *See also* Garvallie.

Garchill—Garrhill, co. Car., [illegible], [illegible].

Gardgrine (co. Westm. ?), [illegible].

Gardener—Gardiner, Bartholomew, vicar of Castleknock, [illegible]; notary, [illegible].

Gardener—Gardiner—Gardner—Gardyner, Robert (knt.), chief justice, [illegible], [illegible]; lord justice of Ireland, [illegible], [illegible]; commissioner, [illegible].

Gardenstown, co. Louth, [illegible], [illegible].

Gardiner—Gardyner, Nicholas, fishing license, [illegible]; surveyor of victual, [illegible].

Gardon, Peirce, pardon, [illegible].

Gardyner. *See* Gardener, Gardiner.

Garegaghe (co. Gal.), [illegible].

Garehlagin. *See* Garryhlain.

Gareydirkye (Garrydork, co. Lim.), [illegible].

Garestown—Garistown (Garristown), co. Dub., 1777, [illegible], [illegible]; grant, [illegible].

Garet, Patrick, [illegible].

Garetstown, co. Meath, [illegible].

Garvanlan, [illegible].

Garey [illegible] (co. Kilk. ?), [illegible].

Gareyll, Daniel m'Gaffrey, pardon, [illegible].

Garinadrey. *See* Garranadray.

Garnagh, Donell, pardon, [illegible].

Garrynywre, co. Kild., [illegible].

Garry [illegible], co. Tip., [illegible].

Garry [illegible], Queen's co., [illegible].

Garyhill (Garryhill, co. Car. ?), [illegible].

Garbithe [illegible] (Garby ? co. Westm.), [illegible].

Garby [illegible], co. Kild., [illegible].

Garby [illegible] alias Loughmore, [illegible].

Garline. *See* Garryroy.

Garlcahoroghe (Garrycahoragh), co. Cork, [illegible].

Garlon Abbey, co. Mayo, [illegible].

Garlowtagart (Garryantaggart), co. Cork, [illegible].

Garigunchough or Garrignanagh, co. Kerry, [illegible].

INDEX TO FIANTS—ELIZABETH.

Garignakighe, co. Kerry, 4014, [illegible].
Garigastell (Garrycastle, King's co.), 6519.
Garlilake (perhaps Garrykeshe, co. Kilk.), 6971.
Garinmaric, co. Lim., [illegible].
Garinkaharagh (co. Cork ?), [illegible].
Garinnae (Gorumna island), co. Gal., [illegible].
Garinelagh, co. Cork, 5131.
Gariston (or Garreston), 3417.
Garistown. See Garrestown, co. Lim.
Garkill—Karkill, co. Car., 838; castle, lands, mill, 5674, 6842.
Garlen, John, pardon, 6877.
Garland—Garlande, Edward. See Gernon.
" George, alias Garnon, grant of land, 298.
" James, knight. See Gernon.
" John, export licence, 6166.
" Nich., pardon, [illegible].
" Patr., pardon, 6444.
" Patrick. See Gernon.
" Roger, sheriff of Louth. See Gernon.
Garlanstoe (co. Meath ?), 3407.
Garlon, James, grant, 5836.
" Patr., pardon, 3817, 4087.
" Roger. See Gernon.
Garlone, Henry, pardon, 6647.
" Margaret, pardon, 6647.
Garlowan, Nich. m'Patrick, pardon, [illegible].
Garmaghe (co. Meath ?), [illegible].
Garmane, co. Gal., [illegible].
Garnagh, Philip m'Shane, pardon, 6181.
Garnan-ton, 6783.
Garnaghshire, co. Tip., 4012.
Garnell, Mullingar, 5628.
Garnells improved for army, 373.
Garnet, Nicholas, 1464.
Garolagh, co. Clare, 1848.
Garonge, James, pardon, 4464.
Garron, Edw., pardon, 3837.
" George, grant of land, [illegible], 1069.
" George, pardon, [illegible], 6738.
" Rob., pardon, 5067.
" Stephen, pardon, [illegible].
" Wm., pardon, 3887.
Garronston (King's co. ?), 6762.
Garoldine, Tho. fitz Wm., pardon, [illegible].
" Wm. fitz Edmond, pardon, [illegible].
Garomlarvey (co. Wat. ?), [illegible].
Garoroughe, co. Ros., 4044.
Garowe (co. Gal ?), [illegible].
Garra James. See Garran James.
Garradaf (co. Gal ?), 5817.
Garraf (co. Gal ?), [illegible].
Garraffe, James fitz Morice, pardon, 4487.
" Wm. m'Edm., pardon, 6702.
Garragh (Gorragh ?), Queen's co., [illegible].
Garraghe, co. Lim., 3144.
Garrahisky (co. Kilk. ?), 1818.
Garrahobock (Garryhubbock, co. Wex.), 6647.
Garra fraghtane (co. Kerry ?), 3[illegible].
Garrald, Davie m'Edm. m'Shane, pardon, 6544.
" John m'James m'Morris, pardon, 6478.
" Nich. m'Edm. m'Shane, pardon, [illegible].
" Tho. fitz Walter, pardon, 6166.
Garramble, Edm. m'Shane, pardon, 6544.
Garraoblinie, 3838.
Garrall, John m'James, pardon, 6783.
Garramowlish (co. Wat. ?), 6478.
Garramore, co. Tip. or Lim., 4694.
Garran, co. Car., 1948.
Garran (co. Cork ?), 2388.
Garran (co. Kerry ?), 8[illegible].
Garran (co. Kilk. ?), 6702.
Garran (co. Lim. ?), [illegible], 6480.
Garran, co. Mon. See Tullagarran.
Garran, Queen's co., 6841.
Garran (co. Tip. ?), 1344, 4638.
Garran, co. Tip., 4[illegible], 5[illegible], 6[illegible], 6[illegible], 6701.
Garran, co. Wat., [illegible], [illegible], 6271.
Garran, co. Westm., 1940.
Garran, co. Wex., [illegible], [illegible], 6160, 6218.
Garran, co. Wex. or Car., 6317.
Garran Anmack (co. Mayo ?), 6768.
Garranban, co. Lim., 6178.
Garranbane, co. Lim. or Cork, 6173.
Garranboy, co. Cork, 6867.
Garranboye—Garran Boy—Garranbuoy—Garranbuy (Garranaboy, co. Lim.), 5874, 6171, 6194, 6478.
Garranamanna—Garrinamanan, co. Kilk., 734, 1946, 1978, 2842. See also Curranacomman.
Garranbane (co. Kilk. ?), 6061.
Garrancinnal, co. Tip., 6169.
Garranconnile (co. Wat. ?), 6623.
Garrancrobally—Garrancrobollie—Garrancrowally—Garran crowally, co. Wat., 1044, 1143, 1234, 2238, 6[illegible].
Garrand (co. Meath ?), 6[illegible].
Garrandarragh—Garrandarraghe—Garranderragh, co. Cork, [illegible], [illegible], [illegible], [illegible], [illegible].
Garrandrallan, co. Cork, 5878.
Garranelrohan, co. Cork, 6647.
Garrane, co. Cork. See Garrans.
Garrane (Garrana), co. Gal., 6486.
Garrane, 1871.
Garrane, co. Lim., 6678.
Garrane (co. Mayo ?), 6788.
Garrane (co. Tip. ?), 6211.
Garrane, co. Wex., 6768.
Garranebane, co. Wat., 436.
Garranedarragh. See Garrandaragh.
Garrane crowally. See Garrancrobally.
Garraneighteraght (Garran Iteragh), co. Mon., 4831.

INDEX TO FIANTS—ELIZABETH.

Garraneskeevna, co. Lim. *See* Garranikyvan.
Garrane Kenefeaky. *See* Garranekenyfeky.
Garranekenagy (co. Cork ?), [illegible].
Garranes, co. Cork, [illegible].
Garraneinonagh — Garranemonagh, co. Lim., [illegible], 4616.
Garrane More and Beg, co. Lim. *See* Graiguenagarrane.
Garrane, co. Kerry, [illegible].
Garraneveddery — Garranewaddery — Garranewaderrig, co. Lim., [illegible], 4616, [illegible].
Garranevally — Garranevelly — Garryvealla, (co. Tip. ?), [illegible], [illegible].
Garranevore (co. Lim. ?), [illegible].
Garranevelly (co. Tip. ?), [illegible].
Garranewaddery — Garranewaderrig. *See* Garranevaddery.
Garranewalerig, co. Cork. *See* Garranewalerig.
Garraneyarlebblane, co. Kerry, [illegible].
Garranfarke, (co. Kilk. ?), [illegible].
Garrangaraun, co. Car., [illegible].
Garrangibbon — Garranegybone — Garrangibbon, co. Tip., 874, 913, [illegible], [illegible], [illegible], [illegible]; grant, [illegible]; rectory, [illegible], [illegible].
Garranground, co. Kilk., [illegible].
Garrangubbon. *See* Garrangibbon.
Garrankarragh (co. Clare ?), [illegible].
Garran Lassie (co. Lim. or Tip.), [illegible].
Garran Reagh — Garran Reagh (co. Lim. ?), [illegible].
Garran Roatty (co. Lim. ?), 6511.
Garran James — Garran James — Garran James — Garran Shames — Garranshames — Garran Tomais — Garrantomasho — Garrantomasho — Garrin James — Garran James (Garranjames), co. Cork, [illegible], [illegible], [illegible], [illegible], 6312, 6477, [illegible], [illegible], [illegible], 6779; grant, 6117.
Garrankenyfeky — Garrane Kenefeaky — Garran kynafeaky, co. Cork, [illegible], [illegible], [illegible].
Garrankeevy — Garranekevy (co. Lim. ?), [illegible], [illegible].
Garrankoyle, co. Gal., [illegible].
Garrankynafeaky. *See* Garrankenyfeky.
Garranikyvan (Garraneskeevna), co. Lim., [illegible].
Garranlaisk (co. Cork ?), [illegible].
Garranmarheary, co. Kilk., [illegible].
GarranmacKarny (co. Kilk. ?), [illegible].
Garranmore, co. Cork, [illegible].
Garranmore, co. Tip., [illegible], [illegible], [illegible], [illegible], 6779; grant, [illegible].
Garrannamanagh, co. Mayo, [illegible].
Garranagowragh, co. Mayo, [illegible].
Garran Ogeany (co. Cork ?), [illegible].
Garran Oyvin (Garranniguvilagh ?), co. Cork, [illegible].
Garranowyhiotaghl (Garran Oira), co. Mon., [illegible].
Garranroe, Queen's co., [illegible].
Garrans [illegible] for army, [illegible], [illegible].
Garrans, the (Garrans), co. Cork, [illegible], [illegible], [illegible].
Garrans, Queen's co., [illegible].
Garran Shames — Garranshames. *See* Garran James.
Garran Tomais — Garrantomasho. *See* Garran James.
Garranuckerly (co. Wat. ?), [illegible].
Garrantarton (Garrantarton, co. Wat. ?), [illegible].
Garranvolley, co. Tip., [illegible].
Garranvillan — Garranvillan, co. Wat., [illegible], [illegible].
Garranwalerig (Garranewalerig), co. Cork, [illegible], [illegible], [illegible].
Garranyvinrighe, co. Cork, [illegible].
Garranyblaney or Garryblaney, co. Dub., [illegible].
Garranes, co. Gal. *See* Garrane.
Garranabey, co. Lim. *See* Garranabeye.
Garrauniguvilagh, co. Cork. *See* Garran Ogyvn.
Garravagh, co. Cork. *See* Garryvaghe.
Garrayne (co. Kerry ?), [illegible].
Garrayne (co. Wex. ?), [illegible].
Garrayarron (co. Tip. ?), [illegible].
Garre (co. Leit. ?), [illegible].
Garre, Owen, pardon, [illegible].
Garrevoe. *See* Garryvoe.
Garrevelughe (co. Lim.), [illegible].
Garrevboyne (Garryboyne), co. Cork, [illegible].
Garreclaffe (Garryclaff), co. Lim., [illegible].
Garreclaffe. *See* Garryduff, co. Tip.
Garrefeyne (Garry Fine), co. Lim., [illegible].
Garredough — Garredughe, co. Wex., [illegible], [illegible].
Garreghe (co. Wex. ?), [illegible].
Garrelaragh (co. Kerry or Lim. ?), [illegible].
Garrelouchie. *See* Garrynouchie.
Garretdowne (co. Lim. ?), [illegible].
Garrokayre, Queen's co., [illegible].
Garrolees, co. Tip., [illegible].
Garret, John fitz Tho., excepted from pardon, [illegible].
" Morris oge fitz Morris, pardon, [illegible].
" Wm. m'Edm., pardon, [illegible].
Garrevlaugh, [illegible].
Garrohighe, co. Wex., [illegible].
Garromore. *See* Garrymore.
Garron, co. Lim., [illegible].
Garron, co. Tip., [illegible].
Garronaiden (co. Gal. ?), [illegible].
Garron Gheryk, co. Lim., [illegible].
Garroneowle (Garryungowle), co. Wat., [illegible].
Garrorsheay — Garriredeny — Garryredeny (Garrendenny), Queen's co., [illegible], [illegible], [illegible].
Garrosquwhil (Garrysagnall), co. Wat., [illegible].
Garrotindale (co. Lim. or Tip.), [illegible].
Garrotoon, Queen's co., [illegible].

INDEX TO FIANTS—ELIZABETH.

Garrvarye, co. Westm., [illegible].
Garr[illegible] (co. Tip. ?), [illegible].
Garr[illegible], co. Cork or Lim., [illegible].
Garr[illegible], co. Lim., [illegible].
Garr[illegible]. See Garran James.
Garr[illegible], co. Wex., [illegible].
Garr[illegible], co. Meath, [illegible].
Garrestown—Garistown—Garreston, co. Lim., [illegible]; parish, [illegible].
Garret, [ ] ny, pardon, [illegible].
„ Ellen ny[illegible], pardon, [illegible].
„ John, pardon, [illegible].
„ alias fitz Thomas, John, pardon, [illegible].
„ Margaret ny, pardon, [illegible].
„ Patrick, comm., [illegible], [illegible].
Garret (co. Tip. or Kilk.), [illegible].
Garr[illegible], co. Car., [illegible].
Garr[illegible] (co. Lim. ?), [illegible].
Garr[illegible] (co. Cork), [illegible].
Garrett, Ellen fitz James, pardon, [illegible].
Garrett, Lionel, pardon, [illegible].
„ Pair, [illegible] comm., [illegible].
„ Richard m'[illegible], pardon, [illegible].
„ Rose ny[illegible], pardon, [illegible].
„ Thomas, [illegible].
Garr[illegible]—Garr[illegible] (Garry[illegible]), co. Wex., [illegible].
Garr[illegible], co. Cork, [illegible].
Garrew, Dermot Byrne, death of, [illegible].
Garr[illegible], co. Gal., [illegible].
Garr[illegible] (co. Tip. ?), [illegible].
Garri[ ]j[illegible] (co. Lim. or Tip.), [illegible].
Garri[illegible], Queen's co., [illegible].
Garri[illegible], co. Wat., [illegible].
Garri[illegible] (co. Cork ?), [illegible].
Garri[illegible], co. Cork, [illegible].
Garricastell (Garrycastle, King's co.), [illegible].
Garri[illegible], Queen's co., [illegible], [illegible].
Garri[illegible] (Garry[illegible]), co. Cork, [illegible]; rectory, [illegible].
Garri[illegible] (co. Kilk. ?), [illegible], [illegible].
Garri[illegible]. See Garryduffe, co. Gal.
Garri[illegible] (co. Ross. ?), [illegible].
Garriduf. See Garryduffe, co. Wat.
Garri[illegible]. See Garrydud, co. Kilk.
Garriduff, [illegible].
Garri[illegible]. See Garryduf, co. Cork.
Garriduff, co. Kerry, [illegible].
Garri[illegible]. See Garryduff, co. Tip.
Garri[illegible]. See Garryduf, co. Cork.
Garriduffe, co. Kilk. or Tip., [illegible].
Garriduffe, co. Lim., [illegible].
Garriduffe (co. Mayo or Gal.), [illegible].
Garriduffe, Queen's co., [illegible].
Garriduffe. See Garryduffe, co. Tip.
Garri[illegible]. See Garry[illegible], Queen's co.
Garri[illegible] (co. Wex. ?), [illegible].
Garri[illegible] (co. Tip. ?), [illegible].
Garrif[illegible], Teige m'[illegible], pardon, [illegible].
Garr[illegible]. See Garry[illegible].
Garri[illegible] (co. Kilk. ?), [illegible].
Garrigan, Bryan ny, pardon, [illegible].
Garrigan, [illegible] m'Donell Y, pardon, [illegible].
Garrigan, Donell m'Donogh Y, pardon, [illegible].
Garrig[illegible]. See Garry[illegible], co. Lim.
Garrig[illegible], Galway, [illegible].
Garrig[illegible]. See Garry[illegible], co. Lim.
Garrig[illegible]. See Garry[illegible], Queen's co.
Garrig[illegible] (co. Sligo or Leit.), [illegible].
Garri[illegible]. See Garry[illegible].
Garri[illegible]. See Garry[illegible].
Garri[illegible], co. Kilk., [illegible].
Garri[illegible] (co. Tip. or Kilk. ?), [illegible].
Garri[illegible]—Garri[illegible]—Garri[illegible]. See Garry[illegible].
Garri[illegible], co. Car. (Garry[illegible], co. Wex. ?), [illegible].
Garri[illegible]. See Garry[illegible].
Garri[illegible] (co. Kilk. ?), [illegible].
Garri[illegible] (co. Cork ?), [illegible].
Garri[illegible]. See Garrymore.
Garri[illegible] (co. Cork ?), [illegible].
Garri[illegible]. See Garra[illegible].
Garri[illegible], [illegible].
Garri[illegible]. See Garry[illegible].
Garri[illegible] (Garry[illegible]), co. Cork, [illegible].
Garran James. See Garran James.
Garri[illegible], co. Cork, [illegible].
Garri[illegible]. See Garry[illegible].
Garri[illegible], co. Tip., [illegible].
Garri[illegible], Owen m'Turlogh, pardon, [illegible].
Garri[illegible] (co. Lim. ?), [illegible].
Garri[illegible] (Garry[illegible], co. Kilk.), [illegible].
Garri[illegible], co. Cav., [illegible].
Garri[illegible] (King's co. ?), [illegible].
Garri[illegible], comm. to provision, [illegible], [illegible].
Garri[illegible], Daniel m'Owen, pardon, [illegible].
Garri[illegible], Mahown m'Donogh I, pardon, [illegible].
Garrivoo—Garrivane. See Garryvoy.
Garro[illegible], Queen's co., [illegible].
Garro[illegible], Queen's co., [illegible].
Garro[illegible] (co. Cork ?), [illegible].
Garrogh, co. Gal., [illegible], [illegible].
Garrogh, co. Ross., [illegible].
Garroghe — Garroke (Garrogh, co. Tip.) rectory, [illegible], [illegible], [illegible].
Garrold, Thos. oge, pardon, [illegible].
Garr[illegible] (co. Ross. ?), [illegible].
Garr[illegible], Nolan m'Gilpatrick, pardon [illegible].
Garr[illegible] (co. Tip. ?), [illegible].
Garr[illegible], co. Cork, [illegible].
Garr[illegible], co. Ross., [illegible].
Garr[illegible], [illegible].
Garr[illegible], Queen's co., [illegible], [illegible].
Garr[illegible]—Garr[illegible] (Garr[illegible]), co. Clare, [illegible], [illegible], [illegible].

INDEX TO FIANTS—ELIZABETH.

Garrowbally (King's co. ?), [illegible].
Garrowe, Dermod m'Rwoghee, pardon, [illegible].
Garrowleash, co. Clare, 4761.
Garrowrie (co. Ross. ?), [illegible].
Garrwagh, co. Clare. *See* Carrowragh, Garvaragha.
Garry (co. Cork ?), [illegible].
Garry — Garrye (Ballingarry ?), co. Lim., [illegible]; rectory, 1716, [illegible], [illegible].
Garry [ ], co. Wex., [illegible].
Garryantaggart, co. Cork. *See* Garrientaggart.
Garrybally (King's co. ?), [illegible].
Garry Blackin (co. Gal. ?), 4767.
Garrybaloghane, co. Kilk., [illegible].
Garrybowe. *See* Garrytroy.
Garrycaddell (Queen's co.), [illegible], 1664.
Garrycahernagh, co. Cork. *See* Garricahernaghe.
Garrycastle, King's co. *See* Garrycastell, Garricastell, Garrycowaynicken.
Garrycloghy — Garrecloghie (co. Tip. ?), [illegible].
Garrycloan, co. Wat. *See* Garrycloon.
Garrycloyne, co. Cork. *See* Garrecloyne, Garricloyne.
Garrycorman, Queen's co., [illegible].
Garry Courty, co. Clare, [illegible].
Garryduf — Garriduff (co. Cork ?), [illegible], [illegible], [illegible], [illegible], [illegible].
Garryduf — Garriduffe, co. Kilk., [illegible], [illegible].
Garryduff, co. Lim. *See* Garreduffe.
Garryduff — Garreduffe — Garriduff, co. Tip., [illegible], [illegible], [illegible]-3, [illegible], [illegible].
Garryduffe (co. Cork or Lim.), [illegible].
Garryduffe — Garriduf, co. Gal., [illegible], [illegible].
Garryduffe — Garriduffe, co. Tip., [illegible], [illegible]-2, [illegible].
Garryduffe — Garriduf, co. Wat., [illegible], [illegible].
Garryduffe (co. Wex. ?), [illegible].
Garrye. *See* Garry.
Garry Ellen (Garryellen), co. Lim., [illegible].
Garryfinnge — Garrifinnge, co. Cork, [illegible], [illegible].
Garryfine, co. Lim. *See* Garrefloyne.
Garrygawill (co. Cork ?), [illegible].
Garrygerry, co. Clare, [illegible].
Garrygloss — Garriglasse (Garryglasse), Queen's co., [illegible], [illegible], [illegible].
Garryglasse — Garriclass, co. Lim., [illegible], [illegible], [illegible].
Garryhande (King's co. ?), [illegible].
Garryhaston, co. Wex. *See* Garrihistie.
Garryhalder, Queen's co. *See* Garryhudder.
Garryhawyn. *See* Garryhiggin.
Garryheenagh — Garrihenaghe (co. Kerry ?), [illegible], [illegible].
Garryhestie, co. Wex., [illegible].
Garryhostye, co. Wex., [illegible].
Garryhiggin — Garehiggin — Garrihigen — Garrihiggine — Garryhawyn (Garryhiggin), co. Kild.), [illegible], [illegible], [illegible], [illegible], [illegible], [illegible].
Garryhill, co. Car. *See* Garyhill, Garchill.
Garryhinde — Garrihinde — Garrihinde (Garryhoody), co. Cork, [illegible], [illegible], [illegible].
Garryhierye, co. Car., [illegible].
Garryimbloock, co. Wex. *See* Garrahoinck.
Garryhudder — Garryhunder (King's co.?), [illegible], [illegible].
Garryhudder — Garryhuder (Garryhelder), Queen's co., [illegible], [illegible].
Garryhunder. *See* Garryhudder.
Garrylecaha, co. Kilk. *See* Garrilicha.
Garrylondry. *See* Garryloundry.
Garryloy (co. Cork ?), [illegible].
Garrylhess, co. Cork, [illegible].
Garrymabowy — Garrymabory — Garrymacvahery, co. Cork, [illegible], [illegible], [illegible].
Garrymadork — Garrymadoke (Garrymaddock), Queen's co., [illegible], [illegible], [illegible].
Garrymanane, co. Cork, [illegible].
Garrymore (co. Car. ?), [illegible].
Garrymore — Garrimore, co. Cork, [illegible], [illegible], [illegible], [illegible].
Garrymore — Garramore — Garriemore — Garrimore, Queen's co., [illegible], [illegible], [illegible], [illegible], [illegible], [illegible], [illegible].
Garrymore — Garremore, co. Tip., [illegible].
Garrymurrilane, Queen's co., [illegible].
Garrynagoragh, co. Wat. *See* Garrynagoragh.
Garrynagowill, co. Wat. *See* Garrenagowle, Garrenagowld.
Garrynagranoge, co. Cork. *See* Garrinegrunagh, Garrynagranoge.
Garrynagrounsie (co. Lim. ?), [illegible].
Garrynamona (co. Tip. or Lim.), [illegible].
Garrynahemalaine, co. Tip., [illegible].
Garrynaheoule, co. Lim., [illegible].
Garrynamoyllroyll wood, co. Car., [illegible].
Garrynardery. *See* Garrendery.
Garrynegeragh — Garrinegaranagh (Garrynegoragh), co. Wat., [illegible], [illegible].
Garrynegroy — Garrynaneri (co. Tip.) ?, [illegible], [illegible].
Garrynegry, co. Clare, [illegible].
Garrynoboloskin, co. Cork, [illegible].
Garrynell, co. Westm., [illegible].
Garrynemomer (co. Ros. ?), [illegible].
Garrynodde — Garrindodde, co. Wex., [illegible], [illegible].
Garrynoyle, co. Tip., [illegible].
Garryoloundry — Garrinloundrye — Garryloundry (Kilgarrylandrey), co. Kerry, [illegible], [illegible]; rectory, [illegible].
Garryoneagel. *See* Garryneneyr.
Garryquarrin, co. Car., [illegible].
Garryrarjo, co. Westm., [illegible].
Garryrorlane, Queen's co., [illegible].
Garryvalle. *See* Garranervally.
Garry ny gowll, co. Cork, [illegible].

INDEX TO FIANTS.—ELIZABETH.

Garrynygrocan, co. Cork, 1494.
Garrynytarpan (co. Leit. ?), 1776.
Garryrickin, co. Kilk. *See* Garrinrickin.
Garryridder alias Kilpatricke (co. Kild.), 1977.
Garryrideralbyns (Queen's or King's co.), 2944.
Garryro, co. Tip., 6468.
Garrywraghe, co. Rosc., 6294.
Garryraghe (Garravragh, co. Cork), 6152.
Garryvan, Donogh m' Melaghlin I., pardon, 2314.
" Donogh m'Teig I., pardon, 2316.
Garryvarren, co. Wex. *See* Garravarran.
Garrytoy—Garthe—Garretoge—Garrivoe—Garrivooe—Garryhowe—Garrvine—Garrin—Garrehoe (Garryvoe), co. Cork, 6168, 4166, 6312, 6469, 6486; rectory, 1258, 1668, 4271, 6244.
Garrywake (co. Kilk. ?), 2068.
Garslew (co. Kilk. ?, perhaps Gracedieu, co. Wat.), 2843.
Gartagh, Donell, pardon, 2378.
Gartheston (co. Westm. ?), 2243.
Gartenabarre (co. Ferm. ?), 6494.
Gartenagh (Gortnagh), co. Mon., 6462.
Gartenearney (co. Rosc. ?), 6284.
Gartenowre—Gortenowre (co. Leit. ?), 6780.
Gartfadd, co. Long. (Gortfaddin, co. Leit. ?), 5544.
Gartin (co. Cork ?), 6816.
Gartines (co. Kilk. ?), 2404.
Gartlanestowne, co. Westm., 3422.
Gartlanestowne, 6704.
Gartlinghrye, co. Gal., 4717.
Gartmakelly (co. Ferm. ?), 4824.
Gartnanoel, co. Cav. *See* Gorte na nabbeil.
Gartnamp (Gortnamp), co. Kilk., 6118.
Gartnolough (co. Leit. ?), 4840.
Gartrowe. *See* Gortroe.
Garvally, co. Gal., 4712.
Garvan, James fitz Morris, pardon, 4781.
Garvaughe. *See* Garvonagh.
Garvagh (co. Long. ?), 6868.
Garvagh, co. Mon., 6881.
Garvaghwe, co. Long., 1798.
Garvaleh (co. Clare ?), 4622.
Garvalle. *See* Garbally.
Garvallagh (co. Clare ?), 4521.
Garvallie alias Garvallo (Garbally ?, co. Gal.), 4188.
Garvally (co. Gal ?), 6718, 6711.
Garvally—Garvalle, King's co., 1101, 1843.
Garvan, Dermod m'Connor, pardon, 6468.
" Donogh m'Conoghor, pardon, 6468.
" Donogh m'Melaghlyn I., pardon, 2316.
" John m'Conoghor, pardon, 6468.
Melaghlin m'Connor, pardon, 6468.
Garvane, Conoghor oge m'Conoghor, pardon, 6494.
" Dermod m'Owen I., pardon, 4318.
" John m'Dermody I., pardon, 2314.
" John m'Owen I., pardon, 4468.
Garvanagha castle (Garvanagh ?), co. Clare, 6791.
Garvaros in the Morros, co. Wex., 188.
Garvaughe (co. Gal.), 3124.
Garve, co. Gal., 4669.
Garve. *See* Garvey.
Garvea (co. Rosc. ?), 4660.
Garvee, Brian, pardon, 6228.
Garvedaher, co. Gal., 6624.
Garven, John (*see* Garvey), 342.
Garveston, co. Kild., 4317.
Garvey—Garve—Garven—Garvie—Garvye—Garvoy—Garwy:
" James, lease, 4248.
" John, archdeacon of Meath, 363; prebendary of Tipperkevin, 366; dean of Christ Church, 711; bishop of Kilmore, 1471; archbishop of Armagh, 4343, 6664; English liberty, 301; commissions, 363, 162, 817, 722, 1434, 1668, 2184, 7818, 2234, 2548, 2646, 2821, 3062, 3084, 3222, 3941–4, 3047, 3166, 3193, 3316, 3323, 3384, 3367, 3374, 3181–2, 3411–2, 3464, 3601, 3633–2, 3617, 3667, 3664, 3667, 3626, 3717, 3826, 3867, 4051, 4169, 4168, 4178, 4430, 4437–8, 4462, 4633, 4689, 4818, 5021, 5182, 5313, 4443, 5367, 5475, 5834, 5778, 6781; pardon, 421, 1868, 2842, 1961; grant to his son, 6737.
" Nicholas, pardon, 3434.
" Robert, commissioner of faculties, 2304, 3432; substitute master of faculties, 3531; appeals from, 3387, 3831; master in chancery, 3818, 3618, 4142; commissions, 3221, 3308, 3428, 3017, 3214, 3322–3; license of absence, 3482.
" William (son of the primate), grant of land, 6737.
Garvgiere (co. Donegall), 6218.
Garvie. *See* Garvey.
Garvik (co. Kilk. ?), 2912.
Garvill, co. Gal., 2848.
Garvilly, co. Gal., 4652.
Garvock—Garvocke, co. Kild., 461; rectory, 3446, 6160.
Garvye, John. *See* Garvey.
Garwale, John, pardon, 4944.
Garwalle. *See* Garbally.
Garwashe, co. Rosc., 4272.
Garwologhy (Garvogue river ?), 6207.
Garwey, John. *See* Garvey.

INDEX TO FIANTS—ELIZABETH.

Garvoke. *See* Garvock.
Garvy, John. *See* Garvey.
Gary, Donell m'Morthirty 1, pardon, 4421.
" Redmund, pardon, [illegible].
Garyeorrogh (co. Clare ?), [illegible].
Garydul (co. Rosc. ?), [illegible].
Garye brandon (co. Car.), [illegible].
Garyen (co. Kerry ?), [illegible].
Garyneonryhelan (Garryeastle, King's co.), [illegible].
Garynegrange (Garrynagrange, co. Cork), [illegible].
Garynoway (co. Lim. ?), rectory, 6347.
Gary Uskan—Garyuskan (co. Lim. ?), rectory, [illegible], 6347.
Garyvo, Owen, indenture, 6790.
[illegible] (Gaskinstown), co. Meath, [illegible].
Gascoyn wines, [illegible].
Gasoue, Awlyn m'Donell Y, pardon, [illegible].
" Dermod and Teig m'[illegible] Y, pardon, [illegible].
Gauger and searcher. *See under* names of ports.
Gaule, Peirs (of Gaulstown), pardon, [illegible].
" *See also* Gall.
Gaule, Teige oy, pardon, 4612.
Gaulstown—Galleston—Galkstowne—Galleston—Galstown — Gaulstowe (Gaulstown, co. Kilk.), 142, 183, 1821, 2417, [illegible], [illegible], [illegible], [illegible], [illegible], 6791.
Gaultier, Stephen, a French merchant, protection, [illegible].
Gauran. *See* Gawran.
Gaurigawige, co. Kilk., [illegible].
Gavel Rarall. *See* Cowlrusell.
Gavavoghe, co. Cork, [illegible].
Gaw, Omor, ss. m'Teig na, pardon, [illegible].
Gawallericke (co. Tyrone ?), [illegible].
Gawar (co. Lim. ?), [illegible].
Gawine, co. Tip., [illegible].
Gawinson, co. Louth, [illegible].
Gawine, co. Tip., 4674.
Gawn—Gawne, John na, pardon, [illegible], [illegible].
Gawne, Wm. m'Donogh 1, pardon, [illegible].
Gaway, Dermod m'Teige oy, pardon, 6791.
Gawran—Gaaran—Gowran — Ballingowran —Ballygawran (Gowran), co. Kilk., [illegible], [illegible], [illegible], 1917, [illegible], [illegible], [illegible], [illegible], [illegible], [illegible], [illegible], [illegible], 6758; [illegible] in, granted, [illegible].
" portrieve and burgesses, pardoned, [illegible].
" castle, [illegible].
" collegiate church of B.V.M., land of the vicar, [illegible]; chaplains in, [illegible], [illegible].
" hospital for lepers, [illegible].
" Hagard street, [illegible].
" new mill, [illegible].
Gaybieston. *See* Gaybieston.
Gaydon, John, 4211.
Gaybieston—Gaylonston—Gaylieston, co. Kild., [illegible], [illegible], [illegible].
Gaylebuy (Galeybuy, co. Down), [illegible].
Gaynard, William, pardon, 1327.
Gaynor, Rob., pardon, [illegible].
Gaynesdaniels by Cullen, co. Wex., [illegible].
Gayrston (Ballygowry ?), co. Wex., [illegible].
Geaghegan, Donell, pardon, [illegible].
" Teig [illegible], pardon, [illegible].
Geaghlagy, co. Mon., [illegible].
Geaghmore, co. Mon., [illegible].
Geall, co. Tip., [illegible].
Geall, Felim m'Morishe oy, pardon, [illegible].
Geallevarridom, co. Tip., [illegible], [illegible].
Geablingle (co. Long. ?), 4168.
Gealeraine, John m'Dermod J, pardon, [illegible].
Geanaghe, Morierlagh, pardon, [illegible].
Gear, Dermod, pardon, 6167.
" Henry, pardon, [illegible].
Gearn, [illegible].
Gearramcloragh, co. Cork. *See* Geyrry Dashahog
Gearranlaue, co. Wat., [illegible].
Geare, Dermod, pardon, [illegible].
" James, pardon, [illegible].
Gearnon. *See* Gernon.
Geagre, King's co., [illegible].
Gearvie, Rob. fitz Edm., pardon, [illegible].
Geatie, Thomas, pardon, [illegible].
Geashill, King's co. *See* Geshill.
Gelson. *See* Gibson.
Gelblach, John, pardon, [illegible].
Geerre, Edmund, pardon, [illegible].
Geelson, David, pardon, [illegible].
Geeyne, Conoghor m'Donill 1, pardon, [illegible].
Geho, John na, pardon, [illegible].
Gefferie, Jeane fitz, pardon, [illegible].
Gelline (co. Kilk. ?), [illegible].
Gelrine, Dermod oge oy, pardon, [illegible].
Gelryn in Keyneagher, [illegible].
Gelliberynlonagh, co. Cork, [illegible].
Gellis, Rich. m'Walter, pardon, [illegible].
Geflowes, Peirce, pardon, [illegible].
Gelly duff, pardon, 4183.
Gelmagh or M'[illegible], Farrell, pardon, [illegible].
Gemis, Cornell, [illegible].
General of array, appointments and powers of, [illegible], [illegible], [illegible], [illegible], [illegible], [illegible], [illegible], [illegible].
Genison. *See* Jenyson.
Genkyns mill, Kilkenny, [illegible].
Gennill, Tho., [illegible].
Gentlemen of county exempt to freedom, [illegible].
Gentlemen exempt from martial law, [illegible].
Genyson—Genysson. *See* Jenyson.
Gerarde, William, [illegible].
Geraghan alias Fitzgerald, Anne, pardon, [illegible].

INDEX TO FIANTS—ELIZABETH.

Geaghanston, co. Wes., 417.
Geamkagh, Teige, pardon, [illegible].
Gearaskeen, co. Wat., [illegible].
Geardyne, Gillpatrick m'Shane M'Cawra, pardon, [illegible].
Gearchyne, Myrogh M'Cawra, pardon, [illegible].
George, John (alias Barington), pardon, [illegible].
" Jenkyn, [illegible].
" Josias or Josiphus, wardship, &c., of son, [illegible].
" Philip, [illegible].
" Robert, commission, [illegible]; grant of land, [illegible]; wardship of heir, [illegible].
" Robert, wardship, [illegible].
" Thomas, wardship and livery, [illegible].
Georgeston—Georgiston—Georgalston, co. Wat., [illegible], 1046, [illegible].
Gerald—Geralde—Gerali—Gerrald—Geraldo:
" David, pardon, [illegible].
" David duff. See FitzGerald.
" Derret ny, pardon, [illegible].
" Edmund, pardon, [illegible].
" Edm. fitz John. See Fitzgerald.
" Edm. fitz Thomas. See Fitzgerald.
" Ellis ne, pardon, [illegible].
" Elis or Ellice ne, pardon, [illegible].
" Gerald or Gerrot, pardon, [illegible].
" Henry fitz Morice, pardon, [illegible].
" James, pardon, [illegible].
" James fitz Tho. (of Conneghie), attainted, [illegible].
" James m'Edm., lands of, in county Kerry, granted, [illegible].
" Johanna, or Jona ny, pardon, [illegible].
" John, pardon, [illegible].
" John oge (of the Island, co. Kerry), commission, [illegible].
" John fitz Edmund. See FitzGerald.
" John oge fitz John. See FitzGibbon.
" Katherine ny, pardon, [illegible].
" Margaret, pardon, [illegible].
" Maurice or Morris, pardon, [illegible].
" Maurice fitz Edm., attainted, [illegible].
" Morris Fitz Knight, pardon, [illegible].
" Morris fitz Redmund (of Brohill), pardon, [illegible].
" Nicholas, pardon, [illegible].
" Onora, pardon, [illegible].
" Patrick, pardon, [illegible].
" Richard, pardon, [illegible].
Gerald—Rosenyte, pardon, [illegible].
" Shane, pardon, [illegible].
" Thomas, pardon, [illegible].
" Thomas fitz Davy, lands of, in co. Kerry, granted, [illegible].
" Thomas oge (of the Island, in Munster), excepted from pardon, [illegible].
" William, pardon, [illegible].
" Wm. fitz John fitz Edm., pardon, [illegible].
Geraldine—Geraldyn—Geraldyne—Geraldin—Geraldine:
" Gerald, pardon, [illegible].
" Maurice or Morris, pardon, [illegible].
" Nicholas, pardon, [illegible].
" Richard, pardon, [illegible].
" Shane, pardon, [illegible].
" Thomas, pardon, [illegible].
" Walter, pardon, [illegible].
" William, pardon, [illegible].
Geraldines—Geraldins—Geraldine—Geraldynes, [illegible].
" Edm. fitz Tho. of the, pardon, [illegible].
" Gerald fitz Gerald of the, pardon, [illegible].
" Gerald fitz John of the. See Fitz Gerald.
" James fitz Edm. roe of the, pardon, [illegible].
" James fitz Redmund roe of the, pardon, [illegible].
" John fitz Edm. of the. See Fitz Gerald.
" John fitz Tho. of the, pardon, [illegible].
" Maurice fitz Edm. of the, [illegible].
" Maurice fitz Tho. of the, wardship and livery, [illegible].
" Thomas cawme fitz John, heir of, [illegible].
" Tho. m'Rich, [illegible].
Geraldston, co. Meath, [illegible].
Geraldstowne, alias Ballingerald, co. Cork, [illegible].
Geraldyn—Geraldyne. See Geraldine.
Gerali. See Gerald.
Geranhane—Gerranelan (co. Wat. ?), [illegible].
Gerranbondy (co. Kilk. ?), [illegible].
Gerarde, Wm. See Gerrard.
Gerardeston—Gerardestowne—Gerardston—Gerardyston. See Garrardeston.
Gerarreston, co. Meath, 1141.
Gerbert, William, [illegible], 1979.
Gerlandston, co. Meath, [illegible].
Geriowston, co. Louth, 42.
Geriowston, co. Meath, [illegible].
Gerrman, William, pardon, [illegible].
Germans, denization of, [illegible].

INDEX TO FIANTS.—ELIZABETH.

Garnon — Garland — Garlon — Garnon — Gernon.
„ Bartholomew, pardon, 763.
„ Edward (of Gerlonstown), sheriff of Louth, 42; comm., 443.
„ James, knight (of Killincoole), comm., [illegible]; livery of, [illegible].
„ James, pardon, [illegible].
„ Patrick (of Killincoole), pardon, 2540, livery to heir, [illegible].
„ Pyrrhus, pardon, 6274, 6314.
„ Roger (of Stabannan), sheriff of Louth, 3480; commissions, 3443, [illegible], 4167, 4448, [illegible]; pardon, 2084, grant of land, 6740.
„ Stephen, pardon, 3497.
„ Thomas (of Killincoole), livery, [illegible].
„ See Garlan, Garland, Garlon, Garloner and Garnon.
Garot, Tho. McWilliam, pardon, 6[illegible].
Garoll, Patr., comm., [illegible].
Gerald—Geralde. See Gerald.
Geraldin—Geraldine. See Geraldine.
Geraldine—Geraldynes. See Geraldines.
Geralte, Wm. fitz Rob., pardon, 6701.
Gerane, Tho. roe m'Maurice, pardon, [illegible].
Gerane begg, co. Lim., 6[illegible].
Gerane Roe (co. Kilk.?), [illegible].
Geran Dowib (co. Lim.?), 6311.
Gerard — Gerarde, Wm., lord chancellor, commissions, [illegible], [illegible], [illegible], [illegible], 3047, [illegible], [illegible], [illegible], [illegible], 4701; licence of absence, [illegible], [illegible], [illegible]; keeper of seal appointed in his absence, [illegible], [illegible]; death, [illegible].
Gerardeston—Gerardeston—Gerardestowne—Gerardeston—Gerardyston—Gerardiston, co. Meath, [illegible], 64, [illegible], 67, 21[illegible], [illegible], [illegible], [illegible], 1[illegible], 1[illegible], 2112.
Gerardeston — Gerardeston (Jarretstown), co. Meath, [illegible], [illegible].
Gerardiston (Gerardstown), co. Dub., 1[illegible].
Gerran, Teig m'Teig I., pardon, [illegible].
Gerrepont. See Jerpoint.
Gerrold, Edm., of [illegible] (co. Lim.), 6[illegible].
Gerripont. See Jerpoint.
Garrod, John, pardon, 6310.
Gerrol, Ellys ayne, pardon, 6781.
„ James, pardon, [illegible], 3[illegible].
„ John, pardon, [illegible].
„ Maurice (of Shian), pardon, (see Fitz Gerald), [illegible].
Gerroldstown (co. Cork?), [illegible].
Gerrold, Mary ni Ricard ny, pardon, [illegible].
„ Tho., [illegible].
Garry, Donell and Gerald m'Owen, pardon, [illegible].
Gertie, co. Car., [illegible].
Gertmalock (Gortmalock, co. Donegal), [illegible].
Geshill — Geshell (Geashill), King's co., manor and whole barony granted, 1[illegible].
„ church of the B. V. M., advowson granted, 1[illegible].
„ vicar presented, 7[illegible].
„ prebendary presented, [illegible].
Gessille, Phelim in (Geashill, King's co.?), [illegible].
Gevell, Cornell, [illegible].
Gewash alias Shanaho, co. Sligo, [illegible].
Gewle, Maurice m'Owen I., pardon, 5766.
GeyBagh, ny. James Roch, [illegible].
Geyrale, Dermot m'Teige I., pardon, [illegible].
Geyre, Thomas no, pardon, 3[illegible].
Geyrie, Morish, [illegible].
Geyry Inskahag (Gearnaskeagh), co. Cork, [illegible].
Geyshell, [illegible].
Ghealey, Donill reagh m'Dermot vic Owen Y., pardon, [illegible].
Ghinnikinnolle (Glenasmole), co. Wick. or Glassmollane, co. Dub.), [illegible].
Gibbenston. See Gibbonston.
Gibbes, Rob., 6131.
Gibbeston Palmer, co. Louth, 3116, [illegible].
Gibbeston—Gibbiston, co. Meath, [illegible], [illegible], [illegible], [illegible].
Gibbestone (Gibstown, co. Westm.), [illegible].
Gibbestowne (Gibbinstown), co. Meath, 1[illegible].
Gibbot mead or meadow, Dublin, [illegible], [illegible], 4[illegible].
Gibbiston. See Gibbeston.
Gibbonston. See Gibbonston.
Gibbockestowne, co. Meath. See Gibbestowne.
Gibbon—Gebon—Gibon—Gybbon.
„ David, pardon, 1[illegible], 4[illegible], 4[illegible], 6[illegible].
„ Edm. fitz John oge, White Knight. See Fitz Gibbon.
„ Edm. fitz John oge (of Ballinakeddy), pardon, [illegible], [illegible].
„ Edm., pardon, [illegible]-1, [illegible], [illegible], [illegible].
„ Ellen or Ellinor, pardon, [illegible], [illegible], 6770.
„ Garrett, pardon, 1[illegible], 6[illegible].
„ Gerald, Gerrold, or Gerot, pardon, [illegible], [illegible], [illegible], 4[illegible], 4[illegible], [illegible], 47[illegible], [illegible], [illegible], [illegible]-7, [illegible], [illegible].
„ Gibbon ro m'Rich., pardon, 4[illegible], 4[illegible].
„ Gibbons, pardon, [illegible].
„ Honora fitz Edm., grant, [illegible].
„ James, pardon, [illegible], [illegible], [illegible].
„ John oge fitz John, White Knight. See FitzGibbon.
„ John, pardon, 1[illegible], 4[illegible], [illegible], [illegible]-8.
„ Jovan or Joan, pardon, [illegible], [illegible].

INDEX TO FIANTS—ELIZABETH.

Gibbon, Maurice or Morice or Morris, pardon, 1484, 2814, 4460-1, 4468, 4478, 6486, [illegible], 5872.
„ Moyller or Moiler, pardon, [illegible], [illegible].
„ Oneriun, pardon, 2282.
„ Philip, pardon, 4461, 4478.
„ Ricard, pardon, 4468.
„ Shane, pardon, 4478.
„ Shanon, pardon, 4464.
„ Shonckie, pardon, 4468.
„ Thomas, pardon, 4460-1, 4462, 4465, 4478, 5362.
„ Tibbold, pardon, 4469.
„ William, death of, 94.
„ Wm., pardon, 627, [illegible], 1894, 4462.
Gibbons, Gibbon m'Rich. of, 5814.
„ Philip fitz Wm. fitz Davy of, [illegible].
Gibbons ditch, Ardcolm, co. Wex., 437.
Gibbonston—Gibbonstown—Gibbicuston, co. Kild., [illegible], 4870, 5424.
Gibbonstown, co. Lim. See Ballygibbons.
Gibbs, John, marshal of courts in co. Wat., [illegible].
Gibeston (Gibstown, co. Meath ?), [illegible].
Giblestown, alias Gibbergeston, co. Kild., [illegible].
Gibney, Tho., pardon, [illegible].
Gibnie, Nich., pardon, [illegible].
Gibny, Dionysius, pardon, [illegible].
Gibsen. See Gibbons.
Gibralmr. See Jubreraltarn.
Gibson, Wm., pardon, [illegible].
Gibston — Gibstowne, co. Meath, [illegible], [illegible], [illegible], [illegible]. See Gibeston.
Gibstown, co. Westm. See Gibbestoun.
Giffenston, co. Car. (Griffinstown, co. Wick.), 5714.
Gifford, Capt. Rich. See Gyfford.
Gageratowne in Upperossorie, [illegible].
Gigeon, Patrick, lands in tenure of, [illegible].
Giggrestowne, co. Kild., 5713.
Gilagh, John, pardon, [illegible].
Gilbart, Godfrey, pardon, [illegible].
Gilbartiston (co. Louth ?), [illegible].
Gilberston. See Gilbertiston.
Gilbert, Edm., pardon, [illegible].
„ (or Jylbert) Humfrey, knt., colonel of Munster, pardon, 1468; service done under him, 1468, 1416.
„ John, grant, 5178.
Gilbertestone, co. Louth, 5416.
Gilbertston — Gilbertstown — Gilbaston, co. Westm., [illegible], [illegible], [illegible].
Gilbeston, co. Meath, [illegible].
Gilbride, Ellinor, pardon, [illegible].
Gilcagh — Gilcoghe — Gilkeagh — Gylkagh (Gilkagh), co. Gal., [illegible], [illegible], 4711, [illegible], [illegible].
Gilcaghmore, co. Kilk., 1648.
Gilcockis (co. Kild. ?), [illegible].
Gilcoghe. See Gilcagh.
Gildersley, John, serjeant-at-arms, Munster, [illegible].
Gilford, Henry, commission, [illegible].
Gilgerie, co. Wat., [illegible].
Gilgrany (co. Car. ?), 6447.
Gilick (co. Wat. ?), [illegible].
Gilkeagh. See Gilcagh.
Gillabbey — Gilley — Gillye abbey — Gille Abby — Gillenboy — Gylley abbey, co. Cork, [illegible], [illegible], [illegible].
„ monastery de Antro of S. Finbar, leased, 3767, [illegible], [illegible], [illegible]; granted, [illegible]; reversion leased, [illegible]; granted, 6714.
Gillam, John, pardon, 738, [illegible].
Gillane, co. Cork, 6416.
Gille Abby—Gillenboy. See Gillabbey.
Gillechriste (name of person), [illegible].
Gillecdyne (name of person) [illegible].
Gilleinffe; Tris O'Flugan, [illegible].
Gillelnffe; John O'Boylan, pardon, [illegible].
Gillegraily, Margaret ny, pardon, [illegible].
Gillegrome, Beanveen ny, pardon, [illegible].
Gilleguolan, co. Mon., [illegible].
Gillegraly, Cormock Brian, pardon, [illegible].
Gillekeylly, Brian roe m'Shane m'Brian, pardon, [illegible].
Gillepatrick, Neale, pardon, [illegible].
Gillerevelagh, Morirtagh m'Donnell, pardon, [illegible].
Gillerorre, Brein, pardon, [illegible].
Gillernewe, Una roe ny, pardon, [illegible].
Gillernaffe (name of person), 5416.
Gillerroe, Mahowne m'Donnell M'Killeroe, pardon, 5418.
Gilleston (co. Meath ?), [illegible].
Gilleston (co. Ross. ?), [illegible].
Gillett—Gillot, John, serjeant-at-arms in Munster, [illegible], [illegible].
„ Nich., pardon, [illegible].
Gilley abbey, Cork. See Gillabbey.
Gilliamstown, co. Meath. See Kylleyreston, [illegible].
Gilliandon (Ballymagillin, co. Meath), [illegible].
Gillicowrabin, Donogho m'Moloughlen vic, pardon, [illegible].
Gillingston (Gillinstown), co. Meath, [illegible].
Gillam, Jaques le, pardon, [illegible].
Gillerane, Patr., pardon, [illegible].
Gilleen, John, pardon, [illegible].
Gillernan, Wm., pardon, [illegible].
Gilltown, co. Kild. See Gillton.
Gilltown, co. Meath. See Gylton.
Gillsbery, Donogho Connis, pardon, [illegible].
Gillye Abbey. See Gillabbey.
Gilmurry, Owen m'Edm., pardon, [illegible].
Gilpatrick, Eloe ny, pardon, 1708.

INDEX TO FIANTS—ELIZABETH.

Gilpatrick, Mahowin oy, pardon, 4602.
Gilpickin, 4780.
Gilragh (co. Gal. ?), [illegible].
Gilrevane—Gilshinan, John, clerk, hospitality, 840; pardon, 8045, 3904.
Gilsenane, Patr., pardon, 3301.
Gilshinan, John. See Gilrevane.
Gilson, Matthew, pardon, [illegible].
Gilsenan, Wm., pardon, [illegible].
Giltown—Gyltone—Gillistowne—Gyltone (Gillistown), co. Kild., 337, 3146, 4060, 4372.
„ rectory, 783, 3516, 4994, 6182.
„ advowson of church, 3146.
Ginger, sickle, 837.
Gingerstone—Ginnestestone, co. Kild., 6109, 6717.
Ginkovery, co. Mayo, 4582.
Girle—Gyrlle, co. Meath, 148, 2[illegible].
Giroffe, a spice, 837.
Girvane, co. Cork, 6516.
Girvagilore (co. Kerry ?), 6482.
Girlinaghilloo, co. Cork, 6182.
Girtesfolbegh, co. Lim., 5171, 5[illegible].
Girton—Girtone, William, pardon, 170; vers., 163, 3780.
Glaaeytemwik (co. Cork ?), 2384.
Glackstown, co. Wexfor. See Glakstowne.
Glacky, co. Long., 4462, 6167.
Glacum (co. Kerry ?), 6182.
Gladdan Iyrvollan, co. Kerry, 6182.
Glaine (co. Tip. ?), 5784.
Glaine (co. Leit. ?), 4787.
Glaineskynran (co. Ross. ?), 4806.
Glaishare, 6372.
Glakstowne (Glackstown, co. Wexfm. ?), 4451.
Glan, co. Clare, 3977, 4602, 6462.
Glan, 3920.
Glan, co. Kerry, 6871.
Glan (King's co. ?), 4627.
Glan—Glann, co. Lim., 3774, 4406.
Glan—Glann, co. Long., 5025, 4681.
Glan, co. Mayo, 5767.
Glan—Glann (Glen), co. Mon., 5610, 5695, 5678.
Glan (co. Tip. ?), 1686, 5776, 6107, 6780.
Glan, co. Wat., 3881, 5784.
Glan (co. Wex. ?), 41.
Glanafrolan (co. Cork ?), 6871.
Glanagan, Gilpatrick oge, pardon, 6761.
Glanamoro, co. Lim., 5522.
Glanamullin (co. Cork ?), 6271.
Glanan (Glanana), co. Mon., 4666.
Glanarme (Glenarm, co. Antrim), vacant, &c., of port, 1960.
Glanballecullenan, 5698, 5761.
Glanballilotle (co. Kilk. or Tip.), 4201.
Glanballiquillan, co. Wat., 3781.
Glanballycollyman, co. Wat., 628.
Glanbane, co. Wat., 6281.
Glanbane weir, co. Tip., 3151.
Glanbannow, co. Cork. See Glanshannowe.
Glanbarraghan, co. Cork, 3604, 6315.
Glanbeg (co. Tip. ?), 4861.
Glanlehie. See Glanbehy.
Glanbehigh—Glanbehagh (co. Tip.), 5817, 4911.
Glanbehy—Glanbehie, co. Kerry, 6386; rectory, 3348, 4171.
Glanbride (co. Tip. ?), 6708.
Glanbrine, co. Kerry, 6183.
Glancapp—Glancap—Glancape—Glancappe—Glancape (Glencap, co. Wick.), 318, 628, 1102, 3960, 4254, 6310; rectory, 1831, 2220.
„ martial law in, 633, 1812, 2166, 2626.
„ seneschal, 2984, 3812.
Glancoury, co. Kerry or Cork, 6378.
Glancowane, co. Cork, 6397, 6532.
Glancoy, Bowdan, indentures of to his land in co. Clare, 4781. See Clancy.
Glancloraven, co. Cork, 4782.
Glancoughe, co. Mayo, 4682.
Glancollumkylly — Glancollumkille — Glancallomkilly — Glancolomkyly (Glencolumbkille), co. Clare, 1317, 2887, 4782, 4781.
Glancountogher (co. Cork ?), 4161.
Glancrotery—Glancrotherie (Glin), co. Lim., manor and lands of, 6182.
Glancormick—Glancormocke (Glencormick, co. Wick.), 6910, 6641.
Glancorme, co. Cork, 3085.
Glan Crane, co. Cork, 6468.
Glancryne, co. Cork, 4460. See Glanncryn.
Glancullen—Glancullinge (Glencullen), co. Dublin, 836, 6181, 6588.
Glancullin (co. Tip. ?), 6682.
Glancullinge. See Glancullen.
Glancollomkilly. See Glancollumkylly.
Glancurre, co. Wat. (perhaps Glanworth, co. Cork), 5622.
Glancurryn (co. Cork or Lim.), 4424.
Glandalagh (co. Cork ?), 4416.
Glandahill (Glandahillin), co. Kerry, 6691.
Glandala [illegible], co. Cork, 4802.
Glandalen (co. Kerry ?), 6182.
Glandeboy. See Clandeboy.
Glandelagh—Glyndelagh (Glendalough, co. Wick.), archdeacon of, 183, 199, 446, 3877, 3687.
Glandile, co. Clare, 4101.
Glandonayne (co. Kerry ?), 6649.
Glandore, co. Cork. See Cloghinnalrally.
Glandonyne, co. Kerry, 6182.
Glandin, 6334.
Glandry, co. Clare, 6688.
Glandulle (co. Wexm. ?), 4642.
Glandyne (co. Kerry ?), 6376.
Glane, co. Gal., 6688.

Glane (Glin), co. Lim., 2877, 3051.
Glane—Glanne, co. Wat., 1788, 3748, 6898, 6822.
Glanehanno wo (Glanheemod), co. Cork, 4586.
Glanebeugh. See Glanbehigh.
Glanebostarbo, co. Tip., 4699.
Glanecomen (co. Kilk. ?), 2061.
Glanecoyn, co. Lim., 6479.
Glanefosshe, co. Mayo, 4844.
Glanegn, co. Lim., 3754.
Glanegoale (Glannagall), co. Kerry, 3844.
Glaneghell, co. Cork, 4685.
Glanegurtine (Glangurtteen, co. Cork), 5699.
Glanegynty, co. Kerry, 3844.
Glaneheaghely (Glennahoghlish, co. Lim.), 4175.
Glaneis, nation of, in M'Dermott's country, 2160.
Glanelane, co. Lim., 2873.
Glanelespe. See Glanneleskpe.
Glanemanaghie, co. Clare, 4761.
Glanenaclash (co. Wick. ?), 3877.
Glanenalevra (co. Clare ?), 6616.
Glanen, Morish: pardon, 6512.
Glanenaghe, co. Clare, 4746.
Glanenurtin (co. Wat. ?), 6478.
Glanenkeaghe. See Glankeagh.
Glanepleah, co. Kilk., 4366.
Glanetempan, co. Cork, 6666.
Glanetiwor, 6473.
Glaneynashe (co. Clare ?), 6047.
Glanfeske—Glanfeskie—Glanfesky—Glennfesky — Glawnyfeske (Glanfesk, co. Kerry), 4062, 4467, 4930, 6153, 6151, 6764.
Glanfuyse (co. Gal. ?), 5969.
Glange (Clonegath ?), co. Kilk., 4561.
Glangowll—Glangowle (co. Tip. ?), 4918, 5481.
Glangella, co. Cork, 6218.
Glangortaherrane, co. Kerry, 6305.
Glangrill (co. Cork ?), 5858.
Glangibbons (co. Cork ?), 4838.
Glangile (co. Cork ?), 6871.
Glangole, co. Tip., 6818.
Glanhirie — Glanbarry — Glanehoyre (Glanbary barony, co. Wat.), 4461; woodshire ground, 1928, 5738.
Glankine, co. Clare, 5469.
Glanknockmesacle, co. Cork, 6131.
Glankugan, co. Kerry, 4122.
Glankyne—Glankyn, co. Clare, 5463, 5713, 5762.
Glanleghar, co. Gal., 3646.
Glanlarn, co. Lim., 6417.
Glanlarty, co. Lim., 5618.
Glanleshane (co. Wick. ?), 4457.
Glanleigh, co. Kerry or Cork, 4476.
Glanlick (co. Cork ?), 6768.
Glanmalirv. See Glanmalire.
Glanmeck, co. Dun., 3161.
Glanmare (co. Cork), 6068.
Glanmore (in Glencap, co. Wick.), 6909, 6319.
Glann. See Glan.
Glannagall, co. Kerry. See Glanegoale, Glannegalty.
Glannaghlenaghe, co. Tip., 6818.
Glannahowe, co. Kerry, 6576.
Glannakilloch (co. Clare ?), 4962.
Glannaleppa, co. Kerry. See Glannacleappa.
Glannan, co. Mon. See Glenan.
Glannbeaura (co. Cork ?), 6011.
Glannerra, co. Cork, named in district in parish of Farnhitine, 6808.
Glanne (Glin), co. Lim., 3747; castle and lands, 2877, 5852.
Glanne, knight of the, 2877, 6317.
Glanne, co. Rosc., 4548.
Glanne, near river Sure, 1538.
Glanne. See Glane.
Glanne in Cabrie, co. Westm., 1373.
Glannecoyne, co. Lim. or Cork, 6588.
Glannegallagh (co. Rosc. ?), 6498.
Glannegalty (Glannagall), co. Kerry, 3844.
Glannemullagh, co. Clare, 2041.
Glannegurrie (Glannagarrane), co. Lim., 6547.
Glannergyntie, co. Kerry, 3843.
Glannehoyre. See Glanhirie.
Glanneleskpe — Glanelespe (Glannaleappa), co. Kerry, 4128, 6566.
Glannerigane, co. Cork, 6458.
Glannerdaliue, co. Kerry, 6427.
Glannoskeagh. See Glenaskeagh.
Glannewydan. See Glanwydan.
Glannidoghie (co. Cork ?), 6616.
Glanmadrine (co. Cork ?), 5849.
Glannomore, co. Lim., 3781.
Glannor—Glannoure—Glannur—Glanor—Glanore (Glanworth, co. Cork, which is written Glanor on Down Survey), 2545, 3305, 3161, 4267, 5722.
" house of friars preachers, lands, 5212, 5516.
Glannwidan. See Glanwydan.
Glaney, Donald in, pardon, 2056.
Glannylenalagh, co. Cork, 6011.
Glanourane (co. Cork ?), 5462.
Glannykonky, co. Cork, 4268.
Glannygorra, co. Lim., 4856.
Glanprvaddon (Glebevadding, co. Wat.), 2210.
Glanprvine (co. Westm. or Cav. ?), 2657.
Glanoger—Glanogerie—Glanogere—Glanogree. See Glenoger.
Glanor—Glanore. See Glannor.
Glanpaddyne, 6431.
Glantoymowe, co. Kilk., 4921.
Glanriougie (Glanreagh), co. Cork, 6011.
Glanrushensloane, co. Kilk., 5264.
Glanscallie, co. Lim., 4858.
Glansised, co. Clare, 4854.
Glansimocurpe (co. Kerry or Lim. ?), 6168.

INDEX TO FIANTS.—ELIZABETH.

Glanshenkin (co. Cork), [illegible].
Glanshagha, co. Kilk., [illegible].
Glanskeagh—Glanskerughe—Glanscoheagh (co. Tip. ?), [illegible], [illegible], [illegible].
Glansland — Glanslaude — Glansknysel, co. Clare, [illegible], [illegible]; castle and land, [illegible].
Glansmale, co. Lim., [illegible].
Glanstalie, co. Lim., [illegible].
Glantancollica, co. Cork, [illegible].
Glanteige (Glenteige, co. Wick.), [illegible].
Glantimeeny, in Munster, [illegible].
Glanbrega, co. Gal., [illegible].
Glantallobern, co. Wat., [illegible].
Glantarin (Glentark), co. Mayo, [illegible].
Glanughrwym (Glenquin), co. Lim., [illegible].
Glanveaghe (co. Tip. ?), [illegible].
Glanvoghe, co. Mayo, [illegible].
Glanwedan. *See* Glanwydan.
Glanwigowe — Glanwigowe (co. Kilk. ?), [illegible], [illegible].
Glanwilliam (Glanwilliam), co. Lim., [illegible].
Glanworth, co. Cork. *See* Glanoer, Glanore.
Glanwydan—Glannowydan — Glanowidan —Glanwedan, co. Wat., [illegible], [illegible], [illegible].
„ rectory, [illegible], [illegible].
Glany, Donell, or Donell M'Owen, pardon, [illegible].
Glany—Glanye, co. Ross, [illegible], [illegible], [illegible].
Glanycrosie (co. Cork ?), [illegible].
Glanycroynie (co. Cork ?), [illegible].
Glanyerym, co. Cork, [illegible].
Glanydan, co. Westm., [illegible], [illegible].
Glanye. *See* Glany.
Glanye m'Moriche nehoyrye, John, pardon, [illegible].
Glanyghenie (co. Wat. ?), [illegible].
Glary, John m'Teig I., pardon, [illegible].
Glasna, co. Wex., [illegible].
Glascarne (Glascarn), co. Meath, [illegible].
Glascara, co. Wex., manor of, [illegible].
Glascarvold, co. Wex., [illegible].
Glascarrick — Glascarricke — Glascarrycke (Glascarrig), co. Wex., [illegible], [illegible], [illegible], [illegible], [illegible].
„ priory leased, [illegible], [illegible], [illegible].
„ rectory, [illegible].
Glasdrumagh, co. Gal., [illegible].
Glasee (co. Kilk. ?), [illegible].
Glasore, rectory, in dio. of Ossory, [illegible].
Glasderregan — Glasderrogane (co. Tip. ?), [illegible].
Glasdrums (co. Leit. ?), [illegible].
Glasduyrskilhoria, brook of, King's co., [illegible].
Glase, Hubbert, pardon, [illegible].
Glasely—Glasheely—Glasholie—Glasheely—Glashelly—Glasholl—Glasholl (Glasealy), co. Kild., [illegible], [illegible], [illegible], [illegible], [illegible], [illegible], [illegible].
Glasevoman (co. Leit. ?), [illegible].
Glasevoyne (co. Leit. ?), [illegible].
Glashare — Glasharye — Glasare — Glasshare, co. Kilk., [illegible], [illegible], [illegible], [illegible], [illegible], [illegible], [illegible], [illegible].
„ rectory, [illegible], [illegible], [illegible], [illegible].
Glashbrow, co. Kilk., [illegible].
Glashealy. *See* Glasely.
Glashoboylenwilor, Queen's co., [illegible].
Glashenaboyne, stream, King's co., [illegible].
Glashine yarraghe in Cwereme, co. Cork, [illegible].
Glashmaskan. *See* Glasmocky.
Glaskarne — Glaskearne (Glascarn), co. Westm., [illegible], [illegible], [illegible], [illegible].
Glaskea, co. Westm., [illegible].
Glaskill, King's co., [illegible].
Glaskin (Glascarn, co. Westm. ?), [illegible], [illegible].
Glasdaghes—Ballaghdagh (Gladoughl, co. Mon., [illegible], [illegible].
Glasloe, co. Cork, [illegible].
Glasmocky — Glashmucke — Glasmocke— Glasmocky — Glasmeenmuckye (Glasmocky, co. Dub.), [illegible], [illegible], [illegible], [illegible], [illegible], [illegible].
Glasmullen, co. Wick. *See* Glaishmocka.
Glasnevin (Glasnevin), co. Dub., [illegible].
Glasse, co. Kilk., [illegible].
Glaspistoll, co. Louth, [illegible].
Glass imported for works, [illegible].
Glass making, monopoly granted, [illegible].
Glascallen, co. Meath. *See* Glassenallyn.
Glassan, Derby, pardon, [illegible].
„ Dermod, pardon, [illegible].
„ Donoghe, pardon, [illegible].
Glassana, [illegible].
Glassare. *See* Glashare.
Glassarnallen, co. Dub. *See* Glassinchanallin.
Glascarrick — Glascarricke. *See* Glascarrick.
Glascragh (co. Tip. ?), [illegible].
Glassdergane, [illegible].
Glasse, Donell, pardon, [illegible].
„ Teig, pardon, [illegible].
„ Wm., pardon, [illegible].
„ (name of person), [illegible].
Glasselowra, co. Clare, [illegible].
Glassecro—Glasse Croo, co. Kilk., [illegible], [illegible].
Glassenallyn (Glassallen, co. Meath), [illegible].
Glassealy, co. Kild. *See* Glasely.
Glassemullagh, co. Mon., [illegible].
Glassemeanmuckye. *See* Glasmocky.
Glassery, Hubert, pardon, [illegible].
Glassinkounge, brook, Queen's co., [illegible].
Glasshare. *See* Glashare.
Glasshegeddi, King's co., [illegible].
Glassboskillcaingell, brook, Queen's co., [illegible].
Glassholie. *See* Glasely.
Glassinorgullenye, Queen's co., [illegible].

INDEX TO FIANTS—ELIZABETH.

Glasheroskin, King's co., [illegible].
Glashkinoban, brook, Queen's co., [illegible].
Glassmarte, brook, Queen's co., [illegible].
Glasnigeniskey, co. Cork, [illegible].
Glassbgarny (Glasingan [illegible]), co. Cork, [illegible].
Glasslacken, co. Lim., [illegible].
Glassycorry, Queen's co., [illegible].
Glasterton, co. Mon., [illegible].
Glasthelly. See Glasely.
Glastragm, co. Mon., [illegible].
Glaughmorry, co. Meath, [illegible].
Glaungeill (co. Cork ?), [illegible].
Glausie, Margaret ny, pardon, [illegible].
Glave, Donogh and Morogh m'Teig ne, [illegible].
Glawnegrowdrey, co. Cork, [illegible].
Glawnecrocme (co. Cork ?), [illegible].
Glawnyfleske. See Glanfleske.
Glayne (co. Donegal), [illegible].
Glaymne (co. Donegal), [illegible].
Glayne, co. Clare, [illegible].
Glaymore—Glaymmore, co. Wat., [illegible].
Glaynhakilgore (Kilgory), Queen's co., [illegible].
Glazier's present, [illegible].
Glebland. See Gibland.
Glean bealagh (co. Fer. ?), [illegible].
Gleancolomkyly. See Glancolinmkylly.
Gleanalabline (co. Kerry ?), [illegible].
Gleanalrier, in Idrone, [illegible].
Gleanaloina, co. Kerry, [illegible].
Gleane, co. Gal., [illegible].
Gleaner, (co. Lim. ?), [illegible].
Gleanetowne, co. Gal. or Mayo, [illegible].
Gleanedane, co. Westm., [illegible].
Gleanfesky. See Glanfleske.
Gleannedane, co. Westm., [illegible].
Gleany, Donogh in, pardon, [illegible].
Gleawan, Ivan ny, pardon, [illegible].
Gleaswyn, John mac Donogho y, pardon, [illegible].
Gleadc Thearnocol Imongain (or Imonglan) river, in co. Tyrone, [illegible], [illegible].
Gleader, John, pardon, [illegible].
Glebise, co. Cork, [illegible].
Glebwne Cowrie (Glencoum, co. Kilk. ?), [illegible].
Gledmorris (co. Westm. ?), [illegible].
Gleeragh alias M'Phillip, Rich., pardon, [illegible].
Glen, co. Mon. See Glan.
Glen (co. Tip. ?), [illegible].
Glenagorlera, co. Cork. See Glanrgartine.
Glenabiry, co. Wat. See Glashirie.
Glenan (co. Kilk. ?), [illegible].
Glenarme, co. Ant. See Glanarme.
Glenavaddire, co. Wat. See Glannyvaddine.
Glencap, co. Wick. See Glancapp.
Glenche. See Glink.
Glencolumbkille, co. Clare. See Glancolumkill, Glancolumkylly.
Glencormick, co. Wick. See Glancormocke, Glancorymac.
Glencoum, co. Kilk. See Glewne Cowrie.
Glencullen, co. Dub. See Glanculllen.
Glendalough, co. Wick. See Glandalogh.
Glendowyne, (co. Kerry ?), [illegible].
Glenfleak, co. Kerry. See Glanfleske.
Glennagowan, co. Lim. See Glannegowne.
Glenmalunghbit, co. Lim. See Glanchageleky.
Glenna, co. Louth, [illegible].
Glennoke. See Glenok.
Glennaybore, co. Mon. See Glanabore.
Glennyrowry (co. Cork ?), [illegible].
Glenoge, co. Car. See Glenok.
Glenogre—Glanogre—Glenogerrie—Glanogre—Glanogrire—Glenogerie—Glynnogry—Glynogry—Glynnogry—Kanegar (Glenogre), co. Lim., 177, [illegible], [illegible], [illegible], [illegible], [illegible], [illegible].
„ manor, castle, and land, [illegible].
„ rectory, [illegible], [illegible], [illegible].
Glenok—Glenoke (Glenoge), co. Car., [illegible], [illegible].
Glenquin, co. Lim. See Glanaghwyne.
Glenragh, co. Cork. See Glanriough.
Glentaige, co. Wick. See Glantaige.
Glenlark, co. Mayo. See Glanlarke.
Glenarkin—Glenarkyne, [illegible], [illegible].
Glenteman, in Munster, [illegible].
Glibland in Tombne (Glabland in Tomin, Queen's co.), [illegible].
Glin (co. Cav. or Long.), [illegible].
Glin, co. Lim. See Glancorbery, Glane, Glanne.
Glin, co. Wat., [illegible].
Glina or Lynna (co. Long. ?), [illegible].
Glingwell (co. Tip.), [illegible].
Glinmalrie—Glinmalirry. See Glanmalire.
Glinnes—Glynnes—Glynnes (in co. Antrim), [illegible], [illegible]; under the governor of Knockfergus, [illegible], [illegible], [illegible], [illegible]; martial law in, [illegible], [illegible], [illegible], [illegible].
Glinsk—Glinske—Glinskie—Glinsky—Glynske (Glynske), co. Gal., [illegible], [illegible], [illegible], [illegible], [illegible], [illegible], [illegible].
Glinsraker, co. Gal., [illegible].
Glisane, John m'Donnell y, pardon, [illegible].
Glisladrevennocke brook, Queen's co., [illegible].
Glismane, in Munster, [illegible].
Glissane. See Glissanke.
Glonivollen (co. Cork ?), [illegible].
Glorie (Glourie), co. Kerry, [illegible], [illegible].
Glorine (co. Rosc. ?), [illegible].
Gloucester—Glouceter, in England, priory of Lanthony near, [illegible], [illegible], [illegible], [illegible], [illegible].
Glowrie, co. Kerry. See Glowrie.
Glover, Henry, commission, [illegible].
Glovers, pardon, [illegible]; mentioned, 177, [illegible], [illegible], [illegible], [illegible], [illegible].

INDEX TO FIANTS—ELIZABETH.

Glovers of Cork, licensed to dress skins, [illegible].
Gloves, rent of, reserved, [illegible], 5761.
Gloves, co. Gal. See Gloes.
Glowrie—Glorie (Glourie?), co. Kerry, [illegible], [illegible], [illegible].
Gloes (Gloves, co. Gal.?), [illegible], [illegible].
Glaie (co. Long.?), [illegible].
Glynmalyre. See Clanmalire.
Glyn, co. Cork, [illegible].
Glyn, Wm., pardon, [illegible].
Glyndelagh. See Glandelagh.
Glyne, co. Gal., [illegible].
Glynnes. See Glinnes.
Glynmallyre—Glynmalyry—Glynmalyrye. See Clanmalire.
Glynn, co. Wat., [illegible].
Glynne, John, Kossoe, [illegible].
Glynnes. See Glinnes.
Glynnes, in Maryborton, co. Meath, [illegible].
Glynnes. See Glinnes.
Glynogray — Glynogrey — Glynogry. See Glinogry.
Glynshie. See Glinsk.
Glynsleame, in Munster, [illegible].
Glynowrie, Donogho, pardon, [illegible].
Gnashill (Nashill), co. Meath, [illegible].
Gnave, Donell [illegible], pardon, 6754.
Gnaw, Conoghor m'Teig [illegible], pardon, 4757.
" Donogho m'Teig [illegible], pardon, [illegible].
Gneevekoel, co. Westm. See Guyvekyell.
Gnevebracke—Guyvebracke (Gneevebrack), co. Westm., 1744, 4578.
Gnobegg—Gnowbeg country (in bar. Moyculleen), co. Gal., 6191; chief rent to earl of Clanrickard, [illegible].
Gnomore country (in bar. Moycullen), co. Gal., 6191.
Gnowbeg. See Gnobegg.
Gnowe (Grove?), co. Meath., [illegible].
Gnoweghbaraght (Grove?), co. Meath., [illegible].
Gnyvebracke. See Gnevebracke.
Gnyvekyell — Knive Kille (Gneevekoel, co. Westm.), 1763, 4578.
Gnyvenamangha — Guyvenemaugh — Goyvenemanagh — Gwynemanagh, co. Westm., [illegible], 1666, [illegible], [illegible].
Goywe (co. Westm.?), [illegible].
Goywlorgomanagh—Guywenamaugh. See Guyvenamangha.
Goagh, Patr., comm., 5761.
Goare, Edw., pardon, 4625.
Goarianory (co. Tip.?), 4627.
Goat felt, illegal export of, [illegible].
Gobe (co. Leit.?), 4794.
Gobbinstown, co. Wex. See Ballygobban.
Gobborne, Geo., [illegible].
Godamonde, co. Dub., [illegible].
Godament — Goddamonde, co. Kild., 1087, [illegible].
Goddall — Goodale — Gondal — Gowdale, John, chief engraver, Exchequer, [illegible], [illegible], [illegible], [illegible]; chief remembrancer, [illegible], [illegible]; commissioner, [illegible], [illegible], [illegible]; pardon, 1784, [illegible]; grant of land, [illegible]; lease, [illegible], [illegible], [illegible].
Goddamonde. See Godament.
Goddergrannage (Grangidder), co. Kild., [illegible].
Godolfyn, Sir William, knt., fishery lease, [illegible].
Goe, Mahn, pardon, [illegible].
Gogh—Goghe. See Gough.
Goell, co. Tip., [illegible].
Goen, Johan ny [illegible], pardon, [illegible].
Goer, Rob., pardon, [illegible], [illegible].
Goele Clonemore (Goffeloonmore), co. Gal., [illegible].
Gogaine, Tho., pardon, [illegible].
Gogan—Gogane, Edm., pardon, [illegible].
" James, pardon, [illegible].
" John, pardon, [illegible], [illegible], [illegible].
" John m'Donogho y, pardon, [illegible].
" Phrow, pardon, [illegible].
" Philip, pardon, [illegible].
" Rich, pardon, [illegible].
" Tho., pardon, [illegible], [illegible], [illegible].
" Wm., pardon, [illegible], [illegible], [illegible].
Goganrath — Gogan Rath, co. Cork, [illegible], [illegible].
Goggan, John, pardon, [illegible].
" William, pardon, [illegible].
Goggan-hill, co. Cork. See Knockygogaine, Knockogogan.
Gogh—Goghe. See Gough.
Goghegan, Elizabeth ny, pardon, [illegible].
" Grany ny, pardon, [illegible].
" Katherine ny, pardon, [illegible].
" Mary ny vy, pardon, [illegible].
Golborne, George, [illegible].
Gold, illegal export of, [illegible], [illegible], [illegible].
Golde—Gold—Goold—Gole:
" James, collector of wine duty in Cork, [illegible]; lease, [illegible].
" James, queen's attorney in Munster, [illegible]; second justice of Munster, [illegible], [illegible]; commissioner, [illegible], [illegible], [illegible], [illegible], [illegible], [illegible], [illegible]; lease, [illegible].
" James (of Limerick), pardon, [illegible].
" [illegible] (John), provost of Cork, [illegible].
" Stephen, pardon, [illegible].
" See Goulde.
Golden, co. Tip. See Gowlyn.
Golden head, river, co. Westm. See La Ware.
Goldeney (Coolderry, co. Louth?) [illegible].
Goldesmythe, Edw., comm., [illegible].
Goldesworth, seignory of, [illegible].
Goldfinch, Henry, comm., [illegible].
Goldinge—Golding—Gowlding:
Elizabeth, widow, [illegible].

INDEX TO FIANTS—ELIZABETH.

Goldinge, Jenet. See Goldynge.
" John, house in Dublin, 1861.
" John (son of Walter of Peirston Laundy), wardship, 2367; wardship of his heir, 6612.
" John, pardon, 6461.
" Katherine, abduction, 2394; matrimonial suit, 2380.
" Maud, surrender by, [illegible].
" Mich. (of Artaine), pardon, 774, [illegible].
" Morish, pardon, (or Goulding), 4561.
" Rich., pardon, [illegible], [illegible], 6543.
" Tho., pardon, [illegible].
" Walter, remembrancer of the Exchequer, 153, 172, 2717, [illegible]; comm., [illegible]; abduction of his daughter, [illegible].
" Walter (of Peirston Laundy), wardship of his heir, 2367; livery, [illegible].
" Walter (son of John, of Peirston Laundy), wardship, [illegible].
Goldings land, co. Meath, [illegible].
Goldsmith, John (or Goldsmyth), 1137.
Goldsmiths mentioned, 177, 1470, 3196, [illegible], 4118, [illegible], 6762.
Goldsmyth—Goldsmith, John, clerk of the council, 31, 116; licence of absence, 21; assignment, 1130; grant of a wardship, [illegible].
Goldynge, lady Jenet, pardon, [illegible].
Gole, James. See Goole.
Goltane, Maurice, pardon, [illegible].
" Tho., pardon, [illegible].
Golril, Julian, protection, [illegible].
Golly (Gully river), Queen's co., [illegible].
Golrie (Golree), co. Mon., [illegible].
Gomaghe, Donell m'William, pardon, [illegible].
Gomeboy, Joan ny, pardon, [illegible].
Gome, Patr., pardon, [illegible].
Gomere, Edmund, pardon, [illegible].
Gomevan, Shane m'Tege I, pardon, [illegible].
Gomell, Tho., pardon, [illegible].
Gonlerrey (Goulterry?), Queen's co., [illegible].
Gonytown, Tho. mac Shane I, pardon, [illegible].
Good, David, vicar of St. John, Kilkenny, [illegible].
" Henry, [illegible].
" Henry, pardon, [illegible].
Goodale—Goodall. See Godall.
Goodburne, ruined abbey, Carrickbegge (Woodburn), [illegible].
Goode, William, 1844, [illegible].
Goodman—Goodmane, George, commissions, 4733, [illegible]; surrender, [illegible]; leases, [illegible], [illegible].
" James (of Loughlinstown), commissions, [illegible], [illegible], 1165, 2345, [illegible]; pardons, [illegible], [illegible]; freedom from subsidy, [illegible]; suit as to his will, [illegible].
Goodman, Rich., pardon, 4758, [illegible].
Goodwyn, Edward, [illegible].
Googe (Gouge), Barnaby, provost marshal of Connaught, [illegible], [illegible], [illegible], [illegible]; commissions, [illegible], 4[illegible]; pardon, [illegible].
Goole, Edmund, mayor of Cork, pardon, [illegible].
" George, pardon, [illegible].
" John, pardon, [illegible].
" Patrick, pardon, [illegible].
" Stephen, pardon, 1043, [illegible].
" William, pardon, 1088.
Goole s, John, pardon, 1470.
Goore, Edward, grant of a wardship, [illegible].
Gooshe, Piers, pardon, 6517.
Goose, Rich., 2343. See Goose.
Goraghill, co. Clare, 1618.
Gorane, co. Louth, [illegible].
Gorevan, Wm., pardon, 4115.
Gorel—Gorill (co. Gal. or Mayo), [illegible], [illegible].
Gorkegrevor (Gortgrevour, co. Lim.), 5171.
Gormaken, co. Mayo, [illegible].
Gormagh—Gormagho (King's co.), [illegible], [illegible].
Gormichane, John, pardon, 6477.
Gorman, Richard, pardon, [illegible].
" Tho., pardon, 4115.
" Wm., pardon, [illegible].
Gormane, Wm., pardon, [illegible].
Gormanston. See Gormanston.
Gormanston, co. Lim., 5472.
Gormanston. See Gormanstown, co. Meath.
Gormanston—Gormanstown—Gormanston
" viscount of, William Preston, alienations by, 5472.
" " Jenico, commissions, [illegible], [illegible], [illegible]; livery to heir, [illegible]; alienations by, [illegible].
" " Christopher, livery, [illegible]; commissions, [illegible], [illegible], [illegible], [illegible], [illegible], [illegible], [illegible], [illegible], [illegible], [illegible], [illegible], [illegible], [illegible], [illegible]; freedom from subsidy, [illegible]; licence of absence, [illegible]; intrusion, [illegible].
Gormanstown—Gormanston, co. Meath, 777, 1476, 5174, [illegible], [illegible], [illegible].
Gormanstown, viscount of. See Gormanston.
Gormanstown, co. Tip., [illegible].
Gormanstowne. See Gormanstown, co. Meath.
Gormegan, Ellen ny, pardon, 6447.

INDEX TO FIANTS—ELIZABETH.

Gormogan, Farlonroughe, pardon, 6161.
" Honora ny, pardon, 6778.
" Michael, pardon, 6158.
" Thady, pardon, 6164.
Gormoyll alias Gormuyll, William, pardon, 534.
Gornakarrikye (near Youghal ?), 6198.
Gorrycrone (co. Cork ?), 6571.
Gorrymagh, co. Cork, 6082.
Gorrouse, Donbio m'Owen I., pardon, 6613.
Gorragh, Queen's co. See Garragh.
Gorrankrorie, co. Wex., 616.
Gorranarrie, co. Wex., 528.
Gorred, co. Tip., 4738.
Gorsse, Richard, 6147. See Gorse.
Gorse, Peter, pardon, 1108. See also Goorsie, Piers.
Gorsin, Michael, pardon, 4201. See Gorse.
Gort—Gorte, co. Gal., 4471, 4707, 4789, 5068, 5428, 5688. See Gortinsgory.
Gort (co. Ross. or Clare ?), 6431.
Gort a Cherraun—Gort a Chearnain (co. Don.), 5952, 6077.
Gortaclosane, co. Kerry, 6163.
Gortacurra (King's co.), 4168.
Gortagort (Gortagort), co. Kerry, 6132.
Gortagh, Feylim m'Donill McCarthy, pardon, 5268.
Gortardagh, co. Wat., 677, 1048.
Gortboffyny (Gortboffinna), co. Cork, 6602.
Gortcardo, co. Kerry, 6013, 6.28.
Gortchill, co. Kerry, 6153.
Gorteclonmore, co. Gal. See Gorte Glonmore.
Gortcomykyn, co. Lim., 4698.
Gortconnecan (co. Clare ?), 6615.
Gortcooghe, co. Lim., toghe of, 5547.
Gortculloe — Gortekullyne, co. Tip., 5627, 6466.
Gortcurrey-Gortnorry, (King's co. ?), 6466.
Gortdromcullie (co. Lim. ?), 6478.
Gortdromlahcullie (co. Kerry ?), 6477.
Gortdrowmydelkeio (co. Kerry ?), 6477.
Gorte. See Gort, co. Gal.
Gortecallagane, co. Lim., toghe of, 5547.
Gortecoullyn, co. Tip., 5651.
Gorte Donoghy Inoyr, co. Cork, 5641.
Gorteen, co. Kild. See Gurtyn.
Gortene, Queen's co. See Gortin.
Gortenaloswill, co. Cav. See Gortin an tairbhe.
Gorteforrekill, co. Clare, 5588.
Gortegobbane. See Gortpolean.
Gortegowne, co. Tip., 5698.
Gortekelle, 1489.
Gortekullyne. See Gortcullee.
Gortellowre (co. Leit. ?), 5748.
Gortemoll, co. Westm., 5846, 5803.
Gortemony (Gortmanny), co. Mon., 5687.
Gortemore. See Gortmore.
Gortemore (Gortmore), co. Mon., 4683.
Gorte na caileall (Garrancoll), co. Cav., 5458.
Gorteneaughe, co. Lim., 4571.
Gorteneclogharre, co. Gal., 4848.
Gortendavie, by Lyons, co. Kild., 6777.
Gortenecka, in Upper Ossory, 6133.
Gorteneclohe in Upper Ossory, 897.
Gorteneccoilmore (co. Kerry ?), 6497.
Gortenedrom, co. Clare, 6401.
Gortenedromny (co. Clare ?), 6818.
Gortene Polye, in Bantry, co. Cork, 6142.
Gortenegeragher, co. Kerry, [illegible].
Gortenehawinge, [illegible].
Gortenehawne, co. Tip., [illegible].
Gortenemacken—Gortenamaclane, in Connaght, 1471, 1482.
Gorteneparre, co. Tip., 4424.
Gortenemackane. See Gortenemacken.
Gortenerathe. See Gortenrathen.
Gortenraghe. See Gortnaskeagh.
Gortenstubbered. See Gortenstubberaid.
Gortenemarry, co. Sligo, 5429.
Gortenyclowny (Gortenmaclonne), co. Cork, 5602.
Gorterane—Gorterane (co. Leit.), [illegible].
Gorterenan, co. Tip., 6813.
Gorteron, co. Tip., 6403.
Gortenerovan (co. Lim. ?), 6490.
Gortenke, co. Lim., [illegible].
Gorteslinghe (co. Leit. ?), 4128.
Gortesaghyle, co. Kerry, 6122.
Gortessa, co. Tip., 3364.
Gortelogher (co. Mayo ?), 4788.
Gortevalle (King's or Queen's co. ?), 5644.
Gortevickery, co. Galway, 5608.
Gortevoler. See Gortvolare.
Gorteynishegory. See Gortinsgory.
Gortfadda, co. Leit. See Gortfadd.
Gortfine (co. Clare ?), 6765.
Gortgallboye, co. Lim., 5687.
Gortglasse, co. Kerry, 5948.
Gortgubban—Gortegobbane (co. Ross. ?), 5848, 5868.
Gorthebiro, co. Gal., 4548.
Gort Lerow, co. Cork, 6128.
Gortillough, co. Tip., 5483.
Gortin, King's co., 6488.
Gortinmadoke, co. Tip., [illegible].
Gortinna (King's co.), 618.
Gortinacorrall, co. Cork, 5555.
Gortinchegory — Gortinchygorye. See Gortinsgory.
Gortinclogh[illegible], co. Cork, 6872.
Gortinadive, co. Gal., 5418.
Gortine, King's co., 5944.
Gortine, co. Tip., [illegible].
Gortinmacknagh (co. Lim. ?), 5698.
Gortinsory, co. Don. See Gortinshogane.

INDEX TO FIANTS—ELIZABETH.

Gortinagrow (co. Cork ?), [illegible].
Gortinbrabalye, co. Cork, [illegible].
Gortinbaugho, co. Lim., 4917.
Gortinacarrig, co. Cork, [illegible].
Gortinacryale, co. Cork, 6514.
Gortinacarrig (co. Kerry ?), [illegible].
Gortineygory—Gortin yaishogory—Gortin-chavary—Gortinchgorye—Gortinagore—Gort Inishgory (Gort, co. Gal.), 1778, [illegible], [illegible], [illegible], 6417, [illegible].
Gort in wage, co. Gal., 4617.
Gortire, co. Cork or Lim., [illegible].
Gortivarrye, co. Gal., [illegible].
Gortkelly (co. Tip. ?), [illegible].
Gortleman (co. Lim. ?), [illegible].
Gortlemalen, co. Mayo, [illegible].
Gortmakellis (co. Tip. ?), [illegible].
Gortmacshira, co. Cork, [illegible].
Gortmistan (co. Ros. ?), [illegible].
Gortmoinan (co. Ros. ?), [illegible].
Gortmoldo (co. Ferm. ?), [illegible].
Gortmonoy, co. Mon. See Gortmoney.
Gortmoore. See Gortmore.
Gortmor, co. Lim., [illegible].
Gortmore—Gortemore—Gortmoore, co. Cork, [illegible], [illegible], [illegible], [illegible], 6314, [illegible], [illegible].
Gortmore (co. Londonderry), [illegible].
Gortmore, co. Mon. See Gortmore.
Gortmore—Gortemore, co Westm., 1366, 1618, [illegible], [illegible], [illegible], 6767.
Gortmoye (co. Cav. ?), [illegible].
Gortmoyma, co. Lim., [illegible].
Gortmuclan, Queen's co. See Gortinecloian, Gortaicle, Gortayele.
Gortna Crapagh, co. Lim., [illegible].
Gortnacraha, co. Cork (see Gortaycrossye), [illegible].
Gortnagap, co. Kilk. See Gortnagap.
Gortnagross, co. Cork. See Gortaygrosse.
Gortnagrow, co. Lim., [illegible].
Gortnagrower, co Lim. See Gortnagrower.
Gortnahorna—Gortan Horney (Gort-horney ?), co. Don., [illegible], [illegible].
Gortnaleck, co. Don. See Gortinaleck.
Gortnamona (co. Gal. ?), [illegible].
Gortnana, co. Mon. See Gortanagh.
Gortnapeanagh (co. Ros. ?), [illegible].
Gortnaraha, co. Mayo. See Gortnaraihae.
Gortnaskegh—Gortnaskeghe—Gortnaskeagh, co. Tip., [illegible], [illegible], [illegible].
Gortnaskehe, co. Kerry. See Gortnaskehie.
Gortnaskerna (co. Clare ?), [illegible].
Gortnecloke (co. Kilk. ?), [illegible].
Gortnecloho (Gortneclea, Queen's co. ?), 4914.
Gortneclogh (co. Kerry ?), [illegible].
Gortnadoghe, co. Cork, [illegible].
Gortnacrossa, co. Kerry, [illegible].
Gortmadin (co. Mayo ?), [illegible].
Gortnelohie, co. Westm., [illegible].
Gortnadoramyle, [illegible].
Gortnadrake, co. Tip., 6317.
Gortnegeranghe, co. Kerry, [illegible].
Gortnegoraghe, co. Lim., [illegible].
Gortnegirvangarde, co. Gal., [illegible].
Gortnenoyall (co. Cork ?), [illegible].
Gortnegrosse (co. Lim. ?), [illegible].
Gortnoherry (co. Mayo ?), [illegible].
Gortneharna—Gortneharny—Gortnyhorey (co. Cork ?), 6514-5, [illegible], [illegible].
Gortnoberine (co. Cork ?), [illegible].
Gortnackleby (Queen's co. ?), [illegible].
Gortnclogo (co. Leit. ?), [illegible].
Gortnelly, Queen's co., [illegible].
Gortnoclonane, co. Cork, [illegible].
Gortnclown (co. Leit. ?), [illegible].
Gortnedyny, co. Kerry, [illegible].
Gortnemrahir, co. Kilk., [illegible].
Gortnemucklagh (co. Cork ?), [illegible].
Gortnemore (Gortnecorne), co. Cork, [illegible].
Gortnerahine—Gortnearaihe (Gortnaraha, co. Mayo), 1[illegible], [illegible].
Gortnerbeagh (co. Kerry ?), [illegible].
Gortnesleamplas, co. Kerry, [illegible].
Gortnesleamphe, co. Kerry, [illegible].
Gortneskeagh. See Gortnaskegh.
Gortneskehie (Gortnaskehe ?), co. Kerry [illegible].
Gortnesskryne, co. Cork, [illegible].
Gortnetober (co. Lim. ?), [illegible].
Gortnetubrid. See Gortnetubbrid.
Gortnetubbrid—Gortnetubbride—Gortnetobrid—Gortnetubbrid, co. Lim., [illegible], [illegible] (castle and land), [illegible], [illegible].
Gortnetubbrid—Gortnetubrid—Gortnytobbred, co. Cork, [illegible], [illegible], [illegible].
Gortnetubbrid—Gortnotuberid, co. Lim. or Cork, [illegible], [illegible].
Gortnetubrid (co. Lim. ?), [illegible].
Gortnohalloy (co. Lim. or Cork ?), [illegible].
Gortnolde (Gortnecloe), Queen's co., [illegible].
Gortolaske, co. Kerry, [illegible].
Gortollagher (co. Mayo ?), [illegible].
Gortosleghie (co. Lim. or Tip.), [illegible].
Gortoskryne (co. Cork), [illegible].
Gortoltoghee (co. Mayo ?), [illegible].
Gortolly (co. Leit. ?), [illegible].
Gortondogh—Gortnodoghe, co. Cork, [illegible].
Gortnyoboholyn, co. Cork, [illegible].
Gortayele (Gortmuclan), Queen's co., [illegible].
Gortnyfoby (co. Cork ?), [illegible].
Gortnyrooly, co. Cork, [illegible].
Gortnygaddorye, co. Cork, [illegible].
Gortaygrosse (Gortnagross), co. Cork, [illegible], [illegible].
Gortayhorny. See Gortanhorne.
Gortay park, co. Cork or Lim., [illegible].
Gortaysloaghy (co. Tip. ?), [illegible].
Gortayskryne, co. Cork, [illegible].

INDEX TO FIANTS—ELIZABETH.

Gortaystelvred. *See* Gortinadaldred.
Gortakoisio, co. Cork, 6567.
Gortemcgalcannilus, co. Kerry, 6128.
Gortcelogh, co. Louth, 4808.
Gortcam—Gortcade, co. Tip., 2284, 6521.
Gorteglleran (co. Cav. ?), 4912.
Gortiquylleyn (co. Tip. ?), 6283.
Gortrodan—Gortirodan, co. Tip., 6464, 6468.
Gortrae—Gartrowe—Kilegortroe, co. Cork, 1628, 6602.
Gortrotingan (near Youghal ?), 3188.
Gortraddaro (co. Tip. ?), 6318.
Gortrue (co. Cork ?), 6696.
Gortrevblo, co. Kerry, 4132.
Gortshighan, co. Lim., 6166.
Gortskeaghan (co. Lim. ?), 6566.
Gortskeagho (Gortskeagh), co. Lim., 4947.
Gortthomakuott, co. Gal., 3519.
Gortvendera. *See* Gortrodan.
Gortnekavgee (co. Cav. ?), 6403.
Gortinmill (co. Westm. ?), 6627.
Gortwallie (co. Lim. ?), 6168.
Gortweilor, co. Cork, 6602.
Gortvelar — Gortovolare, co. Kerry, 6618, 6926.
Gortvoleyre (co. Cork ?), 5084.
Gortwallallo, co. Gal., 6626.
Gortwallie (co. Lim. ?), 6427.
Gortwillowro (co. Cork ?), 6267.
Gortydoyra, co. Clare, 6942.
Gortyno, co. Lim., 6660.
Gortynos, co. Kilk., 612.
Gortynfin — Gortynfyne, King's co., 1803, 1868.
Gorumna, co. Gal. *See* Garrowlirhna in Gartmna.
Gos, Richard, 5211. *See* Gosle.
Goshawks reserved as rent, 4511, 4686, 6103, 6468.
Goslingston — Goslingstown — Goslingstowne (Goslingstown, co. Kilk.), 2679, 3012, 4267, 5666, 5676.
Gossall, Henry, queen's attorney in Munster, 4023, 5365, 6438.
Gosse, Edw., pardon, 4097.
" Michael, pardon, 3468. *See also* Gorsla.
Goste—Gosst—Gorste—Gust, Richard, pardon, 911; commissions, 3147, 3948, 3911.
Gov, Tho., pardon, 4118.
Gouge, Barnaby. *See* Gouge.
Gough — Gorgh — Googhe — Gugh — Goghe — Goughe:
" Edward, sheriff of Cross Tipperary, pardon, 4384; com., 4456; surrender, 4683; grant of land, 4891; land in his tenure, 5691.
" James, 3441; pardon, 31.
" John, alderman of Dublin, 2236.
" Mary, 4281.
Gough, Patrick, trading license, 51; pardon, 128, 438, 791; alderman of Dublin, com. 3460; lessee of customs, 2271.
" Patrick, pardon, 4114.
" Thomas, pardon, 3312.
" William, pardon, 4638; grant of a wardship, 4114.
Goughon, Shoolie sy, pardon, 6574.
Gould, James. *See* Golde.
Gouldin, Philip, archdeacon of Cork, comm., 4626.
" Stephen, pardon, 4704.
Gouldinge, Edmund, wardship, 3461.
" John (of Harbertston), heir of, 6460.
" Morris, pardon, 6494.
" Redmond, pardon, 6544.
" Walter, 4821.
" *See* Goldinge.
Gouk, Edmund, pardon, 1437.
" Pate, Sir John, pardon, 1907.
Gouselnam, co. Louth, 6413.
Goven, Jovan sy, pardon, 6466.
Govere (co. Clare ?), 6673.
Government, appointment of lords justices, 1286, 2676, 4084, 5184, 5340; their powers, 4651.
" commissions during absence of chief governor in remote parts, 279–81, 684, 1422–3, 2118, 3461, 3647, 3750, 4404, 4616, 4760, 4829, 5427, 5353, 5567, 5901–2, 5634, 5941, 6128, 6168, 6202, 6226, 6428, 6477; similar commission for Munster, 888; for Ulster, 3366.
" exceptional powers given to earl of Essex in Ulster, 2463.
" provincial, *see* Connaught, Munster and Ulster.
" district, *see* Clandeboy, King's and Queen's counties (2043), Byrnes country (3617).
" of Irish countries; chiefs appointed by crown, as Captain; authority given to chief by name of seneschal, 1404, 1684, 1760, 3615, &c. *See* Seneschal. *See also* Tanist.
Gowell beg—Gowell beg (co. Don.), 6589, 6567.
Gowell more—Gowell more (co. Don.), 6594, 6567.
Gowell ulrvke (co. Tyr. ?), 6606.
Gowrdale. *See* Godsall.
Gowry, Aleon sy, pardon, 6625.
" Donell m'Teig, pardon, 6548.
" Donyll, pardon, 4469.
" Farrall ogo, pardon, 4469.

INDEX TO FIANTS—ELIZABETH.

Gown, Gilpatrick m'Shane, pardon, [illegible].
" (alias Smith), James, pardon, [illegible].
" John, pardon, 4118.
" Melaghlin m'Conor, pardon, [illegible].
" Mortagh, [illegible].
" Philip, pardon, [illegible].
" Rorie, pardon, [illegible].
" Tirlagh, pardon, [illegible], [illegible].
Gowell (co. Lim.?), [illegible].
Gowell beg. See Gowell beg.
Gowell more. See Gowell more.
Gowen, Brian, Donogho, and Nich. m'Shoryne I, pardon, [illegible].
" Owen m'Hugh I, pardon, [illegible].
" Tho. m'Shoryne I, pardon, [illegible].
Gowlan (co. Kerry ?), [illegible].
Gowld, John, pardon, [illegible].
" Piers, heir of, [illegible].
" Thomas, wardship, [illegible].
Gowlde, Rob., pardon, [illegible].
Gowlding. See Golding.
Gowle, David, livery to brother of, [illegible].
" Dominic, pardon, [illegible].
" Edmund, mayor of Cork, comm., [illegible].
" George, livery, [illegible].
" James, comm. of claims on exchanged lands, [illegible].
" or Golde, James, lease, [illegible].
" John, livery to heir of, [illegible].
" Stephen, pardon, [illegible].
Gowles, James, pardon, [illegible].
Gowles weire, co. Cork, [illegible].
Gowlin, co. Car., [illegible].
Gowloe, co. Gal., [illegible].
Gowlyn castle (Golden ? co. Tip.), [illegible].
Gowna, lough. See Loghgaune.
Gownane, John fitz James Tobine, [illegible].
Gowne, John m'Philip ny, pardon, [illegible], [illegible].
Gowran, co. Kilk. See Gawran.
Gowyre, co. Clare, [illegible].
Goydagh, Philip m'Edward, pardon, [illegible].
Goyer, Cornelius and Wm. fitz Tho. or, pardon, [illegible].
" Rob., pardon, [illegible].
Goyrisle, Owen m'Brien I, pardon, [illegible].
Graan, co. Lim., [illegible].
Grace, Adam, pardon, 1117, [illegible], [illegible], [illegible], [illegible].
" Alaster, pardon, [illegible].
" Alexander, pardon, [illegible], [illegible], [illegible], [illegible], [illegible], [illegible], [illegible], [illegible], [illegible], [illegible], [illegible], [illegible], [illegible].
" Alissone fitz John, pardon, [illegible].
" Amelius, pardon, [illegible].
" Artondre, pardon, [illegible].
" Awnsell, pardon, [illegible].
" Edmund, pardon, [illegible], [illegible], [illegible], 1117, [illegible], [illegible], [illegible], [illegible], [illegible], [illegible], [illegible], [illegible], [illegible], [illegible], [illegible], [illegible], [illegible].
Grace, Ellen, pardon, [illegible], [illegible], [illegible], [illegible].
" Ellis Sampson, war upon, [illegible].
" Fowke fitz Rob., pardon, [illegible].
" Garrett fitz Fowke, pardon, [illegible], [illegible].
" Garrett fitz Rob., pardon, [illegible].
" Geoffrey carragh, pardon, [illegible].
" Gerald (son of Oliver), [illegible]; comm., [illegible].
" Gerald (of Legan), pardon, [illegible], [illegible].
" Gerald, pardon, [illegible], [illegible], [illegible], [illegible].
" Helen, pardon, [illegible].
" Honor, pardon, [illegible].
" James, constable of gaol of Kilkenny, pardon, [illegible].
" James, sheriff of Carlow, [illegible], [illegible].
" James (of Ballylinch), pardon, [illegible], [illegible]; comm., [illegible].
" James, pardon, [illegible].
" Jasper, pardon, [illegible], [illegible].
" John fitz Edm., pardon, [illegible].
" John (son of Oliver), [illegible]; pardon, [illegible], [illegible].
" John, pardon, [illegible].
" Katherine, pardon, [illegible], [illegible].
" Leonard, pardon, [illegible], [illegible], [illegible].
" Marcus or Mark, pardon, [illegible], [illegible], [illegible].
" Margaret, pardon, [illegible], [illegible], [illegible].
" Nicholas, pardon, [illegible], [illegible], [illegible], [illegible], [illegible].
" Oliver, comm., [illegible]; sheriff of Kilkenny, [illegible].
" Oliver (of Grace's court), commissions, [illegible], [illegible], [illegible]; pardon, [illegible], [illegible], [illegible].
" Oliver (of Legan), grant of land, [illegible], [illegible].
" Oliver, land in tenure of, [illegible].
" Oliver, pardon, [illegible], [illegible], [illegible], [illegible], [illegible], [illegible], [illegible], [illegible].
" Onorie, pardon, [illegible].
" Onorina, pardon, [illegible].
" Patrick, pardon, [illegible], [illegible], [illegible], [illegible], [illegible], [illegible], [illegible].
" Peirs or Peirce, pardon, [illegible], [illegible].
" Peirs, or Piers, war upon, [illegible]; evil disposed person, [illegible].
" Peirs, pardon, [illegible].
" Peter (of Brownsbagh), attainted, [illegible].
" Peter, pardon, [illegible], [illegible], [illegible].
" Philip, pardon, [illegible], [illegible], [illegible], [illegible], 1604, 1614, [illegible], [illegible], [illegible], [illegible].

Grace, Redmund, pardon, 1068, 1267, 1648, 2791, 2012, 3720, 6706.
" Richard, son of Oliver, 1834.
" Rich., conveyance of lands to, 6169.
" Richard, pardon, 1063, 2838, 3118, 3807, 4238, 4383, 4399, 4438, 4692, 5373, 6434, 6486, 6577, 6706, 6774.
" Rob., pardon, 1113, 1856, 1664, 2784, 2827, 3064, 3463, 4298, 4747, 4982, 5069, 6140, 6161, 6320, 6419, 6461, 6542, 6706, 6776.
" Roland, pardon, 3795, 4720.
" Shane, pardon, 1062.
" Thomas (son of Oliver), 1838.
" Thomas, rector of Callan, pardon, 1860.
" Thomas, eveillis (or Thos. of the mill) fitz Peirs, a rebel, 4266, 4767.
" Thomas, pardon, 927, 1064, 1312, 1867, 1873, 2764, 2809, 3131, 3628, 3807, 4370, 6110, 6321.
" Uncell als Rowland, pardon, 6162.
" Walter, pardon, 856, 957, 1068, 2807, 3208, 6110, 6320, 6732.
" Walter, son of, 968.
" Wm., land held by, 4879.
" William, hanged, 258.
" Wm., pardon, 4539, 6110, 6410, 6442, 6651, 6677.
Grace of God, house of gauge. See Grace-dieu.
Gracecastle—Gracecastell. See Castlegrace.
Gracecastle (Queen's co.), 6341.
Gracecourt—Gracecourte. See Grangecourt.
Gracedieu—Gracedew—Gracelewe—Grace-diew—Graceline—Gracediwe—Graceelywe — Gracia Dei — Grace of God — Gracelow — Gracia Dei, co. Dub., 280, 567, 749, 782, 846, 1708, 1784, 2724, 4791, 5760, 5788, 6234.
" nunnery, possessions leased, 553, 808, 812, 601, 1181, 1182, 1490, 2494, 2687, 3128, 3316, 4130, 4063, 6166, 6411, 6316; granted, 7632, 6716.
" rectory, 6316.
Gracefories (co. Kilk. ?), 1843.
Gracecastle. See Castlegrace.
Gracecourt — Gracecourt — Gracecourt — Gracecorte—Gracecourte, co. Kilk. 798, 1128, 1683, 1801, 1886, 6117, 6318, 6141.
Gracia Dei. See Gracedieu.
Gracioscastill. See Castlegrace.
Grackaro (co. Kilk. ?), 2966.
Grada, David I, pardon, 6671.
Gradame, co. Cav., 4981.
Graddie, Loughlin m'Ea I, pardon, 4664.
Graddy, Loghlen, pardon, 840.
" William, pardon, 840.
Graddye, Teig m'Donoghe I, pardon, 4682.
Gradom, co. Cav., 4684.
Gradgee (co. Tip. ?), 6468.
Gradie. See Grady, co. Cork.
Gradie, Dermod m'Ea I, pardon, 4462.
" James, pardon, 6845.
" Morierteagh m'Teige I, pardon, 6611.
" Wm. m'Loghlen I, pardon, 6791.
Grady—Gradie alias Granee, co. Cork, 2694, 4964, 4725, 5026.
Grady, Donoghe m'Shane m'Teige I, pardon, 3148.
" Hary m'Mahowny, pardon, 4652.
" Hugh, pardon, 6176.
" John oge, pardon, 6832.
" Loughlin m'Donoghe I, pardon, 4428.
" Onora ny, pardon, 4694.
Graeg, co. Wat., 4157.
Graen, co. Lim., 5862.
Graffe (co. Westm.), 3698.
Graffogh—Graffy, co. Westm., 3347, 6116.
Grafton, Rich., serjeant-at-arms, 5769; comm., 6650.
Grag, co. Cork, 3125.
Gragaddor, co. Kild. See Goldengaugh. Gragaddire.
Graganaghe (co. Cork ?), 6432.
Gragauporell, co. Lim., 6017.
Graganae—Graganae (the barony of Enerchi), co. Clare, 4761.
" seneschal of, 1963.
Graganollen, co. Lim., 6017.
Grag al Ice, co. Kerry, 6182.
Gragantagh, co. Tip. See Carragya.
Gragdranton, co. Kilk., 1289.
Grage. See Craig, co. Cork.
Grage. See Graige, co. Kilk.
Grage. See Graiges, Queen's co.
Grage. See Graige, co. Tip.
Grangebolne, co. Kilk., 1913.
Gragolrisle. See Graigalridy.
Gragebarne (Graigcumneagh), co. Lim., 3471.
Grage I Currie, co. Gal., 3369.
Gragemorie, co. Lim., 6171.
Gragemoyemill, co. Cork or Lim., 6666.
Gragemanydown, co. Car., 1341.
Gragneme, co. Tip., 6334.
Gragenaw. See Graignawe.
Gragenabe, co. Wat., 1976.
Graguee (Graigue More and Beg), co. Wex., 1129, 1786.
Gragevale (Queen's co. ?), 4918.
Gragfestall—Gragfeall (Graigreypoddle), co. Kild., 5643, 6617.
Gragnase. See Gragnae.
Gragghorestane, Queen's co., 2357.
Gragroddan, Queen's co., 1940.
Graghshe (co. Long. or Rosc. ?), 4686.

INDEX TO FIANTS—ELIZABETH.

Craghill, co. Car., 6457.
Craghinacurrie (co. Lim. ?), 6478.
Craghleo (Craigabeccaha, co. Tip. ?), [illegible].
Cragnefynney, King's co., [illegible].
Cragnastehy, Queen's co., 6551.
Cragnecraunte (co. Tip. ?), [illegible].
Cragnekelly, co. Tip., 6457.
Cragnekerrie, Queen's co., 6438.
Cragnoo (co. Kilk. ?), [illegible].
Cragodire (Cragodder), co. Kild., 6217.
Cragrowahan, Queen's co., 1840.
Craidge, Queen's co., 6551.
Craiedown (co. Tip. ?), 6581.
Craig—Crage, co. Cork, [illegible], 4428.
Craig, co. Kild., [illegible].
Craig—Crage—Craige, co. Kilk., 971, 1886, 1763, 4341, 4843, 6719, [illegible], 6704, 6782.
Craig—Craige (Creigue, co. Lim.), 6777, 6847, [illegible].
Craig, co. Sligo, [illegible].
Craig (co. Wat. ?), 6571.
Craigacurragh, co. Lim. *See* Craughurro.
Craigabeccha, co. Tip. *See* Craghleo.
Craigavera, Queen's co. *See* Craigeshowrane.
Craigcurre, co. Wat., [illegible].
Craigdridy—Cragdrisle—Craigedrisle, co. Kilk. 927, 1048, 1278.
Craige, [illegible], 6778.
Craige (co. Car. or Kild. ?), 6778.
Craige, co. Gal., 6868.
Craige, co. Kerry, 6117.
Craige. *See* Craig, co. Kilk.
Craige, co. Lim., 4488.
Craige. *See* Craig, co. Lim.
Craige—Crage (Craigue), Queen's co., 1298, 1432, [illegible], 6438, [illegible], [illegible], 6722.
Craige—Crage, co. Tip., 6634, 6763.
Craige, co. Wat., 6348.
Craige (co. Wex.), 65.
Craigedrisle. *See* Craigdrisly.
Craigehisle, 6378.
Craigenahisle, co. Tip., 6128.
Craigenalowan (co. Tip. ?), 2828.
Craigenflen, co. Kerry, 6128.
Craigenn, co. Tip., 6654.
Craigenue (co. Kilk. ?), [illegible].
Craigenuwe. *See* Craigenwe.
Craigerisle, in Upper Ossory, 6792.
Craigeshowrane—Craigeshowrane (Craig-avera ?), Queen's co., 1823, 2845.
Craigge I Garry (co. Gal. ?), 1841.
Craighinacoirowe (co. Lim. ?), 6481.
Craighnefynney, King's co., [illegible].
Craigilenah (co. Wex. ?), 6417.
Craigkeavyn, co. Tip., 1813.
Craigmagrana (co. Wat. ?), 2868.
Craigmacflee, co. Kerry, 6672, [illegible].
Craigna Howen (Craigueenahown), Queen's co., 1823, [illegible].
Craigncrkyle (co. Tip. ?), 6702.
Craignewmolan (Craignewmolane (Craigne-newmullan), Queen's co., 1823, [illegible].
Craigneo (Craigneo), co. Kilk., 6348.
Craignowe (co. Kilk. ?), 6702.
Craigrawe—Cragraw — Craigraware, co. Kilk., 856, 3164, 1296, [illegible], [illegible], 6702.
Craigrovagher, co. Sligo, 6481.
Craigs, co. Kilk., [illegible].
Craigue, co. Lim. *See* Craig.
Craiguenfulle, Queen's co. *See* Craygephelly.
Craiguealing, co. Car. *See* Crangedrane.
Craigue-arrah, co. Wat. *See* Craigacurrahane.
Craiguenvallagh, Queen's co. *See* Craynevolly.
Craigue More and Beg, co. Wex. *See* Craigue.
Craigueenahown, Queen's co. *See* Craigna Howen.
Craigueenamanagh, co. Kilk. *See* Donah.
Craiguenamullan, Queen's co. *See* Craig-newmolan.
Craigueenaspiddane, co. Car. *See* Craigue ne Spedak.
Craiguepoile, co. Kild. *See* Cragfootall.
Craigvolly, Queen's co., 6581.
Crain, foreign trade in, 1711.
„ illegal export of, 1078, 3080, 6009.
Craines (Carrane More and Beg ?), co. Lim., 6049.
Craisge, co. Kild., 1274.
Craige. *See* Grange.
Craisge by Millome, co. Louth, 2637.
Craisge, Great. *See* Grange.
Craisgeneclashe (perhaps Craigcurranish, co. Wat.), 894.
Craisgeshe, co. Wat. or Cork, 6084.
Cralagh. *See* Crallagh.
Cralagheyatrick, co. Down, 4827.
Craleigh—Craleigh. *See* Crallagh.
Crallagh — Crallaghe— Crallaugh — Crallaghe, co. Dub., 317, 1250, 1478, [illegible], 3318, 3323, 6818, 6488, 6872.
„ chapel, 1480, 3481.
Crallagh—Cralaugh—Crallaghe—Cralogh — Cralogh—Crallagh—Crelagh—Crellagh, co. Tip., 872, 1287, 1942, [illegible], 2381, 6378, 6634, 6636, 6644, 6518, 6622, 6748.
Crallagh, co. Tip. *See* Creaghmore, and Creaghlinmore.
Crallagh, 6401.
Crallagh — Crallaghe, co. Wat., 944, 3138, 6631.
Crallaghe — Crallaugh — Crallaughe. *See* Crallagh.
Crame, Edm., pardon, 4671.
„ Teig, pardon, 4888.
Crame, Wm. m'Richard, pardon, 6780.

Grangegonaghe, co. Cork, 6161.
Grangh, co. Cork, rectory, 3121.
Grangh, co. Lim. See Grangeagh, Grangeghe.
Grangh, John m'Wm., pardon, 4186.
Granghe, co. Ross., 4077.
Grangmore, co. Ross., 1291.
Granard—Granarde, co. Long., 1401, 2888, 5114, 6420, 6672.
„ abbey, possessions leased, 826, 1401, 2348, 3303, 4241, 6416.
„ manor, 4534, 6632.
„ granges, 528, 1401, 6416.
„ termon, 6850.
„ barony. See Clanlane, Moyghery-gwarnel.
Grancagin Maghubrybraghe. See Grange Maghery Rovaghe.
Grandan, Shane, pardon, 6167, 6571.
Grandg. See Grange.
Grandgeclare. See Grangeclare.
Grandge. See Grange.
Grandgemanagh, 4775.
Grandgmoghonse (co. Kilk. ?), 1487.
Grane. See Grany, co. Kild.
Grane, co. Car., 2867.
Grane, John, pardon, 6148.
„ Shane, pardon, 866.
Granell, Donell roe m'Kelan, pardon, 4797.
Granerahy (co. Kilk. or Tip. ?), 4704.
Granesaghbeg, co. Tip., 2564.
Granewhoughe (Grange, par. Fermoy ?), co. Cork, 6668.
Grang. See Grange.
Grangbeg. See Grange beg.
Grangehaghe Maghubryrvagh. See Grange Maghery Revaghe.
Grange—Grangie—Granngh, 878, 884, 6447, 6477, 6684.
Grange, co. Car. (Wick. ?), rectory, 1367.
Grange (co. Car. ?), 5135.
Grange (co. Cork ?), 6151.
Grange, co. Cork, 5668.
Grange alias Grady (Grange in par. Abbeymahon), co. Cork, 4866, 4728, 6084.
Grange in par. Fermoy, co. Cork. See Granewhoughe.
Grange (in Ardes), co. Down, rectory, 1849, 3767.
Grange—Grannge, co. Dub., 2651, 3291, 4114, 4481, 4578.
Grange—Grang—Grawnge, co. Gal., 3965, 4848, 4849, 4898, 4867, 6483.
Grange, co. Kild., 1284.
Grange (co. Kild. or Car. ?), 6775.
Grange—Graingo—Grandge—Grang—Grannge—Granudge, co. Kilk., 463, 1103, 1698, 1698, 1766, 1614, 3463, 3912, 4462, 4468, 4214, 6420, 6484, 6794.
Grange (King's co. ?), 6687.
Grange—Graunge (co. Lim. ?), 2830, 4978, 6465, 6694, 6411. See Granshaghe.
Grange, co. Louth, 2874.
Grange (near Allerdston), co. Louth, 5487.
Grange—Graunge, co. Meath, 378, 2878, 6381.
Grange, co. Meath, rectory, 4231.
Grange alias Rochegrange (Graughermagers), co. Meath, 162.
Grange (co. Mon.), 2408, 6726.
Grange—Grang—Graunge, Queen's co., 463, 3393, 4729, 6497, 6833.
Grange—Grandge—Grang—Granndge—Granngo (co. Ross.), 1166, 3963, 4077, 4107, 6468, 6806.
Grange—Grainge—Grandg—Grandge—Grauudge—Graunge, co. Sligo, 1166, 2160, 3683, 4046, 4708, 5026, 6150, 6434, 6174, 6184, 6397, 6916, 6468.
Grange—Grandge—Grang—Graunge, co. Tip., 2310, 3637, 6974, 4013, 4371, 4447, 6206, 6163, 6622, 6796.
Grange (in Ormond), co. Tip., 1628.
Grange (co. Tip. or Kilk.), 4708.
Grange—Grang—Grannge—Granadge—Graduge, co. Wat., 628, 844, 1371-2, [illegible], 3133, 4368, 4466, 5518, 6121.
Grange—Grang—Granudge—Graunge, co. Westm., 647, 1406, 1465, 1771, 2332, 2694, 3065, 3464, 4151, 4317, 4397, 5760, 6833, 6874.
Grange—Grannge, co. Wex., 117, 514, 4901.
Grange—Graunge, co. Wex. or Car., 6311.
Grange (co. Wick.), rectory, 1367.
Grange, Great, alias Grangmore, co. Kild., 4184, 4298.
Grange, Great (co. Sligo), 1166, 3102, 4107.
Grange—Grainge—Graunge, Great (Grangemore), co. Tip., 381, 834, 3777, 4131, 4165, 6337, 6460.
Grange, Little, 186.
Grange, Little, co. Gal., 1861.
Grange, Little, co. Kild., 5490, 6152.
Grange, Little (co. Sligo), 1166, 3168, 4407.
Grange, Little—Graunge Bittell, co. Tip., 784, 2414.
Grange, Little, co. Westm., 1106, 2019, 4123.
Grange, Nelbor, 206.
Grange, New, co. Lim., rectory, 2411.
Grange, New, co. Tip., 3377, 4114, 4164.
Grange, Old (co. Kilk. ?), 2072, 3882.
Grange, Upper, 206.
Grange by Athassel, co. Tip., 4666.
Grange by Fethard, co. Tip., 6648.
Grange—Graunge by Milton or Myleton, co. Louth, 6837, 6971, 5166.
Grange by Mollingar, co. Westm., 4548.
Grange by Trevett or Tryvet, co. Meath, 5136, 6816.
Grange of Athinab (co. Tip. ?), 1866.
Grange of Ballelugge, co. Westm., 7112.

INDEX TO FIANTS.—ELIZABETH.

Grange of Ballyn, co. Wex., 7[illegible].

Grange of Bectyff, co. Meath, [illegible].

Grange of Cowlshirrie or Coulbarey, co. Sligo, [illegible], 4497.

Grange of Culrevaghe or Cowleraghe, co. Gal., [illegible], [illegible], [illegible].

Grange of Dunbrody, co. Wex., [illegible].

Grange of Inyslawnaght, co. Tip., [illegible], [illegible], [illegible].

Grange of Irre, co. Tip., [illegible].

Grange of Kells, co. Kilk., [illegible].

Grange of Killeggan, co. Westm., [illegible].

Grange of Kilmeri, co. Wex., [illegible].

Grange of Kilrie (Grangekilrey), co. Kilk., [illegible].

Grange of Kiltobber (Grange and Kiltobber), co. Westm., [illegible], [illegible].

Grange of McWilliam Carrighe or Carrog-hen—Grange McWilliam Carraghe (co. Kilk.?), [illegible], [illegible].

Grange of Maghoberraghe. See Grange Maghory Revaghe.

Grange of Mowyawy—Mowawy, co. Gal., 1456, [illegible].

Grange of Moyntervlyn—Grange of Moyntervlyn or Montervllis, co. Leit., 1456, [illegible], 1497.

Grange of Newton, co. Wat., [illegible].

Grange of O'Felan or O'Folan, co. Ros., 1456, [illegible], [illegible].

Grange of Rossalvan (Grangerossolvan), co. Kild., [illegible], [illegible].

Grange of S. Katherine, Waterford, [illegible].

Grange of Trywel or Trevill, co. Meath, [illegible], [illegible].

Grange of Tullomcathane, co. Meath, rectory, [illegible].

Grange of Tulahirrie (co. Ros.?), [illegible].

Grange of Wittocke, co. Kild., [illegible].

Grange beg—Grange begg—Grangebeg; Granng bege, co. Sligo, 4457, [illegible], [illegible], [illegible].

Grangebeg. See Littlegrange.

Grangebregge—Grange bege (co. Sligo ?), belonging to Boyle abbey, 1[illegible], [illegible].

Grangeclare—Granlgclare—Grangeclare, co. Kild., [illegible], [illegible], [illegible], [illegible], [illegible]; castle and land granted, [illegible].

„ rectory, [illegible].

Grangedonane, co. Kilk., [illegible].

Grangeren—Grangeren (co. Wick.), [illegible], [illegible].

Grangecoor, co. Kild. See Canna Ore.

Grange Gorr (co. Kild.?), [illegible].

Grangecorro, co. Wat., [illegible].

Grange Cowlpapple—Grange Cowlefoble, co. Kilk., [illegible], [illegible].

Grange Culreraghe. See Grange of Culreraghe.

Grange edriely, co. Kilk., [illegible].

Grangeford—Grangeford—Grangeforth—Granngeford — Grange-forthe—Grangfort, co. Car., 776, 1567, 1571, [illegible], [illegible], [illegible], 4161, [illegible].

„ church of S. Brigid, [illegible].

Grangeford, co. Kild., [illegible], [illegible].

Grangeforl—Grangeforth. See Grangeford.

Grangegilloe (Grangegooth), co. Meath, [illegible].

Grangegeallin (co. Wick.?), [illegible].

Grangegorman—Grangegorman—Grange Gorman, near Dublin, [illegible], [illegible], 1[illegible], 1704, 1[illegible], [illegible], [illegible], [illegible], [illegible], [illegible], [illegible].

„ manor, [illegible], 1[illegible].

Grangelisse (co. Cork ?), [illegible].

Grangeberrie—Grangeberrye—Grange-birrey—Grangebirre—Grangcoldirrie, co. Tip., [illegible], [illegible], 4161; grant, [illegible].

Grangelliggin, co. Kild. See Grangliggyn.

Grangekilrey, co. Kilk. See Grange of Kilrie.

Grangelyons, co. Kilk., rectory, [illegible].

Grangelinge (Grangemelinge), co. Car., [illegible].

Grange Maghory Revaghe—Grangeghe Maghoberraghe—Grangebaghe Maghoberraghe—Grange Maghoberoraghe—Grangemaghoryeraghe—Grange Neaghrie Revaugh, co. Gal., [illegible], [illegible], [illegible], [illegible].

Grange m'gilpatrick — Grange Mac Gillepatrick, co. Kild., 1131, 1[illegible].

Grange Massmalis, co. Sligo, [illegible].

Grangemell — Grangemaylle (Grangemellon ?), co. Kild., 1[illegible], [illegible].

Grangemellon—Grangemollon—Grangemollyn—Grange Mylln—Grangemollen—Grange Mollyn—Grange Myllen—Grangmullen (Grangemellon), co. Kild., [illegible], 1474, [illegible], [illegible], [illegible], [illegible], [illegible], [illegible], [illegible].

Grange Moclere—Grangemoclyer, co. Tip., [illegible], [illegible].

Grangemollen—Grangemollyn. See Grangemellon.

Grangemore or Great Grange — Mochgrange, co. Kild., 3148, [illegible].

Grangemore—Grainemore, belonging to Boyle abbey, 1[illegible], [illegible], [illegible].

Grangemore—Grainemore, co. Sligo, [illegible], [illegible].

Grangemore, co. Tip. See Grange, Great.

Grange Mowyawy—Grange Mowyawie—Grangmoury, co. Gal., 1455, [illegible], [illegible].

Grange myllen. See Grange mill.

Grange Myllen. See Grangemellon.

Grangenal—Grangenal, co. Meath, [illegible].

Grange Neaghrie Revagh. See Grange Maghory Revagh.

Grangeneconnaghe — Granconnaugh, co. Sligo, 1456, [illegible], 4497.

Grangemonisheagho, co. Tip., 681.
Grangenocroskan, Queen's co., 684.
Grange ne Spedak—Grangenspiddoke (Graig-nenaspiddoge), co. Carl., 664, 4658.
Grange Ore (Grangeover ?), co. Kild., 1161, 1262.
Grangeposelierde, co. Kild., 5012.
Grangee, Thomas, treasurer Waterford cathedral, 4837.
Grange Rosbilvan (Grangerosbolcan, co. Kild.), rectory, 1507. See Grange of Ros-nalvan.
Grangery, co. Tip., 264.
Granges, two (Grangeis, co. Mon.), 4042.
Graniespiddoke. See Grange ne Spedak.
Granneth (co. Meath ?), 5628.
Grangetullaghan in diocese of Ossory, 3441.
Grangewoden (co. Car. ?), 5768.
Grangfort—Grangforte. See Grangeford.
Grangingyn (Grangebeggin, co. Kild. ?), 2674.
Grangipodes, co. Kilk., 5082.
Grangrase, 1844.
Grang-m'William Caragho. See Grange of m'William Carrigiie.
Grangmoure. See Grange Moyrewry.
Grangmore. See Grangemore.
Grangmellon. See Grangemellon.
Grangpadan (co. Lim.), 6179.
Grangredyn, 1806.
Granimore, co. Sligo. See Carrow Grany-more.
Granis, Donell, pardon, 6488.
Granisbery (Queen's co. ?), 1175.
Granagh, co. Kilk., 5060, 5554.
Granagh—Granaghe (Granaigh ?), co. Lim., 5647, 5455; grant, 5590.
Granne, Owen, pardon, 6488.
Granagh, co. Lim., lord of, 5394.
Granege (co. Kilk. or Car. ?), 4484.
Granoge, Tolg m'Fynin, pardon, 6186.
Granagh, co. Cork or Lim., 5808.
Granshe, co. Mon. See Granges.
Granshagh—Granshaghe (Grange), co. Lim., parish of, 5781-3.
" castle, &c., granted, 5782.
Granshagh, co. Rosc., 5326.
Granshough—Granshoghe (co. Gal.), 4707, 6512.
Granstrigh (co. Cork ?), 2316.
Grantey, co. Westm., 2857.
Grant—Grante. See Graunt.
Grantestown—Grantiston—Grannistowyn—Granstiston—Grauntstown, co. Tip., 3457, 3805, 4818, 6180, 4391-3, 5765.
Granistowe—Granston—Grauntestowne, Queen's co., 5885, 3951, 4722.
Grantstown—Grantiston, (co. Wat. ?), 3129.
Granug, Rich. fitz William mc, pardon, 4722.
Granz—Grauze, co. Kild., 2675, 6406, 6686.
Grany, David, pardon, 6404.
" Donell, pardon, 6931.
" Mahown, pardon, 6468.
" Shane, pardon, 5858, 5741.
Granyll, Morear, pardon, 6580.
Granyshaghe (co. Cork ?), 6540.
Granden. See Grandine.
Granlow. See Grawndon, co. Dub.
Grasdine—Grasden—(Grasedion ?), co. Wat., 791, 5404.
Grase, Oliver, pardon, 4393.
Grasseatle, co. Cork or Lim., 3807.
Grate, Edm. fitz Walter, pardon, 6454.
Gratencastle, co. Tip., 6694.
Gratin Dut. See Graceding.
Grandy alias O'Grady, Edmund, pardon, 5108.
Grandley, Daniel, 2802.
Graunage, Old, co. Kilk., 4839.
Graundge—Graung. See Grange.
Graung in Lowyne, co. Cork, 5418.
Graung Little. See Grange Little.
Graungboge. See Grangeboge.
Graunge and names beginning with Graunge—, are indexed Grange.
Graungstowne (co. Tip. ?), 4658.
Graunshaghe. See Granshaghe.
Graunt—Grant—Graunte—Grauntt:
" Arland, pardon, 4385, 4400, 4876, 6192.
" Edmund, pardon, 552.
" Geoffrey, pardon, 4464, 4888, 6561.
" James, pardon, 355, 4250, 4922, 5704, 6808.
" John, pardon, 3667, 5445, 4475-6, 5780.
" Patrick (of Waterford), pardon, 3006; pardon at his suit, 3087.
" Patr., usher to president of Munster, 6067, 5729; marshal of courts, &c., Munster, 5471, 5548, 5445; grants of land, 5408, 5724, 4554.
" Piers, licence for his house at Waterford, 4487.
" Peter, pardon, 3564, 3687.
" Peter, pardon, 4889.
" Philip, 5156.
" Rich., pardon, 3902, 4040, 5146, [illegible], 5094-5, 6685, 4702.
" Rich. (of Waterford), grant of a wardship, 6648.
" Walter, coroner of co. Cork, 5458, [illegible] ; commn., 4468.
" Walter, pardon, 6906, 5504, 6755.
" William, pardon, 3548, 3482.
Grauntestown—Grauntiston—Grauntstowne—Grauntestowne. See Grantestowne, Granistowe.
Grave—Greaves, Rob., A.M., dean of Cork, 3651; precentor, Holy Trinity, Dublin, 3596; made bishop of Fernes and Leighlin, 3417-18.

INDEX TO FIANTS—ELIZABETH.

Grovenor, Rich., gentleman porter, Munster, [illegible]; licence of absence, 6764.
Graver, Ellis, pardon, [illegible].
Grawnge. See Grange.
Gray, Edw., commission, 6614, [illegible].
Grayclogha, co. Wex., 417.
Graygaphofly (Graigneafulla), Queen's co., [illegible].
Grayghane (co. Kild. ?), [illegible].
Graygevally (Graiguenevallagh, Queen's co. ?), 6762.
Grayghanefynne (King's co. ?), 1844.
Graygreagh (Queen's co. ?), [illegible].
Grayneigmore (co. Leit. ?), 4784.
Graynolly (Queen's co. ?), 6762.
Grayge, co. Kild., [illegible].
Graystowne—Graiston—Graistown—Greyston—Greystown, co. Tip., 1103, 4881, 4743, [illegible], [illegible], 4764.
Graugh, co. Mon. See Gryghan.
Graughglasse (Graughglass), co. Mon., [illegible].
Graughnasivine (co. Leit. ?), 6419.
Greallagh—Greallagha. See Grallagh.
Grealliagh, co. Gal., [illegible].
Greana (Grean, co. Lim. ?), 6172.
Greame, George, kern, 4617.
" James, horseman, 6671.
" Rich., capt. (afterwards knight), comm. for martial law, 6743; grant of land, 6378; pardon recommended by, 6187.
" Tho., horseman, [illegible]; his son, 6671.
Grean, co. Lim. See Greana, Greane, Greinegeraghe, Greanagowneghe, Gryan.
Greane (co. Wick. ?), 2838.
Greanagh Dearge (co. Don. or Tyr.), [illegible]; river, 6677.
Greane, co. Lim., [illegible].
Great and Little Arden. See Arden.
Great Briorch alias Bewbrook, co. Meath, [illegible].
Great Burgadge, co. Kilk., [illegible].
Greatcastell, co. Cork, [illegible], [illegible].
Great Connall—Great Connell, co. Kild., 3712, 4114, 6779; rectory, [illegible].
Great Grainge. See Great Grange.
Great Grange alias Grangmore, co. Kild., 4134, [illegible].
Great Grange (co. Sligo), [illegible].
Great Grange — Great Grainge — Great Grannge, co. Tip., [illegible], 6141, 4168, 4857.
Great Grannge, in Tireragh, co. Sligo, [illegible].
Great Island, co. Cork, 1673 [illegible], [illegible].
Great Island (Barry More's), co. Cork, 1167, [illegible].
Great Island of Bearhaven, co. Cork, [illegible], [illegible].
Great rath (co. Wick. ?), [illegible].
Great Seal, keeper of, appointed, 1, [illegible] [illegible].
Great Woods (Kilmore), co. Cork, [illegible].
Greaughmedarougha, co. Cav., [illegible].
Greaves, Rob. See Grave.
Greco, Paul. See Greene.
Greenan (co. Kilk. ?), 6447.
Greenan, co. Wat. See Grenan.
Greenanstown, co. Meath. See Greenanstown.
Greene—Grene—Greno:
" Andrew, keeper of house of Kylmainham, [illegible], [illegible].
" Elizabeth, pardon, 5816.
" Henry, vice constable of Dungarvan, pardon, 6776.
" James, pardon, 117, 6761.
" Julian, [illegible].
" Paul, keeper of the house of Kilmainham, [illegible], 1144, 6709, 6765; surveyor of the deputy's stable, [illegible]; authorised to impress hay, [illegible], [illegible], 4061, 4179; commissions, [illegible], 1186, [illegible]; leases, 1167, 1518, 1739, [illegible], 3118; grant of a wardship, [illegible]; pardon, 1744, [illegible].
" Roger, kern, 1884, 6762.
Greenfield, Sir Richard, or Grenville, [illegible].
Greenoge, co. Meath. See Granoak.
Greenwich, queen's letters and instructions dated at, [illegible], [illegible], [illegible], [illegible], [illegible], [illegible], [illegible], [illegible], 1258, 1267, 1268, [illegible], 1311, [illegible], [illegible] [illegible], [illegible], [illegible], [illegible], [illegible], [illegible], [illegible], [illegible], [illegible], [illegible], 1461, [illegible], [illegible], [illegible], [illegible], [illegible].
Grepagh alias Lyndmarrow, co. Wexm., [illegible].
Greran (co. Kild. ?), 6442.
Greghane (Graugh ?), co. Mon., [illegible].
Gregory—Gregorie, Thomas, 9192, [illegible], [illegible].
" Wm., pardon, [illegible]; his house in Cashel, 2811.
Gregorye, Stephen, [illegible].
Greifin, John, pardon, [illegible].
" Thady, pardon, [illegible].
" Uriace, pardon, [illegible].
Greighvnallagh, co. Mon., [illegible].
Greinegeraghe — Greinegeraghe (Grean), co. Lim., [illegible].
Greinvile, Richard, comm., see Greenfield, 1330.
Greiston—Greistown. See Graystowne.
Greleagh. See Grallagh.
Greleghclone, co. Mayo, [illegible].
Greleaghmore in Muskryquyrck (Grallagh), co. Tip., [illegible].
Grelaughbegge (Grallagh), co. Tip., [illegible].
Grellagh—Grellaghe. See Grallagh.
Grenagh, [illegible].
Grenagh (or Kreanagh, co. Clare), [illegible].
Grenagh, co. Cork. See Grinaghe.
Grenagh—Grenaghe, co. Kilk., 812, [illegible], [illegible], [illegible].
Grenaghan, co. Long., [illegible].
Grenaghe (Grenagh), co. Cork, [illegible], [illegible].

INDEX TO FIANTS—ELIZABETH.

Grenagha. *See* Grenagh.
Grenaght, co. Kilk., 142.
Grenan, John, pardon, 6378.
Grenan (co. Kilk.), 1821, 2022, 2918, 2880, 3962, 4466, 4704; manor, 4710.
Grenan (co. Lim. ?), 2363, 3400.
Grenan, co. Long., 3141.
Grenan, co. Mon., 4824.
Grene—Grenane (Queen's co.), 2274, 4918.
Grenan—Grenane, co. Tip., 948, 4419, 4471, 6704.
Grenan—Grenane (Greenan, co. Wat.), 844, 1484, 2327, 2326, 3182, 3183; grant, 5891.
Grenanbeg (co. Lim. ?), 6490.
Grenanmore (co. Lim. ?), 3148.
Grenane. *See* Grenan.
Grenanston (Grenanstown), co. Meath, 1482.
Grenaston, co. Meath, 4094.
Grenaugha (Granagh, co. Lim.), 5171.
Grenekedagh (King's co. ?), 5157, 5631.
Grene, Paul, &c. *See* Greene.
Grenehill—Grenhill, co. Wex., 815, 4091.
Grenecrogowenagho — Grycugwonaiha (Green), co. Lim., rectory, 2083.
Grenevile—Greneffeld—Greinvile—Greynevile, Rich., knt., comm., 1320; an undertaker, 4461; grant of land, 4465; lease, 4467.
Grenhange, co. Ross., 4741.
Grenhill. *See* Grenehill.
Grennage (co. Cork ?), 6734.
Grenock—Grenocke—Grenok—Grenoke (Greenoge, co. Meath), 647, 849, 854–6, 1280, 1729, 1704, 3960, 3884, 4475, 4914, 4696, 5473: premises in, granted, 4023.
" manor, 848.
" rectory, 624, 2879, 4845, 6707.
" Palmerston near, 2014, 4018.
Grewe, Connoghor roogh m'Owen nic, pardon, 6782.
Grey of Wilton, Arthur, lord, lord deputy, 3487.
Greyabbey, co. Down. *See* Jugo Dei, 4781.
Greyfriars of Kildare, lands of, 4286, 5366, 5742.
" *See* Franciscans.
Greynevile, Sir Rich. *See* Grenevile.
Greystone—Greystown. *See* Graystowne.
Grieghan, Wm., pardon, 6481.
Grieman (co. Tip. ?), 6482.
Griese, James, pardon, 5486.
Griffen, Donogh m'Giolle, pardon, 6444.
Griffen, Daniel m'Dermod Y, pardon, 4474.
Griffen. *See* Griffin.
Griffenston, co. Car. (Griffinstown, co. Wick.) 4088; rectory, 3487.
Griffenstown, 5211.
Griffin — Griffen — Griffine — Gryffen — Gryffyn:
" Daniel, pardon, 4434.
" Donell, pardon, 5444.
" Ellis ogo, pardon, 5484.
" Ellis, pardon, 4502.
" Humfrey, pardon, 5462.
" John, pardon, 2442.
" Maurice, pardon, 6444.
" Mich., chief baron, temp. Hen. VI, 3164.
" Nich., pardon, 6662.
" Peter, pardon, 4032.
" Rich., searcher and gauger of Dublin, 3582, 4847; grant of a wardship, 4088; license of absence, 4882.
" Rob., pardon, 4680.
" Shane m'Teig, pardon, 4448.
" Theobald, pardon, 4488.
" Tho., janitor, Dublin castle, 4822, 5742.
" Tho., pardon, 6468.
" Walter, pardon, 3807, 4080.
" Wm., pardon, 6628.
" Wm. m'Shane, pardon, 6863.
Griffin or Greffen more, pardon, 447.
Griffinrath—Rathegriffen (co. Kild.), 108, 781.
Griffinston (co. Westm.), 2987.
Griffinstown, co. Wick. *See* Griffenston, Ballygriffin; Gillyn-ton.
Grilambill, co. Antrim, 6704.
Grimaliche—Grimealiche, Ralph, 4390; lease, 3182.
Grimaghe (Gronagh), co. Cork, 4228.
Grinanston (co. Meath ?), 4971.
Grimstone, John, dean of Leighlin, 6381.
Grinmane, Donogh O'Galleghure, pardon, 6189.
Groat, white, 2451.
Gronteenakin—Grantemakin (co. Leit. ?), 6788.
Grocery, trade in, 80.
Grogan, Cormock m'Shane I, pardon, 6628.
Grogganstown, co. Westm., 1460.
Grogill (co. Gal.), 4244.
Groin, Brian, pardon, 4117.
Groirfliesh (co. Leit. ?), 6881.
Groinstown, co. Kilk., 2880.
Grom, Wm., pardon, 4588.
Grome, Ferrall, pardon, 4782.
Gromley, Conley, pardon, 2608.
Gromly, Edm., pardon, 4145.
Gromogh, Donell, pardon, 4238.
Gromy, John M'Donell, pardon, 5498.
Gromyn (co. Leit. ?), 4464.
Grontlonagh, Tho. Gention, pardon, 4442.
Groome, Donell, pardon, 4445.
Groonan, co. Lim., 4781.

INDEX TO FIANTS—ELIZABETH.

Grot (co. Gal.?), 6787.
Grot, Rich. Myinter, pardon, 6768.
Grotkylly, 6762.
Grotecologha, co. Cork, 6152.
Groltawne, co. Leit., 6463.
Grove (Grovebeg), co. Kilk., 6288. See Growe.
Groves, co. Meath. See Grawe, Gaowragh-teragh.
Grovetowne, co. Wex., 6787.
Growe, co. Kild., 6758; rectory, &c., 6763.
Growe (Grove, co. Kilk.?), 5914, 6250, 7863, 8144, 6794.
Growe hille, co. Kilk., 1064, 1118.
Growe (co. Wex.), 62.
Growgle, Richard na, pardon, 6698.
Growtan (Growtown), co. Meath, 1469, 5551.
Growtan, co. Wex., 752.
Grraft (Grafty), co Meath, 1462.
Groogalar, Katherine ny, pardon, 6182.
Grougane, Edm. m'Meagle I, pardon, 6162.
Grougayne, Moroce m'Ile 1, pardon, 4611.
Grungogh, Galligh, pardon, 5166.
Gruamy, Donogh, pardon, 5651.
Grutchins, co. Kilk., 852.
Gryan (Grean), co. Lim., vicarage, 94.
Gryengwomaiha. See Greinawgowragha.
Gryffen—Gryffyn. See Griffin.
Grynan (co. Lim.?), 5618.
Guarin, co. Long., 1728.
Gueallye, Nicholas, murdered, 1882.
Guaby, Moriertagh m'Dermod oge ny, pardon, 6752.
Gualy, Mikey m'Dermod oge ny, pardon, 6752.
Guelyne (co. Kerry?), 5451.
Guer, Edmund, pardon, 5154.
Guertine (see Gurtine), 5654.
Guhart (Guhard), co. Kerry, 5152.
Guileagh, co. Wat. See Gyleaghe, Killighe.
Guilds: barbers and surgeons, Dublin, 5136; guild merchant, Dingle, 4816; guild merchants and other guilds, Kilmallock, 4876; shoemakers, Waterford, 5768.
Guillorde, Henry, lease, 1468.
Guin, John. See Gwynn.
Guldcliffe, Edmund more, pardon, 5122.
Guiffoll, Granny duff ny, pardon, 5176.
Gullaine—Gulleyne, co. Cork, 5456, 4671.
Gullevane, Teige m'Conoghor, pardon, 6764.
Gullvane, Dermod m'Shane I, pardon, 6764.
" Donell m'Shane, pardon, 5731.
Gully river. See Golly.
Gullyrynane, Eiken ny, pardon, 6794.
Gully Patrick, Margaret ny, pardon, 6618.
Gulnagnagh, Donogh m'Teig, pardon, 6618.
Gunahan, John, pardon, 6894.
Gunner in Dublin castle, 6948.
Gunner, master, of Ireland, 6964, 6442, 5694.
" master, of the queen's ship, 6012.
Gunners impressed for queen's ships, 5588, 1687.
Gunnocke—Gunuke (Gunnocke), co. Meath, 878, 1777.
Gunnockes—Gunnockes de Plunket (Gunnocke), co. Meath, 874, 4481.
Gunnocks, co. Meath. See Hollywoodde Gunnocke, 878, 4861.
Gunry, Donill m'Moriertagh Y, pardon, 6772.
Gunoke. See Gunnocke.
Gunpowder, accident from, 6171.
Guns, borne by comity levies, 5444.
Guodil, James, pardon, 6771.
Guortinrue, co. Cork, 6761.
Gurlinagh (co. Kerry?), 5444.
Gurline (co. Kerry?), 5454.
Gurion, Shane mo, pardon, 5461.
Gurraigheloughane (co. Tip.?), 6671.
Gurran James. See Garvan James.
Gurren Nabba, co. Mayo, 6458.
Gurtocarryn (co. Mayo or Gal.), 6488.
Gurtevoard, co. Cork. See Gurtinearde.
Gurtemandoona, co. Cork. See Gortany-cloway.
Gurteanroe, co. Cork. See Gurtinearrue, Gurtynarrowe.
Gurtearroe, co. Cork. See Gortnaerowe.
Gurtin, co. Car., 1940.
Gurtenaghkelly (co. Lim.?), 5958.
Gurtenagroane, co. Cork, 5562.
Gurtenphillip (co. Wex.?), 6689.
Gurthen, Queen's co., 5462.
Gurtin, co. Car., 5948, 6467.
Gurtin (co. Kilk.?), 6566.
Gurtin, King's co., 6766.
Gurtin (Gortin), Queen's co., 1827, 5868, 6661.
Gurtin (co. Tip.?), 5179.
Gurtin an labriho (Gurtinalabrill), co. Cav., 5488.
Gurtinenasky (co. Gal.?), 4797.
Gurtinearde (Gurtevoard), co. Cork, 5582.
Gurtine, co. Cork, 5511, 6626, 6642.
Gurtine (co. Kilk.?), 1526, 5144.
Gurtine—Guertine (co. Kilk. or Tip.), 5654, 6704.
Gurtine (co. Long.?), 5459.
Gurtine (co. Sligo?), 4487.
Gurtinenchelly (co. Lim.?), 6615.
Gurtine a Kaill, co. Long., 5664.
Gurtine Malovrane, co. Tip., 5654.
Gurtinegaple, King's co., 556, 1664.
Gurtinegallo, Queen's co., 1829.
Gurtinenahomana, co. Cork, 4561.
Gurtinemoneso—Gurtynamonean, King's co., 556, 1654.
Gurtinenonee—Gurtynamonce, King's co., 556, 1654.
Gurtinamonan, King's co., 5459.

INDEX TO FIANTS—ELIZABETH.

Gurtinemishleigh (co. Lim. ?), [illegible].
Gurtinerowe (Gurtenerroe), co. Cork, [illegible].
Gurtines — Gurtins (co. Kilk. ?), 1894, [illegible], [illegible].
Gurtines (co. Tip. ?), [illegible].
Gurtin Rice, co. Wex., [illegible].
Gurtin Roe, co. Kerry, [illegible].
Gurtins (co. Kerry ?), [illegible].
Gurtins (co. Tip. ?), [illegible].
Gurtintubbered (co. Lim. ?), [illegible].
Gurtinvoline, co. Tip., [illegible].
Gurtinetobred (co. Cork ?), [illegible].
Gurtowenbogan, co. Long., [illegible].
Gurtigan, co. Tip., [illegible].
Gurtyn, co. Gal., [illegible].
Gurtyn (Gortean), co. Kild., [illegible].
Gurtyn, Queen's co., [illegible].
Gurtyn (co. Westm. ?), [illegible].
Gurtyne, co. Kilk., [illegible].
Gurtyne, co. Wex., [illegible].
Gurtynegreno—Gurtyne Gyene, Queen's co., [illegible], [illegible].
Gurtynemenas. See Gurtinemonane.
Gurtynemenan. See Gurtinemane.
Gurtynerowe (Gurtenerrow), co. Cork, [illegible], [illegible].
Gurtynesheanlan — Gurtyneshenlan (King's co. ?), [illegible], 1854.
Gurtyneskeane, co. Wat., [illegible].
Gurtynemane, King's co., [illegible].
Gurtynrohen (Kings co. ?), [illegible].
Gurtynn, co. Kilk., [illegible].
Gurtynn, co. Tip., [illegible].
Gurtyrymshowry (co. Cork ?), [illegible].
Guryleadra (co. Kerry ?), [illegible].
Guydon or standard bearer, [illegible].
Guyn, John. See Gwynn.
Gwaniffe, Donogh, Murogh, and Rory m'Teig [illegible], pardon, [illegible].
Gwallys, Nicholas O'Connor, murder of, [illegible].
Gwere, Nicholas, pardon, [illegible].
„ Shane, [illegible].
Gwerr, Maurice fitz Edmond, pardon, [illegible].
Gwerre, Edmund, pardon, [illegible].
Gwerriestown (co. Tip. ?), [illegible].
Gwerrine, John, [illegible].
Gwery, John, [illegible].
Gwigin, Dermot and Donell m'Connor I., pardon, [illegible].
„ Hugh m'Connor I., pardon, [illegible].
Gwire, Dermot m'Edm. I., pardon, [illegible].
„ Dermot m'Melaughlen I., pardon, [illegible].
„ Donogho m'Philip I., pardon, [illegible].
„ Phill m'Donell I., pardon, [illegible].
„ Teige m'Donogho I., pardon, [illegible].
Gwiade Herbert, co. Kerry, seignory called, [illegible].
Gwoly, Henry oge, pardon, [illegible].
Gwrtynemore, Queen's co., [illegible].
Gwyer, Henry, pardon, [illegible].
Gwy alias Denbrick, Henry, pardon, [illegible].
Gwyn, Tho., pardon, [illegible].
Gwyne, Ellen ny, pardon, [illegible].
„ Onory ny, pardon, [illegible].
Gwyne, Maurice, pardon, [illegible].
Gwyneconnagh, [illegible]. See Gayvoneconnaghe.
Gwynn—Guin—Guyn, John, presentations, [illegible], [illegible], [illegible], [illegible].
Gwynne, John, grant of a wardship to, [illegible].
„ Richard, lease, [illegible].
Gwynneth, Owen, pardon, [illegible].
Gwyre, Redmond, pardon, [illegible].
Gwyroneclynmoriarie, co. Clare, [illegible].
Gybb, John, keeper of gaol at Waterford, [illegible].
Gybbensare, co. Kild., [illegible].
Gybbeston, co. Meath, [illegible].
Gybbon. See Gibbon.
Gybbones, Wm., robbed, [illegible].
Gybbons Shepbotwn, co. Kilk., [illegible].
Gybsey, Tho., pardon, [illegible].
Gybon, Margaret ny Thomas ny, pardon, [illegible].
Gyboon Gibbon duff fitz Tho., pardon, [illegible].
Gybons wood, co. Wex., [illegible].
Gyollagh, Callaghan, pardon, [illegible].
Gyffard—Gifford, Richard, capt., marriage settlement, [illegible]; land surrender, [illegible]; lease, [illegible].
Gyfford's Grove in Kilmainham, co. Dub., [illegible], [illegible].
Gyhenle, Gormely, pardon, [illegible].
Gyleaghe—Gylleaghe—Gylky (Guileagh), co. Wat., [illegible], [illegible]; chapel, [illegible].
Gylgoyre (Kilgabriel), co. Wat., [illegible].
Gylow alias Sylye, pardon, [illegible].
Gyllaagh (or Gilloagh, co. Gal.), [illegible].
Gylleaghe—Gylky. See Gyleaghe.
Gyllreskly, co. Ross., [illegible].
Gyllenalyaly (co. Cork ?), [illegible].
Gylleyabbey. See Gillabbey.
Gylluy, Dorman rowe m'Shane I., pardon, [illegible].
Gylygduffe alias Power, Rowland, pardon, [illegible].
Gylton—Gyltons. See Gilton.
Gylton (Gillitown), co. Meath, [illegible].
Gyltons. See Gilton.
Gyrane (co. Cork ?), [illegible], [illegible].
Gyrtie. See Girte.
Gyrryloe (Garryclone, co. Wat.), [illegible].
Gyrwicaghe, Shane, pardon, [illegible].

INDEX TO FIANTS—ELIZABETH.

Habart—Habard—Habert:
" David, pardon, 3478, [illegible].
" Edm. fitz Morish, pardon, [illegible].
" Francis, pardon to widow of, 1530. *See* Harbert.
" John fitz Morish, pardon, [illegible], [illegible].
" Morish, pardon, 3474.
" Ulliack, pardon, [illegible].
Habbarde, John roe, pardon, [illegible].
Habergeon of mail used in county levies, [illegible].
Habergestowne, co. Louth, [illegible].
Habert. *See* Habart.
Hacket—Hackett—Hacked—Hackole—Hackuth:
" Amiasco, pardon, [illegible], 4744.
" David, pardon, [illegible], [illegible].
" Dermod, pardon, [illegible].
" Edmund, pardon, [illegible], [illegible], [illegible], [illegible], [illegible], [illegible], [illegible].
" Edm., license to make aqua vitæ, [illegible].
" Edw., pardon, [illegible].
" Ellen, pardon, [illegible].
" James, house in Fethard, [illegible]; pardon, [illegible], [illegible].
" John, pardon, 1842, [illegible], [illegible], [illegible], [illegible], 3134, [illegible], [illegible].
" John (son of Wm.), premises in Cashel, [illegible]; pardon, [illegible].
" Meiler, pardon, [illegible], [illegible].
" Morish, pardon, [illegible].
" Nicholas, pardon, [illegible], [illegible].
" Nicholas, license to make aqua vitæ, [illegible].
" Oliver, pardon, [illegible], [illegible], [illegible], [illegible], [illegible], [illegible].
" Patrick, pardon, [illegible], [illegible], [illegible], [illegible], [illegible], [illegible], [illegible].
" Patr., license to make aqua vitæ, [illegible].
" Peirs, pardon, [illegible], [illegible], [illegible].
" Peter, pardon, [illegible]; pardon to son, [illegible].
" Philip, pardon, [illegible], [illegible], [illegible], [illegible], [illegible], [illegible], [illegible].
" Redmond, pardon, [illegible], [illegible], [illegible], [illegible].
" Richard (of Fethard), cosen., [illegible]; a trustee, [illegible]; land in his tenure, [illegible].
" Richard, pardon, [illegible], [illegible], [illegible], [illegible], [illegible], [illegible], [illegible], [illegible].
" Rich. fitz John, pardon, [illegible], [illegible].
" Rob., premises in Cashel, [illegible].
" Rob., pardon, [illegible], [illegible], [illegible], [illegible].
" Theobald, pardon, [illegible].
" Tho., chaplain, [illegible].
" Tho., husband, co. Dub., [illegible].
Hacked, Thomas, pardon, [illegible], [illegible], [illegible].
" Ullick m'Tybbot, alias Machteaske, pardon, [illegible].
" Walter, pardon, 1671, [illegible], [illegible], [illegible], [illegible], [illegible], [illegible].
" William (in-grees of Cashel), [illegible].
" William, pardon, [illegible], 1360, 1364, [illegible], [illegible], [illegible], [illegible], [illegible].
Hackuth—Hackethe. *See* Hacked.
Hackeston, co. Dub., [illegible].
Hacketstown, co. Tip., [illegible].
Hackeston, co. Wat., [illegible].
Hackett. *See* Hacket.
Hackolston, co. Car., 4132.
Hackney, reserved as rent, [illegible].
Hacknosalany[illegible], co. Down, [illegible].
Hacroy, co. Down, [illegible].
Hacroyne, co. Down, [illegible].
Hacy, John, alias Lacy Walo, pardon, [illegible].
Hadgor, Nich., pardon, [illegible].
" Rob., pardon, [illegible].
Hadsor, James, pardon, [illegible].
Hafferton, 6411. *See* Hamerdston.
Hagard, co. Gal., [illegible], [illegible].
Hagbuttier—hagbutter. *See* Arquebusiers.
Haggard (co. Ross.?), [illegible].
Haggard, co. Wex., [illegible], [illegible].
Haggardo, co. Louth, manor, [illegible].
Haggart, [illegible].
Haggart, co. Gal., [illegible].
Haghnus, Jono [illegible] ny, pardon, [illegible].
Haghveyty, co. Tip., [illegible].
Haghyerista, Meragh m'Ownie I, pardon, [illegible].
Hagoilbagh, co. Down, [illegible].
Hahir, Patr., pardon, [illegible].
Hahyn, Margaret ny, pardon, [illegible].
Hale, Stephen, vicar of S. Patrick's, Wexford, [illegible].
" Tho., pardon, [illegible].
Hailly, Cornelius, pardon, [illegible].
Haimston, co. Kild., [illegible].
Hakarford, co. Down or Ant., [illegible].
Hakonus near Kylharnik, King's co., [illegible].
Hakett, John, pardon, [illegible].
Hakill (co. Mayo?, perhaps Achill), [illegible].
Hakoyrnyhallamagho, co. Down, [illegible].
Hakoyrnynmavill (co. Antrim or Down), [illegible].
Hale (Balrounde Hall or Loftus Hall?), co. Wex., 3154.
Halfepeny, Conor, pardon, [illegible].
" Hugh, pardon, [illegible].
" John, pardon, [illegible].
" Mahulin, pardon, [illegible].
" Patr., pardon, [illegible].
" Tirelagh, pardon, [illegible].
Half-face money, [illegible]; value in sterling, [illegible].
Halfpeny or Halpeny, certain of the name excepted from a pardon, [illegible].
" Patr., pardon, [illegible].

INDEX TO FIANTS—ELIZABETH.

Hale. *See* Haly.
Hall, Thomas, pardon, 2761.
" Walter, 3814.
" William, pardon, 1906, 2786.
Hallaghane, Joan ny, pardon, [illegible].
Hallahane, Donogh m'Donell Y, pardon, [illegible].
Halloran, Shane m'Wm. I., pardon, [illegible].
Halligont, Edm., pardon, [illegible].
Halliganiston, co. Kerry, [illegible].
Hallyhan, Edmund, pardon, [illegible].
" John, death of, [illegible].
Halligan, Owen m'Cormock I, pardon, [illegible].
Hallon, Wm., pardon, [illegible].
Hallowston, co. Meath, [illegible].
Hallowside (time of All Hallows, a rent term), [illegible].
Hallorane, Moroe ny, pardon, [illegible].
Hallowe, Anisse ny, pardon, [illegible].
Hally. *See* Haly.
Hally, Richard, sovereign of Kilmallock, pardon, 1469.
Halman, Clement, merchant, [illegible].
Halpenny, John (or Harpenny), pardon, [illegible].
" Patr., pardon, [illegible].
Halpeny, James, pardon, [illegible].
Halpeny or Halfpeny, certain of the name excepted from a pardon, [illegible].
Halpine, John, pardon, [illegible].
Halton, co. Meath, [illegible].
Halverston alias Ballyhallway, co. Kild., [illegible].
Halviston, co. Kild., [illegible].
Halvorston, co. Kild., [illegible].
Halwetson, co. Kild., [illegible].
Haly, Morgho m'Rory Y, pardon (O'Hanly), [illegible].
Haly—Hale—Hally—Halye:
" David, pardon to son, [illegible].
" Edm., pardon, [illegible].
" Katherine, aqua vitae license, [illegible].
" Nicholas, a student, pardon, [illegible]; learned in the law, commissions, [illegible].
" Rich., burgess of Cashel, pardon, [illegible]; comm., [illegible]; premises held by, [illegible].
" Rich., sovereign of Kilmallock, 1458.
" Tho., [illegible].
Halye lough (on Shannon), [illegible].
Halyvaine—Halyvayne—Halyvane, Conoghor m'Teig I, and others of the name, pardon, [illegible].
Haman, Ralph. *See* Hamond.
Hamanstowne, co. Lim., [illegible].
Hamler, John, comm., [illegible].
Hamlen—Hamlyn, Robert, pardon, [illegible].
Hamleston, co. Meath, [illegible].
Hamlyn. *See* Hamlen.
Hammondstown. *See* Hamonston.
Hamond—Hamon—Haman—Hammond—Hamonde—Hamone—Hawmond:
" John, 1714.
" Lawrence, constable of castle of Trim, [illegible]; late controller of customs of Dublin, [illegible]; comm., [illegible]; pardon, [illegible]; pardon at his suit, [illegible]; leases, [illegible].
" Morryce, [illegible].
" Ralph, usher to the president of Munster, [illegible]; grant of a wardship, [illegible]; license of absence, [illegible].
" Rob., lease, [illegible].
Hamonston, co. Louth, 1949.
Hamonston—Thamondston (Hammondstown), co. Meath, [illegible].
Hamorackstown, co. Wat. or Cork, [illegible].
Hampton, (——), comm., [illegible].
Hampton, Rich., [illegible].
Hampton court, letters dated at, [illegible], 1497, 1527, 1543, 1561, 1568, [illegible], 1573.
Hanaghan, Morihirtagh m'Teige I, pardon, [illegible].
Hanaper, clerk of. *See* Allen, Tho.; Alford, Lancelot.
Hanconnelhane, co. Cav., [illegible].
Hanckardston, co. Dub., [illegible].
Hancocke—Hancock—Handcock:
" Katherine, [illegible].
" Nicholas, lease, [illegible]; surrender, [illegible].
" William, license [illegible]; pardon, [illegible].
Handlon, Rob., pardon, [illegible].
Handmaide (queen's ship), capt. of, [illegible].
Hanefran (co. Kerry ?), [illegible].
Haneghan, Conor m'Shane Y, pardon, [illegible].
Hanging, man pardoned who had survived, [illegible].
Hanigloghlane, co. Down, [illegible].
Hankard, John, pardon, [illegible].
Hankes, Thomas, lease, [illegible].
Hanley, Hugh, pardon, [illegible].
" Richard, 1714.
" Una ny, pardon, [illegible].
Hanlon, Owen, [illegible].
Hanlowe (O'Hanlon), country of (co. Armagh), [illegible].
Hanly, Cornelius, pardon, [illegible].
" Derby, pardon, [illegible].
" Richard, pardon, [illegible].
" Gillernew m'Dermott I, and others of the name, pardon, [illegible]. *See* O'Hanly.

INDEX TO FIANTS.—ELIZABETH.

Hanmer, Meredith, S.T.P., presentation, 5867, 6313, 5346.
Hanmoroga, Nich. oge, pardon, 6463.
Hann, Rich., 2914.
Hanny, John, 1782.
Hannyne, Moriah Mac David, pardon, 6487.
Hanragtan, Peter, 2391.
Hanraghane, David, pardon, 5434.
„ Patr., pardon, 5434.
„ Wm., pardon, 5434.
Hanraighane, Donogho m'Conogher Y, pardon, 4472.
Hanrait, Owne oy, pardon, 4217.
Hanregane, Richard, pardon, 2286.
Hanreghan, James, pardon, 5363.
Hanrighane, David, pardon, 1517.
Hanrohayne, Conner oge, pardon, 112.
Hans, John, homicide of, 4834.
Hanse and other liberties granted to Dingle, 4806.
Hanswell grange, co. Kilk., 1175.
Hany rectory, in M'William Bork's country, 1464, 3413.
Hanyo (Annies?), co. Mayo, 5418.
Hanygals, co. Down, 4257.
Hanyn, Onary oy, pardon, 6432.
Hanyne, John, pardon, 6284.
Hap Hazard, seignory called, 6478.
Hare, Folmie m'Cormock I, pardon, 4633.
Harbard—Harbards. See Harbert.
Harbardeston. See Harberiston.
Harbardiston. See Harbertiston.
Harbard's land in Kilmainham. See Harbert's land.
Harbardston, co. Meath. See Harbertiston.
Harbart—Harbarts. See Harbert.
Harbartiston. See Harbertiston.
Harbartiston, King's co., 2912.
Harbart's land. See Harbert's land.
Harbartston. See Harbertston, co. Meath.
Harberd. See Harbert.
Harberdstown. See Harbertston.
Harbersten — Harberstowne. See Harbertiston.
Harbert—Harbart— Harbard — Harbarte — Harberd—Harbart—Herbert:
„ Charles, grant of land, 5215; commission, 5914, 5891.
„ David, pardon, 4232, 5414.
„ Edm., clerk, pardon, 4236.
„ Edm., pardon, 4089, 4471, 4533, 6481, 6475, 6394.
„ Edw., lease to Dublin, 1671.
„ Edw. (afterwards knight), 2619, 5522; sheriff of King's co., 4463; of Cavan, 4481; commissions, 4656, 5128, 5311, 5874, 5931; pardon, 5168, 5782.
„ Ellen, pardon, 6427.
Harbert, Francis, knight, 297; pardon, 11; commissions, 516, 328, 738, 33, 412, 621, 523. See Herbert.
„ Francis (son of Nich.), 2516, 2512.
„ Garrett, pardon, 4468.
„ Henry (of Colbandstown), pardon, 3426; wardship of heir, 5921.
„ Henry (son of Nich.), 2514, 3222; commission, 4980.
„ James, pardon, 6487.
„ Jasper, 2518, 2522.
„ John (of Collandston), wardship, 2093; sheriff of co. Kildare, pardon, 5772, 5778.
„ John, pardon, 6451.
„ Katherine, pardon, 2519, 2222.
„ Maurice, pardon, 4268.
„ Morris, pardon, 6494.
„ Nicholas (of Monasterevin), commissions, 522, 863, 2117, 2243, 2444, 2531, 4785; grants of land, 2519, 2922; surrender, 2915; lease, 443; pardon, 5365.
„ Nich., 2518.
„ Nich. (of Colbandstown), pardon, 6773.
„ Richard, 2518, 2522.
„ Shane, pardon, 1542.
„ Ulig, pardon, 2542.
„ William, 2518, 2523.
Harbertiston—Harbardiston—Harbartiston—Harberstowne, co. Kild., 1216, 1274, 1122, 1275, 3431, 5863; rectory, 3871.
Harbertston—Harbardeston—Harbardston—Harbertiston — Harbertston — Harbartston — Harberdstown (Herbertstown), co. Meath, 279, 1174, 1463, 1777, 3344, 3826, 5873.
Harbert's — Harbard's — Harbart's land, in Kilmainham, 1546.
Hardiman's Statute of Kilkenny, reference to, 5441.
Hardinge—Harding:
„ Edm., pardon, 2030.
„ Ellen, pardon, 6440.
„ John, pardon, 6274.
„ Mich., grant of a wardship, 4485; lease, 5222; lands in his tenure, 5460; grant of lands to his wife, 5611, 6370; pardon, 4238, 6448, 6728.
„ Thomas, grant of land, 1554.
Hardman, Peter, pardon, 3037.
Hardwood — Hardwold — Harwood alias Kilcroe, co. Meath, 673, 946, 1518, 4377-8, 5924.
Hare, Donogh m'Tumultie I, pardon, 4783.
Harem, Nicholas, esq., lease, 636.
„ Wm., pardon, 5438.
Haropony, Anthony, chaplain of Garrne, 2264.

INDEX TO FIANTS—ELIZABETH.

Harosmeadio, co. Wex., 6787.
Harostion. See Harbstowne, co. Wat.
Harostown. See Harristown, co. Kild.
Harry, [car]l, co. Down, 4337.
Harford weal in Wales, 3160.
Harford, James, pardon, 6412.
Hariesion—Harlestone. See Harriston, co. Meath.
Harington—Haringuion. See Harrington.
Hariston. See Harrison.
Haristown—Harruston, co. Car., 878, 6486.
Haristowne—Haroston, co. Wat., [illegible], 3486, [illegible].
Harlestoon (Harlesktowne), co. Meath, 3128.
Harlotlston, co. Meath, 944.
Harman, Nich., [illegible].
„ Rich., pardon, 5142.
Haroan, Moriertagh m'Dermoda, pardon, 4554.
Harnel, Donell m'Nimaul, pardon, 4617.
Harnell, Conoghor m'Donell I, pardon, 4617.
Harnor, John, pardon, 4619.
Harold—Haroide. See Harrold.
Harolds country, co. Dublin, 1581.
Haroll, John. See Harrold.
Harpanny—Harpeny, John, clerk of the castle chamber, 1422, 7148; second chamberlain of exchequer, [illegible], [illegible]; clerk of the ordnance, 2962, 3510.
Harpenny or Halpenny, John, pardon, [illegible].
Harpeny, John. See Harpenny.
Harpersione. See Harpurston.
Harpers to be banished or punished, 1864, 1494, 1565, 1835, 2080, 2312, 3156, [illegible], [illegible].
Harpers pardoned, 784, 1207, 1225, 1728, [illegible], 2351, 3153, [illegible], 4058, 4431, [illegible], 4794, [illegible], 4971, [illegible], 6477, 5104, 6454, 5607, 6136, 6541, 5660, 6383, 5956, 6012, 6416, 6461, 6727, 6734, 6781, 6782.
Harpers lease, co. Meath, 6316.
Harperston—Harparestone—Harpeston, co. Wex., [illegible], [illegible], 1763, 4458.
Harperstone, co. Kerry, 4615.
Harpesion, 1763. See Harpurstun.
Harpmaker pardoned, 5464.
Harpoll—Harpole—Harpolle—Harpoole—Harpooll—Harpoulle—Haripolle—Haripoole:
„ Grane, wife of Rob., [illegible].
„ Helen, 5917.
„ Robert, constable of Carlow castle, 1188, [illegible]; commissions, 963, 1308, 1679, 2101, 2117, 2147, 2178, 2348, 2444, 2776, [illegible], 3450, 5134, 6731; writ discharging from appearance in court, [illegible]; grants of land, &c., [illegible], 613, 1693, [illegible], 5184; surrender, [illegible]; license to alien, [illegible]; leases, [illegible], 1234, 1609, 2173, 4230, [illegible]; pardons, 630, 1168, 1566, 1788, [illegible], 3467, [illegible], 4321, [illegible]; pardon at his suit, 2873; house in Maryborough, [illegible].
„ Thomas, pardon, [illegible].
„ Walter, dean of Leighlin, 3193, [illegible]; alienation to, [illegible].
„ William (son of Rob.), constable of Carlow, [illegible]; license of absence, [illegible]; comm., [illegible]; lease, 4078; pardon, 3467, [illegible], [illegible], 4321, 5161, 6775.
Harporigallon alias Heaby Crany, co. Down, 4337.
Harpper, John, pardon, [illegible].
Harrald, Anne. See Harrold.
Harrels, Edw., pardon, 3434.
Harrelston, King's co., [illegible].
Harrengton alias O'Heagertye, John m'Teige, pardon, [illegible].
Harres, John, lease, 1625.
Harreson, Philip, pardon, [illegible].
Harreston. See Haristown, co. Car.
Harreston. See Harristown, co. Kild.
Harreston. See Harriston, co. Meath.
Harreston Barrel—Harrestonbarrell. See Harristone Barrel.
Harrestowne. See Harristowne.
Harrestowne—Harryestowne (Harristown, co. Louth), 1784, 4883.
Harrighan, Thomas duf m'Richard, pardon, [illegible].
Harries, Wm., pardon, 3494.
Harristown (co. Wex. 7) 81.
Harriestone barrel—Harriestonbarrell. See Harristone Barrel.
Harrington—Harlngton—Harington—Harrington—Harryngton, Henry (afterwards knight), seneschal of O'Byrne's country, 3198, 5612; commissions, 2548, 2912, 3080, 3480, 4418, 4817, 5134, 5178, 6236, 6354, 6452, 6837, 5668; grants of land, &c., 3705-16, 5078-81, 5116; leases, 3698, 3698, [illegible], 5334, [illegible], 5379; grant of a wardship, [illegible]; party to a bond, [illegible]; pardon, 3643, [illegible]; pardon at his suit, 4441; license of absence, [illegible], 5299.
Harrisho, George, pardon, 5162.
Harrison, Joseph, pardon, 5373.
„ Rob., grants of land, 4848, 6877; surrender, 4876; release of money due to him, [illegible]; lease, 6653.
Harriston—Hariston (King's co. 7), 5803, 5267.
Harriston—Hariston—Harlston—Harreston, co. Meath, 3484, 3573, 4157, 5806, [illegible]; grant, 5577.
Harristown—Harstown—Harreston—Harrestowne, co. Kild., 1176, 2644, 4258, 4304, 5761, 6456; castle and lands, [illegible].

Harristone Barret — Harreston Barret — Harriston barret, co. Meath, [illegible]; grant, [illegible]; [illegible], [illegible].

Harristown, co. Kild. See Hourlowton, Harriston.

Harristown, co. Louth. See Harrestowne.

Harrodes country. See Harroldes.

Harroell, Richard, pardon, 1817.

Harrold—Harold—Harolde—Harell—Harrald—Harrolde—Harroll:

" Anne, pardon, [illegible].

" Edm., pardon, 4027, 5181, 5401, [illegible], [illegible].

" Fergananym, pardon, 412, 870, [illegible].

" Geoffrey, pardon, 878, [illegible].

" James, pardon, [illegible], [illegible], 4118, 5736.

" John, pardon, [illegible], [illegible], [illegible], 6101, [illegible].

" Nich., pardon, [illegible], [illegible], [illegible].

" Oliver, pardon, [illegible].

" Patrick, pardon, 1644.

" Redmund, pardon, [illegible].

" Richard, house in Dublin, 1311.

" Rich., pardon, [illegible], [illegible].

" Robert, pardon, [illegible], [illegible].

" Thomas, pardon, [illegible], [illegible], [illegible].

" Walter, pardon, 870, [illegible], [illegible], [illegible], 5737, [illegible].

" Walter, second engrosser of Exchequer, [illegible], [illegible]; lease, [illegible], [illegible]; pardon, [illegible]; security, [illegible].

" William, [illegible], [illegible].

" William, pardon, 117, 870, [illegible], [illegible], [illegible], [illegible], [illegible], [illegible], [illegible].

" Wm., pardon to servant of, [illegible].

Harroldes—Harrodes country, co. Dub., 1691, [illegible].

Harroldes grange (Harolds grange), co. Dub., [illegible], [illegible].

Harroldstown, co. Dub., [illegible].

Harrols, Rich., [illegible].

Harrynstowne. See Harrestowne, co. Louth.

Harryngton, Henry. See Harrington.

Harrold—Harnolde, William, 1772, [illegible].

Harte, Eustace, lease, [illegible].

" John (of Trim), [illegible]; pardon, [illegible].

" —Hart, John (merchant of Cashel), [illegible]; pardon, [illegible].

Hartesdon (co. Meath ?), [illegible].

Hartestowne—Hartestowne alias [illegible] (Hartstown, co. Dub.), [illegible], [illegible].

Hartford, Edw., smith of the ordnance, [illegible], [illegible], [illegible].

Hartpolle—Hartpoole. See Harpoll.

Hartwell—Artwell—Artowell, co. Kild., 1172, [illegible], [illegible], [illegible], [illegible].

Harveston (co. Kilk. ?), [illegible].

Harveston — Horweston, co. Wex., [illegible], [illegible].

Harvey—Harvie—Harvye:

" George, [illegible] by Hugh m'[illegible], 878; constable of Maryborough castle, [illegible], [illegible], [illegible]; comm., [illegible]; house of alnmses, [illegible]; pardon, 4194.

" Johanne, pardon, [illegible].

" Philip, constable of Maryborough castle, [illegible].

" Tho., pardon, [illegible].

Harwood. See Hardwood.

Harynall, John roe, pardon, [illegible].

Haselwoode, Andrew, pardon, [illegible].

Hasquine, John, [illegible].

Hassard, Jenkyn, pardon, [illegible].

Hassolestowne, co. Louth, 1752.

Hassardstowne—Hassardeston (Hassardstown), co. Dub., [illegible], [illegible].

Hassle, Downe, pardon, [illegible].

Hassynaston, co. Lim. or Cork, [illegible].

Hat manufacture, [illegible].

Hatche, Rich., [illegible].

Hathy Casey (probably a ford on Causeway water flowing into Carlingford lough, co. Down), 4317.

Hatton, sir Christopher, lord chancellor of England, a Munster undertaker, [illegible]; grant of land, [illegible].

Haukeeston, co. Meath, [illegible].

Haule, the, co. Down, 4327.

Haule, Edw., pardon, [illegible].

Havering — Haveringe — Haveryng, letters dated at, [illegible], [illegible], [illegible], [illegible], [illegible], [illegible].

Hawallan, co. Down, [illegible].

Hawestowne, co. Kild., [illegible].

Hawey, Philip mo, pardon, [illegible].

Hawghrigan, James, pardon, [illegible].

Hawks, export of, prevented, [illegible], [illegible], [illegible]; license to take to England, [illegible]; those breeding on lands granted, reserved to crown, [illegible]; reserved as rent, [illegible], [illegible].

Hawlaght, co. Mon., [illegible].

Hawmond, Laurence. See Hammond.

Haworth, Nich., pardon, [illegible].

Haws or Haus, John, English liberty, [illegible].

Hay, authority to take up, [illegible], [illegible], [illegible], [illegible], 4172, [illegible], [illegible]; for deputy's horses, [illegible], [illegible], [illegible], [illegible]; rate allowed for making, [illegible], 4172, [illegible], [illegible], [illegible]; hay for deputy, price paid for, [illegible].

Hay. See Haye.

Hay, John m'Hooky I, pardon, 1480.

Haydom, James, pardon, [illegible].

Haydon, John, pardon, [illegible].

Haydon, James, provost marshal for Munster, comm., [illegible].

Haye—Hay:

" Andrew, pardon, [illegible].

" Gemel, [illegible].

INDEX TO FIANTS—ELIZABETH.

Hayo—Hay:
" John, pardon, [illegible], 6217.
" Matthew (of Tacumshane), sheriff of Wexford, 23; comm., 67; pardon, 1749.
" Nich., pardon, 6183.
" Patrick, pardon, 1910.
" Richard, pardon, [illegible], 6128.
" Rob., pardon, 4617.
" Robert, house in Dublin, 1811.
" Stephen, vicar of S. Patrick, Wexford, 437, [illegible].
" Thomas, pardon, 4541.
" Walter, pardon at suit of, 6412.
" Wm., pardon, 3412, 6210, [illegible]41.
Hayes, Griffith, porter, Dublin castle, 6748.
Hayeshaggarde — Hayeshaggort — Hayshaggard, co. Wex., 782, 5180, 6412.
Haylle, Richard, sovereign of Kilmallock, [illegible].
Hayne, William, house in Dublin, 1811.
Haynestown (Hynestown), co. Dub., 1480.
Haynestown, co. Kild. See Haynestown.
Haynston, co. Dub., 831.
Haystown, co. Meath. See Heiston.
Hazardstown, co. Dub. See Hazardston.
Hatowe, George, pardon, 6712.
" Nich., pardon, 6712.
" Patr., pardon, 6712.
" Rob., pardon, 6712.
Hea—Hee:
" Conoghor m'Rowry I, pardon, 4677.
" Conoghor m'Teige Y, pardon, 6566.
" Conoghor m'Tho. Y, pardon, 4616.
" Conor m'Dermod I, pardon, 5071.
" Derby m'Shane I, pardon, 4616.
" Dermod m'Shane I, pardon, 4574.
" Donell m'Dermody I, pardon, [illegible].
" Hellen ny, pardon, 1744.
" John fitz John, pardon, [illegible].
" Mahown m'Conoghor I, pardon, 4626.
" Morris m'Shane I, pardon, [illegible].
" Rich. m'Tho., pardon, [illegible].
" Rob. fitz Edm., pardon, [illegible].
" Teig m'Shane I, pardon, 4616, 4677.
" Wm. fitz Teig, pardon, [illegible].
Head, William, [illegible].
Headon, Henry fitz Mologhlen, pardon, 4977.
Headin, Rich., 6584.
Heaghragh (co. Kilk. ?), [illegible].
Heagirtie, Katherine ny, pardon, 6618.
Healoghane, Conoghor roe m'Mahowne, pardon, [illegible].
Healy, Connor, pardon, [illegible].
" John, pardon, [illegible].
" Wm., pardon, [illegible].
Heargirtie alias O'Heagirtie, Dermod, pardon, [illegible].
Hearne, Henry, pardon, [illegible].
Hearon, Nicholas. See Heron.
Heartie, Dermod, pardon, [illegible].
Heath as fuel, [illegible].
Heath—Heathe, John, registrar of Prerogative court, and of Faculties, and collector of fines, 5344, [illegible], [illegible].
Heatheston (Heathstown, co. Westm. ?), [illegible].
Heath moor—Hethe more, co. Kild., [illegible], [illegible].
Heathton. See Heathtowne.
Heathton—Heighton (Heathtown), co. Meath, 1480, 2464.
Heathtowne or Heathton, co. Dub., 6421.
Heckye, Patr., pardon, [illegible].
Hedan, James, pardon, [illegible].
Hedian, Philip, [illegible], [illegible].
Heding, Nicholas, pardon, [illegible].
Hedles cross near Calragh, co. Dub., [illegible].
H[axlon], Edmund, lands of, granted, [illegible].
Hedrington. See Hetherington.
Hee. See Hea and O'Hea.
Heeman, Wm., pardon, [illegible].
Hegheane, Donogh m'Shane I, pardon, 4772.
Heiden, Wm., treasurer Holy Trinity, Dublin, 6642.
Heiggen, Cornelius, pardon, [illegible].
Heigham, Tho., pardon, [illegible].
Heighton. See Heathton.
Heike, Tho., pardon, 6018.
Heimbie lands, co. Meath, 6747.
Heleyn, Arthur, pardon, [illegible].
Helring, Cairo A., pardon, [illegible].
Helron, Nicholas. See Heron.
Heiston (Haystown), co. Meath, [illegible].
Hekey, Conor, pardon, [illegible].
Helen Horse mead, Dublin, [illegible].
Hellford, Maurice, pardon, [illegible].
Helle, Donnys, pardon, [illegible].
" Elizabeth, pardon, [illegible].
" William, pardon, [illegible].
Helliers impressed for works, [illegible].
Helly, John, pardon, [illegible].
Helmeshore, Bryce, pardon, [illegible].
Helmeshore, Phelym m'Carterie, pardon, [illegible].
Heloighe in manor of Carlow, [illegible].
Holy—Helye, Patrick, vicar of Oschill, 749; vicar of Oughterard, 787.
Helymrowe (co. Gal. ?), [illegible].
Helyn, Patrick. See Holy.
Hemmepare (co. Gal. ?), [illegible].
Hemerpin, Edm., pardon, [illegible].
Hemard (Queen's co. ?), 1178.
Hembery, David. See Hensbery.
Hene, Patr., pardon, [illegible].
Hene( ), Donald, pardon, [illegible].
Hender, John, pardon, [illegible].
Hensbery—Henbury—Henseby—Hensobrew, David, pardon, [illegible], 4527, [illegible], [illegible].
Henebre, Edmund (or Hynebrye), pardon, [illegible], [illegible].

Hemetire, Maurice, pardon, [illegible]; his son, [illegible]
„ Nicholas, pardon, [illegible]
„ Philip, pardon, [illegible]
Hemsley, David fitz Wm., pardon, [illegible]
Hemolie, Conoghor oy, pardon, [illegible]
Henoglantane (co. Tip. ?), [illegible]
Henely, Rich., pardon, [illegible]
Hense, David, pardon, [illegible]
Hensele, Tho., pardon, [illegible]
„ Tho. fitz Rich. E, pardon, [illegible]
Hennessy, David m'Tho. Y, pardon, [illegible]
„ Philip m'Tho. Y, pardon, [illegible]
Hengirtie (co. Cork ?), [illegible]
Henesbree—Hensobry, David. See Hensbery.
Henoleston, co. Meath, [illegible]
Henors, Rob., pardon, [illegible]
Henrys, Wm., pardon, [illegible]
Henreston. See Henrieston.
Henries land, co. Kerry, [illegible]
Henrieston, co. Kild., 1161.
Henrieston—Henreston (Harristown ?), co. Kild., [illegible]
Henrieston alias Haricston. See Harriston, co. Meath.
Henry VI., charter to barbers of Dublin recited, [illegible]
Henry VIII., supplemental fiants of reign, [illegible]
Henry logge, indenture, [illegible]
Henry, Gyellis ny, pardon, [illegible]
Henry—Henrye, John, chief serjeant of Connaught, [illegible]; lease, [illegible]
„ Katherin ny, pardon, [illegible]
Henshaw—Henshawe—Henshae, capt Tho., seneschal of Monaghan, [illegible]; commissions, [illegible]; pardon, [illegible]; lease, [illegible]
Herbard, Wm. boy, pardon, [illegible]
Herbart, Henry. See Herbert.
Herbert, Charles. See Harbert.
„ David, pardon, [illegible]
„ Edward. See Harbert.
„ Francis. See Harbert.
„ Gerald, pardon, [illegible]
„ James, pardon, [illegible]
„ Katherine, pardon, [illegible]
„ Moriah, pardon, [illegible]
„ Redmund, pardon, [illegible]
Herberte, sir William, land grant, [illegible]
Herbertstown, co. Meath. See Harbertstown.
Hereford, viscount. See Essex, W. earl of, [illegible]
Heresies and heretical opinions, cognizance of, by ecclesiastical commission, [illegible]
Heresies and infidelities included in pardon, [illegible]
Herford, Edw., pardon, [illegible]
Herithy, Tho. B[ ] m'Davy Y, pardon, [illegible]
Herman, John, chancellor of Christ church, [illegible]
Hern—Herne, Nicholas. See Heron.
Heron—Haron—Hearon—Heirun—Hern—Herne—Heron—Hoyron:
„ Alice, leases, [illegible]
„ Nicholas (afterwards knt.), sheriff of Carlow, [illegible]; seneschal of Wexford, [illegible]; late constable of manor of Ferns, [illegible]; part of co. Carlow under his rule, [illegible]; commissions, [illegible]; leases, [illegible]; licence to alien, [illegible]; residence of, [illegible]; pardon, [illegible]
„ William, constable, [illegible]; pardon, [illegible]; leases to his wife, [illegible]
Herrois, co. Tip., [illegible]
Herroley, James, pardon, [illegible]
Herrig, Wm., pardon, [illegible]
Herrings taken for army, [illegible]
„ customs payable, [illegible]
„ stolen, [illegible]
Herton, [illegible]. See Hessordston.
Herveston. See Harveston.
Hesko (co. Down or Antrim), [illegible]
Hesketh, Rob., [illegible]
„ Thomas, [illegible]
Hespinoss, Jaques de, denization, [illegible]
Hethe more. See Heath moor.
Hetherington—Etherington—Heirington—Hetherinton—Hetherington—Ithertington:
„ David, livery, [illegible]; grant of land, [illegible]; pardon, [illegible]
„ George (son of Patrick), livery, [illegible]
„ George, pardon, [illegible]
„ George (senior), pardon, [illegible]
„ Joukin, grant of land, [illegible]; lease, [illegible]; livery to heir, [illegible]
„ Patrick, grant of land, [illegible]; livery to son, [illegible]
„ Wm., pardon, [illegible]
Hetheringston, Patrick (see Hetherington), [illegible]
Hetherton, Joynkyn (see Hetherington), [illegible]
Hethoton, co. Westm., [illegible]
Hevarin, Margaret ny, pardon, [illegible]
Heverine, Giles ny, pardon, [illegible]
Hevyne, Grany, pardon, [illegible]
Howes, Rich., pardon, [illegible]

INDEX TO FIANTS—ELIZABETH.

Hewed, Charles, lease, [illegible].
Hewetson, Chr., treasurer, Holy Trinity, Dub., [illegible].
Hewrye, Eugene A., pardon, [illegible].
" Patrick A., pardon, [illegible].
Heydan, Peter, pardon, [illegible].
Heydison, Rich. fitz Peirs, pardon, [illegible].
Heydon, James, lease, [illegible].
" Wm., treasurer, Holy Trinity, Dub., [illegible].
Heykye, Connes, pardon, [illegible].
Heymoihe, Wm., pardon, [illegible].
Heye, Anney ny, pardon, [illegible].
Heyne, Dermot m'Tho. I., pardon, [illegible].
" One, son of, surrender of name of O'Heyne, [illegible].
Heynie, John, pardon, [illegible].
" Rich., [illegible].
Heyron, Nicholas. See Heron.
Heyslome, co. Wex., [illegible].
Heyther, John, pardon, [illegible].
Heyward, c. pardonal, [illegible].
Hiallhie, Donogh m'Tho. Y., pardon, [illegible].
" Wm. m'Donogh, pardon, [illegible].
Hiallhy, John, pardon, [illegible].
Hiallihie, Donogh m'Tho. I., pardon, [illegible].
" John oge, pardon, [illegible].
Hiallihy, Wm. m'Donoghow Y., pardon, [illegible].
Hiallyhy, Ellen ny Donell I., pardon, [illegible].
Hibbard, Morris, pardon, [illegible].
Hickie—Hickey—Hicky—Hickye:
" Anne, pardon, [illegible].
" Anstace, pardon, [illegible].
" Connor, pardon, [illegible].
" David, pardon, [illegible].
" Derby, pardon, [illegible].
" Donell, pardon, [illegible].
" Eneas, pardon, [illegible].
" Ferdorogh, pardon, [illegible].
" Hugh, pardon, [illegible].
" James, pardon, [illegible].
" Joan ny, pardon, [illegible].
" John, pardon, [illegible].
" John, surgeon, pardon, [illegible].
" Mahown, pardon, [illegible].
" Margaret, pardon, [illegible].
" Maurice, comm., [illegible].
" Morgan, pardon, [illegible].
" Morris, surgeon, pardon, [illegible].
" Morris, pardon, [illegible].
" Nane, pardon, [illegible].
" Nich., surgeon, pardon, [illegible].
" Nich., pardon, [illegible].
" Patrick, pardon, [illegible].
" Shane, pardon, [illegible].
" Tho., pardon, [illegible].
" Wm., surgeon, pardon, [illegible].
" Wm., pardon, [illegible].
Hickieston, co. Meath, [illegible].
Hicky—Hickye. See Hickie.
Hide, Arthur. See Hyde.
Hides, trade in, [illegible].
Hidrone. See Idrone.
Hiefinn, James fitz Walter, pardon, [illegible].
Hieralle, co. Wex., chapel, [illegible].
Hierlchie, Conoghor m'Hurly, pardon, [illegible].
Hierlehy, Ellen ny, pardon, [illegible].
Hierlihie, Shane m'Donald Y., pardon, [illegible].
Hifferan. See Ferney.
Hifferan, Conoghor m'Wm. I., pardon, [illegible].
" Feraghor m'Gilkrist, pardon, [illegible].
" Hugh m'Donell I., pardon, [illegible].
" Teig m'Hugh, pardon, [illegible].
" See Hyfferna.
Hifferane, Wm. m'Donogho I., pardon, [illegible].
Hifferaye, [illegible] ynr, pardon, [illegible].
" [illegible] ynr, pardon, [illegible].
Higan, Elly, pardon, [illegible].
Higanstowne, Queen's co., [illegible].
Higort, co. Lim., [illegible].
Higorle, co. Lim., [illegible].
Higgen, John B., pardon, [illegible].
Higgen, Gillerne A., pardon, [illegible].
" Onny ny, pardon, [illegible].
" Shane, pardon, [illegible].
" Shane A., pardon, [illegible].
" Una ny, pardon, [illegible].
Higgenstowne. See Higgenston.
Higgen, co. Ros., [illegible].
Higgensgardinge—Higinsgardins, co. Kilk., [illegible].
Higgenston—Higgenstowne—Higinston—Hygenston (Higginstown, co. Westm.), [illegible]. See also Ballyhiggen.
Higgenstowne, [illegible].
Higgens, Wm., pardon, [illegible].
Higgin, Rouse ny, pardon, [illegible].
" Tully, pardon, [illegible].
" See Higgens.
Higgins, King's co., [illegible].
Higginstown, co. Kilk. See Hyggenston.
Higginstown (co. Tipp.), [illegible]. See also Ballyhiggan.
Higginstown, co. Westm. See Ballyhiggen, Higgenston, Ballyhiggan.
High Commission for ecclesiastical causes. See Ecclesiastical Commission.
High Court Ecclesiastical. See Ecclesiastical Commission.
High Rath, co. Kilk., [illegible].
Hight, Katherine ni, pardon, [illegible].
Higins garden. See Higgensgardinge.
Higinston. See Higgenston.
Hiirdell, Donogh, pardon, [illegible].
Hikan, [illegible].

INDEX TO FIANTS—ELIZABETH.

Hilmeston, co. Meath, [illegible].
Hilsie, Maurice, physician, pardon, [illegible].
,, Nich., pardon, [illegible].
,, William, pardon, [illegible].
Hilrye, James m'Cormell, pardon, [illegible].
,, John, pardon, [illegible].
,, See Hyky.
Hilughne Glanfosky (co. Kerry ?), [illegible].
Hilcock—Hylcock, Anne, 1[illegible], [illegible].
,, Matthew, [illegible].
Hilcoke, Robert, death of, [illegible].
Hill, Geoffry, pardon, [illegible].
,, John, pardon, [illegible], [illegible].
,, Moyses or Moses, provost marshal in Clandeboy, pardon, [illegible]; sheriff of Antrim, lease, [illegible]; commissions, [illegible], [illegible].
,, Rich., burgess, Athlone, [illegible].
,, —Hyll, William, commissions, [illegible], [illegible], [illegible]; pardon, [illegible], 1125, [illegible]; leases, [illegible], [illegible], [illegible]; surrender, [illegible].
Hillelan, co. Mon., [illegible].
Hilliage, Tho., searcher of foreign fishing vessels, [illegible].
Hilltown (co. Kilk. ?), [illegible].
Hilltown. See Hilton.
Hilly, Tho., pardon, [illegible].
Hilton (co. Cav. ?), [illegible], [illegible].
Hilton—Hiltone (co. Dub. ?), [illegible], [illegible].
Hilton (Hilltown), co. Meath, [illegible], [illegible], [illegible], [illegible]. See also Holton.
Hilton villages (Hilltown, great and little), co. Meath, 14[illegible].
Hilton (Hilltown), co. Westm., [illegible], [illegible], [illegible].
Hiltone. See Hilton, co. Dub.
Hiltowden (Holdenstown, co. Wick. ?), [illegible], [illegible].
Himmestown, Nicholas, [illegible].
Himsyn, Scathlan, pardon, [illegible].
Hinderyell, Philip m'Conoghor I., pardon, [illegible].
,, Shane m'Teige I., pardon, [illegible].
,, Shane m'Conoghor I., pardon, [illegible].
Hingardell, John, pardon, [illegible].
Hingardle, John, pardon, [illegible].
Hinnis, Wm., pardon, [illegible].
Hirath, co. Kilk., [illegible].
Hires, Tirrelagh m'Shane I., pardon, [illegible].
Hirine, Donogh m'Dermody I., pardon, [illegible].
Hirrishey, Shane m'Ranell I., pardon, [illegible].
Hirrasin, Dermot mac Teig Y., pardon, [illegible].
Hirtan, Conoghor and Donell m'William, pardon, [illegible].
Hissett, Francis, porter of Maryborough fort, [illegible].
Hitherington — Hitherington. See Hetherington.
Hige, Rosso oge, pardon, [illegible].
Hive (co. Lim. ?), [illegible].
Hoane (co. Cork ?), [illegible].
Hoare, David, pardon, [illegible].
,, Edm., pardon. See Hore.
,, Edm., pardon, [illegible].
,, James, footman in Dublin castle, [illegible].
,, James, pardon, [illegible], [illegible], [illegible].
,, John, pardon, 4114, [illegible].
,, Jovan, pardon, [illegible].
,, Matthew, pardon, 4114.
,, Mich., pardon, 4114.
,, Mich. fitz John, pardon, 4114.
,, Nicholas. See Hore.
,, Nich., pardon, [illegible].
,, Patr., pardon, 4114, [illegible], [illegible].
,, Peter, pardon, 4114.
,, Rob., pardon, 4114.
,, Tho. oge, pardon, [illegible].
Hoare. See Hore, co. Tip.
Hoare abbey. See Hore abbey, co. Tip.
Hoare's mill (Mill), Wexford, [illegible].
Hoaretowne — Horetown, co. Meath, [illegible], [illegible], [illegible].
Hoaretowne. See Horetown.
Hoarne hill, [illegible].
Hoathestown, co. Louth. See Hothestown.
Hoblaurd, Maurice, pardon, [illegible].
,, Ulick, pardon, [illegible].
Hobbertston, co. Kild., [illegible].
Hobbies, illegal export of, [illegible].
Hobbins, John, pardon, 4107.
Hoboldston, co. Kilk., rectory, [illegible].
Hobler pardoned, [illegible].
Hocke. See Hooke.
Hockestone. See Hokeston.
Hocknell, Ralph, [illegible].
Hod, Adam, clerk, pardon, [illegible].
Hodd, Rob., pardon, [illegible].
Hodbrook. See Hodnet.
Hodges, Wm., pardon, [illegible].
Hodo, Rob., pardon, [illegible].
Hodgeston — Hodgiston — Hogeston (Hodgestown), co. Kild., 3157, [illegible], [illegible], [illegible].
Hodgestown, co. Meath. See Hoggeston.
Hodgson, Rich., [illegible].
Hodnet—Hodnoth—Hodnett (or M'Phiarde):
,, James, pardon, [illegible], [illegible].
,, John, pardon, [illegible].
,, Rich., pardon, [illegible].
,, Wm., pardon, [illegible].
Hodney, Rich., pardon, [illegible].
Hoey, John, grant of a wardship, [illegible].
Hogain, Hugh, pardon, [illegible].
Hogaine, Onora ny, pardon, [illegible].
,, Wm., pardon, [illegible].
Hogan, Donice, pardon, [illegible].
,, Donagh, dean of Killaloe, [illegible].
,, Edm., pardon, [illegible].

INDEX TO FIANTS—ELIZABETH.

Hogan, Ellis nyn, pardon, 6611.
" Hugh, dean of Killaloe, 6674.
" Johanna, pardon, [illegible].
" John, pardon, 6177, 6687-8.
" John fitz Edm., clerk, pardon, [illegible].
" John fitz Edm., priest, pardon, [illegible].
" Katherine, pardon, [illegible], 6671.
" Wm., pardon, [illegible].
Hogane, Grany ny, pardon, 6191.
" John, lease, [illegible].
" Philip, pardon, [illegible].
Hogalstowne, (co. Tip. ?) [illegible].
Hoggen green. See Dublin.
Hogeston, co. Meath, 163.
Hogeston alias Hogges by Athboye, co. Meath, 1348.
Hogges by Dublin, house of nuns. See Dublin.
Hogges alias Hoggeston, by Athboye, co. Meath, 1368.
Hoggeston (Hodgestowne), co. Meath, 1480.
Hoggiston. See Hodgeston, co. Kild.
Hoggs, near Dublin, house of nuns. See Dublin.
Hoke. See Hooke, co. Wex.
Hoker, John. See Hooker.
Hokeston—Hookestone, alias Ballyhook (Ballyhook, co. Wick.), 1687, 5718, [illegible].
Holdenstown, co. Wick. See Ballyhallen, Hillcreston.
Hologan alias Mory, Philip, pardon, 1161.
Holer, Wm., alias Maryman, Wm., pardon, [illegible].
Holfen, co. Ros., 4677.
Holgan, Philip m'Olave I, pardon, [illegible].
Holican, Gillicady m'Ricard I, pardon, [illegible].
" John m'Donlee I, pardon, [illegible].
Holle Crosse. See Holy Cross, co. Tip.
Hollo—Holly—Hollo Island (Saints Island in L. Ree, co. Long.), priory leased, 1178, [illegible].
Holivan, Teig m'Dermot I, pardon, 6412.
Holiwod—Holiwodd—Holiwood. See Hollywood, co. Wick.
Holland, James, pardon, 6187.
" Randolph, [illegible].
Hollanda, George, pardon, 6128.
Hollanston—Hollanstown, co. Meath, 2154, 3716.
Hollican, Donell and Edm. m'Donell roe Y, pardon, [illegible].
Hollicrosse. See Holycross.
Hollis, John, [illegible].
Hollo Island (see Hollo Island), 1178.
Hollyhane, Conughor m'Donnoghow I, pardon, [illegible].
Hollinshed — Hollingshead — Hollingshed, Laurence, collector of customs, [illegible]; keeper of records in Bermingham tower, [illegible], [illegible]; clerk of the castle chamber, [illegible], [illegible].
Holliwod, co. Dub., [illegible].
Holliwood, Chr. and Rich. See Hollywood.
Holliwoodrath. See Hollywoodrathe.
Holliwood's acre, co. Westm., [illegible].
Hollohan, Dermod m'Conor I, pardon, [illegible].
Hollohan, Mahowne m'Shane I, pardon, [illegible].
Hollowabor, co. Kilk., 128.
Holly, Donell m'Donogho I, pardon, [illegible].
Hollycrosse. See Holy Cross.
Holly Island. See Hollo Island.
Hollyman, Loghlen m'Cormoll, pardon, [illegible].
Hollywell, Ellen, pardon, [illegible].
" Wm., pardon, [illegible].
Hollywod—Hollywodd. See Hollywood.
Hollywood — Holliwood, Christopher (of Artaine), wardship, 1777; land of, [illegible], [illegible].
" Nich., heir of, 1777.
" Rich., pardon, [illegible].
Hollywood — Hollywoodde, co. Dub., [illegible], [illegible], [illegible]; rectory, [illegible], [illegible]. See also Holywood.
Hollywood—Holywood, Little, co. Dub., 1480, 1777.
Hollywood — Holiwod — Holiwodd — Holiwood—Hollywod —Hollywodd—Holywod —Holywood (co. Wick.), 427, [illegible], 783, [illegible], 1416-8, [illegible], [illegible], 3169, 3199, [illegible], [illegible], 6677.
Hollywood, [illegible].
Hollywoodde. See Hollywood.
Hollywoodisa Gunnocke (Gunnocke), co. Meath, [illegible], [illegible].
Hollywoodrathe—Holliwoodrath, co. Dub., [illegible], [illegible].
Holmegrange rectory, [illegible], [illegible].
Holmepatrie—Holmepatrick—Holmepatrik. See Holmpatrick.
Holmes, Robert, pardon, 104.
Holmpatrick — Holmepatric — Holmpatrik, co. Dub., [illegible], [illegible], [illegible], [illegible].
" priory, leased, [illegible], [illegible], 6811.
Holmastle, co. Cav., 4834.
Hologhane, Conoghor m'Teige Y, pardon, [illegible].
Holohane, Donell m'Dermod I, pardon, 4477.
Holte, Marc, pardon, [illegible].
Holte, Worcestershire, [illegible].
Holtan (Hilltown), co. Meath, [illegible].
Holyman, Conoghor m'Allen I, pardon, [illegible].
Holycross, [illegible].
Holy Cross — Hollo Crosse — Hollicrosse— Hollycrosse, co. Tip., [illegible], [illegible], [illegible], [illegible].
" abbey granted, [illegible]; possessions granted, 5416.
" abbot of, [illegible].
" rectory, [illegible].

Holy Cross priory, Killeigh, King's co., 1294, [illegible].
Holyday, John, soldier, pardon, 1[illegible].
Holy Island. *See* Hollo Island.
Holy Trinity castle, Youghall, co. Cork, [illegible].
Holy Trinity cathedral. *See* Dublin.
Holy Trinity, college, Dublin, charter, [illegible]. *See* Dublin.
Holy Trinity hospital, New Ross, charter, [illegible]; grant of premises, [illegible].
Holy Trinity island (in Lough Key, co. Ross.), monastery of canons leased, 1734, [illegible]; possessions leased, [illegible].
Holy Trinity island (in Lough Oughter, co. Cav.), monastery of canons leased, 1[illegible], [illegible], [illegible].
Holywood—Holywod. *See* Hollywood.
Holywood, Great (Hollywood, Great), co. Dub., [illegible].
Holywood, Little. *See* Hollywood, Little.
Homeston—Homistowne (Holmestown, co. Wex.), [illegible], [illegible].
Homuth (O'Meath, co. Louth), [illegible].
Homistowne. *See* Homeston.
Homsuckstowne (co. Tip.?), [illegible].
Homow — Homowe alias Hyomowe, co. Westm., [illegible], [illegible], [illegible].
Honshre, Edm., pardon, [illegible].
Honorally (co. Cork?), [illegible].
Honoy, first fruits of, [illegible], [illegible].
„ vicar, [illegible].
Honoman, Donell m'Morobe Y, pardon, [illegible].
Honomane, Conoghor m'Donogh Y, pardon, [illegible].
Honraghane, Conoghor and Shane m'Teige Y, pardon, [illegible].
Honrogane, Derbie, pardon, [illegible].
Hoopa, Maurice, pardon, [illegible].
Hoode, James, marshal of the four courts, 1[illegible].
Hooke—Hooko—Hoke—Howke, the (Hook), co. Wex., [illegible], [illegible], [illegible], [illegible], [illegible], [illegible], [illegible].
Hooke alias Hooker, Wm., [illegible].
Hooker — Hoker — Howker alias Vowell, John, commissions, [illegible], [illegible], [illegible], [illegible].
Hooker alias Hooke, Wm., grant of a wardship, [illegible].
Hoope, Walter. *See* Hope.
Hoore Abbey. *See* Hore Abbey.
Hoore, Edm., pardon, [illegible].
„ James, pardon, [illegible].
„ Tibbot m'Edmond, pardon, [illegible].
„ Walter, pardon, [illegible].
Hoorley, Russell, pardon, [illegible].
Hootiho, John, [illegible].
Hope—Hopp—Hoope—Hop—Hoppe—
„ Archo, pardon, [illegible].
„ Edmund, pardon, 1[illegible], [illegible].
„ Edward, pardon, [illegible], [illegible].
Hope—Jonet, grant of a wardship, [illegible].
„ Margaret, pardon, [illegible].
„ Redmond, pardon, [illegible].
„ Richard, pardon, [illegible].
„ Shane, pardon, 14[illegible].
„ Walter, constable of gaol of Mullingar, [illegible], [illegible], [illegible]; constable of the castle, [illegible], [illegible]; commissions, [illegible], [illegible], [illegible], [illegible]; grant of land, &c., [illegible]; grant of fairs, [illegible]; leases, [illegible], [illegible], [illegible]; surrender, [illegible]; pardon, [illegible], [illegible]; house late in tenure of, [illegible].
„ (   ) of Ledwidston, comm., [illegible].
Hopper, Richard, licence of alienation, [illegible].
Hops taken up for army, [illegible], [illegible], [illegible], [illegible], [illegible], [illegible].
„ foreign trade in, [illegible].
Hopton, George, rector of Kilcolmanbane, [illegible].
Hopwood, Rich., clerk of ordnance, [illegible].
Horalay. *See* Hore.
Horagh, Margaret ny, pardon, [illegible].
Horan, Dermod m'Donell I, pardon, [illegible].
Horane, Dermond duffe A, pardon, [illegible].
Hore, Edmund (of Harperstown), wardship granted, 17[illegible]; pardon, [illegible].
„ Gerrott, pardon, [illegible].
„ James, pardon, [illegible], [illegible].
„ John, pardon, [illegible].
„ Nicholas (of Harperstown), murdered, [illegible], [illegible]; wardship of heir, [illegible].
„ Nich., pardon, [illegible], [illegible].
„ Philip, treasurer, co. Wex., [illegible].
„ Philip, pardon, [illegible], [illegible].
„ Rich., pardon, [illegible].
„ Robert, pardon, [illegible], [illegible].
„ Tho., pardon, [illegible], [illegible].
„ Walter, pardon, [illegible].
„ William, pardon, [illegible].
„ Wm. (of Pooke), pardon, [illegible].
„ Wm. (of Harperstown), wardship of his heir, 17[illegible].
Hore Abbey or Jugo Dei (Grey Abbey), co. Down, possessions leased, [illegible].
Hore—Horalay—Hoore—Hoore abbey (Hore abbey), co. Tip., [illegible], [illegible], [illegible]; rectory, gardens, and closes, [illegible].
Hore—Hoore—Hoore abbey or Hope, co. Tip., abbey leased, [illegible], [illegible]; possessions leased, [illegible], [illegible], [illegible], [illegible], [illegible].
Horecock, co. Meath, [illegible].
Horew, co. Westm., 17[illegible].
Hores (Hores) wood, Dublin, [illegible], [illegible], [illegible].
Horetown. *See* Hoaretown.
Horetown—Horeton — Horetowne — Horetowne—Horton—Hortonne, co. Wex., [illegible], [illegible], [illegible], [illegible], [illegible], [illegible], 17[illegible], [illegible], [illegible], [illegible], [illegible], [illegible], [illegible], [illegible], [illegible], [illegible].

INDEX TO FIANTS—ELIZABETH.

Horetown, friary of the B.V.M. leased, [illegible].
Horie, Fulr., pardon, [illegible], [illegible].
Horie, co. Westm., [illegible].
Horiston, co. Meath, [illegible].
Horley, Donogh m'Donell, pardon, [illegible].
„ Margaret, pardon, [illegible].
Horlogho no poke, pardon, [illegible].
Hornehead, co. Don., [illegible]-1, [illegible].
Hornestown (co. Kild.?), [illegible].
Horraine, Morrish, clerk, pardon, [illegible].
Horrell, James, pardon, [illegible].
Horrestenowton, co. Meath, [illegible].
Horriston, King's co., [illegible].
Horrock, co. Meath, [illegible], [illegible].
Horsalhely, co. Wex., [illegible].
Horseman, pardoned, [illegible].
Horse, a chief, to be rendered by m'Wm. Twyhter, [illegible].
Horseboys to have their masters' bill, [illegible].
Horsecrosse—Horsecrosse, at Trim, [illegible], [illegible].
Horsekeeper, manslaughter of, [illegible].
Horsekeepers pardoned, [illegible], [illegible], [illegible], [illegible], [illegible], [illegible], [illegible].
Horseman, John, [illegible].
Horseman appointed, [illegible].
Horsemen, pay of, [illegible].
Horsenewton, co. Meath, [illegible].
Horses of deputy, hay for, [illegible].
Horses, illegal export of, [illegible], [illegible], [illegible].
„ licence to take to England, [illegible].
„ impressed for army, [illegible].
„ (post), impressed for army, [illegible], [illegible].
„ stolen, [illegible].
„ „ value of, [illegible], [illegible].
Horsey—Horsey, Jasper, seneschal of Imokilly, pardon, [illegible]; comm., [illegible]; leases, [illegible], [illegible]-7, [illegible], [illegible], [illegible], [illegible], [illegible], [illegible], [illegible], [illegible].
Horsfall, Cyprian, pardon, [illegible], [illegible].
Horseparke in Odder, co. Meath, [illegible].
Horsnecrosse. See Horsecrosse.
Horsey, Jasper. See Horsey.
Hortayne, Donogh m'Knoghor, pardon, [illegible].
Horton—Hortowne—Hortowne. See Horetown.
Horttowe, co. Wex., [illegible].
Horyman, Conoghor m'Donoghe Y, pardon, [illegible].
Hosberston. See Osberston, co. Kild.
Hospital—Hospitall, co. Lim., [illegible], [illegible], [illegible], [illegible], [illegible], [illegible], [illegible], [illegible].
Hospital or termon, lands granted, [illegible], [illegible].
Hospital founded at New Ross for sick poor, [illegible], [illegible].
Hospitals for leprosy, [illegible], [illegible].
Hospital of S. John of Jerusalem. See S. John.
Hoss, John, pardon, [illegible].
Hostages to be given by O'Farralls pardoned, [illegible]-2.
Hostings, chiefs to serve on or send to, [illegible], [illegible], [illegible], [illegible], [illegible], [illegible], [illegible], [illegible], [illegible], [illegible], [illegible], [illegible], [illegible], [illegible], [illegible].
„ O'Molloy, standard bearer in, [illegible].
„ freedom from subsidy for those charged to go to, [illegible], &c.
„ to be attended by grantees of land in King's and Queen's cos., [illegible].
Hoth. See Howth, Mary.
Hothestowne (Hoathestown, co. Louth), [illegible].
Houghe, Henry, pardon, [illegible].
Houghmarowemple, co. Ant., [illegible].
Houghmestrage, co. Ant., [illegible].
Houses to be built by Undertakers, [illegible].
Houth—Houthe. See Howth.
Hovedon, Maud, pardon, [illegible].
„ Rich, pardon, [illegible].
Hovendon—Hovindon—Hovindene—Hovington—Hovynden—Ovington:
„ Giles, comm., [illegible]; pardon, [illegible]; lease, [illegible].
„ Henry, pardon, [illegible].
„ John, grant of lands, [illegible], [illegible]; pardon, [illegible]; licence of alienation, [illegible].
„ John. See Ovingdon.
„ Piers or Peter (of Tankardstown), grant of land, [illegible], [illegible]; lease, [illegible]; pardon, [illegible].
„ Peter. See Ovingdon.
„ Robert, pardon, [illegible].
Howard—Howarde, Charles, lord Howard of Effingham, lease, [illegible]; earl of Nottingham, grant, [illegible].
„ Nicholas, chamberlain of Exchequer, [illegible].
Howardstown, co. Lim. See Ballyhoarde.
Howel alias Owed, Philip, pardon, [illegible].
Howell, Hugh ap David ap, pardon, [illegible].
Howelleston, co. Kilk., rectory, [illegible].
Howet, Nich., pardon, [illegible].
Howke. See Hooke.
Howker, John. See Hooker.
Howle, Richard, pardon, [illegible].
Howlen, David, pardon, [illegible].
Howling—Howlinge, David, pardon, [illegible], 1914.
„ James, pardon, [illegible], [illegible], [illegible].
„ Nich., pardon, [illegible], [illegible].
„ William, pardon, [illegible], [illegible].
Howlivan, Donogh and Shane m'Dermot I, pardon, [illegible].
Howloghan, Connoghor m'Teige B, pardon, [illegible].
Howlywane, Dermod m'Teig m'Fynyn I, pardon, [illegible].
Howmacshoneick (co. Wex.?), [illegible].
Howman, Donell m'Teige Y, pardon, [illegible].

Howse, Richard, pardon, [illegible].
Howraghan, Mulmorie, pardon, [illegible].
Howry, Ellish ny ne, pardon, 5407.
" Owen ny, pardon, 4402.
Howrith, Wm., pardon, [illegible].
Howrane, Donell m'Donogh Y, pardon, [illegible].
Howson, Tho., pardon, [illegible].
Howth — Houth — Hoathe — Hawthe, co. Dub., [illegible].
haven, [illegible].
Christopher S. Lawrence, baron of, commissions, [illegible], [illegible], [illegible], [illegible], [illegible], [illegible], [illegible], [illegible], [illegible], [illegible], [illegible], [illegible]; grant of a wardship, 1719; livery to heir, [illegible].
Nicholas, baron of, livery, [illegible]; commissions, [illegible], [illegible]; pardon, [illegible]; wife of, [illegible].
Howth—Hoth—Houth—Houthe—Hawthe: Alice or Alsone, grant of wardship, [illegible]; license, [illegible], [illegible], [illegible].
Anne, [illegible].
George, pardon, [illegible].
Jane, [illegible].
John, theft from, [illegible].
Margaret, pardon, [illegible].
Mary, [illegible].
Stephen, pardon, [illegible].
Thomas, lease, [illegible].
Thomas, pardon, [illegible], [illegible], [illegible].
Walter, commissions, [illegible], [illegible], [illegible]; pardon, 197.
Howthston—Howthestone (Howthstown), co. Meath, 187, [illegible].
Hoye—Hoy, John, serjeant at arms, [illegible]; marshal of Four Courts, [illegible]; pursuivant at arms, [illegible]; grant of wardships, [illegible], [illegible]; grant of fines, [illegible]; lease, [illegible]; license of alienation, [illegible], [illegible].
" Patrick, [illegible].
Hoyne, Mr., lord deputy's servant, [illegible].
Hoynestown (Haynestown ?), co. Kild., [illegible].
Hoyre, Richard m'Moriertagh, pardon, [illegible].
Hoys impressed for carriage of victual, [illegible], [illegible], [illegible].
Hubard, John, pardon, [illegible].
" Morish, pardon, [illegible].
Hubarde, Davie fitz Morice, pardon, [illegible].
Hubart, Edm. m'Morice, pardon, [illegible].
" Wm., pardon, [illegible].
Hubbard, Edm., pardon, [illegible].
Hubbard, Ellyn oge, pardon, [illegible].
Hubbard, Katherine, pardon, [illegible].
Hubbert, David fitz Morris, pardon, [illegible], [illegible].
Edmund, clerk, [illegible].
Edm. m'Henry, pardon, [illegible].
Ellis, pardon, [illegible].
Hubbert, John m'Edm., pardon, [illegible].
" Morrys, pardon, [illegible].
" Sesilie ny, pardon, [illegible].
Hubert, Edm. fitz Morice, pardon, [illegible].
" Ellen fitz Garret, pardon, [illegible].
" Gerald fitz Morrish, pardon, [illegible].
" Redmond, pardon, [illegible].
" Shane, pardon, [illegible].
" Ulig fitz Morrish, pardon, [illegible].
Hubertstown (co. Cork ?), [illegible].
Hubord, Davie fitz, pardon, [illegible].
Hudingtonryle (co. Ross ?), [illegible].
Hudd, Rob., pardon, [illegible].
Hue, Elise ny. See Aphugh.
Hue and cry after rebels and robbers, [illegible].
Huestown, co. Kild., [illegible], [illegible], [illegible].
Huet—Hewet, Charles, controller of wine customs, [illegible]; lease, [illegible].
Hugan, Agnes, pardon, 326.
Huggins, Capt. Anthony, pension grant, 6722.
Hugh, Derron ny ne, pardon, [illegible].
" Farrill, pardon, [illegible].
" Owny ny ne, pardon, [illegible].
" Rees ap. See Aphugh.
" Reese ny ne, pardon, [illegible].
" Dulb m'Hugh Duff's country (O'Donnell), [illegible]; martial law in, [illegible].
" oge, slain in rebellion, [illegible].
Hughes, Moire ny ne, pardon, [illegible].
" Rynsh ap. See Aphugh.
" Shelah, [illegible].
Hugole, Andrew, a Frenchman, pardon, [illegible].
Huhacy, Slany ne Carry, pardon, [illegible].
Hulowan, Teig oge m'Teig ?, pardon, [illegible].
Hulkan, Donell m'Shane I., pardon, [illegible], [illegible].
Hulkan (co. Lim. ?), [illegible].
Hullavan, M'Crayth m'Teige I., pardon, [illegible].
Hullyvan, Dermot m'Donill Y, pardon, [illegible].
Hulyvane, Mahowne m'Finnan I., pardon, [illegible].
Humeldore, Nich., [illegible].
Humfreston. See Humfreston.
Humffrey, Nicholas, [illegible].
Humfreston — Humfreston (Humphreystown, co. Wick.), [illegible], [illegible], 4194.
" See also Owyllerystowne.
Humfryes, James, master gunner, pardon, [illegible].
See also Umfrey.
Humpston, Robert, made bishop of Down and Connor, [illegible].
Hunbery, Tho., pardon, [illegible].
Hundred or tughheand, [illegible].
Hungary. See Fanatio.
Hunerendall, Philip m'Teig I., pardon, [illegible].

INDEX TO FIANTS—ELIZABETH.

Hungerford—Hungerfoorde, Anthony, constable, Dungarvan castle, 4180, [illegible]; grant of land, 5778; comm., 4873; pardon, 4785; died without heir male, his lands granted, [illegible], [illegible].
Hunmore, co. Wexford, 1764.
Hunt, John, soldier, pardon, 76.
" Richard, comm., 541; lease, 1407.
Hunte, George, pardon, 3480; pardoner, [illegible], 6312.
Hunterstown—Huntestown (Hunistown), co. Dub., [illegible], [illegible].
Huoneen, David and William m'Dermot I., pardon, [illegible].
Hurpus, Geoffrey A., pardon, 1394.
Hoolachaine, Dermod m'Edm. I, pardon, [illegible].
Hurleighnan, Conoghor m'Shane Y, pardon, [illegible].
Hurlleghane, Ellys ny Awlife I, pardon, [illegible].
Hurleghan, John m'Gillemoubliegh, pardon, [illegible].
Hurnyn, Moris, priest, pardon, 6611.
Hurtnard, Morish og, pardon, [illegible].
Hurden, Peter, pardon, [illegible].
Hurdey, Maurice David I, pardon, [illegible].
Hurdy, Wm. oge, pardon, 3787.
Hurgan, Mahown, pardon, 6671.
Horine—Hurine—Hurine, David, clerk, notary public, 3474, 3811, [illegible], 4161.
Hurlestone—Hurlestowne. See Hurlston.
Hurley—Hurlie—Hurly:
" Conoghor, pardon, 6616.
" Cormock, pardon, 6511.
" David, pardon, [illegible].
" Darby, pardon, 6511.
" Donoghie, pardon, [illegible].
" Donell, pardon, 6511, 6616, [illegible].
" Edm., pardon, [illegible], 6478.
" (alias Browne), Elinor, pardon, [illegible].
" Ellis ny Ranoll, pardon, 6616, 6776.
" Francis, pardon, [illegible].
" John, pardon, [illegible], 6511, 6616.
" Maurice, comm., 1264.
" Moriertagh, pardon, 6616.
" Morris, pardon, 6478, [illegible].
" Owen or Owney, pardon, [illegible], 6511.
" Philip, pardon, 6478, 6511.
" Ranoll, pardon, [illegible], [illegible].
" Shane, pardon, 6616.
" Shilie, pardon, [illegible].
" Teige, pardon, 6616.
" Tho., pardon, 1785, [illegible], 4214, [illegible].
" Wm., pardon, 5646, [illegible], 6511, 6616, [illegible].
Hurlston—Hurlestone—Hurlestowne (Hurlstone), co. Louth, 1196, 1782, [illegible].
Hurly—Hurlye. See Hurley.
Hurnagh, Mortagh m'Connor R, pardon, [illegible].
Hurvenagh, co. Mayo, 1494, [illegible].
Hurrily, Donell m'Teige Y, pardon, [illegible].
Hurryly, Thomas, pardon, [illegible].
Hurrylye, Conoghor m'Donoghe Y, pardon, [illegible].
Hurly, Philip fitz Edm., pardon, [illegible].
Hussey, Laurence fitz Chr., pardon, 6314.
Husse, George, pardon, 4117.
Hussey, James, pardon, [illegible].
" Shilie, pardon, [illegible].
Husse—Hussee. See Hussey.
Hussey—Husse—Husee—Hussee—Husseye—Husey:
" Christopher, pardon, [illegible], [illegible].
" Edmond, pardon, [illegible], [illegible], [illegible].
" George, pardon, [illegible], [illegible].
" Gerald, pardon, 1377, 6412.
" Gerald, pardon, [illegible].
" Gilbert, pardon, 6618.
" Hubert, pardon, [illegible].
" James (of Galtrim), pardon, 3183; commissions, 4118, 4461.
" James, pardon, [illegible], [illegible], [illegible], [illegible].
" Jone (Browne), pardon, 6314.
" Jone or Johanna (Dalahide), grant of lands, [illegible]; pardon of alienation, [illegible]; pardon, 6314.
" John, attainted, [illegible]; slain in rebellion, [illegible].
" John, pardon, [illegible], [illegible], [illegible].
" Mary (Courtney), pardon, [illegible].
" Matthew, pardon, [illegible].
" Meiler (of Mulhussey), commissions, 56, [illegible], 1097; pardon, 109, 776, [illegible]; pardons at his suit, [illegible], [illegible]; lease, [illegible].
" Michael, pardon, [illegible], [illegible].
" Meiler or Mellyrie (of Castlegregory), pardon, [illegible], [illegible].
" Morish m'Shane, his lands granted, [illegible].
" Morris, pardon, [illegible], [illegible].
" Nicholas, pardon, [illegible], [illegible].
" Oliver, pardon, 4477, [illegible]; excepted from pardon, 6773.
" Patrick, knt., baron of Galtrim, commissions, [illegible], [illegible], 2217, [illegible], 2444.
" Patrick, pardon, 376.
" Pieres, pardon, [illegible].
" Peter, pardon, [illegible].
" Raimund, pardon, [illegible].
" Robert, pardon, [illegible].
" Robert (of Castlegregory), pardon, [illegible].
" Thomas, pardon, [illegible], [illegible].
" Walter, house in Dublin, 1491.

INDEX TO FIANTS.—ELIZABETH.

Hussey, Walter, commissions, 4149, 4451.
" Walter, pardon, 4314.
" William, pardon, 4114.
Hussyeston, co. Down, 5401.
Hussie—Husy—Hussye. See Hussey.
Hustie, Ea m'Donogh I, pardon, 5487.
Hustyne, John, pardon, [illegible].
Hutchinson — Hutchinsone — Hutchinsone — Hutchinsone:
" Christopher, lease, 1781, 5377.
" William, lease, 891; license to alien, 408.
Hwasy, co. Cork, 5182.
Hweligham, Ellen ny, pardon, 4671.
Hwone, Wm., pardon, [illegible].
Hyallyby, Honor ny, pardon, 6431.
Hyan (co. Wick.?), 4577.
Hyde—Hide, Arthur, grant of lands, [illegible], 5591; sheriff of Cork, 4578; commissions, 4579, 4575.
" Wm., 5591.
Hyde, Berkshire, 5591.
Hyene, Mary ny, pardon, 5754.
Hyfferaghe, co. Westm., 1461.
Hyfforgan, Edmund, lease, 943.
Hyggenston (Higginstown), co. Kild., 3492.
Hyggeston. See Higgenston.
Hyky, James, pardon, 1253.
" Wm., pardon, [illegible], 4572.
Hyll, Wm. See Hill.
Hyllock, Anne (or Hilcock), 1546.
Hy Masy. See Imasy.
Hytchins, Tho., pardon, 5735.
Hyndsyre, Edmund. See Hansiere.
Hysery, James, pardon, 5494.
Hyssesown, co. Dub. See Haystown.
Hyngerty, Dermot, English liberty, 1394.
Hynie, Joan ny, pardon, 4527.
Hyndebyr, 478.
Hyny, Donell ny, pardon, 5874.
Hyraghtie, Donell, pardon, [illegible].
Hyrrin, Melaghlen m'Tirrelagh I, pardon, [illegible].

Iachoris (see Iagharis), 4234.
Iagharis, Shane m'Morris, pardon, 4440.
Iagharis—Iagharen—Iacharis—Iagh Loren —Iaghioris—Iaharis—Iakanran —Iakaahran—Ieaghires:
" David, pardon, 4477.
" Dermod m'Shane, pardon, 5478.
" Derby m'Shane, pardon, 4778.
" Donell, pardon, [illegible].
" Donogh m'Dermod, pardon, 5964.
" Gerald, pardon, 5374.
" Gerrot, pardon, 5374.
" John, pardon, 4732.
Iagharis, Moriertagh m'Owen, pardon, [illegible].
" Morroghy m'Owen, pardon, [illegible].
" Morris, pardon, 5444.
" Owen, pardon, 5482.
" Teig, pardon, 5374.
" Thomas, pardon, 5374, 4363.
" William, pardon, 5374, 4234, 4712, 6294.
" See also Aghiara, O'Hagharis.
Iaghio, Dermod m'Tho., pardon, 4451.
Iaghiorin — Iagh Loren — Iaharis. See Iagharis.
Iakaoran—Iakaohran. See Iagharis.
Ialio, Dermod m'Tyeokowne, pardon, 5754.
Ialihio—Ialiahio, Ellen ny, pardon, 4467, 4471.
Ialune, Donogh, pardon, 5344.
" William, pardon, 5344.
Ialyerne, Teige, pardon, 5172.
Iagauro—Iawiro (Garrowniro, co. Rosc.), 5741, 6348.
Ianraghan—Ianranghane, Donogh m'Gilcrist, and Moenogh m'Gillcrist, pardon, 4464.
Iar Connaught. See Ieher Connaught.
Iarighion, Sean and Tho. m'Wm., pardon, 5487.
Iaris—Iros—Iryis (Erris), barony, co. Mayo, 4694, 5507, 5577.
Iarian, Melaghlin m'Dave, pardon, 4314.
Iarmoy. See Formoy.
Iawiro. See Iaaauro.
Ibasywally. See Ibasywally.
Ibawno—Ibane—Ybawne (Ibane half barony), co. Cork, 4327, 4131, 4412.
Ibhoaithim, Odo son of Malachy, pardon, 4494.
Ibrenkan—Ibrocane—Ibricane—Ibracane—Ibrakan (Ibrickan barony), co. Clare, 4477, 4761; castle, 4751.
" Donogh O'Brien, baron of, 5454, 4761, 6411.
Ibros, Moriegh, pardon, 1456.
Ibricane. See Ibrenkan.
Icahill. See Cahill.
Icallagh, David, pardon, 4484.
Icallahane. See Callahane.
Ichallan, Donogh m'Shane, pardon, [illegible].
Ichingam. See Itchingham.
Ichoyle, Illoenel m'Donogh, pardon, 4532.
Icheyn, Art, Hugh and Teig m'Teig, pardon, 2313.
" See Iuoyne.
Icbruzie, John m'Morris, pardon, 5484.
Icbyngham, Edward. See Itchingham.
Icouigh, Dermod O'Connell, pardon, 4451.
Icoaill. See Coaill.
Icoonaugh—Iconaugh, co. Tip., 1541, 4512.
Icoanoghor. See Connoghor.

INDEX TO FIANTS—ELIZABETH.

Imaery, Moriagh m'Owen, pardon, 6172.
Iowrage, Teige, pardon, 6615.
Iowhan, John m'Owin, pardon, [illegible].
Iowinane, Morish Tobin, pardon, [illegible].
" Owrygh, pardon, 6411.
" Voughie, pardon, [illegible].
Iowmock, co. Clare, 4761.
Ioyned country (country of O'Quin, or Muntergnigain, co. Long. ?), [illegible], [illegible], [illegible]. See also Oquin, 6121.
Ioronyse. See Oronyse.
Iorughor, Donogh m'Donogh, pardon, 6472.
Iourrigh, Dermod m'Teige, pardon, 6468.
Idirrin, Dermod and Donell, pardon, 6462.
Idle persons to be punished by martial law, 1163.
Idonkeston, co. Down, 3401.
Idogh. See Idonagh.
Idomy, Tirlagh O'Connor, pardon, 6477.
Idorogha (co. Wick. ?), 6677.
Idough — Idogh — Idowghe — Edulf (the barony of Fassadinin, co. Kilk.), country of, 186, 1617, [illegible], [illegible], [illegible], [illegible], [illegible], [illegible].
Idowies, Philip Tobyn, 6477.
Idrone—Idrenie—Ihdrone—Odrone, country of, co. Car., [illegible], 1116, 1267, [illegible], [illegible], [illegible]; barony, [illegible]; martial law, 1303; com. to inquire of boundaries, 7147.
Idrowyne (Endrim ?, King's co.), 1611.
Ie, Shane (see O'Hea), pardon, 5947.
Ieghie, Connor m'Moriertagh, pardon, 6418.
Ieher, Connor m'Dermody, pardon, 4678.
Ieher Connaght — Ieruconaght — Iher Connaght — Ireconaght — Eihir conaghty — Ehyreconaght (Iar Connaught), co. Gal., [illegible], 4773, 5131, [illegible]; captain of, 1432.
Ielande, co. Gal., [illegible].
Ienlasie — Ieuynsie, David m'Shane and others, pardon, [illegible].
Ienerane, Tege m'Donill, pardon, [illegible].
Iensey, Tho. m'Teig, pardon, 4945.
Ierconaght. See Ieher Connaght.
Ieriyhy, Dermod m'Donell, pardon, [illegible].
Iermoy. See Fermoy.
Ieyne, Connoghor m'Owen, pardon, 6917.
Ifelstone, co. Kild., 4811.
Iferkeraan. See Ioorkeran.
Ifernoke—Ifrenoge, co. Wex., 4742, [illegible].
Iffaingho, Conor m'Moriertagh, pardon, 6418.
Ifrenog. See Ifernoke.
Ifanlow—Ifaniwe (a territory in Muskerry), co. Cork, [illegible], [illegible], [illegible].
Igarran, Shane O'Horgan, pardon, [illegible].
Igarvane, Conoghor m'Conoghor, pardon, [illegible].
Igawles, Rob. fitz Wm., pardon, 6631.
Igegyne, Conoghor m'Donill, pardon, 6617.
Igheillygher, Donagh m'Morish, pardon, [illegible].
Igherowre, Marigh m'Brian, pardon, 6311.
Ighoburte, Fayllym m'Righ, pardon, [illegible].
Ighicrmurragh, co. Cork. See Eughlormarren.
Igibine, Shane m'Donell, pardon, [illegible].
Igiamyhy, Shane m'Teige, pardon, 6754.
Iglanny, Donal m'Wm., pardon, [illegible].
Igrangane, Coverdok, Dermot and Hugh m'Shane, pardon, 6464.
Igowregane, Conoghor m'Wm., pardon, [illegible].
Igraogane — Igranganye, Edm. m'Meanis, pardon, 6122.
" Meanis m'Ee, pardon, 6611.
Igryhen, John m'Dae, pardon, [illegible].
Igyllay, Dermod m'Shane, pardon, 4962.
Ihanlowe (co. Cork ?), [illegible].
Ihar Connaght. See Ieher Connaght.
Ihiallyhy, Ellen ny Donell, pardon, 6671.
Ihaghrwe, Muriagh m'Connor, pardon, 6476.
Ihenalin, Ee m'Donogh, pardon, 6487.
Ihngardell, Shane m'Donell, pardon, 6167.
Ihelahagn, co. Leit., 6441.
Ilahard, Peter m'Brien, pardon, 1884.
Ilan, Donell m'Merrish, pardon, [illegible].
Ilan, the. See Iland, co. Gal.
Iland (co. Cork ?), [illegible], [illegible].
Iland—Ilande—Ilan, co. Gal., [illegible], [illegible].
Iland, co. Kilk., [illegible].
Iland (co. Westm. ?), 1170.
Ilandbegg ballymotto (co. Clare ?), 6415.
Ilandbegnow (Begny ?), co. Down, 4490.
Ilande, co. Kerry, 1848, [illegible]; castle of the Island (Castleisland), [illegible].
Ilande, co. Wex., [illegible].
Ilandes. See Ilands.
Iland Hubbuck - Ilanhobuck (Islandbobbuck), co. Wat., 4670, [illegible], [illegible].
Iland Igonenan, co. Clare, [illegible].
Ilandknock (co. Mayo ?), [illegible].
Iland m'Gillevalle (co. Mayo ?), 5760.
Iland m'Ilasket. See Illane m'Hasket
Iland Mnake, co. Down, 4769.
Ilandroe (Illanroe ? co. Mayo), [illegible].
Ilands—Ilandes (barony of Islands), co. Clare, 4761.
Ilane, Hugh m'Shane, pardon, 4672.
Ilane Kiltobert (Kiltobrid Island), King's co., [illegible].
Ilane Ieffymeabine (co. Cork ?), [illegible].
Ilane Eloige in Lough Ree, co. Long., [illegible].
Ilan Iregan (Illanayregan), co. Clare, [illegible].
Ilaninghirin (co. Clare ?), 6715.
Ilnocke, Geo., Nich., Rob., and Tho., pardon, 816.
" See also Ilkeocke.
Ileagh—Ileaghe—Ileah, co. Tip., [illegible], [illegible], [illegible].

INDEX TO FIANTS—ELIZABETH.

Ileagh—Ileaghe, Dermod m'Donogh, pardon, 6473, [illegible].
" Wm. m'Donogh, pardon, 6474.
Ileagh lowir, James fitz Morris, pardon, 6474.
Ileah, co. Tip. (see Ileagh), 4468.
Ileyne, Morierlagh m'Shaghnessie, pardon, 6497.
Ileys, Donogh m'Da., pardon, [illegible].
Iliavie, Donell m'Dermot, pardon, 6665.
Ilidane, Conoghor m'Donell, pardon, 4486.
" Dermod, pardon, [illegible].
Ilig'he (Illagh? co. Donegal), 5186, 6367.
Iliman, Donell m'Teig, pardon, 6418.
Ilane, Owen m'Shane, pardon, 6418.
" Teig m'Shane, pardon, 6468.
Ilainecounisic. See Ilanecounisic.
Ilalor, Donogh m'Neile, pardon, 1874.
" Edm. and Patr. m'Donell, pardon, 6497.
Ilanmoulick, co. Cork (see Ilanmoulick), 6462.
Ilanegawy, co. Long., 4484.
Ilanacoe, co. Kerry, grant, 6512, 6626, 6482.
Ilan Ballenyneill, co. Gal., 6457.
Ilanboge, co. Clare, [illegible].
Ilanecounisic—Ilainecounisic—Ilanicounsic—Ilan Counisic, co. Cork, [illegible], [illegible], [illegible], [illegible].
Ilaned, co. Gal., [illegible].
Ilane Arron (Aran Islands), 6644.
Ilanes (Islands), co. Tip., [illegible].
Ilanebegge, co. Kerry, [illegible].
Ilanegaunnagh (co. Gal.?), [illegible].
Ilane Inisherowane—Ilaned of Inchcrowan (Inchicronan Island), co. Clare, 4761, 4764.
Ilaneknave. See Ilanyknave.
Ilane m'Hacket—Ilaned m'Hacket, co. Gal., 1268, 5143.
Ilanemore, co. Lim., 6047.
Ilane ny fynyn—Ilane neffynenhine (co. Cork?), 5241, 5611.
Ilane ne guntamagh, co. Clare, 4791.
Ilanhobuck. See Ilaned Hobbock.
Ilan I Graddye—Ilane I Grady (co. Clare), 6948, 4468.
Ilan m'Cragh (co. Gal.? perhaps Island magrath co. Clare), [illegible].
Ilanmoulick—Ilanmoulick—Ilanmoulic, co. Cork, 4498, 4646, [illegible].
Ilanmagowne, co. Long., 6484.
Ilanmoulic. See Ilanmoulick.
Ilanmykunagh (co. Gal.?), [illegible].
Ilanrus, co. Mayo. See Ilandrue.
Ilanimarney (Islandmarney, co. Wat.), [illegible].
Ilanykane—Ilanekane—Ilanykane (Islandikane), co. Wat., 1284, 6479; rectory, 1158.
Ilanyvrik, co. Wat., 877.
Ilard. See Ullard.
Ilaneyvegan, co. Clare. See Ilan Iregan, [illegible].
Ilol—Ilyde (Ullid), co. Kilk., rectory, [illegible], 1299.
Ilomurk, co. Cork, [illegible].
Iloghly, Tirrelagh m'Owen, pardon, 6611.
Ilyde. See Ilol.
Ilyman, Owen M'Carty, pardon, 6624.
Ilolanesaghe, Conoghor m'Donell, pardon, [illegible].
Ilealy, Donogh m'Shane, pardon, 6418.
Ilynoluanny, co. Cork, [illegible].
Imackyllye. See Imokilly.
Imaghian, Edm. m'Donogh, pardon, [illegible].
Imahoune, Conoghor m'Dermod, pardon, [illegible].
Imahowragh, Owen m'Finin, pardon, [illegible].
Imale—Imallo. See Imayle.
Imany—Imanny—Omany—Omanny (Hy Many, O'Kelly's country in co. Gal. and Rosc.), 1282, 1685, 2581, 1250, [illegible], [illegible], [illegible], [illegible], [illegible], [illegible], 5618.
Imayle—Imale—Imallo—Imayell—Amayle—Ymale—Omalle—Omayle—Omaylle—Omalll, (co. Wick.), 674, [illegible], [illegible], [illegible], [illegible], 1416, [illegible], [illegible], [illegible], 5111; captain of, [illegible]; seneschal of, [illegible], 1418, [illegible], [illegible]; martial law, [illegible], [illegible], 1194, 1830, 1815, [illegible], [illegible], [illegible].
Imeakine (co. Cork?), [illegible].
Imfleghilie, Donell m'Donogh, pardon, [illegible].
Imill (Emmel, King's co.), [illegible].
Imleghe (Emlagh, co. Rosc.?), [illegible], [illegible].
Imlaghyshell. See Emlaghyshell.
Imlovagger (Emlybeg?), co. Mayo, [illegible].
Imlly (Emly, co. Tip.?), 4744.
Imly (co. Cork?), [illegible].
Immolid (co. Tip.?), 3447.
Immoly, co. Tip., [illegible].
Immoshine, co. Gal., 4448.
Imo (Emo), Queen's co., 1824, [illegible].
Imoghor, Teig m'Donogh, pardon, [illegible].
Imokilly—Imokillie—Imakillie—Imokilly—Imokelly—Imokellie—Imokylly—Imackyllye, cantred or barony, co. Cork, [illegible], 1131, [illegible], [illegible], [illegible], [illegible], [illegible], [illegible], [illegible], [illegible]; cathedral lands in, [illegible].
" seneschal of. See Horsey, Jasper, [illegible], 1815; see Fitzgerald, John fitz Edm., [illegible], [illegible], [illegible], 6477.
Imollaghny, Dermod fitz James, pardon, [illegible].
Imoriertie, Morish m'Teig, pardon, [illegible].
Impor. See Ruyor.
Impressed articles. See Victuals, hay, wheat, wine, &c.
Imrigorum, Rusoe and Teig m'Tho., pardon, [illegible].
" Tho. m'Hoe, pardon, [illegible].
Imrigurimn, Tho. m'Shane, pardon, [illegible].
Imrigurymne, Shane m'Edm., pardon, [illegible].
Imullpatrick, Teig m'Dermot, pardon, [illegible].

INDEX TO FIANTS—ELIZABETH.

Imalrian, Wm. m'Teig, pardon, [illegible].
Imaroghe, Shane m'Donell, pardon, [illegible].
Imamallich (Murlough, co. Down), 4827.
Imarroghow, Donell m'Donogho, pardon, [illegible].
Imaryhowe, Donald m'Shane, pardon, [illegible].
Imaronyne, Brian m'Conoghor, pardon, [illegible].
Imagho (co. Tip. or Lim.), 4694.
Imaghten, John m'Donell, pardon, [illegible].
Ime, co. Meath. See Tyman.
Imne (Imane, co. Tip.?), [illegible].
Imneys, Donell m'Donoghy, pardon, [illegible].
Imrvine, Shane m'Dorenol, pardon, [illegible].
Imsmird, Teig, pardon, [illegible].
Imsogh, Edm. m'Donell, pardon, [illegible].
Ime (see Inche), [illegible].
Imalcoby (co. Leit.?), 4784.
Imamarron (co. Leit.?), 4780.
Imamarraue (co. Leit.?), 4784.
Imoruak (co. Leit.?), 6441.
Imoorowalrie (co. Leit.?), 4780.
Inch. See Inche.
Inch, co. Kerry. See Inches.
Inchaleogh, co. Cork. See Inchrilough.
Inchamakirne, co. Gal. See Insie M'Coyne.
Inchaphace, co. Cav. See Inchinfowhle.
Inchaquire, co. Kild. See Inchemquir.
Incharmaderinot, co. Long. See Inchokarrog Dermid.
Inchbofin, co. Westm. See Inchebofyne.
Inche—Inish—Inse—Inse—Ynche, co. Clare, [illegible].
Inche—Inche of Clonramata. See Ennis, co. Clare.
Inche (Inch), co. Donegal, [illegible].
Inche (Inch), co. Down, monastery, possessions leased, [illegible].
Inche (Inch), co. Kerry, [illegible].
Inche—Inshe—Ynche, co. Kilk., [illegible]; grant, [illegible].
Inche—Inshe—Ynche, co. Wex., [illegible].
Inche, co. Meath, [illegible].
Inche, co. Mon., [illegible].
Inche (Inch), Queen's co., [illegible].
Inche, co. Westm., 1173.
Inchebofyne (Inchbofin, co. Westm.), [illegible].
Incheboyne—Enisbothine (Ennisboyne, co. Wick.), [illegible]; rectory, [illegible].
Inchecalla — Inchecalle (Nuns Island, in Lough Ree, co. Westm.), 1811, [illegible].
Incheconvenirie, co. Kild., 1864.
Inchecronan — Inishcronan (Inchicronan), co. Clare, 4781, [illegible].
Incheguyriagh—Inchegeiniaghe. See Inchigeelagh.
Inchehiggen—Inchehiggen—Inchehyggon, in Lough Ree, 1811, [illegible].
Incheinfierry. See Inchiniferie.
Inchekillyn — Inchekillin. See Enniskillen.
Inchekertog Dermid — Inchokarrog dermayd (Incharmaderinot, co. Long.), 1811, [illegible].
Incheloghreno—Incheloghrene alias Inchmore, in Lough Ree, 1811, [illegible].
" monastery, [illegible].
Inchemacnedder—Inchmacnedder, co. Kild., [illegible].
Inchemequir — Inchemequyn — Inchequire (Inchaquire), co. Kild., [illegible].
Inchemore—Enyshmore (Inchmore, in par. of Columbkille, co. Long.), monastery leased, [illegible].
Inchemore (co. Tip.), 4122.
Inchemore—Inshemore (Inchmore in Lough Ree, co. Westm.), 1811, [illegible].
" monastery, lease, 1811, [illegible]; grant, [illegible].
Inchenagh, co. Long. See Inchenenagh.
Inchenemeo— Inchenemeo — Inchenemeo, alias Island of Life (Inish na mbeo, in townland of Monaincha, co. Tip.), monastery leased, [illegible].
Incheneganmanagho (Canon Island, co. Clare), 1778.
Inchenegoriro, co. Tip. [illegible].
Incheneygran (co. Long.?), [illegible].
Inchenenagh—Inchenenagh (Inchenagh in Lough Ree, co. Long.), 1811, [illegible].
Inche ne cyrire, co. Donegal, [illegible].
Incheneurragh (co. Rosc.?), [illegible].
Inchenewollopp (Inchinaquillib, co. Tip.), [illegible].
Incheqain—Incheqyne—Inchequyne, co. Clare. See Inchiquin.
Inchequin—Incheqnyn— Inchequin—Inchiquye — Enchyquin — Ynchiquyne — Ynchyeoyne (Inchiquin, co. Cork), [illegible]; barony and castle, [illegible].
" See Innehquyny.
Inches—Inshe (Inch, co. Kerry), grant, [illegible].
Inches. See Ynches.
Inchetowrky (Inchturk, co. Long.), 8404.
Inchevoughe (co. Clare?), 4782.
Inchevicahrine — Inchevickrynays—Inchvickrynye (Inisemic Neirin—Church Island, in Lough Key, co. Rosc.), priory or house of canons, leased, [illegible].
Inchicronan. See Inchecronan, Illane Inchecronane.
Inchie (co. Cork or Kerry), [illegible].
" See Inshie, Ynchy.

INDEX TO FIANTS—ELIZABETH.

Inchigilagh — Inchegeyleagh — Inchageela-
 ghe — Inchygyelaghe — Inchigelagh (Inchigeelagh, co. Cork), [illegible], 6131, 6467, [illegible]; rectory, 6121, 6467.
Inchinaluacky, co. Cork. See Inchinfuacky.
Inchistriela, co. Wat. See Inchistrielly.
Inchinilleris—Inchinillorrye—Inchenillorry, co. Leix, 5448.
Inchinsquillib, co. Tip. See Inchonscollopp.
Inchiquin — Inchequin — Inchequyne — Inchequeyne—Inchyquin — Inchiqwin—Inchyquyn — Inchiqwyne, co. Clare, 3041-2, 4763, 5034, 5712, 6562, 6815,
 " barony, 6161. See Tullaghydae.
 " Donnel O'Brien, baron of, 415.
 " Morogh or Maurice, baron of, 415; livery, 1522; a party to the Thomond indenture, 4731; his possessions, 4761; his heir, 5481.
 " Maurice, baron of, livery, 5491; commissions, 5153, [illegible].
Inchiquin, co. Cork. See Inchequin.
Inchimore. See Inchemore.
Inchmory (co. Leix ?), 5463.
Inch ne cane, co. Tip. See Inchenecho.
Inchesfowkie (Inchaghanna), co. Car., [illegible].
Inchofgerelo, co. Tip., 6464.
Inchovelan (co. Clare ?), 6815.
Inchtiork, co. Long. See Inchetowrky.
Inchvickrevye. See Inchevickerine.
Inchycollagh—Inchyerwlaghe—Inyshykilloyle, co. Clare, 4503, 5646, 6817.
Inchycrallaghie (co. Clare ?), 4763.
Inchynecrewnagh — Inchenecranagh — Inchynecrunagh — Inchy ny Crenagh—Inchynecrynagh, co. Cork, 2760, 2738, 4110, 4676, 5407, 5464, 6572.
Inchyowlaghan, co. Kilk. See Inchyowlaghane.
Inchyquin. See Inchiquin.
Incladdy, Donogh m'Teig, pardon, 6526.
Incladig, Donell m'Teig, pardon, 5456.
Incorlacky, co. Kerry, 5158.
Incydon, Edm., pardon, 2748.
Indentures with chiefs, 4450, 4731, 4994, 4848, 4760-62.
Indirrie, Donogh O'Riordan, pardon, 6467.
Ineraghe, Conor m'Donogh, pardon, 6574.
Inesle, Donogh m'Teig, pardon, 5462.
Innyshesyman (Ennistimon ?), co. Clare, 6077.
Inescortie. See Enniscorthy.
Inesshigo, co. Cav., 6627.
Inesherane, in Kinsale harbour, 6351.
Inesheane. See Inishane.
Inesskillen. See Enniskillen.
Inesslowragh. See Innislawnaght.
Inestiog — Inestioke — Inestiok. See Inistioke.
Inferny (Farney, co. Mon.), 1725.
Inga, co. Cork, 6066.
Ingordell, Shane m'Donell I, pardon, 6467, 6671. See O'Hingerduil.
Ingledrigh, Tho. m'Teig, pardon, 6234.
Inglorney, Owen m'Rory, pardon, 6217.
Inghandy, Donell and Donogh m'Shane, pardon, 4432.
Inglisbe, Redmond, pardon, 6572.
Inishaishiny (Inishbofin, co. Mayo ?), 4482.
Iniscarragh. See Inishcarry.
Iniscirean —Inishkirean—Innishirean—Inishirhane—Inishirhane (Sherkin island), co. Cork, 6671.
 " house of friars, located, 6525, 6528, 6638.
Inisowin, 6622.
Inisglymmyne. See Ennistimon.
Inisfallen. See Innisfallen.
Inish (co. Clare ?), 6815.
Inish. See Ennis, co. Clare.
Inishaolaun, co. Clare. See Inyshelane.
Inishammon, co. Mon. See Inismagen.
Inishbeg, co. Cork, 6671.
Inishbofin, co. Mayo. See Innishbofin.
Inishcalira, co. Gal. See Inishkealtera.
Inishcarry — Iniscarragh — Inishcarie — Inishkarry—Inyskarry—Enyskarry (Inishcarra), co. Cork, 5256, 6151, 6467, 6438, 6814, 6763.
Inishcowe — Inishkwoe — Inniskoe (Inishcoe, co. Mayo), 6796, 5553.
Inishcroman, 6526. See Inchecroman.
Inishcrone, co. Sligo. See Inishgrowin.
Inishdadroum, co. Clare. See Innyshdadrome.
Inishdyman. See Ennistimon.
Inishear, co. Gal. See Inishery.
Inishcrimagh, co. Gal., 6634.
Inishery — Inyshearrye (Inisheer, Aran islands), co. Gal., 5563, 6452.
Inishlovicorcity, co. Clare, 4781.
Inishfindy, co. Cork, 6034.
Inishfallen. See Innisfallen.
Inish Free, co. Ferm. See Inishfroye.
Inishgrowin—Inyslargowin (Inishcrone), co. Sligo, 4426, 6562.
Inishirkane. See Iniscirean.
Inishkea, co. Mayo. See Innisskey, Innishkea.
Inishkealtera — Inishkealty — Inyscaltreh (Inishcaltra, co. Gal.), 4663, 6478.
Inishkeen, co. Mon. See Iniskyen.
Inishkillen. See Enniskillen.
Inishkine (Ennisken, co. Cork ?), 6612, 5563.
Inishkine (co. Mayo ?), 5461.
Inishkwoe. See Inishcowe.
Inishloe, co. Clare. See Inyshloch.

Inishloonaght. *See* Innishlawnaght.
Inishmaan, co. Gal. *See* Inishmaany.
Inishmacowney, co. Clare. *See* Inishwickowny.
Inishmaine, co. Mayo. *See* Innishmaine.
Inishmaany — Innyshmanye (Inishmaan, Aran islands), co. Gal. 6443, 6444.
Inishmore, co. Cav. *See* Inismore and Inesmore.
Inishmore. *See* Ynishmore.
Inishnacommighty (co. Tip. or Lim.), 4004.
Inishmore (co. Kerry or Lim. ?) 6489.
Inishnag, co. Kilk., 6443.
Inishowan, co. Cork, 6430, 4404.
Inishowen—Inisowqine, co. Donegal, country surrendered, 6160; regrant, 6307; man of, pardoned, 6883.
Inishtubbrid, co. Clare. *See* Innyshtabbered.
Inishturk, co. Mayo. *See* Inisturke, Enisturk.
Inishwickowny (Inishmacowney, co. Clare), 5683.
Inisowqine. *See* Innishowen.
Iniskarry. *See* Inishcarry.
Iniskattie—Innoskattie, co. Lim. (Scattery Island, co. Clare), 4483.
„ religious house granted, 5394.
Iniskean—Inoskean—Inskeane—Inshkyne—Inyskeane—Iniskeyn—Iniskine—Inneskene—Ennskine—Ynishkine (Enniskean, co. Cork, some of the references may represent Inishkenny), 1086, 2384, 4053, 3636, 4371, 4848, 4880, 6322, 6814, 6839–42, 6871, 6876; manor, 1873, 6430, 6431.
Iniskellin. *See* Enniskillen.
Iniskelly (co. Ferm. ?), 6402.
Iniskeyn. *See* Iniskean.
Iniskillen. *See* Enniskillen.
Iniskine. *See* Iniskean.
Iniskirwan. *See* Inisceirwan.
Iniskyne—Inyskyne (Inishkeen, co. Mon.), 1013.
„ vicar of, 6487.
Inislonkin (Inishlonckan, co. Gal. ?), 4845.
Inis mac Neirin in Lough Key, co. Ros. *See* Inchevicneirine.
Inismore (Inishmore, co. Cav. ?), 4602.
Inismega. *See* Moinemega.
Inisamon (Inishammon), co. Mon., 6601.
Iniseo Tonahar (co. Don. ?), 4833, 6467.
Inisairkane. *See* Inisciruan.
Inistioke—Inistiocke—Inostioge—Inestiok—Innestioke—Innestiock—Inisticoke—Enestioke—Ennestioke—Enaetyock—Ennistiocke—Enystyogue (Inistioge), co. Kilk., 2041, 2716, 2808, 2856, 6342; men of, pardoned, 2764, 2802.
„ portreeve and burgesses, 2674.
Inistioke, provost, 2117, 2444.
„ priory of S. Columba, possessions leased, 1868, 2636, 3081, 3461, 3972, 4086, 4428, 4438, 4183, 6344; grant, 6646.
„ fisheries, mills, &c., 1717.
„ rectory, 3972, 4080, 6344.
Inisturke (Inishturk, co. Mayo), 4844.
Inistymayn. *See* Ennistimon.
Inlon (co. Clare ?), 6719.
Inn, Donogh m'Dermod, pardon, 4179.
Innaghaly, co. Cork, 6444.
Inneen, Owney or m'Donogh, pardon, 4463.
„ Donogh m'Dermod, pardon, 4463.
Inne—Ene—Enaghe—Eny—Ayne—Eshaye—Eiheare (Inny river, co. Westm.), 1039, 1940, 1858, 1448, 1659, 4381, 4890, 4877.
Inncarty. *See* Enniscorthy.
Inneagmore, co. Cork, 6881.
Innealnaly (co. Clare ?), 6914.
Inneskarty (co. Kilk. ?), 2089.
Inneskattie. *See* Iniskattie.
Inneskirolyman mokain, Queen's co., 1916.
Inneslawnaghe. *See* Innislawnaght.
Innestioke—Innestiock. *See* Inistioke.
Innover (Inver ?), co. Mayo, 6817.
Innishcarne (co. Ferm. ?), 4830.
Innisfallen — Inisfallen — Inishfallen, co. Kerry, granted, 4977, 5717.
„ abbey granted, 6647.
Innisfreye (Inish Free, co. Ferm. ?), 4814.
Innishburkan—Innyshbarckane, co. Gal., 6445, 4014.
Innishcoosche (Enniscouch, co. Lim.), 6171.
Innishdyman—Innishdyman. *See* Ennistimon.
Innishe Amnaghe, co. Ros., 4234.
Innishebofin—Inishbafiny—Inshibufyny (Inishbofin, co. Mayo ?), 3080, 4463, 5877.
Innishcoleero (Clare Island ?), co. Mayo, 5877.
Innishekeans (Inishkea), co. Mayo, 6877.
Innishmurraghan, co. Sligo, 5877.
Innishloughe, in Muskerry, co. Cork, 4404.
Innishmaine—Innishmeane (Inishmaine in Lough Mask), co. Mayo, religious house, 4363; granted, 6863.
Innishollen. *See* Enniskillen.
Innishkey (Inishkea ?), co. Mayo, 5817.
Innishoe. *See* Inishowen.
Innislawnaght — Innyslawnaght — Innyslanaghe — Innyslanaghe — Innislanaghe — Innoslawnaghe — Inoslownagh — Inyslownaght — Ennislawnaght — Ennislawnaghe (Inishlounaght, co. Tip.), 1687, 2445, 2849, 3132, 4441; grant, 4492.

Innislawnaght — town, [illegible]; grant, [illegible].
" abbey, lease, [illegible], [illegible]; grant, [illegible]; surrender, [illegible]; grant, [illegible]; remainder, 4141.
" rectory, [illegible], 4121, [illegible].
" grange, [illegible], 4121, 4141, [illegible].
" appendant of lordship, [illegible].
" See Shenaghis, Shenaght.
Innistiman. See Ennistimon.
Innistiocke. See Inistioke.
Innistyvan. See Inisloynan.
Innonistom, co. Kilk., [illegible].
Inns: tenants of manor of Carlow to keep accommodation for travellers, [illegible].
Innsh. See Ennis.
Innshgayny, island of, co. Cork, [illegible].
Insare (Carrowsure), co. Rosc., [illegible].
Inny river. See Inne.
Innyaharrye. See Inisbory.
Innysh barckane. See Inishbarkan.
Innyshdadrume (Inishdadroum, co. Clare), [illegible].
Innyshdyman. See Ennistimon.
Innyshe. See Ennis.
Innyshark, 1775.
Innyshlosh (Inishloe, co. Clare), 1775.
Innyshmanye. See Inishmacy.
Innyshtubberod (Inishtubbrid, co. Clare), 1775.
Innyskillen. See Enniskillen.
Innyslawaghe—Innyslawnaght. See Innislawnaght.
Innysmaghan, co. Gal., [illegible].
Innys scill charney (co. Ferm.?), [illegible].
Inoghwotera, co. Cork, [illegible].
Inowho, Tho. m'Conoghor, pardon, [illegible].
Inowane, Donell m'Dae leigh, pardon, [illegible].
Inper (Emper, co. Westm.?), [illegible].
Inse (see Inche), co. Clare, [illegible].
Inse. See Inshe.
Insegrey. See Insenegrey.
Inselonton (co. Westm.?), [illegible].
Inseloghor. See Insenaloher.
Insemore (Inishmore), co. Cav., [illegible].
Insemore, co. Wat., [illegible], [illegible].
Insenegeane (co. Long.?), [illegible].
Insenegrey—Insegrey, co. Kild., [illegible], [illegible], [illegible].
Insenaloher—Inseloghor, co. Kild., [illegible], [illegible], [illegible].
Insequire. See Inshenaquire.
Insen. See Inchen.
Insrure (co. Tip.?), [illegible].
Inshe. See Inche, co. Kilk.
Inshe—Inse (co. Tip.?), [illegible], [illegible].
Inshe. See Inche, co. Wex.
Inshcale—Inshealle—Inshcall—Inshiall, co. Cork, [illegible], [illegible], [illegible], [illegible].
Insheralls. See Inshcalle.
Inshecurlingh (co. Cork?), [illegible].
Inshed, co. Clare, [illegible].
Inshehanrie—Inshehanrie—Inishehanrie, co. Kerry, granted, [illegible], [illegible], [illegible].
Inshehigon—Inshehygon. See Inchehigon.
Inshekerlagdermuyd. See Inshekerlag Dermid.
Insheloagh. See Inshiloagh.
Inshelonnagdon, Queen's co., 1948.
Inshelogheroe. See Inshelogheroe.
Inshelybe (co. Leit.?), [illegible].
Inshemore. See Inchemore.
Inshemore (co. Leit.?), 4736.
Inshenacranagh. See Inchynacrawnagh.
Inshepregarrie, 5748.
Insheramagh. See Inchamagh.
Insheshaghis, co. Clare, 5077.
Inshequin. See Inchiquin, co. Cork.
Inshewrick, co. Lim., [illegible].
Inshiboge (co. Clare?), [illegible].
Inshillotynny, co. Mayo (see Inishbofin), [illegible].
Inshie. See Inshy, co. Clare.
Inshie (Inch), co. Cork, [illegible], [illegible]. See also Inshye.
Inshie, co. Kerry (see also Insye), [illegible].
Inshie — Insie (co. Cork or Wat.), [illegible], [illegible].
Inshiall, co. Cork (see Inshcale), [illegible].
Inshilough—Inshilleigho—Inshilogh—Inshilagh—Inshiolagh—Insyloho (Inchilough, co. Cork?), [illegible], [illegible], [illegible], [illegible], [illegible].
Inshillignee, co. Cork, [illegible].
Inshinlore, 6477.
Inshinflacky—Inshynyflacky—Inshycobacky—Inshenvacky—Inshinfluckey—Ensytacke—Itoslacke—Itoslako (Inchinabacky), co. Cork, [illegible], [illegible], [illegible], [illegible], [illegible], [illegible]; rectory, [illegible], [illegible], [illegible], [illegible].
Inshinidrisly — Ynshedrisly (Inchigdrisle, co. Wat.), [illegible], [illegible].
Inshiniddeny (co. Cork?), [illegible].
Inshiquin — Inshiqwyne, co. Clare. See Inchiquin.
Inshiquyn, co. Cork. See Inchequin.
Inshkerah (Mutton island? co. Clare), 1775.
Inshkyan. See Inishcan.
Inshmacodder. See Inchemacodder.
Inshnevacky. See Inshinflacky.
Inshohanrie. See Inshehanrie.
Inshonan, co. Mon., [illegible].
Inshy—Inshie, co. Clare, [illegible], [illegible].
Inshy (co. Tip. or Kilk.?), [illegible].
Inshye—Ynshee—Ynshy, co. Cork, [illegible], [illegible], [illegible]. See also Inshie.
Inshycowiaght. See Inchycollagh.
Inshynacrawnagh. See Inchynacrawnagh.
Inshynagaine (co. Clare?), [illegible].

INDEX TO FIANTS—ELIZABETH.

Inchynetmekie. See Inchinilmacky.
Inchyneorryeagh. See Inchyneorrawnagh.
Inchyniclarie, co. Lim., 4404.
Inchyuigieny, co. Cork, 3701.
Inchyrylmacky. See Inchinilmacky.
Inchyny Oranagh. See Inchyneorrawnagh.
Inchyvochy, co. Clare, 5563.
Inchyowleghane (apparently in Munster, but perhaps Inchyolaghan, co. Kilk.), 4466.
Inchyquin—Inchyquyn. See Inchiquin.
Inche (co. Cork or Wat.), 6054.
Inche (Inch, co. Donegal), 5186, 4387.
Inche M'Coyne (Inchemakinna, co. Gal.), 5138-1.
Insigalagh. See Inchiirlagh.
Inshilbacky. See Inchinilmacky.
Inskeane. See Inishkean.
Insiquin (co. Cork ?), 4811.
Insula Canonicorum (Canons' Island, co. Clare), 5434.
Insulamreagha, co. Down, 4037.
Insye (co. Kerry or Cork), 6874.
Insylohe. See Inshilenah.
Insyfygeagh (co. Cork ?), 2823.
Insample (Templetate, co. Mon.), 4641.
Interpreter to the Government, appointed, 2551-4, 2223, 5180.
Istlea, John, pardon, 6498.
Intragh (co. Clare ?), 4605.
Intrusions on lands, assessment of fine for, 6605; commission to inquire for concealed intrusions, 5728.
Inugan—Inwnans—Inwnayn:
" Donagh m'Morish, pardon, 4456.
" John m'Richard, pardon, 6500.
" Richard m'Shane, pardon, 4461.
Inure, Walter, pardon, 1044, 2512, 4714.
Invasion, preparations against, 5918.
Inver, co. Mayo, castle, &c., 4561. See also Innever.
Inveran, co. Gal., 4533, 4854.
Invurrie, Shane m'Teig, pardon, 5671.
Inwnans—Inwnayn. See Inugan.
Inwyre (Carrowmure, co. Rosc.), 1454.
Iny, co. Sligo, 4723.
Inyaerie, Ony, pardon, 4733.
Inykeny, Johanna, pardon, 675.
Inynighrery, co. Cork, 4630.
Inyscallrah. See Inishkealtra.
Inyscholoyne (co. Rosc. ?), 4773.
Inysherowin. See Inishgrowin.
Inyscheiane (Inishmacilane ?), co. Clare, 4781.
Inyskilleys. See Ennisklllen.
Inyshykmaleghe. See Inchycallagh.
Inyskarry. See Inishcarry.
Inyskeane. See Inishkean.
Inyskyne. See Inishkyne.
Inyslawnaght—Inyslowraght. See Inishlawnaght.
Inyspicke (Spike Island ? co. Cork), 2826.
Inysmarryn, co. Mon., 4557.
Iogrsyne, Hugh m'Teig, pardon, 5548.
Iologhan, Morierteagh m'Auliff, pardon, 4884.
Iollighane, Beirie m'Dermod, pardon, 5784.
Ioman, Gilpatrick m'Shane, pardon, 6812.
Iorgan, Donogh m'Teig, pardon, 4459.
Ioriell. See Oriell.
Iowrean, Bernard m'Eoin, pardon, 134.
Ipororyne, Shane m'Donill, pardon, 6817.
Iphan, co. Kerry, granted, 2812, 4893, 5804.
Iplosnoe (co. Kerry ?), 5183.
Iprell, Brian m'Owen, pardon, 6551.
Ipre, in Flanders, 254.
Iprischan—Iprisghane:
" Dermod m'Donogh, pardon, 4467, 4671.
" Donogh m'Teig, pardon, 4467.
Iquilane, Conoghor and Dermot, pardon, 5657.
Iquiylloch, Dermot m'Philip, pardon, 4611.
Iraghilleghe—Iraghelighe (O'Reilly), Bernard, Carallus, Fergall, Hugh and John, pardon, 4464.
Iraght Icoror—Iraghtye Conoghor—Iraught I Knoghor—Iraghte I Knoghor (barony of Iraghticonnor, co. Kerry), 5177, 5183; to be made shire ground, 5783.
Irali (O'Reilly), Geoffrey, son of John, pardon, 4468.
Iraskanie, Dermod, Donell, Philip and Wm. m'Tho., pardon, 4452.
Iraught I Knoghor. See Iraght Icoror.
Irasnaght (see Iohar Connaght), 4707.
Iranloghe, Conoghor, Philip and Shane, pardon, 4458.
Iregan—Aregan—Eregan—Erregan, country of (now barony of Tinnahinch, Queen's co.), 1531, 1537-8, 1579; martial law, 524, 3807; made shire ground, 1534, 3118.
Irogiene (Aragiin river, co. Cork), 1548.
Irelaghe—Irrelaghe—Irilagh, co. Kerry, 4393, 5028.
" abbey, granted, 2947.
Ireland, lords justices and governors appointed, 5184.
" lord chancellor of. See Chancellor.
" lord treasurer of. See Ormond, Earl of.
" secretary of. See Secretary.
" general surveyor. See Surveyor.
" appeals in spiritual causes made to Chancery in England, 1572.
Irell, co. Kerry, 4452.
Irus, the barony of (the barony of Erris ?), co. Mayo, 4545.
Irasheton. See Irishtowne.
Ireyn, Conoghor and Donoghe m'Donell, pardon, 6503.

INDEX TO FIANTS—ELIZABETH.

Irgan, Bryan m'Ferryll, pardon, 5480.
Irgkream, co. Gal., 1[illegible].
Iriell (O'Reilly ?), Donell, Edm., Gillpatrick, Henry, Hugh, John, Moyle Shanghalen, Patr., and Shane, pardon, 6[illegible].
Irien, Donell m'Donogh, pardon, 4[illegible].
Iriordan, Dermod, Donell, Edm. and Owen, pardon, 4[illegible].
Irigall, co. Cav., 6[illegible].
Irilagh. *See* Irelagha.
Irish, not to be maintained by settlers in King's and Queen's co.'s, 474; lands of undertakers not to be alienated to, [illegible]; King's co., planter married to Irish woman, [illegible].
„ rebels, services against, 717, 1[illegible].
„ borderers, Queen's subjects assembled against, [illegible].
„ of Ulster, Earl of Essex to subdue, [illegible], [illegible], [illegible], [illegible].
„ of Munster oppress diocese of Ardfert, [illegible].
„ wild, 17[illegible].
„ customs or exactions proclaimed illegal, [illegible]; renounced, [illegible], [illegible]; specified, [illegible]; permitted under name of seneschal's fee, 1[illegible], 1[illegible]; chief relieved from exactions levied by crown, [illegible]; converted into money payments, [illegible].
„ church, offences against Act of Uniformity, [illegible].
„ manner of building, 4[illegible], [illegible], [illegible].
„ lord not to be enfranchised by borough, 17[illegible].
„ law, new shire ground withdrawn from, 1[illegible].
„ tenure, not to bind English subjects, [illegible].
„ tongue (see Interpreter), [illegible], [illegible].
„ mountains, co. Wick., [illegible].
Irishetown, 7[illegible].
Irishtown—Irisheton—Iryshetowne, co. Dub., 1[illegible], [illegible], [illegible], [illegible], [illegible].
Irishtown—Irishton—Iriston—Irishetowne, Kilkenny, [illegible], 1[illegible], [illegible], [illegible], [illegible], [illegible], [illegible]; incorporated with Kilkenny, [illegible].
Irishtown—Irishtowne—Irishtowne, co. Meath, [illegible], [illegible], 1174, 1[illegible], [illegible], [illegible].
Irishtowne, co. Louth, 17[illegible].
Irishtowne—Irishton—Irishton—Irosheton—Iryshton — Yrishtowne, co. Westmeath, 11[illegible], 1[illegible], 1[illegible], 1[illegible], [illegible], [illegible], 4[illegible], 4[illegible], [illegible], [illegible], [illegible], [illegible].
Iritne—Irtyne, Queen's co., 1[illegible], [illegible].
Irock, Shane m'Brien, pardon, [illegible].
Iron, import trade in, [illegible], [illegible], 1711, 4[illegible]; to be impressed for ordnance, &c., 11[illegible], [illegible], [illegible], [illegible].
Ironhills, co. Kild. *See* Ironhill.
Irow (co. Ros. ?), 4[illegible].
Irr, co. Kild., [illegible], [illegible].
Irragh I Manuon (O'Mannin's country, in bar. Tiaquin), co. Gal., [illegible].
Irraghte I Knoghow. *See* Iraghl I conor.
Irramore, co. Kerry. *See* Irrymore.
Irre, country of (in Queen's co.), [illegible], 1[illegible], [illegible].
Irre, grange of, [illegible]. *See* Erry.
Irroe (Iry ?), Queen's co., 1[illegible].
Irrogane, Teig m'Morroghtow, pardon, [illegible].
Irrolagha. *See* Irelagha.
Irriell, Edm., pardon, [illegible].
„ Walter, pardon, [illegible], [illegible].
Irris (co. Ferm. ?), [illegible].
Irris (Erris), barony of, co. Mayo, [illegible]. *See* Iaris.
Irry. *See* Erry.
Irrymore (Irramore), co. Kerry, granted, [illegible], [illegible].
Irrynaghe (Ironaght), lands granted, [illegible].
Irwirdan, Teig m'Dermody (O'Riordan), pardon, [illegible].
Iry, Queen's co. *See* Irroe.
Irygan, Shane m'Bryan, pardon, [illegible].
Iryshetowne. *See* Irishton, co. Dub.
Iryshton. *See* Irishtowne, co. Westm.
Isam—Isham—Isame, George, pardon, [illegible]; grant of land, [illegible], 4117.
„ John, 1[illegible].
„ Patrick, pardon, [illegible].
„ Philip, seneschal of Wexford, [illegible], [illegible].
„ William, pardon, [illegible].
Iscartmon—Ischartmon—Iscartmon (Ishartmon), co. Wex., 437; rectory, [illegible], [illegible], [illegible], 6114, [illegible].
Isewghtane—Isewghtowne, co. Kild., 11[illegible], 1[illegible].
Ishartmon. *See* Iscartmon.
Isikleran (co. Gal. ?), [illegible].
Iskerleran. *See* Iscriskerane, co. Gal.
Iskerkelly—Ishorkelly (Iskirkelly), co. Gal., 6111, [illegible].
Iskerkoran—Iskirkorane (Iskirkieran), co. Tip., rectory, 1[illegible], 4[illegible], [illegible].
Isknowe—Isknoe—Iskenowne—Iskenowne (Skenowe or Kneknow, co. Rosc.), [illegible], [illegible], [illegible]; market at, [illegible].
Iskriskerane—Iscrleran—Iskirkeyran—Ysherkierane, co. Gal., 4734, [illegible], [illegible], [illegible].
Iskirkelly, co. Gal. *See* Iskerkelly.
Iskirkieran, co. Tip. *See* Iskerkoran.
Isartmon. *See* Iscartmon.
Iskenowne. *See* Isknowe.
Isryn, Dermod m'Tho., pardon, [illegible].
Isham, Geo. *See* Isam.
Ishartmon, co. Wex. *See* Iscartmon.
Ishorkelly. *See* Iskerkelly.

Ichicorroe, Moriertagh m'Teig, pardon, 6686.
Ikerbog (Baker Bog, King's co.), 1347.
Ikerwan, co. Meath. See Rekowan.
Ikker, 1316. See Kaker, Queen's co.
Ikkerowan—Ikkerowne—Ikkerowne—Yek-erowne (co. Sligo?), 5120, 6806, 6762, [illegible], 6616.
Ikkerron (Eckorron, co. Gal.?), 6122.
Iklayne, Peter m'Dermot, pardon, 6182.
Ikkir, co. Gal., 5686.
Ikrowne. See Ikkerowne.
Island, the, in Connaught, 1478.
Island, the, co. Gal., 6187.
Island, the, co. Kerry, 6642.
Island, the, in Munster, 6778.
Island Arren, co. Clare, 6677.
Islandhubbock, co. Wat. See Iland Hubbock.
Islandkilane, co. Wat. See Illanykane.
Island Magee, co. Ant. See Island of Magy, Macgwier Island.
Islandmagrath, co. Clare. See Illan m'Ckragh.
Island of Lile. See Inchenoboo.
Island of Magy (Island Magee, co. Antrim), 4801.
Islands, co. Clare. See Ilands.
Islands, co. Tip. See Illane.
Island Sydney, in Lough Neagh, 1101.
Islandtarsney, co. Wat. See Illantarsney, 1158.
Isle of Canons (Canon Island, co. Clare), 1773.
Isle of Man, 6636.
Isnage, Donill m'Teig vick (see M'Isnok), pardon, 6617.
Isnarowne. See Isornowe.
Isrelly, Wm., pardon, 4634.
Itollord, co. Cork, 6661.
Itanywally—Itanywelly (Coolnanavally), co. Cork, 5626, 6658.
Itarmys, Edm. m'Simon, pardon, 6663.
Itchingham—Itchyngham—Ichyngham—Ichingam:
 „ Charles, 661, 6646.
 „ Edward, livery, 1397; his heir, 6646.
 „ John, suit by, 6624, 6869; pardon, 6642; livery, 6662.
 „ Osborn, knight, grant to, 1677; his heirs, 1387, 6264.
 „ Osborn, pardon, 6642.
Itellor, Teige, pardon, 6467.
Iterman, John Barrie, pardon, 6464.
Itesmacke (see Inchinilnachy), 6306.
Ithell, Thomas, rector of Castleknock, 162, 446, 722.
Ithrunlow (co. Cork?), 6171.
Itirmotrowe, 6174. See Knightermurrow.
Itlanny, Conoghor m'Teige, pardon, 6467.
Iumghtie, Teig m'Tho., pardon, 6606.
Itinaghty, Teig, pardon, 6676.
Itosby, Dermod, pardon, 6606.
Itwoma, Dermod m'Conoghor, pardon, 6618.
Iunghlen, Donogh m'Dermod, pardon, 6684.
Ingun, John m'Dermod, pardon, 6264.
Ivaghain, Shoolie ny Donell, pardon, 6672.
Ivahuny, Conoghor, Dermod, and Moriertagh m'Teig m'Donell, pardon, 6601. See O'Mahony.
Ivallane, Dermod, pardon, 6676.
Ivaltig, Teig, pardon, 6676.
Ivanane, Molaghlin m'Donell, pardon, 6676.
Ivanliine, Donell m'Conghor, pardon, 6666.
Ivanisane, Wm. fitz John, pardon, 1642.
Ivary, Donogh m'Dermod, pardon, 6467.
Ivagh—Evagh—Evagh, country of, co. Down, 1666, 4766, 6767, 6784; to be made shire ground, 1766; captain appointed, 6666; surrendered, 6316; regrant and boundaries, 6627; martial law, 6641. See also Magennis's country.
Ivaghan, co. Cork, 4467.
Iveagher, Donogh m'Shane and Donell m'Donogh (O'Meagher), pardon, 6667.
Ivoghan, Teig m'Cormac, pardon, 2611.
Ivaleary—Iveleary—Yveleary territory, (Ui Laoghaire, parish of Inchigeelagh, co. Cork), 6674, 4764, 6636, 6631.
Ivelston (co. Kild.?), 6166.
Iveragho, co. Kerry, 6678.
Ivurmane, Donogh m'Dermod, pardon, 6676.
Iverling (co. Cork or Lim.), 6666.
Ivers, Barnaby, 1676; commission, 260.
 „ Chr., commissions, 661, 6646.
Ivorum, co. Lim. See Eglise O'Bearde.
Ivirne—Iviro—Ivyrne (Ui Brinin-na-Sinna—O'Beirne's country), co. Ross., 1636, 6166, 6666-4, 6690.
Ivolayne, Donell m'Moriertagh, pardon, 6617.
Ivore, Nich. m'Donell, pardon, 6667.
Ivoreghowe, Mahon m'Conoghor (see Omoreghowe), pardon, 6662.
Ivorys, Donogh m'Rory (see O'Morris), pardon, 2294.
Ivronane, Conor m'Donogh and Conor m'Moriagh, 6674.
 „ Donell, Donogh, and Edm. m'Owen, 1884.
 „ See O'Bronan.
Ivrkillye, Cornelius m'Donogh, pardon, 1072.
Ivrogan, Hew m'Brian, pardon, 6174. See O'Brogan.
Ivryn, Dermod m'Shane, pardon, 6662.
Ivyrne. See Ivirne.
Iwaddigan, Mahon m'Donell, pardon, 5418. See O'Maddogan.

INDEX TO FIANTS—ELIZABETH.

Iwarrymane, Conoghor m'Shane, pardon, 6744.
Iwari de Conaght, 6788.
Iwoman, Donell m'Teig, pardon, 4618.
Iwynaughnane, Dermod m'Conoghor, pardon, 6744.
" Teig m'Dermod, pardon, 6744.
Iyane, Ricard and Wm. m'David, pardon, 6072.
Iyamony, Tho. m'Conhor, pardon, 2638.
Iykye, Laig m'Donell, pardon, [illegible].
Iyurraughnane, Donogh, pardon, 6476.
Iywogane, Sille nyn Dermod, pardon, 6604.

Jack, armour worn by county levies, 2414.
Jackes, Rich. (see Jaques), 4.
Jackestown, co. Westm., 1121.
Jackmaker (or Jack), 4814.
Jackman, Peter, pardon, 678.
Jacob, Edward, pardon, 4232, 6774.
" John, pardon, 4232, 6774.
" Rich., 4239; pardon, 4232, 6773.
" Thomas, pardon, 4232.
" Walter, pardon, 2834, 4206, 4232, 6773.
Jacstowne, co. Meath, 1794.
Jagoe, Wm., 2281.
Jagoeston — Yagoeston — Yeagoiston — Yeaston (Jago ?), co. Kild., 1289, 1664, [illegible], 4537; grant, 5272.
Jakestowne (Jackstown), co. Kilk., 594.
James, Donogh m'Phelim, pardon, 5642.
" Katherine ny, pardon, 6477.
" Wm., controller of customs and searcher of Dublin and Drogheda, 4788, 5184; surrenders, 4651, 4667–69, 4683, 6731.
Jamestone—Jamestone (Jamestown), co. Lim., 5182, 6617.
Jamestowne (co. Kild. ?), 6874.
Jamestowne (Jamestown, co. Kilk. ?), 1140.
Jamestowne (Jamestown, co. Tip.), 4272.
Janing's lands — Jamyg's lands, co. Dub., 1212, 1362.
Jans, Agnes, pardon, 4017.
" Elizabeth, lease, 4838.
" Rob., executors of, 865.
" Tho., surrender, 856.
Jamyg's lands. See Janing's.
Jaques—Jackes, Rich., pardon, 4, 382.
Jardarde, Wm. See Jordarde.
Jarmyn—Jarmyne, John, serjeant at arms, 2454, 6993.
Jarrelstown, co. Meath. See Jorodleston.
Jealotew, Peirs, pardon, 6264.
Jeffords grove, co. Dub., 2084.
Jeffreystown, co. Westm. See Ballyheffray, 1468.
Jellons, Peter, pardon, 4407.
Jenison, Thomas. See Jenyson.
Jenkenstoun (Jenkinstown), co. Meath, 2860.
Jenkins—Jenkyns, Wm., pardon, 6798, 6498.
Jenkinston (Jenkinstown, co. Kilk.), 1623, 1622.
Jenkinstown, co. Meath. See Jenkenstoun.
Jenkyns. See Jenkins.
Jennings — Jenings, Stephen, surveyor-general of ordnance, 6849, 6861–2; clerk-general of works, 6812, 6262.
Jenyson — Jenison — Genison — Genyson, Thomas, auditor-general, license of absence, 842, 1118, 1431, 3470; pardon, 1744, 2062, 3289, 3467; commissions, 2267, 3802, 5498, 4434; grant, 4883; pardon to his servant, 4381.
Jorodleston (Jarrelstown), co. Meath, 1880.
Jordarde—Jardarde—Jorbard:
" Walter, treasurer of Wexford, 1237, 5668.
" William, searcher of Wexford, 878; treasurer, 1237, 6685; collector of wine duty, 1581; commissions, 863, 1836.
Jeripont—Jeripount—Jeripoint—Jeripounde—Jeropont—Jeropounte—Jeroponte—Jeropont—Jerypount—Gerrypont — Gerripont (Jerpoint), co. Kilk., 1605, 1617, 2844, 4440, 4447, 6524, 6704.
" abbey, granted, 594; possessions leased, 383, 938, 2115, 2689, 4602, 6183, granted, 594, 6844.
" rectory, 2683.
" Newtown of, 594.
Jerusalem, hospital of S. John of. See S. John.
Jerypount. See Jeripont.
Jesuits, excepted from pardon, 6461, 6697, 6773.
Jhoanne—Jhoane—Jhones, Tho. See Jones.
Joanes, Elizabeth, pardon, 6602.
" Rich., pardon, 6069.
" Tho., pardon, 6266, 6540.
Jobson, Francis, commission of survey, 6287.
Johnston (Johnstown), co. Dub., 3118, 4147.
Johnstonfeston, co. Westm., 1674.
Johnes, Rob., pardon, 4863.
" Thomas. See Jones.
Johnston. See Johnston.
Johnstone manor (now Castleboy, co. Down), 4432.
Johnstone, Johnestowne. See Johnston.
John Rothestone (co. Kilk. ?), 6837.
Johns, Brian, commission, 122.
" Hugh, 5414.
" Morgan, 6238.
" Nicholas, pardon, 6812.

INDEX TO FIANTS—ELIZABETH.

Johns, Roger, pardon, [illegible].
" Wm., pardon, 6150.
Johnson, Henry, pardon, 44.
" John, grant, 1778.
" John, burgess of Athlone, 6319.
" Justin, vicar of Balrane, 6424; treasurer of Ferns, [illegible].
" Katharine, wardship, 4283.
" Peter, a Fleming, 5007.
" Richard, [illegible]; prebendary of Maynooth, 5367.
" Robert, commission, 4077; pardon, [illegible], 3780, 4473.
" Rowland, 6318.
" Thomas, grant, 626; his heir, 1778.
" Thomas, wardship, 1779; his heir, 4202.
Johnston — Johnstowne (Johnstown), co. Car., 1603, 4431, 6474.
Johnston — Johnstowne (Johnstown), co. Cork, [illegible], 5183, 4256-7, 5376, 5567, 5763.
Johnston — Johnston (Johnstown), co. Kild., 337, 1057, 1344, 2346, 4184, 4186, 4189, [illegible], 4347-8, [illegible], 5727; rectory, 5391, [illegible].
Johnston — Johnstowne (Johnstown), co. Meath, 347, 1260, 1480, 1553, 4110, 4575.
Johnston (Johnstown), co. Westm., 4463, 4641.
Johnston (Johnstown), co. Wex., 3945.
Johnston pingnot, co. Kild., 5797.
Johnstown, co. Wick., 4332.
Johnstown ford alias Avalloy Slaine, co. Ant., [illegible].
Joie, Tho., pardon, 4694.
Joie, James, prebendary of Kilmanagh, 703-4.
Jolly, Henry, master gunner, 5903.
Jones, John, keeper of Cork gaol, 4345.
" Rice, pardon, 3400.
Jones — Jhonnsie — Jhones — Jhoones — Johnes—Joanes, Thomas, chancellor of St. Patrick's, 2716, 3737; dean, [illegible], 4718; pardon of intrusion, 5081; commissions, 2718, 3344, 3516-1, 3434, [illegible], 3717, 3732, 3633, 3807, 4133, 4148, 4176, 4433; made bishop of Meath, 4376. *See* Meath, Bishop of.
" Wm., pardon, 5049.
" Wm., marshal of Castle Chamber, 5830; porter of Dublin Castle, 5344, 6143.
Jonesston (co. Westm.), 4161.
Jonnyn, Rich. m'Ricard, pardon, 5422.
Jonoyes, lands of, in bar. Kilmaine, co. Mayo, 4378.
Jordan, Rob., pardon, 4383.
Jonyn, Margaret ny ne, pardon, 5850.
Joones, Tho. *See* Jones.
Jordan, Barnard, son of John, and others of the name in co. Cavan, pardon, 5464.
Jordan—Jordane—Jordain—Jourdan—Jourdaine—Jurdan:
" Dionysius, pardon, 6314.
" James, pardon, 4715.
" John, pardon, 5365, 6034.
" John (of Hilson), 1600, 6434.
" Lewis. *See* Jurdan.
" Onory, pardon, 6731.
" Tho., pardon, 6313.
" Philip, pardon, 6467.
" Richard, 6006; pardon, 4118.
" Walter, pardon, 6877.
" William, pardon, 5946.
Jordanston—Jordanstown—Jourdanstown, co. Cork, 3487, 6578, 5762.
Jordanston (Jordanstown), co. Dub., 347, 1260, 5612.
Jordanston—Jordanstowne, co. Kilk., 1303, 5387.
Jordanston—Jordanston—Jordanstowne—Jordanstown, co. Meath, 1017, 2187, 2191, 2113, 2823, 2378, 3107, 3444, 5956, 5962, 4214, 4317, 5465, 6312.
Jordanston (co. Tip.?), 5211.
Jordanston, co. Westm., 5356, 6257.
Jurdston (Jordstown, co. Westm.?), 6623.
Jorne, John, pardon, 5703.
" Nich., pardon, 5703.
" Patr., pardon, 5903.
" Rich., pardon, 5904.
" Robert, pardon, 5971.
" Wm., pardon, 2749, 2904.
Jourdan—Jourdaine. *See* Jordan.
Jourdanstown. *See* Jordanston.
Joy, Nich., pardon, 5554.
" Redmond, pardon, 4823.
" *See* Joie, Joye.
Joyce, Rob., pardon, 5454, 5723.
" *See* Joye, Joien.
Joye, Edm., pardon, 6530.
" John, pardon, 4064, 6303.
" Nich., pardon, 6523.
" Redmond, pardon, 6053.
" Tho., pardon, 4026.
" Walter, pardon, 4636.
Joye—Joy—Joys (Joyce of Joyce's country):
" David m'Gilleduff, and twenty-three others of the name, pardoned, 5554.
" Edm. m'Tyboyd, pardon, 4936.
" Thomas oheam, attainted, 5605.
" Wm., pardon, 5753.
" ( ) m'Rory og, pardon, 4623.
Joyes country (Joyce's country, barony of Ross, co. Gal.), 5121, 6344.
Joyner, Roger, 4600.
Joyner's land, co. Kild., 4635.
Joys, Rob., pardon, 538.
" *See* Joye.

INDEX TO FIANTS—ELIZABETH.

Juan, Sawry ny, pardon, [illegible].
Jubcmlare wines (Gibraltar ?), 3102.
Jukkdoard, co. Meath, 1[illegible], [illegible].
Judge appointed temporarily in absence of justices of court, [illegible].
Jugo Dei, abbey de (Greyabbey), in Ards, co. Down, possessions leased, 47[illegible].
Julyanstown—Juliansion (Juliamstown), co. Meath, [illegible], [illegible], [illegible], [illegible], [illegible]; rectory, 14[illegible], [illegible].
Jonnestowne (co. Wex. ?), [illegible].
Jurdan, John, &c. See Jordan.
Jordanston (Jordanstown, co. Westm. ?), [illegible].
Jurdan, Lewis, grant, [illegible].
Juries, exemption from service on, [illegible], [illegible].
Justices of Assize and gaol delivery, functions of committed to chief commissioner of Ulster, [illegible].
Justices (lord) of Ireland, appointments, 11[illegible], [illegible], [illegible].
Justices of Peace. See Peace commissions ([illegible], [illegible], &c.), also Government.
Justices of Peace, [illegible], [illegible]; to take oath of supremacy, [illegible]; none in co. Carlow, [illegible]; chief magistrates of towns made, [illegible], [illegible], [illegible].
Jylbart, Sir Humfrey, colonel, 14[illegible], 1[illegible]. See Gilbert.

Kabrro, Shane m'Donell Y, pardon, 47[illegible].
Kacro, John, pardon, [illegible].
Kagall—Cagall—Kagnlo—Kaggall, co. Gal., [illegible], [illegible], [illegible], [illegible], [illegible].
Kaghreer, Patrick, pardon, [illegible].
Kaharagh, Margaret ny, pardon, [illegible].
Kaharougarry (co. Cork ?), [illegible].
Kahorowmacnoughe or Kaharoucmcnaghe, co. Cork, 47[illegible].
Kahecard, co. Kerry, [illegible].
Kaharrcclaine. See Caharoroban.
Kaherkonlish. See Caherkonlish.
Kahorkroken. See Cahir Crokane.
Kaherowmanagho, co. Cork, [illegible].
Kaharowmonoughe, co. Cork, 47[illegible].
Kaharowe (co. Cork ?), [illegible].
Kaharowgary, co. Cork, [illegible].
Kaherrowmanagho, co. Cork, [illegible].
Kaherysewin. See Cahirsewyne.
Kaharywaleyne, co. Cork, [illegible].
Kahill, Ricard m'Donill Y, pardon, [illegible].
Kahirasele. See Cahirasele.
Kahirologan. See Cahir-logan.
Kahircroggraine. See Cahircroggrane.
Kahirelly. See Caherelly.
Kahiroyare, co. Clare, [illegible].
Kahirgillcweyre (co. Lim. ?), [illegible].
Kahirledegin, co. Mayo or Ross., [illegible].
Kahirkanovane. See Caherkonevan.
Kahirkilloske, co. Lim., [illegible].
Kahirkinlish. See Caherkonlish.
Kahirloppane. See Cahirloppan.
Kahirlavyloye, co. Lim., 57[illegible].
Kahir m'Keon (Caheraderus, co. Clare ?), [illegible].
Kahir m'Ulicke (Caheramaculick, co. Mayo), [illegible].
Kahirmoonyn. See Cahermonan.
Kahirmorehowe. See Cahermorrohowe.
Kahirmally, in Connaght, 14[illegible].
Kaiole, Philip, pardon, [illegible].
Kaler (co. Wex. ?), [illegible].
Kalrofussock—Marrofuwsok (co. Lim. ?), rectory, [illegible], [illegible].
Kallaghe — Kallaghe, monastery, co. Lim., leased, [illegible], [illegible], [illegible]. See Monastery no Keylinsha.
Kallie, co. Long., [illegible].
Kalrirocdnan, co. Cav., 12[illegible].
Kallaghain, Dermot m'Shane Y, pardon, [illegible].
Kallaghan. See Callaghan and O'Callaghan.
Kallaghane (co. Wat. ?), 10[illegible].
Kallan, Tohl m'Malowny Y, pardon, [illegible].
Kallanan, Mologhlin oonlaghe I, pardon, [illegible].
Kallanaferele. See Callanyferoy.
Kallathrane. See Callathran.
Kalle. See Calle.
Kalle, Dionysius, pardon, 1[illegible].
" Patrick, pardon, 1[illegible].
Kallaghane, Dermod m'Teig Y, pardon, [illegible].
Kallohhane, Conor m'Dermod Y, pardon, [illegible].
" Conor m'Teige Y, pardon, [illegible].
Kalligban, Donogh m'Teig I, pardon, [illegible].
Kallighane, Donell m'Connoghor I, pardon, [illegible].
Kallowmagh, co. Clare, [illegible].
Kally, Siban ny, pardon, [illegible].
" Gillaluff m'Conner oo, and Shane roogh, his son, pardon, [illegible].
" John m'Redmond m'Shane Y, pardon, 1473.
" Katherine, pardon, 1[illegible].
" Richard boy, Donald, Edm. and Wm. m'Redm. m'Shane Y, pardon, 1[illegible], 1473.
" Walter m'Redmond m'Shane Y, pardon, 1473.
Kallylaggy, co. Cork, [illegible].
Kallyglasse, Owen m'Teig Y, pardon, [illegible].
Kallykynagher (King's co. ?), [illegible].
Kalogh, co. Lim. (see Calloghe), [illegible].
Kalry (co. Leit. ?), [illegible].
Kalry. See Calry.

INDEX TO FIANTS—ELIZABETH.

Kame ogo, Moriagh, pardon, 4415.
Kamoke. See Camock.
Kamemucky, co. Wat., 4438.
Kame, co. Wat., 5941.
Kankell (co. Rosc. ?), 5468.
Kankilly (co. Cork ?), 5778.
Kanmock. See Kanmock.
Kannarry (co. Cork ?), 6612.
Kannife, Connoghor m'Rinno Y, pardon, 6514.
" Donell m'The. Y, pardon, 6514.
" Shane m'Connoghor Y, pardon, 6514.
Kanny, Moraw oy, pardon, 4494.
Kanywy (co. Cork ?), 4578.
Kanraghenion, co. Meath, 604.
Kanton, Donald oe, pardon, 7341.
Kanierk—Kantork—Kantorke—Kantnirk—Kantnirke—Kontherk, co. Cork, 148, 2348, 2352-3, 2357, 2391, 4513, 6304, 6468, 6505.
Kanty, Donnoghe m'Dermod, pardon, 4444.
Kanwy—Kanvoy—Kanny vie (Cannaway), co. Cork, 3941, 5378, 6130, 6262.
Kapagh. See Cappagh.
Kapaykmockane (co. Cork ?), 6614.
Kapowly. See Capole.
Kapp[ ], co. Lim., 5468.
Kappaenyne, co. Lim. or Cork, 5688.
Kappagh, the (co. Gal. ?), 5684.
Kappagh—Kappagha. See Cappagh.
Kappaghbodya, co. Kilk., 512.
Kappenullan—Kappicullen—Kappoycwllin, (Cappanculleen), co. Lim., 468, 1342, 6304.
Kappanowko — Kappanmocko — Kappanowke — Kappannowke — Kyappanalick (Cappanouk), co. Lim., 461, 6304; grant, 6387.
Kappicullen. See Kappenullan.
Kappinargid (Cappanargid), co. Kild., 471.
Kappoge, co. Kilk. or Tip., 4728.
Kappygane (co. Kerry ?), 4576.
Karagh, Dermot m'Shane, pardon, 4108.
Karde, William, pardon, 678.
Kardiston. See Kardiffeston.
Kardiff. See Kardiffe.
Kardiffton — Kardiliston — Kardiston. See Kardiffeston.
Kardraghe (Cardmah, co. Meath), 698.
Karegine ne Veigh (Queen's co. ?), 6646.
Karell, John, pardon, 5378, 4115.
Kargo, Brian oe, pardon, 4340.
Kargon. See Cargin.
Kargin, co. Tip., 4088.
Kargine—Kargyne. See Cargin.
Karha, co. Clare, 4369.
Karhirelly (Cahorelly, co. Lim.), 4492.
Karickfergus. See Carrickfergus.
Karigeowrien. See Carrigiorian.
Karigekylly. See Carrigokille.
Karigifaky. See Carigifaky.
Karigiakerry, co. Cork, 4458.
Kariginnine, co. Wat. (co. Cork ?), 6062.
Karigifaky. See Carigifaky.
Karigkirryly. See Carrigkirell.
Karignasse. See Carrignassy.
Karignokury. See Carrignecurry.
Karignamock. See Carrignamock.
Karigogunill. See Carrigogrunell.
Karigroughanbegg. See Carrigrowghanbegg.
Karigynowury. See Carrigynoury.
Karigyrrik. See Carrigebrick.
Karkill. See Carkill.
Karkinlish — Karkinliske. See Caharkenlesh.
Karkir. See Carkir.
Karkynlishe. See Caharkenlesh.
Karn. See Carne, co. Mayo.
Karnagh, diocese of Ferns, rector, 5438.
Karne. See Carne.
Karney, John. See Kerny.
" Patrick. See Kernye.
Karnie, Barnaby fitzPhilip, pardon, 6461.
Karny, Connor, pardon, 6404.
" Thomas, pardon, 5128.
" Wm., pardon, 6404.
Karny (co. Mayo ?), 4781.
Karoine, co. Tip., 4371.
Karownamolle (co. Sligo ?), 3160.
Karowebryn (Carrowerin, co. Rosc. ?), 5438.
Karowe ne Corroe—Karowe ne Carroe (co. Donegal), 6362.
Karowenyny—Kearowenyny (Carrowneany), co. Gal., 5468, 5104.
Karowe Rossmylan — Kearowrossmidan (Rossmoylan), co. Gal., 6303, 5168.
Karowglasse, co. Mon., 5838.
Karowkipp, co. Sligo, 4628.
Karowecvor (co. Gal. ?), 5478.
Karowrossmakan, 5168. See Carrowreinbakan, co. Rosc.
Karowroe Lyskeeham—Kearowrow Lyscheeno (Carrowroe), co. Gal., 4688, 5168.
Karowroe ne Dawalone — Kearowrow ne dawelan (Carrowroe), co. Gal., 5362, 5168.
Karr (co. Lim. ?), 4308.
Karragh, Tho., pardon, 6138.
Karraghan, Rich. Condon fitz Davy in, 4481.
Karranbegg (co. Lim. ?), 6048.
Karrolahe, co. Wat., 4618.
Karrofussok. See Kairofussock.
Karricke Knyvloyoke, co. Down, 1828.
Karrickmore (co. Kild ?), 3478.
Karrickorowe, co. Wex., 688.
Karrickforgus. See Carrickfergus.
Karrickgranoge, co. Wex., 6412.
Karrickmayne. See Carrickmaya.
Karrickmogillaghe. See Carrigmogillaghe.
Karrigu[ ]ury (co. Cork ?), 5564.
Karrigfooka. See Carigifaky.
Karrigh Inody. See Carrigeody.

INDEX TO FIANTS.—ELIZABETH.

Karrigindrohit (Carrigadrohid, co. Cork ?), [illegible].
Karrigkattle — Karrykattle — Karykattle (Carrickittle, co. Lim.), [illegible], [illegible].
Karrigkilly. See Carrigakilla.
Karrigleaid (Carriglead, co. Car ?), 5447.
Karrignegloryuye (co. Kilk. ?), [illegible].
Karrignakorie—Karrignakorry — Karrignokory. See Carrignacurry.
Karriguyyvlaghe. See Carrighegulaghe.
Karrigugunacha. See Carrigugonogh.
Karrigrawhane (co. Cork ?), 4878.
Kartigrowghanbegg. See Carrigrowghanbeg.
Karrigyrandy. See Carrigundy.
Karrigyrrich. See Carrigeirick.
Karrikippane, co. Cork (see Carrickcappan), 5878.
Karrickma, co. Louth, 5418.
Karroll, Giles ny, pardon, 4878.
Karrocame (King's co.), 1681.
Karrowban, co. Rosc., 5857.
Karrowgarrowe, by Kilmallock, co. Lim., 5857.
Karrownavanie, co. Gal., [illegible].
Karrowreoghe, co. Lim., [illegible].
Karrveghbane (co. Lim. ?), [illegible].
Karry. See Carra, co. Mayo.
Karrye, a territory in co. Leitrim (Carro in "Iar Connaught," p. 347), [illegible].
Karrykettle. See Karrigkattle.
Karrygnoilly. See Carrignaphilly.
Karrygyndavie alias Templibrydan, vicar of, 54.
Karrywolane (King's co.), 1671.
Karten, Thady ne, pardon, 5436.
Karvylan, Paden, pardon, 5437.
Karya, co. Clare, 4774.
Karykettle. See Karrigkattle.
Karyte, co. Gal., 4856.
Karyny (co. Gal. ?), 4787.
Karwehall, co. Clare, [illegible].
Karwe in Kellymaugh (co. Tip. or Lim. ?), 4887.
Karwraragh, co. Clare, 4283, 4774.
Kashia, Owen oge m'Brien Y, pardon, 5543.
Kashane Ruddery, co. Cork, 5581.
Kashan Nackalt (Castlehacket ?), co. Gal., 1587, 5412.
Kassane, Rorie m'Donogh in, 5461.
Kauny (co. Cork ?), [illegible].
Kavan (see Cavan), 4584.
Kavanagh—Kavanaghe. See Cavanagh.
Kavana. See Cavan.
Kavna, Henry, pardon, 5811.
Kavanagh—Kavenanaghe. See Cavanagh.
Kavagh, Murtagh, pardon, [illegible].
Kawne, Nich., pardon, 5434.
Kawnee, Donogh, pardon, 5434.
„ James, pardon, 5434.
Kaycrourny. See Cahircurnie, co. Lim.
Kayhirglasena—Kayhyrglassen. See Caherglassane.
Kaylagh—Kaylaghe, monastery of S. Katherine, 5118, [illegible]. See Monaster ne Kaylaghe.
Kaylaghton. See Callaghton, co. Louth.
Kayneguil — Knyoegadd (Kinnegad ?, co. Westm.), 4834.
Kaynkye, Shone ny, alienation to, [illegible].
Kayrlay, Rioard m'Shane Y, pardon, [illegible].
Kayrcurny. See Cahircurnie.
Kayr Ely. See Caherelly.
Kayrecurney. See Cahircurnie.
Kee, Connoghor m'Mahowny Y, pardon, [illegible].
Keaddofus, Donald, pardon, [illegible].
Kealagh—Keadraghe. See Kedragh.
Keady, co. Mon., [illegible].
Keagh, Donogh, pardon, 4596.
„ Henry, pardon, 5455.
„ Hugh, pardon, [illegible].
„ John, pardon, 5418.
„ Tirlagh m'Keoghar, pardon, 4441.
Keaghane, Teig, pardon, [illegible].
Keaghe, Ferrall boy m'Edmond, pardon, 5542.
„ William, 2878.
Keagher, 4814.
Keaghyre, co. Rosc., 5818.
Keahe, Shane, pardon, 5554.
Keale, John, pardon, 4564.
Keale m'Enecullis (co. Cork ?), 4778.
Keale, co. Gal. or Clare, 4712.
Keallaghan, Keallaghan m'Woney I, pardon, 5254.
Keallaghane, Dermot m'Teig I, pardon, 5877.
„ Donald m'Shane Y, pardon, 2878.
„ Teig m'Cahir I, pardon, [illegible].
Keallie, Rowrie O'Moell fitz John, pardon, [illegible].
Keallogie, Margaret nyn Owen oy, pardon, 5818.
Keallnymanaghe, co. Tip., 4886.
Keally, Honory yny, pardon, 5116.
„ Katherine ny, pardon, 5551.
Kealtagh, Connor's co., 4881.
Kealtraghdonan, 5478.
Kealtraghe Mycholl, co. Gal., 4836.
Kealy, Edm., pardon, [illegible].
„ Philip m'Moriertagh I, pardon, [illegible].
„ Rorie m'Philip I, pardon, [illegible].
„ Teige m'Philip Y, pardon, [illegible].
Keamanory (co. Lim. or Tip. ?), 5587.
Kean, John, pardon, 5841.
„ Teige, pardon, 5851.

INDEX TO FIANTS.—ELIZABETH.

Keas (or Cahill), Tho., priest, pardon, [illegible].
Keanemtyckin. *See* Kenmuck.
Keanevaine, Conle m'Shane Y, pardon, 6461.
Keanmarrie — Keannaroy (Kenmare), co. Kerry, rectory, 6846, 6172.
Keannalmorhy, co. Cork, 6615.
Keannaroy. *See* Keanmarrie.
Keanry (Kerry ?), co. Lim., 5004.
Keantairke—Keanturke. *See* Kanturk.
Keanyvie. *See* Kanwy.
Keapaghbeg, co. Gal., 5234.
Keapaghe (Cappagh, co. Leit. ?), 5545.
Keapaghe (Cappagh), co. Wat., [illegible], 6122.
Keapaghinoona (Cappaghoon ? co. Gal.), [illegible].
Keapaghkylnnayso, King's co., 1397.
Keapaghmore (Cappagh More), co. Gal., 6228.
Keapaghmadrisye, co. Gal., 4436.
Keapallan (Queen's co. ?), 6762. *See* Capallan.
Keapanagh, co. Gal., 5108.
Keapeycwillin. *See* Kappocullan.
Keapitteige (Cappaidign, co. Kerry ?), 6468.
Keapenighan, co. Lim. (see Cappanighan), 4561.
Keapowle. *See* Capole.
Keappagh—Keappaghe. *See* Cappagh.
Keappaghe ne moddaghe (co. Tip. ?), 4868.
Keappaghiddyn (co. Tip. ?), 6744.
Keappanagh, co. Gal., [illegible].
Keappanagraigy (Cappanagraigue), Queen's co., 4612.
Keappanilane (Cappalane ?), Queen's co., [illegible].
Keappocke (see Keppock), Stephen, livery, 6728.
" Thomas, livery to son, 6788.
Keappey (see Cappoge), [illegible].
Kearntighe, Irish exaction (said by Cox to be a tax of 8s. 4d., a ploughland to maintain the lord's kerne. *See* Carew Cal., vol. III., p. 79), 4467.
Kearde, Donell, pardon, 6761.
" William, pardon, 5361.
Keare, Deirmot, pardon, 6727.
" Moriah, pardon, 6787.
Kearen, Tho. *See* Kearon.
Keadrume, co. Kerry, 6728.
Kearhuny (co. Lim. ?), 6467.
Kearighe, Donell, pardon, 6416.
Kearmor, co. Lim. or Kerry, 6467.
Kearnan, John. *See* Kernan.
Kearne, King's co., 4458.
Kearne, Kilsmary, pardon, 4631.
" Walter Brenagh fitzJohn, pardon, 6440.
Kearnemart. *See* Cahernemarie.
Kearnes, East (see Eastkernes), co. Meath, 543.
Kearny—Kearney—Kearnie—Kearnye:
" Barnaby, pardon, 6156, 6527.
" Conoghor, pardon, [illegible].
" Cornelius, pardon, 6176.
" Daniel, pardon, 6581.
" David, pardon, 5818, 5568.
" Edmund, pardon, 4568, 5496, 6527.
" James, pardon, 6537-8.
" John, burgess of Cashel, 5416.
" John, pardon, 5808.
" Morris, pardon, 6173, 6602.
" Ownie, pardon, [illegible].
" Philip, English liberty, 448.
" Philip, pardon, 1470.
" Richard (of Ballydowagh, co. Tip.), pardon, 6527, 6744.
" Robert, pardon, 4928.
" Thomas m'Donogh I., pardon, 6464.
" Thomas, pardon, 6492.
" Uny ny, pardon, 6467.
" William, pardon, 6421, 6754.
" [ ], (of Ballygibrowre), pardon, 6881.
Kearow Clonaghin. *See* Carrowclonfaghnasy.
Kearowcranagher. *See* Carrow Cranagher.
Kearowe, co. Lim. (see Carrowe), 6152.
Kearowegonn (Carrowgun ?), co. Sligo, 5444.
Kearowkill, co. Long., 6162.
Kearowkillanlagy, 5049. *See* Carrowkillanlagy.
Kearowkillomore, 4658. *See* Carrowkillemore, co. Gal.
Kearow Kilraghnabby. *See* Carrow Enlragh ne boby.
Kearowlare, co. Long., 6152.
Kearowmoghar (see Carrow Clonmagher), co. Gal., 6462.
Kearowneskyllino, co. Mayo, 4672.
Kearownikippy, co. Sligo, 5564.
Kearowny. *See* Karowenyny, co. Gal.
Kearowreogh. *See* Carrowreough, co. Gal.
Kearowrinbackan. *See* Carrowrinbakan, co. Rosc.
Kearowresmidan. *See* Karowe Resmylan, co. Gal.
Kearowrow Lyneahoun. *See* Karowroe Lyshneaham, co. Gal.
Kearowrow nodawelan. *See* Karowroe ne Dawelane.
Kearowrudsell, 6746.
Kearroll or O'Kerroll, Wm. and John, kern, (see O'Carroll), 1518.
Kearrough beg mollaghe, co. Lim., 4594.
Kearrowwroda — Kearowwroilds (Carrowerod, co. Sligo ?), 5456, 5856.
Keartan, Teig ne, pardon, 5557.
Keartin, John m'Nich. ny, pardon, 5452.

INDEX TO FIANTS—ELIZABETH.

Keartin, Nich. m'Wm. ny, pardon, [illegible].
Keary. See Kerry.
Keasigine, Donogh oge, pardon, [illegible].
Kealagh, Ulick m'Tebot, pardon, 4590.
Keateinge. See Keatinge.
Kealgansemuntle (co. Rosc. ?), [illegible].
Keatinge — Keating — Keting — Ketinge — Keateinge — Keathcinge — Keatin—Keatinge—Keetinge—Kette — Ketyn — Ketyng — Ketynge — Keyting — Keytinge:
„ Andrew, pardon, [illegible].
„ Anery, pardon, [illegible].
„ Arthur, grant of land (co. Wex.), [illegible]; a trustee, [illegible].
„ Arthur, pardon, [illegible], [illegible].
„ Edmund, grant of land, [illegible].
„ Edmund, pardon, 191, 1600, 1694, [illegible]; sons of, 2641.
„ Edward M'Nogurred, pardon, [illegible].
„ Edw., pardon, [illegible].
„ Ellenor—Ellenora, pardon, [illegible].
„ Fardorogh, pardon, [illegible], [illegible], [illegible].
„ Garret, pardon, [illegible], [illegible].
„ Geoffrey, pardon, [illegible].
„ Gerald, pardon, [illegible].
„ Gerral — Gerot, pardon, [illegible].
„ Hubert, pardon, [illegible], [illegible], [illegible].
„ James, premises in Kilmainham, 1566.
„ James, pardon, 1646, [illegible].
„ James, livery to heir, [illegible].
„ Jaffrey, pardon, 4162.
„ Jenytria, pardon, [illegible].
„ Joan, pardon, [illegible].
„ John (of Ballymoylerna, Queen's co.), grant of land, [illegible]; pardon [illegible].
„ John, pardon, [illegible].
„ John, sons of, [illegible].
„ Mary, pardon, [illegible].
„ Matthew, pardon, [illegible].
„ Maurice—Morish, pardon, [illegible].
„ Meiler, a thief, [illegible].
„ Meyler, pardon, [illegible].

Keatinge:
„ Michael, livery, [illegible].
„ Nicholas, pardon, [illegible].
„ Oliver, pardon, [illegible].
„ Onory, pardon, [illegible].
„ Patrick, pardon, [illegible].
„ Paul, pardon, [illegible].
„ Peirse, pardon, [illegible].
„ Peter, pardon, 161, [illegible].
„ Philip, pardon, [illegible].
„ Redmund, pardon, [illegible].
„ Richard, (of Ballinkmoyler, Queen's co.), grant of lands, [illegible]; lease, [illegible].
„ Rich., land in his tenure (co. Tip.), [illegible], [illegible].
„ Richard, pardon, 1671, [illegible].
„ Robert, pardon, [illegible].
„ Shane, pardon, [illegible].
„ Thomas, grant of land, [illegible].
„ Thomas, pardon, 749, [illegible].
„ Thomas, son of, [illegible].
„ Walter, grant of land, [illegible].
„ Walter, rector of Tacumshane, pardon, [illegible].
„ Walter, pardon, [illegible].
„ William, commission, [illegible].
„ William, pardon, [illegible].
„ William, sons of, [illegible].
Keatingeston — Ketingston — Ketingstowne (co. Kilk.), [illegible].
Keavan, Cahir m'Donogh, pardon, [illegible].
Keavan, Gerald, pardon, [illegible].
Keavanogh, Donnyn or Donogh M'Dermot, pardon, [illegible].
Keavallonigan (co. Tip. ?), [illegible].
Keavin, Wm. fyn, pardon, [illegible].
Keaughe, Edm. (of Kelman, co. Meath), trailer, [illegible].
Kearoshe, co. Wat., [illegible].
Kedagh, More ny, pardon, [illegible].
Kedaragh. See Kedragh.
Kedlontahyaham, King's co., [illegible].

INDEX TO FIANTS—ELIZABETH.

Keiragh—Keadragh — Kealerash (Keirah, co. Tip. ?), 1268, 3948, 5216, 4525, 6464-5, 6768.
Keal, Manus m'Connor I, pardon, 6752.
Keall, David m'Teig Y, pardon, 6584.
Keagane, Amble ne, pardon, 6108.
Keagon, Patr., pardon, 5558.
Keal, co. Long. See Keyll.
Kealoge, co. Wick. See Kricke.
Kealogue, co. Lim. See Killogue.
Keakegus, co. Wex. See Keylocks.
Kealy, Maurice m'David Y, pardon, 6763.
" Philip m'Teig Y, pardon, 3947.
Keaoge, co. Meath. See Kenaugh, 1460.
Keaogh, John m'Rich. roe, pardon, 6078.
Keane, co. Meath. See Kyran.
Keane—Keane — Keave — Keven, Thomas, marshal of Castle Chamber, 4178, 4459, 4594; chief engrosser, Exchequer, 6014; second chamberlain, Exchequer, 6061, 6161; lease, 4879; licence of alienation, 6167.
Kearine, William, English liberty, 1867.
Keatinge. See Keatinge.
Kegan, Joan, pardon, 6709.
" Katherine ny, pardon, 6565, 6796.
" Wm., pardon, 6160, 6307.
Kegane, Sawe ny, pardon, 4804.
" William, vicar of Kildonoghe, 655.
Keghe, William, vicar of Kilcolme, 757; prebendary of Kilmanagh, 758, 1817; precentor of Kilkenny, 3434.
Keghan, Elizabeth nine, pardon, 4577.
Keghow, Moyragh gare, pardon, 6266.
Kegra, Elizabeth nyne, pardon, 4577.
Kehie, Ellen ny, pardon, 4987.
Kehe, Richard, a pensioner, 4203.
" Capt., constable of Blackwater fort, 6878.
Kell, John fitz Derby, pardon, 6678.
Keiffe—Keif—Keife, Connor m'Owen I,
" Ee m'Owen,
" Sile ny,
" and others of the name pardoned, 4575, 6136, 6466, 6456-6, 6348.
" See O'Keaffe.
Keigan, Katherine ny, pardon, 5702.
" Tho., pardon, 6423.
Keigane, John, pardon, 6734.
Keigh harowe, co. Ross., 4575.
Keigh, Owin, pardon, 6901.
Keighe, Galcranve, riman pardon, 4078.
Keihe (co. Mayo ?), 6462.
Keile (co. Donegal), 6363.
Keilegarvife (Kilgarvife, co. Cork ?), 6612.
Keile m'Keevlis (co. Cork ?), 6770.
Keilenalter, co. Meath, 3430.
Keilleyhaly, in Munster, 6424.
Keilelallo (co. Cork ?), 6770.
Keilienlagh, co. Cav., 6563.
Keilinaloghir, co. Gal., 6603.
Keill (co. Gal. ?), 4681.
Keill, co. Westm., 6452.
Keillaghkery, co. Tip., 4383.
Keillogowne (co. Cav. ?), 6762.
Keillie, Morrish m'Ricard E, pardon, 4923.
Keill m'Phillippoig (co. Tip. ?), 4498.
Keillmeraghar co. Tip. ?), 6664.
Keillmore (co. Long. ?), 6864.
Keillmoroghow (co. Lim. ?), 6496.
Keillmourrie (co. Tip. ?), 6467.
Keillmamanaghe(Kilnamanagh, co. Tip.), 4687.
Keillna Nagno (co. Lim. ?), 6464.
Keillncorolery (Kilnacrana, co. Cav.), 6762.
Keill ne fagye, Rob. M'Kellgoide, pardon, 6467.
Keillnybonnale (co. Cork ?), 6467.
Keilloquirke—Keleguirk (co. Tip.), 4697, et al.
Keillvacknocrane (Kilmacnocrane, co. Cav. ?), 6762.
Keillvell anseo (co. Tip. or Lim. ?), 4807.
Keillvoillin (co. Lim. ?), 4804.
Keillyrve (co. Tip.), 4680.
Keillmore (co. Cork or Lim.), 6616.
Keilnyery in Ormond, co. Tip., 6874.
Keilskeighe, co. Gal., 4628.
Keiran, John m'Donogh I, pardon, 6781.
Keirean (co. Mayo ?), 4603.
Keishill (co. Cav. ?), 6762.
Keleghei (co. Kerry or Cork), 6614.
Keleguirk. See Keilloquirk.
Kelle (co. Kilk. ?), 6488.
Kelbarrenedane. See Kilbarrynoden.
Kelebe, Queen's co., 4681.
Kelekeny, co. Kilk., 6437.
Keld, co. Gal., 6612.
Kele, co. Cork, 6422.
Keleghe r, John m'Teig I, pardon, 6874.
Kelegode, Katherine fitz Richard is, pardon, 6477.
Kelenbregh, 6594.
Keleen, Baron of. See Killeen.
Kelfrush (Kilfrush, co. Lim.), 6611.
Kelhaghre (co. Tip. ?), 6666.
Keljchan, Donell m'Morrice I, pardon, 4564.
Keligrede, Sely ny, pardon, 6458.
Kelinmulreaye (co. Ross. ?), 6465.
Kelke (Kilkea, co. Kild. ?), 4775.
Kelkede, co. Clare, 4048.
Kelkenny. See Kilkenny.
Kellaghan, Connor garraf m'Donogh I, pardon, 4361.
Kellaghir, co. Cork, 4518.
Kellaise, Donnell A, pardon, 6722.
Kellaloughe. See Killaloe.
Kellbegg, co. Gal., 6445.
Kell Donell, Queen's co., 4461.
Kelldromed, Queen's co., 4681.
Kelle, Edm., pardon, 6423.
Kelleyened (Killekenned), co. Clare ?), 6612.

INDEX TO FIANTS—ELIZABETH.

Kelleghan, co. Wat., 677.
Kellen, Katherine, [illegible].
Kellenenral, co. Tip., [illegible].
Kellenoll, Queen's co., 6782.
Kellenenna (co. Rosc. ?), 6477.
Kellenealive (Kilmaslieve ?), co. Gal., 6418.
Kellenoyn (co. Rosc. or Westm. ?), 6474.
Kelles. See Kells.
Kelles, King's co., 6464.
Kelleston — Kellestowne. See Kelliston, co. Car.
Kellestowne, co. Dub., [illegible].
Kellevollphell, Queen's co., [illegible].
Kelley. See Kelly.
Kellfadde, co. Gal., 6453.
Kelliavragh (Killfaragh, co. Kilk. ?), [illegible].
Kelliffigle (Killiffigy ?), co. Gal., 6453.
Kellgedde, Wm. Ferche ne bwale, pardon, 6457.
Kellichan, Conoghor m'Donell I, pardon, [illegible].
Kellie. See Kelly.
Kellies country, Connaught, barriers appointed, [illegible].
„ See O'Kelly.
Kelligheane Teige m'Cahir Y, pardon, [illegible].
Kellin, King's co., 6449, [illegible].
Kellie, Shane, pardon, [illegible].
Kellinaboyan, co. Mayo, [illegible].
Kellinimake (co. Tip. ?), [illegible].
Kellioyode (co. Long. ?), [illegible].
Kellirhoragh (co. Tip. ?), [illegible].
Kelliston—Kelleston—Kellestowne, co. Car., 911, 1644, [illegible], 4556; rectory, [illegible].
Kellistone (co. Kilk. ?), 2467.
Kell m'Kneriliis (co. Cork ?), [illegible].
Kellmadra, [illegible].
Kellmanasaghe (Kilmanaragh, co. Tip. ?), 6447.
Kelloyhune, co. Cork, [illegible].
Kellock. See Kellocks.
Kellog—Kellogy (co. Tip. or Lim.), 6457.
Kellogues (co. Rosc. ?), [illegible].
Kellogy. See Kellog.
Kelloghe, co. Kerry, [illegible].
Kellocks, King's co., [illegible].
Kellocks—Kellock (Queen's co.), [illegible], 1064.
Kellonogue, co. Gal. or Rosc., 6414.
Kellroe (Kilroe), co. Gal., 6129-1.
Kells—Kelles—Kenles—Kenlas—Kenlis—Kenlys, co. Kilk., 59, 64, 107, 191, 1848, [illegible], [illegible], [illegible].
„ priory of the B. V. M. granted, [illegible]; possessions leased, [illegible], [illegible], [illegible], [illegible], [illegible], [illegible], [illegible], [illegible], [illegible], [illegible]; granted, 6414, [illegible].
„ rectory, [illegible].
„ grange, [illegible].
Kells—Kelles—Kellys—Kenles—Kenlys, co. Meath, [illegible], 1189, 1540, [illegible], [illegible], [illegible]; land and messuages in, [illegible].
„ honor and manor, 4874.
„ sovereign of, commissions, [illegible], [illegible], 3444, 3047.
„ abbey, possessions leased, [illegible].
„ hospital of S. John, leased, [illegible], [illegible], [illegible]; procurations, 4797.
„ rectory, [illegible], [illegible].
„ commission of martial law on garrison at, [illegible].
„ barony, martial law, 64, 1412.
Kells, 6170.
Kellsmrolly (co. Rosc. ?), 6445.
Kellyvalswryne (co. Rosc. ?), [illegible].
Kellunyunie (co. Tip. ?), [illegible].
Kelloragh, co. Gal., 4080.
Kellvallinecrenagh, co. Tip., [illegible].
Kelly—Kelley—Kellie—Kellye:
„ Alexander, pardon, [illegible].
„ Annabla ny, pardon, [illegible].
„ Anastace, pardon, [illegible].
„ Brene, pardon, [illegible].
„ Conoghor m'Teig I, pardon, [illegible].
„ Conoghor ne, pardon, 6457.
„ Daniel, lease, [illegible], [illegible].
„ Daniel, pardon, [illegible].
„ David, pardon, 615, 737, [illegible], [illegible], [illegible].
„ Derbie, Darby, Derby, pardon, [illegible], [illegible], [illegible].
„ Dermot, pardon, [illegible].
„ Donell, pardon, [illegible].
„ Donell A, pardon, [illegible].
„ Donell m'Cahir m'Donogh ne, pardon, [illegible].
„ Donell m'Teig I, pardon, [illegible].
„ Donogh, pardon, [illegible].
„ Edmund, pardon, [illegible], [illegible], [illegible], [illegible], [illegible], [illegible], [illegible], [illegible], [illegible].
„ Edm. m'Owen ne, pardon, [illegible].
„ Ellinor ny, pardon, [illegible].
„ Evlin, pardon, [illegible].
„ Gerald, pardon, [illegible].
„ Gillen ny, pardon, [illegible], [illegible].
„ Hugh, gunner in Dublin Castle, [illegible].
„ James, pardon, 4752.
„ John, presentation, [illegible]; suit as to treasurership of Cashel, [illegible].
„ John, pardon, [illegible], [illegible], [illegible], [illegible], [illegible], [illegible], [illegible], [illegible], [illegible], [illegible].
„ Katherine, pardon, [illegible].
„ Laughlin, pardon, 4754.
„ Margaret, pardon, [illegible], [illegible].
„ Maurice, pardon, [illegible].
„ Maurice, premises in Youghal, [illegible].
„ Mollaghlin m'Shane ne, pardon, [illegible].
„ Molaghlen, pardon, 6414.

Kelly:
„ Morgan, pardon, 3434.
„ Mortagh, pardon, 2834.
„ Nelo, pardon, 744.
„ Nicholas, lands of (co. Louth), 1184, 4266.
„ Owen ne, pardon, 6468, 6616.
„ Patrick, pardon, 854, 3434, 3734, 6180.
„ Patrick, house in Naas, 6108.
„ Peirse or Piers, pardon, 5101, 6448, 6694.
„ Peter, pardon, 1888.
„ Randolf, office of Gotcher, 790, 2274.
„ Richard, pardon, 2891.
„ Rory or Rorie m'Philip I, pardon, 6180, 6466.
„ Shane, pardon, 4323.
„ Sowo ne, pardon, 6618.
„ Sysile (wife of Lord Bermingham), pardon, 6747.
„ Teig, pardon, 434, 5101, 6076, 6223, 6311, 6180, 6440.
„ Terence, pardon, 4378.
„ Terrelagh, pardon, 4788.
„ Thady m'Dermod Y, pardon, 2884.
„ Thomas, grant of lands, 6067.
„ Thomas, pardon, 2867, 3714, 6180, 6438, 6494, 6577.
„ Walter, land of (in co. Louth), 1184, 4266.
„ William, license to export wheat, 1718.
„ William, surgeon, 6108; lease, 6747.
„ William, house in Dublin, 4314; suit, 2803.
„ William, house in Trim, 1714.
„ William, a disqualified vicar, 4318.
„ William, land in Clonsilagh, co. Dublin, 6778.
„ William, pardon, 3738, 6493, 6468, 6573, 6689, 6691.
„ Wm. m'Donogh oy, pardon, 5101.
Kelly's country. See O'Kelly.
Kellydane (co. Mayo ?), 5468.
Kellye. See Kelly.
Kellyes, King's co., 6496.
Kellycstown alias Killasnuy, co. Car., rectory, 948.
Kellycston, co. Dub., 1636.
Kellykorran, co. Mon., 5603.
Kellyn, 5612.
Kellynaneugh (co. Tip. or Lim. ?), 6307.
Kellynteemalitt (co. Lim. ?), 6667.
Kellye. See Kelle.
Kellyston (Kellystown, co. Meath), 858.
Kellyvelly, co. Westm., 2567.
Kellyvogher (co. Gal. ?), 6664.
Kelmeyleon (Kilmeeliokin ?), co. Gal., 6903.
Kelnaguenmagh, co. Tip., 6664.
Kelnathlengurt (co. Tip. ?), 6788.
Kelnyeroldy (Kilmerold, co. Cav. ?), 6597.
Kelnylegg (Killenlag, co. Gal. ?), 6603.
Kelogo, 173.
Keloke (Keelogs, co. Wick.), 6664.
Kelrachpurinower (co. Ros. ?), 6612.
Kelsarolle (co. Ros. or Cav. ?), 6548.
Kelsochonaght (Kilacohenagh, co. Cork ?), 6613.
Keltepinne (Kilrinolan ?), co. Tip., 6768.
Keltagh, co. Westm., 4368.
Keltecolle, co. Cav., 4334.
Keltegadda, co. Tip., 6682.
Kelteyman, co. Tip., 6712.
Keltobur, co. Westm., 1486.
Kelucherie (co. Tip. ?), 6758.
Kelue, co. Mon., 6656.
Kely, Dermod m'David I, pardon, 2818.
„ Robert, pardon, 4468.
„ Moriertagh and Philip m'Teig I, pardon, 2818.
Kelyloghan (co. Cork ?), 6816.
Kemlan, Tho., pardon, 1468.
Kemmeess (Kimmins, co. Meath), 4282.
Kemoros (see S. Keran, co. Wex.), 2828.
Kempe, Wm., pardon, 3728.
Kene, Ambrose oge, pardon, 6577.
Kenagh (co. Gal. or Ros.), 4778, 6712.
Kenaghan, 674.
Kenaghestown, co. Meath, 1892.
Kenalagh. See Kinalagh.
Kenalboick, co. Cork, 6614.
Kenale (co. Cork ?), 6568.
Kenalee — Kenalloye (O'Shaughnessy's country), co. Gal., 1778, 6768.
Kenaleagh — Kenaliagh — Kenaliaghe. See Kinaleagh.
Kenall, co. Cork, 6614.
Kenalloye. See Kenalee.
Kenalvie, co. Dub., 1777.
Kenane, Philip, pardon, 1617.
Kenanston (co. Meath ?), 2877.
Kenard (Kinard ?), co. Mon., 6676.
Kenaugh (Kenoage), co. Meath, 1668.
Kenay, Thomas, vicar of Banne, 787.
„ Wm., pardon, 6188.
Kendall — Kendal, Laurence, chaplain of Gowran, 6730.
„ Robert, registrar of causes before the deputy and council, 2648; clerk of the Castle Chamber, Dublin, 2868, 3488, 3784; lease, 3896; pardon, 3842.
„ Wm., marshal of the Castle Chamber, 3437, 3714, 6294; pension, 4151.
Kendelson, Edw., pardon, 2334.
Kendelmarch, Robert, pardon, 2841.
Kene, Margaret, pardon, 1784.

INDEX TO FIANTS—ELIZABETH.

Kene, Patrick, robbed, [illegible].
Kennina, co. Gal., [illegible].
Kenochenno, co. Meath, [illegible].
Kenedie, Brian m'Shane I, pardon, [illegible].
" James, pardon, [illegible].
" Margaret ayne, pardon, 6701.
" More ayn Teige, pardon, [illegible].
" Nich., chaplain, [illegible].
" Rorie, pardon, [illegible].
Kenedigh, Ode, pardon, [illegible].
" Ode m'Philip, pardon, [illegible].
" Owen m'Othney I, pardon, [illegible].
Kenedy, Connor, pardon, [illegible].
" Conor m'Tirrelay I, pardon, [illegible].
" Donogh m'Mahowne buoy, pardon, [illegible].
" Edmund, pardon, [illegible], [illegible].
" Honora, pardon, [illegible].
" James, pardon, [illegible], [illegible].
" Joan, pardon, [illegible].
" John, pardon, [illegible].
" Margaret ny, pardon, [illegible].
" Philip, pardon, [illegible].
" Shane m'Owen, pardon, [illegible].
" Terrietus, pardon to daughter of, [illegible].
" Thomas, chaplain, pardon, [illegible].
" William, pardon, [illegible], [illegible], [illegible].
Kenefeck, Edm., pardon, [illegible].
Kenelaige, John fitz Edm., pardon, [illegible].
Kenele, Conoghor m'Shane I, pardon, [illegible].
Keneleighe, co. Westm., [illegible].
Kenelmeak, co. Cork, [illegible].
Keneleam (co. Ross. ?), [illegible].
Kenett, Patrick, house in Naas, [illegible].
Kenevan, Rob., pardon, [illegible].
Kenien. See Kelle.
Kenleston—Kynleston, co. Dub., [illegible], [illegible], [illegible].
Kenleston, alias Ballykelly, co. Dub., [illegible].
Kenlee — Kenlie — Kenllye — Kenlye. See Kelle.
Kenmare, co. Kerry. See Kenneyre morra.
Kenmuck—Kenmock — Keanemmycke, co. Wat., [illegible], [illegible].
Kennaghe, co. Westm., [illegible].
Kennaghna, co. Meath, [illegible].
Kennaghmore, co. Westm., [illegible].
Kennalleghe. See Kinelagh.
Kennan, Conle m'Shane Y, pardon, [illegible].
Kennane, Katherine, pardon, [illegible].
Kennaugher, More ny, pardon, [illegible].
Kennedie, James, pardon, [illegible].
" John, pardon, [illegible].
" Tho., pardon, [illegible].
Kennedy, Ellis fitz Philip, pardon, [illegible].
" Shily ny, pardon, [illegible].
" Tho., pardon, [illegible].
" Thomas, house in Dublin, [illegible].
Kennegha, co. Car., [illegible].
Kennelle, More ny, pardon, [illegible].
Kennelly, Dermod Y, pardon, [illegible].
Kennelstown, co. Lim., [illegible].
Kennely (co. Mon. ?), [illegible].
Kennery. See Kenny.
Kennetstown, co. Meath. See Kynestown.
Kennett, Patrick, [illegible], [illegible].
Kennett (Kinitty ?), co. Ross., [illegible].
Kenney, Nich. See Kenny.
Kennitte (Kinnitty, King's co. ?), [illegible].
Kennimore, John, [illegible], Athlone, [illegible].
Kenny—Kenney—Kennye:
" Anne, pardon, [illegible].
" John, pardon, [illegible], [illegible].
" Maurice, Macdaibh liberty, [illegible].
" Maurice m'Rory I, pardon, [illegible].
" Nich., clerk of first fruits, [illegible], [illegible]; commr. for valuing benefices, [illegible]; deputy auditor, [illegible], [illegible]; general surveyor, [illegible], [illegible].
" Nich., pardon, [illegible], [illegible], [illegible].
" Rich., pardon, [illegible].
" Robert, pardon, [illegible].
" Thomas, [illegible].
Kenny's mill, Wexford, [illegible].
Kennydy, John, pardon, [illegible].
Kennye morra (Kenmare ?), co. Kerry, advowson of church, [illegible].
Kennye, Nich. See Kenny.
Kennye, James, pardon, [illegible].
Kenoch—Kenocke, co. Meath, [illegible], [illegible], [illegible], [illegible].
Kenocke (Kenogue), co. Meath, [illegible].
Kenowenradde (Carrowcrod ?), co. Sligo, [illegible].
Kenredy, John, pardon, [illegible].
Kenry — Kennory — Kenrye (barony of Kenry), co. Lim., [illegible], [illegible], [illegible], [illegible].
Kensale—Kensall. See Kinsale.
Kenselagh, Donogh, pardon, [illegible].
Kenselle. See Kinsale.
Kenselogh, Edm., pardon, [illegible].
Kenselagh, Donogh m'Edm., pardon, [illegible].
Kenselo, a district in north of co. Wexford, indentures with the chiefs, [illegible].
Kenshelagh, Felim, pardon, [illegible].
" Shan, pardon, [illegible].
Kenshellaugh, Bran m'Donnogh, pardon, [illegible].
" (Gerald) m'Murrough, pardon, [illegible].
Kensham—Kynsham (Keynsham, Somersetshire, England), priory, possessions leased, [illegible], [illegible].
Kent, Nicholas, livery, [illegible]; commission, [illegible].
" Thomas, heir of, [illegible].
Kent's land in Dublin, [illegible].

INDEX TO FIANTS.—ELIZABETH.

Kenis, Edm., pardon, [illegible].
" Patr., pardon, [illegible].
Kenturk—Kenturke. See Kanturk.
Kentiston (Kentstown), co. Meath, manor, [illegible].
Kenton, George, [illegible].
" Janet or Genet, livery, [illegible], 841.
" Patrick, daughter and heir of, 821, 841.
Kenvoire, co. Donegal, [illegible].
Kenvicke, John, pardon, [illegible].
Kenyiske, James, pardon, 4110.
" Rich., pardon, 4169.
Kenyfeel, Richard, pardon, 1816.
Kenyrtusa (King's or Queen's co.), [illegible].
Kenyn, Sawney, pardon, [illegible].
Kenymake, Richard, pardon, 4676.
Keogh—Keoghe, Brian, pardon, [illegible], [illegible].
" Brian carragh m'Edm., pardon, [illegible].
" Collo m'Donogh, pardon, [illegible].
" Conchor m'Hugh, pardon, [illegible].
" Connor m'Maurice, pardon, [illegible].
" David mac William mac Walter, pardon, 847.
" Teig, pardon, [illegible].
" Henry, pardon, [illegible].
" Hugh m'Conchor, pardon, [illegible].
" James, pardon, [illegible].
" Mortagh, pardon, [illegible].
" Moylor m'Walter, pardon, [illegible].
" Owen, pardon, [illegible].
" Salle ny Thomy, pardon, [illegible].
" Wm. oge, pardon, [illegible].
" Wm., pardon, [illegible].
Keoghe, Donald, pardon, [illegible].
" Nich., pardon, [illegible].
" Thos., pardon, [illegible].
Keoghes, Farrcyle m'Farrell, pardon, [illegible].
Keologeleighe—Keologilloghe, co. Mayo, [illegible].
Keonecayllly, co. Kerry, [illegible].
Keonyne, Carolyn oge, pardon, [illegible].
Keopagh, co. Clare, [illegible].
Keopidronnya. See Kepdronnya.
Keoyghe, Anable ne, pardon, [illegible].
Kepagh (co. Clare ?), [illegible].
Kepagh. See Kepanghe.
Kepagh (Cappagh ?), Queen's co., [illegible].
Kepaghe. See Keppaghe, co. Car.
Kepaghe. See Keppagh, co. Wat.
Kepaghe roe (Cappa roe, co. Tip. ?), [illegible].
Kepaghingorran. See Cappagh na gorran.
Kepanloghan (co. Lim. ? see Cappanlaghan), [illegible].
Kepatrick (co. Cork ?), [illegible].
Kepaughe—Kepagh (Cappagh), co. Lim., [illegible]; manor or castle and land, [illegible], [illegible].
Kepdronnya—Keopidronnya (Cappadrummin, co. Tip.), [illegible], [illegible].
Keppaynam, co. Westm., [illegible].
Keppegragy (co. Kild. ?), [illegible].
Keppenrey (see Capparney, Queen's co.), [illegible].
Keppocan (King's co.), [illegible].
Keppogevran—Keppogeran (King's co.), [illegible].
Keppoghney (King's co.), [illegible].
Keppogolen. See Cappaghgollen.
Kepole. See Capole, Queen's co.
Keppaghe (King's co.), [illegible].
Kepowle. See Capole.
Keppach (see Cappagh), co. Clare, [illegible], [illegible].
Keppagh (see Cappagh, co. Tip.), [illegible].
Keppagh—Kepaghe (Cappagh, co. Wat. ?), [illegible], [illegible].
Keppagh (Cappagh, co. Wick. ?), [illegible].
Keppaghe—Keppaghe (Cappagh ?), co. Car., [illegible], [illegible], [illegible].
Keppache (see Cappagh), co. Kilk., [illegible].
Keppaghe duffe (Cappaghduff), co. Mayo, [illegible].
Keppagh krovyn, King's co., [illegible], [illegible].
Keppagh loughane (Cappalough, Queen's co. ?), [illegible].
Keppaghwhinch (co. Kilk. ?), [illegible].
Keppaugh (see Cappagh), co. Tip., [illegible].
Keppock. See Keppoke, co. Dub.
Keppock or Keppocke, Stephen, livery, [illegible].
" " Thomas, livery to son, [illegible].
Keppoge (see Cappock), co. Kild., [illegible].
Keppoke—Keppock, co. Dub., [illegible], [illegible].
Keppoke, William, [illegible].
Keragh alias M'Kally, Moriertagh, pardon, [illegible].
Kerane, co. Meath, [illegible].
Keranestown—Keranston. See Carranstown.
Keraugh—Keraughe. See Carroughe, co. Kild.
Kerbage, co. Kerry, [illegible]. See Kermor.
Kerbrie, Roric, pardon, [illegible].
Kerde, John, [illegible].
Kerde, pardoned, [illegible].
Kerdeston—Kerdestowne. See Kerdiffeston.
Kerdiffe—Cardiff—Cardife—Cardiff—Cardiffe—Kardiff—Kerdif—Kerdiffe—Kerdyf:
" Arthur, [illegible].
" Christopher (Rolleston), wardship, [illegible]; livery, [illegible].
" Christopher (of Pillekston), his heir, [illegible].
" James (of Dunsink), pardon, [illegible]; comm., [illegible].
" James, pardon, [illegible].
" John, treasurer of Christ Church, refuses oath of supremacy, [illegible].

INDEX TO FIANTS—ELIZABETH.

Kerdiffe :
- „ John (of Ralestown), grant, [illegible] ; his heir, 6442, [illegible].
- „ John (of Turvey), livery, 844.
- „ John (of Pillotstown), wardship, [illegible].
- „ Margaret, 4214.
- „ Nicholas, serjeant at law, [illegible] ; comm., [illegible].
- „ Richard, wife of, 182.
- „ Thomas, death, [illegible].
- „ Walter, justice Common Bench, 18.
- „ Walter (of Turvey), his heir, 844.
- „ (   ), house in Waterford, [illegible].

Kerdiffeston—Cardiffeston—Cardifston—Cardifton—Kerdiffton—Kardifston—Cardeston—Cardiston—Kardestone—Kardiston—Kerdiston—Kardestowne (Kerdiffstown), co. Kild., 4137, 4150, [illegible], 4378, 4433, 4834, 5012, [illegible], [illegible], [illegible], [illegible], [illegible], [illegible], [illegible], [illegible].
- „ rectory, [illegible], [illegible], [illegible].

Kerdyf, John. See Kerdiffe.
Keregan, Katherine ny, pardon, [illegible].
Kereheill (co. Kilk. ?), [illegible], [illegible].
Keremody (co. Lim. ?), [illegible].
Keretane, co. Clare, [illegible].
Keren, Tho. See Kearon.
Kerbonkille (co. Cork ?), [illegible].
Kerhill (co. Kilk. ?), [illegible].
Keriane, Owen, pardon, 8447.
Kermode, Teige mac Mahowne I., pardon, [illegible].
Kermor and Kerbegg (Kerries), co. Kerry, [illegible].
Kermore (co. Wex. ?), 1250.
Ker Morvey (Morvey), co. Gal., [illegible].
Kern, to be maintained by O'Maddon, [illegible].
- „ of the Sheriff of Kilkenny, [illegible].
- „ See Kearnetighe.

Kernalvye. See Carnalway.
Kernan—Kearnan—Kernane—Kernon :
- „ Edmund, pardon, 8457.
- „ John, sub-sheriff of Westmeath, [illegible], [illegible], [illegible] ; seneschal of M'Kearnan's country in co. Cavan, [illegible] ; clerk of the pleas Exchequer, [illegible], [illegible], [illegible] ; pardon, [illegible], [illegible], [illegible], [illegible], [illegible], [illegible], [illegible].
- „ John, pardon, [illegible].
- „ Moleghlyn, pardon, [illegible].
- „ Murtagh, pardon, [illegible].
- „ Thady, pardon, [illegible].

Kernanstowne—Ballykernan (Kernanstown), co. Car., [illegible], [illegible], [illegible].
Kerne, Patrick, 1728.
- „ Rosse, pardon, [illegible].

Kerne, William, 1728, [illegible].
Kernes, villages (Carnes East and West), co. Meath, 1460.
- „ See Eastkernes and Westerkernes.

Kerney, James, pardon, [illegible].
Kerney—Kernie, John. See Kerny.
Kerumoury (co. Clare ?), [illegible].
Kernon, John. See Kernan.
Kerny, co. Cork, rectory, [illegible].
Kerny — Kerney — Kurney — Kerneye — Kernie—Curni, John, treasurer, St. Patrick's, commissions, [illegible], [illegible], [illegible], [illegible], [illegible], [illegible], [illegible].
- „ John, pardon, [illegible].
- „ Patrick, pardon, [illegible].
- „ Paul, pardon, [illegible].
- „ Philip, pardon, [illegible].

Kernye—Kerney, Patrick (of Cashel), pardon, [illegible] ; aqua vitae license, [illegible].
Kereyn, co. Tip., [illegible].
Keroy, Moloughlin m'Connor, pardon, [illegible].
Keroggarrowe (see Carrowgarrowe), co. Lim., [illegible].
Kerolan, Patr., pardon, [illegible].
Kerolanston, co. Meath, 418.
Kerorivagho (Carrowreagh ?), co. Rosc., [illegible].
Kerowmoloyle, 1178.
Kerowsboggo (Carrow Bog, co. Long.), 1170.
Kerowmon (see Carrowmon, co. Gal.), [illegible].
Kerowmore (Carrow More, co. Long.), 1170.
Kerowntyfrole, co. Gal., [illegible].
Kerreighan, Edm., pardon, 4118.
Kerreston (Carstown), co. Louth, [illegible].
Kerrey. See Kerry.
Kerroyghan, John, pardon, 4118.
- „ Tho., pardon, 4118.

Kerrie. See Kerry.
Kerries, co. Kerry. See Kermor.
Kerrig ny cassell (co. Cork ?), [illegible].
Kerrikbroghan—Kerrikobroghan, co. Car., [illegible], [illegible].
Kerrollonighe, in Imanny, in Connaght, [illegible].
Kerroughtimoneleaghoghe, co. Westm., [illegible].
Kerrowkoyleu (co. Rosc. ?), [illegible].
Kerrowruyn (Carrowcrin, co. Gal. ?), [illegible].
Kerrowusmen (Carrowusnon, co. Donegal), [illegible].
Kerry—Kerry—Kerrey—Kerrie—Kery—Kiery—Kyery—Kyerye, [illegible], [illegible], 6804, 6811.
- „ comm. to set out county, 1048 ; doubtful lands to be added to, [illegible], [illegible].
- „ clerk of crown, &c., [illegible].
- „ justices of peace, [illegible].
- „ old county of, [illegible], [illegible].
- „ liberty, [illegible].
- „ comm. to hear disputes between people and earl of Desmond, [illegible].
- „ ecclesiastical comm., [illegible].

INDEX TO FIANTS—ELIZABETH.

Kerry:
„ command of soldiers in, 2457, 2566.
„ martial law, 963, 1007, 1580, 1646, 2186, 2696.
„ lands of earl of Desmond in, 4928.
„ grants of land to undertakers, 5043, 5217, 5206, 5373-5, 5701, 5047, 5717; to others, 5034, 5117, 5134, 5494.
bishop of, lands of, 5043.
archdeacon of, 2274.
knight of, John fitz Wm. (Fitz-Gerald), comm., 1846.
knight of, pardon, 2183.
„ knight of, Helen, daughter of, 4744.
Kerry, 4743.
Kerry, Maurice, 1987.
Kerry Castle—Kerrycurrihie (Kerrycurrihy, co. Cork), 4967, 4696.
Kerrye, Margery ny, pardon, 6407.
Kerrye, Robert, 1460.
Kerrslellye—Katrushellye (Carrowneloragh, co. Gal. ?), 4079.
Kerrahey, co. Gal., 6420.
Kerrivann (co. Gal. ?), 4724.
Kery. See Kerry.
Kery, John, 2418.
Kerseghtine, co. Mayo, 4630, 4783.
Kerseghthomas, 878.
Kerryeghter, co. Mayo, 4654, 4609.
Keshea, Shane m'Wm. I., pardon, 4803.
„ Wm. m'Tho. I., pardon, 4605.
Keshe (King's or Queen's co. ?), 6954.
Kessyny wny river, co. Down, 4977.
Kestelltarne, co. Carl., 6540.
Kessnegteen (co. Tip. or Kilk. ?), 3608.
Ketin—Keting—Ketinge. See Keatinge.
Ketingeston—Ketingstowne. See Keatings-town.
Ketjamon, 2816.
Kettewell, Michael. See Kettlewell.
Kettellwell—Kettelwell, Michael. See Kettle-well.
Ketten, Maurice, pardon, 6734.
Kettlewell — Kettiwell — Kettellwell — Ketelwell, Michael, collector of customs, Wexford, 2917; surveyor of the Exchequer 2998, 3446, 4842, 5800, 6014; clerk of works, 3446, 3618; surveyor of ordnance, 4960, 5442, 4841-2; constable of Dublin Castle, 5700; comm., 6771; leases, 2426, 3067, 4461; assignees of, 3547, 4918, 3067.
Ketyn—Ketyng—Ketynge. See Keatinge.
Keugh, Moyler m'Philip, pardon, 6454.
Kevan, Denis, mason, 2717, 5870; widow of, mason, 4366.
Dionysius, house in Dublin, 1611.
Edm., pardon, 6476.
Kahir, pardon, 6476.
Walter, 1714.
Kevan, William, pardon, 1881.
Kevanagh — Kevanaghe — Kevanaigh — Kevaneth — Kevenaagh — Kevenagh — Kevennagh—Kevenaghe. See Cavanagh.
Kevoye, Mare nyne, pardon, 4677.
Kewan, Robert, alias Cavenagh, English liberty, 494.
Kewrsie, Wm., pardon, 6482.
Kewloncoshey (or Coolnahinery), co. Ross., 6858.
Kewlowrin—Kewlrodin, co. Clare, 6164, 5618.
Key, Edm. oge m'Henry, pardon, 4079.
Key, Redmond m'Henry, pardon, 4079.
Key, Lough. See Loughkee.
Keyes, Edward, grant of a wardship, 4103.
Keylogenne (Queen's co. ?), 4498.
Keyle, Dermod, Philip and Tho. m'Dee I., pardon, 4460.
„ Davie m'Shane Kynull I., pardon, 6480.
Keylemalyne, co. Meath, 5544.
Keyll (Kool, co. Long.), 6787.
Keylinevo, co. Tip., 4960.
Keylegowrye, in Connaught, 4478.
Keylinegaull, co. Tip. or Lim., 4748.
Keylivelynycnoyraugh (co. Cork ?), 4495.
Keylly, Teig m'Donnogh I., pardon, 6794.
Keylmadire (co. Mayo ?), 4448.
Keylmaondagh (co. Long. ?), 4498.
Keylmenane (Kilmanan, Queen's co.), 5165.
Keylooke (Keelogue, co. Wex. ?), 81.
Keyloghe (co. Ross. ?), 4484.
Keyly, Tho. m'Teig I., pardon, 4901.
Keynan, Matthew, house in Dublin, 1811.
Keynard (Kinard), co. Lim. (see Kynarde), 6160.
Keyne, Wm., pardon, 4449.
Keynoged (Kinnegad ? co. Westm.), 4624.
Keyrleyne, co. Westm., 1461.
Keyneare, Shane I., pardon, 6486.
Keythelbridge, co. Louth, 1793.
Keyting—Keytinge. See Keatinge.
Keyton, Rich., pardon, 4963.
Khaetine, James oe, pardon, 6477.
Khellob, Sawry ny, pardon, 4851.
Khenes, Ambrose, pardon, 4684.
Kherry (co. Leix. ?), 4790.
Khove, co. Lim., 1143.
Khryegh — Kryshe (Creagh, co. Ross. ?), rectory, 1481.
Khyllcloragh in Connaught, 1406.
Kiaghe, Edm., pardon, 5110.
Kiancwduff. See Carrowduff.
Kinrow ny Wadirye, co. Cork, 4430.
Kiarrowaikeny (co. Ross. ?), 6468.
Kibrock (co. Cork ?), 4411.
Kid-fell, used by glovers, 6811.
Kidd (co. Cork ?), 4871.
Kie, Katherine ny, pardon, 4052.
Kieopinshe, co. Kerry, 4605.

Kiedagha, co. Tip., [illegible].
Kief—Kiefe—Kieff—Kieffe:
„ Art m'Donell Y,
„ Dermot m'Conor I, and others of the name pardoned, [illegible], 3474, [illegible], 4214, [illegible].
„ See also O'Keeffe.
Kiefe, co. Cork, [illegible].
Kieghe, Brian dorogh m'Henry, pardon, [illegible].
„ Rory, pardon, 4467.
Kiehmeagh (co. Wat.?), 5716.
Kielcitagh, co. Cork, [illegible].
Kielcarne, co. Cork, 6744.
Kielcarry (co. Cork ?), 6514.
Kielegurrifle (co. Cork ?), 6770.
Kielellie (co. Kerry ?), [illegible].
Kielelagh (co. Cork ?), 6871.
Kielle (co. Clare ?), [illegible].
Kiellkierane (co. Cork ?), 6814.
Kiellderic (co. Clare ?), [illegible].
Kiellcolla, co. Mayo, [illegible].
Kielloley, co. Kerry, [illegible].
Kielmehoneary (Killmoney), co. Cork, [illegible].
Kielmemartie (Kilmamartery), co. Cork, [illegible].
Kieltervikeegean, co. Clare, 4374.
Kielvillie, co. Cork, [illegible].
Kieppagha, co. Kerry, [illegible].
Kierdane, Moriertagh m'Donogh I, (perhaps for Rierdan), pardon, [illegible].
Kierviagh, Morish, pardon, [illegible].
Kierry, Tho. oge m'Tho. m'Tho., pardon, [illegible].
Kiery. See Kerry.
Kierycurrihie. See Kerry Curhie.
Kiese, Art m'Donell, pardon, 6674.
„ Conchor m'Leighe and Conchor m'Art, pardon, 6674.
„ Gerald, pardon, 6674.
Kif—Kife—Kiff—Kiffe:
„ Owen m'Art I,
„ Teig m'Eig Y,
„ Ellen ny,
and others of the name pardoned [illegible], 6674, [illegible], 4457, [illegible], [illegible], [illegible], [illegible], [illegible].
Kiffe, Donogho m'Conohor I, pardon, 4367.
Kigane, Wm., pardon, 6457.
Kigieman, Thomas, pardon, 6514.
Kihie, Jovan ny, pardon, [illegible].
Kikerine, co. Tip., [illegible].
Kilcragh, Gerrott m'Edm., pardon, [illegible].
Kilachie (co. Tip. ?), [illegible].
Kilagh. See Killaha, co. Kerry.
Kilaghy (King's co. ?), [illegible].
Kilaha. See Killahie.
Kilahegard (co. Tip. ?), [illegible].
Kilahie, co. Cork, [illegible].
Kilalgeo, co. Tip. or Kilk., 6704.
Kilallo in Upper Ossory, 677.
Kilalone. See Killalloe.
Kilardry, co. Tip., 4837.
Kilarighi. See Killarnaght.
Kilarney, co. Kerry, 6070.
Kilasparguolan (Killasparguolan, co. Gal. ?), 4676.
Kilbalcroguen (co. Wick. ?), [illegible].
Kilballaltie (co. Wat. ?) [illegible].
Kilballagh, co. Westm., [illegible].
Kilbalane, in Munster (perhaps Kilbolane), [illegible].
Kilballadaff, Queen's co., 6651.
Kilballane, co. Cork, [illegible].
Kil Balli clement. See Kilvallicloment.
Kilballigorman, [illegible].
Kilballinedie (co. Wat. ?), [illegible].
Kilballiwortlie, co. Cork, [illegible].
Kilballyboyne (co. Clare ?), [illegible].
Killallykilly, co. Wat., 5167.
Kilballyfalsive — Kilballyfahyve (Kilbally-lahiff), co. Kerry, 5016.
Kilballymurrilie, [illegible].
Kilballyveer, co. Meath, 31.
Kilbane, co. Kerry. See Killebane.
Kilbane—Kylbane, Queen's co., [illegible], 1347, [illegible], [illegible].
Kilbane (co. Wick.), [illegible].
Kilbanere (co. Cork ?), 6764.
Kilbaren (co. Tip. or Lim.), rectory, [illegible], 3347.
Kilbarghe, co. Meath, [illegible], [illegible].
Kilbarmedyn. See Kilbarrymedon.
Kilbarrie. See Kilbarry.
Kilbarrimedyne. See Kilbarrymedon.
Kilbarry—Kilbarrie — Kilbury — Kilcbarry, co. Cork, 2677, 3622, [illegible], [illegible], [illegible], 4169, [illegible], [illegible], [illegible], [illegible], 6764. See also Kilwarrye.
Kilbarry—Kilbarrie, co. Wat., [illegible], [illegible].
„ preceptory, [illegible].
Kilbarrymeden—Kolbarrumedane—Kilbarri-medyne—Kilbarmedyn (Kilbarrymeaden co. Wat.), [illegible], [illegible], [illegible], 1346, [illegible].
Kilbarrymorie, co. Cork, [illegible].
Kilbary. See Kilbarry.
Kilbayloe, co. Wick. See Kilbaloe.
Kilbaylie (co. Cork ?), rectory, 5151.
Kilbeacock (co. Kilk. ?), [illegible].
Kilbeagh, co. Kerry or Lim., 4610.
Kilbeaghan, co. Kerry, [illegible].
Kilbeahan (co. Lim. ?), 2470.
Kilbeake— Kilbeakakillagh (Kilbeacon ? co. Kilk.), rectory, [illegible], [illegible], [illegible].
Kilbeacoke—Kylbeacock, in Ossory, vicar of 4910, [illegible].
Kilbeg—Kilbegg (co. Car. ?), 6617.
Kilbeg, co. Cork, [illegible].
Kilbeg—Kilbege, co. Dub., 444.

INDEX TO FIANTS—ELIZABETH.

Kilbeg—Kilbego — Kilbegg — Kilbeggo, co. Gal., [illegible], [illegible], [illegible], [illegible]. See also Killbegg.
Kilbeg (Kylebeg?), co. Kerry, [illegible].
Kilbeg, co. Kerry, [illegible].
Kilbeg—Kilbeggo—Kylbegge, co. Kild., [illegible], [illegible].
„ preceptory or manor, [illegible], [illegible].
„ rectory, [illegible].
Kilbeg—Kilbegg—Kylbeg (co. Lim. ?), [illegible], [illegible]; grant, [illegible].
Kilbeg—Kilbeggo, co. Meath, rectory, [illegible], [illegible].
Kilbeg — Kilbegge — Kylbego — Kylbegg, Queen's co., [illegible], [illegible], 1729.
Kilbeg—Kilbego, co. Wat., 1087, [illegible], [illegible], [illegible].
Kilbeg—Kilbegg, co. Westm., [illegible], [illegible].
Kilbeg—Killbegg (co. Wex. ?), [illegible], [illegible].
Kilbeg (co. Wick.), 1414.
Kilbegan. See Kilbeggan.
Kilbego—Kilbegg. See Kilbeg.
Kilbegg, [illegible].
Kilbeggan — Kilbegan — Kylbegan — Kylbeggan, co. Westm., [illegible], [illegible], [illegible]; lands in, [illegible], [illegible].
„ abbey of the B.V.M., leased, [illegible], [illegible], [illegible], 3143, [illegible], [illegible]; possessions leased, [illegible], [illegible]; granted, [illegible], [illegible].
„ church, [illegible].
„ rectory, [illegible], [illegible], [illegible].
„ grange, [illegible], [illegible], [illegible].
„ mill, [illegible], [illegible].
Kilbeggs, co. Kild., [illegible].
Kilbegh, [illegible].
Kilbegnate (Kilbegnet, co. Gal.), rectory, [illegible].
Kilbegnet—Killbegnett, co. Wex., [illegible].
Kilbeloid — Kilbelled — Kilbellyd, co. Kild., [illegible], [illegible], [illegible].
Kilbelot—Kilbelid—Kylbelilota (Kilmaylot, co. Wick.), 1416, [illegible], [illegible].
Kilbell (Kilmaylot, co. Wick. ?), [illegible], [illegible].
Kilbelled—Kilbellyd. See Kilbeloid.
Kilbennan, co. Gal. See Kilbronan.
Kilberaghan—Kilberoghan — Kilborighan—Kilbarraghan, co. Kilk., [illegible], 1080, [illegible], [illegible], [illegible], [illegible].
Kilberran, co. Kilk., 1816.
Kilberaghan. See Kilboraghan.
Kilberehire (co. Cork ?), [illegible], [illegible], [illegible].
Kilbergin (co. Kilk. ?), [illegible].
Kilberighan. See Kilboroghan.
Kilbernye, co. Wat., [illegible].
Kilberraghan. See Kilboraghan.
Kilbervie (co. Kild. ?), [illegible].
Kilbervie (co. Cork ?), [illegible].
Kilberrie, co. Meath, rector of, [illegible].
Kilbhide, co. Clare, [illegible].
Kilbiny (see Kilvinal, co. Cork), [illegible].
Kilbirtane (Kilbrittain), co. Cork, [illegible].
Kilbixkye—Kilbiskie—Kylbiskye—Kylbyxky (Kilbixy), co. Westm., [illegible], [illegible], [illegible]; rectory, [illegible], [illegible].
Kilblaskore, co. Cork, [illegible].
Kilblasse—Kilblaine — Kilblaye — Kylblaye (Kilbolane, co. Cork ?), [illegible], [illegible], [illegible], [illegible]; castle, [illegible].
Kilbleyn — Kilbleis — Kilbleine, co. Kilk., [illegible], [illegible], [illegible], [illegible], [illegible].
Kilboggie, co. Gal., [illegible].
Kilboght, [illegible].
Kilboght—Kylboghta, co. Gal., [illegible].
„ house of friars, granted, [illegible].
Kilbolan—Kylbolane—Kylbullan (Kilbolane), co. Cork, [illegible], [illegible]; castle, &c., [illegible], [illegible]. See also Kilblane.
Kilbonane, co. Cork. See Kilvenane.
Kilbonane, co. Kerry. See Kilgevenane, Kilvonane.
Kilbonnan (co. Kerry ?), [illegible].
Kilboro—Kylboro, King's co., [illegible].
Kilboran—Kilborin—Kilboryn, co. Wat., [illegible], [illegible], [illegible].
Kilboy, co. Tip., [illegible].
Kilbrack (co. Kilk. ?), [illegible].
Kilbrackan, Queen's co. See Kylbrackan.
Kilbradaine, co. Lim., rectory, [illegible].
Kilbradan, co. Lim., [illegible].
Kilbradan, co. Lim. See Kylbradane.
Kilbradane, co. Lim., [illegible].
Kilbraghe (Kilbraher, co. Cork ?), abbey, possessions granted, [illegible]. See Kylbra.
Kilbraghe, co. Tip., [illegible].
Kilbraghie (co. Tip. ?), [illegible].
Kilbrak—Kilbrake, co. Wat., [illegible].
Kilbramnery, co. Kild., [illegible].
Kilbrayne, co. Meath, [illegible], [illegible].
Kilbre (co. Cork ?), [illegible].
Kilbreckane. See Kilbreckane.
Kilbreck (co. Wat. or Kilk.), [illegible].
Kilbreckan (co. Car. ?), [illegible].
Kilbreckan — Kilbreckane — Kilbrickan, co. Clare, [illegible], [illegible], [illegible].
Kilbreckan — Kilbreckane — Kylbreckan (Kilbrickan), co. Kilk., [illegible], [illegible], [illegible], [illegible].
Kilbreckan (Kilbrickan), Queen's co., [illegible].
Kilbreckane (co. Tip. or Clare ?), [illegible].
Kilbrecktown (Kilbrecktown), co. Meath, [illegible].
Kilbredie (Kilbride ?), Ossory, vicar of, [illegible].
Kilbredye—Kylbredye, [illegible].
Kilbree (co. Car. ?), [illegible].
Kilbree (co. Cork ?), [illegible]. See also Kilbre, Kilbrie, Kilbry.
Kilbreede, co. Gal., [illegible].
Kilbreedy, co. Lim. See Kilbride, Kilbrydy.

Kilbreenan—Kilbreenane (perhaps Kilbrennan), co. Gal., friary leased, [illegible]; granted, [illegible].

Kilbreeny—Kylbreeny, co. Car., [illegible].

Kilbrewy, co. Wex., [illegible].

Kilbrevy, co. Wex., [illegible].

Kilbrew — Kilbrue — Kilbrwe — Kylbrowe — Kylbrue, co. Meath, [illegible], 1780, [illegible], 3446, [illegible], [illegible], [illegible], [illegible], [illegible], [illegible], 6743.

Kilbrey, in Munster, [illegible].

Kilbrickan. See Kilbreckan, Kylbryckan.

Kilbrid. See Kilbride.

Kilbride — Kilbryd — Kylbride, co. Car., [illegible], [illegible], [illegible].

Kilbride—Kylbryde, co. Cork, [illegible].

Kilbride—Kylbride, co. Dub., [illegible], [illegible].

Kilbride — Kilbrid, co. Gal., [illegible], [illegible], [illegible], [illegible].

Kilbride—Kilbryde, co. Kild., [illegible].

Kilbride — Kilbrid, co. Kilk., [illegible], [illegible], [illegible], [illegible], [illegible], 6704. See also Kilbredye.

Kilbride — Kilbrid (King's co.), rectory, [illegible], [illegible].

Kilbride, King's co. or Meath, [illegible], [illegible].

Kilbride (co. Lim. ?), [illegible].

Kilbride (Kilbready, co. Lim.), 6717.

Kilbride (co. Long. ?), [illegible].

Kilbride — Kilbrid, co. Mayo, [illegible], [illegible], [illegible].

Kilbride — Kilbrid — Kilbryde — Kylbride, co. Meath, [illegible], [illegible], [illegible], [illegible], [illegible], [illegible].
" (in parish of Moymet), [illegible], [illegible].
" parish of, [illegible], 1174.
" curacy, [illegible], [illegible].

Kilbride, Queen's co., [illegible], [illegible], [illegible], [illegible], [illegible], [illegible], [illegible].
" rectory, [illegible], [illegible].

Kilbride, co. Ros., rectory, 1814, [illegible].

Kilbride, co. Wat., [illegible].
" rectory, [illegible].

Kilbride (co. Westm. or Meath ?), [illegible].

Kilbride — Kilbryd — Kilbryde — Kylbride, co. Westm., [illegible], [illegible], [illegible], [illegible], [illegible], [illegible], [illegible], [illegible], [illegible].
" rectory, [illegible], [illegible], [illegible], [illegible].

Kilbride—Kylbryde, Pass — Pace — Pace — Paces of (Pass of Kilbride, co. Westm.), [illegible], [illegible], [illegible], [illegible], [illegible].

Kilbride—Kilbrid—Kilbryde, co. Wex., [illegible], [illegible], [illegible], [illegible], [illegible], [illegible].

Kilbride, co. Wick., [illegible], [illegible], [illegible], [illegible].

Kilbridie (co. Kilk. ?), [illegible].

Kilbrie, co. Cork, [illegible].

Kilbrie, co. Wex., [illegible].

Kilbrittaine—Kilbrittayne—Kilbrittan—Kilbrittan—Kilbrittane—Kilcbryttaine—Kylbrittan — Kylbrytaine — Kylbrytane, co. Cork, [illegible], [illegible], [illegible], [illegible], [illegible], [illegible], [illegible], [illegible], [illegible], [illegible], [illegible].

Kilbryckan (co. Car. ?), [illegible].

Kilbrogan, co. Cork, rectory, [illegible].

Kilbrue—Kilbrwe. See Kilbrew.

Kilbry — Kilbrye, co. Cork, [illegible], [illegible], [illegible], [illegible].

Kilbry (co. Kilk. ?), 1614.

Kilbryan, co. Rosc. See Kilbryn.

Kilbryd—Kilbryde. See Kilbride.

Kilbryddy—Kilbride—Kilbryde (Kilbready), co. Lim., [illegible], [illegible], 6717.

Kilbrye. See Kilbry.

Kilbrye, co. Wex., [illegible].

Kilbryn (co. Kerry or Lim. ?), [illegible].

Kilbullan (Kilbolane, co. Cork), [illegible]; castle, [illegible].

Kilbunnane, co. Cork, [illegible].

Kilbuoglee—Kylbuoglee, co. Car., [illegible].

Kilbury, co. Lim., [illegible].

Kilbyreddy — Kylbyreddy (co. Clare ?), [illegible].

Kilbyrne — Kylbyrne (co. Cork ?), [illegible], [illegible].

Kilca — Kilcas (Kilkea), co. Kild., [illegible], [illegible], [illegible].

Kilcack — Kilcacke, co. Kild., [illegible], [illegible], [illegible].

Kilcack (co. Westm. ?), [illegible].

Kilcairill (co. Tyrone ?), [illegible], [illegible].

Kilcaish. See Kilcash.

Kilcale, co. Kild., [illegible].

Kilcallane (Kilcullane, co. Lim.), rectory, [illegible], [illegible].

Kilcallie (co. Kerry ?), [illegible].

Kilcalline (co. Kerry ?), [illegible].

Kilcallotrume (co. Car. ?), [illegible].

Kilcaman (Kilcommon, co. Wick. ?), [illegible].

Kilcamman (co. Car. ?), [illegible].

Kilcamowy (Kilcamvoo, co. Wat.), [illegible].

Kilcannon, co. Wex. See Kilcoman.

Kilcappagh, King's co. See Kylcappaghe.

Kilcartain — Kylcartaine (co. Gal.), [illegible], [illegible].

Kilcargo, co. Car., [illegible].

Kilcarke, co. Car., [illegible].

Kilcarn, co. Meath. See Kilcarne.

Kilcarnen (Killycarnan), co. Mon., [illegible].

Kilcarne, co. Meath, [illegible], [illegible], [illegible].
" little, [illegible].
" rectory, [illegible], [illegible].

Kilcarne (co. Westm. ?), [illegible].

Kilcarny, co. Cork, [illegible].

Kilcaroo—Kilcarowe (Kilcarra, co. Wick. ?), [illegible], [illegible], [illegible].

Kilcarragh (co. Car. ?), [illegible].

Kilcatragh, co. Clare, [illegible].

Kilcarrows, co. Tip. See Kilcharrowntagan.

Kilcartan, co. Wat., [illegible].

Kilcarty, co. Meath. See Kylcarte.

Kilcash, co. Ross. See Kilcasyn.

INDEX TO FIANTS—ELIZABETH.

Kilcash — Kilcaish — Killcaish — Kilcashe— Kilcaishe—Kilchasse—Kylkashe, co. Tip., 128, 1042, 1843, [illegible], [illegible], 6441, [illegible], 6704; rectory, [illegible], 6416.
Kilcaskan, co. Cork, 4721.
Kilcaskin — Kylcaskyn — Kylkaskyne — Kylkaskyne (co. Kild.), 1430, [illegible], [illegible]. See also Kilcaskan.
Kilcashe. See Kilcash.
Kilcashan, co. Kild., 5404.
Kilcavan, Queen's co. See Kilkavan.
Kilcayarin (co. Gal. ?), 4734.
Kilcayne (Kilcash), co. Rosc., 5678.
Kilchan (co. Wat. ?), 5783.
Kilcharcaile, co. Lim., 5171.
Kilcharamtillove, co. Kerry, 6117.
Kilcharantiove, co. Kerry, 5117.
Kilcharolnagry (co. Clare ?), 6486.
Kilcharomeghe. See Kilcharrowaughe.
Kilcharowman (co. Gal. ?), 6478.
Kilcharowne, 616.
Kilcharra—Kylcharra, co. Car., 1477.
Kilcharrowaughe — Kilcharrowaughe (Kilcarroon ?), co. Tip., 5683, 6517.
Kilchasse. See Kilcash.
Kilchavon, co. Lim., 5171.
Kilchide (co. Clare or Gal.), [illegible].
Kilchime, co. Wex., 3652.
Kilchoan, co. Gal., 4587, 5229.
Kilchocke—Kilchogine alias Choghesland, co. Dub., 1894, 4401.
Kilchoan, co. Gal. or Rosc., 4578.
Kilchoscane, co. Tip., 6618.
Kilchoaky, co. Westm., 1788.
Kilchemine yeloy (Kilcummin), co. Kerry, 6377.
Kilchoagh (co. Leit. ?), 6474.
Kilchroane, co. Clare. See Kilcrisle.
Kilchroobane, co. Clare, 5162, 5429.
Kilchrummeragh. See Kilcrummeragh.
Kilchrone (co. Wick. ?), 5541.
Kilchurybyre—Kylchurylyre, co. Cork, 6347.
Kilchy—Kylchy, co. Clare, 4808.
Kilclagh (co. Cork ?), 6319.
Kilclagher (Kilclogh, co. Cork ?), 5632.
Kilclanfert (see Kilclonafert), 5783.
Kilclean, co. Down, 3908.
Kilcloighe—Kilcliogh (Kilclonagh), co. Westm., rectory, 1461, 3300, 4316.
Kilcloggan. See Kilcloggan.
Kilcloghan, co. Westm., 4854.
Kilcloggan—Kilclogan, co. Wex., 1746, 4864.
" preceptory or manor leased, 5697; granted, 5080.
Kilclogh, co. Cork. See Kilclagher, Kilclohy.
Kilclogh, Queen's co., 6453.
Kilclogh—Kylclogh, co. Rosc., 5948.
Kilcloghaghe—Kylcloghmagh, co. Rosc., 1482, 834.
Kilcloghan—Killclaoghan, co. Westm., 1746, 4771.
Kilcloghe, co. Car., rectory, 1387.
Kilclogher, co. Gal., 4431.
Kilclogher—Kylclogher (Clogher), co. Louth, 673, 1812, 2334.
Kilcloghor, co. Rosc., 5213, 5412.
Kilcloghan, co. Westm., 5318.
Kilclohy (Kilclogh, co. Cork ?), 5631.
Kilcloighe, co. Dub., 5314.
Kilcloine (co. Tip. ?), 5704.
Kilclonbrenen. See Kylclonbrenen.
Kilclonecorkry, King's co. See Kylcloncourkey.
Kilclone — Kylclone (Kilcloon, co. Gal.), rectory and vicarage, 1583, 1581.
Kilclone, co. Kilk., 5297.
Kilclone (co. Kilk. ?), 5784, 5704.
Kilclone—Kilcloyne, co. Meath, 5777.
" church, 1356.
" See Culcloyne.
Kilclone (co. Wat. ?), 5748, 6476.
Kilclonafert—Kilclonfert, Queen's co., 657, 5783.
Kilclonagh (co. Wat. ?), 6478.
Kilclonmalaure—Kilclonalowan, co. Westm., 1491, 4306.
Kilcloney (co. Wat. or Cork ?), 5534.
Kilclonfert, King's co., 573, 5853.
" rector of, 4594, 5783.
Kilclonhobard (Kylclonhobert), Queen's co., 3538.
Kilclonie. See Kilclony.
Kilclonway, co. Cork, 5439.
Kilclony—Kylclonye (Kilclooney ?), co. Cork, 5048, 5817.
Kilclopy, co. Gal., 5447.
Kilclowry—Kilclonie (co. Wat. ?), 588, 2369, 6478.
Kilcloon, co. Gal. See Kilclone.
Kilclooney, co. Cork. See Kilclony.
Kilclough or Cloghesland, co. Dub., 1588.
Kilclovo (co. Gal. ?), 4858.
Kilcloyne. See Kilclone.
Kilcluro (co. Kerry ?), 6469.
Kilcnockanagh, 6451.
Kilcondiloe (co. Wex. ?), 6517.
Kilcoman alias Kilcolman, co. Kilk., rectory, 5916.
Kilcoman (Kilcwane), co. Lim., 5878.
Kilcoan, in Ossory, vicar of, 6136.
Kilconane (co. Lim. ?), 5604.
Kilcock — Kilcocke — Kilcok — Kilcoke— Kylcock, co. Kild., 347, 1884, 3886, 4886, 5817, 5781, 6119; licence for a tan house in, 5634; rectory, 5908, 5446, 5426, 5638.
Kilcock (co. Kilk. ?), 5148.
Kilcock (Kilcoke), Queen's co., 5451.
Kilcockan, co. Wat. See Kilcoggan.

Kilcoddane, co. Wex., 6784.
Kilcogyr (co. Tip. ?), 6457.
Kilcoggan (Kilcowkan, co. Wat.), 1687.
Kilcogh, co. Cork, 6818.
Kilcoghlan — Kilcoghlane, co. Cork, 5046, [illegible], 5736, 6816.
Kilcohan (Kilqnane ?), co. Lim., 6731.
Kilcohan (co. Wat. ?), 1046.
Kilcohor, co. Car., 1114.
Kilcoffe—Kylcoffe, co. Lim., 4767; grant, 6634.
Kilcoire, co. Mayo, 5798.
Kilcok—Kilcoke. See Kilcock, co. Kild.
Kilcoke, Queen's co. See Kilcock.
Kilcolgan, co. Gal., castle and land, 6301.
Kilcolgan—Kilcolgen—Killcolgan, King's co., 1461, [illegible], 4353, 4581, 6815.
Kilcolic, co. Cav., [illegible].
Kilcollane, co. Kilk., [illegible].
Kilcollohy—Kylcollehy, co. Cork, rectory, [illegible], [illegible].
Kilcollon, co. Kild., 153.
Kilcolligan (co. Wat. ?), [illegible].
Kilcolligan. See Kilcolman.
Kilcolle, co. Mayo, rectory, 1404.
Kilcollemaloo. See Kilcolmanbane.
Kilcollumbe (Kilcolumb, co. Kilk.), rectory, [illegible].
Kilcollumbilly (co. Cork), 6758.
Kilcolly (King's co. ?), 6462.
Kilcolman — Kilcollman — Kilcolmau — Kylcolman, co. Cork, 3781, [illegible], 5473, [illegible], 6514-5, 6769; granted, [illegible]: patronage of church, 5273, [illegible], [illegible]. See Kilcolman.
Kilcolman, co. Kilk., rectory, 6312.
Kilcolman—Kylcolman (King's co. or Tip.), 971, 6398, [illegible].
Kilcolman—Kilkolman—Kylcolman—Kyllcollman, co. Lim., 5874, 6678, 6751; grant, 6751; parish, 6782, 6847; rectory, 1613, 4612.
Kilcolman—Kylcolman, co. Mayo, 5416, [illegible], 4840; rectory, 1404, 5418.
Kilcolman (co. Rosc. ?), 6412.
Kilcolman—Kylcolman, co. Tip., 632.
Kilcolmanbane — Kilcollemalan — Kylcolmanbane, Queen's co., 485, 871, 1878, 1594, [illegible]; rectory, 1514, 1875, 1594, 5834.
rector of, 801.
Kilcolmane, 6477.
Kilcolmane (Kilcorman ?), co. Kerry, 6128.
Kilcolme, diocese of Ossory (Kilcolumb ?), vicar of, 767.
Kilcolokin — Kilcolokine — Killcolotyn, Queen's co., 632, 4748, 5462.
Kilcolumb, co. Kilk. See Kilcollumbe, Kilcolme.
Kilcolyn, co. Gal., 5948.
Kilcoman, King's co., 4567.
Kilcoman — Kylcoman (Kilcommon), co. Mayo, rectory, [illegible], 5419.
Kilcoman, co. Sligo or Mayo, [illegible].
Kilcoman—Killcomain (co. Tip. ?), 3778, [illegible].
Kilcoman—Kilkoman (co. Wick.), [illegible], [illegible], 6477.
Kilcomon — Kylcomon (Kilcummin), co. Gal., rectory, 1641, 5464.
Kilcomon—Kylcomon, co. Tip., [illegible].
Kilcomoraghe — Killcomoragh — Kilcomrory, co. Wat., 1048, [illegible], [illegible].
Kilcommock, co. Long. See Killcommock.
Kilcommon, co. Mayo. See Kilcoman.
Kilcommon, co. Wick. See Kilcoman.
Kilcommyn in Ely (Kilcomin, King's co.), 4874.
Kilcomocko—Kylcomocke (Kilmacomoge), co. Cork, rectory, 3747, 5467.
Kilcomoslon, co. Lim., 6781.
Kilcomon (Kilcummin), King's co., 6818.
Kilcomyn, co. Sligo, 4878.
Kilcomyn (co. Kerry ?), 6406.
Kilcomyn—Kylcomyn, Queen's co., [illegible].
Kilcomyn (co. Westm. ?), 6160.
Kilcomyne — Kilcomyne Ihie — Kilcomyne Ihoy — Kilcomynythe (Kilcummin, co. Kerry), 6717; rectory, [illegible].
Kilconam—Kilkonam (co. Wick. ?), 1068.
Kilconan, co. Lim., 5432.
Kilconce (Kilconcy), King's co., 1404, [illegible], 4354.
Kilconcogh (Killcoscomagh, co. Cork ?), 6811.
Kilconellier, co. Tip., 4446.
Kilconell, Johanna ny, pardon, 6452.
Kilconell (co. Cork or Lim. ?), 4896.
Kilconell—Kilconill. See Kilconnell.
Kilconieria, co. Gal. See Kylconerye.
Kilconile (Kilconly), co. Kerry, [illegible]. See also Kilcowle.
Kilconnaghe—Kylconnagh, co. Tip., rectory, 1648, 4012.
Kilconnau, co. Cork, [illegible].
Kilconnelo (co. Wex. ?), 6064.
Kilconnell—Kilconell—Killconnell—Kyleconell — Kylconnyll, co. Gal., 1543, 4678, 6781.
house of friars, leased, 4678, 5611.
barony, seneschal of, [illegible], 5734.
Kilconnell — Kilconnell — Kilconill — Kilconill—Killconnell—Kilconill—Killconnell, co. Tip., 547, 1380, 3068, 3538, [illegible], 4453, 4457, 6378, [illegible], 5516, 6364, 6364.
Kilconnalle, co. Wex. See Kilconybb.
Kilconnry (co. Kerry ?), 6468.
Kilconnynythie, co. Cork, rectory (see Kilcomyne), 3428.

INDEX TO FIANTS.—ELIZABETH.

Kilcough (co. Ros. ?), 4782.
Kilcomore (co. Lim. ?), 4487.
Kilcommran (co. Lim. or Kerry), 4832.
Kilcoatiss, co. Wat., 1682.
Kil Conybb (Kilcoonalb, co. Wex. ?), 4517.
Kilcomyll (co. Tip. or Wat.), 4142.
Kilconle, co. Tip., 4637.
Kilconly. See Kilcowle.
Kilcooney, King's co. See Kilcone, Kylchowne.
Kilcoonah, co. Gal. See Kilcoahos.
Kilcoogreagh (co. Kilk. ?), 1816.
Kilcopp, co. Wat., 4164.
Kilcoragh, co. Kerry, 6196.
Kilcorane (co. Wat. ?), 4562.
Kilcorbe, co. Mon., 5551.
Kilcorbeighe (Kilcorbry ?), King's co., 478, 5871, 6171.
Kilcorbrye—Kylcorbre, co. Wex., 1648; rectory, 3448.
Kilcorcre—Kylcorkre, King's co., 1636, 1668.
Kilcordirpane—Kylcordirpane, co. Tip., 542, 1596.
Kilcorgan, [illegible].
Kilcorlham, co. Cork, [illegible].
Kilcorill, co. Westm., 1614.
Kilcorke—Kilkorke, co. Kild., 1627, 5715.
Kilcorleragh—Kylcorleragh (co. Wex. ?), 467.
Kilcorman, co. Clare, 4543.
Kilcormayoke, co. Tip., 4674.
Kilcormick — Kilcormock — Killcormucke — Kylcormuck — Kylcormucke — King's co., 1555; Carmelite friary leased, 1540, 4471, 4158, 5128.
Kilcornain (co. Mayo or Ross.), 4640.
Kilcornan, co. Clare, 3458, 4543.
Kilcornan (co. Gal. ?), 4794.
Kilcornan—Kylcornan, co. Lim., patronage of, 4947.
Kilcornan, co. Westm., 5767.
Kilcorney—Kilcrony—Kylcorne (Kilcorney), co. Cork, rectory, 6131; patronage of church, 4973, 4826, 4214.
Kilcorran, co. Mon. See Killychoran.
Kilcorroll — Kylcorroll — Kylcorroll (co. Wex. ?), 947.
Kilcorry (Kilcourcy, King's co.), 1178.
Kilcortaine — Kylcorteyne (Coriswood ?), co. Wat., 446, 5182.
Kilcoryly (co. Cork or Lim. ?), [illegible].
Kilcossaghe (co. Leit.), 4830.
Kilcosgrane (Kilcosgrave), co. Lim., 5079.
Kilcoshos (Kilcoosh, co. Gal. ?), 4788.
Kilcoskan — Kilkoskan — Kylcoskan (co. Dub.), 162, 950, 4427.
Kilcoslanie, co. Kerry, castle and lands, 4215.
Kilcosy—Kylcosy, King's co., 5811.
Kilcotty (co. Wex. ?), 4769.
Kilcouline (co. Lim. ?), 5140.
Kilcouran (Queen's co. ?), 6744.
Kilcourcy—Killcourcie (Kilcourcy), King's co., barony, 4244, 4342. See Fox's country. See also Kilcorry.
Kilcourty—Kylcourty (Queen's co. ?), 1178.
Kilcoval (co. Wick.), 1245.
Kilcowan, co. Cork, 4131; rectory, [illegible].
Kilcowan—Killcowan (co. Gal. ?), 1902, [illegible].
Kilcowan—Kylcowan, co. Wex., 1283; rectory, 3977, 4168; manor, 1127.
Kilcowane, co. Kilk., rectory, [illegible].
Kilcowanmore—Kylcowanmore, co. Wex., 1283; rectory, 894, 902.
" See Kylcohan.
Kilcowane (co. Tip. ?), 4323.
Kilcowall, co. Car., 4434.
Kilcowen (co. Meath ?), 4468.
Kilcowghan (co. Kilk. ?), rectory, 3877, 5548.
Kilcowle (co. Car. or Kilk. ?), 5454.
Kilcowle (Kilcoely), co. Kerry, rectory, 1545, 4313.
Kilcowle, co. Kilk., 5144.
Kilcowle (Kilcooly), co. Meath, rectory, 1454.
Kilcowle—Kylcowle (Kilcooly), co. Tip., 594, 637, 1048, 1635, 5682, 6745, 6765.
" monastery granted, 504; possessions leased, 3874, 4613.
" rectory, 3874, 4613, 6123.
" grange, 504.
Kilcowle, co. Westm. (Kilcooly, co. Meath ?), 3294.
Kilcowlenaline. See Kilcowlnalyne.
Kilcowlian (co. Tip. ?), 4565.
Kilcowlie, co. Kerry, 6132.
Kilcowlie (co. Kilk. ?), 4964.
Kilcowlie, co. Tip., 5484.
Kilcowlekillie, co. Kerry, 6133.
Kilcowly (co. Leit. ?), 4767.
Kilcowly—Killcowley, co. Westm., 146, 1152.
Kilcowlnalyne—Kilcowlenaline—Kylcoulnalyne—Kylcowlnalien, co. Wex., 1768, 5341.
" customs due from, 4941.
" chief serjeant of, 1562.
Kilcowman—Kylcowman, co. Kilk., rectory, 1765.
Kilcowran, Queen's co., 5551.
Kilcowrane, co. Cork, 5851.
Kilcow[ ]lane (co. Tip. ?), 6323.
Kilcoyer, co. Gal., 4618.
Kilcoyle—Kylcoyle, co. Lim., 1142, 5116.
Kilcoyle—Kylcoyle (co. Wick. ?), 964.
Kilcoynagy, co. Tip., 1698.
Kilcoyr—Killcoyre, co. Mayo, 5452.
Kilcraghe. See Kilcraugh.
Kilcraghe, co. Ross., 4425.
Kilcrancd—Kilcranel—Kilcraneis—Kilcranel, co. Cork, 6287, 6782.

Kilcreagh — Kilcreaghe — Killcreaughe, co. Dub., 1854, 2818; grant, 6780.
Kilcrewe, co. Mayo, chapel, 5325.
Kilcrewe, co. Westm., 6256.
Kilcrea—Killcrea—Kilcre—Kilcreo—Kilcroy, co. Cork, 2564, 2941, 3081, 3280, 4656, 4945, 5180, 5253, 5437, 5508, 5555, 5565, 5672, 6754.
" manor, 3275, 3280, 5133.
" house of friars minor leased, 5114, 6262.
Kilcredan—Kilcreadane—Kilcredan—Kilcridane, co. Cork, 4638, 5455, 4573, 6731, 6708, 6754. See also Kilcreyden, Kilcorydane.
Kilcredaun, co. Clare. See Kilcredon.
Kilcrees, co. Mon. See Kilcryne.
Kilcreevanty, co. Gal. See Kilcreevaght.
Kilcregan — Kilcregane — Kilcreggan—Kilcregaine—Kilcregan (co. Kilk. ?), 960, 1048, 2843, 2858, 4908, 5302, 5448, 6704.
Kilcregane — Kylcregane — Kylcrikan (Kilcreggane), co. Wat., 545, 5133; chapel, 595.
Kilcreghe, co. Cork, 5456.
Kilcrevaght—Kilcrevan is — Kilcreaght—Kylkrevane (Kilcreevanty), co. Gal., 4884, 5903, 6458.
" house of nuns, granted, 1391, 6651.
Kilcrevaun, 6352.
Kilcrewe, co. Westm., 1540.
Kilcreyden — Kilcreydan (Kilcredan, co. Cork ?), 5513, 5504.
Kilcridan (co. Cork ?), 5701.
Kilcrikan, co. Wat., chapel, 5133.
Kilcrill (Kilcurly ?), co. Lim., 5115.
Kilcrina, co. Gal., 6708.
Kilcriste — Kylchriste — Kylcryste (Kilchreest), co. Clare, rectory, 1529, 1775, 5525.
Kilcro (King's co. ?), 4334.
Kilcro. See Kilcrowe, co. Meath.
Kilcro—Kilcroo (Kilcrow, co. Kild.), 6726; wood, 5724.
Kilcroad (co. Gal. or Ros.), 4779. See also Kilcroane, Kilcroan.
Kilcrobin—Kylcrobin, Queen's co., 1150.
Kilcroe. See Kilcro, co. Kild.
Kilcroe. See Kilcrowe, co. Meath.
Kilcroghan — Kylcroghan, co. Cork, 4020, 4781; rectory, 2962.
Kilcroige, co. Cork, 5541.
Kilcrohano (Kilcrohane), co. Kerry, rectory, 2945, 5373.
Kilcromikeraghe, co. Westm., 1543.
Kilcrompor (Kilcrumper), co. Cork, rectory, 1083, 2838; vicarage, 4557.
Kilcromreragh — Kilchromrereagh — Kilcrumrerough (Kilcumreragh), co. Westm., 1750, 2771, 4575.
Kilcrumriough, co. Westm., 6771.
Kilcromane — Kylcromane (Kilcroma), Queen's co., 1523, 5455.
Kilcrono (co. Kilk. ?), 6564.
Kilcronoy, co. Clare, 5517.
Kilcrony. See Kilcorny, co. Cork.
Kilcrony, co. Kilk., 5704.
Kilcrony, co. Louth, 1513.
Kilcroste (Kilcrow), co. Kilk., 1511.
Kilcrowe, co. Wex., 5517.
Kilcrowmton (co. Cork ?), 5606.
Kilcrow, co. Kild. See Kilcro.
Kilcrowe — Kilcro — Kilcroe — Kylcro — Kylcroo (Hardwood), co. Meath, 512, 543, 1515, 4377-8, 6038.
Kilcrowe, co. Westm., 1582.
Kilcrowes (Kilcrow), co. Mon., 5548.
Kilcrowlan, co. Ros., rectory, 4343.
Kilcroys (co. Cork ?), 4152.
Kilcruane (Kilcroan, co. Gal. ?), rectory, 5133.
Kilcrubyne—Kylcrubin (Cruboen), Queen's co., 1178, 1525, 5553.
Kilcrugg—Kylcrugg, co. Cork, 5108.
Kilcrumper, co. Cork. See Kilcrompor.
Kilcruse—Kylcruse (Kilcruise), Queen's co., 1557, 5147.
Kilcrush, co. Clare, 6077.
Kilcrydane (co. Cork ?), 5515.
Kilcryll (Kilcurly ?), co. Lim., 5524.
Kilcrynirie, co. Kerry, 5153.
Kilcuan (co. Lim. ?), 4534.
Kilcuayn, co. Gal., 4080.
Kilcuicyhine, co. Cork, rectory, 4269.
Kilculiane, co. Lim. See Kilcullane, Kilcullan.
Kilcullen—Kilcullin (co. Cork ?), 5147, 5659, 6571.
Kilcullen—Kilcollyn—Kilcollen—Killcullen, co. Kild., 123, 1215, 5407, 6553, 5287, 6791.
" messuages and gardens in, 6791.
" Tho. Eustace, lord of, lease, 6762.
Kilcullen, co. Tip. or Lim., 6742.
Kilculley (co. Cork ?), 5522.
Kilculliheen, Waterford. See Kilkelihin, Kilkilhill.
Kilcolyne—Kylcolyne, co. Lim., 1542.
Kilcumane, co. Wat., 5360.
Kilcummin, co. Gal. See Kilcomen.
Kilcummin, King's co. See Kilcomen.
Kilcumreragh, co. Westm. See Kilcromreragh.
Kilcumyn (Kilcummin), co. Kerry, town, 5277.
Kilcumyn Et la (Kilcummin), co. Kerry, 5277.
" See Kilcomyne.
Kilcurfin, co. Cork. See Kilcurfine.
Kilcurkye, co. Wex., 573.
Kilcurl, co. Kilk. See Kilkirryhill.

Kilcurly, co. Lim. *See* Kilcrill, Kilcryll, Killurlie.
Kilcurnan, co. Lim., 4182.
Kilcurnan, rector of, 160.
Kilcurran, Queen's co., 6661.
Kilcurrie—Kilkurry—Kylcurrie, co. Kilk., rectory, 1188, 1825, 2422, 4394.
Kilcurrish, co. Clare. *See* Kylcurrysshe, 6741.
Kilcurrydane, co. Clare, 6617.
Kilcurryhie, co. Clare, 6786.
Kildacollin (co. Lim. ?), 6677.
Kildacolleen, co. Lim., [illegible].
Kildacommock, co. Long., 4168.
Kildahely—Kildahelly, co. Wat., [illegible], 1078, [illegible].
Kildalbye—Kyldalbye, King's co., 1887.
Kildalkie—Kildalky—Kyldalkey, co. Meath, rectory, [illegible], 3447, 4304, 6013, 6707.
Kildallan, co. Cav. *See* Kyldallon, [illegible].
Kildallone — Kyldalow (Kildalloe, co. Wex. ?), 673.
Kildamas, co. Leit., [illegible].
Kildangin—Kildangyn, co. Kild., 1316, 1676.
Kildare—Kildar—Kyldare, 704, 1216, [illegible], [illegible], [illegible], 4323, 4286, 4373, [illegible], [illegible], [illegible], [illegible], 6064, 6748, 6763, 6760.
" sovereign of, commissions, [illegible], 2117, 3444; murder of, 6760.
" Colliers lands, 5310, 5446, 5570.
" Curragh of, 4863, 5287-8, [illegible], 6745, 6746.
" house of nuns, leased, 3151; granted, 4576.
" house of grey friars, possessions leased, 5310, 5289, 5446, [illegible], 6746.
" house of white friars, lands of, leased, 5228, 5246, 6740.
" Gerald, late (9th) earl of, 1828; attainted, his lands leased, 0783, [illegible]; rent from his lands granted, 2480; commission to enquire as to his lands, 703-4, [illegible].
" Gerald, (11th) earl of, general of the forces, [illegible], 1412, [illegible], [illegible], [illegible]; captain of Leinster, 741; to meet Desmond, 3419; sent to the queen, [illegible]; pardon, 103, [illegible], 1346, [illegible]; commissions to make war on O'Mores and O'Conors and other rebels, [illegible], 1468, 3916; commissions, 50, [illegible], 760, 812-3, 861, [illegible], 894, 1067, 1417-8, 1434, 1848, 2117, 3945, [illegible], 3444-5, [illegible], [illegible], [illegible], [illegible], [illegible], [illegible], [illegible]; grants of land, 1340, 1876, [illegible], [illegible]; grants from Philip and Mary, recited, [illegible]; grant of an advowson, [illegible]; grants

Kildare—Gerald:
of wardships, 167, 1100, [illegible]; leases, 1660, 4370; license to alien, 3440; pardon of alienation, [illegible]; great house in Dublin, 1940; land conveyed by, 404; lease by, recited, [illegible]; custody of his lands, [illegible].
" Henry, earl of, commissions, [illegible], 5228, 5347, [illegible], [illegible], [illegible], [illegible]; grants of land, [illegible], [illegible], [illegible], 5766; surrender, 5764; lease, [illegible].
" Gerald, (14th) earl of, commissions, [illegible], [illegible], [illegible], [illegible].
" earl of, lands of, in co. Limerick, 5173, [illegible]; lands held of, [illegible], tenement occupied by, in Dublin, [illegible].
" Mabel, countess of, [illegible], [illegible].
" Thomas, son of the earl of (Silken Thomas), lease from, recited, [illegible].
" bishop of, Thomas (Leverous) refuses the oath of supremacy, 163.
" " Alexander (Craik), commissions, [illegible], [illegible]; license of alienation, [illegible]; death, [illegible].
" " Robert (Daly) commissions, 2117, 2348, 3414, 3047, [illegible], [illegible], [illegible], [illegible], [illegible], [illegible].
" " Daniel (Neylan), deputy master of Prerogative, 4765; commissions, [illegible], [illegible], 4476, [illegible], [illegible], [illegible], [illegible], [illegible], [illegible], [illegible]; appeal by, [illegible]; lease, [illegible]; presented to benefice, [illegible]; prohibition addressed to, [illegible].
" chapter of St. Brigid's cathedral, [illegible].
" diocese, presentations in, [illegible], [illegible], [illegible], [illegible], [illegible], [illegible], [illegible], [illegible].
" " suits as to benefices in, [illegible], [illegible], [illegible].
" " tithes in, leased, [illegible], [illegible].
" county, oath of supremacy administered to justices and officers, [illegible]; wages of soldiers cessed on, 1911; ploughlands in, [illegible]; towns belonging to lord Gormanston, [illegible]; forfeited lands, [illegible]; sessions of, [illegible].

INDEX TO FIANTS—ELIZABETH.

Kildare county, sheriff, 52-3, 66, 210, 272, 230, 280, 361, 542, 581, 686, 1100, 1214, 1263, 1487, 1678, 1854, 1864, 1946, 2288, 2463, 2634, 2706, 2836, 3013, 3378, 3472, 3786, 4156, 4860, 5125, 6117, 6712.
 sub-sheriff, 3456, 3788, 5678.
 chief serjeant, 1570, 1596, 1718, 3310, 4363.
 general of army in, 4861, 5030, 6113, 6634.
 general cesser, and collector, 3792, 4367.
 clerk of the peace and crown, 7141.
 keeper of the gaol, 6506.
 commissions of peace, 378-81, 384, 543, 661, 1694, 2114, 2446, 2670, 3156, 3693, 3367, 4068, 4408, 4518, 4769, 4880, 5842, 6051, 5297, 6039, 6264, 5283, 6020, 6408, 6427.
 commissions of muster, 280, 3117, 3548, 3448, 4190, 4508, 5126.
 martial law, 66, 218, 333, 443, 591, 793, 804, 866, 963, 1166, 1263, 1422, 1487, 1497, 1637, 1848, 2231, 2259, 2696, 2824, 2830, 2870, 2921, 2981, 3009, 3156, 3786, 3897, 3849, 4047, 4090, 4227, 4489, 5133, 6106, 5217, 6360, 6361, 6498.
 enquiry as to lands forfeited, 703, 753.
 hay taken up, 3886, 4061, 4172, 4434, 6250, 6051, 6412.
 leather tanned in, 1780.
Kildaree, co. Gal. See Kyldarin, 1067, 6129.
Kildaregane—Kildarigan—Kildoregan, co. Kilk., 1848, 3091; grant, 6464.
Kildarirye (Kildorrery), co. Cork, rectory, 3994.
Kildarough, co. Donegal. See Kildorigh.
Kildarrk—Kyldarrk (co. Cork?), 6910.
Kildaton, co. Kilk., 6866, 6804.
Kildea—Kyldeigh—Kyldagho (Kilday, co. Wick.), 314, 3994, 6289.
Kildeglin, co. Wick., 6686, 6793.
Kildelgen, Queen's co., 5651.
Kildemocke, co. Louth, vicar of, 665.
Kildennyn, co. Wex., 3360.
Kilder—Kildir, co. Kilk., 580, 1164.
Kildermot (co. Wex.?), 6547.
Kildergan. See Kildaregane.
Kildergan (co. Kilk.?), 6704.
Kilderkay (co. Kerry?), 6570.
Kilderie (co. Lim.?), 3363.
Kilderemoll (co. Cav.?), 6616.
Kilderrehan, co. Queen's co., 4461.
Kilderrey—Kyldirry (Kildorry), co. Kerry, 3948, 4573.
Kildorry (co. Clare?), 9616.
Kildorry—Kildorrie, co. Kilk., 3164, 6467.
Kildorry (co. Lim.?), 6694. See also Kildyrry.
Kildorryn, co. Long., 4616.
Kildoryn (co. Lim.?), 3948.
Kildasey (co. Wex.?), 6438.
Kildeynon (co. Car.?), 6486.
Kildeyne—Kyldeyne (co. Wex.?), 870, 6817.
Kildigan, co. Meath, 6696.
Kildille, co. Cork, 6986.
Kildimo, co. Lim. See Kyldimo.
Kildimock, co. Meath, 3991.
Kildina (co. Lim.?), 3086.
Kildinegin, co. Tip., 6706.
Kildinogo (co. Tip.?), 6466.
Kildir. See Kilder.
Kildiro (co. Car.?), 6492.
Kildirroe, co. Kilk., 5670.
Kildough, co. Mon. See Kildodowe.
Kildoey (co. Cork?), 3913.
Kildollocke, co. Ross., 4761.
Kildomadarvy—Kyldomadarvy, co. Cork, 5063.
Kildoman. See Kildonan.
Kildonan, co. Car., 4618, 6644.
Kildonan — Kildonane, Queen's co., 169, 6834.
Kildonnell, co. Lim., 5850.
Kildonoghbuy—Kildonoghobuy (co. Cork?), 4197, 6311.
Kildordan, co. Long., 5656.
Kildorigh (Kildarough, co. Donegal), 5583.
Kildorogh—Kyldoroghe, co. Cav., 4654.
Kildorrery, co. Cork. See Kildarirye, Kildirrye.
Kildough in Kill (co. Kilk.?), 4060.
Kildowan—Kyldowan, co. Wex., 126.
Kildownoke, co. Tip., 2601.
Kildraght, co. Wex. or Car., 4627.
Kildrinagh, co. Kilk., 3708, 6120.
Kildriaw (co. Wick.?), 2468.
Kildrogh. See Kildrough.
Kildrolyn (co. Car. or Queen's?), 1467.
Kildromadong (co. Gal.?), 4014.
Kildromma, co. Kild., 1947.
Kildromme (co. Kilk.?), 6068.
Kildromoll in Upper Ossory, 647.
Kildromfarsan—Kildromfarisan, co. Cav., 4678, 4636.
Kildromody, Queen's co., 4651.
Kildroney (co. Kilk.?), 4069, 6784.
Kildroey (co. Tip. or Kilk.?), 5065.

INDEX TO FIANTS—ELIZABETH.

Kildrought—Kildroght—Kildroghte — Kill-droght — Kyldroght, co. Kild., 1620, [illegible], [illegible], 4180, 4314, 4317, 4824, [illegible], [illegible], [illegible], [illegible], 6764.
" manor, 4157, 4314, [illegible].
" castletown of, 796, [illegible], [illegible].
" burgagery of, 796.
" rectory, [illegible], 6182.
Kildrumo (co. Kerry ?), [illegible].
Kildryne (Killydream), co. Mon., [illegible].
Kildryth (co. Wex. ?), [illegible].
Kilduff—Kilduffe—Kylduf, King's co., 814, [illegible], [illegible].
Kilduff, co. Lim., 6132.
Kilduffe, co. Lim., [illegible].
Kildufane (co. Cork ?), [illegible].
Kildume (co. Lim. ?), 6457.
Kildymmo (co. Lim. ?), 6478.
Kildyrry (Kildorry), co. Lim., 4374.
Kileagh, [illegible].
Kilealoughard, co. Lim., [illegible].
Kilcan (co. Ross. ?), [illegible].
Kilcarnie (co. Cork ?), [illegible].
Kilcaskyth, co. Cork, [illegible].
Kilcbarry (see Kilbarry, co. Cork), [illegible].
Kilcbeg, co. Cork, [illegible].
Kilcbrittaine (see Kilbrittaine, co. Cork), [illegible].
Kilcmacnaue (Kilmakan), co. Cork, [illegible].
Kilcnicbanet (Kilgobnet), co. Cork, [illegible].
Kilcoole, co. Cork, 4576.
Kilcolman (see Kilcolman, co. Cork), [illegible].
Kilcomnery (Kilcommoragh, co. Wat. ?), [illegible].
Kilcorany, co. Cork, [illegible].
Kilcorydane (Kilcredan, co. Cork ?), [illegible].
Kilcouromane, co. Cork, [illegible].
Kilcourfine (Kilcurfin, co. Cork ?), [illegible].
Kilegobnet (Kilgobnet), co. Cork, [illegible].
Kilegortroe (Gortroe), co. Cork, [illegible].
Kilchabin in Connaught, 1474.
Kilchanyne, co. Cork, 4764.
Kilchowne in Youghal, [illegible].
Kilchnocke Igowne y, co. Cork, [illegible].
Kileloan, co. Gal., [illegible].
Kilellaine, co. Gal. or Mayo, 4792.
Kilellman. See Killeleman.
Kilelyan, co. Gal., [illegible].
Kilemicholl (co. Cork ?), [illegible].
Kilemihill (Kilmichael ?), co. Cork, [illegible].
Kilemishe, co. Cork, [illegible].
Kilemorchine—Kilemorihin, co. Cork, [illegible], [illegible].
Kilemyrche, co. Meath, [illegible].
Kilen, Queen's co., [illegible].
Kilene, Queen's co., 1818.
Kilenaseurrie (co. Cork ?), [illegible].
Kilennimagye, co. Cork, 4468.
Kilenabeony, co. Cork, [illegible].
Kilenelly, co. Cork, 4463.
Kilesteamarterie (Kilmountmartery), co. Cork, [illegible].
Kilestarye (co. Wick. ?), [illegible].
Kilestrwe, co. Cork, [illegible].
Kileoghe, co. Tip., 4574.
Kilecorre, co. Cork, [illegible].
Kilecougloragh, co. Cork, [illegible].
Kilepatricke, co. Cork, [illegible].
Kilepeddir, co. Cork, [illegible].
Kilera (co. Mayo or Gal. ?), [illegible].
Kilerigan (Killerrigh, co. Car., [illegible].
Kilerame (co. Gal. ?), [illegible].
Kilerary (co. Gal. ?), [illegible].
Kilerone (co. Cork ?), [illegible].
Kilerowe (Kilrone), co. Cork, [illegible].
Kilerasse (Kilbarrah), co. Cork, [illegible].
Kilesbrynsbine (co. Cork ?), [illegible].
Kilestalle, co. Gal., [illegible].
Kilelasy, co. Cork, [illegible].
Kiletouran (co. Cork ?), [illegible].
Kileirobe (co. Clare ?), [illegible].
Kilevalien, co. Cork, [illegible].
Kilevershurie, co. Cork, [illegible].
Kilevonane (Kilbunane, co. Kerry), 4574.
Kilevyalisdae, co. Cork, [illegible].
Kilevyne, co. Cork, 4814.
Kilewoher, co. Gal., 4442.
Kilewyle, co. Cork, [illegible].
Kileyero (co. Cork ?), [illegible].
Kiliader, co. Cork, [illegible].
Kilfaine—Kylfane (Kilfane), co. Kilk., [illegible], [illegible].
Kilfahy, co. Kerry, [illegible].
Kilfarge (Killyfargy), co. Mon., [illegible].
Kilfariske (Killergne), co. Lim., parish, [illegible].
Kilfaughny, co. Westm. See Killenfaghney, Kyllenaughen.
Kilfaunnes (co. Tip. ?), [illegible].
Kilfavin, co. Kerry, [illegible].
Kilfawlloe, co. Cork, 4571.
Kilfeacle, Queen's co. See Kilfeacle.
Kilfeadamer (co. Lim. ?), [illegible].
Kilfeakle, co. Tip. See Kilfekill, Kilfakill.
Kilfenragh, co. Clare. See Kilfenveraghe.
Kilfeagh (co. Leit. ?), [illegible].
Kilfegin, co. Ross., [illegible].
Kilfekill — Kilfekle — Kilfecle — Kilfakill (Kilfeakle), co. Tip., 1748, [illegible], [illegible], [illegible], [illegible]; manor, [illegible].
Kilfollan (co. Lim. ?), [illegible].
Kilfonor (co. Car. or Queen's), 4764.
Kilfenora—Killfynoraghe—Kylfynoragh—Kylfynnoragh — Kylfynnora, co. Clare, 4781.
" Daniel, bishop of, 4782.
" Dean of, 4781.
" Archdeacon of, [illegible], [illegible].
" Diocese, presentation in, [illegible].
" possessions of bishopric, 4781.
" See Fynibour.

INDEX TO FIANTS—ELIZABETH.

Kilfinora, co. Kerry. *See* Kilfinorighe, Kilfynorighe.
Kilfarye (co. Lim. ?), [illegible].
Kilfaragh — Kilfraughe — Kilfreraghe — Kilfferagh, co. Kilk., 1004, [illegible], [illegible], [illegible], [illegible], [illegible]; rectory, [illegible], [illegible].
Kilferdinane (co. Lim. ?), [illegible].
Kilfergus, co. Lim. *See* Kilfarisle, Kyllforris.
Kilferre (co. Tip. ?), [illegible].
Kilfiert (co. Cav. ?), [illegible].
Kilfinele—Kilfinkill. *See* Kilfinkill.
Kilfinlane (co. Kerry ?), [illegible].
Kilfinragh. *See* Kilfaragh.
Kilfinan (Kilfinnane ?), co. Lim., 2578.
Kilfinnane, co. Lim. *See* Kilfynan.
Kilfinny, co. Lim. *See* Kylfynney, Kyllfynen.
Kilfinorighe (Kilfinora, co. Kerry), [illegible].
Kilfithmone, co. Tip. *See* Fithmone, Feth-mayne.
Kilfoyan, co. Kerry, [illegible].
Kilfoslan, co. Kerry, [illegible].
Kilfrekell, co. Tip., [illegible].
Kilfrisle, co. Kerry, [illegible].
Kilfrush — Kilfrushe — Kilfrusse — Kilfrust, co. Lim., [illegible], [illegible], [illegible]; rectory, [illegible], [illegible].
Kilfrushy (co. Lim. ?), [illegible].
Kilfynan (Kilfinnane), co. Lim., [illegible], [illegible].
Kilfynnoraghe. *See* Kilfinora.
Kilfynorighe (Kilfinora ?), co. Kerry, [illegible], [illegible].
Kilgabriell, co. Wat., [illegible]. *See also* Gyl-goyre.
Kilgarvane (co. Westm. ?), [illegible].
Kilgaran, co. Car., [illegible].
Kilgarlaighinaigh (co. Cork ?), [illegible].
Kilgarran, co. Westm., [illegible], [illegible].
Kilgarowphe, co. Cork, rectory, [illegible].
Kilgarrovan (Kilgarvan ?), co. Cork, [illegible].
Kilgarriff, co. Cork. *See* Kellegarriffe.
Kilgarrowe (co. Cork ?), [illegible].
Kilgarrylander, co. Kerry. *See* Garrylaun-dry.
Kilgarvan, co. Cork. *See* Kilgarrovan.
Kilgarvan, co. Wat. or Tip., [illegible].
Kilgarvan (co. Westm. ?), [illegible].
Kilgarvan, 1634.
Kilgatarnaitt, co. Wat., [illegible].
Kilgavan, co. Westm., [illegible].
Kilgawan (co. Kerry ?), [illegible].
Kilgeefin, co. Rosc., [illegible]. *See also* Kilkevine.
Kilgemane—Kilgemme, Queen's co., [illegible], [illegible].
Kilgerran, co. Car., [illegible].
Kilgarrill, co. Gal. *See* Kylkaryll.
Kilgervan, co. Cork, [illegible].
Kilgesoin, Queen's co., [illegible].
Kilgeber, co. Louth, [illegible].
Kilghery (co. Clare ?), [illegible].
Kilghirell, [illegible].
Kilghyll—Kylghyll, in Connaught, [illegible].
Kilgirre, co. Lei., [illegible].
Kilgislane. *See* Kilglass.
Kilglan (co. Kild. ?), [illegible].
Kilgina, co. Lim., [illegible].
Kilglas (Kilglass), co. Rosc., rectory, [illegible], [illegible].
Kilglash (co. Clare ?), [illegible].
Kilglass—Kilglasse—Kilglasse—Kilglaisse—Kilglash—Kylglasshe, co. Sligo, [illegible], [illegible], [illegible], [illegible], [illegible], [illegible], [illegible].
Kilglasse, co. Cork, [illegible], [illegible].
Kilglasse — Kylglasse (Kilglass, co. Long.), [illegible]; rectory, [illegible], [illegible], [illegible], [illegible], [illegible].
Kilglasse. *See* Kilglass, co. Sligo.
Kilglassy — Kylglasse, co. Clare, [illegible], [illegible], [illegible].
Kilglyne—Kylglyne (Kilglin), co. Meath, [illegible], [illegible].
Kilgolan, co. Cork, [illegible].
Kilgolan — Kilgoliane, co. Dub., [illegible], [illegible], [illegible], [illegible], [illegible], [illegible].
Kilgoliane (co. Cork ?), [illegible].
Kilgolihan — Kylgobbinn (co. Cork ?), [illegible], [illegible], [illegible].
Kilgobban, co. Kerry. *See* Kylkobane.
Kilgobanet—Killgobanett. *See* Kilgobnet.
Kilgobennet—Kylgobonett (Kilgobnet), co. Wat., [illegible], [illegible].
Kilgobnet, co. Cork. *See* Kilgobanaltie, Kilkobnet.
Kilgobnet — Kilgobanet — Kilgobanett — Kyllgobynett, co. Kerry, [illegible], [illegible], [illegible]; grant of, [illegible].
Kilgobnett (co. Wat. ?), [illegible], [illegible].
Kilgobonltie—Kilcobnbrnet—Kilgobnet—Kylgobnaltie (Kilgobnet), co. Cork, [illegible], [illegible].
Kilgolban, co. Lim. *See* Kilgallobon.
Kilgolbin (Kilgulbin), co. Kerry, [illegible], [illegible], [illegible].
Kilgome (Kilgowan ?), co. Kild., [illegible].
Kilgore (Kilgory), Queen's co., [illegible], [illegible], [illegible]. *See* Glashchkilgore.
Kilgorenly, co. Mon. *See* Kilgrome.
Kilgoaghy (co. Ferm. ?), [illegible].
Kilgoane, co. Wex., [illegible].
Kilgowan, co. Kild. *See* Kilgome.
Kilgowen, co. Cav., [illegible].
Kilgowrghe, co. Wat., [illegible].
Kilgowne — Kilgowne, co. Wex., [illegible], [illegible], [illegible], [illegible].
Kilgrach (Kilgrogy), co. Mon., [illegible].
Kilgrante, co. Tip., rectory, [illegible].
Kilgreage—Kilgrog—Kilgroge, co. Meath, [illegible].
Kilgreige — Kilgregan (Kilgraigue), co. Meath, [illegible], [illegible]. *See* Newton of Rathgerinloghgreige.

Kilgrellan—Kylgrellan, co. Kilk., 804.
Kilgrenie, co. Wat., [illegible], [illegible].
Kilgreny—Kilgrene—Kylgren, co. Car., [illegible], 1428, [illegible], [illegible], 6447, 6817.
Kilgrige, co. Meath, 6775.
Kilgrogy—Kilgrowgy, co. Tip., 4384, 6471.
Kilgrome (Kilgormly ?, co. Mon.), 5042.
Kilgultin, co. Kerry. See Kilgolbin.
Kilgultom (Kilgollan), co. Lim., [illegible].
Kilgurtine—Kylgurtine, co. Clare, [illegible].
Kilhachlin (co. Cork ?), [illegible].
Kilhagan, co. Tip., [illegible].
Kilhahie abbey (Killagh abbey in parish of Kilcoleman, co. Kerry ?), [illegible].
„ See also Killaha.
Kilhard (co. Wex. ?), 6867.
Kilharmick—Kilharmake, 6872, 4800, [illegible]. See Kilharmick, King's co.
Kilhea—Kylhe, co. Wat., 783; rectory, [illegible].
Kilheale—Kilhele (Kiltoel), co. Kild., [illegible], [illegible], [illegible].
„ prebendary, 1667.
Kilhecky, [illegible].
Kilhelle (co. Wex. ?), 4861.
Kilhelle, co. Kild., [illegible].
Kilhelan, parish, co. Kild., 1814.
Kilhelan—Kylhelan, Queen's co., 1187, 1834, [illegible].
Kilhele. See Kilhealn.
Kilhelan, co. Kild., 6734.
Kilhenneleghe, [illegible].
Kilhervie (Kilmaharvey), co. Mon., 6440.
Kilhevan (co. Kerry ?), 6878.
Kilhoylaghe—Kylhoylaghe, co. Lim., 6741.
Kilhigterowe (co. Kerry), 4873.
Kilhile, co. Wex. See Kylhenle, 1867.
Kilhoroughe, co. Lim., 5781.
Kilhobboge — Kilhobocke — Kilhowbock, country in co. Wex., 5784.
„ chief serjeant of, [illegible], [illegible].
„ customs due from, [illegible].
Kilhyde (co. Clare ?), 4612.
Kiliaby (co. Cork ?), 6784.
Kilidnuffe (co. Lim. ?), 6400.
Kilighe, King's co., 1402.
Kilimyghell (co. Cork ?), 6871.
Kilimmackie (Kilmmacky), co. Cork, [illegible].
Kilingruan, co. Tip., 1848.
Kilinichon, co. Wex., 617.
Kilinorie (co. Cork ?), [illegible].
Kilinyaly, [illegible].
Kilirvarigie (co. Lim. ?), 6804.
Kilinyhon (co. Clare ?), 6790.
Kiliveragh, co. Cork, [illegible].
Kilka—Kilkaa—Kilkae—Kylka (Kilkea), co. Kild., [illegible], [illegible], [illegible]–10, [illegible], 6764; rectory, 1830.
Kilkaa—Kylkan, co. Car., 864.
Kilkale by Connall, co. Kild., [illegible].
Kilkallan, co. Lim., 1808.
Kilkallane in Munster, [illegible].
Kilkalme, co. Gal., 4487.
Kilkaly in O'Birne's country, [illegible].
Kilkandrogh in O'Birne's country, [illegible].
Kilkanewry (Kilcanevoe, co. Wat. ?), [illegible].
Kilkare, co. Wex., 4818.
Kilkarne (Kilcarn), co. Meath, 4487, [illegible].
Kilkarne (co. Wex. ?), 5884.
Kilkarrig (co. Kerry ?), 6487.
Kilkart( ), co. Wat., [illegible].
Kilkashell (co. Rosc. ?), 6428.
Kilkeahine (co. Clare ?), [illegible].
Kilkeakyn (co. Kild. ?), 5866.
Kilkea (Kilcrea ?), co. Cork, 4848.
Kilkea (co. Cork ?), 6794.
Kilkea, co. Kild. See Kilka, Kelka, Kilca.
Kilkealy — Kylkealy (Kilkeady), co. Clare, [illegible], [illegible].
Kilkedy (co. Cork ?), 6414.
Kilkeoran, King's co. See Kylkeoran.
Kilkeovaragh (co. Kerry ?), 5168.
Kilkefolde, Queen's co., [illegible].
Kilkeslea, co. Kilk., 1304.
Kilkelan, co. Lim., 1766.
Kilkellan, co. Kerry, 5018, [illegible].
Kilkellan—Kilkellane—Kilkellain, co. Lim., [illegible], 4526, 6183, 6470.
Kilkellan (Kilcullane ?), co. Lim., [illegible].
Kilkelshin — Kilkelshene — Kilkellshin— Kilkellyn—Kilkyllyn—Kylkillyn, co. Kilk. (Kilcullihene, Waterford), [illegible], 5844.
„ abbey leased, 1508; possessions leased, [illegible].
„ rectory, [illegible], [illegible].
Kilkelley—Kylkelley (King's co.), [illegible].
Kilkellin, co. Kilk., [illegible].
Kilkemeny, co. Car., 6447.
Kilkemmalan, co. Lim., 4890.
Kilken—Kylken, co. Tip., [illegible].
Kilkenan (Kilcannon ?), co. Wex., [illegible], 6816.
Kilkenane—Kylkenan, co. Wex., [illegible], [illegible].
Kilkenny—Kilkennie—Kilkeny—Kylkenny —Kylkeny (mentioned), [illegible], 107, 143, 317, [illegible], 377, 618, [illegible], [illegible], [illegible], [illegible], [illegible], [illegible], [illegible], [illegible], 1031, 1030, 1068, 1078, [illegible], [illegible], [illegible], [illegible], 1848, [illegible], [illegible], [illegible], 1911, 1918, 1918, [illegible], [illegible]–1, [illegible]–8, [illegible]–8, [illegible], [illegible], [illegible]; member of parliament of, [illegible]; sovereign of, [illegible]; charter, [illegible];

INDEX TO FIANTS—ELIZABETH.

Kilkenny:
corporation, similar liberties granted to Kilmallock, 1575; measure of, 4088, 5344; messuages and gardens in, granted, 104, 5654.
sovereign, burgesses, and commonalty, charter, 2461.
sovereign, commissions, 665–7, 2317, 2444, 3047, 3660, 3670, 4758; to proclaim persons indicted of treason, 1544.
recorder comm., 306–7.
burgesses pardoned, 2136, 5745.
merchants pardoned, 2136, 3867; merchants of Irishtown, 1637.
Boyshis lane, 2464.
Frank house, 1349, 6420.
Frerin street, 3468.
High street, 3354.
house of friars, cemetery, 3509.
house of Blackfriars, possessions granted, 3654.
Loslane, 4894.
market cross, 3354.
mill sites near, 5693.
S. John, vicar of, 6712.
S. Kenice cathedral, 2454, 4430.
" parish, 2451.
S. Mary church, 4684.
Thelsel, 2451.
Upperhill by, 1608.
See Irishtown, 2040, 4509.
bishop of (see Ossory), 3868.
dean of, 4128.
archdeacon, 2474.
procurator, 2424.
county, enquiry as to injuries done by men of, 438; persons pardoned, to give security to appear at sessions, 497, &c.; persons indicted of treason in, 1838; lands in to be exchanged by N. White, 3926; plenty of corn, 6316.
sheriff, 94, 68, 61, 138, 410, 588, 734, 838, 1198, 1361, 1831, 2117, 2150, 2417, 2451, 2448, 2841, 2940, 2848, 3409, 3801, 3839, 3980, 4098, 4351, 4368, 4853, 5046, 5302, 5394.
sub-sheriff, 2484, 3980, 4958, 5040, 5394.
clerk of crown and peace, 143, 2409.
escheator, 2831.
general of forces in, 2831, 4880, 6316, 3486.
Kilkenny county, constable of gaol, 1139.
" " overseer of tanning, 2692.
" " commission of peace, 563–4, 1644, 1652, 2457, 2628, 2644, 3254, 3364, 3423, 4457, 4743.
" " commission of muster, 2117, 2346, 3444.
" " comm. to lead inhabitants against rebels, 661.
" " ecclesiastical comm., 560–2.
" " comm. as to earl of Kildare's lands, 758, 763.
" " martial law in, 56, 64, 136, 498, 663, 734, 1193, 1461, 1534, 1621, 2159, 2438, 2461, 2541, 2618, 2918, 3021, 3098, 3144, 3361, 3052, 3880, 4401, 4028, 4770, 5015, 5158, 5694, 6649.
Kilkenny—Kelkenny (Kilkennybeg), co. Tip. 6441.
Kilkenny—Kylkenny—Kylkeny West (Kilkenny West), co. Westm., 1385, 2348, 5290, 6498, 6682.
" hospital of S. John, leased, 863, 1111; granted, 1385, 1582; possessions granted, 2820; pension of, 6797.
" barony, divided into ploughlands, 3535.
" " martial law in, 2006, 5888.
" " seneschal of, 3315, 4886, 4328.
Kilkenniso (Kilkieran), co. Clare, 6319.
Kilkeran (co. Cork?), 6415.
Kilkeran — Kilkeranie (Kilkerranmore, co. Cork), 3380, 4502.
Kilkeran, co. Gal., 4798, 5060.
Kilkeran, co. Mayo, 4808, 5517.
Kilkerane (co. Cork?), 6415.
Kilkerane, co. Kilk., 1965.
Kilkerane (co. Mayo?), 4809.
Kilkerelagh, co. Tip., 4654.
Kilkery, co. Sligo. See Kilkere.
Kilkerill—Kilkeril—Kilkeroll—Kilkervill, co. Kilk., 1985, 2700, 3840, 4007, 6907.
Kilkeron, co. Westm., 3363.
Kilkerynan, co. Kerry, 5018, 6076, 6407, 6698.
Kilkerig (co. Car.?), 6547.
Kilkeryll. See Kilkeroll.
Kilkevill—Kilkervill, King's co., 6436, 6468.
Kilkerumocka (King's co.?), 4162.
Kilkern, co. Wex., 4612.
Kilkern—Kylkern, co. Leit. or Ross., 4788.
Kilkerran, co. Cork, 6638. See also Kilkyrane.
Kilkerranmore, co. Cork. See Kilkeran.
Kilkere (Kilkere?), co. Sligo, [illegible].

INDEX TO FIANTS—ELIZABETH.

Kilkerrill. *See* Kilkeroll, Kilkerrill.
Kilkerrydisy, co. Lim., 5274.
Kilkervyn (King's co. ?), 6496.
Kilkervan, 1664.
Kilkesan—Kylkesan, co. Wex., [illegible], 1877.
Kilkevan (Kilcavan ?), Queen's co., [illegible].
Kilkevan—Kylkevan—Kylkevane, co. Wex., [illegible], 72, [illegible], 6482, 5743.
Kilkevane, 723.
Kilkevin, co. Ross., 4572.
Kilkevine—Kilkevyne (Kilgefin, co. Ross.), rectory, 1464, 3126.
Kilkey—Kylkey, co. Clare, [illegible].
Kilkhy (co. Clare ?), 6414.
Kilkide, co. Clare, 4682.
Kilkidy, co. Clare, 5712.
Kilkie, co. Clare, [illegible].
Kilkienan, co. Clare. *See* Kilkenaine, Kilkeyne.
Kilkienane (co. Cork ?), 4573.
Kilkilasher (co. Tip. ?), 4528.
Kilkilhill (Kilcullihoom), co. Wat., 1896.
Kilkillan, co. Kerry, 5117.
Kilkillen, co. Lim., 3678, 4443.
Kilkillame (co. Lim. or Tip.), 4784.
Kilkilvery, co. Gal. *See* Kilkylwyrroy.
Kilkipp. in Munster, 5615.
Kilkivan, co. Cork or Wat., [illegible].
Kilkimage (co. Gal. ?), [illegible].
Kilkire, co. Cork, [illegible].
Kilkirie, co. Louth, 4396.
Kilkirley, co. Wex., rectory, [illegible].
Kilkirrill (co. Kilk. ?), [illegible], [illegible].
" *See* Kilkerrill.
Kilkirryhaill (perhaps Kilcurl), co. Kilk., [illegible].
Kilkish, co. Clare, 6401.
Kilkissyn—Kilkyshin, co. Clare, [illegible], [illegible].
Kilkiltey—Kylkilny, co. Meath, [illegible].
Kilkeady, co. Kilk., rectory, [illegible].
Kilknock, co. Car., 4273, [illegible], [illegible]. *See also* Kylnocyoke.
Kilknockan (co. Tip. ?), [illegible].
Kilknockan (co. Wat. ?), [illegible].
Kilknockaght, co. Kerry, [illegible].
Kilknocke—Kylknocke, Queen's co., [illegible].
Kilknoke (co. Kilk. ?), [illegible].
Kilkona, co. Wex., 5742.
Kilkonane, co. Gal. or Rosc., 4676.
Kilkobanel (Kilgobnet, co. Cork ?), [illegible].
Kilkonigan. *See* Kilconigan.
Kilkollen. *See* Kilcollen.
Kilkoleman. *See* Kilcolman.
Kilkoman, co. Tip., [illegible].
Kilkoman. *See* Kilcoman.
Kilkommanagh, co. Kilk., [illegible].
Kilkonan. *See* Kilconnan.
Kilkonell. *See* Kilconnell.
Kilkonel, King's co., [illegible].
Kilkore (co. Mayo ?), [illegible].
Kilkorke. *See* Kilcorke.
Kilkorskan. *See* Kilcorskan.
Kilkorwan. *See* Kilcorwan.
Kilkowley. *See* Kilcowly.
Kilkrage, [illegible].
Kilkrayne (Kilkieran), co. Clare, 6316.
Kilkrea. *See* Kilcrea.
Kilkreadane—Kilkredan. *See* Kilcredan.
Kilkredan (Kilcredane, co. Clare ?), [illegible].
Kilkreggane—Kilkregan. *See* Kilcregan.
Kilkrumaght. *See* Kilcrumaght.
Kilkronan, co. Mon., [illegible].
Kilkridane. *See* Kilcredan.
Kilkrile—Kilkrille—Kilkryle—Kylkrille—Kylkrylle (Kilcurly ?), co. Lim., 1148, 4787, [illegible], [illegible].
Kilkrine (co. Kerry ?), [illegible].
Kilkrot (co. Car. ?), 4447.
Kilkryle. *See* Kilkrile.
Kilkryne (Kilcronan), co. Mon., [illegible].
Kilkurry. *See* Kilcurrie.
Kilky—Kilkye, co. Clare, [illegible], [illegible].
Kilkyde (co. Gal. ?), [illegible].
Kilkydy—Kilkyde—Kylkydy, co. Clare, [illegible], [illegible], [illegible], 5735.
Kilkydy, co. Lim., rectory, 3434.
Kilkye. *See* Kilky.
Kilkylly (co. Clare ?), [illegible].
Kilkyllye. *See* Kilkellahin.
Kilkylwyrroy—Kylkilwyrry (Kilkilvery), co. Gal., 1667, 5412.
Kilkypp, co. Wat., [illegible].
Kilkyshin. *See* Kilkissyn.
Kill—Kyll, co. Kild., 1186, 1173, [illegible], [illegible], [illegible], 4431.
" rectory, 1173, [illegible], [illegible], [illegible].
" parish, 1567.
Kill (co. Kilk. ?), [illegible].
Kill—Kyll (co. Sligo or Mayo), [illegible], [illegible].
Kill—Kyll (co. Tip. ?), [illegible].
Kill (co. Wick. ?), [illegible].
Kill, Corbeh of, [illegible].
Kill, Wony, pardon, [illegible].
Killabban, Queen's co. *See* Killeban.
Killabraher, co. Cork. *See* Kylbra.
Killacloure (co. Tip. ?), [illegible].
Killacollon (co. Tip. ?), [illegible].
Killacormog (co. Long. ?), [illegible].
Killaconnenagh, co. Cork. *See* Killcoonagh.
Killaconnigan, co. Meath. *See* Killconogan.
Killadadorie—Kyladorry—Killodadorie (Killaderry), King's co., 6137, [illegible].
" advowson, [illegible].
Killadaran, co. Wex., [illegible].
Killadoon, co. Mayo. *See* Cilladiro, [illegible].
Killaderry, King's co. *See* Killadadorie, Killedory.

Killadirrye (Kildorrery ?), co. Cork, 6617.
Killadoran, co. Kild. See Kylladowne.
Killadowne, co. Rosc., 6191.
Killadowaill, co. Clare, 4868.
Killadroman, co. Wick. See Kylladrymane, 814, 2859.
Killadyart, co. Clare. See Kyllyahyrt.
Killafalla, in Munster, 6467.
Killaferagha, co. Gal., 6[illegible].
Killagarry — Kyllagarrye, Queen's co., 996, 1594.
Killagas (Killag), co. Wex., 1258.
Killagh, co. Kerry. See Killaha.
Killagh—Killagha, co. Kilk., 2611, 2839, 6144.
Killagh—Killahan—Kylaghe—Kyllahie (Killahy in bar. Knocktopher), co. Kilk., rectory, 5572, 5996.
" vicar of, 4718, 6[illegible].
Killagh — Killaughe (Killahy), co. Kilk., rectory, 5[illegible], 4094, 6[illegible]41.
" See Killaghi.
Killagh, co. Tip., 6[illegible]24, 6722.
Killaghaks (co. Leit. ?), 6428.
Killaghamba—Kyllaghamba, co. Rosc., 4245.
Killaghan (co. Cork ?), 6411.
Killaghan (Killyon), co. Meath, 6722.
Killaghdroght, King's co., 6458.
Killagha. See Killagh.
Killagha, co. Lim., 6717.
Killaghara, co. Tip., 4[illegible].
Killaghi in dio. Ossory, vicar (see Killagh), 6[illegible].
Killaghcallaghan (co. Cork ?), 6618.
Killaghiry, co. Tip., 4[illegible].
Killaghy—Kylaghie (co. Cork ?), 5794.
Killaghy—Kilaghy, King's co., 6456.
Killaghy, Queen's co. or Kilk., 6110.
Killaghy, co. Tip. See Killahy.
Killagko—Kyllaghko, vicar of, 718.
Killagly—Kyllagly, King's co., 6798.
Killagowna, co. Wex. See Kyllogowna.
Killagowne—Kyllagowne (co. Sligo ?), 6618.
Killaha—Killagh—Kylaha (Killagh abbey, in Kilcolman demesne near Milltown, co. Kerry), abbey leased, 3948, 4318, 6172, 6814. See also Killahaie, Kyllaha.
" rectory, 3[illegible]48, 6179.
Killaha (co. Kerry ?), 6[illegible], 6[illegible]79.
Killaha (co. Kilk. ?), 4[illegible]72.
Killaha (co. Lim. or Cork), 5[illegible].
Killaha. See Killahie.
Killahaa. See Killagh.
Killahagh (co. Cork ?), 5911.
Killahaly—Killahally — Killahayly — Killahalie, co. Wat., 2944, 3610, 3[illegible]80, 6153, 6472.
Killahane (co. Kerry ?), 5[illegible]94.
Killahayly. See Killahaly.
Killaha. See Killahie.
Killahee (co. Kilk. ?), 6704.
Killahoa. See Killahy.
Killahogard—Killahogard (co. Tip. ?), 6[illegible].
Killahomlo, co. Kerry, 6671.
Killahoro (co. Tip. ?), 67[illegible].
Killahorian (co. Wex. ?), 4174.
Killahlo — Killaha — Killaha — Killahe (co. Tip. ?), 5[illegible]43, 5618, 6[illegible], 6[illegible], 67[illegible]. See Killahy.
Killahine (co. Kerry ?), 6124.
Killaboriane (co. Wex. ?), 5904.
Killalmchare (Killahurler, co. Wick. ?), 5[illegible]4.
Killahower—Kyllahower (co. Cork ?), 2279.
Killahy, co. Kilk. See Killagh.
Killahy—Killahan—Killahoa (Killaghy ?), co. Tip., 966, 1978, 2189, 2761.
Killaine, co. Gal., 6618.
Killala, co. Mayo, 1568.
Killalgow—Killalgowe (co. Tip. or Kilk.), 5[illegible].
Killalleirane, 5[illegible].
Killallaghtan, co. Gal. See Cillalachdan, 5[illegible].
Killallo—Kilallo, in Upperossory, 697.
Killallon—Kyllallon—Killalone—Killalon, co. Meath, 2[illegible]04, 3618, 4149, 6461, 6[illegible].
Killallon, co. Mon., 5[illegible].
Killalo—Kyllalo (co. Mayo ?), 4781.
Killaloe — Killalowe — Kyllalowe — Kalalonghe, co. Clare, 6941.
" bishop of, comm., 6[illegible].
" bishop Maurice (M'Brien Ara), a party to Thomond composition, 4761; comm., 3[illegible]57, 6[illegible].
" bishop of, possessions of see, 47[illegible]; rectory in gift of, 6472.
" dean, 4791, 6474.
" archdeaconry, 6472.
" diocese, commissaries of archb. of Cashel in, 2[illegible]77.
" diocese presentations, 4[illegible].
Killalogu, co. Wex., rectory, 5[illegible].
Killalon—Killalone. See Killallon.
Killalaren—Killalorin — Kyllalaran—Kyllelaryn, co. Westm., 996, 2294, 4[illegible], 6[illegible]; grant, 5[illegible].
Killalowe, co. Lim., 4[illegible].
Killalpoke (co. Wex. ?), 6[illegible].
Killaly—Kyllaly, 759.
Killaly, co. Tip., Franciscan friary, 5[illegible]61.
Killamery—Killamorie, co. Kilk., 4[illegible], 67[illegible].
Killamoran — Kyllomoran (Kilamoran, co. Gal.), 1408, 2408.
Killamoy (co. Sligo ?), 4577.
" ruined chapel, 6[illegible]77.
Killamyan, co. Gal., 4[illegible].
Killan, John m'Donell I., pardon, 4[illegible].
Killan—Killane—Kyllan, co. Louth, 5[illegible], 77[illegible], 17[illegible], 6411.
Killan. See Killane, co. Meath.
Killanahan, co. Lim. See Killenyohan.

INDEX TO FIANTS.—ELIZABETH.

Killecaill (co. Tip. ?), 6766.
Killasaran (co. Lim. ?), 6176.
Killancoll — Killancole (Killincooly), co. Wex., rectory, 1088, 2923.
Killane, co. Car. *See* Killanny.
Killane—Kyllane, co. Clare, abbey, 4761.
Killane—Kyllane (co. Gal. ?), rectory, 1583.
Killane (co. Kerry ?), rectory, 5254, 5347.
Killane—Kyllane, co. Louth, 1747, 1751.
Killane — Kyllane (Killaun, co. Meath ?), rectory, [illegible].
Killane—Killane (Killaney), co. Meath, [illegible], [illegible], 4128, 4467.
Killanin, co. Tip., 4631.
Killanisole, co. Gal., [illegible].
Killanlogo (co. Cork ?), 3511.
Killanire, Queen's co., 2315.
Killanleagho, co. Down, 5572.
Killanlogha, co. Lim. 6171.
Killanny (Killane, co. Car., or Killane, co. Wex.), 272, 2042, 3166.
Killanoghan, co. Lim., 4671.
Killantoke — Kyllantoke (Killanstogo), King's co., 616, [illegible], [illegible].
Killanullye—Kyllanullye (co. Sligo ?), [illegible].
Killaraght—Killaright—Killarighte—Kyllaraght (co. Sligo ?), 4074, 4644.
" religious house, possessions granted, 4826.
Killard (co. Kerry ?), 6464.
Killard (co. Westm. ?), 6533.
Killardarry. *See* Killardorrye.
Killardo—Kyllardo, co. Kild., 872.
Killardo—Kyllardo, co. Meath, 1828, 3442.
" manor, 3446.
Killardorrye — Killardarry — Killardorye, [illegible], [illegible], 6763.
Killardry—Killardry, co. Tip., 4637, 6711, [illegible].
Killardy (co. Kerry ?), 6497.
Killare, co. Westm., [illegible], 6780, 6160.
Killareny (co. Kilk. ?), 5563.
Killargo—Killargan—Killargie. *See* Killarga.
Killargian—Killarglande (co. Kerry ?), 6874.
Killargy. *See* Killorgo.
Killari, rector of, 1671.
Killaridde—Killarid—Killaridi—Killaridy (Killaride), co. Kerry, 5618, [illegible], 6908.
Killarneye. *See* Killarney.
Killarnane — Kyllarnane (Killernane), co. Clare, 4761.
Killarney — Kilarney — Killarneye — Killarney—Kyllarny, co. Kerry, 2778, 3157, [illegible]; church and town, 6277, 6717.
Killarny—Killaryme (Killarn, co. Down ?), rectory, 1656, 3767.
Killarush, co. Cork. *See* Killoruske, [illegible].
Killarvan (Kilsharvan), co. Meath, rectory, 1460.
Killary, co. Kilk., 1626.
Killary, Queen's co., 4461.
Killary—Killarye (co. Tip. ?), [illegible], 6708.
Killary, [illegible].
Killaryme. *See* Killarny.
Killaryoyne—Kyllaryoyne, in Omaey, 1631.
Killashog, co. Kilk., 2417.
Killasaraghe. *See* Killasarough.
Killashandra, co. Cav. *See* Kylshanra.
Killashee, co. Long. *See* Kilsie.
Killasia (co. Clare ?), 4878.
Killaskillen, co. Meath. *See* Killaskeillinge.
Killasnogan, co. Gal. *See* Killasnogan.
Killasnoy or Kellyaston, co. Car., rectory, 398.
Killason. *See* Killasson.
Killaspickoen. *See* Killaspick Oen.
Killaspicklonnan. *See* Killaspocklonan.
Killaspick Oen—Killaspickoen, co. Cork, [illegible], 4128, 6848, 6842.
Killaspocklonan—Killaspoglonan—Killaspicklonan—Kyllaspock Lonnan (Killaspoglonane), co. Clare, 4761, [illegible], [illegible].
Killaspugmoylane—Killaspugmolan (Killaspugmoylan, co. Gal.), 1337, 4872.
Killassaraghe—Kyllassaraghe (Killossaragh), co. Wat., 664, 2128.
Killasser (co. Sligo ?), 5715.
Killassarough—Killassaraghe (Kilhassaragh), co. Cork, [illegible], [illegible].
Killasson—Killasson (co. Long.), 4183, 5274.
Killaster (co. Wat. ?), 2771.
Killatero, co. Lim., 6171.
Killaughe. *See* Killagh, co. Kilk.
Killaught, co. Lim., 2777.
Killaughtcorrig, co. Gal., 6471.
Killauke, co. Wex., 1299.
Killavally, co. Meath, 4684.
Killavie—Kyllavie, co. Car., 504.
Killavoy, co. Cork. *See* Kylowoy, [illegible].
Killayeo, 1598.
Killaynyne (co. Gal. ?), 4712.
Kill——, names commencing so (followed by a consonant) are indexed Kil——.
Kille, co. Donegal, [illegible].
Kille (King's or Queen's co.), 618.
Kille, Queen's co., 4461.
Kille, co. Tip., 6454.
Kille, Donogh mc., pardon, 3868, [illegible].
" Edm., pardon, [illegible].
Killoe, co. Wat. *See* Kylloe, 1627.
Killeagho (co. Cork ?), [illegible].
Killeagha, co. Westm., 1344.
Killean—Kyllean, co. Car., 894.
Killean—Kyllean, co. Meath, 1836.
Killean — Kyllean (Killyon ?), co. Meath, 6767.
Killean—Kyllean (Killiane), co. Wex., [illegible].
" Hiilo, 417.
Killeasman (co. Kilk. ?), 4638.

INDEX TO FIANTS.—ELIZABETH.

Killenane (co. Wat. ?), [illegible].
Killeanne, co. Clare, [illegible], [illegible].
Killenane (co. Leit. ?), [illegible].
Killeany, co. Gal. *See* Killanyn.
Killenay, co. Meath. *See* Killane.
Killenaro — Kylienaro (co. Gal. ?), rectory, [illegible].
Killenarney. *See* Killarney.
Killeban—Kyleban—Killeban (Killabban), Queen's co., [illegible], [illegible], [illegible].
" rectory, [illegible].
" vicarage, [illegible].
Killeinane (Killinane), co. Kerry, [illegible].
Killebegg (co. Wex. ?), [illegible].
Killebegye, co. Gal., [illegible].
Killebrien (Killybreen), co. Mon., [illegible].
Killebyrne (Killyborn), co. Mon., [illegible].
Killecheran, co. Tip., [illegible].
Killechie. *See* Killeshony.
Killechone, co. Long., [illegible].
Killeck—Kyleck, King's co., [illegible].
Killeckie (Killyleck), co. Mon., [illegible].
Killecle — Kylecle (perhaps Killinacle), Queen's co., [illegible], [illegible].
Killecloghan. *See* Killcloghan.
Killecloghe — Kyllecloghe, Queen's co., [illegible], 47[illegible].
Killecoman, co. Lim., [illegible].
Killecrolman (Killcolman), co. Cork, [illegible].
Killecomogan—Killecomogan (Killacommigan), co. Meath, [illegible].
" rectory, [illegible], [illegible].
Killecromgan (Killycromgan), co. Mon., [illegible].
Killecorryth (co. Car. ?), [illegible].
Killecorrell, co. Wex., [illegible].
Killecryan (co. Cav. ?), [illegible].
Killedamm, co. Kilk., [illegible], [illegible].
Kille dorrane, Teig m'Arte oo (Kinsheloagh or Cavanagh), pardon, [illegible].
Killedory—Killedorie (Killadorry), King's co., rectory, [illegible], [illegible].
Killedmond, co. Car., [illegible].
Killedonoghe (Killydonagh), co. Mon., [illegible].
Killedrogh—Kyledrogh, co. Cav., [illegible].
Killedowan, co. Ros., [illegible].
Killedrom, Queen's co., [illegible].
Killeedy, co. Lim. *See* Killekid, Killidy, Kyledie.
Killeef, co. Mon. *See* Killyfe.
Killeek, co. Dub. *See* Killeegh.
Killeen, co. Kild. *See* Killyne.
Killeen, co. Kilk. *See* Kylline.
Killeen, co. Lim. *See* Killyne.
Killeen, co. Meath. *See* Killene, Killane, Kyllane.
Killeen, Queen's co. *See* Killena.
Killeenadeema, co. Kerry. *See* Killynyfynan.
Killeenough, co. Wat. *See* Kyllene.
Killeenagrough, co. Westm. *See* Killeneghrough.
Killeenavarra, co. Gal. *See* Killinvarogh, Killynvarrogh.
Killeenboy, co. Long. *See* Kyllynboy.
Killeenaboy, co. Westm. *See* Killinaboy.
Killeenbrack, co. Westm. *See* Killenbrack, Killenbrick.
Killeentagheo, co. Westm., [illegible].
Killeenmacoog, co. Clare. *See* Killenmacke.
Killeencunnamanagh, co. Cork. *See* Killenamanagh.
Killeenaghty, co. Lim. *See* Killynoghty.
Killeenycallaghan, co. Westm. *See* Killencallahan.
Killeeshal, co. Wat. *See* Killyshell.
Killeevan, co. Mon. *See* Killyvan.
Killegarrd (Killogar, co. Wick.), [illegible].
Killegh (Killeek), co. Dub., 1777.
Killeghlogy (co. Wex. or Car. ?), [illegible].
Killeglan (Killeglaud), co. Meath, [illegible], [illegible].
" church of, [illegible].
Killeglen—Kyleglen, in Omany, [illegible].
Killegney, co. Wex., [illegible]. *See also* Killeighlyn.
Killegrenagh, co. Cork, [illegible].
Killegrine, co. Wex., [illegible].
Killegroome, [illegible].
Killehallagh, co. Lim., [illegible].
Killehoon, co. Lim. *See* Killehine.
Killehobertagh (co. Tip. ?), [illegible].
Killehony, co. Kerry. [illegible], [illegible].
Killehony — Killeohie — Killehinee (Killehenny), co. Kerry, rectory, [illegible], [illegible], [illegible].
Killehide, Queen's co., [illegible].
Killehinee (Killnchlinch ?), co. Westm., [illegible].
Killehine (Killehoon), co. Lim., [illegible].
Killehine—Kyllehine, co. Lim., [illegible].
Killehorin (co. Leit. ?), [illegible].
Killehowlane (co. Wick. ?), [illegible].
Killehyo—Kylehyo, co. Clare, [illegible].
Killeigh, co. Dub., [illegible].
Killeigh—Killeighe — Killighe — Killeighe— Killighe—Kyllyegh—Kylleighe, King's co., [illegible], [illegible], [illegible], [illegible].
" priory of canons of the Holy Cross, leased, [illegible]; granted, [illegible], [illegible], [illegible], [illegible].
" house of friars, leased, [illegible]; granted, [illegible], [illegible].
" house of nuns, leased, [illegible]; possessions granted, [illegible], [illegible].
" parish church, [illegible].
Killeighan, [illegible].
Killeighe, co. Kild., [illegible].
Killeighe, co. Louth, [illegible].
Killeighe, co. Westm., [illegible].
Killeighlyn (Killegny ?), co. Wex., [illegible].
Killeigh Page, co. Tip., rectory, [illegible], [illegible].

INDEX TO FIANTS—ELIZABETH.

Kilcolgan (co. Wexm. ?), [illegible].
Killadagh, co. Clare, 6077.
Killallen, co. Gal., [illegible].
Kille Ivallin (co. Cork ?), [illegible].
Killeloroughe (Killylooragh, co. Mon.), 6042.
Killakhane (co. Clare ?), 6077.
Killekid—Killokidd (Killoody ?), co. Lim., rectory, 1643, 4612.
Killekill (Killcakle ?), co. Tip., rectory, 1643, [illegible].
Killekilla, co. Wex. or Car., 6617.
Killekinly, co. Cork, 4616.
Killekuhan, co. Cork, 4648.
Killekynnue (Killmurvan), co. Cork, [illegible].
Killelane, co. Kerry, [illegible].
Killelanan—Killclolan—Killollyname—Killelymayne—Kiollinan—Kylliolynan, co. Mayo, [illegible], 4467, [illegible], [illegible], 5442-3, 5617, 6614, [illegible]; castle and lands granted, [illegible], 6614.
Killelaraght (Killylaragh), co. Mon., 5672.
Killelayrto (Kinelarty barony), co. Down, woods and mines of, granted, [illegible].
Killelgan (King's co. ?), [illegible].
Killelina, co. Kerry, 5642.
Killellan (King's co. ?), 6428.
Killelles (co. Tip. ?), [illegible].
Killellire, King's co., 5766.
Killellymane. See Killelanan.
Killelongirle (co. Wat. ?), [illegible].
Killeloughvally (Killyloughavoy ?), co. Mon., [illegible].
Killelton, co. Kerry. See Kylkelly, [illegible].
Killelymayne. See Killelanan.
Killemallaghe. See Killemoumallagh.
Killemanaghe (Kilmaganagh), co. Ros., [illegible].
Killemanoghe—Kyllemanoghe (co. Wick.), 1163, [illegible].
Killemardmak, co. Kerry, [illegible].
Killemelle (co. Cork ?), 4704.
Killemodan (co. Leit. ?), 5428.
Killemagher, co. Mayo, [illegible].
Killenace, co. Car., [illegible].
Killenar, 5767.
Killenaugher, co. Gal., [illegible].
Killenaye (co. Wexm. ?), [illegible].
Killen, [illegible].
Killen, co. Gal., 5728, 5712.
Killen. See Killeen, co. Meath.
Killenagh—Killenaghe—Kyllynaghe (Killenagh), co. Kild., 648, 4977-8, 6604.
Killenaghe, 1568.
Killenaghe — Killenaughe (Killenagh), co. Wex., rectory, [illegible], [illegible], [illegible], 5712.
Killenaule—Killenale, co. Tip., [illegible], [illegible].
Killennay, co. Kerry, 5043.
Killenan (Killinane), co. Kild., [illegible].
Killenan (co. Lim. ?), [illegible].
Killenan (co. Tip. ?), 6406.
Killenan (Killynan), co. Westm., [illegible].
Killennane, co. Lim., 1843.
Killenane—Kyllenan, co. Westm., [illegible], [illegible].
Killenany (co. Clare ?), 5766.
Killenarraght (co. Mayo ?), 5767.
Killenaughe. See Killenaghe.
Killenaule, co. Tip. See Kyldenale.
Killenavisha, co. Long., 5444.
Killenawee (Killinawee ?), co. Long., [illegible].
Killenbeg, co. Long., [illegible].
Killenbracke (Killenabrack, co. Westm. ?), [illegible].
Killenbride—Killenbryde (co. Wick. ?), 678, [illegible], 1343.
Killenbryde in Fowartynolane, 471.
Killencallaghan (Killenycallaghan), co. Westm., [illegible].
Killencarge (Killincarrig, co. Wick. ?), [illegible].
Killenchane (co. Wick. ?), [illegible].
Killencoke (Killenacnamanag ?), co. Clare, 6777.
Killencowe (King's co. ?), [illegible].
Killencrewle (Killincoole), co. Louth, [illegible].
„ manor, [illegible].
Killencurtire—Kyllencurtire, King's co., 448, [illegible].
Killendowne, 5748.
Killene (co. Kerry ?), rectory, [illegible], [illegible].
Killene, King's co., [illegible].
Killeen, King's co. or Meath, [illegible], [illegible].
Killeene—Kelene—Killen—Killin—Kyllene—Kyllyune (Killeen), co. Meath, 37, [illegible].
„ rectory, [illegible], 6767.
„ Christopher Plunket, baron, commissions, 64, 733, [illegible].
„ James, baron of, commissions, 1066, [illegible], 4166, 4441.
„ baron of, commissions, 6311.
Killeno—Kylleno (Killeen), Queen's co., [illegible], [illegible], 1668, 1733, [illegible].
Killenoe, co. Kerry, 5078.
Killenochoy, co. Clare, [illegible].
Killenoconnaghe — Kyllenoconnanagh, co. Cork, [illegible], [illegible].
Killenocour (co. Leit. ?), 4767.
Killenocourriggie, co. Wat., [illegible].
Killenoclassie (co. Cork ?), [illegible].
Killenocronaghe—Killenoconoronaghe, King's co., rectory, 1401, [illegible], 4348.
Killenocrone, 4601.
Killenofaghnes. See Killenofaghnoy.
Killenogowre (co. Westm. ?), [illegible].
Killenogragh, co. Tip., 1184.
Killenogranaghe, co. Cork, [illegible].
Killenogroughe (Killenomgrough), co. Westm., [illegible].
Killenobrie, co. Wex. or Car., [illegible].
Killenokarge (co. Wick. ?), [illegible].

INDEX TO FIANTS—ELIZABETH.

Killenckneven — Killuknowen (Kilmacnowen), co. Westm., rectory, 687, [illegible], 3744.
Killowalongarta, co. Tip., [illegible].
Killenmallaghe—Killenallaghe alias Butlyrant, co. Cork, [illegible], [illegible], 4262.
Killygownaghe—Killenaumanaghe (Kilnamanagh), co. Rosc., rectory, 2180, 4407.
Killenamerne (co. Leit.), [illegible].
Killenamoddagh, co. Long., [illegible].
Killenaurry (co. Car. or Wex. ?), [illegible].
Killeneene (Killynenagh), co. Mon., [illegible].
Killenenagh, [illegible].
Killenesaler (co. Kerry ?), [illegible].
Killenanan or Killenyman (co. Dub. ?), 4478.
Killenagrenan, co. Cork, [illegible].
Killepenan, co. Dub., 1838.
Killenerreny, co. Long., [illegible].
Killenery, co. Clare, [illegible].
Killeneric—Killenacriey—Kyllencrie, co. Car., 1477, [illegible], 4617.
Killenerowiks—Kyllenerowike (co. Rosc. ?), [illegible].
Killenerre (Killenerry), co. Kilk., [illegible].
Killendryeand—Kyllenedryeand, co. Mayo, [illegible].
Killenevarle—Kyllenevary, Queen's co., [illegible], [illegible], 1792.
Killenevanke—Kyllenevanke, co. Lim., [illegible].
Killenewarre—Kyllenewarre, Queen's co., 1867.
Killenewre alias Killure, co. Dub., [illegible].
Killenowre, co. Westm., [illegible].
Killenryode, co. Gal., [illegible].
Killenyre—Kyllenayre, Queen's co., 1525.
Killenfaghney — Killenefaghne — Killenfanghne (Killaghny), co. Westm., 1336, [illegible], [illegible], 3718.
Killeng[ ] (King's co. ?), 4778.
Killenbaugh, co. Wex., [illegible].
Killenie in Munster, 4177.
Killenlekiel (co. Rosc. ?), [illegible].
Killenispick—Kylleniepick or Bishopswood (co. Tip. ?), [illegible].
Killenkaan (co. Wick. ?), 1088.
Killenlaben (co. Westm. ?), [illegible].
Killenleigh (co. Tip. ?), [illegible].
Killenloygh (co. Cork ?), 6516.
Killenmor—Killenmore, co. Kild., 444, 4567.
Killenmore, King's co., 6174, [illegible].
Killenmore (co. Westm. ?), 6514.
Killenne Crosse—Kyllenne Crosse, co. Don., [illegible].
Killennane, co. Westm., 1147.
Killennel, co. Kilk., 2518.
Killennineme—Killenanymane or Kilvecine, co. Kilk., rectory, 5116, [illegible].
Killenny, rectory (now included in par. Aghmacart), Queen's co., [illegible].
Killennynane. See Killennineme.
Killenoor, co. Westm., 5716.
Killenogron (co. Clare ?), 5744.
Killenogh—Kyllenoghe, Queen's co., [illegible], 1283, 1790.
Killenogholan (co. Cork ?), 6178.
Killenore, 872.
Killenore—Kyllenore (co. Car. ?), 1868.
Killenounie (Killummod ?), co. Rosc., rectory, 2150.
Killenowrach, co. Car., 1844.
Killenowre (co. Lim. ?), 6460.
Killenparke (co. Wick.), 1168.
Killenquerten—Kyllenqueren (King's co. or Tip.), 678, [illegible], [illegible].
Killenraghte — Kyllenraght (Killinraghty), co. Rosc., [illegible], 6106.
Killenroe (King's co.), 448, [illegible].
Killenm—Kyllenm, co. Tip., 1688, 4871.
Killenshonokon, King's co., 614.
Killenshonokin — Killenshunken — Kyllenshonaken (on Down Survey there is a Killinsonkin occupying the position of the present townland of Rockavra in par. Killare), co. Westm., [illegible], 4672, [illegible].
Killentone—Kyllentone, co. Wat., [illegible].
Killenure—Kyllenure, co. Meath, [illegible].
Killenure — Kyllenure — Kyllenwre, co. Westm., 700, [illegible], 6151, 4883, [illegible].
Killenvyde, co. Car., 618.
Killenwrick (Killenbrack ?), co. Westm., [illegible].
Killenwrycke, King's co., 314.
Killeny—Kylleny, Queen's co., [illegible], 3418, [illegible], [illegible].
Killenyoben (Killenabun), co. Lim., [illegible].
Killenye—Kylleny (Killeany), co. Gal., 1587, 6414.
Killenyle (Killynoill), co. Mon., [illegible].
Killenyn, co. Westm., [illegible].
Killenynan (co. Dub. ?), [illegible], 4878.
Killeomor — Kylleomor in Omany, rectory, 1881.
Killeonanan (co. Lim. ?), [illegible].
Killeovoraghe—Kylleovoragh (Killfearagh), co. Clare, 1848, [illegible].
Killeowley (co. Cork or Kerry), 4518.
Killeqrovaine, co. Kerry, 6183.
Killeran (co. Mayo or Gal. ?), 6178.
Killerashe (co. Clare ?), 5744.
Killeran, co. Mon., [illegible].
Killerasnie (co. Mayo ?), [illegible].
Killerailh, co. Car., 1867.
Killercke. See Killerk.
Killercowle (Killymooly), co. Mon., [illegible].
Killergale (co. Leit. ?), [illegible].
Killergo—Killargo—Killargan—Killargie—Killargy (Killeerig), co. Car., 2148.

Killergo: preceptory granted, [illegible]; possessions leased, [illegible]; granted, [illegible].
„ rectory, [illegible].
„ advowson of church, [illegible].
„ court of, [illegible].
Killerick, co. Tip., rectory, [illegible].
Killerk — Killerake, co. Tip., [illegible].
Killernane, co. Clare. See Killarnane.
Killerman (co. Ros. or Gal.), [illegible].
Killeramoy — Kyllaromoy (co. Kerry ?), [illegible].
Killerry (co. Ross. ?), [illegible].
Killero (co. Westm. ?), [illegible].
Killerragh (co. Westm. ?), [illegible].
Killerogan, co. Tip., [illegible].
„ vicarage, [illegible].
Killerowe, co. Wex., [illegible].
Killerowlagh (co. Tip. ?), [illegible].
Killerro (co. Leit. ?), [illegible].
Killery (co. Leit. ?), [illegible].
Killery, co. Wex., [illegible].
Killescoll—Kyllescoll (Killescully), co. Tip., rectory, [illegible].
Killeshe (co. Car. ?), [illegible].
Killeshill, King's co. See Kyllyswell, [illegible].
Killeshin—Kylleshen, Queen's co., [illegible].
Killeskellinge—Killeskillin—Killeskillinge (Killeskillen), co. Meath, [illegible]; granted, [illegible].
Killeswell, King's co., [illegible].
Killessaragh. See Killeruragh.
Killester, co. Meath. See Collester.
Killesteraghbege—Kyllesteraghbeg, Kyllesteraghmore, Queen's co., [illegible].
„ See also Kyllysheraghbege, &c.
Killesuragh—Killessuragh (co. Lim. ?), [illegible].
Killetloe—Killetle, co. Tip., [illegible].
Killettle—Kyllettle, co. Kerry, advowson of church, [illegible].
Killetovan — Killetovane (Killetovan, co. Ross.), rectory, [illegible].
Killetyrmade, co. Mayo, cell or chapel and land, [illegible]. See also Killemotrymead.
Killeulyn (co. Wat. ?), [illegible].
Killeurban (co. Cork ?), [illegible].
Killevalleche, co. Cav., [illegible].
Killevanny, co. Cav., [illegible].
Killevarriggye — Kyllevarriggye, co. Lim., [illegible].
Killevarrigh (co. Cork ?), [illegible].
Killevehan, co. Long., [illegible].
Killevehane — Killewehane, co. Cav., [illegible].
Killevny—Kyllevny, co. Gal., [illegible].
Killevollane — Kyllevollane (co. Cork ?), [illegible].
Killew (co. Mayo), [illegible].
Killewchane. See Killevehane.
Killewerk, co. Kild., [illegible].
Killewhine, co. Ross., [illegible].
Killewre (co. Gal. ?), [illegible].
Killewryden, co. Westm., [illegible].
Killeylagh, [illegible].
Killeynan, co. Tip., [illegible].
Killeynan (co. Westm. ?), [illegible].
Killeconogan—Killeenogan—Killesonocon alias Killeconogan, co. Meath, [illegible].
Killiaghe (co. Kerry ?), [illegible].
Killian, King's co., [illegible].
Killian, co. Meath, parish, [illegible].
„ manor, [illegible].
Killian—Kyllyane, co. Wex., rectory, [illegible].
Killianan, co. Clare, [illegible].
Killiane, co. Wex. See Killean, Killian, Kyllean.
Killianiskie (co. Cork ?), [illegible].
Killibegg—Kyllebegge (Killbeg), co. Gal., [illegible].
Killicallie, co. Lim., [illegible].
Killicharmy—Kyllicharmy, co. Tip., [illegible].
Killickingarowe (co. Lim. ?), [illegible].
Killickery, Queen's co., [illegible].
Killicloghir, co. Gal., [illegible].
Killiclonaghe, co. Mon., [illegible].
Killicogh (co. Cork ?), [illegible].
Killicorrowe, co. Long., [illegible].
Killicountagh (co. Cork ?), [illegible].
Killiterachia, co. Kerry, [illegible].
Killidy—Kyllydeye (Killeedy), co. Lim., [illegible]; parish, [illegible].
Killie, Morris, pardon, [illegible].
„ Morris fitz David, pardon, [illegible].
„ Peirse, pardon, [illegible].
Killien or Killeaghe, co. Westm., [illegible].
Killieaghterqua, co. Kerry, [illegible].
Killiean—Kyllean, co. Car., [illegible].
Killieghe. See Killeigh.
Killieghterlry, co. Kild., [illegible].
Killieighleragh, [illegible].
Killien, Queen's co., [illegible].
Killienlich, [illegible].
Killieraghteraghe—Killiergteraghe—Killieteragh, co. Tip., [illegible].
Killighe. See Killeigh.
Killighe (Gulleagh), co. Wat., rectory, [illegible].
Killiginae, co. Cork, [illegible].
Killihalle. See Killehaly.
Killihan (co. Westm. ?), [illegible].
Killikinalee, [illegible].
Killile—Kyllely—Kyllilee—Kyllylye (Killile), co. Wex., [illegible]; rectory, [illegible].

INDEX TO FIANTS—ELIZABETH.

Killill, co. Wex., 417.
Killilia, co. Tip., rectory, [illegible], [illegible].
Killilia, co. Wex., [illegible].
Killily (co. Kerry ?), [illegible].
Killima (co. Leit. ?), [illegible].
Killi m'Talerty (Kilmmacancarte, co. Lim. ?), [illegible].
Killimagh, King's co. or Meath, [illegible], [illegible].
Killimartrane (co. Cork ?), [illegible].
Killimecurry (co. Cork ?), [illegible].
Killimegrell (co. Gal. ?), [illegible].
Killimentie (co. Cork ?), [illegible].
Killimurr—Kyllimurr, co. Gal., [illegible].
Killimurrie, co. Kerry, [illegible].
Killimurrie (co. Lim. ?), [illegible].
Killimurrin (co. Cork ?), [illegible].
Killimyale (co. Tip. ?), [illegible].
Killin, co. Car., [illegible].
Killin, co. Gal., [illegible], [illegible], [illegible], [illegible].
Killin, King's co., 1767, [illegible], [illegible].
Killin (co. Long. ?), [illegible].
Killin. See Killone.
Killinagh, co. Kild. See Killonagh.
Killinagh, co. Long., [illegible].
Killinaghmucke (co. Wick. ?), [illegible].
Killinaghton, co. Lim., [illegible].
Killinan—Kyllinan (co. Lim. ?), [illegible], [illegible].
Killinane, co. Kild. See Killonan.
Killinanighane, co. Tip., [illegible].
Killinawas, co. Long. See Killonawas.
Killinabowcher, co. Lim., [illegible].
Killinaboy — Kyllynaboy (Killinamboy), co. Westm., [illegible], [illegible].
Killinabreane. See Cillinabreana, [illegible].
Killincarrig, co. Wick. See Killincarge.
Killinchalli, co. Clare, [illegible].
Killindonaghe, co. Meath, [illegible].
Killinelonachely (co. Car. ?), [illegible].
Killineowle, co. Louth. See Killoncowle.
Killineonly, co. Wex. See Killinecoll.
Killinecowle or Killecowle, co. Tip., rectory, [illegible].
Killinecrell, co. Louth, [illegible].
Killinerevagh (co. Kild. ?), [illegible].
Killinedare (co. Wick. ?), [illegible].
Killinederry (co. Clare ?), [illegible].
Killinelime, co. Gal., [illegible].
Killinee—Kyllinee (co. Cork ?), [illegible].
Killine, in Munster, [illegible].
Killinee—Kylline, in M'Gilpatrick's country, Queen's co., rectory, [illegible], [illegible], [illegible].
Killines, co. Tip., [illegible].
Killinetery, co. Clare, [illegible].
Killinebreanen, co. Mayo, [illegible].
Killinelanry (co. Sligo ?), [illegible].
Killinelogh (co. Tip. ?), [illegible].
Killinenallye (co. Lim. ?), [illegible].
Killinecoweare—Kyllinecoweare, co. Cork, [illegible].
Killinespiede (co. Lim. ?), [illegible].
Killinecrvane, co. Ross., 4108.
Killinees—Kyllinees (co. Tip. ?), [illegible], [illegible], [illegible], [illegible].
Killinecy (co. Meath ?), [illegible].
Killinefehy (co. Westm. ?), [illegible].
Killineycloncrofin, co. Car., [illegible].
Killingarroeburke, co. Long., [illegible].
Killingo wood—Kyllingo wood, co. Louth, [illegible], [illegible], [illegible].
Killingiaiche — Kyllingiaiche (co. Wat. ?), rectory, [illegible].
Killingore—Killingower, co. Westm., [illegible], [illegible].
Killingronan—Killingronan, co. Tip., rectory, [illegible], [illegible].
Killinigeane (co. Tip. ?), [illegible].
Killininnule (Killummod, co. Ross. ?), [illegible].
Killinakelly, co. Gal., [illegible], [illegible].
Killinkerry, co. Sligo, [illegible].
Killinleany—Kyllinleany (co. Sligo ?), [illegible].
Killinlogh—Killinlogh, co. Tip., [illegible], [illegible].
Killinleigh (co. Cork ?), [illegible].
Killinlonahluone, [illegible].
Killinnocarra (co. Long. ?), [illegible].
Killinocgrath (co. Car. ?), [illegible].
Killino (co. Kerry ?), rectory, [illegible].
Killinograghan (co. Cork or Lim.), [illegible].
Killinormody (co. Wat. ?), [illegible].
Killinquirke, co. Ross., [illegible].
Killinraghty, co. Ross. See Killonraghte.
Killinlampie (co. Wick. ?), [illegible].
Killinrayne, King's co., [illegible].
Killinvaraghe — Kyllinvarrah (Killinvarra, co. Gal.), [illegible], [illegible].
Killinvoy, co. Ross. See Kinarboy.
Killinydode, [illegible].
Killiogrich, co. Clare, [illegible].
Killiro, vicarage, 1170.
Killishine (co. Car. ?), [illegible].
Killiskie (co. Long. or Westm.), [illegible].
Killisky (co. Car. or Wex.), [illegible].
Killivenogan—Killivenogan (Killeenaugan), co. Gal., [illegible], [illegible].
Killivarrige, co. Cork, [illegible].
Killiviclary, co. Cork, [illegible].
Killivie, co. Gal., [illegible].
Killo, co. Mon., [illegible].
Killoban. See Killolan.
Killocmock — Killockamocke — Kilcknamocke — Kyllocamock (Kilcommock, co. Long. ?), rectory, [illegible], [illegible], [illegible], [illegible], [illegible].
Killocrie, co. Lim., [illegible], [illegible], [illegible], [illegible]. See Kilmallock.
Killock—Kyllock (King's co. or Kild. ?), [illegible].
Killockamocke. See Killocamock.
Killockine (co. Ross ?), [illegible].
Killockinie (co. Westm. ?), [illegible].
Killockrobert — Kyllockrobert — Kylnkrobert, King's co. [illegible], [illegible].

Killcorbrewry, [illegible].
Killodadoria. See Killadadoghe.
Killodiorgan. See Kyllodirnan, Killordiernan.
Killoe (co. Long.), rectory, 487, 5760.
Killog (co. Wick.?), 2801.
Killogo, Queen's co., [illegible], 4716, 6162.
Killogue (Kenlogue, co Lim.), 6178.
Killogh—Killoghe, co. Tip., 5767.
Killoghe, co. Down, 4163.
Killoghe (co. Wick.), [illegible], 1414.
Killoghgrough, co. Ross., 5777.
Killoghbane, co. Wat., rectory, [illegible].
Killoghtica, co. Westm., 3445.
Killoghkenidie (Killokennedy), co. Clare, [illegible].
Killoghollobane, co. Lim., rectory, 3414.
Killoghy (co. Tip.?), [illegible].
Killogula (co. Gal.?), 4711.
Killogynaghor, [illegible].
Killogynedy — Killoghkenidie (Killokennedy), co. Clare, [illegible]. See also Kylloguned.
Killokene—Kyllokene, King's co. [illegible], 1634.
Killokeny (co. Ross.?), [illegible].
Killolagh, King's co., 6498.
Killolaugh, co. Meath, rectory, 1100, 3264.
Killolman (co. Mon.?), 5042.
Killolle, co. Clare, 5712.
Killolane, co. Tip., [illegible]; rectory, [illegible].
Killomalcon—Kyllomalcan, 1491.
Killomartin, co. Mon., [illegible].
Killommey—Kyllommey, co. Cork, rectory, [illegible].
Killomoda, co. Leit., [illegible].
Killomoran, co. Gal. See Killamoran.
Killonane—Kyllonane (co. Cork?), 2361, [illegible].
Killonan (co. Lim.?), [illegible].
Killona( )e (co. Lim.?), 6143.
Killonayn (co. Lim.?), 6427.
Killone, co Gal. or Ross., [illegible].
Killone—Kyllone—Kylloona, co. Clare, 4781.
" abbey, possessions, 4781.
Killoge—Killone—Kyloone (co. Cork?), [illegible], [illegible], [illegible].
Killone—Kyllon, Queen's co., [illegible], [illegible], [illegible].
Killone, co. Wat., 5746; rectory, [illegible].
Killone, co. Wex., [illegible].
Killonerry, co. Kilk. See Killenerry.
Killongtrie—Kyllongtrie, co. Wat., [illegible], [illegible].
Killonaghan, co. Clare, [illegible], 4774.
Killonoghan—Killonoghou, co. Lim., [illegible], [illegible].
Killonyne (co. Tip.?), [illegible].
" See Killownoyne.
Killooran (Killukin), co. Ross., [illegible].
Killor, [illegible].
Killoran, co. Ross., [illegible].
Killoran—Killoran (co. Car. or Wex.?), [illegible], [illegible].
Killorance—Kyllorance, co. Kild., [illegible].
Killorane—Killoran (Killoran), co. Gal., [illegible], [illegible].
Killorane—Kyllorane—Killorane (co. Sligo?), [illegible].
Killardiorgan (Killodiorgan), co. Tip., [illegible].
Killordy—Kyllordy (perhaps Kilworth, co. Cork), [illegible].
Killorgan, co. Kerry, [illegible], [illegible].
Killorgill (co. Kerry?), 6484.
Killorglin — Killorgina — Killorigiyne—Killorglin — Kyllorglane, co. Kerry, 4877, [illegible], [illegible].
" rectory, [illegible], [illegible].
Killorogh (co. Kilk.?), [illegible].
Killory (co. Tip.?), [illegible].
Killosogathain, co. Tip. or Lim., [illegible].
Killosnylaryn, rectory, [illegible].
Killosombe—Kyllosombe (Killoscobe, co. Gal.), rectory, [illegible], [illegible].
Killosculty, co. Tip. See Killoscull.
Killoskehan, co. Tip., [illegible].
Killoskillin — Killoskilliage. See Killokelliage.
Killoskellane (co. Kilk.?), [illegible].
Killosky—Kyllosky, co. Tip., [illegible].
Killosmony (co. Long. or Westm.?), [illegible].
Killosman (co. Long.?), [illegible].
Killosorry (co. Long.?), [illegible], [illegible].
Killossaragh, co. Wat. See Kyllossarraghe.
Killossery—Killossorie, co. Dub., parish, [illegible].
" Rath of, [illegible].
Killostin, co. Tip., [illegible].
Killostine, co. Cork, 5191.
Killoucvan (Killocan), co. Westm., [illegible].
Killoughe — Kiloaghe (Killough, co. Wick.), [illegible], [illegible].
Killoughert, co. Wat., [illegible].
Killoughrier, [illegible].
Killourrane—Kyllourrane (King's co.?), [illegible].
Killovan. See Killowan.
Killovlaughye — Kyllovlaughye, co. Clare, 4781.
Killovoyr, co. Gal., [illegible].
Killowan, co. Gal., [illegible].
Killowan—Killovan (co. Westm.?), rectory, [illegible], [illegible].
Killowe—Kyllowe, co. Clare, [illegible].
" chapel, [illegible].
Killowen, King's co., [illegible], 4277-8, [illegible].
Killowen (co. Wat.?), [illegible].
Killowghterwyne — Killoghteriine, co. Wat., [illegible], [illegible].
Killowhorine, (co. Leit.?), [illegible].
Killowlanchye — Killowlanchie, co. Clare, [illegible].
" rectory, [illegible].
Killowtery, co. Gal., [illegible].
Killowragh—Kylowragh (co. Cork?), [illegible].

INDEX TO FIANTS—ELIZABETH.

Killowran (co. Car. or Wex. ?), [illegible].
Killowrane (co. Tip. ?), [illegible].
Killowrane, co. Wat., rectory, [illegible].
Killowrie, co. Sligo or Leit., [illegible].
Killowryce (King's co. ?), [illegible].
Killoyne, co. Kerry, [illegible].
Kill Saint Nicholas, co. Wat. See S. Nicholas, rectory of.
Killucan, co. Westm. See Killoucane, Killuckan.
Killuckell alias Killoccan (co. Ross.), [illegible].
Killuckan—Killuckin (Killucan), co. Westm., [illegible], [illegible].
Killucknoy—Kylluckney, co. Ross., [illegible], [illegible].
Killuckin—Killuckyne (Killuckin), co. Ross., [illegible], [illegible], [illegible].
Killuckin. See Killuckan.
Killuckyne. See Killuckin.
Killnalloy (co. Kerry ?), [illegible].
Killugelly—Kyllugelly (co. Gal. ?), [illegible].
Killuglory, co. Cork, [illegible].
Killukin, co. Ross. See Killuckin.
Killukcowan (Kilmacnowan), co. Westm., rectory, 457. See Killcuckcowan.
Killukwillytag, co. Clare, [illegible].
Killukwillymore, co. Clare, [illegible].
Killult, co. Donegal. See Killultagh.
Killultagh—Killultagh—Kilulto—Killultogh—Kilultough—Kylultagh—Kylultogh, a district in barony of Upper Massereene, co. Antrim. See Reeves' Down and Connor, p. [illegible]), [illegible]; woods and mines of, [illegible].
" to be made shire ground, [illegible].
" comn. to punish rebels, [illegible].
" martial law in, 1196, [illegible], [illegible], [illegible], [illegible].
" seneschal of, [illegible], [illegible], [illegible].
" governor, [illegible], [illegible].
Killummod, co. Ross. See Killumonnie, Killimonnie, Kyllummole.
Killumnoy, co. Cork. See Kilnicholomnoy, [illegible].
Killunnure, co. Gal. or Ross., [illegible].
Killumyly—Kylumyly, co. Cork, [illegible].
Killunahane—Killunnane (co. Car. ?), [illegible].
Killunure (co. Lim. or Kerry), [illegible].
Killuro, or Killunowre, co. Dub., [illegible].
Killure—Kyllure—Kyllurye—Killure, co. Wat., [illegible], [illegible].
" preceptory or commandery, leased, [illegible], [illegible], [illegible], [illegible]; granted, [illegible]; possessions granted, [illegible].
Killurren—Kyllurren—Killurin (Killurin), co. Wex., [illegible]; rectory, [illegible], [illegible], [illegible], [illegible], [illegible].
Killuria (Killury), co. Kerry, [illegible], [illegible].
" " advowson, [illegible].
Killurigho (co. Cork ?), [illegible].
Killurin, King's co., [illegible].
Killurine (co. Kerry ?), [illegible].
Killurran, co. Tip., [illegible].
Killurny—Kyllurny (co. Ross. ?), [illegible].
Killury, co. Kerry. See Killuria.
Killurye. See Killure.
Killusky, co. Kild., [illegible].
Killusky—Kyllusky—Kylluskye—Kilusky, co. Wex., [illegible]; rectory, [illegible], [illegible], [illegible], [illegible], [illegible].
Killussy—Kyllussye, co. Kild., rectory, [illegible].
" vicar of, [illegible].
Killy—Killye:
" Brene, pardon, [illegible].
" Donald m'Arte oe (O'Morghoe?), pardon, [illegible].
" John, pardon, [illegible].
" Shane oy, pardon, [illegible].
Killy—Kylly, co. Lim., [illegible].
Killyannor—Kyllyannor, King's co., [illegible].
Killyane—Kyllyan (Killyan), co. Meath, [illegible].
" rectory, [illegible].
Killyballylenyne (co. Ulster ?), [illegible].
Killyborn, co. Mon. See Killubyrne.
Killyboan, co. Mon. See Killuleton.
Killycarnan, co. Mon. See Kilcarnan.
Killycharan (Kilcorran), co. Mon., [illegible].
Killycknogan (co. Lim. ?), [illegible].
Killycunnigan, co. Mon. See Killcrotogan.
Killycooly, co. Mon. See Killcrowle.
Killycowleth—Kyllycowlieth, co. Lim., [illegible].
Killycunnaghane, co. Mon. See Kilcunnanaght.
Killydaragh, co. Mon. See Killadonaghe.
Killydroon, co. Mon. See Kilderyne.
Killye. See Killy.
Killye, co. Westm., [illegible].
Killyearthlane—Kyllyearthlane, co. Cork, [illegible].
Killyen—Kyllyen, or Killeny, Queen's co., [illegible], [illegible].
Killyeno—Kyllyene, King's co., [illegible].
Killyena. See Killyne.
Killyeuldeglowry, co. Lim., [illegible].
Killyfanny, co. Mon. See Killarge.
Killyfe (Killeef), co. Mon., [illegible].
Killygarard, Queen's co. See Kyllegaver.
Killygowan, co. Cav. See Cillagoan, [illegible].
Killyhan (co. Westm. ?), [illegible].
Killyhonan, co. Mon., [illegible].
Killyhygyn, co. Wat., [illegible].
Killykanagh, co. Mon. See Killekanoghe.
Killylea, co. Westm., [illegible].
Killylane—Kyllylane (co. Westm. or King's), [illegible].
Killylaragh, co. Mon. See Killelaraght.
Killyleck, co. Mon. See Killeckie.
Killylir—Kyllylir, King's co., [illegible].

INDEX TO FIANTS.—ELIZABETH.

Killyloughavoy, co. Mon. *See* Killclough-vally.
Killyly, co. Gal., 6324.
Killyly, co. Kerry, 5472.
Killymoke—Kyllymoke, co. Louth, 1722.
Killymoney (co. Cork ?), 6516.
Killymurry, co. Mon. *See* Ballykilmurry, Kilmurry.
Killyn—Kyllyn, co. Cav., rectory, 4264.
Killyn, co. Clare, 6343.
Killyn, co. Gal., 5453, 6814.
Killyn—Kyllyn (co. Kerry ?), 1393.
Killyn (co. Long. ?), 5454.
Killynagh (co. Long. ?), 3494.
Killynan, co. Westm. *See* Killenan.
Killynane—Kyllynane (co. Cork ?), 1057; rectory, 1587.
Killynane (co. Ross. ?), 2322.
Killynaraloghe (co. Longf. or Westm. ?), 6497.
Killynelorry, co. Gal., 3478.
Killynelyme, in Connaught, 1668.
Killyne (Killeen, co. Kild.), 1322.
Killyne—Kyllyne (Killeen), co. Lim., 6377, 6717.
Killynebroome (co. Clare ?), 5064.
Killyneonganaughe, co. Cork, 4444.
Killyneonappy Farrell (co. Gal. ?), 5552.
Killynecrossowrley—Kyllynecrossowrley (co. Gal. or Mayo), 6500.
Killynedyny (co. Gal. ?), 6608.
Killyneshomay, co. Cork, 4318.
Killyneill, co. Mon. *See* Killeneyle.
Killynesa, co. Kild., 4283.
Killynen, co. Lim., 4444.
Killynenagh, co. Mon. *See* Killenena.
Killynenevan, co. Rosc., 3763.
Killyneoghone—Kyllyneoghone (co. Cork ?), 3878.
Killynes—Kyllynes (co. Tip. ?), 5422.
Killynesurvin, co. Cork, 6318.
Killyraine, co. Cork, 5528.
Killyralyne (co. Gal. ?), 4974.
Killyrenalrom (co. Rosc. ?), 4361.
Killyroo (co. Kerry ?), rectory, 5347.
Killynoghty—Killyaghtie (Killconoghty), co. Lim., 4448, 6018.
Killyn Crowgh—Kyllyn Crowgh (co. Kild. ?), 1400.
Killyns (Killeen), co. Kilk., 5454.
Killynatruyme—Kyllynatruyme, King's co., 1688.
Killyavarrogh (Killosnavarra), co. Gal., rectory, 5462.
Killyavrido (co. Car. ?), 180.
Killyvey, co. Kerry, 6122.
Killywyhoye, co. Clare, 4561.
Killyaycanaughe—Kyllyaycanaughe, co. Cork, rectory, 4557.
Killyaychon, co. Lim., 4424.
Killyaylynan — Kyllynalynan (Killenaflamane), co. Kerry, 3149, 6176.
Killyvan, co. Meath. *See* Killaghan, Killean, Killyane.
Killyrowe (co. Westm. ?), 6774.
Killyvall, co. Cork, 5448.
Killyshall (Killoskall), co. Wat., 4349.
Killywhowragh, co. Lim., 3478.
Killyskoroughbege—Kyllyskoroughbege, Kyllyskoroughmore (Queen's co.), 398.
Killyvan (Kilkevan, co. Mon.), termon of, 6762.
Killywarig (co. Cork ?), 5568.
Killywogery, co. Gal., 6612.
Kilmakine—Kilmakyne, co. Cork, 5428, 6473.
Kilmaboy in Ossory, rectory, 5465.
Kilmacahill, co. Kilk. *See* Kilmocahill.
Kilmacalle—Kylmacayle—Kilmackeall, co. Westm., 952.
„ house of friars, leased, 906, 2852, 4163.
Kilmacallan, co. Sligo. *See* Kilmacahallan.
Kilmacaramoney, co. Rosc. *See* Kilmaconanny.
Kilmacanearie—Kilm'canearie, co. Lim., 5171.
„ *See also* Kilm'Inierty.
Kilmacanoge, co. Wick. *See* Kilmacknocck, Kilmakenoge.
Kilmacar, co. Kilk., vicar of, 6676.
„ *See* Kilmakare, Kilmocar.
Kilmacargie—Kylmacargan, co. Dub., 5227, 7622.
Kilmacarron—Kylmacarron—Kylmacharon, co. Westm., 8 (?). 1355, 3381.
Kilmacayle. *See* Kilmacalle.
Kilmacoahill (co. Cork ?), 4492.
Kilmacalistery (co. Tip. or Lim.), 4596.
Kilm'Clyaine (co. Cork ?), 4352.
Kilm'Clyrine (co. Cork ?), 4352.
Kilm'coorh (co. Gal. ?), 5652.
Kilm'dea (co. Kerry ?), 6497.
Kilmacduagh—Kilm'dough—Kilmachogh—Kilmacoughe—Kilmacogh—Kilmacoughe—Kilmacruagh—Kilmachaughe—Kylmackoogh—Kylmachough, co. Gal., 1408, 3152, 6592.
„ monastery of canons, leased, 1488, 3163.
„ cathedral of, 6360.
„ Stephen, bishop of, comm., 2667.
„ Roland Lynch, bishop of, comm., 4080; obtains bishopric of Clonfert, 6625.
„ archdeacon of, 4896.
„ diocese, presentation in, 1752.
Kilmacduane, co. Clare. *See* Kilmacduvan.

INDEX TO FIANTS—ELIZABETH.

Kilm'Eancaice. See Kilm'Eandis.
Kilm'eda, co. Kerry, [illegible] or [illegible], 5117.
Kilmacadovan—Kilmacaddowanny—Kylmacdovan (Kilmacdtane), co. Clare, [illegible]; rectory, 1[illegible], [illegible].
Kilmacrgowne (co. Clare ?), 6712.
Kilm'Eceis—Kilm'Eancaice, co. Cork, [illegible], [illegible].
Kilmacbain (co. Kilk. ?), 6794.
Kilmachallon (Kilmacallan), co. Sligo, rectory, 4[illegible].
Kilmachan (co. Long. ?), 6471.
Kilmachanry (co. Long. or Rosc.), [illegible].
Kilmachenery (co. Cork ?), 6421.
Kilmack—Kylmacke (Kilmanack, co. Wat.), [illegible], 5121, [illegible].
manor, 5171, 5[illegible].
Kilmackaell. See Kilmacoile.
Kilm'hane (co. Kilk. ?), [illegible].
Kilmackdowanny. See Kilmacalowne.
Kilm'kendis, King's co., 6[illegible].
Kilmackomok (Kilmacanoge, co. Wick.), 6[illegible].
Kilmackillo, co. Donegal. See Kilvickillowra.
Kilmackiyto, co. Cork, 6[illegible].
Kilmackogh. See Kilmarduagh.
Kilmacleague, co. Wat. See Kilmacleage.
Kilm'macrbye (co. Lim. ?), [illegible].
Kilm'manny (Kilmacomanny, co. Rosc.), [illegible].
Kilmacnovan, co. Westm. See Killmackrovan.
Kilmacnicholas—Kylmacnicholas, co. Wat., [illegible], 4[illegible]. See Kylmychreoola.
Kilm'sillowe, co. Gal., 64[illegible].
Kilmacnoran, co. Cav. See Kallivackmorrane.
Kilmacoragha. See Kilmacduagh.
Kilmacod, co. Dub., 44[illegible].
Kilmacodrike—Kylmacodrik, co. Dub., [illegible], 3434-5.
Kilmacow (Kilmacow, co. Lim.), castle and land, 6171.
Kilmacogh. See Kilmacduagh.
Kilmacogue, co. Tip. See Kilmacouge.
Kilmacolivor—Kill m'Olivor, co. Kilk., 1[illegible], [illegible], [illegible].
Kilmacollock—Kylmacollok, co. Kerry, 6[illegible], 4718.
Kilmacollock Cester, co. Kerry, rectory, 5172.
Kilmacolmar (perhaps Kilmacoliver, co. Kilk.), [illegible].
Kilmacomma, co. Wat. See Kilmacghoma.
Kilmacomock—Kylmacomok (Kilmacomoge), co. Cork, 3737; rectory, [illegible].
Kilmacomoge (Kilmacomoge ?), co. Cork, rectory, [illegible].
Kilmacoragha. See Kilmacduagh.
Kilmacow, co. Lim. See Kilmacow, Kilmaho, Kilmahho.
Kilmacowe (Kilmacow), co. Cork, 6[illegible].
Kilmacraghe, co. Gal., [illegible].
Kilmacreny, co. Gal., castle and land, 6[illegible].
Kilmacredock, co. Kild., 4[illegible], 4011, [illegible].
Kilmacreeve, co. Wex. See Kilmacorye.
Kilmacrian—Kylmacrian, in Connaught, rectory, 1594.
Kilmacroy, co. Rosc. See Kylmacroe.
Kilm'Eddorie, co. Cork, [illegible].
Kilmacshane, co. Gal., [illegible], 6747.
Kilm'Shane, co. Kilk., 1160.
Kilmacthomas (co. Cork or Lim. ?), 6[illegible].
Kilmacthomas, co. Wat., 1948.
Kilmacthomasine—Kilmacthomasyne—Kilm'thomasin—Kylm'thomashin—Kylmacthomasyne, co. Wat., 6[illegible], [illegible], 1[illegible], [illegible], [illegible], [illegible].
Kilmacdimmy, co. Sligo. See Kylvychoiren.
Kilmaceagh. See Kilmacduagh.
Kilmacuagh, co. Westm. See Kyllmacowgh, Kylmacoghe.
Kilmacullagh, co. Wick. See Kylmacolle, 614.
Kilmacullen, co. Cork, 6[illegible], 6[illegible].
Kilmagally, co. Kild., 1761.
Kilmagarvoh—Kilmagarwogue, co. Car., 1[illegible], [illegible].
Kilmagha, King's co., 6[illegible].
Kilmaghan, in diocese of Meath, 6787.
Kilmaghahir (co. Gal. or Mayo ?), 6[illegible].
Kilmaglisho (co. Car.), 6[illegible].
Kilmagobboke—Kilmagobook—Kilmagoboke, Queen's co., grange and tithes, [illegible], 2[illegible], 5[illegible], 6[illegible], 6793.
Kilmagoragh (Kilmagoum), co. Cork, [illegible].
Kilmagoude—Kilmagoudor—Kylmagoude, Queen's co., 1619, 3[illegible].
Kilmahioke—Kilmahiock, co. Dub., 2[illegible], 1[illegible], 1[illegible].
Kilmaho—Kylmahooo (Kilmacow ?), co. Lim., 5[illegible]; rectory, 5[illegible], 6[illegible].
Kilmaloe, co. Mon., [illegible].
Kilmahounock (co. Cork ?), 6[illegible].
Kilmahorrok, co. Lim., rectory, 6411.
Kilmahowe—Kylmahowe, co. Wex., 1[illegible].
Kilmahune (Kilmanahan, co. Wat. ?), castle and town, 5[illegible].
Kilmahund—Kylmahud, co. Dub., land and rectory, 770.
Kilmaine, King's co. See Kylmaine.
Kilmaine, co. Mayo. See Kilmaye.
Kilmaine larney, co. Mayo. See Moyntermreghan.
Kilmainebeg, Kilmainemore, co. Mayo. See Kilmainebegge, Kilmainemore.
Kilmainham—Kilmaynam—Kilmaynan—Kilmaynhame—Kilmaynham—Kylmaynam—Kilmainham—Kilmaynham

INDEX TO FIANTS—ELIZABETH.

Kilmainham:
—Kilmainghoham—Kylmainam—Kylmaynham—Kylmaynham—Kylmynham—Kylmaynham, co. Dub., [illegible], [illegible], 1072, 1182, [illegible], 1194, 1218, 1649, 1728, [illegible], [illegible], [illegible], [illegible], [illegible], 3418, 3420, 4461; fiants dated at, [illegible], [illegible], [illegible], 1041; highway to, [illegible].
„ manor, 1733, [illegible].
„ profits of court, 1723, [illegible].
„ customs, 1722, [illegible].
„ west gate of town, 1723, [illegible], [illegible].
„ premises and lands leased, 1648, 1722, [illegible], [illegible], [illegible], [illegible], 4180, 4434, [illegible], [illegible].
„ keeper of the queen's house and demesne at, [illegible], 1160, [illegible], [illegible], [illegible], [illegible].
„ queen's and chief governor's house at, [illegible], [illegible], 4772, [illegible], [illegible], [illegible], [illegible].
„ Black hedge, 1649.
„ Churchland, 1648, [illegible].
„ demesne lands, 1649.
„ mill baily, 1722.
„ mills and weirs at bridge, [illegible], [illegible].
„ petty canons land, 1648.
„ Ravings lane, 1649.
„ wood, 4004.
„ lands, [illegible], 4401.
„ hospital or priory, 1447, 1519, [illegible], [illegible].
„ „ prior of, [illegible], [illegible], [illegible], [illegible]. See Saint John of Jerusalem.
„ Newton of, co. Dub., 1488, [illegible], [illegible].
Kilmainham wood, co. Meath. See Kilmaynam wood.
Kilmalcolm, co. Gal., [illegible].
Kilmakelly, King's co., [illegible], 3171.
Kilmakonoge (co. Kerry ?), [illegible].
Kilmakenoge—Kilmakenoch—Kilmakenoke—Kylmakenok—Kilmakynok (Kilmacanoge, co. Wick. ?), [illegible], 1168, 1789, [illegible], [illegible], [illegible]; granted, [illegible].
Kilmakero—Kylmakero (Kilmacar), co. Kilk., rectory, 1788, [illegible].
Kilmakory (co. Lim. ?), [illegible].
Kilmakovoge—Kylmakowoge, co. Kilk., rectory, [illegible].
Kilmakho—Kylmakho (Kilmacow ?), co. Lim., 1716; rectory, [illegible].
Kilmakilloy—Kylmakilloy, King's co., 478.
Kilmakonagh. See Kilmacdonagh.
Kilmakow (co. Lim. ?), 3474.
Kilmakrynam, co. Gal., rectory, 3418.
Kilmakylloke, Queen's co., 1933.
Kilmalaghe—Kylmalaghe, King's co., [illegible], 1084.
Kilmaleghin, Queen's co., 1822, [illegible].
Kilmalchedir—Kilmalchedir (Malahiffe), co. Kerry, 4977, [illegible].
Kilmalenock, co. Gal., [illegible].
Kilmalashe—Kylmalashe (Kilmalash), co. Tip., [illegible], [illegible]; grant, [illegible].
Kilmaleam, co. Cork, rectory, [illegible].
Kilmaled, co. Westm., 1178.
Kilmalodie (Kilmalady), King's co., [illegible].
Kilmaloghes, in Connaught, rectory, [illegible], [illegible].
Kilmaloeke—Kylmaloeke (Kilmalogue ?) King's co., [illegible], 1344.
Kilmallen (co. Cork ?), [illegible].
Kilmalighe, co. Westm., [illegible].
Kilmalin—Kilmalyn (co. Wick.), [illegible], [illegible].
Kilmaliro (co. Clare ?), [illegible].
Kilmalkedar, co. Kerry. See Kilmaelkyedir.
Kilmallock—Kilmallok—Kilmalloke—Kilmalock—Kilmaloke—Kilmallock—Kylmallok—Kylmallog—Kylmalloke—Kilmehalloke—Kylmehalock—Kylmalock—Kyllmallok, co. Lim., 101, 145, [illegible], [illegible], [illegible], [illegible], [illegible], [illegible], [illegible], [illegible], 3144, 4237, 4300, 4144, [illegible], [illegible], [illegible], [illegible], [illegible], [illegible]; premises and land in, granted, [illegible], [illegible], [illegible]; land beside, granted, [illegible]; premises in, leased, [illegible].
„ charter, [illegible].
„ grant to corporation, [illegible]; lease, [illegible].
„ sovereign pardoned, [illegible]; commissions, [illegible], [illegible], [illegible].
„ burgesses pardoned, [illegible].
„ merchants pardoned, [illegible].
„ monastery of friars preachers, leased, [illegible]; granted, [illegible].
„ Court Hinkley castle near, [illegible].
„ river of, [illegible].
„ St. John Street near, [illegible].
„ See Killocle.
Kilmallock, co. Wex. See Kilmalloke.
Kilmallee (King's co. ?), [illegible].
Kilmaloch—Kylmaloghe, co. Wex., 497, [illegible].
Kilmalow, co. Wat. See Kilmacowe.
Kilmalow, co. Wat., [illegible].

INDEX TO FIANTS.—ELIZABETH.

Kilmaloy, in Munster, 6477.
Kilmalogue, King's co. See Kilmalogoke.
Kilmalon (Kilmalton, co. Kild.), 1418.
Kilmalymoriertie (co. Cork ?), 2351.
Kilmalyn. See Kilmallie.
Kilmalyr (co. Wick. ?), 1162.
Kilmanagh—Kilmanaghe—Kylmanagh, co. Kilk., 1513, 6575, [illegible].
" prebendary or rector of, [illegible], 1617.
Kilmanahan, co. Wat. See Kilmanahin.
Kilmanamane (Kilmanmon), Queen's co., 6632.
Kilmanaoghe — Kylmanaghe, co. Tip., [illegible].
Kilmanehame. See Kilmainham.
Kilmancham wood. See Kilmaynam wood.
Kilmanolan, King's co., [illegible].
Kilmanchin (co. Kilk. ?), [illegible], [illegible], [illegible], 6754.
Kilmanahin—Kilmanahyn—Kilmanahon—Kilmanhyne—Killvanahine—Kilvanytyre—Kylmanyhyre (Kilmanahan), co. Wat., 1082, [illegible], 2571, 3471, [illegible], [illegible], 4280, 4337, 6365; grant, 4581; manor, 6033. See also Kilmahon.
Kilmanerusaine (co. Tip. ?), 6714.
Kilmanhen—Kilmanhyne. See Kilmanahin.
Kilmanichelas, co. Wat. See Kylmynicknocheas, Kilmanichelas.
Kilmanman, Queen's co. See Kilmanamane, Kilmanyrya.
Kilmanoughe, [illegible], [illegible].
Kilmanaughe. See Kilmanagh.
Kilmanrachie, co. Cork, [illegible].
Kilmanyhyn. See Kilmanahin.
Kilmanyrya (Kilmanman), Queen's co., rectory, [illegible].
Kilmaog—Kilmaoh—Kilmaoke—Kylmaogo, co. Kild., 1168, 1510, [illegible], [illegible], 6857.
Kilmaone (co. Long. ?), [illegible].
Kilmarigie (co. Lim. ?), 6461.
Kilmarone — Kylmarone (Kilmorony), Queen's co., [illegible], [illegible].
Kilmarouke—Kilmarouske, co. Gal., 4067, 4718.
Kilmarton—Kilmartane—Kilmartyn—Kylmarton (Kilmartin), co. Dub., 846, 1623, [illegible].
" wood of, [illegible].
Kilmartan, Queen's co., [illegible], [illegible].
Kilmartery (co. Cork ?), [illegible].
Kilmartin (co. Wick. ?), 1840.
Kilmartyn. See Kilmarton.
Kilmaroshagh (co. Gal. ?), [illegible].
Kilmasan (co. Wex. ?), 4174.
Kilmasrelly (co. Tip. ?), [illegible].
Kilmastion (co. Wick.), [illegible].
Kilmaster, co. Wex., [illegible], [illegible].
Kilmauslom (co. Kild. ?), [illegible].
Kilmavallwey, prebendary of, [illegible].
Kilmavoigh—Kilmavie, co. Tip., [illegible]; grant, [illegible].
Kilmawrwarke, co. Cork, [illegible].
Kilmayne—Kylmayne—Kilmaine—Kilmaine—Kylmaine—Kylmaine (Kilmaine), co. Mayo, [illegible], [illegible].
" barony, [illegible], [illegible], [illegible], [illegible], [illegible]; lands of, granted, [illegible].
" monastery, [illegible], [illegible].
Kilmaynam wood — Kilmaneham wood (Kilmainham wood), co. Meath, [illegible], [illegible].
Kilmaynam. See Kilmainham.
Kilmaynan—Kylmaynan, co. Meath, [illegible], [illegible].
Kilmaynan—Kylmaynan, Queen's co., [illegible], 1383, 1780.
Kilmaynham. See Kilmainham.
Kilmaynhamwood, co. Meath, 3137.
" preceptory or commandery leased, 4791.
Kilmaynol, co. Long., lands of market at, [illegible].
Kilmead, co. Kild. See Kilmeal.
Kilmeadan—Kilmedan—Kilmeadane—Kylmeadan, co. Wat., [illegible], [illegible], [illegible], [illegible], [illegible], [illegible], [illegible], [illegible], [illegible], 4118, 4143, [illegible], [illegible], [illegible].
" vicar of, [illegible].
Kilmeaghell (co. Wex. or Car. ?), [illegible].
Kilmeaghen (co. Car. or Wex. ?), [illegible].
Kilmean. See Kilmayne.
Kilmeanolege (Kilmainolege, co. Mayo), rectory, [illegible], [illegible].
Kilmeane. See Kilmayne.
Kilmeane, co. Ros. See Kilmyan.
Kilmeanmore (Kilmainmore, co. Mayo), rectory, [illegible], [illegible].
Kilmearo (co. Cork ?), 4107.
Kilmeclogue (co. Wick. ?), [illegible].
Kilmecounoke (Kilmacounoge, co. Cork), [illegible].
Kilmecorry (co. Tip. ?), [illegible].
Kilmedan—Kilmedane. See Kilmeadan.
Kilmedine, co. Ros., [illegible].
Kilmeede, co. Kild., [illegible].
Kilmeedy, co. Wick. See Kilmyde.
Kilmeelickin, co. Gal. See Kelmylocke.
Kilmeghan (co. Westm. ?), [illegible].
Kilmeghlaghlan, co. Tip., [illegible], 4188.
Kilmeghlin, co. Long., lands of market, [illegible].
Kilmehlowlock, Queen's co., 1690.
Kilmekyevoke (Kilmakevoge), co. Kilk., rectory, [illegible].
Kilmeklagh, co. Tip., 4141, [illegible].
Kilmelagie, co. Lim., [illegible].
Kilmelappoke—Kilmelpog — Kilmelappoge, co. Car., 1438, 1748, [illegible].
Kilmeleigh, co. Cork, [illegible].
Kilmelane (co. Cork ?), [illegible].

INDEX TO FIANTS—ELIZABETH.

[illegible] — Kylmalowe (Kilmaloo), co. Wat., [illegible], [illegible].
Kilmacow, co. Gal., [illegible].
Kilmacrath, co. Wex., [illegible].
Kilmaery, co. Kerry, [illegible].
Kilmacry[illegible] (co. Cork ?), 4769.
Kilmacrye—Kylmacrayn, co. Wat., [illegible].
Kilmacyrenan alias Kilvernice (Kilvem-nos, co. Tip. ?), rectory, [illegible].
Kilmalaghyr, co. Tip., [illegible].
Kilmaqawde — Kylmaqawde, Queen's co., [illegible].
Kilmarerne, co. Tip., [illegible].
Kilmarrie—Kylmarrie, co. Meath, [illegible].
Kilmarton — Kylmarton (Kilmurry ?), Queen's co., [illegible].
Kilmarton, co. Rosc., [illegible].
Kilmasane, co. Car., 756-1.
Kilmasan — Kylmasan — Kylmesan, co. Meath, [illegible], [illegible], [illegible], [illegible]; rectory, [illegible], [illegible].
Kilmasie, co. Long., rectory, [illegible].
Kilmavogh (co. Rosc. or Gal.), [illegible].
Kilmaylin, co. Lim., parish, [illegible].
Kilmichell (Kilmichael, co. Cork), [illegible]; rectory, [illegible]. See Kilmihill, Kilmihile.
Kilmichell — Kilmichill — Kilmihile (Kilmichael, co. Wex.), [illegible], [illegible], [illegible], [illegible], [illegible], [illegible].
Kilmichill, co. Kerry, [illegible].
Kilmickinogane—Kilmickilinogane, co. Tip., rectory, [illegible], [illegible].
Kilmiddie (co. Cork ?), [illegible], [illegible].
Kilmighlasan, co. Tip., rectory, [illegible].
Kilmihill, co. Clare. See Kyllomyle.
Kilmihile, co. Cork, [illegible], [illegible].
Kilmihillie. See Kilmichell.
Kilmihy—Kylmihy, co. Cork, [illegible].
Kilmilage, co. Tip., rectory, [illegible].
Kilmillicaster, co. Tip., [illegible].
Kilminchy, Queen's co. See Kilvinsico.
Kilmine, co. Cork, [illegible].
Kilmirwin, co. Wat. See Kilmaycin, Kilvinise, Kylmaysnacyena.
Kilmirry—Kylmirry, co. Meath, [illegible].
Kilmiskon—Kylmiskon, co. Westm., [illegible].
Kilmoashill (Kilmashill), co. Kilk., [illegible].
Kilmocar — Kilmocarr — Kilmokar — Kilmoker (Kilmacar, co. Kilk. ?), [illegible], [illegible], [illegible], [illegible], [illegible], [illegible], [illegible].
Kilmacho, Queen's co., 493.
Kilmochorwe, co. Cork, [illegible].
Kilmocko—Kilmochwe—Kilmochowe (co. Cork ?), [illegible], [illegible], [illegible].
Kilmockriske (Kilmockridge), co. Wex., rectory, [illegible], [illegible].
Kilmockrye. See Kilmocrye.
Kilmocloge—Kilmocloig—Kilmocllog (Kilmaclongan, co. Wat. ?), [illegible], [illegible], [illegible].
Kilmoclery (co. Cork ?), [illegible].
Kilmoclyne (co. Cor. ?), [illegible].
Kilmocroge (Kilmacogue), co. Tip., [illegible].
Kilmocroge — Kilmoconoge — Kylmocoogho, co. Wat., [illegible], 734, [illegible].
Kilmocollorniegh (co. Tip. ?), [illegible].
Kilmocomoge (co. Cork ?), [illegible]. See also Kilcomoke, Kilmocomoke.
Kilmocowake—Kilmacowacke (co. Wat. ?), [illegible], [illegible].
Kilmocrye—Kilmackrye—Kylmakre (Kilmacree), co. Wex., rectory, [illegible], [illegible], [illegible], [illegible], [illegible].
Kilmocrum, [illegible].
Kilmodalle (co. Kilk. ?), [illegible].
Kilmodally (co. Lim. or Cork ?), [illegible].
Kilmoelkyadir—Kylvoylkadire (Kilmalkedar, co. Kerry), [illegible], [illegible].
Kilmoell, co. Lim., [illegible].
Kilmoellaghayn, co. Tip. or Lim., [illegible].
Kilmoer, co. Gal., [illegible].
Kilmoore O'Rusheline (co. Tip. ?), [illegible].
Kilmoerery, co. Tip., [illegible].
Kilmog (Kilmogue ? co. Kilk.), [illegible].
Kilmogar (co. Tip. ?), [illegible].
Kilmoge, Queen's co., [illegible].
Kilmoghmenock—Kylmoghonpenk, Queen's co., [illegible].
Kilmoghoine—Kylmoghoyne (co. Mayo), [illegible], [illegible].
Kilmoghome (Kilmacomma, co. Wat. ?), [illegible], [illegible].
Kilmoghoo (co. Westm. ?), [illegible].
Kilmogyltronock, Queen's co., [illegible].
Kilmogrange (co. Wat. ?), [illegible].
Kilmogue, co. Kilk. See Kilmog.
Kilmoheallock—Kylmohalock. See Kilmallock.
Kilmohide—Kylmohide, Queen's co., [illegible].
Kilmohine, co. Wat., [illegible].
Kilmole, Queen's co., [illegible], [illegible].
Kilmolle, co. Clare, rectory, [illegible].
Kilmokar—Kilmoker. See Kilmocar.
Kilmokillye, co. Tip., [illegible].
Kilmokyn (co. Tip. ?), [illegible].
Kilmokynok. See Kilmunkenoge.
Kilmolapon—Kylmolapon, co. Car., [illegible].
Kilmolappoge. See Kilmolappocke.
Kilmolaro (Kilmolara, co. Mayo), rectory, [illegible], [illegible].
Kilmolash—Kilmolash—Kilmolaisly (co. Sligo ?), [illegible].
Kilmolashe—Kilmolasse—Kilmolassye, co. Tip., [illegible], [illegible], [illegible].
Kilmolaugh, co. Wex., [illegible], [illegible].
Kilmoleagher — Kilmolegher (co. Tip. ?) [illegible], [illegible].
Kilmoleane, co. Kerry, [illegible], [illegible].
Kilmolody—Kilmolodie, co. Cork, [illegible].

Kilmolee (co. Wat. ?), [illegible].
Kilmolerher. *See* Kilmuleagher.
Kilmolgan, Queen's co., 482.
Kilmolkmarisho (co. Tip. ?), [illegible].
Kilmollocke—Kilmelloke—Kylmolonge—Kyllmollocke (Kilmollock), co. Wex., 866, 4002, 6116, [illegible]; rectory, [illegible].
Kilmolocke—Kilmolocke (co. Wex. ?), 6647.
Kilmologe—Kylmologe, co. Tip., parsonage, [illegible], 6841.
Kilmolrone (Kilmorony), Queen's co., 6676.
Kilmona, co. Gal., [illegible].
Kilmonagha, co. Lim., 6171.
Kilmonane—Kylmonan, co. Kerry, [illegible], [illegible]; rectory, 6172.
Kilmone—Kylmone, co. Cork, 3747, [illegible].
Kilmone, co. Meath, 4477.
Kilmonen — Kylmonen, co. Westm., 866, 6934.
Kilmonemun, co. Wat., 6117.
Kilmoney—Kilmonie—Kilmoney, co. Cork, [illegible], 6437, [illegible], 6749; rectory, [illegible].
Kilmonie, co. Tip., 6786.
Kilmonock (co. Cork ?), [illegible].
Kilmonoge, co. Cork. *See* Kilmaconoge.
Kilmoory. *See* Kilmoory.
Kilmoory (co. Westm. ?), 4623.
Kilmoyn, co. Westm., [illegible].
Kilmoyne, co. Wat., 1587.
Kilmoryvoke—Kylmooryvoke, King's co., 1691.
Kilmoog, co. Kilk., 4115.
Kilmoor—Kilmoore. *See* Kilmore.
Kilmoore (co. Leit. ?), 4794.
Kilmoory — Kilmoraithe — Kilmore—Kylmorey — Kylmorre (Kilmurry, co. Wick.), 814, 1307, 3745, [illegible]; rectory, 1307.
Kilmor. *See* Kilmore.
Kilmoraithe. *See* Kilmoory.
Kilmore, co. Car. *See* Kilmoory, co. Wick.
Kilmore—Kilmoore, co. Cav., [illegible].
" John Garvey, bishop of, commissions, [illegible], 6139, [illegible].
Kilmore (co. Clare ?), [illegible].
Kilmore—Kilmoore—Kyllmore, co. Cork, [illegible], [illegible], [illegible], [illegible], [illegible]; grant, [illegible].
" *See* Kylmore.
Kilmore—Kylmore, barony, co. Cork, made shire ground, [illegible]; lands in, granted, [illegible]. *See* Great Woods.
Kilmore—Kylmore, co. Dub., [illegible], 4418.
Kilmore, co. Dub. or Kild., 4744.
Kilmore, co. Gal., 6816.
Kilmore, co. Gal., rectory, 1328, [illegible].
Kilmore—Kilmoore, co. Kerry, [illegible], [illegible]; rectory, 6172.
Kilmore — Kylmore — Kyllmore, co. Kild., 617, 1348, 1567, 3167, 4878, [illegible].
Kilmore (co. Kilk. or Tip.), 1602.
Kilmore—Kilmor—Killmoore—Kylmor, co. Lim., [illegible], [illegible], 6171, [illegible].
Kilmore, co. Lim. or Cork, [illegible].
Kilmore—Kylmore, in Tyrawley, co. Mayo, rectory, 1728, [illegible].
Kilmore—Kylmore, co. Louth, [illegible].
Kilmore, co. Meath, rectory, 1343, [illegible].
Kilmore, co. Mon., [illegible], [illegible]; lordship, [illegible].
Kilmore—Kylmore, Queen's co., [illegible], [illegible], 1782.
Kilmore—Kylmore, co. Ros., [illegible], [illegible], [illegible], [illegible], [illegible].
" rectory, [illegible], [illegible].
" monastery, leased, [illegible], [illegible], [illegible], [illegible].
Kilmore, co. Tip., 1912, [illegible], [illegible]; rectory, 4912.
Kilmore (co. Tip. ?), 4236, [illegible], [illegible].
Kilmore (co. Wat.), 1637.
Kilmore—Kyllmore (co. Westm. ?), [illegible], [illegible].
Kilmore—Killmor—Kylmore, co. Wex., [illegible], 1359, 6731.
" rectory, [illegible].
" vicarage, [illegible].
" Grange of, [illegible].
Kilmore Brennaghe—Kylmorebrenaghe, co. Kild., [illegible], [illegible].
Kilmore Magdalen (Kilmurry), co. Lim., rectory, 1443, 4912.
Kilmoredoll, co. Gal., [illegible].
Kilmorecumlam—Kylmorecumlam, co. Cork, [illegible].
Kilmoreghe—Kylmoreghe, Queen's co., [illegible], 1964.
Kilmoric, co. Dub. or Kild., 4782.
Kilmoric, co. Kilk., [illegible].
Kilmorn, co. Ros., [illegible].
Kilmorogh (co. Sligo ?), 6516.
Kilmoroney, Queen's co. *See* Kilmarone, Kilmolrone.
Kilmorre—Kylmorre—Kyllmorre or Kylmorre, Queen's co., [illegible], 1363, 1728.
Kilmorrie, co. Cork, [illegible].
" rectory, [illegible].
Kilmorrie. *See* Kilmurry.
Kilmorry. *See* Kilmurry.
Kilmorry, co. Wex., 417.
Kilmorrymanig, co. Lim., [illegible].
Kilmory—Kylmory, co. Cork, rectory, [illegible].
Kilmory (Kilmurry, co. Kild.), [illegible].
Kilmoryo—Kylmorye, co. Car., [illegible].
Kilmorye in Byrne's country, 1162.
Kilmow (co. Cork ?), [illegible].
Kilmoyemany—Kilmoyemie, co. Kilk., rectory, [illegible], [illegible].
Kilmoyly, co. Kerry. *See* Kilwille.
Kilmoynis (co. Mayo or Ros.), [illegible].
Kilmoyrye (co. Wat.), [illegible].
Kilmuckridge, co. Wex. *See* Kilmockriske.

INDEX TO FIANTS.—ELIZABETH.

Kilmane (co. Cork ?), [illegible].
Kilmuke—Kyllmukin (co. Lim. ?), [illegible].
Kilmukilloak, co. Cork, [illegible].
Kilmullin, co. Cork, [illegible].
Kilmulloghoy (co. Clare ?), 4463.
Kilmulpody (co. Cork ?), [illegible].
Kilmurey, co. Cork, rectory, [illegible].
Kilmurey, co. Rosc., chapel or cell, [illegible].
Kilmurie (co. Cork ?), [illegible].
Kilmurie, co. Lim., [illegible].
Kilmurre—Kylmurre, King's co., 1566, [illegible].
Kilmurre, co. Lim. or Kerry, [illegible].
Kilmurre, in Munster, [illegible].
Kilmurre (Kilmurry, co. Wick.), [illegible].
Kilmurrey. See Kilmurry, co. Cork.
Kilmurri. See Kilmurry, co. Lim.
Kilmurrie. See Kilmurry, co. Cork.
Kilmurry, co. Clare, [illegible].
Kilmurry — Kilmurry — Kilmurrie — Kilmurrey — Kilmury — Kylmurrey, co. Cork, [illegible], [illegible], [illegible], [illegible].
„ rectory, [illegible], [illegible].
Kilmurry, co. Gal., [illegible].
„ chapel, [illegible], [illegible].
Kilmurry, co. Kild. See Kylmurre, [illegible]; also Kilmury.
Kilmurry (co. Kilk. ?), [illegible].
Kilmurry, King's co. See Kylmurre, [illegible].
Kilmurry—Kilmurry—Kilmurri, co. Lim., [illegible], [illegible], [illegible].
„ rectory, [illegible].
Kilmurry, co. Lim. See Kilmore Magdalen.
Kilmurry — Kilmurrie — Kylmurrie — Kylmurry—Kylmurry, co. Meath, [illegible], [illegible], [illegible], [illegible], [illegible], [illegible], [illegible], [illegible].
Kilmurry (Killymurry), co. Mon., [illegible].
Kilmurry, Queen's co. See Kylmurhen.
Kilmurry, co. Tip. See Kilvoro.
Kilmurry, co. Wat. See Kilwenane.
Kilmurry, co. Wick. See Kilmoory, Kilmurre.
Kilmurrye (co. Lim. ?), [illegible].
Kilmury. See Kilmurry, co. Cork.
Kilmyan (Kilmeanan), co. Rosc., rectory, [illegible].
Kilmychell (co. Wex. ?), [illegible].
Kilmyshroyre, co. Sligo, [illegible].
Kilmyde—Kylmikle (Kilmicaly), co. Wat., [illegible], [illegible].
Kilmydie (co. Cork ?), [illegible].
Kilmyhine (co. Wex. ?), [illegible].
Kilmyhieog (co. Cork ?), [illegible].
Kilmylane, [illegible].
Kilmymore, co. Gal. or Rosc., [illegible].
Kilmyn (co. Tip. ?), [illegible].
Kilmynane, co. Dub., [illegible].
Kilmyne—Kylmyne (co. Cork), [illegible], [illegible], [illegible], [illegible].
Kilmyne (co. Leit. ?), [illegible].
Kilmyrale (Kilmirrie, co. Wat. ?), [illegible].
Kilmynyn, co. Tip., [illegible].
Kilnyvine, co. Cork or Lim., [illegible].
Kilnacarriga, co. Tip. See Kilnacarrigye.
Kilnacash, Queen's co. See Kylnacaysbill, Kilnykinnaghe.
Kilnacask, co. Tip. See Kilnecaskan.
Kilnacloshe (co. Cork ?), [illegible].
Kilnacloy, co. Mon. See Kilnecleigh.
Kilnacorragh, co. Cav. See Kyllcorranaghe.
Kilnacross, co. Cav. See Kilnacrossy.
Kilnacrott, co. Cav. See Kilnacroit, Kelnycrotty.
Kilnadrea, co. Lim., parish, [illegible].
Kilnagarvanagh — Kilnagarvanagh — Kilnagorvagh — Kilnagurvough — Kilnagurvanagh — Kylnagarranaghe — Kylnagorranaghe (Kilnagarragh, King's co.), [illegible], [illegible], [illegible], [illegible]; grant, [illegible].
Kilnage—Kilnag, co. Lim., [illegible], [illegible], [illegible].
Kilnaghtin —Kilnaghtan —Kilnaghty (Kilnaughtin, co. Kerry), [illegible].
„ rectory, [illegible].
„ advowson, [illegible].
„ vicarage, [illegible].
Kilnaglory, co. Cork. See Kilnagloarie.
Kilnagranaye—Kylnagranaye, co. Wat., [illegible].
Kilnaharvey, co. Mon. See Kilharvie.
Kilnahinch, co. Wexm. See Kilnahinch.
Kilnaing, co. Gal. See Carrowkilleniogy, Kelloyleagg.
Kilnalo (co. Tip. ?), [illegible].
Kilnalmochi, [illegible]. See Kinalmochi.
Kilnamack, co. Wat. See Kilmack, Kilnemack.
Kilnamuddy, co. Mon. See Kilnemaddy.
Kilnamanagh (Killoonamannagh ?), co. Cork, [illegible].
Kilnamanagh, co. Rosc. See Killenmanaghe, Killemmanaghe, Kilnomanagh.
Kilnamanagh, co. Tip. See Keilenmanagho, Kellemanaghe, Kilnemanagh.
Kilnamartery, co. Cork. See Kilnamartine.
Kilnamucky, co. Cork. See Kilnamuckie, [illegible].
Kilnamurry, co. Kild., [illegible].
Kilnanoila, co. Cork, [illegible].
Kilnanlock, King's co., [illegible].
Kilnanloge, King's co. See Kilnaniske.
Kilnarath, co. Tip. See Kilnam.
Kilnasmor, Queen's co. See Keylnamore Kilnamore.
Kilnashruo, Queen's co. See Kilnesean.
Kilnasilty, co. Long., [illegible].
Kilnasleve, co. Gal. See Kellnasleeve.
Kilnathboogari (co. Tip. ?), [illegible].
Kilnaulory (co. Cork ?), [illegible].
Kilnaulora (Kilmalooro ?), co. Cork, [illegible].
Kilnaughtin, co. Kerry. See Kilnaghtin.

INDEX TO FIANTS—ELIZABETH.

Kilnevale (King's co. ?), [illegible].
Kilmacatoge, King's co., [illegible].
Kilnebolemuntaney—Kilnebolemuntane (co. Kilk. ?), 611, [illegible].
Kilnebrenan, [illegible]. See Kilbrenan.
Kilneby (co. Kilk. ?), [illegible], [illegible].
Kilnecanagho—Kylnecarmanagho, co. Cork, 3747, 4070.
Kilnecannaghe—Kylnecannaghe—Killecannaghe (co. Wat. ?), 1637, [illegible].
Kilnecappe, co. Lim., 6761.
Kilnecarr, co. Tip., [illegible].
Kilnecarigge (Kilnacarriga, co. Tip. ?), [illegible].
Kilnecarre, co. Long., [illegible].
Kilnecarriggye (co. Wat. ?), [illegible].
Kilnecarygan (co. Cork ?), [illegible].
Kilnecasse — Kylnecasse (Kilnacask), co. Tip., [illegible], [illegible].
Kilnecashy (co. Cork ?), 4114.
Kilnecaryshill — Kylnecaryshill (Kilnacash ? Queen's co.), 1716.
Kilneclassie (co. Cork ?), [illegible].
Kilnecleigh (Kilnecley), co. Mon., [illegible].
Kilnecloragh, [illegible].
Kilnecolone, co. Cork or Lim., [illegible].
Kilneconyne (co. Lim. or Tip. ?), [illegible].
Kilnecorcragh (King's co.), [illegible].
Kilnecorti, co. Cav., [illegible].
Kilnecourte—Kilnecort—Kilnecorrie—Kylnecorrie—Kyllnecourte—Kylnecorty (Courtwood ? Queen's co.), 437, [illegible], [illegible], [illegible], 3170, [illegible], [illegible], [illegible].
Kilnecrynaghe (Killycronaghan), co. Mon., [illegible].
Kilnecroke (co. Long. ?), [illegible].
Kilnecroit — Kilnecroin — Kylnecroit—Kyllnecroit (Kilnacroit), co. Cav., [illegible], [illegible], [illegible], [illegible], [illegible].
Kilnecurry, co. Tip., [illegible].
Kilnemur, Queen's co., [illegible].
Kilnecurie, Queen's co., [illegible].
Kilnedry (co. Cork ?), [illegible].
Kilnedwan, co. Ross., [illegible].
Kilnedy, co. Kilk., rectory, [illegible].
Kilnefarrilocy, [illegible].
Kilnefreickin, [illegible].
Kilnegananagh, co. Wat., [illegible].
Kilnegannagh (co. Tip. ?), [illegible].
Kilnegaragh, co. Wat., [illegible].
Kilnegarvan, co. Mayo, vicarage, [illegible].
Kilneglenagh—Kilnygleraghe (co. Cork ?), 2941, [illegible].
Kilneglory, co. Cork, [illegible].
Kilnegloorie—Kilnyglory (Kilnaglory, co. Cork), [illegible], [illegible].
Kilnegolman, co. Kerry, [illegible].
Kilnegranaghe—Kylnegranaghe, co. Cork, 3747.
Kilnegorranagh—Kilnegornagh. See Kilnegarranagh.
Kilnegurtin (King's co. or Kild. ?), [illegible].
Kilnehorny —Kilnehornay, co. Cork, [illegible].
Kilnehornay — Kylnehornoy — Kilnehornay—Kylnehornyny (co. Cork ?), 4791; rectory, 5151.
Kilnekannanagha. See Kilnecannaghe.
Kilnekerpagh, in Munster, [illegible].
Kilnekneck — Kylneknock, co. Gal., [illegible], [illegible], [illegible].
Kilnelago (co. Tip. ?), 4874.
Kilnelaquiert (co. Tip. or Lim.), [illegible].
Kilnelyawo — Kylnelyawo (co. Ferm. ?), 4816.
Kilnemack (Kilnamack), co. Wat., [illegible], 4141.
" rectory, [illegible].
Kilnemaddy (Kilnamaddy), co. Mon., [illegible].
Kilnemalloghe or [illegible], co. Cork, [illegible].
Kilnemanagh — Kylnemanaghe, co. Gal., [illegible].
Kilnemanagh — Kylnemanaghe, (Kilnamanagh, co. Ross.), [illegible]; rectory, 1144.
" religious house, [illegible].
Kilnemanagh—Kilnemanaghe—Kilnemanaghe — Kylnymanagh (Kilnamanagh), co. Tip., [illegible], [illegible], [illegible].
" country or cantred of, [illegible], [illegible], [illegible].
Kilnemanagh (co. Wick.), [illegible].
Kilnemanaghe (co. Wick. ?), [illegible].
Kilnemartine—Kilnemartirie—Kilnemartorie — Kilnymartery — Kylnymartirie (Kilnamartery), co. Cork, [illegible], [illegible], [illegible], [illegible], [illegible].
Kilnemeolagh—Kilnemoldaghe, co. Long., [illegible], [illegible].
Kilnemona, co. Clare, [illegible], [illegible], [illegible], [illegible].
Kilnemore, Queen's co., [illegible], [illegible], [illegible].
Kilnenan (King's co. ?), [illegible].
Kilnenon (co. Wat. ?), [illegible].
Kilnenowan (King's or Queen's co. ?), [illegible].
Kilneneyn, Queen's co., [illegible].
Kilnenyne, co. Wexf., [illegible].
Kilnenynte — Kylnenynyn — Kilnenynten (co. Wexf. ?), [illegible].
Kilnequvel o, co. Dub., 1143.
Kilnera (Kilnamath), co. Tip., rectory, [illegible].
Kilnerie—Kylnerie (co. Car. ?), [illegible].
Kilnerray—Kylnerray, co. Cav., [illegible].
Kilnerbokahan (co. Kilk. ?), [illegible].
Kilneroan (Kilnashane), Queen's co., [illegible], [illegible].
Kilnesere—Killneshyre (Kilnaseer, Queen's co. ?), 4818, [illegible].
Kilnesure, co. Tip., [illegible].

INDEX TO FIANTS—ELIZABETH.

Kilnasye, co. Long., rectory, 6131.
Kilnatne, King's co., 6816.
Kilnavalley—Kylnavalley, co. Cork, 5472.
Kilnavannagho. *See* Kilnamanvrvah.
Kilnavenage—Kylnavenagh, co. Lim., 6001.
Kilnekilkagh. *See* Cillakilkeagh, 4472.
Kilneighill — Killnighane, co. Lim., parish, [illegible].
Kilnihall (co. Cork ?), 6529.
Kilnimanye, co. Lim., 3117.
Kilnodichevagh ?, co. Meath, 6287.
Kilnon (co. Wex. ?), 6947.
Kilnamar—Kylnamar, vicarage, 1170.
Kilnamanan, co. Clare, 5352.
Kilnamill (co. Tip. ?), 5361.
Kilnarnyd (co. Wat. ?), 1016.
Kilnyan (co. Gal. ?), 4072.
Kilnydy (co. Cork ?), 6675.
Kilnyfernake — Kylnyfernake, Queen's co., [illegible].
Kilnyglorogha. *See* Kilnadoornagh.
Kilnyglory. *See* Kilnaglooria.
Kilnykeranyay. *See* Kilnakeranoy.
Kilnyhone (co. Cork ?), 6147.
Kilnyhuny (co. Cork ?), 6467.
Kilnykeanaghe (Kilnacash), Queen's co., [illegible].
Kilnymartery—Kylnymartirie. *See* Kilnomartine.
Kilnymonagh — Kylnymonagh, co. Tip., [illegible].
Kilnyngale—Kylnyngale (co. Kerry ?), 6162.
Kilnyurse—Kyllnyurse (co. Kerry ?), 3870.
Kilnyvreghan—Kilnyvrelane (co. Wat. ?), [illegible].
Kilogavolin, co. Long., 6104.
Kiloghtolnine. *See* Kilowghtorwyne.
Kiloghtermoy — Kyloghtermoy — Kiloughtermoy (Kilwatermoy, co. Wat.), 1697, 2782, [illegible].
Kilogramee—Kylogramee, co. Long., 6106.
Kilohannoke. *See* Killoonmock.
Kilone. *See* Killone.
Kiloran—Kilorane. *See* Killoran, Killorane.
Kilorgin. *See* Killorglin.
Kilorne (King's co. or Westm. ?), 3109.
Kilosky, co. Tip., 5677.
Kiloughe. *See* Killougha.
Kiloughtermoy. *See* Kiloughtermoy.
Kiloumagh, co. Cork, [illegible].
Kilowine (co. Cork ?), 6315.
Kilowmoyne, co. Tip., 6797.
Kilowyghe, co. Tip., [illegible].
Kilowragh —Kylowragh (co. Cork ?), 2691.
Kilpadar—Kilpadirr — Kilpeador, co. Cork, [illegible], [illegible].
Kilpatrick — Kylpatrick, co. Cork, [illegible], [illegible].
„ rectory, 3747, [illegible], [illegible].
Kilpatrick, co. Kild., [illegible].
Kilpatrick (co. Leit. ?), 4736.
Kilpatrick — Kilpatrike — Kylpatrick, co. Meath, 1414.
„ rectory, [illegible], 1401, [illegible], [illegible], [illegible].
„ vicar of, [illegible].
Kilpatrick—Kilpatrike—Kilpatryk—Kilpatrick, co. Westm., 775, 1465, [illegible], [illegible], [illegible], [illegible], [illegible], 6141, 6590. *See also* Dardingill.
Kilpatrick (co. Wex. ?), [illegible].
Kilpatricke, co. Wex., rectory, 1060, [illegible].
Kilpeador. *See* Kilpadar.
Kilpeacock, in Ossory, vicar of, 4318.
Kilpoore — Kilporie — Kilporishe (Kilpierran, co. Wex. ?), [illegible], 4749.
Kilphillipce (Kilphillipbeen), co. Cork, [illegible].
Kilpoole—Kilpolle—Kylpole—Kylpoole (co. Wick.), [illegible], [illegible], 6744; granted, [illegible].
Kilpowly alias Kipowle, [illegible]. *See* Capole.
Kilpursell (Kilpurcell ?), Queen's co., 6461.
Kilquane, co. Lim. *See* Kilquan, Kilcohan.
Kilquiggin (co. Wick.), 6616.
Kilraghtmahby, co. Gal., [illegible].
Kilrahenagh, co. Lim., [illegible].
Kilramore—Kilramery, co. Kild., 6777.
Kilrane—Kilrian, co. Wex., [illegible].
Kilranelaghe (co. Wick.), [illegible].
Kilrash (Ranelagh, co. Wick.), martial law in, [illegible]. *See* Cahiral Raghmill.
Kilrass, co. Sligo, church and rectory, [illegible].
Kilrekree, co. Gal., [illegible].
Kilrntyry (co. Gal. ?), 4731.
Kilrathmoy, [illegible].
Kilreaghe (co. Ross. ?), [illegible].
Kilree, co. Kilk. *See* Kilrie.
Kilreekill, co. Gal. *See* Ballykilrekill.
Kilrolyn—Kyrolyn, [illegible].
Kilromayn—Kilromayne, co. Kerry, [illegible], 5172.
Kilronagh, [illegible].
Kilrondoge, 4872.
Kilrondony — Kilr[ ]ondowne — Kilrindoine—Kilriedowne—Kilryndowine, co. Kilk., 1117, [illegible], 4287, 4803, 6704.
Kilroske, [illegible].
Kilroyon—Kylroyon, co. Wat., 1673.
Kilrian or Kilrane, co. Wex., [illegible].
Kilrie (co. Cork ?), 6117.
Kilrie—Killrie—Kilry—Killry—Kyllsie (Kilree), co. Kilk., 1028, 4876.
„ rectory, [illegible], [illegible].
„ grange of, [illegible].
Kilrindoine — Kilriedowne. *See* Kilrondony.
Kilrobyn—Kylrobyn, co. Kilk., [illegible], [illegible].
Kilrodane, co. Lim. *See* Kilrodane.
Kilroe, co. Clare, [illegible].
Kilroe, co. Cork. *See* Kilcrowe, [illegible].
Kilroe, co. Gal. *See* Kelfroe.

INDEX TO FIANTS—ELIZABETH.

Kilros—Kylros, co. Meath, 4401.
Kilrosanagh (co. Cork ?), [illegible].
Kilrosan (Kilrosané), co. Cork, [illegible].
Kilrosan (Kilrosan, co. Gal. ?), rectory, [illegible].
Kilrosan (co. Ross. ?), 4737.
Kilrosan—Kilrosan, co. Wat., 1045, [illegible], 2744, [illegible], [illegible].
Kilrosan, vicarage, 1170.
Kilrosse, in Munster, [illegible].
Kilrossy, co. Westm., 4279.
Kilrory. See Kilrowry.
Kilroshrestran (King's co. ?), [illegible].
Kilrosha. See Kilroshe.
Kilroslaghen—Kilroshlaghen, co. Kild., 1181, [illegible].
Kilrossan—Kylrossan, co. Cork, 1873.
Kilrothery—Kylrothery—Kylrodry (Kilroddery, co. Wick.), [illegible], [illegible], 1144, [illegible], [illegible].
Kilrowan—Kylrovayn, co. Cork, rectory, [illegible], [illegible].
Kilrowane—Kilrowan, co. Cork, 4816, [illegible].
Kilrowe—Kylrowe, co. Meath, [illegible], [illegible], 1791, [illegible], [illegible], [illegible], 4312, [illegible], [illegible].
Kilrowe, lordship (described as in O'Molloy's country, but lands named appear to be in parish of Killare, co. Westm.), 314, [illegible], [illegible].
Kilrowry—Kylrory—Kylrowry (Kilrory), Queen's co., [illegible], 1182, [illegible], [illegible].
Kilroytane—Kylroytane, co. Wat., [illegible], [illegible].
Kilruain, co. Tip., [illegible].
Kilruane, co. Tip. See Kylleruane.
Kilrudane (Kilrodane), co. Lim., [illegible].
Kilruddery, co. Wick., See Kilrothery.
Kilruffed (co. Tip. ?), [illegible].
Kilruishe. See Kilruyshe.
Kilrus. See Kilrushe.
Kilrushe—Killrushe—Kilrushe, co. Clare, [illegible], [illegible], [illegible].
Kilrushe—Kilrus, co. Cork, [illegible], [illegible].
Kilrushe—Kylrushe, co. Kild., [illegible].
 " rectory, 1894.
Kilrushe—Kylrush—Kilrusse, co. Kilk., [illegible], [illegible], 1098, 1118, [illegible], 4933, [illegible]; rectory, [illegible].
Kilrushe—Kylrushe, co. Wex., 1139, [illegible].
Kilrusse—Kilrussed. See Kilrushe.
Kilruyshe—Kilreyske—Kilruiske, Queen's co., 1421, [illegible].
Kilry—Kilry. See Kilrie.
Kilryn, co. Kild., 1818.
Kilryndowine. See Kilrondowy.
Kilsaghan, [illegible].
Kil saint Nicholas—Kyl saint Nicholas, co. Wat., [illegible], 877, [illegible]; rectory, [illegible].
Kilsaint lawrence—Kylsaintlawrence, co. Wat., [illegible]; rectory, 4150.
Kilsalchane—Kilsalaghan. See Kilsaighan.
Kilsalan, co. Ross., rectory, 4342.
Kilsaight [ ], 181.
Kilsaighan—Kilsalchane—Kylsaighan—Kylsalaghan—Kilsalaghan (Kilsallaghan, co. Dub.), [illegible], [illegible], 4144, 4410, 4875; rectory, [illegible], [illegible].
Kilsallagh, co. Mayo. See Kilsalache, [illegible].
Kilsallaghan, co. Tip., [illegible].
Kilsallaghe, co. Kerry, [illegible].
Kilsaran—Kylsaran, co. Louth, [illegible], [illegible], 9414, [illegible].
 " prompiary, 1485.
Kilsaro, co. Westm., [illegible].
Kilscanlan, co. Wex. See Kilstanley.
Kilscannell—Kilskannell—Kilsknell—Kilshanell—Kylscanell—Kylscannell, co. Lim., 6810, [illegible], [illegible], grant, [illegible]; parish, [illegible], 5781.
Kilscohagh, co. Mayo. See Kilskeveagh.
Kilscohonaght (Kilsonhanagh), co. Cork, [illegible]. See Kulsculanaght.
Kilscroly, [illegible].
Kilseany—Kylseany—Kilsonane (Kilshanny, co. Clare), religious house, [illegible]; possessions leased, [illegible], [illegible].
Kilsegan. See Kilsheelan.
Kilsenan (Kilsenankett ?), co. Clare, [illegible].
Kilsevell—Kilsowell (co. Wick. ?), [illegible].
Kilsharane, co. Tip., [illegible].
Kilshanclonae, co. Car., [illegible].
Kilshanoloe, co. Kild. See Kylshanagh, [illegible].
Kilshane, co. Lim., house of friars minor, [illegible].
 " abbey granted, 6171.
Kilshane—Kylshane, co. Tip., [illegible], [illegible], [illegible].
 " rectory, [illegible], [illegible], [illegible].
Kilshannell. See Kilscannell.
Kilshanny, co. Clare. See Kilseany, Kilsonane.
Kilsharvan, co. Meath. See Kilsarvan.
Kilshaunaght (co. Cork ?), [illegible].
Kilshanedan. See Kilshenshiam.
Kilsheelan—Kilselan—Kylselan—Kilshelane—Kylshelan (Kilsheelan), co. Tip., [illegible]. See also Kelshelane.
 " rectory, [illegible], [illegible].
 " vicar of, [illegible], [illegible].
Kilshenell (co. Tip. ?), [illegible].
Kilshenne (Kilshine, co. Meath), church, [illegible].
Kilshenshiam—Kilshanshian—Kilshenshian—Kylsenshyam—Kylsynsham, co. Cork, [illegible], [illegible], [illegible], [illegible], [illegible].
Kilshroughe (co. Long. ?), [illegible].
Kilsie—Kilsy—Kylsy (Kilshalsee, co. Long. ?), rectory, [illegible], [illegible], [illegible].
Kilskannell—Kilskanell. See Kilscannell.

INDEX TO FIANTS—ELIZABETH.

Kilskeagh — Kylskyagh, co. Gal., 1499, 4393, 6514.
Kilskyr—Kilskyrr, co. Meath, 148, 6291.
Kilsonwaghe (Kilsonbagh, co. Mayo ?), 5481.
Kilspillaghe (co. Cav. ?), 6818.
Kilsenane (Kilsbanny), co. Clare, abbey, 6731. See Kilsbany.
Kilsonlay — Kylsonloy (Kilsonlan, co. Wex.), 5642, 5868.
Kilsowghane (co. Kilk. ?), 6564.
Kilsale, co. Clare, 5943.
Kilsy. See Kilsale.
Kilsylan (co. Tip. ?), 2304.
Kilsyaye (co. Cork ?), 6548.
Kiltaarke (co. Leit.), 4732.
Kiltalery (co. Long. ?), 6296.
Kiltagaran, co. Dub., 414.
Kiltagh, Forogh (O'Mauldon ?), attainted, 6286.
Kiltaghan, co. Kild., 6748, 6773.
Kiltaile. See Kiltale.
Kiltain, co. Clare, 5077.
Kiltale—Kyltale—Kyltalle—Kiltalle, co. Meath, 636-1, 649, 1247, 2051, 4987.
rectory, 664, 2363, 6088.
Kiltalagh, co. Kerry. See Kiltallaugh.
Kiltallagh—Kiltallagh (co. Cork ?), 2270, 6828.
Kiltalow (co. Cork ?), 6871.
Kiltample, co. Tip., rectory, 1643, 4018.
Kiltane, co. Tip., 6543.
Kiltanna, co. Lim. See Kiltynanan.
Kiltanny (co. Cork ?), 5068.
Kiltaragh (the barony of Kiltartan, co. Gal., 6824.
Kiltaragh (King's co. ?), 6619.
Kiltaraghts—Kyltaraghts, co. Gal., rectory, 1628, 5112, 5332, 6412.
Kiltarahan, in Munster, 6477.
Kiltardum, co. Gal., 4587.
Kiltartan, co. Gal. See Kiltaragh.
Kiltashell (co. Wex. ?), 4015.
Kiltaughoroke, co. Leit., 4793.
Kiltavany—Kyltavany, co. Cork, 5098.
Kiltavikangtan, co. Clare, 4968.
Kiltaale, Queen's co. See Kiltill.
Kiltean (Kiltsean), co. Kerry, 5018, 6290, 6506.
Kilteanm, co. Lim., 5777.
Kilteanne, 6276.
Kiltearane (co. Wick. ?), 6677.
Kiltebeg (Kiltybege), co. Mon., 5671.
Kiltedogha, Queen's co., 406, 6047.
Kiltedowe (Kildough ?), co. Mon., 5660.
Kilteean, co. Kerry. See Kiltean.
Kilteely, co. Lim. See Kiltelly.
Kilteevan, co. Rosc. See Kiltetovan.
Kilteadde—Kyltadde (co. Sligo ?), 6818.
Kiltegan—Kyltegan (co. Kerry ?), 4677.
Kiltegane (co. Tip. ?), 6742.
Kilteghan—Kilteghane, co. Kild., 6891, 5694, 6786.
Kilteghan (co. Meath ?), 5458.
Kilteghame. See Kilteighan.
Kilteel, co. Kild. See Kilteele.
Kilteigo, co. Rosc., 1614, 2798.
Kilteighan, Queen's co., 3836.
Kilteighan—Kilteighnan — Kiltegham, co. Tip., rectory, 168, 2367, 2578.
Kiltefolde, co. Clare, 5401.
Kiltell—Kiltelle, co. Wex., 168, 6682.
Kiltele (co. Clare ?), 6082.
Kiltely, co. Cav., 5685.
Kiltelloyny, co. Sligo, 5604.
Kiltemoan. See Kiltimon.
Kiltemplane, co. Lim., 5170, 6604.
Kilteman, co. Lim., 5791.
Kiltenan—Kyltenan, co. Tip., 1008, 2210, 6782.
Kiltenanlea, co. Clare. See Kilnenan.
Kiltenbeen (co. Cork ?), 4840.
Kiltennanloghe—Kyltennanloghe, co. Lim., 6781.
Kiltennell, co. Car. See Kilteynan.
Kilteragh (co. Wex. ?), 6624.
Kilterirooke, co. Mayo, 5563.
Kiltevan—Kyltevan, co. Rosc., 4078.
Kiltewnoy—Kyltewny (Kiltivna), co. Gal., 6498, 5308.
Kilteynam, co. Tip., 5461.
Kilteynan (Kiltennell), co. Car., rectory, 1640, 2834.
Kilteynan, co. Lim., 5777.
Kilteynan — Kylteynan — Kilteynane (Kiltinan, co. Tip. ?), 1876, 1900, 2306, 2310, 2368, 6189, 6144.
Kilteyne, 567.
Kilteyne, co. Mayo, 1828.
Kiltbomas, co. Gal., 4778.
Kiltibrowne, Queen's co., 5160.
Kilticollo—Kylticollo, co. Mayo, 1404, 6418.
Kiltie, Maloghlan duff a, pardon, 4940.
Kiltiernan, co. Dub., 6808.
Kiltiegane, co. Wat., 5616.
Kiltill (Kiltaale), Queen's co., rectory, 1324.
Kiltille—Kyltille (Kiltilly), co. Wat., 1132, 6768.
Kiltilly—Kiltillie—Kiltilly—Kiltylle—Kyltilly (Kilteely, co. Lim. ?), 4743, 4697, 5088, 5098, 6184, 6190.
Kiltimon—Kiltimony—Kiltamone (co. Wick.), 6263, 6208, 6417.
Kiltimun, co. Kerry, 6817.
Kiltinan—Kyltinan—Kiltynan (co. Tip.), 6823. See also Kilteynan
Kiltine (co. Tip. ?), 1988.
Kiltinehe, co. Tip., 6544.
Kiltivna, co. Gal. See Kiltewnoy.
Kiltiso, co. Tip., 6823.
Kiltivan, co. Mon., 5678.

INDEX TO FIANTS.—ELIZABETH.

Kiltober—Kiltobber—Kyltober, co. Westm., 1314, 1402, 1760, 1763, [illegible]-13, [illegible], [illegible], [illegible], [illegible].
" grange of, [illegible], [illegible], [illegible], [illegible]; grant, [illegible].
Kiltockeglassed (co. Kilk. ?), [illegible].
Kiltofaddo—Kiltofaddie, co. Sligo, [illegible], [illegible].
Kiltoghan (co. Kilk. ?), 913, [illegible].
Kiltoghor, co. Gal., [illegible].
Kiltoboraghe, co. Clare, [illegible].
Kiltoleghane—Kiltolleghane—Kyltoleghane, co. Kilk., [illegible], [illegible], [illegible].
Kiltolgane, King's co., 1612.
Kiltolkin, Queen's co., [illegible].
Kiltollagh—Kiltollanghe. See Kiltullagh.
Kiltolleghane. See Kiltoleghane.
Kiltome—Kiltom (Kiltomy, co. Kerry ?), rectory, [illegible], [illegible].
Kiltome (Kiltoom), co. Rosc., rectory, [illegible].
Kiltomes—Kyltomes, [illegible].
Kilton, [illegible].
Kilton. See Kiltome.
Kiltoom, co. Rosc. See Kiltome.
Kiltorkan—Kiltorkin (Kiltorcan), co. Kilk., [illegible], [illegible].
Kiltorman, co. Gal., [illegible].
Kiltoronte—Kiltorance, co. Gal., [illegible], [illegible].
Kiltorry—Kyltorry (co. Sligo ?), [illegible].
Kiltorych—Kyltorych, co. Lim., 1341.
Kiltotan, co. Westm., [illegible].
Kiltowin, co. Tip. or Kilk., [illegible].
Kiltowne or Kiltowen, King's co., 474, 4278, [illegible].
Kiltraghe of Pallice (Caltrapallas, co. Gal.), friary leased, 1541, [illegible].
Kiltrochane, co. Kilk., [illegible].
Kiltrone, co. Mayo, [illegible].
Kiltrasken—Kiltrasane—Kiltresken, co. Rosc., [illegible], 4741, 4914, [illegible], [illegible], [illegible]; parish, [illegible].
Kiltryne (King's co. ?), [illegible].
Kiltubbrid island, King's co. See Bane Kiltubbert, [illegible].
Kiltubret (Kiltubbrid), co. Mon., [illegible], [illegible].
Kiltullagh—Kiltollagh—Kiltollanghe—Kyltolagh — Kyltullagh, co. Gal., 1474, [illegible], [illegible], [illegible], [illegible], [illegible].
" rectory, [illegible].
" See Templemoll.
Kiltullaugh — Kiltulaghe — Kyltullaughe (Kiltallagh ?), co. Kerry, [illegible], [illegible].
" rectory, [illegible], [illegible].
Kiltultoke — Kyltultoge (Kiltultoge), co. Rosc., [illegible], [illegible].
Kiltumerogh (co. Cork ?), [illegible].
Kiltumnile — Kyltumnile, King's co., [illegible], [illegible].
Kiltarhe, co. Wex., vicarage, [illegible].
Kiltwrike (Kiltwrik), co. Wex., rectory, [illegible].
Kiltwrock (co. Cork ?), [illegible].
Kiltwoge (co. Lim. ?), [illegible].
Kiltwyne, co. Gal., [illegible].
Kilty, Dermot m'Donell y, pardon, [illegible].
Kiltyanna (Kiltanna), co. Lim., [illegible].
Kiltyborne, co. Mon. See Kiltober.
Kiltyleowrnyne — Kyltyleowrnyne, Queen's co., 1642.
Kiltyconnor (co. Rosc. ?), [illegible].
Kiltyhane, co. Cork, [illegible].
Kiltyll, co. Tip., [illegible].
Kiltylle (co. Clar. ?), [illegible].
Kiltylle. See Kiltilly.
Kiltynvine—Kiltynvyn (co. Wex. ?), [illegible].
Kiltyrnan. See Kiltinan.
Kiltyrin, King's co., [illegible].
Kiltulaster (co. Cork ?), [illegible].
Kilulagh—Kilule—Kilulagh—Kiltulagh. See Kiltullagh.
Kilulteagh (Kilull, co. Donegal), [illegible].
Kilunyly—Kylunyly, co. Cork, [illegible].
Kilure, co. Gal., [illegible].
Kilure. See Killure.
Kilurcan, co. Kerry, [illegible].
Kilurie (co. Kerry ?), [illegible].
Kilurie. See Kilurin.
Kilushurygh (co. Lim. ?), [illegible].
Kilusky. See Killusky.
Kilvane (Kylvanemurragh ?), co. Lim., [illegible].
Kilvalum, Queen's co. See Kilvean.
Kilvalin (co. Westm. ?), [illegible].
Kilvalebigh, co. Kerry, [illegible].
Kilvaldaluffe, co. Kerry, [illegible].
Kilvalian, in Munster, to be made shire ground, [illegible].
Kilvalian—Kylvalian, [illegible]; rectory, [illegible].
Kilvalloconra, King's co., [illegible].
Kilvalleconremedan, co. Cork, [illegible].
Kilvallelomane, co. Cork (Kill Ballelomand, in parish of Clonpriest, in Book of Survey and Distribution), [illegible].
Kilvallikillie. See Kilvallykilly.
Kilvallumgleveyrik, co. Tip., [illegible].
Kilvallytowne, King's co., [illegible].
Kilvallykilly — Kilvallikillie (co. Wat. ?), [illegible], [illegible].
Kilvanaline, co. Cork, [illegible].
Kilvanoline. See Kilmanoline.
Kilvanolane, co. Cork, [illegible].
Kilvanny—Kylvanny, co. Wat., [illegible], [illegible].
Kilvanyhyn. See Kilmanoline.
Kilvartyn. See Kilwartin.
Kilvarned (co. Sligo ?), [illegible].
Kilvarraghane — Kylvarraghane, co. Wat., [illegible].
Kilvasdaine (co. Clare ?), [illegible].
Kilvellan (Kilvellane), co. Tip., rectory, [illegible].

INDEX TO FIANTS—ELIZABETH.

Kilvane — Kylvane — Kylvayne — Kylvane (Kilvelane), Queen's co., 617, 1167, [illegible], [illegible], [illegible].
Kilvechane—Kylvechane, co. Gal., rectory, [illegible], [illegible], [illegible], [illegible].
Kilverne, co. Kerry, [illegible].
Kilvesiagh (co. Kerry ?), 6477.
Kilvegiallie, co. Gal., [illegible].
Kilvegond, co. Sligo, ruined church, [illegible].
Kilvegonne — Kilvegoone, co. Ross., [illegible], [illegible].
Kilvehane, co. Lim., [illegible].
Kilveick—Kylveick, Queen's co., [illegible].
Kilvein (co. Cork ?), [illegible].
Kilvekeragh — Kylvekeragh (co. Clare ?), [illegible].
Kilvelogher—Killwollogher (co. Tip. ?), [illegible], [illegible].
Kilvemine — Kilvemine (Kilvemmon, co. Tip. ?), rectory, [illegible], 9118, [illegible].
Kilvenn, co. Kerry, [illegible], [illegible].
Kilvenane — Kilvenan (Kilbonane ?), co. Cork, parsonage of church, 2373, [illegible], [illegible].
Kilvenient, alias Kylvenyll, co. Cork, [illegible].
Kilvenie (co. Mayo ?), [illegible].
Kilvenien. See Kilvemine.
Kilvenaghe—Kyllvenaghe (co. Tip. ?), [illegible].
Kilvervan (co. Tip. ?), [illegible].
Kilveyrane, co. Clare, [illegible].
Kilvickadowne, co. Cork. See Kyllmack Rome, [illegible].
Kilvickeenan (co. Ross. ?), [illegible].
Kilvickmone—Kylvickmone (co. Ross. ?), 1734.
Kilvickillowe (Kilmacnkillen), co. Donegal, [illegible].
Kilvickrikie—Kyllvickrikie, co. Clare, [illegible], [illegible].
Kilvickowrall, co. Ross., [illegible].
Kilvid—Kylvide (Kilmead), co. Kild., 676, [illegible].
Kilvidi, co. Cork, 4467.
Kilvickill—Kilvyhille—Kylvihille, co. Cork, [illegible], [illegible], [illegible].
Kilvin (co. Gal. ?), [illegible].
Kilvino, co. Cork, [illegible].
Kilvincyn—Kilvinlyn. See Kilvrudne.
Kilvinl (Kilmeen ?), co. Cork, rectory, [illegible].
Kilvinine — Kylvynine (Kilminnin ?), co. Wat., [illegible], [illegible].
Kilvinsine — Kilvinsin — Kilvincyn — Kilvinlyn—Kylvynsyn (Kilmainchy), Queen's co. [illegible], [illegible], [illegible].
Kilviryty, co. Cork, [illegible].
Kilvoichoriane, co. Tip., [illegible].
Kilvolne (co. Cork ?), [illegible].
Kilvolbyne, co. Lim., [illegible].
Kilvolen, co. Cork, [illegible].
Kilvonane—Kilvonan (Kilbonane), co. Kerry, rectory, [illegible], [illegible].
Kilvore—Kilwore (Kilmurry ?), co. Tip., [illegible], [illegible].
Kilvory (co. Cork ?), [illegible], [illegible].
Kilvoy, co. Lim., [illegible].
Kilvoyle—Kylvoyle (co. Cork ?), rectory, [illegible].
Kilvrectain, co. Tip. or Lim., [illegible].
Kilvren (co. Kild. ?), [illegible].
Kilvrin—Kylvrye (King's co. ?), [illegible].
Kilvrone (co. Kilk. ?), [illegible].
Kilvronill, co. Cork, rectory, [illegible].
Kilvry—Kylvry, co. Cork, [illegible], [illegible].
Kilvry, King's co., [illegible].
Kilvryn—Kylvryne (Kilbryne), co. Ross., 1794, [illegible].
Kilvughlormoy (Kilwatermoy), co. Wat., [illegible].
Kilvullane (co. Cork ?), [illegible].
Kilvyclustrone — Kylvyclustrone (Kilmaclenany ?), co. Sligo, 1734.
Kilvyly—Kylvyly (co. Wat. ?), [illegible].
Kilvyhille. See Kilvichill.
Kilvynille—Kylvynille, co. Cork, [illegible].
Kilvynyne (co. Wat. ?), [illegible].
Kilwaragined (co. Kerry ?), [illegible].
Kilwarden, co. Kild. See Kilwarnyng.
Kilwardoran, co. Lim., rectory, [illegible], [illegible].
Kilwarglase, co. Kilk., [illegible].
Kilwarlin — Kilwarlen — Kilvarlyn — Kilwarlinge, country of (parish of Hillsborough and neighborhood in barony of Lower Iveagh, co. Down), surrender and regrant, [illegible].
" to be made shire ground, [illegible].
" pass of, [illegible].
" woods and mines in, [illegible].
" captain and chief of, [illegible].
" governor of forces in, [illegible].
Kilwarnyng—Kylwarnyng (Kilwarden), co. Kild., [illegible].
Kilwarron—Kylwarron, [illegible].
Kilwarrigan, co. Cork, [illegible].
Kilwarryo (Kilbarry), co. Cork, [illegible].
Kilwatermoy, co. Wat., [illegible]. See also Killoghlormoy.
Kilweare—Kylweare (Kilmurry ?), co. Wat., [illegible], [illegible].
Kilwehan, co. Clare, [illegible].
Kilwelogher. See Kilvelogher.
Kilwey (co. Cork ?), [illegible].
Kilwille—Kilwyle (Kilmoyly, co. Kerry ?), rectory, &c., [illegible], [illegible], [illegible].
Kilwilliam (co. Cork ?), [illegible].
Kilwilline (co. Cork ?), [illegible].
Kilwoan—Kylwoan, co. Clare, [illegible], [illegible].
Kilwoldmole, co. Wat., [illegible].
Kilwony, co. Clare, [illegible].
Kilwoonn, co. Clare, [illegible].

INDEX TO FIANTS.—ELIZABETH.

Kilwoorusky, co. Gal., [illegible].
Kilwore. *See* Kilvore.
Kilworby, co. Cork, [illegible].
Kilwurile—Kylworyle, co. Wat., [illegible], [illegible].
Kilworrigho (co. Lim. or Cork), [illegible].
Kilwurib, co. Cork. *See* Killerdy.
Kilworyne, co. Wat., 4142.
Kilwris, co. Wex., 417.
Kilwyle. *See* Kilwille.
Kilwylie, co. Cork, [illegible].
Kilynalougtard—Kylynalougtard, co. Tip., [illegible].
Kilyne—Kylinoe Deboraghe (co. Meath ?), [illegible], [illegible].
Kimmuid, co. Donegal. *See* Carned.
Kimmine, co. Meath. *See* Kenmoine, Kynnyne.
Kinegad — Kynnegad (Kinnegad), co. Westm., [illegible]; castle and land, [illegible].
Kinaloa. *See* Henalea.
Kinalagh—Kenaliagh—Kenaliaghe—Kenaliagh — Kenalagh — Kenaleaghe—Kinaliaghe—Kinnaliagh—Kinnalleaghe—Kynaliagh—Kynaliyaghe—Kynaleagh—Kynnaleigh — Kynyleaghe (Macgeoghegan's country, at this time corresponding with the barony of Moycashel), co. Westm., 1348, [illegible], 1788; chief rent from, to earl of Kildare, 1348; made shire land, 1361; rebels in, [illegible]; surrendered by chief, [illegible]; bounds between it and King's co., [illegible].
„ marital law, [illegible], [illegible], [illegible].
„ seneschal, [illegible], [illegible].
Kinallen, co. Down. *See* Ballinahenmien, [illegible].
Kinalmeaki (Kinalmeaky barony), co. Cork, granted, [illegible].
Kinalmeaky—Kinalmeky, co. Cork, [illegible].
Kinard (co. Long. ?), [illegible].
Kinard, co. Lim. *See* Kynarde.
Kinarde (co. Kerry ?), [illegible].
Kinaye, Margaret fitz Tho., pardon, [illegible].
Kinckhullie (Kinkillew, co. Long. ?), [illegible].
Kincloro—Kyncro (Kincrow, co. Wat. ?), [illegible].
Kinelongo (co. Lim. ?), [illegible].
Kincnan—Kyncone, co. Mayo, [illegible].
(Kincora)—Kyncore—Kyncora, King's co., [illegible], [illegible].
Kincorra (Kincoraugh), co. Mon., [illegible].
Kindelan — Kindelane — Kindellan — Kyndelan:
„ John, pardon, [illegible].
„ Nich., pardon, [illegible].
„ Roland, pardon, [illegible].
„ Tho., pardon, [illegible], [illegible].
Kinderry, co. Kilk., [illegible].
Kindlemorche, Hich., kern, [illegible].
Kinelaff or Blackroll, Diversi Irish exaction, [illegible], [illegible].
Kinearde, co. Kild. *See* Kynnegha.
Kinegh, co. Tip., [illegible].
Kinegh (co. Wex. ?), [illegible], [illegible].
Kinelarty, co. Down. *See* Killelarty, Kynnalerty.
Kinelmeakie, co. Cork, [illegible].
Kinerboy (Killinvoy ?), co. Ross., rectory, [illegible].
Kinestone — Kynneston, grant and title, Queen's co., [illegible], [illegible], [illegible].
King—Kinge—Kyng:
„ Barnaby, lease to, radical, [illegible], [illegible].
„ Broyn, pardon, [illegible].
„ Constance, lease, [illegible].
„ Elizabeth, lease, [illegible].
„ Henry (of Dublin), [illegible], [illegible].
„ Henry (of Ardnurcher, co. Westm.), [illegible], [illegible].
„ Henry (of Castletown in Ossory), pardon, [illegible].
„ John, pardon, [illegible]; commission, [illegible]; pardon of alienation, [illegible]; deputy vice treasurer, [illegible]; grant of a wardship, [illegible].
„ Matthew, comm., [illegible]; lease to, radical, [illegible], [illegible], [illegible]; widow, [illegible].
„ Simon, pardon, [illegible].
„ Thomas, marshal of the Castle Chamber, [illegible]; horseman, [illegible], [illegible].
„ Wm., pardon, [illegible].
Kinges mill, Milton, co. Dub., [illegible].
Kingestone (Kingstown), co. Meath, [illegible].
King's county, commission and return setting out the bounds of county, [illegible]; commissions to reduce to shire ground Fircal, Ely O'Carroll, and other districts not included in original county, [illegible], [illegible], [illegible]; parts formerly included in Westmeath, [illegible], [illegible].
„ lieutenant of, [illegible], [illegible], [illegible].
„ seneschal of, [illegible], [illegible], [illegible], [illegible], [illegible], [illegible], [illegible].
„ lieutenant of fort of Philipstown, [illegible].
„ constable of Philipstown to govern co., [illegible].
„ general of army in, [illegible], [illegible].
„ governor of forces in, [illegible].
„ sheriff, [illegible], 1310, [illegible], [illegible], [illegible], [illegible], [illegible], [illegible], [illegible], [illegible], [illegible], [illegible], [illegible], [illegible].
„ sub-sheriff, [illegible].
„ clerk of crown and peace, [illegible].
„ overseer of tanning, [illegible].

INDEX TO FIANTS.—ELIZABETH.

King's county:
„ commissions of the peace, [illegible], [illegible], [illegible], [illegible], [illegible], [illegible], 4618, [illegible], [illegible], [illegible], [illegible], [illegible], [illegible], [illegible], [illegible], [illegible], [illegible], [illegible].
„ commission of gaol delivery, [illegible].
„ commissions for musters, 2117, [illegible], [illegible], [illegible].
„ martial law, [illegible], [illegible], [illegible], 1190, [illegible].
„ rebels in, [illegible], [illegible].
„ soldiers in, [illegible].
„ earl of Kildare's lands in, [illegible].
„ conditions attached to grants of land in, 474.
„ pardon to men of, [illegible], [illegible], [illegible], [illegible], [illegible], [illegible], [illegible], [illegible], [illegible], &c.
„ gentlemen and inhabitants petition for pardon of certain O'Conors, &c., [illegible].
„ O'Conors excepted from pardon, [illegible], [illegible].
Kingsale. See Kinsale.
King's gardens in Kilmainham, [illegible].
King's highway in Kilmainham, [illegible].
King's Island, Limerick, [illegible], [illegible].
King's meadow in Ballydoud, co. Dub., [illegible], [illegible].
King's mill in manor of Newcastle, co. Dub., [illegible], [illegible].
King's mills, Limerick, [illegible], [illegible].
King's Milton—Mylton, co. Dub., [illegible], [illegible].
King's moor—More, co. Kild., [illegible], [illegible].
Kingstown, co. Meath. See Kingstown.
King's way in Carrick, [illegible].
King's way, co. Kild., [illegible].
Kingswood (co. Westm.?), [illegible].
Kinitty, co. Rosc. See Kennagh.
Kinkanywirisacrect (co. Lim.?), [illegible].
Kinkelly—Kinkellie, co. Mayo, [illegible].
Kinkillew, co. Long. See Kinckhullie.
Kinnakeighane — Kynnakeighan, co. Gal., rectory, [illegible], [illegible].
Kinnalagh—Kinnalloaghe. See Kinaleagh.
Kinnegad, co. Westm. See Kinnegad.
Kinnet — Kynnet — Kynnettie — Kynnitte — Kynnitte—Kynnyte (Kinnitty, King's co.), [illegible], [illegible], [illegible].
Kinnoul, co. Dub. See Kynnewood.
Kinraght, Tho., pardon, 1470.
Kinricke (co. Clare?), [illegible].
Kinsalagh. See Kinsalagh.
Kinsale—Kynsale—Konsale—Konsall—Konsalle—Kingsale—Kinsall—Kinsalle—Kinsalle—Kynsale—Kynsall, co. Cork, [illegible], [illegible], [illegible], [illegible], [illegible], [illegible], [illegible], [illegible], [illegible], 4111, [illegible], [illegible], [illegible], [illegible], [illegible], [illegible], [illegible]; house in, granted, [illegible]; bounds of the franchises of the town, [illegible].
„ sovereign and commons, charter, [illegible].
„ sovereign, commissions, [illegible], [illegible], [illegible], [illegible], [illegible].
„ merchants of, [illegible], [illegible], [illegible], [illegible], [illegible], [illegible], [illegible], [illegible], [illegible], [illegible], 6751.
„ rectory, [illegible], [illegible], [illegible], [illegible].
„ house of friars of B. V. M., [illegible]; leased, [illegible], [illegible].
„ spittle house, [illegible].
„ port, [illegible], [illegible].
„ port, supervisor of, [illegible].
„ suit as to prise wines, [illegible].
„ wine impost leased, [illegible].
„ wine impost collector, [illegible], [illegible], [illegible], [illegible], [illegible], [illegible].
„ wine impost controller, [illegible], [illegible], [illegible], [illegible].
„ gauger and searcher, [illegible], [illegible], [illegible].
„ water and ferry, [illegible].
„ Old head of, [illegible], [illegible].
Kinsalo—Kinsalle—Kynsalle (Kinsalebeg), co. Wat., [illegible], [illegible]; chapel, [illegible], [illegible].
Kinsallagh. See Kinselagh.
Kinsalle. See Kinsale.
Kinselagh — Kinselaghe — Kinshelaghe — Kinshelaughe — Kinsellaghe — Kynselaghe — Kynselo — Kynsellagh — Kynsellaghe (a district in N.E. of co. Wexford), [illegible], [illegible], [illegible], [illegible], [illegible].
„ customs due from, [illegible].
„ surrender of, [illegible].
„ chief serjeant of, [illegible], [illegible].
Kinselagh—Kinselaghe—Kinsellagh—Kinselaugh — Kinsellagh — Kinshelagh —Kinsheloghe—Kinshelagh — Kinslagh—Kynselagh:
„ Arthur m'Donogh, pardon, [illegible].
„ Cowne, pardon, [illegible], [illegible].
„ Donald m'Morogh, attainted, [illegible].
„ Donogh, pardon, [illegible], [illegible], [illegible], [illegible].
„ Edm., pardon, [illegible].
„ Fahy, pardon, [illegible].
„ Gerald or Gerrot, pardon, [illegible], [illegible].
„ John, pardon, [illegible], [illegible], [illegible].
„ Kirrow, pardon, [illegible].
„ Owen or One, pardon, [illegible], [illegible], [illegible].

Kinsalagh:
" " Phelim, pardon, [illegible].
" Teig, pardon, 1897, [illegible].
" Thomas, pardon, [illegible].
Kinsella. See Kinsale.
Kinsalagh—Kinshalaghe—Kinshelaughe—Kinshelagh—Kinsillaghe—Kinselagh. See Kinsalagh.
Kinsalon—Kynsalon, King's co., [illegible].
Kintarke (co. Westm.?), [illegible].
Kintogre, co. Cork. See Kyntyre.
Kintilarrevighe, co. Gal., [illegible].
Kinlogher (Ganlogher), co. Lim., [illegible].
Kinturke (co. Westm.?), [illegible].
Kinturke—Kynturke, co. Mayo, [illegible].
Kintavke—Kintark (co. Sligo?), [illegible].
Kinturley (co. Gal.?) [illegible].
Kinur, co. Cork, [illegible].
Kinvilshin, Queen's co., [illegible].
Kinwelmershe, Rich., general clerk of musters, 4817, 5418.
" See Kinillmershe.
Kioghtegarrol, co. Tip. or Kilk., [illegible].
Kiolstion—Kyolistion, co. Westm., 1448, 1877.
Kippagh (co. Wat.?), [illegible], 2771.
Kippane—Kippan—Kyppane, co. Cork, [illegible], 6488; grant, [illegible].
Kipplheden, [illegible]. See Copyrhodyn.
Kirbe, John, grant of a wardship, [illegible].
Kirck. See Kirke.
Kiryleison. See Kyrieleison.
Kirikle (co. Wick.?), [illegible].
Kirke (co. Mayo?), [illegible].
Kirke—Kirck—Kyrck—Kyrke:
" John m'Gerrot, pardon, [illegible].
" Nich. fitz Wm., pardon, [illegible].
" Thomas, pardon, [illegible].
Walter, lands of, granted, [illegible]; pardon, [illegible].
" Wm., pardon, [illegible], [illegible].
Kirky, Tho., pardon, [illegible].
Kiroan, Andrew fitz David, pardon, [illegible].
Kiroyne, Stephen, dean of Clonfert, [illegible].
Kirowan, Ambrose, pardon, [illegible].
Kirrane (co. Cork?), [illegible].
Kirvane, Mahon m'Donogh, pardon, [illegible].
Kirrchye—Kyrreky (co. Wick.?), 1038, 1846.
Kirrehill, co. Kilk., [illegible].
Kirwan, Patrick fitz Edm., pardon, [illegible].
" Robuck, pardon, [illegible].
Kirwick, Derby, pardon, [illegible].
Kissequrin. See Kissickurk.
Kishane, Wm., pardon, [illegible].
Kishawarny, co. Kild. See Cashawran.
Kissane, Donell m'Teig I., pardon, [illegible].
" John m'Wm. I., pardon, [illegible].
" See Kysseyn.

Kissickurk—Kissonrirke—Kissourke—Kisshourirke—Kyshourke, co. Lim., [illegible], [illegible], [illegible], [illegible], [illegible].
Kisillagmore, co. Wex., 417.
Kittagh, Conner, Dermod and Donogho, pardon, [illegible].
" Dermod, pardon, [illegible].
" John m'Dermodie, pardon, [illegible].
" Redmund, pardon, [illegible].
Kivagh, David m'Wm., pardon, [illegible].
Kivalalie, co. Lim., [illegible].
Kive, Donogh m'David I., pardon, [illegible].
Klancolleman. See Clancoleman.
Klankonealy, Donald m'Donell m'Tirlagh of, pardon, [illegible].
Klanlish. See Clanlish.
Klanrery, Teig m'Mortiherty m'Rory, pardon, [illegible].
Klinbrisloghes (Clanbrassalagh), co. Armagh, 4877.
Klincolman. See Clancolman.
Klinkarill (co. Car.?), [illegible].
Klinvolium (co. Cav.?), [illegible].
Klongro (co. Mayo?), [illegible].
Kloghlond (Cloghlond?), co. Tip., [illegible].
Kloghran—Kloghrane, co. Gal., [illegible], [illegible].
Kloinlomane, co. Wat., [illegible].
Klonowlan in Thomond, [illegible].
Klonloite. See Clondoty.
Klonobolge. See Clonbolge.
Klonchorke. See Clonchorke.
Klonkurillen (Cloncurlin), co. Kild., [illegible].
Klonkar (co. Lim.?), [illegible].
Klonkrevyn (Clonreven), King's co., [illegible].
Klonlishard. See Clonlishard.
Klonmwin. See Clonmadie.
Klonsast—Klonsasto. See Clonsast.
Kloynkyne. See Cloynekyne.
Klyntrusselagh (Clanbrassalagh, co. Armagh, 4877.
Klynkonny. See Clankonny.
Knabilly (Knawbill, co. Cork), [illegible].
Knapoke. See Knappock.
Knapp, Thomas, pardon, [illegible].
Knappagh, co. Mayo, [illegible].
Knappock—Cnappock—Knapoke—Knappock, co. Clare, 1840, 4781, [illegible]; castle, [illegible].
Knappog, co. Clare, [illegible].
Knawbill, co. Cork. See Knabilly.
Knenaghe, Moriah, pardon, 1710.
Kniho—Knoy (Knigh?), co. Tip., [illegible], [illegible].
" See also Ceeyaghe.
Knighan (King's co.?), [illegible].
Knight, Ralph, lease, [illegible]; assignee of, [illegible], [illegible].
Knight Marshal, [illegible].
Knight of the Valley or Knight of the Glenn (Thomas Fitzgerald, Knight of Glin, attainted, [illegible], [illegible], [illegible], [illegible], [illegible], [illegible].

INDEX TO FIANTS—ELIZABETH.

Knight of the Valley, Edm. fitzTho. Gerald, excepted from pardon, 6774.
Knightleston—Knightliston, co. Meath, [illegible], [illegible], [illegible].
Knights Cowrte, co. Lim., 3478.
Knight's fee, the quantity of an ancient[illegible], [illegible].
Knight's free land, co. Lim., [illegible].
Knights' lands in Magino, co. Kerry, [illegible].
Knight's street (Knightstreet), co. Lim., granted, [illegible].
Kniltstown, co. Meath, 4714.
Knive Kille (see Goyvokyall), co. Westm., 4378.
Knivan sidon, 497.
Knocnalyagh (co. Tip. ?), [illegible].
Knocbracke. See Knockbrake.
Knocbrek, Queen's co., 871.
Knochry, co. Meath, 464.
Knocrun, co. Lim., 4690.
Knock, John, pardon, 618.
Knock, co. Armagh. See Knockballydonnaboy.
Knock (co. Clare ?), [illegible], 6401, [illegible].
Knock—Cnock (co. Fermanagh), [illegible].
Knock—Cnock—Cnocke, co. Gal., [illegible], [illegible], [illegible].
Knock (King's or Queen's co. ?), [illegible].
Knock (co. Long. ?), [illegible].
Knock—Knocke—Knoke, co. Louth, 714, 1781, [illegible], [illegible], [illegible].
„ abbey of, possessions leased, [illegible], [illegible], [illegible].
Knock—Knocke, co. Meath, 1843, 1412, [illegible], [illegible], [illegible].
Knock—Knocke, Queen's co., [illegible].
Knock (co. Tip. ?), [illegible].
Knock, co. Westm. or King's, [illegible].
Knock—Knocke, co. Westm., [illegible], [illegible].
Knockabeany, co. Mon. See Knockbilein.
Knockacuttig, co. Cork, [illegible].
Knockaderry, co. Lim. See Knockaderry.
Knockaderry, co. Wick. See Knockaderrie.
Knockadoo, co. Sligo. See Knockadowe.
Knockagh (Knocker), co. Antrim, [illegible].
Knockagh (co. Kilk. ?), [illegible].
Knockagh — Cnockagh, co. Tip., [illegible], [illegible], [illegible], [illegible].
Knockagh, co. Wex., [illegible].
Knockagho (co. Long.), 1032.
Knockaghae—Cnockaghan (co. Fermanagh ?), [illegible].
Knockainy, co. Lim. See Aney.
Knockaird—Knokeird, co. Westm., [illegible].
Knockakirwan, co. Mon. See Knockyrvan.
Knockamanyne, in Arra, co. Tip., [illegible].
Knockamore, co. Meath, [illegible].
Knockampar (Knockampower), co. Wat., [illegible], [illegible].
Knockan, David in, pardon, [illegible].
Knockan, co. Gal., in O'Flaherty's country, [illegible].
Knockan, King's co., [illegible].
Knockan (co. Tip. or Lim.), [illegible].
Knockan (co. Tip. ?), [illegible].
Knockan (co. Wat. ?), [illegible].
Knockan, co. Westm., [illegible].
Knockane—Cnockane, co. Gal., [illegible].
Knockanallany (co. Clare ?), [illegible].
Knockanatan (co. Long. ?), [illegible].
Knockanbranshan (co. Wat. ?), [illegible].
Knockan brogagh, King's co., [illegible], [illegible].
Knockanbroghe (Knocknagreagh ?), Queen's co., [illegible].
Knockan[illegible] (co. Wat. ?), [illegible].
Knockanconer—Cnockan[illegible] (co. Leit. ?), [illegible].
Knockananne, Queen's co., 871.
Knockan[illegible] (co. Lim. ?), [illegible].
Knockancowskore—Cnockancowskore, co. Clare, [illegible].
Knockandillon, Queen's co., [illegible].
Knockandontork — Knockandontorek, co. Wat., [illegible], [illegible].
Knockane, Donell Y, pardon, [illegible].
Knockane (co. Tip. ?), [illegible], [illegible].
Knockane—Cnockane (Knockanne), co. Wat., [illegible], [illegible].
Knockanecroghe in manor of Carlow, [illegible].
Knockane Eoltie, co. Kerry, 6717.
Knockaneclonerie, co. Kerry, [illegible].
Knockanegall (Knockangall), co. Wex., 5794.
Knockanegole or Knockingwodd, co. Meath, [illegible].
Knockaneo in Vodity, co. Lim., [illegible].
Knockane[illegible] (co. Cork ?), [illegible].
Knockanepearinge in Munster, [illegible].
Knockan Brelly, co. Kerry, [illegible].
Knockanesluske, co. Kerry, [illegible].
Knockaney, co. Cork, [illegible].
Knockaneyvye, co. Wat., [illegible].
Knockangall, co. Wex. See Knockanegall.
Knockangarrowe — Knockancaroghe — Knockanganwen — Knockangoregh, co. Wex., [illegible], [illegible], [illegible], [illegible], [illegible], [illegible].
Knockanilbuige, co. Kerry, [illegible], [illegible].
Knockan in O'Flaherty, co. Gal., [illegible].
Knockanlouhim, co. Kerry, [illegible].
Knockannityrie—Knockannityrre, Queen's co., [illegible].
Knockanmore, co. Cork, [illegible].
Knockan na lailgeagh — Cnockan nalailgeagh (co. Tyrone ?), [illegible], [illegible].
Knockannarogoo, co. Tip., [illegible].
Knockanneagan, co. Westm., [illegible].
Knockannegow, Queen's co., [illegible].

Knockaniemle—Caonkanacmle (co. Tip. or Lim.), [illegible].
Knockanpower, co. Wat. See Knockampar, Knockpower.
Knockanquin—Knockanquyne, King's co., 617, [illegible].
Knockanmawne, co. Wex., 1677.
Knockansmore alias Knockanmore, co. Wex., [illegible].
Knockanstickan (Knockanstickane), co. Cork, [illegible].
Knockantemaker, Queen's co. [illegible].
Knockanihyneslery, co. Cork, [illegible].
Knockanure, co. Kerry. See Knockanure.
Knockanvallemastyn, co. Cork, [illegible].
Knockaswig (co. Wat. ?), 5746.
Knockanycaner, co. Ross. See Knockyn-canagher.
Knockanybeige, co. Kerry, [illegible].
See also Knockanibeige.
Knockanyvarody (co. Cork ?), [illegible].
Knockapireaghann, co. Clare. See Knockoy-preghane.
Knockaphubble, co. Mon. See Knockpubble.
Knockardagur, Queen's co. See Knockard Khorre.
Knockardibleghiane, co. Cork, [illegible].
Knockardo, co. Cork, [illegible].
Knockardoblenghane, co. Cork, [illegible].
Knockard Khorre (Knockardagur), Queen's co., [illegible], [illegible].
Knockargua, co. Cork, [illegible].
Knockarigg, co. Wick. See Crockwriek, Knockoricke, Knockwricke.
Knockarny, co. Tip., [illegible].
Knockasha (co. Tip. ?), [illegible].
Knockast (co. Westm. ?), [illegible].
Knockastickane, co. Cork. See Knockan-stickan.
Knockastye, mountain (co. Westm. ?), [illegible].
Knockath, co. Westm. (co. Long. ?), [illegible].
Knockane, co. Mayo. See Carironknockane.
Knockaum, co. Wat. See Knockane.
Knockaunbane, co. Mayo. See Cnocano-bane, [illegible].
Knockavilly, co. Cork. See Knock Ivilla.
Knockavulla, co. Mon. See Ballyknockan-[illegible].
Knockballebreanboy (perhaps Knock, par. Seagoe, co. Armagh), 4277.
Knockballenan, co. Tip., [illegible].
Knockballiephowreen—Knockballiphowreen (co. Lim. or Tip. ?), [illegible].
Knockbarron, co. Kilk. See Knockwar-rowre.
Knockbegg, co. Meath, [illegible].
Knockborragh (Knockbarragh), co. Down, [illegible].
Knockbogtagh—Knockboghan, [illegible], [illegible].
Knockboy, co. Car. See Knockroy.
Knockboy — Knockeboy, co. Meath, [illegible], 3162.
Knockboy — Cnockboy, co. Long., [illegible], 3771.
Knockbrawlran, co. Lim., [illegible].
Knockbrack—Cnockbrack (Knockbrack), co. Lim., [illegible].
Knockbracke—Knockbracke (Knockbrack), co. Wat., [illegible].
Knockbreyn, 671.
Knockbride, co. Cav., [illegible].
rectory, [illegible].
Knockbryanegarrowe (co. Ross. ?), [illegible].
Knockburden, co. Cork. See Knockybur-denaghe.
Knockbury, co. Long., [illegible].
Knockbyllandyn, rectory in co. Lim., [illegible].
Knockcame (co. Westm. ?), [illegible].
Knockcaurd, co. Westm., [illegible].
Knockcowgan—Cnockcowgan (Coggansbill, co. Cork ?), [illegible].
Knockcraffan —Knockcraffan. See Knock-graffan.
Knockcroghery, co. Ross. See Knockrogh-ery.
Knockdallye, co. Cork, [illegible].
Knockdallin (co. Sligo ?), [illegible].
Knockdlorke (co. Lim. ?), [illegible].
Knockdloe, co. Gal. See Leighcarrowe Knockdwe.
Knockdowe (co. Ross. ?), [illegible].
Knockdowe (perhaps Knockedoe, co. Gal.), [illegible].
Knockdromon, co. Dub., [illegible].
Knockduffeleny, co. Lim., [illegible].
Knocke. See Knock.
Knocke, Ellen, [illegible].
Knockeagliane (Knockcabane ? co. Ross.), [illegible], [illegible].
Knockeangdon, co. Dub. (Wick. ?), [illegible].
Knockearnaywle, in Munster, [illegible].
Knockearnagh, co. Kerry. See Knockmaghe.
Knockeawarde—Knockeaward (co. Meath ?), 5157, [illegible].
Knockeballi Loghvany, co. Tip., [illegible].
Knockeballynaslinan, co. Clare, [illegible].
Knockebanakeneferyn, co. Clare, [illegible].
Knockeboy. See Knockboy.
Knockebride. See Knockbride.
Knockecashel—Cnockeacashe, co. Long., [illegible], 4607.
Knockeahill (co. Cork ?), [illegible].
Knockecloghpell — Cnockcohappell (co. Mon. ?), [illegible].
Knockeloran, co. Wat., [illegible].
Knockederrie, in Ymale (Knockaderry, co. Wick.), 6111.
Knockederry (Knockaderry, co. Lim.), [illegible].

INDEX TO FIANTS—ELIZABETH.

Knocke Drenie (co. Rosc. ?), [illegible].
Knockeen, co. Cav. See Knockyne.
Knockearkey (co. Lim. ?), [illegible].
Knockeferguis. See Carrickfergus.
Knockegan (co. Wick. ?), [illegible].
Knockeheallo—Knockeballe, co. Tip., [illegible], [illegible].
Knocke Idowe (co. Rosc. ?), [illegible].
Knockeirghbery (co. Rosc. ?), [illegible].
Knocke Ivilly. See Knock Ivilla.
Knockekillie, co. Tip., [illegible].
Knockelaghe (co. Rosc. ?), [illegible].
Knockelaghte, co. Rosc., [illegible].
Knockelegan—Cnockelogan (co. Lim. ?), [illegible].
Knockelegan (co. Mayo or Rosc. ?), [illegible].
Knockelly—Knockelli—Cnockelly, co. Tip., [illegible], [illegible], [illegible].
Knockelonge (see Kno[illegible]), [illegible].
Knockemeane—Knockemean. See Knockeman.
Knockemore — Knockemorne (Knockmorne), co. Cork, rectory, [illegible], [illegible].
Knockemoy. See Knockmoy.
Knocken—Knockene—Cnocken—Knockin—Cnoken, co. Car., 1477, [illegible], [illegible], [illegible], [illegible], [illegible].
See also Knockyn, and Knockyne.
Knockenaghe (Knockenaagh), co. Kerry, [illegible].
Knockenanam, co. Tip., [illegible].
Knockenanymy, co. Tip., [illegible].
Knockenarte, co. Mayo (Gal. ?), [illegible].
Knockenbein (co. Kilk.), [illegible].
Knockencallagh—Cnockencaylinghe alias Callaughton, co. Kild., [illegible], [illegible].
Knockencasher, co. Lim., [illegible].
Knockeneen. See Knockeen.
Knockenemarragh — Knokenemarragh, co. Wat., [illegible], [illegible].
Knockenergappoll — Cnockenegappull, co. Cork, [illegible].
Knockenough (co. Lim. ?), [illegible].
Knockenogarton — Knockenegarton. See Knockenegarlone.
Knockenemanagh. See Knocknemanagh.
Knockenemnemolagh, [illegible].
Knockenemango (co. Clare ?), [illegible].
Knockenegan, co. Dub., [illegible], [illegible].
Knockenskilly—Knockenskylly, co. Kilk. or Tip., [illegible], [illegible].
Knockenmalyn, [illegible].
Knockenore (co. Lim. ?), [illegible].
Knockenrodie (co. Tip. ?), [illegible].
Knockenasho (co. Cork ?), [illegible].
Knockenmall (co. Tip. ?), [illegible].
Knockentemoycastlen, co. Lim., [illegible].
Knockenure—Cnockenowre (Knockanure), co. Kerry, [illegible]; grant, [illegible]; rectory, [illegible].
Knockenvar, co. Kerry, [illegible].
Knockenville — Cnockenville (co. Cork ?), [illegible].
Knockenyn (Knockinean, co. Wick. ?), [illegible].
Knockenyrre (co. Tip. ?), [illegible].
Knocker, co. Ant. See Knockagh.
Knocker—Cnocker (co. Lim. ?), [illegible].
Knocker (co. Wick. ?), [illegible].
Knockeraffre, co. Wat., [illegible].
Knockeridge, co. Kerry, [illegible].
Knockernoghtie, co. Kerry, [illegible].
Knockeston — Knockestone (Knockstown), co. Wex., [illegible], [illegible].
Knocketonegeneline (co. Lim. ?), [illegible].
Knocketogher, co. Kilk., [illegible].
Knockevillig, co. Kerry, [illegible].
Knockeville—Cnockeville (co. Cork ?), [illegible], [illegible].
Knockeville — Cnockeville (co. Cork ?), [illegible], [illegible], [illegible].
Knockewirgyn, co. Kild., [illegible].
Knockeyproghane (Knockaphroghane), co. Clare, [illegible].
Knockfind, co. Cav. See Cnokfade.
Knockfad — Cnockfadd (Knockfadda, co. Wick.), [illegible], [illegible].
Knockfargus. See Carrickfergus.
Knockfarrin, co. Mayo, [illegible].
Knockfergus, [illegible].
Knockfergus—Knockfirgus. See Carrickfergus.
Knockfin — Knockfyn — Knockfynne, co. Clare, [illegible], [illegible], [illegible].
Knockforie (co. Wat. ?) [illegible].
Knockfynne. See Knockfin.
Knockgarrancrahyn, co. Tip., [illegible].
Knockgur (co. Lim. ?), [illegible].
Knockgormanagh (co. Don.), [illegible].
Knockgurragh—Cnockgurragh (co. Wick. ?), [illegible].
Knockglasmony (co. Wex. ?), [illegible].
Knockglass — Knockglasse, co. Mayo, [illegible], [illegible].
Knockglasse (co. Kerry or Lim. ?), [illegible].
Knockglasse — Cnockglasse, co. Rosc., [illegible], [illegible].
Knockglenwony (co. Wex. ?), [illegible].
Knockgogna (co. Cork ?), [illegible].
Knockgraffon — Knockgraffan — Knockgraffon — Knockgraffin — Knockgraffine — Knockgraffan — Knockgraffon — Cnockgraffin — Cnockgraffyn — Cnockgraffune, co. Tip., [illegible], [illegible], [illegible], [illegible], [illegible], [illegible], [illegible], [illegible], [illegible], [illegible], [illegible], [illegible]; rectory, [illegible], [illegible].
Knockhaveglash — Cnockhaveglash (co. Wat. ?), [illegible].
Knockheale, co. Tip., [illegible].
Knockhibla (Knockabeaty ?), co. Meath, [illegible].

INDEX TO FIANTS—ELIZABETH.

Knockiawo (co. Cork ?), 6632.
Knocki Garrigne—Knockicarignae—Cnocki-carrigne, co. Cork, 6[illegible], [illegible], 6571.
Knock Iearna, co. Down, 4237.
Knockiorna, co. Wick. See Knockcoyrn.
Knockigogane—Knockigogaine. See Knock-ygogaine.
Knockikhiriell—Knockikhirell, co. Cork, [illegible], [illegible].
Knockillan (Knockiclland), co. Meath, 1460.
Knockillogenan (co. Tip. ?), [illegible].
Knockilwhohle (co. Cork ?), [illegible].
Knockin. See Knockon.
Knockinagh, co. Kerry, [illegible].
Knockinabo, co. Kerry, [illegible].
Knockinalkie, co. Clare, [illegible].
Knockinboske (co. Tip. ?), [illegible].
Knockinoshilogra, co. Gal., [illegible], [illegible].
Knockinespull (Knockongnypolo), co. Cork, [illegible].
Knockine, co. Car., 1744.
Knockine, Shane o, pardon, [illegible].
Knockinsigh (co. Lim. ?), [illegible].
Knockinskiev, co. Down. See Ballyknock-maliar, Knockmyllar.
Knockinomeraghi, 6574.
Knockingwold or Knockinnegolo, co. Meath, [illegible].
Knockinlonky, co. Tip., [illegible], 6760.
Knockinnagrow (Knocknagraugh), Queen's co., [illegible].
Knockiaros (co. Lim. ?), [illegible].
Knockiquenmalins (co. Lim. ?), 6[illegible].
Knockiginafe (co. Cork ?), [illegible].
Knockievalley, co. Sligo, 4[illegible].
Knockishell—Knockishall, co. Wex., [illegible], 4[illegible].
Knockislaud, co. Meath. See Knockillan.
Knockitoma (co. Cork ?), 6[illegible].
Knock Ivagan—Cnock Ivagan (co. Long. ?), [illegible].
Knock Ivillo—Knockivillio—Knockivilly—Knocke Ivilly—Knockyvillie—Knockno-villo—Knocyvillio—Cnocky villy (Knocke-villy, co. Cork), 4[illegible], 4418, 4457, [illegible], [illegible], [illegible], [illegible], 6764; patronage of church, [illegible], [illegible], [illegible].
Knockivilly (co. Cork ?), [illegible].
Knockkeanagown—Cnock keanagown—Cnocke-keanagown (Crockmacunny ?, co. Don.), [illegible], [illegible].
Knockkeaghan (co. Lim. ?), [illegible].
Knocklaga, co. Mayo, 4[illegible].
Knocklegan—Cnocklegan (co. Lim. ?), [illegible].
Knockling (co. Wick. ?), [illegible].
Knocklisaragh, co. Mayo, [illegible].
Knocklinghie, co. Tip., [illegible].
Knockloghly (Knock ofly, co. Tip.), 6763, 67[illegible].
Knockloghy (co. Cork ?), [illegible].
Knocklonghy, co. Tip., [illegible].
Knockloghlit (co. Cork or Tip.), 67[illegible].
Knocklongy—Knocklonge—Knocklongy—Knocklongie—Knocklungy—Knocklonge—Knocklongie—Cnocklonghy—Cnocklongy—Cnocklonghy—Cnocklungie—Cnock-longy, co. Lim., 10[illegible], 12[illegible], 1760, [illegible], [illegible], [illegible], 4176, 4712, [illegible], [illegible], [illegible], [illegible], [illegible], [illegible]. See also Lolage, Loyage.
Knocklown, co. Car., [illegible].
Knockloy (co. Car. ?), [illegible].
Knocklunny, [illegible]. See Knocklongy.
Knocklyne—Cnocklyne, co. Dub., [illegible], [illegible], 4678.
Knockmagillan, co. Kerry, [illegible].
Knockmanline, co. Kilk., 6764.
Knockmanon, co. Wat. See Knockmoan.
Knockmarke—Knockmarke—Knockmarke—Knockmark, co. Meath, [illegible], [illegible], [illegible], [illegible], [illegible], [illegible]; rectory, [illegible]; parish, [illegible].
Knockmaria, co. Mayo (Gal. ?), [illegible].
Knockmaroan, co. Rosc., 4567.
Knockmoelan—Cnockmoelan, co. Kilk., 1[illegible].
Knockmonan, co. Kerry, [illegible], [illegible].
Knockmonel, co. Westm., 1[illegible].
Knockmallry, co. Kild., [illegible].
Knockmiehie—Cnockmiehie (co. Lim. ?), [illegible].
Knockminé, co. Westm., [illegible].
Knockmoan—Cnockmoan, co. Kilk., [illegible].
Knockmoane—Knockmoune—Knockmone—Knockmoane—Knockmone—Knock-mowan—Knockmoyo (Knockmoan ?), co. Wat., [illegible], [illegible], 1914, [illegible], [illegible], [illegible], [illegible], [illegible], [illegible], [illegible], 4587, [illegible].
Knockmockylyne, co. Cork, [illegible].
Knockmockylyne, co. Cork, [illegible].
Knockmoelan, co. Kilk., 4794.
Knockmone. See Knockmoane.
Knockmony (co. Kerry ?), 4576.
Knockmonoyne, co. Lim., [illegible], 6751.
Knockmor, co. Sligo, house of friars, leased, [illegible].
Knockmore, co. Sligo, 6476.
Knockmorny—Cnockmorney, co. Cork, 4676.
vicar of, 5136.
Knockmorran, Queen's co., [illegible].
Knockmowan. See Knockmoan.
Knockmoy—Knockmoy—Knockmoye—Cnockmoy (Abbey Knock-moy), co. Gal., [illegible], [illegible], [illegible].
abbey, called Collis Victoriae, [illegible], [illegible]; leased, [illegible], [illegible], [illegible]; its possessions leased, [illegible], [illegible], [illegible]; granted, [illegible].

INDEX TO FIANTS—ELIZABETH.

Knockmoylan — Cnockmoylan, co. Kilk., [illegible], [illegible], 6704.
Knockmoyle, co. Gal., [illegible].
Knockmoyn. See Knockmonn.
Knockmullion — Knockmullvin, co. Sligo, [illegible].
Knockmunihie (co. Lim. ?), 5042.
Knockmylle, co. Louth, bridge of, 1188.
Knockmyne — Cnockmyne (co. Kild. ?), [illegible].
Knocknabooly, co. Lim. See Knocknobwolly.
Knocknaclough—Cnocknaclough, co. Long., 5712.
Knocknagapple, co. Cork. See Knocknacapell.
Knocknagaul, co. Lim. See Cnocknegall.
Knocknagortecny, co. Lim. See Cnocknogortyn, Knocknegradone.
Knocknagranshy, co. Lim. See Knocknogransie.
Knocknagrough, Queen's co. See Knocknagroghe, Knockhanegrew.
Knocknagulshy, co. Mayo. See Knocknogulshe.
Knocknamarriff, co. Cork. See Knocknomarolfe.
Knocknamona, co. Cork. See Knocknymonye.
Knocknamore, co. Sligo, 6430.
Knocknobwolly — Cnocknobuolly (Knocknabooly, co. Lim. ?), 6473, 6504.
Knocknotemple, co. Cork, 5547.
Knocknoeigh (co. Lim. ?), 4512.
Knocknofough (co. Wick. ?), 2202.
Knocknogappe—Cnocknogappe (co. Cork ?), [illegible].
Knocknogappell — Knocknogaple (Knocknacappull), co. Cork, [illegible], 6792.
Knocknogh, [illegible].
Knocknogippaghe, co. Cork, 6117.
Knocknogirvane, co. Cav., 4834.
Knocknogowle (co. Cork ?), [illegible].
Knocknogransie—Knocknogranshy—Cnocknagransie—Cnocknogranshy (Knocknagranshy), co. Lim., 4185, 4518, 6457, [illegible].
Knocknogulshe—Knocknogulshie (Knocknagulshy), co. Mayo, [illegible], 6018.
Knocknogradone — Knocknogurtion — Knocknogurtion—Cnocknogurtyn (Knocknagortecny), co. Lim., 455, 6034.
Knocknomanagh — Knocknomanaghe —Knocknomanagh, co. Gal., [illegible], [illegible], 4816, [illegible] ; grant, [illegible].
Knocknomarolfe—Knocknomarolfe (Knocknamarriff), co. Cork, 5941, 6161.
Knocknomuck — Cnocknomuck, co. Wat., 2779, 2783, [illegible].
Knocknomurry, co. Westm., 1340.
Knocknomulbough — Cnocknomulbough, (co. Gal. ?), [illegible].
Knocknonirrie, co. Kerry, [illegible].
Knocknoscahire—Knocknoscaharie, co. Wat., [illegible], 6132.
Knocknoskennoke (co. Ross. ?), 5462.
Knocknose, co. Ross., 6344.
Knocknosh (co. Ross. ?), [illegible].
Knocknosparre, co. Clare, 4562.
Knocknoshiby, co. Ross., 1340.
Knocknoshy (co. Ross. ?), 6346.
Knocknosille — Knocknosilaghe (Wilkeyhill ?), co. Cork, 5767, [illegible].
Knocknoskagh — Knocknoskeagh (co. Ross. ?), 2841, 4778.
Knocknosse, co. Cork, 5747.
Knock ne skeagh — Cnocke ne skeagh, co. Dun., 4278.
Knocknotory (co. Wat. ?), [illegible].
Knocknosulock, co. Wex., 5047.
Knocknosure, 1286.
Knocknosy—Cnocknosy, co. Ross., 4332.
Knocknotyniell, co. Tip., [illegible].
Knocknovilla. See Knock Ivilla.
Knocknowille or Rockville courte, co. Wat., [illegible].
Knocknoy Callen (co. Kerry ?), 4408.
Knocknurnanagh (co. Cork ?), [illegible].
Knocknobwolly (Knocknabooly), co. Lim., 4478.
Knocknybrerdownaghe (Knockburden, co. Cork), 5152.
Knocknyleagh (co. Cork ?), [illegible].
Knoc nykeasy, co. Cork, 5714.
Knocknyller (Knockinckiller ? co. Down), [illegible].
Knocknymanagh, co. Cork, 5941.
Knocknymogh (co. Cork ?), 6518.
Knocknymonye (Knocknamona), co. Cork, 5804.
Knocknyshypane, co. Cork, 1878.
Knockogronyne, co. Cork, 5573, [illegible], [illegible].
Knockomer, co. Meath, 674.
Knockonye, co. Louth, 1722.
Knockorolan (co. Tip. ?), 6678.
Knockorkiko (Knockartgg, co. Wick.), 594, 6061.
Knockorn, [illegible].
Knockorne, [illegible].
Knockoryn (co. Mon. ?), 6563.
Knockoskehane (Knockskehan), co. Ross. 6342.
Knockowgan, co. Cork, 5747.
Knockowlusy (co. Clare or Tip. ?), 5765.
Knockowrane (co. Cork ?), 5571.
Knockpatrick — Cnockpatrick, co. Lim., 1923, 5073, 6401, [illegible].
Knockpoore (Knockanpowry, co. Wat. ?), 1667.

INDEX TO FIANTS—ELIZABETH.

Knockpuble (Knockaphubble), co. Mon., 6465.
Knockra—Knockrae. See Knockraith, co. Wick.
Knockragen (co. Wick. ?), 1098.
Knockragh. See Knockraith.
Knockrahie—Cnockrahie (co. Cork ?), 6405.
Knockran (co. Wick.), 2842.
Knockraith—Knockra—Knockrae—Knockragh (co. Wick.), 1845, 2202, 4164, 6077.
Knockraith—Cnockraith, rectory, 1820.
Knockrawre (co. Cork ?), 4784.
Knockrawre—Cnockrawre (co. Cork ?), 6457, 6671.
Knockre—Cnockre in Fartry (co. Wick.), 6540.
Knockrea (co. Wick.), 1346.
Knockrine (co. Cork or Kerry), 6070.
Knockro—Cnockro (co. Gal. ?), 6478.
Knockro, co. Kilk., 4528.
Knockrochery. See Knockrogeory.
Knockroe, co. Lim., 6873.
Knockroe, 5490.
Knockroghery—Cnockrochery (Knockcroghery, co. Rosc.), 3459, 6478.
Knockroo (co. Car. ?), 878, 6155.
Knockroe—Cnockroe (co. Leit. ?), 5473.
Knockroray, mountain, co. Kilk., 1617.
Knockrua, co. Gal., 4580.
Knockrewry—Cnockrewry (co. Rosc. ?), 5428.
Knockullighane, co. Cork, 6122.
Knockawry—Cnockawry (Knockaruna ?), co. Lim., 2781.
Knockacuro, 6541.
Knockesamhane (co. Kilk. ?), 2044.
Knockeequer (Knockycosker), co. Westm., 6289.
Knockshanavoie—Knockshanvole—Knockshaevoy (Knockshanawee), co. Cork, 5373, 6260, 6298.
Knockshehan, co. Rosc. See Knockonghane, Knockoshehane, Knockohehane.
Knockshill—Knocksnyll, co. Louth, 7027, 3961, 5697.
Knocksawne, co. Lim. See Knockawry.
Knockquar, co. Car., 1746.
Knockslowre, co. Wex. See Knocktown.
Knocktalane, co. Mayo, 5784.
Knocktane—Knocktane, co. Sligo, 5524, 5601.
Knocktincher (co. Westm. ?), 6596.
Knocktofer—Knocktofter—Knocktogher—Knoctoire—Cnoctofer—Cnoctofer (Knocktopher), co. Kilk., 60, 628, 685, 1018, 1618, 2529, 2331, 3944, 3650, 3940, 4850, 5268, 6447, 6537, 6704.
" provost and commonalty, pardoned, 5575.
" priory, 109, 1066.
Knocktom, 718.
Knocktoughter, co. Wex., 4091.
Knocktowne, co. Wex., 6018, 6759.
Knocktwo (Knocktelope), co. Gal., 5810.
Knockurke (co. Kilk. ?), 6167.
Knockvallisdaun (co. Lim. ?), 6190.
Knockvievarie (Knockvicar), co. Rosc., 5486.
" house of friars, leased, 6191, 6420.
Knockvillie (co. Cork ?), 6824.
Knockvoy (Knockloy), co. Car., 4314.
Knockvrin (co. Lim. or Cork ?), 6348.
Knockwarrowe (Knocklaurvan ?), co. Kilk., 5784.
Knockwrickyn, Car. (Knockaring, co. Wick.), rectory, 1567.
Knockywargan, co. Cork, 1476, 6252.
Knockyrattie, co. Cork, 5518.
Knockyconoghur—Cnockyconoghor, co. Mayo, 5158.
Knockycosker, co. Westm. See Knockeequer.
Knockydowne, co. Rosc., 5447.
Knockyeran, co. Meath, 1890.
Knockygirrane, 6514.
Knockygowlane—Knockigowlane—Knockigowlane—Knockygowney (Goggansmill ?), co. Cork, 2364, 3373, 6138, 6333.
Knockyn, 780-1, 878, 4712.
Knockynagh, co. Kerry, 6041.
Knockyndryn (co. Wat. ?), 1046.
Knockyncconoghor (Knockanyconor), co. Rosc., 6078.
Knockyno (Knockeen), co. Car., 1496.
Knockyno (co. Tip.), 6573.
Knockynonyladyry, co. Cork, 5904.
Knockynkeldin, co. Tip., 4755.
Knockynure (co. Cork ?), 6081.
Knockyrran (Knocksakirwan), co. Mon., 1698.
Knockynowle—Cnockynowle, 5628.
Knockyvenilly (co. Lim. ?), 6430.
Knockyvenan—Cnockyvenan, co. Long., 6168.
Knockyvanighane, co. Cork, 6003.
Knockyvillie—Cnockyvilly. See Knock Iville.
Knockgran, co. Gal., 5230.
Knocloghter, co. Wex., 614.
Knoclonsie. See Knockloagy.
Knocloughe (co. Lim. or Tip.), 4734.
Knocmark. See Knockmark.
Knocmeanalboric. See Knockmeanabire.
Knoctofre. See Knocktofer.
Knocyville. See Knock Iville.
Knodes, James, pardon, 6460.
Knoegher, Brian m'Owen I, pardon, 5575.
Knoghe (co. Meath ?), 4082.
Knogher, Donald mac Tadg I, pardon, 5977.
" Donill mcRory I, pardon, 5977

INDEX TO FIANTS—ELIZABETH.

Knoghor, Gillydufe m'Diarmodie Y, pardon, [illegible].
Knokaird, co. Westm., 2318.
Knockanbally, co. Tip., 6141.
Knokn abbey. *See* Knock, co. Louth.
Knokefergus. *See* Carrickfergus.
Knokmonarragh. *See* Knockmonasragh.
Knokealchane (Knockaloghan), co. Rosc., [illegible].
Knoknaskeagh. *See* Knocknaskeagh.
Knokroban, co. Kild., [illegible].
Knokyichiwell, co. Cork, 3373.
Knollis, Henry, commission, 3940.
Knolls, Oliver, pardon, [illegible].
Knopogo, co. Clare. *See* Knappock.
Knoppock, co. Kerry, 4313.
Knorlagh (co. Lim. ?), [illegible].
Knowde, Elizabeth, pardon, 8018.
Knowle, James, pardon, [illegible].
Knowle, Walter, pardon, [illegible].
Knowgher, Margaret ny, pardon, 8407.
Knowles, Francis, knt., [illegible].
" John, grant, 5701.
Knowre (co. Cork ?), 6457.
Knoyth (Knowth, co. Meath), [illegible].
Knyghe, co. Tip., [illegible].
Knynagim, 6747.
Knywyr, co. Cork, [illegible].
Kod, Katherine, pardon, [illegible].
Koffe, Hugh m'Thick E, pardon, [illegible].
Koirryhowny, co. Cork, [illegible].
Kolirydo, Queen's co., 1170.
Kolmore (co. Long. ?), 5143.
Kologht, co. Car., 1477.
Kollaghtowne. *See* Collaghton.
Kolleknock. *See* Colleknock, [illegible].
Kollenoge, co. Wex., 4434.
Kolligan, Hough A, pardon, [illegible].
Kollompoy (see Colompoy), [illegible].
Komenaso (co. Rosc. ?), [illegible].
Komen, Nich., pardon, 4534.
Konloe, Dervle m'Teas I, pardon, [illegible].
Konnyrghanan, 5740.
Konogh (co. Lim. ?), [illegible].
Koonbye, co. Tip., [illegible].
Kochelillyh, co. Cork, [illegible].
Kortally. *See* Cortally.
Korkemoye (Corca Mogha or Corcamoe, in parish Killkerrin, co. Gal.), 1478.
Korkerne, Ranoll m'Dermod I, pardon, [illegible].
Korkinolare (co. Westm. ?), 4018.
Korkipmologe, co. Rosc., [illegible].
Korlok, co. Cav., [illegible].
Korngarwe, co. Wex., [illegible].
Korone (co. Mon. ?), [illegible].
Kornah, co. Cork, [illegible].
Korrankrowye (co. Wex. ?), 4741.
Korrasmore (co. Leit. ?), [illegible].
Korroghlont (King's or Queen's co.), [illegible].
Korrokne grant, Karrokon Nalo (Carroge), co. Down, [illegible].
Korrowill. *See* Corrowill.
Kosso (co. Lim. ?), 5436.
Kottle, Teig I, pardon, [illegible].
Koulelnalle. *See* Cullbally, [illegible].
Koulthpynone, in Upper Ossory, [illegible].
Koumboy, co. Cork, [illegible].
Kowell, co. Wex., 1362.
Kowlaghe, Shane oy, alias Shane O'Cullane, pardon, [illegible].
Kowle Dassywally — Kowle Dassywally. *See* Coull y tarywally.
Kowlohewle, co. Car., 1477.
Kowlekoldrye (co. Rosc. ?) [illegible].
Kowlgarlo (co. Rosc. ?), [illegible].
Kowllowtyn, a territory in co. Leitrim, [illegible].
Kowlmonkle (Coolmundry, co. Cork ?), [illegible].
Kowrale, Connor y, pardon, [illegible].
Kowry, Richard, pardon, [illegible].
Koylloheary, co. Car., [illegible].
Koyllmore (co. Mon. ?), [illegible].
Koyllequyrek (co. Tip. ?), [illegible].
Koyllyhoenige (co. Lim. ?), [illegible].
Koyllyn, co. Tip. or Lim., [illegible].
Koylmare (co. Lim. ?), [illegible].
Koyrolly, co. Kerry, [illegible].
Krahe, Margaret ny, pardon, [illegible].
Kraigbrien. *See* Craighrenan.
Kraigy (co. Gal. ?), 4734.
Kranaghe, co. Gal. or Mayo, [illegible].
Kranolach, co. Westm., [illegible].
Kranoshwaghe, Nicholl, lease, [illegible].
Krealane (Cruadan, co. Wat. ?), [illegible].
Kreg. *See* Cregg, co. Cork.
Kregan, in Connaught, 1478.
Kregna grogey (co. Rosc. ?), [illegible].
Krogiul (co. Mayo ?), [illegible].
Krogo (see Crogo, co. Gal.), [illegible].
Krogirne, co. Mayo, 1484, 8412.
Krogg. *See* Cregg, co. Cork.
Kregy (co. Rosc. ?), 5112.
Kreggle (co. Rosc. or Leit.), [illegible].
Krobgnagh, [illegible].
Kroiglanrrige, co. Gal., [illegible].
Kroightaroaly (co. Gal. ?), 4734.
Kroigintarty, co. Gal., [illegible].
Kroigymulgrony, co. Gal., [illegible].
See also Crogymulgrony.
Kronoconre (Cronnaconar, co. Don.), [illegible].
Kronokoulagh — Kryanagoulaghe, in Offaly, rectory, [illegible], 6747.
Kronghone, co. Rosc., 6452.
Krowndan, co. Tip., 1843.
Krowaghe. *See* Crovagh.
Krowaghlane. *See* Crovaghlane.
Krowyquin — Krowyquyne — Krowoquyne, co. Rosc., [illegible], [illegible], [illegible].
Krowaghe. *See* Crovagh, co. Meath.

INDEX TO FIANTS—ELIZABETH.

Krowedon, co. Tip., 4618.
Krowogh. See Crowagh.
Kroy (King's or Queen's co. ?), [illegible].
Kriel. See Grieve.
Krieghe (co. Gal. ?), 2573.
Krigdaffe, co. Mayo, 5427.
Krigmitaria, co. Gal., [illegible].
Krinagh (co. Long. ?), 5143.
Krivagh (co. Westm. or King's), [illegible].
Krivathe—Krivath—Kryvaghe, co. Louth, [illegible], 6411.
Krivis, co. Rosc., 6467.
Krivath. See Krivathe.
Kroeghfee—Kroughffee (co. Cork ?), [illegible].
Krydane, Wm., harper; pardon, [illegible].
Krye, co. Mayo, [illegible].
Krymore, co. Wex., 1387.
Krynane, Patrick, pardon, 1617.
Krynockdaghe. See Kranokdagh.
Kryroe, Queen's co., 6351.
Kryne (Cruobh, O'Cahan's country, in co. Londonderry), grant of, [illegible].
Kryvaghe (see Krivathe), [illegible].
Kuallynaghane manyo, co. Cork, [illegible].
Kuinte, Wm. fitz David, pardon, 4672.
Kulcam (Coolcamm), co. Cork, [illegible].
Kulkirvic. See Coolkeria.
Kullaghe (see Cullagh), 1848.
Kullenagh (Cullenagh), co. Clare, [illegible], 4374.
Kullfyne (Coolfin, co. Gal. ?), 4794.
Kullebeill (co. Tip. ?), [illegible].
Kullmeny (co. Cork ?), 4871.
Kullynagh (see Cullenagh), co. Cork, [illegible].
Kullynaghe (Cullenagh ?), co. Wat., [illegible], 1846.
Kulmylaghe, co. Wex., 1138.
Kuneilon, John, pardon, 6477.
Kuoleryrye, co. Cork, [illegible].
Kuonymy (co. Sligo ?), [illegible].
Kurkreane, co. Westm., [illegible].
Kurkmilagh in the Moroes, co. Wex., [illegible].
Kuriare, co. Gal., 3148.
Kurragh duff (Curraghduff), co. Tip., 4712.
Kurvine. Owen roe m'Teige I., pardon, [illegible].
Kusyhy (co. Lim. or Tip. ?), 6743.
Kuryboy (co. Cork ?), [illegible].
Kwillocan—Kwillicanam, co. Lim., [illegible], [illegible].
Kwohin, co. Mon., [illegible].
Kwrrighwoy (co. Cork ?), 4734.
Kwyllballyspillan (Ballyspillane, co. Cork ?), [illegible].
Kwyllnygan (Coolnagun, co. Tip. ?), [illegible].
Kwyllyn, co. Mayo, [illegible].
Kyappandick (Cappanuck ?), co. Lim., [illegible]. See Kappanuwke.
Kyarowtegowl. See Carrownagowle.
Kyarowvedye, [illegible].
Kyarrowenkinane, co. Gal., [illegible].
Kyarrowneyleagh (Carrowneleagh, co. Gal. ?) [illegible].
Kyn, Katherine ny, pardon, 6418.
Kyeff, Jane ny, pardon, [illegible].
Kyeffy, Fynin m'Laghe, pardon, [illegible].
Kyvane, John m'Dermod, pardon, [illegible].
Kyellmadyrroe, 6147.
Kyolean (co. Kerry ?), [illegible].
Kyoramede, Donogh ny, pardon, [illegible].
Kyorane, Ilyle ny, pardon, [illegible].
Kyorryvane, Andrew fitz David, pardon, [illegible].
Kyorvick, Wm., pardon, [illegible].
Kyory. See Keery.
Kyffe—Kyf—Kyfe—Kyff:
— Art m'Donill I., pardon, [illegible].
— Conoghor m'Art I., pardon, [illegible].
— Donogh m'Teige I., pardon, [illegible].
— Finin m'Art Y., pardon, [illegible].
— Jane ny, pardon, [illegible].
— Lwyeh m'Art I., pardon, [illegible].
— Morrin ny, pardon, [illegible].
— Owen m'Art I., pardon, [illegible].
— Teige m'Fynin I., pardon, [illegible].
— See O'Keeffe.
Kyman, Katherine ny, pardon, 4787.
Kylaghe. See Killagh.
Kylaghie. See Killaghy.
Kylale. See Killaile.
Kylartry (co. Tip. ?), [illegible].
Kylarneck, co. Cork, grant, [illegible].
Kylauke (co. Kilk. ?), [illegible].
Kylballigibbon (Ballygibbon ?), co. Kild., [illegible].
Kylbally Valladiery, co. Cork, [illegible].
Kylbane. See Kilbane.
Kylbarock. See Kilbarocke.
Kylbeg. See Kilbeg.
Kylbeggan. See Kilbeggan.
Kylbego—Kylbogy. See Kilbogy.
Kylboggan. See Kilboggan.
Kylbogee. See Kilbeg.
Kylbolkil. See Kilbolkil.
Kylbolkye. See Kilbolkye.
Kylblayne. See Kilblane.
Kylboghle. See Kilboghle.
Kylbolane. See Kilbolan.
Kylbone, King's co., [illegible].
Kylbra—Kilbraghe (Killabraher), co. Cork, abbey, granted, [illegible]; possessions granted, 5171.
Kylbracken—Kylbrecan (Kilbracken, Queen's co.), [illegible], 1584.
Kylbracken. See Kilbrackan.
Kylbradye (co. Tip. ?), [illegible].
Kylbrany, co. Car., [illegible].
Kylbrewe. See Kilbrew.
Kylbride. See Kilbride.
Kylbrittan. See Kilbrittain.

INDEX TO FIANTS.—ELIZABETH.

Kylbryckan (Kilbrickan), co. Car., 104.
Kylbryd—Kylbryde. See Kilbride.
Kylbrylaine—Kylbrylium. See Kilbritaine.
Kylbolkin. See Kilbokin.
Kylbnoglen, co. Car., 104.
Kylbyrkilly (co. Clare ?), 1733.
Kylbyrne. See Kilbyrne.
Kylbysky. See Kilbokye.
Kylcaslaine. See Kilcaslain.
Kylcarte—Kylcartie (Kilcarty), co. Meath, 1408, 1541.
Kylcaskyn. See Kilcaskin.
Kylcharra, co. Car., 1477.
Kylchowan (co. Cork ?), 3840.
Kylchowne (Kilcooney), King's co., 508, 1804.
Kylchriste. See Kilcriste.
Kylchurybryn, co. Cork, 2247.
Kylclry. See Kilcly.
Kylcloghagh. See Kilcloghaghe.
Kylclogher. See Kilclogher.
Kylclonbrenon—Kylclonbrenane—Kylclonebrenane — Kylclonebrenan — Kylclonbrenan—Kylclonbrenyn, King's co., 596, 1488, 1599, 1400, 1454, 3346.
Kylclonecurkey—Kylclonkourky—Clynecurkie (Kilclonecurky, King's co.), 595, 1487.
Kylclone. See Kilclone.
Kylclonebrynnan. See Kylclonbrenan.
Kylclonkourky. See Kylclonecurkey.
Kylclonye. See Kilcleny.
Kylclonbrennan. See Kylclonbrenon.
Kylcoch—Kylcoche. See Kilcoch.
Kylcolan (Kilcowannaone?), co. Wex., rectory, 1389.
Kylcolle. See Kilcole.
Kylcollony. See Kilcollony.
Kylcoleman. See Kilcoleman.
Kylcolmanbane. See Kilcolmanbane.
Kylcomen. See Kilcomane, co. Gal.
Kylcoman. See Kilcoman, co. Mayo.
Kylcoman, co. Tip., 145.
Kylcomocka. See Kilcomocka.
Kylcomyn or Kylcmocke, Queen's co., 520.
Kylcomnagh. See Kilcomnaghe.
Kylconnell—Kylconnyll. See Kilconnell.
Kylcorbie. See Kilcorbye.
Kylcorlimane, co. Tip., 892, 1284.
Kylcorkre. See Kilcorore.
Kylcormock—Kylcormucke. See Kilcormick.
Kylcorne. See Kilcorny.
Kylcorrell (co. Wex. ?), 157.
Kylcorbeyne. See Kilcorleine.
Kylcoshan. See Kilcoshan.
Kylcorty, King's co., 1811.
Kylcowinalyne. See Kilcowinalyne.
Kylcourty (Queen's co. ?), 3171.
Kylcovoryn (Kilconierin, co. Gal. ?), rectory, 1881.
Kylcowen. See Kilcowan.
Kylcowannere. See Kilcowannere.
Kylcowen (Ballycowan, co. Kild. ?), 818.
Kylcowle. See Kilcowle.
Kylcownes, co. Kilk., rectory, 1746.
Kylcowinalyon. See Kilcowinalyne.
Kylcoyle. See Kilcoyle.
Kylcoyle (co. Wick. ?), 824.
Kylcregane—Kylcrighen. See Kilcregane.
Kylcre. See Kilcrowe.
Kylcrobin, Queen's co., 1336.
Kylcroghan. See Kilcroghan.
Kylcromane. See Kilcromane.
Kylcrow. See Kilcrowe.
Kylcruhin. See Kilcruhyne.
Kylcruny, co. Cork, 5400.
Kylcrune. See Kilcrune.
Kylcrysse. See Kilcriste.
Kylcullyne, co. Lim., 1143.
Kylcumbrennan, King's co. (see Kylclonbrennan), 1206.
Kylcuwrie. See Kilcurrie.
Kylcurryche (Kilcurrish), co. Clare, 4761.
Kyldallane, King's co., 1337.
Kyldalloy. See Kildalloe.
Kyldallen (Kildallan), co. Cav., termon or hospital, 4831.
Kyldare. See Kildare.
Kyldarin (Kildaren, co. Gal.), 1067, 1419.
Kyldarrk (co. Cork ?), 3610.
Kyldeigh—Kyldeighe. See Kildea.
Kyldeniale (Kildenniale, co. Tip.), 4287.
Kyldimo (Kildimo, co. Lim. ?), 6472.
Kyldirry. See Kildorrery.
Kyldondanvy, co. Cork, 5904.
Kyldoroughe. See Kildorough.
Kyldowan, co. Wex., 130.
Kyldroght. See Kildroght.
Kylduf. See Kilduff.
Kyldysharte Murhullo (Kildysart, co. Clare), rectory, 1778.
Kyle, co. Westm., 1351.
Kyleamarrogh, co. Lim. See Kilvrage.
Kylebegg, co. Cork, 5928.
Kyleclonhobert, Queen's co. See Kilclonhobert.
Kylecridane (co. Cork ?), 6818.
Kyledie (Kilmeady ?), co. Lim., castle and lands, 5908.
Kylemore (Kilmore), co. Cork, 4039.
Kylentyre (co. Cork ?), 5773.
Kyletanny—Kiletony, co. Cork, 3902, 5486.
Kylevey (Kilvey ?), co. Cork, 5903.
Kyleymane, co. Kerry, 5621.
Kylfane. See Kilfaine.
Kylfynnan, co. Clare, 4767.
Kylfyntey (Kilfinny ?), co. Lim., 5906.
Kylfynoragh—Kylfynanagh. See Kilfenora.
Kylgloyll, in Connaught, 1586.

INDEX TO FIANTS.—ELIZABETH.

Kylglasha. *See* Kilglass, co. Sligo.
Kylglassen. *See* Kilglassy, co. Clare.
Kylglasse. *See* Kilglassen, co. Long.
Kylglyne. *See* Kilgline.
Kylgobban. *See* Kilgobban.
Kylgobonnell. *See* Kilgobonnel.
Kylgobonilla. *See* Kilgobonilla.
Kylgren. *See* Kilgreny.
Kylgwyrtine, co. Clare, [illegible].
Kylhaba Prior (co. Kerry), [illegible].
Kylharmik — Kylharmike or Killcormok 1080. *See* Killcormick.
Kylheale (Kilhile), co. Wex., 1427.
Kylhelan. *See* Kilhelan.
Kylharylagha, co. Lim., 6791.
Kylhin Doboragha, co. Meath, [illegible].
Kylka. *See* Kilka.
Kylkan, co. Car., 804.
Kylkapagh. *See* Kylkapaghe.
Kylkartia. *See* Kylkarle.
Kylkatha. *See* Kilkeah.
Kylkealy. *See* Kilkealy.
Kylkelley, King's co., [illegible].
Kylkem, co. Tip., [illegible].
Kylkeman. *See* Kilkeman.
Kylkenny—Kylkenny. *See* Kilkenny.
Kylkepaghe — Kylkapagh (Kilcappagh), King's co., [illegible], 1094, 1461.
Kylkeran (Kilkeran), King's co., [illegible], 1054.
Kylkerryll in Omany (Kilgerrill, co. Gal. ?), vicarage, 1082.
Kylkeman. *See* Kilkeman.
Kylkestid, Queen's co., [illegible].
Kylkevan—Kylkevan. *See* Kilkevan.
Kylkey, co. Clare, [illegible].
Kylkillyn. *See* Kilkellehin.
Kylkilwyrry. *See* Kilkylwyrry.
Kylkinny, co. Meath, 6467.
Kylkoncke, Queen's co., [illegible].
Kylkobone (Kilgobbane ? co. Kerry), [illegible].
Kylkrenaha. *See* Kilcrenaght.
Kylkrille—Kylkrylle. *See* Kilkrile.
Kylkrydy. *See* Kilkydy.
Kyll. *See* Kill.
Kyll, Shane, pardon, 1183.
Kylladorry. *See* Killadaderle.
Kylladowne (Killadoon ? co. Kild.), 1883, [illegible].
Kylladrynane—Kyllydrynyn (Killadreenan, co. Wick.), [illegible], [illegible].
Kyllagarryn. *See* Killagarry.
Kyllagowne (co. Sligo ?), [illegible].
Kyllaghnamba, co. Ross, rectory, 4345.
Kyllaghe, vicar of, 718.
Kyllagly, King's co., 6726.
Kyllahle. *See* Killagh.
Kyllahowyr (co. Cork ?), 2276.
Kyllallon (*see* Killallon), 4462.
Kyllala (co. Mayo ?), 4781.
Kyllaloran—Kyllalorya—Kyllaloryne. *See* Killaloran.
Kyllalowe. *See* Killaloe.
Kyllaly, 763.
Kyllan. *See* Killan.
Kyllane, co. Clare, abbey, 6761.
Kyllane (co. Gal. ?), rectory, 1881.
Kyllane. *See* Killane, co. Louth.
Kyllane (Killeen, co. Meath ?), rectory, [illegible].
Kyllanlooke. *See* Killanlake.
Kyllanallye (co. Sligo ?), [illegible].
Kyllanaghil. *See* Killanaght.
Kyllarde, co. Kilk., [illegible].
Kyllarde. *See* Killarde, co. Meath.
Kyllarnane. *See* Killarnane.
Kyllarny. *See* Killarney.
Kyllarynyne, in Omany, 1681.
Kyllaspuck Lonnan. *See* Killaspuckloman.
Kyllassaraghe (Killossaragh), co. Wat., [illegible], 8128.
Kyllavie, co. Car., 801.
Kyllaymalon (Gillamalown), co. Meath, 1466.
Kyllclogh, co. Hosr., 3748.
Kyllcollman. *See* Kilcolman.
Kylloorman, co. Lim., patronage, [illegible].
Kyllcorroll (co Wex. ?), 857.
Kylldalow. *See* Kildallowe.
Kylldoyn. *See* Kildoyne.
Kylle, Teig m'Donoghe ne, pardon, 6785.
Kyllean, co. Car., 804.
Kyllean, co. Meath, 1028.
Kyllean (Killyon ?), co. Meath, church, 6767.
Kyllean (Killeane), co. Wex., rectory, [illegible].
Kylleare (co. Gal. ?), rectory, 1881.
Kyllelan. *See* Killelan.
Kyllelagga. *See* Killilagh.
Kyllbuck, King's co., 1464.
Kyllerle. *See* Killerle.
Kyllealogh. *See* Killeclogha.
Kyllecrannoghe (Kilnacranagh, co. Cav.), 1881.
Kyllealoragh, co. Cav., 1824.
Kylleganer (Killygarard), Queen's co., [illegible].
Kyllegine, in Omany, 1881.
Kyllegowne (Killagowan ?), co. Wex., 2978.
Kylleh (Killen, co. Wat.), 1687.
Kyllebine, co. Lim., 6047.
Kyllehye, co. Clare, [illegible].
Kylleighe. *See* Killeigh.
Kyllelly (Killelton), co. Kerry, 6048.
Kylleldy. *See* Killitle.
Kyllelynan. *See* Killeleman.
Kyllemacowgh (Kilmacanagh, co. Westm.), 1694.
Kyllemanoghe. *See* Killemanagha.
Kylleman. *See* Killenane.
Kyllemeratire. *See* Killemeraire.
Kylleme. *See* Killeme.

INDEX TO FIANTS—ELIZABETH.

Kyllene (Killenaugh, co. Wat.), 1487.
Kyllenecammagh. See Killenecammaghe.
Kyllencorie (Dourtwood ?), Queen's co., 1854.
Kyllengarie. See Killencarie.
Kyllenerowske (co. Ross ?), 6250.
Kyllengairfnond, co. Mayo, 6016.
Kyllengovary. See Killengovarie.
Kyllenevonekn, co. Lim., 453.
Kyllenewarre, Queen's co., 1347.
Kyllenyre, Queen's co., 1473.
Kyllenispicke or Bishopswood (co. Tip. ?), 3928.
Kyllenne Crowe, co. Donegal, 6452.
Kyllenoghe. See Killenogh.
Kyllenore (co. Car. ?), 1880.
Kyllenperson. See Killenperson.
Kylleoraght. See Killcarraghte.
Kylleons. See Killeons.
Kylleoanghan (Killoanghny ?), co. Westm., 849.
Kylleshonnokon. See Killoushonokin.
Kyllesloma, co. Wat., 1487.
Kyllesnure, co. Meath, 831.
Kyllesmore—Kyllemore. See Killemore.
Kylleny. See Killeny, Killenye.
Kyllemner in Ossory, rectory, 1481.
Kylleovoragh. See Killeovoraghe.
Kylleorumoy (co. Kerry ?), 3070.
Kylleruwane (Killrusane), co. Tip., rectory, 843.
Kylleshin (Killeshin), Queen's co., 549.
Kyllesteraghbege, Queen's co., 1454.
Kyllesteraghmore, Queen's co., 1454.
Kyllestoll. See Killswooll.
Kylleucle, co. Kerry, advowson of church, 4947.
Kyllevarrigayo, co. Lim., 6767.
Kyllevay. See Killevay.
Kyllevollane. See Killevollane.
Kylliondymore (Fedamore), co. Lim., 6371.
Kyllforris (Killoforus ?), co. Lim., 6947.
Kyllfynan (Killfiny, co. Lim.), castle and lands, 4171.
Kyllfynnan—Kyllfynnoraghe. See Killfinnan.
Kyllgobynett. See Kilgobnet.
Kyllgrellan, co. Kilk., 804.
Kyllholmrony, co. Tip., 5408.
Kylliecon, co. Cav., 801.
Kyllilloe. See Killilla.
Kyllimur, co. Gal., 6332.
Kylliman. See Killiman.
Kylline (co. Cork ?), 6834.
Kyllina. See Killina, Queen's co.
Kyllinecurrare, co. Cork, [illegible]
Kyllinan. See Killinan.
Kyllingo wood. See Killingo wood.
Kyllingbaloe (co. Wat. ?), rectory, 6188.
Kyllipleasy (co. Sligo ?), 5948.
Kyllisse (Killosse), co. Kilk., 5844.
Kyllisvarragh. See Killisvaraghe.
Kyllkayskiggo—Kyllkayskyne. See Killmakin.
Kyllkovn (co. Leit. or Ross.), 4783.
Kyllklembrenan. See Kylclembrenan.
Kyll m'Kenny (Kilmacgeagnanny, co. Ross.), 5804.
Kyllmack Ennes (Kilvickennane), co. Cork, 6113.
Kyllmacolle (Kilmacullagh, co. Wick.), 2828.
Kyllmacn. See Kilmayn.
Kyllmalock—Kyllmallok. See Kilmallock.
Kyllmaynam—Kyllmaynham. See Kilmainham.
Kyllmayne. See Kilmayn.
Kyllmeenan. See Kilmeenan.
Kyllmellcke. See Kilmellocke.
Kyllmoore. See Kylmorre.
Kyllmore. See Kilmore.
Kyllmorre. See Kilmorre, Queen's co.
Kyllmorre. See Kilmory, co. Wick.
Kyllmuke (co. Lim. ?), 3917.
Kyllnecroll. See Kilnecroll.
Kyllnocknock. See Kilnocknock.
Kyllnorie (co. Car. ?), 878.
Kyllnorny, co. Cav., 4651.
Kyllnyness (co. Kerry ?), 6070.
Kyllobean alias Killoban, which see.
Kyllocannock. See Killocannock.
Kyllock (King's co. or Kild.), 1454.
Kyllockrobert—Kyllokebrobart, King's co., 896, 1454.
Kyllodirnane (Killodiernan), co. Tip., rectory, 462.
Kylloghtyrmoy (Kilwatermoy, co. Wat.), 1487.
Kyllokebrobart. See Kyllockrobert.
Kyllokone, King's co., 896, 1454.
Kyllomaleon, 1481.
Kyllomnoy, co. Cork, rectory, 6131.
Kyllomoran (Killomoran, co. Gal.), 1455.
Kyllomylo (Killmihil), co. Clare, rectory, 1482.
Kyllon. See Killone.
Kyllonane. See Killonan.
Kyllone. See Killowe.
Kyllongirie. See Killongirie.
Kyllonne. See Killone.
Kylloranco, co. Kild., 491.
Kyllorane. See Killorane.
Kyllordy (perhaps Kilworth, co. Cork), 6083.
Kyllorglane. See Killorglin.
Kyllorotte. See Killorotte.
Kylloskey, co. Tip., 1283.
Kyllowran (King's co. ?), 6078.
Kylloveragh (Coill Ua bhFiachrach), or O'Heynes country (in bar. Killartan, co. Gal.), tanist appointed, 5534.

INDEX TO FIANTS—ELIZABETH.

Kyllovlaughyre, co. Clare, 4761.
Kyllowe. See Killowe.
Kyllrie. See Killrie.
Kyllrowe. See Kilrowe.
Kyllsamlloremoe. See Kilsamlloweenea.
Kyllsconell. See Kilsconnell.
Kyllsery (co. Sligo ?), 1614.
Kyllteiloch. See Kiltallagh.
Kyllnckony. See Killnockony.
Kyllagolly (co. Gal. ?), 3863.
Kylltomnache (Kiltummond, co. Rosc. ?), 1465.
Kyllture. See Killture.
Kyllturen. See Killuren.
Kyllurny (co. Rosc. ?), 2940.
Kylluryn. See Killure.
Kyllusko—Kylluskye. See Killusky.
Kyllussye. See Killussy.
Kyllvennaghe (co. Tip. ?), 1698.
Kyllvickrilie. See Kilvickrilie.
Kyllyradune (Kilbrodran), co. Lim., parish 1947.
Kylly, co. Lim., 6444.
Kyllymaney, King's co., 6041.
Kyllyan. See Killywan.
Kyllyane. See Killian.
Kyllyeowlath, co. Lim., 6767.
Kyllydnye. See Killidy.
Kyllydrynyn. See Kyllwdrynean.
Kyllynmartinane, co. Cork, 4868.
Kyllyagh. See Killeigh.
Kyllyan. See Killyan.
Kyllyone (King's co.), 1504.
Kyllyhane (Westm. or King's co.), 3644.
Kyllyllir, King's co., 1268.
Kyllyllye. See Killilie.
Kyllymoke, co. Louth, 1722.
Kyllyn, co. Cav., rectory, 4066.
Kyllyn (co. Kerry ?), 1268.
Kyllynagh. See Killonagh.
Kyllynane (co. Cork ?), 1667; rectory, 1697.
Kyllynboy (Killeentierry), co. Long., 5108.
Kyllynboy. See Killinboy.
Kyllyne. See Killyne.
Kyllynecooowiley (co. Gal. or Mayo), 1600.
Kyllyneoghone (co. Cork ?), 3578.
Kyllynes (co. Tip. ?), 6622.
Kyllynilyean. See Killynylyean.
Kyllyn Orawgh (co. Kild. ?), 1400.
Kyllynbrayne, King's co., 1509.
Kyllynycomanogie, co. Cork, rectory, 4067.
Kyllykanaghboge, Kyllykonaghmore, Queen's co., 396.
Kyllyzell or Kyllyshell (Killeshill), King's co., 631.
Kylmacongen. See Kilmacorgh.
Kylmacarron. See Kilmacaron.
Kylmacoyle. See Kilmacoyle.
Kylmacbovan. See Kilmacbovan.
Kylmackeyron. See Kilmacairan.
Kylmaeke. See Kilmack.
Kylmacknogh—Kylmacknogh. See Kilmacknogh.
Kylmacmichaim. See Kilmacmichaim.
Kylmacmdrik. See Kilmacmdrike.
Kylmacotte (Kilmacottinch, co. Wick.), 614.
Kylmacolloe. See Kilmacollock.
Kylmacomock. See Kilmacomock.
Kylmacrtan, in Connaught, rectory, 1354.
Kylmacrane (Kilmacrony ?), co. Rosc., 1487.
Kylmacthomyn. See Kilmacthomaine.
Kylmacride or Kylmagroder. See Kilmagriede.
Kylmaiood. See Kilmain.
Kylmahowe, co. Wex., 1627.
Kylmahuil, co. Dub., 770; rectory, 778.
Kylmainam—Kylmainham. See Kilmainham.
Kylmalcnoe. See Kilmalcnoge.
Kylmaltcon. See Kilmakon.
Kylmaltewoke, co. Kilk., rectory, 719.
Kylmakha. See Kilmakha.
Kylmakelly, King's co., 478.
Kylmakeo. See Kilmacrye.
Kylmalogmedo, King's co., 804, 1664.
Kylmalocoke, King's co., 803, 1891.
Kylmallanbe. See Kilmalande.
Kylmallock—Kylmallor—Kylmallohe. See Kilmallock.
Kylmalogho. See Kilmalock, co. Wex.
Kylmanagh. See Kilmanagh.
Kylmanmoghe, co. Tip., 2445.
Kylmanehin—Kylmanchyn—Kylmanghyn. See Kilmanehin.
Kylmanagh. See Kilmanap.
Kylmarone. See Kilmarone.
Kylmarton. See Kilmarton.
Kylmayn. See Kilmayn.
Kylmaynam—Kylmaynam. See Kilmainham.
Kylmaynam. See Kilmaynam, Queen's co.
Kylmaynham—Kylmaynham—Kylmaynham. See Kilmainham.
Kylmaydnerome (Kilmanain), co. Wat., 4340.
Kylmean (Kilmeaden, King's co.), 694.
Kylmeadan. See Kilmeaden.
Kylmeadowe. See Kilmeadowe.
Kylmeadyn, co. Wat., 4500.
Kylmeagawde, Queen's co., 1439.
Kylmeareig—Kylmairy, co. Meath, 886, 1668.
Kylmearam (Kilmurry ?), Queen's co., 606.
Kylmeanan. See Kilmeanan.
Kylmedo. See Kilmeyde.
Kylmelly, co. Cork, 3100.
Kylmelry. See Kylmeoria.
Kylmekan. See Kilmickea.
Kylmeoaghe. See Kilmeonage.
Kylmeogne (Kilmaenagh, co. Westm.), 1491.
Kylmeghnemock, Queen's co., 551.

INDEX TO FIANTS.—ELIZABETH.

Kylmoghoyne. See Kilmoghinine.
Kylmohalock. See Kilmallock.
Kylmohilo, Queen's co., 2183.
Kylmolapon, co. Car., 1010.
Kylmologe. See Kilmoloam.
Kylmologen. See Kilmolloske.
Kylmoman. See Kilmoname.
Kylmono. See Kilmone.
Kylmonen, co. Westm., 908, 923.
Kylmonyvoke (King's co.), 1401.
Kylmore—Kylmor. See Kilmore.
Kylmore, co. Louth, 1146.
Kylmore bronaghe. See Kilmore Bronaghe.
Kylmoreoneland, co. Cork, 5911.
Kylmoney. See Kilmoney.
Kylmorghe, Queen's co., 514, 1081.
Kylmorro (Kilmurry), co. Kild., 4063.
Kylmorre—Kylmoure (Kilmurry), King's co., 465, 473.
Kylmoure. See Kilmorre, Queen's co.
Kylmorrie—Kylmorry. See Kilmurry.
Kylmoriloomsoyne. See Kilmorellimaystne.
Kylmory, co. Cork, rectory, 5181.
Kylmorye, co. Car., 491.
Kylmurre, King's co., 1800, 1801.
Kylmurrey. See Kilmurry, co. Cork.
Kylmurry—Kylmurrye. See Kilmurry, co. Meath.
Kylmyckonedus (Kilmanicholas, co. Wat.), 1037.
Kylmyne. See Kilmyne.
Kylmaymurye, co. Wat., 1078.
Kylnecunnaghe. See Kilnecunaghe, Kilnecunaghe.
Kylnecasle. See Kilnecasken.
Kylnecyndill (Kilnagash? Queen's co.), 1016.
Kylnecorte—Kylnecorty—Kylnecourt. See Kilnecourte.
Kylneerott. See Kilnecrote.
Kylnegarranaghe—Kylnegorranaghe. See Kilnagarranagh.
Kylnegraunaghe, co. Cork, 5717.
Kylnehonnoy—Kylnehannyhy (co. Cork ?), 4731; rectory, 5181.
Kylnelyawe (co. Ferm. ?), 4616.
Kylnemanaghe, co. Gal., 4962.
Kylnemanaghe. See Kilnamanagh, co. Ross.
Kylneynyn (co. Westm. ?), 6818.
Kylneyilloe, co. Cork, 5173.
Kylnevonoge, co. Lim., 6001.
Kylnomer, vicarage, 2170.
Kylnoycke (Kilnock), co. Car., 504.
Kylnyforoche, Queen's co., 498.
Kylnymurtrie (Kilnamartery). See Kilnamartine.
Kylnymonagh. See Kilnamanagh.
Kyloghtermoy. See Kiloghtermoy.
Kyloguamoo, co. Long., 6103.
Kylone. See Killone.
Kylowragh (co. Cork ?), 5684.
Kylpatrick. See Kilpatrick.
Kylpole—Kylpoole. See Kilpoole.
Kylquygan (Colligan, co. Wat.), 1087.
Kylrullym, 604.
Kylroyon, co. Wat., 1676.
Kylrobyn. See Kilroban.
Kylrodery—Kylrodry. **See Kilrothery.**
Kylroe, co. Meath, 4154.
Kylrory. See Kilrowry.
Kylrosse, co. Cork, 1673.
Kylrowan. See Kilrowan.
Kylrowry. See Kilrowry.
Kylroylane. See Kilroylane.
Kylruish—Kylruske. See Kilrush.
Kylsaint Nicholas. See Kilsaint Nicholas.
Kylsalghan. See Kilsalghan.
Kylsaran. See Kilsaran.
Kylsanell. See Kilseanell.
Kylsany. See Kilsany.
Kylselan. See Kilshelan.
Kylsealyman. See Kilshenahan.
Kylshalghan. See Kilshalghan.
Kylsinan. See Kilsinan.
Kylsinagho (Kilsinaghen), co. Kild., 6081.
Kylskanna (Kilskanahan, co. Cav.), rectory 1681.
Kylsleelan. See Kilsheelan.
Kylskyagh. See Kilskeagh.
Kylstanley. See Kilstanley.
Kylsy. See Kilsie.
Kylsynchan. See Kilsynchan.
Kyltale—Kyltalle. See Kiltale.
Kyltaraghta. See Kiltaraghta.
Kyltareny, co. Cork, 5658.
Kyltatuide (co. Sligo ?), 5635.
Kyltegan (co. Kerry ?), 4877.
Kylteman (co. Tip. ?), 2318.
Kyltemanaloghe, co. Lim., 5782.
Kyltevan, co. Ross., 4478.
Kyltowny. See Kiltownoy.
Kyltaynan—Kyltaynane. See Kiltaynane.
Kyltecolla. See Kilticolla.
Kyltilla. See Kiltilla.
Kyltilly. See Kiltilly.
Kyltinan. See Kiltinan.
Kyltober. See Kiltober.
Kyltologhan. See Kiltoloughane.
Kyltoloagh. See Kiltolagh.
Kyltomos (co. Gal. ?), 1460.
Kyltorrick, co. Lim., 1362.
Kyltullaughe. See Kiltullagh.
Kyltullage. See Kiltullage.
Kyltumulle. See Kiltumulle.
Kyltylmoveayon, Queen's co., 1013.
Kyltulagh. See Kiltullagh.
Kyltunyty, co. Cork, 5190.

INDEX TO FIANTS—ELIZABETH.

Kylvallan, 1637; rectory, 1637.
Kylvane. See Kilvann.
Kylvarraghane, co. Wat., 6536.
Kylvayne—Kylvann. See Kilvann.
Kylveckane. See Kilveckane.
Kylvelick, Queen's co., 871.
Kylvekenagh (co. Clare ?), 1609.
Kylvenytt or Kilvenoton, co. Cork, 6782.
Kylveylledre. See Kilmoelkyadir.
Kylvickeone (co. Rosc. ?), 1734.
Kylvida. See Kilvid.
Kylvihile. See Kilvichill.
Kylvoyle (co. Cork ?), rectory, 5131.
Kylvry. See Kilvry.
Kylvryn. See Kilvrin.
Kylvryne. See Kilvryn.
Kylvyckatrone (Kilmacteranny ?, co. Sligo), 1734.
Kylvydy (co. Wat. ?), 2573.
Kylvynine. See Kilvinine.
Kylvynillie, co. Cork, 4387.
Kylvynsyd. See Kilvinsion.
Kylwanny. See Kilvanny.
Kylwaruyng. See Kilwaruyng.
Kylwarran, 1238.
Kylwanra. See Kilwanra.
Kylwona. See Kilwoan.
Kylworyle. See Kilworilo.
Kylymalongford, co. Tip., 2162.
Kymdelan, Roland, pardon, 4573.
Kymoghill alias Killnogan, co. Cork (which see), 5171.
Kymmane, John, pardon, 4288.
Kyme, co. Cav., 4694.
Kymalowruyoll, co. Clare, 4761.
Kymaley, 5318.
Kymaise, co. Tip. or Wat., 3171.
Kymaldoony (co. Clare ?), 5808.
Kynaliagh—Kynallyaghe. See Kinalough.
Kynard, co. Kerry or Lim., 6432.
Kynarde—Keynard (Kinard), co. Lim., 4274, 6186.
Kynawood (Kinwood), co. Dub., 1460.
Kynoon, pass of, co. Down, 4837.
Kynoona. See Kinooan.
Kynorevyra, co. Sligo, 6488.
Kynachan (co. Westm. ?), 1139.
Kynafeake, John, pardon, 6434.
Kynallan, co. Gal., 4787.
Kynalle, Edm. fitz Wm. I, pardon, 4143.
Kynoro (Kinnrow), co. Wat., 1637.
Kyneroith, Donald and Matthew vic, English liberty, 5157.
Kynoore—Kynoorn. See Kinoore.
Kyndolan. See Kindolan.
Kyneaxlor, Great and Little, Queen's co., 837, 1484.
Kynfealm, Rich., pardon, 3478.
Kyniackemlowne, co. Cork, 3472.
Kyng. See King.
Kyngalowne, co. Wex., 4787.
Kyngogan, John m'Tho. I, pardon, 4451.
Kynkeston. See Konkeston.
Kynnamonowe (co. Gal. ?), 4874.
Kynny, Wm., pardon, 6178.
Kynmalowruyoll, co. Clare, 4761.
Kynnagad. See Kinnegad.
Kynnaghe, co. Car., 4778.
Kynnalough. See Kinalough.
Kynnaloorty—Kynnaloortie—Kynnaloorty (Kinelarty barony, co. Down), 1422, 5767, rectory, 1639.
Kynnanleigh. See Kinalough.
Kynnakelghane — Kynnakelghan, co. Gal., rectory, 1823, 3418.
Kynnaloorty. See Kynnaloorty.
Kynnally, co. Gal., 4491.
Kynnaloghan (co. Lei. ?), 4800.
Kynnaughe, co. Car., 1236.
Kynne, Darby, pardon, 810.
Kynnarfenke, John, pardon, 6177.
Kynnefeck, James, pardon, 6162.
Kynnegahan, co. Gal., 4684.
Kynneghe (Kineagh), co. Kild., rectory, 479, vicar of, 743.
Kynneligho, 792.
Kynnoe. See Kyunyne.
Kynnot—Kynnotte—Kynnite—Kynnitte. See Kinnect.
Kynnyne—Kynnune (Kinnalea ?), co. Meath, 5342, 6128.
Kynoalestowne (Kennoalestowne), co. Meath, 1468.
Kynolowrhan (Conol Lanvelain, territory in bar. Carrigallen, co. Leit.—Ann. I. C.), 4682.
Kynsale—Kynsall—Kynsalle. See Kinsale.
Kynsalagh — Kynsalaghe — Kynsellaghe — Kynsolo—Kynsellagh. See Kinsalagh.
Kynshame. See Konsham.
Kynshonder, King's co., 4341.
Kynlagh, co. Down, 5401.
Kyntolagonna, 81.
Kyntire (co. Lim. ?), 4488.
Kyniston. See Kinston.
Kyntorke, co. Mayo, 5707.
Kyntyre (Kinleorn), co. Cork, 5946.
Kynyn, co. Cav., 4831.
Kynyleagh. See Kinloach.
Kyoghe, Donogh m'Donogh, pardon, 4872.
Kyolleton. See Kioleston.
Kypnagho Coynu, co. Wat., 5344.
Kyppe, Edm., pardon, 3880.
Kyppena. See Kippana.
Kyrna—Kyrnan (Kournan), co. Meath, 837, 2948.
Kyrokile, John, 4772.
Kyrok, Wm., 4366. See Kirke.
Kyrkeleane — Kirkeleson — Kirkelelane — Kyrykleam abbey (Odorney, co. Kerry), 2812, 3769, 5708, 6122.

INDEX TO FIANTS—ELIZABETH.

Kyrke, Wm., 5346. *See* Kirke.
Kyrkeslon—Kyrkysion, co. Meath, 1630.
Kyrnan, Matthew fitz Davy, 4722.
Kyrrangho, Henry, 1723.
Kyrroby. *See* Kirroby.
Kyrrenbey, co. Clare, 4791.
Kyrrye. *See* Kerry.
Kyrywood, co. Meath, 6603.
Kyry, 4706.
Kyryleison. *See* Kyrkleison.
Kyrys, David, pardon, 2494.
Kylmcorke. *See* Kiechburk.
Kywayn, Ph., pardon, 4100.
Kyshewan (Kisha wanny), co. Kild., 837.
Kytnany (co. Cork ?), rectory, 8171.
Kyvan, Oran m'Morgh, pardon, 1161.
Kyvard, Katherine ny, pardon, 4699.
Kywane, Donas, pardon, 5434.
" John, pardon, 1817.

La, Walter (co. Lim.), 6774.
Laariane, co. Mayo, 1604.
Laawghe (Leagh ?), Queen's co., 640.
Labasagho, co. Lim., 4286, 6283.
Labelleconor, co. Gal., 6816.
Lable, Rob., pardon, 6282.
Labourers, charge for making hay, 4528.
" impressed for army, 875, 3461, 3458.
Lacan (co. Wick. ?), 6620.
Lacagh. *See* Lackaghe.
Lacagh (Lackagh), co. Mon., 5621.
Lacaghe. *See* Lackaghe, 4874.
Lacan, 762.
Lacovallyvory (co. Wick.), 1415.
Lacey, Hugh. *See* Limerick, bishop of.
Lacey, Joan. *See* Lacy.
Lacie. *See* Lacy.
Lacka Bog, co. Kerry. *See* Lackybogo.
Lackafyn (Lackafinna, co. Gal. ?), 4878. *See* also Lockaghfine.
Lackagh—Lackaghe—Lakagh—Lockagh—Loyeaghe, co. Kild., 1316, 1374, 2117, 2308, [illegible], [illegible], 3714, 4180, [illegible].
Lackagh (co. Kilk.), 6794.
Lackagh, co. Mon. *See* Lacagh.
Lackagh (co. Tip. or Kilk.), 6703.
Lackaghe—Laccagh—Lacaghe—Lokaghe, co. Gal., 4088, 4874, 6512.
" prebend, 997.
Lackaghe. *See* Lackagh, co. Kild.
Lackaghe (Lackagh, King's co.), 1401.
Lacka More, co. Kerry. *See* Lackymore.
Lackan (co. Cav. ?), 6517.
Lackan, in Connaught, 1868–9.
Lackan, co. Rosc., 4608, 5601.
Lackan, co. Sligo. *See* Locan.
Lacken, co. Westm. *See* Lenkine, Lackyn, Lyn de Leighon.
Lackandarragh, co. Wick. *See* Lakindarra.
Lackane, co. Rosc., 5681.
Lacke, 5272.
Lacke (co. Clare ?), 6814.
Lackechronan, co. Kerry, 6188.
Lackengranan, co. Lim., 5274.
Lackenullagh, co. Wat. *See* Liskohillaghe.
Lackensleneyne, co. Cork, 6431.
Lackenthamen, co. Cork, 5161.
Lackoyne, co. Tip., 6794.
Lackfin (co. Gal. ?), 5161.
Lackiboge—Lackiboge. *See* Lackyboge.
Lackicullagh (co. Wat. ?), 6177.
Lackimore. *See* Lackymore.
Lackin, co. Tip., 6519.
Lackine, co. Tip., 6810.
Lackinicine (co. Lim. or Cork ?), 6465.
Lackinn, Queen's co., 4798.
Lackome, co. Cork, 4816.
Lacky (co. Tip. or Kilk. ?), 6584.
Lackyboge—Lackiboge—Lackiboge—Lackybogue (Lacka Bog), co. Kerry, 2818, 3720, 4504.
Lackygarragh, co. Cork, 6602.
Lackymackerish, co. Tip., 4584.
Lackymore—Lackimore—Lakymore (Lacka More), co. Kerry, 2819, 3740, 4388.
Lackyn (co. Tip. ?), 6784.
Lackynovintan, co. Lim., 4186.
Lackyngrufyman, co. Lim., 4186.
Lackyntonyne (co. Cork), 4578.
Lackyavintan, co. Lim., 4814.
Lackynworay, co. Tip., 8102.
Lacy—Lacey—Lacie—Lacye:
" David, pardon, 6178, 6452, 6462, 6497, 6868.
" Davie, pardon, 6028.
" Eady (of Bruree), pardon, 6263, 4665, 6444.
" Eady or Edy, pardon, 3478, 4597, 6478, 6477, 6822.
" Eady or Eddie oge (of Bruree), pardon, 6444, 6487.
" Edm., pardon, 6408, 4111, 4476, 6168, 6487, 6534.
" Ellen, pardon, 6464.
" Ellice, pardon, 6178, 6414.
" Ellinor, pardon, 6487, 6468.
" Hugh, pardon, 1694.
" Hugh. *See* Limerick, bishop of.
" James fitz Rob., pardon, 1694, 2117, 4666, 6461–2.
" Joan, pardon, 6406, 6485, 6511.
" John, pardon, 1604, 1786, 4827, 4303, 6448, 6461. *See* Wale.
" John, rector of Kilcloufert, 6758.

Lacy, John fitz David, pardon, 1304, 1467, 6462.
„ John fitz Wm., pardon, [illegible]; attainted, [illegible], [illegible].
„ Katherine, pardon, [illegible].
„ Mary, pardon, [illegible], [illegible].
„ Morris, pardon, [illegible].
„ Oliver, pardon, [illegible], [illegible], [illegible].
„ Patr., pardon, [illegible].
„ Peirs (of Bruff), pardon, [illegible], [illegible].
„ Peirs, pardon, [illegible], [illegible], [illegible], [illegible], [illegible]; [illegible].
„ Philip, pardon, [illegible].
„ Redmond, pardon, [illegible].
„ Rich., license to make aqua vitae, [illegible].
„ Rich., pardon, [illegible], [illegible].
„ Rob., pardon, [illegible], [illegible], [illegible].
„ Tho., pardon, [illegible], [illegible], [illegible], [illegible], [illegible], [illegible], [illegible].
„ Ullagh, pardon, [illegible].
„ Ullick, Ulyg, or Willige, pardon, [illegible], [illegible], [illegible], [illegible].
„ Wm., sheriff of Limerick, [illegible]; pardon, [illegible], [illegible].
„ William, junior (of Bruff), pardon, [illegible]; commission, [illegible].
„ Wm. (of Lismakeery), pardon, [illegible], [illegible].
„ William, pardon, [illegible], [illegible], [illegible].
„ *See* Lacey, Lasy.
Lacy svoye, Wm., pardon, [illegible].
Lacystown, co. Meath. *See* Leceston.
Ladder, Donald, [illegible].
Ladeaher, Dermot, pardon, [illegible].
Ladie Abbey. *See* Lady Abay.
Ladiecastell—Ladiecastell. *See* Lady Castle.
Ladie land by Ryvers crosse, co. Meath, [illegible].
Ladiestowne. *See* Ladytowne.
Ladir, Edm. m'Shane, pardon, [illegible].
„ Gerrott m'Shane, pardon, [illegible].
„ Morrish m'Tho., pardon, [illegible].
Ladirath. *See* Ladyrathe.
Laditon. *See* Ladytowne, co. Kild.
Laditone. *See* Ladytowne, co. Car.
Ladnifo, co. Lim., [illegible].
Lady Abay—Ladie Abbey, co. Tip., [illegible], [illegible].
Ladycastell (co. Meath ?), [illegible].
Lady Castle—Ladiecastell—Ladiecastell, co. Kildare, [illegible], [illegible], [illegible], [illegible].
Ladyrathe — Ladirathe, co. Meath, [illegible], [illegible].
Ladytowne—Ladiestowne—Laditone (Ladyetown), co. Car., [illegible], [illegible]; rectory, [illegible].
Ladytowne—Laditon—Ladyton—Ladytone (Ladytown), co. Kild., [illegible], 7[illegible], [illegible], [illegible], [illegible]; rectory, [illegible], [illegible].
Laeght Iwedan (co. Mayo ?), [illegible].
Lafally (co. Tip. or Lim.), [illegible].
Lafan, Rich., pardon, [illegible].
Laffallo, in Connaught, [illegible].
Laffallye (co. Tip. or Lim.), [illegible].
Laffaly, co. Lim., [illegible].
Laffan, Henry, pardon, [illegible].
„ James, pardon, [illegible], [illegible], [illegible], [illegible], [illegible], [illegible], [illegible].
„ James (of Ballingree), pardon, [illegible], [illegible].
„ James, prebendary of Whitechurche, [illegible].
„ James (of Graystown), sheriff of Tipperary, [illegible]; pardon, [illegible], [illegible], [illegible].
„ John, pardon, [illegible], [illegible].
„ Peirce or Peirs, pardon, [illegible], [illegible], [illegible].
„ Peter, pardon, [illegible], [illegible].
„ Tho., pardon, [illegible], [illegible], [illegible], [illegible].
„ Walter, pardon, [illegible], [illegible], [illegible].
Laffane, James, [illegible]. *See* Laffan
„ Peirse, [illegible]. *See* Laffan.
„ Rich., pardon, [illegible].
Laffanestowne (co. Tip. ?), [illegible].
Lafferrion—Lafferryen, co. Clare, [illegible], [illegible].
Lagan—Laggan river (co. Antrim), [illegible]; fishing of, [illegible].
Lagan, co. Kilk., [illegible].
Lagane, the, co. Long., [illegible].
Lagein (co. Kerry ?), [illegible].
Laggagine, co. Meath, [illegible], [illegible].
Laggan river. *See* Lagan.
Laggan, co. Leit. or Rosc., [illegible].
Laggan, co. Rosc., [illegible].
Laggaustown, co. Tip. *See* Ballinlogane.
Laghan (co. Leit. ?), [illegible].
Laghanaght (see Lahenaght), [illegible].
Laghanstown, co. Westm., [illegible].
Laghard (Lahard, co. Leit. ?), [illegible].
Laghardan (Lahardan, co. Clare), [illegible].
Laghardan (Lahardan, co. Tip.), [illegible].
Laghbally (co. Cav. ?), [illegible].
Laghbunrowranle, co. Clare, [illegible].
Laghcroit (co. Cork ?), [illegible].
Laghean (co. Leit. ?), [illegible].
Laghein (Lahuen ? co. Leit.), [illegible].
Laghell (co. Tip. ?), [illegible].
Laghenaght—Laghenat—Laghenaught. *See* Lahenaght.
Laghes in Munster, [illegible].
Laghin (co. Long. ?), [illegible].
Laghkey, Thady or Teige bane m'Teo I, pardon, [illegible].
Laghlen—Laghlin. *See* Leighlin.
Laghlin, Owen ny Shane ny, pardon, [illegible].
„ Patr., pardon, [illegible].
Laghlinbridge. *See* Leighlinbridge.

Laghlin doone, More ny, pardon, 5624.
Laghlyn. See Leighlin.
Laghnanstowne, 4820.
Laghrne—Lahran (Laragh, co. Westm.?), 5728, 4732.
Laghtnaike (Laghtcanak?), co. Rosc., 6151.
Laghvalla, co. Tip., 5342.
Laghvallie (co. Tip.?), 6334.
Laghvane, co. Lim., 5460.
Lagkaghe (co. Tip.?), 4826.
Lagragh (co. Cork?), 6764.
Lahanaght, co. Cork. See Lahenaght.
Laharne, co. Kerry. See Leaharnum.
Lahard, co. Leit. See Laghard.
Lahardan, co. Kerry, 4152.
Lahardan. See Laghardan.
Laharie (co. Kerry?), 6184.
Lahenn, co. Leit. See Laghoine.
Lahenaght — Laghanaght — Laghenaght — Laghenaht—Loghenaught (Lahenaght, co. Cork), 6613, 6080.
Laherty, Margaret ny, pardon, 4658.
Lahie, Nich., pardon, 6417, 5732.
Lahil, Rich., (or Lacie), aquavitae license, [illegible].
Lahies in Connaught, 1562.
Lahirigh in Munster, 5477.
Lahive, Rich., 4822.
Lahrae. See Loghrae.
Lakagh—Lakaghe. See Lackagh.
Lakdoran (co. Wat.?), 1687.
Lakan, co. Westm., 4912.
Laken (co. Wick.?), [illegible].
Lakill (co. Long.?), 5808.
Lakindaro (Lacknadarragh? co. Wick.), [illegible].
Lakymore. See Lackymore.
Laley, Edmund, pardon, 591, 6232.
" James, pardon, 5594.
" Nich., pardon, 5482.
" Pall, pardon, 4002.
" Patr., pardon, 5482.
" Richard or Ristin, pardon, 6094.
Lalor, Donchowe, pardon, 4692.
Lally, Daniel, pardon, 5410.
" Patrick, pardon, 1564.
Lalor, David, pardon, 5594.
" Donell, pardon, 5795.
" Henry, pardon, 5432.
" More ené, pardon, 6110.
" Patr., pardon, [illegible].
" Richard, pardon, 5098.
" Tho., pardon, 5458.
" See Mlalor.
Lambarte. See Lambert.
Lambay—Lambey island, co. Dub., 194, 1028, 1258, 1611; rectory, 4310.
Lambe, Chr., commissions, 5587-8.
Lamben—Lambane. See Lambyn.
Lambert — Lamberte, Sir Oliver, governor of Connaught, 6640; lease, 4489, 6591.
" Rob., pardon, 5448, 5462.
Lambestone (Lambstown, co. Wex.), 6617.
Lambey. See Lambay.
Lambin. See Lambyn.
Lambs, tithe of, 1720.
Lambyn — Lamben — Lambane — Lambin, Tho., sheriff of Queen's co., 3348, 5343; commissions, 3174, 3348, 5123; grant of lands, 1498, 1869; leases, 4282, 4474, [illegible]; his message in Maryborough, 1628, 5624; pardon, 2348, 3077; security, 4277.
Lamerstown (co. Kilk.?), 3072.
Lames lands in Ardmulchan, co. Meath, 4804.
Lammas, 1594.
Lampard—Lamparte. See Lampart.
Lampton, John, pardon, 1838.
Lamport—Lampard—Lamparte—Lamporde —Lamporte:
" James, wardship, 6732.
" Matthew, overseer of tanning, 5830; pardon, 2708.
" Nich., pardon, 2833.
" Patrick, his heirs, 5944, 6720.
" Philip, pardon, 5735; pardon of alienation, 5615; wardship of grandson, 6730.
" Philip, livery, 5944.
" Philip, pardon, 6647.
" William, pardon, 4434.
Lamy, Abbey of (Abbeylara, co. Long.?), 5857.
Lancaster, Anne (daughter of archbishop Lancaster), 4451.
" Rebecca (daughter of the archbishop), 4452.
" Tho., archbishop of Armagh, pardon, 1808, 6237; his will, 4452. See Armagh.
Lancaster county, undertakers from, for land in Munster, 4963.
Land, Gerald, pardon, 408.
Landanstown, co. Kild., 4717.
Lander, Gerald fitz Edm. fitz Piers, pardon, 8102.
" John riogh, pardon, 4898.
Landon, Maurice, pardon, 4112.
Londra, Gerrott, pardon, 6494.
Lands, claims to by subjects, not to be barred by grant to Irish chief, 1860.
" claims on escheated lands in Munster to be considered, 5251.
" customary division abolished, 4781.
" of malefactors and attainted persons to be enquired for, 5408-48, 6138, 4314.

INDEX TO FIANTS—ELIZABETH.

Lands of co. Monaghan granted in freehold to the inhabitants, [illegible], [illegible].
„ mortgage, amount for which lands were mortgaged, [illegible], [illegible]; custom as to, [illegible].
„ in Munster, plot for planting with undertakers, [illegible].
„ persons pardoned to submit to conditions as to their lands, [illegible], [illegible], [illegible], [illegible], [illegible].
„ tenants' services to be fixed, [illegible].
„ tenure, forfeitures for failure to sue livery, [illegible]; first livery sued in co. Galway of a long time, [illegible].
„ tenure. See Freeholders, Tenants.
„ waste from rebellions and difficulty of obtaining occupiers, [illegible].
Lane, Clement, pardon, [illegible].
„ John, dean of Waterford, [illegible].
„ Ralph, comm., clerk of the cheque of the army, [illegible]; muster master, [illegible], [illegible]; governor of Belfast castle, [illegible]; commissions, [illegible], [illegible], [illegible], [illegible].
„ Thomas, 1722, 3418.
Lanegain, Dermot mac Conoghor I, pardon, [illegible].
Lanegane or O'Lanegane, William, English liberty, [illegible].
Lanegirtie (co. Kilk. ?), [illegible].
Lang, Wm., pardon, [illegible].
Langan, Bartholomew, pardon, [illegible].
„ (or Dalton), Ellinor, pardon, [illegible].
„ John, [illegible].
Langarnes, co. Meath, [illegible], 1462, [illegible], [illegible].
Lange, David fitz Wm., pardon, [illegible].
„ James, freedom from subsidy, [illegible].
Langewyell (Longueville), co. Cork, [illegible].
Langford, Owen, surveyor of works, Carrickfergus, [illegible].
„ Rich. gunner, Dublin castle, [illegible].
„ Roger, constable, Carrickfergus castle, [illegible].
Langrage (co. Wex. ?), [illegible].
Langraige (co. Wex. ?), [illegible].
Langton, Arthur, pardon, [illegible].
„ Edw., pardon, [illegible].
„ Joan or Johanna, pardon, [illegible], [illegible].
„ Tho., pardon, [illegible].
„ Walter, pardon, [illegible].
„ Wm., pardon, [illegible].
Lanhegnisey, [illegible].
Lanirgan, Flolo or Florence, pardon, [illegible].
„ Thomas macDavid, pardon, [illegible].
Lans, Geoffry, pardon, [illegible], [illegible].
Lanie, Edm. fitz Wm., pardon, [illegible].
„ Gerald, pardon, [illegible].
Lanthony—Lanthonie priory, by Gloucester, in England; its possessions in Ireland, leased or granted, 165, [illegible], 1165, [illegible], [illegible], [illegible], [illegible], [illegible], [illegible], [illegible], [illegible].
Lany, Conoghor oge ny Y, pardon, [illegible].
Lany—Lanye, Francis, surveyor of victual, [illegible]; grant of land, [illegible]; alienation licence, [illegible].
„ John, marriage settlement, [illegible].
„ John, pardon, [illegible].
„ Richard, son of, [illegible].
Lanye, John, smith of the ordnance, [illegible], [illegible].
Lanyore Roogho. See Laynyarn Roogh.
Lapan (Lappan), co. Mon., [illegible].
Lappane, co. Cav., [illegible].
Lara. See Laragh.
Laracor—Laraghcore—Laracor—Laricor—Lorraghcor, co. Meath, [illegible], [illegible]; rectory, 1842, [illegible].
„ vicar of S. Mary of, [illegible].
Laragh, [illegible].
Laragh (co. Car. ?), [illegible].
Laragh—Laragho, co. Cork, [illegible], [illegible].
Laragh (co. Rosc. or Gal.), [illegible].
Laragh—Lara—Laragho, co. Westm., [illegible], 4161, [illegible], [illegible], [illegible]. See also Laghrus, Lelaluath, Layghrath, Loyrath.
Laragh, the (co. Wick.), [illegible].
Laraghcore. See Laracor.
Laragho. See Laragh, co. Cork.
Laragho, co. Sligo, [illegible].
Laragho—Laraghe (Learagh), co. Wat., [illegible], [illegible], [illegible].
Laragho. See Laragh, co. Westm.
Laraghes—Laraughes—Larochs, co. Kild., [illegible], [illegible], [illegible], [illegible].
Laraghminche, co. Louth, 1512.
Laraghteige, co. Car., [illegible].
Larah, co. Cav. See Larrae.
Larane, Tho., pardon, [illegible].
Larans. See Lawrence.
Larass, co. Sligo. See Lairas.
Laraugh (co. Westm. ?), [illegible].
Laraughes. See Laraghes.
Larayho, co. Gal., [illegible].
Larbrick, lord of, co. Antrim, [illegible].
Larckeshill alias Carnaltushocke, [illegible].
Lard, illegal export of, [illegible], [illegible], [illegible].
Larecor. See Laracor.
Laregh, in Munster, [illegible].
Lareign, [illegible].
Larence. See Lawrence.
Largay, co. Cav. See Learge, Leragge, Large.
Largo, John, supervisor of exports, [illegible].
Larghibrack (Larguibrack, co. Donegal), [illegible].
Largi s, Pair, pardon, [illegible].

Largye, territory in co. Leitrim, 4052.
Laries, co. Kerry. *See* Lahrey.
Larise (co. Long. ?), 4148.
Lariour. *See* Larnour.
Larimbill alias Lighill, co. Westm., 1069, 6479.
Larne, co. Antrim. *See* Learne.
Laroche (*see* Loroghes), 6400.
Larrao (Larah), co. Cav., townon, 5636.
Larraes (co. Sligo ?), 6918.
Larragh, the (co. Cav. ?), 5762.
Larragh—Larro monastery (Abbeylara, co. Long.), 1401, 1480, 6800. *See also* Greanard, abbey.
Larraghour. *See* Laracur.
Larraghe. *See* Laraghe, co. Wat.
Larraghe, Queen's co., 438.
Larray (co. Long. ?), [illegible].
Larrhe, co. Westm., 4181.
Larris, co. Sligo, 5348.
Larro. *See* Larragh.
Larroke, co. Car., 788.
Larty, Donald m'Rory I, pardon, 5872.
Larygho (Lauragh, Queen's co.), 1718.
Laryn—Laryne, co. Gal., [illegible], 5158.
Lasalemn, co. Car., 5541. *See* Lismalinan.
Lasartane, co. Westm., 1701.
Lase, Edm., pardon, 4018.
Lasey, Edm., pardon, [illegible].
" John m'Ulyke, pardon, [illegible].
" William, pardon for felonies (*see* Lacy), 1584.
Lashy, Hiliner, pardon, [illegible].
Laskya, church of, 5787.
Lasmaline—Lasmalyn. *See* Lismalin.
Lasmolan—Lasmollon. *See* Lesmollon.
Laspopall. *See* Lispopall.
Laspydell, co. Gal., 1631, 5458.
Lassaden, co. Louth, 1480.
Lassmollen. *See* Lesmollon.
Lastertoe (co. Tip. ?), 5844.
Lasie, Rob., pardon, 4830.
Lastery, the (co. Gal. ?), [illegible].
Lasmallin. *See* Lismallin.
Lasmillean, [illegible]. *See* Lismallenan.
Laste, Francis, pardon, 4100.
Lasion, co. Meath, 4149.
Lasy, John, pardon, [illegible].
Lasye, Rob., pardon, 4817.
" Wm., pardon, [illegible].
Lateo, King's co., [illegible]. *See* Laloy.
Latem. *See* Latten.
Lateraghe—Laterogh. *See* Leitragh.
Latey—Laten—Latiedronkey, King's co., 478, [illegible], 5471, 4188, [illegible].
Latgallen, co. Mon. *See* Lattycallan.
Latheragh. *See* Latteragh.
Latherokley chapel, 84.
Lathe, customs of, 5788; impressed for works, 9488.

Lattro—Latyro, co. Louth, [illegible], 5162.
Latenard (Latenanard), co. Mon., [illegible].
Laten (co. Clare ?), 6918.
Latoun, co Clare. *See* Lattowne.
Lattacrossan, co. Mon. *See* Lattercrossan.
Lattiedronkey, King's co., 418. *See* Latoy.
Lattomerstowne, co. Wex., 1310.
Latten — Laten — Lattyn (Lattin, co. Tip.), 5787, 4748, [illegible], 6190, [illegible].
" prebendary of, 84.
Latteragh—Latoraghe—Latoragh — Latheragh, co. Tip., 5810, 4878, [illegible], 6706, 6744.
Lattercrossan (Lattacrossan), co. Mon., 6647.
Lattinge, John, 5104.
Lattelcrottl (co. Cav. ?), 5788.
Lattycallan (Latgallen, co. Mon.), 6943.
Lattyn. *See* Latten.
Lattyne, John, 5108.
Lature, co. Westm. (Long. ?), 1884.
Latyra. *See* Lattro.
Lauder, Wm. m'Tho., pardon, [illegible].
Laulir, Gerald fitzEdm., pardon, 5030.
Laughnam, Edward, lease, 1970.
Laughan, John, 6817.
Laughbegg, co. Lim., 5781.
Laughe, John, 1732.
Laughelenan (co. Leit. ?), 4788.
Laughkant (Loughkant, co. Tip. ?), [illegible].
Laughlen. *See* Leighlin.
Laughlenbridge. *See* Leighlinbridge.
Laughlin, Clan-, in Inishowen, men of, pardoned, 6423.
Laughlin, Old (*see* Old Laughlin), [illegible].
Laughlin. *See* Leighlin.
Laughlinbrig. *See* Leighlinbridge.
Laughlinston—Laughlinstone (Laughlinstown ? co. Kild.), 1628, [illegible].
Laughmore, co. Lim., 5781.
Launder, John, pardon, 5962.
" Thomas duf fitz Edmond, pardon, [illegible].
Launt, Edm., pardon, [illegible].
" Gerot, pardon, 5857.
" Petrus, pardon, 4504.
Launt—Launte, Richard, pardon, [illegible], 3434, 4378, 5394.
Laury, Donell m'Conoghor oy I, pardon, 6560.
Lauragh, Queen's co. *See* Larygho.
Lauragh, co. Wat. *See* Laraghe.
Lavalstion, co. Westm., 3168.
Lavallo, co. Rosc., 4844.
Lavalles, co. Rosc., 4844.
Lavallen—Lavallin, Richard, pardon, [illegible], [illegible].
" Tho., pardon, 3158.
Lavally, co. Mayo, 4688.
Lavally, co. Rosc., 4044.
Lavane, Patrick, pardon, 158.

Laviorg—Lavyrog, Dowling and Maurice m'Dermot, pardon, 4015.
Law, executions, &c., under, suspended by prerogative, [illegible].
Lawally (co. Gal. ?), [illegible].
Lawarghil, river and weir of (The Silver-hand, the stream from Lough Gwol to Lough Iron), 1340.
Lawcholl, co. Leit., [illegible].
Lawdrig, Maurice m'Dermod, pardon, 1745.
Lawe (Queen's co. ?), 4318.
Lawen, William, pardon, 14[illegible].
Lawghocure, co. Gal., [illegible].
Lawghill, river (Loghill), co. Lim., 6073.
Lawles, Adam, pardon, 1317, 3434.
„ Donagh, pardon, 4[illegible].
„ Edm., pardon, 6773.
„ Hugh, pardon, [illegible].
„ James, pardon, 1317.
„ John, chaplain, lease, 1343.
„ Morris, pardon, [illegible].
„ Nich., pardon, [illegible], [illegible], [illegible].
„ Paul, pardon, [illegible], [illegible].
„ Peter, pardon, 6377, 6378.
„ Rob., pardon, 6314.
„ Thomas, pardon, [illegible].
„ Walter, pardon, [illegible].
„ Wm., pardon, [illegible], [illegible].
„ land of, in Clonmel, [illegible].
Lawless, Shan roe, pardon, [illegible].
Lawleston, co. Westm., [illegible].
Lawlis, Wm., pardon, [illegible].
Lawlor, David, pardon, [illegible].
„ Edm. m'Shane, pardon, [illegible].
„ Patr., pardon, [illegible].
Lawnder, Maurice, pension, 1[illegible].
„ Morrish, pardon, [illegible].
Lawndleston, [illegible].
Lawnie, Tho., pardon, [illegible], [illegible].
La Wore, water called (The Golden hand, the southern outlet of Lough Owel), 1340.
Lawraugh (Laragh), co. Kild., [illegible].
Lawrence—Laranc—Larence:
„ James, pardon, [illegible].
„ Lewis, water bailiff of Shannon, [illegible]; pardon, [illegible]; pensioner, [illegible].
„ Richard, serjeant-at-arms, [illegible], [illegible]; marshal of Four Courts, [illegible].
„ Walter, house in Maryborough, [illegible].
„ Walter, pardon, [illegible]; keeper of Naas gaol, [illegible], [illegible].
Lax weirs. See Leix la weres.
Layles, David, pardon, 1470.
Layles, John, pardon, [illegible].
Layman, deprived of rectory, [illegible].
Layncheslowne (co. Tip. ?), [illegible].
Layne, co. Dub., [illegible].
Layne—Layon. See Loyne, co. Sligo.
Laynearboy — Laynorraghboy (part of barony of Loyny, O'Hara boy's country), co. Sligo, [illegible].
Laynes. See Loyne.
Laynycara Reogh — Lanyora Reoghe (part of barony of Loyny, O'Hara Reogh's country), co. Sligo, [illegible].
Layon. See Loyon.
Layragh, co. Gal., [illegible], [illegible].
Le, Tho. See Lea.
Lea, Dermot m'Morris, pardon, [illegible].
„ Donell m'Conoghor m'Donogh, pardon, [illegible].
„ Donell m'Donogh m'Owen, pardon, [illegible].
„ Edm., pardon, 4[illegible], [illegible].
„ Gerrott, pardon, [illegible].
„ Gilpatrick, pardon, [illegible].
„ John, pardon, [illegible].
„ Margaret, pardon, [illegible].
„ Maurice, pardon, [illegible].
„ Morris m'Owen, pardon, [illegible].
„ Owen, pardon, [illegible].
„ Teige m'Morishe, pardon, [illegible].
„ Capt. Tho. See Lea.
„ Thomas, pardon, [illegible].
Lea alias Lee, Walter, pardon, [illegible].
Lea, Queen's co. See Leye.
Leabeg, co. Wick. See Le Begge.
Leabymkidde, co. Cork, [illegible].
Leacarraghan (co. Don.), [illegible], [illegible].
Leacowe (co. Sligo ?), [illegible].
Leackan, co. Rosc., [illegible].
Leacone, co. Cork, 4418.
Leadiffe (co. Cork ?), [illegible].
Leaffeny, co. Sligo. See Lowthine, Liefeny, Liehveny.
Leagan (co. Tip. ?), [illegible].
Leaganeo (co. Tip. or Kilk.), [illegible].
Leaggaytyvmy Ile, co. Down, [illegible].
Leagh, Onoghor m'Donell, pardon, [illegible].
„ Connoghor m'Dairmound, pardon, [illegible].
„ David garragh m'Shane, pardon, [illegible].
„ Donell m'Shane, pardon, [illegible].
„ Ellen ny Tone, pardon, [illegible].
„ Morrish, pardon, [illegible].
„ Murrogh, pardon, [illegible].
„ Wm., pardon, [illegible].
Leaghan, Teig m'Conoghor I, pardon, [illegible].
Leaghane, Donell m'Dermot I, pardon, [illegible].
Leaghassy river, co. Don. See Liashasagh.
Leahbaliymoydan, co. Rosc., [illegible].
Leaghe, in Connaught, 1[illegible].
Leaghe, Dermod m'Gilleconne, pardon, [illegible].

INDEX TO FIANTS.—ELIZABETH.

Leaghe, Donogh m'Donogh, pardon, [illegible].
" Donogh m'Dermod I, pardon, [illegible].
" John m'Donogh I, pardon, [illegible].
" Teig m'Dermod I, pardon, [illegible].
Leaghlin. *See* Leighlin.
Leaghoro, co. Long., [illegible].
Leaghlenkroname, [illegible].
Leaghvally (co. Tip. ?), [illegible].
Leaharoum (Laharan ?), co. Kerry, [illegible].
Leakmadrongh, co. Cav., [illegible].
Leahrahe, co. Gal., 4879
Leakagh (Queen's co. ?), 6731.
Leakane (co. Rosc. ?), [illegible].
Leakee (co. Tip. ?), [illegible].
Leakeyvallye, co. Westm., 1371.
Leakine (Leckan), co. Westm., rectory, [illegible].
Leales, Rich., pardon, [illegible].
Lealex, Maloghlin, pardon, 6737.
Lealor, Edmund, pardon, [illegible].
Lealgaide, co. Lim. or Cork, [illegible].
Lealy alias O'Mullaly, William, dean of Tuam, [illegible].
Leam — Leame, co. Mayo, [illegible]; castle and land, [illegible].
Leamchevog (co. Tip. ?), 6707.
Leamcon, co. Cork. *See* Lemcon.
Leamcor, co. Cork, [illegible].
Leame. *See* Leam.
Leame Ivanan — Leame Evanan — Leamevanan — Leamovanan — Lem Ivanan — Lemyvanan (Leim Ui Bhanain, Leap castle, King's co.), 1741, [illegible], 4136, [illegible], [illegible].
Leamaleam, co. Cork, [illegible].
Leamovanan. *See* Leame Ivanan.
Leam Iyn, Wm. M'Morish, pardon, [illegible].
Leam Inneagh, co. Clare, [illegible].
Leamnemihe, co. Clare, [illegible].
Leamneaih, co. Clare, [illegible].
Leamore, co. Rosc. *See* Lyemor.
Leamore, co. Wick. *See* Le Moore.
Lean, Doughow m'Conor Y, pardon, [illegible].
Leanach, Geoffrey, pardon, [illegible].
" Tho., pardon, [illegible].
Leannamore, co. Kerry. *See* Lyannamore.
Leannmore, [illegible].
Lean, Peter, pardon, [illegible].
Leary, Tho., pardon, [illegible].
Leare, co. Cav., [illegible].
Learga (Largay, co. Cav.), [illegible].
Learie, Awliffe m'Donogh I, pardon, [illegible].
" Connoghor m'Art I, pardon, [illegible].
" Conoghor m'Dermod I, pardon, [illegible].
" Ellen ny, pardon, [illegible].
" Tho. m'Awliff, pardon, [illegible], [illegible].
Learne (Larne), co. Antrim, [illegible].
Learne, co. Cav., [illegible].
Learrise, Wm., pardon, [illegible].
Leary, Conoghor m'Awliff I, pardon, [illegible].
" William, pardon, [illegible].
Learye, Wm., pardon, 4070.
Leas, Rich., pardon, [illegible].
Lease, Edm. fitz Morice, pardon, [illegible].
Leases of lands, conditions attached to, [illegible], [illegible], [illegible], [illegible], [illegible], [illegible], [illegible], [illegible], [illegible], [illegible].
Leasnabane, co. Gal., [illegible].
Leakmyn, co. Gal., [illegible].
Leather, illegal export of, [illegible], [illegible], [illegible].
" impressed for army, [illegible].
" not to be sold until examined and sealed by say-master, [illegible], [illegible], [illegible], [illegible].
" shoemakers of Waterford and Cork licensed to tan, [illegible], [illegible].
" *See* Tanning.
Leatrym (Leitrim, co. Cork ?), [illegible].
Leatrym. *See* Leitrim, co. Leit.
Leaugh, Queen's co., [illegible].
Leaugh, David Gall, [illegible].
Leawes, Brian, pardon, [illegible].
Leawgh, Thomas, pardon, [illegible].
Leayor, co. Cav., [illegible].
Leayaley, Tho. m'Donoghow, pardon, [illegible].
Lebalboye, Evan, pardon, [illegible].
Leban, Gillecalle m'Morris, pardon, [illegible].
Lebbale, co. Mayo, [illegible].
Le Beggo (Lambeg, co. Wick.), [illegible].
Lecaghe, King's co., [illegible].
Lecale—Lecaile—Lecayle—Leycall, co. Down, [illegible], [illegible], [illegible], [illegible]; to be made shire ground, [illegible]; martial law in, [illegible], [illegible], [illegible].
Lecan (Leckan), co. Sligo, [illegible].
Lecan, co. Wex., [illegible].
Lecanny (co. Mayo ?), 6767.
Lecarrowe, co. Rosc., [illegible]. *See also* Leigh-learrow.
Lecayle. *See* Lecale.
Leccan, co. Wex., [illegible].
Leckan, co. Sligo, [illegible].
Lecester, George, commissions, [illegible], [illegible].
" Rob. *See* Leicester.
Lecestown (Lecystown), co. Meath, [illegible].
Lechaghe, King's co., [illegible].
Lechannaghe (co. Kilk. ?), [illegible].
Leche. *See* Leech.
Lechmoe, co. Meath, [illegible].
Leckagh (see Leckagh, co. Kild.), [illegible].
Leckaghfine (Leckafinna), co. Gal., castle and land, [illegible].
Leckan, co. Sligo, [illegible].
Leckano, co. Cav., [illegible].

Lackane, co. Ross., 4678.
Lackane, co. Sligo, [illegible].
Lacke, John, clerk of ordnance, 5418.
Lacke (Leck), co. Mon., [illegible].
Lackes (co. Cork ?), 2368.
Ledgrenagh, co. Gal., [illegible].
Ledigan, co. Gal., 4518.
Ledwich—Ledwech—Ledwiche—Ledwyche—Ledwytche—Leedwyche:
" Edm. (of Carick), pardon, [illegible]; commissions, 4161, 4463.
" Edm. (of Ballimallake), [illegible].
" Edm., pardon, 4631.
" Gerald, pardon, [illegible], 6367.
" Henry, pardon, 4632.
" Katherine, 4623.
" Marion, pardon, 4682.
" Nich., pardon, 2468, 4778, 5143, 6697.
" Patrick, pardon, 4596.
" Peter, coroner, co. Westm., 4948.
" Piers, pardon, 4637.
" Richard, wardship of his heir, [illegible].
" Richard, pardon, 5818.
" Tho., pardon, [illegible].
" Walter, widow of, [illegible].
" Wm., pardon, [illegible].
Ledwychstown, co. Westm., 2318.
Ledwytche. See Ledwich.
Lee, Arthur, pardon, 5782.
" Connor m'Donoghow, pardon, 4781.
" Donell oge m'Donell, pardon, 4868.
" Edm., pardon, 5763.
" Henry, first sch., T.C.D., 5718.
" James, pardon, 1317.
" John, lease, [illegible].
" John (of Clonmel), pardon, 2801, 3782.
" John, pardon, [illegible], 4872.
" Knoghor, pardon, 4576.
" Nich., sheriff of Waterford, 5742.
" Teig, pardon, 4875, 5748.
" —Lee-Le, Tho. (of Castlemartin), pardon, 3873; commissions, 4150, 4464; lease, 4184; captain, pardon, [illegible]; provost marshal of Connaught, 4578, [illegible]; commissions, 4771, 5155; grant of a wardship, 5108.
" Tho., junr., pardon, [illegible].
" Wm. m'Thomas, pardon, 4383.
" Wm. oge Duffe m'Walter, pardon, 4878.
" See Ley.
Leech—leche, surgeon, 4028, 4804. See Physicians.
Leedwyche, Edm. See Ledwich.
Leek, co. Mon. See Licwe.
Leeke, John, controller of wine duty, 3768; clerk of the ordnance, 5437.
Leekyn (Lechan), rectory, co. Westm., 467.
Leen (Leny), co. Westm., rectory, 467, 5762.
Leery, Teige m'Donell ny killy Y, pardon, 4791.
Leffe, Melaughlen, 4914.
Leffelane, John, pardon, 4737.
Leffan, James, 1659. See Laffan.
le Ginke, Francis, protection, 1318.
Legan, [illegible].
Legan, barony, co. Down (the denominations mentioned are in parishes of Clonallon and Kilbroney), 1609, 4637.
Legane, co. Gal., 3185.
Legan, co. Kilk., [illegible], 5191.
Legan, grange of, co. Kilk., 594.
Legan (co. Ross. ?), 4340.
Loganlake (Logganhill), co. Meath, 1462.
Legane, co. Kilk., 6778.
Legganlane (co. Cork ?), [illegible].
Leggaule, co. Clare, 4408.
Leggoy, co. Mon., 5648.
Leggunhill, co. Meath. See Loganlake.
Leghan, Wm. m'Rimrie Y, pardon, 5782.
Leghanyneleylan (co. Clare ?), 5815.
Leghlinarrow Fearry, co. Mayo, 4268.
Leghlen—Leghlin. See Loughlin.
Leghlin, Ph., harper, 5104.
Leghmanaghan (Lemanaghan), King's co., 1848.
Leghnenan (co. Leit. ?), 6482.
Leghraneil (co. Kerry ?), 6477.
le Gilhem, Jacques, a Frenchman, pardon, [illegible].
Legin (co. Ferm. ?), 5402.
Legline or the Glinne (co. Long. ?), [illegible].
Legnie (co. Ross. ?), 6694.
Legreconn (co. Leit. ?), 4808.
Legrowle (co. Wick. ?), 6677.
Legrenan or the Grenan (co. Kilk. ?), 6794.
Legroghe, Teige O'Shanaghan, pardon, 934.
Legra, Donoghow m'Davy, pardon, 4811.
Lehannagh, co. Gal. See Lobonnoyn.
Lehane, Cormock O'Trantyman, pardon, 1823.
Lehannagh (co. Kilk. ?), 6042.
Lehe, Knoghor, pardon, 4874.
Lehenaghe alias Lenaghe (Lohonagh), co. Cork, 4328, 4736, 5784.
Lehennoyn (Lohanagh), co. Gal., 5418.
Lehedalmahin bury, co. Lim., 6468.
Lehillayn, co. Gal., 5804.
Lehin, Muriagh m'Donogh, pardon, 118.
Lehinch, co. Gal. See Lohynnh.
Lehinch—Lehinchie, King's co., [illegible], [illegible], 6152.
Lehinshe, co. Meath, 578.
Lehinchie. See Lehinch.
Lehen, co. Car., 4818.
Lehrny (Larha), co. Kerry, 4232.
Lehrally (co. Mon. ?), 5402.
Lehrally (co. Sligo ?), 6818.

INDEX TO FIANTS.—ELIZABETH.

Lehysch (Lohinah), co. Gal., [illegible].
Leighe, John ny, pardon, 6516.
Leicester — Leceter — Loycester, Robert, controller of customs, Drogheda, [illegible], 4781; clerk of crown and peace in Ulster, 4374, [illegible]; usher of Philipstown fort, [illegible], [illegible]; surveyor general of the ordnance, [illegible]; licence of absence, [illegible], [illegible], 6760.
" See Lecester.
Lehi (co. Cork ?), 6467.
Leidigan (Lydacan), co. Gal., 4970, 4471, [illegible], [illegible]-7.
Leigh, Conoghor m'Donogh, surgeon, pardon, 597.
" Dermod leigh m'Teige, pardon, [illegible].
" Donogh, pardon, 6516.
" Edm. m'Loghlin m'Shane, pardon, 6110.
" Edm. m'Shane, pardon, 6541.
" Katteline ny Dermod m'Teig, pardon, 6671.
" Moleghlin, pardon, 6707.
" Morieghe m'Donogh, pardon, 6110.
" Rob., pardon, 6477.
" Shane m'Conor m'Shane, pardon, 6640.
" Teig, pardon, 6578.
" Teig m'Dermot, pardon, [illegible].
" Teige fitz John, pardon, 6511.
" Thomas, pardon, 5372.
Leighballincclough, co. Mayo, 6911.
Leighbally Ardmunassan, co. Ross., [illegible].
Leighballyneeloy, co. Mayo, [illegible].
Leigh Carowe Rowgham. See Leigh Carrowroughan.
Leigharro—Leigharroe. See Leigharrow.
Leigharrow—Leighcarro—Leigharroe, co. Ross., 1462, 3341, 4948, 6016.
Leigh Carrow Arraghe—Leigh Ccarrowe arraghe, co. Ross., 6190, 6016.
Leigh Carrowhogrughell, co. Gal., 6911.
Leighcarrow brackloweo Aghleage—Leighe Carrowe Brackloweo — Liegh Carrow Brockloeo (Brackloonagh ?), co. Mayo, [illegible], 6911, 6616.
Leigh Carrow Carrovagan — Leighe Carrowe Corrovogan (Corravoggaun), co. Mayo, [illegible], 6911.
Leigh Carrow Clonde Killie Boallick—Leighcarrow Clondekille boalick—Leighe Carrowe Clondekilly Ballick (Cloonty-killew), co. Mayo, [illegible], 6911, 6616.
Leigh Carrow Cownele — Leighcarrow Cownyell — Leighe Carrowe Cowoneyle (Connell), co. Mayo, [illegible], 6911, 6016.
Leighcarrowoboggowghell, co. Gal., 4610.
Leighcarrowe Carran Reighe, co. Gal., 4610.
Leighcarrowe Knockiwe (Knockdoe), co. Gal., 4610.
Leighcarrowfarren Sleight Moyler in Bealick—Leigh Carrow forrensleighte Molline Beallick — Leighe Carrowe Farrensleighte Moyle in Boallicke, co. Mayo, [illegible], 6911, 6016.
Leigh Carrow Knoigin. See Leighcarrowneknoigen.
Leighcarrow ne Cloghe (Carrowcloghagh), co. Mayo, 6016.
Leighcarrowneknoigen — Leigh Carrow Knoigin — Leighe Carrowe ne Knoigyn, co. Mayo, [illegible], 6911, 6016.
Leigh Carrowroughan — Leigh Carowe Rowgham (Roogheun), co. Mayo, [illegible], 6911.
Leigh Ccarrowe arraghe. See Leigh Carrow Arraghe.
Leigh Ccarrowungeraghe, co. Ross., 4190.
Leigh Ccarrowneisterte, co. Ross., 4190.
Leigh Ccarrow wardaghe, co. Ross., [illegible].
Leighe (Greyabbey ?), co. Down, [illegible].
Leighe, Conoghor m'Shane, pardon, [illegible].
" Donald, pardon, 5567.
" Donogh roe m'Donoghe, pardon, [illegible].
" Gerald m'Tho., attainted, 6117.
" Honora ent Tane, pardon, 6110.
" Rob., pardon, [illegible].
" Teige, pardon, 672.
" Tho., attainder of, 6117.
" William, pardon, 872.
Leighobbay. See Lichie.
Leighe Carrowe Brackloweo. See Leighcarrow brackloweo aghleage.
Leighe Carrowe Clondekilly Beallick. See Leighcarrow Clondekillie Boallick.
Leighe Carrowe Corrovogan. See Leigh Carrow Carrovagan.
Leighe Carrowe Cowoneyle. See Leigh Carrow Cownele.
Leighe Carrowe Farrensleighte Moyle in Boallicke. See Leighcarrowfarren Sleight Moyler in Bealick.
Leighe Carrowe Knappee, co. Sligo, [illegible].
Leighe Carrowe Moytlerwyn (Muniorowen, co. Gal.), [illegible].
Leighe Carrowe necladdy, co. Mayo, [illegible].
Leighe Carrowe ne Knoigyn. See Leighcarrow neknoigen.
Leighe Carrowe Tullaghe, co. Sligo, [illegible].
Leighomackemaske, church of, 697.
Leighie, Donogh m'Craghie I, pardon, [illegible].
" Wm., pardon, 6312.
" Wm. m'Donogh Y, pardon, 4782.
Leighill, 6478.
Leighkcarrow Clondowro, co. Mayo, [illegible].

Leighlen. *See* Leighlin.
Leighlen, in province of Connaught, 1478.
Leighlenbridge. *See* Leighlinbridge.
Leighlin—Leighlen—Laghlen—Laghlin—Laghlyn—Laughlen—Laughlin—Lechlin—Leighlene—Leighlyn—Loughlen, 94, 63, 818, [illegible], [illegible], 1114, 1447, [illegible], [illegible], [illegible], [illegible], [illegible], [illegible]; burned by rebels, [illegible]; possessions of earl of Ormond in, surrendered, [illegible], [illegible], [illegible], [illegible], [illegible], [illegible], 8411. *See* Old Leighlin, Leighlinbridge.
„ castle, constable of, 15, 1444, [illegible].
„ fort, garrison at, [illegible].
„ hospital or mansiohouse for lepers, [illegible].
„ bishop Thomas (O Fihel), commission, [illegible]-7.
„ bishop Daniel or Donell (Cavenagh), commissions, [illegible], [illegible], [illegible], [illegible], [illegible].
„ bishop Richard Meredith, [illegible]; fined by star chamber, [illegible]; pardon of alienation, [illegible]. *See* Meredith.
„ bishop (*see* Ferns), [illegible]-9, [illegible], [illegible].
„ bishop and chapter, letter of, [illegible].
„ dean, [illegible], [illegible], [illegible], [illegible], [illegible].
„ prebendary, [illegible]-6.
„ diocese, [illegible], [illegible], [illegible]; advowsons granted, [illegible], [illegible], [illegible]-6, [illegible]-8, [illegible].
Leighlinbridge—Laghlinbridge—Laughlenbridge—Loughlinbrig—Leighlenbridge, co. Car., [illegible], [illegible], [illegible].
„ castle, [illegible]. *See* Leighlin.
„ house of Carmelites leased, [illegible], [illegible].
Leighno, John, pardon, [illegible].
Leigh ny Dermodie, Honora, pardon, [illegible].
Leighragh (Laragh? co. Westm.), [illegible].
Leighterrow—Leightenrowe (Lowarrow?), co. Rosc., [illegible], [illegible].
Leighy, Donnogh, pardon, [illegible].
Leigne, Dermod m'Connoghor I, and others of the same, pardon, [illegible].
Leilaugh, co. Tip., [illegible].
Leim Ui Bhanain, King's co. *See* Leame Ivanan.
Leinagh, Moragh m'Shane, pardon, [illegible].
„ Oliver, pardon, [illegible].
„ Shane, pardon, [illegible].
Leinaghe, Dermitius or Derbo, pardon, [illegible].
„ Tho., attainted, [illegible].
Leinaghenton (co. Tip.?), [illegible].
Leine, Donell m'Awlyve I, pardon, [illegible].
Leingir (co. Rosc.?), [illegible].
Leinster—Leynster, lord deputy occupied in government of, [illegible], [illegible]-4; commissions for government of, [illegible]-8, [illegible].
„ east of Barrow to be surveyed for a shire, [illegible]; land not shire ground to be divided into shires, [illegible]; rebels in, [illegible], [illegible]; proctors of leper houses may ask for alms in, [illegible]; concealed lands, [illegible].
„ general of the forces in, [illegible], [illegible], [illegible].
„ escheator, [illegible].
„ provost marshal, [illegible], [illegible], [illegible], [illegible], [illegible].
„ martial law, [illegible], [illegible], [illegible].
Leiriagane, co. Westm., [illegible].
Leirgo—Loyrgo, co. Down, rectory, [illegible], [illegible].
Leirgin, co. Gal., [illegible].
Leirige, Donogh m'Donell, pardon, [illegible].
Leirie, Donell, pardon, [illegible].
„ Philip ny, pardon, [illegible].
Leirue (Larne?), co. Sligo, [illegible].
Leirvey, co. Meath, [illegible].
Leis. *See* Leix.
Leisaghe, Nich., pardon, [illegible].
Leiter, co. Kerry, [illegible].
Leitheragh, [illegible].
Leitry, co. Cork. *See* Fonaghe Beghitry.
Leitrim, co. Clare. *See* Leotrym.
Leitrim, co. Cork. *See* Leatrym, Letrim, Leitrome, Loytrim.
Leitrim, co. Gal. *See* Letrim.
Leitrim, co. Kerry. *See* Loytrim, Lietrim.
Leitrim, King's co. *See* Loytrym.
Leitrim—Leatrym—Leotrym—Letrim—Leirym—Leytrom, co. Leitrim, [illegible], [illegible], [illegible], [illegible]; manor, [illegible].
„ county, commission to set out, [illegible], [illegible]; pardon to men of, [illegible], [illegible]; martial law, [illegible]; commission to prosecute rebels, [illegible].
„ „ sheriff, [illegible].
„ „ otherwise Breny[illegible], [illegible].
„ *See also* Lynkrinyche.
Leitrim, co. Lim. *See* Lietrem.
Leitrim, co. Mon. *See* Leotrymboga, Leotrymmore.
Leitrim, co. Rosc. *See* Lotrem, Librim.
Leiwe, Hugh, pardon, [illegible].

INDEX TO FIANTS.—ELIZABETH.

Leix—Leis—Leixe—Lex—Leyse—Lies (a district in Queen's co.), 11, 18, 62, 122, [illegible] 1084, [illegible]; survey of bounds, [illegible]; O'Moores of, excepted from pardon, [illegible]; martial law in, [illegible]; commission to treat with people of, 182.
„ lieutenant of, 133, 2843.
„ commander of, 4044.
„ governor of forces in, 0808.
„ sheriff, [illegible]. See Queen's co.
„ abbey of (Abbeyleix), [illegible]; site and possessions of the abbey granted, 687.
„ castle of Maryborough in, constable of, [illegible].
„ fort of, 8, 98.
„ „ lieutenant of, 4, 10, [illegible], [illegible], 2843, [illegible], [illegible].
„ „ commander of, 4044.
„ „ victualler of, [illegible].
Leix (Abbeyleix), Queen's co., 467.
Leix in wevre fishery—Lex weir (Lax weire) Limerick, 1806, [illegible].
Leixlip — Leixlipp — Leixlippe — Lexlip— Lexlipp—Lexlippe—Leyslip, co. Kild., 487, [illegible], [illegible].
„ provost of the town, [illegible].
„ manor, castle, lands, &c., leased, [illegible]; granted, [illegible]; alienation of, [illegible].
„ monastery of, granted, [illegible].
„ rectory, 1877, [illegible], [illegible], [illegible].
„ land of parish church, [illegible].
Lekaghe prebend, [illegible]. See Lockaghe, co. Gal.
Lekeeve, co. Sligo, [illegible].
Lelandiston, co. Kilk., 912.
Leleno, co. Meath, [illegible].
Lelenabeale, co. Tip., [illegible].
Leleson, Hugh, pardon, [illegible].
Lelesse, co. Gal., [illegible].
Lelee, David, clerk, pardon, 4475.
Leling, co. Gal., [illegible].
Lem (King's co. ?), [illegible]. See Leame Ivanan.
Lemagh (co. Car. ?), [illegible].
Lemanaghan, King's co. See Loghmanaghan, Lethmanaghan, Lovanaghan, Lyvanaghan.
Lemcon—Lemcoune (Lemcon, co. Cork), [illegible].
Lemeneaghe, co. Clare, castle and land, [illegible].
Lemenagh (co. Clare), [illegible].
Lemericheall—Lemerycahill (in par. Ballymacelligott), co. Kerry, castle and lands, [illegible]. See Lemhorenhold.
Lemevanan. See Leame Ivanan.
Lemyvore, co. Mon., [illegible].
Lemgare—Lemgaare (co. Ross. ?), [illegible].
Lemgor, co. Ross., [illegible].
„ See Lymagar.
Lemhorenhold, co. Kerry, [illegible].
Lem Ivanan. See Leame Ivanan.
Lemlare—Lemlarie, co. Cork, [illegible]. See Lymlary.
Lemlemoneilleran — Lemliemoneilleran, co. Tip., [illegible].
Lemnah, co. Clare, [illegible].
Le Moore (Lemmore, co. Wick.), [illegible].
Lemy. See Inylemy.
Lemyvanan. See Leame Ivanan.
Lenagh—Lenaghe alias Lebenaghe (Lebenagh), co. Cork, [illegible].
Lenagh, Andrew, pardon, [illegible].
„ Patrick, [illegible].
„ Tho. oge, pardon, [illegible].
Lenaghe m'Gerrot glays, Mayo, pardon, [illegible].
„ Peter, pardon, [illegible].
Lenaghe. See Lenagh, co. Cork.
Lenaghmore — Lenaghmore, co. Westm., [illegible].
Lenam, Thomas, commission, [illegible].
Lenamarron, King's co. See Lynamarron.
Lenan, Edmund, wife of, pardon, [illegible].
„ Elizabeth, pardon, [illegible].
„ Robert, pardon, [illegible].
Lenane (co. Gal. ?) [illegible].
Lenaughe, Patrick, [illegible].
Lenche, Stephen, pardon, [illegible].
Lenchie, Dermod m'Shane, pardon, [illegible].
„ Morertagh m'Gilleel, pardon, [illegible].
Lendoneilyeare, co. Westm., 1480.
Lenghlemayne, co. Ross., [illegible].
Lenoheaghe, co. Lim., [illegible].
Lenall, Redmund m'Philbek, pardon, [illegible].
Lenegon (co. Leit. ?), [illegible].
Lenreaghe, co. Gal., [illegible].
Lenham, Thomas (son of Rich. of Adamstown), wardship, [illegible].
Lenifeck, John, pardon, [illegible].
Lenigier (co. Ross.), [illegible].
Lennaghmore. See Lenaghmore.
Lennan, John, pardon, 8, [illegible]; house at Dublin, [illegible].
„ Patrick, pardon, 8.
„ Rich., pardon, [illegible].
Lennane, Nich., pardon, [illegible].
Lenroge (co. Car. ?), [illegible].
Lenshie, Donogh m'Teig I, pardon, [illegible].
„ Teig m'Teig Y, pardon, [illegible].
Lensky, Dermod m'David I, pardon, [illegible].
„ Tho., pardon, [illegible].
Lensye, Margaret, pardon, [illegible].
Lenton, Edw., lease, [illegible].
Lenus, Fynine m'Conoghor m'David, pardon [illegible].

INDEX TO FIANTS—ELIZABETH.

Leavicke, John, coroner of Drogheda, [illegible].
Leaver, Dougagh, pardon, [illegible].
Leay, Molaghlin and Teig mac Mahowny Y, pardon, 4478.
Leay, co. Wexf. See Leam, Lyn de Leighlin
Leayeagh (co. Lim.?), 6507.
Lee, Edmund, pardon, 3303, 3467, 4453, 4471, 6497.
" James, pardon, 3467, 4471, 6478.
" John, pardon, 3217, 3478, [illegible].
" Katherine, pardon, 6452.
" Morrish, pardon, 6478.
" Rich., pardon, [illegible], 4471, 6469.
" Tho., pardon, 6197.
" alias Lea, Walter, pardon, 3467, 3784, 6470.
" William bay, pardon, 3467.
" Wm. buoy m'Nich., pardon, 6464.
Leeffyane, co. Sligo, 6478.
Leeghill, King's co. (Leghill, now co. Kild.), [illegible], 1444.
Leenagh, James oge m'James, pardon, 4140.
Leonard, Alex., pardon, [illegible].
" Elis, widow, [illegible].
Leonard—Leonarde, George, grant of land, 610; his widow, [illegible].
Leonardstown, co. Meath. See Leynaghstown.
Leopardstown, co. Dub. See Ballinlowen, Ballynalowre.
Leorum (Lorum), co. Car., rectory, 1880, [illegible].
Lees, Edm., pardon, 6453.
" James, pardon, 6453.
" John, pardon, [illegible], 6194.
" Morish m'Gerrot, pardon, 6634.
" Rich., pardon, [illegible].
" Shane fitz Rich., pardon, [illegible].
" Simon fitz John, pardon, 6464.
Leotarry—Leotory (Lettery), co. Gal., [illegible], [illegible].
Leotrim. See Leitrim, co. Gal.
Leotrym (Leitrim, co. Clare?), [illegible].
Leotrym. See Leitrim.
Leotrymhoge (Leitrim), co. Mon., [illegible].
Leper house, Cashel, 6514.
" Leighlin and Gowran, [illegible], [illegible].
" Youghal, [illegible].
Leperstone (co. Wat.?) [illegible].
Lequarrown, co. Sligo, [illegible].
Le reggan (Largay or Redhon in N.W. of co. Cav.?), [illegible].
Lerayo, co. Gal., 4078.
Lerbecke, co. Westm., 1480.
Lere, Honor ny, pardon, [illegible].
Lerga (Largay, co. Cav.?), [illegible].
Lerganboy (Larganboy), co. Cav., termon, [illegible].
Lerie, Conoghor m'Teig m'Donogh I., pardon, [illegible].
" Dermod leigh m'Donogh, pardon, [illegible].
" Donell m'Shane, pardon, [illegible].
" Donogh m'Conoghor m'Teig, pardon, [illegible].
" Ellen ny, pardon, 6487.
" Eylyne ny Diermody Y, pardon, [illegible].
" Granie ny, pardon, 6467.
" Helen ny, pardon, 6487.
" Mahown m'Awliff Y, pardon, [illegible].
" Teig m'Shane I, pardon, [illegible].
Le Rode, co. Wick., [illegible].
Lerra, co. Gal., lordship and manor, [illegible].
Lerradie, co. Sligo, 6484.
Lerry, co. Gal., 5334.
Lery, Brian ogo Y, pardon to wife of, [illegible].
" Conoghor m'Teige I., pardon, [illegible].
" Dermod m'Donell I., pardon, [illegible].
" Donell m'Diermod Y, pardon, [illegible].
" Donogho m'Dermody Y, pardon, [illegible].
" Donogho m'Teige Y, pardon, [illegible].
" Ellen ny Diermody Y, pardon, [illegible].
" Manus m'Cahall, pardon, 4727.
" Margaret ny Connor Y, pardon, 4781.
" Teige m'Dermod Y, pardon, [illegible].
Les —, most place names commencing so, are indexed Lis —.
Leshanestown—Lyshinestown (Leshanestown?) co. Meath, 1230, 1124.
Lesiton, King's co., 6214.
Le Skin, [illegible].
Leskin — Leskyn, co. Wex., rectory, [illegible], 1577.
Leskyn, co. Kilkenny, 977.
Lesmullen — Lesmalen — Lesmolen — Lesmollen—Lessemollen—Lesmollen — Lesmollin — Lesmollyn — Lismolle — Lysmollen (Lismullin), co. Meath, [illegible], [illegible], 1484, [illegible], [illegible], [illegible], 4119, 4[illegible], [illegible], [illegible]; rectory, [illegible].
" house of nuns of the Holy Trinity, possessions leased, [illegible], 1401, 4199; granted, [illegible]; premises, 6797.
Lessy, James, pardon, 810.
Le Strange, Hamond, heir of Nich., 6710.
" lady Margaret Bath, wife of Sir Thomas, 748, [illegible].
" Nicholas, knt., custody of his lands, 6710.
Le Strange — le Straunge — le Strang — le Straung — le Strange — Strang—Strange — Straunge, Thomas (of Ballymore Loughsudy, afterwards knt.), Sheriff of Westm., [illegible], 118, 178.

INDEX TO FIANTS—ELIZABETH.

Le Strange:
441; seneschal of Dalton's country, 1415; constable of Roscommon castle, [illegible]; chief commissioner of Connaught, [illegible]; commissions, [illegible], 216, 261, 860, [illegible], 643, [illegible], 652, 1106, [illegible], [illegible], 1417-8, 1434, 1498, 1624, [illegible], 2345, 2464, [illegible], [illegible], 2376, 2737, 2764, [illegible], [illegible], 3117, 3687-8, [illegible], 4151, [illegible], 4190, 4428, 4514, 4783, 4744, [illegible], 5426, 5178, 5182, [illegible], 5349, [illegible], [illegible]; pardon, 118, 441, [illegible], 1147, 1744; pardon at his suit, 3429; leases, [illegible], 1179, 1814, 2159-4, 2737-8, [illegible], [illegible], [illegible], 4590; his wife, 748, 3811, [illegible].

Leitire, co. Gal., [illegible].
Leteyle, co. Louth, [illegible].
Letercane, co. Sligo, [illegible].
Letermakee—Lyttermackloo (Lettermuckoo), co. Gal., [illegible], [illegible].
Leteruellan, co. Gal., [illegible].
Lethe (co. Kerry ?), [illegible].
Letherim, co. Wick. or Dub., [illegible].
Lethmanaghan (Lemanaghan), King's co., [illegible].
Letherime (Leitrim, co. Cork), grant, [illegible].
Letrim—Liatrom—Listrim—Lytrim (Leitrim, co. Cork), [illegible], [illegible], [illegible], [illegible].
Letrim—Letrym—Leatrim (Leitrim), co. Gal., castle and lands, [illegible]; manor, [illegible].
" John Bourke [illegible] baron of, 4137; marriage suit, [illegible].
Letrim. See Leitrim, co. Leit.
Letrim (co. Rosc. ?), 4777.
Letrom, co. Cav., [illegible].
Letrugh (co. Kerry ?), [illegible].
Letrym. See Letrim, co. Gal.
Letrym. See Leitrim, co. Leit.
Letrymo (Leitrim, co. Rosc. ?), 4777.
Letter—Lettyr—Lyter—Lytter—Lyttyr, co. Kerry, [illegible], [illegible], [illegible], [illegible], [illegible], [illegible], [illegible].
Letteren, co. Gal. See Lecterry, Leyderry.
Letterbrock, co. Mayo. See Litterbrock.
Lettergeish (Lettergesh, co. Gal. ?), [illegible].
Letter Gorman, co. Cork, [illegible].
Letteringeighe (co. Gal.), [illegible].
Letterlicky, co. Cork. See Litterlicky.
Letteriume, King's co. See Lettyur.
Lettey m'Ubenhon, co. Kerry, [illegible].
Lettermaclaue, co. Gal., [illegible], [illegible].
Lettermullen, co. Clare, [illegible].
Lettermuckoo, co. Gal. See Letermackoo.

Lettirro (co. Gal. ?), [illegible].
Lettertinlis — Lettirtinlis — Littertinlis — Littirtinlis (Lettertinlish, co. Cork), [illegible], [illegible].
Lettir—Littir (co. Cork ?), [illegible], [illegible].
Lettir, co. Kerry, [illegible].
Lettirtinlis (see Lettertinlis), 6770.
Lettowne (Letown), co. Clare, [illegible].
Lettrom, co. Clare, [illegible].
Lettrum (Leitrim, co. Rosc. ?), [illegible].
Lettyer — Litter — Lyttyre — Lyttyure (Letterlum, King's co. ?), 673; rectory, 673, [illegible], [illegible].
Lettyr. See Letter.
Levorocks. See Leverocks.
Leughlen. See Leighlin.
Louth, Shane m'Geoghegan, pardon, [illegible].
Levalentine, [illegible].
Le valley (co. Wat. or Cork ?), [illegible].
Levally, co. Rosc., [illegible].
Levallyrough, co. Down. See Levallyriagh.
Levan (Liffane), co. Lim., [illegible].
Levanaghan—Lyvanaghin (Lemanaghan, King's co.), [illegible], [illegible].
Levedisstowne. See Lovelistown.
Leveg, co. Kerry, [illegible].
Levallyriagh (Levallyrough), co. Down, [illegible].
Leverett, William, pursuivant, [illegible], [illegible].
Leverett, Edmund, chamberlain of the Exchequer, [illegible], [illegible].
Leverocks—Leverock—Levorocks (co. Car.), country of, [illegible], [illegible], [illegible].
Leverton ( ), preacher, ecclesiastical causes commission, [illegible].
Levory, in Youghal, [illegible].
Levus, Nich., pardon, 1784. See Lewes.
Levetiston — Lovelistown — Levetston — Levidston, co. Kild., 14, 1684, [illegible], [illegible].
Levo, Donell m'Gerowill Y, pardon, [illegible].
Levoney, co. Long., [illegible], [illegible].
Levore, near Ardcallen, co. Kerry, [illegible].
Levorance, Robert, pardon, [illegible].
Lewally (co. Mon. ?), [illegible].
Lewes, David, pardon, [illegible].
" Edmund, pardon, 1684.
" James, pardon, 1634.
" John, pardon, [illegible], 1684.
" Nicholas, son of, pardon, [illegible]. See Lewes.
" Thomas, lease, 2378; second engrosser of the Exchequer, [illegible], [illegible].
" Walter, house in Naas, [illegible].
" Walter, pardon, 1694.
Lewhime (Loughbeey), co. Sligo, [illegible].
Lewice, Thomas, grant of wardship, [illegible].
Lewis, Francis, pardon, [illegible].
" Nich., chief engrosser, Exchequer, [illegible].
" Teig, pardon, [illegible].

INDEX TO FIANTS—ELIZABETH.

Lywlos, Wm., pardon, [illegible].
Lowragh [ ], 4780.
Lowry, co. Gal., [illegible].
Lowraith Loys (Lowraith, co. Louth), 1312.
Lox. See Leix.
Leslip—Leslipp—Leslippe. See Leixlip.
Loxwery or Common weir, Limerick, [illegible].
See Leix in weres.
Loy, captain, men serving under, [illegible].
" Edward, murder of, 437.
" Emericus, pardon, 487.
" James, pardon, 3494.
" John, pardon, 3079.
" John, pardon at suit of, 3452.
" Maurice, pardon, 3034.
" Nicholas (of Kilkenny), pardon, 1078, 2434.
" Nicholas, wardship, 5344.
" Rob., 4152.
" Shane, pardon, 441.
" Simon, heir of, 5344.
Loy[ ] (co. Car. or Wex.), 878.
Loybin, Donogh m'Shane ny, pardon, 4742.
Loyaghe. See Leckagh, co. Kild.
Loycall. See Loxale.
Loycester, Robert. See Leicester.
Loycester, Peter, grant of land, [illegible].
Loydegare, co. Gal., [illegible].
Loydery (Lettera ?), co. Gal., 4642.
Loydican—Loydigane, co. Gal., 4575, [illegible].
See Lidegane, Lydecane.
Loye, Teig, pardon, [illegible].
Loye (Lea, Queen's co.), town of, [illegible].
Loyes, Tho., pardon, 4891.
Loyeston. See Loytowne.
Loygayne I Hanly, co. Ross., 4648.
Loyghraith (Laragh ?), co. Westm., [illegible].
Loyland, co. Dub., 262.
Loyles, John, pardon, 3457.
" Nychol fitz Philip, pardon, [illegible].
" Tho. fitz Nicholas, pardon, 4462.
Loym, co. Gal., [illegible].
Loymeeny, co. Lim., [illegible], 4618.
Loymlary (Carrigleamleary ?), co. Cork, [illegible].
Loymnaih (co. Clare ?), 6817.
Loyn, Awliff, pardon, [illegible].
" Derby, or Dermicius, pardon, 118.
" John, pardon, 4467, 6467, 6871.
" Shane m'Donoghowe Y, pardon, 4781.
" See Loyne.
Loynagh—Loynaghe:
" Edm., pardon, 648.
" Edw., pardon, 4777.
" Geoffrey, pardon, 3817, 3941, 4137.
" Gerald roe, pardon, 3817.
" Gilbert, pardon, 3818.
" James, pardon, [illegible].
" John, pardon, [illegible].
" Maurice, pardon, 3818, 3941.
Loynagh, Morris, pardon, [illegible].
" Moyler, pardon, 3814.
" Olo m'Shane, pardon, 4418.
" Oliver, pardon, [illegible], 3941.
" Peirs, pardon, 1134, 4117, [illegible], [illegible].
" Peter, pardon, 3408, 4100, [illegible].
" Redmund, pardon, [illegible].
" Richard, pardon, 3814, 3443, [illegible].
" Rob., pardon, 4462.
" Sheffyne, pardon, 642.
" Theobald, pardon, 3721, [illegible].
" Tho. m'Rich., pardon, 3777.
" Tho., captain of footmen, pardon, 3794.
" Tho., pardon, 4117.
" Tho., attainted, 4378, 4462. See Lynagh.
" Walter, pardon, 842, 1[illegible].
" Wm. m'Shane, pardon, 4418.
Loynaghes, sept of, martial law in their land 3032.
Loynaghton (co. Meath), [illegible].
Loynan's lands in Kilmainham, 3418.
Loynes, John, pardon, 3440.
Loynaughton (Leonardstown ?), co. Meath, 3342.
Loyne, Awliffe m'Mahowne I, pardon, [illegible].
" Brene of Awly I, pardon, [illegible].
" Conoghor m'Shane I, pardon, [illegible].
" Donoghow m'Donell Y, pardon, [illegible].
" Enos, pardon, 6467.
" Gormaly ny, pardon, 6467.
" John, pardon, [illegible].
" John m'Donogh I, pardon, [illegible].
" Teige m'Shane, pardon, [illegible].
" William, pardon, 1018.
Loyne (King's co. ?), 4022.
Loyne—Layne—Laynes—Layon—Loyn—Mughery Loynye (barony of Leyny), co. Sligo, [illegible], 4860, 5161, 5724, [illegible], [illegible]. See also Laynmoriny, Laynyecare Rengh O'Hyn
Loynogh, James m'William m'Shane, pardon, 678.
" Piers m'William m'Shane, pardon, 676.
" Tho., pardon, [illegible].
Loynoh—Loynolh, co. Clare, 6817.
Loyne, Walter, pardon, [illegible].
Loynoygh, Wm., pardon, 4104.
Loynagh, Richard, pardon, 1400.
" Sheffyn, pardon, 1401
Loyns, Alexander, pardon, [illegible].
Loyns (co. Mayo ?), 5787.
Loyseter. See Leicester.
Loyny, co. Sligo. See Loyne.
Loyragh, Cormock m'Donogh, pardon, [illegible].
" Teige O'Hallowan, pardon, [illegible].
Loyraith (Laragh), co. Westm., [illegible].

INDEX TO FIANTS—ELIZABETH.

Leyrge (see Leirge), co. Down, 1888.
Leyris, Ellen ny, pardon, 6461.
Leyris, co. Kerry, 8467.
Leyrreg, co. Meath, 887.
Leyry, Dermod roe m'Conoghor Y, pardon, 6781.
Leyraghe, Nich., sub-sheriff of Kildare, pardon, 3452.
Leys. See Leix.
Leyse, Mowe ny, pardon, 4182.
Leyslip. See Leixlip.
Leytragh, co. Long., 3083, 5157.
Leytriemmaghe, co. Kilk., 1717.
Leytrimtoes, co. Louth, 1723.
Leyton (Laytown), co. Meath, 1460, 3879, 3888.
Leyton, great, co. Meath, 1777.
Leytowne—Leyoton, co. Meath, 64, 871.
Leytrim — Leytryme (Leitrim, co. Cork), rectory, 1088, 2828.
Leytrim (Leitrim), co. Kerry, 8123.
Leytrom (co. Leit.), 4794.
Leytryn (Leitrim), King's co., 2516.
Leytryn, 6102.
Leytryme. See Leytrim, co. Cork.
Lezquarryne, co. Rosc., 4741.
Liagh, John fitz Darby, pardon, 6875.
" Niall, pardon, 2017.
Liagh Garrow Brunkloan. See Leigh Garrow Bracklown.
Liaghmokovoge (co. Tip. ?), 6863.
Liakeilliaghe (Lackendilagh ?), co. Wat., 188, 8132.
Liales, Wm., pardon, 6878.
Liathmagh (Leaghany river, co. Donegal), 4896, 5687.
Lietrum. See Leitrim.
Libbie—Leisboblay—Lighbley (Lickbla, co. Westm.), 4889; rectory, 1088, 3478.
Libbronagh (Lisronagh), co. Tip., rectory, 1142.
Liche, Rich., pardon, 6616.
Lick (co. Lim. or Kerry), 4612.
Lickadowne — Lickidowne — Likadown (Lickadoon), co. Lim., 3767, 4021, 5487, 6594. See also Lickydwne.
Lickbearagan (Lickbarrahane, co. Cork), 6611.
Lickbla, co. Westm. See Licbla.
Lickdowne. See Lickadowne.
Lickinfovan, co. Kerry, 6868. See Likfavin.
Lickelly—Likellie—Likellye, co. Lim., 6363, 4871, 6626, 6121.
Lickoly, 5483.
Licksidstown, co. Kilk. See Likedisten.
Lickliane (Lickleash, co. Cork ?), 6942.
Lickley, co. Gal., 4416.
Licklyenrane (co. Gal. ?), 4878.
Lickonawe. See Lixnaw.
Lickydwne (Lickadoon, co. Lim. ?), 6478.
Lidegane, co. Gal., 3447.
Liecarra, co. Cav., 4824.
Liefuny (Lenfony), co. Sligo, 4728.
Liego (Loch ?), co. Mon., 5492.
Liegh, Tho. m'Shane, pardon, 6488.
Lieghe, Melaghlin, pardon, 1892.
Liehiry, co. Long., 5106.
Liehvony — Liehwony (Lenfiny ?), co. Sligo, 2891.
Liemarton, King's co., 2818.
Lienhen, co. Sligo, 6436.
Lietennemaynn, King's co., 4181.
Lieter m'crnoen, co. Kerry, 6468.
Lietrom (Leitrim), co. Long., 5083, 5157.
Lietrim. See Leitrim.
Lietrim, co. Kerry, 6123.
Lietry (co. Cav. ?), 5783.
Lieutenant of the army, 6981, 6825.
Liewe, Ellice, pardon, 6828.
Liewiane, Pat., pardon, 6675.
Liex. See Leix.
Liffane, co. Lim. (see Lovane), 6873.
Liffie—Liffy—Lyffie—Lyffye river, 1783, 6416 6819; mills and fishing at Kilmainham, 626, 2884; at Leixlip, 2898; country south of, 142, 6941. See Anlyffe, Anliffie, Ayliffe.
Liffiecaghan, 6642.
Liffy. See Liffie.
Ligard in Thricene, co. Clare, 6877.
Ligcarde (co. Clare ?), 5784.
Lighbley. See Lichbla.
Lighill alias Lorkehill, co. Westm., 1088.
Lighters impressed for army, 1861, 5481, 5991, 3028.
Liman, Donogh m'Teig Y, pardon, 4418.
Likarre (co. Long. ?), 5576.
Likadown. See Lickadowne, 6487.
Likedisten — Lykidiston (Licketstown, co. Kilk.), 427, 6664.
Likeholewir (co. Kilk. ?), 1878.
Likellie—Likellye. See Lickelly.
Likenny, co. Mayo, 5777.
Likfavin, co. Kerry, 6123.
Likisnawe—Likesnawe. See Lixnaw.
Lillieghmore (Lullymore), co. Kild., 431.
Lime impressed for the army, 378, 1182.
Limeskilpill, co. Down, 4887.
Limeonarragan, King's co., 1782.
Limerick—Limeric—Limericke—Limerik—Limerike—Limric—Limrick—Limrike — Lymbrick — Lymbrike—Lymbrycke—Lymerick — Lymericke — Lymerik — Lymeryck — Lymrick (mentioned as a description), 79, 177, 187, 191, 204-6, 691, 2482, 2184, 2317, 2830, 2884, 2891, 3941, 4168, 4187, 4478, 4817, 5784, 6088,

Limerick:
6462, 6461, 6498, 6197, [illegible]; sessions at, 3484, 4347; imports of wine, &c., 6746; illegal exports, [illegible]; land near, 6477; premises in, 6347; rock of Asgeaston near, 1[illegible] 6113; men of, spoil French ship, 1518.
„ mayor, 6541; commissions, [illegible], 620-7, 828, 2150, 2480, [illegible], 4186, 4468, [illegible], 6916, 6661.
„ mayor, bailiffs, and citizens, authorised to appoint gauger, [illegible]; grant of lands, [illegible].
„ bailiffs, commission, 4186.
„ recorder, 620-7, 828, 1948, 2768, 2771, 3032, [illegible], 4186, 4498.
„ alderman, 4186.
„ merchants, 1288, 3008, [illegible], [illegible], [illegible], 4761, 4805, [illegible], 6194, 6074, 6704, 6461.
„ constable of the castle, 1326, 3803, 3846, [illegible], 4744, 4791, 6107, [illegible], 6164.
„ archdeacon's court, house called, 6941.
„ Back lane, 3943
Gardewarr, 3937.
„ Dominican friary granted, [illegible]
„ gaol, escape from, 4837.
„ Kings island, 1294, [illegible].
„ Kings mills, 3377, [illegible], 6106-8.
„ Lazarets—Laix in worros, 1224, [illegible].
„ Mill lane, 6576.
„ Millshore, 6942.
„ Monkslands near, 3902.
„ Rock of the Shannon, 5186.
„ S. John, rectory, 5414.
„ S. Mary, parish, 6578.
„ S. Nicholas, parish, 6941, 6376; cemetery, 3941.
„ S. Peter, church or cell, possessions leased, [illegible]; granted, 6728, 6131.
„ weirs, 1258, 2989, 6201.
„ port, supervisor, 6659.
„ gauger, searcher, and surveyor, 161, [illegible], 2218.
„ gauger and searcher, 603; right of appointment conceded to corporation, 3937.
„ surveyor or surveyor, 603.
„ collector of wine impost, 1490, 2128, 3767, 3816, 4026, 6031, 6916.
„ comptroller, 1494, 3157, 3768, 3843, 3596, 3875, 3689, 4322, 6917.
„ wine impost leased, 4020.
„ bishop Hugh Lacy, commissions, 808, 620-7, 828; lease, 6184.
Limerick, bishop William (Casey), commissions, 1840, 2768, 2771, [illegible], 3186; appeal from, 4186.
„ bishop John (Thornburgh), commissions, [illegible], 4616, [illegible], [illegible], 6144, [illegible].
„ bishop, reservation to, of liberties due to his church, 1676.
„ precentor or chanter, [illegible], 6418; manor of, 6134-5.
„ chancellor of cathedral, 6364, [illegible], 6961.
„ treasurer, 5384.
„ prebend in cathedral, 6418.
„ official principal, 5394.
„ ecclesiastical commission in diocese, 5683, 6918.
„ county, doubtful lands to be made shire ground, 1946, 2768, 2840; disputes between inhabitants and earl of Ormond, [illegible]; command of soldiers, 3457, [illegible]; great and small cocries, [illegible].
„ county, justices of peace, [illegible].
„ „ general escheator, 4772.
„ „ sheriff, 43, 837, 1322, 1828, 1784, 2404, 2768, 2771, 2818, 3941, 4442.
„ „ clerk of the crown, [illegible].
„ „ general cessor, [illegible].
„ „ ecclesiastical commission, 620-7.
„ „ martial law, 968, 1037, 1338-40, 1630, 1842, [illegible], 2404, [illegible], [illegible].
„ „ lands of White Knight surrendered, [illegible]; lands of earl of Desmond granted by custodiam, [illegible]; escheated lands allotted to undertakers, [illegible]; grants to the undertakers, [illegible], [illegible], [illegible], 6171, 6179, 3974, [illegible], [illegible], 6444, [illegible], [illegible], 4717, 4791-2, [illegible], [illegible], 6186.
Limerkarrie (co. Lim.?), 6461.
Limrie—Limrick—Limrike. See Limerick
Linagh, Dorothy, pardon, 6152.
Linse—Linch—Linche. See Lynch.
Linshin, Morierigh m'Conoghor I., pardon, 6183.
Lincole, Andrew fitz John, pardon, 6677.
Lincoll, Katherine, wardship, 6114.
„ William, his heiress, 6114.
Linoy, Cahell m'Edm., pardon, 6670.
Linogh, John, pardon, 6748.

INDEX TO FIANTS.—ELIZABETH.

Linen draper in Naas, 1489.
Linen drapery, trade in, 58.
Linen yarn, illegal export of, 5068.
Ling impressed for army, 1169.
Linham, Rich. (of Adamston), wardship of his heir, 5783.
Linmoune (co. Ferm. ?), 4810.
Linseed, growth and export of, 4661.
Lionadon, co. Wex., 4654.
Lioskie, Donell m'Shane I, pardon, 6458.
Lion, Margaret, pardon, 6567.
Lions. See Lyons.
Lippyatt—Lipiot — Lyppyattie, Hugh, grant of land, 636 ; commissions, 843, 5784.
Liraoh Ille, co. Cork, 5963.
Liradien, co. Down. See Ballyliesdougan, 1682.
Lisagh, Giles nine, pardon, 6440.
" Honora ny, pardon, 6440.
" James, pardon, 6567.
" Katherine nyn, pardon, 6440.
" Uny nyn, pardon, 6440.
Lisaghe, Redmund, pardon, 6948.
Lisaghenedan, co. Westm., 5565.
Lisalakan—Lysalycan. See Lisallican.
Lisalvye—Lysalvye (Lisealway, co. Rosc.), 6777.
Lisalycan. See Lisallican.
Lisamlak, co. Cav. See Lisamlake.
Lisanaronaghe, co. Cav., 6582.
Lisanloghwe—Lysanloghwe (Lisanloughe? co. Clare), 4678.
Lisanover — Lysanover—Lysanower (Lisanover, co. Cav. ?), 4816, 6657.
Lisanelle, co. Tip., 6765.
Lisarblagh, co. Cork, 6782.
Lisard—Lysard (Lisnard ?), co. Long., 6969.
Lisardspanla, co. Kerry, 6123.
Lisbane (Lisbane), co. Lim., 2874.
Lisballagh, co. Tip., 6512.
Lisballabar, co. Cav., 4891.
Lisballagh, co. Tip., 6681.
Lisballimore, co. Gal., 6718.
Lisballinardan, co. Rosc., 6777.
Lisballo, co. Cav., 4891.
Lisbally, co. Cav., 4891.
Lisbalo, co. Cav., 6667.
Lisbane (co. Cav. ?), 1677.
Lisbane, co. Down, 4890.
Lisbane, co. Lim. See Lisbaen.
Lisbane (co. Tip. ?), 6708.
Lisbany (co. Tip. or Kilk. ?), 5163.
Lisbeg—Lysbeg (co. Gal.), 4678, 6722.
" See also Lisgog.
Lisbeghan—Lisbeghane, co. Lim., 6678.
Lisbelled (Lisbealad), co. Cork, 6426.
Lisbigne (Lisbigney), Queen's co., 1692, 6424.
Lisboman (co. Leit. ?), 4768.
Lisboyne alias Lisbigne, Queen's co., 6826.
Lisbryoyn (Lisbrannan), co. Mon., 6666.
Lisbony, co. Tip., 1714.
Lisbyaly (co. Cork ?), 5270.
Liscaghe—Lescaghe, co. Kerry, 4828.
Liscadonan—Lyscadonan, co. Long., 6648.
Liscahane — Lyscahane — Lyskahane, co. Kerry, 6648.
Liscanamann, co. Gal. See Liskmoman.
Liscand, co. Lim., 6123.
Liscanill—Liskanill, co. Lim., 6840, 6117.
Liscannor, co. Clare. See Liskanowre.
Liscapple, 5927.
Liscarney, co. Mon., 6666.
Liscarragh, 4768.
Liscarroll—Lescarroll — Lesmarroll—Liscarrowll—Lisnarroll—Liskarroll—Lyskaroll, co. Cork, 1084, 6814, 6426, 6829, 6763 ; manor, 6827 ; rectory, 4862. See also Lish Carvell.
Liscartan—Lescartan, co. Meath, 1184, 6118.
Liscartie—Lescartin, 478.
Liscaylagh—Lescaylagh, King's co., 1884.
Liscecarle, co. Gal., 6447.
Lischowill, co. Ferm., 6002.
Liscloghev, co. Westm. See Lisloghev.
Lisclunes (King's co. ?), 6874.
Liscolle—Lescolle (co. Leit. ?), 6428.
Liscollan (co. Kerry ?), 4714.
Liscollyn—Lyscollyn (co. Gal. ?), 4874.
Liscolyn (co. Kilk. or Tip. ?), 6736.
Liscoman — Lyscoman (Lismagomman), Queen's co., 1686, 6824.
Liscomyskie (Liscumasky), co. Mon., 1629.
Liscon, co. Long., 6962.
Lisconagh—Lesconagh — Lysconagho—Lysconnogh — Lysconowe (Liscony ?), co. Sligo, 5486, 6816, 6566.
Lisconduff, co. Mon. See Listonduff.
Liscordan—Lyscordan (Lisgordan), co. Lim., 6626.
Liscormake—Lyscormake, chapel, 84.
Liscore — Lescore — Lyscorey, co. Kerry, 4678, 6126.
Liscreagh, co. Tip., 6812, 6568.
Liscrisnaghan — Lyscrisnaghan, co. Gal., 6062.
Lisdalin (co. Kilk. ?), 4952.
Lisdavonya, co. Cork, 4486.
Lisdomasky, co. Mon. See Liscomyskie.
Lisdalou (co. Cork ?), 6701.
Lisdalone, co. Rosc., 4891.
Lisdaragan — Lesdargan, co. Kerry, 3482, 4677, 4678.
Lisdawny, co. Kilk., 6363.
Lisdeasragane (co. Kerry ?), 4484.
Lisdorg, King's co. See Lisdarge.
Lisdiche. See Lisdugh.
Lisdoan—Lysdoan, co. Gal., 4687.
Lisdoan — Lesdoan (Lisduane, co. Lim.), 6171.

INDEX TO FIANTS.—ELIZABETH.

Lisdoogan, co. Sligo. See Carrow Lisdowgan.
Lisdoonvarna, co. Clare. See Lisdunvarny.
Lisdornan, co. Meath. See Lisbernon.
Lisdowan — Losdowan — Lysdowan, co. Westm., [illegible], [illegible]. See Losdowan.
Lisdoufe—Lysdoufe (co. Cav. ?), 4812.
Lisdough. See Lisinah.
Lisdough—Lysdough, co. Long., [illegible].
Lisdowny—Lisdony—Lisdonye—Lisdownie—Lysdony, co. Kilk., 847, 1583, 2189, 4180, 6494.
Lisdoyn (co. Rosc. ?), 6344.
Lisdrolin (co. Kilk. ?), 1874, 6302.
Lisdrowmno — Lysdrowmno, co. Ferm., 6043.
Lisdrumallein, co. Armagh. See Drumkeelan.
Lisduane, co. Lim. See Lisduan.
Lisduf—Losduf—Lysduffe—Lisduff — Lysduff, co. Gal., 4313, 4591, 5416, 6565.
Lisduf, co. Long., 6082.
Lisduf—Lisduff—Lysduf—Lysduff, Queen's co., 977, 5844, 6461.
Lisduf—Lysduffe (co. Rosc. ?), 6308, 6542.
Lisduf—Lysdul (co. Tip. ?), 4807.
Lisduff—Lisduffe, co. Clare, 1258, 6802.
Lisduffe—Lysduffe (co. Gal. ?), 4874.
Lisduffe (co. Long. ?), 6642.
Lisduffe—Lysduffe (co. Rosc. ?), 6842.
Lisduffe (co. Westm. ?), 6487.
Lisdugh — Lysdiche — Lysdough, co. Gal., 1041, 1881, 6488.
Lisduh rectory, co. Gal., 3455.
Lisduller (Lisdullere), co. Rosc., 6873.
Lisdargo—Lysdargo (Lisdarg, King's co. ?), 6312.
Lisdromlom—Lesdromlome (Drumlom), co. Mon., 6649.
Lisegare—Lysegare, co. Cav., 4834.
Lisegugine—Lysgugine, co. Gal., 4730.
Lisegomey (Lismagonwny), co. Mon., 6649.
Lisknoghur — Lesknoghor, co. Kerry, 5961.
Lislltin—Lisellin—Lysellton—Lysaltyne — Lysseltyn (Lisselton), co. Kerry, 4718, 5457; rectory, 5980, 5768, 5886; advowson, 6235.
Lismane—Lysmane, co. Kilk., 1184.
Lismoby—Lysmoby, co. Rosc., 6741.
Lismore—Lysmore, 6747.
Lismoyran (Lismoyran, co. Tip.), 2311.
Lismucky. See Lismucky.
Lisnyskis, co. Mon., 5625.
Lisnaania, co. Gal., 5514.
Lisnamirore (co. Gal. ?), 5632.
Lisnalake—Lysnalake (Lisnalah), co. Cav., 4501.
Lisnarie, co. Mon., 5594.
Lisnonaghan, co. Mon., 6601.
Lisnoolaugho — Lysnoolaugho, co. Lim., 6783.
Lisnospyran. See Lisnospyran.
Lisneaskey (co. Cork ?), 4152. See Lisknoghe.
Lisnosky—Lisnouske—Lysnoskey—Lysnosky (Lisnnisky), co. Tip., 4087, 4288, 4809, 6443.
Lisnower. See Lisnovor.
Lisnuskee—Lysnuskee, co. Kilk., 4502.
Lisophobill (Lisophobbie, co. Rosc.), 6784.
Lisordowly, co. Long., 6282, 5107.
Lisoraghaine — Lysorochane (Lisoraghann, co. Gal.), 4808, 4876.
Lisornonogh, co. Tip., 6422.
Lisoserlinge (see Listorlyn), 6684.
Lisovarry—Lysovarry—Lysovarye, co. Cork, 4298, 4734.
Lisovoyrane — Lysovoyrane (co. Wat. ?), 6623.
Lisfada—Lysfada, co. Gal., 4884.
Lisfinni—Lisfynie—Lisfyny—Lysfyny (Lisfinny), co. Wat., 5941, 5624; allotted to undertakers, 4871; castle and lands granted, 5048. See also Lisfynen.
Lisfarbie—Lysfarbie, co. Clare, 4266, 4874.
Lisfoinsbie (Lisfunshion ?), co. Tip., 6188.
Lisfolyn, 6412.
Lisfynon—Lisfynine—Lysfynyn (Lisfinny ?) co. Wat., 1046, 2198, 2475, 5774, 6229.
Lisfynie (co. Cork ?), 6563.
Lisfynie. See Lisfinni.
Lisfynine, co. Waterford. See Lisfynon.
Lisfyny. See Lisfinni.
Lisfynyn. See Lisfynon.
Lisgarvan, co. Car. See Lisbogarvan.
Lisgoinan — Losgoinan — Lysgoinan — Lysgoynam (Lisgenan), co. Wat., [illegible], [illegible]; chapel, [illegible], 3183.
Lisgibbon—Lysgibbon, co. Tip., 5668.
Lisgoban—Losgobbon — Lysgoban (Lisgobban, co. Rosc.), 4848, 4741, 5867.
Lisguigy (co. Mon. ?), 6622.
Lisgordan, co. Lim. See Liscordan.
Lisgormaloo—Losgormalee, 5440.
Lisgowle rectory (Lisgoold ?), co. Cork, 4352.
Lisgowre, co. Mayo, 6759.
Lisgriffin — Lysgriffyn, co. Cork, 3352, 4614, 6464.
Lishardill (Lisardill ?), co. Sligo, 6848.
Lishahane (co. Kerry ?), 5477.
Lishalloonyne, co. Cork, 6358.
Lishane (co. Cork ?), 6516–6, 6773.
Lisbarroll (Lisnarulla ?), co. Gal., 5423.
Lisballinardan (co. Rosc. ?), 5083.
Lish Carroll (Liscarroll, co. Cork ?), 5946.
Lisboulfe (co. Leit. ?), 5468.

INDEX TO FIANTS.—ELIZABETH.

Lishdoffe, co. Long., 3612.
Lishaugh, co. Mon., 5647.
Lishealane (co. Cork ?), 5516.
Lishebidalye (co. Cork ?), 6816.
Lishecorro—Lyshecoro, co. Lim., 5761.
Lishena, co. Tip. *See* Lisheene, Lisleine.
Lisheenataggart, co. Tip. *See* Lissin Itagart.
Lishegarron—Lyshogarron (Lisgarvan ?), co. Car., 554.
Lisheleyvane (Lislevane, co. Cork ?), 4524.
Lisheenarch (co. Tip. ?), 5745.
Lishenhall—Lesheenhall (Lissenhall), co. Dub., 2597.
Lishenoshigo, co. Cork, 6778.
Lishenorhig—Lyshonorhig—Lyshonorhige (co. Cork ?), 6518.
Lishervaliane, co. Gal., castle and land, [illegible].
Lishetrey (co. Cork ?), 6516.
Lishew, co. Rosc., 5437.
Lishgowre, co. Mayo, 5765.
Lishiansion—Lyshiansion. *See* Lesheenasion.
Lishin—Leshen, King's co., 2714.
Lishin—Lyshin (King's or Queen's co.), [illegible].
Lishinkelly—Lyshinkelly (co. Lim. ?), 6451.
Lishione (co. Rosc. ?), 6453.
Lishkonult—Leshkonult, co. Lim., 4534.
Lishle—Lyshle (co. Cav. ?), 4165.
Lishles (co. Long. ?), 6398.
Lishlevane, co. Cork, 4524.
Lishmore (co. Wat. ?), 6534.
Lishmorarthy—Lyshmorerthy, co. Tip. or Lim., 4768.
Lishmotty, co. Lim. or Cork, [illegible].
Lishnoynane, co. Tip., 4594.
Lishnahayrde (co. Cork ?), 6940.
Lishnogan (co. Leit. ?), 6452.
Lishnagonyne (Lismagonnorty, co. Kerry ?), 5477.
Lishnomaddry—Lyshnomaddry (co. Wat.), 1557.
Lishnorhige (co. Cork ?), 6518.
Lishnoselie. *See* Lisnaselie.
Lishnoshiele (co. Gal. ?) (*see* Lisnoyyole), 4573.
Lishnotollaghie—Leshnotollaghie, co. Leit., [illegible].
Lishride (co. Lim.), 6461.
Lishroosh, co. Gal. or Rosc., 5514.
Lishrwe—Lyshrwe, co. Lim., 5698.
Lishinhill. *See* Listowell.
Lishtrey, 6516.
Lishvickyre, co. Lim. or Cork, 6565.
Lishynaghie—Lyshynaghie (co. Rosc. ?), 6452.
Lishyonghane, co. Clare, 5617.
Lishyvane, co. Cork, [illegible].
Lisiergaill, co. Long., 5063, 6167.
Lisighane Swyane, 5158.
Lisin—Lysin (co. Clare ?), 4876.
Lisin—Lysin (co. Gal. ?), 4784.
Lisinan, co. Mon. *See* Lisseynan.
Lisinnahane—Lysinnahane, co. Gal., 4567.
Lisinnakoy—Lislsnakie (co. Cork ?), 6561.
Lisiqunkye—Lysinnakye, co. Tip., [illegible].
Liskdie, co. Tip., 6163.
Liskahane. *See* Liscahane.
Liskallie, co. Kerry, 6576.
Liskane, co. Kerry, 6942.
Liskamill. *See* Liscannill.
Liskaneowre (Lissanmore ? co. Clare), 4562.
Liskarie, co. Gal., 5421.
Liskarrell—Lyskaroll. *See* Liscarroll.
Liskarrye—Lyskarrye, co. Lim., [illegible].
Liskart—Leskart (co. Cork ?), 6512.
Liskaryo, co. Gal., 5421.
Liskayolaghe—Leskayolaghe, King's co., [illegible].
Liskeenan—Lyskeeneane—Lyskeenane—Lyskeynan—Lyskynan, co. Gal., castle and land, 4533, 4541, 4549; river of, 4518.
Liskehen—Leskehen, co. Wes'm., 1504.
Liskellin, co. Mayo, 4412.
Liskelleane—Leskelleane (co. Lim.), 6178.
Liskellye—Lyskellye, co. Mayo, 4573.
Liskennenan—Lyskennanain (Liscananann, co. Gal. ?), 4474, 4578.
Liskemet (co. Lim. ?), 5598.
Liskenlan, 6477.
Liskeon (co. Tip. ?), 6457.
Liskerry—Leskerry (co. Car. ?), 1557.
Liskeynane. *See* Liskeenane.
Liskillen—Lyskyllin, co. Lim., 5647, 6946, 6578.
Liskillin—Liskillyne, co. Mayo, [illegible].
Liskoteil—Lyskoteil, in Connaught, 1662.
Liskmawe. *See* Lixnaw.
Liskolcrean, co. Leit., 5445.
Liskreagh, 5692.
Liskyllin. *See* Liskillin.
Liskymon—Lyskymon, co. Lim., 6192.
Liskynan. *See* Liskeenan.
Liskyngorough, co. Mon., 6481.
Liskywin, co. Tip., 1557.
Lislagastaghe, co. Lim., 5411.
Lislaghtie—Lislaghtin—Lislaughty (Lislaughtin), co. Kerry, 5125.
house of Franciscan friars leased, 5177.
church of, 5177.
Lisle, Tho., marshal, Ecclesiastical High Court, 5348.
Lisleagh—Lysleagh, co. Gal., 4517.
Lisloe, co. Cork. *See* Lislie.
Lisleeye—Lysleeye, co. Rosc., 5435.
Lislennaghan, co. Clare, 6514.
Lislotrim—Lyslotrim, co. Cork, [illegible].

INDEX TO FIANTS—ELIZABETH.

Lislevan—Lislivan—Lyslevan—Lyslivan—Lyslyvan (Lislevane), co. Cork, [illegible], 4169, 4722, [illegible]. See also Lisheslevane.

Lislie, co. Cav., [illegible].

Lislie, co. Cavan, [illegible].

Lislie — Lisly — Lysly (Lisloe), co. Cork, [illegible], [illegible]; rectory, [illegible], 4169, 4778, [illegible].

Lislie, co. Gal., 5106.

Lislie, Tho. (see Lisle), 5340.

Lislihaugh, co. Mon., 6409.

Lislin—Leslin, [illegible].

Lislivan. See Lislevan.

Lisloghor—Losloghor, co. Westm., [illegible].

Lisloniue—Lysloune. See Lisloyne.

Lislonskeaghan—Lyslonskeghan, co. Rosc., [illegible], 5102.

Lisloyne—Lesloniue—Lesloynyne—Lysloune—Lysloyne, co. Kilk., 3069, [illegible], 4237, [illegible]; rectory, [illegible].

Lisly—Lysly, co. Cork, [illegible]. See also Lislie.

Lislycobahan, co. Mon. See Lissnakeygan.

Lismacallye — Lysmacallye (co. Mon.?), [illegible].

Lis m'Ea (co. Tip.?), [illegible], [illegible]. See also Lismackhee.

Lismackdonaghy — Lysmackdonaghy, co. Gal., [illegible].

Lism'Kery — Lismikire — Lysmackyrye — Lysmakery—Lysmikerie — Lysmykerry — Lysmykire—Lysmykyre, co. Lim. (Lismakeery), 1718, [illegible], [illegible], [illegible], [illegible]; castle and lands, [illegible]; rectory, [illegible], [illegible].

Lismackhee—Lismakee—Lismaky (Lismasee?), co. Tip., [illegible], [illegible]; grant, [illegible]. See also Lis m'Ea.

Lismacnole, [illegible].

Lismacorek, co. Mon. See Lisveacorin.

Lismacteig — Lysmacteige (Lismateig, co. Kilk.), [illegible], [illegible], [illegible], [illegible].

Lismafadda, co. Gal. See Lismyfadda.

Lismagham—Lysmagham, co. Clare, [illegible].

Lismagunway, co. Mon. See Lisegunney.

Lismahon, co. Meath. See Lismochon.

Lismakagan (Lismakeegan, co. Leit.), [illegible].

Lismakee. See Lismackhee.

Lismakeery, co. Lim. See Lism'Kery.

Lismakeige, co. Kilk., [illegible].

Lismakerke, co. Mon., [illegible].

Lismaky. See Lismackhee.

Lismalin—Lismallin—Lismalyn—Lysmallen—Lysmallyn — Lysmalyn — Lesmallen — Lesmalyn—Lesmallin, co. Tip., [illegible], [illegible], [illegible], [illegible], [illegible], [illegible]; rectory, [illegible], [illegible].

Lismarrog—Lysmarrog, co. Westm., [illegible].

Lismayne—Lesmayne, co. Westm., [illegible].

Lismavoltney (co. Gal.?), [illegible].

Lismealcomy—Lysmealcomy, [illegible].

Lismeckenan, co. Gal., [illegible].

Lismeiough, co. Rosc., [illegible].

Lismoilleryde (Lismulleryde?), co. Clare, [illegible].

Lismikire—Lysmikirke. See Lism'Kery.

Lismoleare, co. Gal., [illegible].

Lismochon — Lysmochone (Lismahon), co. Meath, [illegible], [illegible].

Lismoile—Lysmoile, co. Westm., [illegible].

Lismoill—Lysmoill, co. Gal., [illegible].

Lismolyrynoy (co. Clare?), [illegible].

Lismone—Lysmone, co. Gal., [illegible].

Lismoghe—Lysmoghe, co. Gal., [illegible].

Lismoile—Lysmoile, co. Gal., [illegible].

Lismolan—Lismolane—Lismollan—Lesmolane—Lysmoleyn, co. Lim., [illegible], [illegible], [illegible], 5112, [illegible].

Lismollin—Lismullen—Lismollyn. See Lesmullen.

Lismollen (or Lismolan), [illegible].

Lismonurn (co. Long. or Westm.?), [illegible].

Lismonanuse—Lysmonanuse, in Connaught, [illegible].

Lismony—Lesmony (co. Westm.?), [illegible].

Lismor. See Lismore.

Lismore—Lesmore, co. Cork, [illegible].

Lismore—Lesmore (co. Gal.?), [illegible].

Lismore, Queen's co., [illegible], [illegible].

Lismore—Lesmore (co. Tip.?), [illegible].

Lismore—Lismor—Lesmore—Lysmore, co. Wat., [illegible], [illegible], [illegible], [illegible], [illegible]; houses and gardens in, [illegible]; burgage of, [illegible], [illegible].

" Archdeacon's lands, [illegible].

" Christ's Church and cemetery, [illegible].

" S. Mochod's cathedral, vicars choral, [illegible].

" bishop Patrick, [illegible], [illegible]. See Waterford.

" bishop commendatory (archbishop Miler Magrath), [illegible], [illegible], [illegible].

" archdeacon Donogh M'Cragh, [illegible]; Donat called pro archdeacon, [illegible].

" diocese, benefices in, [illegible], [illegible], [illegible].

Lismortiltrie—Lismortiltride—Lysmortiltry—Lysmorehortie— Lysmorterty — Lysmorteriagh, co. Tip., 1296, [illegible], [illegible], [illegible], [illegible], [illegible].

Lismoyle — Lismoily — Lysmoyle — Lysmoly (Lismoyle?), co. Lim., [illegible], [illegible], [illegible].

Lismoyfine—Lysmoyfine, co. Gal., [illegible].

Lismoyneas, co. Tip. See Lisemoynan.

Lismoyny, co. Westm. See Lismoynoy.

Lismucky — Lysmucky (Lismuck?), co. Lim., [illegible], [illegible].

Lismulloreale, co. Clare. See Lismoilleryde Liswolwrikly.

Lismullen—Lysmullen, co. Lim., [illegible], [illegible].

Lismultin, co. Meath. See Lesmullen.

INDEX TO FIANTS—ELIZABETH.

Lismullin — Lismullin (co. Wex. ?), 6647, 6681.
Lismyfadda — Lismyfaddae (Lismafadda), co. Gal., 4718, 6421.
Lismykerry—Lysmykire—Lysmykyre. See Lismakerry.
Lisna—Lysna, co. Tip., 4660.
Lisnabryny (co. Cork), 2088.
Lisnacoyme—Lysnacoyme (co. Cork), 6471.
Lisnacullie, co. Lim. See Lisnakilly.
Lisnagalbraghe—Lysnagalbraghe (co. Ross. ?), 6182.
Lisnagall (co. Tip.), 6681.
Lisnagallaghe—Lesnagallaghe (co. Ross. ?), 5457.
Lisnagaul, co. Tip. See Lisnegall.
Lisnagumman, Queen's co. See Lisnegunan.
Lisnagonarny, co. Kerry. See Lishnagonayne.
Lisnagonoge, co. Tip. See Lisnegonok.
Lisnahedorne, co. Cav. See Lisnahoydirney.
Lisnalea, co. Mon. See Lisnale, Lisnilea.
Lisnamanamy — Lysnamanamy, co. Ross., 4571.
Lisnamrocke—Lisnamrock (co. Tip.), 6363, 6551.
Lisnamuck, co. Lim. See Lisnamucky.
Lisnanagh—Lysnanoagh, co. Long., 6499.
Lisnarode, Queen's co. See Lisnerode.
Lisnasallagh, co. Cork. See Lisnefallaghe, Lisnesalla.
Lisnaselle — Lishnaselle—Lisnaselle (Lisnaselle), co. Tip., 6348, 6463, 6764.
Lisnashannagh, co. Mon. See Lisnashinnagh.
Lisnashoner—Lysnashoner, stream, 6630.
Lisnaspoare, co. Mayo. See Lisnaspoory.
Lisnatibberd (co. Tip. ?), 6748.
Lisnavolinoyo—Lysnavolina—Lysnavoltay, co. Gal., 4078, 4780.
Lisnebynner—Lysnebynner (co. Westm. ?), 6637.
Lisnecarrowkielle — Lisnecarrowkilly (Carrowkeel), co. Mon., 6661.
Lisnache — Lysnache (Lisnanagh ?), co. Sligo, 6544, 6562.
Lisnecamyne — Lysnecamyne (co. Kerry ?), 6497.
Lisnecrine—Lysnecrine, co. Car., 604.
Lisnecroughe—Lysnecroughe (co. Mon. ?), 6043.
Lisnefallaghe (Lisnasallagh), co. Cork, 6667.
Lisnegall—Lysnegall (Lisnagaul, co. Tip. ?), 6376.
Lisnegaynin (co. Long. ?), 6112.
Lisnegnare, co. Cav., 4592.
Lisnegasin (co. Sligo ?), 6207.
Lisnegaraghe—Lisnegaraagh, co. Wat., 677, 1944.
Lisnegobaslane—Lysnegobaslane (co. Cork ?), 6421.
Lisnegonok—Lesnegonok (Lisnagonoge), co. Tip., 662.
Lisnehoydirney—Lysnehoydirney, co. Meath (Lisnahedorne, co. Cav. ?) 1040.
Lisnehoan, co. Clare, 4563, 4571.
Lisnekany—Lysnekany (co. Kilk. ?), 6072.
Lisnekilly, co. Mon., 6652.
Lisnele (Lisnalea ?), co. Mon., 6667.
Lisnemanamrahy—Lysnemanamae, co. Ros., 5797, 6428.
Lisnemrock. See Lisnamrocke.
Lisnemucky—Lysnemucky, co. Cork, 6478.
Lisnemukey — Lysnemukey (Lisnamuck), co. Lim., 5781.
Lisnenean—Lysnenean (co. Long. ?), 6499.
Lisnerode (Lisnarode), Queen's co., 4622.
Lisnesalla — Lysnesalla (Lisnasallagh), co. Cork, 6392.
Lisnesella. See Lisnaselle.
Lisneshinnagh (Lisnashannagh), co. Mon., 6642.
Lisnesilley—Lysnesilley, co. Tip., 4117.
Lisnespoory—Lysnespoory (Lisnaspoare, co. Mayo ?), 5476.
Lisnespyman—Lisnespyman, co. Mon., 6645, 6478.
Lisnespyle, co. Gal., 6780. See also Lishneshiele.
Lisnespyle—Lysnespyle, co. Ross., 4577.
Lisnetane — Lesnetan — Lesnetane — Lisnetany—Lysnetany, co. Kilk., 44, 63, 1803, 1811, 2062, 2284.
Lisnevagh, co. Car. See Lisnevoy.
Lisnevan—Lesnevan, 911, 5767.
Lisnevir (co. Car. ?), 1676.
Lisnevoliny. See Lisnavolinoyo.
Lisnevyn—Lysnevyn (co. Tip. ?), 5010.
Lisnicoll—Lysnicoll, co. Gal., 4664.
Lisnigaddy, co. Lim., 5079.
Lisnikaleo (co. Cork or Lim.), 6628.
Lisnilea—Lysnilea (Lisnalea, co. Kilk. ?), 6310.
Lisnoanagh — Lysnoanagh, co. Long. 6499.
Lisnodanaghe, co. Cav., 6687.
Lisnykillye, co. Lim., 6682.
Lisnylie—Lysnylie (co. Tip. ?), 6123.
Lisnyne, co. Mon., 5637.
Lisnynoharran — Lysnynoharran, co. Cork, 5428.
Lisnyskyo — Lysnyskyo (Lisnasiska), co. Lim., 5763.
Lisomohy—Lysomohy, co. Ross., 4741.
Lisonavarny — Lysonavarny (co. Clare ? perhaps Lisdoonvarna), 4763.
Lisoowo—Lysoowe, co. Ross., 4072.
Lispeg (Lisbeg), co. Gal., 4718.
Lispobbele — Lespoble — Lyspobele (Lispopple), co. Westm., 6294, 6467, 6486.
Lispolle—Lyspolle (co. Ross. ?), 6642.

INDEX TO FIANTS—ELIZABETH.

Lispopell—Laspopell—Lasypio—Lespoppell (Lispopple, co. Dub.), 784, 780, [illegible], 841, [illegible], [illegible], [illegible].
Lisquillins (co. Cork ?), 4791.
Lisrahoune (co. Tip. ?), [illegible].
Lisriogy, co. Long., 6404.
Lisro—Lisroe, co. Gal., 6447, 6612.
Lisronagh, co. Tip. See Liosronagh, Tullagh-Hironaghe.
Lisroyn—Lysroyne, co. Rosc., 4944.
Lisrushaggo—Lysrushaggo, co. Gal., 4944.
Lisruyn—Lysruyn, co. Rosc., [illegible].
Lisryan, co. Long., 6657.
Lisryoe—Lysryoe (Lisrivis ?), co. Gal., [illegible], [illegible].
Lissaboye—Lessaboye (Lisboy), co. Rosc., 4777.
Lissadill, co. Sligo. See Lissondall, Lishadill.
Lissaghncadan—Lysaghncadan, co. Cav., [illegible].
Lissaiore—Lesaiore, co. Gal., 5162.
Lissalican—Lesalican—Lessallican—Lysalakan—Lysalyman—Lysalikan, co. Cav., 1677, [illegible], [illegible], [illegible], [illegible].
Lissaloughe, co. Clare. See Lisanloghwe.
Lissalway, co. Rosc. See Lisslvye.
Lissamaron, co. Long. See Lissmaherne.
Lissamoia, co. Lim. See Lissamuntia.
Lissaniske, co. Lim. See Lisnyskye.
Lissanisky, King's co. See Lisinnskie.
Lissanisky, co. Tip. See Lisnosky.
Lissanode, co. Westm. See Lisnode.
Lissanover, co. Cav. See Lisanover.
Lissaphobble, co. Rosc. See Lisphobill.
Lissaphuca, co. Rosc. See Lisserphuca.
Lissard, co. Long. See Lisard.
Lissardowne—Lysardowne, co. Long., 4418.
Lissaroaghann, co. Gal. See Lissaroghane.
Lissarte, co. Mayo, 4[illegible].
Lissarty, co. Mon. See Lissarowarte.
Lissarnla, co. Gal. See Lisharroll.
Lissbrin, co. Gal., 6618.
Lisscarne—Lescarne (co. Leit. ?), 6708.
Lisscoylilire (co. Leit. ?), [illegible].
Lissdowne bryme—Lysdowne bryme, co. Cav., 6684.
Lissdoff. See Lisdal, co. Gal.
Lissduff—Lysduff (Lisduff), co. Lim., 6647.
Lissduff. See Lisluff, Queen's co.
Lissduffe (Lisduff, King's co. ?), 6422.
Lisseagh, co. Mon., 4678.
Lissehilly, co. Westm., 2234.
Lissehoneochor—Lysehoneochor (Lissyconor), co. Gal., 5105.
Lissenanowe (co. Sligo ?), 4678.
Lissendall—Lysendall, co. Sligo, 4702.
Lissendaryghe—Lysendaryghe (King's co.), 1402.
Lissodill—Lysodill (co. Gal.), 6478.
Lissolonvroo, co. Cav., 4634.
Lissdowncelchan—Lysdowncelchan, co. Cav., 4881.
Lissduffe, co. Rosc., 6933.
Lissdulloe, co. Westm., 4[illegible].
Lissefin, co. Clare, 4[illegible].
Lissegarian—Lysegarian (Lissgarian, co. Mon.), [illegible].
Lissoken—Lesoken, co. Gal., 6478.
Lisseltno, co. Gal., [illegible].
Lisselton, co. Kerry. See Lisleitn.
Lisseltyn—Lyseltyn. See Lisultin.
Lissemoarie, co. Mon., 6[illegible].
Lissemockagan—Lessemockagan (co. Leit. ?), 4768.
Lissemotte—Lysemotte (Lissamota ?), co. Lim., 1710.
Lissemoyny—Lysemoyny (Lismoyny), co. Westm., 2317.
Lissenachart—Lysenachart, co. Gal., 4444.
Lissenchonghor—Lysenchonghor (Lissyconor), co. Gal., [illegible].
Lissendall—Lesendall (Lissadill ?), co. Sligo, 4660, 4704.
Lissenogoway, co. Tip., [illegible].
Lissenolan (co. Clare ?), 6616.
Lissenolle—Lysenolle (co. Clare ?), [illegible].
Lissenosy, co. Cav., 4[illegible].
Lissenhall, co. Dub. See Lisfenhall.
Lissenilt—Lysenilt, co. Wat., [illegible].
Lissenlee, co. Mayo, 5[illegible]1.
Lissenkoyll—Lysenkoyll (co. Tip. ?), [illegible].
Lissenol (co. Rosc. ?), 4604.
Lissenode (Lissanode, co. Westm.), [illegible].
Lissenosky. See Lisnosky.
Lissennake, co. Westm., 1172.
Lissenyne—Lysenyne, co. Mayo, [illegible].
Lissephoonke—Lessephoonke (Lissaphuca), co. Rosc., 5620.
Lisserame—Lyserame (co. Mon. ?), [illegible].
Lisseroe—Lesseroe, co. Gal., 4[illegible].
Lisserowarte—Lyserowarte (Lissarty, co. Mon. ?), 5[illegible].
Lissetane (co. Mayo ?), 5707.
Lissetanvallye—Lysetanvally (co. Mon. ?), 5[illegible].
Lissevarrie, co. Cork, [illegible].
Lissevarrin, co. Cork, [illegible].
Lisseyoghane, co. Gal., [illegible].
Lisseynan (Lisdman), co. Mon., [illegible].
Lisshine (Lisheen, co. Tip. ?), [illegible].
Lisshinhuskye, co. Gal., [illegible].
Lisshillo, co. Cav., 5762.
Lissichurrig—Lissicurrigo (Lissycurrigh), co. Kerry, 5184, 5[illegible].
Lissiculligan—Lysiculligan, co. Cork, [illegible].
Lissicurringo (co. Kerry ?), 5184.
Lissidogan—Lysidogan, co. Gal., 4[illegible].

INDEX TO FIANTS.—ELIZABETH.

Lisilanmine, co. Clare, 6677.
Lisin—Lysnin (co. Tip. or Lim.), 4694.
Lisinnaine (co. Tip.?), 6568.
Lisindall. *See* Lisnendall.
Lisine—Lysine, co. Clare, 6617.
Lisine—Lesmine, co. Tip., 6510, 6561, 6562.
Lismo—Lysmine (Lisboen), co. Tip., 6694.
Lisinliffe, co. Rosc., 6172.
Lisin Itaggart (Lishenmataggart, co. Tip.) 6148.
Lisinmanmragh, co. Gal., 6664.
Lisinmarigid (co. Tip. or Lim.), 4694.
Lisinowen—Lysmoowle, co. Wat., 6182.
Lisnowskry—Lesinowskey, 6489.
Lisinnskie—Lysinnskie (Lismanisky), King's co., 6381.
Lisiny (co. Leit.?), 4794.
Lisloriahe, co. Tip., 6631.
Lismaconnegan — Lysmaconnagan (Lismacanigan?), co. Cav., 4834.
Lismaikin, co. Kerry, 6284.
Lismeal—Lesmeal, 6458.
Lismolian (co. Lim.), 6492.
Lismorievtagh. *See* Lismorahirie.
Lismoity. *See* Lismoie.
Lismollin. *See* Lismullin.
Lismygeill—Lysmygeill, co. Gal., 4697.
Lismard—Lysmard, co. Gal., 1681.
Lismgeragh. *See* Lismogeraghe.
Lismakilly — Lysmakilly (Lismacullie), co. Lim., 6478.
Lismavoy—Lysmavoy (Lismovagh), co. Car., 4834.
Lismoyd, co. Westm., 6682.
Lismycarrigie (co. Kerry ?), 6679.
Lismbwick, co. Mon., 6698.
Lismfyn (co. Rosc. ?), 6628.
Lismlaughe—Lesmolaughe, co. Meath, 6673.
Lismaine—Lesmanan—Lysmomine (Lismanon), co. Long., 6363, 6546.
Lismdiff, co. Rosc., 6628.
Lismnow—Lysmnow (co. Rosc. ?), 4340.
Lisrony—Lysrony, co. Down, 4677.
Lisrirroroaughe, co. Rosc., 6777.
Lisrickee, co. Tip., 1078-1.
Lisyogan, co. Gal. *See* Lismachongher, Lismahonechor.
Lisycronyn — Lysycrotnyn (co. Cork ?), 6948.
Lisycurrig, co. Kerry. *See* Lisdchurrig.
Lisyhollans—Lysyhollane, co. Cork, 6606.
Lisyliseyn, co. Clare, 6463.
Lisycarrogud—Lysymarregud, co. Tip., 6583.
Lisynboyn — Losynboyne (Lisboy ?), co. Meath, 287, 2943.
Lisynoalony — Lysymmalony, co. Clare, 6677.
Lisynowvin—Lysynowvin, co. Wat., 604.
Lisynunke—Lysyunske, King's co., 6468.
Lisyeyalley—Lysyeyalley, co. Cork, 6162.
Listamnoctanesdraghe — Lysvamnocamnoseraghe, co. Wat., 861, 6188.
Listanyne, co. Mayo, 4678.
Listarallie, co. Cork, 6567-8.
Listawne—Lesiawne, co. Leit., 6489.
Listen—Losten (co. Wat. ?), 3663.
Listdogher (Lisdogher ?), co. Westm., 1468.
Listelyn—Lestelyn, co. Westm., 1468.
Listen alias Liston, Rich., pardon, 6487.
Lister alias St. Leger, Patr., pardon, 4391.
" Rob., pardon, 6324.
Listerin, co. Gal., 1698.
Listerlyn—Listerlinge, co. Kilk., 6804, 6768.
Listernoe — Lesternon (Listernan), co. Meath, 1460.
Listerolin—Lesterolen (co. Kilk. ?), 6644.
Listicongher, 2943.
Listbany, co. Mon. *See* Listymnie.
Listoist—Lystoist, co. Long., 5404.
Liston, Ellen fitz Gerroit, pardon, 4487.
" Garrot, pardon, 4463.
" Gerald, pardon, 6183.
" Gerroit, pardon, 6478.
" Honora, pardon, 6473.
" alias Sellinger, John, pardon, 6179.
" John, pardon, 4423, 6363.
" Morris, pardon, 6478, 6363.
" alias Listen—Lyston—Lystown, Rich. or Ricard (of Kilmcannell, co. Lim.), pardon, 6616, 6487; his lands granted, 5047.
" Rich., pardon, 4537.
" Rob., pardon, 4538.
" Senlie, pardon, 6487.
Liston's lands in Youghal, 4898, 6034.
Listondaff (Liscondaff), co. Mon., 6834.
Listor, Edm. fitz Philip, pardon, 6487.
Listosty—Lysiosty, co. Rosc., 6463.
Listowell—Lestowell—Lestowell—Lishtohill — Listwohill (Listowel), co. Kerry 4698, 6883, 6788, 6180; rectory, 6634.
Listownie (co. Kilk. ?), 6484.
Listrey (Listry, co. Kerry ?), 6489.
Listrim — Lestrym — Lystrim, co. Kerry, 6014, 4838.
Listriesaghan—Lystrisaghan, co. Gal., 6109.
Listrolyn — Lestrolen (Listrolin, co. Kilk.), 6484, 6584.
Listry, co. Kerry. *See* Listrey.
Listwohill. *See* Listowell.
Listymnie (Listimny), co. Mon., 6634.
Lisynchegan (Lisynchahan), co. Mon., 6437.
Lisvann, 1918.
Lisvalon (co. Tip. ?), 1878.
Lisvicky, co. Tip., 6144.
Lisvolin, co. Cav., 6637.
Lisvote—Lesvote (Lismanote, co. Lim.), 6371.
Liswacorke (Lismacrork), co. Mon., 5648.

INDEX TO FIANTS.—ELIZABETH.

Lisvadigge—Lysvadigge, co. Cork, [illegible].
Liswalwridy (Lissnalbrenda ?), co. Clare, [illegible].
Lisyehwill—Lysychwill, co. Gal., [illegible].
Lisynyvill - Lysynyvill, co. Ross., [illegible].
Lisyvoghsly, co. Cork, [illegible].
Litirbrock (Letterbrock, co. Mayo), 6700.
Litle Bolies. See Little Bolies.
Litle Down—Litledown. See Little Downe.
Litlegrange. See Little Grange.
Litlegrove—Litle Growe (co. Kilk.), [illegible], [illegible].
Litle Ilande (Little Island), co. Wat., 118.
Litleton (Littletown), co. Kild., 6473, [illegible].
Litrime (Leitrim, co. Ross. ?), 4777.
Littell Graung. See Grange, Little Grange.
Littellgraunge (Littlegrange, co. Louth), [illegible].
Littell Riverston. See Little Riverston.
Littelton by Grangeford, co. Car., rectory, [illegible].
Litter (co. Gal. ?), [illegible].
Litter, co. Wex., [illegible].
Litterlicky—Litterlycky—Littyrlicky (Letterlicky, co. Cork), [illegible], [illegible], [illegible].
Litterlyrkle (co. Cork ?), [illegible].
Litter m'Phillipp — Lytter m'Phillipp, co. Mayo, [illegible], [illegible].
Litterrawhan (co. Clare ?), 6416.
Littertinlis (see Lettertinlis), [illegible].
Littier. See Lettyer.
Littir. See Lettir.
Littirtinlis. See Lettertinlis.
Little Arden, co. Down, [illegible], [illegible].
Little Beberk alias Bewbeck, co. Meath, [illegible].
Littlebole — Little Bolee — Little Boolys—Little Bulley, co. Kild., [illegible], 4673, [illegible], [illegible].
Littlebolies—Little Bolles—Little Bolyes—Litle Bolies, co. Meath, 211, 642, 1344, [illegible].
Little Boolys—Little Bulley. See Littlebole.
Little Downe—Litle Down—Litledown (co. Westm. ?), [illegible], [illegible].
Little Grandge, 158.
Little Grange—Lyttlegrange (Grangebeg ?), co. Kild., [illegible].
Littlegrange, co. Louth. See Littellgraunge.
Littlegrange, Queen's co., [illegible].
Little Grange—Litlegrange—Littell Graung (Grangebeg), co. Tip., [illegible], [illegible], [illegible], [illegible].
Little Grange, co. Westm., [illegible].
Little Graunge (co. Sligo), [illegible], 6407.
Littlegraunge, co. Tip., 6711.
Little Island, co. Wat. See Litle Ilande.
Little Newtown, [illegible].
Littlepace, co. Dub. See Pace.
Littlerath—Little Rathe, co. Kild., [illegible], [illegible].
Littlerath, co. Meath, [illegible].
Little Rologhe, co. Cav., [illegible].
Little Riverston — Littell Riverston, co. Meath, [illegible], [illegible].
Littletown, co. Kild. See Litleton.
Littyrlicky. See Litterlicky.
Livane, Thomas, 742.
Liverpooll, in England, 427.
Livery of lands, forfeitures for want of, [illegible]; note as to assessment of fine, [illegible].
Livery. See Lyvory, Coyne.
Livotiston, [illegible].
Living Spring of Largho, co. Tip., [illegible].
Livott, Philbocke fitz Tho., pardon, [illegible].
" Tho. roe fitz Tho., pardon, [illegible].
" See Lyvott.
Lixnaw — Lickenawe — Likienawe—Liknawe—Licknawe — Lixnawe —Lixnawe, co. Kerry, [illegible], 6457, [illegible], [illegible].
" Thomas, baron of, commission, [illegible]; pardon, [illegible].
" Patrick, baron of, [illegible]; pardon of son, [illegible]; his heir excepted from general pardon, [illegible].
" Joan, lady of, pardon, [illegible].
Loaln, co. Kerry, [illegible].
Loaghgarr (co. Lim. ?), 6457.
Loaghlineston, co. Cork, [illegible].
Locrkan, Barnaby, grant of land, [illegible].
Lochannsholme (co. Ross. ?), [illegible].
Locharewa. See Loegharewa.
Lochga, co. Cav., [illegible].
Lochmilkeryne, co. Ross., [illegible].
Lock, Martin, 842.
" Patrick, pardon, 6577.
" Walter, pardon, [illegible], 6477.
Lockardeston — Lockardiston — Lockartstowne (Lockardstown), co. Westm., [illegible], [illegible], [illegible]. See also Ballylockard.
Locke, John, rector of Old Ross, [illegible].
" Pats., pardon, [illegible].
Lockrt, Giles ny Canne, pardon, [illegible].
" Ralph, pardon, [illegible].
Lockwod—Lockowod—Lockwodde:
" James, pardon, [illegible].
" Thomas, dean of Christ Church, Dublin, takes oath of supremacy, 237; commissions, [illegible], [illegible], [illegible], [illegible], [illegible].
Lockwoode, Egidius roo Cann, pardon, [illegible].
Lodyne, John fitz Wm., pardon, [illegible].
Lossyllyne, co. Cav., [illegible].
Loddoragh, David m'Donogh, pardon, [illegible].
Loddowne (Ludden), co. Lim., rectory, [illegible], [illegible].
Loddeyn, co. Lim., 1680.
Lodge, George, lease of customs of Dublin, [illegible]; authorized to seize illegal exports, [illegible]; collector of wine duties, Dublin, [illegible]; premises in Dublin late in his tenure, [illegible].
Lodiragh, Donogh, pardon, [illegible].
Lodum, Wm., pardon, [illegible].

INDEX TO FIANTS—ELIZABETH.

Ladymacre, co. Lim., 5767.
Ladyshegg, co. Lim., 5767.
Lafin, Piers, pardon, 4178.
Laftehouse—Lofthowse, Adam, 486, 462. See Loftus.
Loftus, Adam, doctor of Theology, nominated archbishop of Armagh, empowered to act in the diocese and take the temporalities, 480, 487; styled archbishop, 543; made dean of S. Patrick's, Dublin, 697; archbishop of Dublin, 1185; keeper of the great seal, [illegible], 3169, 3406, 3611, 5784; lord chancellor, 4148; lord justice of Ireland, 3875, 4684, 5184, [illegible], 5546, [illegible]; master of court of Prerogative, 4765; judge of Prerogative court, 6611, 6735; judge of court of Faculties, 5177, 5186, [illegible], [illegible], 6769; commissary of diocese of Ossory, 4816; his surrogate or general substitute for Faculties and Prerogative, 4196, 4483; his vicar-general, 5547; writ to, [illegible]; first provost of T.C.D., 5718; licence of absence, [illegible], 674, [illegible], 1063, 5443; commissions, 485, 642, 547, 1417–18, 1494, 2117, 2345, 3444–5, 3818, 3574, 3933, 3784, [illegible], [illegible], [illegible], [illegible], 4647, 5118, 5182, 3596, 3641, [illegible], [illegible], [illegible], 3740, 4148, [illegible], 4490, [illegible], 4515, 4754, [illegible], [illegible], [illegible], 5194, [illegible], [illegible], [illegible], [illegible], [illegible], [illegible], [illegible], 5851, [illegible], [illegible], [illegible], [illegible], [illegible], [illegible], [illegible], [illegible], [illegible], [illegible], 6125, 6457, 6677, [illegible]; pardon, 1065, 7210, [illegible], [illegible], 4257; pardon at suit of, 1540; signs a fiant, 1459; letter to, 1534; his son-in-law, 5164; his son, 6166.
" Adam, A.M., judge of the marshal court, 6146, [illegible]; master in Chancery, [illegible], [illegible]; licence of absence, [illegible], 6475; commissions, [illegible], [illegible].
" Adam, captain, alienation to, [illegible]; commission, 6512.
" Anne, widow of Henry Colley, grant of a wardship, [illegible].
" Edward, marries heiress of Henry Duke, [illegible]; lease, 6030-1; alienation to, 6156; serjeant at laws, 6144, 6548; commissions, 6125–6, 6344.
" sir Edward, knt., commission, 6547.
" Edward, rector of Delgany, [illegible].
" Robert, leases, 576, 1548, [illegible], 5581.
" Thomas, constable of Wicklow castle, [illegible]; commission, 5945; sir Thomas, pardon at his suit, 6763.
Log (King's co.?), 6512.
Logacurry, 5112.
Logan (co. Rosc.?), 6754.
Logan park al Mallinat, co. Louth, [illegible], 3971, 5375.
Logganstown, co. Meath. See Longhanston.
Loggan, Hugh m'Teige a, pardon, [illegible].
" Rich., pardon, 4031.
Loggireyray—Loggtreynay (Logairyna, co. Wick.?), 4158, [illegible].
Logina, Dermod, pardon, 5488.
Loghanane, John, pardon, [illegible].
Logherteyne, co. Westm., 5547.
Logherte (Lohert?), co. Cork, 5405.
Loghie, Tirelagh m'Owen Y, pardon, 4784.
Loghill, co. Lim. (see Lawghill), 5578.
Loghill, co. Long. See Longhill.
Loghlen, Anne m'Conoghor Y, pardon, 4418.
Loghlin, Anlan, dean of Clonfert, 5194.
" Ellane ny, 4210.
" James m'Wm., pardon, [illegible].
" Slany uyne, pardon, 5447.
Loghly. See Illoghly.
Loghmane, Joan ny, pardon, 6527.
Loghnan, John, pardon, 5424.
Loghnane, Nichol, pardon, [illegible].
Loghortcasan (Lohercannan), co. Kerry, 5446.
Logh——, other place names commencing so, are indexed Lough——.
Loughegowne (Loughnagowna, co. Clare?), 5712.
Logowogn, co. Cav., 4834.
Lohercannan, co. Kerry. See Loghortcasan.
Loherviane — Lohirtane (Lowertown), co. Westm., 1760, 4578, 5145.
Lohertgysin (co. Cork or Lim.), 5567.
Lohinagh (co. Kerry?), 5464.
Lohirt—Lohirte (Lohort?), co. Cork, 4814, 5567. See also Logherte.
Lohirtane. See Loherviane.
Lohirte. See Lohirt.
Lohort, co. Cork. See Lohirt.
Loingo rectory (Knocklong?), co. Lim., 5956.
Loimmanaghe, Conoghor m'Donell I, pardon, 5488.
Lokar—Loker. See Luker.
Lollardies and assisting Lollards, pardoned, 67, 211, 265.
Loma, John, pardon, 1517.
Lombard—Lombarde:
" Anne, pardon, 5572.
" Ellice, pardon, 5442.
" Elinor, pardon, 5443.
" James (of Buttevant), pardon, 3341, 4814, 4836.
" James, pardon, 3941.
" Jasper, pardon, 6536.
" See Lombard.
Lombards, Peter, pardon, 234.

INDEX TO FIANTS—ELIZABETH.

Lomcloone, King's co., [illegible].
Lomerton, co. Westm., [illegible].
Loncurt (see Longford), [illegible].
Loncurt (Longford), King's co., 674.
Loncurt, co. Westm., house of friars of (Longford, co. Longford). [illegible].
Londergan, David oge, pardon, [illegible].
" Edm. fitz Wm., pardon, [illegible].
Londey, Edm., pardon, [illegible].
London, 473, [illegible], [illegible], [illegible].
London diocese, notary of, in Dublin, [illegible].
London, Richard de, attainted, co. Lim., lands granted, [illegible].
" Wm. fitz Edm., pardon, [illegible].
Londowne (co. Cork ?), [illegible].
Londra, Gerrott oge, pardon, [illegible].
Londragh, Gerrott m'Thomas, pardon, [illegible].
" Gerrott oge, pardon, [illegible].
Londres, Peirs, pardon, [illegible].
Londroy, David, pardon, [illegible].
" Wm. duff, pardon, [illegible].
Londry, Gerrot fitz Edmond, pardon, [illegible].
" Wm. duffe fitz Garret, pardon, [illegible].
Londrys, Edm., pardon, [illegible].
Lonelsman (co. Rosc. ?), [illegible].
Lonergan, Edmund fitz William, pardon, [illegible].
Lonergan, David oge m'David, pardon, [illegible].
" Thomas, pardon, [illegible].
Lonergan, Brian, pardon, [illegible], [illegible], 6404.
" Daniel fitz David, pardon, [illegible].
" David, pardon, [illegible], [illegible].
" Derby, pardon, [illegible].
" Edm., pardon, [illegible].
" John fitz Tho., pardon, [illegible], [illegible].
" John m'Teig, pardon, [illegible].
" John fitz Wm., pardon, [illegible].
" Kenedy, pardon, [illegible].
" Simon, pardon, [illegible].
" Tho., pardon, [illegible], [illegible], [illegible].
" Wm., pardon, [illegible], [illegible].
Lonergane, Donogh, pardon, [illegible].
" Edm., pardon, [illegible].
" John fitz David, pardon, [illegible].
" Kenedy m'Davie, pardon, [illegible].
" Philip oge, pardon, [illegible].
" Teige, pardon, [illegible].
" Tho., pardon, [illegible].
" Wm., pardon, [illegible].
Lonerigan, David fitz Wm., pardon, [illegible].
" Philip m'Rory, pardon, [illegible].
Long, James, murder of, [illegible].
" John, murder of, [illegible].
" Rob., pardon, [illegible].
" Thomas, pardon, [illegible].
Longaston, co. Westm., [illegible].
Longe, Bartholomew, pardon, [illegible]; commissions, [illegible], [illegible].
Longe, alias O'Longe, Dermod, pardon, [illegible], [illegible].
" Dr., pardon at suit of, [illegible].
" James, 2nd engrosser, Exchequer, [illegible].
" Patr., pardon, [illegible].
" Richard, house in Dublin, [illegible]; pardon, [illegible].
" Rob., commission, [illegible].
" Rob., constable of Limerick castle, [illegible], [illegible].
" Rob., pardon, [illegible].
" Rob., overseer of tanning, [illegible], [illegible].
" Symon, pardon, [illegible].
" Tho., pardon, [illegible], [illegible].
Longeloord (co. Kilk. ?), [illegible].
Longeford. See Longford.
Longeford, [illegible]. See Longford, co. Mayo.
Longefordo. See Longford, co. Gal.
Longefordo. See Longford, co. Meath.
Longefordo. See Longford, co. Sligo.
Longegorte (Longford, co. Galway), [illegible].
Longemylewade, co. Dub., [illegible].
Longeston, co. Kild., [illegible].
Longetioth. See Longtitho.
Longewood. See Longwood, co. Kildare.
Longewood alias Moyderwy, co. Meath, [illegible], [illegible].
Longfoord, co. Cork, [illegible].
Longford—Longeforde—Longegorte—Longhart, co. Gal., 917, 4716; country (barony of Longford, in co. Galway), [illegible], [illegible], [illegible], [illegible].
Longford, King's co. See Loncurt.
Longford—Longeford—Loncurt, co. Longford, [illegible], [illegible], 4152, [illegible], [illegible], [illegible], [illegible].
" castle and gaol, constable of, [illegible], [illegible], [illegible].
" gaol, constable of, [illegible], [illegible], [illegible].
" house of friars, leased, [illegible]; granted, [illegible].
" county, commission to set out, [illegible]; annual rent of [illegible] payable by inhabitants, [illegible]; appointments of captains and seneschals of districts in, [illegible], [illegible], [illegible], [illegible], &c.; wardship of heir of chief, [illegible]; men of, pardoned, [illegible], [illegible], [illegible], &c.; tithes in leased, [illegible]. See also Annaly.
" county, commission of peace, [illegible].
" " " of musters, [illegible].
" " " of martial law, [illegible], [illegible], [illegible], [illegible], [illegible], [illegible], [illegible], [illegible], [illegible], [illegible].

INDEX TO FIANTS—ELIZABETH.

Longford county, general of the army in, [illegible].
„ „ sheriff, 1789, 1863, 2914, [illegible], [illegible], 4040, 4088, 5127, 6108.
„ „ clerk of the crown and peace, 5991, 6131, 6612, 6144.
„ barony. *See* Clanhugh.
Longford—Longesford (co. Mayo or Sligo), 5078, 5942.
Longford—Longesforde, co. Meath, [illegible], 1468, 1469, 5456, 5482.
Longford, Queen's co., 6117.
Longford—Longeford (co. Ross. ?), 6044, 6600, 6614. *See* Longport.
Longford — Longeforde — Lowngford (co. Sligo ?), 4548, 4620, 4804, [illegible], [illegible], 6615.
Longport (Longford, co. Ross. ?), 6600.
Longha, Donogho m'Shane I., pardon, [illegible].
Longhart. *See* Longford, co. Gal.
Longind (co. Westm. ?), 6069.
Longirin, co. Wat., 1014.
Longnamuck, co. Ross. *See* Loughnamuck.
Longport (co. Lim. ?), 6508.
Longrage (co. Wex. ?), 6847.
Longth, Owen alias Teig M'Donogh, pardon, 6544.
Longtithe — Longetiloah, co. Meath, 116, [illegible].
Longwood—Longewood, co. Kild., 2792, [illegible], 5428, 6481.
Longwood — Longewood, co. Meath, [illegible], 5482.
Lonie, Donald m'Tho. Y, pardon, 2828.
„ Tho. m'Donough, pardon, 2828.
Lonngford. *See* Longford, co. Sligo.
Lonorogan, Edm. fitz Wm., pardon, 1486.
Lonran, Mortorough I., pardon, [illegible].
Lontan (Lowran ?), Queen's co. 6391.
Lonrogan, Edm., pardon, 3774, 6304.
„ Kennedy, pardon, 6304.
„ Kynedie fitz David, pardon, 3774.
„ Morgan, pardon, 6304.
„ Philip m'Edm., pardon, 3776.
„ Wm., pardon, 6304.
Loot, Wm., pardon, 4008.
Loote, Robert, pardon, 1074.
Loty, Edm., pardon, [illegible].
Looker, John. *See* Luker.
Looker, Richard. *See* Luker.
Lootrymmore (Leitrim), co. Mon., 4461.
Lopan, Philip, pardon, 4084.
Loppi( ), John fitz David, pardon, [illegible].
Lora, co. Tip., 4665.
Lora, co. Westm., 6464.
Loran (co. Tip. ?), 4488.
Loraan, Daniel, pardon, 3482.
„ Walter, pardon (or O'Loran), 3482.
Lorcot, John, house in Dublin, 1611.
Lord Lieutenant's guard, [illegible].
Lorgan, co. Gal., 4676, 4897.
Lorgane, Wm., pardon, 6784.
Lorghalle, 4830.
Lorgo (co. Tip. or Kilk.), 6764.
Lorgeyn, co. Westm., 1298.
Lorghe (Lorrha), co. Tip., vicarage, 5472.
Lorgie (co. Leit. ?), 5428, 5442.
Lorgin (Lorgan ?), co. Westm., 5704.
Lorgine, King's co., [illegible].
Lorgon, co. Mayo, 5740.
Lorgyn (King's co.), 814.
Lorkan, Monier, co. Gal., 4716.
Lorne, co. Long., 5143.
Loro, Peter, pardon, [illegible].
Lorrha, co. Tip. *See* Lorghe.
Lorton (co. Westm. ?), 5613.
Lorum, co. Car. *See* Leorum.
Lory, co. Tip., 4680.
Losdoman (Lisdoman), co. Westm., 6787.
Losn, Richard, pardon, 640.
„ William, pardon, 848.
Loshan, Brian m'Thirrely verraly I., pardon, 6917.
Loshlin, Rowe m'Morroghy warry I., pardon, 6417.
Loshlyn, Conoghor m'Loshlyn I (O'Loghlin), pardon, 6417.
„ Donogh m'Rosby I., pardon, 6417.
Loshewell (co. Lim. or Cork ?), 6806.
Losnes, co. Mon. *See* Noloshe.
Losseloughe—Losselloghe—Loseullough, co. Meath, [illegible], 1790, [illegible], 4673.
Lotashe (co. Cork ?), 3974.
Lothrugh, co. Mon., 1372.
Loudon, Edm., pardon, 1818.
„ John, absolved, 6153.
„ John fitz Wm., pardon, 6508, 6464.
„ Rich. fitz Gerrot, pardon, 6179.
Loudon (co. Kilk. ?), 5968.
Loudon begg, co. Lim., 6173.
Loughfoyle. *See* Loughfoile.
Louggorole, co. Clare, 4628.
Loughagar Beg, co. Westm. *See* Loughgarbeg, Loughgarbeg.
Loughagarmore, co. Westm. *See* Lougharmore.
Loughaghry · Loghaghrya co. Down, 4915, 4950.
Loughan—Loghan, co. Cork, 6528, 6871.
Loughan—Loghan, co. Down, 4712.
Loughan—Loghan, co. Ross., 5648.
Loughanaghi — Loghanaghi (co. Cork ?), 6486.
Loughanagore, co. Westm. *See* Loughanecore, Loughanecorr.
Loughane (co. Cork ?), 6871.
Loughane—Loghane co. Sligo, 6684.

INDEX TO FIANTS.—ELIZABETH.

Loughane ne Shynaghe. See Loughan ne Shemagh.
Loughanevanna—Loghanevana (co. Ros. ?), 6428.
Loughanknis—Loghanknoght (Loughan-lowaght), co. Westm., 1948, 6839.
Loughan ne Shemagh—Loghane ne Shyn-aghe—Loghhaneynagh (King's co. ?), 1175, 2234, 5486.
Loughanra—Loghanra, co. Meath, 148.
Loughanston (Logonstown), co. Meath, 1449.
Loughanstown — Loghanstown, co. Dub., 1161.
Lougharban — Loughartegge (Loughagar Beg), co. Westm., 1468, 2564.
Loughards—Loghards (co. Cork ?), 6468.
Loughballiegra, in Ulster, 1825.
Loughbeggy—Loghbegg, co. Tip., 5948.
Loughboe—Loghboe (co. Sligo or Rosc.), 4727.
Loughbollykin. See Loughbollygin.
Loughbowne—Loghbowne, co. Gal., 4278.
Loughbraghe, co. Dub., 891.
Loughbraiske — Loghbraiske, co. Kild., 6751.
Loughbricklin — Loughbrenlyn (Lough-bricklaud), co. Down, 1858, 4618. See also Loghbreghan.
Loughbollygin — Loghballykin, co. Clare, 5977, 5756.
Lough Cane (co. Tip. ?), 6528.
Lough Carra, co. Mayo. See Loughkera.
Loughclea, co. Rosc., 4682.
Loughclee—Loghclie—Loghcliogh, co. Rosc., 4741.
Loughcoir — Loghcoir (Lough Owel ? co. Westm.), 1948.
Loughcoldaleagh—Loghcoldaleagh—Logh-coll Daleagh, co. Leit., 6442.
Loughcomocke—Loghconocke, co. Cav., 6962.
Loughconvy — Loghconwaye — Loughe-comowy (Loughconway, co. Leit.), 4769, 4782, 5443.
Loughcoor—Loghcoor (co. Leit.), 6442.
Loughcore — Loghcore (Loughcrew ?), co. Meath, 1942.
Loughcrewe.—Loghcrewe — Loghcrew — Loghcrowe — Loghcrive — Loghcru — Loughcrue—Loughcrue—Loghcriewe — Loghcrane — Loghkrew — Loughkrive (Loughcrew), co. Meath, 288, 1164, 1938, 2117, 2841, 2876, 3444, 3404, 3380, 3468, 3474, 4143, 4338, 4481, 5491.
Loughcrot — Loghcrott — Loghcroitt, co. Cork, 6814.
(Loughcroter)—Loghcotra, co. Gal., 6961.
Lough Derg, co. Don. See Red logh.
Loughdonche — Loghdonche (co. Leit.?), 6436.
Loughdoncurre—Loghdonecorrey (co. Leit. ?), 6438.
Loughdowan — Loghdovan—Loghdowhin—Loughdoyne, co. Wat., 477, 2843, 2850.
Loughdoyin—Loghdoyin (co. Wat. ?), 6474.
Loughe or Phillipstown, King's co., 481.
Lough Earne — Logh Earne (Logh Erne), 4693, 6097.
Loughcalcary—Loghcalcary, co. Gal., 4687.
Lougheclochir (co. Leit. ?), 4782.
Loughecomowy. See Loughconvy.
Lougheriowe—Loghorriowe. See Lough-crowe.
Loughcroite—Loghcroitt. See Loughcrot.
Loughcrue—Loghcrue. See Loughcrowe.
Loughcur (co. Lim. ?), 6470.
Loughgill (Loughguile, co. Antrim), trugh, 4684.
Loughokeraghe — Loghokeragha. See Loughkeragh.
Loughokerman, co. Down.
Loughole—Loghole (co. Lim. ?), 6467.
Lougholoyn — Logholoyn (Lough Lene, a lake in co. Westm.), 1099.
Lougholl—Loghcll (co. Lim. ?), 6008.
Loughom, co. Tip., 2184.
Loughomnaek. See Loughmnak.
Loughomynevrake — Loghomynevrake (co. Leit. ?), 4811.
Loughon—Loghon (co. Leit. ?), 6468.
Loughonaght—Loghonaght (co. Cork ?), 5815.
Loughonegoro (Loughanagore), co. Westm., 2364.
Loughonny, co. Dub., 5910.
Loughonny—Loghonny, co. Tip., 4862.
Lougher—Logher, co. Lim., 6462, 6467.
Lougher—Logher—Loghir, co. Meath, 1148, 1160, 1428, 2814, 2968, 3761, 4830, 6562.
Loughe Reddy — Loghe Reddy (co. Leit. ?), 5184.
Loughermore (Loughagar More), co. Westm. 1481.
Lougriset (co. Wat. ?), 2854.
Loughorinyne. See Loghorinyne.
Loughoric. See Loghoric.
Loughocurry — Loughoskure (Loughesk, co. Leit. ?), 4769, 4798.
Loughoswdy. See Loughsowdy.
Loughshynne—Loghshinny. See Lough-shinny.
Loughskure. See Loughocurry.
Loughfoyo—Loghfoye, co. Kild., 5818.
Loughford—Loghford, co. Sligo, 6587.
Loughfoile—Loghfoyle—Lougfoyle.
" commander of forces at, 6873-1, 6874.
" governor of, 6887.
" supervisor of part, 6488.
" river and fishing of, 6497.

INDEX TO FIANTS—ELIZABETH.

Loughgarboy — Loghgarbagge (Loughagar Bog), co. Westm., 2048, 5813.
Loughgowna —Loghgawne (Lough Gowna, lake, in co. Long.), 818, 1061.
Loughgur—Loghgor (co. Cork ?), 6858.
Loughgur—Logher—Loghgere—Loghgar—Loghgir—Loghgir (Loughgure), co. Lim., 1879, 3862, 4859, 5464, 5478, 6387, 6806; castle, lands, and lough, 6369.
Lough Gowna. See Loughgowna.
Loughgowre, co. Meath, 644, 6358.
Loughguile, co. Antrim. See Loughegill.
Loughhamoynnagh. See Loughan na Shee-nagh.
Loughill—Loghill, co. Long., 6088.
Loughillparke — Loghillparke, Queen's co., 466, 2528, 2837.
Loughinchcorrive—Loghinchcorrive (co. Leit. ?) 6112.
Loughintogh (co. Lim. ?), 5502.
Loughir—Loghir, co. Cork, 5088.
Loughir—Loghir. See Lougher, co. Meath.
Loughkarve—Loghkarve (co. Tip. ?), 3081.
Loughkee. See Loughkee.
Loughkeen—Loghkeen (co. Tip.), 3368.
Loughkeent—Loghkeent (co. Tip.), 5469.
Loughkee—Loghkee—Loghkee — Loghkey—Loghkie (Lough Key), co. Rosc., 4582.
priory of canons on isle of the Holy Trinity, leased, 1724, 5070; possessions, 5877.
priory of Inchevickrynye—Inchvickrynye—Inchevickrine (Inis mac Neirin, now Church Island, in L. Key), leased, 4997, 5018; possessions leased, 6151.
Loughkeele—Loghkeele (co. Tip.), 5755. See also Loughkeent.
Loughkeragh—Loghkeraghe — Loghekearaghe—Loghekeraghe—Loughkiraghe, co. Tip., 2048, 3131, 5461.
Loughkeere (Lough Carra), co. Mayo, 4777.
Lough Key, co. Rosc. See Loughkee.
Loughkiraghe—Loghkiraghe. See Loughkeragh.
Loughkirwill—Loghkirwill (co. Leit. ?), 4746, 5456, 5978.
Loughkewe—Loghkewe. See Loughcrewe.
Loughlahan, co. Rosc., 4074.
Loughlaghery, 4861. See Loughleghery.
Loughlakinge, King's co., or Meath, 3187, 5691.
Lough Leane. See Loughlino.
Lough Lene, co. Westm. See Loughaleyn.
Loughline—Loghleane (Lough Leane, Killarney), 4677, 5717.
Loughlinstown, co. Dub. See Ballyloghlins, Ballyloghnan.
Loughlistown, co. Kild. See Loughlinston.
Loughlinstown, co. Meath. See Balmaloghlan.
Loughlogherbuy—Loghlogherbegg, co. Tip., 6521.
Loughloghery—Loughloghery (Loughlohery, co. Tip. ?), 4625, 5492.
Loughlore—Loghlore, co. Tip., 511; rectory, 4176.
Loughlyn, co. Rosc., 4076.
Loughma—Loghma. See Loughmoye.
Loughman, Margaret Inny, death of, 888.
Loughmask — Logh Muske — Loghmeske — Loughemask:
" manor (Loughmask castle, in parish of Ballinchalla), co. Mayo, 4777-8.
" islands in, 4935, 5595.
" See also Ballyloughmask.
Loughmey—Loghmey (Loughmoe, co. Tip. ?), 5143.
Loughmie — Loghmie — Loghmore. See Loughmoye.
Lough Mowneyinght, King's co., 5786.
Loughmorne—Loghmorne (Lough Morne near Carrickfergus), 3541, 4626.
Loughmoye—Loghma—Loghmie—Loghma—Loghmore — Loghmoye—Loughma— Loughmy—Lowmgma (Loughmoe), co. Tip., 1878, 4493, 5211, 6325, 6708; rectory, 1793, 3512.
" baron of, 888, 1868, 4417, 6826.
" See also Loughmey.
Loughmoyliagh — Loghmoyliagh, co. Leit., 4409.
Loughnagh — Loghnaghe (Lough Neagh), 4647.
Loughnaderwan, King's co., 5786.
Loughnagage—Loghnagage (co. Donegal), 4941, 5487.
Loughnakeirge — Loghnakeirge (co. Leit. ?), 4735.
Loughnamuck — Loghnamuck (Lougnamuck), co. Rosc., 6626.
Loughnanegowna — Loghnanegowna (co. Donegal or Tyrone), 5458, 5957.
Loughnagowen, co. Clare. See Lagnagowne.
Loughnamuton—Loghnamuton, co. Dub., 5674.
Loughna. See Loughmoye.
Loughnee (co. Tip. ?), 6788.
Lough Neagh. See Loughnagh.
Loughneer, co. Leit., 4867.
Loughnecur—Loghnecure (Loughanagure), co. Westm., 265, 3324, 5493.
Loughnecoute—Loghnecoute — Loghnecote, co. Leit., 5439.
Loughnegalkrie—Loghnegalkrie (co. Meath ?), 5008.

INDEX TO FIANTS—ELIZABETH.

Loughnagowrie — Loghnagowrie (co. Clare ?), 6764.

Loughmegore—Loghmegore, King's co., 4891.

Loughmcheill—Loghmcheill, co. Mayo, 6487.

Loughnakumwhy (co. Leit. ?), 4788.

Loughnalephinrie — Loghnalephinrie, co. Mon., 1468.

Loughnemorragho — Loghnemorragho, co. Tip., 6966.

Loughnaey—Loghaey, co. Tip., 6666.

Loughnagowrye—Loghnagowrye, co. Sligo, 6488.

Loghnay. See Loughmoyo.

Loughnonry, co. Mon. See Loughowne.

Loughoughter — Loghoughter — Loughowghter, co. Cav., 1681, 4818, 4926. See Holy Trinity island monastery.

Lough Owel, co. Westm. See Loughwolr.

Loughowne — Loghowne (Loughonry, co. Mon.), 6961.

Loughporte—Loghporte, co. Rosc., 6638.

Loughrawyre—Loghrawyre (co. Cav. ?), 4161.

Loughreaghe — Loghreagh — Loghreaghe — Loghriegh — Loghriegh — Loghrieghe — Loughreoghe (Loughrea), co. Gal., 2736, 4678-80, 4473, 6864, 8143, [illegible]; manor, 6901.

„ rector, 6961.

„ See Ballyloghreagh.

Loughrie — Loghrie — Loghry — Loughrye (Lough Ree on the Shannon), 1464, 1482, 1611, 2163, 4183, 2941, [illegible], 6441, 6348, 6484, 6494, 6495, 6614.

Loughrire (co. Leit. ?), 6428.

Loughroddy—Loghradda—Logh Roddo (co. Leit. or Rosc. ?), 4780, 4877, 6468, 6478.

Loughrye—Loghry. See Loughrie.

Loughsallaghe — Loughsallaughe (Loughsallagh), co. Meath, 175, 3861.

Loughsanneghan — Loghsanneghan, Queen's co., 1981.

Loughseur, co. Leit. See Loughsentry, Loughskur.

Loughsellyern—Loghsellyern (co. Rosc. ?), 6006.

Loughsewdy — Loghsewdy — Loghsewdie — Loghsewdy — Loghsewdye — Loughsewdy — Loughsewdie — Loughsewdye — Longsowdy — Lowghsewdie (Ballymore), co. Westmeath, 21, 134, 673, 748, 1147, 2284, 6493, 6224.

priory or abbey leased, 673, 2154, 2698, 6873, 6130-1; possessions leased, 6871, 6875, 6180; granted, 6836, 6844; proxies, 6777.

Loughsewdy priory, site granted, 6844.

„ parish church erected into cathedral for Meath, 6797.

„ church of S. Thomas, 6797.

„ rectory, 6461, 6797.

„ chapels, 6797.

„ parson, 1171.

(Loughshinny) — Loghsheoney — Loghshonan—Loughsanbyane, co. Dub., 1448, 6316, 6600.

Loughsuille — Loghswillie — Loughswilly — Loughsuille (Lough Swilly, co. Donegal), 6370-1, 6376, 6454.

Loughskur (Loughseur, co. Leit.), 6787.

Loughswilly—Loughsuelle. See Loughsuille.

Loughsollian · Loghsollian, co. Cav., 6865.

Lough Swilly, co. Donegal. See Loughsuille.

(Loughteoge)—Loghteoge, Queen's co., 861.

Loughtecassian ·Loghtecassian (co. Meath ?), 5062.

Loughtie — Loghtie — Loughtiy (Loughtee, co. Mon.), 4863, 4981, 6704.

Loughtikerraghe -- Loghtikeraghe — Loghtikerraghe, co. Tip., 3131, 4141, 6691.

Loughton, co. Dub., 6341.

Loughtone—Loughtone (King's co. ?), 6167, 6331.

Loughtown—Loghtown, co. Meath, 648, 654.

Loughton — Loghton, co. Wex., 616, 4691, 6316.

Loughtowne — Loghtowne (co. Car. or Wex. ?), 6541.

Loughtreiney — Loughtroyny — Loghtreyny — Loghtrony (Laghtryna, co. Wick. ?), 4189, 6611.

Loughtrodden—Loghtrodden, Queen's co., 641.

Loughtly. See Loughtie.

Loughurt (co. Cork), 6688. See Loughorte.

Loughvony—Loghvony, co. Cav., 4941.

Loughwarch, co. Wex., 948.

Loughwaylinghe (co. Leit. ?), 6297.

Loughworth—Loughwortie, co. Wex., 6785, 6363, 6718.

Loughwillda onghe—Loughwillda Eaghe—Loughwikleroghe (co. Leit. ?), 4762.

Loughwieghe, King's co., 6768.

Loughyn—Loghyn, Queen's co. 987.

Loughyny—Loghyny (co. Tip. ?), 6661.

Loughyrty—Loghyrty (co. Cork), 6666.

Lougowdy. See Loughsewdy.

Lounargan, Morgan, pardon, 4180.

Loundorstoe (Lundorstown), co. Meath. 1462.

Lounghirt — Loungturt (co. Wat. ?), 6328, 6371.

Loury (co. Kilk. ?), 4348.

Lourgan, co. Cav., 4892.

Lourgne, Philip fitz John, 6765.

INDEX TO FIANTS—ELIZABETH.

Louth—Lowth—Lowthe—Lovid, [illegible], 6105; rectory, 1518.
„ priory, possessions of, 1811, [illegible], 6418, [illegible], [illegible].
„ Thomas Plunket, baron of, commissions, [illegible], 843, [illegible], [illegible], 1657, 1656; freedom from subsidy, 841; leases, [illegible], 1486; his heir, 3672.
„ Patrick, baron of, commissions, 3137, [illegible], 3444-5, 3751, [illegible], [illegible], 4616; his successor, 5673.
„ Patrick, baron of, son of preceding, 3673; (not mentioned by Lodge or Burke).
„ Oliver, baron of, livery, 3672; commissions, 4147, 4485, 5125, 5943, 5353, 5257, [illegible].
„ county, excepted from government of Ulster, [illegible], 4453; ploughlands in, [illegible]; cessions of, 4811; gaol of, 1453; lands of earl of Kildare in, 783; forfeited lands, 4018; wages of soldiers cessed on, 1521; treaty with Tyrone in, [illegible], 5672, [illegible].
„ „ commissions of peace, 678-81, [illegible], 443-5, 3448, 3182, [illegible], [illegible], 4017, 4458, 4818, 4785, [illegible], 5342, [illegible], [illegible], [illegible], [illegible], [illegible], [illegible], 6429, [illegible].
„ „ commissions of muster and array, 3117, [illegible], 3444, 4147, 4468, 5125.
„ „ commissions for martial law, 67, 218, 443, [illegible], 1623, 2364, 3731, 3621, 3163, [illegible], [illegible], [illegible], [illegible].
„ „ authority to impress hay in, [illegible], 4061, 4173, 4468, [illegible], [illegible], 6413.
„ „ general of army in, 3672.
„ „ sheriff, 43, [illegible], 848, [illegible], 1522, [illegible], 2344, [illegible], 3484, 3918, 4147, 5126, 6100.
„ „ sub-sheriff, 6100.
„ „ clerk of the crown, &c., [illegible], 3151, 5818, 6144.
„ „ chief serjeant, 811, 1812, 1280.
„ „ cess collector, 3791.
„ „ general cessor, 4267.
„ „ searcher of tanning, 2213.
Lovayne, lord. See Essex, earl of, 3048.
Lovell, Francis, sheriff of co. Kilkenny, 1960, [illegible], 4864, [illegible]; commissions, 3918, [illegible], [illegible]; pardon, [illegible], 4720, [illegible]; lease, 4267; pension, [illegible].
Lovell, Wm., pardon, [illegible], [illegible].
Lovet, Nich., pardon, 5918.
Lovett, Brian O'Connell m'Thomas, pardon, 5842.
Lovid. See Louth.
Lowagum (Loughmoe), co. Tipperary, baron of, [illegible]. See Purcell, Tho.
Lowbutlerston — Lowbutlerstown (co. Wat. ?), 3748.
Lowcha, co. Leit., [illegible].
Low Countries, pension for services in, [illegible].
Lowe, Anthony, leases, 1357, 1378, [illegible], [illegible], [illegible], 1837, 1884, [illegible], 2071, 2161, [illegible], [illegible].
„ Elizabeth ny, pardon, 4811.
„ John, carpenter, [illegible].
Lowe Grange (co. Kild. ?), 6464.
Lowertown, co. Westm. See Laherlann.
Lowes, James m'Rob., pardon, [illegible].
„ John, pardon, [illegible].
„ Richard, pardon, [illegible].
„ William, pardon, [illegible].
Lowesion. See Lowestowne.
Lowesion (co. Kild. ?), [illegible].
Lowestowne—Loweston—Lowiston—Lowistowne, co. Kild., [illegible], 1515; rectory, 3671.
Lowetowne (co. Kild. ?), [illegible].
Lowgad, co. Leit., [illegible].
Loughantan, King's co. (perhaps Annaghmore Lough), [illegible].
Lowghsewdie. See Loughsewdy.
Lowinge, Conogher m'Donell I. pardon, [illegible].
Lowiston—Lowistowne. See Lowestowne.
Lowndon, William m'John, pardon, [illegible].
Lowngle, Donogho m'Moriah I. pardon, 4576.
Lowrale, More ny, pardon, 4318.
Lowny (co. Mayo ?), [illegible].
Lowran, Queen's co. See Loraran.
Lowrath, co. Louth. See Lowrath.
Lowran, James, pardon, [illegible].
Lowth. See Louth.
Lowth, Tho., pardon, [illegible].
Lowton (co. Kild.), [illegible].
Lowtye (co. Cork ?), [illegible].
Loynally. See Lynally.
Loyneagho, Wm., pardon, [illegible].
Loyngo (Knocklong), co. Lim., rectory, 5347.
Loys, James, pardon, [illegible].
Loyal, co. Mon. See Nelocke.
Lubrothe, co. Dub., [illegible].
Luby, John, pardon, [illegible].
Lucan—Lucane—Lukan—Lukane, co. Dub., 347, 1063, 1180, 1260, [illegible], [illegible], [illegible], [illegible], [illegible], 3124, 4480, 4466, 4675, 5718, [illegible], [illegible]; messuage and land granted, 4773.
„ rectory, [illegible], 1781, 4489, 4870, 4918, [illegible]; tithes, 1129, [illegible].
„ vicar of, [illegible].

INDEX TO FIANTS—ELIZABETH.

Lucas, Fercinus, pardon, a Frowdrusse, [illegible].
„ Roger, pension, [illegible], 4648, 4867; pardon, [illegible]; commission, 5614.
„ Wm. oge, pardon, 6762, 6767.
Lucot, John, pardon, 6563.
„ Fillip, pardon, [illegible].
„ Rich., pardon, [illegible].
Luckan, co. Dub., 1574.
Luddan, co. Lim. *See* Luddowne.
Luddenbeg (co. Lim.), 6190.
Lucadunegan, co. Mon., 5571.
Luffertaun, co. Gal. *See* Lyrtane.
Lugalryne, co. Wick. *See* Loggiircymy. Loughirelmey.
Lugbroghen (Loughbrickland? co. Down), 4357.
Lughill, co. Kild. *See* Loughill.
Lughyn, Queen's co., 537.
Lukan—Lukane. *See* Lucan.
Lukar—Lokar—Loker—Lookar—Lonkar—Luker:
John, controller of wine duty, Waterford, 2128; pardon, 880; leases, 1162, 4093; house of, 4402.
Richard, sheriff of co. Waterford, 1046, 1167, 1196; controller of wine duty, 1466; commissions, 683, 1158, 1322, 1857, 1683, 1856; lease, 636; pardon, 880, 1127, 1196, 1828.
Lull, George, pardon, [illegible].
Lullymore, co. Kild. *See* Lilloghmore, 151.
Luman, Donogh and Owen m'Teig Y, pardon, [illegible].
Lumbard, Ellen, pardon, [illegible], 6754.
„ James, pardon, 2267.
„ John, 1824.
„ Patr., pardon, 2646.
„ Thomas, robbed, 662.
„ William, 1828.
Lumbardes lands, Waterford, 2378, 1162.
Lumbert, Oliver, lease, 6129.
Lumyn, Teige m'Rorie I, pardon, 6467.
Lundenstown, co. Meath. *See* Lounsdorstown.
Lune—Luyne barony, co. Meath, martial law in, [illegible], 6810.
Lung, vicarage, 84.
Lunighane, John m'Theige I, pardon, 6801.
Lunnane, Conor m'Teig m'Conor alias m'Teig Y, pardon, 6496.
„ Cormock and Fyneen m'Conor m'Teig Y, pardon, 6498.
„ Owen m'Teig Y, pardon, 6468.
Lunnyn, Teig m'Rorie Y, pardon, 6471.
Lurce (co. Gal.?), 5562.
Lurgabrack, co. Donegal. *See* Lurgighbrack.
Lurgan, John, pardon, 3631.
„ Tho. fitz John, pardon, 6761.
Lurgan, co. Mon., 5571.
Lurgan, co. Westm. *See* Lurgin.
Lurganboy, co. Mon. *See* Ballymakurgan, Lurganboy.
Lurganville, co. Down. *See* Ballylurgan Evill.
Lurghe—Lurghoo—Lurhoe (Lorrha), co. Tip., house of canons leased, 5573, 6472, 6810.
„ house of Dominican friars, leased, 5773, 6472, 6810.
Lurgyn, co. Louth, 162.
Lurhoe. *See* Lurghe.
Lurkan, Brian, pardon, 6467.
Lurkane, Donogh m'Donell I, pardon, 6714.
Lusk, co. Dub., 288, 1464, 1758, 2284, 2178, [illegible], 6572.
Lusloe (Lustown), co. Meath, 674, [illegible], [illegible], 6672.
Lutroll. *See* Luttrell.
Lutrollston. *See* Luttrellston.
Luttarell. *See* Luttrell.
Luttrelleston. *See* Luttrellston.
Luttrell—Lutrell—Lotterell:
„ Alexander, pardon, 6468.
„ Andrew, merchant, 237; suit concerning will of, 3030.
„ Henry, 3060, 3618.
„ Isabella, 2384.
„ John, house in Dublin, 181.
„ John, merchant, of Dublin, [illegible].
„ John, heir of Rich. (of Luttrellston), 3146.
„ John, pardon, [illegible], 6522.
„ Mary, jointure of, [illegible].
„ Nicholas (of Clonsilla), surrender by, 654-6.
„ Richard (of Luttrellstown), livery to heir, 6798.
„ Richard (of Luttrellstown), pardon to son, 3146.
„ Rich., surgeon, 2104.
„ Robert, archdeacon of Meath, refuses oath of supremacy, 124; deprived, 183.
„ Robert, clerk, surrender, 654-6.
„ Robert (of Tankardstown), freedom from subsidy, 1414.
„ Robert, 3030.
„ Rob., pardon, 3563, 6508.
„ Rob., widow, 642.
„ Simon (of Luttrellstown), commissions, 3117, 3414, 4163, 4480; pardon, [illegible].
„ Thomas (of Luttrellstown), knt., chief justice of Common Bench, livery, 3764.
„ Thomas, knt., leases, 1126, 2366, [illegible], 6704.
„ Thomas, lands of, 1126, 1326, 2626, 6861.

INDEX TO FIANTS.—ELIZABETH.

Luttrelleston—Luttrellston—Luttrellston—Luttrelston, co. Dub., 2117, [illegible], 3444, 4146, 4148, 4462, 6794.
Luttrill, Katherine, pardon, 6464.
Luyne. See Lune.
Lurys, Shane m'Teig I., pardon, [illegible].
Ly, Nicholas, alderman of Waterford, commission, [illegible].
Ly Dolphin, Walter, pardon, [illegible]. See Dolfin.
Lyagh, John, pardon, [illegible].
Lyamamore (Leamomore), co. Kerry, 4121.
Lyarie, Thady m'Connor I., pardon, [illegible].
Lyartane (Lafertown), co. Gal., [illegible].
Lyath, Gillpatrick, pardon, [illegible].
Lyaideyme (Loitrim, co. Leitrim ?), [illegible].
Lycarythoghish (co. Cork ?), 4414.
Lycknafeirean, co. Gal., [illegible].
Lyckeyne, co. Clare, [illegible].
Lyckidwne (co. Lim. ?), [illegible].
Lyckin (co. Wick. ?), [illegible].
Lyckloniran (co. Gal. ?), [illegible].
Lydacan, co. Gal. See Leidigan.
Lyde, Robert, prebendary of Christchurch, refuses oath of supremacy, [illegible].
Lydeacon, co. Gal., [illegible].
Lydagaine (co. Gal. ?), 4767.
Lydoan, co. Gal. or Rosc., [illegible].
Lydyard, Wiltshire, [illegible].
Lye, Arthur, pardon, [illegible], [illegible].
,, Emery (son of John), pardon, [illegible]; leases, 4408-10, [illegible]; mortgage, [illegible].
,, John (of Ballina), his son, 4408-10.
,, John, junior, pardon, [illegible].
,, John, commission, [illegible]; grant of land, [illegible]; leases, [illegible], [illegible], [illegible], [illegible]-11, [illegible], [illegible], [illegible]; surrenders, [illegible], [illegible]; pardon, [illegible], [illegible].
Lyen, Niall, pardon, [illegible].
Lyegh (co. Tip. ?), [illegible].
Lyemaren. See Lynemarven.
Lyeme, Joan ayne Tayne uyne, pardon, [illegible].
Lyemor (Leamore, co. Rosc. ?), [illegible].
Lyen, Derby, pardon, [illegible].
Lyene, Donogh m'Teig I., pardon, [illegible].
Lyenemarven. See Lynemarven.
Lyenky, co. Long., [illegible], 5107.
Lyerin, Dermot, pardon, [illegible].
Lyetrom (co. Leit. ?), [illegible].
Lyetrym, in Connaught, [illegible].
Lyeltony, co. Gal., [illegible].
Lyevanaghin. See Levanaghan.
Lyevonye (co. Sligo ?), [illegible].
Lyfevar, co. Cav., [illegible].
Lyffe—Lyffye. See Liffe.
Lykallie—Lykelly, co. Lim., [illegible], [illegible].
Lykidiston, [illegible]. See Likadiston.
Lykyany (co. Rosc. ?), [illegible].
Lylly, Florence, chaplain, lease, [illegible].
Lymbrick—Lymbrike—Lymbrycke—Lymerick. See Limerick.
Lymerick, John, rector of Derver, [illegible].
Lymericke — Lymerik — Lymeryck. See Limerick.
Lymgar, co. Rosc., [illegible].
Lymlary (Carrigleamleary), co. Cork, [illegible].
Lymrick—Lymricke. See Limerick.
Lyn, co. Westm., [illegible].
Lynagh, Edw., pardon, [illegible].
,, James, pardon, [illegible].
,, Richard, pardon, [illegible], [illegible].
,, —Lynaghe, Thomas, attainted, possessions leased, [illegible], [illegible], 1813. See Leynagh.
Lynaghe, Thomas, premises of, [illegible].
Lynaigh, James oge m'James, pardon, [illegible].
Lynallow (King's co.), [illegible].
Lynally—Loyually, King's co., [illegible], [illegible].
Lynam, Chr., pardon, [illegible].
,, Richard, commission, [illegible].
,, Thomas, house in Dublin, [illegible].
Lynamngardinge (Lynamsgarden), co. Kild., [illegible].
Lynan, Philip m'Shane I., pardon, [illegible].
Lynanoghe, John, pardon, [illegible].
Lynce. See Lynch.
Lyne's park, [illegible].
Lynch—Linch—Linche—Lynche—Linse—Lynce:
,, Anthony, lease, 4100.
,, Arthur, pardon, [illegible].
,, Cecily, pardon, [illegible].
,, Christopher, commission, [illegible].
,, Christopher, pardon, [illegible].
,, Donnys, pardon, [illegible].
,, Derby, pardon, [illegible].
,, Dominick, collector of wine duty at Galway, &c., [illegible].
,, Geoffry, [illegible].
,, John, official principal, Limerick, [illegible].
,, John, bishop of Elphin, [illegible].
,, John, pursuivant at arms, [illegible], 4412, [illegible]-10.
,, Jonamr, [illegible].
,, Margaret, [illegible].
,, Mark, controller of wine duty, Galway, [illegible].
,, Marcus, alderman of Galway, [illegible].
,, Mark or Marcus, pardon, [illegible], [illegible], [illegible], [illegible].
,, Nicholas, pardon, [illegible], [illegible].
,, Oliver, pardon, [illegible].
,, Patrick (of Knock), livery, [illegible]; lease from him, [illegible].
,, Patrick, pardon, [illegible].

INDEX TO FIANTS—ELIZABETH.

Lynch, Peter (of the Knock), 1343, [illegible]; his heir, 1418.
" Philip, 4878.
" Richard, land of (co. Kild.), 8414.
" Richard, deputy auditor general, [illegible]; commissioner of exchequer, 6278.
" Richard, pardon, 1141, [illegible], 6740.
" Roback, pardon, 5870.
" Roland, bishop of Clonfert and Kilmacduagh, 5496.
" Stephen, pardon, 4673, 4763, 5740, [illegible].
" Thady, land of (in co. Kild.), 8414.
" Thomas (of Waterford), debt to him [illegible]; lease, 6422.
" Thomas, pardon, 5740, 4877.
" Ulick, mayor of Galway, 5737.
" Ullick, pardon, 5495, 5716.
" Walter (of Doncro), commissions, [illegible], 4148, 4441; pardon, [illegible].
" Walter, land of, at Trim, 66, [illegible].
" Walter, pardon, 5777, 5817.
" Wm., pardon, 6431.
Lynchy, Donogho, pardon, 5808.
" Hugh and Teig m'Donell oge, pardon, 6857.
Lyncy, Donnell m'Conor, pardon, [illegible].
Lyn do Leighim, church (Lany and Lackan), co. Westm., 6797.
Lyndover, Rich., constable of Longford gaol, 2564, [illegible]; grant of a wardship, 5461.
Lyne, Joan ny, pardon, 6762.
Lyneghan, David, pardon, [illegible].
Lynemurren—Lynemaron—Lynemmaaron—Lynemmarraghan (Lomenarron, King's co.), [illegible], 2900, [illegible], 4971.
Lyaid, Walter, pardon, 4830.
Lynean, Rene duff ny, pardon, [illegible].
Lynean, Newetown of (Newtownlennan), co. Tip., [illegible], 5774; rectory, [illegible].
Lynnan gardon, co. Kild., 6152.
Lynemmarraghan. See Lynemurren.
Lyned, Gillegrome, pardon, 6761.
" Walter, pardon, 6763.
Lynold, Tho., pardon, 4850.
Lynamoe' land, in Kilmainham, 1348.
Lynol, Tho. m'Ulick boy, pardon, 4781.
" Voder m'Tho., pardon, 4781.
Lyncles, lands of, in Thrawley (Lynolt), 4878.
Lynolt, Hubert crone, pardon, [illegible], 5407.
" Ulick, pardon, 4781, 6046.
Lyns, Garrett, pardon, 6462.
Lynsey, Donogh m'Dermody, pardon, 4867.
Lynstadwello, co. Gal., [illegible].
Lynt—Lynte, or Skelton:
" Martin, Svery, [illegible].
" Matthew, grant of lands, [illegible], 1448; commission, 5107.
Lyon, John, pardon, 4873.
Lyons, John, pardon, 6694.
" Katherine, 1422.
Lyons, co. Dublin (see Newcastle Lyons), [illegible], 5718.
Lyons—Lions, co. Kild., [illegible], 438, 543, [illegible], [illegible], [illegible], 5444, 1482, 3620, 6796, 4152, 4446, 5777, [illegible], 8484.
Lyppyaile, Hugh, grant of land (or Lipplail), 606.
Lyre (co. Cork?), 4571.
Lyroke (Lyrogo?), Queen's co., 6951.
Lyrros, co. Gal., [illegible].
Lys—, Names of places commencing so in Calendar are indexed Lis—.
Lysley, Martin, pardon, 5461.
Lyswell, Nich., 5746.
Lytawne, James, pardon, 6611.
Lytdon, Richard. See Liston.
Lytlowne, Ricard. See Liston.
Lyter. See Lotter.
Lytlegrange. See Littlegrange.
Lytlenowton (see Newton), 5148.
Lytleton, co. Car., 5146.
Lytloye, Owen, pardon, [illegible].
Lytrim. See Leitrim, co. Cork.
Lyttler. See Lotter.
Lyttlerfynyn, co. Cork, grant, [illegible].
Lyttermackloe (Lettermackloe), co. Gal., 6014. See Lettermackoo.
Lytter m'Phillipp. See Litter m'Phillipp.
Lyttermacphillippe, co. Ross., 4873.
Lytteyre—Lyttyore. See Leityre.
Lyttyr. See Letter, co. Kerry.
Lyvanaghan—Lyvanaghane (Lemanaghan), King's co., rectory, 1401, [illegible], [illegible].
Lyvanelan, King's co., [illegible].
Lyvery, illegal custom, 3771.
Lyvelderton, co. Kild., 1938.
Lyvoll, Tho. fitz Ullick boy, pardon, [illegible].
" Ullick boy fitz Tho., pardon, 5657.

Mabo, Tho., pardon, [illegible].
Mabrge (co. Cork?), 4574.
Mabrelon, co. Wat., 8632.
Mabilerton, co. Wat., 714.
Mabbleston or Mapraton, co. Dub., [illegible].
Macabe—Macabbo—M'Abe, persons of the name, pardoned, 4810, 4881-3.
M'aBhrohink, Dermod, pardon, [illegible].
M'Abie, Edm., pardon, 6467.
M'Abe, Donogh, pardon, 1728.
M'Abey—Abeye—Abeie, persons of the name, pardoned, 196, 168, 618, 1930, [illegible].
M'aBrenkinok, Owen, pardon, 6824.
M'abrohan, Gillegrome, pardon, 5762.
M'aBrolick, Eneas, pardon, [illegible].
M'aOatwe, Gillepatrick, pardon, [illegible].

INDEX TO FIANTS—ELIZABETH.

M'aCallaogh, Walter, pardon, [illegible].
M'aCaRogh, Dermot, pardon, [illegible].
M'Acharta, Edm., pardon, [illegible].
M'Adam—Addam, persons of the name, pardoned, [illegible], [illegible], [illegible], [illegible], [illegible], [illegible], [illegible], [illegible]. See Macadam.
M'Adegany, Tuahill, pardon, 4314.
M'Adon, Johnack, pardon, [illegible].
M'aDonaltie, persons of the name, pardoned, [illegible].
M'Adrwy, Tho., pardon, 4777.
M'Agayll, Rob., pardon, [illegible].
M'Aghy (M'Kena?), persons of the name, pardoned, [illegible].
M'Agyre, Donald, pardon, [illegible].
M'Agardo, Gerot, pardon, [illegible].
M'Agoyle, David, pardon, [illegible].
M'Alg Oyn, pardon, [illegible].
M'aKernan, Ferall, pardon, [illegible].
M'Akelly, Shane, pardon, [illegible].
M'Alester, Randall, pardon, [illegible].
M'Alestrum, Philip, pardon, [illegible].
M'Aleame, Manus, pardon, [illegible].
M'Alea duff, How boy, pardon, [illegible].
M'Alester, persons of the name, pardoned, [illegible], [illegible].
M'Alexander, Tirlagh (of Ballyboy, co. Wick.—M'Donnell), pardon, [illegible], [illegible], [illegible]; captain of gallowglas, indenture with, [illegible].
" others of the name, pardoned, [illegible], [illegible], [illegible], [illegible], [illegible], [illegible], [illegible], [illegible], [illegible], [illegible], [illegible].
M'Alexander roe, Hugh boy, pardon, [illegible].
M'Alexandre, persons of the name, pardoned, [illegible].
M'Alexster, Alexster and Colla, pardon, [illegible].
M'Alin, Callogh, pardon, [illegible].
M'Aline, Moylor, pardon, [illegible].
M'Allestran, Rich., pardon, [illegible].
M'Allaster, Donell, pardon, [illegible].
M'Allastrum, Tho., pardon, [illegible].
M'Allester, Nico., pardon, [illegible].
M'Allexander, Edm., pardon, [illegible].
M'Allister, persons of the name, pardoned, [illegible].
M'Allye, Fiacha, pardon, [illegible].
M'Alowe, David, pardon, [illegible].
M'Alpen, Rich., pardon, [illegible].
M'Altin, Murogh, pardon, [illegible].
M'Alvarte, persons of the name, pardoned, [illegible].
M'Alyan, Thady, pardon, 4072.
M'Alylly, Patrick, pardon, 1798.
M'Amester, Maloghlen, pardon, [illegible], [illegible].
M'Amely, Edm. and Rich., pardon, [illegible].
M'aMilla( ), Donald, pardon, [illegible].
M'Amley — Amly, persons of the name, pardoned, [illegible].
M'Amore—Amor (M'Damore), country of, co. Wex., rents and customs due from, [illegible], [illegible]; captain of, [illegible].
M'anAbba, Emuys, pardon, [illegible].
M'Anaba, Conghor, pardon, [illegible].
M'Anaboy, Calo and Shane, pardon, [illegible].
M'Anabar, Dermot O'Solyvan, pardon, [illegible].
M'Anallie, Melaghlin, pardon, [illegible].
M'Anally, Brian (of Tullyboy), pardon, [illegible].
" Edm. and Walter, pardon, [illegible].
" See M'Enally, M'Inally.
M'Anally, Donell, pardon, [illegible].
M'Anbard, Brian, pardon, [illegible].
M'Ancleery, Gilpatrick and Teig, pardon, [illegible].
M'an Coyllew, Donell, pardon, [illegible].
M'Ancrasino, Donogh, pardon, [illegible].
M'Andowalty, Con and Gorman, pardon, [illegible].
M'Andrew — Andrew — Andrews (of co. Mayo):
" Charles, pardon, [illegible]; attainted, [illegible], [illegible].
" John or Shane, pardon, [illegible]; attainted, [illegible], [illegible].
" others of the name, pardoned, [illegible], [illegible], [illegible], [illegible].
M'Andrewe (of co. Kerry):
" Adam, attainted, [illegible].
" David, attainted, 4117.
" Wm., attainted, [illegible].
M'Ane, Edm., pardon, [illegible].
" M'Anea. See M'Canea.
M'Anellye — Anellie, persons of the name, pardoned, [illegible].
M'Anenany, Shane, pardon, [illegible].
M'Anerie, Follomy, pardon, [illegible].
M'Anfer merohe, Romus, pardon, [illegible].
M'Anfhir Dhorcha, Feilim, pardon, [illegible].
M'Angawnery, Brian, pardon, [illegible].
M'Angawney, Gilpatrick, pardon, [illegible].
M'Anghemo, Neil, pardon, [illegible].
M'Anhogey, Cahill, pardon, [illegible].
M'Anis, Donell and Owen, pardon, [illegible].
M'Aniocno, Hugh and Gillernow, pardon, [illegible].
M'Aniocyne, persons of the name, pardoned, [illegible].
M'Aniowe, Tirrelagh, pardon, [illegible].
M'Anioyous, Donell, pardon, [illegible].
M'Anioghie, Melaghlin, pardon, [illegible].
M'Anioyne, Brian and Milloconnie, pardon, [illegible].
M'Anmochan, Melaughlen, pardon, [illegible].
M'Anna (M'Canna), persons of the name, pardoned, [illegible], [illegible], [illegible].
M'Annany, Owen, pardon, [illegible].
M'Annonany, Melaghlen and Wm., pardon, [illegible].

M'Ammovoia, Hugh, pardon, 6448.
M'Ammovoia, Rorie, pardon, 6448.
M'Ammovoy, Teig, pardon, 6448.
M'Amollie, Owen, pardon, 4628.
M'Amomasy, Jeffrey, pardon, 6477.
M'Amovoy, persons of the name, pardoned, 6448.
M'Amrack, persons of the name, pardoned, 4617.
M'Amteggurte, Teig, pardon, 6448.
MacAnthony, Walter, traitor, [illegible].
M'Anally, James and Owen, pardon, 4486.
M'Anyerkayo, John, pardon, 5711.
M'Aogain, Owin, brehon, pardon, 4679.
M'Araghayo, Terence, pardon, 6602.
M'Ardill—Macardell—M'Ardell—M'Ardill:
,, Colle Hugh, grant of land, [illegible]; pardon, 6751.
,, Cormack, grant of land, [illegible]; pardon, 6751.
,, Cormack ogo, grant of land, [illegible]; pardon, 6751.
,, Gilpatrick, grant of land, [illegible].
,, Gilpatrick ogo, grant of land, [illegible].
,, Henry, grant of land, [illegible].
,, Manus, grant of land, [illegible]; pardon, 6751.
,, Philip, grant of land, [illegible]; pardon, 6751.
,, Philip m'Gilpatrick, grant of land, [illegible]; pardon, 6751.
,, Thiegh, grant of land, [illegible]; pardon, 6751.
,, others of the name, pardoned, [illegible], [illegible], [illegible], 5794, [illegible], 6751. See also M'Cardell.
Macarmack, Hubert, pardon, [illegible].
Macarmacke, Nich., pardon, 2912.
Macarmick—Macarmyck, persons of the name, pardoned, [illegible], 4557, 6444, 6621, 6574.
Macarnycke, Pair., pardon, 4737.
M'Arre, Ferragh, pardon, 4887.
M'Arrebiddie alias m'Thomas, Wm., pardon, 6921.
M'Arrye, Owen, pardon, 5752.
M'Art—Arte:
,, Cahir, indenture, [illegible].
,, Eugene, chaplain, Eng. liberty, 1914.
,, Hugh, indenture, 4718.
,, Owen, claims proctorship of Ross, [illegible].
,, Pair. (M'Mahon ?), grant of land, [illegible].
,, others bearing this name, or patronymic, pardoned, 19, 787, 813, [illegible], 831, 867, 1702, [illegible], 2166, [illegible], 2348, [illegible], [illegible], [illegible], [illegible]-4, [illegible], [illegible], [illegible], 4626, 4162, 4163, 4624, [illegible], [illegible], [illegible], [illegible], 6109, 5178, [illegible], [illegible], [illegible], [illegible], 6433, 6487, 6417, [illegible], [illegible], [illegible], [illegible], 6446, 6541, 6571, 6577, [illegible], [illegible], [illegible].
M'Art ogo—Arte ogo, Felim duffe, pardon, [illegible], [illegible].
M'Arte ne Kille, Teig, pardon, 4647.
M'Artie, Florence. See M'Carty.
,, Moriertagh, pardon, [illegible].
M'Arter, Mollmurry, pardon, 6718.
M'Arte ogo. See M'Art ogo.
Macarty Eoragh, [illegible].
Macary, Teig, pardon, [illegible]-4.
M'Asse, Teig, pardon, [illegible].
M'Athony, Ulick, traitor, [illegible].
M'Auley, Bernard, pardon, [illegible].
M'Aulaghan, Tho., pardon, [illegible].
M'Auley—Aulie. See M'Awliff, M'Awly.
M'Auliff—Auliffe. See M'Awliff.
M'Aullin, Ewer, pardon, [illegible].
M'Auly. See M'Awliff, M'Awly.
M'Aulye, Rorie (of Aghnagar, co. Long.), attainted, 6648.
M'Aulyve. See M'Awliff.
M'Avoey, Brian, pardon, [illegible].
M'Avir, Murtagh, pardon, 4447.
M'Avoye, Teig, pardon, 2548.
M'Award—Awaird—Awarde, persons of the name, pardoned, 4572, 4657, [illegible], [illegible], [illegible], 6751.
M'Awemory. See Awmorye.
M'Awihr, Brian, pardon, 4447.
M'Awleff. See M'Awliff.
M'Awley—Awlie. See M'Awliff, M'Awly.
M'Awliff—Awliffe—Awlide—Auliff—Auliffe—Aulyve—Awleff—Awlive—Awliff—Awly—Auley—Aulie—Auly—Awley—Awlie:
,, "M'Awlie," pardoned, [illegible].
,, Dermot (of Castlemcauliff), "M'Awly," attainted, 6714.
,, Molaghlen, pardon, [illegible], [illegible]; M'Awliffe, and captain of his name, pardon, 4727, [illegible]: his wife, 6464.
,, Moregh—Morragh, pardon, [illegible], [illegible], 4[illegible], 4642.
,, Owen, pardon, [illegible], [illegible], [illegible], 4498, 4533, 4626, 4781.
,, Thady m'Conner, pardon, [illegible].
,, others of the name (in co. Cork and neighbourhood), pardoned, [illegible]-7, [illegible], [illegible], [illegible], [illegible], [illegible], 4712, 4497, [illegible], [illegible], [illegible], [illegible], [illegible], [illegible], 6457, [illegible], [illegible], [illegible]-8, [illegible], [illegible], [illegible], [illegible], [illegible], [illegible], 6764.
M'Awline, Teig, pardon, [illegible].

INDEX TO FIANTS—ELIZABETH;

M'Awliff. See M'Awliff.
M'Awley, Donagh, pardon, 6422.
M'Awly—Auley—Aulie—Auly—Awlie—Awlye:
- „ persons of the name in co. Westm., pardoned, 4686, 6871. See also M'Gawly.
- „ in co. Cork. See M'Awliff.
- „ persons of the name in Connaught and elsewhere, pardoned, 3768, 4697, 5478, 6597, 6803, [illegible], [illegible], [illegible].

M'Awnerye—Awnerey, David O'Connery, pardon, [illegible], 5708.
M'Awney, Parres, pardon, 4887.
M'Balke, Donogh M'Donell, pardon, 4879.
M'Banne, Donogh, pardon, 1881.
M'Barde, Wm., pardon, 6917.
M'Barlly, John, pardon, 1922.
M'Barrowe, Owen, pardon, 6149.
M'Bartre, John, pardon, 6746.
M'Baugh, Shane, pardon, 2165.
M'Bolan, persons of the name, pardoned, 6437.
M'Berwickerey, Oliver or Gillopenodin, pardon, 6762.
M'Birabegroe, Boshallagh, pardon, 6029.
M'Birne, Tirlagh, pardon, 6677.
M'Biragne, Peter, pardon, 4894.
M'Birrekry, Peaddirus, pardon, 6762.
M'Birryhaggerey, Donell, pardon, 6060.
M'Boddoyge, Teig, pardon, 6794.
M'Boe, Wm., pardon, 6697.
M'Boelagh, Carrilore and Conne, pardon, 6462.
M'Boelle, Conne, pardon, 6486.
M'Bowrke, Shane, pardon, 6482.
M'Boy—Boye, persons of the name, pardoned, 618, 1821, 4832, 6448.
M'Boykin, persons of the name, pardoned, 5436.
M'Boyke, John, pardon, 6492.
M'Boyle, persons of the name, pardoned, 6762.
M'Braddye, Donell, pardon, 6671.
M'Brade, persons of the name, pardoned, 4885, 5828, 6682.
M'Brady—Bradie—Bradye:
- „ Brian m'Cormac, attainted, 6848.
- „ others of the name, pardoned, 3861, 4610, 4685, 6460, 5608, 6762, 5806, 6681, 6676, 6618, 6867, 6734.

M'Braine, Owen, pardon, 6678.
M'Bran, persons of the name, pardoned, 868, 2744, 3610, 5408, 6102, 6412, 6867.
M'Branan—Branane, persons of the name, pardoned, 1550, 4073, 4075-7, 5028, 5479, 5611, 5616, 5681, 6036, 6626, 6867.
M'Brandon, John, pardon, 6468.
M'Brandone, pardon, 3482.
M'Branne, Pardorogh, pardon, 4417.
M'Brannane, persons of the name, pardoned, 6682.
M'Branne, persons of the name, pardoned, 1966, 4897, 6617.
M'Braten, Dallagh, pardon, 5887.
M'Brany, Shane, pardon, 5898.
M'Brasell—Brasill—Brassill—Brassill, persons of the name, pardoned, 446, 961, 1104, 1834, 4287, 5432, 6113, 6717, 6774.
M'Breen—Breene, persons of the name, pardoned, 871, 3146, 3251, 4160, 6578, 6784.
M'Broassill, Cahill, pardon, 6425.
M'Bregne, Rich., attainted, 6404.
„ Shane, pardon, 6576.
M'Brehan, Donogh, pardon, 4817.
M'Brehowne, Shane, pardon, 6434.
M'Brehon, Tege O'Carvell, pardon, 6542.
M'Brehowne, Connor, pardon, 6616.
„ See also M'Ebrehowne, M'Evrehon, M'Inbrehone.
M'Brehune, Malachias, archdeacon of Kilmacduagh, 6066.
M'Brein—Breine:
- „ Rory, grant of land, 6606.
- „ Toole, grant of land, 6646.
- „ others of the name, pardoned, 1880, 2287, 6022.

M'Bren, persons of the name, pardoned, 2882, 3712, 3868, 4028, 4127, 6574.
M'Bren Ogonagh, pardon, 3470.
M'Brenan, persons of the name, pardoned, 4948, 4944, 4968, 5427, 5417, 6667.
M'Brenoyne, persons of the name, pardoned, 4761.
M'Brene, persons of the name, pardoned, 165, 614, 1662, 2082, 2164, 2470, 3321, 3608, 3043, 4696, 4747, 4613, 6025, 6160, 6296, 6486, 6617, 6942, 1822. See Mic Brene.
M'Brenelle, Donell, pardon, 4661.
M'Brewne, Murtertagh, pardon, 6918.
M'Breyn—Breyne, persons of the name, pardoned, 1068, 2294, 2298, 4407.
M'Brian—Brien—Briane—Briene:
- „ Conoghor—Connor (of Cloghdallen), attainted, 4777; pardon, 5187.
- „ Donogh m'Kenedy (of Arlow), pardon, 5478.
- „ Donogh O Loghlen, pardon, 6321.
- „ Kenedy, priest, 6179; dean of Emly, 6487.
- „ Kenedy, attainted, 6276, 6540.
- „ Kenedy m'Richard, clerk, pardon, 6794.
- „ Matthew, son of Cornelius, clerk, pardon and protection, 28-4.
- „ Maurice, son of Matthew, clerk, pardon and protection, 23-4.

INDEX TO FIANTS.—ELIZABETH.

M'Brian, Morogh m'Teig (or M'Bryn), (of Ballybrackry, co. Lim.), pardon, [illegible].
Teig m'Brian, 4884.
Thady m'Donill, attainted, 5777.
Tirlagh, archdeacon of Emly, 6497.
Wm. (in co. Gal.), attainted, 5038.
Wm. m'Tirlagh (in co. Lim.), pardon, [illegible].
others of the name, or patronymic, pardoned, [illegible], 451, 1176, [illegible], 1533, 1740, 1747, [illegible]. See also M'Brean, M'Brein, M'Bren, M'Brene, M'Bryen, M'Bryn.
M'Brian boy, Rory oge, attainted, [illegible].
M'Brian oge (M'Mahon ?), Hugh, &c., pardon, [illegible].
M'Brickey, Moriegh, pardon, [illegible].
M'Brien—Briene. See M'Brian.
M'Brien revagh, Manus, pardon, [illegible].
M'Brin. See M'Bryn.
M'Brinan, Molmery, pardon, [illegible].
M'Britin, Shane, pardon, [illegible].
M'Broaddie, Mollon, pardon, [illegible].
M'Brodee, Wm., pardon, [illegible].
M'Brodie, Teig, pardon, [illegible].
M'Brodire, Conoghor, pardon, [illegible].
M'Brody, persons of the name, pardon, [illegible].
M'Brodyn, John, pardon, [illegible].
M'Brodyne, Gilbride, pardon, [illegible].
M'Broonn, persons of the name, pardoned, [illegible].
M'Bronane, Dermot, pardoned, [illegible].
M'Brounan, Owen, pardoned, [illegible].
M'Broumaghe, John, pardoned, [illegible].
M'Browman, persons of the name, pardoned, [illegible].
M'Bruan, Donald, pardoned, [illegible].
M'Bruney, Conolior, pardoned, [illegible].
M'Bruny, Teig, pardoned, [illegible].
M'Bruodyne, Wm., pardoned, [illegible].
M'Bruyck, Morris, pardoned, [illegible].
M'Brwyn, Donell, pardoned, [illegible].
M'Bryan—Bryane—Bryen—Bryene:
" Conoghor O'Loghlin, pardon, [illegible].
" Donoulie (in co. Lim.), his lands granted, [illegible].
" Morogh M'Torrelagh, lord of Granneogh, [illegible].
" Morogh oy (of Fallis, co. Lim.), pardon, [illegible].
" Terence (O'Connor ?), pardon, [illegible].
" Terence (of Fanne, co. Clare), attainted, 5777.
" others of the name, pardoned, [illegible].
" See also M'Brian.
M'Brynnne, Ferdorogh, pardon, [illegible].
M'Bryn—Brin:
" Morogh m'Teig (see M'Brian), [illegible].
" others of the name, pardoned, [illegible].
MacBrynane, Wony, pardon, [illegible].
MacBryne, Hugh, pardon, [illegible].
M'Bryne, Teig, pardon, [illegible].
M'Bryny, Teig, pardon, [illegible].
M'Bucllige, Carbery, pardon, [illegible].
M'Bucllyet, Conoy, pardon, [illegible].
M'Bullis, Cunnah, pardon, [illegible].
M'Bynny, Owen and Rory, pardon, [illegible].
M'Byrne, Art, pardon, [illegible].
M'Byrredin, Donagh, pardon, [illegible].
M'Byrrybeagorey, Rorilagh, pardon, [illegible].
M'Caagan, Hyne, pardon, [illegible].
M'Caall, Laughlin, house in Arklow, [illegible].
M'Cabe, persons of the name, pardoned, [illegible].
M'Caish, persons of the name, pardoned, [illegible].
M'Cabbe, persons of the name, pardoned, [illegible].
M'Cabbo, Tirlagh, pensioner, [illegible].
" others of the name, pardoned, [illegible].
M'Cabbey, Mulmory, pardon, [illegible].
M'Cabboy, Allestrerius, pardon, [illegible].
M'Cabby, persons of the name, pardoned, [illegible].
M'Cabe, Alexander, grant of land, [illegible]; pardon, [illegible].
" Brian fitz Alexander, grant of land, [illegible].

INDEX TO FIANTS—ELIZABETH.

M'Cabe, Druine kiagh, grant, 4654; pardon, 5654.
Braine m'Donell, grant, 5663.
Brohan m'Foly, grant, 5663.
Edm. boy, grant, 5654.
Edm. m'Alexander, grant, 5664; 5663.
Faly, pardon, 5663.
Fuly, grant, 5663.
Gilpatrick, grant, 5064.
James, grant, 5064.
Owin, grant, 5663.
Patr., grant, 6371.
Rosse, grant, 5665; pardon, 5663, 6788.
Rosse m'Moloughlin, grant, 5654.
Shane, grant, 5665.
Tirlough, lease, 1842, 2874; license to alien, 2882, 3697; pension, 4473. See also M'Cabbe.
Tirlagh, grant, 5663.
Toole, grant, 5664.
others of the name, pardoned, 3063, 4806, 4816, 4877, 5356, 5663, 5664, 5763, 5763, 5698, 6400, 6546, 6503, 6784.
" See also Macabe.
M'Caben, Moriertagh, pardon, 3665.
M'Cabie. See M'Caby.
M'Caboye, Murtagh, pardon, 1923.
M'Caby—Cabie, persons of the name, pardoned, 1604.
M'Cabye, James, pardon, 4623.
M'Cade, Brian, pardon, 5406.
M'Caell, Gilpatrick, pardon, 4577.
" Owin, pardon, 3911.
M'Caffecky, Hugh, pardon, 6761.
M'Caffre, Phelym, chief of his name, 5719.
M'Caffrady, Donald, pardon, 4698.
M'Caffrie—Caffre—Caffroy—Caffry:
Felim, pardon, 4816. See also M'Caffra.
Teig alias Parson, pardon, 5718.
others of the name, pardoned, 3313, 4819, 4821–2, 4824, 5602, 5716, 6378, 6631.
M'Cagan, Edm. (or M'Kagan), pardon, 1863.
others of the same, pardoned, 1654, 5440, 6616, 6548.
" See M'Kagan.
M'Cagane, Turlagh, pardon, 4692.
M'Caggaine, Tirrelagh, pardon, 4626.
M'Cagans, persons of the name, pardoned, 4816, 5419.
M'Caghia, Callo, pardoned, 5734.
M'Caghie, Edm. (or M'Kaghie), pardoned, 5644.
" Philip, pardoned, 5644.
M'Cahall, persons of the name, pardoned, 5462.
M'Cahan, persons of the name, pardoned, 6370, 6798.
M'Cahane, persons of the name, pardoned, 5478, 6617.
M'Caharlagh, Morierteagh and Teig, pardon, 6017.
M'Cahartie, Donogh, pardon, 6611.
M'Cahrille, Donald and Phelym, pardon, 6642.
M'Cahuir, Phelym, pardon, 6119.
M'Cahell—Cahelle. See M'Cahill.
M'Caher—Cahire. See M'Cahir.
M'Cahill—Cahell—Cahelle:
" Edm. (of Ballologe, co. Long.), pardon, 6104.
" Shane reogh (in co. Cav.), attainted, 5648.
" others of this name, or patronymic, pardoned, 3162, 3297, 3342, 3539, 4665, 4027, 4702, 4768, 4808, 5431, 5439, 5693, 5784, 5708, 5802, 5815, 6106, 6100, 6168, 6302, 6418, 6404–5, 6460, 6490, 6615, 6356, 6558, 6574, 6628, 3657–8, 4540, 6698.
M'Cahir—Caher—Cahier—Cahire:
" Art (of Cangort, co. Tip.?), pardon, 5662.
" Donogh (of Piercetown, co. Wex.), pardon, 6737.
" Moreh (Cavanagh?), pardon, 376, 1825, 1903.
" Morertagh duffe, indenture, 6786.
" Moragh or Morierragh oge, (Cavanagh?), pardon, 376, 1803.
" Wm. (of Balloboy, King's co.), pardon, 5580.
" others of the name, or patronymic, pardoned, 185, 633, 611, 931, 1102, 1899, 1418, 1767, 1864, 1575, 1882, 2014, 2309, 3060, 3482, 3931, 3440, 4018, 4019, 4036–4, 4174, 4182, 4540, 4505, 4596, 4748, 4777, 4852, 5199, 5449, 5814, 5818, 4569, 6110, 6160, 6179, 6191–2, 6222, 6223, 6262, 6288, 6338, 6401, 6404, 6458, 6196, 6614, 6617, 6598, 6541, 6548, 6277, 6647, 6668, 4706, 6765.
" See M'Kahir.
M'Cahirr, Donogh, pardon, 4813.
M'Caholl, Tho., pardon, 4685.
M'Cahyle, Brone, pardon, 6617.
M'Cahyr—Cahyre, persons of the name, or patronymic, pardoned, 2682, 4800, 6617.
M'Caior, Donell, pardon, 6189.
" Edm., pardon, 6164.
M'Cale, Phelym, pardon, 6625.
" Teig, pardon, 717.
M'Cale balle, Thady, pardon, 4844.
M'Caloage, Roris, pardon, 4635.

INDEX TO FIANTS.—ELIZABETH.

M'Calciro, Dermot, pardon, [illegible].
M'Calery—Calerie, persons of the name, pardoned, [illegible], [illegible], [illegible].
M'Caligham, Teig, pardon, 6600.
M'Call, Owen, pardon, [illegible].
M'Callaghan—Callaghane—Callahan—Callaghan—Callaghane, persons of the name, or patronymic, pardoned, 4273, [illegible], 6167, 4511, 6515-6, [illegible], [illegible], [illegible], 6701, 6784, 6767, 6770.
M'Callaghe, John m'Donell, pardon, 6784.
M'Callahan. See M'Callaghan.
M'Callan, persons of the name pardoned, 745, 1167, 4144, [illegible].
M'Callavard, David, pardon, 6421.
M'Calle, Thady, grant of land, 422.
" others of the name, pardoned, [illegible], [illegible].
M'Calleghan—Calleghane. See M'Callaghan.
M'Callenan, Conoghor, pardon, 6143.
M'Callorie, Patr., pardon, 6706.
M'Calloy, Edm., pardon, 4814.
M'Callo, Dermot, pardon, [illegible].
" Rory (of Brackland, co. Gal.), pardon, 5718.
" Shane (M'Mahon ?), grant, [illegible].
M'Callogh—Calloghe—Callough—Callough—Callow—Callowe—Callowgh:
" Hugh (M'Donell ?), grant of land, [illegible].
" Hugh boy M'Donell, captain of galloglasses, sheriff of Mayo, [illegible]; indenture, [illegible], 4716; surrender, 4768; pardon, [illegible], [illegible], [illegible]; his daughters, Elizabeth and Mary, [illegible]. See M'Icallowgh.
" others of the name, pardoned, 345, [illegible], [illegible], 4678, [illegible], [illegible], [illegible], [illegible], [illegible], [illegible], [illegible], [illegible].
M'Calloighan, Dermot, pardon, [illegible].
M'Callon, Ea, pardon, [illegible].
M'Callough—Calloughe—Callow—Callowe—Callowgh. See M'Callogh.
M'Callredocker, Owin, pardon, 4811.
M'Cally, Mochmery, pardon, 4534.
M'Calradocker, Brian, pardon, 4540.
M'Calreaghe, James, pardon, [illegible].
M'Callen, Donell, pardon, [illegible].
M'Callin, Con, pardon, 5801.
M'Camoelill, Hugh, pardon, [illegible].
M'Camly, Bryne, pardon, [illegible].
M'Can, persons of the name, pardoned, [illegible], 6146, [illegible], 6714.
M'Cane, Donell, pardon, 6761.
M'Canne, Donell (now M'Anne), pardon, [illegible].
M'Cangellye, Teig, pardon, [illegible].
M'Canne, persons of the name, pardoned, [illegible], [illegible], 6710, 6712. See also M'Anne.
M'Cannayn, Shane, pardon, [illegible].
M'Canny, persons of the name, pardoned, [illegible], [illegible], 6170, 6172.
M'Canraghi, Callough and Philip, pardon, [illegible].
M'Canrick, Wm., pardon, 6118.
M'Canrye, Donogh, pardon, [illegible].
M'Cany, persons of the name, pardoned, [illegible].
M'Cara, Conoghor, pardon, 4618.
M'Caragh, Owen, pardon, [illegible].
M'Caranty, Shane reogh, pardon, [illegible], [illegible].
M'Carbrie—Carberie—Carberrie—Carbery—Carbreo—Carbri—Carbry:
" Donogh (of Clananly, co. Long.), pardon, 6794.
" Knoe (co. Mon.), grant of land, [illegible].
" others of the name, pardoned, [illegible], [illegible], [illegible], 4434, [illegible], [illegible], 4271, 6440, [illegible], [illegible], [illegible], [illegible], 6104, [illegible], [illegible], [illegible], [illegible], 6490, [illegible].
M'Cardell—Cardill—Cardlo:
" Patrick, priest, pardon, [illegible].
" others of the name, pardoned, [illegible], [illegible], [illegible], [illegible], [illegible]. See also M'Ardill.
M'Care, Coramoke, pardon, [illegible].
M'Cargy, Donogh, pardon, [illegible].
M'Carhaghe, Fynes, pardon, [illegible].
M'Carhan, Dermot, pardon, [illegible].
M'Carhie—Karhie, persons of the name, pardoned, [illegible], [illegible], [illegible].
M'Carhig, Donell, pardon, 6518.
M'Carhigo, Owen, pardon, [illegible].
M'Carie, Donogh, pardon, [illegible].
M'Carie, Loughlin, pardon, [illegible].
M'Carloy, Teig, pardon, [illegible].
M'Carmack—Carmacke—Carmaick—Carmick—Carmicke—Carmuck—Carmoick—Carmoke—Carmyck—Carmycke—Karmack—Maccarmack:
" Brian (of Ardcoagh, co. Long.), pardon, [illegible].
" others of the name, pardoned, 1191, [illegible], [illegible], [illegible], [illegible], 5771, 5784, [illegible], [illegible], [illegible], [illegible], [illegible], [illegible], 5740, [illegible], [illegible], [illegible], [illegible], [illegible], [illegible], [illegible], [illegible], [illegible]. See Maccarmack, Mocarmoyke.
M'Carmody, Conoghor and Moriertagh, pardon, [illegible].
M'Carmoick—Carmoke—Carmyck—Carmycke—Carmyck—Carmycke. See M'Carmack.
M'Carmycke, Phelim, pardon, [illegible].
M'Carny, Teig, pardon, 6704.

INDEX TO FIANTS—ELIZABETH.

M'Caron, Hobbert, made chief serjeant of his nation, [illegible].
„ lands belonging to chief (in bar. Kilkenny West, co. Westm.), [illegible].
M'Caroule, Caroule and Daniel, pardon, [illegible].
M'Carr, Brian, pardon, [illegible].
„ Dermot (M'Carty), Eng. liberty, 672.
M'Carragh, Teig, pardon, [illegible].
M'Carraighan, Teig, pardon, [illegible].
M'Carrall, Morgh, grant of land, [illegible].
M'Carraly, Owin, pardon, 5754.
M'Carre, persons of the name, pardoned, [illegible], [illegible].
M'Carrell, Rory, pardon, [illegible].
M'Carrelly, persons of the name, pardoned, [illegible], [illegible], [illegible].
M'Carrie, Owen, pardon, [illegible].
M'Carrigh—Karrighe, Shane, pardon, [illegible].
„ Teig, pardon, 6477.
M'Carrigle, Connor O'Cahoosy, pardon, [illegible].
M'Carrigillasse, John, pardon, [illegible].
M'Carroghan, Keadagh and Shane, pardon, [illegible].
M'Carroll, Donill (of Clontescongh, Queen's co.), pardon, [illegible].
„ Gillekeagh (of Bally m'carroll, co. Cav.), lands of, embezzled, [illegible].
„ others of the name, pardoned, [illegible], [illegible], [illegible], [illegible], [illegible], [illegible], [illegible], [illegible].
M'Carrolle, Finn, pardon, [illegible].
M'Carroly, Owen, pardon, [illegible].
M'Carrowle, Davie, pardon, [illegible].
M'Carrylle, Farryle, pardon, [illegible].
M'Carta, Avartagh, pardon, [illegible].
M'Cartan—Kartan, persons of the name, pardoned, [illegible], [illegible], 4614, [illegible], [illegible], [illegible], [illegible], [illegible], 6577, [illegible].
M'Cartan—Carton—Cartayne's country (the barony of Kinelarty, co. Down), [illegible], [illegible], [illegible]; made shire ground, [illegible]; martial law in, [illegible], [illegible], [illegible].
M'Cartane, John, pardon, [illegible], [illegible].
M'Cartayne. *See* M'Cartan.
M'Carte—Cartey. *See* M'Cartie.
M'Carthane, Edm., pardon, [illegible].
M'Cartie—Carty—Artie—Cart—Carte—Cartey—Carthie—Carthy—Carti—Cartye—Macarty;
„ Callaghan m'Teig, pardon, [illegible], [illegible], [illegible], [illegible].
„ Cormac m'Dermod m'Teig (of Blarny), surrender and regrant of land, [illegible], [illegible]; pardon, [illegible], [illegible].
M'Cartie, Cormac m'Teig (afterwards knt., of Blarny), sheriff of Cork, [illegible]; commissions, [illegible], [illegible]; grants of land, [illegible], [illegible]; lease, [illegible]; pardon, [illegible], [illegible], [illegible], [illegible], [illegible]; his brother and attorney, [illegible].
„ Cormock m'Teig, pardon, [illegible].
„ Cormock m'Donell, pardon, [illegible], [illegible].
„ Cormock don or downe, pardon, [illegible], [illegible]; attainted, [illegible].
„ Cormock oge m'Cormock (of Blarny), pardon, [illegible].
„ Dermod m'Cormock (of Cosinagple, co. Kerry), pardon, [illegible].
„ Dermod m'Donyll, land in occupation of, [illegible].
„ Dermod m'Owen alias M'Donogh (of Kanturk), pardon, [illegible].
„ Dermod m'Teig, knight, captain of Muskerry, [illegible]; commissions, [illegible], [illegible]; pardon, [illegible].
„ Dermot (of Duhallow). *See* M'Carr, 672.
„ Donald or Daniel (of Kilgobban, co. Cork), pardon, [illegible], [illegible].
„ Donell alias M'Carty Reogh, pardon, [illegible].
„ Donell or Donald, bastard son of earl of Clancar, pardon, [illegible], [illegible].
„ Donell, bastard brother of earl of Clancar, [illegible].
„ Donald m'Cormock (of Cloghan), pardon, [illegible]; attainted, [illegible].
„ Donell m'Teig (of Carrignamuck), pardon, [illegible], [illegible], [illegible].
„ Donell ny Counley m'Teig, pardon at his suit, [illegible].
„ Donogh M'C. Reogh, captain of Carbery, comn., [illegible]; pardon, [illegible]; claimant under, [illegible]; deceased, [illegible]; wardship of heir, [illegible].
„ Donogh, pardon, [illegible].
„ Donogh m'Cormock oge, pardon, [illegible].
„ Donogh m'Teig, pardon, [illegible].
„ Donogh m'Teig alias Dryny, pardon, 4414.
„ Donogh M'Ny Gally, pardon, [illegible].
„ Donoghe, bastard brother of earl of Clancar, [illegible].
„ Donoghe (of Killbrittain), pardon, [illegible].
„ Donoghe m'Cormock (of Kanturk), pardon, [illegible].

M'Cartie, Florence or Fynen, son of sir Donogh, wardship, [illegible]; pardon at his suit, [illegible]; alienation to, [illegible]; grant, [illegible]; pardon, [illegible].
" Florence juvenis, pardon, 3034.
" Finian m'Donell oge (of Dunderick), pardon, 6467.
" Fynen duff m'Cormock, lands of granted, 6123.
" Fynen moriagh, pardon, [illegible], 6778.
" John m'Teig, Eng. liberty, 112.
" John alias m'Teig Ellan, pardon, 6773.
" Owen or Eugene, knt., M'C. Reogh, pardon, 1567, [illegible]; seneschal of Carbery, [illegible]; alienation to, [illegible].
" Owen m'Donogh alias M'Donogh, pardon, [illegible]. See Wohny m'Donogh m'Teig, 2361.
" Owen, son of viscount Clancarty, pardon, [illegible].
" Owen m'Teig lohman or Illyman, pardon, [illegible], [illegible].
" Owen m'Fynen oge, lands of, granted, [illegible].
" Teig m'Dermod or Teig O'Norse, pardon, 4414.
" Teig m'Dermod, pardon, 4764; grant of land, [illegible].
" Teig m'Donell ny Countie, pardon, [illegible].
" Teig m'Owen, pardon, [illegible], [illegible], 6784.
" Thady, pension, [illegible]. See M'Charie.
" others of the name, pardoned, [illegible], [illegible], [illegible], [illegible], [illegible], [illegible], [illegible], [illegible], [illegible], [illegible], [illegible], [illegible], [illegible], [illegible], [illegible], [illegible], [illegible], [illegible], [illegible], 4416, [illegible], 6701, [illegible], [illegible], [illegible].
M'Cartie Reogh. See M'Cartie, Donogh, Owen, and Donell.
" " country of, [illegible]. See Carbery, co. Cork.
M'Carton. See M'Cartan.
M'Carty—Cartye. See M'Cartie.
M'Cartye, Philip, pardon, [illegible].
M'Carwell, persons of the name pardoned, [illegible].
M'Cary, Cormac, pardon, [illegible].
M'Carye, Conor, pardon, [illegible].
M'Cashelin, Phelim, pardon, [illegible].
M'Cashlin, Gilpatrick, pardon, [illegible].
M'Cashidy, Wm., pardon, [illegible].
M'Cashin, Edm., pardon, [illegible].
M'Cashin, Tho., surgeon, pardon, [illegible].
M'Cashine, persons of the name pardoned, [illegible], [illegible].
M'Cashyn, persons of the name pardoned, 6110.
M'Casie, persons of the name pardoned, [illegible].
M'Casane—Kasane, persons of the name pardoned, [illegible], [illegible].
M'Caserie, persons of the name pardoned, [illegible].
M'Caserlie, persons of the name pardoned, [illegible].
M'Casson, Gilpatrick, surgeon, pardon, [illegible].
" others of the name pardoned, [illegible], [illegible].
M'Caserie, Brian, pardon, [illegible].
M'Casmorty, persons of the name pardoned, [illegible], [illegible].
M'Cashide, Tirrelagh, pardon, [illegible].
M'Casluen, Owen, surgeon, pardon, [illegible].
M'Casshine—Kasshine, persons of the name pardoned, [illegible], [illegible], [illegible].
M'Cassidie, Peirse, pardon, [illegible].
M'Cassigan, Donogh, pardon, [illegible].
M'Cassin, persons of the name pardoned, [illegible].
M'Cassine, Donogh, pardon, [illegible].
M'Casye, John, surgeon, pardon, [illegible].
" others of the name pardoned, [illegible].
M'Castile, Shane, pardon, [illegible].
M'Caughlan, John (see M'Coghlan), [illegible].
M'Caurick—Caurick, persons of the name pardoned, [illegible], 1072.
M'Cavell, Donell, pardon, [illegible].
M'Caveal, Edm., pardon, [illegible].
M'Cavill, Cormock, pardon, 6741.
" Eugene or One, pardon, [illegible].
M'Cavoyle, Colle, pardon, [illegible].
M'Cavy, Jeffrey, pardon, [illegible].
M'Cawell—Cawill:
" Manus, vicar, pardon, 6712.
" others of the name pardoned, [illegible], 6713–4.
M'Cawile, persons of the name pardoned, [illegible].
M'Cawly, Edm., pardon, [illegible].
M'Cawny, persons of the name pardoned, 4471–2.
M'Cawole boy, Edm. and Ullike, pardon, [illegible].
M'Cawque, Jonock, pardon, [illegible].

INDEX TO FIANTS.—ELIZABETH.

M'Cawyn, Donogh, pardon, 6761.
M'Cawyshe, Donogh, pardon, 6104.
M'Cay — Caye, persons of the name pardoned, [illegible], 4697, [illegible], 6518.
M'Caybior, Donald, pardon, [illegible].
M'Ceagharan, Ferryll, pardon, 6761.
M'Cerbrogh, Donchie, pardon, [illegible].
M'Chaghen, Guillasbog, pardon, 6126.
M'Chaball, Brein, pardon, [illegible].
" Edm., pardon, 5425.
M'Chaier, Donogh, pardon, [illegible].
M'Chairo, Ferdoragh, pardon, [illegible].
M'Chaleni, Randulph, pardon, 6126.
M'Chaleelon, Donogh, pardon, [illegible].
M'Charna, Owen, pardon, [illegible].
M'Charte, Thady, land of (in co. Cork), [illegible].
M'Chartey, Teig, pardon, 6611.
M'Chartie, persons of the name pardoned, [illegible], [illegible], [illegible], [illegible].
M'Chaseane, Tirlagh, pardon, [illegible].
M'Chay, Guillas, pardon, [illegible].
M'Cheghan, Kahell, pardon, 6168.
M'Cheneill, Randulph and Sorle, pardon, [illegible].
M'Cheony, Hugh, pardon, 6612.
M'Chrahe, Enyas, pardon, 6162.
M'Christiane, Bryan, pardon, 6770.
M'Christick, Shan, pardon, 5456.
M'Chrubyne, Hugh, pardon, 6162.
M'Cilladyick, Wm., pardon, [illegible].
M'Claaghy, Conor, pardon, [illegible].
M'Claghlen, Tho., pardon, 6120.
M'Claghlyne, Meloghlin, pardon, [illegible].
M'Clanachy, persons of the name pardoned, [illegible], [illegible].
M'Clanaghan, Donell and Donoghe, pardon, [illegible].
M'Clanaghe, Donell, pardon, [illegible].
M'Clanaghie, Wm., pardon, 6704.
M'Clanaghy, Tho., pardon, 4462.
M'Clanaghye, Cosnagh, pardon, [illegible].
M'Clanchy—Clanchie—Canchye:
" Donogh (of Dromore), pardon, [illegible], [illegible].
" others of the name pardoned, [illegible], [illegible], [illegible], [illegible], [illegible], [illegible], 4878, [illegible], [illegible], [illegible], [illegible], [illegible], [illegible], [illegible], 6617, 6768.
" See M'Glanchy.
M'Clancy—Clancie, persons of the name pardoned, 4610, 4714, [illegible], 6400, [illegible], [illegible].
M'Clanechan, Wm., pardon, [illegible].
M'Clanechy—Clanechie, Donell, pardon, [illegible], 6712.
M'Claneghey, Conoghor, pardon, 3078.
M'Claneghi, Owen, pardon, 4438.
M'Claneghie, John, pardon, 3782.
M'Clanghey, Conoghor, pardon, 3078.
M'Clanghie, persons of the name pardoned, [illegible], [illegible], [illegible], [illegible].
MacClanky, Donogh (of Urlin, co. Clare), pardon, [illegible].
M'Clanky, John, pardon, [illegible].
M'Clannahy, Connoghor, pardon, 6762.
M'Clannaghan, Donogh and Teig, pardon, 6511.
M'Clannchy, Donell, pardon, 6763.
M'Clannchy, Cosnagh, pardon, [illegible].
M'Clanoghie, Donogh, pardon, [illegible].
M'Clanowe, Donogh, pardon, [illegible].
M'Clanque, Tho., pardon, [illegible].
M'Clansey, Tho. (of Bolowtoun), pardon, [illegible].
M'Clansie, Dorby, pardon, [illegible].
M'Clansy, Donogh, pardon, [illegible].
" Teig (of Ballyrobert), pardon, [illegible].
M'Cleary, persons of the name pardoned, [illegible].
M'Cleefe, John, pardon, [illegible].
M'Clemane, Thady, pardon, [illegible].
M'Clery, persons of the name pardoned, [illegible], [illegible], 6794, [illegible], 6108.
M'Cleyry drowne, Gillepy, pardon, [illegible].
M'Cloane, Morogh, pardon, [illegible].
MacCloghiren, Wm., pardon, [illegible].
M'Cloghlen, Murtagh, pardon, [illegible].
M'Cloister—Cloyster, persons of the name pardoned, [illegible], [illegible], [illegible].
M'Clomes, persons of the name pardoned, [illegible].
M'Clone, persons of the name pardoned, [illegible], [illegible].
M'Cloonye, Morogh, pardon, [illegible].
M'Closhe, Morris, pardon, 6768.
M'Closkie, Tirrelagh, pardon, 6736.
M'Closter, John, pardon, [illegible].
M'Clowes, John, pardon, [illegible].
M'Clowne, Loughlin and Morogh, pardon, [illegible].
M'Cloyskey, Dermot, pardon, [illegible].
M'Cloyster, Dennis (see M'Cloister), pardon, [illegible].
M'Clume, Dermod, pardon, [illegible].
" Tho., pardon, [illegible].
M'Clunane, Dermod, pardon, [illegible].
M'Clwoe, Rob., Esq. liberty, [illegible].
M'Clwune, Donell Dyvine, pardon, [illegible].
M'Clyanyeane, Teig, pardon, [illegible].
M'Clynyeane, Conoghor, pardon, [illegible].
M'Cnauyne, Donell oge, pardon, 4160.
M'Cnavin, Donell beg, pardon, [illegible].
M'Cnollsie, Owen, pardon, [illegible].
M'Cnoghor—Coughor, persons of the name, or patronymic, pardoned, [illegible], [illegible], [illegible], [illegible], [illegible], [illegible], 6676, [illegible].
M'Cnoghoure, Cahir, pardon, [illegible].

INDEX TO FIANTS.—ELIZABETH.

M'Comber, Moyler, pardon, [illegible].
M'Coad—Coade, persons of the name (in co. Mon.), pardoned, [illegible], 6734.
M'Coag, Rich., pardon, [illegible].
M'Coagh, Ogby, pardon, 5416.
M'Cochogrye — Coghogerie — Cocogroy — Cocogrye, persons of the name pardoned, 1767, [illegible], [illegible].
M'Cochoeaght, Edm. (M'Mahon ?), grant of land, [illegible].
M'Cocogroy—Cocogrye. *See* M'Cochogrye.
M'Coda, David (*as* Archdeacon), pardon, [illegible].
" Shane, pardon, [illegible].
M'Codd, Wm., pardon, 6442.
M'Coddane, Shane, pardon, [illegible].
M'Codde, persons of the name pardoned, 1884, [illegible]-7.
M'Coddie, persons of the name pardoned, [illegible], 4364, [illegible].
M'Coddes, Garret, pardoned, 5412.
M'Cody—Coddy—Coddye—Code—Codey—Codie—Codoo—Codye:
" David, slain, [illegible].
" others of the name pardoned, [illegible], [illegible], 1078, [illegible], [illegible], [illegible], 1615-4, [illegible], [illegible]-9, [illegible], [illegible]-6, [illegible]-8, [illegible], 5870, [illegible], 6123, 6170, [illegible], [illegible], 6515, [illegible], [illegible], [illegible]-6, 6677, [illegible], [illegible], [illegible].
" *See* Archdeacon Mack Cody.
M'Coogye, Shane, pardon, [illegible].
M'Coogh, Tho., pardon, [illegible].
M'Coemyll—Coenill:
" Hugh boy (of Balaclan, co. Mayo), attainted, [illegible].
" Marcus m'Enabb (of Togher), pardon, [illegible]. *See* M'Coonell.
" others of the name pardoned, [illegible].
M'Coestilo, Rich., pardon, 1874.
M'Coevaye, Donald, pardon, [illegible].
M'Coevye, Donald, pardon, [illegible].
M'Cogan, Dermod, pardon, 4544.
" Wm., pardon, [illegible].
M'Cogerane, Donogh, pardon, 4871.
M'Cogh, Donagh, pardon, 4864.
M'Coghegan, Donche, pardon, [illegible].
M'Coghegrie, Malaghlin, pardon, 6512.
M'Coghegry, Tirlagh, pardon, [illegible].
M'Coghelane, Coochogerie, pardon, [illegible].
MacCoghelane, Wm., pardon, [illegible].
M'Coghie, Hough, in O'Maddens country, co. Gal., 6712.
" Tho., pardon, [illegible].
M'Coghlan—Coghlain—Coghlane—Coghlie—Coglan—Canglan—Coughlan—Macoclan.
" Arthur, pardon, 1680, [illegible], [illegible].
" Edm. oge, pardon, [illegible].
" Gerald, son of sir John, pardon, [illegible].
" John (of Cloghane), knt., seneschal of M'Coghlan's country, grant of land, [illegible]; pardon, [illegible], 1680, [illegible], [illegible], [illegible], [illegible]; pardon of his son, [illegible]; murder of his son, 6734, [illegible].
" John, son of sir John, [illegible].
" Shane m'Donell, entitled lands of, 6777.
" Teig, son of sir John, pardon, 1680, [illegible].
" Teig m'Shane (of Moyclare), pardon, [illegible].
" others of the name pardoned, 1694, 1848, [illegible], [illegible], 4167, 4474, [illegible], [illegible], 5611, [illegible], [illegible], [illegible], [illegible], [illegible], [illegible], [illegible], [illegible], [illegible].
M'Coghlan — Coglan — Macoghlan — Macoughlan — Macowghlan — Macoclan's country (the barony of Garrycastle, King's co.), 161, [illegible], [illegible], [illegible]-4, 6577, [illegible]; seneschal of appointed, 4031.
M'Coghran, Rory, pardon, [illegible].
M'Coghogry, Donell and Hugh, pardon, 1771.
M'Coghn. *See* M'Coghlan.
M'Cohan, Rory, pardon, 1084.
M'Cohy, Donogh, pardon, [illegible].
M'Coigne, Shane and Thady, pardon, [illegible].
M'Coime, James, pardon, [illegible].
M'Coine, Cone, dona, pardon, [illegible].
" others of the name pardoned, [illegible], [illegible].
M'Coinny, Shane, pardon, [illegible].
M'Coisht, Moyler, pardon, [illegible].
M'Coiste, Sherowne, pardon, 5461.
M'Coistigyn, Shane, pardon, [illegible].
M'Coke, persons of the name pardoned, [illegible].
M'Cole, Teig, pardon, [illegible].
M'Colain, persons of the name pardoned, [illegible].
M'Colgan, Donell and Shane, pardon, [illegible].
M'Colitan. *See* M'Collatan.
M'Coll, Donagh, pardon, 4464.
M'Colle, persons of the name pardoned, [illegible], [illegible], [illegible], [illegible].
M'Collae, Edm. and Walter, pardon, [illegible].
M'Collagh, Donell, pardon, [illegible].
M'Colloghane, Riccard, pardon, [illegible].
M'Collel, Edm., pardon, [illegible].
M'Collein, Pholem, pardon, [illegible].
M'Collen, Donell and Tirlagh, pardon, [illegible].

INDEX TO FIANTS.—ELIZABETH.

M'Colletan—Colletane—Colitan—Collitan—Collytan, persons of the name pardoned, [illegible], [illegible], 5046, 5184, 6084, 4871, [illegible], 6641.
M'Collerre, Owen, pardon, 6404.
M'Colley, Edm., pardon, 6490.
M'Colligan, Patrick, pardon, [illegible].
M'Collie, Walter, pardon, [illegible].
M'Collimet, Donell, pardon, [illegible].
M'Collin, Phelim, pardon, 6761.
M'Collitan, Molaghlin, 6641. *See* M'Colletan.
M'Collman—Collmane, Hugh duff, pardon, [illegible], [illegible].
M'Collo—Colloe, persons of the name pardoned, 1778, [illegible], 4074, 4076, [illegible], 4487, [illegible], [illegible], 5478–4, [illegible], 6540.
M'Collochan, persons of the name pardoned, [illegible].
M'Colloo. *See* M'Collo.
M'Collow—Collowe, persons of the name pardoned, [illegible], [illegible].
M'Colloy, Ferrell, pardon, 4162.
M'Collrick, Phelim, pardon, 6816.
M'Collitan, Edm., pardon, 6641.
M'Colly, persons of the name pardoned, 6918.
M'Collyn—Collynn, persons of the name pardoned, 4021, 6761.
M'Collytan. *See* M'Colletan.
M'Colman, Garbry, pardon, 1621.
„ Walthesar, pardon, 5457.
M'Cologhain, Meloghlin, pardon, 6616.
M'Colomet, Cowconaght, pardon, [illegible].
M'Coltan, Edm., pardon, 6712.
„ Meloghlin, pardon, 6641.
M'Com, Hugh, pardon, [illegible].
M'Comaloyne, Tho., pardon, 6542.
M'Come, Gelpatrick, pardon, 6441.
„ Mordaugh, [illegible].
M'Comegatee, Mare, pardon, 4946.
M'Comoghe, Shane, pardon, [illegible].
M'Comyn, persons of the name pardoned, 1946, 2744, [illegible], 5641, 6179, 6497, [illegible].
M'Con, Gilpatrick (M'Mahon ?), grant of land, [illegible].
„ Shydy, pardon, 1640.
M'Conalayn, Rowry, pardon, [illegible].
M'Conall, Fear, pardon, [illegible].
M'Conalye, Brian, pardon, [illegible].
M'Conave, Teig, pardon, [illegible].
M'Conbue, Donell, pardon, 5511.
M'Conedyne, Mahon, pardon, 4471.
M'Conchan, persons of the name pardoned, [illegible].
M'Conchor—Conchore, persons of the name pardoned, [illegible], 1473, 2146, 2374, 5046, [illegible], [illegible], [illegible], 6477.
M'Conchor ne dom, Brien, pardon, [illegible].
M'Conchydyne, persons of the name pardoned, 4471.
M'Concor, Moris, pardon, [illegible].
M'Concron, Shane, pardon, 6712.
M'Con Croygh, Donogh, pardon, [illegible].
M'Cone, Meloghlen, pardon, 1674.
M'Conechore moyle, Feragh, pardon, 1472.
M'Conelieg, Awliffe, pardon, [illegible].
M'Conell. *See* M'Connell.
M'Conella, Donogh, pardon, 6778.
M'Coneliane, Dermod, pardon, 6779.
M'Conellye, Cunnghor, pardon, 6648.
M'Conemarre, Donell, pardon, 5183.
M'Coneo, persons of the name pardoned, 4581, [illegible].
M'Congher, Owen and Teig, pardon, 616.
M'Conghore, Thady, pardon, 5151.
M'Congiane, Wm., pardon, 5114.
M'Congianie, Shane, pardon, 6113.
M'Conher, Cormac, pardon, 6646.
M'Conick, Gillernow, pardon, [illegible].
M'Conigan, persons of the name pardoned, 2946, [illegible], [illegible], 4487, 5618, 6734.
M'Conigher, Dermot, pardon, 1673.
M'Conine, Shane, pardon, 6794.
M'Conle, Owen, pardon, 42.
M'Conloy, Brian, pardon, 4814.
M'Conly—Conlye, persons of the name pardoned, [illegible], [illegible], 4284, 6317.
„ Cornelius m'Dermot (of Cloghtredvally, co. Cork), [illegible].
M'Connarre, Donogh and Shane, pardon, [illegible].
„ *See* M'Conemarre.
M'Connarroghe boy, Shane, pardon, [illegible].
M'Connay, Donogh, pardon, 1549.
M'Conmas, Hugh, pardon, [illegible].
M'Con mac riagh, Cornelius m'Donoghe, pardon, [illegible].
M'Connigiane, Donell, pardon, 6764.
M'Conny, Mulmory, pardon, [illegible].
M'Cona, Dermot, pardon, [illegible].
„ Garret, pardon, 6642.
M'Conne, Mohon, pardon, 4478.
M'Connally, Teig m'Ardell, pardon, [illegible].
M'Conne, Rosse, pardon, 4111.
„ Toole, pardon, 6779.
M'Connell—Conell—Conill—Connel—Connill:
„ Alexander, pardon, [illegible].
„ Alexander m'Donell ballagh, pardon, 5762.
„ Alexander m'Hugh boy, pardon, [illegible]; attainted, 6016.
„ Allen, attainted, 6844.
„ Donell gorm, pardon, [illegible].
„ Farrigh, pardon, [illegible]; attainted, [illegible], 6911.
„ James, son of Sawrley, pardon, 6597.

INDEX TO FIANTS—ELIZABETH.

M'Connell, Marcus m'Enabbo, pardon, 4573, [illegible], [illegible] (M'Conyll).
" Morieragh, grant of land, 508.
" Sorley boy, pardon, 5414.
" Sawrdey, English liberty, [illegible]; surrender and indenture, [illegible]; pardon, 4517.
" Sowrly, pardon, [illegible].
" others of the name pardoned, 2348, [illegible], 3406, [illegible], [illegible], [illegible], [illegible], [illegible], [illegible], [illegible], 4[illegible], [illegible], [illegible], [illegible], 5431, 5448, 5451-3, [illegible], [illegible], 5417, 5778, 5797, [illegible], [illegible], [illegible], [illegible], [illegible], [illegible], [illegible], [illegible], [illegible], [illegible], [illegible], 5744.

M'Connellon, Teig, pardon, 5467.
M'Connoy, Bren, pardon, 5574.
" Donogh, pardon, 6534.
M'Connigan, Hugh, pardon, 5761.
" Mulmory, pardon, 4542.
M'Conull. See M'Connell.
M'Connoloy, Brian, pardon, 5115.
M'Connour, Connoor, pardon, [illegible].
M'Connoghor, persons of the name pardoned, 91, [illegible], [illegible], [illegible], [illegible], 6444, 6478, 6467, [illegible], 5611, [illegible], [illegible], 6571, [illegible], [illegible], 6761, 6762, 6784, 6778.
M'Connoghor ne prack, Fynine, pardon, 6571.
M'Connoghor ny Sawny, Dermod, pardon, 6762.
M'Connoly, persons of the name pardoned, 6768.
M'Connor, Donell m'Thriogh, attainted, [illegible].
" others with this patronymic pardoned, 1[illegible], 1380, [illegible], [illegible], 4915, [illegible], 4[illegible], [illegible], [illegible], [illegible], 4[illegible]-4, 4711, 4778, 4783, [illegible], [illegible], 4844, [illegible], [illegible], [illegible], [illegible], 6415-6, [illegible], 6130, 6374, [illegible], 6426-[illegible], 6465, [illegible]-78, 6477, [illegible], [illegible], [illegible], 6311, 6318, [illegible], [illegible], [illegible], 6474-7, [illegible], 6788.
M'Connor mctan, Hugh boy, pardon, 5474.
M'Connor ny Sawnie, Conoghor, pardon, 6496.
M'Connor og, Cahill and Rory, pardon, 3941.
M'Connorogh, Donogh, pardon, 5[illegible].
M'Connovan, Morgh and Morieragh, pardon, 5144.
M'Connoy, Malachy and Thady, English liberty, 548.
M'Connry, Donoho, pardon, 5184.
M'Conny—Conye, persons of the name pardoned, 5[illegible], [illegible], [illegible].
M'Connygan, Tyrlagh, pardoned, [illegible].
M'Connyll, persons of the name pardoned, 4416, [illegible], [illegible].
M'ConnyUigho, Donogho, pardoned, [illegible].
M'Conoghe, Brian, pardon, [illegible].

M'Conoghor, persons with this patronymic pardoned, 618, 1078, 1378, 1718, [illegible], [illegible], [illegible], [illegible], [illegible], [illegible], 4484, [illegible], [illegible], [illegible], [illegible], 4618, [illegible], [illegible], 4678, [illegible], [illegible], [illegible], [illegible], 4734, 4751, 4752, [illegible], [illegible], [illegible], [illegible], 5408, 6447, [illegible], [illegible], [illegible], [illegible], [illegible], [illegible], [illegible], [illegible], [illegible], [illegible], [illegible], 6311, 6185, [illegible], [illegible], [illegible], 6511, 6516-7, [illegible], [illegible], [illegible], [illegible], [illegible], [illegible], 6791, 6782, 6784, 6770.
M'Conoghor boy, Donald, alienation to, [illegible].
M'Conoghor caragh, Donell, pardon, [illegible].
M'Conoghor inquilliane, Shane, pardon, [illegible].
M'Conoghor ny Sowragh (or ne Seowry), Donogh, pardon, [illegible], 4743.
" Conoghor and Fyn, pardon, 6743. See M'Connor ny Sawnie.
M'Conoghor ny sliologh, Teig, pardon, [illegible].
M'Conogry, Conchor, pardon, 6[illegible].
M'Conor, Lisagh, surrender of his lands, 3811.
" others with this patronymic pardoned, 3478, 1763, 3041, [illegible]-46, [illegible], 4248, 4518, [illegible], [illegible], [illegible], [illegible], [illegible], 6472, 6444, [illegible].
M'Conor ny grohir, Donogh, pardon, [illegible].
M'Conor og, Teig, pardon, 1281.
M'Conough, Murtagh, pardon, [illegible].
M'Conowe, Molaghlin, pardon, 1641.
M'Conraghe, Wm., pardon, [illegible].
M'Conrayo, persons of the name pardoned, [illegible].
M'Conroy, persons of the name pardoned, 4[illegible], [illegible].
M'Conrie, persons of the name pardoned, 6476, [illegible], 6540, [illegible].
M'Conrowe, Brian, pardoned, 6[illegible].
M'Conry, persons of the name pardoned, [illegible], [illegible], [illegible], [illegible], [illegible], 6418, [illegible].
M'Conryde, Donell and Morieragh, pardon, [illegible].
M'Conrye, Mahon, pardon, [illegible].
M'Consmelyne, Mahon, pardon, [illegible].
M'Considon, persons of the name pardoned, [illegible].
M'Considin, persons of the name pardoned, 6766-[illegible].
M'Considine, persons of the name pardoned, [illegible].
M'Conskilyn, Donell, pardon, [illegible].
M'Consly, Dermod, pardon, [illegible].
M'Consydiyn, Donell, pardon, [illegible].
M'Consyly, Donogh duff, pardon, 1343.
M'Consylyn, Mahon m'Donogh duff, pardon, [illegible].
M'Convae, Teig, pardon, [illegible].
M'Convay, Donogh, pardon, [illegible].
M'Convre, Thady M'Nemaroff, pardon, 1257.
M'Convoy, Teig, pardon, [illegible].

INDEX TO FIANTS.—ELIZABETH.

M'Conwall, persons of the name pardoned, [illegible], [illegible].

M'Conway, persons of the name pardoned, [illegible], [illegible].

M'Conwayle, Hugh and Kayle, pardon, [illegible].

M'Conwell, Phelim, pardon, [illegible].

M'Conwye, Rory, pardon, 6714.

M'Cony, Fonnell, pardon, [illegible].

„ Wm., pardon, 6487.

M'Conyma, Tirrelagh, pardon, [illegible].

M'Conyl, Daniel, pardon, [illegible].

M'Conyll, Turelagh, messuage in Ardee, 17[illegible].

„ others of the name pardoned, [illegible], [illegible], [illegible], [illegible].

M'Conyllan, Gillebride, pardon, [illegible].

M'Conyn, Connor (of Termon M'Conyn), pardon, 4874, [illegible].

„ persons of the name pardoned, [illegible], [illegible].

M'Conyne, persons of the name pardoned, [illegible], [illegible].

M'Coochogurle, Conoghor, pardon, [illegible].

M'Cooichonaght, Pair. and Teoll, pardon, [illegible].

M'Coole, Edm., pardon, 6784.

M'Coon, Shane, pardon, 10.

M'Coog, Redmund, pardon, 6611.

M'Coole, Ever, pardon, 6770.

M'Coole, Rosse (M'Mahon?), grant of land, [illegible].

M'Coomyn, Nich. and Walter, pardon, [illegible].

M'Coonghe, Donell, pardon, [illegible].

M'Cor, Donell and Gilleduf, pardon, 4[illegible].

M'Cortan, John, pardon, [illegible].

M'Corby, Shane, pardon, [illegible].

M'Corkran—Corrane—Corkrane, Moloughlin, pardon, 1178, [illegible], 57[illegible].

M'Corishe or Bermingham, Shane, pardon, 714.

M'Corkrane. See M'Corckran.

M'Cormack—Cormacke:

„ Ferdorogh (of Cloynmore, King's co.), pardon, [illegible].

„ Teig m'Dermoda, of the Glancarties, lands of (in co. Kerry), granted, [illegible], 6717.

„ others of the name pardoned, [illegible], [illegible], [illegible], [illegible], [illegible].

M'Cormain, John, pardon, [illegible].

M'Cormaine, Don, pardon, 6712.

M'Cormak, Cormak oy (O'Conor?), pardon, [illegible].

M'Cormake, Conoghor, pardon, [illegible].

„ Donald, pardon, [illegible].

M'Corman, persons of the name pardoned, [illegible], [illegible], [illegible], [illegible], [illegible], [illegible].

M'Cormane, persons of the name pardoned, [illegible], [illegible], [illegible], [illegible], [illegible].

M'Cormaye, Donogh, pardon, [illegible].

M'Cormeck, Donoghe (of Loghir, co. Cork), pardon, [illegible].

M'Cormick—Cormicke, persons of the name pardoned, 1178, [illegible], [illegible], [illegible], [illegible], [illegible], [illegible], [illegible], [illegible], [illegible].

M'Cormock—Cormocke:

„ Callaghan m'Teig, 6764. See M'Carty.

„ Conor (of Clonkeine, King's co.), pardon, [illegible].

„ Donald (of Boghem). See M'Cartie.

„ Donogh (M'Carty), desires to surrender his lands, [illegible].

„ Fynine, abbot of Gilley, pardoned, [illegible], [illegible].

„ others of the name pardoned, [illegible], 6770.

M'Cormuk, persons of the name pardoned, [illegible], [illegible], [illegible], [illegible].

M'Cormoucke, Dermot, pardon, [illegible].

M'Cormuck—Cormucke—Cormuk:

„ David, English liberty, 148.

„ Kalleghan m'Teig, [illegible]. See Callaghan M'Cartie.

„ others of the name pardoned, 10, 782, [illegible], 4108, 4[illegible], 4741, [illegible], [illegible], [illegible], [illegible], [illegible], [illegible].

M'Cormyck, Donogh, pardon, 2970.

„ Hugh, pardon, [illegible].

M'Cormycke, Owen, pardon, [illegible].

M'Cormyke, Hugh, pardon, [illegible].

M'Corrbry, Laughlin, pardon, [illegible].

M'Corroman, Teig, pardon, [illegible].

M'Correy, Moleghlin, pardon, [illegible].

M'Correyrie, Conoghor and Shane M'Donogh, pardon, [illegible].

M'Corrigan, Teig, pardon, 441.

M'Corrine, persons of the name pardoned, [illegible].

M'Cory, Oo, pardon, [illegible].

M'Corrie, Dermot, pardon, [illegible].

M'Cosey, Redmund, pardon, 1474.

M'Cosdallowe, Wm., pardon, [illegible].

M'Cosdigine, Donoghe, pardon, [illegible].

M'Cosgrove, Gay, pardon, 172.

M'Cosgryr, Tho., pardon, [illegible].

M'Cosin, Shane, pardon, [illegible].

MacCosny, Kahir, pardon, [illegible].

M'Cosnigin, Donell, pardon, [illegible].

INDEX TO FIANTS.—ELIZABETH.

M'Cossichan, Donogh, pardon, 6014.
M'Cosrichon, Aghidie, pardon, 5012.
M'Costallighe, Donagh, pardon, 5086.
M'Costall, Redmund, pardon, 1467.
M'Costo, Hubert, pardon, 4687.
" Shernan, pardon, 4287.
M'Costedyry, Wm., pardon, 4621.
M'Costegan, Donell, cruse, and others of the name, pardon, 6551.
M'Costegane, Dermod, pardon, 5148.
M'Costegine, Donell, pardon, 3818.
" Donogh, pardon, 3780.
M'Costela, Meyler, pardon, 3380.
M'Costelle, Tole, pardon, 6498.
M'Costell—Costello:
Hugh, death of, 183.
others of the name pardoned, 876, 5417, 6237, 6777.
M'Costello — Costellow — Costellowe — Costellowe—Costelo—Costelor—Costello—Costilloe—Costillo—Costilloe.
John (of Tulrahan), pardon, 6677.
Shane, surrenders lands and title, 4368; lands regranted, 4383.
others of the name pardoned, 1387, 4665, 2536, 4995, 4877, 5481, 5890, 5414–5, 5517, 5748, 6700.
title of, renounced, 4698.
territory of (barony of Costello), co. Mayo, 4368.
M'Costelly, Edm., surgeon, pardon, 5817.
" Meiler, pardon, 2408.
M'Costelo—Costelos. See M'Costello.
M'Costely, persons of the name pardoned, 4443, 6700.
M'Costigin, persons of the name pardoned, 2444, 6120.
M'Costigine, Carroll, pardon, 443.
M'Costilleyn, Shane, pardon, 3607.
M'Costille, Cnick, pardon, 5658.
M'Costillo—Costilloe—Costilo—Costiloe. See M'Costello.
M'Costogina, Wm., pardon, 3898.
M'Costogyn, Donell, pardon, 5551.
M'Costolly, David, pardon, 3290.
M'Costy, Shurdie, pardon, 6712.
" Walter, pardon, 5935.
M'Costygan, Fynin, pardon, 6182.
M'Costygyn, Donogh, pardon, 690.
M'Cotter—Cotter—Cottir—Coltier—Cottyr:
persons of the name pardoned, 3116–7, 2348, 2354–63, 4076, 3864, 3874, 4107, 4673, 4288, 4434–6, 6494, 6761.
MacCough: Shorown M'Kough, pardon, 2491. See M'Cowck, M'Kough, M'Quist.
M'Cough, Edm. and Shane, pardon, 5408.
M'Coughegrye, James and Roe, pardon, 2480.
M'Coughlen—Coughlane. See M'Coghlan.
M'Coukellie, Teig, pardon, 5177.
M'Coulroy, Donogh, pardon, 2754.
M'Couman, Morris, pardon, 3890.
M'Counly, Brian, pardon, 5684.
M'Counnoylly, Dermod, pardon, 5418.
M'Counsully, Shoney, pardon, 5428.
M'Courcie, persons of the name pardoned, 4483.
M'Coutrilo, Donell, pardon, 4487.
M'Cou[ ] Thady, pardon, 1388.
M'Cowan—Cowane, persons of the name pardoned, 6663.
M'Cowck, Knight alias, pardon, 4671. See M'Cough.
" Henry moile, pardon, 1866, 4571.
M'Cowdre, Geoffrey, pardon, 1652.
M'Cowoogry, Donell, pardon, 4861.
M'Cowge, Edm., pardon, 5179.
" Redmund, pardon, 4871.
M'Cowkoggry, Tolk, pardon, 5654.
M'Cowhoran, Wm., pardon, 4953.
M'Cowiooma, Tole, pardon, 6679.
M'Cowlag, Dorrick, pardon, 4893.
M'Cowlick, Moriris, pardon, 6574.
M'Cowlin, Gillyes, pardon, 5465.
M'Cowlooma, Molaghlin and Shane, pardon, 6622.
M'Cowlon, Cormick, pardon, 6480.
M'Cowloye, John, pardon, 1996.
M'Cowly, Brone, pardon, 6813.
M'Cowlyn, Conchonaght, pardon, 5658.
M'Cowna, Conn, pardon, 6618.
M'Cowran, Mathew, pardon, 6438.
M'Cowrel, Henry, pardon, 5623.
M'Cowrell, Hugh, pardon, 4007.
M'Cowrky, Connor, pardon, 4781.
M'Cowrly, Pair, pardon, 6438.
M'Cowrya, Connor, 6606.
M'Cowrycke, Theobald, pardon, 2790.
M'Cowrylo, Alyn, pardon, 4900.
M'Coyn, James, pardon, 6736.
M'Coyn—Coyne, persons of the name pardoned, 618, 2888, 2838, 3888, 4360, 3641, 4396, 4508, 4888, 5600, 5406, 5615, 6062, 6408, 6478, 6468, 6818.
M'Cra, Tho., pardon, 6827.
M'Crabinck, Gilladuf, pardon, 5698.
M'Crach, persons of the name pardoned, 4604, 4061.
M'Cracho, Donly m'Teig, pardon, 671.
M'Crach—Craghe:
Dermod, harper, pardon, 4871.
Donogh (or Donoghe M'Crah of Gallolly), pardon, 4007; attainted, 6179.

INDEX TO FIANTS—ELIZABETH.

M'Cragh, Donogho, archdeacon of Lismore, [illegible].
" Eneas m'Morogh, attainted, [illegible], [illegible].
" Fian, rymor, pardon, [illegible].
" John m'Hera, rymor, pardon, [illegible].
" Philip m'Rory (see Cragh), pardon, [illegible], [illegible].
" Philip fitz Thomas, son of the rector, pardon, [illegible], [illegible].
" Philip m'Tho. (of Castleconnery), pardon, [illegible].
" Thomas (of Castlemanagh), pardon, [illegible].
" Tho. fitz John fitz Pierce, pardon, [illegible].
" Tho. m'Rory, pardon, [illegible].
" Tho. oge m'Tho. m'Rory, pardon, [illegible], [illegible], [illegible], [illegible].
" Tho. m'Shane m'Donell, pardon, [illegible], [illegible].
" Wm. O'Fernan, pardon, [illegible].
" others of the name pardoned, [illegible], [illegible].
M'Craghor, Owen, pardon, [illegible].
M'Craght, Philip, pardon, [illegible].
M'Craghy, Dermot and Shane, pardon, [illegible].
M'Crah—Crahe:
" Donogho. See Donagh M'Cragh.
" Tho. oge Pierce, pardon, [illegible].
" others of the name pardoned, [illegible], 1617, [illegible], [illegible], [illegible], [illegible], [illegible], [illegible], [illegible], [illegible], [illegible].
M'Crahin, John, pardon, [illegible].
M'Crahin, Morris, pardon, [illegible].
M'Craigh—Craighe, persons of the name pardoned, [illegible], [illegible], [illegible], [illegible], [illegible], [illegible], [illegible], [illegible].
" See M'Kraigh, Mocraighe.
M'Crahe, Baris, pardon, [illegible].
M'Craith, Donogh, pardon, [illegible].
M'Craly, Shane, pardon, [illegible].
M'Crath, Donell, pardon, [illegible].
MacCraven, Philip, clerk, pardon, [illegible].
M'Cravia, Fair. and Philip, pardon, [illegible].
M'Crawe, John, pardon, [illegible].
M'Crawyle, Gillymoyle, pardon, [illegible].
" See Macrawell.
M'Crayn, Gillarayne, pardon, [illegible].
" See M'Kray.
M'Craythe, Teig, pardon, [illegible].
M'Credan, Donogh and Shane, pardon, [illegible].
M'Creffon, Donogh, pardon, [illegible].
M'Crefford, Edm., pardon, [illegible].
M'Creghte, Teig, pardon, [illegible].
M'Crele, Mologhlin, pardon, [illegible].
M'Crell, Donell, pardon, [illegible].
M'Cremoyne, Wm., pardon, [illegible].
M'Cremyne, Hubert m'Moiler, and others of the name pardoned, [illegible].
" See M'Remon.
M'Crener, Fair., pardon, [illegible].
M'Crenir, Cale, pardon, [illegible].
M'Creobin, Conoghor, pardon, [illegible].
M'Crephin, Edm., pardon, [illegible].
M'Crephon, Donagh (Cavanagh ?), [illegible].
M'Cressogan, Donell, pardon, [illegible].
M'Crere, Donell, pardon, [illegible].
M'Creverty, Conoghor, pardon, [illegible].
M'Creyale, persons of the name pardoned, [illegible].
M'Cridan—Cridane, persons of the name pardoned, [illegible], [illegible].
M'Criffon, Donell, pardon, [illegible], [illegible].
M'Crigan, Teig, pardon, [illegible].
M'Crichin, Donell, pardon, [illegible].
M'Criphon, Tirrelagh, pardon, [illegible].
M'Crinian, Tirlagh, pardon, [illegible].
M'Cristie, Shane, pardon, [illegible].
M'Crobock, Edm., pardon, [illegible].
M'Crobocke, Moyler and Redmond, pardon, [illegible].
M'Crodin, Teig, pardon, [illegible].
M'Crohir, Conoghor, pardon, [illegible].
M'Crole, Fair. and Phelim, pardon, [illegible].
M'Crolin, Donell, pardon, [illegible].
M'Crongally, Rich., pardon, [illegible].
M'Crongoly, Tho., pardon, [illegible].
M'Crosile, Feagh, pardon, [illegible].
M'Crossie, Tege, pardon, [illegible].
M'Crosson, Aghowlie, pardon, [illegible].
M'Crosson, David and Maurice, pardon, [illegible].
M'Croughan, Brian, pardon, [illegible].
M'Crowane, Naile, pardon, [illegible].
M'Crowne, Owen, pardon, [illegible].
M'Croy, Dermod, pardon, [illegible].
M'Cruyn, Donogho, pardon, [illegible].
M'Cruffin, Tirlagh, pardon, [illegible].
M'Crughan, Owen, pardon, [illegible].
M'Cruhen—Cruhin, persons of the name pardoned, [illegible], [illegible], [illegible].
M'Crusie, persons of the name pardoned, [illegible].
M'Cruttan—Crutten, persons of the name pardoned, [illegible], [illegible], [illegible].

INDEX TO FIANTS—ELIZABETH.

M'Crydan, Donogh, pardon, 1297.
M'Crykow, Dermod, pardon, [illegible].
M'Cryor, Teig, pardon, [illegible].
M'Cryphon, Edm., pardon, 5481.
M'Crycuhy, Teig, pardon, 5804.
M'Cong, persons of the same pardoned, 4078, [illegible], [illegible].
M'Cuaga, Edm., pardon, 4078.
M'Coak, Edm., pardon, 4080.
M'Cuan, Morish, pardon, [illegible].
M'Cushanoghl, Brian, pardon, [illegible].
M'Cudy, Teig, pardon, [illegible].
M'Cugg, Edm., pardon, [illegible].
M'Cugin, Maurice, pardon, 134.
M'Cuilline—Cullines—Culling—Cullinge, persons of the same pardoned, [illegible].
" See M'Quilline.
M'Cullie, Teig, pardon, [illegible].
M'Cullmart, Hugh, pardon, 6741.
M'Cultagly, Kennedas, dean of Clonfert, [illegible].
M'Cumigan, Tirlagh, pardon, [illegible].
M'Cunigane, Gobarry, pardon, 5784.
M'Cunaya, persons of the same pardoned, [illegible].
M'Cunigan, persons of the same pardoned, [illegible], [illegible], [illegible].
M'Cunnegane, Teig, pardon, [illegible].
M'Cunnigan, Tirlagh, pardon, 6467.
M'Cunny, Fair., pardon, [illegible].
M'Cuntayn, Hugh, pardon, [illegible].
M'Cunye, Mohla, pardon, [illegible].
M'Cuog, Rich., pardon, [illegible].
M'Curin—Curine, persons of the same pardoned, [illegible].
M'Currera, persons of the same pardoned, 4761.
M'Curryn, Wm., pardon, [illegible].
M'Curtaine, Teig merregagh, pardon, [illegible], [illegible].
M'Curtayne, Wm., pardon, [illegible].
M'Cusack, persons of the same pardoned, [illegible], 6613.
M'Cusoge, Donogh, pardon, 6747.
" Thady, pardon, [illegible].
M'Cusoke, Dermod, pardon, [illegible].
M'Cusuy, Edward, pardon, [illegible].
M'Cwlie, Brian and Shane, pardon, [illegible].
M'Cynolig, Teig, pardon, [illegible].
M'Da, persons of the same pardoned, 1118, [illegible], [illegible], 4818, 6448.
M'Da more. See M'Damore.
M'Da oge, Edm. (Barry?), pardon, 2871.
M'Dae, Dermot and Shean, pardon, [illegible].
M'Dae Kierry, Tho., pardon, 4446.
M'Dae, persons of the same pardoned, 2281, [illegible], [illegible].
M'Dae Iriotane, Tho., pardon, 6477.
M'Dae oge, John, pardon, [illegible].
M'Dale, persons of the same pardoned, 18, 6467.
M'Dallo—Dallee—Dallawe, Shane duorog or John shorogh, pardon, [illegible], 4881, 6100.
" Gerald, pardon, 3784, 4180.
M'Dalogh, Donell, pardon, [illegible].
M'Dallon, Hugh and Shane, pardon, [illegible].
M'Dallough, Cahir, pardon, [illegible].
" Donell, pardon, 5121.
M'Dallow—Dallowe, Gerod, indenture, [illegible].
" others of the same pardoned, [illegible], 5116, [illegible], 6408, [illegible], [illegible].
M'Damore, Phelym, indenture, [illegible].
" See M'Amore, M'David More, M'Dayo Moore, Macdamore.
M'Daniell—Daniel, persons of the same pardoned, [illegible], [illegible], [illegible], 6217, [illegible], [illegible], [illegible].
M'Darragh, Tho., pardon, [illegible].
M'Darnell, Morice, pardon, [illegible].
M'Darcy, Thady, pardon, [illegible].
M'Dave, Tho., pardon, [illegible].
M'Daved. See M'David.
M'Davon. See M'Davy.
M'Davoyd, Shane (of the Clan David in Inishowen), pardon, [illegible].
M'David—Daved—Davy:
" Hubert boy Bourk (of Glinsk), seneschal of his country, [illegible]; grant of lands, [illegible].
" Hubert, surrenders land and name, [illegible]; grant, [illegible].
" title abolished, [illegible], 5104.
M'David, Edm., tenant of seignory of Castletown, co. Lim., [illegible]; pardoned, 6457.
" John, land in tenure of, [illegible].
" Manus (of country of Kinselagh, co. Wex.), indenture, [illegible].
" persons of the same pardoned (in co. Galway and neighbourhood), 1867, 4848, [illegible]; elsewhere, [illegible], 1668, 1913, [illegible], [illegible], [illegible], [illegible], [illegible], [illegible], 4814, [illegible], [illegible], [illegible], 6470, [illegible], [illegible], [illegible], [illegible], [illegible], [illegible], [illegible], [illegible], [illegible]. See also M'Davy.
M'David More's country (co. Wex.), chief serjeant, [illegible]. See M'Damore.
M'David og, Edm. (Barry?), pardon, [illegible], [illegible].
" Tho., pardon, [illegible].
M'Davie. See M'Davy.
M'Davog, Rich. (of Portumna, co. Gal.), and others of the same pardoned, [illegible].
M'Davy—Davie—Davye:
" Gerald (in co. Lim.), attainted, [illegible].

M'Davy, Hubert boy. *See* M'David.
,, others of the name pardoned (in co. Gal. and neighbourhood), 4660, 4682, 4697, 4724, 4777, 4868, 5147-8, 5152, 5476, 5484, 5810, 5817, 5747, 5906, 6084; elsewhere, 106, 397, 1290, 1804, 2063, 2148, 2302, 2426, 3084, 3108, 3960, 4169, 4543, 4660, 5098, 5688, 5687, 6110, 6163, 6213, 6338, 6159, 6488, 6478, 6506, 6517, 6873, 6555, 6604.
M'Davy, title abolished, 6104. *See* M'David.
M'Davy — Daveo — Davie's country (the barony of Ballymoe, co. Gal. and Rosc.), 4498, 5134.
,, seneschal of, 3604.
M'Davy duff, John or Shane (Bourk, of Caraigunagh, co. Mayo), pardon, 2866, 3709, 6906.
M'Davy mere, Caver, pardon, 1066.
Helena, dau. of Gillpatrick (in co. Wex.), pardon, 5712.
M'Davy oge, Edm. owny or wony (of Killalonan, co. Mayo), attainted, 4568, 6614.
M'Davyd, persons of the name pardoned, 1748, 5392, 5864, 4908.
M'Davye. *See* M'Davy.
M'Dawllowe, Gerald, pardon, 5110.
M'Dawyre, Gwilliamall, pardon, 4907.
M'Day, Dermod, pardon, 6457.
M'Daye, Fardorogh, pardon, 11.
,, Teig, pardon, 10.
M'Daye Moore's country (co. Wex.), 2544. *See* M'David more, M'Damore.
M'De, Shane, alias the parson, pardon, 4468.
M'Deane, Cahill, pardon, 4666.
M'Deermonde roe, Edm., 6429. *See* M'Dermot Ro.
M'Deermote sgarragh, Hugh and Owen, pardon, 1446.
M'Degone, Cormuck and Neyl, pardon, 6483.
M'Deirmod. *See* M'Dermot.
M'Deirmoda gall, Cahill, 5807. *See* M'Dermot gale.
M'Deirmodie—Deirmody. *See* M'Dermody.
M'Deirmot—Deirmott. *See* M'Dermott.
M'Demige, Donogh, pardon, 4665.
M'Denis—Denise, persons of the name pardoned, 4826, 4752, 5677.
M'Derby, Donogh, pardon, 4728.
,, Wm., pardon, 2542.
M'Dermed, Donogh, pardon, 6213.
M'Dermedy. *See* M'Dermody.
M'Dermide, Teig, pardon, 11.
M'Dermille's (M'Dermott's) country, 4466.
M'Dermod — Dermoda — Dermodi — Dermode. *See* M'Dermot.
M'Dermod galdow. *See* M'Dermot gale.
M'Dermod reogh, Owen, harper, pardon, 6782.
M'Dermodille, Mulmorry, pardon, 5494.
M'Dermodily, Donogh, pardon, 6407.
M'Dermode. *See* M'Dermot.
M'Dermodo, Ouin, pardon, 4210.
M'Dermody—Dermodie—Detrmodie—Deirmody—Dermody—Diermody—Diermodi — Diermodie — Diermody:
,, Fynen m'Owen, pardon, 4473, 4897.
,, others of the name pardoned (in cos. Cork, Lim. and Kerry), 2545, 2747, 2869, 2901, 2970, 3078, 3070, 3460, 4237, 4586, 4710, 4742, 4760, 4781, 4814, 4966, 5004, 5460, 5622, 6270, 5408, 6473, 6486, 6187, 6407, 6404, 6511, 6514-8, 6626, 6660, 6676, 6731, 6732, 6744; in co. Rosc., 1259, 4978, 6147, 6472, (see M'Dermot); elsewhere, 2090, 2140, 4037, 4064, 4976, 5407, 6506, 6424, 6502, 6677, 6624.
M'Dermod Y'Aeshiesh, Donogh, pardon, 6479.
M'Dermody roe. *See* M'Dermot ro.
M'Dermond, persons of the name pardoned, 4601, 5623, 5612, 6454, 5434, 6530, 6165.
M'Dermonde, Connor, pardon, 6410.
M'Dermonde roe, Tounltagh, pardon, 6420.
M'Dermot—Dermod—Dermoda—Dermote—Dermott — Dermond — Diermod — Diermoda — Diermot — Diermott — Dermody — Diermody;
Brian m'Rory (of the Carrick), appointed seneschal of Moylurg, 1617; comm., 3667; lease, 3970; pardon, 5168, 6626.
Brian m'Mulrony, pardon, 5447.
Cahill m'Tirrelagh (of Oughterhavey), pardon, 3702; attainted, 6913.
Cahill duff m'Brian (of Carrig m'Dermot), pardon, 4728.
Conchor (of Aghaghauen), pardon, 4762.
Conor og (of Aghaghane), pardon, 5409.
Conor og m'Teig (of Inchonsseragh), pardon, 4728.
Diermod, pardon, 1869.
Donogh (co. Kerry), attainted, 5036.
Edm. m'Toumltagh, pardon, 6126.
Hugh m'Teig (of Cambo), pardon, 4726.

INDEX TO FIANTS.—ELIZABETH.

M'Dermot, Hugh oge (of Killevny, co. Gal.), pardon, [illegible].
" Melaghlin m'Cormock, attainted, [illegible].
" Mahony m'Brian, pardon, [illegible], 5447.
" Mulrony m'Hugh, pardon, [illegible].
" Mulrony m'Tirrelagh, pardon, [illegible].
" Rory m'Brian, pardon, [illegible].
" Rory kiegh, pardon, [illegible].
" Teig (in co. Kerry), attainted, [illegible].
" Tomultagh, pardon, 3744, [illegible], 5447.
" Tomultagh oge (of Croghan), pardon, [illegible], 5112, 5447.

M'Dermot—Dermod—Deirmod—Deirmot—Dermoda — Dermodd — Dermodde—Dermode — Dermote —Dermott — Diermod—Diermode—Diermond—Diermoda—Diermot—Diermott, persons of the name pardoned (in co. Ross. and neighbourhood), [illegible]; elsewhere, 11, [illegible], 1874, [illegible], 4610, [illegible], 4711, [illegible], 6161-8, [illegible], 6764-6, [illegible], 6777.

M'Dermot's country — M'Dermotte — Dermoyd—Dermoyde — Dermoyt—Dermyt—Dermyti—Dermitte's country or Moylurg (in bar. of Boyle, co. Ross.), [illegible], 1794, [illegible]. See Moylurge.

M'Dermot carragh — Dermote acarragh, Donogh, pardon, [illegible], 1644, [illegible].
" Owen, pardon, [illegible].

M'Dermot gale — Dermod galdow — Deirmoda gall—Diermott galta, persons of the name pardoned, [illegible].

M'Dermot grany—Diermot grane:
" Cahall duff, pardon, [illegible].
" Teig keogh, pardon, [illegible].
" Teig reagh, pardon, [illegible].

M'Dermot oge, Edm. m'Melaghlin, pardon, [illegible].

M'Dermot owre, Cahir m'Brien, pardon, 4015, [illegible].
" Hugh, pardon, [illegible].

M'Dermot reogh, Conchor oge and Rory (of Cortiove, co. Ross.), pardon, [illegible].

M'Dermot Ro—Dermot roe—Dermot roy—Dearmondo roe—Deirmod roe —Deirmott roe—Dermod roe—Dermody roe—Dermode rowe —Dermondo roe—Dermott roe —Diermod roe—Diermot roye —Diermott roe:
" Brian m'Dowaltagh, pardon, [illegible].
" Dowaltagh, pardon, [illegible], 5447, [illegible].
" Edm. m'Tomaltagh, pardon, [illegible].
" Ferall, pardon, [illegible].
" Ferdorohow m'Hugh, pardon, [illegible].
" Kedo, pardon, [illegible].
" Magnus m'Edm., pardon, [illegible], 5447.
" Murtagh m'Conor og, pardon, 5447.
" Owen m'Dowaltagh, pardon, [illegible].
" others of the name pardoned, [illegible], 5447, [illegible].

M'Dermot ruddo, Baill, pardon, 5447.

M'Dermoud. See M'Dermot.

M'Dermoyd — Dermoyde — Dermoyt's country. See M'Dermot's country.

M'Dermydy, Wm., pardon, [illegible].

M'Dermyte—Dermyt's country. See M'Dermot's country.

M'Dey, Farryll, pardon, [illegible].

M'Dicll, Donogh grana, pardon, [illegible].

M'Diermod—Diermode. See M'Dermot.

M'Diermody. See M'Dermody.

M'Diermond, Cormuck, lands of (in co. Cork), [illegible].

M'Diarmod—Diermoda. See M'Dermot.

INDEX TO FIANTS—ELIZABETH.

M'Diermod baddy, John, pardon, [illegible].
M'Diermod boy, Conoghor, pardon, [illegible].
M'Diermod roe. See M'Dermot Ro.
M'Diermodi—Diermodie — Diermody. See M'Dermody.
M'Diermot—Diermott. See M'Dermot.
M'Diermot roye—Diermott roe. See M'Dermot Ro.
M'Diermott galte. See M'Dermot gale.
M'Dillon, John, pardon, [illegible].
M'Doaltagh, Fardorogh, pardon, [illegible].
M'Dobhmill, Mulloroe and Thady, pardon, [illegible].
M'Doell, persons of the name pardoned, [illegible], [illegible], [illegible], [illegible], [illegible].
M'Dolle, Cormock, pardon, 6178.
M'Doll, persons of the name pardoned, [illegible], [illegible].
M'Dole, Mare, pardon, [illegible].
M'Donagn, Neile, pardon, [illegible].
M'Donagh—Donagho:
„ Brian (of Castlebrack, Queen's co.), pardon, [illegible].
„ or Baye, John, physician, [illegible].
„ persons of the name in co. Sligo or Ross. See M'Donogh.
„ others of the name, pardoned, [illegible], [illegible], 1161, 1177, 1414, [illegible], [illegible], [illegible], [illegible], [illegible], [illegible], [illegible], [illegible], [illegible], [illegible], [illegible], [illegible], [illegible], [illegible], [illegible], [illegible], [illegible], [illegible], [illegible].
M'Donagh Roarbe, Owin (in co. Kerry), attainted, [illegible].
M'Donagh evallo, Donald owre (of Ballintereeny, co. Wex.), pardon, 1092, [illegible].
M'Donagh Sheron's country. See M'Donogh.
M'Donagho, Edm. and John, pardon, [illegible].
M'Donall, Donoho Oaghe, pardon, [illegible].
M'Donalde, Rowe boy, pardon, [illegible].
M'Donall, Wm., pardon, [illegible].
M'Donawie, Patrick, pardon, [illegible].
M'Doncha, Gilleduf and Hugh, pardon, [illegible].
M'Donchoe—Donchey. See M'Donogh.
M'Donche, Brian, pardon, [illegible].
M'Donchie, Philip, pardon, [illegible].
„ persons of the name in co. Sligo, see M'Donogh.
M'Doncho, Uhney, pardon, [illegible].
M'Donchye, Brian, pardon, [illegible].
M'Donovan, Wm., pardon, [illegible].
M'Done, Dermot, pardon, [illegible].
„ Mokmore, pardon, [illegible].
„ Thady, pardon, [illegible].
M'Donegh, or M'Garveyrie, Conoghor and Shane (in co. Cork), pardon, [illegible].
„ others of the name pardoned, [illegible], [illegible].
M'Doneghe, Teig and Wm., pardon, [illegible].
M'Doneghy, persons of the name pardoned, [illegible], [illegible], [illegible].
M'Doneghy bane, Teig (of Dunmoylin, co. Lim.), pardon, [illegible].
M'Donel—M'Donell. See M'Donnell.
M'Donell duf, Donogh m'Edm., pardon, [illegible].
M'Donell oge, Donogh m'Dermot, pardon, [illegible].
M'Donell reagh, Oberr, pardon, [illegible].
M'Donell roe, Tirlagh, pardon, [illegible].
M'Donellane, Owen, pardon, [illegible].
M'Donevan, Donell, pardon, [illegible].
M'Doney, Donogh and Owley, pardon, [illegible].
M'Dongh, Dermot, pardon, [illegible].
MacDongh, Hugh, pardon, [illegible].
M'Dongh oig, Mohroney, pardon, [illegible].
M'Donghe, Edm., pardon, [illegible].
„ Mahon, pardon, [illegible].
M'Donghie, Tho. (co. Sligo), [illegible]. See M'Donogh.
M'Donghe, persons of the name pardoned, [illegible].
M'Donhie, Connor (co. Sligo), [illegible]. See M'Donogh.
M'Donigh, Donill, pardon, [illegible].
M'Donil—Donill. See M'Donnell.
M'Donill owre, Art or Arthur, pardon, [illegible], [illegible].
M'Donill roe, Dermot, pardon, [illegible].
M'Donill roe, Reyry, pardon, [illegible].
M'Donilleny, Shane, pardon, [illegible].
M'Donistre, Teig, pardon, [illegible].
M'Donleve, Gilpatrick, pardon, [illegible].
M'Donnagh—Donnaghe:
„ Thady, surgeon, grant of land, 491.
„ persons of the name in co. Sligo. See M'Donogh.
„ others of the name, pardoned, [illegible], [illegible], [illegible], [illegible], [illegible].
M'Donneghy, Owen, pardon, [illegible].
M'Donnell—Donell—Donill—Donel—Donil—Donnel — Donnill — Donnyll—Donyl—DonylI:
„ Alexander, pardon, [illegible].
„ Alexander. See M'Randal boye.
„ Alexander m'Hugh boy, pardon, [illegible], [illegible], [illegible].
„ Alexander oge m'Alester chaery, pardon, [illegible].
„ Alexander, pardon, [illegible], [illegible], [illegible], [illegible], [illegible].
„ Allister oge, pardon, [illegible].
„ Allye, pardon, [illegible], [illegible].
„ Anne m'Conoghor, pardon, [illegible].
„ Anny or Amiliia, pardon, [illegible].
„ Archibald, pardon, [illegible].
„ Art m'Manus, grant of land, [illegible],

INDEX TO FIANTS—ELIZABETH.

M'Donnell, Art boy, pardon, [illegible]; grant of land, [illegible].
" Art, pardon, [illegible], 6417 (?), [illegible].
" Auliffe, pardon, [illegible], [illegible], [illegible].
" Awlim, pardon, [illegible].
" Awlee Ferganoquyrry, pardon, 4414 (?).
" Awly, pardon, [illegible].
" Barnard, pardon, [illegible].
" Brasnell, pardon, [illegible].
" Brelan, grant of land, [illegible].
" Brian—Brene—Bryne, pardon, [illegible], [illegible], 1676 (?), [illegible], [illegible], [illegible], [illegible], [illegible], [illegible], [illegible], [illegible], [illegible], [illegible], [illegible], [illegible], [illegible], [illegible].
" Cahill—Kahell, pardon, [illegible], [illegible], [illegible].
" Cahir—Cahier—Cahiro—Kahier—Kayer, pardon, 1746 (?), [illegible], [illegible], [illegible], [illegible], [illegible], [illegible], [illegible], [illegible], [illegible], [illegible], [illegible], [illegible], [illegible].
" Callaghan, pardon, [illegible].
" Callogh or Charles m'Tirlagh. See M'Tirrelagh.
" Calloogh or Calvacius m'Tirlagh (of Slievemargy), surrender, [illegible]; indenture, [illegible].
" Callough m'Tirlagh m'Alexander (of Ballyboy), pardon, [illegible], [illegible], [illegible].
" Callough—Kallwagh, pardon, 1390 (?), [illegible], [illegible], [illegible], [illegible], [illegible], [illegible].
" Carroll, pardon, [illegible].
" Chaler, pardon, [illegible].
" Chriffin, pardon, [illegible].
" Cohegery, pardon, [illegible].
" Coll, pardon, [illegible].
" Colle—Colle—Collo—Colly—Cheoles, pardon, [illegible], [illegible], [illegible], [illegible], [illegible], [illegible], [illegible].
" Con, pardon, [illegible], [illegible].
" Conell—Connill, pardon, [illegible], [illegible], [illegible].
" Conor—Conchor m'Gerald, pardon, 1084 (?), 1845 (?), [illegible], [illegible].
" Conyr—Conoghor, pardon, [illegible], [illegible], [illegible], [illegible], [illegible], [illegible], [illegible], [illegible], [illegible], [illegible], [illegible], [illegible], [illegible], [illegible].
" Coochonaght, pardon, [illegible].
" Conquigorey—Cowrogry, pardon, [illegible], [illegible].
" Cormack m'Art, grant of land, [illegible].
" Cormock—Cormac, pardon, [illegible], [illegible], [illegible], [illegible], [illegible], [illegible].
" Cornelius, pardon, [illegible], [illegible].
" Costragh, pardon, [illegible].
M'Donnell, Cowmara, pardon, [illegible].
" Cryan, pardon, [illegible].
" Dallaugh—Dalvagh, pardon, [illegible], [illegible].
" Dallon, pardon, [illegible].
" Daniel, pardon, [illegible], [illegible].
" David, pardon, [illegible].
" Dorby, pardon, [illegible], [illegible].
" Durmod—Dermot—Dairmod—Dermond—Dormyd, pardon, [illegible], 416 (?), [illegible].
" Don, pardon, [illegible].
" Donald—Donnald, pardon, [illegible], [illegible], [illegible], [illegible], [illegible], [illegible], [illegible].
" Donoghy oy barrnye, pardon, [illegible].
" Donell m'Tortagh (of Craig m'Togo, co. Lim.), attainted, [illegible].
" Donell—Donall—Doniel—Donill—Donyll, pardon, [illegible].
" Donogh, son of Donald M'Cormack, pardon, [illegible].
" Donogh M'Balka, pardon, [illegible].
" Donogh m'Shane, grant of land, [illegible].
" Donogh m'Thomas, land of, [illegible].
" Donogh—Donagh—Donnogh, pardon, [illegible].
" Donoghe, pardon, [illegible], [illegible], [illegible].
" Doroghe, pardon, [illegible].
" Dowell, pardon, [illegible], [illegible].
" Dowill or Dowicus m'Edmond ballagh, pardon, [illegible], [illegible].
" Durry oy vic donnell, pardon, [illegible].
" Dwaltagh m'Gollyaspig, pardon, [illegible].
" Edm. kytiagh, son of Donell m'Edm., attainted, [illegible].

INDEX TO FIANTS—ELIZABETH.

M'Donnell, Edm. m'Mulmorie (of Moone), pardon, 6864.
Edmund, pardon, 148, 831, 1026-a, 1176, 1344, 1582, 1989, 2002, 2253, 4456, 4030, 4164, 4308, 4512, 4671, 5030, 5454, 5574, 5062, 5814, 5688, 5745, 4181, 6223, 6467, 6517, 6647, 6727, 6754.
Ellice m'Donell, pardon, 4878.
Eneas—Eneah—Enis—Enos—Ennys—Enyne, pardon, 4592, 5056, 5574, 5647, 5740, 5790.
Enestlis, pardon, 6518.
Falle—Fellighe—Phalle, pardon, 14, 142, 881.
Faragh m'Ferlagh (of Newcastle, Queen's co.), livery, 5526; fathers of heirs to, 6503.
Farriegh m'Torlagh roe (in co. Mayo), pardon, 4075, 5032, 5799.
Ferragh—Fariagh, pardon, 4146, 4731, 5607, 5740.
Feollino, pardon, 4879.
Fordorogh—Fardoragh—Feardoragh, pardon, 4015, 4086, 4567, 4731, 5436, 5662.
Fergananym—Farganamom, pardon, 4446, 4731, 5368, 4624, 5815.
Fergus, pardon, 5465.
Feylum, pardon, 4474.
Fynine—Fynan, pardon, 2879, 4624, 5566, 5511, 5515, 5831, 6878.
Fynine M'Cartie, pardon, 4485.
" M'Fyne, pardon, 4589.
Fynwall or Nyn duff, wife of O'Donell, pardon, 4614.
Gerald, pardon, 4617.
Gillasbuicke, pardon, 5065.
Gilleduff—Guylly'duffe, pardon, 1341, 6518.
Gillegrome, grant of land, 5548.
Gillepatrick, pardon, 586, 2136.
Gillernew, pardon, 4867.
Gillereow, pardon, 5628.
Godfrey, surrender, 4758; indenture, 4744.
Goghrow—Gorye m'Tirelagh oge, pardon, 3441, 4747.
Gorry—Gorre, pardon, 3585, 5796.
Gullycaddy (of Aghadoe), pardon, 5079.
Guyly ny Flan—Gwllyane-fane—Gallinywlan, pardon, 1820, 4658, 6811.
Henry, pardon, 4658.
M'Donnell, Hugh m'Gerald (of Kilcommon, co. Wick.), pardon, 1082, 1145, 2002.
Hugh boy m'Callough, pardon, 1037; surrender, 4748; indenture, 4768. See M'Callogh.
Hugh boy m'Taig (of Iar Connaught), pardon, 4058, 4707, 4739.
Hugh duff (of Knocknell, co. Wick.), pardon, 471, 1616, 1818, 2909, 4161; his wife, 4161.
Hugh Mansen, pardon, 4566.
Hugh, pardon, 2363, 4727, 4814, 4876, 5442, 5456, 5216, 5511, 6550.
Henden, pardon, 2856.
Ive, pardon, 4168.
James, pardon, 1085, 3156, 4806, 5848, 6817, 6341.
Jasferie, pardon, 6798.
John, pardon, 1178, 2360, 4684, 4694, 4743, 5405, 5484, 6461, 5463, 5575, 5996, 5511, 6578, 6770.
Kathleline, pardon, 6744.
Keadagh, pardon, 5614.
Kyen, pardon, 4874.
Loghlin, pardon, 3914, 4883, 5602.
Lodovick, pardon, 6632.
Lauder—Lovder, pardon, 5455, 5606.
Lynhugh, pardon, 1106.
Maoiagh, pardon, 4366, 4475.
Mahon—Mahowne, pardon, 1141, 4782, 5068, 5457, 5495, 6606.
Marcus, pardon, 4498, 5075, 5706; Marks m'Mawre vacle (M'Donnell?), 4876.
Margaret, pardon, 6784.
Maurice—Morrice—Moris—Morysh, pardon, 2064, 4431, 4620, 5463, 6617.
Melaghlin—Melaghlin—Mellaghlyn—Myllaghlen, pardon, 1696, 1882, 2348, 4050, 4834, 4545, 5474, 5602, 6106, 4467, 6817, 6580, 6700.
Molrony, pardon, 5615.
Moriertagh, pardon, 5465, 6613.
Mors, pardon, 5670.
Moriertagh—Morrotagh—Morriartagh, pardon, 3168, 3568, 3904, 4164, 5095, 6140, 4406, 5317, 4589.
Morogh—Morrogh—Murrogh, pardon, 2328, 3162, 4102, 4580, 4869, 5461, 6484, 5529, 5714.
Moroghe, pardon, 3975.

INDEX TO FIANTS.—ELIZABETH.

M'Donnell, Malmory — Moylmory — Molomorro — Molmory, pardon, 4071, 6428, 6474, 6406, 6161, 6628.
„ Murtagh — Mortagh, pardon, 4828, 6428, 6484, 6501, 6417, 6641, 6677.
„ Murtagh leagh — Mortagh lya — Mortaugh lea, pardon, 1428, 1845, 2644, 6528.
„ Neale, pardon, 6616, 6614, 6628, 6621.
„ Neave — Nice — Nyce, pardon, 6644, 6621.
„ Nich., pardon, 6787.
„ Obearen, pardon, 6628.
„ Owin m'Alester (or Alexander), pardon, 6628; grant of land, 6646.
„ Owin Nupoota, pardon, 6611.
„ Owen—One, pardon, 2287, 4016, 4781, 5463, 5471, 5482, 5614, 5627, 5718, 5948, 6166, 6168, 6468, 6494, 6517, 6545, 6576, 6628, 6764.
„ Owny, pardon, 2828.
„ Owstian m'Ranyl, pardon, 5814.
„ Patrick, son of M'Donnell of Clankelly, co. Ferm., pardon, 5718; chief of his name, 6687.
„ Patr. m'Hugh, grant of land, 6641.
„ Patr. m'Manus, grant of land, 6641.
„ Patr. m'Shane, grant of land, 6641.
„ Patrick, pardon, 6602, 6328, 6453, 6654, 6694.
„ Peter, pardon, 449, 661.
„ Phelim, pardon, 4768, 4781, 5463, 5614, 5780, 6168, 6528, 6649, 6687.
„ Philip, pardon, 4058, 4812, 4694, 6485, 6477.
„ Portaine, pardon, 6683.
„ R[ ], pardon, 6771.
„ Randall—Rannyll, pardon, 5814, 6148, 6628.
„ Redmond, grant of land, 6645.
„ Richard, pardon, 4836, 6168, 6787.
„ Riurdan, pardon, 6457.
„ Robert, pardon, 6787.
„ Rory — Rorie — Rori — Rury, pardon, 2288, 5478, 5487, 5607, 6728, 4747, 4821, 4860, 5478, 5486, 6628, 6461, 6515, 6868.

M'Donnell, Shane, pardon, 396, 1695, 1848, 2686, 2866, 2667, 4025, 4386, 4422, 4537, 4836, 5063, 4828, 6407, 6511, 6518, 6612, 6582, 6548, 6681, 6571, 6627, 6623, 6647.
„ Teige m'Dermod (of Crookevilly), pardon, 6497.
„ Teige m'Dermodie (of Tooghl Carbrig), pardon, 6406.
„ Teige ne Cashy, pardon, 6504, 6408.
„ Teige ne Skell, pardon, 6467.
„ Teige reriagh, pardon, 6614.
„ Teige — Teig — Tady, pardon, 918, 2278, 2626, 2974, 3867, 4271, 4612, 4698, 4748, 4780, 4824, 5447, 5460, 6647, 6174, 6187, 6460, 6611, 6618, 6617, 6534, 6540, 6561, 6566, 6556, 6549, 6571, 6626, 6627, 6647, 6616, 6766, 6784, 6786, 4778.
„ Terence, grant of land, 488, 4743–4.
„ Terence og, pardon, 1297.
„ Thady, pardon, 186, 236, 1170, 1346, 2626, 3063, 3376, 6314.
„ Thorlagh ro m'Minous, pardon, 5793.
„ Thomas, pardon, 6176, 6467, 6428, 6671.
„ Tirlagh (of Ballaghmoon), pardon, 690.
„ Tirlagh (of Craigmastrig), his son attainted, 4498.
„ Tirlagh m'Alexander (of Ballyboy). See M'Alexander.
„ Tirlagh oge (of Ballaboy), captain of the gallowglas, pardon, 3441, 4747; security for his son, 4477.
„ Tirlagh moyngagh m'Edm. ballagh. See M'Edmond ballagh.
„ Tirlagh—Tirrelagh—Tyrlagh, pardon, 358, 4476, 4728, 5401, 5462, 6190, 6440, 6451, 6497, 6592, 6617, 6538, 6647, 6688.
„ Tirrelagh oge, pardon, 5590.
„ Toole, grant of land, 6646.
„ Towhill—Towall, pardon, 1688, 6489.
„ Turlough (of Newcastle, Queen's co.), livery to heir, 3638.
„ Uny, pardon, 6498.
„ Ustion — Uston, pardon, 4321, 5078, 5874.
„ Walter m'Edm. ballagh — m'Edm. welly, pardon, 5962, 5477.

INDEX TO FIANTS.—ELIZABETH.

M'Donnell, Walter m'Edmond, pardon, 6409 ; pension, [illegible].
" Walter, pardon, 5734, 5476, 5740, [illegible].
" Wm. O'Gowne, pardon, [illegible].
" Wm. or Donoghy ny Vody, pardon, [illegible].
" William, pardon, [illegible], 1103, 1178, 1470, [illegible], 3567, [illegible], 4121, 4127, 4280, [illegible], 5468, 6465, 6478, 6494, 6457, 6511, 6517, [illegible].
" ( ), pardon, [illegible].
" [ ] no Caple, pardon, 6414.
" of Clankelly, chief of his name, 6710.
" See M'Gownyll, M'Connell.
M'Donnells. See Clandonill, Clandonylles.
M'Donnochie—Donnochy—Donnoghie, persons of the name pardoned (co. Kerry), 4718.
M'Donnogh. See M'Donogh.
M'Donnoghare Imane, Farrall, pardon, [illegible].
M'Donnogho. See M'Donogh.
M'Donnoghie. See M'Donnochie.
M'Donnogho—M'Donnoghoe. See M'Donogho
M'Donnough. See M'Donogh.
M'Donnougho. See M'Donogho.
M'Donoho. See M'Donogho.
M'Donochy, Darby and Tho. (co. Cork), pardon, [illegible].
M'Donogh—Donnogh—Donogh—Donchae—Donnchay—Donchie—Donhie—Donnagh — Donnogho —Donnough—Donogho—Donough.
" Cahall oge (of co. Sligo), pardon, [illegible], 4727, 6484.
" Carbry, pardon, [illegible], 4787, [illegible].
" Conor m'Molaghlin, pardon, [illegible].
" Cormack (of Tirerrell), chief of his nation, [illegible].
" Ferdorogh (of Cowlen), pardon, [illegible] ; attainted, [illegible].
" Gillenbreeze (of Roscrib), died without heirs, 6610.
" Hugh (of Corran), chief of his nation, [illegible].
" Molaughlen (of Cowronye), pardon, [illegible].
" Mortertagh keagh, pardon, [illegible].
" Morish, pardon, [illegible], [illegible].
" Mulrony, pardon, [illegible], [illegible].
" Rory (son of Hugh), pardon, [illegible], 4787.
" Shane glasse, pardon, [illegible], 4787, 5424.
" others of the name, in cos. Sligo and Roscommon, pardoned, [illegible], [illegible], 4179, 4267, [illegible], [illegible],
M'Donogh :
4578, 4678, [illegible], 4708, 4777, [illegible], [illegible], [illegible], [illegible], [illegible], [illegible], [illegible], [illegible], [illegible], [illegible], [illegible], [illegible], [illegible], [illegible], [illegible], [illegible], [illegible], [illegible].
" Dermot m'Owen (of Kanturk), livery, [illegible] ; pardon, [illegible].
" Dermod. See M'Donoghowe.
" Owen m'Donogh (of Kanturk), pardon, [illegible], [illegible] ; livery to heir, [illegible].
" others of the name in co. Cork, pardoned, [illegible], [illegible], [illegible], [illegible], [illegible], [illegible], [illegible], 6170, 6173, [illegible], [illegible], [illegible], [illegible], [illegible], [illegible], [illegible], [illegible], [illegible], [illegible], [illegible], [illegible].
" Brian (of Ballinloughey, co. Car.), pardon, [illegible].
" Brian (of Lickeforan, co. Kerry), pardon, [illegible].
" Brian m'Donnell (of Templeal-egan), pardon, [illegible].
" Conoghor m'Brien (of Lirgach, co. Clare), pardon, [illegible].
" Dermod Mangarlye (co. Kerry), pardon, [illegible].
" Donald riogh m'Conway — m'Gowmaye, pardon, 1040, 1041.
" Donogh m'Teig (of Lisdonragan, co. Kerry), pardon, 6484.
" Gerrat (of Rathkeale, co. Lim.), his lands granted, [illegible].
" Hugh, grant of land, [illegible].
" Owen carragh m'Gillyduff, pardon, [illegible], [illegible], [illegible].
" others of the name (elsewhere than in cos. Cork, Sligo, or Rosc.), pardoned, [illegible], [illegible], [illegible], [illegible], [illegible], [illegible], 728, [illegible], [illegible], 1037, [illegible], [illegible], 1161, [illegible], [illegible], [illegible], 1641, 1745, 1787, 1771, 1810, [illegible], [illegible], [illegible], 2146, [illegible], [illegible], [illegible], [illegible], [illegible], [illegible], [illegible], [illegible], [illegible], [illegible], [illegible], 2617, [illegible], 4707, 4711, [illegible], [illegible], [illegible], [illegible], [illegible], 4871, [illegible], [illegible], [illegible], [illegible], [illegible], [illegible], [illegible], [illegible], [illegible], [illegible], 5474, [illegible],

INDEX TO FIANTS.—ELIZABETH.

M'Donogh:

[illegible], 6678, 6477, 6178, [illegible], 6464, [illegible], 6601, 6526, 6517, [illegible], 6638, 6641, 6646-51, 6652, 6655, [illegible], [illegible], 6669, 6674-7, 6612, 6628, 6647, 6680, 6684, 6706, 6737, 6752, 6785.

M'Donogh's country, co. Sligo, 1724.

M'Donogh Corren—M'Donogh Khoron—M'Donnough Khoner's country (the barony of Corran, co. Sligo), 1445, 3105, 4467.

M'Donogh's country (barony of Duhallow), co. Cork, 2235.

M'Donogh kittagh, Donogh oge, pardon, 1151.

" Feedorogh, pardon, 1152.

M'Donogh more, Donell (M'Mahon ?), grant of land, 5638.

M'Donogh oge, Art, pardon, 4494.

Donell dorogh (Cavanagh ?), pardon, 3016, 4036, 4517.

Hugh ballagh, pardon, 3150, 4640, 3377; (of Ballidonnan in Kinshelagh), pardon to him and followers, 4461.

Shane glas (of Kinshelagh), pardon, 875.

M'Donogh roagh, Owin, pardon, 5248.

M'Donogh roe, Tho., pardon, 5516.

M'Donogh romo, James (in Kinshelagh), indenture, 3760; pardon, 3733.

Mark, pardon, 4463.

M'Donogh roy, Owen, pardon, 2351.

M'Donoghan, Morice, pardon, 4454.

" Tho., grant of land, 3731.

M'Donoghean.cahill, Brien, pardon, [illegible].

M'Donoghon, Shane, pardon, 5457.

M'Donoghey, persons of the name pardoned, 5560.

M'Donoghie, Morish, pardon, 4401.

M'Donogho—Donoche—Donnoghe—Donnoghoe—Donnaugho—Donoghoe—Donoughe:

John Walshe (of Kilmoleigh, co. Cork), pardon, 6058.

others of the name pardoned, in co. Cork, 1628, 3032, 3616, 3036, 3076, 3565, 3636, 3327, 4367, 4688, 5001, 4576, 4751, 4763, 4834, 5460, 5511, 5596, 5588; in co. Kerry, 3150, 4876, 4964-5, 5460, 4878; in co. Sligo, 4464, 4470; elsewhere, 10, 2778, 3346, 3537, 4543, 4648, 4655, 4667, 4709, 4724, 4740, 4742, 5056, 5040, 5476, 5365, 5466, 5387, 5373, 5536, 5582.

M'Donoghe mahone, Shane, pardon, 3704.

M'Donoghie caragh, Edm. and Hubert, pardon, 5309.

M'Donoghoe roe, Morice, pardon, 4456.

M'Donohoe, Owen, pardon, 4870.

M'Donoghor, Fintan, pardon, 5496.

M'Donoghow, Rory, pardon, 4811.

M'Donoughowe, Dermot m'Donogh O Cary, lord of Duhallow, co. Cork, pardon, 344. See M'Cary. See also M'Donogh.

M'Donoghy, persons of the name pardoned, 2347, 5645, 4617.

M'Donouch. See M'Donoch.

M'Donoughe. See M'Donoughe.

M'Donoughoe, Dermot, pardon, 4456.

M'Dony, Cahill, pardon, 3960.

M'Donyll. See M'Donnell.

M'Donyll moile, Wm. (of Kinsalagh), indenture, 4740-43.

" Gilpatrick, indenture, 4740.

M'Donyn—Dohyne, Fynine, pardon, 5557, 5571.

M'Doole, Donell, pardon, 3818.

M'Dorbyfyn, William, pardon, 3143.

M'Dorogho, John, pardon, 5240.

M'Dorogh, Brian, pardon, 5403.

M'Dowall, persons of the name pardoned, 5442.

M'Dowlagh, Owen, pardon, 3075.

M'Downey, Kenelagh, pardon, 5526.

M'Dowdall, Rich., slain in rebellion, 5508.

M'Dowde, Rory, pardon, 5555.

M'Dowe, Donell, pardon, 5464.

M'Dowell—Dowll—Dowle—Dowyle—Dowll—Dowyle:

Alexander, pardon, 4471, 4467, 5438, 5438, 5465, 5747, 6108.

Allyne, pardon, 3765, 5633.

Colloch m'Allen, pardon, 5276, 5520, 5502.

Gilbert, pardon, 3784, 5423, 5661, 5396.

Owen, pardon, 3751, 4508, 4412, 5466, 5651.

(of Killscanlan, co. Louth), attainted, 5772.

Tirlagh or Terence, pardon, 5787, 5452, 5484.

Wm. oghragh, pardon, 5445, 6106.

others of the name, pardoned, 1356, 3716, 3714, 3755, 3374, 4577, 4644, 5001, 5421, 5439, 5448, 5487, 5408, 5470, 5486, 5500, 5603, 5663, 5406, 5365, 6061.

M'Dowley, Moughe, pardon, 3064.

M'Dowlin—Dowling—Dowlinge:

" Art m'Brian (Cavanagh ?), pardon, 5641.

" others of the name pardoned, 3058, 4025, 4712, 4645, 4461, 5405, 5232, 5163, 5328, 5437, 5461, 5565.

M'Dowlagh, Teig, pardon, 4524.

M'Downdey, Tho., pardon, 5736.

M'Dowell, James, pardon, 3160.
M'Downey—Downie—Downy, persons of the name pardoned, 4583, 4654, 4828, 5008, 5422, 5448, 5478, 5477, 5528.
M'Dowyle. See M'Dowell.
M'Dowyll (of Ballymcdowell, co. Kerry), pardon, 3461.
M'Doyen, persons of the name pardoned, 1914.
M'Doyll. See M'Dowell.
M'Doyn, Mologhlin, pardon, 6617.
M'Doyne, Wm., pardon, 5458.
M'Doynlowe, James, pardon, 3859.
M'Drig, Mologhlen, pardon, 2144.
M'Drolld, Teig, pardon, 4270.
M'Dualtagh, Ferdorogh, pardon, 6515.
M'Duaney, Teig, pardon, 5704.
M'Duffe, Molmory, pardon, 6153.
M'Duffer, Moroghe, pardon, 1436.
M'Duffie, persons of the name pardoned, 6082.
M'Duffy, persons of the name pardoned, 5734.
M'Duffye, Edm., pardon, 2963.
M'Dulltage, Edm., pardon, 5603.
M'Dun, Edm., pardon, 5308.
M'Dunrill, Donell, pardon, 6906.
M'Duyne, Gillechuff, pardon, 6651.
M'Dwaltagh, Richard and Ullick, pardon, 6515.
M'Dwdarn, Rogan and Moyles, pardon, 4806.
M'Dwile, Owen oge, pardon, 6611.
M'Dwill, Felim, pardon, 4306.
M'Dwyle. See M'Dowell.
M'Dyer, persons of the name pardoned, 5811.
M'Dyermod, Bryen, pardon, 4282.
" Donald, pardon, 1694.
M'Dyermod roe, Dwaltagh, pardon, 5804. See M'Dermot.
M'Dyerye, Donill, pardon, 6238.
M'Dyrmots, Wm., pardon, 6931.
M'Ea, persons of the name pardoned, 5003, 5182, 4494, 4621, 5923, 5624, 6170, 6497, 6420, 6615, 6529, 6575, 6564, 6576, 6828–4.
M'Ea ne brulla, Owen, pardon, 6497.
M'Eabuoy, Donogh, pardon, 6566.
M'Eae, Teig, pardon, 6464.
M'Eagan, Patrick, mule [illegible] of Corrobeg in co. Long., 4628.
M'Eagan—Eagines—Eagane, persons of the name pardoned, 4276, 5411, 6489, 6400, 6518, 6490, 6688, 6791. See M'Egan.
M'Eally, Hugh, pardon, 5888.
M'Eamon garne, Hugh and Tomelyn, pardon, 6489.
M'Eamalla, Richard, pardon, 6610.
M'Eamolis, Teig, pardon, 6640.
M'East, Kenedy, pardon, 4731.
M'Eavan, Morogh, pardon, 4894.
M'Eavare, Hugh, pardon, 5164.
M'Eballagh, Gerald, pardon, 6432.
M'Eboy—Eboye:
" Donald (of Ballyfin, Queen's co.), livery, 5806.
" Morogh, his heir, 5806.
" others of the name pardoned, 168, 4858, 4831, 5307, 5601, 6773.
M'Ebrehowne, Hugh, pardon, 6148.
M'Ebwy, Thady, pardon, 6152.
M'Ecalloghe, Owen, pardon, 3830.
M'Ecallough, persons of the name pardoned, 4304.
M'Ecallowy, Rory, pardon, 3354.
M'eChre, Shough, in O'Madden's country, 4718.
M'EChollaghane, Rory, pardon, 4818.
M'Echaffe, Hugh, pardon, 6462.
M'Echalway, Rory, pardon, 4682.
M'Echols, Dermod, pardon, 6377.
M'Echoran, Donill, pardon, 6692.
M'Echorane, Tirlagh, pardon, 6681.
M'Echry—Echie—Echy—Echye:
" Edm. m'Connagh (of Ennishone, co. Cav.), pardon, 4946, 4908.
" Tirlagh m'Brene (of Cabragh), pardon, 6038, 6568.
" others of the name pardoned, 3427, 4286, 4808, 5142, 5408, 5702, 6362.
M'Echre. See M'Echrye.
M'Echroe, Conor and Mologhlin, pardon, 6876.
M'Echrye—Echre—Echroye, persons of the name pardoned, 3427, 4968.
M'Echyle, Une, pardon, 6180.
M'Eclagale—Eclagoly, Nich. and Tho., pardon, 3344, 4333.
M'Eclearie—Eclery, persons of the name pardoned, 4663.
M'Eclere, persons of the name pardoned, 4634.
M'Eclery, persons of the name pardoned, 5702, 6620, 4794.
M'Ecoigne, Teig, pardon, 6480.
M'eColaghen, Shough, co. Gal., 4718.
M'Ecorte, Gilleduff, pardon, 5428.
M'Ecorffe, Shane, harper, pardon, 5734.
M'Ecowgrie, Tirlagh, pardon, 6775.
M'eCowlye, Shough, in O'Madden's country, co. Gal., 4718.
M'Ecre, Teig, pardon, 6704.
M'Ecren, persons of the name pardoned, 6348, 6564–5.
M'Ecrosan, Muriagh, pardon, 6567.
M'Ecruthan, Edmond Pair., pardon, 6483.
M'Ecrvy, persons of the name pardoned, 4906, 5611.
M'Ecumbe, Owen, pardon, 5904.
M'Edall, Edm., pardon, 4877.

INDEX TO FIANTS.—ELIZABETH.

M'Edallo, persons of the same pardoned, [illegible].
M'Edde, Donoghe, pardon, 4654.
M'Ede, Walter, pardon, 1862.
M'Edegane, Hugh O'Donell, 4904.
M'Edell, Donell (of Ballym'edell, co. Kerry), and others of the same pardoned, 5194.
M'Edill, Carrowl and Donald, pardon, 834.
M'Edmond — Edmund — Edmonde — Edmound—Edmunde:
" (of Tradvally, co. Kerry), pardon, 5460.
" Cahir (of Clonkine, King's co.), pardon, 4034.
" Cahire rowe (of Kinselagh), indenture, 4780.
" Donald duff (Cavanagh ?), English liberty, 740 ; pardon, 751, 1677.
" Donell (co. Gal.), attainted, [illegible].
" Egnechan (of Lisnamanay, co. Ross.), pardon, 4074.
" Garrett m'Shane (co. Cork), lands of, 5432.
" Gilleduff (co. Kerry), attainted, 4122.
" Hubert (in co. Long.), pardon, 1828, 5108, [illegible].
" James (in co. Kerry), attainted, 3812, 4030, 4117.
" James m'Morogh (in co. Wex.), pardon, 4174, 4581.
" John (in co. Lim.), attainted, [illegible].
" Maurice (in co. Lim.), attainted, 3360.
" Mulmory — Mulmorry (M'Donnell), grant of land, 357 ; captain of galloglas, indenture, 2191 ; pardon, 620, 2617, 3123, 3947.
" Robert (in co. Kerry), attainted, 4122.
" Thomas (of Clontokillo, co. Mayo), attainted, [illegible].
" Walter (M'Donnell), pardon, 2621, [illegible], 4747.
" William m'Philip, pardon, 3917, 3947, 4752.
" others of the name, or patronymic, pardoned, 198, 378, 441, 471, 418, 530, 557-8, 578, [illegible], 887, [illegible], 947, 1028, 1038, 1082, 1164, 1278, 1308, 1346, 1389, 1478, 1744, 1746, 1812, 1887-8, 2062, 2080, 2108, 2145, 2202, 2280, 2317, 2343, 2408, 2434, 2534, 2617,

M'Edmond:
[illegible], 2709, 2778, [illegible], [illegible], 3043, 3172, 3631, [illegible], 3784, 3837, [illegible], [illegible], 3881, 3894, 3960, 4015, 4022, 4028, [illegible]-4, 4071, 4082, 4132, 4142, 4183, 4183, 4198, 4230, 4241, 4288, 4292, 4307, 4318, 4371, 4410-1, 4413, 4467, 4676, 4531, 4626, 4637, 4644, 4652, 4673, 4674, 4682, 4698, 4707, 4714, 4736, 4742, 4812, 4814, 4863, [illegible], 4918, 4944-5, 5066, [illegible], [illegible], 5113-8, 5142, 5173, [illegible], [illegible], 5427, 5432, 5437, 5452, [illegible], 5611, 5618, 5652, [illegible], [illegible]-4, [illegible], [illegible], 5735, 5747, 5784, 5789, [illegible], [illegible], [illegible], [illegible], 6108, 6150, 6174, [illegible], [illegible], 6189, 6192, [illegible], [illegible], [illegible], 6329, [illegible], [illegible], [illegible], [illegible], 6413, 5458, 6452, [illegible], 6467, 6477-8, 6487, 6494, 6497-8, 6501, 6504-5, 6511, 6515, [illegible], 6531, [illegible]-4, [illegible], [illegible], [illegible]-51, 6555, [illegible], 6564, [illegible], 6568, 6576-7, [illegible], 6615, [illegible], 6647, [illegible], 6667, [illegible], 6727, 6734-6, 6742, 6744-5, 6775.
M'Edmond ballagh, Tirlagh mergagh (M'Donnell), pardon, 3651, 5477.
M'Edmond bane, Thomas, pardon, 6182, 6437.
M'Edmond duff, Dermot (of Kinsellagh), pardon, 4494, 4547 ; his wife and sons, 4494.
" Arthur duff, son of Dermot, pardon, 4494.
" Donell, pardon, 4884.
" Hugh ballagh, son of Dermot, pardon, 4494.
" Shane, pardon, 3020.
M'Edmond duff's country, in co. Wex., chief serjeant of, 1696, 2244.
M'Edmond moyle, Moriagh, pardon, [illegible].
M'Edmond oge, Morroghe, land of, granted, 6482.
" Morogh and wife, pardoned, 4170.
" Teig, pardon, [illegible], 4822.
" Theobald, pardon, 1848.
M'Edmond rivagh, Teig, pardon, 4026.
M'Edmond's lands, co. Kerry, 4804.
M'Edni, Shane, pardon, 2278.
M'Edoire, Shane, pardon, 6421.
M'Edonaltagh, Gillaspick, pardon, 5616.
M'Edornan, Moriagh, pardon, 6163.
M'Edewlinge, Patrick, pardon, 3086.
M'edrivre, Gillecoym, pardon, 4653.
M'edrwe, Patrick, pardon, 4603.

INDEX TO FIANTS.—ELIZABETH.

M'Edrwye, Thomas, pardon, 6618.
M'Edwally, Cormock, pardon, 4741.
M'Edward—Edwardis, persons of the name pardoned, 1848, 4838, 4884, 4612, [illegible].
M'Ee, persons of the name pardoned, 1084, [illegible], [illegible], 5044, [illegible], 4874, 6439.
M'Eegane, Owny, pardon, 4811.
M'Eemy, Cormuck, pardon, [illegible].
M'Efe, Kenedy, pardon, [illegible].
" Moragh, pardon, [illegible].
M'Efferson, Hubert, pardon, [illegible].
M'Effe, persons of the name pardoned, 3045, 5304, 6433, 6647.
M'Egal( ), Donell, pardon, [illegible].
M'Egaine, Carbrie, pardon, 6454.
M'Egan—Egane:
" Bebeflagh (of Clonelahe), pardon, [illegible].
" Boetagh duf, pardon, 4474, [illegible].
" Carrig, pardon, 4636, 5139, 6467.
" Constantine (of Aghinagh, co. Cork), pardon, 6467.
" Dermot (of Brittas), pardon, [illegible], [illegible].
" Hugh (of Brittas), pardon, [illegible].
" Owen ballagh, pardon, [illegible], [illegible].
" Shane, chaplain, pardon, [illegible].
" Solly, pardon, 4874.
" others of the name pardoned, 812, 1476, 3741, 4884, 4876, 4887, 4447, 4487, 4808, 5188, 5413, [illegible], [illegible], 6467, [illegible], [illegible], [illegible], 6762.
" *See* M'Hegan, M'Keigna, M'Kigna, M'Kygan.
M'Egan's country, [illegible].
M'Egarkie—Egarky, John or Shane, pardon, [illegible], [illegible], [illegible].
M'Egeill, Redmond, pardon, 4836.
M'Egelle, Tirlagh, pardon, 6477.
M'Egeire, Donell and Hugh, pardon, 6577.
M'Egell, Rob., pardon, [illegible].
M'Egere, Gillipatrick, pardon, 6477.
M'Eggan, John, pardon, 6762.
M'Eggane, Constance, pardon, 6768.
M'Eghule, Donchie and Patr., pardon, [illegible].
M'Eghir, Brian, pardon, [illegible].
M'Eghire, Aghie and Patr., pardon, [illegible].
M'Eghlagowly, Nich., pardon, 6178.
M'Eghee, Rory, pardon, 3783.
" John and Tho. m'Rory, pardon, 6762.
M'Egilleduf, Conoghor and Rory, pardon, [illegible].
M'Egimagauny, Margaret ny, pardon, [illegible].
M'Ego—Egoe, persons of the name pardoned, 6467.
M'Egovin, Brian, pardon, [illegible].
M'Egowin, Gillicony and Hugh, pardon, [illegible].
M'Egowne, Carbry, pardon, 5712.
" Edward Smythson, pardon, [illegible].
" Mahon, pardon, [illegible].
M'Egyll, Tho., pardon, [illegible].
M'Egyllne, Tho., pardon, [illegible].
M'Ehowgrie, Hew, pardon, [illegible].
M'Eigan, persons of the name pardoned, 4780, 6702.
M'Eiver, persons of the name pardoned, 1507.
M'Ekelloghe, Brian, pardon, 1182.
M'Ekelly, Cahell, piper, pardon, 6477.
M'eKewghe, Shough, in O'Madden's country, 6718.
M'Ekey—Eky—Ekye:
" Cahir bane, slain, [illegible].
" Shane etotan, slain, [illegible].
" others of the name pardoned, 1640, 4718, 5563, 5447, [illegible].
M'Ekibe, John, death of, [illegible].
M'Eky—Ekye. *See* M'Ekey.
M'Ele, persons of the name, pardoned, [illegible], 6577, 6764.
M'Elahray, Conoghor and Shane, pardon, 6762.
M'Elane, Ekie and Owe, pardon, [illegible].
M'Elarren, Rich., pardon, 6404.
M'Elcharne, Nics, pardon, 4714.
M'Elderay, Evan, pardon, 6763.
M'Elchowleboey, Molaghlin, pardon, [illegible].
M'Elchrive, Hugh, pardon, 6652.
M'Eldony—Eldonie, persons of the name pardoned, [illegible].
M'Elea, Fynyn, pardon, 5606.
" Nich., pardon, 6678.
M'Elenan, Cormick, pardon, [illegible].
M'Elenny, alias Butler, Theobald, pardon, 6478.
M'Elearny—Elearney, persons of the name pardoned, 5791, 6463.
M'Elearne, Teig, pardon, 6618.
M'Elearne, Wm., pardon, 6618.
M'Elelle, Shane, pardon, 6577.
M'Elena, Conologh, pardon, [illegible].
M'Elewne, Hugh and Tirelagh, pardon, 6612.
M'Elewnane—Elewnan, persons of the name pardoned, [illegible].
M'Elome, Rich., pardon, 6184.
M'Ellgott, Edm., pardon, 6432.
M'Ellinan, Phelim, pardon, [illegible].
M'Ellinnan, Hugh and Tirlagh, pardon, 5714.
M'Elle, Dormot and Ullec, surgeons, pardon, 4738.
M'Ellory, Mortagh, rector of Ballymoney, pardon, 4897.
M'Ellogert, Tirrelagh, pardon, [illegible].
M'Ellogod (of Ballymcelligott), pardon, 5631.

INDEX TO FIANTS—ELIZABETH.

M'Elne, Owen, pardon, 3766.
M'Elstrom—Ellestrome:
" Garret, pardon, 5048.
" Thomas, pardon, 4625, 4656.
M'Elrowbe, Phelim and Shane, pardon, 5649.
M'Elvoolen, Moragh, pardon, 5482.
M'Elvridie, Feleni, pardon, 6788.
" Shane, pardon, 5687.
M'Elyvoon, Dermod, pardon, 4434.
M'Elyre, Maghlon and Patk., pardon, 5085.
M'Elyragh, Loghlin, pardon, 5010.
M'Emeryrad, pardon, 5489.
M'Emerrow, Shane, pardon, 5478.
M'Emdyll, Tirlagh, pardon, 6694.
M'Emalley, Maine, pardon, 5460.
M'Emoyne, Leinagh and Thady, pardon, 1179.
M'Ena, Art (M'Vadock), pardon, 6617.
" Melaghlin, pardon, 5563.
M'Enals—Enalls, persons of the name pardoned, 4453, 5456, 5970.
M'Enalcreen, persons of the name pardoned, 1973.
M'Enaine, persons of the name pardoned, 4490.
M'Enallan, Moyler and Shane, pardon, 4156.
M'Enallew—Enallewe, persons of the name pardoned, 6490.
M'Enally—Enallye, persons of the name pardoned, 2464, 3477, 3767, 5796, 6464, 6763.
M'Enalye, Edm., pardon, 6150.
M'Enanan, Geoffrey, pardon, 3085.
M'Enanhis, Dermot, pardon, 5434.
M'Enanne, Owen, pardon, 4153.
M'Enanny, persons of the name pardoned, 4897, 5740, 5648.
M'Enard, Cathirie, pardon, 4603.
M'Enarkin, Tirlagh and Wm., pardon, 5603.
M'Enarneny, Robert, pardon, 6798.
M'Enarrick, Connoghor, pardon, 5817.
M'Enaspicke, Donogh, pardon, 581.
" Edm., pardon, 5825.
M'Enawe, Morertagh, pardon, 6080.
M'Enawe boye, Owen, pardon, 4366.
M'Enaultie, persons of the name pardoned, 6798.
M'Enceigh, persons of the name pardoned, 5763.
M'en Cargie, Shane oge, pardon, 5457.
M'Encarige, Moriertagh, pardon, 6746.
M'Encarnighe, Shane oge, pardon, 5410.
M'Encarrigy, Moriertagh, pardon, 6746. See Vickenolarrigge.
M'Enchun, Farrall and Multrony, pardon, 5814.
M'Enchusan, Tho., pardon, 4845.
M'Enchugy, John, pardon, 4749.
" Murogh, pardon, 5984.
M'Endrogy, Gilpatrick, pardon, 5814.
M'Enduirochane, Wm., pardon, 5803.
M'Eneswell, Gilpatrick, pardon, 5425.
M'Enetee, persons of the name pardoned, 5662, 6580.
M'Enerogh, Donogh, pardon, 6851.
M'Enereghan, Donell, pardon, 4576.
M'en Crohane, Melaghlan and Teig, pardon, 5411.
M'Ene, Callagh and Tirrelagh, pardon, 5451.
M'Enee, Gerald, pardon, 5646.
M'Eneilsine, Donell, pardon, 4854.
M'Enee, Cahir, pardon, 5181.
M'Enellie, Conchor, pardon, 2817.
M'Enele, Edm. and Shellie, pardon, 6817.
M'Enelle, Owen, pardon, 6429.
M'Enellen, persons of the name pardoned, 5498.
M'Enelly, persons of the name pardoned, 4668, 6817. See M'Enilly, M'Enylle.
M'Enemy, persons of the name pardoned, 5482.
M'Enen, Kallagh and Tirlagh, pardon, 6514.
M'Enenos, Brian and Wm., pardon, 4676.
M'Eneney, Manis, pardon, 4505.
M'Enery, persons of the name pardoned, 5686, 5734.
M'Ener, Gerald, attainted, 5011.
" Liseagh and Rich., pardon, 5044.
" See M'Enyr.
M'Enerquogh, Gilpatrick, pardon, 4138.
M'Enerkina, David, pardon, 6298.
M'Enerie. See M'Enery.
M'Enerkine, Cormock, pardon, 5963.
M'Enerin, David, pardon, 5745.
M'Enerine, Shane, pardon, 5615.
M'Enerny, Donell and Manus, pardon, 5421.
M'Enerr, James and Melaghlin, pardon, 5817.
M'Enerran, Donoghe and Mahon, pardon, 5444.
M'Enerrye, Morris, pardon, 4380.
M'Enery—Enerie, persons of the name pardoned, 5477, 5694.
" See M'Kenery, M'Keuney.
M'Enerylane, Cahill O'Brenan, pardon, 5952.
M'Ennes, Callagh, pardon, 4778.
" Edm., pardon, 4178.
M'Enradoline, Pyers, pardon, 6651.
M'Enselle. See M'Enoslie.
M'Enoslie Kavanagh, Teig, pardon, 5446.
M'Enoslee, Dermod, pardon, 6453.
M'Enosly, Donogh, pardon, 4848.
M'Enoslye, Florence Kavanagh (of Kilm'Enoslie), pardon, 2024.
M'Enoseo, Geary, pardon, 5561.
M'Enoslie — Enoslie, persons of the name pardoned, 4488, 4814-6, 5545, 5471, 5641, 6876.
M'Enoghye, Moriertagh, pardon, 5817.
M'Engane, Donell, pardon, 5821.
M'Enganan, Phelim, pardon, 4142.

INDEX TO FIANTS—ELIZABETH.

M'Eaganny, Teig, pardon, [illegible].
M'Eagrume, Conor, pardon, 4163.
M'Ea gawne, Gillcreow and Owen, pardon, [illegible].
M'Eaga wney, Carbery, pardon, [illegible].
M'Eagertagh, Thady, pardon, [illegible].
M'Eaghtighny, Molaghlin, pardon, [illegible].
M'Eaille, Owen, pardon, [illegible].
M'Eaillowe, Gillcchrist, pardon, [illegible].
M'Eaffy, Manus, pardon, [illegible].
„ Owen, pardon, [illegible].
M'Eair, Carbry, pardon, [illegible].
M'Eairo, Dermot, pardon, [illegible].
M'Eaiwe oge, Farragh, pardon, [illegible].
M'Eakelly, Donell, pardon, [illegible].
M'Ealawe, Pair., pardon, [illegible].
M'Ealey, Edm. and Laughlen, pardon, [illegible].
M'Ealen, Conor, pardon, [illegible].
M'Ealevie, Rory, pardon, [illegible].
M'Ealeu, Shane, pardon, [illegible].
M'Ealowe, Owen, pardon, [illegible].
M'Ealowie, persons of the name pardoned, [illegible].
M'Ealowe, Cormock, pardon, [illegible].
M'Ealey, Cormock, pardon, [illegible].
M'Eallove, Loghlin, pardon, [illegible].
M'Eamble, Owen, pardon, [illegible].
M'Eameloane, Owley, pardon, [illegible].
M'Eamen, Ferre, pardon, [illegible].
M'Eameile, Fynin, pardon, [illegible].
M'Eamelle, persons of the name pardoned, [illegible].
M'Eaneghmer, Owen, pardon, [illegible].
M'Eanhane, Morghe, pardon, 471.
M'Eanllow—Eanllowe, persons of the name pardoned, [illegible].
M'Eanokery, Collo, pardon, [illegible].
M'Eanrmoyole, Cahell, pardon, [illegible].
M'ea Cryyan, Redmund, pardon, [illegible].
M'Eanore, Terence, pardon, [illegible].
M'Earaghtie, Teig, pardon, [illegible].
M'Eare, Gullo, pardon, [illegible].
M'Earen, Donell and Owen, pardon, [illegible].
M'Earidorth, Rickard, pardon, [illegible].
M'Earie, persons of the name pardoned, [illegible].
M'Earily, Hugh, pardon, [illegible].
M'Eary, persons of the name pardoned, [illegible].
M'Earyckty, Thomas, pardon, [illegible].
M'Eatedo, Tho., pardon, [illegible].
M'Eatie, Hugh, [illegible].
M'Eatighe, Gillcttereman, pardon, [illegible].
M'Eatoayen, Donell, pardon, [illegible].
M'Eatewynoy, Edm., pardon, [illegible].
M'Eatyo, Brien and Cormac, pardon, [illegible].
M'ea Tye, Mahy, pardon, [illegible].
M'Eaulen, Dermot, pardon, [illegible].
M'Eaully, Ever, pardon, [illegible].
M'Eauske, Coull and Wm., pardon, [illegible].
M'Eavie, Tho., pardon, [illegible].
M'Eavoy, Teig, pardon, [illegible].
M'Eaypeamhin, Mohrone O'Carroll, pardon, [illegible].
M'Eayvrny, Wm., pardon, [illegible].
M'Eayley, Brian and Rory, pardon, [illegible].
MacEaylle, Finn, pardon, [illegible].
M'Eaylle, Owen, pardon, [illegible].
M'Eayllo—Eaylly, persons of the name pardoned, [illegible].
M'Eayly, Downe, pardon, [illegible].
M'Eayny, Teig, pardon, [illegible].
M'Eayr, persons of the name pardoned, [illegible].
M'Eayre, Tirlogh, pardon, [illegible].
M'Eayreche, Manus, pardon, [illegible].
M'Eogaine voir, Brien and Mahon, pardon, [illegible].
M'Eogane voir, Donell, pardon, [illegible].
M'Ep( ), Wm., pardon, [illegible].
M'Eparson, Murtagh, vicar, and others of the name pardoned, [illegible].
M'Eperson—Eparsone, persons of the name pardoned, [illegible]. *See* M'Person, M'Pyerson.
M'eprior, Brian O'Molloy, [illegible].
M'e prioro, Arthur and Nolan, pardon, [illegible].
M'Eraghtin, Brian, pardon, [illegible].
M'Erchedy, Wm., pardon, [illegible].
M'E Reddery, David, pardon, [illegible].
M'Erefearile, Gillo, pardon, 4777.
M'Erehie, Conogher, pardon, [illegible].
M'Erkierie, Walter, pardon, [illegible].
M'Erklery, Teig, pardon, [illegible].
Macgrana, Farrall, pardon, [illegible].
M'Erailry, Tho., pardon, [illegible].
M'Erowe, Donogh, pardon, [illegible].
M'Erroffy, Cahill, pardon, [illegible].
M'e Reiddery, Edm., pardon, [illegible].
M'Ereddrie, or Fitzsymons, Rob., pardon, [illegible].
M'Erviese, Cormock, pardon, [illegible].
M'Eryddan, Hugh, [illegible].
M'Erydericy, Tho., pardon, [illegible].
M'Erydarry, James, pardon, [illegible].
Marewon (co. Dub. ?), [illegible].
Macedon, co. Meath, [illegible].
„ rectory, [illegible].
Macedon, co. Westm., [illegible].
M'Etamolie, Teig, pardon, [illegible].
M'Eteany, Con, pardon, [illegible].
M'Etegert, Hugh, pardon, [illegible].
M'Eteny, Murtagh, pardon, [illegible].
M'Etero, Tho., pardon, [illegible].
M'Etowmane, Donogh and Teig, pardon, [illegible].
M'Etisen, Pharell, pardon, [illegible].
M'Etresie, Molaghlen, pardon, [illegible].

INDEX TO FIANTS—ELIZABETH.

M'Eyer, persons of the name pardoned, [illegible].
M'Eyre, Donill and Mabyd, pardon, 5771.
M'Eury, persons of the name pardoned, [illegible].
M'Eustace, John Poor, pardon, 677.
M'Eustic, Mulmorrie, pardon, 4400.
M'Evadde, Brene and Teig, pardon, 5075.
M'Evaddye, Teig, pardon, 5789.
M'Evage, Donell, pardon, 5770.
M'Evagher, William, pardon, 1866.
M'Evain, Owen, pardon, 6142.
M'Evaird, Cochonoght and Hugh, pardon, [illegible].
M'Evairde, Teig, pardon, 6401.
M'Evaleer, Edm., pardon, 5542.
M'Evaister, persons of the name pardoned, 4743, 5142, 5563, 6698.
M'Evard—Evarde, persons of the name pardoned, [illegible], 4042, 4467, 4692, 4711, 5512, [illegible], [illegible], 6662, [illegible], 5794.
M'Evarder, Mahon, pardon, 6128.
M'Evaster, Brian, pardon, [illegible].
" Carbery, pardon, 6642.
M'Evegre, Teig, pardon, [illegible].
M'Eveighe, Hugh, pardon, [illegible].
M'Evelly, Donogh, pardon, 5740.
M'Ever, Moriertagh, pardon, [illegible].
M'Everrelly, Donogh, pardon, [illegible].
M'Everyn, Teig, pardon, 2870.
M'Evoy, Molaghlin, pardon, [illegible].
M'Evie, persons of the name pardoned, [illegible], 5144.
M'Evile—Evilo—Evill—Evyle's country (barony of Carra, co. Mayo), 1404, 2416, 3462.
M'Evilee, Brian and Edm., pardon, 5075.
M'Eville, Walter and Wm., sons of M'Eville, pardon, [illegible].
M'Eville—Evill. *See* M'Evile.
M'Evincho, Manus, pardon, 5770.
M'Evire, persons of the name pardoned, [illegible], [illegible].
M'Evoy, Mortagh, pardon, 4430.
M'Evoy, Gilpatrick, pardon, 2551.
M'Evore, Ferdoragh, pardon, 6194.
M'Evoy—Evoye, persons of the name pardoned, 1112, 1878, [illegible], [illegible], [illegible], 4461, [illegible], 6364.
M'Evrahowee, David, pardon, 1617.
" Donell pardon, [illegible].
M'Evreleva, Dermot, pardon, 5597.
M'Evrahowne, Conoghor, pardon, [illegible].
M'Evrenne, Amy my, pardon, 5428.
M'Evrybwine, Donill, pardon, 5771.
M'Evyle. *See* M'Evile.
M'Ewaldy, Tho., pardon, 5798.
M'Ewmerowly, Donogh, pardon, 4880.
M'Eward, persons of the name pardoned, 6734.
M'Eward—Ewarde, persons of the name pardoned, 1826, [illegible], 4711, 5675, [illegible], [illegible], 5734, 5416, [illegible], 6148, 5914, [illegible], [illegible].
M'Ewaseller, Richard, pardon, 5434.
M'Ewaster, Cormock, pardon, 1908.
M'Ewnyster, Cormock, pardon, [illegible].
M'Ewery, persons of the name pardoned, 6592.
M'Ewey, Jeffrey, pardon, 4784.
M'Ewhir, Teig, pardon, 6812.
MacEwire, Ewyre oge, pardon, 1828.
M'Ewire, Ferall, pardon, 4073.
M'Ewoy, Edm., pardon, 2179.
" Moriertagh, pardon, 1096.
M'Ewry, Owen, pardon, 4805.
M'Ewy, persons of the name pardoned, [illegible], 6110.
M'Ewyre, Shane, pardon, [illegible].
M'Eyrch, John, pardon, 4978.
M'Eynpany, Rob., pardon, 5454.
M'Eyppuny, Donald and Mulmorry, pardon, 5482.
M'Eyre, Nele, pardon, 5940.
M'Eyerto, Edm., pardon, 6728.
M'Ezvoye, Moriagh, pardon, [illegible].
M'Faghany, Rory, pardon, 840.
M'Faghoy, Dermot, pardon, 5464.
M'Faghine, Irell (O'Ferrall), pardon, 5428.
" Lynagh, pardon, 5740.
" Turlagh, pardon, [illegible].
M'Faghney, Gerald, pardon, 6288.
M'Faghnie, Lenagh, pardon, [illegible].
M'Faghny, Gillernowe. *See* O'Ferrall.
" Ivinre, pardon, [illegible].
M'Fahy, persons of the name pardoned, [illegible], 5100, 6612.
M'Faley, Arthur, pardon, [illegible].
M'Faller, James, pardon, 4945.
M'Falley, Morish, indenture, 6760.
M'Fally, Art, pardon, 6174.
" Lynnoh, pardon, [illegible].
M'Falronia, Olliver, pardon, 1144.
M'Fallogh, Conoghor, pardon, 5481.
M'Faly—Falye, persons of the name pardoned, [illegible], 1863, [illegible], [illegible], 4020, [illegible], [illegible].
M'Fanuyn fyn, Connly, pardon, [illegible].
M'Fararch, Coghmorry, pardon, [illegible].
M'Fardorogh, Tibbot, pardon, 6547.
M'Fardorrogh, Thady, pardon, 6180.
M'Fardurrough, Hugh, pardon, 6047.
M'Fardullo, Morogh, pardon, 6724.
M'Fargamanym, Rich. and Rory, pardon, 4914.
MacFariell, Donogh, pardon, [illegible].
M'Fariell, Oan, pardon, 5578.
M'Farrell, persons of the name pardoned, 4694, 5815, 6461.
M'Farre, persons of the name pardoned, 4475, 6687.

INDEX TO FIANTS—ELIZABETH.

M'Farren, Thady, pardon, 6108.
M'Farrell, Tho., pardon, 6576.
M'Farrey, Donell, pardon, 6437.
M'Farriagh, Cahill and Murche, pardon, 4484.
M'Farris, Donogh, pardon, 6461.
M'Farriell, Edm., pardon, 6605, 5768.
M'Farrill, persons of the name pardoned, [illegible], [illegible], [illegible], 6447, 6648, 6532.
M'Farroll, Connor and Tho., pardon, 6461.
M'Farry, persons of the name pardoned, 4497, [illegible], 6458.
M'Farran, Diermod, pardon, 4538.
M'Farrey, Donogh, pardon, [illegible].
M'Faryne, Tege, pardon, [illegible].
M'Faughlen, Feren, pardon, 2948.
M'Fayly, Dormot, pardon, [illegible].
M'Feagh—Feaghe, persons of the name pardoned, [illegible], 2494, 2498, [illegible], 4622, 4096, 4278, [illegible], 4572, 4614, 6452, 6517, 6660.
M'Feaghe, Tho., pardon, 4078.
M'Feaghny, David and Feardorohy, pardon, [illegible].
Mac (sir) Fealme, Fyrogymanyn, pardon, [illegible].
M'Fear, Manus, pardon, 4494.
M'Fearis, persons of the name (in co. Kerry) pardoned, [illegible].
M'Fearrall, Dermot, pardon, 4403.
M'Feary, persons of the name pardoned, 4630, [illegible], 5740, 6128.
M'Feigh, Hubert, pardon, 6182.
M'Feighie, Terence, pardon, 1482.
M'Feighny, Geras, pardon, 6489.
M'Feilem, Thady, pardon, [illegible].
M'Felam, Leisagh, pardon, 2504.
M'Felem, Thady, pardon, [illegible].
M'Felemy, Donell, pardon, 6467.
M'Felim, persons of the name pardoned, [illegible], [illegible], 4143, 4431, 4584, 6448.
M'Fellemy, Dermod and Fynyn, pardon, [illegible].
M'Fellem, David, pardon, [illegible].
M'Fellymovie, Davy, pardon, 4417.
M'Felym's (Bryan) country, co. Antrim, 1448.
M'Felym, persons of the name pardoned, [illegible], [illegible], 6108.
M'Femine, James, pardon, 6677.
M'Fenoe, Brene, pardon, 5677.
M'Fenline, Mihoory, pardon, 4679.
M'Feoren, Donogh, pardon, 4404.
M'Fer, John, pardon, 4701.
M'Feraile, Leighlen, pardon, 4403.
M'Ferall, Chaire, pardon, [illegible].
M'Ferdinando, persons of the name pardoned, [illegible].
M'Ferdinandow, Headagh, pardon, 4614.
M'Ferdoragh — Fardorogh — Fordorough, persons of the name pardoned, 3146, 3779, 4741, 4611, [illegible] [illegible].
M'Fer duff, Geoffrey and Neill, pardon, 4701.
M'Fere, Mortagh, pardon, 4304.
M'Ferganahen, Patr. Owere and Wm., pardon, 4164.
M'Ferganenim, persons of the name pardoned, 4647.
M'Ferganenim, Richard, pardon, 4480.
M'Ferganenym, Leynagh, pardon, [illegible].
" Mortertagh, pardon, [illegible].
M'Ferganenyme, Donell, pardon, 5517.
M'Ferganeo, Shane, pardon, 4164.
M'Ferganenim, Tho. Enold, pardon, 4877.
M'Ferganenyn, Tirlagh, pardon, 4573.
M'Ferganenim, Cahell, pardon, 4404.
M'Fergrall, Thady, pardon, 184.
M'Fergus, Gilpatrick, pardon, [illegible].
" Tirrelagh, pardon, [illegible].
M'Ferlagh, Donogh, pardon, 5767.
" Farlagh, pardon, 4842.
M'Ferill, John, pardon, [illegible].
M'Ferr, Terence, pardon, 3804.
" Thady, pardon, [illegible].
M'Ferradore, Patr., pardon, 4462.
M'Ferrago boy, Edm., pardon, 5611.
M'Ferragh, Walter, pardon, 4593.
M'Ferrall, persons of the name pardoned, 4440, 4918, 6190, [illegible], 6466, 4437.
M'Ferres, Connell, pardon, 4773.
M'Ferre, persons of the name pardoned, 4124.
M'Ferrick, Petre, attainted, [illegible].
M'Ferriell, Fordorogh, pardon, 1878.
M'Ferrill, Dwaltagh, pardon, 6436.
M'Ferroll, Cahir, pardon, 3844.
M'Ferry, persons of the name pardoned, 5759, 4457, 6494.
M'Fery, Calloagh, pardon, 4467.
M'Feylym, Conoghor, pardon, 3694.
M'Feyrick, Meiler, pardon, 6447.
" Walter, pardon, 6452.
Macffird, Capt. (Mackworth ?), pardon at his suit, 3949.
M'Fiagh, Redmund and Shonag, pardon, 4082.
M'Fiaghe — Fieagh, Walter oge m'Walter, pardon, 4873, 5779.
M'Fiaghra, persons of the name pardoned, 4080.
M'Fiaghy, Ferrall, pardon, 2310.
M'Fibbin owry, Shane and Walter, pardon, 6173.
M'Fieagh. See M'Fiaghe.
M'Fighnie, David, pardon, 4099.
M'Fihie, Shane, pardon, 5748.
M'Filbine, Tibbott, pardon, 4861.
M'Finine — Finon — Finin, persons of the name pardoned, 2574, 4697, 6457, 6611, 6158, 6562.

INDEX TO FIANTS.—ELIZABETH.

M'Fir, Edm. m'Art (Cavanagh ?), pardon, 847. See Mackie.
M'Fir, persons of the same pardoned, 1672, 1697, 2750, 3451, [illegible], 4261, 4263, 5193.
M'Firbishy, Donogh, pardon, [illegible].
M'Firbisey, Fynnoyny and Dubhdary, pardon, [illegible].
M'Fitchedan, Gillernewe, pardon, [illegible].
M'Finlough, Edm., pardon, 4914.
M'Fingaughlin, Teig and Tirlagh, pardon, [illegible].
M'Firr, persons of the same pardoned, 1623, 2418, 2931, 4742, 5799, 6111, 3194, 6500, 6617, 6777.
M'Firre, persons of the same pardoned, 2810, [illegible].
M'Flaill, Edm., pardon, 6737.
M'Flyn, John, pardon, 3774.
M'Flynn, John, pardon, 1770.
M'Folane, Rowrdough, pardon, 4171.
M'Fullegan, Conch, pardon, 1407.
M'Furyn, Phillip, pardon, [illegible].
M'Fowbie, Ounadour, pardon, [illegible].
M'Fowrre, Hugh, pardon, 1463.
M'Fory, Cahir, pardon, 6181.
M'Furrire, persons of the same pardoned, 6173.
M'Feylyr, Ullic, pardon, 1357.
M'Fyn, persons of the same pardoned, [illegible].
M'Fynan, Donell and Gillycuddy, pardon, 6714.
M'Fynes, Fynyne, pardon, 4528.
M'Fynlan —Fynan—Fynlan:
" Dermot roe, lands of, 6123.
" Owen (M'Clerly ?), lands of, 6717.
" others of the same pardoned, [illegible], 3079, [illegible], 4446, 4607, 5181, [illegible], 6110, 6148, 6107, [illegible], 6427, [illegible], 6514–5, 6523, 6520–21, 6541, [illegible], [illegible], [illegible], 6571, 6734.
M'Fynine leyffe, Conoghor, pardon, [illegible].
M'Fynne, Teig, pardon, 2401, [illegible].
M'Fynnen, persons of the same pardoned, 4667, 4378, [illegible].
M'Fynnin, Dermot riogh, attainted, [illegible].
M'Fynyne—Fynyn:
" persons of the same pardoned, 897, 911, 2548, 2779, [illegible], [illegible], [illegible], [illegible], [illegible], 5183, 4528, [illegible], [illegible], 4673, 4781, 6016, 6719, 6189, 6763.
M'Fyon, Teig, pardon, 2337.
M'Fyr, Owen, pardon, 6618.
M'Fyre, persons of the same pardoned, 1110, 2394–5, [illegible], 6617, 6822.
M'Fyrre, Teig, pardon, 1522.
M'Fyvine, Teig, pardon, 4037.
M'Gir, Owen O'Keefe, pardon, 2285.
M'Gall, Molaghlin and Owen, pardon, 1717.
M'Gallaulagh, Teig, pardon, 4094.
M'Gallaghowyll, Owen, pardon, [illegible].
M'Galla. See M'Gawly.
M'Galloglasse—Galloglagh, persons of the same pardoned, 4823.
M'Gan, Cahall, pardon, 6712.
M'Gan, Charles, pardon, 4038.
M'Gambley, Henry, pardon, [illegible].
M'Gamble, Cormock, pardon, [illegible].
M'Ganan, Edm., pardon, [illegible].
M'Gan, persons of the same pardoned, [illegible].
M'Gandel, Shane, pardon, [illegible].
" Tirrelagh, pardon, [illegible].
MacGaraldbuy, Cahir, intrusion, [illegible]. See M'Donald buy.
M'Garagh, Morogh, pardon, [illegible].
M'Garan, persons of the same pardoned, [illegible].
M'Garathie, Morogh, pardon, [illegible].
MacGarald, Morogh, pardon, 48.
M'Garell, Redmond, pardon, [illegible].
M'Gargan, Phillip, clerk, pardon, [illegible].
" others of the same pardoned, 4718, [illegible].
M'Garlegan, Molaghlin, pardon, [illegible].
M'Garill. Garillt:
" Maurice buy. See FitzGerald.
" others of the same pardoned, 4540, [illegible], [illegible].
M'Garod, Wm., pardon, 991.
M'Garr, persons of the same pardoned, 49, 6411, [illegible].
M'Garraghan, Owen, pardon, 2147.
M'Garraghey, persons of the same pardoned, 6761.
M'Garralt—Garralde—Garrall, persons of the same pardoned, 30, 1515, [illegible], [illegible], [illegible], [illegible], [illegible].
M'Garrel—Garrald, persons of the same pardoned, [illegible], [illegible], [illegible].
M'Garry, persons of the same pardoned, [illegible], 4761, 5111, 6618.
M'Garrod—Garrold, persons of the same pardoned, 12, 2709, 3225, [illegible], [illegible], [illegible], [illegible], 6377.
M'Garrey, Art, pardon, [illegible].
" Geoffrey, pardon, [illegible].
M'Garraghty, Brian, pardon, 6761.
M'Garrill, John, pardon, 6576.
M'Garrow, Owen, pardon, 5169.
M'Garrold, Thos. and Wm., pardon, [illegible].
M'Garromaine, Conner, pardon, 4753.
M'Garrul, persons of the same pardoned, [illegible], 6617.
M'Garrold, persons of the same pardoned, [illegible], 4912, 6238, [illegible].
M'Garry, persons of the same pardoned, 4824, 6274, 6180, [illegible].
M'Garryn, Owen, pardon, [illegible].
M'Garteen, Phillip, 3132.
MacGarvey, Donald, pardon, 1498.

INDEX TO FIANTS—ELIZABETH.

M'Garvey, persons of the name pardoned, [illegible].
M'Gasie, Connor, pardon, 4914.
" James, pardon, 5768.
M'Gaskie, persons of the name (in co. Ross.), pardoned, 4477.
M'Gasley, Cormock, pardon, 4873.
M'Gaslie, Murtagh, pardon, 4460.
M'Gaspan—Gaurroyn. See M'Gawran.
M'Gawkie, Neil, pardon, 6874.
M'Gawly—Gawle—Gawlie—Gawllie:
" Brian (of Carne, co. Westm.), pardon, 4014, 6874.
" Chr. (of Donygan), pardon, [illegible].
" Wm. (of Carne), pardon, 4014.
" others of the name pardoned, 947, 4014, [illegible], [illegible], [illegible].
" See also M'Awly.
M'Gawly — Gawle—Gallo's country (the parish of Ballyloughloe, co. Westm.), 1401, [illegible]; martial law, 2163; rebels in, 2164.
M'Gawm, Rob., pardon, 6874.
M'Gawny, Carbry, pardon, [illegible].
M'Gawran—Gauran—Gaurroyn, persons of the name pardoned, [illegible], [illegible], [illegible], [illegible], [illegible], [illegible], [illegible], [illegible], [illegible].
M'Gawry, Donill, pardon, [illegible].
M'Gay, Gillernew, pardon, 6437.
M'Gaegroyne, John, clerk, pardon, 5766.
M'Gearald, Rich., pardon, 6729.
M'Gearahie, Edm., pardon, 4618.
M'Gearne, Rich., pardon, [illegible].
M'Geariayne, Wm., pardon, [illegible].
M'Gehmay, Irgna, pardon, [illegible].
M'Geffrey—Geffarie—Geffray—Geffry, persons of the name pardoned, [illegible], [illegible], 4760, [illegible], [illegible], [illegible], 6110, 6170, [illegible], [illegible], [illegible], [illegible].
M'Gegan, Feilim and Murtho, pardon, [illegible].
M'Gegane, Sallo, pardon, [illegible].
M'Gegher, Donnot, pardon, [illegible].
M'Geichon, Molmurry, pardon, 6310.
M'Geiero, Malagiln and Thomas, pardon, [illegible].
M'Geligod, Shane and Ulick, pardon, 4810.
M'Geline, Gilleduff, pardon, 6437.
M'Gell, Sonog, pardon, 1450.
M'Gellenheane, Shane, pardon, [illegible].
M'Gellegromell, Edm., pardon, 6148.
M'Gellehowly, Teig, pardon, 4741.
M'Gelleqaloyo, Rory, pardon, [illegible].
M'Gelleviell, Edm., pardon, [illegible].
M'Gelain, Hugh, pardon, [illegible].
M'Gemiane, Eugene, bishop of Down, 157.
M'Gemly, Donogh and John, pardon, 6718.
M'Gennan, persons of the name pardoned, [illegible], [illegible].
M'Genney, Hugh, harper, pardon, 1465.
M'Gennelie, Dermod, pardon, 1671.
M'Gennoly, Hugh, pardon, [illegible].
M'Gennan, Dermod, pardon, [illegible].
M'Gennies—Gennys—Gynnes—Gynnose:
" Arthur, protection, 6187.
" Arthur oge, pardon, 1448.
" Edm. m'Price, pardon, 5178.
" Hugh, chief of his nation, pardon, 1450; knight, pardon, [illegible].
" —Gennyes—Gennys—Genys—Ghenes country, co. Down, [illegible], 1609, 1624, 6787; marle shire ground, 1726.
" See Magenise.
M'Gennor. See M'Genore.
M'Gennyes. See M'Gennies.
M'Gennyle, Owen and Shane, pardon, [illegible].
M'Gennys. See M'Gennies.
M'Genor, Moleghlin, pardon, [illegible].
M'Genore—Connor, lands of the lord of, co. Long., [illegible], 1402, [illegible].
" See M'Gynnowar, Magenniure.
M'Genure, Edm., pardon, [illegible], [illegible].
M'Genury, Hobert and Rowe, pardon, [illegible].
M'Genys, Philom, pardon, [illegible].
" See M'Gennies.
M'Geochegan—Geochegan. See M'Geoghegan.
M'Geoffrey, Edm., pardon, [illegible].
M'Geoghan, persons of the name pardoned, [illegible], [illegible].
M'Geoghegan — Geochegan — Geoehgan — Geoghegaine—Geoghegayne—Geoghogan—Geoghegan—Geohegan — Geoghegan—Goghagan — Goghegan—Goghegane—Gogheghan—Golughan:
" Art or Arthur (of Killcober), pardon, [illegible], [illegible], [illegible], [illegible], [illegible].
" Brian, pardon, 1408, [illegible], [illegible], [illegible], [illegible], [illegible]; attainted, [illegible], [illegible].
" Brian, pardon, [illegible]; comn., [illegible].
" Calleogh, pardon, [illegible]; attainted, [illegible].
" Con (of Sheenan), pardon, [illegible], [illegible], [illegible].
" Conghor, late captain of Kynaleagh, [illegible].
" Conley (of Donore), chief of his nation, [illegible]; appointed seneschal of his country, 3418, [illegible]; commissions, [illegible], 4181; pardon, [illegible], 2711, [illegible], [illegible]; surrender, 4234.
" Ferrall, attainted, [illegible].
" Gylos, grant of land, [illegible].

INDEX TO FIANTS.—ELIZABETH.

M'Geoghegan, Neill m'Rosse, heir to M'Geoghegan, 4079; commission, 4467; wardship of his son, 4964.
Rogew, lord deputy's servant, 1362.
Rosse, seneschal of his country, 1742; sheriff of Westmeath, 1852, 3438, 2791; commissions, 1683, 2767; pardons, 3426, 3547; surrender, 338, 3228; leases, 968, 1304, 3284; grant of land, 2913; licence to alien, 3443-4; slain, 4988; his widow, 4986; his son, 4978.
Rosse, son of Nolan, wardship, 3634.
Thomas (of Lanagh), pardon, 3612, 3733; commission, 4151.
others of the name pardoned, 745, 1692, 1693, 1747, 1752, 1771, 2116-1, 2384, 2400, 2426-9, 2728, 2861, 3242, 3247, 3048, 3404, 3712, 3726, 3776, 3897, 3884, 3903, 3998, 4202, 4567, 4290, 4308, 4730, 4778, 5072, 5166, 5291, 5888, 6121, 6903, 5274, 5402, 5537, 6354, 5632, 5861.
„ See Magnoghegan.
M'Geoghegan's country (the barony of Moycashell, co. Westm., 168, 3147, 3231, 4769; seneschal appointed, 1768, 2452, 4278.
M'Geoughe, John, pardon, 6798.
M'Gerald, Maurice (of Shean), 1068. See Fitzgerald.
Shan m'Gerot, attainted, 6193.
Tirlogh m'Donoghie, attainted, 6968.
others of the name, or patronymic, pardoned, 1886, 1678, 1881, 2878, 2948, 2985, 2404, 2733, 3367, 3378, 3484, 3622, 3904, 3061, 2572, 4080, 4332, 4902, 4371-3, 4602, 4661, 4712, 4787, 4813, 4806, 5175, 5444, 5822, 6022, 5427, 6604, 6496, 6517, 3648.
M'Gerald bity, Cahir, pardon, 6736, 6817; indenture, 6790.
Donald or Donell roe, pardon, 6784, 6817; indenture, 6793.
Morigh oge, pardon, 6784; indenture, 6790.
M'Geraldo, Gerrott, pardon, 4714.
M'Geraldin, Morice, pardon, 4641.
M'Geralt, Redmond (of Brohill), pardon, 3374, 4511; attainder, 5368. See Fitzgerald.
others of the name pardoned, 316, 694, 3648, 4393, 5110, 5841, 5977, 6633.
M'Geran, Morogh, 5737.
M'Gerald, Redmond. See M'Geralt.
M'Gerenaght, Teig, pardon, 1307.
M'Gerett, Donogh, pardon, 4464.
M'Gergan, Edm. and Tho., pardon, 6336.
M'Gerigane, Patr., pardon, 3543.
M'Gerigan, Murtagh, pardon, 6545.
M'Gerighty, Farsy, pardon, 4014.
M'Germod, Rory, pardon, 6108.
M'Gerod, James fitzMorish (of Ballyodulayne, co. Cork), pardon, 3990.
„ others of the name pardoned, 2012, 4107-8, 4876.
M'Gerodd, Donogh, pardon, 6136.
M'Gerode, Moriche, pardon, 2227.
M'Geron, Melaghlin, pardon, 3183.
M'Gerot — Gerott, persons of the name pardoned, 103, 1121, 1334, 2537, 2498, 2919, 4088, 4492, 6168.
M'Gerraghty, John, pardon, 3362.
M'Gerralt — Gerralde, persons of the name pardoned, 2296, 4508, 4793, 5040, 5499, 5232, 5902, 6339, 6487, 1317, 5922, 6645, 6465, 6648, 6540, 6547.
M'Gerralt, Cayer, pardon, 6727.
„ James, pardon, 6742.
M'Gerrat, Phelim, pardon, 2862.
„ Tho., pardon, 5428.
M'Gerratt, Hugh, pardon, 2404.
M'Gerratt boy, Morogh oge, pardon, 1305.
M'Gerraghty, Manus, pardon, 5498.
M'Gerrebey, Patr., pardon, 6568.
M'Gerrith, Phelim, pardon, 6652.
M'Gerrolde, Tirlogh, pardon, 6347.
M'Gerrot — Gerrott:
„ Hugh (of Listoograyvin, co. Long.), pardon, 5142.
„ Thomas (of Dingle), 3462.
„ others of the name pardoned, 61, 1477, 1912, 2828, 2855, 2467, 2811, 3164, 3592, 3844, 3862, 4364, 4571, 4712, 4834, 4139, 4462, 4749, 5787, 3887, 5137, 6230, 6198, 6260, 6302, 6362, 6435, 6425, 6477-8, 6482, 6496, 6517, 6536, 6526, 6574, 6575.
M'Gerry, persons of the name pardoned, 4698.
M'Gewre, Hugh, pardon, 6337.
M'Geyre, Donagh, pardon, 6193.
M'Ghoilon country. See M'Gonnies.
M'Ghy, Enuys and Wm., pardon, 6752.
M'Gibbon — Gibbone — Gibon — Gybbon — Gybon:
David ciaoagh, pardon, 5466; his lands granted, 5366.
Edmund, pardon, 2187.
Edmund, his lands, in co. Lim., 2872, 3613.
Gerald, his lands, 2872.

INDEX TO FIANTS—ELIZABETH.

M'Gibbon, Philip (of Mahownagh, co. Lim.), attainted, [illegible]; pardon, 6461.
" Thomas (of Mahownagh), attainted, [illegible].
" Thomas m'Philip (of Mohawny), pardon, [illegible], [illegible]; attainted, [illegible].
" Thomas m'Philip (of Ballynily-nie), pardon, [illegible].
" Thomas m'Shane, attainted, [illegible], [illegible].
" (of Mohanagh), pardon, [illegible].
" others of the name (in Munster) pardoned, [illegible], [illegible], [illegible], [illegible], [illegible], [illegible], [illegible], [illegible], 5418, [illegible], [illegible], [illegible], [illegible], [illegible], [illegible], [illegible], [illegible], [illegible], [illegible], [illegible].
" Shorown (of Ballinknock, co. Mayo), traitor, [illegible].
" Wm. m'Jonyck, traitor, [illegible].
" Wm. oge, traitor, [illegible].
" others of the name (in co. Mayo) pardoned, [illegible], [illegible], [illegible], [illegible], [illegible], [illegible], [illegible].

M'Gie, Alexander, pardon, [illegible].
" Dwolie, pardon, [illegible].
M'Giermody, Cahall, pardon, [illegible].
M'Gige, Gildúf and Melaghlen, pardon, [illegible].
M'Gilbaw, Gilber, pardon, [illegible].
M'Gilbard, David, pardon, 19.
M'Gilberie, Maylor, pardon, [illegible].
M'Gilboy, Laurence, pardon, [illegible].
M'Gilbride, Dermot, pardon, [illegible].
M'Gilbridie, Owen and Fair., pardon, [illegible].
M'Gilbryd, Shane, pardon, [illegible].
M'Gilcondell, Edm., pardon, [illegible].
M'Gilcombell, Edm., pardon, [illegible].
M'Gilconnell, Manus, pardon, [illegible].
M'Gilconyll, Connor, pardon, [illegible].
M'Gilcosker, Peirse and Redmond, pardon, [illegible].
M'Gildaf, Wm., pardon, [illegible].
M'Gildusie, Phelim, grant, [illegible].
M'Gilfadrick, David, pardon, [illegible].
" Teig (in co. Clare), pardon, [illegible].
M'Gilfadrik, Mahon (in co. Clare), pardon, [illegible].
M'Gilgowiye, Shane, pardon, [illegible].
M'Gilkelly, John, pardon, [illegible].
M'Gilkely, Farigh, pardon, [illegible].
M'Gilkeghe, Wm., pardon, [illegible].
M'Gilkerkley, Donell, pardon, [illegible].
M'Gilkenlie, Gillernow and Murtagh, pardon, [illegible].
M'Gill, persons of the same pardoned, [illegible].
M'Gille, Teig, pardon, [illegible].

M'Gillacahir, Eneas and Tirlagh, pardon, [illegible].
Macgillachair, Mulmorie, pardon, [illegible].
M'Gillachombaill, persons of the same pardoned, [illegible].
M'Gillachoyme, Owen, pardon, [illegible].
M'Gillachriest—Gillacriest, persons of the same pardoned, [illegible]. See also M'Gillechrist.
M'Gillackeyne, Tho., pardon, [illegible].
M'Gillacullom, Donagh, pardon, [illegible].
M'Gillacrist. See M'Gillachriest.
M'Gilladuf, John, pardon, [illegible].
M'Gilladuff, Rich., pardon, [illegible].
M'Gilladuffe, Hugh, pardon, [illegible]. See also M'Gilduf, M'Gilleduf, M'Gillinduffe, M'Gillyduff, M'Gullyduf.
M'Gillaghiran, persons of the same pardoned, [illegible].
M'Gillagh Leigh, Rory, pardon, [illegible].
M'Gillaghlen, Edm., pardon, [illegible].
M'Gillaghoy, Moriertagh and Shane, pardon, [illegible].
M'Gillaghee, Tirlagh, pardon, [illegible].
M'Gillakelly, persons of the same pardoned, [illegible].
M'Gillakier, Edm., pardon, [illegible].
" See also M'Gillakier.
M'Gillakioyne, Donell, pardon, [illegible].
M'Gillalea, Teig, pardon, [illegible].
M'Gilla Leigh—Gilla Ley, persons of the same pardoned, [illegible].
M'Gillallen—Gillallen, persons of the same pardoned, [illegible].
M'Gillamartin, Owen, pardon, [illegible].
M'Gilla ny neod, Donogho, pardon, [illegible].
M'Gillapatrick, persons of the same (not of Upper Ossory), pardoned, [illegible], [illegible], 6181.
" See M'Gilpatrick, M'Gillepatrick, M'Gillopatrick, M'Gillephatrik, M'Kilpatrick, M'Kylpatryrke.
M'Gillaphoill, Cughogrithy, pardon, [illegible].
M'Gillareoige, Keoghor and Teig, pardon, [illegible].
M'Gilla Roe—Gillaroe—Gillarowe, persons of the same pardoned, [illegible], [illegible], [illegible].
M'Gillaroya, Edm., pardon, [illegible].
M'Gillaspick, Feragh, pardon, [illegible].
M'Gillavearnoge, Donle and Ever, pardon, [illegible].
M'Gillaweyre, Gillpatrick, pardon, [illegible].
M'Gillawred, Owen, pardon, [illegible].
M'Gillbride, Morris, pardon, [illegible].
M'Gilldonell, persons of the same pardoned, [illegible].
M'Gilldogher, Cormock, pardon, [illegible].
M'Gilldogherd, Laughlin, pardon, [illegible].
M'Gillebaliagh, Shane, pardon, [illegible].

INDEX TO FIANTS—ELIZABETH.

M'Gillichert, David, pardon, 681.
M'Gilleboy, persons of the name pardoned, 4737, 5607, 5748.
M'Gillebride, persons of the name pardoned, 3604, 4237, 5441, 6565.
M'Gillebridy, John, pardon, 2902.
M'Gillebrowny, persons of the name pardoned, 6781.
M'Gillecallyn, John, pardon, 5532.
M'Gillecaslayne, James, pardon, 5841.
M'Gillechallyn, Donell, pardon, 5875.
M'Gillecharry, Brian and Cormock, pardon, 4945.
M'Gillechlonyny, Donell, pardon, 5808.
M'Gillechline [ ], pardon, 6533.
M'Gillechollo, Brian, pardon, 5098.
" Tirrelagh, pardon, 5815.
M'Gillechreaste, Laughlin, pardon, 5715.
M'Gilleciarini — Gillcarin, persons of the name pardoned, 1863, 3066, 4158, 4766, 5374, 5541, 6090.
M'Gillechry, Tweoll, pardon, 5581.
M'Gillechyny, Brian, pardon, 4903.
M'Gilleclehin, Cahill, pardon, 4302.
M'Gilleclehyn, Tan, pardon, 4250.
M'Gillecleyne, Gillecuff, pardon, 4845.
M'Gilleclyne, Donogh, pardon, 5540.
" Boris, pardon, 5406.
M'Gillecoell, Neale, pardon, 5048.
M'Gillecoell, Teig, pardon, 6487.
M'Gillecoman, Morrough, pardon, 5808.
M'Gillecomeatell, Rory, pardon, 5013.
M'Gillecoell, Lauhlen, pardon, 4245.
M'Gillecoell, Cormack, pardon, 5407.
M'Gilleconeell, Donell, pardon, 5145.
M'Gillecoone, Dermot, pardon, 4372.
M'Gillecoonye, Owen and Shane, pardon, 4747.
M'Gillecoscle, **Cormock**, harper, pardon, 6701.
M'Gillecoskie, Donell, pardon, 6490.
M'Gillecrist. *See* M'Gillechrist.
M'Gillecryne, Edm., pardon, 6462.
M'Gillecudd, Donald Gunldagh, attainted, 5602.
M'Gillecuddee, John, pardon, 6488.
M'Gillecuroughe, Donald, land of, 5778.
M'Gilledufe — Gilleduff — Gilleduffe, persons of the name pardoned, 1884, 4076, 4766, 4781, 5107, 1911, 5693, 6538, 6487, 5492, 6806, 6761.
M'Gillefadrick, Bewlian (in co. Clare), pardon, 5540.
M'Gillefaghin, Shane, pardon, 4783.
M'Gilleffin, Teig, pardon, 5546.
M'Gilleffoyle, Dermot and Owen, pardon, 6627.
M'Gillefoile, Donell and John, pardon, 4136.
M'Gillegall, Owen, pardon, 4679.
M'Gillegallingen, Edm., pardon, 5895.
M'Gillegan, Phelim and Boris, pardon, 4887.
M'Gillegan, persons of the name pardoned, 6781.
Macgillegowrym, Brian, pardoned, 5688.
M'Gilleghole, Rorie, pardon, 4781.
M'Gilleghin, Donogh, pardon, 6781.
M'Gilleglasse, Art and Donogh, pardon, 5611.
M'Gilleglasslione, Kedagh, pardon, 5494.
M'Gilleglisse, Teig, pardon, 4473.
M'Gillegongall, Wm., pardon, 4174.
M'Gillegony, Edm., pardon, 4781.
M'Gillegowly, Wm., pardon, 5806.
M'Gillegroma—Gillegrome :
" Owen, pardon, 5061 ; grant of land, 5298.
" others of the name pardoned, 4741, 5295, 5687.
M'Gillegromell, Edm., pardon, 6145.
M'Gillegroome. *See* M'Gillegrome.
M'Gilleguffe, Donogh, pardon, 4776.
M'Gillehoke, John, pardon, 5432.
M'Gillehole, persons of the name pardoned, 5460.
M'Gillehully, persons of the name pardoned, 5442.
M'Gillehowe, Edm., pardon, 4768.
M'Gillekelly — Gillekelley, persons of the name pardoned, 4596, 4471, 4687, 4676, 4810, 4864, 5658, 5180, 5958.
M'Gillekene, Dermot, pardon, 5161.
M'Gillekennie, Donell, pardon, 4130.
M'Gillekeyre, Bryen, pardon, 5486.
M'Gillekier, persons of the name pardoned, 5466.
M'Gillekinny, persons of the name pardoned, 5468.
M'Gillekirre, Morogh, pardon, 5469.
M'Gillekole, Teig, pardon, 5483.
M'Gillekolle, Shane, pardon, 4488.
M'Gillekyne, Owen, pardon, 4686.
M'Gillekylle, Gilpatrick, pardon, 6828.
M'Gillekyne, persons of the name pardoned, 5498.
M'Gillelaghlin, Moriegh, pardon, 6466.
M'Gilleley, Rory, pardon, 4943.
M'Gillelolin, Conor and Donogh, **pardon**, 4898.
M'Gillemarten—Gillemartin, persons of the name pardoned, 4616, 5791, 5908, 5816, 6857.
M'Gillemartine, Conor, pardon, 5428.
M'Gillemartyne, John, pardon, 4897.
M'Gillemichell, persons of the name **par**doned, 5459.
M'Gillemergude, Dowaltagh, pardon, 4794.
M'Gillemoncoffe, Morogh, pardon, 4713.
M'Gillemornel, Pers and Wm., pardon, 3981.
M'Gillemurrea, Teig, pardon, 2146.
M'Gillemymode, Feragher O'Hiffernan, pardon, 6456.

INDEX TO FIANTS.—ELIZABETH.

M'Gillenyrlan, Owen, pardon, 2998.
M'Gillepatrie, Donald, pardon, [illegible].
Mac Gillepatrick, Marighe (in Mineelagh), indenture, [illegible].
M'Gillepatrick, persons of the name (in co. Clare) pardoned, [illegible], [illegible], [illegible], [illegible]; elsewhere (not in Ossory), [illegible], [illegible], [illegible], [illegible], [illegible], [illegible].
M'Gillepatrike, Donald, pardon, [illegible].
M'Gillepindrick, persons of the name pardoned, [illegible].
M'Gillephode, persons of the name pardoned, [illegible], [illegible], [illegible], [illegible], 6712.
M'Gillephoill, wife of, [illegible].
M'Gillepholla, Cowchogry, pardon, 6810.
M'Gillephoyll, Owny, pardon, [illegible].
M'Gillequiayo, Gilleduffe, pardon, 5495.
M'Gilleriagar, Brian and Rory, pardon, [illegible].
M'Gillerogh, Philip, pardon, [illegible].
M'Gillerough, Conell (of Kilglassie), pardon, [illegible], [illegible].
Ony, pardon, [illegible].
Richard m'Doyn, pardon, [illegible], [illegible].
See McGyllerough.
M'Gillerowe, Donogho, pardon, [illegible].
M'Gillerowagh, Owen, pardon, [illegible].
M'Gillerowy, Brian, pardon, [illegible].
M'Gillerane, Bryan, pardon, [illegible].
M'Gillernaue, Borie, pardon, [illegible].
M'Gillerneve, Teig, pardon, [illegible].
M'Gillernawe, persons of the name pardoned, [illegible], [illegible], [illegible], [illegible].
M'Gillerno — Gillernoe, persons of the name pardoned, 6874.
M'Gillernane, Shean, pardon, [illegible].
M'Gillernow — Gillarnewe, persons of the name pardoned, [illegible], [illegible], [illegible], [illegible], [illegible], [illegible], [illegible], [illegible], [illegible], [illegible].
M'Gillerny, Phelem, pardon, [illegible].
M'Gillernyff, persons of the name pardoned, [illegible].
M'Gilleroe — Gillore, persons of the name pardoned, [illegible], [illegible], [illegible], [illegible].
M'Gillerecell, Donogh, pardon, [illegible].
M'Gillerogh, Morirtagh, pardon, [illegible].
M'Gillerore, Dean and Teig, pardon, [illegible].
M'Gillerry or Thaio, Farrell and Wm., pardon, [illegible].
M'Gillerrya, Conoghor, pardon, [illegible].
M'Gilleryowe, Don, pardon, [illegible].
M'Gillesaghie, Rob., pardon, [illegible]. See Macgyllysaghta.
M'Gillesaghtie, Rich., pardon, [illegible].
M'Gillestheane, Tho., pardon, [illegible].
M'Gillevane, Dermod, pardon, [illegible].
M'Gillevarrie, Donell, pardon, [illegible].
M'Gillevonan, Simon, pardon, [illegible].
M'Gillewony, Moriertagh, pardon, [illegible].
M'Gillewy, Donell, pardon, [illegible].
M'Gillfoile, Tho., pardon, [illegible].
M'Gilligowne, Manus and Hugh, pardon, [illegible].
M'Gillichome, Brian, pardon, [illegible].
M'Gillienin, Donell, pardon, [illegible].
M'Gillicomell, Edm., pardon, [illegible].
M'Gillidiffe, Hubert, pardon, [illegible].
M'Gillduffe, persons of the name pardoned, [illegible], [illegible], [illegible], [illegible], [illegible].
M'Gillfoole, Donell, pardon, [illegible].
M'Gilliglass, Donogh, pardon, [illegible].
M'Gillienenave, Donogh, pardon, [illegible].
M'Gillinapatrick, Edm., pardon, [illegible].
M'Gillinsherin, John, pardon, [illegible].
M'Gillisheha, Rory, pardon, [illegible].
M'Gillivenayne, John, pardon, [illegible].
M'Gillkine, Dermot, pardon, [illegible].
M'Gillmartin, Ennis, pardon, [illegible].
M'Gillmorogh, Mahon, pardon, [illegible].
M'Gillpatrick. See M'Gilpatrick.
M'Gillreokill, Adrian, priest, pardon, [illegible].
Bernard and Malachy, pardon, [illegible].
M'Gillnicothoyr, John, pardon, [illegible].
M'Gilltrane, Eugenius and Geoffrey, pardon, [illegible].
M'Gillychiesock, Fain, pardon, [illegible].
M'Gillyclenye, Edm., pardon, [illegible].
MacGillyfaughly, Donogh, pardon, [illegible].
M'Gillyduff, Brian and Donogh, sons of M'Tyrell, pardon, [illegible].
M'Gillykovery, Owen, pardon, [illegible].
M'Gillykorry, Niall, pardon, [illegible].
M'Gillykiery, Edm., pardon, [illegible].
M'Gillynacra, Donell, pardon, [illegible].
M'Gillyole, Meyll, pardon, [illegible].
M'Gillypatrick, Donll (in Offaly), pardon, [illegible].
Fyrre, pardon, [illegible].
M'Gillysaghtie, Wm., English liberty, [illegible].
M'Gilmartin — Gilmartan, persons of the name pardoned, [illegible], [illegible], [illegible].
M'Gilmor, John, lands of, in Wexford, [illegible].
M'Gilmore, Gilbert, pardon, [illegible].
M'Gilpatrick — Gillpatrigh — Gillpatrycke — Gillpatteryke — Gilpatricke — Gilpatrike — Gilpatricke — Gylpatricke — Gylpatricke.
Donald m'Shane (of Kilmacar), pardon, [illegible], [illegible].
Donald, grant of land in Queen's co., [illegible].
Florence. See Upper Ossory, lord, also Fitzpatrick.
others of the name pardoned, (in Upper Ossory), [illegible], [illegible], [illegible]; in Queen's and King's counties, 10, 15, [illegible].

M'Gilpatrick:
373, [illegible], [illegible], [illegible], [illegible]-4, [illegible], [illegible], [illegible], [illegible], [illegible], [illegible], [illegible], [illegible], [illegible], [illegible]; elsewhere, 847, 864, [illegible], [illegible], [illegible], 1857, 1873, [illegible], [illegible], [illegible], 2462, [illegible], [illegible], [illegible], [illegible], [illegible], [illegible], [illegible], [illegible], [illegible], 4164, [illegible], [illegible], [illegible], [illegible], [illegible], [illegible], 6111, [illegible], [illegible], [illegible], 6169, [illegible], [illegible], [illegible], [illegible], [illegible], [illegible], [illegible], [illegible], [illegible], 6417, [illegible], [illegible], [illegible], [illegible], [illegible], [illegible], [illegible]-0, [illegible], [illegible], [illegible], [illegible].
M'Gilpatrick — Macgillpatrick — M'Gilpatrick — M'Kilpatrick's country (Upper Ossory, now the baronies of Clandonagh, Clarmallagh, and Upper Woods, Queen's co.), [illegible], [illegible], [illegible], [illegible], 4012, [illegible], [illegible], [illegible].
M'Gilpholle, persons of the name pardoned, [illegible], [illegible].
M'Gilprior, Art and Neil, pardon, [illegible].
M'Gilrough, Patrick, pardon, 194.
M'Gilroie, persons of the name pardoned, [illegible].
M'Gilrusker, Patr., pardon, [illegible].
M'Gilrowe, Edm., pardon, [illegible].
M'Gilroy, Art and Tirlagh, pardon, [illegible].
M'Gilsenan — Gilsenane — Gilsenan's — Gilshenan:
— Edm. breddie, slain, [illegible].
— Owen boy, pardon, [illegible], [illegible], [illegible].
— The stranger, slain, [illegible].
— others of the name pardoned, [illegible], [illegible], [illegible], [illegible], [illegible], [illegible].
M'Gilsteffan, Shane, pardon, [illegible].
Macgilsynan, persons of the name pardoned, [illegible].
M'Gilvartin, Thady, pardon, [illegible].
M'Gilwarten, Donill, pardon, [illegible].
M'Gilyf, Tho., pardon, 6111.
M'Gimane, Teig, pardon, [illegible].
M'Ginidale, Molaghlin, pardon, [illegible].
M'Ginis, Art, pardon, [illegible].
MacGireightie, Donogh, pardon, [illegible].
M'Girlernow, Teig, pardon, [illegible].
M'Girne, Dermot, pardon, [illegible].
M'Girraght, Tho., pardon, [illegible].
M'Girraly, Brian, pardon, [illegible].
M'Glacan, Donald and Tirrelagh, pardon, [illegible].
M'Glade, Gogkra, harper, pardon, [illegible].
M'Glaghlen — Glaghlin — Glaghlyn, persons of the name pardoned, [illegible], [illegible], [illegible], [illegible].
M'Glanna, Donogh, pardon, [illegible].
M'Glanchie, Connor and Teig (of Tullagh, co. Sligo), pardon, [illegible].
— Donell (in co. Lim.), pardon, [illegible], [illegible].
M'Glanchy, Donogh, chief of his name (in co. Clare), indenture, [illegible].
— Dermod and John, pardon, [illegible].
M'Glancky, Donoghe and Murtagh, pardon, [illegible].
M'Glanghe, Donogh, pardon, [illegible].
M'Glanghey, Owen, pardon, [illegible].
M'Glanaghie, Cosnige and Hugh, pardon, [illegible].
M'Glaneye, Conor, pardon, [illegible].
M'Glarent, Mulrehlen, pardon, [illegible].
M'Glashir, Art, pardon, [illegible].
M'Glasney—Glasny:
— Patrick, grant of land, [illegible].
— others of the name pardoned, [illegible], [illegible], [illegible], [illegible].
M'Glasne, Tirrelagh, pardon, [illegible].
M'Glaughlin, John, pardon, [illegible].
M'Glaudhye, Flannagh, pardon, [illegible].
M'Glavyn, Brian, pardon, [illegible].
M'Glawe, Owen, pardon, 1677.
M'Glaweye, Donell, pardon, [illegible].
M'Glane, Gillolpatrick, pardon, [illegible].
M'Glennan, Muriagh, pardon, [illegible].
M'Glensie, Neill, pardon, [illegible].
M'Glesgie, Donell, pardon, [illegible].
M'Glove, Molaghlen, pardon, [illegible].
M'Glin, Owen, pardon, [illegible].
M'Glone, Patr., pardon, [illegible].
M'Glonone, Teig, pardon, [illegible].
M'Glory, Morgh, pardon, [illegible].
M'Glockie, persons of the name pardoned, [illegible].
M'Glockir, persons of the name pardoned, [illegible].
M'Glyn, persons of the name pardoned, [illegible], [illegible], [illegible], [illegible], [illegible].
M'Glyne, persons of the name pardoned, [illegible], [illegible], [illegible].
M'Glynn, Hugh, pardon, [illegible].
M'Gnavyne, Arth, pardon, [illegible].
M'Gnew, Donoghe and Kallagh, pardon, [illegible].
M'Gnewe, Fardorogh, pardon, [illegible].
M'Galove, Walter, pardon, [illegible].
M'Goende, Gerrot, pardon, [illegible].
M'Goan, Brian, pardon, [illegible].
M'Goawne, John, pardon, [illegible].
M'Gochegan — Geoghegan. *See* M'Geoghegan.
M'Goffrie, chief of his name, pardon, [illegible].
M'Goghegan — Goghegan — Goghegane — Goghgan. *See* M'Geoghegan.
M'Goghegan, Brian, [illegible]. *See* M'Geoghegan.

INDEX TO FIANTS—ELIZABETH.

M'Goigan, Donogh and Melaghlin, pardon, [illegible].
M'Goine, persons of the name pardoned, 4574, 6507.
M'Gokiane, Dorrack, pardon, [illegible].
M'Gosceggrey, Chaell, pardon, 6534.
M'Gone, Conill, pardon, 2572.
M'Gosmyle, Teig, pardon, 6741.
MacGory, Dermot, pardon, [illegible].
M'Goragho, Dermot, pardon, 1161.
M'Gorch—Gorche, persons of the name pardoned, [illegible].
M'Goreman, Conoghor, pardon, 5748.
M'Goren, Edm., pardon, 4174.
M'Gorghe, Ferragh, pardon, 6464.
M'Gorhee, Fardorogh and Walter, pardon, [illegible].
M'Gorhy, Farrall, chief of his name, pardon, 6714.
M'Gorman—Gormane, persons of the name pardoned, [illegible], 3043, [illegible], 4580, 5724, [illegible], [illegible], 6764.
M'Gormayne, Donogh, pardon, 5719.
M'Gormoly—Gormley, Phelim (of Naas), 1138, 4737, 6215.
M'Gormyle, Moragh, pardon, [illegible].
M'Goraghan, Neil, pardon, [illegible].
M'Gorneghane, persons of the name pardoned, [illegible].
M'Gorremane, Teig, pardon, 5746.
M'Gorrhee, Tirlagh, priest, pardon, 5762.
M'Gorre, Donogh, pardon, 6464.
M'Gorremanye, Connor, pardon, [illegible].
M'Gortne, Wm., pardon, 6742.
M'Gonghegan, Fardorogh and Laghlin, pardon, 4567.
„ Ross. *See* M'Geoghegan.
M'Gourk, Neil, pardon, [illegible].
M'Gourroe, Dermod, pardon, 6452.
M'Gowan, persons of the name pardoned, 4788, 6761.
M'Gowe, Shane, pardon, 461.
M'Gowffer, Donell, pardon, 5448.
M'Gowricke, Donell, pardon, 5468.
M'Gowyre, Brian and Donell, pardon, [illegible].
M'Goyre, Moragh, pardon, 5151.
M'Grade, Donagh, pardon, 871.
M'Grady, Dermot, pardon, 6374.
M'Grah, Teig, pardon, [illegible].
M'Graky, Mary, pardon, 6918.
M'Graige, William, pardon, 1523.
M'Graigh, persons of the name pardoned, 6761.
M'Grain, persons of the name pardoned, 5427.
M'Graine, Tirlagh, pardon, 4505.
M'Gralle, Tho., pardon, 1239.
M'Graly, Donogh, pardon, 5447.
M'Gramank, Rorie, pardon, [illegible].
M'Granagh, Tho., pardon, 4636.
M'Granaghan, Shane, pardon, 4761.
M'Granall, Edm., pardon, [illegible].
M'Granan, Johanne, pardon, 187.
„ Kalle, pardon, 4784.
M'Granell—Granill—Granell:
„ Kalle (of Inconnorran), pardon, 4788.
„ Tirlagh. *See* M'Granide.
„ others of the name pardoned (in co. Leitrim and neighbouring districts), 5762, [illegible], 4755–6, 4782–4, 4797, [illegible], [illegible], [illegible], 5497, 5720, [illegible]; elsewhere, 574, [illegible], [illegible], 6464, [illegible], [illegible], [illegible], [illegible].
M'Granell—Granill's country, 6150; to be made shire land, 1652.
„ *See* Magranill.
M'Graney, Donogh and Owen, pardon, 6172.
M'Granide, Gerald and Tirlagh, pardon, 4788.
M'Granill—Grannell. *See* M'Granell.
M'Granilles country. *See* M'Granell's country.
M'Granny, Hubert, pardon, [illegible].
M'Grany, Andrew fitz James, pardon, 4789.
„ Shane, pardon, 4734.
M'Granye, Dermot, pardon, 5497.
M'Granyl, Brene, pardon, [illegible].
M'Grath, Neil and Tirrelagh (in co. Tip.), pardon, [illegible]. *See* Magrath.
M'Grawise, Laughlin, pardon, 5712.
M'Greals, persons of the name pardoned, 4576.
M'Grealle, Teig, pardon, 4573.
M'Greave, Dermot, pardon, 4915.
M'Greene, Brian and Gerrie, pardon, 4573.
M'Greyne, Shane, pardon, 5449.
M'Gree, Riccard and Teig, pardon, [illegible].
M'Greewe, Dwalagh, pardon, 5752.
M'Grevain, Tho., pardon, [illegible].
M'Grevan, Allen, pardon, [illegible].
M'Grevy—Grevye, persons of the name pardoned, 4711, [illegible], [illegible], [illegible].
M'Grewe, persons of the name pardoned, 4473, [illegible], 6517, 4477.
M'Griffen, Ogiry, pardon, 5448.
M'Griffe, Nich., pardon, 4475.
M'Griffine, Nich., pardon, 6162.
M'Grime, Odine, pardon, 5497.
M'Grime, persons of the name pardoned, 6761.
M'Grittine, Fynine, pardon, [illegible].
M'Grogan, Melaghlin, pardon, [illegible].
M'Groicke, Cormock, pardon, 1782.
M'Groirk, Owin, pardon, [illegible].
M'Groirke, Cormock, pardon, 5712.
M'Grogan, Connor, pardon, 5762.

M'Graghe, Kalle, pardon, 4781.
M'Graike, Rich., pardon, 6954.
M'Graye, Gillypatrick, pardon, 6714.
M'Grawo, Mulrony, pardon, 4474.
M'Grearick, Owen, pardon, 6218.
M'Grey, Brine, pardon, 4290.
M'Greye, Conlo, pardon, 4380.
M'Greyrke, Rinond, pardon, 4874.
M'Greyrick, Farrall, pardon, 6232.
M'Grepll (M'Gonnell?), Eyve, pardon, 4793.
M'Grewolyne, Brian, pardon, 5996.
M'Gribon, Garbill, pardon, 5787.
" Philip, pardon, 3687.
M'Grebowne, Philip, pardon, 4784.
M'Grudl, Laughlen, pardon, 4028.
M'Grudla, persons of the name pardoned, 6960.
M'Gugyne, Connor, pardon, 6781.
M'Guiales, Teig, pardon, 5706.
MacGuiles Island (Island Magee, co. Antrim), 5703; captain of, 5768.
M'Guill—Guills, persons of the name pardoned, 4498, 4586.
M'Guigine, Rowaine and Tirlagh, pardon, 6453.
M'Guillameyell, Gullindey, pardon, 4149.
M'Guillikirrigian, Edm., pardon, 4580.
M'Guirak, Tirlagh, pardon, 5463.
M'Guire—Gayre—Gwire—Gwyre;
the archtraitor, proscription of, 6111, 6290.
Connor roe, chief of his nation. See Maguire.
Sir Hugh. See Maguire.
Hugh (of Gyrica), pardon, 8749.
Tirrelagh, galloglas, pardon, 671, 1874.
others of the name pardoned; in Fermanagh, 4483, 6743; elsewhere, 1622, 3694, 3861, 4776, 4494, 5266, 5475, 6225, 6183, 6106, 6456, 6506, 6611, 6762. See Maguire.
M'Guire—Gwyires country, commission to prosecute rebels in, 6379-1. See Fermanagh.
M'Guires, Ee and Donogh, pardon, 6906.
M'Guiseruah, Farroll, pardon, 5675.
M'Gullednff, Barevan, pardon, 4065.
M'Gullenduffe, Morterragh, pardon, 6090.
M'Gullidmoyle, Donoghe, pardon, 6761.
M'Gullemaflayne, Donogh and Owen, pardon 4714.
M'Gullenieghe, Donogh, pardon, 4808.
M'Gullawryle, Mahon, pardon, 4467.
M'Gullelenff, Tirelagh, pardon, 4656.
M'Gullin, persons of the name pardoned, 6963.
M'Gullin Oakrye, Brenoun, pardon, 4984.
M'Gullin Christ, Teig, pardon, 4477.
M'Gullinagrihe, Donogh, pardon, 4475.
M'Gullane, John, pardon, 6494.
M'Gullin duf, Edm., pardon, 4414.
M'Gullenean, Ferdarach, pardon, 6488.
M'Gullenduel, Donogh, pardon, 4421.
M'Gullennure, Owen, pardon, 6828.
M'Gullin ny Flan, Owen, pardon, 4891.
M'Gullyvrida, Gullyvoie, pardon, 4966.
M'Gullyduf, Edm., pardon, 5677.
M'Gullyduff, Tirelagh, pardon, 5718.
M'Gullyduffe, Owen, pardon, 5870.
M'Gullyane, Phelim, pardon, 6414.
M'Gullyghbirry, Edm., pardon, 5484.
M'Gullymarten, Melaghlin, pardon, 4506.
M'Gullymartin, Boric, pardon, 6439.
M'Gullyneane, John, pardon, 6781.
MacGullypatrick, Donald, pardon, 451.
M'Gnode, Adam, pardon, 687.
" Conneloghi, pardon, 5507.
M'Gunire, Teig O'Neal, pardon, 6464.
M'Guoleleock, Gilpatrick, pardon, 5478.
M'Gurhrynck, Felym, pardon, 4479.
M'Gurril, Conoghgrie, pardon, 4884.
M'Gnoole, Oohegro and James, pardon, [illegible].
Macguyes Island (Island Magee, co. Antrim) 5768.
M'Guytin, Edm., pardon, 6758.
MacGuyllin (M'Quillin), lands of, 4664.
M'Guylin duf, Donogh, pardon, 4414.
M'Gwyheyne, Piers, pardon, 3698.
M'Gwyly ny Flan, Donell, pardon, 6911.
M'Gwymaes, Arthur, pardon, 6714.
M'Gwyn, John, clerk, commission, 4624.
M'Gwyre. See M'Guire.
M'Gwyreddine, Donoghnena, pardon, 5086.
M'Gwan, Farrall, pardon, 5108.
M'Gwain, Edm., pardon, 6761.
M'Gwecha, Teig, pardon, 6463.
M'Gwibon, Shane, pardon, 3861.
M'Gwill, Wm., pardon, 6628.
M'Gwigon, Wm., pardon, 4667.
M'Gwire. See M'Guire.
M'Gwivir, Donell, pardon, 6627.
M'Gwilleyeoroilaine, John, pardon, 6448.
M'Gwilyghirry, John, pardon, 2084.
M'Gwnegh, Dermod, pardon, 4449.
M'Gwnrick, Phelim, pardon, 4761.
M'Gwyer, Tirelagh. See M'Guire.
M'Gwyff, Dermod, lease, 6114.
M'Gwyghne, Boric, pardon, 4443.
M'Gwyres country. See M'Guire.
M'Gwyly, Teig, pardon, 4635.
M'Gwyleghenan, Tirlagh, pardon, 848.
M'Gwyna, Gillecomyn, pardon, 4816.
M'Gwyre. See M'Guire.
M'Gwyrin, Donogh, pardon, 6667.
M'Gybbon—Gybon. See M'Gibbon.
M'Gye, persons of the name pardoned, 4868, 5873, 6144, 4628, 4464.

INDEX TO FIANTS—ELIZABETH.

M'Gyrsmoty, Tuit. pardon, [illegible].
M'Gyl, Neal, pardon, 6148.
M'Gylikoly, persons of the name pardoned, [illegible], 5287.
M'Gylliegh, Murtoriagh, pardon, [illegible].
" Teig, pardon, [illegible].
M'Gyll, Duncan, pardon, [illegible].
M'Gyllamooke, Hugh, pardon, 6487.
M'Gyllarulyne, Connor, pardon, 5740.
M'Gyllavryne, John, pardon, [illegible].
M'Gylleobriste, Brene, piper, pardon, 6617.
M'Gyllephadrick, Dermod, pardon, [illegible].
M'Gyllerough, Connor, chief of his name, indenture, 4781.
" Dermod, pardon, [illegible].
M'Gyllduffe, Mahon, pardon, 6817.
M'Gyllliegh, Terelagh and Tho., pardon, [illegible].
M'Gyll-Kelly, John, pardon, 4872.
M'Gyllpatrick. *See* M'Gilpatrick.
M'Gyllyeaghta, Moriertagh, pardon, [illegible].
M'Gyllykerry—Gyllykeyrry—Gyllykiry—Gyllykyrry, persons of the name pardoned, 4781.
M'Gyllypatryeke, Dermol, pardon, 1174.
" Neill, pardon, 1172.
M'Gyllyrran, Mahon, pardon, 6461.
M'Gylpatrick. *See* M'Gilpatrick.
M'Gylpatrike, Donald, grant of land, 510.
Macgylsyman, Owen boy, pardon, [illegible].
MacGylypatrick, Gerald (Cavanagh ?), 987.
M'Gymare, Cormock, pardon, [illegible].
M'Gynilye, persons of the name pardoned, [illegible].
M'Gynnan, Donell, pardon, [illegible].
M'Gynnarra, Rorie, pardon, [illegible].
M'Gynnes—Gynnesse. *See* M'Genniss.
M'Gynnowar, Hubert, hostage for O'Ferrall Bane, [illegible]. *See* M'Gohara.
M'Gyrreght, Donogh, pardon, [illegible].
M'Hackett, persons of the name pardoned, [illegible].
M'Hackett, persons of the name pardoned, [illegible].
M'Hales, Edm., pardon, [illegible].
M'Hanrach—Hanrick, persons of the name pardoned, [illegible], [illegible].
M'Hanry, persons of the name pardoned, [illegible], [illegible], [illegible], [illegible].
MacHartard, Shane, pardon, [illegible].
Machaynsdewan (co. Fermanagh ?), [illegible].
M'Heale, Owen, pardon, [illegible].
M'Heall, Shemane, pardon, [illegible].
M'Hebbert, Garret, pardon, 6817.
M'Hebert, Shane, pardon, 5405.
M'Hee, persons of the name pardoned, [illegible], [illegible], [illegible], [illegible].
M'Hegan, persons of the name pardoned, 4877, [illegible].
M'Hegane, Gillenenewe and Thady, pardon, 1178.
M'Heig, Hugh, pardon, 6158.
M'Helle, David, pardon, [illegible].
M'Heille, Heylle, pardon, [illegible].
M'Heligotte, Richard, pardon, [illegible].
M'Hely, Moyler, pardon, [illegible].
M'Heney, Barnaby, pardon, [illegible].
M'Henis, Fargananim, pardon, 1748.
M'Henley, Brian, pardon, 4707.
M'Henry—Henrie—Henrye:
" James Roche, pardon, [illegible].
" Owen (M'Mahon ?), grant of land [illegible].
" persons of the name pardoned, in co. Galway and Mayo, [illegible], [illegible], [illegible], [illegible], [illegible], [illegible], [illegible], [illegible], [illegible], 4874, [illegible], [illegible], [illegible], 5740, [illegible], [illegible]; elsewhere, [illegible], [illegible], [illegible], [illegible], [illegible], [illegible], [illegible], [illegible], [illegible], [illegible], [illegible], [illegible], [illegible], [illegible], [illegible], 4554, [illegible], [illegible], [illegible], [illegible], [illegible].
M'Henry crone, Moyler (co. Mayo), slain in rebellion, [illegible].
M'Henry duff, Donald (co. Clare), attainted, [illegible].
M'Herbert, persons of the name pardoned, [illegible], [illegible].
M'Hesteght, Brian, pardon, [illegible].
M'Hew, Edm., pardon, [illegible].
M'Hough, persons of the name pardoned, [illegible], [illegible].
M'How—Howe, persons of the name pardoned, [illegible], [illegible], [illegible], 4474, [illegible], [illegible], [illegible], [illegible], [illegible], [illegible].
M'Howgh, Edm., pardon, [illegible].
" Philip, pardon, [illegible].
MacHley, Arthur, pardon, [illegible].
M'Hibard, Wm., pardon, [illegible].
M'Hibare, John, pardon, [illegible].
M'Hibart boy, Shane and Fiagho, pardon [illegible].
M'Hibard, persons of the name pardoned, [illegible].
M'Hibert or M'Hynard, Hugh, pardon, [illegible].
M'Hifferman, Ilarie, pardon, [illegible].
M'Higan, Mortogh, pardon, [illegible].
M'Higgan, Dermot, pardon, [illegible].
M'Highene, Tomoltagh, pardon, [illegible].
M'Hirbert, Shan, pardon, [illegible].
M'Hobart, Wm. oge, pardon, [illegible].
M'Hobbard, Edm., pardon, 1761.
M'Hobert, Ferdorgh, pardon, [illegible].
M'Hoine, persons of the name pardoned, [illegible].
M'Hommys, Connor, pardon, 10.
M'Hone, persons of the name pardoned, [illegible].
M'Honie, Teig, pardon, [illegible].

INDEX TO FIANTS.—ELIZABETH.

M'Horbowe, Karall, pardon, [illegible].
M'Horishs country. *See* M'Orish.
M'Hosie, Rich., pardon, [illegible].
M'Hostie, persons of the name pardoned, [illegible].
M'Howell, John, pardon, [illegible].
M'Howay, Cahir, pardon, [illegible].
" Rosse, pardon, [illegible].
M'Hoyne, Fardorogh and Shane, pardon, [illegible].
M'Hung, Redmond and Thomas, pardon, 4061.
M'Hubert—Hubbert—Hubarde—Hubert—Hubbart:
" Peirs (of Ballannlogh, co. Westm.), pardon, [illegible], [illegible].
" Ullyk (of Isborkeally, co. Gal.), appointed seneschal of M'Hubert's country, 5111.
" Walter or M'Kreman, [illegible]. *See* M'Kreman.
" William (of Isorkelly), pardon, [illegible].
" others of the name pardoned, in cos. Galway and Mayo, 4140, [illegible], 4618, [illegible], [illegible], [illegible], [illegible], [illegible], [illegible], [illegible], [illegible], [illegible], [illegible], [illegible], 6414; elsewhere, [illegible], [illegible], [illegible], [illegible], [illegible], [illegible], [illegible].
M'Hubert's country (co. Gal.), 5111.
M'Hubert boy, Tho. (of Tounagheroyne, co. Gal.), pardon, [illegible].
M'Hue, persons of the name pardoned, [illegible], [illegible], [illegible], [illegible], [illegible], [illegible], [illegible], [illegible], [illegible], [illegible], 4744, [illegible], [illegible], [illegible], [illegible], [illegible].
M'Hugan, Owley, pardon, [illegible].
M'Hugh—Hughe:
" Art m'Neill boy, pardon, [illegible], [illegible].
" Farrigh, excepted from general pardon to men of Connaught, 4112.
" Feragh—Farragh, pardon, 4780, [illegible], [illegible].
" John boy (in co. Gal.), pardon, [illegible].
" Moriertagh (co. Wex.), indenture, [illegible]; pardon, [illegible], [illegible].
" Mulmorie, pardon, [illegible].
" Owen, pardon, [illegible].
" Owen or Oey. *See* O'Dempsie.
" others of the name, or patronymic, pardoned, [illegible], [illegible], [illegible], [illegible], [illegible], 1477, [illegible], [illegible], [illegible], [illegible], [illegible], [illegible], 2701, [illegible], [illegible], [illegible], [illegible], [illegible], [illegible], [illegible], [illegible], [illegible], [illegible], 4374, [illegible], 4170, [illegible], [illegible], [illegible], [illegible], [illegible], [illegible], [illegible], [illegible], [illegible], [illegible], [illegible], [illegible], [illegible], [illegible], 4780, [illegible], [illegible], [illegible], [illegible], 4810, [illegible], [illegible], 4874, [illegible], [illegible], [illegible], [illegible], [illegible],
M'Hugh:
[illegible], 5716, 5740, [illegible].
M'Hugh boy, Alexander. *See* M'Donnell.
M'Hugh boy, Manus, Rory, and Shane (O'Donell ?), pardon, [illegible].
M'Hugh boy, Fergus (M'Donnell ?), pardon, [illegible].
M'Hugh bwoy, Nele, pardon, [illegible].
M'Hugh moyle, Dermot, pardon, [illegible].
M'Hugh oge, Brien, commission to treat with, [illegible].
" Conkorry, pardon, [illegible], [illegible].
M'Hugh roe, Edm., grant of land, [illegible].
M'Hugin, Gerbard and Ulleg, pardon, [illegible].
M'Hugyn, Cowny, pardon, [illegible].
M'Hullickn, Hubbord, pardon, [illegible].
M'Hurryly, Dermod, pardon, [illegible].
M'Hust, Redmund, pardon, [illegible].
M'Hys, Edm., pardon, [illegible].
M'Hyrriyenyvin, [illegible].
M'Hyw, Gillpatrick and Morgh, pardon, [illegible].
M'Iame, persons of the name pardoned, 194.
M'Ibey—Ibooy, persons of the name pardoned, [illegible].
M'Ibrohowne, Hugh, pardon, [illegible].
M'Ibrien Arra, commission, [illegible]; pardon, [illegible].
" country of (Arra, co. Tip.), [illegible].
M'Ibrien Ogownagh, country (Connagh, co. Tip.), [illegible].
" *See* M'Ibren Ogonagh.
M'Ibuyne, Moyler, pardon, [illegible].
M'Icallowe, Edm., clerk, pardon, [illegible].
" Kahill and Tole, pardon, [illegible].
M'Icallowgh—Icballie, Hugh boy, [illegible]; pardon, [illegible].
M'Icallie, Donell, pardon, [illegible].
M'Icaloghe, Owey, pardon, [illegible].
M'Icarggy, Hugh, pardon, [illegible].
M'Icholie, Hugh boy. *See* M'Icallowgh.
M'Ichanin, Rory, pardon, [illegible].
M'Iclieary, How, clerk, pardon, [illegible].
" others of the name pardoned, [illegible].
M'Iconnoly—IConoly, persons of the name pardoned, [illegible].
M'Icrowghan, Moriagh, pardon, [illegible].

INDEX TO FIANTS—ELIZABETH.

M'Idigany, Thady, pardon, 4418.
M'Idill, Kariell, pardon, 4677.
M'Igallagh duff O'Dowaine, pardon, [illegible].
M'Igan, Mortogh, pardon, [illegible].
M'Igane, Carbre, pardon, [illegible].
M'Igarkle, Donell, pardon, [illegible].
M'Igaryveigh, Donell, pardon, [illegible].
M'Igillyreogh, Hugh, pardon, [illegible].
M'Iguyre, alias Smith, John, license, [illegible].
M'Igrane, Donogh, pardon, [illegible].
M'Illullykiere, Mooleroony, pardon, [illegible].
M'Igullykierre, Turrelagh, pardon, [illegible].
M'Ihoole, John, pardon, [illegible].
M'Ilhorigane, Dermod, pardon, [illegible].
M'Ilchavioke, Brene and Tho., pardon, [illegible].
M'Ilean, Rich., pardon, [illegible].
M'Ilerenne, Maurus and Paul, pardon, [illegible].
M'Ilissady, Dermod, pardon, [illegible].
M'Illey, Henry, pardon, [illegible].
M'Illegane, Nics, pardon, [illegible].
M'Ellicon, John and Nics, pardon, [illegible].
M'Ilre, Edm., pardon, [illegible].
M'Ilmarten, Donoghy, pardon, [illegible].
M'Ilmarton, Tirlagh, pardon, [illegible].
M'Ilytoghy, Melaghlen, pardon, [illegible].
M'Imaister, Melaghlen, pardon, [illegible].
M'Imolvihill, Laghlin, pardon, [illegible].
M'Imylle, Thady, prison, [illegible].
M'Inallie, Owny, pardon, [illegible].
M'Inally, persons of the name pardoned, [illegible], [illegible], [illegible].
M'Inante, Donald, pardon, 124.
M'Inarowky, Teig, pardon, [illegible].
M'Inarrowicky, Conoghor, pardon, 6517.
M'Inbrahir, Edm., pardon, [illegible].
M'Inbrehone, Wm., pardon, [illegible].
M'Incarny, Hugh boy, pardon, [illegible].
M'Incarrigy, Moriertagh, pardon, 5077.
M'Incarrygey, Donell, pardon, 6517.
M'Incallie, Dermot, pardon, [illegible].
M'Inchelly, Art, pardon, [illegible].
M'Inchoge, Joffery, pardon, [illegible].
M'Incrogh, John duf M'Cragh, pardon, [illegible].
M'Incrome, Donogho, pardon, 4749.
M'Incroy—Incroye, persons of the name pardoned, [illegible].
M'Incirie—Incirye—Incyrie, land of (co. Cork and Lim.), [illegible].
M'Iner, Moriertagh, pardon, [illegible].
" Mortogh Duon, pardon, [illegible].
M'Incrygoreghe, Tho., pardon, 6577.
M'Inertim, Mahon, pardon, [illegible].
M'Inerrany, Dermot, pardon, [illegible].
M'In Erriaine, Mahon, pardon, [illegible].
M'Incyrie. See M'Incirie.
" Philip, pardon, [illegible].
M'Ingarky, persons of the name pardoned, [illegible].
M'Ingasno, Philip, pardon, [illegible].
M'Ingawny, persons of the name pardoned, [illegible], [illegible].
Macingill, pardon, [illegible].
M'Inhire, Tirlagh, pardon, [illegible].
M'In Lerligh, Donell, pardon, [illegible].
M'Inilly, Fardaragh and Owen, pardon, 5447.
M'Inishch, Daniel, pardon, [illegible].
M'Inkerrie, Gillpatrick, pardon, [illegible].
Macinlanghe, Thomas, pardon, [illegible].
M'Inlenvin, Dermod, pardon, [illegible].
" Morogh, pardon, [illegible].
M'Inlone—in Lane, persons of the same pardoned, 134.
M'Inlyshane, Owen, pardon, [illegible].
M'Inmerony, Ferrall and Owen, pardon, [illegible].
M'Inmler, Dermot and Moriagh, pardon, [illegible].
M'Innir, Gilleduffe, pardon, [illegible].
M'Inreght, Tho., pardon, 6477.
M'Inrie, persons of the name pardoned, [illegible], [illegible].
M'Inrighhigbe, Dermot, pardon, [illegible].
M'Inry, Brian, pardon, [illegible].
M'Inty, Mahn, pardon, [illegible].
M'Inullie, Nich., pardon, [illegible].
M'Inuyre, Tirlagh, pardon, [illegible].
M'Inwry, country of (co. Down or Armagh), [illegible].
M'Inychie, Donell, pardon, [illegible].
M'Inylly, or Stanton, Wm., pardon, [illegible].
M'Inyne, Donogh, pardon, [illegible].
M'Inyrr, Morietagh, pardon, [illegible].
M'Inyrryny, Mahon, pardon, 6517.
M'Iphrierie, persons of the name pardoned, 6517.
M'I Riourdane, Dermod, pardon, [illegible].
Macirreddery, Gibbon m'Shane, death of, [illegible].
M'Irodderie, Edm., pardon, [illegible].
" Morris, pardon, [illegible].
M'Iruddery, John fitz Morris, pardon, [illegible].
M'Ishoche, Ferdorogh, pardon, 4457.
M'Isnock, Teig Dorroghane, pardon, 6517.
M'Isock, Teig, pardon, [illegible].
M'Isock, Ferdorogh, pardon, [illegible].
M'Isteyon, Teig, pardon, [illegible].
M'Itamnye, Moriagh, pardon, [illegible].
M'Itany, Brian, pardon, [illegible].
M'Item-pnaye, Brian and Tho., pardon, [illegible].
M'Item praye, James, pardon, [illegible].
M'Itrosybora, David, pardon, [illegible].
M'Ivagh, James, pardon, [illegible].
M'Ivanaye, Knoghor m'Doyne, attainted, [illegible].
" Mahon m'Doyne, attainted, [illegible].
M'Ivile, Wm. Stanton, pardon, [illegible].
M'Ivoye—Ivoy, Donell, pardon, [illegible].
" Teig, pardon, [illegible], [illegible].
M'Ivylly Stanton, [illegible].
M'Iward, Hugh, pardon, [illegible].

INDEX TO FIANTS.—ELIZABETH.

M'Iwaterig, alias Waler, James, pardon, [illegible].
M'Iyarke, John, pardon, [illegible].
M'Iyarky, Conoghor and Gilpatrick, pardon, [illegible].
M'James, Edmund (in co. Kerry), attainted, [illegible], [illegible].
  Gerrott keock (of Moorllop), pardon, [illegible].
  John m'Gerod, pardon, [illegible].
  Rich. fitz James Barry, pardon, [illegible].
  Rich. duff (in co. Kerry), attainted, 6174.
  See Barry, M'Shonnie, M'Shyaneis.
  others of the name, or patronymic, pardoned, 72, 104, 280, 717, 871, 878, 1238, 1730, 1848, 2016, [illegible], 6574-5, [illegible], [illegible], [illegible], [illegible].
M'James bréa, Brian and Edm., pardon, [illegible].
M'Jeames, Gerald keock, and others of the name, [illegible].
M'Jefferie, persons of the name pardoned, [illegible], [illegible], [illegible], [illegible].
M'Jeffree, Edm., pardon, [illegible].
M'Jenkine, Owen, pardon, [illegible].
M'Jerman, Rich., pardon, [illegible].
M'Johain, Walter, pardon, [illegible].
M'Johim, persons of the name pardoned, [illegible].
M'John, persons of the name pardoned, [illegible], [illegible], [illegible], [illegible], [illegible], [illegible], [illegible], [illegible], [illegible], [illegible], [illegible].
M'John Fiore, pardon, [illegible].
M'Johnon. See M'Jonine.
M'Joinick—Johnigg. See M'Jonick.
M'Johnyn—Johnyne. See M'Jonine.
M'Jonack. See M'Jonick.
M'Jonen. See M'Jonine.
M'Jonick — Johnick — Johnigg — Junack — Jonock, persons of the name pardoned, [illegible], [illegible], [illegible], [illegible], [illegible], [illegible], [illegible].
M'Jonine — Johnen — Johnyn — Johnyne — Jonen — Jonin — Jonyn — Jonnyn — Jonyn — Jonyne — Jolin:
  Theobald boy (of Tobberkeagh), pardon, [illegible], [illegible].
  others of the name pardoned, [illegible].
M'Joning, Edm., pardon, [illegible].
M'Jonne, Shonnyne, pardon, [illegible].
M'Jonnin—Jonnyn. See M'Jonine.
M'Jonock. See M'Jonick.
M'Jonyn—Jonyne. See M'Jonine.
M'Jordan—Jordaine—Jurdan:
  Edmund, duffe (in co. Mayo), excepted from a general pardon, [illegible].
  Edm. evaghary, pardon, [illegible]. See Edm. Wughtery, [illegible].
  others of the name pardoned, [illegible], [illegible], [illegible], [illegible], [illegible], [illegible], [illegible], [illegible], [illegible].
  —M'Jordans country (barony of Gallen, co. Mayo), [illegible].
M'Jordan's land, co. Cork, [illegible].
M'Jordane, Edm., pardon, [illegible].
M'Jorden. See M'Jordan.
M'Jorkane, Hugh, pardon, [illegible].
M'Jurdan. See M'Jordan.
M'Justice, Rich. Mistogs, pardon, [illegible].
Mackabe, Donald, pardon, 1131.
M'Kaall, Firolagh, pardon, 1181.
M'Kagan, Gerald, murder of, 1611.
M'Kaghurne, Neil, pardon, [illegible].
M'Kaghoo, Karroll, pardon, [illegible].
M'Kailler, persons of the name pardoned, [illegible].
M'Kahill, Murgh, pardon, [illegible].
M'Kahir, persons of the name pardoned, [illegible], [illegible], [illegible].
M'Kahyr, Edm., pardon, [illegible].
M'Kaill, Brian, pardon, [illegible].
M'Kaille, Thady, pardon, [illegible].
M'Kaine, Donogh, pardon, 871.
M'Kalle, Rory, pardon, [illegible].
M'Kallaghan, Dermot, pardon, [illegible].
M'Kalloh, Edm., pardon, [illegible].
M'Kallone, Brian, pardon, [illegible].
M'Kallowgh, Rich., pardon, [illegible].
M'Kallway, Farish, pardon, [illegible].
M'Kallyn, Donogh, pardon, [illegible].
Mackamores — Mackamoores country, co. Wex., [illegible]. See M'Damore.
M'Kanoloh, Follymy, pardon, [illegible].
M'Karell, Edm., pardon, [illegible].
M'Karhie, Thady, pardon, [illegible].
M'Karmack, Tho., pardon, [illegible].
M'Karrighe, Shane, pardon, [illegible].
M'Karrye, Donogh, pardon, 1774.
M'Kartan. See M'Cartan.
M'Kartie, Teig, pardon, [illegible].
M'Kassan, Teig, pardon, [illegible].
M'Kaschine, Edm., pardon, [illegible].
M'Kaye, Ferlagh, pardon, [illegible].
M'Kavill, Pole, pardon, [illegible].
M'Kaveng, Richard, pardon, [illegible].
M'Kay, Wm., pardon, [illegible].
Mack Coily, pardon, [illegible]. See M'Coily.
Macke, John m'Tho. oy, pardon, [illegible].

INDEX TO FIANTS—ELIZABETH.

M'Kee, persons of the name pardoned, [illegible], [illegible], [illegible].

M'Keadagh, persons of the name pardoned, 1478, [illegible], [illegible].

M'Keaday, Gerald, pardon, [illegible].

M'Keagidie, Dermot, pardon, [illegible].

M'Keady — Keadie, persons of the name pardoned, 2146, 2348, 4717, [illegible], [illegible], [illegible], [illegible].

M'Keagan, persons of the name pardoned, [illegible], [illegible], [illegible].

M'Keagard, Neyle, pardon, [illegible].

M'Keagh, Carroll, pardon, [illegible].

" Rory, pardon, [illegible].

M'Keaghan, persons of the name pardoned, [illegible], [illegible], [illegible], [illegible].

M'Keaghane, persons of the name pardoned, [illegible], [illegible], [illegible].

M'Keaghell, Marcus, pardon, 1939.

M'Keaghlie, Conogher, pardon, [illegible].

M'Keagho, persons of the name pardoned, [illegible].

M'Keaghry, persons of the name pardoned, [illegible].

M'Kealan, Moriertagh and Tirlagh, pardon, [illegible].

M'Keale, persons of the name pardoned, [illegible], [illegible].

M'Kealie, Gillepatrick, pardon, [illegible].

M'Keally, persons of the name pardoned, [illegible], [illegible].

M'Kean, Wm., pardon, [illegible].

M'Keane, persons of the name pardoned, [illegible], [illegible], [illegible], [illegible], [illegible].

M'Keanedy, Conoghor, pardon, [illegible].

M'Keanaghane, Loghlin, pardon, [illegible].

M'Keanghane, Hector, pardon, [illegible].

M'Kearly, Owen, pardon, [illegible].

M'Kearmoda, Rory, pardon, [illegible].

M'Kearnan's country, co. Cavan, [illegible]. See M'Kernan.

M'Kearnan, Cormock and Laghlen, pardon, [illegible].

M'Kearole, Tirlagh, pardon, [illegible].

M'Kearrane, Phelim and Teig, pardon, [illegible].

M'Kearrowle, Charles or Kearowle, pardon, 1878.

M'Keartan, Nich., pardon, [illegible].

M'Keaven, persons of the name pardoned, [illegible].

M'Keaveny, Molmory, pardon, [illegible].

M'Keavine, Shane, pardon, [illegible].

M'Keay, persons of the name pardoned, [illegible], [illegible].

M'Keebon, Ferriagh and Wm., pardon, [illegible].

M'Keelare, Donell, pardon, [illegible].

Mackeelear, Patr., pardon, [illegible].

Mackeeleare, Hugh, pardon, [illegible].

M'Keeleare, Patr., pardon, [illegible].

M'Keelagh, Conell (of Ballamon in Connaught), pardon, 1478.

" others of the name pardoned, [illegible], [illegible], [illegible], [illegible], [illegible].

M'Keelaigh, Conoy and Rich., pardon, [illegible].

M'Keele, Faghny, pardon, 56.

" James, pardon, [illegible].

M'Keelen, Kellough, pardon, 10.

M'Keelough, Shane, pardon, [illegible].

M'Keen, Shane and Wm., pardon, [illegible].

M'Keeny, Ewer, pardon, [illegible].

M'Keenye, Naghtin, pardon, [illegible].

M'Keerle, Shane, pardon, [illegible].

M'Keegh, John, pardon, [illegible].

MacKeeigane, Donogh, pardon, [illegible].

M'Keely, Wm., parson, pardon, [illegible].

M'Kegan, Bohillagh (of Gregan), pardon, [illegible].

" Carbery (of Aghrim), pardon, [illegible].

" Carbery (of Carrowvadyn), pardon, [illegible].

" Solio, rector of Ardpatrick, [illegible].

" others of the name pardoned, [illegible], [illegible], 1462, 1848, [illegible], [illegible], [illegible], [illegible], [illegible], [illegible], [illegible], [illegible], [illegible], [illegible], [illegible], 4153, [illegible], 4447, [illegible], [illegible], [illegible], [illegible], 4779, [illegible], [illegible], [illegible], [illegible], [illegible], [illegible], [illegible], [illegible], [illegible], [illegible], [illegible], [illegible], 6440, [illegible], [illegible], [illegible], [illegible], [illegible], [illegible], [illegible].

" See M'Egan, M'Keegan, M'Hygan.

M'Kegane, persons of the name pardoned, 1178, 1787, 1848, [illegible], [illegible], [illegible], [illegible], [illegible], [illegible], [illegible], [illegible].

M'Keganne, Brain, pardon, [illegible].

" Conneagh, pardon, [illegible].

M'Kegovan, Wm., pardon, [illegible].

M'Keggan, Brian, pardon, [illegible].

" Teig, pardon, 4787.

M'Keghan, persons of the name pardoned, [illegible], [illegible], [illegible].

M'Keghane, persons of the name pardoned, [illegible], [illegible], [illegible].

M'Keghe — Keghes, persons of the name pardoned, [illegible], [illegible], 3441, [illegible], [illegible], [illegible], [illegible].

M'Keghrie, Peter and Shane, pardon, [illegible].

M'Kegin, Melaghlen, pardon, [illegible].

M'Kego, Laghlen, pardon, 4944.

M'Kegoe, persons of the name pardoned, [illegible].

M'Kegye, Wm., pardon, [illegible].

M'Keho, Cheroie, pardon, [illegible].

M'Keherne, persons of the name pardoned, [illegible].

M'Kehewe, Donill and Shane, pardon, [illegible].

M'Kehile, Thady, pardon, [illegible].

M'Kehoughe, Molmory, pardon, [illegible].

INDEX TO FIANTS—ELIZABETH.

M'Keloghty, Dongh, pardon, [illegible].
MacKeddogh, Callogh, pardon, [illegible].
M'Keigan, persons of the name pardoned, [illegible], [illegible], [illegible], [illegible], [illegible], [illegible], [illegible], 6767, [illegible], [illegible], [illegible].
M'Keigane, Ferall, pardon, 6707, [illegible].
M'Keige, Carbery, pardon, [illegible].
M'Keigh, persons of the name pardoned, [illegible], [illegible], [illegible].
M'Keighagan, Daniel, pardon, [illegible].
M'Keighan, persons of the name pardoned, [illegible], [illegible].
M'Keighely—Keighly, persons of the name pardoned, [illegible], 6514.
M'Keighe, persons of the name pardoned, [illegible], [illegible], [illegible].
M'Keighowe, Morrow, pardon, [illegible].
M'Keigin, Gillernow, pardon, [illegible].
M'Keilkie, Donogh, pardon, [illegible].
M'Keiogheiy, Dermod, pardon, [illegible].
M'Keirvore, James, pardon, [illegible].
Macke Jeame, Tho., pardon, [illegible].
M'Keigod, Tho. (of Galey, co. Kerry), attainted, [illegible]. See M'Kilgod.
M'Keligode, Morris (of Ballym'keligod, co. Kerry), and others of the name pardoned, [illegible].
M'Kelkenye, Donnlagh, pardon, [illegible].
M'Kellagn, persons of the name pardoned, [illegible], [illegible].
M'Kelle, Dermot, pardon, [illegible].
M'Kelleher, Roris, pardon, [illegible].
M'Kelleghane, Teig, pardon, [illegible].
M'Kellegulie, Maron, pardon, [illegible].
M'Kellgowle, Ulliegh, pardon, [illegible].
M'Kellgoide, Rob. Kell ne ferge, pardon, [illegible].
M'Kelligott, Wm. alias Fwohe ne bwoly, pardon, [illegible].
M'Kelligotte, Maurice, pardon, [illegible].
M'Kellogullie, persons of the name pardoned, [illegible].
M'Kelly—Kellye, persons of the name pardoned, [illegible], [illegible], [illegible], [illegible], [illegible], [illegible], [illegible].
M'Kellyn, persons of the name pardoned, [illegible].
M'Kelpatrick, Rich., pardon, [illegible].
M'Kellyn, persons of the name pardoned, [illegible].
M'Kemyne, Shane, pardon, [illegible].
M'Kenn—Kenne—Kenna—Kenaie:
" Ardell, grant of land, [illegible]; pardon, [illegible], [illegible].
" Art, grant of land, [illegible]; pardon, [illegible], [illegible].
" Brian, grant of land, [illegible].
" Brian m'Edm. oge, grant of land, [illegible].
" Brian m'Gromyn, grant of land, [illegible].
M'Kenn, Brian boy, grant of land, [illegible].
" Brian carragh, grant of land, [illegible]; pardon, [illegible].
" Cochanaght m'James, grant of land, [illegible]; pardon, [illegible].
" Cormock, grant of land, [illegible]; pardon, [illegible].
" Cormock m'Patr., grant of land, [illegible].
" Don, grant of land, [illegible]; pardon, [illegible], [illegible].
" Donslowe, grant of land, [illegible]; pardon, [illegible].
" Edmund, grant of land, [illegible]; pardon, [illegible], [illegible].
" Ferdoragh, vicar, pardon, [illegible].
" Giffeduff, grant of land, [illegible].
" Gillegrome, grant of land, [illegible].
" Gilpatrick, grant of land, [illegible].
" Hugh, grant of land, [illegible].
" James, grant of land, [illegible]; pardon, [illegible].
" Mooey, grant of land, [illegible].
" Monny, grant of land, [illegible].
" Nele, grant of land, [illegible]; pardon, [illegible].
" Owin, grant of land, [illegible].
" Owin m'Melaghlin, grant of land, [illegible].
" Owin m'Patrick, remainder man, [illegible].
" Patrick, chief of his name, grant of land, [illegible]; pardon, [illegible], [illegible].
" Patr. m'Gillegrome, grant of land, [illegible], [illegible].
" Patr. m'Nele, grant of land, [illegible].
" Patr. buddy, grant of land, [illegible].
" Patr. Penny, grant of land, [illegible]; pardon, [illegible].
" Phelly, grant of land, [illegible].
" Phelim carragh, grant of land, [illegible]; pardon, [illegible], [illegible].
" Shane m'Gilpatrick roe, grant of land, [illegible].
" Shane, son of Patr., remainder man, [illegible].
" Shane ballagh, grant of land, [illegible].
" Tirlagh duff, grant of land, [illegible]; pardon, [illegible].
" Toole, grant of land, [illegible]; pardon, [illegible].
" Toole boy, grant of land, [illegible]; pardon, [illegible].
" Toole oge, grant of land, [illegible]; pardon, [illegible].
" others of the name pardoned, [illegible], [illegible], [illegible], [illegible], [illegible], [illegible], [illegible].
M'Kenale, Dermot, pardon, [illegible].
M'Kenan, Donogh, pardon, [illegible].

INDEX TO FIANTS—ELIZABETH.

M'Keenane, John, pardon, 4[illegible].
" Moriertagh, pardon, [illegible].
M'Keenchawle, Conacius, pardon, 40[illegible].
M'Keneile—Kenedy—Kenedye:
" Matthew more m'Wm., attainted, 6123.
" others of the name pardoned, 1098, 2347, 2941, 3041, 3076, [illegible], 4694, 4733-4, 4743, 4786, [illegible], 5408, [illegible]-2, 5797, 6437, 6604, 6511.
M'Kenegan, Everven, pardon, 4807.
M'Kenely, Donel, pardon, [illegible].
M'Keneo, persons of the name pardoned, 6310, 6[illegible].
M'Kener, Gillernoe, pardon, [illegible].
M'Kenerie, Tho., pardon, 2511.
M'Kenery, persons of the name pardoned, 4143, 4611, 6478.
M'Keneile, Donell, pardon, [illegible].
Mackenet, Twig, pardon, [illegible].
M'Kenny, Teig, pardon, [illegible].
M'Keneyrry, Brian, pardon, 4736.
M'Kengewey, Owen, pardon, 4201.
M'Kenill, Morghe, [illegible].
M'Kenlagh, Neil and Rorie, pardon, [illegible].
M'Kenna. See M'Kena.
M'Kennedy—Kennedie, persons of the name pardoned, 2776, 4[illegible], [illegible], 5421.
M'Kennetrie, Shane, pardon, 6464.
M'Kennelle, Dermot, alias M'Kennelle, and others of the name pardoned, 4518.
M'Kennely, Dermot, pardon, 6464.
M'Kennery—Kennerie—Kennerey:
" Garrett (of Ballywalleagh), pardon, 4411, 6422.
" Shane alias M'Kenery or M'Kennetrie (of Castletown, co. Lim.), pardon, 4411, 6464.
" Shane (of Balleoghennilly), pardon, [illegible].
" others of the name pardoned, 6464.
" See M'Enery.
M'Kennelie, Thady, pardon, 4997.
M'Kenney, Connor, pardon, 5418.
M'Kenny, persons of the name pardoned, 1[illegible], 4[illegible], 6418, [illegible], [illegible].
M'Kennydy, Wm. (of Cloughbrendagh, co. Lim.), attainted, 6777.
M'Kennye, Gilleduffe, pardon, 4874.
M'Kennyn, Donogh, pardon, 6732.
M'Kennyne, Dermot, pardon, 4782.
M'Kenoy, Owen, pardon, [illegible].
M'Kenraghde, Maurice, 6[illegible].
M'Kenraght, persons of the name pardoned, 5418, 6714.
M'Kenraghrie, Dermot, pardon, 5002.
M'Kenraghile, persons of the name pardoned, 6478, 6437.
M'Kenrathe, Mahon, pardon, 5418.
M'Kenraughtagh, Moriertagh, pardon, 6461.
M'Keonry, Edm., pardon, 6648.
M'Kevy, Hugh, pardon, 4340.
M'Kenyn—Kenyne, persons of the name pardoned, 4738, 6641, 6732.
M'Keo, Owen and Shane, pardon, 614.
M'Keogan, Shane, pardon, 5483.
M'Keogh. See M'Keoghe.
M'Keoghan, Collen, pardon, 6371.
M'Keoghan, Donogh, pardon, 4748.
M'Keoghe—Keogh:
" Shane (of Corrigh, co. Ross.), pardon, 6104.
" others of the name pardoned, 866, 1080, 4008, 4170, 4[illegible], 4[illegible], 4694-6, 4786, 5423, 5447, 6[illegible], 6175, 6183, 6480, 6[illegible], 6[illegible], [illegible].
" See Mecough.
M'Keoghian, Fergananim, pardon, 3874.
M'Keogho—Keoghoe:
" Donald, son of M'Keogho, rhymer pardon, 4873.
" others of the name pardoned, 3478, [illegible], 4874, 4[illegible], [illegible], [illegible], 6[illegible], 6877, 6[illegible].
M'Keogo, Fair., pardon, 5641.
M'Keone—Keon, persons of the name pardoned, 4891, 4463, 4[illegible], 6784.
M'Keonis, Wm., pardon, [illegible].
M'Keorish or Brimigham, John and Rich., pardon, 6765.
M'Keoughe, Donoghe, pardon, [illegible].
M'Keown, Donell, pardon, [illegible].
M'Keoygh, Shane, pardon, 5[illegible].
M'Keoyn, Sawerly, pardon, 4077.
Macker, Edmund mac Art, pardon, [illegible].
M'Keraghane, Duncan, pardon, [illegible].
M'Kerterie, Philip, pardon, 6[illegible].
MacKeraghl, Tho., pardon, [illegible].
M'Kergan, Wm., pardon, 4894.
M'Kertale, Donell, pardon, [illegible].
M'Kermody, Donogh, pardon, 6146.
M'Kernan, persons of the name pardoned, [illegible], 1131, 1433, 4787, 4[illegible], 4614, [illegible], [illegible], [illegible], [illegible].
" See M'Kearnan, M'Kiernain, Mekighearnan.
M'Kernan's country (barony of Tullyhunco), co. Cavan, 6498.
M'Kernane, Geohogria, pardon, [illegible].
" Owthny, pardon, 4[illegible].
Mackerneshe, Queen's co., [illegible].
M'Kerrell, persons of the name pardoned, 4163, [illegible].
M'Kerrightie, Donagh, pardon, [illegible].
M'Kerrighty, James, pardon, [illegible].

INDEX TO FIANTS—ELIZABETH.

M'Kerry, Archibald, pardon, 6633.
" Oo, pardon, [illegible].
M'Kerryle, Gilpatrick, pardon, 6422.
M'Kervan, Molaghlen, pardon, 6465.
M'Kerwell, Shane, pardon, 6661.
Maskerysho, co. Clare, 4781.
M'Kesker, Brien, pardon, 6794.
M'Keyll, Walter, 1722.
Macke Ullick, John, pardon, 4678.
M'Kevan, persons of the same pardoned, 2047, 4163, 6584, 6622, 6614.
M'Kevane, Brian, pardon, 5414.
M'Kevinahi, Teig, pardon, 4548.
M'Kevinahi, Edm., pardon, 4765.
M'kEvoye, Gillpatrick, pardon, 6377.
M'Kevy, Tho., pardon, 6467.
M'Kevyn, persons of the same pardoned, 6472, 6696.
M'Kew, Eugene, pardon, 1367.
M'Kewer, Edm., pardon, 4682.
M'Key, persons of the same pardoned, 638, 2343, 3854, 4841, 4944, 4512, 6696, 6618, 6633.
M'Keye, persons of the same pardoned, 2228, 4724.
M'Keyinan, persons of the same pardoned, 2346, 3773, 6188, 6615.
M'Keylie, Moregh, pardon, 6742.
M'Keylkey, Tho., pardon, 4521.
M'Keyne, Tirlogh, pardon, 6548.
" Wm., pardon, 4729.
M'Keyuyne, Molaghlen, pardon, 697.
M'Keyve, Tho., pardon, 4663.
Mackhacket or Hacket, Ullig, pardon, 1693.
M'Kiadagh, Shane, pardon, 6494.
M'Kian, persons of the same pardoned, 4351, 6441.
M'Kibon, Gerald, pardon, 5294.
M'Kiegan, Donill, pardon, 6626.
" Patr., pardon, 3329.
MacKiegane, Connor, pardon, 481.
M'Kieghan—Kieghane, persons of the same pardoned, 6161, 6204, 6454.
M'Kieginly, Gyllyse, alias M'Kieginly, and others of the same pardoned, 6414.
M'Kiego, Diermod, pardon, 1255.
M'Kiermodie, Dermod, pardon, 4796.
M'Kiernain—Kiernan—Kiernane—Kyernan, persons of the same pardoned, 1694, 4163, 6436, 6548, 6864, 6623, 6724.
MacKiernie, Molaghlin, pardon, 6698.
M'Kierrin, Edmund, attainted, 4013, 6032.
M'Kiernane, Brian, pardon, 6668.
M'Kigan, Patrick (of Currabeg), broken, pardon, 4168, 6682.
" others of the same pardoned, 3723, 4368, 4223, 4133, 6487, 6541, 6640.
M'Kigane, persons of the same pardoned, 3668, 4160, 6478.
M'Kigann, persons of the same pardoned, 1320, 4687, 6420-1, 6428.
M'Kignane, Teig, pardon, 6698.
M'Kiglin, Cohonagh, pardon, 6324.
M'Kiho, persons of the same pardoned, 4140, 6548.
M'Kilavye, Cahill, pardon, 4564.
M'Kilbryde, Moragh, pardon, 1598.
M'Kilchy, Conoghor and Donell, pardon, 4563.
M'Kilcormock, Mahown, pardon, 6663.
M'Kilgool—Kilgool, Thomas (of Unley, co. Kerry), slain in rebellion and attainted, 4613, 6976, 6117. See M'Holand.
M'Kill, Branna, pardon, 1378.
M'Killaghane, Obnia, pardon, 4784.
M'Killbrisly, Naves, pardon, 6792.
M'Killbrelyan, Molaghlin, pardon, 6643.
M'Killbrenla, Derbie, pardon, 6312.
M'Killcoad—Killegrodd, persons of the same pardoned, 6497.
M'Killdoully, Edm., pardon, 4684.
M'Killever, Mahon, pardon, 6412.
M'Killigot, Ullick, pardon, 6642.
M'Killitoll, Conoghor, pardon, 6644.
M'Killmdwill, Shane, pardon, 6328.
M'Killpatrick, persons of the same pardoned, 681, 1161, 6962.
M'Killpatrick country, 6378. See M'Gilpatrick.
M'Killpatrike, Cahill, pardon, 642.
M'Killiane, John, pardon, 4632.
MacKilvanl, Hugh, pardon, 448.
M'Kinderlon, Donogh, pardon, 6678.
M'Kinge, James, pardon, 6867.
" Teig, pardon, 6867.
M'Kinles, Perry, pardon, 6463.
M'Kinna, John, pardon, 6468.
M'Kinnirlen, Dermod, pardon, 4362.
M'Kinny, Neie, pardon, 6625.
M'Kinnaght, Phillip, pardon, 6477.
M'Kinnaghlin, John, pardon, 6628.
M'Kinnola, Donogh, pardon, 6422.
M'Kinlaghlin, Hugh, pardon, 1762.
M'Kirasigh, John, pardon, 4570.
M'Kirrone, James, pardon, 6467.
M'Killagh, Donogh, pardon, 6438.
M'Kirghan, Callagh, pardon, 5472.
M'Klaughin, Cahir and Donill, pardon, 6604.
Macklilaughane—Macklilaghan, Dermod, pardon, 6467, 6871.
" Donogh, pardon, 6467, 6871.
Macklowneigh (co. Cork?), 6638.
Mackmine, co. Wex. See Maghmayn.
M'Knavin—Knavyn—Knawyn:
" John, priest, pardon, 4794.
" Muriagh, priest, pardon, 4482, 4724.
" Teig, priest or clerk, pardon, 4481, 4794.

INDEX TO FIANTS.—ELIZABETH.

M'Kenvin, others of the name pardoned, 4014, 4618, 6791.
Macknehanny—Macknehany, co. Gal., [illegible], [illegible], 6740, [illegible].
M'Keian, Donell and Wm., pardon, 6742.
M'Keoghoe—Keogher, persons of the name pardoned, 1045, 5446, 6781, 6214, 6477, 6480, 6490, 6571, 6476, 6484.
Mackeny (Mackney, co. Gal.?), 2250. See also Mackny.
M'Kean, Tho., pardon, 4114.
M'Keonne, persons of the name pardoned, [illegible].
M'Keddy, or Archdeacon, James, pardon, 6467.
M'Keogh—Keoghe, persons of the name pardoned, 6480.
M'Koge, Donell, pardon, 6440.
M'Keoghow, Donogh, pardon, 6416, 6400.
M'Kelly, Meloghlin and Wm., pardon, 6541.
M'Kemyrgyn or M'Kenmyrgyn, Tho., pardon, 5798.
M'Keo, Syda, pardon, 1827.
M'Keon, Mahon, pardon, 4707.
Mackeomare, John, pardon, 1817.
M'Keonbyrham, Thirelagh, pardon, [illegible].
M'Keonyrgyn, Tho., pardon, 5798.
M'Keoughor, Dermod, pardon, 6479.
M'Keoygan, Dermod, pardon, 1480.
M'Keoyngham, John, pardon, [illegible].
M'Kerchrane, Kowconnaght, pardon, 4807.
M'Kergran, Meloghlin, pardon, 60.
M'Kerron, Donogh, pardon, 5852.
M'Kesdelle, Henry, pardon, 4707.
M'Keogh—Kowgh, Shorown, alias M'Gough, pardon, 3464.
" others of the name pardoned, 3465, 3468-9.
M'Kowse, Jordan, pardon, 6740.
M'Kowrek, Joneck, pardon, 4671.
M'Kowe, Ricard and Shoron, pardon, 4767.
M'Kowgh, Henry, pardon, 3465.
M'Kowne, Conoghor, pardon, 2894.
M'Koyn, Mulmory, pardon, 4736.
M'Kraigh, Wm. iownaght, pardon, 5196.
M'Kray, Donogh and Gillcrnow, pardon, 4707.
M'Kraye, John, pardon, 6813.
M'Kreaner, Gillepatrick, pardon, 4881.
M'Kreary, Daniel, pardon, 6822.
M'Kreghane, persons of the name pardoned, 6821.
M'Krahin, Owen, pardon, 4477.
M'Kroll, Hugh and Patr., pardon, 6814.
M'Kremen, Walter m'Hubert, seneschal of Muster morghe, 2978. See M'Gromyne.
M'Kremure, Brian and Owen, pardon, 6782.
M'Kremore, Keale and Phillip, pardon, 5784.
M'Krenilie, Hugh, pardon, 4823.
M'Kretine, Daniel, pardon, 6432.
Mackrove, co. Lim., 1716.
M'Kroghowre, Mulmory, pardon, 5494.
M'Krohan, Teig, pardon, 4383.
M'Kroo, Philip, pardon, 6203.
M'Krydan, Durby, pardon, 4726.
M'Kryny, Donogh and Teig, pardon, 6581.
Macke, Thomas, pardon, 766.
Mackdowne, co. Tip., 2962.
M'Kuecker, persons of the name pardoned, 6731.
Mackus, Gilpatrick and Wm., pardon, 6447.
M'Kwgan, Dermod, pardon, 6221.
M'Kwick, Jenick, pardon, 5148.
M'Kwirke, Owen, pardon, 6462.
M'Kwolin—Kwoline—Kwolyne, persons of the name pardoned, 5014.
M'Kwoly, Oyne, pardon, 4062.
Mackworth — Macworth — MacWoorth — M'Worthe, Elizabeth or Elice, 4234; lease, 4026.
" Gerrat, son of Humfrey, 4771; grant of land, 5330.
" Humfrey, captain, commissions, 2828, 3081, 3148; pardon, 3480; pardon at his suit, 3483; slain in the queen's service, 4528; widow, 4234; son, 4771, 4726. See also Mackford.
M'Kyan, persons of the name pardoned, 5441.
M'Kyell, Finn, pardon, 4676.
M'Kyen, Wm., pardon, 6479.
M'Kyeren, Donell, pardon, 6456.
M'Kyernan. See M'Kiernain.
M'Kyernane, Owny, harper, pardon, 6081.
M'Kyoshan, Conor, pardon, 4781.
M'Kyewony, Teig, pardon, 5784.
M'Kygan, Carbery (of Moyrath, co. Westm.), pardon, 5762.
" others of the name pardoned, 3400, 4787, 6527, 6458, 6418.
M'Kygane, persons of the same pardoned, 3044, 4460, 6616.
M'Kyggan, persons of the name pardoned, 2957.
M'Kyghan, John, pardon, 6421.
M'Kygo — Kygon, persons of the name pardoned, 4880.
M'Kylleroy, John, pardon, 5633.
M'Kyllyndlom, Owen, pardon, 5418.
Mac Kylpatricke, Conoghor, pardon, 1808.
M'Kylpatryke, John, pardon, 848.
M'Kyon, persons of the name pardoned, 6486.
Mackynaghe, Queen's co., 5786.
Mackynnvoith, Donald and Matthew, English liberty, 3187.
M'Kyne, Tho., pardon, 5157.

INDEX TO FIANTS—ELIZABETH.

M'Kymdie, Thrrolagh, pardon, 4[illegible].
M'Kyrmlyn, Donill, pardon, 5757.
M'Kyrine, Teig, pardon, [illegible].
M'Kyrnnolie, Conall, pardon, [illegible].
" John, pardon, 3778.
M'Kynnoy, Shane, pardon, 3794.
M'Kynny, Donogh and Neal, pardon, 4751.
M'Kyrreghulo, Dermod, pardon, 5478.
M'Kyrroght, Dermod, pardon, 6477.
M'Kyrryne, persons of the name pardoned, [illegible].
M'Kyo, William, pardon, 1878.
M'Kyoghe, Dermot, pardon, 4612.
M'Kyraghan, Rory, pardon, [illegible].
M'Kyraghan, Brian, pardon, [illegible].
M'Kyrraghi, Brian, pardon, [illegible].
M'Kyrrell, Gillpatrick, pardon, 5612.
M'Kyrrelly, Cahill, pardon, [illegible].
" Donogh, pardon, 5[illegible].
M'Kyrock—Kyroge, Teig or Thady, pardon, 1517, [illegible].
M'Kyruke, Dunshy, pardon, 6761.
M'Lagan, Nich. and Teig, pardon, 5[illegible].
M'Laghlen — Laghlin, persons of the name pardoned, [illegible], 4[illegible], [illegible], [illegible], 6171, [illegible], [illegible], [illegible], [illegible], [illegible], [illegible], [illegible], [illegible], [illegible], [illegible], 6614.
M'Lakelen, Macom (of Rosroe, co. Clare), pardon, 3077.
M'Lackie, Cahir, pardon, [illegible].
M'Laghlin—Laghlen:
" Brian (of Ballym'laghlin, co. Leitrim), chief of his name, pardon, [illegible].
" others of the name pardoned, 151, [illegible], [illegible], 4776, [illegible], [illegible], [illegible], [illegible], [illegible], [illegible], [illegible], [illegible], [illegible].
M'Laughlin bane, Shane (O'Conor?), of Shankill, co. Ross, attainted, 3777.
M'Laughlins, Wm., pardon, [illegible].
M'Lawrene, Teig, pardon, [illegible].
M'Lawrence, persons of the name pardoned, [illegible], [illegible], [illegible].
M'Layne, Phely, pardon, [illegible].
M'Lea, Ollan and Wm., pardon, [illegible].
M'Leadyne, Conoghor, pardon, [illegible].
M'Leghilline, Neill, pardon, [illegible].
M'Leice, Phelim, pardon, [illegible].
M'Leish, Patr., pardon, [illegible].
M'Leishagh, Gerald, pardon, [illegible].
M'Leisse, Patrick, pardon, 1[illegible].
M'Leistie, Hepbert, pardon, [illegible].
M'Lemmoicin, Shane, pardon, [illegible].
M'Lenice, Teig, pardon, [illegible].
M'Lenie boye, Rory, pardon, [illegible].
M'Levan, Donagh, pardon, 3734.
M'Levenne, Patr., pardon, 3718.
M'Levane, Paul, pardon, 3145.
M'Leaugh, Owin, pardon, [illegible].
M'Leaugh, Phelim, pardon, [illegible].
M'Levis, Edm. and Loisagh, pardon, [illegible].
M'Lewe, Donell and Patr., pardon, [illegible].
M'Leyce, Cahir, pardon, [illegible].
M'Lice, Donogh, pardon, [illegible].
M'Liece, Dermot, pardon, [illegible].
" Owen, pardon, [illegible].
M'Liesgh — Lieaghe — Lyeagh — Lyeaghe, persons of the same pardoned, [illegible], [illegible], [illegible], [illegible], [illegible], [illegible], [illegible], [illegible], [illegible], [illegible], [illegible], [illegible], [illegible].
M'Lieaigh, Lieagh, pardon, [illegible].
MacLimy, Cahir, pardon, 481.
M'Lishlo, Gerald, pardon, [illegible].
M'Lisie, Phelim, pardon, [illegible].
M'Lissagh, Patr. and Wm., pardon, [illegible].
M'Lisse, Farrell, pardon, [illegible].
M'Llo alias M'Hugh, John, pardon, [illegible].
M'Loughling, Walter, pardon, [illegible].
M'Loghlen—Lochlin:
" Fynen (of Roeroe, co. Clare), 1504. See M'Namara.
" Loughlin oge (of Clonlosrtie, co. Clare), pardon, [illegible].
" others of the name pardoned, 3040, 3077, [illegible], [illegible], [illegible], [illegible], [illegible], [illegible], 3794, [illegible], [illegible], [illegible], [illegible], [illegible], [illegible], [illegible].
M'Loghoro, Moroghe, pardon, [illegible].
M'Lone, Edm. m'Tho. V., pardon, [illegible].
Maclonohie—Maclonochy, co. Cork, [illegible], [illegible], 3794.
M'Loone, Gillaspuck, pardon, [illegible].
M'Loran, Boris, pardon, [illegible].
M'Lorean, Dermot, pardon, [illegible].
M'Loughlen—Loughlin, persons of the name pardoned, [illegible], [illegible], [illegible], [illegible], [illegible].
M'Low, David, pardon, 1103.
M'Lowe, persons of the name pardoned, [illegible], [illegible], [illegible], [illegible].
M'Lowig, Physico, pardon, [illegible].
M'Loyrane, Gillpatrick, pardon, [illegible].
M'Lucas, Redmund, indenture, [illegible].
M'Lurkain, Donell, pardon, [illegible].
M'Lurkan, Moriertagh, pardon, [illegible].
M'Lay, Fardorogh, pardon, [illegible].
M'Lyolm, Tho., pardon, [illegible].
M'Lyll, Tirlagh, pardon, [illegible].
M'Lynagh, Cahir, pardon, [illegible].
M'Lynan, Conolagh, pardon, [illegible].
" Edm., pardon, [illegible].
M'Lyne, persons of the name pardoned, [illegible], [illegible], 3794.
M'Lynot, Edm. (of Dowran, co. Kerry), attainted, 4193.
M'Lyeagh—Lyeaghe. See M'Lieagh.
M'Lyne, persons of the name pardoned, [illegible], 171, [illegible], [illegible].

INDEX TO FIANTS—ELIZABETH.

M'Lynagh, Donogh, pardon, [illegible].
M'Lysky, Conill and Edm., pardon, [illegible].
MacLyssy, James (Cavanagh ?), pardon, [illegible].
M'Machan, Gillepatrick, pardon, [illegible].
M'Maconnell, Murtough, clerk, pardon, [illegible].
M'Macomygane, Donell, pardon, [illegible].
M'Mage or Goodon, Rich., pardon, [illegible]. See M'Mang.
M'Mahowne, persons of the name pardoned, [illegible].
M'Maghowny, Brian, pardon, [illegible].
M'Magoe, Cormick, pardon, [illegible].
M'Magonell, Owin, grant of land, [illegible].
M'Mahae, Owen, pardon, [illegible].
M'Mahallon, persons of the name pardoned, [illegible].
M'Mahony, Dermot, pardon, [illegible].
M'Mahries, Dermod, pardon, [illegible].
M'Mahon—Mahone—Mahoun—Mahound—Mahounde—Mahoune—Mahown—Mahowne:
„ Aghy m'Gilpatrick, pardon, [illegible], [illegible]; grant of land, [illegible].
„ Ardell, grant of land, [illegible].
„ Ardell m'Colla, pardon, [illegible], [illegible].
„ Art m'Art moyle, remainder man, [illegible]; pardon, [illegible].
„ Art m'Brian, grant, [illegible]; pardon, [illegible], [illegible].
„ Art m'Colla, grant, [illegible]; pardon, [illegible].
„ Art m'Edm., grant, [illegible].
„ Art m'Ever, grant, [illegible].
„ Art m'Gilpatrick, grant, [illegible].
„ Art m'Hugh, grant, [illegible], [illegible].
„ Art m'Hugh roe, grant, [illegible], [illegible]; pardon, [illegible], [illegible].
„ Art fitz Marcus, grant, [illegible].
„ Art fitz Molaghlin, grant, [illegible].
„ Art m'Melaghlin, grant, [illegible].
„ Art m'Phelim, grant, [illegible].
„ Art m'Rory, grant, [illegible]; pardon, [illegible].
„ Art oge m'Rorie, pardon, [illegible], [illegible], [illegible].
„ Art m'Rosse, remainder man, [illegible].
„ Brian (of Farney), pardon, [illegible], [illegible].
„ Brian m'Colla, grant, [illegible]; pardon, [illegible], [illegible].
„ Brian m'Con, grant, [illegible]; pardon, [illegible].
„ Brian m'Edm., grant, [illegible].
„ Brian m'Ever, pardon, [illegible], [illegible].
„ Brian m'Gilpatrick, remainder man, [illegible]; pardon, [illegible].
„ Brian m'Hugh oge, grant, [illegible]; pardon, [illegible]; protection, [illegible].
M'Mahon, Brian m'Hugh roe, grant, [illegible], [illegible]; pardon, [illegible], [illegible], [illegible].
„ Brian fitz James, grant, [illegible]; pardon, [illegible].
„ Brian or Breene fitz Patr., grant, [illegible]; pardon, [illegible].
„ Brian or Breine m'Phelym, grant, [illegible].
„ Brian m'Redmond, grant, [illegible]; pardon, [illegible], [illegible].
„ Brian m'Rory, grant, [illegible], [illegible]; pardon, [illegible], [illegible].
„ Brian ballagh, grant, [illegible].
„ Brian or Breine vally, grant, [illegible].
„ Brian boy, grant, [illegible]; pardon, [illegible].
„ Brian—Breine ne Tuabart, grant, [illegible].
„ Brian or Breene oge, brother of Sir Ross, [illegible]; grant, [illegible]; pardon, [illegible], [illegible].
„ Brian oge m'Hugh, grant, [illegible].
„ Brian roe, grant, [illegible].
„ Chonconaght m'Phelim, grant, [illegible].
„ Cochonaght m'Hugh, grant, [illegible].
„ Coll m'Art, pardon, [illegible].
„ Colla—Cowle—Cowle m'Cowle, grant, [illegible]; remainder man, [illegible]; pardon, [illegible], [illegible].
„ Colla m'Toole, grant, [illegible].
„ Collo m'Bryan, captain of Ferney, pardon, [illegible].
„ Collo—Cowle m'Ever, grant, [illegible], [illegible]; pardon, [illegible].
„ Collo, son of Gilduff, remainder man, [illegible].
„ Collo m'Rosse, grant, [illegible].
„ Con m'Colla, grant, [illegible], [illegible]; pardon, [illegible], [illegible], [illegible].
„ Con m'Gilpatrick, grant, [illegible]; pardon, [illegible], [illegible].
„ Con m'Hugh, grant, [illegible], [illegible]; pardon, [illegible].
„ Con m'Marcus, grant, [illegible].
„ Con m'Redmond, pardon, [illegible], [illegible], [illegible].
„ Con m'Rory, grant, [illegible]; pardon, [illegible].
„ Conoghor m'Conoghor (of co. Clare) pardon, [illegible].
„ Constantin m'Gilpatrick, grant, [illegible].
„ Covenay—Coweaye (of co. Clare) pardon, [illegible], [illegible].
„ Edm. m'Edm., grant, [illegible].
„ Edm. m'Ever, grant, [illegible]; pardon, [illegible].

INDEX TO FIANTS.—ELIZABETH.

M'Mahon, Edm., son of Gildufl, remainder man, [illegible].
„ Edm. m'Molaghlin, grant, [illegible]; pardon, 6761, 6842.
„ Edm. m'Owen, grant, [illegible].
„ Edm. ogo, grant, 6614; pardon, [illegible].
„ Ever, grant, [illegible], [illegible].
„ Ever m'Brian, grant, [illegible]; pardon, 6794.
„ Ever m'Cooly, grant, [illegible]; captain of Farney, 6794; pardon, [illegible], [illegible].
„ Gildufl m'Hugh, grant, 6631; pardon, [illegible].
„ Gildufl fitz Patr., grant, [illegible].
„ Gilleduf m'Edm., grant, [illegible].
„ Gilleduf m'Ever, grant, [illegible]; pardon, [illegible].
„ Gillepatrick m'Molaghlin, grant, [illegible].
„ Gillepatrick m'Philip, grant, [illegible]; pardon, [illegible].
„ Gilpatrick m'Hugh, grant, 6631, [illegible].
„ Gilpatrick ogo m'Gilpatrick, grant, [illegible].
„ Glasney m'Manus, grant, [illegible]; pardon, 6794.
„ Hugh, brother of Sir Ross, [illegible]; attainder, his lands, [illegible], [illegible].
„ Hugh, grant, [illegible].
„ Hugh m'Brian m'Art, grant, [illegible].
„ Hugh m'Brian m'Hugh ogo, grant, [illegible]; remainder man, [illegible].
„ Hugh m'Cowley, grant, [illegible]; pardon, 6794.
„ Hugh m'Coverla, grant, [illegible].
„ Hugh m'Ever, grant, [illegible].
„ Hugh m'Gilpatrick, grant, [illegible].
„ Hugh m'Owen, grant, [illegible]; pardon, [illegible], 6794.
„ Hugh m'Thelym, grant, 6614, [illegible].
„ Hugh m'Rory, grant, [illegible]; pardon, [illegible].
„ Hugh m'Ross, pardon, [illegible]; remainder man, [illegible].
„ Hugh bane, grant, [illegible], [illegible]; pardon, [illegible].
„ Hugh boy, grant, [illegible].
„ Hugh en Killy, grant, [illegible].
„ Hugh ogo, grant, [illegible]; pardon, [illegible], 6794.
„ Hugh roo, grant, [illegible].
„ Hugh roo m'Manus ogo, pardon, 6794, [illegible].
„ James, grant, [illegible].
„ James m'Cowle, grant, [illegible].
„ James m'Edm., grant, [illegible].
M'Mahon, John, grant, [illegible], [illegible].
„ Laghlen m'Brian, grant, [illegible].
„ Magnus og, chaplain, pardon, [illegible].
„ Manus, grant, [illegible].
„ Manus m'Philip, grant, [illegible].
„ Molaghlin, grant, [illegible]; pardon, 6761.
„ Molaghlin m'Brian, grant, [illegible].
„ Molaghlin m'Gilpatrick, grant, [illegible], [illegible]; pardon, 6794.
„ Molaghlin m'Molaghlin, grant, [illegible].
„ Molaghlin fitz Rory, grant, [illegible].
„ Owen m'Agby, grant, [illegible].
„ Owen or Owe m'Brian, grant, [illegible]; pardon, 6794, [illegible], 6794.
„ Owen m'Brian m'Donogh, grant, [illegible]; pardon, [illegible].
„ Owen m'Colla, grant, [illegible]; pardon, [illegible].
„ Owen m'Edm., grant, [illegible]; pardon, 6794, [illegible].
„ Owen m'Gillepatrick, grant, [illegible]; pardon, [illegible].
„ Owen m'Hugh, grant, [illegible]; pardon, [illegible].
„ Patrick m'Agby, grant, [illegible].
„ Patr. m'Art, grant, [illegible]; pardon, 6764.
„ Patr. m'Art moyle, grant, [illegible]; pardon, [illegible].
„ Patr. m'Brian ogo, appointed seneschal of Farney, [illegible]; grant of land, [illegible].
„ Patr. m'Colla, grant, [illegible]; pardon, [illegible], 6794, [illegible], 6794.
„ Patr. m'Con, grant, [illegible]; pardon, [illegible], 6794, [illegible].
„ Patr. m'Edm., grant, [illegible], [illegible]; pardon, 6794.
„ Patr. m'Ever, grant, [illegible]; pardon, [illegible].
„ Patr. m'Hugh, grant, [illegible]; remainder man, [illegible]; pardon, [illegible], [illegible].
„ Patr. m'Hugh ogo, grant, [illegible]; pardon, 6794.
„ Patr. m'Hugh roo, grant, [illegible]; pardon, [illegible].
„ Patr. m'Owen, grant, [illegible], [illegible]; pardon, 6794.
„ Patr. m'Phelim, grant, [illegible].
„ Patr. m'Philip, grant, [illegible]; pardon, [illegible], 6761.
„ Patr. m'Philip ogo, grant, [illegible].
„ Patr. m'Rory, late captain of Farney, pardon to sons of, [illegible].
„ Patr. m'Ross, grant, [illegible], [illegible]; pardon, [illegible], 6794, [illegible].

INDEX TO FIANTS—ELIZABETH.

M'Mahon, Patr. m'Shane, grant, [illegible]; pardon, [illegible].
" Patr. duff, grant, [illegible]; pardon, [illegible].
" Phelim m'Hugh, grant, [illegible]; pardon, [illegible].
" Phelim m'Patr., grant, [illegible]; pardon, [illegible].
" Phelim Skippie, grant, [illegible]; pardon, [illegible].
" Philip m'Edm., grant, [illegible].
" Philip, son of Gildiff, remainder man, [illegible].
" Philip m'Moloughlen, grant, [illegible].
" Philip m'Patr., grant, [illegible].
" Redmond m'Brien, grant, [illegible].
" Redmond m'Gilpatrick, grant, [illegible].
" Redmond m'Rory, late captain of Farney, pardon to his sons, [illegible].
" Redmond m'Rosse, grant, [illegible]; pardon, [illegible].
" Rory, grant, [illegible]; pardon, [illegible].
" Rory m'Art, grant, [illegible].
" Rory m'Cowle, grant, [illegible]; remainder man, [illegible]; pardon, [illegible], [illegible].
" Rory m'Gildiff, remainder man, [illegible].
" Rory m'Hugh oge, grant, [illegible]; remainder man, [illegible].
" Rory m'Hugh roe, grant, [illegible]; pardon, [illegible].
" Rory m'Owen, grant, [illegible], [illegible].
" Rory fitz Redmond, pardon, [illegible].
" Rory m'Rosse, grant, [illegible]; pardon, [illegible].
" Rory m'Tole, grant, [illegible]; pardon, [illegible].
" sir Rosse, commission, [illegible]; surrender and regrant of his lands, [illegible], [illegible].
" Rosse m'Colla, grant, [illegible]; pardon, [illegible], [illegible].
" Rosse m'Manus, grant, [illegible]; pardon, [illegible].
" Rosse m'Patr., grant, [illegible]; pardon, [illegible].
" Rosse m'Rory, grant, [illegible], [illegible]; pardon, [illegible].
" Rosse bane, grant, [illegible]; pardon, [illegible].
" Rosse, pardon, [illegible].
" Shane m'Hugh, grant, [illegible]; pardon, [illegible].
" Shane m'Hugh roe, grant, [illegible].
" Shane duff, grant, [illegible]; pardon, [illegible].
" Teig m'Morogh, seneschal of Corcovaskin, co. Clare, [illegible]; indenture, his lands, [illegible].
M'Mahon, Teig keigh (in co. Clare), pardon, [illegible].
" Thady m'Dermod (of Inchanlie, co. Cork), [illegible].
" Tho. m'James, grant, [illegible].
" Tirlagh (of Moyarta, co. Clare), chief of his name in West Corcovaskin; indenture, his lands, [illegible]; pardon, [illegible].
" Tirlagh m'Aodey, grant, [illegible].
" Toole, grant, [illegible].
" Toole m'Arte, remainder man, [illegible]; pardon, [illegible].
" Toole m'Gildiffe, grant, [illegible].
" Toole m'Meloghlen, grant, [illegible].
" Toole m'Owen, grant, [illegible]; pardon, [illegible].
" Toole m'Phelim, grant, [illegible].
" Toole—Twohill boy, grant, [illegible], [illegible]; pardon, [illegible].
" Toole boy m'Ardell, grant, [illegible].
" Toole boy m'Hugh oge, grant, [illegible]; pardon, [illegible].
" others of the name pardoned (in co. Monaghan), [illegible]; in co. Meath, [illegible]; in co. Clare, [illegible]; elsewhere, [illegible].
" title forbidden, [illegible], [illegible].
" his vice-marshal, [illegible].
" his country (county Monaghan), commission to examine offences committed in [illegible]; customary lands in, [illegible].
" in co. Clare, his lands, [illegible].
M'Mahona boy, Dermod, pardon, [illegible].
M'Mahone. See M'Mahon.
M'Mahonie — Mahony — Mahonye, persons of the name pardoned, [illegible], [illegible], [illegible], [illegible].
M'Mahowne — Mahound — Mahounde — Mahowne. See M'Mahon.
M'Mahounry, Onnaghan, pardon, [illegible].
M'Mahown. See M'Mahon.
M'Mahowne, Tirrelagh roe m'Teig (of Clonderalaw, co. Clare), and others of the name pardoned, [illegible]. See also M'Mahon, Teig.

M'Mahowndo, Callogh, pardon, 4665.
" Tirrelagh (of Moyarta, co. Clare), lands of, 4761.
M'Mahowne. See M'Mahon.
M'Mahowny — Mahowne — Mahowney — Mahownie:
" persons of the name pardoned, 2245, 2764, 2876, 3633, 3787, 3874, 4622, 4722, 4744, 4763, 4781, 4800, 4878, 4818, 4887, 5988, 5789, 6176, 6123, 6238, 6477, 6478, 6488, 6457, 6511, 6527, 6528-48, 6575, 6762, 6764.
M'Maighister, Forgal and Maginimus, pardon, 5166.
M'Malryk, Owen, pardon, 4259.
M'Maister, persons of the name pardoned, 1417, 2271, 4418.
M'Malaghlan—Malaghlin, persons of the name pardoned, 891, 2934, 3942, 4164, 4556, 6174, 6800, 6232.
M'Mulaghlyn, Arthur, pardon, 687.
M'Malaughlin, Shane, pardon, 2894.
M'Malaughlins, Morogh, pardon, 1667.
M'Malcicroragh, Taig, pardon, 4662.
M'Mallaghlin — Mallaghlen, persons of the name pardoned, 1367, 2244, 4626, 6468, 5626.
M'Mallrony, Dermot, pardon, 6467.
M'Mahnoghory, Conner, pardon, 6440.
M'Malrogh, Theobald, pardon, 12.
M'Maltuly, Wm., pardon, 6612.
M'Magannis, Neyne, pardon, 6428.
M'Manes, persons of the name pardoned, 2894.
M'Maneen, persons of the name pardoned, 4578, 6440.
M'Manchan, Gillernow, pardon, 4581.
M'Manw, Wm., pardon, 4967.
M'Manes. See M'Manus.
M'Mangan, Donell, pardon, 4361.
M'Manig Conlon, Richard, attainted, 6173. See Conlon, M'Mang.
M'Manish, Toig, pardon, 5578.
M'Manough, Edm., pardon, 6212.
M'Manny, persons of the name pardoned, 6767.
M'Manus—Manes:
" (of Court, co. Sligo), pardon, 4842.
" Brian m'Art, grant, 5621.
" Patrick oge, chief of his name, pardon, 6714.
" others of the name pardoned, in Fermanagh, 6715; in co. Ross., 4087, 4578, 4798, 6474-6; elsewhere, 448, 656, 871, 1516, 1763, 3387, 4163, 4767, 4793, 4794, 4767, 4843, 4934, 5457, 5494, 5782, 5788, 6478, 6485, 6549, 6558, 6568, 6576, 6583, 6724. See M'Mounus.
M'Mannsroe, Hugh, grant, 5672.
M'Manus, Donald and Hugh, pardon, 5543.
M'Many—Manye, persons of the name pardoned, 4844, 5763, 5682.
M'Manys, Rory, pardon, 3441.
M'Maogre, Dermot, pardon, 3964.
M'Maogh Conlon, pardon, 4357. See M'Mang.
M'Maolillollie logh, Gawen, pardon, 4563.
M'Marcus — Marcinis, Enrias or Hogries, pardon, 6454, 6633.
M'Marcus—Markus:
" Enless or Anyas, pardon, 6731, 6768.
" others of the name pardoned, 2328, 4392, 4549, 4650.
M'Markos—Markos, Brian, pardon, 1851, 5427.
M'Markus, Anyas. See M'Marcus.
M'Marnaght, Hugh, pardon, 6343.
M'Marriell, Cahill, pardon, 444.
M'Marrowy, Concoghor more, pardon, 6562.
M'Martin, Rich., pardon, 6453.
M'Master, Donald lower, pledge for O'Farrall, 5362.
" others of the name pardoned, 4143, 4371.
" See M'Maister, M'Mayster, Mesmaighster.
M'Mastyne, Fems, pardon, 4650.
M'Mathowne, Maurice, pardon, 4484.
M'Maug—Mago—Maugho—Maugo—Maogh—Manig—Mawige—Makmawe Conlon:
" Richard, pardon, 2257, 3484, 3513, 4237, 4408, 4788, 5418; attainted, 6173.
" John, pardon, 6486.
M'Maughono, Morrowe, pardon, 6484.
" Shane, pardon, 2806.
M'Maune, Art, pardon, 4650.
M'Maurice, persons of the name pardoned, 2628, 4832. See M'Morris, &c.
M'Mauric alias Roche, James, pardon, 6928.
M'Mavid, Hugh roe, pardon, 2841.
M'Mawhown, Brien and Donogho, pardon, 3337.
M'Mawhowne, Conor, pardon, 5876.
M'Mawige, Rich. See M'Mang.
M'Mayle, Shane, pardon, 6764.
M'Maylor, Shane, pardon, 4671.
M'Maystor, Morgh, pardon, 4622.
M'Mealmorry — Mcallmorye — Mealmory, persons of the name pardoned, 4354, 4622.
M'meck Bryen, Donogho, pardon, 3164.
M'Meeleke —Mecleke, persons of the name pardoned, 6452.
M'Megnaraght, Toig, pardon, 1807.
M'Mellor, persons of the name pardoned, 101, 1626.
M'meck Bryen, Kennedy, pardon, 6104.

INDEX TO FIANTS—ELIZABETH.

M'Melachlim, Hue, pardon, 4944.
M'Meleghlin—Meleghlen ;
„ Agby m'Donogh, grant, 5642 ; pardon, 5784.
„ Donogh m'Breine, grant, 5642.
„ Philip m'Breine, grant, 5642.
„ Rorie, grant, 5645.
„ Rowe m'Breine, grant, 5642.
„ Rosse m'Donogh, grant, 5642 ; pardon, 5704.
„ Tole m'Breine, grant, 5642.
„ others of the name pardoned, 577, 1479, [illegible], [illegible], [illegible], [illegible], [illegible], [illegible], [illegible], [illegible], [illegible], [illegible], 4018, 4174, [illegible], [illegible], 4441, [illegible], [illegible], 4691, [illegible], [illegible], [illegible], 5163, [illegible], [illegible], [illegible], [illegible], [illegible], [illegible], [illegible], 5516, 5294, 5710, [illegible], [illegible], [illegible], [illegible], [illegible], [illegible], [illegible], [illegible], [illegible], [illegible], [illegible], [illegible], [illegible], [illegible], [illegible], 6374, 6377, [illegible], [illegible], 6704, 6761.
M'Meleghlyn, Cahir, pardon, [illegible].
„ Nelan, pardon, [illegible].
M'Melaughlen—Melaughlin, persons of the name pardoned, 169, [illegible], [illegible], [illegible], [illegible], [illegible], [illegible], [illegible], [illegible], [illegible], 6174, [illegible].
M'Melery, John, pardon, [illegible].
„ Owen, pardon, [illegible].
M'Melleghlen — Melleghlin, persons of the name pardoned, [illegible], [illegible], [illegible], [illegible], [illegible], 5517, [illegible].
M'Mellercy—Mellery, Richard, pardon, [illegible], [illegible].
M'Mellmurrie, Donell and Ferganamin, pardon, [illegible].
M'M.lmogby, Donogh, pardon, [illegible].
M'Melmory, Cole, pardon, 138.
M'Memane, Wm., pardon, [illegible].
M'Menlinilly, Ireall, pardon, [illegible].
M'Menus, persons of the name pardoned, [illegible].
M'Meraine, Rorie, pardon, [illegible].
M'Meran, Bren, pardon, 4944.
M'Meter, Brian, pardon, [illegible].
M'Mewiocke, Laughlin, pardon, [illegible].
M'Meyler, persons of the name pardoned, [illegible], [illegible], [illegible], [illegible].
M'Meylery, Richard, pardon, [illegible].
M'Mic Brian, Conoghor, pardon, [illegible].
M'Mic Con, Donill, pardon, [illegible].
M'Mickle Allester, Ranna, pardon, [illegible].
M'Mighbran, Morertagh, pardon, [illegible].
Mac Milaughlen, Donall, pardon, 1346.
M'Milo, Callogh, pardon, [illegible], [illegible].
„ Walter, pardon, [illegible].
M'Miler, Brien, pardon, [illegible].
M'Millaghalen, Donogh, pardon, [illegible].
M'Mirirle, Hugh, pardon, [illegible].
M'Mloghlin, Rory, pardon, [illegible].
M'Mloghlin cam, Donell, pardon, [illegible].
M'Mohoo, Gillen, pardon, [illegible].
M'Mocloghlen, Cornelius and Thady, pardon, [illegible].
M'Moclemorra, Donogh, pardon, [illegible].
M'Moclmory, Cahill, pardon, [illegible].
M'Moritelly, Cormock and Morietagh, pardon, [illegible].
M'Moel:ally, Hugh, pardon, [illegible].
„ Thady, pardon, 1477.
M'Moeltwly, Dermot, pardon, 4741.
M'Moremen, Magonius, pardon, [illegible].
M'Mornis, Owin, pardon, [illegible].
M'Moenus, Cornelius and Donogh, pardon, [illegible].
M'Moseys, Patrick, pardon, [illegible].
M'Mohowne, Conoghor, pardon, [illegible].
M'Moiertagh, persons of the name pardoned, [illegible].
Mac Moilor, Edm., pardon, [illegible].
M'Moiller, Walter, pardon, [illegible].
„ Wm., pardon, [illegible].
M'Moilmorie, Feariegh and Tirrelagh, pardon, [illegible].
M'Moilmory, Geffry, pardon, [illegible].
M'Moleagh, Wm., pardon, [illegible].
M'Moleghlin, Farr, slain in rebellion, [illegible].
„ others of the name pardoned [illegible], [illegible], [illegible].
M'Moleg, Shane, pardon, [illegible].
M'Molie, Shane, pardon, [illegible].
M'Molloghlen, Art, pardon, 287.
„ Mackrahe, pardon, [illegible].
M'Molmoghery, Gilpatrick, pardon, [illegible].
M'Molmorra, persons of the name pardoned, [illegible].
M'Molmorry, persons of the name pardoned, [illegible].
M'Molmory, persons of the name pardoned, [illegible], [illegible].
M'Molronie oge, Daniel, pardon, [illegible].
M'Molrony, persons of the name pardoned, [illegible], [illegible], 5791.
M'Moltollier, Phyneen, pardon, [illegible].
M'Molsolly, Iroll, pardon, [illegible].
M'Molrilly, Ulleen, surgeon, pardon, [illegible].
M'Mony, Brian and Owin, pardon, [illegible].
M'Moore, Brian, pardon, 5441.
M'Moorne, Dermond, pardon, [illegible].
M'Morache, Morogh, pardon, [illegible].
M'Moragh, persons of the name pardoned, [illegible], [illegible], [illegible], [illegible], [illegible].
M'Moraghe, Hugh, pardon, [illegible].
M'Morasky, Conor, pardon, [illegible].
M'Morch, James and Tirrelagh, pardon, [illegible].
M'Morche, Coreme, pardon, [illegible].
„ Lisagh, pardon, [illegible].

INDEX TO FIANTS—ELIZABETH.

M'Morchie, persons of the same pardoned, 6735.
M'Morcho, Daniel, pardon, 2362.
" Hugh, pardon, [illegible].
M'Morchoe, persons of the same pardoned, 6517.
M'More, Donogh, pardon, 5432.
" Edw., pardon, 6494.
M'Moremrtagh, Teig, pardon, 6403.
M'Morees, Richard, pardon, 1264.
M'Moren, Connor, pardon, 5441.
M'Morertagh, Coghegry, pardon, 4153.
M'Moregh, Hugh, pardon, 5412.
M'Moreigh evacy, Donell, pardon, 6122.
M'Morertagh, Donald, pardon, 2281.
M'Moreogh, Hugh or Effe, pardon, 2972.
M'Morey, persons of the same pardoned, 4794.
M'Morgh, persons of the same pardoned, 155, 3172, 6231, 6451.
M'Morghe, David, grant, 631.
" Lowagh, grant, 671; wounded, 717; pardon, 647, 3798.
" Thady duf, grant, 608.
" others of the same pardoned, 18, 82, 103, 338, 723, 871, 924, 931, 1027, 1832, 3172, 2310, 2745, 4968, 5111, 6170, 6360.
M'Morghie, Teall, pardon, 4729.
M'Morgho, persons of the same pardoned, 894, 1462, 2239, 2561, 3464, 4438, 5069, 6312.
M'Morghane yan, Wm., pardon, 432.
M'Morice, Edm. (in co. Kerry), attainted, 5912.
" Gerald (in co. Kerry), attainted, 6913, 6623.
" James (in co. Kerry), attainted, 6912, 6623.
" Nich. (in co. Kerry), attainted, 6612, 6623.
" Richard, chief of his nation (of Clanmorris, co. Mayo), surrender and regrant of his lands, 4457, 4458.
" Walter oge, late captain of his nation, 4404.
" others of the same pardoned, 448, 1769, 1941, 2254.
M'Morice oge, James, attainder of, 6117.
M'Morice, Edm., pardon, 6497.
M'Moriert, Bran, pardon, 263.
MacMoriert, Cahir, pardon, 287.
M'Moriertie, persons of the same pardoned, 6407, 6623.
M'Moriertagh—Moriertaghe:
" Morogh m'Wm., attainted, 6634.
" others of the name, or patronymic, pardoned, 11, 272, 1482, 1692, 1707, 1884, 2043, 2308, 2377, 2373, 2394,
M'Moriertagh:
2550, 2656, 3431, 3711, 3718, 3773, 3894, 3948, 4013, 4085, 4307, 4454, 4481, 4485, 4584, 4638, 4728, 4752, 4831, 4852, 4970, 4838, 5408, 5428, 5482, 5507, 5485, 5487, 5782, 5888, 6106, 6181, 6183, 6223, 6272, 6184, 6446-7, 6477, 6454, 6505, 6511, 6513-7, 6501, 6503, 6553, 6571, 6577, 6587, 6752-3, 6754-6, 6767.
M'Moriertagh fin, Teig, pardon, 4451.
M'Moriertagh leigh, Ed. balbagh, pardon, 3807.
M'Moriertaugh, David, pardon, 141.
M'Moriertay, persons of the same pardoned, 6741.
M'Moriertie, Arthur, pardon, 2183.
M'Moriertoighe, Morish, pardon, 2394.
M'Moriertih, persons of the same pardoned, 1294, 1353-4.
M'Moriertie, persons of the same pardoned, 1141, 3714, 3830, 4256, 4325, 4452, 4794, 4853, 4163, 4793, 6554.
M'Moriertin, persons of the same pardoned, 6353, 6453.
M'Moriertough, Donald and Shane, pardon, 3660.
M'Morierty, persons of the same pardoned, 3508, 4021, 4373, 6460, 6763.
M'Mories, persons of the same pardoned (in co. Mayo), 5431.
M'Moriety, Donogh, pardon, 6141.
M'Morighe, Cahire (in co. Wex.), indenture, 6796.
" Donogh (in co. Wex.), indenture, 6794.
" Tirrelagh (in co. Wex.), indenture, 6796.
" others of the name pardoned, 6541.
M'Morihertie, Hugh, pardon, 3420.
M'Moriheriagh, Owin, pardon, 4794.
M'Morihertie—Moriherty, persons of the name pardoned, 6462, 6633.
M'Morihie, Thady, pardon, 5088.
M'Morine, Cahill, pardon, 6516.
M'Moririartie, Gerald, pardon, 4321.
M'Moris, persons of the name pardoned, 3497, 3734, 4741, 5014.
M'Morisey, Thos., pardon, 4794.
M'Morish—Morishe:
" a certain (in co. Kerry), attainted, 4862.
" John (of Castle Gerald, co. Mayo), pardon, 4522.
" Morrice m'Morogh (Cavanagh?), attainted, 6620.

INDEX TO FIANTS—ELIZABETH.

M'Morish, others of the same pardoned, [illegible], [illegible], [illegible], 1104, 1184, 1718, 1884, [illegible], [illegible], [illegible], [illegible], [illegible], [illegible], 3161, [illegible], 4018, [illegible], 4028, 4076, [illegible], 4818, [illegible], [illegible], [illegible], [illegible], [illegible], [illegible], [illegible]-3, [illegible], [illegible], [illegible], [illegible], [illegible], [illegible], [illegible], [illegible], [illegible], [illegible], 5614, [illegible], 5797, [illegible], [illegible], [illegible], 6477, [illegible], [illegible], [illegible], [illegible], [illegible], [illegible], 6704. *See* Morish.

M'Morish garo, Ferall, pardon, [illegible].

M'Morisho oge, James (in co. Kerry), attainted, [illegible].

M'Morishoy, persons of the same pardoned, [illegible].

M'Morilagh, Moilor, pardon, [illegible].

M'Moritagh, Garol, pardon, [illegible].

M'Mornylle, Daniel, pardon, [illegible].

M'Morogh—Moroghe:

" Moriertagh (Cavanagh ?), attainted, [illegible].

" Thady or Teag (of Bally Inenagh, co. Gal. or Mayo), attainted, [illegible].

" others of the same pardoned, [illegible].

M'Moroghe, persons of the same pardoned, [illegible], [illegible], [illegible], [illegible], [illegible].

M'Moroghoe, persons of the same pardoned, [illegible], [illegible].

M'Moroghan, Dermot, pardon, [illegible].

M'Moroghowe, Tirlagh, pardon, [illegible].

M'Moroghy, Conor, pardon, [illegible].

M'Moroho, Donogh, pardon, [illegible].

M'Morough—Moroughe, persons of the same pardoned, [illegible], [illegible], [illegible], [illegible], [illegible], [illegible], [illegible], [illegible], [illegible], [illegible], [illegible], [illegible], [illegible], [illegible], [illegible], [illegible].

M'Morough reagh, persons of the same pardoned, [illegible].

MacMoroughoe, Phelym, English liberty, [illegible].

M'Morragh, Brian, pardon, [illegible].

" Teig, pardon, [illegible].

M'Morre, persons of the same pardoned, [illegible], [illegible].

M'Morren, Donell and Marge, pardon, [illegible].

M'Morrece, James, pardon, [illegible].

M'Morren, Owen, pardon, [illegible].

M'Morreo, Fardoragh, pardon, [illegible].

M'Morreragh, persons of the same pardoned, [illegible], [illegible].

M'Morrerty, Teig, pardon, [illegible].

M'Morrey, Edm., pardon, [illegible].

M'Morrghy, Allice, pardon, [illegible].

M'Morrice, persons of the same pardoned, [illegible], [illegible], [illegible], [illegible], [illegible].

M'Morrie, Gilleduff, pardon, [illegible].

M'Morriertagh, persons of the same pardoned, [illegible], [illegible], [illegible], [illegible].

M'Morriertagh backagh, Dermod oorre (of Old Ross), pardon, [illegible].

M'Morrierroghe, Shereboe, pardon, 11.

M'Morries, Phelim, pardon, [illegible].

M'Morrig, Donogho, pardon, [illegible].

M'Morris:

" Thomas, alias ne Marie, pardon, [illegible], [illegible].

" Thomas ne Scarte (Fitzgibbon ?), grant to his granddaughter, [illegible].

" others of the same pardoned, [illegible], [illegible], [illegible], [illegible], [illegible], [illegible], [illegible], [illegible], [illegible], [illegible], [illegible]-8, [illegible], [illegible], [illegible], [illegible], [illegible]-8, [illegible], [illegible], [illegible], [illegible].

" *See* M'Maurice, M'Morice, M'Morice, M'Moris, M'Morish, M'Morrice, M'Morrys, M'Moryah.

M'Morrish, Thomas, son of lord of Lixnaw excepted from pardon, [illegible].

" others of the same pardoned, [illegible], [illegible], [illegible], [illegible], [illegible], [illegible], [illegible], [illegible].

M'Morrishe, Thomas (of Clanmorrice, co. Mayo), pardon, [illegible].

" others of the same pardoned, [illegible], [illegible], [illegible], [illegible], [illegible], [illegible].

M'Morriugh, Donogho, pardon, [illegible].

M'Morritok, Meyler, pardon, [illegible].

M'Morrogh, persons of the same pardoned, [illegible], [illegible], [illegible], [illegible], [illegible], [illegible], [illegible], [illegible], [illegible], [illegible], [illegible], [illegible].

M'Morroghe, Thady or Teig, slain in rebellion and attainted, [illegible], [illegible].

" others of the same pardoned, 18, [illegible], [illegible], [illegible].

M'Morroghin, Donell, pardon, [illegible].

M'Morroghe, persons of the same pardoned, [illegible], [illegible], [illegible], [illegible].

M'Morroho, Dermot, pardon, [illegible].

M'Morrough—Morroughe, persons of the same pardoned, [illegible], [illegible], [illegible], [illegible], [illegible], [illegible], [illegible], [illegible].

M'Morroughe, Donill, pardon, [illegible].

M'Morry, Morogh, pardon, [illegible].

M'Morrye, Tirelagh, pardon, [illegible].

M'Morrys, Edm., pardon, [illegible].

" Garrett, [illegible].

M'Mortagh—Mortaghe, persons of the same pardoned, [illegible].

INDEX TO FIANTS—ELIZABETH.

M'Moriaugh, Gillernow, pardon, [illegible].
M'Moriaughe, Toroneo, pardon, 6718.
M'Morihe, Lysaugh, pardon, 10.
M'Morish, Edm. m'Morish (Cavenagh, of Rathpadisboy), pardon, 6841.
M'Morogh, Morough m'Dermot, attainted, 6634.
„ others of the same pardoned, [illegible], 6118.
M'Moringhe, Fergonandus, pardon, [illegible].
M'Mory, Donell, pardon, 4613.
M'Moryce, Loyragh, pardon, 16.
M'Moryo, Donagh, pardon, 4697.
M'Moryertagh, Dermot, pardon, [illegible].
„ Moylery, pardon, 4611.
M'Moryeh, persons of the same pardoned, [illegible], 6807.
M'Moughe, Dermond, pardon, [illegible].
M'Moulially, Shane, pardon, 5464.
M'Moulinilly, Hugh and Wm., pardon, 4600.
M'Moragh, Hugh, pardon, [illegible].
M'Mourrough, persons of the same pardoned, [illegible].
M'Moville, Donogh, pardon, 4781.
M'Mowllane, Donell and Neil, pardon, [illegible].
M'Moylaghe, Edm., pardon, [illegible].
M'Moylaghlin, Donald, pardon, 170.
M'Moyle, Redmond, pardon, 4443.
M'Moyley, Caell and Moyleghlen, pardon, [illegible].
M'Moyleghe, Maloghlin, pardon, 4578.
M'Moylek, Owen, pardon, [illegible].
M'Moyler, persons of the same pardoned, [illegible], [illegible], [illegible], 4707, 4734, 4781, 4734, 4780, [illegible], 4873, 5457, 5461, [illegible], 5740, [illegible], [illegible], [illegible], [illegible], [illegible], [illegible].
M'Moylere, Ricard, pardon, 4618.
M'Moyleree, Garrett, pardon, 634.
M'Moylesheghlin, Gerald, pardon, 4188.
M'Moylie, Wm., pardon, [illegible].
M'Moylior, Neil, pardon, 1788.
M'Moylmurry, Donell, pardon, 6617.
M'Moyloyde, Wm., pardon, 4078.
M'Moyre, Rich., pardon, 4657.
M'Moyry, James, pardon, [illegible].
„ Shane, pardon, [illegible].
M'Moytholle, Mologhlen, pardon, 4071.
M'Moynes, Morihiriagh, pardon, [illegible].
M'Moyniolly, Donell, pardon, [illegible].
M'Moyriman, Tho., pardon, 4878.
M'Muicheel, Daniel, pardon, [illegible].
M'Muichorrey, Moyiyne, pardon, 4877.
M'Mulbmore. See M'Mulmore.
M'Mulmorie. See M'Mulmory.
M'Mulmory. See M'Mulmory.
M'Mulrone, Teig, pardon, 4602.
M'Mulrony fyne, Laughlen, pardon, 5497.
M'Mulrony. See M'Mulrony.
M'Multully. See M'Multully.
M'Mulmore—Mulmore, persons of the same pardoned, [illegible], [illegible], [illegible], [illegible].
M'Mulmory—Mulmorie—Mulmory—Mulmorye:
„ Edm., attainted, [illegible].
„ others of the same pardoned, [illegible], [illegible], [illegible], [illegible], [illegible], [illegible], 6777.
M'Mulrian, Shane, pardon, [illegible].
M'Mulrone, Cheill, pardon, 4267.
M'Mulrony—Mulrony—Mulronie, persons of the same pardoned, 5475, [illegible], [illegible], [illegible].
M'Mulrony boy — Mulrony boy, Mulrony oge, pardon, 5474, [illegible], [illegible].
M'Mulrony fyn, persons of the same pardoned, 5476, [illegible].
M'Mulronye, Connor, pardon, 6804.
„ Moriaugh, pardon, [illegible].
M'Mulshaughlin, Hugh, pardon, 5111.
M'Multally, Hugh, pardon, [illegible].
M'Multolley, John and Teig, pardon, [illegible].
M'Multolly, Arrtully, pardon, [illegible].
M'Multoly, Thady, pardon, [illegible].
M'Multulloy, Manus, pardon, [illegible].
M'Multully—Multully:
„ Murtagh, surgeon, pardon, [illegible].
„ others of the same pardoned, [illegible], 4648, 5474.
M'Muragh, Edm., pardon, 5461.
M'Murchie—Murchy, persons of the same pardoned, 6774, [illegible].
M'Murgh, persons of the same pardoned, [illegible].
M'Murghe, persons of the same pardoned, 615, [illegible], [illegible].
M'Murghe, Murtagh, pardon, [illegible].
M'Murhie, Teig, pardon, 6777.
M'Murtertagh, persons of the same pardoned, [illegible], [illegible], [illegible], [illegible].
M'Murice, Rorie, pardon, [illegible].
M'Murighe, Torelagh, pardon, [illegible].
M'Murihirle, Diermod, pardon, [illegible].
M'Murine, persons of the same pardoned, [illegible].
M'Murishe, James, pardon, [illegible].
M'Murky, Conoghor and Hugh, pardon, [illegible].
M'Muroghe, Dowghe, pardon, [illegible].
M'Muroghrouhan, Mologhlin, pardon, [illegible].
M'Murragh, Donell, pardon, [illegible].
„ Fear dufie, pardon, [illegible].
M'Murraghe, Shane, pardon, 4101.
M'Murroghy, Murtagh, pardon, [illegible].
M'Murrey, Donogh, pardon, [illegible].
M'Murriartagh, persons of the same pardoned, [illegible].
M'Murrie, persons of the same pardoned, [illegible].
M'Murriortagh, persons of the same pardoned, [illegible], [illegible], 6411, [illegible], [illegible], [illegible].

INDEX TO FIANTS—ELIZABETH.

M'Murrogh, persons of the same pardoned, [illegible], 6334, [illegible], [illegible], [illegible], 6467, 6477, [illegible], [illegible], [illegible], [illegible], [illegible], 6797.
M'Murroghe, Hugh, pardon, [illegible].
M'Murroghe — Murroghoe, persons of the same pardoned, [illegible], [illegible], 4449, 4471, [illegible].
M'Murroghowe, Teig, pardon, [illegible].
M'Murrough, persons of the same pardoned, [illegible], [illegible], 6647, [illegible], 6797.
M'Murrugh, Awlif, pardon, [illegible].
M'Murry, persons of the same pardoned, [illegible], [illegible], [illegible].
M'Murryson, Fellagh, pardon, [illegible].
M'Murtage, Phelim, pardon, [illegible].
M'Murtagh, persons of the same pardoned, [illegible], [illegible], 4476, 4481, 4718, [illegible], [illegible], [illegible], 4797, [illegible], 6181–3, [illegible], [illegible], [illegible], [illegible], [illegible], [illegible], 6511, 6517, [illegible], [illegible], [illegible], [illegible], [illegible], [illegible]–[illegible], [illegible], 6647, [illegible], [illegible], [illegible], 6772.
M'Murtaghe, Lisagh, pardon, [illegible].
M'Murtaigh, Gerald, pardon, [illegible].
M'Murthoe, Neile, pardon, 6710.
M'Murtagh, persons of the same pardoned, [illegible], [illegible], [illegible].
M'Murtaghe, Wm., pardon, 6747.
M'Murtaugh, Art, pardon, [illegible].
M'Murye, Shane, pardon, [illegible].
M'Muitolly, Fynyn, pardon, [illegible].
M'Muti, Donogh, pardon, 6647.
M'Mwrighe, Thady, pardon, [illegible].
M'Mwrihirtagh, Murihirtagh, pardon, [illegible].
M'Mwrihirtie, Teig, pardon, [illegible].
M'Myle, persons of the same pardoned, [illegible]–[illegible].
M'Myler, Theobald, pardon, [illegible].
M'Myles, James, pardon, [illegible].
M'Myline, Donell, pardon, [illegible].
M'Mylinghelen, Donell, pardon, [illegible].
M'Mykel, Wm., pardon, [illegible].
M'Naggagy, Edm., pardon, [illegible].
M'Nahannanghine, Gillepatrick, pardon, [illegible].
M'Nahne, Mahony, pardon, [illegible].
MacNale, Hugh, pardon, [illegible].
M'Nales, Davi, pardon, [illegible].
M'Na Madder, Dermot, pardon, [illegible].
M'Namara, persons of the name in co. Down pardoned, 6712.
„ Teig, pardon, 6474.
„ See M'Namara, M'Namare.
M'Namarro, Donogh, [illegible].
M'Narbenyck, Conoghor, pardon, [illegible].
M'Narye, Dermot and Laghlen, pardon, [illegible].
M'Narym, Gillenanorwe, pardon, [illegible].
M'Nashle, Denis and Edm., pardon, 6711.
M'Naughlane, John, pardon, [illegible].
M'Neal—Neale, persons of the name pardoned, [illegible]–[illegible], [illegible], [illegible], [illegible], [illegible], [illegible], [illegible]–[illegible], [illegible], [illegible].
M'Nealye, Rich., pardon, [illegible].
M'Nehne, Gillepatrick, pardon, [illegible].
M'Nebrye, Dermot, pardon, [illegible].
M'Necollen, Brian, pardon, [illegible].
M'ne Gormane, Bryne, pardon, [illegible].
M'Ne Oranagh, Cormock, pardon, 4741.
M'Ne Croghan, Thady, pardon, [illegible].
M'Neale, Donill and Hugh, pardon, [illegible].
M'Neall, Daniel, pardon, [illegible].
M'Neamee, Clare, pardon, [illegible].
M'Nearall, Neal, pardon, 6647.
M'Negarred, Edw., pardon, [illegible].
M'Negange, Cahell and John, pardon, [illegible].
M'ne Gowne, Carbrie and Conor, pardon, [illegible].
M'Negawne, Gelene, pardon, [illegible].
MacNegawney, Morogh, pardon, [illegible].
M'Negawny, Gillegrome, pardon, [illegible].
M'Negawnye, Felym, pardon, [illegible].
M'Negowny, Melaghlin, pardon, [illegible].
Macnehnanie, co. Gal., [illegible].
M'Neil, Donell, pardon, [illegible].
M'Neile, persons of the name pardoned, [illegible], 1786, [illegible], [illegible], [illegible], [illegible], [illegible], [illegible], [illegible], [illegible], [illegible], [illegible], [illegible].
M'Neill, persons of the name pardoned, [illegible], [illegible], [illegible], [illegible], [illegible], [illegible], [illegible], [illegible].
M'Neille, persons of the name pardoned, [illegible].
M'ne Kelly, Daniel and Dermot, pardon, [illegible].
M'ne Killeh, Donogh, pardon, [illegible].
M'Nele, Toole, grant, [illegible].
„ others of the name pardoned, [illegible], [illegible], [illegible], [illegible].
M'Nell, Hugh, pardon, [illegible].
M'Nely, Donell and Owen, pardon, [illegible].
M'Nema, Brian and Donel, pardon, [illegible].
M'Nemara, persons of the name in co. Down pardoned, [illegible].
„ See M'Nemarra, M'Nemara.
M'Ne Mara—Nemarol. See M'Nemarra.
M'Nemaren, Rowre, pardon, [illegible].
M'Nemarye, Wm., pardon, [illegible].
M'Nemario — Nemaro — Ne maroe. See M'Nemarra.
M'Nemeroff, Thady, pardon, 1297.
M'Nemarra—Ne marra—ne Mara—Ne Mare —Nemarol — Ne marie—Nemaro — Ne maroe — Nemarrey — Nemarraghe — Ne marre—Ne marrow—ne Marrow—Nemarrow—Nemarrow —Nemarry — Ne mary — Ny marie—Nymarry;
„ Donell reogh M'N. Reagh, sheriff of Clare, commission, [illegible]; pardon, [illegible]; indenture, his lands, &c., [illegible]; his heir, [illegible].
„ Donald oge, wardship, [illegible].

INDEX TO FIANTS—ELIZABETH.

M'Nemara, Finen m'Loghlen (of Rosroe), pardon, 1004, [illegible], [illegible].
„ Gilladuf (of co. Down), pardon, [illegible].
„ John (of Moriallen), indenture, [illegible]; wardship of John his heir, [illegible].
„ Shane or John, M'N. Fyn, chief of his name, appointed seneschal of his country, [illegible]; pardon, 1340, 1640, [illegible]; indenture, [illegible]; commission to enquire of his lands, [illegible].
„ Shyda (of Rossroe), pardon, [illegible], [illegible].
„ others of the name pardoned, 1640-1, [illegible], 3046, [illegible].
„ country of (baronies of Tullagh and Bunratty, co. Clare), [illegible], [illegible].
M'Nemarra Fynne, lands belonging to, [illegible]. See M'N., Shane.
M'Nemarra Reagh, lands belonging to, [illegible]. See M'N., Donell.
M'Nemus, Shane, pardon, [illegible].
M'Nemee, persons of the name pardoned, [illegible].
M'Nemy, persons of the name pardoned, [illegible], [illegible], [illegible].
M'Ne Myagh, Teig, pardon, [illegible].
M'Nemye, persons of the name pardoned, [illegible], [illegible].
M'ne Mye, Thady, pardon, [illegible].
M'Neney, Pedreke, pardon, [illegible].
M'ne roy, Edm., pardon, [illegible].
M'Nele, Rorie, pardon, [illegible].
M'Neveslee, Rich., pardon, [illegible].
M'Newen, Loue, pardon, [illegible]. See MacNyvyne.
M'Neyle, Donell, land of (co. Lim.), [illegible].
„ Hugh, murder of, 410.
„ others of the name pardoned, [illegible], [illegible], [illegible], [illegible].
M'Neyle Oighe, Conaiiths, 1008. See O'Neill, Con m'Neile oge.
M'Neyll, Owen, pardon, [illegible].
M'Neylle, Chaill, pardon, [illegible].
„ Owen ... , a Scotsman, English liberty, [illegible].
M'Nicholas, Wm., land mortgaged by, [illegible].
„ others of the name pardoned, [illegible], 2946, [illegible], [illegible], [illegible], [illegible], [illegible], [illegible], 4715-6, 4716, [illegible], [illegible], [illegible], [illegible], [illegible], [illegible], [illegible], [illegible], [illegible], [illegible], [illegible], [illegible].
M'Nicholl, persons of the name pardoned, 1848, [illegible], [illegible], [illegible], [illegible].
M'Nigoyll, Wm., pardon, [illegible].
M'Nikorrie, Donogh, pardon, [illegible].
M'Nobno, Gillise, pardon, [illegible].
M'Nogly, Daniel and Bowl, pardon, [illegible].
M'Nonne, Conchor, pardon, [illegible].
M'Nulae, Donell O'Shelly, pardon, [illegible].
M'Nulle, Art, pardon, [illegible].
M'Nully, Edm., pardon, [illegible].
M'ny Banie, Oyne, pardon, [illegible].
M'Nyca, Kyrrine, pardon, [illegible]. See M'Kyrne.
M'Ny Chertagh, Cahill, pardon, [illegible].
M'Ny Colly, Donogh, pardon, [illegible].
M'ny Fiske, Shane, pardon, [illegible].
M'ny Guby, Shane O'Kellaghan, pardon, [illegible].
M'Nyscarak, Teig, pardon, [illegible].
M'Nyrogy, Donell, pardon, [illegible].
M'Nymarie—Nymarry. See M'Nemarra.
M'ny Moiey, Rob., pardon, [illegible].
M'Nymye, Owen, pardon, [illegible].
M'Nyrin, Mahon, pardon, [illegible].
M'ny Rowe, Brian, pardon, [illegible].
M'Nyese, Kyrroy, pardon, [illegible].
MacNyvyne, Lowe, pardon, [illegible].
M'Oboy—Oboie—Oboye, persons of the name pardoned, 812, [illegible], [illegible].
Macocklan. See M'Coghlan.
M'Ocklore, Murtagh, pardon, [illegible].
M'Oderie, Andrew and Farrall, pardon, [illegible].
M'O'Clery, Hugh, pardon, [illegible].
M'O'Clerye, James, pardon, 1743.
M'Ocanne, Tho., pardon, [illegible].
M'Ode alias Archdeacon, Redmund, pardon, [illegible].
M'O'Donighane, Shane, pardon, [illegible].
M'O'Doran, John, pardon, [illegible].
M'O'Doyle, Gerrot, pardon, [illegible].
M'Oen, Dermod and Donogh, pardon, [illegible].
M'O'Gallavan, Cornelius, pardon, [illegible].
M'Ogmaye, Royney, pardon, [illegible].
M'Oge, Edm., pardon, [illegible].
M'Ogen, Donogh, pardon, [illegible].
M'Oghon, Wm., pardon, [illegible].
Macoghlan. See M'Coghlan.
M'Oyire, Kormock, pardon, [illegible].
MacOgwaynan, Dermod, pardon, 10.
M'O'Hara, Hugh, pardon, [illegible].
M'Oile, Owen, pardon, [illegible].
M'Oin, Owen, pardon, [illegible].
M'O'Kenny, Donogh, pardon, [illegible].
M'O'Kormadie, Dermot, pardon, [illegible].
M'olasie, Henry, pardon, [illegible].
M'Oley, persons of the name pardoned, [illegible].
M'Oliver, James, pardon, 1675.
M'Olivorus, John, pardon, [illegible], [illegible].
„ Nich., pardon, [illegible].
Macollopp—Macolop. See Macollop, co. Wat.

INDEX TO FIANTS—ELIZABETH.

M'O'Molconnere, Oliseh, pardon, 5426.
M'Omore, Rich., pardon, 4677.
M'O'Mollowan, pardon, 1618.
M'One, persons of the name pardoned, 182, 579, 618, 2891, 4704, 4944, 5178, 5628, 6577, 6662.
m'One roe, Teig, pardon, 2102.
M'Oney, Donell, pardon, 6190.
M'Ouffes country (see Slught M'O'Neile), 1782.
M'Oney, persons of the name pardoned, 2148, 2600, 3632, 6402.
M'Onhie, Brien, pardon, 6364.
M'Onhy, Donogh, pardon, 2210.
M'Onhye, Donald, pardon, 2848.
Maconill, Brien, pardon, 6429.
M'Onill, Rory, pardon, 4522.
Maconche, Cormock and Donogh, pardon, 4747.
M'Onnion, Henry, pardon, 5708.
M'Ony, Cormick, pardon, 6761.
" Owen, pardon, 2852.
M'Onye, Conall, pardon, 4129.
Maconoge, Ellinor, pardon, 4676.
M'Onnery, Gohnny, pardon, 1462.
M'Oone, persons of the name pardoned, 2698.
M'Oriesh — M'Hortabo or Dermingham's country (barony of Dunmore, co. Gal), 2278, 3418.
M'Oroncho, Shane, pardon, 1561.
M'Otholin, Rich., pardon, 2364.
M'Oone, Hugh, grant, 4841.
" Molaghlin, grant, 4672.
" Rory, pardon, 4823.
Macouge, Joneek, pardon, 4071.
Macoughlan's country, King's co., martial law in, 2182. *See* M'Coghlan.
Macoughland, Edm., pardon, 2221.
M'Ouin, Morogh, pardon, 1528.
M'Oulmartin, Gillepatrick and Shane, pardon, 4281.
M'Oury, Teig, pardon, 4206.
M'Ovendon, Mulmurre, pardon, 2863.
M'Ovin, Hugh, pardon, 2297.
M'Overrowe (of Oulloc), pardon, 2481.
M'Owan, Tirlagh, pardon, 4900.
M'Owane, Donell, pardon, 6614.
M'Owayle, Maurice, pardon, 3442.
M'Owen, Edm., grant, 5432.
" Loughlen, chief of his name (in co. Leitrim), pardon, 5297.
" others of the name pardoned, 10, 481, 618, 717, 812, 857-8, 884, 887, 857, 841, 894, 1057, 1346, 1416-20, 1540, 1780, 1747, 1880, 2146, 2203, 2208, 2348, 2346, 2387, 2777, 2422, 2584, 2887, 2400, 2820, 3342, 3752, 3828, 3848, 3878-8, 4079, 4059, 4088-70, 4077, 4088, 4101, 4146, 4361, 4403, 2343-4, 3782, 3841, 3884, 3904, 3948-50, 3873-3, 4047, 4058, 4086, 4090, 4152, 4287, 4318, 4433, 4510-1, 4532-4, 4546, 4568, 4576, 4618, 4621, 4631, 4663, 4648, 4672-3, 4678, 4670, 4698, 4691, 4763, 4716, 4734, 4742, 4751, 4780, 4777, 4778-80, 4798, 4885, 4819, 4871, 4886, 4886, 4894, 5028, 5088, 5108, 5112, 5122-3, 5128, 5141-2, 5189, 5167, 5168, 5173, 5196, 5197, 5219, 5427, 5456, 5618, 5633, 5662, 5792, 5902-3, 5916, 5988, 6108, 6110, 6180, 6173, 6181, 6182, 6190, 6197, 6216, 6252, 6262, 6266, 6322, 6336, 6378, 6383, 6406-8, 6440, 6443, 6464-6, 6457, 6468, 6477, 6483, 6487, 6494, 6498-9, 6506-8, 6511, 6517, 6521, 6523, 6532, 6526, 6524, 6541, 6552, 6546, 6558, 6564, 6568, 6565, 6571, 6576-7, 6617, 6648, 6668, 6690, 6680, 6701, 6708, 6731, 6762, 6764-5.
M'Owen oge, Donald, lands of, in co. Kerry, 6152.
M'Owena, Donogh, pardon, 1828.
M'Oweryt, Wm., pardon, 4690.
M'Owoyr, Connor, pardon, 6807.
Macowghlan. *See* M'Coghlan.
M'Owhne, Gerrott, pardon, 6432.
MacOwhney, Teig, pardon, 5561.
M'Owin, Donell m'Fynin, attainted, 5950.
" others of the name pardoned, 1164, 1582, 2148, 2817, 1848, 4069, 5308, 5238, 5173, 5208, 6317, 6349, 6567, 6584, 6629.
M'Owine, persons of the name pardoned, 6448, 6479, 6511.
M'Owle, Mulmorie, pardon, 6532.
M'Owley, Gilleduf and Molaughlin, pardon, 4587.
M'Owly, persons of the name pardoned, 4140, 5458, 6128.
M'Owre, persons of the name pardoned, 312, 2202, 4902.
M'Owne, persons of the name pardoned, 3776, 4462, 5276.
M'Owney, persons of the name pardoned, 2423, 3547, 4106, 4620, 4627, 4723.
M'Owni, Teig, pardon, 5059.
M'Owrale, persons of the name pardoned, 4478, 5180, 5164.
M'Owraigh, Dermod, pardon, 2618.
M'Owraly, Donogh, pardon, 4686.
M'Owralye, Shane, pardon, 4717.
M'Owray, persons of the name pardoned, 1148, 1874, 2708, 4798, 4898, 5078, 6162, 6519, 6784.
M'Owrye, Shane, pardon, 6714.
M'Owry, Brian, pardon, 1818.

INDEX TO FIANTS—ELIZABETH.

M'Owyn, persons of the name pardoned, 6346, 6478, 6562.
M'Owyne, Donell and Henry, pardon, 6714.
M'Owyny, Edm., pardon, 6614.
M'Oyen, Oyen, pardon, 4987.
M'Oygane, Donell, pardon, 4918.
M'Oyne, Donell, pardon, 4814.
" Donogh, pardon, 6818.
M'Paden, persons of the name pardoned, 611, 2867, 4037, 4361.
M'Padin, Moylion, pardon, 6346.
M'Padrykyn, Peter, pardon, 2966.
M'Padyn, persons of the name pardoned, 4286, 6617, 6761.
M'Palyne, Dermot, pardon, 1178.
M'Pally, Bruno, pardon, 6317.
M'Parlane, Guy, pardon, 6736.
M'Parlon, persons of the name pardoned, 6446.
M'Parralan, Moyleasurry, surgeon, pardon, 6617.
M'Parrholan, Pharrell, pardon, 6158.
MacParson, Donogho and Moirrors, pardon, 1771.
M'Parson, Tho., pardon, 6464.
M'Patrick, persons of the name pardoned, 2146, 4411, 4780, 5412, 5827, 6326, 6464, 6727.
M'Patrigin, Edm., attainted, 6117.
" John, attainted, 6117.
M'Pattrick, persons of the name pardoned, 6412, 6318, 6571, 6847.
M'Pattrickine, Shane, pardon, 6488.
M'Peake, Dermot and Manus, pardon, 6761.
M'Peiron, Edm., pardon, 6768.
" Edmond, pardon, 6384.
M'Peires, Philip, pardon, 4843.
M'Peirs, persons of the name pardoned, 4812, 4672, 6483, 6617.
M'Peres, Kedenseb, grant of land, 614.
M'Pers, Donell, pardon, 1864.
" Edm., pardon, 2864.
M'Persemon, Patr., pardon, 5488.
M'Person, persons of the name pardoned, 1868, 4468, 4761, 6363, 6617. See M'Eparson.
M'Phaderough, Cahir and Neyle, pardon, 6462.
M'Phale, James, pardon, 4814.
M'Phally, Shane, pardon, 1868.
M'Phaly, Brian, pardon, 4152.
M'Phelan, Thady, pardon, 5836.
MacPhelim, Murtagh boy, indenture, 6788.
M'Phelan, persons of the name pardoned, 839, 4283, 6271, 6548.
M'Phelemy, Dermod roe, 4673, 6467.
" Donell, pardon, 6762.
M'Phelim, James, lands of, 6326.
" persons of the name pardoned, 63, 1748, 2765, 3723, 3844, 3978, 5641, 4207, 4406, 4826, 4863, 4818, 4820,
M'Phelim:
5408, 6661, 5764, 5368, 6182, 6261, 6464, 6468, 6617, 6532, 6566, 6371, 6647, 6782, 6784.
M'Phelime, Teig, pardon, 4914.
M'Phelimey, Fynine, pardon, 6761.
M'Phelimy, Dermod, pardon, 6511.
" Donell, pardon, 6871.
M'Pheline, Shane, pardon, 4740.
M'Phelm, Ferdoragh, pardon, 3660.
M'Phelym, persons of the name pardoned, 22, 717, 1626, 5462, 2377, 3381, 5763–4, 3886, 4198, 4266, 4686, 5478, 5766, 6617.
M'Phelym boy, Rory and Tyrrelagh, pardon, 6672.
M'Phelym reogh, Toole, grant, 5428.
M'Phelyme, persons of the name pardoned, 4187, 6404, 6517.
M'Phelymie, Donell, pardon, 6811.
M'Phelymy, Donell, pardon, 6946.
" John, pardon, 6823.
M'Pheylyme, Cormack, pardon, 6482.
M'Philabbune, Tho., pardon, 6678.
M'Philbin, Walter, pardon, 6866.
M'Philbyn, Walter, pardon, 2884.
M'Phillibane, Edm., Gilleduff, and Richard, pardon, 6678.
M'Phillibaren, Reward, pardon, 6678.
M'Philip, Bruine m'Morogh (M'Mahon?), grant, 5424.
" Gerrott, attainted, 4123.
" Henry (M'Mahon?), grant, 5424.
" Nele (M'Mahon?), grant, 5426.
" others of the name pardoned, 3076, 4464, 4618, 4510, 4578, 4584, 4684, 5643, 5608, 5814, 6366, 6368, 6447, 6467, 6470, 6187, 6497, 6562, 6534, 6566, 6571, 6577, 6847, 6737.
M'Philipp, Edm., pardon, 3542.
M'Phillabbane, Lyshagh, pardon, 6678.
M'Phillan, Donell, pardon, 4161.
M'Phillemie, Cormock, pardon, 6418.
M'Phillip, Ardell, grant, 5643.
" Edmund, attainted, 6447.
" others of the name pardoned, 677, 2842, 2465–6, 2263, 2752, 2517, 2514, 2780, 4364, 4621, 4762, 5861, 5414, 4768, 6363, 6464–6, 6467, 6563, 6576, 6567, 6784.
M'Phillipe, Donald, pardon, 2078.
M'Phillipen, Shane, pardon, 4581.
M'Phillipp, John boy, slain in rebellion (co. Mayo), 4864.
" Morris, land of (co. Cork), 4626.
" others of the name pardoned, 3674, 4184, 4381, 4866, 5408, 5467, 5488, 6467.
M'Phillippe, persons of the name pardoned, 1036, 4073, 4466, 4534, 4843, 6470, 6678.

INDEX TO FIANTS—ELIZABETH.

M'Phillippine, Walter roe, pardon, 5677.
M'Phillips, Teig, pardon, 6166.
M'Philliots, Davy, pardon, 4630.
M'Phillipine, Walter, pardon, 6793.
M'Phorice, Donogh, pardon, 1883.
M'Phylip, Gerald, pardon, 5784.
M'Phyllippine, Meylery, pardon, 6452.
M'Phylye, Rory, pardon, 5621.
M'Pierce, Donell, pardon, 4318.
" Farrell, pardon, 5428.
M'Piers, persons of the same pardoned, 578, 1944, 5482, 4021, 4111, 5517.
M'Pilbin, Meyler, pardon, 4028.
M'Piris, Moris, pardon, 5718.
M'Prior, persons of the name pardoned, 1474, 5078, 4818, [illegible], 6164, 5523, 6110, 6528, [illegible].
M'Qoaid, Maurice, pardon, 4742.
M'Qoanrgan, Colle, pardon, 6348.
M'Qoigean, Donell, pardon, 6784.
M'Quiegon, persons of the name pardoned, 6452, 6616.
M'Quiegin, Phelim, pardon, 6818.
M'Quigine, Donill, pardon, 5736.
M'Quilline, Rich., pardon, 6651.
" *See* M'Quilline, MacQuyllis, M'Quylly, M'Ullin, Maquillyne.
M'Quin, Gillpatrick, pardon, 4831.
" Owen, pardon, 5401.
M'Quine, Murrogh, pardon, 6112.
MacQuire, Murtagh, pardon, 2894.
M'Quirke, Rob., pardon, 6452.
M'Quist, Sherrone, pardon, 4587.
M'Quoad, Art and others of the name, grant of land, 5471.
M'Quoade, John, pardon, 6452.
" Nele, pardon, 4823.
M'Quoine, Keler, pardon, 3738.
M'Quoyne, persons of the name pardoned, 547, 4571, 6146.
M'Qurokan, Taig, pardon, 5494.
M'Quyggine—Quyggine, persons of the name pardoned, 6718.
M'Quylline, Cormock and Rorie, pardon, 6632.
M'Quylly, Tibbott, chief of his nation, appointed seneschal of the Rowte, co. Antrim, 4232.
M'Quyllyne, Folym and Wm., pardon, 6828.
M'Quyn, Owin, grant, 5607.
" others of the name pardoned, 4081, 4680, 4768, 4083, 5713, 6314, 6188, 6478, 6513, 6452, 6762.
M'Quyne, persons of the name pardoned, 461, 6082, 6478.
M'Quynegan, Wm., pardon, 6412.
M'Quynn, Tho., pardon, 6488.
M'Quynne, persons of the name pardoned, 85, 6226.
M'Qwier, Connor, pardon, 5361.
M'Qwin, Murogh duff, attainted, 5660.
M'Qwoyne, Shane, pardon, 6648.
M'Qwyn, Edm., pardon, 5718.
M'Qyrike, Ullyck, pardon, 6494.
M'Rabe, Edw., pardon, 6188.
M'Raigell, Donell, pardon, 5423.
MacRandal boye—Ranell boye, Alexander, captain of the Scots, pardon, 188, 583.
" Gillespick, pardon, 188, 583.
M'Ranell. *See* M'Donnell.
M'Ranell boy. *See* MacRandal boye.
M'Ranill, Mollymory, pardon, 4832.
M'Rannell—Ranell:
" Cahill (of Inchmory, co. Leitrim), pardon, 5442.
" Tirlagh (of Dromard), pardon, 5441.
" others of the name pardoned, in co. Leitrim, 5441-2; elsewhere, 4828, 4397, 5444, 6180, 6177, 6516, 6523, 6540, 6577, 6734.
M'Ranold, James, pardon, 6486.
M'Ranyle, Naghten, pardon, 5762.
M'Rame, Donald, pardon, 1883.
Macraweil, Shane, pardon, 6711.
M'Reall, Edm., pardon, 6204.
M'Reard, Callagh and Henry, pardon, 5678.
M'Rerkard, Shane, pardon, 6462.
M'Red, Henry, pardon, 6612.
M'Redie, Donogh, chaplain, pardon, 6668.
M'Redmond—Redmund—*Redmonde*:
" Hubert boy (of Castleton, co. Gal.), grant of land, 4807; pardon, 6002.
" Hubert boy, pardon, 4878.
" Richard Ena, son of M'R., pardon, 4081.
" Wm. fitz Richard M'Redmond, pardon, 3484, 4071; his son, 4081.
" of Bally Ily, sept of, co. Gal., 4807.
" others of the name pardoned in cos. Gal. and Mayo, 3494, 4083, [illegible], 4396, 5471, 4578, 4616, 4778, 6795, 4474, 5000, 5401, 5518, 6523, 6108, 6096; elsewhere, 871, 1145-6, 2228, 3728, 3768, 4485, 4876, 4871, 5023, 5468, 5615, 5318, 6417, 6460, 6484, 6488, 6498, 6580, 6623-4.
M'Redmond kieghe, Shane, attainted, 6137.
M'Regan, Teig, pardon, 6851.
M'Reilly, Donell, pardon, 6816.
M'Reirie, persons of the name pardoned, 5488, 6183, 6618.

INDEX TO FIANTS.—ELIZABETH.

M'Remon, persons of the same pardoned, 4[illegible], 5[illegible].
" See M'Creamyne, M'Kremon.
M'Remond, Edm., pardon, 4[illegible].
M'Reoghan, Moregh, pardon, 4[illegible].
M'Reorie, Teig, pardon, 6[illegible].
M'Reory, Teig, pardon, [illegible].
M'Reorye, Donell, pardon, 6[illegible].
M'Reyle, Breen, pardon, 6[illegible].
" Conoghor, pardon, 6[illegible].
M'Rery, Donell, pardon, 6[illegible].
" Teig, pardon, 4[illegible].
M'Rerye, Philip, pardon, [illegible].
" Wm., pardon, [illegible].
M'Reynal, Theobald, pardon, 6[illegible].
M'Reynie, Mahon, pardon, 6[illegible].
M'Reynol, Tibbot, pardon, [illegible].
M'Reyry, Eugene or Owen, chaplain, pardon, [illegible].
" others of the same pardoned, 4[illegible], 4[illegible], 6[illegible].
M'Reyske, Conoghor, pardon, 4[illegible].
M'Rhideane, Gerrott, pardon, 6477.
M'Ricard, Everan (of Inver, co. Mayo), slain in rebellion, [illegible].
" Rich. (of Garranmuck, co. Mayo), traitor, [illegible].
" others of the same pardoned, [illegible], [illegible], 4[illegible], [illegible], [illegible], [illegible], [illegible].
M'Ricarde, persons of the same pardoned, 4[illegible], 4[illegible], 4[illegible], 4[illegible], 4[illegible].
m'Ricard ogo, Thady m'Dermod (M'Charlie ?), pardon, [illegible].
M'Ricard, Tho. duff (co. Kerry), attainder of, [illegible].
" others of the same pardoned, [illegible], [illegible], [illegible], 4[illegible], [illegible], [illegible], [illegible], [illegible], [illegible], [illegible].
M'Rievanie, Cornelius, pardon, [illegible].
" Giliduff, pardon, 4[illegible].
" Kenelie, scholar, pardon, 4[illegible].
M'Ricort, Fair, pardon, 6[illegible].
M'Richard—Richarde, Gerald, lands of (in co. Lim.), [illegible], [illegible].
" John, attainder (in co. Kerry), [illegible].
" others of the same pardoned, 16, 17[illegible], 1[illegible], [illegible], [illegible], [illegible], [illegible], [illegible], [illegible], [illegible], 4[illegible], 4[illegible], 4171, 4[illegible], 4[illegible], [illegible], [illegible], [illegible], [illegible], 4[illegible], [illegible], [illegible], 4[illegible], [illegible], [illegible], 4[illegible], 6[illegible].
M'Richard boy, Redmund, pardon, 4[illegible].
M'Richin, Dermot, pardon, [illegible].
M'Rickard, Eugenius or Onby (of Arlen), pardon, [illegible].
" Rich., attainted (co. Mayo), [illegible].
" others of the same pardoned, 4[illegible], [illegible], [illegible], [illegible], [illegible], [illegible], [illegible], [illegible], [illegible], [illegible], [illegible], [illegible].
M'Rickarde, Morris, pardon, [illegible].
M'Rickerd, Wm., pardon, 4412.
M'Rickdery, Walter, pardon, [illegible].
M'Riddrie, David and Wm., pardon, [illegible].
M'Rierie, Dermod, pardon, [illegible].
M'Rikerd, Shane, pardon, 4[illegible].
M'Rikerd ogo, Wm. duff (of Dromkyne, co. Lim.), pardon, [illegible].
M'Rinkey, Gerrot, pardon, 4[illegible].
M'Rinkie, John, pardon, [illegible].
M'Riory, Teig, pardon, 4[illegible].
M'Ristard, persons of the same pardoned, [illegible], [illegible].
M'Ristere, James, pardon, [illegible].
M'Risterd, persons of the same pardoned, 1176, [illegible].
M'Riddick, Donill and Edm., pardon, [illegible].
M'Robert, persons of the same pardoned, [illegible], [illegible], 4[illegible].
M'Robin, Moragh, pardon, 1747.
M'Robin killogh, Edm. and Shane, pardon, [illegible].
M'Robert, Shane, attainder (co. Kerry), [illegible].
" others of the same pardoned, [illegible], [illegible], [illegible], [illegible], [illegible], [illegible], 4[illegible], 4[illegible], [illegible], [illegible], [illegible], [illegible], [illegible], [illegible], [illegible], [illegible], [illegible], [illegible], [illegible].
M'Robinson, Edm. Barry, pardon, [illegible].
M'Robinson, John fitz Edm., pardon, [illegible].
M'Robinstowne, Gerrot, pardon, [illegible].
M'Robistone, Gerald, pardon, 4[illegible].
M'Robistowne, Wm., pardon, [illegible].
M'Robistowne, Wm. m'Edm., pardon, [illegible].
M'Robuck, persons of the same pardoned, [illegible], [illegible].
M'Robug, Ricard, pardon, [illegible].
M'Robuge, John fitz Wm., pardon, 6[illegible].
M'Robye, Murgh, pardon, [illegible].
" Shane, pardon, [illegible].
M'Rochtery, Edm. and James (co. Mayo), pardon, 6[illegible].
M'Roddry, Fair, pardon, [illegible].
M'Rodery, Gerald FitzGerald, pardon, [illegible].
" Wm., pardon, [illegible].
" persons of the same pardoned (co. Mayo), [illegible].
M'Roery, Teig, pardon, [illegible].
Macromp—Macrowny (Macroom), co. Cork, [illegible]; manor, 6[illegible]. See Mocrome, Muckrampy, Muckromby.
Macroney, co. Cork. See Moyerum, Mocronagho, Moghroney, Muckrony.

INDEX TO FIANTS—ELIZABETH.

M'Roury, Wm., pardon, [illegible].
M'Roory, Rome, pardon, 4331.
M'Rorie, Ever, captain of Kilwarlin. *See* M'Rory.
" Moroogh, indictment of, 5[illegible].
" others of the name pardoned, 451, [illegible], 4[illegible], 4[illegible], 4[illegible], 4[illegible], 4[illegible], 4[illegible], 4[illegible], 4[illegible], 4[illegible], 4[illegible], 4[illegible], 4[illegible], 4[illegible], 4[illegible], 4[illegible], 6[illegible], 5[illegible], 5[illegible], 5[illegible], 5178, 5814, [illegible], 5667, 5712, 5747, 5[illegible], 6612, [illegible], 6[illegible], 6[illegible], 6[illegible], 6[illegible], 6[illegible], 6[illegible], 6[illegible], 6[illegible], 6477, 6[illegible], 6[illegible], 6511, [illegible], 6[illegible], 6[illegible], 6641, [illegible], 6[illegible], 6[illegible], 6[illegible], 6674, [illegible], [illegible], [illegible], 6[illegible], [illegible], 6[illegible], [illegible], 6724, 6794.
M'Rorrie, Teig, pardon, 6[illegible].
M'Rory—Roryo:
" Ever, chief of Kilwarlin, co. Down, surrender and regrant of his land, 4[illegible]-[illegible].
" others of the name pardoned, [illegible], 9[illegible], [illegible], 1279, 1[illegible], [illegible], [illegible], [illegible], [illegible], [illegible], [illegible], [illegible], [illegible], [illegible], [illegible], 3677, [illegible], [illegible], [illegible], [illegible], [illegible], [illegible], [illegible], [illegible], [illegible], [illegible], 4183, [illegible], [illegible], [illegible], [illegible], 4701-2, 4[illegible], 4731, 4[illegible], 4[illegible], 4777, 4[illegible], 4[illegible], 4944, 5073, 5100-1, 5[illegible], 5[illegible], 5[illegible], 5[illegible], 5[illegible], 5311, 5[illegible], 5[illegible], 5[illegible], 5[illegible], 5797, 5[illegible], 6[illegible], [illegible], [illegible], 6[illegible], [illegible], [illegible], 6[illegible]-7.
M'Rory oge, Teig, pardon, [illegible].
M'Rory rioogh, John, pardon, [illegible].
M'Rory roe, Rome, pardon, [illegible].
M'Rory roe, Owen and Tirrelagh, pardon, [illegible].
M'Ross, Ferdorogh, pardon, [illegible].
M'Rosse, Rory (M'Mahon ?), grant, [illegible].
" others of the name pardoned, 1[illegible], 481, 812, [illegible], [illegible], [illegible], [illegible], [illegible], [illegible], [illegible], 3776, [illegible], [illegible], [illegible], 4[illegible], [illegible], [illegible], [illegible].
M'Rosse roe, Edm., pardon, [illegible].
M'Rossey, persons of the name pardoned, [illegible].
M'Rossie, Donaghie Enecasmaton, pardon, [illegible].
M'Rosyp—Rosyn, persons of the name pardoned, [illegible], [illegible], 4[illegible], 6[illegible], [illegible].
M'Rothero, Shilie, pardon, [illegible].
M'Roury, Donald, pardon, [illegible].
M'Rowrie, Wm., pardon, [illegible].
Macroway (Macroom), [illegible]. *See* Macroomp.
M'Rowrie, persons of the name pardoned, [illegible], [illegible], 4[illegible], [illegible], [illegible], [illegible], [illegible].
M'Rowry, persons of the name pardoned, 1[illegible], [illegible], [illegible], [illegible], [illegible], [illegible], [illegible], [illegible], [illegible].
M'Rowrye, Cahell, pardon, [illegible].
M'Roynhe, Cormock, pardon, 748.
M'Ruddorie, Gerrot, pardon, [illegible].
" Margaret, pardon, [illegible].
M'Ruddery, Edm., pardon, [illegible].
" Thomas, Knight of the Valley, his lands granted to his heir, [illegible].
" Thomas fitz John, Knight of the Valley, attainted, [illegible].
" Thomas, attainted (co. Lim.), [illegible].
" Thomas macDavid, his lands custodiam (co. Lim.), [illegible].
M'Rory, Donell and Donogh, pardon, [illegible].
M'Ruchiell, Ruchiell oge, pardon, [illegible].
M'Ruskien, Shanchastie, pardon, [illegible].
M'Russick, Edm., pardon, [illegible].
M'Ruyley, Mulaghlin, pardon, [illegible].
M'Rwory, Shane, pardon, [illegible].
M'Ryeard, Teig, pardon, [illegible].
M'Ryeard, Hebbert and Shane, pardon, [illegible].
M'Rydery, Edm. and John, pardon, [illegible].
M'Rykard, Auly, pardon, [illegible].
M'Rynode, Shane, pardon, [illegible].
M'Sabirribe, Conogher, pardon, [illegible].
M'Sakerran, Donell, pardon, [illegible].
M'Saoraly, persons of the name pardoned, [illegible].
M'Sarlen, John Roche, pardon, [illegible].
M'Savall, persons of the name pardoned, [illegible], [illegible].
M'Sawerty, Rory, pardon, [illegible].
M'Sawerty, Randall, pardon, [illegible].
M'Scally, Donell, vicar, pardon, [illegible].
" Gillegrume, pardon, [illegible].
" Thady, pardon, [illegible].
M'Scally, Hugh, pardon, [illegible].
M'Seen, persons of the name pardoned, [illegible].
M'Searnan, Donogh, pardon, 4[illegible].
M'Sehaye, Teig, pardon, 471[illegible].
M'Senaghan, Donell, pardon, [illegible].
M'Seonyn, Tho., pardon, [illegible].
M'Sere, Murtagh, pardon, [illegible].
M'Seraly, Connor, pardon, [illegible].
M'Shane, Wm. (of Lisnageran, co. Gal.), pardon, [illegible].
M'Shaffrie, Wm., pardon, [illegible].
M'Shaharan, Conoghor, pardon, [illegible].
M'Shain, Teig, pardon, [illegible].
M'Shaine, persons of the name pardoned, [illegible], [illegible].
M'Shaine boye, land in tenure of, [illegible].
M'Shanaca, Shane, pardon, [illegible].
M'Shanrowe, Wm., pardon, [illegible].
M'Shan, persons of the name pardoned, [illegible], [illegible], [illegible], [illegible], [illegible].
M'Shan vale, Maurice, pardon, [illegible].

INDEX TO FIANTS.—ELIZABETH.

M'Shane, Dermot, robbery from, [illegible].
" Donald, attainted (co. Gal.), [illegible].
" Edm., indenture (co. Wex.), [illegible].
" Edm. oge m'Edm. (of Killoscurragh, co. Lim.), pardon, 6774, [illegible].
" Gibbon roe, attainted (co. Lim.), [illegible].
" Hugh, lands in co. Cork, [illegible].
" Moriah m'Edm., attainted, [illegible].
" Owen, indenture, [illegible].
" others of the name, or patronymic, pardoned, 10, [illegible] … 6765, [illegible], 6769, 6770, 6775, 6777.
M'Shane, Slough, in O'Madden's country, co. Gal., [illegible].
M'Shane bane, Wm., pardon, [illegible].
M'Shane boddy, Tirrelagh, pardon, [illegible].
M'Shane bog, Gerald or Garrett, [illegible], 4671.
M'Shane boye's lands (in co. Lim.), [illegible].
M'Shane boy, Shane oge, pardon, [illegible].
M'Shane boy, Shane boy m'Wm., attainted (in co. Gal.), [illegible].
M'Shane bwye, David and others, pardon, [illegible].
M'Shane duff, Derby, pardon, [illegible].
M'Shane glas, Hugh duff, pardon, [illegible].
" Philip and others, pardon, [illegible].
MacShane glasse, Conall, war upon, [illegible]; pardon, [illegible].
M'Shane les—lyogh, Rich., pardon, [illegible].
M'Shane maniagh, Thady, pardon, [illegible].
M'Shane oge, Gibbon roe, attainted (in co. Lim.), [illegible].
" Hubert, and others of the name in co. Gal., [illegible], 5112.
" Morris, land of (in co. Lim.), [illegible].
" Maurice, and others of the name in co. Kerry, [illegible].
M'Shane sallagh, Wm., pardon, [illegible].
M'Shane's lands, co. Kerry, [illegible].
MacShanekyne, Tho., pardon, [illegible].
M'Shanelay, persons of the name pardoned, [illegible].
M'Shanely, persons of the name pardoned, [illegible].
M'Shanew, John, pardon, [illegible].
M'Shanley, persons of the name pardoned, [illegible].
M'Shanly, persons of the name pardoned, [illegible].
M'Shore, Melaughlen, pardon, [illegible].
M'Sharra, persons of the name pardoned, [illegible].
M'Sharrie, Donogh, pardon, [illegible].
" Teig, pardon, [illegible].
M'Sharran, Cahill, pardon, [illegible].
M'Sharry, Hugh and Redagh, pardon, [illegible].
M'Shea, persons of the name pardoned, [illegible].
M'Sheain, Henry and Shane, pardon, [illegible].
M'Shremes, Rich., pardon, [illegible].
" Wm., pardon, [illegible].
M'Shean, persons of the name pardoned, [illegible].
M'Sheane, persons of the name pardoned, [illegible].
M'Sheane more, John oge, pardon, [illegible].
M'Shenaicke, Dermot, pardon, [illegible].
M'Sheuran, Redmund, pardon, [illegible].
M'Sheary, persons of the name pardoned, [illegible].
M'Sherrie, Conohor, pardon, [illegible].
M'Sheurie, persons of the name pardoned, [illegible].
M'Sheriby, Gullypatrick, pardon, [illegible].
M'Sherry, Wm., pardon, [illegible].
M'Shenyn, Melaghlin, pardon, [illegible].
M'Shesloy, Dave and Tho., pardon, [illegible].
M'Shedie, Matthew or Malon, pardon, [illegible].
M'Shee, Owen m'Brien, attainted, [illegible].

INDEX TO FIANTS—ELIZABETH.

M'Shee, Owen m'Edm. oge, attainted, [illegible].
„ Rorry, English liberty, 14[illegible].
„ Rory, lands of (co. Lim.), [illegible].
„ others of the same pardoned, [illegible], [illegible], [illegible], [illegible], 6178, [illegible].
M'Sheehe, Tirlagh m'Edm. oge, land of, co. Lim., [illegible].
M'Sheehie, Donogho, pardon, [illegible].
M'Shehegham, Donell, pardon, [illegible].
M'Shehey, Ferdorough, pardon, [illegible].
M'Shehi, persons of the same pardoned, [illegible], [illegible].
M'Shehie, Conoghor oge, land of, co. Lim., [illegible].
„ John, land of, co. Lim., [illegible], [illegible].
„ Manus megiegan m'Edm. oge, pardon, [illegible].
„ Manus oge, pardon, [illegible].
„ others of the same pardoned, [illegible], [illegible].
M'Shehy, Manus, indenture, [illegible].
„ others of the same pardoned, [illegible], [illegible], 4844, [illegible], 4712, [illegible], [illegible], [illegible], [illegible].
„ See also M'Shiehie, M'Shihie, M'Shihy, M'Shyhy.
M'Shehye, Manus knogh, pardon, [illegible].
M'Shei, persons of the same pardoned, [illegible], [illegible].
M'Sheikish, John, pardon, [illegible].
M'Sheman, Oale, pardon, [illegible].
„ William, pardon, [illegible].
M'Shenitta, Owin, pardon, [illegible].
M'Shenus, Cormock, pardon, [illegible].
M'Sheoagh, Conor, pardon, [illegible].
M'Sheoaghan, Owen, pardon, [illegible].
M'Sheoeigh, Edm., pardon, [illegible].
M'Sheonlermine, Tho. roe, pardon, [illegible].
M'Sheomaghe, Tyrlagh, pardon, [illegible].
M'Sheonin, John, pardon, [illegible], [illegible].
M'Shere, Gillpatrick, pardon, [illegible].
M'Sheragh, Owen and Teig, pardon, [illegible].
M'Shere, persons of the same pardoned, [illegible], [illegible], [illegible], [illegible].
M'Sheres, William, pardon, [illegible].
M'Sherhown, Richard and Ulick, pardon, [illegible].
M'Sheroon, Gillpatrick, pardon, [illegible].
M'Sherotn, Hubert, pardon, [illegible].
M'Sheron, persons of the same pardoned, [illegible], [illegible], [illegible], [illegible], [illegible], [illegible].
M'Sherone, Moleghlin and Teig, pardon, [illegible].
M'Sherowen, Ulick, pardon, [illegible].
M'Sherowne, Gerald, pardon, [illegible].
M'Sherrin, Redmond, pardon, [illegible].
MacShoyzy, Donill and Eugenius or Owen, pardon, [illegible].
M'Shiames, Rich., pardon, [illegible].
M'Shiarhie, persons of the same pardoned, [illegible], [illegible].
M'Shiarhy, Teig, pardon, [illegible].
M'Shiarie alias Hodnet, James, pardon, [illegible].
M'Shiarihie, alias Haddenot, James, pardon, [illegible].
M'Shiarry, Awlitte, pardon, [illegible].
M'Shiclie, Donell and Wm., pardon, [illegible].
M'Shide, Donell, pardon, [illegible].
„ Teig, pardon, [illegible].
M'Shidan, Shane, pardon, [illegible].
M'Shide, persons of the same pardoned, [illegible], [illegible].
M'Shidie, Dermod, pardon, [illegible].
M'Shie, Manus and Morgh, pardon, [illegible].
M'Shiede, Morertagh, pardon, [illegible].
M'Shieh, Owen, pardon, [illegible].
M'Shiehie, Tirlagh m'Edm. oge, attainted, [illegible].
„ Murogh m'E[ ] oge, pardon, [illegible].
„ Owen, pardon, [illegible].
M'Shiemis, Nich. Barry, pardon, [illegible].
M'Shighie, Dermod, pardon, [illegible].
„ Edm. yvalligh, pardon, [illegible].
M'Shihe, persons of the same pardoned, [illegible], [illegible], [illegible].
M'Shihi, Edm. and Moriertagh, pardon, [illegible].
M'Shihie, Donogh, attainted, [illegible].
„ Edm. oge fitz Edm., pardon, [illegible].
„ Manus Naglogguis, pardon, [illegible]. See M'Shehy.
„ Miler or Molmory, pardon, [illegible].
„ Morogh (of Ballyaliman), pardon, [illegible].
„ Owen or Eugenius m'Edm. oge, attainted, [illegible], [illegible].
„ Rory (of Ballyalinan), pardon, [illegible].
„ Rory (of Blarny), pardon, [illegible].
„ Rory or Ferdorogh, pardon, [illegible].
„ Rory m'Murogh, pardon, [illegible].
„ Tirlagh m'Edm. oge, attainted, [illegible].
„ others of the same pardoned, [illegible], [illegible], [illegible]-7, [illegible], [illegible], 4734, [illegible], [illegible], [illegible], [illegible], [illegible], [illegible], [illegible], [illegible], [illegible], [illegible]-[illegible], [illegible], [illegible], [illegible]-[illegible], [illegible], [illegible], [illegible], [illegible], [illegible], [illegible], [illegible], [illegible], [illegible], [illegible], [illegible], [illegible]-[illegible].
M'Shihy—Shihye:
„ Edm. oge (of Robertstown, co. Lim.), pardon, [illegible].
„ Moanas m'Ferdorogh, pardon, [illegible].
„ Moriertagh m'Edm., pardon, [illegible].
„ Moriertagh m'Morghe (of Malla), pardon, [illegible].
„ Rory (of Ballyaliman), pardon, [illegible], [illegible]. See M'Shihie.

INDEX TO FIANTS—ELIZABETH.

M'Shiby, Thriagh m'Edm. oge, pardon, 2274. See M'Shichie, M'Shyby.
" others of the name pardoned, 2274, 6810, 2780-1, 3842, 4462, 4614, 6467, 6464, 6497. See M'Shehy, M'Shichie, M'Shyby.
M'Shichie, Manus, pardon, 6958.
M'Shilie, Murogh, pardon, 6176.
M'Shin, John, pardon, 6408.
M'Shittorie—Shittrie, Donogh, pardon, 6515, 6770.
M'Shittery, Teig, pardon, 6568.
M'Shoong, Henry, pardon, 4678.
M'Shone, Shane, pardon, 6541.
M'Shonoken, Hugh and Thomas, pardon, [illegible].
M'Shonokyn, Owen, pardon, 4857.
M'Shonikin, persons of the name pardoned, 6458.
M'Shonyne, Dermod, pardon, 6469.
M'Shooryn, Donill, pardon, 5728.
M'Shordane, Edward and Rory, pardon, 5075.
M'Shorry, Gillepatrick, pardon, 6478.
M'Shordan, Donogh, pardon, 2784.
M'Shorrim, persons of the name pardoned, 4584, 4733, 6682.
M'Shoriayne, Conan, pardon, 6817.
M'Shorton, Cahir, pardon, 4733.
M'Shyane (M'James), James Barry, pardon, 2947.
M'Shydae, persons of the name pardoned, 6615.
M'Shyddy, persons of the name pardoned, 6462.
M'Shyde, Teig, pardon, 6618.
M'Shydye, Rory merigagh, pardon, [illegible].
M'Shyn, Don, pardon, 4462.
M'Shyhie, Manus, pardon, 2778.
" Moriertagh, pardon, 6782.
M'Shyby—Shyhye:
" Fardorogh, pardon, 6472.
" Manus og, pardon, [illegible]. See M'Shehy.
" Morogh m'Edm., pardon, 2846, 5468.
" Owen m'Edm. oge, pardon, 6468.
" Tewage m'Edm. oge, pardon, 6468.
" others of the name pardoned, 2268, 2274, 6468, 6476, 6482.
M'Shymon, persons of the name pardoned, 6467.
M'Shyanan, Brian, pardon, 6628.
M'Shyumc, Collaogh, pardon, 4718.
M'Sid, Brian, pardon, 188.
M'Side, Donoghe, pardon, 4734.
" Hugh, pardon, 4674.
M'Sidie, Donald, pardon, 3042.
M'Sihi, Owen, pardon, 2274.
M'Sihi, Wm., pardon, 4264.
M'Sihie, Rowry, pardon, 2274.
M'Siby, Moroghe m'Edm. oge, pardon, 2274.
" Muriagh m'Edm., pardon, 2846.
" others of the name pardoned, 2271, 2846.
M'Simon, Farall, pardon, 6450.
M'Senckine, Rich., pardon, 6612.
M'sir Fualime, Fyrogynanye, pardon, [illegible].
M'Sirry, Rorie, pardon, 6652.
M'Skulle, Brian, pardon, 6674.
M'Skallamol, Shane, pardon, 6894.
M'Skallie, Donell, pardon, 4467.
" Teig, pardon, 5740.
M'Skelly, Gyrive, pardon, 6652.
M'Skealtin, Teig, pardon, 6462.
M'Skoly, Conchor, pardon, 2884.
M'Skolog, Eugenius, priest, pardon, 4698.
M'Sleredden, Shane, pardon, 6470.
M'Slevyn, David, pardon, 4108.
" Gerald, pardon, 1057.
M'Sonrly, Rory, pardon, 5768.
M'Soine, Morogh na mart, pardon, 6423.
M'Soirly, Cormock, pardon, 6738.
M'Sowny, persons of the name pardoned, 4671, 4668, 4683, 4868.
M'Sowaye, Browne and Donell, pardon, 4585.
M'Sowykeyll, persons of the same pardoned, 4683.
M'Stephen, persons of the name pardoned, 5768.
M'Stephin, Dermot, pardon, 6681.
" Gilpatrick, pardon, 2268.
M'Steyney, Dermot, pardon, 2881.
MacStino, Conoghor, pardon, 4682.
M'Suffe, Oyle, pardon, 2212.
M'Suine, Cavatius or Collre, pardon, [illegible].
M'Sulevan, Dermond, pardon, 6460.
M'Sulligulle, Donell, pardon, 6811.
M'Surley, James, pardon, 6708.
M'Suyn, Donell, pardon, 4727.
M'Suyny, Brian oge (of Courthrack), pardon, 2941.
" Molmory, pardon, 4482.
M'Swayne, Morroghe, pardon, 4444.
M'Swenagh, Moyle moriorogh, pardon, [illegible].
M'Swine. See M'Sweyne.
M'Swinie, Donell and Molmorie, pardon, 6811.
M'Swiney, Owen, pardon, 5468.
M'Swiny, Rory, pardon, 6467.
" Thriagh, pardon, 6814.
M'Swny, Brien, pardon, 4101.
M'Swnye, Manus and Rorie, pardon, 6460.
M'Sweyne, Brien, pardon, 6288.
M'Swyne, Connor, pardon, 4686.
" Thriegh, pardon, 6468.
M'Swyllyhugh, Shane, pardon, 4698.

INDEX TO FIANTS—ELIZABETH.

M'Swyn, persons of the same pardoned, [illegible], [illegible], 4727, 6434.

M'Swyne—Swine:

" Brian (of co. Sligo), pardon, [illegible], [illegible].

" Brian m'Moylemory, pardon, [illegible], [illegible].

" Brian ballagh, pardon, [illegible].

" Brian oge dal., pardon, [illegible].

" Collo (of Killishy, co. Clare), pardon, [illegible]. See M'Swyny.

" Donald m'Morogh, pardon, [illegible].

" Donell, M'S. Fanad, pardon, [illegible].

" Donell m'Owen keoghy, pardon, [illegible].

" Donell oge (of Ballycashan), pardon, [illegible].

" Edm. (of Rowelrum, co. Cork), pardon, [illegible].

" Edm. doroho or doragh (co. Gal.), pardon, [illegible], [illegible].

" Hugh (of Cloghcromman), pardon, [illegible].

" James (of Ballicottle, co. Sligo), pardon, [illegible].

" Maurice or Morogh, pardon, [illegible].

" Mailmory m'Donogh baccagh, pardon, [illegible], [illegible].

" Molmory m'Ony, pardon, [illegible].

" Moylmory m'Edm., pardon, [illegible].

" Mulmory or sir Myles, M'S. of Toe, surrender and regrant of his lands, [illegible], [illegible]; obtains custody of adjoining country, [illegible]; pension, [illegible].

" Mulmory (in co. Sligo), pardon, [illegible], [illegible], [illegible].

" Naslaerus, pardon, [illegible].

" Owen og, M'S. na Duah, pardon, [illegible].

" Owen m'Tirlagh (of Kanturk), pardon, [illegible].

" others of the same pardoned, [illegible], [illegible], [illegible], [illegible], 2045, [illegible], [illegible], [illegible], [illegible], [illegible], [illegible], [illegible], [illegible], [illegible], [illegible], 4075, [illegible], [illegible], [illegible], [illegible], [illegible], [illegible], [illegible], [illegible], [illegible], [illegible], [illegible], [illegible], [illegible], [illegible], [illegible], 4777, [illegible], 6761.

M'Swyne Banaght — M'Swine Banaghie, country of, [illegible], [illegible].

" See M'Swyne bamy.

M'Swyne Fanad — Fanat — Faunott — Fanaghte, Donel, pardon, [illegible]; his son hostage for O'Donell, [illegible].

" country of, [illegible], [illegible], [illegible], [illegible].

M'Swyne na Duah—ne doe—Edoe—Doghe, Owen og, pardon, [illegible]; his son hostage for O'Donell, [illegible].

Mulmory, knight, surrenders his land, [illegible]; regrant, [illegible]; grant of custody of neighbouring countries, [illegible]; pension, [illegible].

" country of, [illegible], [illegible].

M'Swyne ny Bryn, Gildaf, pardon, [illegible].

M'Swynes galloglasses, pardon for, [illegible], [illegible].

M'Swynoo, Mulmorry, pardon, [illegible].

M'Swyney, Mary, pardon, [illegible].

" Owen, pardon, [illegible].

M'Swynie. See M'Swyny.

M'Swyne bamy, Donagh, pardon, [illegible].

M'Swyny—Swynie—Swyuye:

" Brian m'Donell (of Kadirid), pardon, [illegible].

" Brian m'Owen y leghie, pardon, [illegible].

" Brian ballagh m'Moelmory, pardon, [illegible].

" Brian oge m'Brian duffe, pardon, [illegible], [illegible].

" Brian og duffe, pardon, [illegible].

" Collo (of Killey), pardon, [illegible].

" Crevan, pardon, [illegible].

" Donald or Donell m'Owen (of Macroom), pardon, [illegible], [illegible].

" Donell m'Owen y leskie (of Macroom), pardon, [illegible].

" Donell m'Owen (of Moscmghan), pardon, [illegible].

" Edmund (in co. Cork), pardon, [illegible]; a pardon granted at his suit, [illegible].

" Edm. m'Gullaluff, pardon, [illegible].

" Erevan—Barywan m'Morogh, pardon, [illegible], [illegible].

" Gohyre m'Donoughy, pardon, [illegible].

" Hugany (of Cloghrowan, co. Gal.), pardon, [illegible].

" Owen m'Tirrelagh backagh, pardon for his men, [illegible].

" Tirrelagh oge, pardon, [illegible], [illegible].

INDEX TO FIANTS—ELIZABETH.

M'Swyny, others of the name pardoned, 2148, 2234, 2364, 2334, 2841, 3081, [illegible], 3941, 4728, 4418, [illegible], 4297, [illegible], 4397, 4414, 4416, 4427, 4481, 4487, 4462, 4494, [illegible], 4616, 4647, 4714, 4734, 4752, 4764, 4807, 5050, [illegible], 5178, 5632, [illegible], 6168, 6305, 6314, 6465-7, 6468, 6175, 6423, 6468, 6465, 6512, 6514-6, 6516, 6528, 6542, 6534, 6544, 6563, 6568, 6571, 6615, 6626, 6635, 6695, 6704, 6763, 6765, 6767, 6770.
M'Sy, Rory, pardon, [illegible].
M'Syda, persons of the name pardoned, 1817, 4736, 4651.
M'Sydy, Owen, pardon, [illegible].
M'Sydy wanty, Donald, pardon, 1548.
M'Sye, Darby, pardon, 4810.
M'Syhy, Rory, lease, 3417.
M'Symon, persons of the name pardoned, 878, [illegible], 3792, [illegible], 4544, [illegible].
M'Syno, Collo, pardon, 4678.
M'Sythy, Manus and Morogh, pardon, 4418.
Mac-taggard, pardon to all of the name, [illegible].
M'Tane, Ellen, pardon, 4764.
M'Tarellagh, Terellagh, pardon, 5152.
M'Tarvale, James, pardon, [illegible].
M'Terrean, Tirrelagh, pardon, [illegible].
M'Tearrelly, Kenalle, pardon, [illegible].
M'Tebbot, persons of the name pardoned, 6152.
M'Tebot, Edm., pardon, [illegible].
M'Tobote, John, pardon, 4690.
M'Tobot, Redmund, pardon, 4425.
M'Tee, Cormack, pardon, 4667.
MacTege, Mahon, freehold of, [illegible].
M'Tege, persons of the name pardoned, 144, 1613, 2760, [illegible], 3602, 4164, 4731, 6691, 6794.
M'Teig—Teige:
„ Awly (of Glanfleak), pardon, [illegible].
„ Donogh roe, slain in rebellion, [illegible].
„ Donyll, indenture, 6708.
„ Garrett, vicar, pardon, 6510.
„ Matthew, pardon, 5797.
„ Morris m'Owen, lands of, granted (co. Kerry), 4943.
„ Morris m'Owen (of Ballymore, co. Kerry), pardon, 6464.
„ Tho. oge m'Brien, attainted, [illegible].
„ Wolstey m'Donogh, pardon, 2241.
„ others of the name, or patronymic, pardoned, 11, 83, 144, [illegible], 615, [illegible], 478, 446, 481, 912, [illegible], 997, [illegible], 1183, 1621, 1870, 1575, 1626, 1663, 1697, 2085, 2148, 2293, 2336, 2348, 2387, 2304, 2338, 2348, 2512, [illegible], [illegible], [illegible], [illegible], 2446, 3069-70, 3094, 3151, [illegible], [illegible], 3413, 3476, 3438, 3542, 3783-4, 3787, [illegible], 3844, 3851, 3843, 3924, [illegible], 4694,
M'Teig:
4654, 4095, [illegible], 4014, 4049, [illegible], [illegible], 4092, 4186, 4349, [illegible], 4316, [illegible], 4414, 4416, 4424, [illegible], 4427, [illegible], 4612, [illegible], 4542, [illegible], [illegible], 4574, [illegible], [illegible], [illegible], 4610, 4619-3, 4616-20, [illegible], 4642, [illegible], 4650, 4673, 4678-6, 4679-80, [illegible], [illegible], 4699, 4700, 4707, 4711, 4714, 4716, 4727, 4743, 4761, 4763, [illegible], [illegible], [illegible], [illegible], 5022, 5094, [illegible], 5075, 5161, [illegible], 6443, 6447, 5600, 6607, [illegible], [illegible], [illegible], 6094, 5608, 5614, [illegible], 5657, [illegible], 5740, 5759, [illegible], [illegible], [illegible], 6108, 6116, [illegible], 6178-4, 6182, 6189, 6191-2, [illegible], [illegible], 6214, [illegible], [illegible], 6278, [illegible], 6457, 6478-8, 6436, 6450, 6453-3, [illegible], 6462, 6465, 6467, 6468-70, 6477, 6478, [illegible], 6494, 6497-8, 6500-1, [illegible], [illegible], [illegible], 6617, 6618, [illegible], [illegible], [illegible], [illegible], [illegible], 6646, [illegible], 6648, [illegible], [illegible], [illegible], 6664, [illegible], 6671, 6676-7, [illegible], 6617, 6634, 6637, 6647, [illegible], [illegible], [illegible], [illegible], [illegible], 6702, 6708, 6727, 6733, 6761, 6763, 6764, 6768, 6778.
M'Teige duf, Gallough and Donald m'Cahir owre, pardon, 6894.
M'Teige high, Tirrelagh duff M'Dermot, pardon, 4448.
M'Teige leagh, Brien and Edm., pardon, 5161, 5451.
M'Teige oge, Cahire, indenture, 6766.
„ Melaughlen, attainted, [illegible].
„ Teig m'Dermodie, pardon, 6418.
M'Teige riough, Donyll duff, indenture, [illegible].
M'Teige ryogh, Donell, pardon, [illegible], [illegible].
M'Teigg, Cahir and Tirrelagh, pardon, [illegible].
M'Teirnan, Farrice and Teirnan, pardon, 5452.
M'Terrolagh, Thady, pardon, 4467.
M'Terrligh, Torrlagh, pardon, 3468.
M'Terlagh—Terlaghe, persons of the name pardoned, 4316, 5488, 5418, [illegible], [illegible].
M'Terlagh, Mahon, pardon, 6178.
M'Ternan, persons of the name pardoned, 4677, 5428-40.
M'Terrane, Teig, pardon, 6408.
M'Terrelagh, Morogh M'Bryan, lord of Granagh, lands of, [illegible].
„ persons of the name pardoned, 2617, 3768, 4394, 4743, [illegible], 6401, 6451, 6667.
M'Terrelaghe, Owen, pardon, 4657.
M'Terrellagh, Hugh, pardon, [illegible].
M'Terrelly, Patr., pardon, [illegible].
M'Terrens, Patrick, pardon, 3744.
M'Tey, Owen and Shane, pardon, 4497.
M'Theobald, persons of the name pardoned, [illegible], 4038, 6078.

M'Theobald, persons of the name pardoned, [illegible].
M'Therelloke, Donoghe, pardon, [illegible].
M'Thirelagh, Brein, pardon, [illegible].
M'Thirrelagh, Conoghor, pardon, [illegible].
M'Thirrely, persons of the name pardoned, [illegible], [illegible].
M'Thomas, Donogh, tenement of, 6117.
„ Edm., [illegible]. See Fitzgerald, Edm. fitz Tho.
„ Garrot, attainted, 5171.
„ Gerald (of Ballygohan), pardon, [illegible].
„ Gerald, lands of, [illegible], 6317.
„ Gerald (Dillon?), pardon, [illegible].
„ Gibbon, land of, [illegible].
„ John, attainted (co. Kerry), 5012, [illegible].
„ John m'Ulick, lands granted (co. Kerry), 4042.
„ John oge, attainted (co. Kerry), 5012.
„ John oge, lands granted (co. Wat.) [illegible].
„ Jordan, pardon (co. Mayo), [illegible].
„ Ricard attainted (co. Kerry), 6117.
„ Richard fitz Tho. (Fitzgerald) (of the Palace, co. Lim.), slain in rebellion with Desmond, [illegible]; attainted, 5140, [illegible], [illegible], [illegible].
„ Shane oge m'Shane, attainted (co. Kerry), [illegible], [illegible], 6117. See John oge.
„ Thomas m'Richard (Fitzgerald), of the Palace, co. Lim., pardon, [illegible], [illegible]; mortgage by, [illegible].
„ Ulick, attainted, co. Kerry, [illegible].
„ Wm. alias M'Arrenbeddie, pardon, [illegible].
„ of the Pallyne, co. Lim., lands of, granted, [illegible]. See M'T., Richard and Thomas.
„ others of the name pardoned, [illegible], [illegible], [illegible], [illegible], 1708, [illegible], 1690, [illegible], [illegible], 2144, [illegible], [illegible], [illegible], [illegible], [illegible], [illegible], [illegible], [illegible], [illegible], [illegible], 2734, [illegible], [illegible], [illegible], [illegible], [illegible], [illegible], [illegible], [illegible], [illegible], [illegible], [illegible], [illegible], 4109, [illegible],
M'Thomas: [illegible], [illegible].
M'Thomas duffe, Theobald, attainted (co. Mayo), [illegible].
M'Thomas oge, Edm. (of Skrine, co. Ross.), attainted, [illegible].
M'Thomas roo[illegible], Richard (co. Lim.), attainted, 5171.
M'Thomas, persons of the name pardoned, 4361.
M'Thyrrelye, Nyell, pardon, [illegible].
M'Tibali, Pierse and Rob., pardon, [illegible].
M'Tibbald, Gilleduff, pardon, [illegible].
M'Tibbalde, Shane and Tho., pardon, [illegible].
M'Tibbot, Hubert boy, pardon, [illegible].
M'Tibbold, Tho., pardon, [illegible].
M'Tibbot, Walter (of Cruagh, co. Mayo), pardon, [illegible]; attainted, [illegible].
M'Tibbot—Tibbott, persons of the name pardoned, [illegible], [illegible], [illegible], [illegible], [illegible], [illegible], [illegible], [illegible], [illegible], [illegible], [illegible], [illegible], [illegible]. See also Slight vic Tibbot.
M'Tibbot reagh, Moyler, a traitor, [illegible].
M'Tibbot's land, co. Gal., [illegible].
M'Tibold, Walter, pardon, [illegible].
M'Tibot, Shane, pardon, [illegible].
M'Tibott, Hubert, pardon, [illegible].
M'Tiege, Edm., pardon, [illegible].
M'Tierane—Tiernain, Ferrall (of Clinloghe), pardon, [illegible].
„ Hugh (of Loghreddy), pardon, [illegible], [illegible].
„ others of the name pardoned, [illegible], [illegible], [illegible], [illegible], [illegible], [illegible], [illegible].
M'Tiernane, Joffrey and John, pardon, [illegible].
M'Tiernayn, Teig, pardon, [illegible].
M'Tiernayne, Con, pardon, [illegible].
M'Tiraller, Hugh, pardon, [illegible].
M'Tirelagh, Ferragh, attainted, [illegible].
„ others of the name pardoned, [illegible], [illegible], [illegible].
M'Tirelaugh, Donogh and Edm., attainted, [illegible].
M'Tirelogh, Donogh and Shane, pardon, [illegible].
M'Tireloghe ro, Hugh. See M'Tirrelaghe roe.
M'Tirlagh, Donogh (M'Donnell?), pardon, [illegible].
„ Morogh m'Brien, attainted, [illegible].
„ others of the name pardoned, [illegible], [illegible], [illegible], [illegible], [illegible], [illegible], [illegible], [illegible], [illegible], 4143, [illegible], [illegible], [illegible], [illegible], [illegible], [illegible], [illegible], [illegible], [illegible], [illegible], [illegible], [illegible], [illegible], [illegible],

INDEX TO FIANTS—ELIZABETH.

M'Tirlagh; 6219, 6352, 6453, 6459, 6461, 6464, 6473-4, 6478, 6487, 6488, 6494-6, 6523, 6578, 6536, 6560, 6577, 6583, 6627, 6647, 6660.
M'Tirlagh roe, Hugh, 2804. See O'Connor.
M'Tirlaghe, Charles or Callagh, grant of land, 498.
" Diermot, pardon, 671.
" Morogh, pardon, 2108.
M'Tirlaugh, persons of the same pardoned, 4518, 5128, 6408, 4533, 6658.
M'Tirlay, Gillernow, pardon, 4104.
M'Tirlogh, persons of the same pardoned, 6912, 5174, 4976, 6184, 6765, 4680.
M'Tirloghe, Donogh, pardon, 1767.
" Rory, pardon, 1767, 3480.
M'Tirnane, Connor, pardon, 1486.
M'Tirrolagh, Tirlagh, pardon, 6102.
M'Tirreghe, Mochmarrie, pardon, 6704.
M'Tirrelagh—Tirlagho—Tyrrelagh, Callogh, Callough, or Charles (M'Donnell) (of Tinnakilly, Queen's co.), grant of land, 498; pardon, 668, 1094; livery to his heir, 1715.
M'Tirrelagh, Callogh. See M'Donnell.
" Calogh, pardon, 2817.
" Omlaghe m'Wm., attainted, 6993.
" Molaghlin, indenture, 6782.
M'Tirrelagh—Tirrelaghe, others of the same pardoned, 423, 857, 867, 1044-5, 1169, 1179, 1258, 1874, 2520, 2362, 2461, 2845, 2784, 3739, 3834, 3977, 3804, 4149, 4287, 4412, 4944, 4584, 4783, 4860, 5088, 5842, 6323, 6400, 6480, 6727.
M'Tirrelagh meriagh, Dermod (of Arran island), pardon, 6977.
M'Tirrelaugh, Connor, pardon, 845.
M'Tirrelaughe, Edm., pardon, 671, 6162.
" James, pardon, 6162.
M'Tirrelaughe roe—Tirelaghe ro, Hugh (O'Connor?), leases, 5166, 6180. See also O'Connor.
M'Tirrelogh, Teig m'Donogh, pardon, 6077.
M'Tirreloy, Edm., pardon, 4783.
M'Terrelig, Mahon, pardon, 4462.
M'Turell, persons of the same pardoned, 6464.
M'Tirrelly, Muriertagh, pardon, 6464.
M'Tirrely, Donogh and Phelim, pardon, 6765.
M'Tirrilogh, persons of the same pardoned, 1964.
M'Tirvlagh, Bren, pardon, 5642.
" Tomoltagh, pardon, 6480.
M'Tivrelaughe, Farrell, pardon, 678.
M'Tlen, Shane, pardon, 6460.
M'Toholl, Wm., pardon, 5075.
M'Tohill, persons of the same pardoned, 5173.
M'Tomalagh, Donald, pardon, 6112.
MacTomcon, Fair., pardon, 1890.
M'Tomelyn, Tomelyn oge, pardon, 6761.
M'Tomen, Maur. and Morogh, pardon, 5401.
M'Tomlin, Fulim, pardon, 6656.
M'Tomock, Rich. more Burke, pardon, 4402.
M'Tomolin, Donell, pardon, 4617.
M'Tomoltagh, Owen and Tho., pardon, 6814.
M'Tomolin, Thady, pardon, 4444.
M'Tomolty, persons of the same pardoned, 3842, 4890.
M'Tomultagh, persons of the same pardoned, 6941, 5147, 6488, 5818.
M'Tomulty, Morogh, pardon, 4780.
" Tomultagh, pardon, 4702.
M'Tomylin, Cahir and Hugh, pardon, 6761.
M'Tomyn, persons of the same pardoned, 5078, 6174.
M'Toole, persons of the same pardoned, 4444.
M'Tornie, John, pardon, 4764.
M'Torrilagh, Donogh, pardon, 4088.
M'Torrine, John, pardon, 6158.
M'Towchie, Nele, pardon, 6062.
M'Towle, Manus, pardon, 4868.
M'Trione, Marchow, pardon, 4860.
M'Trughtie, Henry, pardon, 6078.
M'Tuahell, Onnarlagh, pardon, 6108.
M'Tulogh reoch, Dudmund, pardon, 4538.
M'Tumolagh, Owen m'Teig, pardon, 5841.
M'Tumultagh, persons of the same pardoned, 5447, 5481, 6824, 6160, 6779.
M'Tumyn, Ricard, pardon, 5078.
M'Tuney, Donell, pardon, 6671.
M'Turlaghe, Morogh ballagh, pardon, 5478.
M'Turlo, Brian, pardon, 6640.
M'Turlogh, Shane, pardon, 5944.
M'Turlough, Donogh, pardon, 5964.
M'Twaill, Brian, pardon, 4482.
M'Twelowgh, Phelim, pardon, 10.
M'Twayne, Owyn, pardon, 4778.
M'Twohell, Donell, pardon, 6761.
M'Twohill, Tirlagh, pardon, 4604.
M'Twolagh, Conoghor m'Teig I Moretagh, pardon, 6638.
M'Twey, James, pardon, 4780.
M'Tybbot reoghe, Moyler, attainted, 6636.
M'Tybbott, Nich., pardon, 6382.
" Rob., pardon, 4674.
M'Tybole, Tho., pardon, 4880.
M'Tyorman, Geoffrey, pardon, 4470.
" Tirlaugh, pardon, 6761.
M'Tymolly, Edm., pardon, 4288.
M'Tympany, persons of the same pardoned, 2264.
M'Tyrelagh, Dermot, attainted, 6890.
M'Tyrell, Donogh, pardon, 4183.
M'Tyrlagh, persons of the same pardoned, 4169, 4602, 4817.

INDEX TO FIANTS—ELIZABETH.

M'Tyriaugh, Lisagh, pardon, 168.
M'Tyriough, Colley, pardon, 6168.
M'Tyrrelagh, Callowagh, 1718. See M'Tirrelagh.
" Hugh, livery, 1718.
" others of the name pardoned, 847, 2292, 2818, 4182.
M'Tyrrely, Donogh, pardon, 5808.
M'Uilin, Rorie (M'Quillin), pardon, 4188.
" See M'Uin.
M'Uisigiom, Teig, pardon, 5740.
M'Ulick, persons of the name pardoned, 4078, 4698, 4874, 5467, 5488, 6418, 5689, 5956, 6477-8, 6486, 6427-8, 6518.
M'Ulick barye, Edm., pardon, 4596.
M'Uligo, Redmund, pardon, 4348.
M'Ulik, Tho., pardon, 6914.
M'Ulkn, Walter, pardon, 4842.
M'Ulin, Rory oge, pardon, 2413.
M'Ullemoi, Cormlagh, pardon, 5388.
M'Ullerdyne, Ullick, pardon, 5768.
M'Ullio, Moyler, pardon, 4474.
M'Ullick—Ullicke:
" Shane m'Edm., attainted, 4898, 6172.
" others of the name pardoned, 4078, 4140, 4396, 4484, 4598, 4628, 4646, 4662, 4734, 4777, 4874, 5088, 5112, 5184, 5466, 5416-8, 5798, 6488, 6323, 6368, 6742.
M'Ullig, Geoffrey, escaped from Limerick gaol, 4287.
" Ricard, pardon, 4621.
" Richard, pardon, 5848.
M'Ulligo, Shane, pardon, 6518.
M'Ullock, John, pardon, 3470.
Macully. See Mukylly.
M'Ullyck, Edm., pardon, 4680.
" Moyler, pardon, 4082.
M'Ullyg oge, Shane, pardon, 1478.
M'Ulvryne, Rich., pardon, 4281.
M'Ulyck, John, pardon, 2564.
M'Umack, Walter, pardon, 5068.
M'Ure, Art, pardon, 5488.
" Gerald, &c. m'Art, pardon, 967.
Macurvin, Donill, pardon, 4800.
M'Va, Teig boy, pardon, 4578.
M'Vadogho, Torrelagh, pardon, 4948.
M'Vadock—Vadick—Vadicke—Vadocke:
" Eyne mac Theobald, indenture, 5700.
" Fergananymo, pardon, 3784, 6317, 6377; indenture, 6780.
" Gerald m'Theobald, pardon, 3784; indenture, 6780.
" Theobald mac Morish, indenture, 6780.
" others of the name pardoned, 5878, 6317, 6377, 6848.
M'Vadock—Vadog's country, customs from, 2121, 4343.
" chief serjeant of, 1468, 3344.
M'Valrumie, John, pardon, 4697.
M'Valtiman, Tho., pardon, 4980.
M'Vanie, Edm. and John, pardon, 4080.
M'Vany, Edm., pardon, 4707.
M'Vengh, Mulmorry, pardon, 4808.
M'Veha, Gilla Coloym, pardon, 4617.
M'Vehey, Hugh, pardon, 4797.
M'Vic Arte, Neill, pardon, 4603.
M'Vic Cragh, Donell O'Dee, pardon, 5758.
M'Vic Dermody, Morierrugh and Tourlagh, pardon, 6447.
M'Vic Mahowny, Threlagh, pardon, 4482.
M'Vic Teige, Teige, pardon, 5084.
M'Vanie, Donogh, pardon, 6984.
M'Vany, Donell, pardon, 5964.
M'Varie, Donald, pardon, 5630.
M'Voulrowny, Brian and Shane, pardon, 4788.
M'Voyne, Rosse, pardon, 82.
M'Vroildie, Philip, pardon, 3948.
M'Vraheorne, John, pardon, 6519.
M'Vyenre, Donogho, pardon, 6568.
M'Vyckyny, Teig, pardon, 4882.
M'Vye, Neyl, pardon, 3780.
M'Wade, Wm., pardon, 5678.
M'Walter reagh, Tho., pardon, 6488.
M'Walrick, Teig, pardon, 6880.
M'Walter, Conoghor (of Agheris, co. Wick.), pardon, 4877.
" Knoghor, indenture, 6789.
" others of the name pardoned, 158, 981, 1477, 1480, 1974, 2079, 2084, 2490, 2960, 3084, 3404, 3507, 4082, 4184, 4328, 4387, 4608, 4707, 4711, 4874-6, 5078, 5178, 5481-6, 5488, 5813, 5874, 5812, 5917, 5988, 6083, 6189-90, 6221, 6408, 6841, 6727.
M'Walter's country in barony Ballymoe, co. Rosc., 4108.
M'Walter boy, James, pardon, 4088.
M'Ward, Owen, pardon, 691.
M'Warde, Shane reagh, pardon, 4731, 5894.
" Teige, pardon, 5988.
M'Ware, Cormac and Shane, pardon, 6814.
M'Water, persons of the name pardoned, 1168, 4108, 4731, 6448.
M'Watten Barred, country of, co. Mayo, 5080.
M'Wheole, Cahir, pardon, 4828.
" Donell, pardon, 4679.
M'Wherie, Dermod, pardon, 5711.
M'Willelowe, Thady, pardon, 7884.
M'William, Gerald, attainted (co. Kerry), 6894.
" Nich. (of Garryglas, co. Lim.), attainted, 4777.
" Philip (co. Kild.), robbery from, 444.

INDEX TO FIANTS—ELIZABETH.

M'William. See Bourke.
" others of the name, or patronymic, pardoned, 162, [illegible], [illegible], [illegible], 1[illegible], 1104, 1158, 1307, 1[illegible], 1494, [illegible], [illegible], [illegible], [illegible], [illegible]-7, [illegible], [illegible], 3160, [illegible], [illegible], [illegible], [illegible], 3101, 3160, [illegible], [illegible], [illegible], [illegible], [illegible], [illegible], 3560, 4018, [illegible], [illegible], [illegible], 4071, 4074, [illegible], 4111, [illegible], [illegible], [illegible], [illegible], 4416, [illegible], [illegible], [illegible], [illegible], [illegible]-30, [illegible], [illegible], [illegible], [illegible], [illegible], 4712, 4794, [illegible], [illegible]-1, [illegible], [illegible], [illegible], [illegible]-8, [illegible], [illegible], 4907, [illegible], [illegible], [illegible], [illegible], [illegible], [illegible], 5110, [illegible], [illegible], [illegible], [illegible], [illegible], [illegible], [illegible], [illegible], [illegible], [illegible], [illegible], [illegible]-2, [illegible], [illegible], [illegible], [illegible], [illegible], [illegible], 6110, 6150, [illegible], [illegible], [illegible], [illegible], [illegible], [illegible], [illegible], [illegible]-8, [illegible], [illegible], [illegible], [illegible], [illegible], [illegible]-5, [illegible], [illegible], [illegible], [illegible], [illegible], [illegible], [illegible], [illegible]-1, [illegible], [illegible], [illegible], [illegible], [illegible]-7, [illegible], [illegible]-8, [illegible], [illegible], [illegible], [illegible], [illegible], [illegible], [illegible], [illegible], [illegible], 6777.
M'William Bourke, 1494, 1800, 3419, [illegible]. See M'W. Eighter; Bourke, Rich.
M'William boy, Edm., pardon, 6777.
" Garrald, pardon, [illegible].
M'William carne, Gerrot, pardon, [illegible].
M'William Carraghe—Carrighe—Carraghan. Grange of, [illegible].
M'William Cruan, Fergus Angill (co. Mayo), slain in rebellion, [illegible].
M'William duff, Edm. boy (co. Mayo), slain in rebellion, [illegible].
" Maurice and Shane, pardon, [illegible].
M'William Eagher — Eighter — Enghier — Ewghter—Ewghiry—Eyghiyr—M'Wyliam Eighter—M'Wylliam Ewghter — M'Wyllyam eighitery — M'William Bourke —M'W. of Nether Connaught (M'W. Iochtair or the Lower), made chief of his race, [illegible]; pardon at suit of, [illegible]; grant to son of, [illegible]; title abolished, [illegible]; proposes to surrender his lands, [illegible]. See Bourke, John m'Oliverus, [illegible]; Bourke, Richard, [illegible], [illegible].
" country of, co. Mayo, [illegible], 1404, [illegible], [illegible], 3419, [illegible], [illegible], [illegible]; sheriff, [illegible].
M'William grana, Feagh, pardon, [illegible].
M'William greny, Teig, pardon, [illegible].
M'William oge, Donogh (co. Lim.), attainted, [illegible].
M'William oge, Donogh grana (of Killboggie, co. Gal.), pardon, [illegible].
" Gerald, pardon, [illegible].
" Morogh, pardon, [illegible].
" William, pardon, [illegible].
M'William reagh, Donogh m'Shane, pardon, [illegible].
M'William roe, John, pardon, [illegible].
M'William roe, William m'Ricard, pardon, [illegible].
M'William's country, [illegible]. See M'William Eughter, country of.
M'Wobaie, Lisagh, pardon, [illegible].
M'Wolloghan, Molloghlan, pardon, [illegible].
M'Wollothan, Donell, pardon, [illegible].
M'Woory, Cahill, pardon, [illegible].
M'Woshy, Donogh, pardon, [illegible].
M'Wony, Brian, pardon, 4416.
" Cahall, pardon, [illegible].
M'Workam, Hugh, pardon, [illegible].
Macworth—Macwoorth, capt. Humfrey. See Mackworth.
M'Worthe, Ellen, widow, lease, [illegible]. See Mackworth.
M'Wyliam Eighter—M'Wylliam Ewghter, [illegible], [illegible]. See M'William Eaghter.
M'Wylliam, Garett, pardon, [illegible].
M'Wyllime, Shane, pardon, [illegible].
M'Wyllow, Thomas, pardon, [illegible].
M'Wyllyam eightery, [illegible]. See M'William Eaghter.
Macwyre, [illegible]. See Maguire.
M'Wyrie, Owny, pardon, [illegible].
M'Yboy, Moriertagh, pardon, [illegible], [illegible].
M'y Callaghe, Brian, pardon, [illegible].
M'Y Callowe, Donagh, Hugh and Walter, pardon, [illegible].
M'ycarry, Tirrelagh, pardon, [illegible].
M'Y Conell, Dermod and Shane, pardon, 4791.
M'Ydiole, Moiroula, pardon, [illegible].
M'y Dorlour, Conoghor, pardon, [illegible].
M'Ydoyle, Conoghor, pardon, [illegible].
M'Yeamie, Donell, pardon, [illegible].
M'Yeamond, Gonnolagh, pardon, [illegible].
M'Ygnill, Wm., pardon, [illegible].
M'Ygowne, Teig, pardon, [illegible].
M'Ygullykierre, Oyne, pardon, [illegible].
M'Ygullykierry, Phillypp, pardon, [illegible].
M'Y Layne, Thady, pardon, [illegible].
M'Ymaster, Edm., pardon, [illegible].
M'Ynoine, Donill, pardon, [illegible].
M'Ynew, Offyrpatryke, pardon, [illegible].
M'Ynnon Randall, pardon, [illegible].
M'Ynir, Mortagh, pardon, [illegible].
M'Ynlagh, Tho., pardon, [illegible].
M'Ynlowe, Tho., pardon, 144[illegible].
M'Ynner, persons of the name pardoned, [illegible].

INDEX TO FIANTS—ELIZABETH.

M'Ynully, persons of the name pardoned, [illegible].
M'Tuyede, Donell, pardon, [illegible].
M'Yperson, persons of the name pardoned, [illegible], [illegible].
M'Yprior, Neyl, pardon, 1477.
M'Yrraghe, Shane, pardon, [illegible].
M'Yscollog, Shane, pardon, [illegible].
M'yrewsiner, John and Tho., pardon, [illegible].
M'Ycarybynie, Donogh, pardon, [illegible].
M'y Vallirey, Dermod O'Crowly, pardon, [illegible].
M'Yvallowilge, John, pardon, [illegible].
M'Yvarthynie, Teig, pardon, [illegible].
Mac Yvar, Tirrelagh, pardon, [illegible].
M'Y Vergele, Dermot, pardon, 4512.
M'yvicarie, Carribre and Tho. O'Culrike, pardon, [illegible].
Madaine (co. Cork ?), [illegible].
Madan, James, commission, 4448.
Madan—Madane, Nich., land in Waterford, [illegible], [illegible].
Madane, Patr., merchant of Waterford, [illegible].
Maddadoo, co. Westm. See Mcdade.
Maddan, James, mortgage in Waterford, [illegible], [illegible].
,, Patr., mortgage in Waterford, [illegible], [illegible].
,, Wm., chaplain, [illegible].
Maddane, Katherine, pardon, [illegible].
,, Thomas, pardon, [illegible].
Maddan, Anastasia, pardon, [illegible].
,, Denis (of Athy), pardon, [illegible].
,, Dionysius (of Waterford), English liberty, [illegible].
,, James, pardon, [illegible].
,, Shely ny, pardon, [illegible].
,, Shough Cahell I, [illegible].
,, ,, Donell I, [illegible].
,, ,, Morogh I, [illegible].
,, ,, Morough duff I, [illegible].
,, ,, Owen I, [illegible].
,, ,, Shane I, [illegible].
,, See Vaddon, O'Madden.
Maddenston—Madenston—Madenstone, co. Kild., [illegible], [illegible], [illegible]. See Ballymaddon, [illegible].
Madder, growth and export of, [illegible].
Madder, Owen m'Donell Y, pardon, [illegible].
Maddigane, Tho. m'Morice Y, alienation to, [illegible].
Maddin, James and Owen (co. Cork), pardon, [illegible].
Maddoge, Gibbon. See Madoge.
Madegane, Joan, pardon, [illegible].
Madellin (Mandlings), co. Kild., [illegible].
Madenston—Madenstone. See Maddenston.
Madery, Teig ua, pardon, [illegible].
Madgan, Shane m'Tho. I, pardon, [illegible].
Madigan, John, pardon, [illegible].
Madin, Anable ny, pardon, [illegible], [illegible].
Madock, Rob. and Wm., pardon, [illegible].
Madocke, Rob., pardon, [illegible].
Madoge—Maddoge, Gibbon, pardon, [illegible], [illegible].
,, Philip and Shane, pardon, [illegible].
,, Wm., pardon, [illegible].
Madrine (co. Cork ?), [illegible].
Madry, Conell ne, pardon, [illegible].
Maducheston, co. Kilk., [illegible].
Magaffe (co. Down or Arm.), [illegible], [illegible].
Magahe, co. Wat. See Moge.
Magan, Tho., pardon, [illegible].
Maganny, Wm., pardon, [illegible].
Maganole, Hugh, [illegible]. See Magenisse.
Maganhagy, Caoll, pardon, [illegible].
Magannyn, Teig, pardon, [illegible].
Magaran, Owen, pardon, [illegible].
Magargan—Magargane, persons of the name pardoned, [illegible], [illegible].
Magarnan, Turlagh, pardon, [illegible].
Magarr, Teig, pardon, [illegible].
Magarre, persons of the name pardoned, [illegible].
Magarrie, Neil, pardon, [illegible].
Magarry, Connor, pardon, [illegible].
Magarvey, James, pardon, [illegible].
Magarvie, Patr., pardon, [illegible].
Magary, Farrell, pardon, [illegible].
Magaurane, Tho., pardon, [illegible].
Magauraye, Gillernanie, pardon, [illegible].
Magaurien, Charles, pardon, [illegible].
Magawan, Fargwuneghye, pardon, [illegible].
Magawell, Hubert and James, pardon, [illegible].
Magawie. See Magawley.
Magawle, James, pardon, [illegible].
Magawley — Magawle — Magawlie — Magawlly — Magawly:
,, Awley, chief of his name, commissions, 4151, [illegible].
,, William, commissions, 4151, [illegible], [illegible].
,, country of, co. Westm., [illegible].
,, See M'Awly and M'Cawlie.
Magawran, Andrew, vicar, pardon, [illegible].
,, Edmund, clerk, pardon, [illegible].
,, others of the name pardoned, [illegible], [illegible], [illegible], [illegible].
Magenwracktowne (Ballymagauran, co. Cav.?), [illegible].
Magdalotines—Maudlens, or Hospitals, [illegible], [illegible].
Magdalens near Waterford, [illegible].
Magregan, Fergus, pardon, [illegible].
Magaughrane, Philip, pardon, [illegible].
Magcarrie—Magcarrye, persons of the name pardoned, [illegible], [illegible].
Magcullie, co. Cork, [illegible].
Magenan, Wm., pardon, [illegible].
Magenor, Phelim, pardon, [illegible].
Magenill, Hugh, pardon, [illegible].

INDEX TO FIANTS—ELIZABETH.

Magenisse—Maguisse—Magannis—Magennise—Magennyse—Magenys—Magnuis—Magnnye—Magnisse—Magnyse—Masynnes:
,, Arthur, son of sir Hugh, 4237; chief of his name, pardon, 6818, 6794; pardon of his followers, 6818.
,, Eugene, bishop of Down, 71.
,, sir Hugh, chief of his nation, made captain of Iveagh, 1545; surrender and regrant of his country, 6818, 4237; commissions, 3812, 6817, 3644, 6791; matrimonial suit, 5647; pardon, 6823; his daughter, 6794.
,, Hugh, son of sir Hugh, 4237.
,, Mary, daughter of sir Hugh, pardon, 6794.
,, Murtagh, son of the bishop, pardon, 6818.
,, Phelim, pardon, 1583.
,, Phelym, son of sir Hugh, 4237.
,, others of the name pardoned, 6403, 6818, 6794.
,, country of (Iveagh, co. Down), 4237; pardon to inhabitants, 6818.
,, See Maguenissa, M'Gennise, M'Genisse.
Magennaeye, Brian, pardon, 1687.
Magennis, Owen, pardon, 6452.
Magenmore, Cormock, pardon, 6523.
Magenoure, Dermot, made seneschal of Montergarvan, [illegible].
,, See M'Genore.
Magennure's country, co. Long., [illegible].
Magennoche, Carbery, pardon, 4747.
Magennor, Gillepatrick, pardon, 6643.
,, James, pardon, 5543.
Magenore, Rosse, pardon, 6142.
Magenure, Cormock, pardon, [illegible].
Magenyne, Conor, pardon, 5542.
Magenys, sir Hugh. See Magenisse.
Magennogh, Henry, pardon, 6794.
Mageoghegan—Magoghegan—Mageoghegan—Maggohagan—Mageoghegan—Mageoghegan—Mageoghegane—Mageoheghan—Magoheghan—Mageoghegan—Magowghegan:
,, Art (of Conmaston), pardon, 6637.
,, Brian pension, 5118; pardon, 6637.
,, Conley or Conlaurus, pardon, [illegible]; chief of his name, commission, 4463. See M'Geoghegan.
Mageoghegan, Hugh, son of Conlaurus, pardon, 4798.
,, Hugh, commission, [illegible].
,, Hugh boy, pardon, 6647.
,, James (of Castletown), pardon, 5637, 5148.
,, Neil (of Moycashel), commission, 4441. See M'Geoghegan.
,, Rosse, sheriff, 1837; commissions, 1837, 3122, 3545; his lands preyed, 5164. See M'Geoghegan.
,, Thomas, commission, 4463.
,, captain of that name, 1709; his sons rebels, 5164.
,, others of the name pardoned, 1848, [illegible], [illegible], [illegible], [illegible], 4614, 4694, [illegible], 5118, [illegible], 6486, 6496, [illegible], 6647, 6512, 6642.
,, country of, 163, 1894, 3153-4, 3873, 6744.
,, See M'Geoghegan.
Magenn, persons of the name pardoned, 6823-4.
Magevaily, Bren, pardon, [illegible].
Magevenne, Phil., pardon, [illegible].
Mageraght, Donaltagh, pardon, [illegible].
Magoghagan, Rose. See Mageoghegan.
Maghair faltagh (co. Gal. ?), 4875.
Maghan, Molaghlen, pardon, [illegible].
Maghane, Pat., pardon, 6792.
Maghary boy (Magheraboy, co. Ferm.), [illegible].
Maghery Stinfinagh (Magherastephana, co. Ferm.), 5661.
Magh Brenaraighe. See Moybreckre.
Magh Breaghmaighe. See Moybraven.
Maghebeserverraghe, co. Gal., 3461.
Maghinbarvaghe, grange of, co. Gal., [illegible].
Maghenmorie (co. Meath), [illegible].
Maghecall (co. Gal. ?), 4476.
Magher, Denis fitz Tho., pardon, 4744.
,, Ellice ny, pardon, [illegible].
,, Hugh m'Teig E, pardon, [illegible].
,, John, pardon, [illegible].
,, Katherine ny, pardon, 6180.
,, Margaret ny, pardon, 6627.
,, Onoria fitz Tho., pardon, 4744.
,, Teig m'Teig E, pardon, [illegible].
,, Wm., pardon, 6637.
Magheran, co. Wexford. See Marra.
Magheraboy, co. Ferm. See Magharyboy.
Magheraclone, co. Mon. See Maghyrcloin.
Magheracoulcan, co. Down. See Ballymaghor Clonlishe, 4640.
Magheradartin, co. Down. See Ballyraghcraghdarvan, 4658.
Magheraliagho, castle of, co. Gal., [illegible].

INDEX TO FIANTS—ELIZABETH.

Magheramenagh, co. Don. *See* Magherevenagh.
Magheramore, co. Mon. *See* Mowllaugh-magheronover.
Magheraghagry, co. Mon. *See* Maghere Jaffrey.
Magherastephana, co. Ferm. *See* Maghary Staghanagh.
Magherecuirk — Magharcburk — Magherewirke — Magherecuirk —Maghirie Quirk — Maghirkuyrk (Machaire Cuirene, the barony of Kilkenny West), co. Westm., 1940, [illegible], [illegible], [illegible], [illegible].
„ seneschal appointed, 2718.
„ captain of, [illegible].
Maghere, Derby, pardon, [illegible].
„ Nicholas, house in Dublin, 1911.
Magherecuirk. *See* Magherecuirk.
Maghere Jaffrey (Magheraghagry), co. Mon., [illegible].
Magherenakilly (Magheranakelly), co. Mon., [illegible].
Magherecloskagh in Upper Ossory, 677.
Magherenawre, co. Cav., [illegible].
Magherecroshe (Magherosse, co. Mon.), 1973.
Magherie Oderney, co. Kerry, 4152.
Magheris Quirk, co. Westm., [illegible].
Magherikilliterdagh in O'Conor Dun's country, co. Rosc., [illegible].
Magheranaharny, co. Mon. *See* Magherneharnan.
Magheranakelly, co. Mon. *See* Magheranakilly.
Magheranekeagh, Queen's co. *See* Maghernockeagh.
Maghernaharnan (Magheranaharny), co. Mon., 2644.
Magheranamore, co. Cav., [illegible].
Maghernockeagh — Mahernockagh — Mahernykagh (Maghernakeagh, Queen's co.), [illegible], 6773.
Maghernawre, co. Cav., [illegible].
Magherosse, co. Mon. *See* Magherecroshe, Maghycrossa.
Maghereradowne, co. Cav., [illegible].
Magherygragh in Connaught, 1581.
Magheryvenagh (Magheramenagh, co. Donegal), [illegible].
Magheryvenagher (King's co.), 1401.
Magherywale (in bar. Athenry), co. Gal., [illegible].
Maghery, co. Mon., [illegible], [illegible].
Maghery, or O'Conor Dun's country, co. Rosc., [illegible], [illegible].
Magherye Loyney (Loyny bar., co. Sligo), seneschal of, [illegible].
Magherytarpaghe, co. Clare [illegible].
Magherygranard — Maghirt Granard, co. Long., [illegible], 1401, [illegible], [illegible].
Maghery Kenrey, co. Clare, [illegible].
Maghir, Dermot, pardon, 1768.
„ Donogho, pardon, [illegible].
„ Hugh m'Dermod, pardon, [illegible].
Maghiroowarcke (co. Donegal or Tyrone), [illegible].
Maghirkuyrk. *See* Magherecuirk.
Maghirt Granard. *See* Magherygranard.
Maghiry, David O'Kenllie, pardon, [illegible].
Maghmayn — Maghmain — Maghmayne — Maighmaine — Moghmayne (Mackmine), co. Wex., 1403, 1748, [illegible], [illegible], [illegible]; the house at, 1742.
Magh na Oowarcke (co. Donegal ?), [illegible].
Maghoneonan, John and Meleghlen, pardon, [illegible].
Maghowne, Dermod m'Conoghor I., pardon, [illegible].
Maghreragh, or barony of Clare, co. Gal., seneschal of, 2201.
Maghrie, Brian, pardon, [illegible].
Maghyrean, Dermot, pardon, [illegible].
Maghyrelow (Maghereclogan, co. Mon.), rectory, 1732.
Maghyrrosse - Magherrosho (Magherose, co. Mon.), rectory, 1314, 1723.
Magie, persons of the name pardoned, [illegible], [illegible], [illegible], [illegible].
Magiernade, Brien (of Moreyn, co. Long.), [illegible].
Magierright, Brien, pardon, [illegible].
Magigan, Amlon, pardon, [illegible].
Magillodyne, Cahill, pardon, [illegible].
Magillaghan, and others of the same, in O'Cahan's country, pardon, [illegible].
Magillie (co. Cork ?), [illegible].
Magilligan, persons of the name pardoned, [illegible].
Magilleyman, persons of the name pardoned, [illegible], [illegible].
Magin, persons of the name pardoned, [illegible].
Magion, Tho., pardon, [illegible].
Magirne, Gillernew, pardon, [illegible].
Magislon — Magistoun — Magistowne, co. Kilk., [illegible], [illegible], [illegible].
Magkeman, Farall, pardon, [illegible].
Maglanna, Maurice, pardon, [illegible].
Maglarne, Brian, pardon, [illegible].
Maglare, co. Kild., [illegible].
Maglare (Moyglare), co. Meath, 6914, [illegible].
Maglaroad, Hugh, pardon, [illegible].
Maglass, knight's lands in (Maglasse), co. Kerry, [illegible].
Maglaughy, Brian and Wm., pardon, [illegible].
Maglavan, Edm., pardon, [illegible].
Maglavoy, Dermot, pardon, [illegible].
Maglavyne, Patr., pardon, [illegible].

INDEX TO FIANTS—ELIZABETH.

Maglawry, Conor, pardon, 6141.
Maglen, Padin, pardon, [illegible].
Maglin, Fedy, pardon, 6712.
„ Teig, pardon, 6712.
Maglisane, Gilpatrick, pardon, [illegible].
Maglyn, persons of the name pardoned, 4287, 6612, 6468, 6712.
Maglynn, Morogh, pardon, 6463.
Magmore, Donill, pardon, 5146.
Magnels—Magneise. See Magenise.
Magner, David gancogh, pardon, 5378, 4564.
„ Edm., pardon, 5746, [illegible], 6573.
„ Ellen, pardon, 3614.
„ James, pardon, 4115, 6482.
„ John, pardon, 4115, [illegible], [illegible].
„ Nich, pardon, 4115.
„ Philip, pardon, 6462.
„ Redmond, pardon, 4109, [illegible].
„ Robert, pardon, 3574, 4111, [illegible].
„ Shane, pardon, 6514.
„ Thomas, pardon, 4115, 5711.
„ Ullig, pardon, 5078.
„ Walter, pardon, 3387, 6478.
„ William, pardon, 3387, 4115.
„ See Maigner, Mangner, Mangnor.
Magners Castleton (co. Cork ?), 3574.
Magnerstowne (co. Cork ?), 5076.
Magnoys. See Magenise.
Magogan, Owen, pardon, [illegible].
Magoimo—Maguyes. See Magenise.
Mago (co. Kerry), [illegible].
Magoe, William, pardon, 842.
Magoeghegan. See Magoeghegan.
Magoegane, Rich., pardon, 4740.
Magoeghegan—Magogheghan—Magoghegane—Magohegan—Magoheghan. See Magoeghegan.
Magohen, Kogowey, pardon, 471.
Magoie, Tho., pardon, 6572.
Magomibie, co. Kerry, 6161.
Magonill, Henry, pardon, 4017.
Magonnowrey, Cormoc and Moroghow, pardon, 4682.
Magonyble (co. Kerry ?), 6162.
Magonyhy (co. Cork ?), 6763.
Magorban, co. Tip. See Mogorban, Moygarbarrye.
Magoreighte, Dermod, pardon, 5806.
Magorman, Manus and Patr., pardon, 5763, 6741.
Magorney (co. Cork ?), 6578.
Magoron, Dermot, pardon, 6412.
Magorran, Tege, pardon, [illegible].
Magoughogan. See Magoeghegan.
Magoughran, Philip and Tirrelagh, pardon, 4818.
Magoumy, co. Kerry, [illegible].
Magourke, Donald, pardon, 6498.
Magouyre, Hugh, pardon, 4760.
Magowan—Magowen, persons of the name pardoned, 4760, 5227.
Magowghogan. See Magoeghegan.
Magowin, Marcus, pardon, 6612.
Magowne, Shane, pardon, [illegible].
Magowyre, Redmond, pardon, 1[illegible].
Magoy, Donogh, pardon, 6422.
Magoye, Dermod, pardon, 4287.
Magoyny, Forshy and Philip, pardon, 6412.
Magoyre, Cormock, pardon, 4281.
Magra—Magragh—Magraghe. See Magrath.
Magramchan, Conor, pardon, [illegible].
Magranill, persons of the name pardoned, 6099.
Magraneechan, persons of the name pardoned, 6654.
Magrannell, persons of the name pardoned, 4764, 4767, 5132.
Magranill—Magranyll's country (co. Leitrim), 1464, 4407. See M'Granell.
Magrannell, Edm., pardon, 6453.
Magrath—Magra—Magragh—Magraghe—Magrathe:
„ Barnaby, 5[illegible], 5087; pardon, 6767.
„ Donogh or Gillegrony, English liberty, 3813; indenture of surrender, 5006; regrant of his lands, 5297.
„ James, son of archbishop, [illegible], 5807.
„ John, priest, pardon, 4678.
„ Marcus, son of archbishop, [illegible], 5297.
„ Meiler. See Cashel, archbishop.
„ Mihell, brother of archbishop, 5483.
„ Neill, 5487; pardon, 6707.
„ Redmond, [illegible], [illegible]; pardon, 6767.
„ Terence, 5484, 6767; pardon, 6707.
„ others of the name pardoned, 5002, 6707.
Magrawley, Thady, pardon, 6942.
Magrein, Cormock and Hugh, pardon, [illegible].
Magrewe, Dermot, pardon, 6617.
Magrine, Tirlagh, pardon, 6701.
Magrodie, Brian and Shane, pardon, [illegible].
Magroice, Redmond, pardon, 6450.
Magroirke, Thomas, pardon, 5158.
Magrorick, Rich., pardon, [illegible].
Magrourtie, Brian, pardon, 6714.
Magroworke, Neall, pardon, [illegible].
Magrowry, Patr., pardon, 4581.
Magruraye, Donagh, pardon, 5602.
Magueniss—Magynnes, Eogain, bishop of Down and Connor, 71, 167.
„ Ferdorogh or Chorrus, pardon, 124.

INDEX TO FIANTS—ELIZABETH.

Magmoclam, Ineras and Donald, pardon, 184.
Magner, Philip fitz John (Magner?), pardon, [illegible].
Magnelle, Darby, burgess of Athlone, [illegible].
Magnier, Downe, pardon, [illegible].
Magnir, Brian, pardon, 4109.
Maguire—Magwire—Maguyer—Maguyre—Magwier—Magwir—Magwyer—Magwyr—Magwyre:
„ Bernard, pardon, 6402.
„ Brian, son of Conor roe, pardon, 6607.
„ Connaght—Cowchonaght—Coconnor—Conellus, captain of Fermanagh, 1081; surrender and regrant of his country, 4983, 4909; commissions, 4782, 5077; pardon, 4810; late chief, 6462.
„ Conor roe, chief of his name, pardon, 6607; surrender and grant of Fermanagh, 6462.
„ Couconnaght, pardon, 6607.
„ Edm., priest, pardon, 5021.
„ Hugh, son of Cowconnaght, knight, and chief of his name, pardon, 4810, 5603, 5716, [illegible]; submission, [illegible], protection, 6187.
„ James, priest, pardon, 5602.
„ John, rector of Uisk, 749; prebendary of Donlovan, commissions, [illegible], [illegible], [illegible], 2257, 2294, 5912, [illegible], 6617.
„ John, son of Maguire, pardon, 4810.
„ Nigar Dacnal, student, pardon, 6602.
„ others of the name pardoned, 671, 896, [illegible], 3037, [illegible], 4630, 5410, 5482, 5602, 5716, 5798, 5917, [illegible], 6607. See M'Guire.
„ pardon to son of, 4810; O'Neill's superiority over, 5013; service done upon, 5847; messenger of, 5847. See M'Guire.
„ country of (the county Fermanagh), 4670, 4909, 6272, 6462. See Fermanagh.
Maguirin, persons of the name pardoned, 6626.
Magullaman, persons of the name pardoned, 6478.
Magunde, Mohuary, pardon, 5132.
Magunde, James, pardon, 5890.
Magunechan, Molaughlen, pardon, 4862.
Maguyer—Maguyre. See Maguire.
Magwain, Brian, pardon, 4626.
Magwire—Magwier—Magwir—Magwaire—Magwyer—Magwyr—Magwyre. See Maguire.
Magy, Maures, pardon, 6711.
Magy, island of (Island Magee, co. Antrim), 4762.
Magyane, Gillduff and Laurence, pardon, 6713.
Magye, persons of the name pardoned, 4464, 6610, 6711.
Magyran, Owyn, pardon, 5890.
Magyllin, Donell, pardon, 6519.
Magylsiman, Donald, pardon, 2457.
Magyrunes, Hugrue. See Magonniwe.
Magyrone, sir Hugh. See Magonlane.
Mahn gon, pardon, 6572.
Mahallagh (co. Cork?), 6459. See Mohallaghe Bwe.
Mahallon—Mahallone, persons of the name pardoned, 5709.
Mahawnagh—Mahawnigh—Mahawny (Mahoonagh?), co. Lim., 5848, 6479, 6457.
Maher, Sarra ny, pardon, [illegible].
„ Wm., pardon, 6622.
Maheroonkagh—Maherayakagh. See Maghernonkagh.
Mahill (co. Clare?), 6712.
Mahind, Florence, vicar of Mothell, 707.
Mahir, Rory, pardon, 6421.
Mahon, Thady fitz Knohor, pardon, 2926.
Mahone, Dermod m'Donell I, pardon, 6941.
Mahoneston—Mahownston (co. Westm.), 3967, 6452.
Mahony, Dermod m'Fynyn m'Teig Y, and others of the name pardoned, 6414-5.
„ See Mahownie, Mahowny.
Mahoonagh, co. Lim. See Mahownagh, Mahawnagh, Mohownagh.
Mahownagh (Mahoonagh, co. Lim.?), 6461, 6571.
Mahound, John and Maurice, pardon, 6446.
Mahoune, Dermod m'Shane Y, and others of the name pardoned, 6459, 6571.
Mahow, Donell m'Teig, pardon, 6457.
Mahown, Any nyn Teig ny, pardon, 6505.
„ Ellice ny, pardon, 4624.
„ Honora ny, pardon, 4466.
„ John m'Conoghor I, pardon, 6459.
Mahownagh—Mahowneghe—Mahowne (Mahoonagh, co. Lim.), 6457, 6366; manor granted, 5769; patronage of church, 5947. See Mahawnagh, Mahoonagh.
Mahownagh, Connor m'Fynyn I, pardon, 6808.
Mahowne, Finolagh nyn Fynine Y, pardon, 6571.
„ Honor ny, pardon, 6467.
„ Teig m'Hearne I, pardon, 6469.

Mahowne boy, cook, murdered, 710.
Mahowne Fin, wardship of heir, 6442. *See* O'Mahowny, Donogh.
Mahowney, Donogho m'Dermody I, pardon, [illegible].
„ Ellen ny Tane ny, pardon, 6518.
Mahownie, Conogher m'Dermot I, pardon, [illegible].
„ Daniel m'Shane I, pardon, 6671.
„ Dermod m'Conogher I, pardon, [illegible].
„ Ellen ny, pardon, 6514.
„ Finola ny, pardon, 6518.
„ *See* Mahowny, Mahony.
Mahowne's park, in Youghal, [illegible].
Mahownsion. *See* Mahonsion.
Mahowny, Teig m'Dermody I, Fynyno m'Conogher m'Da Y, and others of the name pardoned, [illegible], [illegible], 3163, 4467, 4678, 4677, 4702, [illegible], [illegible], [illegible], [illegible], [illegible], [illegible], [illegible], 6764.
Mahulagh (co. Cork ?), [illegible].
Mahuna, Owny ny, wife O'Roly, [illegible].
Maiddle boy, [illegible].
Maign (co. Ross. ?), 6777.
Maighmaine. *See* Maghmayn.
Maigner, Wm., pardon, [illegible].
Maigue, river. *See* Maye.
Maillarde. *See* Maylard.
Maine, co. Cork. *See* Mounes.
Mainham, co. Kild. *See* Manham, Maynam.
Mainothe. *See* Maynothe.
Maintirfandaghin (Mintir Feorachain, a territory in bar. Clanawly, in co. Ferm.), [illegible].
Mainwaring — Mainwaringe. *See* Manwaring.
Maio. *See* Mayo.
Maiode (co. Ross. ?), 4113.
Maiton, Edm., pardon, [illegible].
Maiocco—Maiorcastle, co. Wexf., 3136, 4232.
Maiore — Maior, Wm., marshal of Castle Chamber, 6714, [illegible].
Maistgreen. *See* Mastgreen.
Makadawre, Queen's co., 1664.
Makagan, Fergus more, pardon, 4794.
Makarily, Loghlin, pardon, [illegible].
Makarmane, Cobunaghe, pardon, [illegible].
Makaran, Torlagh, pardon, 2276.
Makarone, James, pardon, 2274.
Makarrill, Patrall, pardon, [illegible].
Makaughine, Neill boye, pardon, [illegible].
Makeon, James, murder of, 1158.
Makenn, Donslowe oge, grant of land, [illegible].
„ Tirlogh roe, grant of land, [illegible].
Makeo, Wm., pardon, 6476.
Makeogh, Donogh oge, pardon, [illegible].
Makey, Patr., pardon, [illegible].
„ Shane m'Teye I, pardon, [illegible].
Makgarrohan, Wm., pardon, [illegible].
Makigo, Donald m'Donkaha, pardon, [illegible].
Makmewe alias Condon, Richard. *See* M'Mang.
Makoffy, Donald m'Moragh, and others of the same pardoned, 6641.
Makonygham, Rairy carraigh, pardon, [illegible].
Malaoh. *See* Mallahow.
Malatuna, co. Meath, 766.
Malaghid. *See* Malahide.
Malaghlen, Annable ny, pardon, [illegible].
„ Cormac, pardon, 4942.
Malahell—Malahoyffe. *See* Molahyffe.
Malahiddert (Mulhuddert, co. Dub.), prebendary of, 1582.
Malahide—Malahyde—Malaghid—Mallahid—Mallahoid—Mollaghid—Mollaghide, co. Dub., 642, 728, 3117, 3348, 3444, [illegible], [illegible], [illegible], 6784, 6818, 6341-6; haven, [illegible].
Malahiffe (co. Cork ?), [illegible].
Malahiffe. *See* Molahyffe.
Malaier, Wm. A., pardon, [illegible].
Malalye, Nich., pardon, [illegible].
Malardston — Malardeston (Mallardstown), co. Kilk., 1481, [illegible].
Malathone alias Molayre, Donald, murdered, [illegible].
Malaughelan, co. Meath (Mullaghlan), 1668.
Malavan. *See* Malathone.
Malbie—Malboy—Malby—Mallbye:
„ Henry, son and heir of Sir Nicholas, 4756; wardship, 4768; commission, [illegible].
„ John, commission, [illegible].
„ Nicholas (afterwards knight), sergeant major of the army, 1161; collector of customs, 1772; principal commissioner of Connaught, [illegible]; governor of Connaught, [illegible], [illegible]; constable of castle of Athlone, 4325; his secretary, [illegible]; composition with chiefs, [illegible], [illegible], 4718; commissions, 1161, 1166, [illegible], 2344, [illegible], [illegible], 4047-8, 3117, [illegible], [illegible], 4467-8, [illegible]; pardon, 1787, [illegible]; pardons on his recommendation, 1471, [illegible], [illegible], [illegible], 2716 (see note), [illegible], [illegible], 4714, [illegible], [illegible], 4074-7, [illegible]; grant of land, &c., 3850, [illegible]; lease, 3164; grant of a wardship, [illegible]; his lands in Connaught, 4786; his rights in co. Longford, [illegible], [illegible]; his heir, 4768, [illegible].
Male, Walter fitz Rich., pardon, 6477.
Malefant, James, pardon, [illegible].
„ Philip, pardon, [illegible].
Malefonte, Robert, pardon, [illegible].
Malefoune, Philip, pardon, [illegible].

INDEX TO FIANTS—ELIZABETH.

Malcho, Richard O'Mulcahel, pardon, 4112.
Malfont, Robert, pardon, 5748.
Malie, Rich., pardon, 6771.
" Tho., pardon, 6772.
Malkester (co. Leit. ?), 5423.
Mall, Torlagh, pardon, 6446.
Malla, co. Cork, 5780-1, 5784.
Mallagh, Dermod, pardon, 4574.
" Donogh, pardon, 6573.
Mallaghemore, co. Gal., 5421.
Mallaghmast (Mullamast), co. Kild., 574.
Mallaghmore (Mullaghmore), co. Gal., 5901, 5971, 5711.
Mallaghmaharne, co. Mon., 4658.
Mallaghoyne, co. Dub., 251.
Mallahid—Mallahide. See Malahide.
Mallahiffe. See Molahyffe.
Mallahold. See Malahide.
Mallahow—Mullahowe—Malauh, co. Dub., 1469, 2708, 3861.
Mallardston (co. Car. ?), 804.
Mallardstown, co. Kilk. See Malardston.
Mallefont, Elice ny Robert, pardon, 4914.
Mallifonte, Philip, pardon, 4284.
Mallifont, Ellis, pardon, 6516.
Mallismany (co. Cork or Wat. ?), 5668.
Mallon, co. Cork, 4466, 6761. See also Malla.
Mallone, Patrick, lease, 1152.
Mallot, Tho. duffe, attainted, 6777.
Mallow, co. Cork. See Moalla.
Mallowin, John, pardon, 1470.
Mallranean — Mallranegan. See Malran-kan.
Mally—Maly, Grany ny (Granualle), pardon, 6173; sons of, 6948.
Mallyroy, 6478.
Malodd, Richard bug, attainted, 4942.
Malode, Rich. oge m'Thomas, pardon, 6436.
Malon, John, pardon, 4794.
" Thomas, pardon, 954.
Malone, Edm., pardon, 4874.
" James, house in Dublin, 4314.
" James, pardon, 6250, 6251.
" James, proctor, 2900.
" John, pardon, 2682, 6362.
" Morish, pardon, 6488.
" Moriagh, pardon, 4443, 4690.
" Patr. premises in Dublin, 1311, 4314, 4416.
" Rich., pardon, 6282, 6877.
" Shane A, pardon, 5928.
" Wm., pardon, 4474, 6272.
Malone, co. Antrim. See Moyelion.
Malond, Edm., pardon, 6842.
Maloy, Wm., pardon, 4526.
Maloye, Gilliduffe, pardon, 6468.
Maloye, Edm., pardon, 6518.
Malphant, Robert, pardon, 2166.
Malrankan—Malranean—Mallranean—Mall-ranegan — Malracan — Malrankane (Mul-rankin), co. Wex., 154, 336, 1618, 1748, 2294, 2371, 4864, 5782, 5821, 5895, 6086, 6786.
Malt impressed for army, 438, 1196, 1453, 1461, 2522.
" reserved in lease, 230.
Maly, Grany ny (see Mally), 6173.
" Maurice, 7004.
Malye, Tho., pardon, 5454.
Malyghanye (co. Cork ?), 2770.
Malyvandervohe, co. Meath, 922. See also Molyhondryvohe.
Mamayne, co. Wex., 5413.
Man, Isle of, 4549; a rectory in, leased, 1458, 5767.
Man, William, house in Dublin, 1311.
Manachan, 4654, 4941. See Monaghan.
Managhan, John (see Monaghan), 1714.
Manahowe, co. Clare, island of, 4142.
Manamayne alias Marmayne, Thomas, English liberty, 111.
Manamston, co. Meath, 4707.
Mandevill, Walter, pardon, 3394.
Mandevill, Edm., pardon, 6657.
Mandowe, Thomaston, lease, 169.
Mando, a man of Drogheda, 4214.
Mandeston, co. Meath, 5457.
Mane, Wm. ogu, pardon, 4190.
Manen (co. Cork ?), 4467.
Manere, Thomas. See Manners.
Manering—Manerings. See Mainwaring.
Manere—Maneres, Thomas, brother of earl of Rutland, commission, 283; lease, 287.
Maneryng. See Mainwaring.
Manecribe (Monmacribe), co. Gal., 5884.
Manastercvorlahe, 5832. See Monastercvoris.
Manastire no feolle. See Monastery of Nophelaugh.
Maneytron (co. Cork ?), 5914.
Manfild, Henry, pardon, 3478.
Mangan, Hugh, pardon, 4868.
" John fitz Edm., pardon, 4874.
Mangan, co. Wex. See Mangane.
Mangancowlin (co. Wex. ?), 5817.
Mangartyn or m'Dermogh, Dermod, pardon, 6574.
Manger Tereloighe — Mangartoniaughe — Mannger Tirreloghe (Manger, co. Wick.), 3744, 6051; rectory, 1887.
Mangner, Philip, pardon, 6362.
" Tho., pardon, 6392.
Manham (Mainham), co. Kild., vicar of, 5997.
Manim (co. Cork ?), 4658.
Manim, co. Gal., 4473.
Manicge (co. Cork), 5761.
Manism (co. Cork ?), 4671.
Manle, Maurice m'Shane, pardon, 6334.

INDEX TO FIANTS.—ELIZABETH.

Manister an Imharie — Manister canhorry. *See* Monaster Imharrie.
Manister ne moyo, co. Cork, preceptory, 5161. *See* Morne.
Manister ne Srehourry—Manister ne Srehurre — Manister neurohurry. *See* Monaster Imharrie.
Manisteradorny—Manister Odorne (Abbeydorney, co. Kerry), 5497.
Manisteraris. *See* Monasteraris.
Manistragh, Shane mc., pardon, [illegible].
Manistrah, Philip m'Shane ne, pardon, 6311.
Mann, George, pardon, [illegible], [illegible].
Mannachan. *See* Monaghan.
Mannagh, David, pardon, 6576.
Mannaghan, John, [illegible].
Mannaghe, Grange of, co. Sligo, 3184.
Manton (co. Cork ?), 6539.
Mannanstown, co. Meath, 1183, 3186, [illegible]
Manne, Edm., pardon, 6497.
Manneen (co. Cork ?), 6487.
Mannen (Mannin), Queen's co., [illegible].
Mannering. *See* Manwaring.
Manneringe, Edmund, grant of land, 6376.
Mannger Tirrelaghe. *See* Maagor Torelaghe.
Mannin, co. Mayo. *See* Mannyn.
Mannin, Queen's co. *See* Mannen.
Manning, co. Cork, [illegible]. *See* Mannynge.
Manninge, Walter, pardon, 173.
Mannon Croughe. *See* Mannynghterreighe.
Mannoryngs, Richard. *See* Manwaring.
Mannyn (co. Cork ?), [illegible].
Mannyn (co. Sligo ?), 6548.
Mannyne, Dermott, pardon, 4837.
Mannynge, Walter, killed, 887.
Mannynge, co. Cork, 6762.
Mannynghterreighe—Mannon Croughe, co. Cork, 4113, 6794.
Mannynvicke Jordan (Manning), co. Cork, 6763.
Manoge, co. Cork, 4361.
Manor, co. Kerry. *See* Newmanor.
Manors to be formed in Connaught, 6746.
Manowe, Shane m'Thomas ne, attainted, 5019, 6'[illegible].
Mansertown, co. Tip. *See* Mounselston.
Mansfieldstown, co. Louth. *See* Mansfeldston.
Mansfild, Edm., pardon, 4114.
„ Henry, pardon, 4115.
„ Rich., pardon, 4116.
Mantach, Philip, pardon, 3874.
Mantagh, Dermod m'Rannell, pardon, 6516.
„ Donogh m'Rannell, pardon, 6516.
„ Fynyn, pardon, 6464.
„ alias Bayos, James fitz Edm., pardon, [illegible].
„ John m'David oge, pardon, 6173, 6539.
Mantagh, Rich. m'David oge, pardon, 6173.
„ Teig m'Fynine, pardon, 6464, 6472.
„ Teige m'Rannell, pardon, 6516.
„ Tirrelagh, pardon, [illegible].
Mantaghe, David oge, pardon, 6173.
„ Moriertagh, pardon, [illegible].
Mantigh, Geffre oge O'Conell, pardon, [illegible].
Manufacture of glass, 6671.
Manwaring —Mainwaring—Mainwaringe—Mannering — Manneringe — Manoryng — Manwering — Mannoryngs —Manwaringe —Manwarynge — Manwayringe — Maywaring — Maynwaringe:
„ Edmund. *See* Manneringe.
„ Edward, gauger of Dublin and Drogheda, 5953-5, 6367.
„ Margaret, surrender, [illegible].
„ Ralph, land of, 6672.
„ Randolf or Randall, pardon, 2817, [illegible], [illegible].
„ Richard, commissions, [illegible], [illegible], [illegible], 1186; pardon, [illegible]; leases, 1077, [illegible], [illegible], 2314-5, 3331, 3416, [illegible], [illegible], [illegible], 4465, [illegible]; his widow, [illegible].
„ Richard, pardon, [illegible], [illegible].
„ Robert, commissions, [illegible], [illegible], 1190; pardon, [illegible]; lease, 636.
„ Roger, chief remembrancer, 2762, 3448, 4188; third baron of Exchequer, 4189; commissions, [illegible], 3811, [illegible], [illegible], 3847, [illegible], 3480; licence of absence, [illegible], 3436; pardon, [illegible].
Manydaffe, co. Long., [illegible].
Manygorymy (co. Lim. ?), 6348.
Many monyo, preceptory, co. Cork, 5161. *See* Morne.
Manyn, co. Gal., 4676-8, 4618, 6414.
Manyn (Mannin), co. Mayo, [illegible], [illegible], [illegible].
Manyshebuge, co. Clare, 4781.
Manyster (Monastery, co. Wick.), 1758.
Mao, John, pardon, 4871.
Maomtraany (Maomltuaan), co. Gal., 4414.
Maorrie (co. Gal. ?), 4679.
Mapasstowne (Mapastown), co. Louth, 1723. *See* Mapestown.
Mape, James, 863.
Mapeston, John, pardon, 2892.
Mapeston, co. Dub., 6363.
Mapestowne (co. Dub. ?), 6604.
Mapestown bridge to be rebuilt, 6044.
Mapleadon, John, constable of Dublin Castle, 4314, 4676, 4700; commissions, 4336, 6981.
Mapperstowne (Mapestown), co. Louth, 1723.

INDEX TO FIANTS—ELIZABETH.

Maquillin, Rowrie m'Cormock, pardon, [illegible].
Maquillyne, Enero, pardon, [illegible].
" Jenkyn m'Cormock, pardon, [illegible].
" Rowrie ogo, pardon, [illegible].
" See M'Quillino.
Maragh, John, pardon, [illegible]67.
Maragh (co. Cork ?), 6371.
Maraghie (co. Cork ?), [illegible].
Marahe, co. Cork, [illegible]41.
Marahan (co. Cork ?), 6418.
Marne, Walter, pardon, 4917.
Marasmall, Hubert m'Donogh, pardon, [illegible]7.
Marbury, John. See Merbury.
March, Anthony. See Marche.
Marchall, Simon, pardon, 4522.
" Thomas, pardon, 4523.
" Wm. oy Reilye fitz Gerot, pardon, [illegible].
Marchandisfield, co. Meath, 4177.
Marchbanke, Thomas, [illegible].
Marche — March, Anthony, grant of land, 637; his heir, [illegible], 6037.
" Christopher, livery to brother, [illegible].
" Edw., pardon, 6418.
" Oliver, pardon, [illegible].
" Robert, pardon, [illegible].
" Thomas, livery, [illegible]; license of alienation, [illegible].
Marches of Dublin, [illegible].
Marcom, Honora ny, pardon, [illegible].
Marcborough — Marchrogh — Marchroughe. See Maryborough.
Marcman, John, pardon, [illegible].
Marcy, Maurice, pardon, [illegible].
" Redmund fitz John, pardon, 4311.
Marcsholm, Trim, [illegible].
Marcward. See Merward.
Maragh, co. Donegal. See Varragh.
Margalian — Margallin — Margalyn barony (Morgallion), co. Meath, [illegible]; martial law, 94, 1412.
Margetson, John, leases, [illegible], [illegible], [illegible]; license to alienate, [illegible].
" John, gunner in Dublin castle, [illegible].
" — Margetson, John, second chamberlain of the Exchequer, [illegible], [illegible]; clerk of first fruits, [illegible], [illegible], [illegible], [illegible].
Marghell, Hubert m'Donoghy, [illegible].
Marhelly, Ellen ny Ronell, pardon, [illegible].
Marlburghe — Marlborough — Marlboroughe — Marlborowe — Marlburroghe — Marlborroghe — Marlborogh — Marlbourghe — Marlbroghe — Marlbrough — Marlbroughe — Marlburgh — Marlburghe. See Maryborough.
Marler, Tho., pardon, 5412.
Marles or Marle, Tho., [illegible].
Marine hwoy alias Margaret, [illegible].
Marimerston. See Marimerston.
Mariners impressed, [illegible], 1411, 2411, [illegible], [illegible], [illegible].
Marimerston — Marimeraton — Marinerstown — Marinerstowne — Marinerton — Mariverton — Marlingstown — Marmanion — Marymerton — Marymerton — Maryverton (Morrington), co. Meath, 163, 178, 241, [illegible], [illegible], [illegible], 1516-7, 1777, 1783, [illegible], [illegible], 3774, [illegible], [illegible]. See Mormerston.
Marle or Marion, Tho., [illegible].
Mariscall, James, attainted, [illegible].
" Ulig, pardon, [illegible].
Marishmore, little, co. Kild., [illegible].
Marishoke, superbe, co. Meath, [illegible].
Marishall, James m'Gerrais duf, pardon, [illegible].
Marishoke, little, co. Meath, [illegible].
Mariverton, co. Meath, 1149. See Marimerston.
Mark, letter of, [illegible].
Markam, Capt., [illegible].
Market, clerk of, duties of, given to corporation of town, [illegible].
" " general, to exercise office throughout Ireland, [illegible], [illegible], [illegible], [illegible].
Market place and tolls leased to corporation of Trim, [illegible], [illegible].
Marlingstown (see Marimerston), [illegible].
Marlinstown, co. Westm. See Ballymarlin.
Marmelot, confection called, [illegible].
Marmanion, co. Meath, [illegible]. See Marimerston.
Marmyne, Tho., English liberty, 111.
Marneglasse, co. Wex., [illegible].
Marnell, pardon, [illegible].
" James, pardon, [illegible].
" Thomas, pardon, [illegible].
Marne (Magbarn ?, co. Westm.), [illegible].
Marroroghe, co. Cork, [illegible].
Marreagh (co. Kilk. ?), [illegible].
Marres, Jordan, pardon, [illegible].
" Oliver, pardon, [illegible].
" Redmund, pardon, [illegible].
Marriage of daughters of burgesses free of royal control, [illegible].
Marriage with Irish, forbidden to settlers, 474.
" second, bar to benefit of clergy, [illegible].
" cognizance of, by eccl. comm., [illegible].
Marriborrowe. See Maryborough.
Marrice, Robert, pardon, [illegible].
Marris, Richard, pardon, [illegible], [illegible].
" William, pardon, [illegible].
Marristowne alias Lattedronkey, King's co., 478.

INDEX TO FIANTS—ELIZABETH.

Marryborough. *See* Maryborough.
Marryonall, James, pardon, 6755.
Marryslowneobiller, co. Kild., 4842.
Marshal of the army, Stanley, 67, 201; sir Nich. Bagnal, 808, 4196; sir Henry Bagnall, 4186, [illegible]; sir Rich. Bingham, [illegible]; sir Chr. Blunt, [illegible]; sir Rich. Wingfield, [illegible].
" his powers and salary, [illegible]; warrant of, 6763.
" called Mr. Marshal, 683.
" to receive book of names of men for whom their chief would answer, 4844.
Marshal, earl, Walter earl of Essex, 2224.
Marshal, under, (John Sankey), 683.
Marshal, vice, under M'Mahon, 4884.
Marshal's court and gaol, 761, 808, 4578.
Marshal Court, judge of, 6148.
Marshall, James fitz Gerrald, pardon, 3042.
" James m'Gerrott duffe, attainted, 4878.
" John, pardon, 3434.
" John fitz Wm., pardon, 6308.
" Michael, 3463, 5408.
" Tho., pardon, 3434, 6167, 6183, 6463.
" Walter, pardon, 3434.
" Wm., pardon, 3434.
" William, rent from his lands in co. Lim., 4532.
" Wm. m'Gerrott, pardon, 3347, 4644.
" Wm. alias Wm. ni booly (of Cloghbullies, co. Lim.), pardon, [illegible].
Marshallescourt, co. Kilk., 504.
Marshallestowne. *See* Marshalstown.
Marshalliston, co. Kild., 1486.
Marshallstown — Marshalls Towne — Marshalston. *See* Marshalstown.
Marshalstown, co. Dub., [illegible].
Marshalstone, co. Antrim, grant, 6628.
Marshalstown — Marsholleistowne — Marshallstown — Marshalston — Marsheliston — Marswhiellston (co. Cork), 2516, [illegible], [illegible], 4878, 4284, 5231, 6488. *See* Ballymarisceall.
Marshalstowne, co. Wex. *See* Ballymarisceall.
Marshialston—Marshialstone, co. Meath, 1983.
Marsk (Murrisk?), co. Mayo, 4878.
Marswhiellston. *See* Marshalstown, co. Cork.
Mart—Marte, Henry, pardon, 1751, 2234, 2926.
Marragh (co. Clare?), 4373.
Marte, Henry (*see* Mart), 2926.
Martell, Chr., pardon, 6778.
" David, 1714.
" Francis, pardon, 2941.
" John, 1714.
" Katherine, 1714.
" Patr., pardon, 5454.
" Peter, pardon, 4297.
" Philip, pardon, [illegible], [illegible], 4428.
Marten. *See* Martin.
Marten's mill (*see* Martin's mill), 5444.
Marteon, William. *See* Martin.
Martener, Robert, pardon, 726.
Martenston (Martinstown), co. Meath, 1124, 4286.
Martenstone, co. Louth, 743.
Martenstowne, co. Kild., 5761.
Marterton, co. Westm., 4161, 4463.
Marterstowne—Martirstowne, co. Cork, [illegible], 4641.
Martery (co. Cork?), 1494.
Martery. *See* Martry.
Martial law commissions. *See* under the several counties and districts.
" power to execute throughout Ireland committed to the marshal of the army, or sergeant major of the army, 726, 683, 1101, 1124, 1382, 1515, 2182, 4297.
" commission for gaol delivery by, 6214-6, 6231, 6344-5, 6294.
" powers conferred on commissioners, 218, 218, 1101, 1828.
" instructions accompanying commissions, 1198.
" limitations to its exercise, 218, 294, 442, 1334, 2832, 1100, 2128, 2281, 3437, 3458, 3631, [illegible].
" commission without usual limitations, 2292.
" pardon to persons engaged in execution of, 618, 639, 635-7, 640-1, 645, 651, 656, 657-8, 658, 2378, 3827, 6662, 4447.
Martin—Marten—Marteon—Martyn:
" Dominick, lease, 1994.
" Dominick, recorder of Galway, commission, 4394.
" Edm., pardon, 2881, 4058.
" Henry, pardon, 1838, 3434.
" James, pardon, 4189.
" Nich., pardon, 4628.
" Piers, merchant of Galway, 3428, 1889.
" Robert, pardon, 5576.
" Tho., pardon, 6467, 4372.
" Thomasin, matrimonial suit, 5652.
" Wm., pardon, 3434.
" Wm., sheriff of co. Galway, 4046; gentleman porter of province of Connaught, 5789; pardon, 3482, 5716, 4862.
" Wm., mill of, at Galway, 5787.
Martingestowne, 648.
Martin's mill, Galway, 5444, 5787, 4183.

INDEX TO FIANTS—ELIZABETH.

Martinstown, co. Meath. *See* Marlestown.
Martinstowne (Queen's co. ?), 6721.
Martinstowne, co. Westm., 1460. *See* Martenston.
Martirie, co. Meath, 2140. *See* Martry.
Martrestown, co. Cork (*see* Marlerstowne), [illegible].
Mortlands, equivalent in acres, 4014, 5341.
Martry—Marteryo—Martirie—Martro—Martrie—Martrys, co. Meath, 180, 2140, 5426; manor, 494; rectory, 1429, 3104, 3814, 3731, 5786, 5426.
Marts or beeves, custom payment, 2319; fine payable in, 1480; rent in, 6785-00.
Marta, Moragh ne, pardon, 5418.
Marty (co. Lim. ?), 4784.
Martymell, Patrick, 622.
" Robert, 622.
Martyn. *See* Martin.
Martynell, Patrick, 51.
" Robert, 51.
Marward—Mareward—Marwarde—Mawrwarde, Jenet or Genet, wardship, 651; pardon, 1487, 5254.
" Walter, baron of Scryne, license of absence, 114; freedom from subsidy, 330; wardship of his heiress, 651; daughter of, 1420.
Marwoode, Henry, 1439.
Mary, Gawen roagh ne, pardon, 5421.
Maryborough—Marohorough—Marobrogh—Marobroughe—Marlborghe—Marlborough—Marlborowe—Marlborroghe—Marlburroughe—Marlburgh—Marlbourghe—Marlbroghe—Marlbroughe—Marlburgh—Marriborrowe—Maryborough—Maryboroughe—Maryborowgh—Marybourgh—Marybrogh—Marybrough—Marybroughe, 490, 1421, 1778, 2124, 2178, 2410, 3346, 3788, 3424, 4298, 4703-4, 4774, 5834-5, 6203, 6354, 6594.
charter of incorporation, 1510.
premises in, granted, 1434, 1377, 1534, 1548, 1561, 1283, 1408, 1544, 1534, 1642, 1643, 1680, 1774, 1823, 2350, 2423, 3400, 5834, 5933; leased, 1846, 5494.
" fort or castle, 653, 1157; lands held of castle, 1825, 2521.
" fort, lieutenant of, 183, 2843.
Maryborough fort, constable of, 612, 1166, 3422, 4161, 4673, 4369; services due to, 430, 2540, 5834, 4573.
" fort, porter of, 2001, 5437.
" commons of pasture of town, 5400.
Mary Gallons, custom so called, at Cashel, 298; at Kilmainham, 1792, 5415; at Mullingar, 5543.
Mary Magdalene, guild of, in Dublin, 2154.
Maryman, John, vicar of Kilpatrick, 1830.
" Wm., alias Holer, pardon, 5577.
Marynerston — Marynerton — Maryverton. *See* Marinerston.
Maryvendriske, co. Meath, 4327.
Mascall alias Rice, Marian, 2824.
Mascally, Gillegowin, pardon, 5542.
" Teige m'Dermot, pardon, 4787.
Masenke, Thomas, pardon, 946.
Masero field, co. Cork, 6473.
Masselon, co. Meath, 8144.
Mashanaglasse—Mashanaglishe—Mashonoglasse—Moshanglashie—Mashanglasse (co. Cork), 5456, 5482, 6447, 6371.
Mashe, Philip, pardon, 3043.
Mason, Bartholomew, treasurer of Christ Church, Dublin, 771.
" Laughlin, pardon, 5302.
" Peter, 5516.
" Rich., land in his tenure, 3318.
" Thomas, treasurer of Christ Church, Dublin, licenses of absence, 481, 704; his successor, 771.
Masons impressed, 1451, 2451, 3485, 3770; pardoned, 4562.
Maspole, co. Wex., 168.
Mass, persons who heard or celebrated, excepted from a pardon, 4317, 5101. *See* Priest.
Masson, Wm. Browne, pardon, 6154.
Masshanoglasse, co. Cork, 4371.
Massingberd, Oswald, knt., prior of S. John of Jerusalem, leases from, 2318, 5484; proclamation for his surrender, 6784.
Mastamaglasse (co. Cork ?) 5452.
Masters (ship), impressed, 1443, 2483, 3078.
Master's field, co. Cork, 1854.
Masterson—Maisterson—Masteranne—Masteranne—Masterton—Mastirson:
" Henry, chief serjeant of Kinselagh, 2344; pardon, 1138, 1342, 3238, 4713.
" Henry, son of Thomas, pardon, 2838, 4012, 4845.
" John, pardon, 2838, 4012, 4845, 5182.
" Nicholas, sheriff of Wexford, commission, 2731; pardon, 2838, 4016, 4845, 5182.

INDEX TO FIANTS—ELIZABETH.

Masterson, Owen, pardon, [illegible].
 " Richard, seneschal of Wexford, [illegible]; constable of Ferns, 4160; commission, [illegible]; lease, [illegible]; pardon, [illegible], 4016, 4646, 6160; knight, his lieutenant, 6441.
 " Thomas, sheriff of Kilkenny, 1196; seneschal of Wexford, 2214, 2401, [illegible]; constable of castle of Ferns, 4517; commissions, [illegible], [illegible], 1126, [illegible], [illegible], [illegible], [illegible], [illegible], [illegible], [illegible], [illegible], 4791; pardon, 016, 1136, [illegible], 1622, [illegible], [illegible], [illegible]; licence to alien to, [illegible]; leases, 1677, [illegible], [illegible], 4342, [illegible]; pardons at his suit, [illegible].
Masterstowne alias Ballymamaistraghe, co. Tip., [illegible].
Masterton, Tho., [illegible]. See Masterson.
Mastin—Mastine, Rich. fitz James, pardon, [illegible], [illegible].
Mastirson, Thomas. See Masterson.
Mastocks—Marrocks—Mastokes, lands in Cromlin, co. Dublin, [illegible], [illegible], [illegible].
Mastokiston, co. Meath, [illegible].
Maston, co. Meath, [illegible].
Mastrome (Mostrim, co. Long.?), rectory, [illegible].
Mateby, co. Cork. See Matheby.
Matholucthy, co. Cork, [illegible].
Matholuoyethy, co. Cork, [illegible].
Matheby (Mateby), co. Cork, [illegible]. See also Teampleanaiche.
Mathewe or Mathewes, Henry, lease, [illegible].
Mathoms, Kyan m'Fyeyn I, pardon, [illegible].
Maudelen land—Maudelen's lands—Mawdelyns land, (Maudlin) near Trim, 1714, [illegible], [illegible].
Maudelenston. See Maudlenestou.
Maudlen chapel and cemetery, Trim, [illegible].
Maudlenestou—Maudelenston, co. Wex., [illegible], [illegible].
Maudlens, co. Meath, [illegible], [illegible].
Maudlens of Wicklow or Spittle house, [illegible].
Maudlin, co. Meath. See Maudelen land, Mawdleyusfield.
Maudlings, co. Kild. See Madellin, Mawdlens.
Maudlins, Trim, [illegible].
Maudlynge (co. Meath?), [illegible].
Maudlyn—Mawdlen—Mawdlin meadow (at Duleek, co. Meath), [illegible], 1462, [illegible], [illegible].
Maudnestown, co. Meath, [illegible].
Maugaurie, Turenne, pardon, [illegible].
Maughanne, Margaret duff ny, pardon, [illegible].
Maugner, Edmund, pardon, [illegible].
 " Philip Iwohir, pardon, [illegible].
Maulaigh (Maulagh), co. Kerry, [illegible].
Mauleycorane (co. Cork?), [illegible].
Mauleygaullo (co. Cork?), [illegible].
Maunetrame, co. Gal. See Macmtramy.
Maunn, Morrish m'Richard, pardon, [illegible].
 " Wm. fitz Nich., pardon, [illegible].
Maunegarrowe (co. Wex. or Car.?), [illegible].
Maunsickston (Mansfieldstown, co. Louth), 1723.
Maunsefeild, Edm., pardon, [illegible].
Maunselston (co. Tip.?), [illegible].
Maunsefelde, Edm. fitz Water, pardon, [illegible].
 " Walter fitz Edm., pardon, [illegible].
Mauntagh, John fitz David oge, pardon, [illegible].
Maurice oge, grant of land, [illegible].
Maurice oge (of Ballytemple co. Cork, FitzGerald?), pardon, [illegible].
Mauris (co. Kilk.?), [illegible].
Maurro, Shane, pardon, [illegible].
Mavna, Morrice, pardon, [illegible].
Maverickston, co. Westm., [illegible].
Maw, Rich., pardon, [illegible].
Mawdeleons. See Mawdlens.
Mawdelens, co. Louth, 182.
Mawdelyn's land. See Maudelen land.
Mawdlen meadow. See Maudlyn meadow.
Mawdlens—Mawdeleness (Maudlings), co. Kild., 6100, 6117.
Mawdleyusfield—Mawdlyusfeild, Trim, [illegible], [illegible].
Mawdlin meadow. See Maudlyn meadow.
Mawdlynsfeild. See Mawdleyusfield.
Mawe—Mawer—Mawne—Mawre (Abbeymahon), co. Cork, [illegible], [illegible], [illegible]; rectory, [illegible], [illegible], [illegible].
 " abbey de Fonte Vivo, leased, [illegible], [illegible], [illegible]; granted, [illegible].
Mawe, Redmund, pardon, [illegible].
Mawer. See Mawe.
Mawgate, Wm., commission, [illegible].
Mawgham near Cork, [illegible].
Mawle, Morish fitz William, pardon, [illegible].
Mawlame, Briane A, pardon, [illegible].
Mawne, co. Cork, rectory, [illegible]. See Mawe.
Mawne, Geoffrey, pardon, [illegible].
 " Gerrod fitz John, pardon, [illegible].
 " Morris, pardon, [illegible].
 " Rob., pardon, [illegible].
Mawre. See Mawe.
Mawrwarde. See Marward.
Maxe, James, vicar of Killpoorok, 4210.
Maxwell, John, a Scotchman, English liberty, [illegible].
May, Humfrey, grant of a wardship, [illegible].
 " John, pardon, [illegible].
 " Walter, 1762.
May. See Maye.
Mayenston, co. Meath, 1460.
Maydarfyme, Owny O'Carroll (of Medrossy?), pardon, [illegible].

INDEX TO FIANTS—ELIZABETH.

Maye, Morris, pardon, [illegible].
Maye—May (river Maigue), co. Lim., [illegible]; salmon weir, 6118, [illegible].
Maye monastery, co. Lim., possessions granted, 5414.
Maynell, Rich., pardon, [illegible].
Mayrh, the, co. Sligo, 4794.
Mayhin alias O'Gallagan, Conoghor, pardon, 4675.
Maylard — Mallarde, Paul, record keeper, Dublin Castle, 1630; registrar ecclesiastical commission, [illegible], [illegible].
Maylardeston — Maylardstone, co. Kilk., [illegible], 4972.
Maynaghille (co. Westm. ?), 6574.
Maynam—Mayman alias Mayne (Mainham), co. Kild., rectory, 614, [illegible].
Mayne, co. Clare, 1048.
Mayne. See Maynam.
Mayne, co. Kilk., rector of, 1617.
Mayne, co. Lim. See Trean meane.
Mayne (co. Louth ?), 1818.
Mayne, co. Meath, 973, 2851.
Mayne, co. Westm., 1611, [illegible], [illegible]; rectory, [illegible], 5478.
„ vicar of, [illegible].
Maynam, co. Cork, [illegible].
Maynothe — Mainothe — Maynoth — Maynoth—Maynowth — Moynothe—Moynooth—Mynoth (Maynooth), co. Kild., [illegible], [illegible], 1148, 1786, 1818, [illegible], [illegible], [illegible], 6567.
„ College of, possessions leased, 6118.
„ Newton by, 789.
„ prebendary of, [illegible].
Maynlayne, Edmund, pardon, 1894.
„ John fitz Rob., pardon, [illegible].
Maynitr Ieodaghin (Muintir-Feodachain, in co. Ferm.), [illegible].
Maynwaring. See Manwaring.
Mayo (co. Leit. ?), [illegible].
Mayo—Maio, co. Mayo, [illegible].
„ abbey or priory of canons, leased, 1494; granted, 5419; possessions leased, [illegible].
„ county: commission to form county, 1584; barony of Ross, a part of, 5121; surrender and regrant of bar. Clanmorris, 4057, [illegible]; martial law, [illegible], [illegible]; gaol, [illegible]; crimes committed outside the county excepted from pardon, 5797, [illegible]; rebels in, [illegible]; pardon to all queen's subjects in, 5782.
„ sheriff, [illegible], [illegible], [illegible].
Mayon, James fitz Tho., pardon, [illegible].
Mayon, Redmund fitz Edm., pardon, [illegible].
Mayor, exemption from serving as, 6771.
Mayors, to take oath of supremacy, [illegible].
Mayrh, Philip, pardon, [illegible].
Mayston (Macetown), co. Westm., [illegible].
Maze, co. Down. See Mow.
Meadstown, co. Cork, [illegible].
Meagh, in Connaught, 1807.
Meagh—Meaghe:
„ David, pardon, [illegible], [illegible], [illegible], [illegible].
„ Garrett fitz Tho., pardon, [illegible].
„ George, house in Kilmallock, [illegible].
„ George, pardon, 4459.
„ James (of Clenlish), pardon, [illegible]; grant of a wardship, [illegible].
„ James (of Kinsale), pardon, [illegible].
„ James fitz Patr. (of Cork), sheriff of Desmond, pardon, [illegible].
„ John. See Myagh.
„ John fitz James, pardon, [illegible].
„ Nich., land grant, [illegible].
„ Patrick, pardon, [illegible], [illegible].
„ Patrick, alienation to, [illegible].
„ Richard, pardon, [illegible].
„ Robert, lease, [illegible].
„ Rob. fitz Rich., pardon, 4448.
„ Stephen, pardon, [illegible].
„ Thomas (of Athy), pardon, 4447.
„ William, pardons in Cork in his tenure, [illegible].
„ William, executed for murder, [illegible].
Meaghair, John, pardon, [illegible].
Meaghan, co. Lim., towghe of, [illegible].
Meaghe. See Meagh, Myagh.
Meaghe's lands, Youghal, [illegible].
Meagher, Anstace fitz Wm., pardon, [illegible].
„ Cornelius, pardon, [illegible].
„ Donogh m'Donill I, pardon, [illegible].
„ Edm., pardon, [illegible].
„ James, [illegible].
„ Mallady fitz Thomas I, pardon, [illegible].
„ Margaret fitz Conoghor, pardon, 4674.
„ Richard fitz John I, pardon, [illegible], [illegible].
„ Teig m'Donogh I, pardon, [illegible].
„ William, pardon, [illegible].
Meaghere, Cornelius, pardon, [illegible].
Meaghill (co. Clare ?), [illegible].
Meaghir, Conoghor m'Teig, pardon, [illegible].
„ Donogh m'Thomas I, pardon, [illegible].
„ John m'Conoghor I, pardon, [illegible].
Meaghiris, Gerralt m'Teig I, pardon, 4734.
Mealstown, co. Dub. See Moteckystown.
Mealaghamor (Mellaghmore), co. Kilk., [illegible].
Mealaugh (co. Rosc. ?), [illegible].
Meale, Gerrott and Rich. fitz James fitz John, pardon, [illegible].

INDEX TO FIANTS.—ELIZABETH.

Meale, Philip fitz Rich. fitz John, pardon, [illegible].
„ Tho. and Wm. m'Shane, pardon, [illegible].
Mealer, John, pardon, 6748.
Mealicke, co. Gal., 5974.
Meallage, John, lease, [illegible].
Meallaghmore, co. Kilk. See Moalaghemor, Molaghmore.
Mean (co. Lim.?), [illegible].
Meane (co. Lim.?), [illegible].
Meane, alias Mahowragh, co. Lim., [illegible].
Meanes (Maine), co. Cork, [illegible].
Meanes—Meanis, co. Lim., 6169.
Meanus, co. Kerry. See Mianus.
Meara, Giles ny, pardon, 6707.
Meargaleagh — Meargalaghe (co. Donegall), [illegible], [illegible].
Mearis, Morish, pardon, [illegible].
Meary, Philip, pardon, [illegible].
Measures of capacity, peck of wheat, oats, or malt, number of gallons in, [illegible], [illegible].
„ measure of butter, [illegible].
„ of Drogheda, [illegible].
„ Kilkenny, [illegible].
„ Wexford, [illegible].
„ false, to be inquired of, [illegible].
Measures of land:
„ See Acres.
„ See Ballybetagh.
„ Gabalti, [illegible].
„ See Carew or quarter.
„ See Cartron.
„ See Carucate.
„ Gallon, [illegible].
„ Martland, [illegible]. See Martland.
„ See Ploughland.
„ Poll, Pole, Pull, 1651, [illegible].
„ Pottle, [illegible].
„ Rood, [illegible].
„ Stang, [illegible].
„ See Taie.
Meat, export of, [illegible], [illegible].
Meath—Methe—Methe—Mydhe:
„ bishop William (Walsh), refuses oath of supremacy, 184.
„ bishop Hugh Brady, license of absence, 646; commissions, [illegible], [illegible], 1417-8, 1496, 1664, [illegible], [illegible], [illegible], 1846, [illegible], [illegible], [illegible], [illegible], [illegible], [illegible], [illegible], [illegible], [illegible], [illegible], [illegible], [illegible], [illegible], [illegible], [illegible], 4148, 4173, [illegible]; pardon, 1729, [illegible], [illegible]; pardon at his suit, [illegible], [illegible], [illegible]; lands allotted to, [illegible]; appeal from, [illegible]; vicar general of, [illegible]; son and heir of, [illegible].
„ bishop, commission, [illegible].

Meath, bishop Thomas Jones, [illegible]; commissions, [illegible], [illegible], [illegible], 4479, [illegible]; pardon of intrusion, [illegible]; license of alienation, [illegible]; grant made at his suit, [illegible]. See Jones, Thomas.
„ bishop, rent to, [illegible]; possessions of See granted during vacancy, [illegible]; church united to bishopric, [illegible].
„ archdeacon Rob. Luttrell refuses oath of supremacy, [illegible]; deprived, [illegible].
„ archdeacon John Garvey, [illegible], [illegible], [illegible], [illegible], [illegible], 712, [illegible], [illegible], [illegible]. See Garvey.
„ vicar general, [illegible], [illegible].
„ official, 3134, [illegible].
„ cathedral, [illegible].
„ diocese, presentations in, [illegible], [illegible], [illegible], [illegible], [illegible]; sequestration in, [illegible].
„ province, ecclesiastical commission, [illegible].
„ East Meath—Meath county, oath of supremacy administered to justices and officers, [illegible]; lord deputy occupied in government of, [illegible], 1417-8; instruction for defence, [illegible]; pardon to be pleaded before queen's commissioners in, [illegible]; excluded from government of Ulster, [illegible]; wages of soldiers against O'Mores cessed on, [illegible]; ploughlands in, [illegible].
„ commission of the peace, [illegible].
„ commission of musters, [illegible], [illegible], [illegible], [illegible], [illegible], [illegible], [illegible].
„ commission to keep watch and ward, [illegible].
„ commissions for martial law, [illegible], [illegible], [illegible], [illegible], [illegible], [illegible], [illegible], [illegible], 1847, [illegible]; martial law on the borders, [illegible].
„ commission to inquire of forfeited lands, [illegible], [illegible]; concealed wardships, &c., [illegible].
„ authority to impress hay, [illegible], [illegible], [illegible], [illegible], [illegible], [illegible], [illegible].
„ general of the army in, [illegible].
„ provost marshal, [illegible], [illegible].

INDEX TO FIANTS—ELIZABETH.

Meath, sheriff, 33, 37, 64, 672, 1828, 3176, 3848, 3360, 3389, 3874, 3978, 3183, 3182, 4304, 5708, 6710, 6714, 6744, 6364.
" clerk of crown and peace, 3634, 6131, 4383, 6818, 3872, 6148.
" cess collector, 6781.
" general cessor, 4387.
" searcher of tanning, 1797, 3018.
Meaye (co. Rosc. ?), 6498.
Meandam, Philip, son of Tho., English liberty, 177.
Mearmoyke, Geoffry m'Broyne, pardon, 1768.
Mearogh, Edmund, son of Donagh, English liberty, 177.
Mearyllyanghtis, Donald, son of Edm., English liberty, 177.
Meckary (Mackrery, co. Gal. ?), 2878.
Meemaighter, Thady, son of Fergal raffus, pardon to son, 6498.
Meeraighe, Moriertagh m'Donell, pardon, 6694.
Medder, a measure, amount of, 4830.
Medicos, pardoned, 6138.
Meeagh, Jasper, comm., 5678.
Meede, James, 2818; pardon, 2888.
Meehan, co. Westm. See Maillmoonaghane.
Meeldrum, co. Westm. See Meyldrome, Mildrom, Moyldrom.
Meellick, co. Gal. See Melock, Nylekn.
Meelick, co. Rosc. See Mellyke.
Meeltamagh, co. Long. See Moyltemy.
Meenaghter, co. Cork. See Minnaghter, Mynooughter.
Megabir, Thady Odolne, pardon, 6604.
Megawlin, co. Kerry, 6498.
Megher, Gillesenewe, pardon, 3941.
Megherrnahe. See Maghyrrowe.
Meghowny, co. Clare, 6462.
Megillne, Cooaghor m'Owen, pardon, 6418.
" Donogh, pardon, 6818.
Megiare. See Moygiare.
Megoge, King's co., 488, 1464.
Megoge, Queen's co., 537.
Mehill, co. Clare, 6988.
Mei, Thomas, 948.
Meiaghe. See Myagh.
Meiraleaboll. See Moyranbol.
Meiaighearnain, Gorman, son of Donaith, pardon, 6464.
" Pelimeus flavus, son of Malachy, pardon, 6462.
" John, son of Felim, pardon, 6462.
Meighearnan, Goyneolpe, son of Donald, pardon, 6462.
Meighearnain, Garbricius, son of Felom, pardon, 6462.
Meigh, co. Cavan, 6464.
Meigher, Wm., pardon, 6042.
Meiler. See Meyler.
Meilerrinton (co. Tip. ?), 6978.
Meilerston (Mylerstown, co. Kild.), 6761, 6498.
Meiltrenage—Mellieman (co. Kilk. ?), 3638.
Meind, co. Lim., 2378.
Meithe, Hugh, bishop of. See Meath.
Melagh, co. Kilk., 4388.
Melagh (co. Tip. ?), 6788.
Melaghoffe, co. Kerry, 6498.
Melaghme mead, co. Dub., 3488.
Melaghlen, Margaret (ny), pardon, 4744.
" Patrick Morcho alias, pardon, 3064.
Melaghlin, Jane ny, pardon, 6457.
" Sealy ny, pardon, 6812.
" Sowe ne, pardon, 6128.
" Sowry ny, pardon, 6418.
" Teige m'Moriertaghe, pardon, 6438.
Melaghl [illegible] (co. Kilk. ?), 3631.
Melaghmore—Mellaghmore (Mcallaghmore ? co. Kilk.), 1904, 3848, 3948, 4903, 6144, 6368.
Melaughan, Arthur, attainted, 6777.
Melay, James m'Conagery A, pardon, 692.
Melaye, Cahyre m'Fir A, pardon, 692.
" Owen m'Conagery A, pardon, 692.
" Rorye m'Conagery A, pardon, 692.
" Rosse m'Conegery A, pardon, 691.
Melchiocke (co. Wex. ?), 78.
Meldrome Meldrome (Meldrum, co. Tip.), 1888, 6916.
Melecke—Meleeke—Mileck—Mileeke—Milyke—Myleeke—Myleck—Myleeke—Mylike—Mylyck (Meelick), co. Gal.), 1661, 3880, 4458, 4684, 5438.
" castle or manor, 1661, 3879, 4458, 5438.
" castle, victualling of, 41; land belonging to, 41.
" village, 1661, 3879, 5438.
Melefant—Meleford—Meltfant—Melifont. See Mellifont.
Melig, Edm. m'Morris, pardon, 6467.
Meligan, Wm. m'Tho. I, pardon, 6197.
Mell, co. Louth, 498.
Mellaghelon, 1763.
Melleghlin, Cahill glaswe, pardon, 6674.
" Joan ny, pardon, 6674.
Mellaghmore. See Melaghmore.
Mellane, John, pardon, 6494.
Mellaughercrowe, 6318.
Mellake, co. Rosc., 6777.
Mellifont—Meleafant—Meleford—Meltfant—Melifont—Mellefont—Mellefount—Mellefounte—Mellifonte—Mellifounte—Mellyfant—Mellyfaunt—Mellyfont—Mellyfonte—Mellyfount—Melly-

INDEX TO FIANTS—ELIZABETH.

Mellifont :
fonnte — Molyfunt — Melyfont — Mellyfont, co. Louth, 641-2, 662, 668, 1780-1, 1987, 2134, 2343, 2345, 2372, 2378, 2604, 2806, 2841, 3362, 3368, 3874, 3876-7, 3887, 4226, 4733, 6008, 6601.
abbey of B. V. M., leased, 690, 2871, 2872, 6547; proxies from churches of, 4787.
parish, 869.
„ wood, 666, 2071, 2872.
Meltyke (Mellick, co. Ross. ?), 4777.
Malad, Rich., pardon, 4481.
Maley, Cahyne roe A. (O'Malley), pardon, 1494.
„ Hugh A., pardon, 1418.
„ John m'Brian A., pardon, 1418.
„ Teig A., pardon, 1418.
Meloy, Patrick rioughe m'Morie A., pardon, 1418.
Melton (co. Wexm. ?), 4467.
Malbone, co. Ross., 3440.
Mellowne, King's co., 4608.
Melyfont—Melyfont. See Mellifont.
Menyan — Menyane — Meinyran, co. Wat., 300, 3123; chapel, 300, 3123.
Menagh, Bren, pardon, 4190.
„ Pheleme, pardon, 4190.
Menagh, co. Tip. or Kilk., 3768.
Menaloan (Moynillan ?), co. Down, 4427.
Menane (co. Cork ?), 6610.
Menane, John, 6063, 6514.
Menarde (Minard), co. Kerry, 4606.
Menarishe, Tirlagh, attainted, 4127.
Menchorin, co. Kerry, 6124.
Menecrie, co. Kerry, 6124.
Menenmore, 741.
Menoochiy, co. Kerry, 6124.
Menovegh, co. Kerry, 6124.
Menoverine, co. Kerry, 6124.
Mongane (Mangan), co. Wex., 4706.
Menlagh (Menlough, bar. Tiaquin, co. Gal. ?), 4671. See also Mynloghe.
Mennarde (co. Kerry ?), 1265.
Meniane, Conchor, pardon, 4617.
Meniargroan, co. Long., 6148.
Menitrnie, in Munster, 4826.
Menlorgh—Meotmraghe, co. Ross., 3160, 6015.
Meny, the, co. Wex., 6161.
Menehan, Thomas, English liberty, 496.
Moory, Margaret, pardon, 1365.
Meranagh, Donogh roo, pardon, 4417.
Mologhlin m'Shane, pardon, 4183.
Meranaghe, Donogh roe m'Teige, pardon, 6716.
Meranagh, Donogh, pardon, 4484.
Merbury — Marbury, John, commissions, 4490, 4731, 4745, 5265; pardon, 4562.
Merchandise, illegal export of, 448.
Merchant guild at Dingle, 4816; at Kilmallock, 4874.
Merchant, Erick, and family, pardoned, 4398.
Merchants who had suffered losses protected from the Government victuallers, 4740.
Merchant tailor, 673, 1387.
Merchants, foreign, protection for, 1718.
Meredeth, Evan, house in Dublin, 1422.
Meredith — Meredeth — Meredithe — Meridith :
„ John, trustee, 6064.
„ John, chaplain of Gowran, 6730.
„ Richard, dean of S. Patrick's, 4718; rector of Loughrea, 4451; licence of absence, 4133; bishop of Leighlin, 5319; commissions, 5708, 4890, 4922; fined by Star Chamber, 6090; pardon of alienation, 6061.
„ Rich., pardon of alienation, 6061.
„ Tho., rector of Delgany, 6732.
Meroeagh, Donogh m'Muriertagh, pardon, 6764.
„ Murkiertagh, attainted, 6133.
Merogan alias m'Shane, Donell, pardon, 4898.
Merriman, Edm. m'Richard, pardon, 4882.
Merrsfield, co. Meath, 1463.
Mercyong—Meroyonge. See Meryong.
Mergagh, Canner, pardon, 4878
„ Connor O'Callvane, pardon, 4874.
„ Donogh, pardon, 6473.
„ Hugh, pardon, 6647.
Mergenstan, co. Dub., 2384.
Mergine, David, pardon, 4323.
„ Morrish, pardon, 4323.
Merginstown, co. Wick. See Ballymurgin.
Mergyghe, Donell, pardon, 6616.
Mergyne, Rob., pardon, 6614.
Merhija, co. Clare, 4608.
Meriall, Richard, pardon, 610.
Merick, Edward fitz Hobert, pardon, 6064.
Meridoth, Richard. See Meredith.
Meris, Tho., pardon, 6434.
Merigagh, David, pardon, 6634.
Donell m'Conoghor, pardon, 4884.
Donell m'Mahowne, pardon, 6634.
Donogh, alias m'Conoghor, pardon, 6513.
John m'Teig, pardon, 4484.
„ Tirlagh m'Donell, pardon, 4484.
Mirigh, Donogh m'Teige, pardon, 4409.
Merighagh, Donell ogo, pardon, 6464.
„ Mollmuro m'Teig, pardon, 6466.
Merighaghe, Fynine m'Teig, pardon, 6458.
Merighi alias M'Shithie, Edm., pardon, 6468.
Merigh alias O'Hoeflaghune, John, pardon, 6179.
Merion—Merionge. See Meryong.
Merlory, John, commission, 1967.

INDEX TO FIANTS—ELIZABETH.

Merreagh, Merrieragh, indenture, [illegible].
Merreghy, Awliffe m'Shane I, pardon, [illegible].
Merrenagh, Calloagh, pardon, [illegible].
Merrick, Ricard, pardon, [illegible].
" — Merryck — Mirrick — Myrrick, Thomas, sheriff of Queen's co., [illegible]; commissions, [illegible], [illegible], [illegible]; pardon, [illegible]; surrender of his lands, [illegible].
" See Mirrick.
Merrikeston, Queen's co., [illegible].
Merrieagh, John, pardon, [illegible].
Merrigtag, Fynyn, pardon, [illegible].
Merrigeagh, Manus fitz Edm., pardon, [illegible].
Merrieigh, Donagh m'Thomell, pardon, [illegible].
Merrion, co. Dub. See Meryonge.
Merriwall, co. Kild., [illegible].
Merry, Katherine ny's Wm., pardon, [illegible].
" Morris fitz Wm., pardon, [illegible].
" Richard alias O'Howlaughan, pardon, [illegible].
" Tho. (of Callan), pardon (see Mary), [illegible].
" Thomas fitz Wm., pardon, [illegible].
Merryck, Art, pardon, [illegible].
" Hubbert oge, pardon, [illegible].
" Tho. See Merrick.
Merryman, capt. Nicholas, pension, [illegible]. See Meryman.
" Peter, pardon, [illegible].
Merugagh, Owen m'Teig, pardon, [illegible].
Mery alias O'Wolighan, John, pardon, [illegible].
Mery alias Holoman, Philip, pardon, [illegible].
Mery, Tho. (of Callan), pardon, [illegible].
Merye, Wm., pardon, [illegible].
Meryyragh, Donogh, pardon, [illegible].
Meryman, Nich., pardon, [illegible].
Meryong — Mereyong — Mereyonge — Merion — Merionge — Meryon — Meryonge — Mirreyonge — Mirryonge — Mirryyoun — Myrreyonge (Merrion, co. Dub.), [illegible], [illegible], [illegible], [illegible], [illegible], [illegible], [illegible], [illegible], [illegible], [illegible], [illegible], [illegible], [illegible]-1.
Meskill, William, pardon, [illegible].
Messenger, Butler's, [illegible].
Messenger of Maguire, pardon, [illegible].
Metcalf, Richard, gunner, [illegible], [illegible].
Methe co. See Meath.
Mevagh, co. Donegal. See Myvaugh.
Mew, five towns of the, (Mase), co. Down, [illegible].
Mey (Moy), co. Gal., [illegible].
Mey, Patr., [illegible].
" Rob., killed, [illegible].
" Thomaston, [illegible].
Meyghaishell. See Moycashel.
Meyldrume (Muldrum, co. Westm.), [illegible].
Meyler — Meller — Meylere:
" Anne, widow, [illegible].
Meyler, John m'Rich., pardon, [illegible].
" Nicholas (of Dunmoremock, co. Wex.), his heir, [illegible].
" Walter, pardon, [illegible], [illegible].
" Walter (of Dunmoremock), wardship, [illegible]; pardon, [illegible].
" William (of Dunmoremock), [illegible].
" Wm., pardon, [illegible], [illegible], [illegible].
Meylerston, co. Kild., [illegible], [illegible].
Meylerstown (co. Kilk.?), [illegible].
Meylerstowne (Mylerstown), co. Kild., [illegible].
Meyll, John, pardon, [illegible].
Meylodstown (co. Tip.?), [illegible].
Meyn, co. Lim., [illegible].
Meynarde (Minard, co. Kerry?), rectory, [illegible], [illegible]. See also Monnarde.
Miaghill, co. Tip., rectory, [illegible].
Miagh — Miaghe, Anne, pardon, [illegible].
" David, son of George, pardon, [illegible], [illegible].
" David, pardon, [illegible].
" Edw., pardon, [illegible].
" George (of Kilmallock), pardon, [illegible], [illegible]; his son, [illegible].
" George, pardon, [illegible], [illegible].
" Gerald, son of George, pardon, [illegible], [illegible].
" Gerald or Gerod, son of Henry, pardon, [illegible], [illegible].
" Henry, son of, pardon, [illegible].
" James, pardon, [illegible], [illegible].
" James. See Myagh.
" John. See Myagh.
" John, son of George, pardon, [illegible], [illegible]-70.
" John, son of Henry, pardon, [illegible], [illegible].
" John, son of Robert, pardon, [illegible], [illegible].
" John, pardon, [illegible].
" Manus groome, pardon, [illegible].
" Margaret, pardon, [illegible].
" Owen boy, pardon, [illegible].
" Patrick (of Kilmallock), pardon, [illegible], [illegible].
" Patrick (of Kinsale), pardon, [illegible].
" Richard, son of Henry, pardon, [illegible], [illegible].
" Richard, son of James, pardon, [illegible], [illegible].
" Robert (of Kilmallock), pardon, [illegible], [illegible].
" Robert (of Kinsale), pardon, 4524, [illegible], [illegible].
" Stephen, pardon, [illegible], [illegible], [illegible].
" Thomas (of Drogheda), [illegible].
" Thomas. See Myagh.
" William, senior, pardon, [illegible].
" William, son of Henry, pardon, [illegible], [illegible].

INDEX TO FIANTS—ELIZABETH.

Miagh, William, son of Robert, pardon, 640, 1470.

" See Meagh, Myagh.

Miagho, vicar of Castellknock, 6910.

Mialogo alias M'Justice, Rich., pardon, 6152.

Miames (Menames), co. Kerry, 5312.

Mic Bran, Donoghe oge, pardon, [illegible].

Mic Brunn, Conogher m'Donoghe, pardon, [illegible].

" Dermod m'Donoghe, pardon, [illegible].

" Donoghe m'Dermod oge, pardon, [illegible].

" Teige m'a Donoghe, pardon, [illegible].

Mic Bryen, Matthew and Maurice, 64. See M'Brien.

Miche Cahraghe alias Cabraghe, Dublin, 708, 1764.

Micheleston. See Michelston.

Michell—Mychell, Francis, [illegible]; grant of a wardship, 6452.

Michelleston. See Michelston.

Michelleston (Michelstown), co. Meath, 4730.

Michellston — Michelleston — Michellstown. See Michelston.

Michelschurche, 1078.

Michelston — Micheleston — Michelleston — Michellston—Michelleton — Michellstown —Michelestone—Michelstowne— Michelton —Mychelleston (Michelstown), co. Cork, 287, 2366, 3784, 3046, 3476-7, 4743, [illegible], 6406, 6567, 6638; manor, 3016, 3283, 3738, 4346, 6718.

Mich Riverston, 734.

Mickmasstown, co. Meath. See Myckmaston, Mylkemaston.

Middle Calfe, island of the, (co. Cork ?), 4426.

Middleton, John, treasurer of Christ Church, Dublin, 6464.

Middleton, co. Cork. See Chore and Castrocore.

Middletowne (co. Tip. ?), 6764.

Mienhill (co. Cork ?), 6615.

Mighan, Wm., pardon, 2410.

Might—Mighte—Myghte, Thomas, authorised to impress victual for army, 677; surveyor of victuals for army, 926, 1168, 1692, 2061, [illegible], 6728; licence to alien, 1890; matrimonial cause, 2821.

Migiare. See Moygiare.

Mileaghy, Teige m'Donnogh I, pardon, 5421.

Mildrom (Mieldrum, co. Westm.), 6607.

Mile, Thomas, commission, 864.

Milecke—Milecke. See Melack.

Miles, Alexander, pardon, 4468.

" John, smith of the ordnance, 6158, 6590.

" See Myles.

Mileston, co. Dub. (co. Wick.), 4621.

Mileston—Myleston (Milestown), co. Meath, 672, 1661.

Milowne (co. Tip. ?), 2208.

Milestowne (co. Cork ?), 6308.

Milstone, co. Louth, beside Termonfeighen, 5416.

Milforen—Myfforen, co. Westm., 467, 3708.

Milhousy—Milhouse. See Moylhussie.

Milick, co. Clare, 3082.

Mill, the (co. Wex. ?), 6161.

Mill to be built by lessee, 1454.

Mill: horse-mills to be impressed for army, 642.

Millaghe (co. Kilk. ?), 4302.

Millbeler, in Kilmainham, 5416.

Millcastle, co. Westm. See Mylcastellon, Mylkastle.

Millen, Margaret, 6162.

Miller pardoned, 4434.

Miller, Wm., burgess, Athlone, 4916.

" Wm., searcher and gauger of Dublin, 6963, 6387.

Millers impressed for army, 676, 1661, 2431.

Miller's half acre, co. Kild., 1347.

Milles, Edward, grant of a wardship, 4064.

Milleston by Rabran, co. Car. (co. Wick.), rectory, 1367.

Mille[towne] alias Ballon Willan, co. Tip., 4648

Millstownewood. See Milltownewood.

Millhorne park. See Mylhorne.

Millmont, Maurice, protection, 1818.

Millmahaught (co. Westm. ?), 6622.

Millston (co. Tip. or Lim.), 6006.

Millo bstowne, co. Kild., 6762.

Millshore, Limerick, 6042.

Millton—Milton, King's co., 4861, 6418.

Milltown, co. Cork. See Ballinvullen.

Milltown (co. Lim.), 6478, 6497.

" See Ballymullen.

Milltown, co. Ross. See Mylton.

Milltown. See Milton.

Milltowne—Milltowne—Mylton, co. Tip., 4652, 6461, 6621. See Milton.

Milltowne, 6534.

Milltownewood—Millstownewood, co. Wex., 6139, 6172.

Mindestown—Myledodan, co. Tip., 4383, 6337.

Milotaston — Millotaston — Myloteston, co. Kild., 1164, 1963, 4363.

Milstown (co. Cork ?), 6166.

Milstowne, mill, co. Kild., 6117.

Mildowne (co. Kilk. ?), 6644.

Milton (co. Cork or Tip. ?), 1368.

Milton, co. Dub., 826, 6663.

Milton, co. Dub. (Wick.), 5745.

Milton—Myllton, co. Dub., in Newcastle manor, 2465, 6347.

Milton—Milltowne (Milltown), co. Gal., 4363, 6164, 6969.

INDEX TO FIANTS—ELIZABETH.

Milton, co. Kild., [illegible].
Milton. See Millton, King's co.
Milton (co. Lim. ?), 6464.
Milton—Miltone—Mylton, grange by, co. Louth, [illegible], [illegible], [illegible].
Milton (in par. Termonfeckin), co. Louth, [illegible].
Milton—Miltone, co. Louth, 5416, [illegible].
Milton, co. Meath, 143.
Milton—Mylton, co. Meath, [illegible], [illegible], [illegible], [illegible].
Milton, alias Killinquirke, co. Rosc., [illegible].
Milton—Mylton, co. Tip., 647, [illegible], 4110, [illegible].
Milton—Miltowne—Mylton — Myltowne, co. Westm. 6, 1618, 1744, [illegible], 3911, [illegible], 3782, 4141, 4281.
Milton, little, co. Westm., 1310.
Miltone, grange by. See Milton, co. Louth.
Miltone, co. Louth. See Milton, co. Louth.
Miltowne. See Milton, co. Westm.
Miltown (co. Westm.), 6443.
Miltowne, 5615.
Miltowne. See Millton, co. Gal.
Miltowne, Queen's co., [illegible].
Miltowne. See Milltowne.
Miltowny. See Moyltrowle.
Milverton, co. Dub. See Myllwardston.
Minakaragh river (co. Donegal), [illegible], [illegible].
Minalvy, co. Meath, [illegible].
Minard, co. Kerry. See Monarde, Moynarde, Mynard.
Minchem farm in Crumlin, co. Dub., 6188.
Minck, co. Tip. or Wat., [illegible].
Mineston — Minstowne (Ministown), co. Meath, [illegible], [illegible].
Minig, Shane, pardon, [illegible].
Minion, Patr., pardon, [illegible].
Minister, a, pardoned, 4487; on appeal commission, [illegible].
Ministown, co. Meath. See Mineston, Mynestowne.
Minitor, David, pardon, 3042.
" David oge, pardon, 3042.
" James. See Mynitor.
" Nich., pardon, 3042.
" Nich., pardon, [illegible]. See Mynatore.
" Teig oge m'Davie oge, pardon, [illegible].
" Tho., pardon, 3042.
" Wm., pardon, 3041.
Minster (Moitenland ?), co. Lim., 5047.
Minughter, in Imokilly (Mounaughter), co. Cork, [illegible].
Minne, Rowland, pardon, [illegible].
Minstowne. See Mineston.
Minteirfondaghis (Mointir Foodachain, co. Ferm.), [illegible].
Mintercheonaki, co. Cav., 4834.
Minyfaigh (Moneyfinagh), co. Cork, [illegible].
Minvale, co. Down, [illegible],
M'Wright, Bryan m'Edm., pardon, [illegible].
Mirre, Philip, pardon, [illegible].
Mirreyonge. See Meryong.
Mirrick, Richard, pardon, [illegible].
" Thomas. See Merrick.
Mirricke, Gillis, knt. (of Radnorshire), grant of a wardship, [illegible].
Mirryong — Mirryonge — Mirryyoung. See Meryong.
Mischell, Shane, pardon, [illegible].
Missell, co. Car., 1740.
Misset, Edw., pardon, [illegible].
Mishell, co. Car., [illegible].
Misset—Myset, Edmund, commission, [illegible]; pardon, 1184; livery to son, 3112.
" Rich., livery, 3112.
Missett, Tho., pardon, [illegible].
Mitcholstown, co. Cork. See Michelston.
Mitchelstowne, co. Meath. See Michellestón, Mychelstone.
Mitchelstowndown, co. Lim. See Ballinvistellanedowne.
Mivernagh, Teige boy, pardon, [illegible].
Mnocklin, Donell m'Shane vic, pardon, [illegible].
Mnowey, Teig, son of John, pardon, [illegible].
Moaghan, co. Clare, manor, [illegible].
Moailne (co. Mayo ?), [illegible].
Moallo—Moalle—Moalley—Moally—Moiallo —Moyallo (Mallow), co. Cork, [illegible], [illegible], [illegible], [illegible], [illegible], [illegible]; inquisition taken at, [illegible], [illegible]; castle and lands granted, [illegible]; rectory, [illegible].
Moanery (co. Cork ?), 5476.
Moanleame, co. Lim. See Moneleenaghe.
Moare, Morrys, pardon, [illegible].
Moarte. See Moyarta.
Moel, co. Kerry, [illegible].
Moelle, co. Gal., [illegible].
Moene, co. Kerry, 5512, [illegible].
Moello (co. Rosc. ?), [illegible], [illegible].
Moelle, co. Westm. See Mooly.
Moey, co. Sligo, [illegible].
Mobernan—Mobernayne, co. Tip., [illegible], [illegible].
Mocallop, [illegible].
Mocare, co. Mayo, [illegible].
Mocarke, co. Tip., [illegible].
Mocorr, co. Mayo, [illegible].
Mocorompy—Mocorompye. See Morrome.
Mocho Marwicke, Trim, [illegible].
Mochincho (Mochinagh, co. Louth), [illegible].
Mochler, Peter, pardon, [illegible].
" Rich., pardon, [illegible].
Mocbrompy, co. Cork, [illegible].
Mockelly (Moiclaise), co. Kild., rectory, [illegible].
Mockenes, co. Clare, [illegible].
Mockerveh. See Mockreah.
Mockbowne, co. Kild., grange of, [illegible].
Mockler, Edm., pardon, [illegible].
" James fitz Nich., pardon, [illegible].

INDEX TO FIANTS.—ELIZABETH.

Mockler, Katherine, pardon, 6476.
" Nich., pardon, 6477.
" Nich. fitz Jeffery, pardon, 6466.
" Tho., pardon, 6766.
Mocklerston—Mocklerston—Mocklerstowne—Mowclerstowne, co. Tip., [illegible], 1648, [illegible], 6477.
Mockley—Mocly, Edw., pardon, 2510, 4907.
Mocler, Melchior, pardon, 6466.
Moclere. See Moyglare.
Moclearc, Redmund, 4923.
Mocler, Edm., pardon, 6462.
" Jacques, pardon, 6466.
" Tho., pardon, 6166.
Mocler—Mowclere, Edmund (of Mocklerstown), pardon, [illegible], 5258.
" John, pardon, [illegible].
" Redmund, 6317.
" Rich. m'Redmund, pardon, 6464.
Moclere (co. Tip. ?), 6644.
Moclerston—Moclerstowne. See Mocklerston.
Mockery, co. Tip., 6437.
Mocly, Edw. See Mockley.
Moclyston (co. Tip. or Lim. ?), 4957.
Mocnagh (co. Wick.), 6477.
Mocollen. See Moycullen.
Mocollop—Mocollopp—Mocolop—Mocollopp—Mocollappe—Moycolpe, co. Wat., 2471, [illegible], 5163, [illegible], 6454, [illegible], [illegible]; castle and lands granted, 5044. See also Mocolpe.
Mocully, co. Kilk., 4734.
Mocurrin, co. Mayo. See Mokarha.
Mocrome — Mocrompy — Mocrompyre — Mocrompe—Mocrompny — Mocrompne — Mocrompy — Mocromy — Mocroome — Mocrowme — Mocrowmy — Mocrowny — Mocroymy (Macroom), co. Cork, 3100, 4467, 4468, 4784, 4914, 6256, 6304, 6167, 6628, 6671; manor, 5371, 6130; patronage of church, 5371, 6128, 6130; rectory, 6131. See Macromp.
Mocronaghe (Macroney), co. Cork, vicarage, 6467.
Mocrowle—Mocrownle, co. Cork, 4528.
Mocroome — Mocrowme — Mocrowmy. See Mocrome.
Mocrowne, co. Cork, 6634.
Mocrowny—Mocroymy. See Mocrome.
Mocullen. See Moycullen.
Modde Duff alias Black wood, co. Westm., 1568.
Moddeseill. See Modeseill.
Moddullie (Moudellby), co. Lim., 6114, 6464.
Moddwrine alias Grefan, Connoghor, pardon, 6138.
Modado (Maddadoo), co. Westm., 5462.
Moderane, co. Tip., 6464.
Moderony—Moderynye (Modreeny?), co. Tip., 4628, 4629.
Modorghe, Marcus, pardon, 6494.
Moderheny, co. Tip., 6532.
Moderion, Dorle, pardon, 6361.
Modore (co. Kilk. ?), 4968.
Modrynye. See Moderony.
Modeseill—Moddeseill (Modeshil ? co. Tip.), 6768. See also Moudeseshell.
Modollaghie—Modologhie (Mondellihy), co. Lim., 6116, 5694.
Modrameetown, co. Westm. See Ballymadren.
Modriniby (Modreeny, co. Tip. ?), 4694.
Modryne (Modreeny, co. Tip.), 5764. See also Moderony, Maydertynne.
Moe, Gerald or Gerrot oge, attainted, 6117.
Moeler, Edm., pardon, 6632.
" Jeffrey, pardon, 6621.
Moel, the (co. Kild. ?), 6332.
Moehill (co. Clare ?), 6908.
Moelidaane, co. Wat., 4714.
Moell, Dermod m'Donogh oge, pardon, 6671.
" Tho., pardon, 6481.
Moelnagh (co. Lim. or Tip.), 6137.
Moellally ( ), pardon 6328.
Moemanymy. See Montanymy.
Moena (co. Donegal), 6381.
Moen Ros (co. Tip. or Queen's), 6711.
Moere (co. Long. ?), 6574.
Moey, in Connaught, 1770.
Moffenstown, co. Meath, 4573.
Mofidde, co. Westm., 4181.
Mogan, the (co. Kilk. ?), 6108.
Mogan (co. Lim. ?), 3178.
Mogamer—Mogramer, co. Tip., 547, 1598.
Mogare, co. Tip., rectory, 632.
Mogawrie (co. Tip. ?), 6381.
Mogawrye, co. Tip., 6383.
Mogo (Magoha ?), co. Wat., 646, 5163.
Mogealy, co. Cork, 6471.
Mogealy, co. Cork. See Mogelly, Mogille, Moygelly.
Mogellogo, co. Wat., 5346.
Mogellie (Mogealy ? co. Cork), 6487.
Mogelly, co. Cork, 1066, 6520. See also Mogyley.
Mogely (co. Cork ?), 6172.
Moghan, co. Clare, manor, 528.
Moghan (Moohane), co. Kerry, 6152.
Moghan, co. Wex., 1577.
Moghan, Honor ny, pardon, 6421.
Moghane, James, pardon, 6477.
" Rich., pardon, 2814.
Moghanvieghillovick (co. Clare ?), 2677.
Moghaloey (co. Clare ?), 3677.
Moghar, co. Tip., 6531.
Moghill (Mohill, co. Leit.), priory of canons, granted, 4836; possessions granted, 5645.
Moghmayne, 6743. See Maghmayn.
Moghnaghe (Muckenagh, co. Westm.), 6767.
Moghobbur (Mohober, co. Tip. ?), 6702.
Moghoreston (Muckerstown, co. Meath), 551.

INDEX TO FIANTS.—ELIZABETH.

Moghorey (co. Leit. ?), 6412.
Moghrompie—Moghrompy, co. Cork, 5941.
Moghrowny (Macrony, co. Cork), mode shire land, 1555.
Moghunogh, co. Lim., 6461.
Mogilie (Mogerly), co. Cork, castle and lands, 5614.
Mogiehill, co. Carlow, 5[illegible].
Mogiane, co. Tip., 5527, 6366, 6784.
Mogoliye, co. Wat., 4180.
Mogorime (Magorban, co. Tip. ?), 6551, 6[illegible].
Mogorrebane (Magorban, co. Tip. ?), 3118.
Mogorye, co. Tip., 5378.
Mogowra, co. Tip., rectory, 1[illegible].
Mogowry (co. Tip. ?), 9[illegible].
Moguirse, co. Clare, 6817.
Mogyolly rectory. See Moygully.
Mogylye, co. Cork, 5478.
Mohalaghe—Mohallagh (Mohallagh, co. Cork ?), 2281, 6761.
Mohallaghe Ewe—Mohullaghe in Ewe—Moballaghe in Ewe (Mahallagh), co. Cork, 1373, 5[illegible], 5[illegible].
Mohannaghe (co. Lim. ?), 3494.
Mohar, co. Long., 8111.
Mohawnagh, co. Lim., 6627.
Mohcrueelyn, co. Clare, 4[illegible], 4774.
Mohie, co. Lim., 3777.
Mohill, 6794.
Mohill, co. Leit. See Moghill, Moyhell, Moyhill.
Mohine (co. Mayo ?), 6[illegible].
Mohinerly, co. Lim., 5[illegible].
Mohnogreaghy, co. Lim., 6[illegible].
Mohober, co. Tip., 5[illegible]. See Moghobber.
Mohoicolum, Derby, pardon, 6[illegible].
Moholker (Mohober), co. Tip., 5[illegible].
Mohonn, co. Cork. See Mwhonnye, 5[illegible].
Mohonagh, co. Lim., 6[illegible].
Mohownagh—Mohownaghe (Mahoonagh), co. Lim., parish, 5[illegible], 5947.
Mosaghy (see Moyaghy), 4[illegible].
Moialie. See Moalie.
Moially. See Moyallie.
Moiasker, co. Meath, 148.
Moiashill barony. See Moyashell.
Moibolge. See Moybolge, co. Cav.
Moibolge, co. Meath, 5[illegible].
Moiclare. See Moyglare.
Moicurke, co. Tip., 1[illegible].
Moide, co. Cork, 5[illegible].
Moidena. See Moydens.
Moiderraghe (co. Leit. ?), 5[illegible].
Moidrume. See Moydrum.
Moiclare. See Moyglare.
Moielly. See Moyelan.
Moifeagher (Moyfeagher), co. Meath, 5[illegible].
Moig, co. Lim. See Moye.
Moigaddy. See Moygaddy.
Moigaddye, great. See Moygadde.
Moigaddye, little. See Moygadd.
Moigarbarie, 4918. See Moygarbarrye.
Moigh, co. Cav., 6[illegible].
Moigiare. See Moyglare.
Moiglasse, co. Tip., 6[illegible].
Moiglimbane (co. Kilk. ?), 1[illegible].
Moigullin (co. Westm. ?), 3341.
Moilaghmore (co. Kilk. ?), 6[illegible].
Moilnagho, co. Tip., rectory, &c., 3115.
Moiklougne, King's co., 6[illegible]1.
Moilkirogo, 5[illegible]. See Moykirum, co. Westm.
Moile, John fitz Rob., pardon, 5[illegible].
Moile, co. Mayo, 5[illegible].
Moilegranson, co. Westm., 6[illegible]1.
Moileloughe (King's co. or Meath), 6[illegible].
Moill, Conoghor oge, pardon, 6[illegible].
Moilre, Hubert roe m'Wmon, pardon, 6[illegible].
Moilrunde, Shillie ny, pardon, 6[illegible].
Moilnesy—Moilnesle. See Moylhansle.
Moimarde (Moynerard ?), co. Tip., 3[illegible].
Moinealness, Hugh, pardon, 5[illegible].
Moinaghan, John, vicar of Tharragh, 5[illegible].
Moinentallen (Mountallen), co. Clare, 5[illegible].
Moinervensine (co. Long. ?), 5[illegible].
Moinglen, co. Wex., 6[illegible].
Moinloghe (Moymlough), co. Sligo, 4[illegible].
Moinragh. See Moyntagh.
Mointerchonaly. See Moynter connaght.
Mointercroghane. See Moynter croghan.
Mointergerane. See Moyntergarane.
Mointer melane quarter (Munter madian, co. Donegal), 5[illegible].
Mointerolas—Mointerolishe. See Moynter-olys.
Mointeregan (Munter Tadhgain, Fox's country, barony of Kilcoursey), King's co., seneschal appointed, 5[illegible].
Mointer wyrane. See Moynter bryrane.
Moiraly (co. Rosc.), 6974.
Moiockestown (Moakstown), co. Dub., 5[illegible].
Moire, co. Clare, 5[illegible].
Moireghe, Queen's co., 6727.
Moistonhillir (Morristownbiller), co. Kild., 1316.
Moiragh, co. Lim., 5[illegible].
Mokarhe (Mocorha), co. Mayo, 5417.
Mokellie, Katherine ny, pardon, 5[illegible].
Mokennaghan (co. Westm. ?), 6374.
Mokerle (co. Cork ?), 5[illegible].
Mokhowne alias Rathlyn, co. Kilk., 504.
Mokilly, 5[illegible].
Mokiriske (Muckridge), co. Cork, 5[illegible].
Mokolop (co. Wat. ?), 5[illegible].
Molanlum (co. Rosc. ?), 6[illegible].
Molagh castle, co. Gal., 4[illegible].
Molaghan, John, pardon, 5427.
Molaghcoisle. See Mullaghcoisle.
Molaghe (Mullagh ?), co. Cav., 5[illegible]7.

INDEX TO FIANTS.—ELIZABETH.

Molaghinsmy, co. Tip., 2775.

Molaghlyn, Turlogh m'Connor E, pardon, 1528.

Molaghmoone, Gildaraigo of, 812.

Molaghmore. See Mullaghmore, co. Gal.

Molahyffe—Malaboif—Malaboyffe—Malahiffe—Mallahiffe—Molahaffe (Molahiffe), co. Kerry, 4658; manor and lands granted, 4977, 4717; rectory, 3818, 5768, 5206. See also Malahiffe and Kilmalahoif.

Molan, John, pardon, 67.

" Morice, 3468.

Molana—Molanaffe—Molaranna—Molanna, co. Wat., abbey or priory leased, 1637, 3161; granted, 4944.

Molana, co. Kerry, castle granted, 4977, 4717.

Molanna. See Molana.

Molaughlen, Donagh fitz William, pardon, 6471.

Molcahy, Shane m'Owen I, pardon, 4714.

Molchan, Donill m'Da I, pardon, 3178.

Moldthie, Brian m'Shane I, pardon, 2929.

Molcomry, Margaret filz Torum I, pardon, 4674.

Moldrumforaghe (co. Leit. ?), 4917.

Moldowy, Wm., pardon, 3494.

Moldrome. See Muldrome.

Molemlaghe (co. Gal. ?), 4656.

Molerdy, Swaney, pardon, 4169.

Molerfane, 6364.

Moleghane, Nicholas, English liberty, 781.

Moleghine, Philip, pardon, 6498.

Molenston—Molenstowne (Mullanstown ?), co. Louth, 1723, 3876.

Molensaught, co. Meath or Westm., 6671.

Molenveghan, co. Westm., 4440.

Molerick, co. Meath. See Molricke.

Molesvane, co. Tip., 6341.

Molestorney, co. Kild., 699.

Molleran (co. Westm.), 2989.

Molgan, Pate., 4402.

Molgine alias Purcell, Thomas, pardon, 6, 1531.

Molgurron, Tho. m'Shane Y, pardon, 5836.

" See Volgurrine.

Molimaghe, co. Meath, 5566.

Moline, Evena, Pate., and Wm. m'Donogh E, pardon, 3168.

Molinesdolan (co. Wex. or Car. ?), 4949.

Molineux. See Molyneux.

Molingar—Molingare—Molingary—Mollingaar—Mollingar. See Mullingar.

Molinloy, co. Westm., 2348.

Molkahy, Teige m'Mahowny I, pardon, 4714.

Molkalygh, Donnagh A, pardon, 3233.

Molkeryn, Mahon m'Donogh Y, pardon, 4418.

Molkeryne, John m'Donogh I, pardon, 4418.

Mollache (Mullagh ?), co. Cav., 4634.

Mollagh. See Mullagh, co. Tip.

Mollaghaygh ( ), co. Cav., 4634.

Mollaghenlowe. See Mullaghwalsh.

Mollaghe. See Mullaghe, co. Gal.

Mollaghe (Mullagh ?), co. Meath, 609.

Mollagh Enseme—Mollaghensme—Mollaghenony (Mollaghmoney ?), co. Tip., 4234, 6457, 6768.

Mollaghgolline (Mullygollen, co. Ros. ?), 4608.

Mollaghmoremaighie (co. Ros. ?), 4638.

Mollaghrome, King's co., 617, 650.

Mollaghmakeloughe (Mullaghmakem, co. Mon.), 6683.

Mollaghtrury, co. Louth, 4463.

Mollan (co. Sligo ?), 3478.

Mollane (co. Lim. ?), 6681.

Mollaughloney, co. Ros., 3794.

Mollemeaghe, co. Westm., 6918.

Mollenaymadhe (Mullenmeehan ?), co. Westm., 5707.

Molleman (Mollinam), co. Meath, 2978.

Mollenlaro—Mollendaro, co. Kilk., 2188.

Mollenmakneswer, Queen's co., 6647.

Mollenostanfelde, co. Meath, 6763.

Mollengar. See Mullingar.

Mollenly, co. Westm., 4239.

Mollenmakmawer, Queen's co., 696.

Mollenoppan (co. Mon. ?), 6613.

Mollenyleght (co. Kild. ?), 4132.

Mollenrn (co. Tip. ?), 4464.

Molleghewan (Mullaghewan), co. Mon., 4861.

Mollinmeaghane—Mollynaghan (Mullinagan ?), co. Westm., 1504, 4703.

Mollineux—Mollinex. See Molyneux.

Mollingar—Mollingar—Mollingare—Mollingar. See Mullingar.

Mollogimony. See Mollagh Enseme.

Mollogirume, King's co., 2914.

Molloy, John, pardon, 6858.

" Margaret, pardon, 6812.

Mollortie (Moylurg, co. Ros.), 1293.

Molloy, Anthony, pardon, 4438.

" Mow co, pardon, 4838.

" See Moyloye.

Molloye, Neillanus or Neile, rector of Kilcloniert, 6764.

Mollylonl. See Mollilont.

Mollynaugh, co. Meath, 3680.

Mollynaghan. See Mollinmeaghane.

Mollynell, Tho., 6718. See Molyneux.

Mollyneux, Edm. See Molyneux.

Mollynger. See Mullingar.

Mollyns, Timothy, pardon, 6764.

Molmorestown, co. Meath, 6288.

Molmory, Owen ny, pardon, 6764.

Molognaston, co. Westm., 4398.

Mologhcomshe. See Mullaghwalsh.

Moloeboloe. See Mullaghboloe.

INDEX TO FIANTS—ELIZABETH.

Mologhmor (co. Ross. or Leit.), [illegible].
Molom. *See* Molom.
Molony, Malachy Y, clerk, pardon, [illegible].
Moloske (co. Clare ?), [illegible].
Molosky, co. Clare, [illegible].
Molough (co. Long. ?), [illegible].
Moloughabbey, co. Tip. *See* Moylagh.
Moloy, Owny oy, pardon, [illegible].
Molrancan—Molrenckan—Molrankan. *See* Mulrenckan.
Molrane, Conhor A. pardon, [illegible].
Molrian, Fenaolle oy, pardon, [illegible].
Molricke (Molerick), co. Meath, [illegible].
Molroney, William fitz John, pardon, [illegible].
Molroo (co. Clare ?), [illegible].
Molryan, Mahown m'Wm. m'Teige I, pardon, [illegible].
Molsagho, co. Gal., [illegible].
Molteferman—Molliferman—Molighferman. *See* Multeferman, co. Westm.
Molum—Molom (co. Kilk.), [illegible], 141.
Molwill, [illegible].
Molybondryssha, co. Meath, [illegible]. *See also* Molyvondertaghe.
Molyne Iniryman, co. Cork, [illegible].
Molyneux—Molinex—Mollineux—Mollinex — Mollyneli — Mullyneux — Molynex — Mullieux — Mulliex:
— Daniel, Ulster king at arms, [illegible].
— Edmund, secretary to lord deputy Sydney, 1444, [illegible]; clerk of Castle Chamber, [illegible], [illegible], 1483; notes on fiants, 1441, 1454, 1600; lease, [illegible]; pardon, [illegible].
— Samuel, marshal of the Castle Chamber, [illegible], [illegible]; clerk of works, [illegible].
— Thomas, surveyor of victuals, [illegible], [illegible]; obtains charter for Swords, [illegible].
— Thomas, chancellor of the Exchequer, [illegible], [illegible]; collector of wine impost, [illegible], [illegible].
Molynnevan, co. Westm., [illegible].
Molynex. *See* Molyneux.
Molyngar—Molynger. *See* Mollingar.
Molynloy, co. Westm., 1546.
Momorie (district in bar. of Cary, co. Antrim, including the par. of Ramoan. *See* Reeves, Down and Connor, p. [illegible]), [illegible].
Mompesson, Rich., grant, [illegible].
Monachan, [illegible]. *See* Monaghan.
Monaferrick, Queen's co. *See* Moniferrick, Monyferricke.
Monagallagh, co. Meath. *See* Monygallagh.
Monagarrow, co. Wex. *See* Monegarrowe.
Monagay, co. Lim. *See* Monaghare.
Monagonaghe (co. Clare), [illegible].
Monagh—Monaghe, King's co., [illegible], [illegible].
Monaghan — Monachan — Manachan — Monachan — Monoghan — Monoghan, co. Mon., [illegible], [illegible], [illegible]; town, [illegible]; rectory, [illegible]; justices of assize at, [illegible].
— castle and manor surrendered and regranted, [illegible], [illegible].
— castle, [illegible]; lands held of, [illegible], [illegible].
— friary, [illegible].
— county, commission to form, [illegible]; lands to be granted in freehold to the inhabitants, [illegible]; grants of land, [illegible]; grants of termon lands, [illegible], [illegible], [illegible], [illegible], [illegible]; men of, pardoned, [illegible], [illegible], [illegible], [illegible], [illegible]; persons not living in, excluded from a pardon, [illegible]; martial law, [illegible].
— seneschal, [illegible], [illegible].
— barony, grants of land in, [illegible], [illegible], [illegible], [illegible].
Monaghan, John (or Managhan), [illegible].
Monaghare — Monaghdare — Monaghdare (Monagay), co. Lim., [illegible], [illegible], [illegible].
Monaghe. *See* Monagh.
Monahowe, co. Clare, [illegible].
Monaleche, co. Tip. *See* Inchemeber.
Monaleran priory, [illegible]. *See* Molana.
Monaley, co. Westm., 1678.
Monalin, co. Wick. *See* Monaline, Moynalin.
Monaltie, co. Meath, [illegible].
Monamolin, co. Wex. *See* Monamolin, Monamolinge, Monamolin.
Monamore, co. Louth, [illegible].
Monamolane, co. Wex., [illegible].
Monanile, co. Cork, [illegible].
Monanige (co. Cork ?), [illegible].
Monanimy, co. Cork. *See* Monanymy.
Monanmony, [illegible].
Monanreie, [illegible].
Monanymy—Monangymy—Monanymay—Moneanymy, (Monanimy), co. Cork, [illegible], [illegible], [illegible], [illegible]. *See also* Monemymy, Moynanymy, Moynanymy.
Monarie (co. Wex.), [illegible].
— *See also* Moynart.
Monasterlaghan, co. Long. *See* Monaskallaghan.
Monastereden, Queen's co. *See* Monasterbane.

INDEX TO FIANTS—ELIZABETH.

Monasteranenagh, co. Lim. See Nenagh.

Monasterboyce (Monasterboice, co. Louth), rectory, [illegible].

Monaster de Beantry (Bantry, co. Cork), [illegible].

Monasterdergo — Monasterdirg — Monasterdirgo — Monasterorig — Monaster Borick — Monaster Berike — Monasterorike — Monaster Boryck (Abbeyderg, co. Long.), 1033, 1787, [illegible], [illegible], [illegible].

— monastery of S. Peter de Rubia, 1033, 1787, [illegible], 4175, [illegible].

Monasteroddan (co. Cork ?), [illegible].

Monasterevin, co. Kild. See Evin, Monasterevan.

Monasterle Evan. See Monaster Nenan.

Monaster Inshorrie—Manister an Inshorie—Manister enshorry—Manister ne Srohourry Manister ne srahurre—Manister nestrohurry (Abbeystrowry), co. Cork, a cell called, [illegible], [illegible], [illegible], [illegible].

Monasterkerry, co. Long., 4175.

Monaster Macgormacan (Abbeygormacan, co. Gal.), 1471.

Monaster ne Keylaghe—Monasternagalloghe—Monaster of Kallagh — Monastery of Kaylagh, co. Lim., house of nuns. 1143, [illegible], [illegible], [illegible], [illegible], [illegible]; granted, [illegible].

Monaster Nenan — Monasterle Evan alias Kennett, co. Ross., [illegible], [illegible].

Monasternokery, great moor (Curry, bar. Moydow, co. Long.), [illegible], 1737.

Monasteroris — Monasterorishe — Manistir oris — Monasterorre — Monasteoris — Monystirorishe—Monaster oris, King's co., [illegible], [illegible], [illegible], [illegible], [illegible], [illegible], [illegible]. See also Moynesterorish.

— house of friars, granted, [illegible]; possessions granted, [illegible]; leased, [illegible].

Monaster Berick — Monaster Bericke — Monaster Berike — Monasterrerike — Monaster Boryck — Monasterrike. See Monasterderga.

Monasterwalle m'Idane (Ballymacadane abbey on townland of Oldabbey), co. Cork, possessions granted, [illegible].

Monastery, co. Wick., [illegible]. See Macgyaler.

Monastery. See Ackerne, Adare, Aghavo, Aghamart, Aghmore, Aghrim, Annagh, co. Mayo; Annaghdown, Ardcarne, Ardee, Ardfert, Ardlygan, Ardkeyn, Ardtarin, Asherowe, Askeaton, Athassel, Athenry.

Monastery:

Athlone, Athy, Ballinahancone, Ballinasmall, Ballindown, co. Sligo; Ballindrohed, Ballinaggart, Ballinskelligs, Ballinsmaler, co. Mayo; Ballyamullary (Ballysadare), Ballybeg, co. Cork; Ballybogan, Ballyclare, co. Gal.; Ballylonghroogh (Loughrea), Baltimore, Baltinglas, Bangor, Bantry, Bath in England, Bush, co. Gal.; Bealaneny, Boyle, Bristol in England, Buttevant, Caher, Callan, Canon Island, Carrickfergus, Carrike, co. Wat.; Cartmell in England, Cashel, Castledermot, Castlelyons, Cavan, Clare, Clane, Clare, Claregalway, Cloghdunmale, Clonard, Clonmacnoghan, Clones, Clonkeene, co. Gal.; Clonroughan, Clonbamoyle, Clonturmakert, co. Ross.; Clontuskert, co. Gal.; Cong, Connell, Corke O'Mollegane (Templemolaga ?), Corcomroe, Cork, Court, co. Sligo; Cowleveraugge, Creveghbane, Derrane, Donegal, Down, co. Down; Downe, co. Wex.; Drogheda, Drumlahan, Dublin, Duleek, Dunbrody, Dundalk, Dungarvan, Dunmore, co. Gal.; Durrow, Elphin, Enniskerry, Ennis, Enniscorthy, Exeter (in England), Fermoy, Ferns, *Furtnegeracha* (Fortagh), Fethard, co. Tip.; Fore, Furness in England, Fryshour (Kilfenora), Gallen, Galway, Gilabbey, Glanner, Glascarrick, Gowran, Graceduieu, Granard, Holmpatrick, Holy Cross, Holy Island in L. Ree, Holy Trinity island, co. Cav.; Holy Trinity island, co. Ross.; Hore abbey, Horetown, Inche, co. Down; Incheloughrene, Inchemore, co. Long.; Inchemore, co. Westm.; Inchenabee, Inchevickerine, Inishcrone, Inishmattie, Inishlokin, Innisfallen, Innishmaine, Inishlawnaght, Irelagh, Jerpoint, Jugo Dei, Kells, co. Kilk.; Kells, co. Meath; Keynsham in England, Kilbeggan, Kilbegin, Kilbrenan, Kilconnell, co. Gal.; Kilcormick, Kilcowle, co. Tip.; Kilcrea, Kilcrenaght, Kildare, Kilkenny, Kilkenny, Kilkenny West, Killaloe, Killaly, Killane, co. Clare; Killaraght, Killeigh, King's co.; Killone, co. Clare; Kilmacallan, Kilmacduagh, Kilmainham, Kilmallock, Kilmore, co. Ross.; Kilmurey, co. Ross.; Kilmananagh, co. Ross.; Kilcony, Kilshane, co. Lim.; Killeagh of Fallis, Kinsale, Knock, co. Louth; Knockmoy, Knockanure, Knockvicar, Kylbra, Lanthony, (in England), Leighlinbridge, Leix, Leixlip, Lismullen, Limerick, Lisloghtin, Longford, co. Long.; Loughkee, Loughrea, Louth, Lurgho, Maws, Mayo, co. Lim.; Maynooth, Mayo, Mellifont, Moghill, Molana, Moesgian, Monasterdergo, Monaster Inshorrie,

INDEX TO FIANTS—ELIZABETH.

Monastery :

Monaster na Kayllaghe, Monasterevin, Monastervalle m'Iliane, Mothill, co. Wat.; Moycarkey, co. Tip.; Moyne, co. Mayo; Mullingar, Muraske, Naas, Navan, Nenagh, co. Lim. (Monasternenagh), Nenagh, co. Tip.; Nephelaugh (Abbeyfeale), New Abbey, co. Kild.; Odder, Odorney, Osney, Quin, Rathbrasse, Rathkeale, Rathmullan, Ratowe, Roscrea, Roscommon, Ross, Rosscarbery, Rosse, co. Wex.; Rosserelly, Rustricke, S. John the Baptist, co. Drog., S. John of Jerusalem, Sawle, Selsker, Shrowell (Abbeyshrule), co. Long.; Skreen, Sruthair, Strade, Synekevan, Teghmoy (Timahoe), Templenoffi Kilculloghe, Termonfeighan, Thome, Thurles, Timolage, Timolin, Tintern, Tobberownock, Tobbervelley, Toomevara, Tracton, Tralee, Trim, Tristeldermot, Tristernagh, Tuam, Tullaa, co. Clare; Tullaghfelim, Tulske, Vonnlee (Ranelagh ?), Waterford, Wexford, Wicklow, Wony, Youghal

Monastery, grantee of, to build stone fortresses on site, [illegible].

" prior, bellringer and [illegible], still in occupation at [illegible], [illegible].

Monastery of Nephelaugh — Mainistir na feile (Abbeyfeale), [illegible]; parish, co. Lim., [illegible].

Monastic lands, Inquisition to enquire of, [illegible], [illegible], [illegible], 4454.

Monatray, co. Wat. See Monamintra.

Moncalvan, co. Wat. See Moneytrayne.

Moncreagheen, co. Cork. See M[illegible].

Moncrill, Edm., pardon to wife, [illegible].

Monckeland, co. Wex., martial law in barony, [illegible].

Mounckeslande near Limerick, [illegible], [illegible].

Moncke's meadow, co. Dub., [illegible].

Monckton alias Carrickbrenan. See Monkton.

Moncktown (see Monkstown), [illegible].

Moncktown, co. Westm., [illegible].

Moncronock, co. Kild., [illegible], [illegible].

Mondaveshill (Modeshil, co. Tip. ?), rectory, [illegible], 2114, [illegible].

Mondollihy, co. Lim. See Moddollis.

Mondre and weke, King's co., [illegible].

Mondobber, co. Tip., [illegible].

Mondrehid, Queen's co. See Moydrehid.

Monduvane, co. Tip. or Lim., [illegible].

Mone, Jenet, pardon, [illegible].

" John, [illegible].

" John, pardon, [illegible].

Mone (co. Tip. ?), [illegible].

Moneaghdare (Monagay), co. Lim., parish, [illegible], [illegible]. See Monaghaire.

M[illegible] alias [illegible], co. Wex., [illegible].

M[illegible], [illegible].

Mone an Tearmoind—Mone an Thearmond (co. Donegal), [illegible], [illegible].

Moneanymy — Moneanymy. See Moneanymy.

Moneard, co. Long., [illegible].

Moneatirre (Monatray), co. Wat., [illegible], [illegible].

Monebolle (co. Kilk.), [illegible].

Mone Catherlange (co. Car. ?), [illegible].

M[illegible] (co. [illegible] ?), [illegible].

Moneclare (Moneyclare), Queen's co., [illegible], [illegible].

Moneclore (co. Wex. ?), [illegible].

Monedonoghe—Monedonough, great moor of, a bog on the borders of co. Long. and Westm. (see Inquisitions, Chancery, Longford, 1 Jas. I.), [illegible], [illegible].

Monedowicke (co. Wex. ?), [illegible].

Monedul. See Moneduff, Queen's co.

Moneduff. See Moneyduff, co. Gal.

Moneduff—Monedul, Queen's co., [illegible], [illegible].

Monefaild, Queen's co., [illegible].

Monefadde (King's co. ?), [illegible].

Moneicloghe, co. Kerry, [illegible].

Moneffidde, co. Westm. (see Moneyfidd), [illegible].

Monelowre (co. Kilk. ?), [illegible].

Monefyn—Monfyn (co. Wick.), [illegible], [illegible].

Monegariffe, co. Lim., [illegible].

Monegarowe (Monegarrow, co. Wex. ?), [illegible].

Monegenaghe (co. Clare ?), [illegible].

Monegeyre (King's or Queen's co. ?), [illegible].

Moneyghan, Joan ny James, pardon, [illegible].

Monekenemoney, co. Tip., [illegible].

Monekilleckymoe, Queen's co., bog, [illegible].

Monelargo—Monelargie, co. Wat., [illegible], [illegible].

Monelaughe, co. Westm., [illegible].

Monelaurge (co. Wat. ?), [illegible].

Moneleigh. See Moneley.

Monelewaghe (Moanlewane), co. Lim., [illegible].

Moneley—Moneleigh—Moneyley (Moneylea), co. Westm., [illegible], [illegible], [illegible], [illegible].

Moneline—Monelyne (Monelin, co. Wick.), [illegible], [illegible].

Monelodane, Queen's co., [illegible].

Monelyne. See Moneline.

Monemenane, co. Gal., [illegible].

Monemodhame, co. Lim., [illegible].

Monemole, co. Kerry, [illegible].

Monemore, co. Wex., [illegible].

Monemolin — Monemolyne (Monamolin, co. Wex.), [illegible], [illegible].

Monemolline, co. Car. (Monamolin, par Templeudigan, co. Wex. ?), [illegible].

Monemolyne. See Monemolin.

Monemore, co. Cork, [illegible].

Monemore, (Moneymore), Queen's co., [illegible].

Monemore. See Moneymore, co. Wex.

INDEX TO FIANTS.—ELIZABETH.

Monamore, in Byrnes country (co. Wick.), 1823.
Monavaurry (Moaruurry), co. Mea., 6968.
Monanclo, co. Wex., 6799.
Monanebolcy — Monanebolio, Queen's co., 1774 ; grant, 6978.
Monanebolio (Moneynabonia), co. Tip., 6091.
Monanemny (Monanimy, co. Cork), 2591.
Monaneauck (Moneynampck, co. Kilk. ?), 6704.
Monanicarrevo, 6867.
Monarvary (co. Wat. ?), 2073.
Monare, co. Cork, 1583.
Monare, co. Cork, manor, 6152.
Monaril (co. Lim. ?), 6477.
Monaro, 867.
Monaro (co. Kilk. ?), 2295, 4582.
Monarode (Monarod), co. Wat., 654, 3163.
Monaroe (co. Kilk. ?), 6672.
Monaroo, co. Tip., 6189.
Monarum, co. Meath, 2913.
Monaryedie (co. Tip. ?), 6782.
Monaseggarde, Queen's co., 6786.
Monasertane (Monaseraisan), Queen's co., 6158.
Monasorovagh (co. Long. ?), 6153.
Monasehallighan (Monaseallaghan), co. Long., 6524.
Monaseskyll, in manor of Carlow, 1682.
Monasterevan—Monasterevan, co. Kild., 1834, 6867.
Monasteris, King's co., 2981. See Monasteroris.
Monastrowne, co. Wat., 4328.
Monevane, co. Gal., 6446.
Monevell, John reogh, pardon, 6946.
Money—hallaca, equivalent in English, 6818.
Money, loss in the exchange, 61.
Money, Donell, pardon, 6592.
„ Edmund, pardon, 165.
„ James, pardon, 6177.
„ Rich., vicar of Carougho, Kildare, 6314.
„ Richard, pardon, 1617, 2494, 3442.
„ Wm., pardon, 6457.
Money, the (King's co. ?), 4468.
Money, Queen's co. See Moane.
Moneyclare, Queen's co. See Monaclare.
Moneycrossa, co. Wex. See Moneycrossane.
Moneyro, James, pardon, 6362.
Moneyfingh, co. Cork. See Minyfinigh.
Moneylanan, co. Long. See Monlagane, Monylagane, Moynylagane.
Moneyloe, co. Westm. See Monaloy.
Moneymohill, co. Lim. See Monymohell.
Moneymore, Queen's co. See Monamore.
Moneynahools, co. Tip. See Monanebolio.
Moneynamuck, co. Kilk. See Monaneauck.
Moneyneileagh, co. Tip., 6963.
Monfolde, Nicholas, killed, 6688.
Monfield, Edm., pardon, 6162.
Monfilde, Maurice, pardon, 6761.
Monfyn (see Monsfyn), 6327.
Monga, Edm., pardon, 6594.
Mongagh—Mongaghe, Queen's co., 867, 6963, 6782.
Mongagh—Mongaghe, co. Ross., 4944, 6814.
Mongaghe river (Mongagh), King's co., 6784.
Mongaghe. See Mongagh.
Mongaghmore, in Upperossory, Queen's co., 6117.
Mongaho (co. Ross. ?), 1803.
Mongan, co. Kilk., 1046.
Mongan (Mungan), co. Kilk., 6626.
Mongan (co. Tip. or Kilk.), 3268, 6798.
Mongan, co. Wex., 6452.
Mongan (co. Wex. or Kilk. ?), 6464.
Mongan, co. Wick. See Mongane.
Mongan, Owen, pardon, 6607.
„ Patrick, pardon, 1163.
Monganachone (Mungan), co. Kilk., 6276.
Mongane (Mongan, co. Wick.), 6641.
Mongansfyn, co. Wex., 4915.
Monganston (Monganstown), co. Westm., 6287.
Mongariff (co. Lim. ?), 6594.
Mongory (co. Lim. ?), 4478.
Mongforn — Mongfine — Mongfoyne (Mongfune), co. Lim., 4466, 4511 ; grant, 6683.
Mongg (Munga), co. Gal., 4129-1.
Mongha (Queen's co. ?), 6782.
Monghan, co. Clare, 1065.
Monghan (co. Kilk.), 6704.
Monghan, Dermod m' Tuig I. pardon, 6652.
„ Edm., pardon, 6642.
Monghan keill (perhaps Mongnacoil), co. Wick., 6612.
Monghoy, Owen fitz Donoho an, pardon, 6611.
Mongiome, co. Car., 5165.
Mongnacoil, co. Wick. See Monghan keill.
Monguigh, co. Ross., 4614.
Mongrett (Mungret), co. Lim., 4838.
Monhila, co. Kild., 72.
Monhowen, co. Kilk., 1651.
Monie (Moone, co. Kild.), 3674.
Monianimmy, co. Cork, 4468.
Monibroe (co. Cork ?), 6594.
Monibrin, 6671.
Monicappan, co. Clare, 6568.
Monichore, 6677.
Monie, Lancellot, F.T.C.D., 6716.
Monio (co. Mayo ?), 4469.
Monishore (co. Wex. ?), 6666, 6763.
Moniair (co. Lim. ?), 6511.
Monierigan (co. Kerry or Lim. ?), 6462.
Monifarick (Monafarrick), Queen's co., 2898.
Monifyne (see Monsfyn, co. Wick.), 6144.

INDEX TO FIANTS.—ELIZABETH.

Monigurry, 673.
Monigeane, Kniberine, pardon, 4814.
Monighore, 6377.
Monilagane (Moneylagan, co. Long.), 6229.
Monine, Queen's co., 601.
Moniquite, alias Moyrdone, 1884.
Moniro (co. Tip. or Lim.), 1868.
Moniowor (co. Wex. or Car.), 6942.
Monivamedy (Monivanahere, co. Cork), 6273.
Monkegrange (co. Tip. ?), 6765.
Monkes grange, Queen's co., 5,986.
Monkesland, 6177.
Monkesland, co. Wat., 4026.
Monkeston—Monkestoune (Monkstown), co. Tip., 5791, 6763.
Monketon — Monckton (Monktown), co. Meath, 890, 1804, 7309.
Monketon—Munckinstone, co. Westm., 407, 5780.
Monketown. See Monkton.
Monkrocmoke, co. Kild., 452.
Monkstown, co. Dub. See Monkton.
Monkstown, co. Tip. See Monkeston.
Monkton—Monckton—Monketon (Monkstown), co. Dub., 465, 2880, 3146, 4184. See Carrickbrenan. Mounton.
Monktown, co. Meath. See Monketon.
Monlogragh (co. Wex. or Car. ?), 6510.
Monnahemock. See Drummahamock.
Monmurry, co. Mon. See Mountmurry.
Monnegane (co. Kerry or Lim. ?), 6492.
Monne (Money ?), Queen's co., 1718.
Monnedowneclocks, co. Wex., 6172.
Monnemore (co. Car. ?), 6817.
Monnemedmoke (co. Wex. ?), 2901.
Monnetchame (co. Tip. ?), 6708.
Monnemurragh, co. Clare, 4128, 4274.
Monnetrane, co. Leit., 5489.
Monnerid (co. Lim. ?), 6583.
Monney, Connor, pardon to wife of, 6765.
Monnorowe (co. Kilk. ?), 1914.
Monnymucke. See Moneymuck.
Monoye, Morris A., pardon, 2229.
Monochan. See Monaghan.
Monncree (co. Cork ?), 4511.
Monoghan. See Monaghan.
Monoghan, co. Wex., 882, 1877.
Monoley (co. Westm. ?), 2842.
Monomolin—Moemolyne, co. Wex., 6286.
Monopoly of export of sheepskin, wool and tallow, from Dublin and Drogheda, granted, 5974.
" of glass making, 4571.
Monrragh, co. Clare. See Morye.
Monrvetown (co. Tip. ?), 2558.
Monroe, co. Lim., 4630.
Monse, co. Tip., 6708.
Monsee, co. Tip. See Mosey.
Monsiall, Peter, pardon, 2234.
Monsell, Edm., pardon, 3434, 5165.
Monsell, John fitz Wm., pardon, 6227.
Monsdale, John, pardon, 6770.
Monshall, John m'Pierce, pardon, 6878.
Monshickmane (co. Ross. ?), 4250.
Monsdyallytowne, co. Cork, 1672.
Monster. See Munster.
Monstereven. See Monasterevan.
Mont, Tirrelagh m'Gilleduf, pardon, 6878.
Montagh (co. Gal.), 1420.
Montaghe (co. Ross. ?), 4905.
Montaine, John m'Hob, pardon, 6108.
" Hob oge, pardon, 6203.
Montallen — Mountallon, co. Clare, 4781, 4789, 6401.
Mont Carbre — Montcarbery. See Mount Carbre.
Monten, John, pardon, 899.
" Nich., pardon, 4323.
Monterchany (Muinter Cnaith — Munterkenny, territory in bar. Rosclogher, co. Leitrim), 4580.
Montercomaghie (see Moyntercomaght), 6562.
Monterdowiyn (in Fox's country), King's co., 6562.
Montergarran (Magcarran's country), co. Long., 4468. See Moymergaram.
Montergalgan. See Muntergaligayn.
Montergaren. See Moyntergarane.
Monterloghery, co. Kerry, 6127.
Monter Larkan, co. Gal., 6714.
Montermorcho. See Moyntermargho.
Monteroine (Munterowen), co. Galway, 4521.
Monteruleme — Monteroilis. See Moyntercolys.
Monter Oran, co. Gal., 4718.
Monter Trasey, co. Gal., 4718.
Montcyne castell. See Mountaine castle.
Montoyne, Garot fitz David, pardon, 4472.
" Maries fitz Davied, pardon, 4492.
Montyarrel. See Mountgarret.
Montine (co. Cork ?), 4415.
Montirewarie, co. Cork, 3625.
Montirigan (Muinter Tadhgain, Fox's country), 1104.
Montrath, co. Westm. See Monyrahy, Moyrrath.
Monturne, in Munster, 6829.
Montrome (co. Ross. ?), 4940.
Montroyn, co. Wat., 2941.
Montyne, co. Cork, 6814, 6770.
Monwill, co. Wat., 865.
Mony, Donald, pardon, 6878.
" Edm., pardon, 2788.
" John, clerk, pardon, 1468.
" John, pardon, 5521.
" Onory ny, pardon, 6180.
" William, pardon, 1817.
Monyard, co. Long., 6168, 6686.

INDEX TO FIANTS.—ELIZABETH.

Monycoppan, co. Clare, 6[illegible].
Monyreaghe, co. Cork, lease, [illegible].
Monydale, co. Gal., castle and land, [illegible].
Monyduff—Monaduff, co. Gal., [illegible], [illegible].
Monyduff (King's or Queen's co.?) [illegible].
Monydime alias Moniquine, 4[illegible].
Monye, Donnell A., pardon, 3[illegible].
„ Patr. A., pardon, [illegible].
„ Wm. A., pardon, [illegible].
Monyferricke (Mounferrick), Queen's co., [illegible].
Monyfild, co. Westm., [illegible].
Monygallagh (Monegallagh), co. Meath, 6164.
Monygeelhane (co. Clare?), 67[illegible].
Monyghan, Katherine ny, pardon, [illegible].
Monylagane—Monylaggane (Moneylagan, co. Long.), [illegible], [illegible].
Monyloy, 7[illegible]. See Moneloy.
Monylogan, co. Long., 61[illegible].
Monymohill (Moneymohill), co. Lim., [illegible].
Monymore, co. Gal., [illegible].
Monymore (co. Ross?), [illegible].
Monymore—Monamore, co. Wex., [illegible].
Monymuck—Monymucke, co. Ross, [illegible], [illegible].
Monynaragh, co. Clare, [illegible].
Monyne (co. Cork?), [illegible].
Monyne, co. Kilk., [illegible].
Monynecrosse (Moneycross), co. Wex., [illegible].
Monynge, Wm., [illegible].
Monytallown (co. Westm.?), [illegible].
Monyvahy (Montrath? co. Westm.), 176[illegible].
Monysalrverishe. See Monasterevis.
Monske, co. Westm., 1[illegible].
Moonrony (co. Cork), 6[illegible].
Moodale, co. Westm., [illegible].
Moosne (co. Donegal), [illegible].
Moohane, co. Kerry. See Moghane.
Moole, Agnes, [illegible].
„ Patrick, suit to administer the goods of, [illegible].
Mooly, David m'Mahowne, pardon, 6116.
„ Margaret, pardon, [illegible].
„ Nich., pardon, [illegible]74.
Moorecktown salmon weir on the Boyne, co. Meath, [illegible].
Moone, co. Kild., [illegible], [illegible], [illegible]. See also Moonie, Mowne.
Mooney, Dermot, pardon, [illegible].
„ Wm., pardon, [illegible].
Moonie, John m'Philip no, pardon, [illegible].
Moonygorny, co. Cork, [illegible].
Moor, Honora, pardon, [illegible].
Moor (old), in Kilmainham, [illegible].
Moore, Conoghor, pardon, [illegible].
„ Donell, pardon, [illegible].
„ Donogh, pardon, [illegible].
„ —More, Edward (of Mellifont, afterwards knight), sheriff of Louth, [illegible]; commission to make war on

Moore:
the O'Conors, [illegible]; constable of Philipstown castle, [illegible], 4[illegible], [illegible]; commissions, [illegible], 6537; leases, [illegible], [illegible], [illegible], [illegible], [illegible], [illegible], 4776; surrender, [illegible]; a surety, [illegible]; pardon, [illegible], [illegible], [illegible], [illegible], [illegible], [illegible]; pardon at his suit, [illegible].
„ Edward (of Barmeath), pardon, [illegible], [illegible].
„ Edward, vicar of Clonecurry, [illegible].
„ capt. Garret, commission, [illegible]; sir Garret, or Gerald (son of sir Edw.), made constable of Philipstown, [illegible]; pardon, [illegible].
„ George, grant of lands, [illegible], [illegible], [illegible], [illegible], [illegible], [illegible], [illegible], [illegible], [illegible], [illegible].
„ Gerald, registrar ecclesiastical commission, [illegible], [illegible], [illegible].
„ sir Gerald. See Moore, Garret.
„ Henry (of Ballynocknagh, co. Meath), [illegible]. See More.
„ —More, John, clerk of the crown in Connaught, [illegible], [illegible], [illegible], [illegible]; pardon, [illegible].
„ John, pardon, [illegible], [illegible].
„ Knogher, pardon, [illegible].
„ Melchior, son and heir of Michael, wardship, [illegible].
„ Michael (of Ashboy), [illegible]. See More.
„ Mother, pardon, [illegible].
„ Murogh, pardon, 4174, [illegible].
„ Morrish, pardon, [illegible].
„ Murtogh (of Rahinduff), livery to heir, [illegible].
„ Owen (of Dublin), pardon, 17[illegible].
„ Owen, clerk of the check, [illegible], [illegible]; commissions, [illegible], [illegible], [illegible]; pardon, [illegible], [illegible]; grant of a wardship, [illegible].
„ Patrick, pardon, [illegible], [illegible].
„ Richard, pardon, [illegible].
„ Rosse, pardon, [illegible].
„ Shane, pardon, [illegible].
„ —More, Thomas (of Mellifont, afterwards of Croghan, knight), commissions, [illegible], [illegible], [illegible], [illegible], [illegible], [illegible], [illegible], [illegible]; grant of land, [illegible]; lease, [illegible]; land in his occupation, [illegible]; pardon, [illegible], [illegible], [illegible].
„ Thomas (of Dublin), pardon, [illegible].
„ Thomas, pardon, [illegible], [illegible].
„ William (of Rosmyde), pardon, [illegible].
„ William (Barmeath), commissions, [illegible], [illegible].
„ William m'Donell, pardon, [illegible].

INDEX TO FIANTS—ELIZABETH.

Moore, co. Ross, 6134. *See* More, Moremoc-karnan.
Moore Aghrime. *See* More Aghrym.
Moorechurch, co. Meath. *See* Morechurch.
Moorecrofte, Hector, collector of wine duty, [illegible]
Moores (O'Mores of Leix.), country of, 2871, [illegible]
" depredations of, [illegible]
Moores lands, Ardmulchan, co. Meath, [illegible]
Moorestown, co. Kerry, [illegible]
Mooreton — Mooretown — Mooretoun, co. Kild., 2714, 2763.
Mooreton—Mooretown, co. Meath, 765, [illegible], [illegible]
Mooreton, little, co. Meath, [illegible]
Mooreton—Mooretowne, co. Wex., 4287, 6647.
Mooretowne, co. Westm., [illegible]
Moorton, co. Kild., 2716.
Moortown, co. Kild. *See* Moreton.
Moosbry, [illegible]
Moot, co. Rosc., [illegible]
Mooto, co. Gal., [illegible]
Mooto, co. Long., 5104.
Morey (Monta, co. Westm.), 1[illegible]
Mora, prebendary of (diocese of Lismore), [illegible]
Mora or Nabolters, co. Mayo, [illegible]
Moraghan, co. Clare, 6168.
Moraghe, Rich., pardon, 5742.
Moraghanyshean, co. Down, [illegible]
Morahowe, John m'Moriertagh Y, pardon, [illegible]
Moran, John, pardon, [illegible], [illegible]
" Wm., pardon, [illegible], [illegible]
Morane, Patr., slaying of, 6794.
" Wm., 4214.
Moranghan, Moriert A., pardon, [illegible]
Morcho, Patrick, pardon, [illegible]
Morcompy (Macroom?), co. Cork, [illegible]
Mordant—Mordon, Nicholas, commissions, [illegible], [illegible]
Morderrye alias Longwood, co. Meath, [illegible]
More, co. Rosc., [illegible] *See* Moore.
More, Anne, pardon, [illegible]
" Christopher, prebendary of Christchurch, Dublin, [illegible]
" Conoghor oge, pardon, [illegible], [illegible]
" David, pardon, 470[illegible]
" Dermod m'Conor, pardon, [illegible], [illegible]
" Edm., pardon, [illegible]
" Edward. *See* Moore.
" Edw. (or M'More), pardon, [illegible]
" Elizabeth, pardon, [illegible]
" George, pardon, [illegible]
" Gerald, pardon, 18.
" Gerott, pardon, [illegible]
" Gilpatrick, pardon, [illegible]
" Gullyduf, pardon, [illegible]
More, Henry, pardon, [illegible]
" Henry, sheriff of Louth, comm., [illegible]
" Honora, pardon, [illegible]
" John, death of, [illegible]
" John, pardon, [illegible]
" Lysagh, pardon, [illegible]
" Melaghlin, pardon, [illegible]
" Michael, freedom from subsidy, [illegible]
" Nicholas, lease, 1[illegible]
" Nich., chaplain, [illegible]
" Nich., pardon, [illegible], [illegible], [illegible]
" Patrick, clerk of the crown, Cavan and Down, [illegible]
" Petrus, pardon, [illegible]
" Richard, pardon, [illegible], [illegible], [illegible], [illegible]
" Rich. alias M'Omore, pardon, [illegible]
" Rosse, pardon, [illegible]
" Slane, pardon, [illegible], [illegible]
" Thomas. *See* Moore.
" Tho., pardon, [illegible], [illegible]
" Tirlogh, pardon, [illegible]
" William, premises in Ashbury, [illegible]
" Wm. (of *Drogheda*), pardon, [illegible]
" Wm. (of Ballymore and Ballybeg, co. Kerry), pardon, [illegible]
More Aghrym—Moore Aghrime, co. Gal., chapel, [illegible], [illegible]
Morean (co. Clare?), [illegible]
Morechurch—Morechurche (Moorechurch), co. Meath, rectory, 1460, [illegible]
" vicar, [illegible]
Moreculliope, co. Wat., [illegible]
Moregh, Margaret ny, pardon, [illegible]
Moreghan, Joan ny, pardon, [illegible]
" *See* O'Moreghe, Vorenghowe.
Morehowelande, co. Kilk., [illegible]
Moreisle, the, co. Wex., [illegible]
Moreis, Tho., alienation licence, [illegible]
More moc-karnan (Moore in Moycarn, co. Rosc.?), [illegible]
Morerenan, co. Kerry, [illegible]
Moregeate, co. Lim., [illegible]
Mores, Anthony, [illegible]
" Edw., pardon, [illegible]
" John, pardon, [illegible]
" More, daughter of, [illegible]
" Oliver, pardon, [illegible]
" Rob., pardon, [illegible], [illegible]
" Wm., pardon, [illegible]
Mores, nation of the (O'More of Leix), rebels, [illegible], [illegible], [illegible]; lands not to be alienated to, [illegible] *See* Moores, O'More.
Moresho, Edw., pardon, [illegible]
Morestile, Darchan, pardon, [illegible]
Moreston, King's co., [illegible]
Morestowne, co. Kild., [illegible]
Morestowne, co. Lim. or Kerry, [illegible]
Morestowne, co. Tip., [illegible]
Morewy, Joann ny, pardon, [illegible]

INDEX TO FIANTS—ELIZABETH.

Moreton, co. Kild., 1394.
Moreton (Mooretown), co. Kild., 1467.
Moreton by Ellea (Ballymanona ?), co. Kild., 1467.
Moreton—Moretown (Ballymanona, co. Lim.), 1388; rectory, 1388, [illegible], 4367.
Moreton, co. Louth, 6418, 6657.
Moreton, co. Meath, 1880.
Moreton—Morton, land of, in Clonmel, co. Tip., [illegible].
Moreton (co. Wex. or Kilk. ?), 6494.
Moretonbey (co. Wex. ?), 6541.
Moreton Curragh, co. Meath, [illegible].
Moreton parva, co. Meath, 6010.
Moretone, co. Tip., [illegible].
Moretown. See Moreton, co. Lim.
Moretown, co. Tip., [illegible], 6427.
Moretown, co. Meath, [illegible].
Morett—Moyret—Moyrett, Queen's co., 2722, 5701, 6443.
Morfowe, Wm. fitz John, pardon, 1714.
Morfie, Elizabeth fitz Nich., pardon, 6447.
„ Gerrot fitz John, pardon, 6447.
„ Patr. and Rich. m'Gerrot m'John, pardon, 6447.
Morgadg, co. Wexm., [illegible].
Morgallion, co. Meath. See Margallion.
Morgan, David, chief serjeant, co. Louth, 1311; co. Kildare, 1718; paymaster of leather, 1707.
„ Hugh, pardon, [illegible].
„ James, grant of a wardship, 5074.
„ John, chief smith of the ordnance, &c., [illegible], [illegible], [illegible]. See Morgane, Morgin.
„ Lawrence, pardon, 6430.
„ Matthew, knt., commander of the forces at Ballyshannon, 6072.
„ Patr., his land at Waterford, 3130.
„ Patr., constable of gaol at Ennis, 6794, [illegible]; wardship of son, 6607.
„ Robert, lease, [illegible].
„ Tho., land of, in Queen's co., 1400.
„ Thomas, wardship, [illegible].
„ Walter, pardon, [illegible].
„ William, knt., marshal of army in Clandeboy, 2349; assistant commander of forces in Munster, 2741; constable of Dungarvan castle, 4138; pardon, 3910; his testament, 1100.
Morgane, John, grant of a wardship, [illegible].
„ Tho., pardon, 6445.
Morgans, co. Lim., 4876.
Morganston, co. Kild., 4280.
Morghan, Patr., pardon, 3434.
Morgho, Conoghor oge m'Conoghor I, pardon, 6941.
Morgho, Patrick roe, pardon, 341.
„ Tho. m'Morrierlagh I, pardon, 3941.
„ Wm. fitz Edm. I, pardon, 3941.
Morghoon, Wm., pardon, 6764.
Morghowe, Wm. m'Donogh Y, pardon, 6376.
Morght, John, controller of wine duties, Dublin, 3166.
Morholly, Katherine ny, pardon, 6318.
Moriarterto marcgagh, attainted, [illegible].
Morhow, Dermod oge m'Dermod I, pardon, 5768.
„ Shane m'Morierlagh I, pardon, 6764.
Morion, Any ny, pardon, 4877.
„ David, pardon, [illegible].
„ Richard, pardon, [illegible].
„ Simon, pardon, [illegible].
Moriell, Richard, pardon, 1118.
Moriertagh, alias ny Devin, Denis, 4617.
„ Donogh m'Teige m'Owen, pardon, 4583.
„ Granye ny, pardon, 6138.
„ Mary ny, pardon, [illegible].
Morhertaghe, More ny, pardon, 4372.
„ See Voriertagh.
Morierrie, Onie ny, pardon, 3772.
Moriertie, Donell m'Donell, pardon, 6349.
„ Donell oge, pardon, 6444.
„ Donogh m'Kee m'Donogh, pardon 6344.
„ Donogh m'Teig, pardon, 6864.
„ Edm. m'Donogh, pardon, 6384.
„ Morish m'Teig, pardon, 4912.
„ Moriagh m'Donell, pardon, 6348.
„ Owen m'Donell, pardon, 6344.
„ Teig m'Donell, pardon, 6344.
„ Teig m'Owen, pardon, 6344.
Morierty, Katherine ny, pardon, [illegible].
Morighane pilerre, indenture, 6788.
Morighowe, James, pardon, 3028.
Morihie, Shane m'Donogh Y, pardon, 6814.
Morihyo, co. Clare, 4468.
Moririgane (co. Lim. ?), 6487.
Moris, Ellen inio, pardon, 1607.
„ Kathleen alias Katherin, pardon, [illegible].
„ Tho., aquavitae license, 3149.
Morisamyng (co. Wex. ?), 4626.
Moriso, Tho., pardon, 4118.
Morish, Ellen ny, pardon, 4328.
„ James fitz Donnyshe, pardon, [illegible].
„ Onory ny, pardon, 4214.
„ Owney ni Vic (M'Morish), pardon, 6789.
„ Wm., pardon, 6430.
Morisho, Elizabeth, pardon, 4328.
„ Ellen and Onora ni vic, pardon, 5792.
„ Ellen ny, pardon, [illegible].

INDEX TO FIANTS—ELIZABETH.

Morishe, James, chaplain, pardon, 4637.
„ James, pardon, 5046.
„ Tho., grant to, recited, 5746.
Morishe cgarrane, Margaret ny, pardon, 4714.
Morisholl, Peirs m'Richard, pardon, 4428.
Morishorishillorelagh (see Maghorishillerelagh), 4538.
Morishoton. See Morishton.
Morishie, Donogh fitz Edm., pardon, 6611.
Morishton—Morisheton, King's co. 3471, 4182, 4998.
Morishtonhiller. See Morishtownhiller.
Morishtone, co. Kild., 3416.
Morishtownhiller — Morishtonhiller—Moryshtonhiller (Morristownhiller), co. Kild., 4111, 5782, 5745.
Morishtowne, Little, co. Kild., 5611.
Morison, sir Richard, commission, 6516.
„ Tho., pardon, 6517.
Moriston, King's co., 3471.
Morisson (co. Tip.?), 1300.
Morisowne Moyaaghe—Moristonmoinagh—Moryston Moynagh, co. Kild., 4114, 4127, 5778.
Moriey, Donnell, pardon, 5858.
„ Sh. or Hugh, pardon, 5809.
„ Mary, pardon, 6515.
Morly, Pyrsins m'Conoghor m'Teig, pardon, 4588.
Mormada, co. Cav., 4802.
Mormod, co. Cav., 5857
Mornan, co. Lim., 5777, 6481.
Mornane, co. Lim., 6464.
Mornanton (Mornington), co. Meath. See Marinerston), 1647, 3434, 3538, 5480.
Morne (Mournabbey), co. Cork, 3131.
„ preceptory, granted, 3131.
Morne. See Mourne, co. Down.
Morgan, co. Cor., 804.
Morain—Moraine—Morninge—Mornyn, co Long., 2813, 3431, 3830, 4565–6, 4880, 6188, 6838. See also Morringe.
Morninge. See Mornyne.
Mornington, co. Meath. See Mornanton.
Mornyn. See Mornyne.
Mornye. See Morain.
Mornyne — Morninge — Mornyn (Murreen, co. Mayo), 4868, 5488, 5514; castle and lands, 4868.
Morovow, co. Cav., 5637.
Morowe. See Morrowe.
Morowz (co. Gal.?), 5874.
Moregh, Dermot m'Shean I, pardon, 4468.
„ Donell m'Dermot I, pardon, 5545.
„ Katherine ny, pardon, 6516.
Moregha, Conor fitz John, pardon, 4600.
„ Dermod, Donogh, Edm. and Wm. m'Donell I, pardon, 5838.
Moregho, Conoghor m'Dermod oyle Y, pardon, 4781.
„ Dermod m'Donell I, pardon, 6764.
„ Donell m'Dermod oyle Y, pardon, 4781.
„ Donell m'Wm. Y, pardon, 4678.
„ Hellen inine ny, pardon, 4744.
„ Teig m'Diermody Y, pardon, 4864.
„ Wm. m'Donell Y, pardon, 4781.
Moreghoe, Donell m'Shane I, pardon, 6458.
„ Donnoghoe m'Donnell Y, pardon, 4814.
„ Margaret ny, pardon, 6518.
„ Thady m'Edm. I, pardon, 4408.
Moreghow, Arthur m'Teig I, pardon, 4015.
„ Cahir m'One I, pardon, 4016.
„ Conoghor m'Donell I, pardon, 6764.
„ Dermot m'Donell I, pardon, 4015.
„ Dermod m'Donogh I, pardon, 6764.
„ Dermod m'Donoghow Y, pardon, 4781.
„ alias M'Kiltagh, Donogh m'Wm., pardon, 5528.
„ Edm. m'Donogh moro I, pardon, 4015.
„ Edm. m'Donoghy I, pardon, 6764.
„ James m'One I, pardon, 4015.
„ John m'Dermod I, pardon, 2577.
„ One m'Donill, pardon, 4016.
„ Shan m'Donogh Y, pardon, 5944.
„ Shane m'Dermod Y, pardon, 4781.
„ Shillie ny, pardon, 6518.
„ Tho. m'Teig Y, pardon, 4782.
„ Tirlagh m'Doall, pardon, 4016.
„ Wm. m'Teig I, pardon, 2577.
Moreghowe, Conor and Dermod m'Shane Y, pardon, 6868.
„ Donell m'Tho. I, pardon, 6764.
„ Edm. m'Connoghor I, pardon, 6764.
„ John oge m'Shane I, pardon, 3944.
„ Shane m'Morierlagh I, pardon, 6412.
„ Teige m'Shane Y, pardon, 4858.
„ Wm. m'Gylleduff Y, pardon, 4814.
Moreho, Shane m'Donoghe I, pardon, 6764.
Morehoe, Patrick, pardon, 6646.
Morehony, Dermond m'Moryertie Y, pardon, 4487.
Morehow, Teige m'Dermond Y, pardon, 4487.
Morehowe, Shane m'Donell I, pardon, 6764.
Morone, Nicholas, pardon, 1668.
„ Wm., pardon, 4256.

INDEX TO FIANTS.—ELIZABETH.

Morough alias M'Teolath, Conoghor m'Teig I, pardon, [illegible].
Morough, Donell buoy m'Donogh Y, pardon, [illegible].
Moroughe, Elizabeth nine, pardon, [illegible].
Moroughoe, Conoghor m'Donogh I, pardon, [illegible].
" Shane oge I, pardon, [illegible].
Moroughowe, Teig, pardon, [illegible].
Morowghowe, Teige m'Donogh I, pardon, [illegible].
Morowho, Edm. and Tho. m'Donoghow Y, pardon, [illegible].
Morphe, John, pardon, [illegible].
" Tho., pardon, [illegible].
" Wm., pardon, [illegible].
Morphen, John, pardon, 2434.
" Rob., pardon, 2434.
Morphey, Wm., pardon, [illegible].
Morphie, Patrick, attainted, [illegible].
Morphie, Philip, pardon, [illegible].
" Richard, pardon, [illegible].
Morphy, David, pardon, [illegible].
" Thomas, pardon, [illegible].
Morragan, co. Lim., castle and land, [illegible].
Morran, Edm., pardon, [illegible].
" John, pardon, [illegible].
" Wm., pardon, [illegible].
Morre, Conor, pardon, [illegible].
" William, pardon, [illegible].
Morreghowe, Donell farahjuga, pardon, [illegible].
Morreis, the, co. Wex., [illegible].
Morreis's land, co. Tip., [illegible].
Morrell, Wm., pardon, [illegible].
Morres, Edm., pardon, [illegible].
" Ennstes, pardon, [illegible].
" Geoffrey, pardon, [illegible].
" John, pardon, [illegible], [illegible].
" Jordan fitz Oliver, pardon, [illegible].
" Walter, pardon, [illegible].
Morrevis, John, pardon, [illegible].
Morrey, Conoghor, pardon, [illegible].
" Morogh, pardon, [illegible].
" Morrogh, pardon, [illegible].
" Rich. m'Moyler, pardon, [illegible].
" Tho., pardon, [illegible].
Morreys — Morris — Morryes — Morrys, Thomas, grant of land, 475; surrender, [illegible]; grant, [illegible]; commission, [illegible]; license of alienation, [illegible].
Morrghe, Shane, murder of, 147.
Morrice, Anne, wardship, [illegible].
" Ellen, pardon, [illegible].
" dame Ellen ny, pardon, [illegible].
" Philip, wardship of daughter, [illegible].
" Rob., pardon, [illegible].
" Sanly ny, pardon, [illegible].
" Tho., land grant, [illegible].
Morrietagh morrogagh, indenture, [illegible].
Morrigh boy, indenture, [illegible].
Morrigan (Morain?), co. Long., [illegible].
Morris, Anstace, pardon, [illegible].
" Denis, pardon, [illegible].
" Edm. fitz Wm., pardon, [illegible].
" Edm. m'Adam, pardon, [illegible].
" Ellen ny, pardon, [illegible].
" Ellen, pardon, [illegible].
" Ellis, pardon, [illegible].
" James, pardon, [illegible], [illegible].
" John, grant, [illegible].
" John, pardon, [illegible].
" Mary, pardon, [illegible].
" Oliver, pardon, [illegible].
" Redmund (of Knockagh, co. Tip.), pardon, [illegible], [illegible].
" Redmund, pardon, [illegible], [illegible], [illegible].
" Rich., pardon, [illegible].
" Simon, pardon, [illegible].
" Thomas, 475. See Morreys.
" Tho., pardon to wife, [illegible].
" Walter, pardon, [illegible].
Morrisca, Dermod m'Shane I, pardon, [illegible].
Morrish, Margaret, pardon, [illegible].
Morrisho, Ellis ny, pardon, [illegible].
" John, pardon, [illegible].
" Tho., pardon, [illegible].
Morrison, Fierce, lease, [illegible].
Morrisowneblilor, co. Kild. See Morishtownbiller, Moistownbiller.
Morristowne (co. Tip.?), [illegible].
Morroes — Moroes — Morros — Morrowes country (O'Murchadha or O'Murroughoe's country), co. Wex., 130, [illegible], [illegible], [illegible], [illegible], [illegible], [illegible], [illegible], [illegible], [illegible]; martial law, 61, 67.
Morrogh, Dermod m'Donogh I, pardon, [illegible].
" Edm., pardon, [illegible].
" Ivey, pardon, [illegible].
" Morrogh oge ny (of Callow, co. Long.), pardon, [illegible].
" Tho., pardon, [illegible].
Morroghe, Donell m'Donoghe Y, pardon, [illegible].
" Ellish ny Shane Y, pardon, [illegible].
" Joan ny, pardon, [illegible].
" Philip m'Donell Y, pardon, [illegible].
" alias Baddy, Shane m'Wm. I, pardon, [illegible].
" Teige m'Wm. Y, pardon, [illegible].
Morroghoe, Honora ny Conoghor ny Bierny ny, pardon, [illegible].
" Shane m'Conoghor I, pardon, [illegible].
" Shelie ny, pardon, [illegible].
" Teig m'Donell Y, pardon, [illegible].
Morroghow, Donogh m'Shane I, pardon, [illegible].
" Ellen ny, pardon, [illegible], [illegible].

INDEX TO FIANTS—ELIZABETH.

Morroghow, Honor ny, pardon, 6431.
" Joan ny Donell I. pardon, 6761.
" Katherine ny, pardon, 6431.
" Tho. m'Connoghor I. pardon, 6764.
" Tho. m'Teige I. pardon, 4997.
Morroghowe, Connoghor m'Donnogho I. pardon, 6764.
" Connor E. pardon, 6378.
" Donell m'Connoghor I. pardon, 6764.
" Edm. m'Donogh I. pardon, 4997.
" Mary ny, pardon, 6764.
" Murtagh m'Connor E. pardon, 6378.
" Shane m'Connoghor I. pardon, 6764.
" Teige m'Connoghor I. pardon, 6764.
" Tho. m'Teige I. pardon, 6764.
" Wm. m'Donogh I. pardon, 6764.
Morron, Tho., pardon, 3412.
Morros, the, 158. See Morrowes.
Morroshe, Conoghor m'Dermond Y, pardon, 4467.
Morrough, Onory oge, pardon, 6368.
" Patr., pardon, 6432.
Morroughe, Donald m'Donoughe I. pardon, 5941.
" Donald m'Edm. I. pardon, 5941.
" Wm. m'Donough I. pardon, 5941.
Morroughowe, Dermod m'Shane I. pardon, 6764.
" Donell m'Edm. I. pardon, 6764.
Morrowes, country of the. See Morroes.
Morrowhow, Donogh m'Donell I. pardon, 6764.
Morryes, Tho. See Morreys.
Morrynett (Mungret ?), co. Lim., castle and lands, 6283.
Morrynett de Temple, co. Lim., 6282.
Morrys, Thomas. See Morreys.
Morstown, co. Louth, 1732.
Mortagh, Donagh, pardon, 6457.
" Donell, pardon, 6457.
" Edm., pardon, 6457.
" Goffray, pardon, 6457.
" Gill Patrick, pardon, 6457.
" James, pardon, 6457.
" Mortagh roe, pardon, 6457.
" Owen, pardon, 6457.
" Rory, pardon, 6457.
" Shane, pardon, 6457.
" Teige, pardon, 6457.
" Wm., pardon, 6457.
Mortagh oge, Innory enuyn, pardon, 4132.
Mortaghe, Carmick m'Edm., pardon, 4643.
Mortaghe, Edm., pardon, 4617.
" John, pardon, 4617.
Mortallon (perhaps Monmallon, co. Clare), 4478.
Mortarstown, co. Car. See Mortellestown.
Mortelleston. See Mortellestown, co. Car.
Mortelleston. See Morteleston, co. Tip.
Mortell, Phillip, pardon, 4180, 4728.
Mortelleston — Mortelleton — Mortellston (Mortarstown, co. Car. ?), 1340, 1408, 6764.
Mortellestown. See Morteleston.
Mortellinton. See Mortelleston.
Morteleston — Mortelinton — Mortellestoe — Mortellston — Mortells towne — Mortelston — Mortelstown — Morteltowne — Morteylston — Mortleston — Mortlestowne, co. Tip., 1869, 1986, 2036, 2691-9, 2877, 3289, 3238, 6463, 6527, 6604, 6535, 6764; rectory, 2294, 2709, 6347, 6541.
Mortonstowne (co. Tip. ?), 6328.
Mortgage, accounts of, 6488, 6631, 6133.
Mortin, co. Long., 6394.
Mortines, Nich., pardon, 6617.
Mortle, Patr., pardon, 6639.
Mortleston — Mortlestoune. See Morteleston, co. Tip.
Mortmain, Statute of, lands granted contrary to, 4777, 6836, 4878, 6040; lands devolved to crown by, 5814, 6834, 6181.
Mortogh, Johanne and Sawcoell, pardon, 6606.
Morton (Ballymascanlan ?, co. Louth), 1488.
Morton (see Mordon), 6251.
Morty's lands, Youghal, 6691.
Mortymer, Katherine, 1714.
Morrymore leez, co. Meath, 3318.
Morvorragh — Morvorragh, Brian reogh, pardon, 4340, 4834.
Morvorragh, Edm., pardon, 4348, 6424.
" Feragh, pardon, 6414.
" Gillecollum, pardon, 4348, 6814.
" Rory, pardon, 4340, 6414.
" Wm. duff, pardon, 4342.
" Wm. oge m'Wm. duffe, pardon, 6615.
Morvornaghe, Henis, pardon, 6418.
Morvorragh, Grany, pardon, 6478.
Morvorry, Breene reogh, pardon, 6516.
Morwghwe, Shane m'Teige I, pardon, 4823.
Mory, co. Long., 6689.
Mory, Donogh, pardon, 6464.
" Moriertagh m'Owen Y, pardon, 1162.
Morye (Monreagh ?), co. Clare, 6163.
Moryn, Tho., pardon, 4637.
Morys, Morgan, pardon, 432.
" Una eyck, pardon, 6768.
Moryse, John, pardon, 548.
Morychtowbiller. See Morishtowbiller.
Moryston Moymach. See Morismwne Moymaghe.

INDEX TO FIANTS.—ELIZABETH.

Mossingtan, co. Cork, 4764, 4948.
Mossy, rectory, diocese of Killaloe (Mosseta, co. Tip.?), [illegible].
Mostoha, co. Clare, 4457.
Moskry, co. Tip., [illegible].
Moskrye. See Muskery, co. Cork.
Moskryloghry, 6514. See Muskrie Loghrie.
Mosse, co. Lim., 1428.
Moston—Mostan—Mostian—Mostian—Mostian—Mostyan:
" Edward, sheriff of Roscommon, [illegible], [illegible]; commissions, [illegible], [illegible]; pardon, [illegible].
" Hugh, controller of wine duty, Galway, [illegible]; customer of Dublin, [illegible]; sheriff of Galway, [illegible].
" Robert, sheriff of Westmeath, [illegible]; commissions, [illegible], 1198, 2161, [illegible], [illegible], [illegible], [illegible], 2764; pardon, [illegible].
" Thomas, sheriff of Galway, [illegible]; pardon, [illegible], [illegible].
" William, pardon, [illegible].
" William, junior, pardon, [illegible].
Mostra (co. Long.?), [illegible].
Mostrim, co. Long. See Mastrim.
Mostyan, Rob. See Moston.
Mota, co. Long., [illegible], [illegible].
Motan, Tho. m'Shane, pardon, [illegible].
Mota, co. Dub., 1777.
Mote (co. Meath?), [illegible].
Mote (co. Rosc.?), 6113.
Mote, Wm., pardon, [illegible].
Motell, Arthur, pardon, [illegible].
Mothell, John, pardon, [illegible].
Mothell, co. Car., 914.
Mothell—Motbill, co. Kilk., [illegible]; rectory, [illegible].
Mothell—Mothill—Mothell (Mothel), co. Wat., [illegible], 1914-5, 1151, [illegible], 1378, 1794, [illegible], 4144, [illegible], [illegible]; rectory, [illegible].
" abbey, leased, [illegible].
" vicar of, 707.
Mothery, co. Cork, [illegible], [illegible].
Mothill, 787.
Mothill. See Mothell.
Mothill, John, pardon, [illegible].
" Rob., pardon, [illegible].
Mothinge, Peter, pardon, [illegible].
Mothrogwir (co. Ferm.?), [illegible].
Motle (co. Wex.?), [illegible].
Mott, Wm., pardon, [illegible].
Mott—Motte (co. Rosc. or Gal.), 4474, 6138.
Moucho Ballyfinnok, co. Wex., [illegible]. See Ballyfinnok.
Mouchegrange (Grangemore), co. Kild., [illegible].
Mouchewood (Muchwood), co. Meath, [illegible], [illegible].
Mouffe, co. Gal., 4657.
Mougaure alias Mogowre, co. Tip., rectory, [illegible].
Mougely (co. Cork?), 4178.
Mough—Moughe (co. Cork?), [illegible], [illegible].
Mough, Queen's co., [illegible].
Moughane, co. Clare, 6764.
Moulahogga no grannagie, co. Watm., [illegible].
Moulleston, co. Meath, 1800.
Moullodarrugh (co. Leit.?), [illegible].
Mounckes grange, Queen's co., [illegible].
Mounckeswoode (co. Wick.?), [illegible].
Mounckman, Robert, pardon, [illegible].
Mounce, John, keeper of the house of Kilmainham, [illegible].
Mounford, Francis, pardon, [illegible].
Moungart, in the Duffry, co. Wex., [illegible].
Mounkesgrang (co. Tip.?), [illegible].
Mounkesland (co. Tip.?), [illegible].
Mounkesland, co. Wat., [illegible].
Mounkeswood (co. Wick.?), [illegible].
Mounsell, Theobald, pardon, [illegible].
" William, pardon, [illegible].
Mounselstown (Manselstown, co. Tip.?), [illegible].
Mounslowe, Fulco, [illegible].
Mounster. See Munster.
Mounster oris, [illegible]. See Monasteroris.
Mountague, capt. Charles, commission, [illegible].
Mountaine, John, marshal of Castle Chamber, [illegible].
Mountaine castle—Mountayne castell — Mountayne castell—Mountene castell—Mountayne castell, co. Wat., [illegible], [illegible], [illegible], [illegible], [illegible], [illegible], 6451.
Mountainestown, co. Wex., 4081.
Mountallon, co. Clare. See Molustallon. Mortallon.
Mountarlog, co. Wex., [illegible].
Mountaynecastell—Mountayne castell. See Mountainecastle.
Mount Carbre—Mont Carbre—Monteckerbery (hills in N.W. of co. Longford, called on Petty's Map, Slievecarbragh), [illegible], 1401, [illegible], [illegible]. See also Sliewcarbry.
Mountdagio Loiell, seignory called, co. Kerry, [illegible].
Mountenrobbin, co. Cork, [illegible].
Mountegarret. See Mountgarret.
Mountenecastell. See Mountainecastle.
Mounter Connaght, co. Cav., [illegible].
Mounterhagan, King's co., Fox's country, [illegible], [illegible].
Mounter Lough (probably in Tyrone), [illegible].
Mounterwarghe (Muinter Murchada, in bar. of Clare, co. Gal.), [illegible].
Mountoyne castell. See Mountainecastle.
Mountgarret—Montgarret—Mountgaret—Mountgarrett — Mountegarret, co. Wex., 1613, 6704.

INDEX TO FIANTS.—ELIZABETH.

Mountgarret, Richard, viscount, commissions, 51, 66, 81, 513, 604-7, 603; lease to, 3157; his son, 851; his son and heir, 844, 3851.
" Edmund, viscount, commissions, 3117, 3345, 3114, 3916, 5133; livery, 3361; pardon, 3153, 4423, 4390; submission, 4309; brother of, 3826; daughter of, 6140; son of, 6020, 6424.
" dame Grany, lady of, pardon, 6302.
" See Moyngarr.
Mountjoye, Charles, lord, arrives as lord deputy, 6761; absent in remote parts, 6128, 6427; orders on fiants, 6433, 6775; servant of, 6778.
Mountjoye, co. Tyrone, 6712.
Mounton (Monkstown, co. Dub.), 3118.
Mountrath, Queen's co. See Moycarrath, Moyrath, Moyrraghe.
Mountrie Doubliagre, in Tyrone, 6713.
Mounteribe, co. Gal. See Mountscribe.
Mount Trenchard, co. Lim., 5078.
Moure, co. Rosc., 3788, 3493.
Moure Moycharne, co. Rosc., 3788.
Mourett (co. Lim. ?), 6107.
Mourne—Morne (barony of Mourne, co. Down), martial law, 48; to be made shire ground, 1728; Sir Nich. Bagenall's country, 4237.
Mourne abbey, co. Cork. See Morne.
Mousrimowneen. See Muskerye Nowneen.
Mousktrie Quirke. See Muskrey, co. Tip.
Mouskry. See Muskery.
More, Moyle m'Teige, pardon, 6460.
Moviddy—Moveddy—Movedy—Movidde—Movidde—Movidie—Movyddy—Muvide, co. Cork, 5066, 5191, 5337, 5373, 4781, 5330, 5332, 6946; patronage, 5373, 5460, 6202.
Moveydo, co. Cork, 2891.
Movroghe (co. Mayo ?), 4686.
Movyddy. See Moviddy.
Mowclere, Edmund. See Mowlere.
Mowclerstowne. See Mocklerstown.
Mowclogheen, co. Clare, 6462.
Mowelone (Muckloon, co. Gal. ?), 2591.
Mowfore townsend, 2961.
Mowgan (co. Kilk. ?), 1961.
Mowghane, co. Clare, 1941.
Mowghane, Teige m'Donogh I., pardon, 6473.
Mowgowny (co. Clare ?), 6794.
Mowlike (co. Mon. ?), 6013.
Mowlleaghmore. See Mullaghmore, co. Gal.
Mowllaughmaghoremowre (Magheramore, co. Mon. ?), 5062.
Mowmakr, Matthew fitz John, pardon, 4606.
Mowne (Moone ?), co. Kild., 3141.
Mowne Dongdy, co. Cork, 2817.
Mownecowre in Shrahagrin, Queen's co., 6766.
Mowrmion, co. Westm., 1474.
Mowrolecrolan, co. Cork, 2878.
Mowrwry, Grange of, in Clanrickard, 1488.
Mowragine, co. Louth, 628.
Mowre, Nich., pardon, 5788.
Mowreagh, Cormock, pardon, 6798.
Mowree, Wm. fitz Philip, pardon, 4793.
Mowerye. See Muskrey, co. Tip.
Mowskerryloweyther. See Muskrie Logharte.
Mowskery. See Muskrey, co. Tip.
Mowlling, Peter, pardon, 4388.
Mowlinge, James, pardon, 6025.
Mowynewy, Grange of, co. Gal., 1484, 5110.
Moy, co. Clare, 4941.
Moy, co. Gal. or Rosc., 5008.
Moy (co. Gal. ?), 6718.
Moy, co. Gal. See Moy.
Moy, co. Mon., 6692.
Moy, co. Sligo, 5434.
Moyacom—Moyacoe—Moyacione, co. Car., rectory, 673, 1136, 1686, 5456, 4941.
Moyaddo—Moyadu (Moyadd), Queen's co., 1653, 6385, 6788.
Moyagh, Newton of (Newtown moyaghy, co. Meath), 5908.
Moyaghe (co. Meath ?), 4868.
Moyaghen (co. Westm. ?), 6767.
Moyagher, co. Meath, 5925; rectory, 682, 2306, 5542, 6181.
Moyaghy—Mologhy (King's co. ?), 4182.
Moyaliffe (co. Tip.), 6763.
Moyalian, co. Down. See Megalmane.
Moyallie—Moially—Moyally (Moyaliff, co. Tip. ?), 616, 6848, 6704.
Moyalie. See Moalle.
Moyally. See Moyallie.
Moyaly (co. Meath ?), 6631.
Moyamagh (co. Westm. ?), 6463.
Moyamaghe. See Moyamagh.
Moyane alias Moylynne, co. Meath, tithes, 608, 3163, 6403.
Moyanne. See Tworeannane.
Moyannagh—Moyanaghe—Moyanaghe—Moyrcheny (Moyanna), Queen's co., 683, 3382, 6937.
" rectory, 1316.
Moyardo, co. Gal., 6120-1.
Moyarta—Moaria—Moyaria—Moyartie, co. Clare, 4741, 6401. See Moyfarta.
Moyarta barony. See Corckovaskine, Corcowaskyne.
Moyashell—Moiashill (Moyashel), co. Westm., barony, 6346, 6618.
Moyaskarrag, co. Gal., 4688.
Moyasker, co. Gal., 4862.
Moyasiraghe, co. Gal., 5816.

Moyaughay, co. Meath, [illegible].
Moybian, co. Lim., 6124.
Moybilley, co. Gal., 6123-4.
Moybillie, co. Kerry, 6128.
Moybillie, co. Kerry, [illegible].
Moybillye, co. Kerry, 6487.
" See Moyeboilly.
Moybolge — Moibolge — Moybolge — Moybolgo, co. Cav., 4[illegible]1, 6464.
Moybologe, co. Cav., [illegible].
Moybraven — Moybrevany — Moyvrawin — Moywraven (Magh Breaghmhaine or Moybrawne, a district in baronies of Shrule, Moydow and Ardagh—see Inquisitions—part of O'Ferrall Boy's country), co. Long., [illegible], 6[illegible]1.
" captain of, 1108, 1871.
Moybrecke alias Moybrecke, lordship (Magh Breacraighe, the west part of barony of Moygoish), co. Westm., [illegible], [illegible]6-7.
Moybrevany. See Moybraven.
Moybrick, co. Down. See Ballymoyvricke, [illegible].
Moycally (co. Kilk. ?), [illegible].
Moycarkye, co. Tip., 1878.
Moycashel—Maicaishell — Moychaishell — Moycashall — Moycashill — Moycassell — Moycashell — Moycassell, co. Westm., 1427, 3458, 3737, 3347, [illegible], 3774, [illegible], 6151, [illegible].
" manor, &c., surrendered, [illegible].
" barony, 1780.
" martial law in, 3152, 6[illegible].
" seneschal, 4378.
Moycawe (co. Gal. or Sligo ?), 5474.
Moycharnan, co. Rosc., [illegible].
Moycharnan, Moore, co. Rosc., 3783.
Moycloroy, co. Wex., [illegible].
Moyclare—Moyglare, King's co., 1401, 6612.
Moyclare, co. Meath, 846.
Moyclare. See Moyglare, co. Meath.
Moycloine, co. Wex., 3734.
Moycolpe. See Mocollop.
Moycrom—Moycromer (Macroney, co. Cork), rectory, 10[illegible], [illegible].
Moycruse, co. Kerry, [illegible].
Moycullen—Mocollen—Moculion, co. Gal., 4711, [illegible], [illegible]-1.
" castle, [illegible].
" barony, 6150-1, [illegible], [illegible], [illegible], [illegible].
" See also Macoullin.
Moydawe (Moydow), co. Rosc., [illegible].
Moyden—Mokleme, co. Rosc., [illegible], [illegible].
Moydervy alias Longwood, co. Meath, [illegible].
Moydollan, co. Gal., [illegible]-1.
Moydow, co. Long. See Moygowe.
Moydow barony, co. Long. See Clanawly, Clanconnogher, Clangilkerne, Moybraven.
Moydow, co. Rosc. See Moydawe.
Moydrohitt (Mondrohid ?), Queen's co., [illegible].
Moydrohed in Upper Ossory, Queen's co., [illegible].
Moydrum—Moidrome, co. Westm., [illegible], [illegible].
Moye, co. Gal., [illegible].
Moye, King's co., land surrender, [illegible].
Moye, co. Lim., 3377.
Moye (Moig ?), co. Lim., 5717.
Moye, co. Rosc., 1880.
Moyeboilly (co. Kerry ?), 6478.
Moyeghteragh (Moy Bira), co. Mon., [illegible].
Moyehanny. See Moyeanagh.
Moyeloe—Moielly, co. Westm., 6512, [illegible].
Moyell, Kellagh m'Teige, pardon, [illegible].
Moy-Ilon, near Belfast (identified by Bishop Reeves with Malone, co. Antrim), [illegible].
Moyelly, King's co. (Westm. ?), 6777.
Moyelly, co. Westm., 1884.
Moyely, co. Cork, [illegible].
Moyemlagh, co. Sligo, [illegible].
Moyenny (Moyhenna), co. Mayo, 3777.
Moyeurath (Mountrath), Queen's co., 1878.
Moyeragh (co. Donegal), [illegible].
Moy Bira, co. Mon. See Moyeghteragh.
Moyfadda, co. Clare, [illegible].
Moyfarta (Moyarta ?), co. Clare, [illegible].
Moyfeagher, co. Meath. See Moikeagher, Moyeagher.
Moyfenragh — Moyfenraghe barony, co. Meath, martial law in, [illegible], [illegible].
Moyfine — Moyfyune alias Moyane, co. Meath, [illegible], [illegible], 4409.
Moygadd — Moigaddye — Moygadde, little, (Moygaddy, co. Meath), [illegible], [illegible].
Moygaddie, Myche — Great Moigaddye (Moygaddy, co. Meath), [illegible], [illegible].
Moygaddy — Moygaddie — Moigaddy, co. Meath, [illegible], [illegible], [illegible]. See also Moygarde.
Moygan alias Myggan (co. Kild. ?), 3144.
Moygannie, co. Car., [illegible].
Moygannon, co. Down. See Moyogannon.
Moygarbarrye — Moigarbarie — Moygaribarrie (Magorban), co. Tip., rectory, 1[illegible], 4012, [illegible]1.
Moygarde, great (Moygaddy), co. Meath, [illegible].
Moygarde, little (Moygaddy), co. Meath, [illegible].
Moygare—Moygeare, co. Meath, manor, [illegible], [illegible], 1[illegible], [illegible].
Moygaribarrie. See Moygarbarrye.
Moyganure, co. Tip., [illegible].
Moygawna, co. Cork, [illegible].
Moyge, co. Cork, [illegible]. See also Nomoyge.

INDEX TO FIANTS—ELIZABETH.

Moygare. *See* Moygara.
Moygelly—Mogyelly (Mogeely), co. Cork, rectory, [illegible], [illegible].
Moygh, co. Sligo, [illegible].
Moygher by Kelles, co. Meath, [illegible].
Moygherye in the Duffrye, co. Wex., [illegible].
Moyglare, co. Kild., [illegible].
Moyglare alias Boolaclachare (see Moyclare, King's co.), 1471.
Moyglare — Maglare—Moglare — Miglare — Moclare—Moiclare—Moieclare — Moiglare — Moyclare, co. Meath, [illegible], [illegible], [illegible], [illegible], [illegible], 6124, 4976-7, [illegible], 6416, [illegible], 6777.
" manor, [illegible], [illegible].
" rectory, 1677, [illegible], [illegible].
Moyglas—Moyglasse, co. Ross., [illegible], [illegible].
Moyglosse (co. Ross. ?), [illegible].
Moygoise barony (Moygoish, co. Westm.), martial law in, [illegible]. *See also* Moybrackre.
Moygow, co. Clare, [illegible].
Moygowe (Moydow, co. Long. ?), rectory, [illegible], [illegible], [illegible], [illegible], [illegible].
Moyh, co. Clare, [illegible].
Moyhall, co. Clare, [illegible].
Moyheddan, [illegible].
Moyhell. *See* Moyhill.
Moyhell (Mohill, co. Leit. ?), [illegible].
Moyhell (co. Lim. ?), [illegible].
Moyhenna, co. Mayo. *See* Moyenny.
Moyhery, [illegible].
Moyhie, co. Clare, [illegible], [illegible].
Moyhill—Moyhell, co. Clare, [illegible], [illegible].
Moyhill (Mohill, co. Leit.), [illegible], [illegible].
Moyhowragho, King's co., [illegible].
Moyiele, co. Wat., [illegible].
Moyinlaken, co. Clare, 1817.
Moykeell (co. Cor. ?), [illegible].
Moylagh (co. Donegal), [illegible].
Moylagh, co. Gal., [illegible], [illegible].
Moylagh—Moylaghe—Moyllagh, co. Meath, [illegible], [illegible], 4149, [illegible].
Moylagh, Castleton of (Castletown, in parish of Rathmolyon, co. Meath), [illegible], [illegible], [illegible].
" lordship of (see Mylagh), [illegible].
Moylagh — Moylaghe — Moylaugho alias Mullough (Molough abbey), co. Tip., abbey or house of nuns, leased, [illegible], [illegible], [illegible].
" rectory, [illegible], [illegible].
Moylagh—Moyllaghe, co. Westm., [illegible], [illegible], [illegible].
Moylaghe (Moylough, co. Gal.), rectory, [illegible], [illegible].
Moylaghe. *See* Moylagh, co. Meath.
Moylaghe, co. Ross., [illegible].
Moylaghe. *See* Moylagh, co. Tip.
Moylaker (co. Long. ?), [illegible].
Moylaloghry (co. Ross. ?), [illegible].
Moylarge. *See* Moylurge.
Moylaughe. *See* Moylagh, co. Tip.
Moylaughlyn (Mullaghlaulin ?), co. Meath, [illegible].
Moyldrom—Moildrome—Moyldrian—Moyldrume — Moyldrynn (Moeldrum), co. Westm., [illegible], [illegible], [illegible], [illegible].
Moyle, Donald, pardon, [illegible].
" Donogh (of Dromlara, co. Lim.), attainted, [illegible], [illegible].
" Henry, sheriff, co. Cork, commission, [illegible].
" John, pardon, [illegible].
" Manus m'Teig, pardon, [illegible].
" Maurice, capture of, 717.
" Morris m'Edm., pardon, [illegible].
" Shane ne, pardon, [illegible].
" Thady m'William, pardon, [illegible].
" Tho., pardon, [illegible].
" William, pardon, [illegible].
Moylehussy. *See* Moylhussie.
Moylerston, co. Kild., [illegible].
Moylerston (Mylerstown), co. Kild., [illegible].
Moyletraugh, co. Ross., [illegible].
Moyley, John ne, pardon, [illegible].
Moylhussie — Milhussy — Milhussie — Milussey—Moilussey—Moilussie — Moylehussy—Moylussy (Mulhussey), co. Meath, [illegible], [illegible], [illegible], [illegible], [illegible], 3412, [illegible], [illegible].
Moyllhycragh (co. Cork ?), [illegible].
Moylin, co. Westm., [illegible], [illegible].
Moylis, co. Gal., [illegible].
Moylis, co. Mayo, [illegible].
Moyllagh. *See* Moylagh, co. Meath.
Moyllaghe. *See* Moylagh, co. Westm.
Moyloe (co. Mayo ?), [illegible].
Moylorge. *See* Moylurge.
Moyloyston, co. Kild., [illegible].
Moylough, co. Gal. *See* Moylaghe.
Moyloye's (Molloy's) country, [illegible].
Moylurey (Meelionagh ?), co. Long., [illegible].
Moylyclarran. *See* Mullclarran.
Moylurge — Moylarge — Moylorge (M'Dermot's country), co. Ross., [illegible], [illegible], [illegible].
" seneschal of, appointed, 1817.
" *See* Mollurg.
Moylussy. *See* Moylhussie.
Moylyurogh, co. Ross., [illegible].
Moymed, [illegible].
Moymed—Moymede. *See* Moymet.
Moymen, co. Kerry, [illegible].
Moymet—Moymed—Moymete—Moymeth, co. Meath, 761, [illegible], [illegible], [illegible], [illegible], [illegible], [illegible], [illegible], [illegible], [illegible]; rectory, [illegible], [illegible], [illegible].
Moymlough, co. Sligo. *See* Moinlaghe.

Moymor (co. Clare ?), [illegible].
Moymore, co. Gal., [illegible].
Moymore, co. Lim., [illegible].
Moymore—Moymoyre, co. Westm., rectory, [illegible], [illegible], [illegible]. *See also* Moyvore.
Moyn, barony of (Tirawley), co. Mayo, [illegible].
Moyn, co. Mayo, [illegible].
Moynagh, Phelim, pardon, [illegible].
„ Shane m'Moriarty, pardon, [illegible].
„ Teige, pardon, [illegible].
Moynaghe, Peter, pardon, [illegible].
Moynaghmore (co. Ross. ?), [illegible].
Moynalin (Monalin, co. Wick. ?), [illegible].
Moynallgeler (co. Wex. ?), [illegible].
Moynallestrim (co. Wick. or Wex.), [illegible].
Moynalthe, co. Meath, [illegible], [illegible].
„ rector or parson of, [illegible], 1448, [illegible], [illegible], [illegible].
Moynalvy, co. Meath. *See* Monalvy.
Moynamy, co. Cork, [illegible].
Moynananny, co. Cork, [illegible].
Moynanny, co. Cork, [illegible].
Moynanyvany, co. Cork, [illegible].
Moynard, co. Meath, [illegible].
Moynart—Moynarte, co. Wex., [illegible], [illegible].
Moyne, co. Cav., [illegible].
Moyne, co. Gal., castle and land, [illegible].
Moyne (co. Mayo ?), [illegible].
Moyne, co. Mayo, S. Francis monastery, [illegible].
„ *See* Moyn.
Moyne, Queen's co., [illegible].
Moyne (co. Wick. ?), [illegible].
Moyneaffrin, [illegible].
Moynealestrome (co. Wex. or Car.), [illegible].
Moynealestrom (co. Wex. or Car. ?), [illegible].
Moyneard, co. Tip. *See* Moinarde.
Moyneart in the Duffrye, co. Wex., [illegible].
Moynebeg (co. Wex. or Car.), [illegible].
Moyneeish, co. Wex., [illegible].
Moynegroneye, co. Lim., [illegible].
Moyne Inirye, co. Down, [illegible].
Moynekenle, co. Westm., [illegible].
Moynemore (co. Car. ?), [illegible].
Moynenelarge (co. Wat. ?), rectory, [illegible].
Moyneoguenagh. *See* Moynogyranagh.
Moyneraithe (Mountrath), Queen's co., [illegible].
Moyneraith, co. Wat., [illegible].
Moynerly (co. Tip. ?), [illegible].
Moynesterwish (Mounsterwris ?), King's co., [illegible].
Moyneart in the Duffrye (perhaps Mountgarret), co. Wex., 1744.
Moynfie (co. Cork ?), [illegible].
Moynkerie in the Duffre, co. Wex., [illegible].
Moynlaugh, co. Sligo, [illegible].
Moynloh (co. Wex. ?), [illegible].
Moynmanny, co. Cork, [illegible], [illegible].
Moynogh, Brian, pardon, [illegible].
Moynogyranagh—Moyneoguenagh, co. Clare, [illegible], [illegible].
Moynoire, co. Rosc., [illegible].
Moynoke (King's co. ?), [illegible].
Moynoco (Moynoe), co. Clare, [illegible].
Moynore, co. Mon., [illegible].
Moynothe—Moynouth. *See* Maynothe.
Moyrure. *See* Moyrath.
Moyrraghe (Mountrath ?), Queen's co., [illegible].
Moyrath — Moyrraithe (Mountrath), Queen's co., [illegible], [illegible].
Moyrath—Moyrre (Montrath), co. Westm., [illegible], [illegible].
Moyrro (co. Tip. or Lim.), [illegible].
Moyntagh (co. Rosc. ?), [illegible].
Moyntagh — Mointagh (co. Sligo ?), [illegible], [illegible].
Moyntaymston, co. Wex., [illegible].
Moyntle, co. Rosc., [illegible].
Moynterargagh, co. Clare, [illegible].
Moynterbryan — Mointerwryane (a sept in Kenaliagh, co. Westm.), [illegible].
Moyntercunnaght — Mointerchonaly — Moynterconnaghe — Monterconaghte (Muintereonnaght), co. Cav., [illegible], [illegible], [illegible].
Moyntercroghan—Mointercroghane (district in barony of Kilmaine), co. Mayo, [illegible]; seneschal of, [illegible].
Moynterdaybe, in O'Conor Don's country, co. Rosc., [illegible].
Moynterdowlle, co. Gal., [illegible].
Moynterdwan (see Munterduln), [illegible].
Moyntergarane — Mointergowan — Muntergarran — Muntergeran (Muintir Geradhain, co. Long.) (see Am. I. Co, index), [illegible], [illegible], [illegible], [illegible].
„ seneschal appointed, [illegible].
Moyntergeigan. *See* Muntergeiganye.
Moyntermarghe—Montermorohe—Moyntermorhe (originally more extensive, but here the northern and western part of bar. Clare, co. Galway), [illegible]; chief rent to earl Clanrickard, [illegible]; rectory, [illegible], [illegible].
Moynterolys—Mointerolee—Mointerolishe — Monterolesse — Monterollis (Muinter Eolais, M'Ranall's country in co. Leit.), to be surveyed and formed into shire ground, [illegible]; surrendered, [illegible].
„ grange of, [illegible], [illegible], [illegible].
Moyntervarye, co. Cork, [illegible].
Moyntwor (Moyntore), co. Rosc., [illegible].
Moyntyoylany — Moyntymoilany (co Kilk. ?), [illegible], 1173.
Moynully—Moynullie, co. Mayo, [illegible].

INDEX TO FIANTS—ELIZABETH.

Moyruare—Myruire, co. Rosc., 6423, 6486.
" See also Moyruwre.
Moyruy (co. Cork), [illegible], 4942.
Moyrylagans (Moncylagan, co. Long. ?), 6760.
Moyrodkeston, co. Dub., 4434.
Moyrogamon (Moygannon), co. Down, 1604.
Moyrure (co. Mayo ?), 4173.
Moyra, co. Don. See Moyren.
Moyraih, Queen's co., 1623.
Moyraih—Moyrathe, co. Westm., 3464, [illegible], [illegible], 6773.
Moyrathe, co. Meath, 4266.
Moyrathe. See Moyraih, co. Westm.
Moyrene (Moyren), co. Clare, 4741.
Moyret—Moyreth. See Moreti.
Moyrharro, co. Kerry, 6162.
Moyris, co. Gal., 4443.
Moyroo (Murroe or Moyra, co. Donegal), 6282.
Moyrslagher (Moylaghor), co. Meath, 6948.
Moystown, King's co. See Muryster.
Moytaugh, co. Sligo, 5026.
Moythall (co. Kilk. ?), 4220.
Moytra (a district in bar. Longford), co. Long., 4253, 6043, 6767.
Moytren, co. Long., 6453.
Moyvaghille (Moyvoughly, co. Westm. ?), 6423. See also Myvaghell.
Moyvallagh, co. Kild., 6383.
Moyvallin (co. Westm. ?), 6425.
Moyvally, co. Gal., 5618.
Moyvally—Moyvaly—Moyvayle, co. Kild., 1744, 4623, [illegible], 6239.
Moyvanan (Moyvannan), co. Rosc., 6781.
Moyvanio (co. Donegal), 4887.
Moyvayle. See Moyvally.
Moyvuroe — Moywuroe (Moyvure ?), co. Westm., 1618, 5431.
Moyvoly, co. Gal., 5518.
Moyvore, co. Westm., 4150, 6368. See also Moyenore, Moyvurroe.
Moyvoughly, co. Westm. See Moyvaghille.
Moyvrawin—Moywrawen. See Moybrawen.
Mrone, Owen m'Donogh oy, pardon, 4784.
Mroyvallin (Moyvullen, co. Gal.), 1428.
Much Ardene, co. Kild., 2742.
Much Ballyphemock, co. Wex., 2393. See Ballyfinnok.
Much Ballibyn (Ballybiln), co. Meath, 2578.
Much Dericks (Derrockstown), co. Meath, 1578.
Muchefelde—Mychefeld, at Trim, co. Meath, 88, 622.
Muchegranege (co. Kild. ?), manor, 5745.
Muchelly, 6766.
Muche Riverston, co. Meath, 159, 2547.
Muchwood, co. Meath. See Munchewood.
Muckalee, co. Kilk. See Mockolly, Mukylly.
Muckanagh, co. Westm. See Moghnagho.
Muckarnan, 4753.
Muckcrownchy, co. Cork, 2384.
Muckamagh (co. Rosc. ?), 2834.
Muckamagho Edardahalye—Mukanaghe Edardahalie (Muckanaghederdanhaulie), co. Gal., 4555, 6014.
Muckcongher (co. Lim. ?), 6604.
Muckenes, co. Clare, 6863.
Muckennagh (co. Gal. ?), 4752.
Muckenerys, co. Clare, 6857.
Muckerin, co. Kerry, 4888.
Muckerstown, co. Meath. See Mogherreston, Mughoreston.
Muckherys, co. Gal., 5698.
Mucklagh, co. Louth. See Mochlache.
Muckland (Mucklon), co. Kild., 6063, 6438.
Mucklechan, co. Leit., 5442.
Muckloy, Edw., pardon, 4712.
Mucklon, co. Kild. See Muckland.
Muckloon, co. Gal. See Mowloon.
Mucklowe, co. Gal., 5108.
Muckmoe alias Muckme (Muckno), co. Mon., country, territory and termon, 4752.
Muckonaghe (co. Long. ?), 6266.
Muckrumpy—Muckrampyn (Macroom, co. Cork ?), 2858.
Muckridge, co. Cork. See Mokiriahe.
Muckrie, co. Kerry, 4888.
Muckromby (Macroom ? co. Cork), 3463.
Muckromy, co. Wat. (Macromy, co. Cork ?), 6018.
Muckrownchy (co. Cork ?), 2384.
Muckrush — Mockerush (Muckross), co. Kerry, 6277, 6717.
Muckston, 6468.
Muckully (co. Kilk.), parson of, 6221.
Mucle A korne, Cahir, pardon, 618.
Mucolpe (Mocollop, co. Wat. ?), 4024.
Mucromoy, co. Cork, 6708.
Mucromchie, co. Cork, 6761.
Mucrompe, co. Cork, 6764.
Mucromy, co. Cork, 6764.
Mucrompe, co. Cork, 6764.
Mueniterchonaght (Muntercomaught, co. Cav.), 2394.
Mugnaily, Cormock m'Teige, pardon, 6482.
" Hewe m'Cormock, pardon, 6423.
Mugelligie (co. Cork ?), 6498.
Mugheraston (Muckerstown), co. Meath, 2168.
Muicke, co. Wat., 4687.
Mulngarivhal, co. Cork or Lim., 5028.
Muintercolms, co. Leit., 4474. See also Moyntercolye.
Muintir Creaith. See Montercheny.
Muintir Fandachain, co. Ferm. See Maintrisnlaghin.
Muintir Geradhain. See Moyntergerane.
Muintir Oilgain. See Muntergaligayn.
Muintir Murchada, co. Gal. See Mountermorghe, Moyntermorghe.

INDEX TO FIANTS—ELIZABETH.

Muintir Tadhgain. *See* Mointorngan, Montirtagan, Monsterlagan.
Muintir—. *See* Moinier—, Moynier—.
Muko Rush, co. Cork, 4783.
Mukrenghe Ederdabalie. *See* Muckroaghe Ederdabelyn.
Mukkerys (Muckrush, co. Gal.), 1881.
Mukris, co. Kerry, [illegible].
Mukylly (Muckaloo or Macolly), co. Kilk., rectory, [illegible]. *See also* Muckully.
Mulbrian, Donell m'Melaughlen I, pardon, 4418.
Mulcahagh, Donell m'Donogh Y, pardon, [illegible].
Mulcahee, Conoghor m'Mahowne Y, pardon, [illegible].
Mulcahy, David m'Teig Y, pardon, [illegible].
Mulcayle, More ny, pardon, [illegible].
Mulchae, Donogh m'Donell I, pardon, [illegible].
Mulchahae, Shane m'Donell I, pardon, [illegible].
Mulchahy, Teige mac I, pardon, [illegible].
Mulchirvill, Rowe ny, pardon, [illegible].
Mulconrie, Dermod m'Senighane I, pardon, [illegible].
Mulcorry, Donill m'Shane, pardon, [illegible].
Mulcroyly, Donogh m'Royry I, pardon, [illegible].
Mulcrugy (co. Gal. ?), [illegible].
Muldowny, Dermot, John and Owen m'Knoghor I, pardon, [illegible].
Muldownie, Shane m'Morrish I, pardon, [illegible].
Muldowneys, Daniel and Owen m'Teig I, pardon, [illegible].
Muldoyne, Patrick, pardon, [illegible].
Mulghe, river, co. Antrim, [illegible].
Mulgorum, Teig and Shane m'Tho. I, pardon, [illegible].
" Tho. m'Ker I, pardon, [illegible].
Mulgorrom (co. Tip. or Lim ?), [illegible].
Mulguirme, Tho. m'Shane I, pardon, [illegible].
Mulgrryne, Shane m'Edm. I, pardon, [illegible].
Mulhussey, co. Meath. *See* Moyithmede.
Muligh cowle, constable of, 148.
Mulingar. *See* Mullingar.
Mulhuddart, co. Dub. *See* Malahiddert.
Mulkahy, John m'Donogh I, pardon, [illegible].
" John m'Mahowny I, pardon, [illegible].
" Maurice m'David I, pardon, [illegible].
" Richard m'Mahony I, pardon, [illegible].
" S( ) m'Ricard Y, pardon, [illegible].
" Tho. m'Tenyll I, pardon, [illegible].
Mulkerrie, Connoghor m'Morris I, pardon, [illegible].
Mulkerrie, Hey m'Shane I, pardon, [illegible].
Mulkyry, Wm. mac Donogh ny, pardon, [illegible].
Mullacash, co. Kild. *See* Mullaghcaish.
Mullachiredan (co. Mon. or Cav. ?), [illegible].
Mullacloe, co. Louth. *See* Mullaghcoloe.
Mullacurry, co. Louth. *See* Mullaghcourre.
Mulladrillen, co. Louth. *See* Mullaghdrisslone.
Mullagarry, co. Mon. *See* Mullaghgarry.
Mullagh, co. Cav. *See* Molaghe, Mollache.
Mullagh, co. Meath. *See* Mollaghe.
Mullagh—Mollagh (co. Tip. ?), [illegible], [illegible].
Mullagh (co. Tip. ?), [illegible].
Mullagha, co. Meath. *See* Mylaugha.
Mullagharosh, King's co. *See* Mcllaghecrosse.
Mullaghbboy, co. Mon., [illegible].
Mullaghcaish — Molaghcaishe — Mollaghcaisse — Mologhcasshe (Mullacash), co. Kild., [illegible], [illegible], [illegible], [illegible].
Mullaghcloe—Mologhcloe, co. Westm., [illegible], [illegible].
Mullaghcorran (Mullaghcor), co. Mon., [illegible].
Mullaghdrin, co. Down. *See* Ballymolaghdrum, [illegible].
Mullaghdrisslone (Mulladrillen, co. Louth), [illegible].
Mullaghe — Mollaghe, co. Gal., 1474, [illegible], [illegible].
Mullaghe, co. Ros., 1380, [illegible].
Mullaghe (co. Tip. ?), [illegible].
Mullaghcoloe (Mullacloe), co. Louth, [illegible].
Mullaghcourre (Mullacurry ?), co. Louth, 763.
Mullaghenesloe. *See* Mullaghmaeloe.
Mullaghfin, co. Meath. *See* Malaughsion.
Mullaghgarry (Mullagarry), co. Mon., [illegible].
Mullaghhurtan, co. Mon., [illegible].
Mullaghid—Mullaghide. *See* Malahide.
Mullaghmartin, co. Mon., [illegible].
Mullaghmaste — Mollaghmast (Mullamast), co. Kild., [illegible], [illegible].
Mullaghmore, [illegible].
Mullaghmore — Molaghmore — Mowllaghmore, co. Gal., 1476, [illegible], [illegible], [illegible], [illegible], [illegible], [illegible], [illegible]. *See* Mullaghmore.
Mullaghmore, co. Mon., [illegible], [illegible], [illegible].
Mullaghmorybeneght, co. Mon., [illegible].
Mullaghmaeloe—Mollaghenesloe, alias Ballinlobar, co. Rosc., chapel, [illegible], [illegible].
Mullaghmeldwre, co. Wexm., [illegible].
Mullaghnorry, co. Tip. *See* Mollagh Enorre.
Mullaghny, Dermod m'James I, pardon, [illegible].
Mullaghshalahanagh, co. Mon., [illegible].
Mullaghsalenne, co. Mon. *See* Mollaghsalshenaghe.
Mullaghsowe, co. Mon., [illegible].
Mullaghshillock, co. Mon., [illegible].
Mullaghtelin, co. Meath. *See* Moylaughlye.
Mullaghen, Honore ny James I, pardon, [illegible].
Mullaglasan, co. Mon. *See* Molliglasan.
Mullamast, co. Kild. *See* Mullaghmaste.

INDEX TO FIANTS—ELIZABETH

Mullamock—Mullamocke (Mullymucks, co. Ross.), 1814, 3784.
Mullanamak, co. Mon. See Mullanakeaske.
Mullane, Donell m'Teige Y, pardon, 6767.
Mullanokeaske (Mullanamak), co. Mon., [illegible].
Mullanlary, co. Mon. See Mullolary.
Mullanstown, co. Louth. See Molesworton.
Mullave (co. Cork ?), 6452.
Mullawerna (co. Long. ?), [illegible].
Mullody, Rory, pardon, [illegible].
Mulleigh (co. Tip. ?), 6421.
Mullolary (Mullanlary), co. Mon., 6471.
Mullen, Rich. m'Donogh, pardon, 1782.
Mullencross, co. Louth, 6[illegible].
Mullemmochan, co. Westm. See Mollemy-aghe.
Mullgwiren, ( ) m'Tho. I, pardon, 6610.
Mullhabella, co. Kerry, 6469.
Mullichaghe (co. Kerry ?), 6374.
Mullick, co. Clare, 3784.
Mullinam, co. Meath. See Mollinan.
Mullineux—Mullinex. See Molyneux.
Mullingar—Mollingar—Mollingare—Mollingar—Mollinger—Mollengar—Mollingnar—Molliagar—Mollingare—Mollinger—Mollyngar—Molyngar—Molyngar—Mullingor, 144, 194, 1482, 1638, 1377, 1853, 2946, 3828, 4[illegible], 4613, 4684, 4694, 5281, 6274, 6104, 6[illegible], 6[illegible]; fine to be paid at, 1108-10, 1171, 1271; security to be given at, [illegible]; sessions at, 6343; custom of Mary gallons, 4546; houses and gardens leased, 1488, 3289, 4330, 5[illegible], 5438, 5[illegible]; rectory, 1449, 3[illegible], 5384-5; fortification of town, 4564.
" provost, [illegible], 2117, 3444.
" provost, burgesses and commonalty, grant of fairs, 4[illegible].
" constable of the castle, [illegible], 4364.
" abbey or priory, granted, [illegible]; possessions leased, 418, 1174, 1448, 1[illegible], 2[illegible], 3[illegible], 3418, 4317, 4[illegible], 5[illegible], 5[illegible], 5540, 6370; granted, 2718, 6548.
" " prior of, 1145, 1[illegible], 6[illegible].
" house of friars preachers, 582.
" Balor Seligro, [illegible], [illegible], 6434.
" Bridge, 5[illegible].
" the Faigh, 2[illegible], 6434.
" Frank house, 6318, [illegible], 5[illegible].
" gaol, to be built, [illegible]; fines bestowed on, 1623-3, 1763, 1771; prisoners to be committed to, 1[illegible]; to be
Mullingar; delivered by martial law 6216, 6345, 6256; prisoners in, pardoned, 6[illegible].
" " constable of, [illegible], 5767, 4[illegible].
" market, robbery at, 5[illegible].
" Spittell house, [illegible], 4[illegible], 4[illegible].
Mullkerrin, Conoghor m'Shane I, pardon, 6457.
Mullmoy, Edmund, pardon, 182.
Mullmory roe (M'Gibbon ?), attainted, 6[illegible].
Mullocmahinna, co. Cav., 6[illegible].
Mullogudan, 6672.
Mullomy, Connor m'Shane ny hiller I, pardon, 6[illegible].
Mullough. See Moylagh, co. Tip., 6411.
Mullpatrick, Teig m'Dermot I, pardon, 6[illegible].
Mullrian, Molaghlin reogh m'Wm. I, pardon, 6478.
" Wm. m'Reedy I, pardon, 6490.
Mullurge, co. Ross., 6[illegible].
Mullyggollane, co. Ross. See Molleghgollane.
Mullymucks, co. Ross. See Mullamock.
Mullyn, Dermot m'Donogho I, pardon, 4[illegible].
Mulmorey, Shanchan, pardon, 4[illegible].
Mulmorie, Ellen nyne, pardon, 4[illegible].
Mulowey, William, son of Donald Y, English liberty, 117.
Mulpatrick, Connor and Teig m'Connor I, pardon, 4753.
Mulranckan—Molranean—Molranekan—Molrankan (Mulrankin), co. Wex., 4[illegible], 4[illegible], 5[illegible], 6727.
Mulrean, Donill m'Donogh roe I, pardon, 6[illegible].
" Ossory ny, pardon, 4[illegible].
" Philip m'Shane glishe I, pardon, 6[illegible].
Mulrenane, Derby oige, alias Ryan, clerk, pardon, 4[illegible].
Mulregan, co. Lim., 5[illegible].
Mulreis, Wm. m'Teige I, pardon, 4[illegible].
Mulrian, Connor m'Shane I, alias annoreg, pardon, 6[illegible].
" Conoghor m'Shane I, pardon, 6[illegible].
" Derby, pardon, 6[illegible].
" Donald m'Shane glish I, pardon, 6[illegible].
" Donogh m'Laghlin I, pardon, 6[illegible].
" Donogh lader m'Mahown I, pardon, 6[illegible].
" Donogh m'Teige I, pardon, 6[illegible].
" Donogh m'Wm. leigh I, pardon, 6[illegible].
" Edm. duv Tho. I, pardon, 6[illegible].
" Gillen ny, pardon, 6[illegible].
" Henry m'Leisye I, pardon, 5[illegible].
" Henry m'Teig I, pardon, 4786.
" Margaret ni, pardon, 5[illegible].
" Owne m'Rorie I, pardon, 6[illegible].

Muirian, Rory m'Conoghor Y, pardon, [illegible].
„ Rorie m'Donell oge I, pardon, [illegible].
„ Rorie m'Owne I, pardon, 4504.
„ Shane m'Rory Y, pardon, [illegible].
„ Teig m'Dermody I, pardon, 4478.
„ Teig m'Melaghlin I, pardon, [illegible].
„ Teige m'Shane I, pardon, [illegible].
„ Tho. m'Wm. I, pardon, [illegible].
„ Wm. m'Teig Y, pardon, [illegible], 4504.
Muiriane, Dermod m'Melaghlen I, pardon, [illegible].
Mulronie, Daniel m'Shane Y, pardon, [illegible].
Mulrony, Tho. m'Shane I, pardon, [illegible].
Mulrough (co. Gal. ?), [illegible].
Mulryan, Cornell m'Shane I, pardon, [illegible].
„ John ny, pardon, [illegible].
„ Mahir m'Shane glish I, pardon, [illegible].
„ Philip m'Wm., pardon, [illegible].
„ Shane m'Donell I, pardon, [illegible].
Mulryan, Fynola I, [illegible].
Multifarnan—Molteferan—Moltifernan—Mollighfarnan—Moyltyfarnan—Multifornane (Multyfarnham), co. Westm., [illegible].
Mulvurrian, Donogh m'Shane I, pardon, [illegible].
Mumane (co. Cork ?), 4418.
Munckhowgan, Robert, provost marshal, 1830.
Munchstown. See Monkstown.
Muncygurran (co. Lim. ?), [illegible].
Munegurra, co. Lim., [illegible].
Munessyngallagh, in Munster, [illegible].
Munga, co. Gal. See Monga.
Mungan, co. Kilk. See Mongan, Mongansheharn.
Mungart, co. Wex., [illegible].
Mungerrill (co. Lim. ?), [illegible].
Mungret, co. Lim. See Mongrett, Monrygrett.
Munkeneston, co. Meath, [illegible].
Muns, John, pardon, [illegible].
Munsell, Wm., pardon, [illegible].
Munschtowne (co. Tip. ?), [illegible].
Munster—Mounster—Mouster, land not yet shire ground to be divided into counties, [illegible]; lord deputy engaged in, [illegible]; sessions held in counties, [illegible]; casual revenues, [illegible]; similar government extended to Ulster, [illegible]; trade in, [illegible], 1819; capt. Zouche in, 4044; cows given for support of army in, [illegible]; expedition under earl of Ormond, [illegible]; province unable to support garrisons, [illegible]; soldiers in, [illegible]; government to raise forces and complete fortifications, [illegible]; wasted by war

Munster:
and rebellion, 1819; coshes and exactions, [illegible]; commissions to determine the rents and services by which tenants hold, [illegible]; persons pardoned to bring their goods and cattle within the protection of the army, [illegible]; Irish oppression, [illegible]; persons pardoned to submit and give security before the president, &c., [illegible]; pardon limited to persons born in, [illegible]; pardon of all the poor inhabitants of the province, [illegible]; patent for dividing the escheated lands among undertakers, [illegible]; conditions imposed on grantees, [illegible]; grants to undertakers—see under counties Cork, Kerry, Limerick, Tipperary and Waterford; commission to consider claims on escheated lands, and disputes between undertakers, [illegible]; lands passed by commissioners to undertakers not invalidated by subsequent grant to another, [illegible]; petition pending a grant of lands in Munster, [illegible].
„ commission of peace and civil government (including Thomond), [illegible]; excluding Thomond, [illegible]; commission for government in military affairs, [illegible]; commission for muster and array, [illegible].
„ commission for ecclesiastical causes, [illegible].
„ commission to enquire for concealed lands of monasteries and attainted persons, [illegible]; commission of survey, [illegible].
„ commission for martial law, [illegible].
„ lord president, sir John Perrot, [illegible].
„ chief commissioner, Francis Agarde, [illegible].
„ „ „ James Dowdall, [illegible], 2771.
„ lord president, sir William Drury [illegible].

INDEX TO FIANTS.—ELIZABETH.

Munster, general of the army in the absence of the governor, T. earl of Ormond, 4608.
" lord general and governor of province, T. earl of Ormond, 4602.
" lieutenant-general of province, T. earl of Ormond, 4452.
" lord president, sir John Norreys, 4462, 4490, 4516, 4620, 5113, [illegible], [illegible], 5428, [illegible], [illegible], [illegible], [illegible], [illegible], 6139, 6144.
" vice president, sir Thomas Norreys, 4887, 5066, 6797, 5479, 5834, 6062, 5991.
" chief commissioner, sir Tho. Norreys, 6144.
" lord president, sir Tho. Norreys, 6167.
" lord president, sir George Carew, [illegible], [illegible], 6421–2, [illegible], 6464.
" president, security for rent to be given to, 2610; captain of country to attend, 5648; authority of, 4574; suspected treasons to be reported to, 4825; diet at the board of, 5379; persons pardoned, to appear before president, justice, or attorney, and give security, 6431, 5451, 6404–5, 6497.
" president and council, fine at discretion of, [illegible]; persons pardoned, to submit before, 6768.
" council, decree of, and proceedings before, [illegible]; recognizances to be entered in council book, 6487, 6768.
" " clerk of, [illegible], &c. See below.
" colonel of the whole province, sir Humfrey Gilbert, 1462.
" James Dowdall to have charge of soldiers of the province, [illegible].
" general of the army, T. earl of Ormond, 4602. See above among governors of the province.
" chief colonel and general commander, sir Warham St. Leger, 6748–1.
" provost marshal, 1463, 5103, 1856, [illegible], 4087, 4191, 4465, 4879, 5215, 5876, [illegible], [illegible], 6144.
" chief justice (Fettiplace), 1846; (Walshe), [illegible], [illegible], 4115, 4186, [illegible], 4499, 4807; (Smythes), [illegible], [illegible], 5187, 5441, 5479, 5876; (Saxey), [illegible], 5615, [illegible], 6144, [illegible], 6497, 6768, 6772.
Munster, second justice (Walshe), 1846, [illegible]; (Myagh), 4115, 4771, [illegible]; (Golde), [illegible], 5479, [illegible], [illegible], 6144, [illegible]; (Comerford), 6444, 6497, 6764, 6772.
" queen's attorney (Myagh), 3788, 3771; (Golde), 4134; (Becon), 4675, [illegible], 5641, [illegible], [illegible]; attorney general of the province (Ashfield), 5707; (Robinson), [illegible]; queen's principal attorney, (Gosnall), [illegible], [illegible]; (Barsfield), [illegible], 6497, 6768, 6772.
" clerk of the council (Burgate), [illegible]; (Bryskett), 4226, [illegible]; (Boyle), [illegible].
" clerk of the crown and peace, 4457, 4986, 6148, 6167.
" marshal of the courts and gaols, 5471, 6167, 6448.
" general escheator, [illegible].
" collector of fines, [illegible].
" cessors and collectors of cess, [illegible].
" victualler of the garrison, 1518.
" serjeant at arms, [illegible], 3795, [illegible], 4458, [illegible], 5734.
" usher or gentleman porter, [illegible], 5159, 5702, 6734.
" constable of Castlemaine castle, [illegible], 6159, 6451.
Munstercounaught, co. Cav. See Moyntercoonaght, Munterconaught.
Munterdalin—Moynterdwlin, people called, in Glanmolman, co. Westm., 1340. See also Monterdowlyn.
Muntergeligayn—Montergeigan—Moyntergalgan (Muintir Gilgain, a district in baronies of Ardagh, Moydow, and Shrule—Inq. Lagenia), co. Long., [illegible], [illegible], 6107.
" seneschal of, [illegible].
Munterkenny, co. Leit. See Monterchenry.
Muntermellan, co. Donegal. See Muinter melan.
Munterowen, co. Gal. See Leighe Carrow Moyeterown, Montercoin.
Muntir Banlaghan in Inishowen, men of, pardoned, [illegible].
Muntir—. See Mointer—, Monter—, Moynter—, Muintir—.
Munyneagh, co. Clare, 5617.
Munymaraghe, co. Clare, 6617.
Munytruym (Mocantrim, co. Wat.), [illegible].
Muny royine (co. Gal. ?), 4707.
Mocrilly, Donell m'Tho., pardon, 4652.
Muraghie (co. Cork ?), 5942.
Murchan, Dermot oy, pardon, 4117.

INDEX TO FIANTS—ELIZABETH.

Murcho, Mary, pardon, 6649.
Murchowe, Donell, Shane, and Teig m'Teig I, pardon, [illegible].
Murder excluded from pardons, 6102.
Mureghu, Shane m'Donell I, pardon, [illegible].
Murffy deanery in diocese of Dublin (Ui Muireadhaigh or Omurthy in S. of co. Kildare), 6474.
Murfie, Tho., pardon, 6511.
" Wm., pardon, 6594.
Murghee, Shane, pardon, [illegible].
Murhally, Ellen ny Donnell, pardon, 6918.
" Ranell oge brg, pardon, 4810.
Murhely, Conoghor oge m'Conoghor m'Teige, pardon, 6514.
Murher—Murhir, co. Kerry, 6159; rectory, 6391.
Murhillya, John m'Teige Y, alienation to, 5028.
Murhir. See Murher.
Murhulle, co. Clare, 1774.
Muriariagh, Donogh m'Shane I, pardon, 6764.
Murlherty, Morris m'Teig I, pardon, 4877.
Murlhie, Ellen ny, pardon, 6314.
Murrigan, co. Kerry, 6491.
Murley, Donell and Shane m'Diarmody m'Conoghor, pardon, 6514.
" Shane m'Shane m'Teige, pardon, 6514.
" Teige m'Conoghor m'Shane, pardon, 6514.
Murlough, co. Down. See Insturallich, 4887.
Murly, Conoghor and Dermod m'Teig m'Shane, pardon, 6464.
" Leaffe m'Conoghor m'Teige, pardon, 6514.
" Owen m'Wm. m'Conoghor, pardon, 6514.
" Shane m'Teig m'Shane, pardon, 4808.
" Teig m'Wm. m'Donell, pardon, 6808.
" Teige m'Wm. m'Conoghor, pardon, 6514.
Murneen, co. Mayo. See Morrayne.
Murogh alias Boyerlagh, Hugh, pardon, 6831.
Murcups, co. Cork, 6764.
Murough, Shane roe, pardon, 4883.
Murphe, Robert, pardon, 4163.
Murphee, Tho., pardon, 8481.
Murphie, Crohin, English liberty, 2898.
" Edmund fitz John fitz Thomas, pardon, 482.
" James, alias O'Moroghe, English liberty, 2898.
" Richard, alias O'Moroghe, English liberty, 2898.
Murphie, Wm., pardon, 4115.
Murphy, Philip fitz David, pardon, 5078.
Murraghey (co. Cork ?), 6640.
Murraghie (co. Cork ?), 6640.
Murroghie, John m'Donoghie, pardon, 6640.
" Moriertie m'Donogh Y, pardon, 6571.
" Teig m'Donoghie, pardon, 6640.
Murroghoo, Dermod m'Donoghie, pardon, 6640.
" Donoghie m'Teig m'Shane I, pardon, 6640.
" John and Teig m'Donoghie, pardon, 6640.
Murroghowe, Conoghor fitz Edm., pardon, 6640.
Murroy, Edm. lye m'Edm., pardon, 4724.
" Moylor m'Loghlyn boy, pardon, 4058.
" Owen m'Toole, pardon, 4844.
" Tomultagh m'Tomultagh, pardon, 4467.
Murrie, Felim, pardon, 8066.
Murrish (co. Kerry ?), 6404.
Murrisk barony, co. Mayo. See Owll O'Mallie, also Marsk, Murske.
Murroane, Owen ny, pardon, 6671.
Murroe, co. Donegal. See Moyroe.
Murrom, co. Wex., country, 6080.
Murroghe, Dermod m'Teig I, pardon, 6462.
" Donoghe m'Shane Y, pardon, 6100.
" Katherine ny, pardon, 6767.
" Richard, pardon, 1874.
Murroghoe, Connor m'Shane I, pardon, 6468.
" Dermot m'Donell, pardon, 6578.
" Dermot m'Donoghoe, pardon, 4828.
" Donell m'Donogh, pardon, 4820.
" Edm. m'Donell, pardon, 4820.
" Mahowne m'Connor I, pardon, 6468.
" Shane m'Conoghor Y, pardon, 6671.
" Teig m'Shane Y, pardon, 6671.
Murroghow, Donell m'Donogho I, pardon, 6467.
Murroghowe, Edm. m'Shane, pardon, 6640.
" John m'Donell roe I, pardon, 6764.
Murroghow, Philip m'Donyll Y, pardon, 5882.
Murry, John, 1722.
" Patr., pardon, 6430.
Murryo, Neylo, pardon, 6480.
Murryrygane (co. Kerry), 6494.
Murske (Murrisk), co. Mayo, barony of, 5985.
" friary leased, 6002.

INDEX TO FIANTS—ELIZABETH.

Murtagh, Donogh, pardon, [illegible].
„ Edmund, pardon, [illegible].
„ Geoffrey, pardon, [illegible].
„ Hubert, pardon, [illegible].
„ John, pardon, [illegible].
„ Maurice ny Kelly, pardon, [illegible].
„ Murghe, pardon, [illegible].
„ Owen, pardon, [illegible].
„ Owen m'Teig, pardon, [illegible].
„ Teige reagh, pardon, [illegible].
„ William, pardon, [illegible].
Murtogh, Denis, pardon, [illegible].
Murrughe, Philip m'Donald Y, pardon, [illegible].
Murvey, co. Gal. See Kor Morvey.
Muryhirty, Donoghe m'Teig m'Donoghe I, pardon, 6677.
„ Murtagh, Owen, Shane and Teig m'Teig m'Donell I, pardon, 6677.
Murykowe, Donald m'Shane I, pardon, [illegible].
Muscrilmoherrye (see Muskrie Loghrie), 6784.
Muskereye Nowman—Moscuri nowman, co. Lim., [illegible], [illegible].
Muskery—Muskrye—Monskry—Muskrey—Muskrie—Muskry—Muskrye (Muskerry), co. Cork, 1064, [illegible], [illegible], [illegible], [illegible], [illegible], [illegible], [illegible], [illegible], [illegible], [illegible]; surrender of country, [illegible]; grant of country, [illegible], [illegible]. See Glenconnoghor.
„ captain of, 1019, 1194.
Muskrey—Mowscrye—Mowskery—Mouskerie Quirke—Muskrey Kuricke—Muskriquirk—Muskryquirk—Muskryquyrck (the barony of Clanwilliam, co. Tip.), [illegible], [illegible], [illegible], [illegible], [illegible], 6977.
„ captain of, 1978.
Muskrey (co. Tip.?), [illegible].
Muskrie. See Muskery, co. Cork.
Muskrie Loghrie—Moskryloghry—Mowskerryloghter—Muscrilmoherrye (co. Kerry?), [illegible], [illegible], 6764; 13 carucates in, granted, [illegible].
Muskriquirck—Muskriquirk. See Muskrey, co. Tip.
Muskry. See Muskery, co. Cork.
Muskry. See Muskrey, co. Tip.
Muskryagh, Donill m'Dermod, pardon, [illegible].
Muskrye (see Muskery, co. Cork), [illegible].
Muskrye, co. Cork, [illegible].
Muskryquirk—Muskryquyrck. See Muskrey, co. Tip.
Mustart, Morrish ogn m'Morish, pardon, [illegible].
Muster and array, commissions for, [illegible], [illegible], [illegible], [illegible], [illegible]; instructions for taking, [illegible]; power included in higher commissions of peace, [illegible], &c.
Muster:
Muster of barony of Newcastle, co. Dub., [illegible]; of men of city of Waterford, [illegible]; of Athenry by magistrates of the town, [illegible]. Quarterly musters of the army to be held before clerk of check and special commissioners, [illegible].
Muster master of the army, [illegible], [illegible], [illegible].
Mustrisse, Irish exaction, [illegible].
Mutton island, co. Clare. See Inishkerah.
Muttons impressed for army, [illegible].
Muvide (Moviddy), co. Cork, [illegible].
Muyckinagh, co. Kerry, [illegible].
Muyge, co. Cork, [illegible].
Muylerrye, Ellen fitz Diermod, pardon, [illegible].
Muynoo (co. Clare), [illegible].
Mwhonaye (Mohana), co. Cork, [illegible].
Mwyder (Moyestown? King's co.), [illegible].
Myagh—Meaghe—Meaghe, Dominick fitz Gerrot, pardon, [illegible], [illegible], [illegible].
„ —Meaghe—Mioghe, James fitz Rich., pardon, [illegible], [illegible], [illegible].
„ —Meagh—Meaghe—Meaghe—Miagh—Mieghe—Myaghe, John, recorder of Cork, [illegible], [illegible]; queen's attorney of Munster, [illegible], [illegible]; second justice of Munster, [illegible], [illegible]; general escheator of counties Cork and Limerick, [illegible]; commissions, [illegible], [illegible], [illegible], [illegible], [illegible], [illegible], [illegible], [illegible], [illegible], [illegible]; pardon, [illegible]; leases, [illegible], [illegible]; pardon of alienation, [illegible]; land in his occupation, [illegible]; custodiam grant, [illegible]; grant of a wardship, [illegible].
„ Philip, pardon, [illegible].
„ Teig, pardon, [illegible].
„ —Mieghe, Thomas, constable of Naas gaol, [illegible], [illegible].
„ See Meagh, Miagh, Myaghe.
Myaghan, William, pardon, [illegible].
Myaghe, David fitz Stephen, pardon, [illegible].
„ James, or O'Mora, pardon, [illegible].
„ John. See Myagh.
„ John fitz Robert, pardon, [illegible].
„ Tho. (of Woodstock, co. Kild.), pardon, [illegible].
„ William, [illegible].
Myalleryll, co. Tip., [illegible].
Mycart, John, son of William, English liberty, [illegible].
Mychaellicall (Coolycall), co. Wex., [illegible].
Mychefeld. See Mucheleldin.
Mychell, Francis. See Michell.
Mychelleston. See Michelston.
Mychelstowne (Michelstown?), co. Meath, [illegible].
Mykenneston (Mickenestown), co. Meath, [illegible], [illegible].

INDEX TO FIANTS—ELIZABETH.

Mydda, co. Wex., [illegible].
Myddynaigstowne (co. Tip. ?), [illegible].
Myothe (see Meath), [illegible].
Mygan—Mygann (co. Car. ?), 5148.
Mygan or Moygann (co. Kild. ?), 5146.
Mygell, Rich., commission, [illegible].
Myghte, Tho. See Might.
Myhimer, Nich., pardon, 6417.
Myincerdry (co. Westm. ?), [illegible].
Myinter Gro., Rich., pardon, [illegible].
Mylacke, co. Ross., [illegible].
Mylagh, co. Clare, [illegible].
Mylagh lordship, martial law in, 1162. See Moylagh, Castleton of.
Mylamaghan, [illegible].
Mylaughe (Mollaghe), co. Meath, [illegible].
Mylcastillon—Mylcastellowne (Millcastle, co. Westm.), [illegible], 2678.
Mylaaghe (co. Ross. ?), [illegible].
Mylecke—Myleck—Mylecke. See Molock.
Myler, Rich., pardon, [illegible].
Mylerstown, co. Kild. See Mollerston, Moylerstowne, Moylerston.
Myles, John, archdeacon of Kilmacduagh, [illegible].
" Robert, [illegible]; lease, [illegible].
Myleston. See Milestan, co. Meath.
Myleton, Grange near, co. Louth, [illegible].
Mylestowne, co. Ross., [illegible].
Mylfaren, co. Westm., [illegible].
Mylhill, co. Meath, [illegible].
Mylhousye, co. Kild., [illegible].
Mylick, co. Clare, [illegible].
Mylick, Queen's co., [illegible].
Mylig, [illegible].
Mylike. See Molock.
Mylkastle (Millcastle, co. Westm. ?), [illegible].
Mylkenanestown (Mickmanstown), co. Meath, 1460.
Myll, [illegible].
Myll, Thomas of the.—Tho. Grace, [illegible].
Myller, Thomas, [illegible].
Mylleagh, co. Gal., [illegible].
Myllare alias Myllhorse park, co. Dub., 6416.
Myllen, Edward, grant of a wardship, [illegible].
" Rob., deputy clerk of the council, [illegible].
Myllhill, co. Meath, [illegible].
Myllhorse park, co. Dub., 6416, [illegible].
Myllmaedebryke, [illegible].
Mylliericke, [illegible].
Myllton. See Milltowne, co. Tip.
Mylltown. See Milton, co. Dub.
Myllwardstown (Milverton ?), co. Dub., [illegible].
Mylode, Rich., pardon, [illegible].
Mylodeston. See Mlodestown.
Mylesston. See Milteston.
Myloti, seignory called, [illegible].
Mylshake, co. Wex., 1768.
Mylston (co. Lim. ?), [illegible].
Mylton. See Milton.
Mylton, co. Dub., [illegible].
Mylton (co. Kild. ?), [illegible].
Mylton — Myltone (Milltown), co. Ross., [illegible], [illegible], [illegible].
Myltona. See Myltan, co. Ross.
Myltowne, co. Lim., 1494.
Myltowne. See Milton, co. Westm.
Myltyn, co. Louth, [illegible].
Mylyck. See Molock.
Mymer, James, pardon, [illegible].
Myn, Tho., pardon, 4918.
Mynaragh, Morogh, pardon, [illegible].
Mynard — Mynarde (Minard, co. Kerry), [illegible], [illegible], [illegible].
Mynce, Jonas, commission, [illegible].
Myne, co. Gal., [illegible].
Mynesbone, co. Kerry, [illegible], [illegible], [illegible].
Mynduff, co. Cork, [illegible].
Mynemore, co. Kerry, [illegible], [illegible].
Myneoghan, co. Kerry, 6117.
Mynaughter (Mosonaghter ?), co. Cork, [illegible].
Mynestowne (Ministown), co. Meath, 1460.
Mynetown, Rich., pardon, 5712.
Mynoteman, co. Meath, 1576.
Myntier, James, pardon, [illegible].
Mynive (co. Cork ?), [illegible].
Mynlagh, co. Gal., [illegible], [illegible].
Mynloghe (Menlough), co. Gal., [illegible], [illegible], [illegible].
Mynne, commissioner, temp. Henry VIII [illegible].
Mynne, Tho., clerk of crown in Munster, 4457.
Mynohahan (co. Kerry ?), [illegible].
Mynoth (see Maynooth), [illegible].
Mynshall, Wm., grant of a wardship, [illegible].
Myrure. See Moyture.
Myrory, Redmund m'Thomas, pardon, [illegible].
Myre, co. Down, [illegible].
Myrgagh, Tirlagh, pardon, [illegible].
Myrreyonge. See Moryong.
Myrrick, Thomas. See Merrick.
Myrry, Rowland, surgeon, [illegible].
Mysell (Myshall), co. Car., [illegible].
Myset, Edmund. See Missel.
Myshall, co. Car. See Mishell, Mysell, Mysell.
Myshell, co. Cork, [illegible].
Myshill, co. Wex., [illegible].
Myskelye, Edm., pardon, [illegible].
Myskuran (co. Cork ?), [illegible].
Myvaghell, co. Westm., [illegible].
Myvaugh (Movagh, co. Donegal), [illegible].
Mywny (co. Cork ?), [illegible].
Myxell (Myshall), co. Car., [illegible].

INDEX TO FIANTS.—ELIZABETH.

Naace. *See* Naas.

Naall—Naal (Naal), co. Dub., 1777, 3180, 6136; rectory, 6464. *See also* Nall.

Naas—Naase—Naasse—Nace—Nas—Naso 412, 690, [illegible], 918, 1087, 1404, 1576, 1800, 1875, [illegible], [illegible], [illegible], 4294, 4711, 4735, 4875, [illegible], 6372, 6380, 6744, 6771; corn measure, [illegible]; similar customs granted to Philipstown, 1800; customs at, 2014; inquisitions taken at, [illegible], 6118.

" premises and land in, leased, 1354, 1480, 2811, 4177, 4188, 6106, 6428, 6785, granted, 6787, 6611, 6318, 6117; land near, granted, [illegible].

" charter, 1410.

" sovereign, 4, 254, 940, 2117, 3444, [illegible].

" castle, constable of, 3479.

" " escape of prisoners, 484.

" " or gaol, constable and keeper, [illegible].

" keeper of gaol, 1046, 4463.

" a castle in, leased, 1430, 1670; granted, 6787, 6818.

" garrison of, 4891.

" faly green, customs of cattle sold on, 4137, 4183; messuage upon, [illegible].

" frank house, 4818, 6324.

" hospital of S. John, leased, 1864, 6417, 6786; possessions granted, 6777.

" house of Augustinian or Austin friars, leased, 1184, 4431; possessions granted, 6117.

" rectory or tithes, 3464, 6704.

" tower, barony, [illegible].

Naas, William, pardon, 1443.

Nabardo, co. Ross., 4473.

na boyllye, William, pardon, [illegible].

na brahle, Shane, pardon, 6487.

Naco. *See* Naas.

Nacomtowne (co. Kild. ?), 3082.

Nacpinialla, co. Mayo, [illegible].

Nacplanie alias Ackmycke, co. Mayo, 4761.

Nacplanyrowre, co. Mayo, 4616.

Nackelta. *See* Kasleen Nackelt, co. Gal.

Nadanoble (co. Ross. ?), 5432.

Naddie, Rich., pardon, 6431.

Naddy, Anstace, pardon, 6765.

" Rob., pardon, 6765.

Nadenora, co. Clare, [illegible].

Nadired—Nadired—Nadiret—Nadirid, co. Cork, 4408, 4467, 4862.

Naesmh, John m'David, pardon, 6783.

Nagann, Shane oy, pardon, 6469.

na gaw, Conor, Moroghe, and Rory m'Teig, pardon, 4792.

Nagell, David, pardon, [illegible].

" David fitz George, pardon, [illegible].

" George, pardon, 4487.

Nagell, Gerrot, pardon, 3346, 3894, 4364.

" James, pardon, 4234.

" Maurice, pardon, 4387.

" Nich., alias Nicholas, alias M'Griffine, pardon, 6183.

" Phillip fitz Garrett, pardon, 6302.

" Rich. fitz Garret, pardon, 6323.

" Wm., pardon, 1287.

Nagelle, George, pardon, 4371.

Naghell, James fitz Rich., pardon, 6367.

Nagherim (co. Wick. ?), 6577.

Naghill, co. Mon. *See* Guaghill.

Naghten, John, pardon, 2310.

" John, pardon, 6968.

" John m'Donell I, pardon, 6157.

" Katherine, pardon, 6621.

Naghtie, Tho., pardon, 4163.

Naghtin, Edm., pardon, 4388.

" Wm., pardon, 6858.

Naghton, Walter, surgeon, 6186.

Nagill, David, pardon, 2346, 6157.

" George, pardon, 2345.

" Gerot, pardon, 2341.

" Gerrot beg, pardon, 2344.

" Gybon, pardon, 2343.

" John, pardon, 2314.

" John oy Hilly, pardon, 2346.

" Maurice oy cargy, pardon, 2341.

Nagle, Edw., pardon, 4432.

" Gybbon roe, pardon, 3464.

" James, pardon, 3961.

" John, pardon, 6484.

" John, pardon, 4511.

" Maurice oy carrigey, pardon, 3864.

" Nich., pardon, 6411.

" Philip, pardon, 6763.

" Rich., pardon, 6511, 6762.

" Rich. ne Coonnle, pardon, 3861.

" Rob., pardon, 4403.

" Sander oge, pardon, 6437.

" Tho., pardon, 4460, [illegible].

" Wm., pardon, 4461.

Naglotrin alias M'Shihie, Magnus, pardon, 6178.

na gnaw, Doughe m'Teig, pardon, 4286.

Nagraga, co. Cork, 4049.

Naglen, Derby, pardon, 4074.

Nagyll, John, pardon, 2334.

" Hyny, pardon, 2344.

Nahallgh, co. Cork, 4426.

Nahenve, Donall grany m'Teige, pardon, 6478.

Nahallora alias More, co. Mayo, 4741.

Nahowrye (co. Cav.), 1681.

Nails impressed for public works, 3458.

Nalse (co. Lim. ?), 4069.

Naishe, Edm., pardon, [illegible].

" Philip, pardon, 1641.

" Wm., 4633.

INDEX TO FIANTS.—ELIZABETH.

Naishtown, co. Kilk., 6441.
Naissa (co. Lim. ?), [illegible].
Naish, David fitz John, pardon, [illegible].
„ John fitz David, pardon, [illegible].
Nale, John fitz Oliver, pardon, 6451.
Nall (Naul), co. Dub., 687, 770, 1898, 1830, 2117, 3848, [illegible], 4148, 4462, 6779; rectory, 1460.
Nall (Naul), co. Meath, 1460, [illegible].
Namoney, Philip, pardon, [illegible].
Nanaughe, 1976.
Nange, Murtagh and Moyler m'Dermod og, pardon, [illegible].
Nangell, Margery, pardon, [illegible].
„ Richard, lease, [illegible].
Nanger, co. Dub., 1498.
Nangill, David fitz John, pardon, [illegible].
„ Robert, chancellor of St. Patrick's, takes oath of supremacy, [illegible].
Nanglanye, co. Mayo, 6014.
Nangle, Christopher, pardon, [illegible].
„ David, pardon, 6476.
„ Edm., pardon, [illegible].
„ Edw., pardon, [illegible], 6764.
„ Elinor, pardon, [illegible].
„ Garret, pardon, [illegible].
„ George, pardon, [illegible].
„ Gerald, pardon, [illegible], [illegible].
„ James, pardon, [illegible], [illegible].
„ James Laffyn, pardon, [illegible].
„ John fitz David, pardon, [illegible].
„ Maurice ny cargy fitz John, pardon, [illegible].
„ (or de Angulo), Patrick, baron of Navan, livery, 459; commissions, [illegible], 2117, 3464, 4169, 6441.
„ Patrick, pardon, [illegible].
„ Petres, pardon, [illegible].
„ Pers, pardon, [illegible].
„ Peter (of Abbeyshrule), pardon, [illegible]; sheriff of Longford, commissions, [illegible], 4040.
„ Peter, pardon, [illegible].
„ Peter (of Bishopstown), sheriff of Westmeath, pardon, [illegible].
„ Peter, pardon, [illegible].
„ Peter, clerk, pardon, [illegible].
„ Peter (of Stokestown), pardon of intrusion, [illegible].
„ Richard, alienation of land, [illegible].
„ Richard (of Ballacorky), pardon, [illegible], [illegible].
„ Rich., pardon, [illegible], [illegible], [illegible].
„ Rich., alias ny Cownte, pardon, [illegible].
„ Robert, pension, [illegible]; leases, [illegible], [illegible], [illegible], [illegible], 6774, [illegible].
„ Rob., pardon, [illegible].
„ Thomas, pardon, [illegible].
Nangle, Walter, sheriff of Down, commission, [illegible].
„ Walter, pardon, [illegible].
„ William, alienation by, [illegible].
„ William, pardon, [illegible], [illegible], [illegible].
Nantenan—Nantynan, co. Lim., [illegible]; parish, [illegible].
Nantyne, co. Cork, [illegible].
Napper, Robert, knt., chief baron of the Exchequer, [illegible], [illegible]; commissions, [illegible], [illegible], [illegible], [illegible], [illegible], [illegible], [illegible], [illegible], [illegible], [illegible], [illegible], [illegible], [illegible], [illegible], [illegible]; lease, [illegible]; pardon, [illegible]; his servant receives an appointment in the Exchequer, [illegible].
Napton, co. Dub., 1777.
Narahery, Morrowe (M'Brien), pardon, [illegible].
Naraya, Donell m'Donoghy I., pardon, [illegible].
Narbon, Nicholas, Ulster King of Arms, [illegible], [illegible].
Nare, Nich., pardon, [illegible].
Narlaghe, rectory, [illegible].
Narlee (Arlee), Queen's co., [illegible], [illegible], [illegible].
Narowater. See Narrow water.
Narragha. See Norragh.
Narraghmore, co. Kild. See Norragh.
Narroure, co. Cork, [illegible].
Narrowe, co. Kild., [illegible].
Narrow water — Narowater — Narrows water, co. Down, [illegible], [illegible], [illegible], [illegible], [illegible].
Narrw, Wm., pardon, [illegible].
Narte (Nort), co. Mon., [illegible].
Narvine, Shane m'Dermod I., pardon, [illegible].
Nas—Nass. See Naas.
Nase, Edm. m'Thomas, pardon, [illegible].
Nash, David, pardon, [illegible].
„ Edw., pardon, [illegible].
„ Redmund, pardon, [illegible].
„ Shane boy, pardon, [illegible].
„ Wm. oge, pardon, [illegible].
Nashe, David, pardon, [illegible], [illegible], [illegible], [illegible].
„ Edm., pardon, [illegible], [illegible].
„ Edw. fitz Rich., pardon, [illegible].
„ James, pardon, [illegible], [illegible], [illegible].
„ John, pardon, [illegible], [illegible].
„ Leonard, pardon, [illegible].
„ Morish, pardon, [illegible].
„ Nich., pardon, [illegible].
„ Philip, pardon, [illegible], [illegible].
„ Raimund, pardon, [illegible], [illegible].
„ Rich., pardon, [illegible], [illegible], [illegible].
„ Tho., pardon, [illegible], [illegible], [illegible].
„ Tibbott, pardon, [illegible].
Nashe—Naashe—Naysh—Nayshe (Naish), co. Wex., [illegible], [illegible], [illegible], 6541.
„ rectory of, [illegible], [illegible].
Nashestown, co. Kilk., [illegible], [illegible].
Naside, Shane, pardon, [illegible].
Naspocucke, co. Cav., [illegible].
Nasriske (Astrish), co. Mon., [illegible].

Naas, David, pardon, 6464.
„ Edm., pardon, 6464.
„ Rich., pardon, [illegible].
Naase. See Naas.
Naase, James oge, pardon, 4481.
„ Philip, pardon, 6804.
„ Rich. do, pardon, 4478.
Naasha. See Nasshe, co. Wex.
Nasey, William, pardon, 61.
Nastogogy, Donell, pardon, [illegible].
Navy, Henry, pardon, [illegible].
Nathmerney (co. Ross. ?), [illegible].
Nailrum, co. Leit., [illegible].
Naughtin, Dermod and John m'Teig I, pardon, [illegible].
Naul, co. Dub. See Naall, Nall.
Naul, co. Meath. See Nall.
Navan—Navon—Novan—Novane—Nowan, co. Meath, [illegible], [illegible], 947, [illegible], [illegible], [illegible], [illegible], [illegible], 41[illegible], [illegible], [illegible], [illegible], [illegible], [illegible], 64[illegible], [illegible], [illegible]; measure of corn of, [illegible]; rebellion at, [illegible]; houses in, [illegible], [illegible], [illegible]; rectory, 4186.
„ provost or portrieve, commissions, [illegible], [illegible], [illegible], [illegible].
„ monastery or abbey, proxies from, [illegible]; possessions leased, [illegible], [illegible].
„ baron of, [illegible], [illegible], [illegible], [illegible]. See Nangle, Patrick.
„ barony, martial law, [illegible].
Naveagh, Morrish m'Donell m'Shane, pardon, [illegible].
Navigation of Shannon to be facilitated by removal of weirs, [illegible], [illegible].
Naviwater. See Navy Water.
Navon. See Navan.
Navy (co. Cork ?), [illegible].
Navy: Authority to press men for queen's service at sea, [illegible], [illegible], [illegible]; fishermen to be pressed for defence of coast, [illegible]. See also Ships.
Navy Water—Naviwater, co. Westm., Priors weir on lough called, [illegible], [illegible].
Nayland, David, [illegible].
Naylands, James. See Nelland.
Naysh, [illegible]. See Nashe.
Nayshe, Rich., pardon, [illegible].
Nayshe, [illegible]. See Nashe.
Nea, Shane m'Teige na, pardon, [illegible].
Neachowre (co. Kilk. ?), [illegible].
Neaddinagh (Nedimagh), co Cork, [illegible].
Neadd ne viagh, co. Rosc., [illegible].
Neaaghe, co. Tip. or Lim., [illegible].
Neagh, Lough. See Eaghe.
Neaghe, Shane de, pardon, [illegible].
Nealan, James. See Nelland.
„ Nich., pardon, [illegible].
Nealanstowne, co Clare, [illegible].
Neale, Conoghor m'Donogh I, pardon, [illegible].
„ Donell m'Teige I, pardon, [illegible].
„ Donell oge m'Donell I, pardon, [illegible].
„ Donogh m'Conneor I, pardon, [illegible].
„ Edm., pardon, [illegible].
„ Joanne ny, pardon, [illegible].
„ John (of Carlingford), commission, [illegible].
„ John (in Munster), pardon, [illegible], [illegible], [illegible], [illegible].
„ Margaret, pardon, [illegible], [illegible].
„ Margery ny, pardon, [illegible].
„ Neal m'Teig I, pardon, [illegible].
„ Onor nyn, pardon, [illegible], [illegible].
„ Ona duf O'Dowell I, pardon, [illegible].
„ Philip, pardon, [illegible].
„ Sara ny, pardon, [illegible], [illegible].
„ Sarowe ny, pardon, [illegible].
„ Shane, pardon, [illegible].
„ Wm., pardon, [illegible].
„ —Neale, Wm., premises in Dublin, [illegible], [illegible], [illegible], [illegible].
„ Wm. m'Dowill I, pardon, [illegible].
Neale—Nelle, co. Mayo, [illegible], [illegible], [illegible], [illegible].
Neallane, John, pardon, [illegible].
Nealle, Feyllym, Henry, and Hugh m'Donell Y. (in co. Wat.), pardon, [illegible].
Neabrory, Giles, pardon, [illegible].
Neanagh, co. Tip., [illegible].
Neanstown (co. Gal. ?), [illegible].
Neasy, Philip m'Shane Y, pardon, [illegible].
Neay Clonvard (co. Rosc. ?), [illegible].
ne bally, Teige, pardon, [illegible].
ne barten, Philip m'Thomas, pardon, [illegible].
Neboke, David, pardon, [illegible].
ne boyle, James m'William, pardon, [illegible].
Neboyle, Rickard m'Shane Barett, pardon, [illegible].
ne broeke, Thady m'Conoghor, pardon, [illegible].
ne bually, Edm. fitz Thomas, pardon, [illegible].
Necale (King's co.), [illegible].
Necarigyn. See Necarrigen.
Necarthy, Edm., pardon, [illegible].
Necarrigen—Necarigyn—Necarygyn, co. Cork, [illegible], [illegible].
Necarrigyn, Morris fitz Tho., pardon, [illegible].
Necarygyn. See Necarrigen.
ne Connie, Rich. Nagle, pardon, [illegible].
ne courte, Shane m'William, pardon, [illegible].
Nedalle, Donogh oge, pardon, [illegible].
Nedan, the (co. Wat. ?), [illegible].
Neddans—Neddanes, co. Tip., rectory, [illegible].
„ vicar, [illegible].
Nedden, Fynen, pardon, [illegible].
Neddestowne, co. Tip., [illegible].
Nedarti (co. Cork ?), [illegible].
Nedimagh, co. Cork. See Neaddinagh.
Neele, Henry, pardon, [illegible].
„ Thomas, house in Dublin, [illegible].

INDEX TO FIANTS.—ELIZABETH.

Neale, Wm. *See* Neale.
Nefeiddane (Fiddane), co. Cork, 5098.
ne foellie, Hugh m'Teig, pardon, 4717.
negna, William, pardon, 6457.
Negaylagh — Negaylaghe — Neguilaghe, co. Lim., monastery of S. Katherine, 4757, 6118, 6964. *See* Monaster ne Hayllaghe.
ne gobe, John, pardon, [illegible].
ne Gobe, John m'Gerald (O'Hagherin ?), [illegible].
Neguilaghe. *See* Negaylagh.
Negeylagh, Teige, pardon, [illegible].
Neggarvame, co. Tip., 6817.
ne glavo, Donogh and Morogh m'Teig, pardon, 6518.
Neglegan, Manus (M'Shebie), pardon, 6418.
Neglihy, Hugh, pardon, [illegible].
ne gnave, Donell, pardon, 6784.
Negunlagh, Hugh, pardon, 6452.
Negurtyny (co. Kerry ?), 2452.
Nehallerne, co. Mayo, 6918.
Nehanie — Nehanny (Annies ? co. Mayo), 1404, 5418.
nehenaye, Donell ower and Donogh m'Arte, pardon, 4586.
Nehoghillie, co. Kerry, 6984.
Nehyny, Shane, pardon, 6571.
Neigham — Nighome (Neigham, co. Kilk.), 1979, 6802.
Neile. *See* Neale, co. Mayo.
Neile, Clement, 6757.
„ Derbe, pardon, 5826.
„ John, pardon, 1577.
„ John, chancellor of Ossory, pardon, 1517.
„ John, 6182.
„ Patrick, 436.
„ Tho., pardon, 2648.
Neill, Conoghor m'Donogh roe A., pardon, 6354.
„ Malachias m'Conoghor I, pardon, 6544.
„ Manus m'Tho. I, pardon, 6976.
„ Neall m'Shane B, pardon, 6452.
„ Phelim duff m'Hugh, pardon, 4573.
„ Phelim m'Shane B, pardon, 4452.
„ Rorie m'Melaghlin B, pardon, 6452.
„ Shane m'Phelim B, pardon, 6452.
„ Teig roe m'Donell I, pardon, 6454.
Nelagh, co. Kerry, 6042.
Nelan, James, pardon, 6325.
„ John fitz Flin, pardon, 6942.
„ John fitz Teige, pardon, 5462.
„ Nich., pardon, 4682.
„ Wm., pardon, 6842.
Neland, David fitz Edm., pardon, 6418.
„ John, pardon, 6454.
„ Wm., doctor, pardon, 6416.
Nelande, John, pardon, 4698.
Nelane, David, pardon, 6122. *See also* Neland.
Nelane, James, pardon, 6623, 6617.
„ John, pardon, 4186.
ne lappen, Tho. alias Tho. oge [ ]oy, pardon, 5608.
Nele, Donell oge m'Teige Y, pardon, 4682.
„ John, pardon, 3414.
„ Teige m'Connor Y, pardon, 4682.
„ Teige m'Farrall Y, pardon, 4682.
„ Tho. m'Connor Y, pardon, 4682.
„ Walter, pardon, 6452.
„ Wm., pardon, 5434.
Nele, the, co. Gal., 4652.
Nelegh, co. Lim. (perhaps Mullagh), 6078.
Nell, Sara, pardon, 6818.
Nellan, John, physician, 3777.
„ Shane Y, pardon, 4678.
Nelland, Donell, pardon, 4687.
„ Edm., pardon, 1687.
Nelland — Neylande — Nealan — Neyland, doctor, James, protection, 318; commission, 2769; leases, 1466, 4785; surrender, 4744; lands confirmed to him by composition, 4761.
Nellard, James, pardon, 4687.
„ Robert, pardon, 1417.
„ William, pardon, 1517, 3942, 4687.
Nellane, David, pardon, 4968.
Nellie, alias Onlor, James, pardon, 6337.
Nelosie (Lossot or Loyed), co. Mon., 5654.
Nelson, Tho., pardon, 1117.
Nelva (Elvey), co. Mon., 6871.
Nemaddery — Nemadre (Carrownamaddy, co. Ross.), 1482, 6015.
Neman, Morghe m'Dermot, pardon, 140.
Nemoe, John, pardon, 842.
Ne Monasteraghe, Shane, pardon, 678.
ne monne, Teige, pardon, 4628.
Nemore (Emy ?), co. Mon., 6477.
Nenagh — Nenagho — Nownagh (Monasternenagh), co. Lim., abbey leased, 1143, 3174, 4134, 4757, 6118; granted, 6964.
Nenagh (Enagh), co. Mon., 4457.
Nenagh—Nenagho, Queen's co., 1278, 1694, 6874.
Nenagh—Enagho—Nenagho—Nenaugh, co. Tip., 852, 4438, 6947, 5687, 6818, 6782.
„ abbey of S. John, granted, 842, 1526.
„ rectory, 442.
Nenagho, co. Westm., 1689, 3673.
Nenagle, co. Tip., 4437.
Nenaugh, co. Tip., 6247.
Nenevagh, Shane m'Teig, pardon, 6814.
Neniggart, John, pardon, 6528.
Nentoman, 4148.
Nerry, co. Cav., 4863.
Nephalangh, parish of monastery of (Abbeyfeale), co. Lim., 4588.
Nerkarty—Nerkartye, Thomas, attainted, 6962.
Nesker, co. Kilk., 2969, 4813.

INDEX TO FIANTS—ELIZABETH.

Nether (Eshor), co. Mon., [illegible].
[illegible], Donagh rowe m'Teig, pardon, 1068.
Netervile—Netervyle. See Nettervyll.
Nether Conell, co. Cav., [illegible].
Nether Conaght (Lower Connaught), [illegible].
Nettervyll —Netervile—Netervyle—Netherfelde — Nethervill — Netterfeld—Nettervelde —Nettervill — Nettervild — Nettervilde — Nettervile — Nettervill — Nettervyld — Nettervyle—Nettirvile — Nettirvill —Newtervyle:
„ Christopher, wardship of his son, [illegible].
„ John (of Castleton of Kilpatrick), freedom from subsidy, 1518.
„ John (of Dowth), commissions, [illegible], [illegible], 4340, 4401, [illegible].
„ Luke, second justice of Chief Place, 168, [illegible]; commission, 216.
„ Richard, lease, [illegible].
„ Richard (of Kilsallaghan), commissions, [illegible], [illegible], [illegible], [illegible], [illegible]; leases, [illegible], [illegible], [illegible], [illegible], [illegible], [illegible], [illegible], [illegible], [illegible], [illegible]; license to alien, 346-7; party in a suit, [illegible].
„ Richard (of Dowth), pardon of alienation, [illegible].
„ Richard, son of Christopher, wardship, [illegible].
Netoyiane, Donagh (of Graan, co. Lim.), attainted, [illegible].
Netumyd, Donagh Carry, pardon, [illegible].
Networypny, co. Clare, [illegible].
Nenechurch. See Newchurch.
Neuston (Newstown, co. Car. ?), [illegible].
Neuston (Newmoore ?), co. Meath, [illegible].
Newton, co. Westm. (see Newton), [illegible].
Nevesle, David, attainted, [illegible].
Nevell—Nevill:
„ John, pardon of son of, [illegible].
„ Marcus, wardship, [illegible].
„ Margaret (or Manwaring), surrender, [illegible].
„ Piers or Peter, pardon, [illegible], [illegible], [illegible], [illegible].
„ Richard, pardon, [illegible], [illegible].
„ Richard, wardship of heir, [illegible].
„ Robert, pardon, [illegible].
„ Thomas, surrender, [illegible].
„ Walter, pardon, [illegible].
„ Walter, livery, 1517.
„ William, heir of, 1517.
Neviewe, Gillpatrick, pardon, [illegible].
Nevill, Rich., [illegible]. See Nevell.
Nevody, Teig, pardon, [illegible].
New Abbey—New Abay—Newabaye—New Abbeie — Newe Abbeie — Newe Abbaye (Newabbey), co. Kild., [illegible], [illegible].
„ house of friars, leased, [illegible], [illegible], [illegible], [illegible], [illegible], [illegible].
Newbawde (Newbawn ?), co. Wex., [illegible].
Newbawn — New Bawn — Newbawne, co. Wex., [illegible], [illegible], [illegible], [illegible].
Newbay, co. Wex., [illegible], [illegible]. See Nubay.
Newbridge (co. Kild.), [illegible].
Newbridge, co. Wex., [illegible].
Newcastle, [illegible], [illegible], [illegible].
Newcastle—Newe Castell, Cosslog's (co. Cork), 1444.
Newcastle (co. Donegal), [illegible], [illegible].
Newcastle — Newcastell — Newcastle by Lyons, co. Dub., 97, 444, [illegible], [illegible], [illegible].
„ castle and lands, [illegible].
„ manor, 1891, [illegible], [illegible].
„ „ seneschal, 173, 377, [illegible], [illegible].
„ barony, [illegible], [illegible].
„ prebendary of, 180, 446.
Newcastle—Nucastle—Nuncastle, co. Gal., [illegible], [illegible], [illegible].
Newcastle, co. Kild., [illegible].
Newcastle (co. Kilk. ?), [illegible].
Newcastle (co. Leit. ?), [illegible].
Newcastle—Newcastell, co. Lim., [illegible], [illegible], [illegible], [illegible], [illegible], 6464, [illegible], [illegible], [illegible].
„ parish, [illegible].
„ seignory called, [illegible].
„ See also Castletown.
Newcastle—Newcastell, co. Long., [illegible], [illegible], [illegible].
Newcastle — Newcastell — Neucastle, co. Mayo, [illegible], [illegible], [illegible], [illegible].
Newcastle — Newcastell — Newe Castle, co. Meath, [illegible], [illegible], [illegible], [illegible], [illegible].
Newcastle—Newcastell, Queen's co., [illegible], [illegible].
Newcastle—Newcastell—Nua Castle—Nywecastell, co. Tip., [illegible], [illegible], [illegible], [illegible], [illegible], [illegible], [illegible], [illegible], [illegible], [illegible], [illegible], [illegible], [illegible], [illegible], [illegible].
Newcastle — Newcastell, co. Wat., rectory, [illegible], [illegible].
Newcastle—Newcastell, co. Westm., [illegible], [illegible], [illegible], [illegible], [illegible], [illegible], [illegible], [illegible], [illegible], [illegible], [illegible].
Newcastle—Newcastell, co. Wex., [illegible], [illegible], [illegible], [illegible], [illegible], [illegible].
Newcastle — Newcastell m'Kynnegan — Newcastell Macynegan — Newcastle M'Kynneghan, co. Wick., [illegible], [illegible], [illegible], [illegible], [illegible]; grant of castle, manor, &c., [illegible]; rectory, [illegible]. See also Castle Macynegan

INDEX TO FIANTS.—ELIZABETH.

Newcastletown (co. Lim. ?), [illegible].
Newcomen, Samuel, serjeant at arms, 6762.
New chapel or Aghnoe, rector of, 6774.
Newehouse, co. Kilk., 5512.
Newchurche—Newechyrche or Templenoe, co. Kerry, 5640, 6172.
Newchurche—Nenenchurch, co. Kilk., [illegible], 6704.
Newchurche—Newechurch (co. Tip. ?), [illegible].
" vicar of, [illegible].
Newcomen, Robert, surveyor general of victuals, [illegible], 6730.
Newe Abbaye, Newe Castle, &c. See New-abbey, Newcastle, &c.
Neweman, William, lease of rectories, 1831, 6770.
Newenagh, Queen's co., 1940.
Neweraghe (Newrath, co. Wick.), 1573.
Newerathe (Newrath, co. Wat.), 1569.
Newe Rathe. See New Rathe.
Newerie. See Newry.
Newestan—Newestowne. See Newston.
Newetou—Newetowne. See Newton.
Newetowne by Trim. See Newtown by Trim.
Newetown of Lynman. See Newton of Lynman.
Newetown juxta Mare—Newetowne by the Strond. See Newton by the Strond.
Newetowne by Trym. See Newtown by Trim.
Newfield of Knockmark, co. Meath, 5719.
New fort in Leix, 4, 86.
Newgarden—Newe garden, co. Kilk., 4570, [illegible].
Newgate, Dublin. See Dublin.
Newgent. See Nugent.
Newghown, co. Kilk., [illegible].
Newgraig, co. Kilk., [illegible].
Newgrang—Newegrange—Newgrannge, co. Dub., [illegible], [illegible].
Newgrange, co. Kilk., [illegible].
Newgraunge. See Newgraunge.
New grange—Newe Grange—Newegraunge—New Graunge, co. Tip., 181, 3277, 4141, 4162.
Newgraunge—Newegraunge, co. Car. (co. Wick.), 1367, 3745, [illegible].
Newgraunge, co. Dub., 631.
New Graunge rectory, co. Lim., 1114.
Newgraunge (Newgrange, co. Meath), [illegible], [illegible].
New Graunge. See New grange.
Newhaggard, co. Dub., 1758.
Newhaggard—Newehaggard, co. Meath, 1465, 6436, 6804.
Newhaggard, co. Wex., 1577.
Newhaven, passage for serviceable, 5916.
Newhois—Newehayes, co. Kild., [illegible].
New hillman, 4762.
Newhome. See Newhouse.
Newhouse—Newehouse—Newhose—Newhowse, co. Kilk., [illegible], [illegible], [illegible], [illegible], [illegible], 6564.
Newhouse—Newehouse—Newhowse, co. Louth, 245, 611, 5416, [illegible].
Newhowse—Newehouse or Ballyxure (co. Wick.), 3716, 6071.
Newhowse. See Newhouse.
Newland—Nuland (co. Kild.), [illegible], 4130, 4464.
Newman, Donoghow, pardon, [illegible].
" James, grant of a wardship, [illegible].
" sir Thadye, clerk, master of spital house of Wicklow, 1381.
" Tho., surgeon, 6104.
" Wm., messuage in Dublin, [illegible]. See Neweman.
" Wm., pardon, [illegible].
" Wm., sub sheriff of Kilkenny, [illegible].
Newmanor (Manor ?), co. Kerry, 5042.
New mill of Earl of Ormond, [illegible].
Newnagh. See Nenagh, co. Lim.
New Rathe—Newe Rathe (Newrath), co. Meath, 187, 2042.
Newra (Newrath ?), co. Wick., 372. See Neweraghe.
Newrie. See Newry.
New Ross—New Rosse. See Ross, co. Wex.
Newry—Newerie—Newrie—Newrye—Nury, co. Down, 1736, [illegible], [illegible], [illegible], [illegible]; merchant of, [illegible]; martial law in, 46; rent of northern chiefs payable at, [illegible], [illegible], [illegible]; lands of, to be made shire ground, 1734.
Newston—Newestan—Newestowne, co. Car., 140, 1123, 1420. See also Nouston.
Newstone, co. Meath. See Nouston.
Newstowne, co. Meath, [illegible].
Newtemple (co. Kerry ?), 4578.
Newterwyle, John. See Netterwyll.
Newther, Morogh duff, pardon, 4702.
Newton. See Newtown.
Newton, capt. John, pardon, [illegible]; pardon at his suit, 4366; leases, [illegible], [illegible], [illegible]; land held by, [illegible].
" Rich., pardon, 6458.
" Wm., pardon, 6456.
Newton, co. Car., 3787, 6842.
Newton, co. Dub., 656, 1460, [illegible].
Newton—Newtown (by the river Dodder), co. Dub., 4178.
Newton (Blackrock or Newtown Blackrock), co. Dub., 3148, 4254. See Newton by the Strond.
Newton (co. Dub. or Wick.,), 3494.
Newton. See Newtown, co. Gal.
Newton (co. Gal. ?), 4793.
Newton—Newton—Newtowne, co. Kild., 112, [illegible], 4590, 6111, 6771, [illegible].

INDEX TO FIANTS—ELIZABETH.

Newton—Newtone, in manor of Leixlip, co. Kild., 1588, [illegible]

Newton—Newtowne, King's co., 278, [illegible], 3471, 4132, [illegible], 4454, [illegible]

Newton or Ballenewet, co. Leit., manor, [illegible]

Newton, co. Lim., 6484.

Newton, co. Long., 3281, [illegible], [illegible], [illegible]

Newton—Newtown or Ballenewe, co. Long., [illegible]

Newton—Newtone, co. Louth, 6416, [illegible]

Newton—Newtowne, co. Mayo, [illegible], [illegible]

Newton (in bar. Tyrawley), co. Mayo, castle, 4873.

Newton—Nuton, co. Meath, 781, [illegible], [illegible], 1126, 1560, [illegible], [illegible], [illegible], [illegible], [illegible]; rectory, [illegible]

Newton (Newtown, par. Colp), co. Meath, 1448, [illegible]

Newton—Newtown (Newtown, par. Duleek), co. Meath, 148, 1460, [illegible], [illegible]

Newton, co. Ross., [illegible], [illegible], 4750. *See* Newtown.

Newton, co. Ross. or Sligo, 6727.

Newton (co. Ross. or Long. ?), 4642.

Newton, co. Tip., 1763.

Newton, co. Wat., 1784, [illegible], [illegible], [illegible]; grange of, [illegible]

Newton, co. Westm., 1498, 1768, 2234, [illegible], [illegible], [illegible], [illegible], [illegible]. *See* Newtown.

Newton—Newtown, co. Wex., [illegible], [illegible], [illegible], [illegible]

Newton (co. Wick. ?), 6748.

Newton—Newtown, [illegible], [illegible]

Newton, little, co. Dub., 847, 1250.

Newton—Newton, little (Little Newtown), co. Kild., 1037, 3144, [illegible]

Newton near Ardare (co. Lim. ?), rectory, 6347.

Newton by Blackhall, co. Kild., [illegible]

Newton of Clane, co. Kild., 4162.

Newton of Dernidall near Cowinke, co. Dub., [illegible]

Newton of Garrendon, co. Meath, 4477.

Newton of Kilmaynham. *See* Newtown by Kylmaynham.

Newton (little) by Kylmacrey (co. Wick.), rectory, 1527.

Newton of Lyman—Newetown of Lyman—Newton Loman (Newtownlemman), co. Tip., rectory, [illegible], [illegible], 6774; vicar, 6177.

Newton by Maynoth, co. Kild., 782.

Newton by Moate, co. Long., [illegible]

Newton of Moyagh (Newtownmoyaghy), co. Meath, [illegible]

Newton of Rathgorinloglgreige (perhaps Newtown rathganley and Kilgreige), co. Meath, [illegible]

Newton of Rathgoranley (Newtownrathganley ?), co. Meath, [illegible]

Newton by the Strond—Newton juxta Mare—Newetowne by the Strond (Blackrock or Newtown Blackrock), co. Dub., 1722, [illegible], [illegible]. *See* Newton, co. Dub.

Newton of Termonfeghen, co. Louth, 742.

Newton by Trym. *See* Newtown by Trim.

Newtone of Kilmainham. *See* Newtown by Kylmainham.

Newtone. *See* Newton.

Newtone, alias Kilgrenie, co. Wat., [illegible]

Newtown, co. Wex., 6742.

Newtowne. *See* Newton, co. Mayo.

Newtowne by Trim. *See* Newtown.

Newtowne, co. Wex., [illegible]

Newtowne (co. Wick. ?), [illegible]

Newtowne Anor (Newtownanner, co. Tip.), 4785.

Newtown, co. Dub., [illegible]

Newtown—Newton—Newtowne, co. Gal., [illegible], 4677, 5431, [illegible]

Newtown, King's co., [illegible]. *See also* Ballyrane.

Newtown, [illegible]

Newtown or Ballyrane, co. Lim., [illegible]. *See also* Ballyrane.

Newtown, co. Long., 5142.

Newtown, co. Meath. *See* Newton.

Newtown, Queen's co., 5551.

Newtown—Newtowne, co. Ross., [illegible], [illegible], [illegible], [illegible]

Newtown, co. Wat., [illegible]. *See* Ballenewe, [illegible]

Newtown—Newton, co. Westm., [illegible]. *See also* Ballyrane.

Newtown (co. Wick. ?), [illegible]

Newtown. *See* Newton, Newtowne.

Newtown—Newton of Clane, co. Kild., 4162, [illegible]

Newtown of Jerpoint, co. Kilk., [illegible]

Newtown by Kylmaynham—Newton by Kilmaynam—Newtone of Kilmainham, co. Dub., 1428, [illegible], [illegible], [illegible]

Newtown — Newetowne — Newetowne — Newton—Newtowne—Newtowne, of or by Trim (Newtown Clonbun), co. Meath, 97, 149, 774, [illegible], [illegible], [illegible], 1291, 1528, 2428, 3122, [illegible], [illegible], [illegible], [illegible]

" church, 6727.

" rectory, 1171, [illegible]

" abbey of S. Peter, [illegible], [illegible], [illegible], 3281, 3129, [illegible], [illegible], [illegible], [illegible], [illegible], 6134, [illegible]

" hospital of S. John, [illegible], 1512, [illegible], 2719, 3431.

" *See* Trim.

Newtownanor, co. Tip. *See* Newtowne Anor.

Newtown Blackrock. *See* Newton by the Strond.

INDEX TO FIANTS—ELIZABETH.

Newtownlemman, co. Tip. *See* Newton of Lyman.
Newtownmoyaghy, co. Meath. *See* Newton of Moyagh.
Newtown rathganley, co. Meath. *See* Newton of Rathgornsley, Newton of Rathgurtalogilgroige.
Newtownstalahan, co. Louth. *See* Stalahan, [illegible].
Neyland, Doctor James. *See* Nelland.
Neylande, Daniel, bishop of Kildare. *See* Kildare.
" John, physician, Limerick, [illegible].
Neyle, Clement, 1578.
" John, [illegible].
Neyleston, co. Dub., [illegible].
Neylestone, co. Dub., [illegible].
Neyll, Teig m'Tho. A., pardon, [illegible].
Neymemore, co. Wex., [illegible].
Niall, John m'Garret I., pardon, [illegible].
Nicholas, Roger ny, pardon, [illegible]1.
Nicholas, John, pardon, [illegible].
Nicholaston — Nicholleston. *See* Nicholston, co. Kild.
Nichollstowne. *See* Nicholston, co. Tip.
Nichols, alias Nagell, alias M'Griffine, Nich., pardon, [illegible].
Nicholston — Nicholeston — Nicholliston — Nicolstowne — Nicholstowne — Nicoliston — Nicolliston — Nicolston — Nicolstowne (Nicholastown), co. Kild., 1884, 3452, [illegible], [illegible], [illegible], [illegible], [illegible], [illegible], 1484, [illegible], 6775.
Nicholston (co. Kilk.), [illegible].
Nicholston — Nichollstowne — Nicholstowne — Nicholstown — Nicolliston — Nicolstowne (Nicholastown), co. Tip., [illegible], [illegible], [illegible]1-3, [illegible]4-5, [illegible].
Nicholstowne. *See* Nicholston, co. Kild.
Nicholstown. *See* Nicholston, co. Tip.
Nicholstowne. *See* Nicholston, co. Kild.
Nickerath (co. Louth ?), [illegible].
Nicogn, Rich. m'Shane, pardon, [illegible].
Nicoleston. *See* Nicholston, co. Kild.
Nicoll, More enyne, pardon, [illegible]04.
Nicolliston. *See* Nicholston.
Nicolson, Thomas, grant of a wardship, [illegible].
Nicolston — Nicolstowne, co. Kildare. *See* Nicholston, co. Kild.
Nicolstowne. *See* Nicholston, co. Tip.
Niddtowen, co. Rosc., [illegible].
Nighome. *See* Neighom, 1570.
ni glack, Dermod m'Owen, pardon, [illegible].
Nihirly (co. Tip. ?), [illegible].
Nikippagha, co. Cork, [illegible].
Nilenre, Margaret, pardon, [illegible].
Ninche — Nynche (Ninch), co. Meath, 14[illegible], [illegible], 1[illegible].
Ninche — Nynche, co. Westm., 10[illegible], [illegible].
Nivynagh, Teig, pardon, [illegible].
Noagh (Fough, co. Gal.), 1[illegible].
Noan (co. Tip.), [illegible].
Noaskerry, co. Gal. or Mayo, [illegible].
Nobber — Nobbir, co. Meath, [illegible], [illegible], [illegible], [illegible], [illegible].
" rectory, [illegible].
" sermon, 4718.
Nobber, co. Mon., [illegible].
Nobbir. *See* Nobber.
Noddlestown, co. Tip., [illegible].
Noddle, Rich., pardon, [illegible].
Nodirets (co. Cork ?), [illegible].
Nodolane, Mulmory and Turralto m'Rory, pardon, [illegible].
Noeanagh, co. Clare, [illegible].
Noer — Nyoure — Ore (river Nore), [illegible], [illegible], [illegible]; several fishery, 1[illegible].
Noffoyro (Fiories ?), co. Kerry, [illegible], [illegible].
Nogell, Rich., pardon, [illegible].
Nogholl, Rich., pardon, [illegible].
Noghomall — Noghomole (Oughavall?), Queen's co., [illegible], [illegible].
Noghovally, co. Cork, [illegible].
Noghvalle, co. Kerry, [illegible].
Noghwall — Noghwale. *See* Noughwall.
Nogill, James, pardon, 4118.
" Philip, pardon, 4118.
Nogle, Garret m'Philip, pardon, [illegible].
" Gilbert, pardon, 4218.
" James, alias ykhollin, pardon, [illegible].
" John, pardon, [illegible].
" Nich., [illegible].
" Philip, pardon, [illegible].
" Rich., pardon, [illegible].
" Walter, pardon, [illegible].
Nogle's land, Youghal, [illegible].
Nogropogy, Donell, pardon, [illegible].
Nograwre alias m'Thomas, Donogh, pardon, [illegible].
Nohanall. *See* Noughwall.
Nohaval, co. Kerry (see Oghvalle), [illegible].
Noiughevale (Noughaval, co. Clare), [illegible].
Nolan, Gerald, pardon, 5111.
" James, pardon, [illegible], 5111.
" Margaret nyne, pardon, [illegible].
" Morogh riagh m'Gilpatrick I., pardon, [illegible].
" Patrick, pardon, 5111.
" Rich., [illegible].
" Rich., burgess, Athlone, [illegible].
" Rob., pardon, [illegible].
" Shane, robbery of, [illegible].
" Thadeus, pardon, [illegible].
" Tho., burgess, Athlone, [illegible].
" Walter, pardon, [illegible].
Nolande, Tho., pardon, [illegible].
Nolane, Edm. m'Dermody, pardon, [illegible].
" James, pardon, [illegible].
" More ny, pardon, [illegible].

Nolane, Fair., pardon, [illegible].
„ Tho., pardon, 6494.
„ William, pardon, 140, 6494.
Nolcaine, Rich. m'( )orie m'James, pardon, [illegible].
Nollan, Grany, pardon, 6462.
„ Thomas, house in Dublin, 1211, 1844.
Nomaddrye — Nonaddrie (Garrownamaddy ?), co. Rosc., 5341, 5342.
Noman's land, in Kilmainham, 1842.
Nomoyge (Moyge), co. Cork, [illegible].
Nomoyne, co. Cork, [illegible].
Nonaddrie. See Nomaddrye.
Nogedaff (co. Gal. ?), [illegible].
Nordan, Wm., pardon, [illegible]1.
Nore river. See Noer.
Norfolk, duke of, his possessions leased, 464, 1736, 2412, [illegible], 3167, [illegible], 4346, 5184; granted, 3167.
Norghar, co. Cav., 4801.
Norian, James, pardon, 4467.
Norumyly, Wm. fils James, pardon, [illegible].
Norunyle, Katherine fils Davie, pardon, [illegible].
„ Tho. fils Davie, pardon, [illegible].
Norney—Norny—Norsye. See Nurney.
Norragh—Narraghe—Norogh—Norraghe—Norraihe (Narraghmore), co. Kild., 642, 1340, [illegible], [illegible], [illegible], 4272.
„ rectory, 678, 1942, 6114.
„ baron of, his son, 671.
„ Walter Wesley, baron of, 4160, 4464. See Wesley.
Norraghbeg, co. Kild., [illegible].
Norreis. See Norreys.
Norreston, co. Wex., 162, 342.
Norroy (co. Tip or Lim. ?), [illegible].
Norreys—Norreis—Norrice—Norrice—Norris—Norryes—Norrys;
„ sir John, lord president of Munster, [illegible], 4489, [illegible], 6144, 6167; general of the army, 6488, [illegible]; commissions, [illegible], [illegible], [illegible], 6122, [illegible], [illegible], [illegible], [illegible], [illegible], [illegible], [illegible]; party to an indenture with chief, [illegible]; deceased, 6144.
„ sir Thomas, vice president of Munster, 4287, [illegible], [illegible]; chief commissioner of Munster, 6144; lord president of Munster, 6167, [illegible], 4843; lord justice of Ireland, [illegible]; commissions, [illegible], [illegible], [illegible], [illegible], [illegible], [illegible], [illegible], [illegible], [illegible], [illegible], [illegible], 6144, [illegible]; grant of land, [illegible]; license to alien, [illegible]; dead, [illegible].
Norris, William, commission, [illegible].
Norrowne, Edm., pardon, [illegible].
Norry, Morris o, pardon, [illegible].
Norryes—Norrys. See Norreys.
Norryshe (co. Car. ?), 6617.
Northfolke, duke of, 1712. See Norfolk.
Norton, Dudley, collector of wine duty, [illegible], [illegible]; provost marshal of Connaught, [illegible], [illegible].
„ Gregory, pardon, [illegible].
„ John, commission, 3847; pardon, [illegible].
Norwiche, Ralph, grant of wardship, [illegible], [illegible].
Noryn, co. Long., [illegible]1.
Notary public, [illegible], [illegible].
Notession, co. Dub., 1777.
Notiston (Nuistown ?), co. Meath, [illegible].
Notnell, Fouke, pardon, [illegible].
Note, Katherine, [illegible].
Notteston, co. Dub., [illegible].
Nottingham, Charles Howard, earl of, custodiam grant, [illegible].
Nottleton, Tho., 4714.
Noughaval, co. Clare. See Nolughevale.
Noughaval, co. Westm. See Noughwall.
Noughe (co. Cork ?), [illegible].
Noughwall—Noghvall—Noghwale—Nohewall—Nowghwall—Oghewalle (Noughaval), co. Westm., [illegible], [illegible], [illegible], [illegible], [illegible], 6797.
Novaghe, co. Gal., [illegible].
Novan—Novane—Nowan. See Navan.
Nowne (co. Tip. ?), 6742, 6744.
Nowane, Donell m'Tee ?, pardon, [illegible].
„ Mullmory fils Marish ?, pardon, 6477.
Nowenan, Mary ny, pardon, [illegible].
Nowery (Newry), town of, 4327.
Nowgawle, in Munster, 6477.
Nowghwall, 6977. See Noughwall.
Nowhamell, co. Westm., [illegible].
Nowire (Garrowoure ?, co. Rosc.), [illegible].
Nowlan, Grany ny, pardon, [illegible].
Nowlane, Daniel m'Moroghoe, pardon, [illegible].
Nowman, Conoghor m'Edm. ?, pardon, [illegible].
„ Dorogh and John m'Tuis ?, pardon, [illegible].
Nowrice, Tho. ?, pardon, [illegible].
Nowrey (Urney), King's co., [illegible], 1861.
Nuan, co. Tip., [illegible].
Nubey (Newbay, co. Wex. ?), [illegible].
Nucastle. See Newcastle, co. Gal.
Nudgent, Maurice (in co. Kerry), pardon, [illegible].
Nuecastle. See Newcastle.
Nueman or Neman, Nich., incumbent of Kilcaslan, [illegible].
Nueton Lessed. See Newton of Lymmie.
Nuge (co. Wex. ?), [illegible].

INDEX TO FIANTS.—ELIZABETH.

Nugent—Newgent—Nugente: -
" Andrew, pardon, 617, 1[illegible], 1446, [illegible], [illegible], [illegible], [illegible], 6740.
" Anne, widow, [illegible].
" Anne, pardon, 6667.
" Balthazar, pardon, [illegible].
" Brandon, pardon, 4341.
" Christopher, knt., baron of Delvin, livery, [illegible]. See Delvin, baron of.
" Christopher, death of, [illegible].
" Christopher (of Moyrath), wardship, [illegible]; commissions, [illegible], [illegible]; pardon, 6778.
" Christopher, commission, [illegible].
" Christopher (of Carolanston), heir of, 2911.
" Christopher fitz Oliver, pardon, [illegible].
" Christopher, pardon, 11[illegible], 1141, [illegible], [illegible], [illegible], [illegible], [illegible].
" Edmund (of Carolanston), wardship, 2911.
" Edm., rebellion, [illegible].
" Edm., pardon, [illegible], [illegible], [illegible], [illegible], [illegible], [illegible], [illegible].
" Edward (of Ballymahranagh), wardship and livery, 197, 218, 6011.
" Edw. (of Ballymahranagh), his son pardoned, [illegible].
" Edw. (of Brakllin), livery, 316; commissions, [illegible], [illegible].
" Edw. (son of Tho. of Brackkan), wardship, [illegible].
" Edw. (of Carolanston), commission, [illegible].
" Edw. (of Collamber), pardon, [illegible].
" Edw. (of Derrynagarragh), pardon, [illegible].
" Edw. (of Disert), pardon, [illegible]; commissions, [illegible], [illegible], [illegible], [illegible], [illegible]; livery to his heir, [illegible].
" Edw. (of Gilbertston), pardon, [illegible].
" Edw. (of Marlestown), commissions, [illegible], [illegible].
" Edw. (of Moorstown), pardon, [illegible].
" Edw. (of Ross), pardon, [illegible].
" Edw., commissions, [illegible], [illegible].
" Edw. (Newgent) messuage in Trim, 1714.
" Edw. (or Winsldon), pardon, [illegible].
" Edw., pardon, 1446, [illegible], [illegible], [illegible], [illegible].
" Elenor, [illegible].
" Elenor or Ellen, grant of land, [illegible].
" Elizabeth, pardon, [illegible].
Garret, pardon, [illegible], [illegible].
Nugent, Garrett fitz Edw. (of Newcastle), pardon, [illegible].
" George fitz Peter (of Foyalle or Oyalea, co. Ross.), pardon, [illegible], [illegible], [illegible], [illegible].
" George (of co. Ross.), pardon, [illegible], [illegible].
" Gerald (of Ballebranagh, knight), wardship and livery, 197, 216, 6011.
" Gerald, pardon, 411, [illegible], [illegible], [illegible], [illegible], [illegible], [illegible], 6776.
" Gerrot, pardon, [illegible], [illegible], [illegible], [illegible].
" Ismay, pardon, [illegible].
" James, son of Christopher (of Coolamber, uncle of baron of Delvin), commissions, [illegible], [illegible], [illegible], 1681, [illegible], [illegible], [illegible], [illegible]; hostages of the O'Farralls to be placed in his hands, [illegible]-2.
" James, sheriff of Westmeath, [illegible].
" James, commissions, [illegible], [illegible]. (The three preceding references probably relate to James of Coolamber.)
" James (of Dysart), pardon, 191.
" James (of Donore), commissions, 1658, 3117, [illegible].
" James (of Donamore, recte Donore?) comm., [illegible].
" James (of Donaran, recte Donore?), comm., [illegible].
" James, house in Trim, [illegible].
" James, issue, [illegible].
" James, son of Edw., pardon, [illegible], [illegible], 1162.
" James (of Carne), pardon, 11[illegible]; murder of, 1[illegible].
" James (of Carne), pardon, [illegible].
" James fitz Gerald, commission, [illegible].
" James (of Leslogher), pardon, [illegible].
" James, sheriff of Westmeath, [illegible].
" James (of Killrush, co. Lim.), attainted, [illegible].
" James, pardon, [illegible], [illegible], [illegible], [illegible], [illegible], [illegible], [illegible], [illegible].
" Jeffery, pardon, [illegible].
" Jonet, pardon, [illegible], [illegible].
" John (of Waterford), theft from, 411.
" John (of Clonconnekeran, co. Wat.), wardship of heir, [illegible].
" John, pardon, [illegible], 1446, [illegible], [illegible], [illegible], [illegible].
" Katherine, pardon, [illegible], [illegible], [illegible].
" Lavalin (of Drumarde), livery, [illegible]; pardon, [illegible]; commissions, [illegible], [illegible].
Lewellyn fitz Edm., pardon, [illegible].

INDEX TO FIANTS—ELIZABETH.

Nugent, Margaret, pardon, [illegible], [illegible], 6973.
,, Margery, pardon, [illegible], [illegible].
,, Mary, pardon, [illegible], [illegible], [illegible].
,, Mauris, pardon, 4712.
,, Morish—Morris, pardon, [illegible], [illegible], [illegible].
,, Nicholas, principal solicitor, [illegible], 1[illegible]; second baron Exchequer, [illegible], [illegible]; chief justice Common Bench, [illegible], [illegible]; commissions, [illegible], [illegible], 1417–12, 1434, 1[illegible], 1[illegible], [illegible], 2343, 3444, [illegible], [illegible], [illegible]; lease, [illegible].
,, Nich. (of Kilcarne or Killrane), commission, [illegible]; widow of, [illegible], 4614.
,, Nich., pardon, [illegible], [illegible], [illegible], [illegible], [illegible], [illegible], [illegible].
,, Nich. fitz Edw., pardon, [illegible].
,, Nich. ro, pardon, [illegible], [illegible].
,, Oliver (of Dromeran, knt.), wardship of his heir, [illegible].
,, Oliver (of Dromcroe), wardship, [illegible]; his heir, [illegible].
,, Oliver (of Boladowncmeys), pardon, [illegible].
,, Oliver, alienation to, [illegible].
,, Oliver, pardon, 1153, 1[illegible], [illegible], [illegible], [illegible], [illegible], [illegible].
,, Philip, pardon, [illegible].
,, Pierce, alderman, [illegible].
,, Ralph, pardon, [illegible].
,, Richard. See Delvin, baron of.
,, Richard (of Dysore), pardon, [illegible], [illegible]; commissions, [illegible], [illegible], [illegible].
,, Richard fitz Tho., commission, [illegible].
,, Rich. (son of Nich., of Kilcarne), grant in remainder, 4614.
,, Rich., land of, near Cork, [illegible], [illegible].
,, Rich., land in his tenure, [illegible].
,, Rich. (of Clonmorkeran, co. Wat.), wardship, [illegible].
,, Rich., pardon, 1159, 1[illegible], [illegible], [illegible], [illegible], [illegible], 6511-2, [illegible], [illegible], [illegible], [illegible].
,, Robert (of Dromcroe), his heir, [illegible].
,, Robert (of Disart), commission, [illegible]; livery, [illegible].
,, Rob. (of Killenchonmakin), livery, [illegible].
,, Rob. (of Carolanston), wardship of heir, [illegible].
,, Robert (described as of Carrick, Tulsk, Gillestown, and Ballinegille, co. Rosc., but apparently one man), sheriff of Roscommon, [illegible]; sheriff of Leitrim, [illegible]; pardon, [illegible], 4974, [illegible], [illegible], [illegible]; commission, [illegible].

Nugent, Robert, pardon, [illegible], [illegible], [illegible], [illegible], 6772.
,, Simon, pardon, [illegible].
,, Theobald, heir of, [illegible].
,, Theobald, pardon, 11[illegible].
,, Thomas, knt. (of Moyrath, according to Lodge), sheriff of Westmeath, [illegible], [illegible]; commissions, [illegible], [illegible], [illegible], [illegible], [illegible], 2344, 3444.
,, Thomas, esquire, commission, [illegible].
,, Thomas (of Moyrath), esquire, commission, 3484; wardship of heir, [illegible].
,, Thomas, commissions, [illegible], [illegible].
,, Thomas (of Bracklin), livery to heir, [illegible].
,, Thomas (of Brackland), wardship of heir, [illegible].
,, Thomas (of Ballorogh), death of his son, [illegible].
,, Thomas (of Taghmon), commissions, [illegible], 3444.
,, Thomas (of Carne), heir of, [illegible].
,, Thomas (of Dardiston), commissions, [illegible], [illegible].
,, Thomas, land in his tenure, [illegible].
,, Thomas, pardon, [illegible], 1141, 1[illegible], 1[illegible], 1[illegible], [illegible], [illegible], [illegible], [illegible], [illegible], [illegible], [illegible], [illegible].
,, Walter, pardon, [illegible], 1073, 1[illegible], [illegible], [illegible], [illegible], [illegible], [illegible], [illegible].
,, William, son of Theobald (of Newhaggard), wardship, [illegible].
,, William fitz Theobald, pardon, 11[illegible].
,, William (of Clonon), livery, [illegible]; rebellion, [illegible], [illegible], [illegible], [illegible]; pardon for rebellion, [illegible].
,, William, lands in co. Lim., [illegible].
,, William, pardon, 1[illegible], [illegible], [illegible], [illegible], [illegible], [illegible], [illegible], [illegible].
Nugent's lands in Hotstown, co. Meath, [illegible].
Nugentrath (co. Louth ?), [illegible].
Nugurtiny, co. Tip., [illegible].
nuillyn, Edm. Doyle, pardon, 1[illegible].
Nuland. See Nowland.
Nully, Margaret, [illegible].
Numan or Nneman, Nich., incumbent of Kilshelan, 6177.
Numane, Donoghy m'Morris I., pardon, [illegible].
nunan, John m'Rickard I., pardon, [illegible].
Nungintiagh (co. Cav. ?), [illegible].
Nuns Island, in Lough Ree, co. Westm. See Inchcatta.
Nunly, co. Cavan, [illegible].
Nupanto, alias M'Donell, Owen, pardon, [illegible].
Nure (Carrowmore), co. Rosc., [illegible], [illegible]. See Nowire.
Nuregare, [illegible]. See Uregare, co. Lim.

INDEX TO FIANTS.—ELIZABETH.

Nurten, co. Wexford, [illegible]4.
Nurtey—Kornoy—Norey—Nortye—Nurrie, co. Kildare, [illegible], 3448, 3214, [illegible], [illegible], [illegible], 6784.
Nury. See Newry.
Nutmegs stolen, [illegible].
Nuson. See Newton, co. Meath.
Nuttstown, co. Meath. See Notiston.
Nuyvoye (co. Cav. ?), 6587.
Nwyre, alias Inwyre (Carrowmore, co. Rosc.), 1682.
ny cahirvaghe, Donogh, pardon, 1[illegible].
ny Carregie, John, pardon, 4[illegible].
ny cluy, Ross, pardon, 5486.
ny cogge, Murtagh, pardon, [illegible].
ny courty, Maurice m'Thomas, pardon, 4192.
Nydon, co. Kerry, 6[illegible].
Nyeveryn, Elizabeth or Ezabelle, pardon, [illegible].
Nygarvan, co. Cork, [illegible].
Nygurvane, alias Fitz Morice, James, pardon, [illegible]7.
ny harpe, Jovane, pardon, 6404.
ny byrry, Donell, pardon, 6876.
ny Hoartin, John m'Nich, pardon, [illegible].
Nylake (Morlick ?), co. Gal., 4[illegible].
Nylan, Onoghor, pardon, 6[illegible]7.
Nyllayn, Dionysius Y, English liberty, 177.
" Donogh Y, sons of, 177.
" John Y, English liberty, 177.
" John Y, English liberty, 177.
" William Y, English liberty, 177.
Nymcomane, co. Cork, [illegible].
Nymaghe, co. Tip., [illegible].
Nymane, Tho. pardon, [illegible], [illegible].
Nymcho. See Nimcho.
Nyner, Murragh m'Teig Y, pardon, [illegible].
Nynshore, in Kilmatalaway, [illegible].
Nynsye, co. Cork, [illegible].
Nyoure river. See Nore.
Nyrowe. See Nyrrowe.
Nyrr, Gaye nyne, pardon, [illegible].
Nyrrowe—Nyrowe, co. Rosc., [illegible], [illegible].
Nyselyrath — Nyselyrathe — Nyslcrath, co. Louth, [illegible], 6418, [illegible].
Nyskreowen, co. Sligo, [illegible].
Nyslerath. See Nyselyrath.
nyraddy, Donogh m'Shane, pardon, [illegible].
Nyvrry, alias Daniell, Morris, pardon, [illegible].
ny twoe, Dermod m'Teig, pardon, [illegible].
Nytany, Donell, pardon, [illegible].
ny voukhowne (M'Cowan ?), Honora, pardon, 4917.
ny veroll, Giles, pardon, 4917.
ny verchane, Doren, pardon, [illegible].
Nywcastell. See Newcastle.
Nywtowne, co. Dub., [illegible].
nywtowne, James riogh m'Shane, pardon, [illegible].

O'Aghoherin — Aghorion — Aghierin — Aghierny, persons of the name pardoned, [illegible], [illegible], [illegible], 6763. See also Agherne, O'Haghierin.
O'Aghoyne, Tho., pardon, [illegible].
Oakearne, Tirrelagh, pardon, [illegible].
O'Aulone, Donogh, pardon, [illegible].
O'Archelane, Fynnyn, pardon, [illegible].
Oaten malt, price of, [illegible].
Oats impressed for army, 14[illegible], 14[illegible], [illegible]; customary payments in, [illegible], 1[illegible]4, 1[illegible]; price of, 1[illegible], [illegible].
Oawhhle, Tho. O'Henry, pardon, [illegible].
O'Bagayn, John, pardon, [illegible].
O'Baghan, Teig, pardon, [illegible].
O'Baghly, Shane, pardon, [illegible].
O'Bahillye, John, [illegible].
O'Ballohen, Donogh, pardon, [illegible].
O'Ballevan, Donnoghe, pardon, [illegible].
O'Banan—Banane—Bannan, persons of the name pardoned, [illegible], [illegible], [illegible], [illegible], [illegible], 4167, [illegible], [illegible], [illegible], [illegible], [illegible]. " See also Ivanane.
O'Banan, Hugh, pardon, [illegible].
O'Bardan, Shan (of Tisiny, co. Long.), pardon, [illegible].
O'Bardan — Bardane, others of the name pardoned, 1[illegible], [illegible], 7[illegible], [illegible], [illegible], 1[illegible], [illegible], [illegible], 4174, [illegible], [illegible], [illegible], [illegible], [illegible].
O'Barr—Barre—Barre, John or Shane, commissions, [illegible], [illegible], [illegible].
O'Barran, Dermot, and others of the name pardoned, [illegible].
O'Barre, John. See O'Barr.
O'Barrenagh, Donogh, pardon, [illegible].
O'Barrel, Conleyh, pardon, 6[illegible].
O'Barry, James, surgeon, pardon, [illegible].
O'Barry—Barrie, persons of the name pardoned, [illegible], [illegible], [illegible], [illegible], [illegible], [illegible], [illegible], [illegible], [illegible], [illegible], [illegible], [illegible].
O'Beaghain, Owen, pardon, [illegible].
O'Beaghan—Beaghane, persons of the name pardoned, 1[illegible], 1[illegible], 4117, [illegible], [illegible], [illegible], [illegible], [illegible].
O'Beagly, Donoghy, pardon, [illegible].
O'Beanaghane, Owen, pardon, [illegible].
O'Bearne, Dermod, pardon, [illegible].
" Morris, pardon, [illegible].
O'Becan, persons of the name pardoned, [illegible], [illegible].
O'Beehan — Beohane, persons of the name pardoned, [illegible], [illegible].
O'Began, Connor, pardon, [illegible].
O'Begayne, Maurice, English liberty, 177.
O'Begelly — Begely — Begrolly — Beggilly — Beglile — Beglile — Begilly — Biggely, persons of the name pardoned, [illegible], [illegible], [illegible], [illegible], [illegible], [illegible], [illegible], [illegible].

INDEX TO FIANTS,—ELIZABETH.

O'Begelly. *See also* Begellie, Vegily.
O'Began, Donogh, attainted, [illegible].
O'Beggahan, Donogh, pardon, 6447.
O'Beggelly—Beggilly. *See* O'Begelly.
O'Beggily. *See* O'Begly.
O'Beggin, Donogh, pardon, 6576.
O'Beghan—Beghane, persons of the same pardoned, 3744, 4778, 6210, 6406, 6743.
„ *See also* Iveghan.
O'Begin, Connor, pardon, [illegible].
O'Begillie—Begilie—Begilly. *See* O'Begelly.
O'Begkehan, Donell, pardon, 6447.
O'Begler, Donoghe, pardon, [illegible].
O'Begloyn, Tho., pardon, 3749.
O'Beglie. *See* O'Begly.
O'Begline, Donogh, pardon, [illegible].
O'Begly—Beglie—Beggily, persons of the same pardoned, [illegible], [illegible], 6736, 6763.
O'Behan, Cahill and Ferall, pardon, 3443.
O'Beheghone, Teig, pardon, 6733.
O'Beichan, Dermot, pardon, [illegible].
O'Beirn, Donogh boy, pardon, [illegible].
„ *See* O'Birne.
O'Beirnes country. *See* Ivigne.
O'Bekan—Bekane—Beknyn, persons of the same pardoned, 615, [illegible], [illegible], [illegible].
O'Beman, Gillepatrick, pardon, 6713.
O'Benachain—Benachane—Benaghan—Benahan—Benaghan—Benechan, persons of the same pardoned, [illegible], [illegible], 5434, 5428, [illegible], [illegible].
O'Bengane, Owen, pardon, 6751.
O'Benaghan—Benechan. *See* O'Benachain.
O'Benlane—Benlaine—Benlain—Benlan—Benlayne, persons of the same pardoned, [illegible], [illegible], [illegible], [illegible], 5740, 6708, [illegible], [illegible].
O'Beola, Gilleduff and Rich., pardon, 6751.
O'Beolin, Teig, pardon, [illegible].
O'Beollaine (alias M'Enllowe), Gillcokrist, pardon, [illegible].
O'Beollan, persons of the same pardoned, [illegible], [illegible].
O'Bergin — Bergine — Bergan — Bergyn—Birgin—Birgyn—Byrgin, persons of the same pardoned, 547, [illegible], [illegible], [illegible], [illegible], [illegible], [illegible], [illegible], [illegible], [illegible], 6110, [illegible], [illegible], [illegible], [illegible], [illegible], [illegible], [illegible].
O'Beriekehane—Berickhane, persons of the same pardoned, [illegible].
O'Bern, Brym, pardon, [illegible].
O'Berne. *See* O'Birne.
O'Bernes, Dermot and Kahier (see O'Birne), 6118.
O'Berren, Brian, pardon, [illegible].
O'Berrie, Donogh, pardon, [illegible].
O'Berry, James, pardon, [illegible].
O'Bevany, Donogh, pardon, [illegible].
O'Bey, John, pardon, [illegible].
O'Boyclane Mortagh, pardon, 3572.
O'Boyll, Teig, pardon, [illegible].
O'Biche, Donell or Ferdinand, pardon, 6447.
O'Biggoly, Hugh (see O'Begilly), pardon, [illegible].
O'Biglean—Biglane—Bigloyn, persons of the same pardoned, [illegible], 3740, [illegible].
O'Birdan, Conor, pardon, [illegible].
O'Birgin, Teige, student, pardon, [illegible].
O'Birgin—Birgyn. *See* O'Bergin.
O'Birn. *See* O'Birne.
O'Birne—Byrn—Byrne—Byrn—Berne:
„ Cahir m'Hugh m'Shane, pardon, [illegible].
„ Cahir m'Hugh duff, pardon, [illegible], [illegible].
„ Cahir m'Teig (of Rowragh), pardon, [illegible].
„ Cahir m'Teig oge, pardon, [illegible], [illegible], [illegible].
„ Callagh m'Bran (co. Car.), pardon, [illegible], [illegible], 6817.
„ Conell m'Hugh m'Shane, pardon, [illegible].
„ Dermot, clerk, lease, 4311.
„ Edmund m'Teig oge (of Tibberlaughe), pardon, [illegible], [illegible], [illegible].
„ Edmund m'Shane m'Redmund, pardon, 1848, [illegible].
„ Edmund (of Tullaghfergus), pardon, 1616, [illegible].
„ Elizabeth ny Hugh, wife of Phelim O'Toole, pardon, 6716, [illegible].
„ Feagh m'Hugh m'Shane (of Ballinacor), pardon, 471, 473, 1026, 1848, [illegible], 4518, [illegible]; pardon at his suit, [illegible]; pardon of his men, 4511-13; his rebellions, [illegible], [illegible], [illegible], [illegible]; his wife pardoned, [illegible]; his sons evil disposed persons, 6116, [illegible].
„ Gerald m'Murogh m'Edm. (of Kilmeston), pardon, [illegible].
„ Hubert m'Fyrr, pardon, [illegible].
„ Hugh m'Shane m'Redmund (of Ballinacor), pardon, 471, 473, [illegible], 1848, [illegible].
„ James, soldier, pardon, [illegible].
„ John m'Hugh m'Shane, pardon, [illegible].
„ Morogh m'Teig oge (of Blind Wood), pardon, [illegible], 4441, 5482, 6197.
„ Morogh m'Edm. (of Simonswood), pardon, [illegible], [illegible].
„ Owen m'Fyrr (of Bumberstown, co. Car.), pardon, [illegible], [illegible].
„ Patr. m'Tirlagh, pardon, [illegible], [illegible].
„ Phelim m'Feagh m'Hugh (of Ballinacor), pardon, [illegible], [illegible], [illegible], [illegible].
„ Phelim m'Feagh m'Redmund, pardon, 471, 473.

O'Birne, Redmond m'Feagh m'Hugh, pardon, [illegible], 6377, [illegible].
„ Redmond oge m'Redmond m'Brian, pardon, [illegible], [illegible].
„ Rose, wife of Feagh m'Hugh, pardon, [illegible].
„ Shian, robbery from, 444.
„ Teig oge, chief of his name (co. Wick.), [illegible], [illegible], [illegible]; grant of the customs due to the chief, [illegible]; his sons, [illegible], [illegible], [illegible], [illegible], [illegible].
„ Tirlagh, son of Feagh m'Hugh, pardon, [illegible].
„ Tirlagh or Terence, grant of land, 6401, [illegible].
„ Walter boy m'Gerald, pardon, [illegible].
„ persons of the name in Wicklow, Carlow, and adjoining counties pardoned, 140, 124, 126, [illegible], 670, 611, [illegible], [illegible], [illegible], 1008, [illegible], 1159, 1124, 1648, [illegible], [illegible], 1687, 1741, [illegible], 1877, [illegible].
„ Carbry (of Dungin, co. Rosc.), pardon, [illegible], [illegible], [illegible]; commission, [illegible].
„ Dualtagh, pardon, [illegible], [illegible].
„ Teig, chief of Tir Briuin (in co. Roscommon), leases, [illegible], [illegible]; appointed seneschal of his country, [illegible].
„ Teig oge (of Dungen, co. Rosc.), pardon, [illegible].
„ Teig roe, pardon, [illegible], [illegible]; attainted, [illegible].
„ —by Vyrn—Vyrne, persons of the name in co. Roscommon and adjoining districts, pardoned, [illegible].
„ persons of the name in other parts of Ireland, pardoned, [illegible]. *See also* Byrne.

O'Birne, rebels, [illegible].
O'Birnes country. *See* Byrnes country.
O'Birnes country (co. Rosc.), [illegible].
O'Birrain — Birrane, persons of the name pardoned, [illegible], [illegible].
O'Birren—Birrin—Birryn—Byrran — Byrren —Byrrin, persons of the name pardoned, [illegible], [illegible], [illegible], [illegible], [illegible], [illegible], [illegible], [illegible], [illegible].
Obleige, Donell, pardon, [illegible].
O'Bile, Cahill, pardon, [illegible].
O'Blyn, Hugh, pardon, [illegible].
Obo, Philip, pardon, [illegible].
O'Boden, Donogho, pardon, [illegible].
O'Boe, Philip and Rich., pardon, [illegible], [illegible].
O'Boelane, Wm., pardon, [illegible].
O'Boelle, John, pardon, [illegible].
O'Bogaine, Patr., pardon, [illegible].
O'Boghan, Donogho and Wm., pardon, [illegible], [illegible], [illegible], [illegible].
O'Boghilly—Boghelly—Boghillie — Bohillie—Bowghylly, persons of the name pardoned, [illegible], [illegible], [illegible], [illegible].
O'Boghola, Patr., pardon, [illegible].
O'Bohan, Magus, pardon, [illegible].
O'Boherane, Shane, pardon, [illegible].
O'Bohery, Brian, pardon, [illegible].
O'Bohillie, Donell, pardon (see O'Boghilly), [illegible].
O'Boilane, Shane, pardon, 10.
O'Boile, persons of the name pardoned, [illegible], [illegible], [illegible], [illegible].
O'Boillan, Teige, pardon, [illegible].
O'Bolaine, Dermod, pardon, [illegible].
O'Bolan, Teig, pardon, [illegible].
O'Bolan, persons of the name pardoned, [illegible], [illegible], [illegible].
O'Bolane, persons of the name pardoned, [illegible], [illegible], [illegible].
O'Bolger, Morghoo, English liberty to daughter of, [illegible].
O'Bolge, Patrick down, pardon, [illegible].
O'Bolger—Bolgier—Bolgir—Bolgire:
„ Dermod, surgeon, pardon, [illegible].
„ Gillopatrick, surgeon, pardon, [illegible].
„ James, leche, pardon, [illegible].
„ Walter, surgeon, pardon, [illegible].
„ others of the name pardoned, 1917, 1748, [illegible], [illegible], [illegible], [illegible], [illegible], [illegible], [illegible], [illegible], [illegible], [illegible], [illegible], [illegible], [illegible], [illegible], [illegible], [illegible], [illegible], [illegible].
O'Bolgie, Donell and Nich., pardon, [illegible], [illegible].
O'Bolgier—Bolgir—Bolgire. *See* O'Bolger.
O'Bollgir, Walter, pardon, [illegible].
O'Bolkyre, Dermod, pardon, [illegible].
O'Bollighly, David, pardon, [illegible].
O'Bolyer, Donogh, pardon, [illegible].
O'Bon, Walter, pardon, [illegible].

INDEX TO FIANTS.—ELIZABETH.

O'Boolan, Banyoco, pardon, [illegible].
O'Borget, Owoly, pardon, 1828.
O'Boughale, Donogh, pardon, 6412.
O'Boughan—O'Boughane, persons of the name pardoned, 5041, 6424.
O'Bouhillane, John, pardon, 6456.
O'Bouk, Philip, pardon, 4628.
O'Bourke, Shane, pardon, 5408.
O'Bow, John, pardon, 2028.
Obowe, Edm., pardon, 6162.
O'Bowghellan, Cormuck, pardon, 4581.
O'Bowghylly, Donell, pardon (see O'Boghilly), 5763.
O'Bowigo, Dermod, and others of the name pardoned, 5614.
O'Bowile, Brian, pardon, 6504.
O'Bowill, Shane, pardon, 2028.
O'Bowlain, Morogh, pardon, 5878.
O'Bowlan—Bowlane, Rich. and Rory, pardon, 5403.
O'Bowrowe, Gerrol, pardon, 1881.
O'Boy—Boye, persons of the name pardoned, 567, 2043, 5457, 5377, 6761.
O'Boyell, Brian and Rory, pardon, 6476, 6571.
O'Boylane — Boylan, persons of the name pardoned, 18, 4029, 5458, 6067, 6464.
O'Boyle, Cornelius, chaplain, English liberty, 1814.
" Teig oge, pardon, 4501, 6761.
" others of the name pardoned, 4208, 4543, 5516, 6408, 5764, 6762, 6741, 6771. *See* O'Baile.
O'Boyle's country (co. Donegal), commander of the forces in, 4572.
O'Boyll—Boylle, persons of the name pardoned, 1800, 5208, 5443.
O'Bracane. *See* O'Brackane.
O'Brachan. *See* O'Brackane.
O'Brackane—Brachan—Bracane — Brakane, persons of the name pardoned, 1767, 2813, 5541, 6414, 6383.
O'Bradegan—Bradegane—Bradigan, persons of the name pardoned, 4631, 4885, 5131, 5484, 5468, 6611.
O'Bradan, persons of the name pardoned, 4435, 4838, 6062.
O'Braddan, persons of the name pardoned 6761.
" *See* Vraddan.
O'Bradegan—Bradegane. *See* O'Bradagan.
O'Brader, Melmorie, pardon, 4857.
O'Bradigan. *See* O'Bradagan.
O'Bradile, Wm., pardon, 6465.
O'Bradine, Meloghlin, pardon, 4577.
O'Brady, Morish and Owen, pardon, 6636, 6662.
O'Braen, Donogh, baron of Ibrakan (*see* O'Brien), 5428.
O'Bragan, Shane, pardon, 5465.
O'Bragane, Fearshey, pardon, 5468.
O'Brahye, Rob., pardon, 6152.
O'Brakane. *See* O'Brackane.
O'Bran, Tirlagh, pardon, 6734.
O'Branagan — Brannagan, persons of the name pardoned, 59, 6714.
O'Branaine, Patr. and Philip, pardon, 4734.
O'Branan, Cahill m'Marcus M'Enerybane, pardon, 4623.
" others of the name pardoned, 584, 4621.
O'Brannagan. *See* O'Branagan.
O'Brannon, Wm., pardon, 4890.
O'Branyll, Dermot, pardon, 5698.
O'Braonain, Meloghlin, harper, pardon, 4734.
O'Braonan, Hugh, pardon, 2594.
O'Braonan, Knoghry or Connor, pardon, 4707.
O'Brasill, John, pardon, 5868.
O'Brassall, persons of the name pardoned, 5714, 6362.
O'Bray, Donogh, pardon, 4858.
O'Breya, Edm., pardon, 4711.
O'Breyne, Rich., pardon, 4719.
O'Breman, Melaghlin, pardon, 6574.
O'Brenckan, Morgh, pardon, 6423.
O'Bren, sir Tirlagh or Terence. *See* O'Brien.
" Tege. *See* O'Brien.
" —I Brean, others of the name pardoned, 4894, 5641, 4366, 6424.
O'Brenain, Neil, pardon, 4883.
O'Brene, Conor and Murtagh, pardon, 5541, 6578.
O'Bresale, Murtagh, pardon, 6464.
O'Bresall, Dowell, pardon, 6363.
O'Breskan—Breane—Brekan, persons of the name pardoned, 949, 1418, 2393, 2323-4, 3881, 4626, 6367, 6438.
O'Bresler, Edm., pardon, 4728.
O'Breon, Mahon, attainted, 6578.
" Morghe (*see* Inchiquin, baron), 1823.
O'Breone, Barnaby (O'Brien), pardon, 1842.
" Morgh, attainted, 4873.
O'Bregan, persons of the name pardoned, 2883, 6761.
O'Breghan, Coll, pardon, 6469.
O'Bregine, persons of the name pardoned, 5868, 6488.
O'Brehonknaghe, Shane, pardon, 5031.
O'Brein, Terence or Tirlagh. *See* O'Brien.
" —Breine, persons of the name pardoned, 1678, 5304, 4838, 4581.
O'Breine—I Breine, Mahon (*see* O'Brien), 1438.
" Wolhney, pardon, 6048.
O'Brekan. *See* O'Breskan.
O'Bren, Teig (*see* O'Brien), 6470.
O'Bren, persons of the name pardoned, 187, 2883, 5408, 6108, 6457, 6463.
O'Brenagh, Walter, pardon, 6868.

O Brenaghan, Donogh, pardon, 6454.
O'Brenan, chief of his name in co. Westm., commissions, 4151, 4488 (see O'Breinane).
" Donald (of Inchiquin, co. Clare), pardon, [illegible].
" Donill ballagh, attainted, [illegible].
" Edm. m'Gillepatrick oge, pardon, 442, 911, [illegible].
" Geoffrey, pardon, [illegible], [illegible]; attainted, [illegible].
" Hugh m'Shane, attainted, [illegible].
" James m'Donogh more, attainted, [illegible].
" Owen, called O'Brenan, pardon, 1874.
" Patrick, murder of, [illegible].
" Rory, pardon, [illegible], attainted, [illegible].
" Thady (of Grevagh, co. Westm.), pardon, [illegible], [illegible].
O'Brenan — Brenane — Brennan — Brenain Brinan — I Vrenane, persons of the name in co. Kilkenny and adjoining districts, pardoned, 442, 616, 672, 911, 1274, [illegible], [illegible], 1617, [illegible], [illegible], [illegible], [illegible], [illegible], 1917, [illegible], 5477, 5708, [illegible].
" persons of the name in co. Westmeath, pardoned, [illegible], 1673, [illegible], [illegible], [illegible], [illegible], [illegible], [illegible], [illegible], [illegible], [illegible], [illegible], [illegible], [illegible], [illegible], [illegible], [illegible], [illegible], [illegible], [illegible], [illegible].
" —Brenaye — I Vrenan — I Vroy-nane, persons of the name in cos. Kerry and Cork, pardoned, [illegible], [illegible], [illegible], [illegible], [illegible], [illegible], [illegible], [illegible], [illegible].
" persons of the name in other districts, pardoned, [illegible], [illegible], [illegible], [illegible], [illegible].
O'Breno, Aulone (of Whitestown), pardon, [illegible].
" Dermot (see Inchiquin, baron), 918.
" Donogh (see Thomond, earl), [illegible].
" Donogh m'Murogh, attainted (see O'Brien), [illegible].
" Margaret, wife of earl of Clanricard (see O'Brien), [illegible].
" Murogh (see Inchiquin, baron), 918.
" sir Tirlagh (see O'Brien), [illegible].
O'Breno, others of the name pardoned, [illegible], [illegible], [illegible], [illegible], [illegible], [illegible], [illegible], [illegible], [illegible].
O'Brengan, Art, and others of the name pardoned, [illegible].
O'Brenie, Donogh, and others of the name pardoned, [illegible].
O'Brean, Hugh, pardon, [illegible].
O'Brennan. See O'Brenan.
O'Brenon, Molaghlin, pardon, [illegible].
O'Breoyne, Pohilim, pardon, 6178.
O'Breskiane, Nich., pardon, [illegible].
O'Bressnih, Dermod, pardon, [illegible].
O'Brossell, Murtagh, pardon, [illegible].
Obresloe, [illegible].
O'Broyen, Wm. fitz Tho., pardon, [illegible].
O'Broyn, Mahon m'en Aspog, slain (O'Brien), [illegible].
" See O'Broyne.
O'Broynane, Molaghlin, pardon, [illegible].
O'Broyne—Broyn, persons of the name pardoned, 1204, 1873, [illegible], [illegible], [illegible], [illegible], [illegible], 4448, 4715-6.
O'Brian—Briane. See O'Brien.
O'Bridane—Bridan, persons of the name pardoned, [illegible], 5761.
O'Bricone, Rory, pardon, [illegible].
O'Brien—Brien—Briene — Bryan — Bryen — [illegible] — [illegible] — Y Brien — I Vrien:
" Auver, pardon, 3112, 4476, [illegible]; mortgage to, [illegible].
" Brian duble, attainted, [illegible].
" Brien duffe (of Carrigogunnell), chief of his nation in Pobblebrien, pardon, 4475; surrender and regrant of his lands, [illegible], [illegible]; his brothers, [illegible]; pardon, [illegible].
" Brien m'Donogh (of the Curraghe, co. Wat.), attainted, [illegible].
" Conoghor, attainted, [illegible].
" Conor, indenture, 4791.
" Cornelius or Conoghor (of Carrigogunnell), [illegible]; pardon, [illegible], [illegible].
" Dermod (of Pobblebrien), [illegible]; pardon, [illegible], [illegible].
" Dermot. See Inchiquin, baron of, 918, [illegible].
" Donald m'Conie (of Greangonogh), attainted, [illegible].
" sir Donill (of Ennistimon), [illegible]; pardon, 1984, [illegible]; lease, [illegible]; commissions, [illegible], [illegible]; his sons, 1934, [illegible], [illegible].
" Donell (of Ennistimon), pardon, [illegible].
" Donogh. See Thomond, earl of, [illegible].
" Donogh. See Ibrackan, baron, [illegible], [illegible], [illegible].

INDEX TO FIANTS.—ELIZABETH.

O Brien, Donogh m'Morogh (of Dromoleane), pardon, 1840; attainted, [illegible], [illegible].
„ Donogh (of Ballyvesy), indenture, 4752.
„ Donogh, attainted, 6711.
„ Donogh m'Kennedy (of Kilecommary), pardon, [illegible].
„ Mahon (of Clondowan), pardon, [illegible]; indenture, 4751; slain in rebellion, 5151, [illegible], 6777.
„ Mahon fitz Mortagh, attainted, [illegible].
„ Margaret, wife of earl of Clanricarde, 2117.
„ Mortagh m'Conor (of Dromleyne), indenture, 4751; his lands, 4761.
„ Murogh, great grandfather of lord Inchiquin, and first earl of Thomond, his heirs male, 4752.
„ Murogh. See Inchiquin, baron of, 819, 1858, 6491.
„ Morogh m'Conor (of Cahirmenan), pardon, 6077; his lands, 4751.
„ Morogh, attainted, 6317, 6777, [illegible].
„ Morogh m'Enaghor (of Castlegar in Arra), attainted, [illegible].
„ Patr., lands of, in co. Kild., 4414.
„ Thady m'Conoghor, brother of sir Donell, lease, 1582, 3448, 4774.
„ Taig m'Morogh, his man pardoned, 1640.
„ Taig m'Morogh (of Ballingown), wardship of his heir, 3470; his daughters and co-heiresses, 4751; his lands, 4751.
„ Taig (of Roghmolle, esq.), pardon, [illegible].
„ Taig (of Carrigogunnell), 1518; pardon, 4475.
„ Teig or Taddeus (of Newry, co. Down), pardon, [illegible].
„ sir Tirlagh or Terence (of Ennistymon), pardon, 1034, 3077; seneschal of Corcumroe and Burren, [illegible], [illegible]; lease, [illegible]; surrender, 4364, 4373; regrant of his lands, 4374; pardon, 4753; party to indenture of composition, 4751; his demesne lands, &c., 4751; grant of land, [illegible]; commissions, 4480, 4746, [illegible], 5183, [illegible], [illegible], [illegible], [illegible]-4.
„ Tirlagh m'Taig (of Beallcorrig), pardon, 4684, 4753; indenture, 4751; his lands, 4751.
„ Tirlagh, alias M'IBrien Arra, pardon, [illegible].
O Brien, Wm. m'Tirlagh, pardon, 5118; attainted, [illegible].
„ others of the name pardoned, [illegible], 964, 1076, 1078, 1183, 1304, 1340-2, 1840, 1694, 1818, 1863, [illegible]-4, [illegible], [illegible], 7394, 3464, 3427, [illegible], 3814, 3834, 3040-2, 3777-4, [illegible], 3691, 5118, [illegible], [illegible], 3670, [illegible], [illegible], [illegible], [illegible], 4011, [illegible], 4478, 4483, [illegible], [illegible], [illegible], [illegible], [illegible]-6, 4618, [illegible]-1, [illegible], [illegible], [illegible]-6, 4717, 4734, 4743, 4753, 4780, [illegible], [illegible], [illegible], [illegible]-6, [illegible], [illegible], 5151, [illegible], [illegible], 5419, [illegible], [illegible], [illegible]-4, [illegible], 5712, 5726, [illegible], [illegible], [illegible], [illegible], 6170, 6175, 6179, 6186, [illegible], [illegible], [illegible], [illegible], [illegible], 6440, 6464-6, 6478, 6487, [illegible], [illegible], [illegible], [illegible]-6, [illegible], 6514, [illegible], [illegible]-3, [illegible], [illegible], [illegible]-3, [illegible], 6775, [illegible], [illegible], 6816, 6817, [illegible]-4, [illegible]-5, 6705, 6785, 6765. See also O'Brean, O'Breen, O'Breene, O'Brein, O'Breine, O'Bren, O'Brene, O'Broyn, O'Brin, O'Brine, O'Bryn, O'Bryne, O'Brynn.
„ country of, 6761.
O'Brienan, Rory, pardon, [illegible].
O'Briensbridge, co. Clare. See Bridge, castle of the.
O'Briggin, Teig, pardon, [illegible].
O'Brin, persons of the name pardoned, 140, [illegible], 1041, 1124, 1748, [illegible], [illegible], 6211, 3467, [illegible], 6448, 6447, [illegible], [illegible], [illegible], 6618.
O'Briman—Brimane. See O'Breman.
O'Brine, persons of the name pardoned, [illegible]-4, 1873, 1874, 1876, [illegible], 1890, 3067, 3348, [illegible], [illegible], 5714, 6447, [illegible], 6577, 6706.
O'Briode, Hugh, pardon, [illegible].
O'Briody, Brian and Maure, pardon, [illegible].
O'Brislenayn, James, pardon, [illegible].
O'Bristian or Bristan, Brian, pardon, [illegible], [illegible].
O'Broader, Shane, pardon, 4717.
O'Broder, James, pardon, 89, 141, [illegible].
„ —Y Broder, others of the name pardoned, [illegible], [illegible], 6348, 6447, [illegible], [illegible], [illegible], 6794.
„ See O'Brother.
O'Broe, Teig, pardon, 6447.
O'Brogan—Ivrogan, persons of the name pardoned, [illegible], 6781.
O'Broghan, persons of the name pardoned, [illegible], [illegible].
O'Broghe, persons of the name pardoned, [illegible], [illegible], 6773.
O'Broghie, persons of the name pardoned, [illegible], 6464.
O'Broha, persons of the name pardoned, [illegible], [illegible], [illegible].

INDEX TO FIANTS—ELIZABETH.

O'Brohe, persons of the name pardoned, [illegible], [illegible], [illegible].
O'Broher, Philip, pardon, 6706.
O'Brohy—Brohie—Brohey, persons of the name pardoned, [illegible], [illegible], 4787, 4796, [illegible], [illegible], [illegible], 6110, [illegible], [illegible], [illegible], [illegible].
O'Broin, Rickard, pardon, 4874.
O'Brohane (O'Brenan), Edm. and Owen, pardon, [illegible].
O'Brollan, Shane, pardon, [illegible].
O'Broman, Conor, pardon, [illegible].
O'Broman, Wm., pardon, [illegible].
O'Brome, Dermot, pardon, [illegible].
O'Bronie, Edm. and others of the name pardoned, [illegible].
O'Brony, Tibbot, pardon, [illegible].
O'Broo, Conor and Wm., pardon, [illegible], [illegible].
O'Broader, Donogh and Moriertagh, pardon, [illegible].
O'Brosnaghan—I Brosnaghan—I Vrosnaghane, persons of the name pardoned, 4677, [illegible].
O'Brotall, Conor, persons of the name pardoned, 4887.
O'Brother, persons of the name pardoned, 1049, 1471, 3427, [illegible], [illegible].
O'Brouder, Conor, pardon, [illegible].
O'Broughillaghan, John and Gilpatrick, pardon, [illegible].
O'Browder, Donell, pardon, 4870, [illegible].
O'Browdire, Owen and Rich., pardon, [illegible].
O'Brown—Browne, John or Shane, pardon, [illegible], [illegible].
O'Browodyn, Wm. oge, pardon, [illegible].
O'Broy, Wm., pardon, [illegible].
O'Broyn, Gilpatrick, pardon, [illegible].
O'Broynne, Melaghlin, pardon, [illegible].
O'Bruadar—Bruadir—Bruader, persons of the name pardoned, 4078-80, 4418, 4794.
O'Bruadoir, Harry buy, pardon, 4734.
O'Bruck, John, pardon, [illegible].
O'Bruen—Bruyen, persons of the name pardoned, 4461.
O'Brughallan, Donell and Teig, pardon, [illegible].
O'Bruhilligan, Donell and Teig, pardon, [illegible].
O'Bruoder—Bruodir, persons of the name pardoned, [illegible], [illegible].
O'Bruyan, Laghlin, pardon, [illegible].
O'Bruyn, Harwell, pardon, [illegible].
O'Bruyne, Shane, pardon, [illegible].
O'Brwoder, Melaghlin, pardon, [illegible].
O'Brwynnian, Melaghlin, pardon, [illegible].
O'Bryan. See O'Brien.
O'Bryn, Tirlagh, pardon, 1078.
O'Bryen. See O'Brien.
O'Bryn—Ivryn, persons of the name pardoned, [illegible], 1697, [illegible], [illegible], 1907, [illegible], [illegible], [illegible], [illegible], 4371, [illegible], [illegible], [illegible], [illegible], [illegible], [illegible], [illegible].
O'Bryman, persons of the name pardoned, 1633—4, 4818, [illegible], [illegible], [illegible].
O'Brymane, Patr., pardon, 6775.
O'Bryne, Thady and Donogh (of Inchiquin, co. Clare), sons of Murroghoe, late chief of his nation, pardoned, 1108, [illegible].
„ (O'Brien), Murogh m'Conor, and Mahon, 4761.
„ others of the name pardoned, [illegible], 911-2, 1085, [illegible], 1748, [illegible], [illegible], 1648, 1672, 1677, 1687, [illegible], [illegible], [illegible], [illegible], [illegible], [illegible], 4742, [illegible], [illegible], [illegible], [illegible], [illegible], [illegible], [illegible].
O'Bryne's country, co. Westm., divided into ploughlands, 1498.
O'Brynn, persons of the name pardoned, [illegible], [illegible], [illegible], 6512, [illegible], [illegible], [illegible].
O'Brynnane, Teig, pardon, [illegible].
O'Brynne, Edm., pardon, [illegible].
O'Brypde, Manus, pardon, [illegible].
O'Bryody, Brene, pardon, [illegible].
Observantine friars. See Youghal, [illegible], &c.
O'Buggim, Murtagh, pardon, [illegible].
O'Buhy, persons of the name pardoned, [illegible].
O'Bull, Rory, pardon, [illegible].
O'Bulger, Dermot and Hugh, pardon, [illegible].
O'Buoghaly—Buoghilie—Bwoughaley—Bwoghelie, persons of the name pardoned, 6407, [illegible], [illegible], [illegible].
O'Burder, Tho., pardon, [illegible].
O'Burn, Hugh, slaying of, [illegible].
O'Burrin, Cormock, pardon, [illegible].
O'Buylane—Bwylane, persons of the name pardoned, [illegible], [illegible].
O'Buyle, Teig, pardon, [illegible].
O'Buyll, Rory, pardon, [illegible].
O'Bwaghane—O'Bwagh[ ], persons of the name pardoned, [illegible].
O'Bwile, persons of the name pardoned, [illegible].
Obwony, Edm., pardon, 4718.
O'Bwoghan, Rich., pardon, [illegible].
O'Bwoghaley. See O'Buoghaly.
O'Bwoghane, John, pardon, 6571.
O'Bwoghelie. See O'Buoghaly.
O'Bwoy—Bwy, Twoll, pardon, 4786, [illegible].
O'Bwylane, Magnes (see O'Buylane), pardon, [illegible].
O'Bwyle, persons of the name pardoned, [illegible].
O'Byayn, Eylard, pardon, 4718.
O'Byrane, Donogh, pardon, [illegible].
O'Byrgin, Dermot and Wm. (see O'Burgin), pardon, 6732.
O'Byrne. See O'Birne.
O'Byrne's country. See Byrne's country.
O'Byrne's country in co. Roscommon, [illegible].
O'Byrrin—Byrren—Byrran, persons of the name pardoned, [illegible], [illegible], [illegible], [illegible]. See also O'Birren.

O'C[illegible]lan, Donoghe, pardon, 6761.
O'Ca[illegible]well, Shane, pardon, 6639.
O'Caane, Bryan and Dermot, pardon, [illegible].
O'Cadane, Hugh, pardon, [illegible].
O'Caerny, Art, chirurgeon, pardon, 5768.
O'Caffarky, Owen, pardon, 5761.
O'Caffo, Teig, pardon, 6703.
O'Caffoo—Caffoe—Calo, Darby, and others of the name pardoned, [illegible], [illegible], [illegible].
O'Caffowe, John and Wm., pardon, [illegible].
O'Caffoye, Teig, pardon, [illegible].
O'Calo, Darby, pardon, [illegible].
O'Cafoygh, Conor, pardon, [illegible].
O'Caghelane, Shane, pardon, 6414.
O'Caghan, James, pardon, 6766, 6766.
O'Caghane, Owen, pardon, 4671.
O'Cahacie, Donell, pardon, 6412.
O'Cahaie, Wm., pardon, 6407.
O'Cahaine, Dermot, pardon, [illegible].
,, Shedine (O'Cahan), pardon, [illegible].
O'Cahalan, Donell, pardon, [illegible].
O'Cahallan, Donogh and Wm., pardon, 6414, [illegible]. See O'Kahallan.
O'Cahallane, Laghlin and Wm., pardon, 4707.
O'Cahan, Coyne Ballough (Coney ballagh), his lands, [illegible].
,, Donald or Daniel, chief of his name, O'Neill's superiority over, [illegible]; protection for, [illegible]; grant of O'Cahan's country, [illegible]; pardon to him, his family and followers, [illegible].
,, Nich. (of Kilrush, co. Clare), pardon, 6416.
,, —Cahane, others of the name in Ulster, pardoned, [illegible], [illegible], [illegible], [illegible], [illegible], 6741.
,, persons of the name in other districts, pardoned, 677, [illegible], 4779, [illegible], [illegible], [illegible], 5746, [illegible], [illegible], [illegible], [illegible], [illegible], 4517, [illegible], [illegible], [illegible], 6415.
,, See O'Cane, O'Kahan.
O'Cahan's country regranted to the chief, [illegible]; general pardon of the inhabitants, [illegible]. See O'Cane's country.
O'Cahanie, Conghor, pardon, [illegible].
O'Cahasie, persons of the name pardoned, [illegible], [illegible].
O'Cahassie—Cahassy, persons of the name pardoned, [illegible], [illegible], 4470, [illegible], [illegible], [illegible], 6571.
O'Cahe, Wm., pardon, 6713.
O'Cahelan, Wm., pardon, 6412.
O'Cahell, Philip, weaver, pardon, [illegible].
,, others of the name pardoned, [illegible], [illegible], [illegible], [illegible], [illegible], [illegible], 6764.
O'Cahellane, Donell, pardon, [illegible].
O'Cahesie, persons of the name pardoned [illegible], [illegible], [illegible].
O'Cahessie—Cahessy—Chahessy, persons of the name pardoned, [illegible], [illegible], [illegible], [illegible], [illegible], [illegible].
O'Cahill, sir Donald, English liberty, [illegible].
,, others of the name pardoned, 1417, 1890, [illegible], [illegible], [illegible], [illegible], [illegible], [illegible], [illegible], [illegible], 4712, [illegible], [illegible], 6440, [illegible], 6417, [illegible], [illegible], [illegible], [illegible], [illegible], [illegible], [illegible], [illegible], 6744.
,, See O'Hahill.
O'Cahillaine, Dermod, pardon, 6571.
O'Cahin, Nich., pardon, [illegible].
O'Cahine, persons of the name pardoned, [illegible], [illegible].
O'Cahir, Donell, pardon, [illegible].
O'Cahisie, Conoghor, pardon, [illegible].
O'Cahhig, Teig, pardon, [illegible].
O'Cahisee, Rory, pardon, [illegible].
O'Cahissie—Cahissy, persons of the name pardoned, [illegible], [illegible], [illegible], [illegible], [illegible].
,, See O'Hahissy.
O'Cahisy, John, pardon, [illegible].
O'Caine, Mahon, pardon, 6511.
O'Cahyry, Tho., English liberty, 177.
O'Caloine, Finin, pardon, 6511.
O'Calan—Calane. See O'Callan.
O'Caleghan, Dermot, pardon, [illegible].
O'Calenyan, Mahon, pardon, 4616.
O'Calghan or O'Calighan, Conoghor, pardon, [illegible].
O'Calgie, Gillernow, pardon, [illegible].
O'Calhan, Donell, and Morris, pardon, 4416, [illegible].
O'Calien, Wm., pardon, [illegible].
O'Callaghan—Callaghan—Callaghane—Challaghan—Hallaghan—Kallaghane—Kellaghan:
,, Cahir moddery (of Dromnyne), pardon, [illegible], 6762.
,, Conoghor (of Clonmeen), surrender and regrant of lands, [illegible], [illegible]; pardon, 6407.
,, Dermot m'Owen, baron of Dromore, pardon, [illegible].
,, Dermot alias Squyney, pardon, 4447.
,, Donogh or Donald, wardship, 6407.
,, Kellaghan m'Conoghor, pardon, [illegible], [illegible], [illegible]; chief of his nation, his heir, 6407.
,, others of the name pardoned, [illegible], [illegible], [illegible], [illegible], [illegible], [illegible], 4414, [illegible], [illegible], [illegible], [illegible], 4751, 4784, [illegible], [illegible], [illegible], [illegible], [illegible], [illegible], [illegible], [illegible], [illegible], [illegible], [illegible], [illegible], [illegible], 6764.

O'Callaghan. *See also* Callaghan, Challaghan, O'Heallaghan.
O'Callahane, Dermod, pardon, 4[illegible].
O'Callaine, Teig and Wm., pardon, 5470.
O'Callan — Calane — Calan — Callano — Kallan:
„ Donogh (of Farney), pardon, 54[illegible], 6[illegible]4.
„ others of the name pardoned, [illegible], 644, 1175, [illegible], [illegible], [illegible], 4[illegible], [illegible], 5784, [illegible], [illegible], 64[illegible], [illegible], [illegible], [illegible], [illegible], [illegible], [illegible]7, 6714.
O'Callenalan, John, pardon, [illegible].
O'Calleman—Callamane, persons of the name pardoned, [illegible], [illegible], [illegible], [illegible], [illegible], 6440, [illegible], 6770.
O'Cal[illegible], Brene or Bernard, pardon, 1[illegible].
O'Callegan, Conoghor, pardon, 5[illegible].
O'Calloghan. *See* O'Callaghan.
O'Callon, Noyle, pardon, 64[illegible].
O'Callemane—Calleman, persons of the name pardoned, 4[illegible], [illegible], 5142, [illegible], 67[illegible].
O'Calleran, Shane, pardon, 6512.
O'Callie, Wm., pardon, 4477, 6[illegible].
O'Calligane, Teig, pardon, [illegible].
O'Callighane. *See* O'Callaghan.
O'Calliman, persons of the name pardoned, [illegible], [illegible], [illegible].
O'Callo, Edm., pardon, [illegible].
O'Callon, Conor and Laghlin, pardon, [illegible], [illegible].
O'Calloman, Gillegerry, pardon, [illegible].
O'Calloughan—Callowghan, persons of the name pardoned, 5[illegible], [illegible].
O'Cally, How and John, pardon, 1179, 4[illegible]0.
O'Callyman, Conoghor, pardon, [illegible].
O'Calnon, Con, pardon, [illegible].
O'Calon, Patr., pardon, 1761.
O'Caman, Conoghor, pardon, [illegible].
O'Camane, Donogh, pardon, [illegible].
O'Camenan, Dermod, pardon, 5418.
O'Camman, Rory, pardon, [illegible].
O'Canally, Conor and Phelim, pardon, [illegible], 5714.
O'Canan, Malachy, pardon, [illegible].
O'Cananan, persons of the name pardoned, 6712.
O'Cane, protection for, 5167.
„ Matthias, pardon, [illegible].
„ others of the name pardoned, [illegible], [illegible], [illegible].
„ *See* O'Cahan.
O'Cane's country (co. Londonderry), [illegible]; commander of the forces in, [illegible]-1; martial law in, [illegible]. *See* O'Cahan's country.
O'Canevan, Mallerie, pardon, [illegible]. *See* O'Kanavan.
O'Cangelly, Wm., pardon, [illegible].
O'Canie, Wm., pardon, 1447.
O'Canlon, Donald, pardon, [illegible].
O'Cannan, Conor and Donell, pardon, [illegible].
O'Cannane, Tho., murder of, 1[illegible].
O'Cannon, Shane and Wm., pardon, [illegible].
O'Cannovane, Rich., pardon, [illegible].
O'Cannyn, Ennys, pardon, [illegible].
O'Canolan, Donell, pardon, [illegible].
O'Canoran, John or Shane, pardon, 6411.
O'Cantle, Donogh, pardon, [illegible].
O'Canty, Dermot, pardon, [illegible].
O'Cany, Thady, pardon, 14[illegible].
O'Canyn, James, pardon, [illegible].
O'Canyve, Tho., pardon, [illegible].
O'Caphowagh — Capphowagh, persons of the name pardoned, [illegible], [illegible].
O'Capphowe, Tho., pardon, [illegible].
O'Caran, Teig, pardon, [illegible].
O'Carban, Teig, alias O'Heavane, pardon, [illegible].
„ Owen, pardon, [illegible].
O'Carbane, Loghlin, pardon, [illegible].
O'Carbery — Carberie—Carbry, persons of the name pardoned, [illegible], [illegible], [illegible].
O'Carbie, Morinus or Morrow, English liberty, [illegible].
O'Carborie, Rich., pardon, [illegible].
O'Carbry. *See* O'Carbery.
O'Care, Hugh, pardon, [illegible].
O'Carell, Tirrelagh, pardon, [illegible].
O'Carhe, Donogh, pardon, [illegible].
O'Carhie, Neill, pardon, [illegible].
O'Carhy, Conoghor and Hugh, pardon, [illegible], [illegible].
O'Carie, Wm., pardon, [illegible].
O'Carmacle, Dermot, pardon, [illegible].
O'Carmodie—Karmody, persons of the name pardoned, [illegible], [illegible], [illegible], [illegible].
O'Carne, Melaghlin, pardon, [illegible].
O'Carnahe, Donogh, pardon, [illegible].
O'Carny—Carnie, persons of the name pardoned, [illegible].
O'Carolan. *See* O'Carrolan.
O'Caroll. *See* O'Carroll.
O'Carr, persons of the name pardoned, [illegible], [illegible].
O'Carrain, Conoghor, pardon, [illegible].
O'Carraine, Donald, pardon, [illegible].
O'Carralan, Hugh and Wm., pardon, [illegible].
O'Carrall. *See* O'Carroll.
O'Carran — Carrane, persons of the name pardoned, [illegible], [illegible], [illegible]-10, [illegible], [illegible], [illegible], [illegible], [illegible], [illegible], 5144, [illegible], [illegible], 5178, [illegible], [illegible], [illegible], [illegible], [illegible], [illegible], [illegible], [illegible].
„ *See* O'Carron.
O'Carre, Donogh, pardon, [illegible].
O'Carroll. *See* O'Carroll.
O'Carren, Melaghlin roe, lands of granted, [illegible].

INDEX TO FIANTS—ELIZABETH.

O'Carrie, Brian, pardon, [illegible].
O'Carrol. *See* O'Carroll.
O'Carrolan—O'Carolan, persons of the name pardoned, 4716, [illegible], [illegible], [illegible].
" *See* O'Karrulan.
O'Carrole, Mulronie (O'Carroll), pardon, [illegible].
O'Carroll—Caroll—Carrall—Carvell—Carrol—Karoll—Keroll—Karroll—Kearowell—Kearoll—Kerrall—Kerrolle—Kerrole—Kerrall—Keroll:
" Charles (of Leamonvanan), chief of his name, and knight, commission 4117; pardon, 4120, 4101, [illegible], [illegible]; pardon at his suit, 4187.
" Donogh and Thady, English liberty, [illegible].
" Donoghane, alias M'Guyskine (in co. Rosc.), pardon, [illegible].
" Johanna, claims to be wife of baron of Leitrim, 4478.
" John, lease, 978–4, 1618, [illegible]; chief of his name, [illegible].
" Mulrone M'Euycashin, pardon, [illegible].
" Mulrony m'Wm. (of Leam Ivanen), chief of his name, pardon, [illegible]; commission, [illegible].
" Owny m'Mulrony (of Modreeny), pardon, [illegible], [illegible], [illegible], [illegible].
" William owre, chief of his nation and knight, made captain, 41; pardon, 40, 874, 1741, [illegible], [illegible]; lease, 973, 1618; his son, [illegible], 3788; surrender and regrant of his possessions, [illegible].
" Wm., alias O'Hally, pardon, [illegible].
" others of the name pardoned, [illegible], [illegible], [illegible], [illegible], 910, [illegible], [illegible], [illegible], 1741, [illegible].
" lordship of, 973, [illegible], [illegible].
" country of, [illegible], 978–4, [illegible], [illegible], [illegible], [illegible]; excepted from government of president of Munster, [illegible].
O'Carron, Cahir, pardon, [illegible].
O'Carrooll, persons of the name pardoned, [illegible], [illegible], [illegible].
O'Carrovan, Denis, pardon, [illegible].
O'Carrovell, Daniel, pardon, [illegible].
O'Carrowill, Wm., pardon, 1517.
O'Carrowyll, Brian, pardon, [illegible].
O'Carrulan, Owen, pardon, [illegible].
O'Carrule, persons of the name pardoned, [illegible], [illegible], [illegible].
O'Carrull, Donell, pardon, [illegible].
O'Carryhane, Owny, pardon, [illegible].
O'Carryhin, Dermod, pardon, [illegible].
O'Cartan, persons of the name pardoned, [illegible], [illegible], [illegible], [illegible].
O'Cartayne—Cartaine, Shane, pardon, [illegible], [illegible], [illegible].
O'Cartie, Donell and Saly, pardon, [illegible], [illegible].
O'Cartry, Edm., death of, [illegible].
O'Carvell, Bryn and David, pardon, [illegible], [illegible].
O'Carvan, Wm., pardon, [illegible].
O'Carwell, Wm. (*see* O'Carroll), [illegible].
O'Cary, Dermot, alias M'Donoghow, pardon, [illegible].
O'Caryn, Dermot, pardon, [illegible].
O'Case, Shane, pardon, [illegible].
O'Casedye, Teig, pardon, [illegible].
O'Casey, persons of the name pardoned, [illegible], [illegible], [illegible].
O'Cashede—Cashedee, Hugh and Moriah, pardon, [illegible].
O'Cashedin, Edm., pardon, [illegible].
O'Cashedy, persons of the name pardoned, [illegible].
O'Cashine, Owen, pardon, [illegible].
O'Cashely, Neal, pardon, [illegible].
O'Casie—Casy:
" a son of, [illegible]
" Conor, priest, pardon, [illegible].
" Donell duff (of Castlereagh, co. Long.), pardon, [illegible].
" others of the name pardoned, [illegible], [illegible], [illegible], [illegible], [illegible], [illegible], [illegible], [illegible], [illegible], [illegible], [illegible]. *See* O'Casye.
O'Cassedie, Patrick, sergeant, pardon, [illegible].
O'Cassen, Feghar, pardon, [illegible].
O'Cassedie, Cornelius, pardon, [illegible].
O'Cassedy—Cassydie—Cassiddy, persons of the name pardoned, [illegible], [illegible].
O'Cassey, persons of the name pardoned, [illegible].
O'Casshell, persons of the name pardoned, [illegible].
O'Casshid, persons of the name pardoned, [illegible].
O'Cassidie, persons of the name pardoned, [illegible].
O'Cassidie, persons of the name pardoned, [illegible], [illegible].
O'Cassidy (*see* O'Cassedy), [illegible].
O'Casie, Tho., pardon, [illegible].
O'Casein, Tho., pardon, [illegible].
O'Casey, persons of the name pardoned, [illegible], [illegible], [illegible], [illegible].

INDEX TO FIANTS—ELIZABETH.

O'Casrydie (see O'Cassidy), [illegible].
O'Casryne, Rory, pardon, [illegible].
O'Caste, Dermod, pardon, 6377.
O'Castigne, Wm., pardon, [illegible].
O'Casy. See O'Caste.
O'Casydy, Neill or Nolanus, pardon, 1577.
O'Casye, persons of the name pardoned, [illegible], [illegible].
O'Caifroth, Donogho, pardon, 6100.
O'Cathane—Cathaine—Cathine, persons of the name pardoned, [illegible].
O'Cawertie, Moleghlin, pardon, [illegible].
O'Caye, Wm., pardon, [illegible].
O'Ccaine, Ocohonaght, pardon, [illegible].
O'Ccarroll. See O'Carroll.
Occhonghor, Terence, English liberty, 71.
O'Cchonor. See O'Connor.
Occkelly—Ocinkiley, persons of the name pardoned, [illegible].
O'Cconnor—O'Ccenor. See O'Connor.
Occupations of the persons pardoned, stated with special frequency, 6487, [illegible], [illegible], [illegible], [illegible], 6737, [illegible].
O'Ccurren. See O'Curren.
O'Ceallaghan, Donogh, pardon, [illegible].
O'Celly, Derby, pardon, [illegible].
O'Cercolde, Owen, pardon, [illegible].
O'Cesertie, Owen, pardon, [illegible].
O'Cestie, co. Kerry, [illegible].
O'Chaell, Finin, pardon, [illegible].
O'Chaardyne, Hugh, pardon, [illegible].
O'Chagell, Cnnoghor, pardon, 6802.
O'Chahessy. See O'Cahessie.
O'Chabriane, Donne, pardon, 4744.
O'Challaghan. See O'Callaghan.
O'Chan, 6015. See O'Cahan.
O'Chanchoune, Dalogh, pardon, [illegible].
O'Chane, Tho., clerk, lease, [illegible].
O'Chanty, Dermod, pardon, 5784.
O'Charnie, Bryan, pardon, [illegible].
O'Charry, Brian, pardon, [illegible].
O'Chary, Manus, pardon, [illegible].
O'Chasse, Conoghor, pardon, [illegible].
O'Chasse, Shane, pardon, [illegible].
O'Cheligham, John and Wm., pardon, [illegible].
O'Chelm, Hugh, pardon, [illegible].
O'Chonchonan, Donald, pardon, [illegible].
O'Chere, Hugh and Wm., pardon, [illegible].
O'Choghes, Caroll, pardon, [illegible].
O'Chohere, Mahon, pardon, [illegible].
O'Chonchanin—Chonchanya. See O'Concannon.
O'Chone, Morice, pardon, [illegible].
O'Choughor. See O'Connor.
O'Chonor, Rory, pardon, 10. See O'Connor.
Ochony, Patr., clerk, pardon, 6441.
O'Choogan (or O'Hoogan), Conohor, pardon, [illegible].
O'Chorne, Dionysius, English liberty, 14.
O'Chorcran, Hugh, pardon, 4310.
O Chorrhan, Wm., pardon, [illegible].
O'Choyne, Morgh., pardon, [illegible].
O'Clabby, Shane, pardon, [illegible].
O'Clackeryt, Teig, pardon, [illegible].
O'Clamper, Gerald, pardon, [illegible].
O'Clanahan, John, pardon, [illegible].
O'Clancie, Donogh, pardon, [illegible].
O'Clancy, Fyhill, pardon, [illegible].
O'Clanchey, Tho., pardon, [illegible].
O'Clanlowe—Clanlow, persons of the name pardoned, [illegible].
O'Clanmolaghlin, persons of the name pardoned, [illegible].
O'Clare, Oliver, pardon, [illegible].
O'Clavan, Edm., pardon, [illegible].
O'Cleanchane, Ferall, clerk, pardon, [illegible].
O'Cleare, Ennis, pardon, [illegible].
O'Clearie—Cleary. See O'Clery.
O'Cleere, Edw., pardon, [illegible].
O'Clearie, Owen, pardon, [illegible], [illegible].
O'Cleeran, Wm., pardon, [illegible].
O'Clere, persons of the name pardoned, 1343, 1617, 2021, 2026, [illegible], [illegible], [illegible], [illegible], [illegible], [illegible].
O'Cleroghe, Gilpatrick and Simon, pardon, [illegible].
O'Clerian, Con, Brein, Patr., Shane, and Thomas, grant of land, [illegible].
O'Clerie. See O'Clery.
O'Clerky, Thady, pardon, [illegible].
O'Clery—Clerie—Cleary—Clearie—Clerye—Klery—Y Clerie:
Gilleduff, attainted, [illegible], [illegible], [illegible].
others of the name pardoned, 1319, 1617, [illegible], 2357, [illegible], [illegible], 2348, [illegible], 4370, [illegible], [illegible], [illegible], 4731, [illegible], [illegible], [illegible], [illegible], [illegible], [illegible], [illegible], [illegible], [illegible], [illegible]-[illegible], [illegible]-[illegible], [illegible].
O'Clie, Donell, pardon, [illegible].
O'Clirie, James, pardon, 4737.
O'Clivan, Murtagh, murder of, [illegible].
O'Cloan—Cloane, Conor and Finn, pardon, [illegible], [illegible].
O'Clohaine, Brian, pardon, [illegible].
O'Cloghane, Morogh, pardon, [illegible].
O'Clogherie, David, pardon, [illegible].
O'Cloghessy, Edm., pardon, [illegible].
O'Cloghus, Donogh, pardon, [illegible].
O'Clognie, Teig, alias O'Bryn, pardon, [illegible].
O'Clohessy, Owen, pardon, [illegible].
O'Clondowill, Cormic, robbed, [illegible].
O'Cloogh, Dermot, pardon, 4174.
O'Clory, Henry and Murtagh, pardon, [illegible], [illegible].
O'Cloven, persons of the name pardoned, [illegible], [illegible].

INDEX TO FIANTS—ELIZABETH.

O'Clovane, persons of the name pardoned, [illegible], [illegible].
O'Clowan, Donald, English liberty, 112.
" others of the name pardoned, [illegible], 6798.
O'Clowne, Dermot, pardon, 4517.
O'Cluan, Dermod, pardon, [illegible].
O'Cluane, Moylmory, [illegible].
O'Clniwyne, Conoghor, pardon, 3150.
O'Cnochour, Gerald, pardon, 3444.
O'Cnoghor, Donogh, pardon, 6448.
O'Cnoghor, Donoghe, pardon, 6170.
O'Coam, Brian, pardon, 4818.
O'Coan, Hugh and Teig, clerks, pardon, 4447.
" others of the name pardoned, 5448.
O'Coanye, Donell and Brasill, pardon, 6901.
O'Coayn, Brian, pardon, 4081.
O'Cockhlan, Cormock and Moriertagh, pardon, [illegible].
O'Coddie, James, pardon, 6704.
O'Codihie—Coddihie—Codyhie—Kaddyhy, persons of the name pardoned, 1048, 3048, [illegible], 6704.
O'Cody, Donogh, pardon, 2462.
O'Codyhie. See O'Codihie.
O'Cougly—Coogllo, persons of the name pardoned, [illegible].
O'Coell, persons of the name pardoned, [illegible].
O'Coely, Conoch, surgeon, pardon, 4084.
O'Coffie—Coffy—Coffye—Coffee—Koffie:
" Con, lessee, [illegible], [illegible]; grant, 4470.
" Donell, clerk, pardon, 6978.
" others of the name pardoned, 848, 874, [illegible], 1294, 1308, [illegible], 1764, [illegible], [illegible], [illegible], [illegible], [illegible], [illegible], 6014, [illegible], [illegible], [illegible], [illegible], [illegible], [illegible], [illegible], [illegible], [illegible], [illegible].
O'Cogan, Dermot, pardon, 2378, [illegible].
O'Coghane, Wm., pardon, 6812.
O'Coghelane, Teig, pardon, 6616.
O'Coghie, persons of the name pardoned, [illegible].
O'Coghlan, Philip, pardon, [illegible].
O'Coghlaine, Donell, pardon, 6811.
O'Coghlane—Coghlan, persons of the name pardoned, [illegible], 4678, [illegible], [illegible], 6191, [illegible], [illegible], [illegible], [illegible], 6770.
O'Coghy, Hugh, pardon, 6702.
O'Cogran, Donogh, pardon, 4712, [illegible].
O'Cohallan, Conoghor, pardon, 6914.
O'Cohane, Hugh, pardon, [illegible].
O'Cohy, Cormock and Wm., pardon, [illegible], [illegible].
O'Coillane—Coilane, Morice, pardon, 6467, [illegible].
O'Coine, persons of the name pardoned, [illegible], [illegible], 6764.
O'Coinall, Rich., pardon, 977.
O'Coinnill, Thos., pardon, [illegible].
O'Coishe, Wm., pardon, 10.
O'Colan—Colane, persons of the name pardoned, 6118, [illegible], 6977.
O'Coleyman, Rory, pardon, [illegible].
O'Colgan—Colgane—Colgin—Kolgan—Kolgane, persons of the name pardoned, 10, [illegible], [illegible], [illegible], 1327, [illegible], [illegible].
O'Colgy, Art, pardon, [illegible].
O'Colin, Laghlin, [illegible].
O'Collaine. See O'Collane.
O'Collan, persons of the name pardoned, [illegible], [illegible], [illegible], [illegible], [illegible], 6714.
O'Collanan, John, pardon, 6770.
O'Collanane, John and Onory, pardon, 6707.
O'Collane—Collaine, persons of the name pardoned, 10, 4467, [illegible], [illegible], [illegible], 6770.
O'Colle, Hugh, pardon, 4844.
O'Collena, John, pardon, 4618.
O'Collerane, Shane, pardon, 6784.
O'Collevane—Collevain, persons of the name pardoned, [illegible], 6764-6.
O'Collewarn, Henry, pardon, 1749.
O'Colleran—Colleriane, persons of the name pardoned, 1862, [illegible], [illegible], [illegible], 6727.
O'Collhane, Donogh, pardon, 6460.
O'Colliaghe, Tirlogh, pardon, 6460.
O'Collian, Ferall and Une, pardon, 6448.
O'Colliman—Collimaine. See O'Colman.
O'Colline, persons of the name pardoned, [illegible], 6977, 6616.
O'Collogan, Dermot and Rich., pardon, [illegible], 6174.
O'Collomayne, Morish, pardon, [illegible].
O'Collon, Ferall and Morgh, pardon, [illegible], [illegible].
O'Collomayne, Gillepatrick, pardon, 4627.
O'Collone, Morogh, pardon, 6727.
O'Colloupy, Wm., pardon, [illegible].
O'Colly, Nich., clerk, pardon, [illegible].
" others of the name pardoned, [illegible], 4763.
O'Collymane, Teig, pardon, [illegible].
O'Collymane, John, pardon, 6747.
O'Colman—Colliman—Collimaine, persons of the name pardoned, 1147, [illegible], [illegible], 6478, [illegible], [illegible], 6766.
O'Colmane, Teig, pardon, [illegible].
O'Comain — Comaine, persons of the name pardoned, 4714, [illegible], [illegible], [illegible].
O'Coman, persons of the name pardoned, [illegible], [illegible], [illegible], [illegible], [illegible], [illegible], 4712, [illegible], [illegible], [illegible], [illegible], [illegible], [illegible], [illegible], [illegible], [illegible], [illegible], [illegible], [illegible], [illegible].
O'Comane, persons of the name pardoned, 1048, 6467, 6765.
O'Comain, Philip and Rory, pardon, [illegible].
O'Comman, Walter, pardon, [illegible].
O'Comon, Dermot, pardon, [illegible].
O'Cony, Edm., pardon, [illegible].

O'Conyle, Moriah, pardon, 4412.

O'Conyn, Cormack and Dermot, pardon, [illegible].

O'Con, Edm. and Shane, pardon, 4216, 6466.

O'Conaghinine, Rory, pardon, 5183.

O'Conaill, Riccard, pardon, [illegible].

O'Conalane, Henry (see O'Connalane), pardon, 5781.

O'Conally. See O'Connally.

O'Conally, Gilleroew, pardon, 4891.

O'Cogan, persons of the name pardoned, 1312, 4944, 5718.

O'Conahan, Gerald and Wm., pardon, 5460.

O'Conane, James, pardon, [illegible].

O'Conbu, persons of the name pardoned, 2928, [illegible], 6121, 6763.

O'Concannon — Conchanon — Conchanin — Conchonyne — Conkennon — Conkenain — Chonchanin — Chonchanyn:
- Cahill, pardon, 1475; tanist of Corcamoy, co. Gal., 6318.
- others of the name pardoned, 1474, 1476, 4074, [illegible], 4732, 4780, 5113, [illegible], [illegible], 5711, [illegible].

O'Conchor, Brian and Gilletuff, pardon, [illegible]. See O'Connor.

O'Conchonyne. See O'Concannon.

O'Cone, persons of the name pardoned, 2173, 6784.

O'Conegan, Teig, pardon, 5109.

O'Conelan. See O'Connellan.

O'Conell. See O'Connell.

O'Conelan—Conelaine. See O'Connellan.

O'Conely, Tuole, pardon, 6794.

O'Coner. See O'Conor.

O'Conerau, Edm. (see O'Connoran), 6517.

O'Conery—Conerie—I Conerie—Y Conerye:
- David, alias M'Awnorye, pardon, 625, [illegible].
- others of the name pardoned, [illegible], 1073, [illegible], [illegible], [illegible], [illegible], [illegible], [illegible], [illegible], 5714.

O'Conew—Conewe:
- Dermod, clerk, pardon, 4497.
- others of the name pardoned, [illegible].

O'Coneye, Shane, pardon, 5116.

O'Congan, Shane, pardon, [illegible].

O'Conghor—Conher. See O'Connor.

O'Conie, Shane, pardon, 4946.

O'Conigan—Y Conigane, persons of the name pardoned, [illegible], [illegible], 5748.

O'Conighan, Brian, pardon, 4516.

O'Conilan. See O'Connellan.

O'Conill. See O'Connell.

O'Conillan. See O'Connellan.

O'Conkenain—Conkennon. See O'Concannon.

O'Conlagh, [illegible], pardon, [illegible].

O'Conlan, Laughlin, pardon, 6904.

O'Conlin, Philip, pardon, 5785.

O'Connaghiane, Thady, pardon, 6416.

O'Connalane—Conalane, Henry and Philip, pardon, 5781.

O'Connell. See O'Connell.

O'Connalloy. See O'Connally.

O'Connallo, persons of the name pardoned, 4944, 4878.

O'Connally—Connalloy—Conaly, persons of the name pardoned, 4944, 4468, 5781, 6612.

O'Connane, Donogh, pardon, 4571.

O'Connchor, persons of the name pardoned, 6784.

O'Conne, persons of the name pardoned, 3548, 5778.

O'Connoghane, Hugh, pardon, [illegible].

O'Conneiane. See O'Connellan.

O'Connell—Conell—Connill—Conill—Conall—Connyll—Conyll—Konell—Konill—Konnell—Konnyll—I Conell—Y Conell—I Conell—Y Connell:
- Owen, kearn, 4182.
- others of the name pardoned, 445, 1648, 1237, [illegible], [illegible], [illegible], [illegible], [illegible], 2297, [illegible], [illegible], [illegible], [illegible], 2806, [illegible], [illegible], [illegible], [illegible], [illegible], [illegible], [illegible], [illegible], [illegible], [illegible], [illegible], [illegible], [illegible], [illegible], [illegible], [illegible], [illegible], [illegible], [illegible], 4677, [illegible], [illegible], 4744, [illegible], 4781, [illegible], [illegible], [illegible], [illegible], 5178, [illegible], [illegible], [illegible], [illegible], [illegible], 5745, 5784, [illegible], [illegible], [illegible], [illegible], [illegible], [illegible], [illegible], [illegible], [illegible], [illegible], [illegible], [illegible], [illegible], 6407, [illegible], [illegible], [illegible], [illegible], [illegible], [illegible], [illegible], [illegible], [illegible], [illegible], [illegible], [illegible], [illegible], [illegible], [illegible], [illegible], [illegible], [illegible], 6571, [illegible], [illegible], [illegible], [illegible], [illegible], [illegible], 6710, [illegible], 6764–5.

O'Connellan—Connelane—Conelan—Connellaine—Conellan—Conilan—Conillan—Konylan—Konylan, persons of the name pardoned, [illegible], [illegible], 5713, [illegible], 4702, [illegible], 4741, [illegible], 5108, 5614, [illegible], [illegible], [illegible], [illegible], [illegible], [illegible], [illegible], [illegible], [illegible], 6571, [illegible], [illegible]. See O'Conelan, O'Connellayne.

O'Connollie. See O'Connolly.

O'Connollen, persons of the name pardoned 5481.

O'Connolly—Connollie—Conoly, persons of the name pardoned, [illegible], 5183, [illegible].

O'Connor. See O'Conor.

O'Connoran—Conoran, Dermot and Edm., pardon, 6456, 6517.

O'Connory—Connorie—I Connorie—Y Connory, persons of the name pardoned, 4612, [illegible], 6466, 6473, 6614.

INDEX TO FIANTS—ELIZABETH.

O'Connigaine, John, pardon, 6417.
O'Connigan, Ervin, pardon, [illegible].
O'Connigane, Hugh, priest, pardon, 6448.
O'Connill. *See* O'Connell.
O'Connly, Cormock, pardon, 6374.
O'Connoe, Shane, pardon, 4118.
O'Connogh, Owen, pardon, 6427.
O'Connoghor, persons of the name in co. Clare pardoned, 4743, 6363, 6617, 6773.
" *See* O'Connor.
O'Connole—Connolay. *See* O'Connolly.
O'Connoll, Cormock, pardon, 5494.
O'Connollane—Connollayne, Donogh, pardon, 4451, 6374.
O'Connolloy. *See* O'Connolly.
O'Connollayne. *See* O'Connollane.
O'Connolly—Connole—Connolay—Connollay—Connoly:
" Tirlogh, chief of his name and vice-marshal to M'Mahon, grant of lands, 4664.
" others of the name pardoned, 5402, 6722.
O'Connor—Conor—Conoghor—Connoghor—Conchor—Conghor—Conhor—Conner—Oconor—Choughor—Knogher—Knoghor—Konchour—Kunnor—Konor—I or Y Connoghor, Conoghor or Connor:
" Callogh m'Tirrelagh (of Cloonmurry, co. Rosc.), attainted, 6285.
" Dermot: O'Conor Don, pardon, 433, 1688; appointed captain of his country, 1683; chief lord of O'Hanly's country, 1562.
" Dermot m'Carbrey keigh, attainted, 6243.
" Donell, knight: O'Conor Sligo, surrenders name of O'Conor Sligo, regrant of his lands, 4830; agreement with, 4841; pardon, 4869; pardon at his suit, 6068; commissions, 4687, 4733, 4748.
" Donell m'Shane Bgyn, attainted, 6302.
" Hugh m'Dermot: O'Conor Don, pardon, 1294, 4644, 4616; regrant of his possessions after surrender, 4484; composition with, 4464.
" Hugh m'Tirlagh roe, appointed tanist of O'Conor Roe, 4827; pardon, 4884, 4944; attainted, 6160, 6160, [illegible], 6616.
" Maowe, alias Bourke, pardon, 6666.
O'Connor, Owen, pardon, 4706; commission, 4732.
" Rory grane m'Phelim boy, attainted, 5844; pardon, 6158, 6621.
" Teig oge: O'Conor Roe, appointed captain of his country, 1591, pardon, 1888-90, 6484; attainted, 6606.
" Teig boy, pardon, 4741, 6411.
" Thady, father of O'Conor Sligo, 4461.
" Tirlagh roe, pardon, 4741, 6611; attainted, 6777.
" Tirrelagh roe: O'Conor Roe, 1591; son of, 6140, 6160.
" others of the name in counties Rosc. and Sligo, pardoned, 1589-90, 3753-4, 3834, 3924, 4031, 4073-4, 4076-7, 4078, 4340, 4544, 4663, 4647, 4673, 4686, 4708, 4741, 4777, 4878, 4873, 4877, 4944, 5009, 5038, 5112, 6158, 5430, 5428, 6464, 5462, 5463, 5478, 5473, 5486, 5488, 5604, 5634, 5648, 5597, 5606, 5611, 5616-8, 5662, 5684, 5715, 5740, 5802, 5806, 5808, 5815, 5848, 6460.
" Brian, attainted, 614, 2890, 6798.
" Brian m'Cahir, son of, 610.
" Brian, son of Callogh roe (of Derrymollan), wardship, 3909, livery, 4400; pardon 6777.
" Callagh roe m'Teig, grant of land, 589; pardon, 717; his heir, 3909, 4400.
" Callagh or Charles, son of Brian m'Cahir, grant of land, 610, 3838, pardon, 618.
" Callagh, murder of, 717.
" Charles, grant of land, 672.
" Con, English liberty, 1502.
" Cormock boy, murder of, 6748.
" Cornelius, English liberty, 148.
" Margaret, English liberty, 228.
" Morogh carrogh, pardon, 3934.
" Moriagh O'Cogy, pardon, 3834.
" Nicholas Gwenllys, murder of, 1083, 1360.
" Phelim, house in Trim, 1714.
" Teig or Thady m'Cahir, grant of land, 589; pardon, 717.
" Teig m'Gillepatrick, pardon, 432, 814, 2884, 4388, 5174.
" Terence, English liberty, 74.
" others of the name in Offaly and adjoining districts, pardoned, 10, 98, 254, 549, 449-51, 574, 618, 662, 750, 763, 810, 847, 1084, 1143, 1144-6, 1373, 1387, 1408, 1458, 1761, 1808,

O'Connor:
[illegible], [illegible], 2900, [illegible], 3084, [illegible], [illegible], 3410, [illegible], 4280, [illegible], 4580, 4581, 5146, 5274, 5189, [illegible], [illegible], [illegible], 6472, [illegible], 6454, 6714, [illegible], 6776, 6777.
" Brian (of Carrigafoile, co. Kerry), attainted, 6128.
" Conoghor (of Carrigafoile, co. Kerry), attainted, 6128.
" Knoghor (of Ireghticonnor), his heir, 4816.
" John, wardship, 4816; pardon, 6471; excepted from pardon, 6772.
" others of the name in co. Kerry, pardoned, [illegible], 4512, 4677, 4718, [illegible], [illegible], 5610, 6183, 6477, 6479, [illegible], [illegible], [illegible], 6578.
" Teig na gall (in co. Clare), attainted, 4872.
" others of the name in co. Clare pardoned, [illegible], 4728, [illegible], [illegible], [illegible], [illegible].
" persons of the name in other districts, pardoned, 1747, 1751, 2834, 2847, [illegible], [illegible], [illegible], 4274, [illegible], [illegible], 4418, 4418, 4419, [illegible], 4761, 4764, 4768, 4864, [illegible], [illegible], 4897, 5049, 5416, 5170, [illegible], [illegible], [illegible], [illegible], 6476, 6484, 6487, [illegible], [illegible], 6514–5, [illegible], [illegible], [illegible], [illegible], 6671–2, [illegible], [illegible], 6707, 6714, 6724, [illegible].
" *See also* O'Conchor and O'Connohor.
O'Connor Don. *See* O'Connor, Dermot and Hugh.
" country of, 1681, 6131, [illegible], [illegible], [illegible].
O'Connor Roe. *See* O'Connor, Tirrelagh roe, and Teig oge.
" country of, 1446, 4457, 6120–1, [illegible], [illegible], [illegible], 6777, [illegible], [illegible]; chief of, [illegible]; tanist of, [illegible], [illegible].
O'Connor Sligo. *See* O'Connor, Donell.
" " —Sligagh—Slygogh, country of, 1446, [illegible], [illegible], 5160, 6341, [illegible], 4407, [illegible], [illegible].
O'Connors (of Offaly), war made on, [illegible], [illegible], 2144, [illegible], [illegible], 2872, [illegible], [illegible], [illegible], [illegible]; excluded from pardons, [illegible], [illegible], [illegible], [illegible], [illegible].
O'Connorde, Rory, pardon, [illegible].
O'Connoran, Owny (of the Fivagh, co. Antrim), pardon, 6716.
O'Connoure, Dermod, pardon, [illegible].
O'Connour, Cahine, English liberty, [illegible].
" Donald and Kedagh, pardon, [illegible].
O Connow—Connowe—Conowe—Konowe—I or Y Connowe, persons of the name pardoned, 2048, [illegible], [illegible]–8, [illegible], [illegible], [illegible], [illegible], 4731, [illegible], 5118, [illegible], [illegible], [illegible], [illegible], [illegible], [illegible], [illegible], [illegible], [illegible], [illegible], [illegible].
O'Connugh, Morris, pardon, [illegible].
O'Connyll. *See* O'Connell.
O'Connys, Rory and Tho., pardon, [illegible].
O'Conogan, Mulmorie, pardon, [illegible].
O'Conoge, Knoghor and Rory, pardon, [illegible].
O'Conoghan—Conoghane, Donogh, pardon, [illegible], [illegible].
O'Conoghance, John, pardon, [illegible].
O'Conoghor. *See* O'Connor.
O'Conolan—Conolane—Conollan—Konlloyne—Konolloyne, persons of the name pardoned, [illegible], 1257–8, 3412, [illegible], [illegible], [illegible], [illegible], [illegible].
O'Conoloy, Phir., pardon, [illegible].
O'Conolie, Art, pardon, 6734.
O'Conollan. *See* O'Conolan.
O'Conor. *See* O'Connor.
O'Conorne, persons of the name pardoned, [illegible], [illegible], [illegible].
O'Conorogh, Wm., pardon, [illegible].
O'Conorey, Owen, pardon, [illegible].
O'Conover, Gerald, pardon, [illegible].
O'Conoughan, Donell, pardon, [illegible].
O'Conovor, Wm., English liberty, [illegible].
O'Conowe—Conow. *See* O'Connow.
O'Conowghaime, Hugh, pardon, [illegible].
O'Conra, persons of the name pardoned, [illegible], [illegible].
O'Conrahy, Donogh, pardon, 2146.
O'Conran, Donagh, pardon, [illegible].
O'Conrey, John or Shane more, pardon, [illegible].
O'Conrie—Conry—Conrye, persons of the name pardoned, [illegible], [illegible], [illegible], [illegible], [illegible].
O'Contreyney, Denis or Donogh, pardon, [illegible].
O'Conty, Cormock and Dermod, pardon, [illegible], [illegible].
O'Convun, Mologhlin, pardon, [illegible].
O'Conway—Conwaie, persons of the name pardoned, [illegible], [illegible].
O'Conwey, persons of the name pardoned, [illegible].
O'Cony, Walter, pardon, [illegible].
O'Conye, Geoffrey, pardon, [illegible].
O'Conygan—I Conygan, persons of the name pardoned, [illegible], [illegible], [illegible].
O'Conygay, Shane, pardon, [illegible].
O'Conylane, Edm., pardon, [illegible].
O'Conyll. *See* O'Connell.
O'Conyllane, Shane, pardon, [illegible].
O'Conyn, Conoghor and Tho. (of Tralee), pardon, [illegible].
O'Conyne, John, pardon, [illegible].
O Coony, Shane, pardon, [illegible].

INDEX TO FIANTS—ELIZABETH.

O'Coran, Rich. Bourk m'Doyll (= m'Donlevan an chorain, or son of "Devil's Hook"), pardon, 6783.
O'Corane, Teig, pardon, 6671.
O'Corbac, Tho., pardon, 6671.
O'Corban — Corbane, persons of the name pardoned, 674, 1063, 3234, [illegible], [illegible], 5448, [illegible], [illegible], 6466, 6477, 6617, 6630, 6703, 6762, 6766.
O'Corbin, Dermod, pardon, 4773.
O'Corcheran — Corkran — Korcrane, persons of the name pardoned, 4844, 4980, 6484, [illegible], [illegible]. See O'Corkeran, O'Corkran, O'Corkrane.
O'Corcran — Corcrane — Korkraine — Korkran, persons of the name pardoned, 676, 3707, 4018, 4693, 4888, 6718, 6421.
„ Cornelius, priest, pardon, 5802.
O'Coregan—Coregane, persons of the name pardoned, [illegible], 6776, 4780.
O'Corer, persons of the name pardoned, 4622.
O'Corerane, Tirlagh, pardon, 6788.
O'Corgan, persons of the name pardoned, 4347, 4078, 6623.
O'Corhane, Owen, pardon, 6630.
O'Corin, Donogh and Henry, pardon, 4494, 6492.
O'Coringe, Moriah, pardon, 4522.
O'Corkan, Wm. and Walter, pardon, 6674.
O'Corkeran — Corkerane, persons of the name pardoned, 3324, 6331, 6468, 6516, 6438–8, 6676.
O'Corkery — Corkerie—Corkirie— Korkerie —Korkyrye—I or Y Corkery, persons of the name pardoned, 6022, 4467, 6467, 6479, 6615, 6668, 6571, 6783, 6784.
O'Corkran, Conconagh and Florence, pardon, 4638, 6064.
O'Corkrane, persons of the name pardoned, 3483, 3743, 4161, 4498, 6848.
O'Corkyrane, John, pardon, 6672.
O'Cormack — Cormak, Edm. and Rich., pardon, 4672.
O'Corman, Mahon, pardon, 3082.
O'Cormane, David, pardon, 4279.
O'Cormocan, Donell, pardon, 6834.
O'Cormick—Kormick, persons of the name pardoned, 3281, 4468, 6679, 6708, 4773.
O'Cormock—Cormacke, persons of the name pardoned, 4442, 6673, 6678, 6764–6.
O'Cormocke, Donogho, pardon, 4768.
O'Cormokan, persons of the name pardoned, 4484, 6842.
O'Cormoke, Humfrey and Tho., pardon, 3068, 3089.
O'Cornor, Gildaff, pardon, 4678.
O'Cornamkan, Shane, pardon, 6634.
O'Cornally, Cahell, pardon, 5630.
O'Cornayoke, Dermot, pardon, 3499.
O'Cornin, John, pardon, 6561.
O'Cornmackan, Conoghor, pardon, 6467.
O'Corobnin, Tho., pardon, 4718.
O'Corohan, Teig, pardon, 6674.
O'Corogan, Donagh, pardon, 1418.
O'Corokane, Patr., pardon, 6328.
O'Corr—Corre, persons of the name pardoned, 6346, 6713–4.
O'Corraine, Donogh, pardon, 4806.
O'Corran, John and Philip, English liberty, 14.
„ —Corrane, others of the name pardoned, 3637, 4767, 6003, 6381, 6166, 6576.
O'Corre, Rory, pardon, 6718.
O'Corregan—Corrigane—Corrogane—Horrogan, persons of the name pardoned, 4036, 4330, 6642, 6130, 6468, 6682.
O'Corren, persons of the name pardoned, 6373, 6694, 6116, 6577.
O'Corrhan, Conor and Hugh, pardon, 1430, 6434.
O'Corrihane, persons of the name pardoned, 3347, 6660, 6761.
O'Corrie. See O'Corry.
O'Corrigane. See O'Corregan.
O'Corrin, Wm., pardon, 6483.
O'Corrugane. See O'Corregan.
O'Corry—Corrie, persons of the name pardoned, 1698, 6642.
O'Corryn, Teig and Dermod, pardon, 1038, 1741.
O'Cortly, Donell, pardon, 6872.
O'Corulayn, Gille-Isa and Wm., pardon, 4081.
O'Corvolan, Hugh, pardon, 1438.
O'Cory, Maleghlin, pardon, 6081.
O'Coryn—Coryne, persons of the name pardoned, 4036, 4823.
O'Cose, Shane, pardon, 6477.
O'Cosedy, Donell and Donogh, pardon, 4681.
O'Cosedy, Donagh and Maurice, pardon, 4161.
O'Cosgre, Harry, pardon, 4783.
O'Coshe, John, pardon, 6874.
O'Coshene, John, pardon, 1848.
O'Cosker, Edm., pardon, 6304.
O'Coskirr, Wm., pardon, 6440.
O'Coskry, Donogh, pardon, 6671.
O'Costegan, Gilpatrick, pardon 4481.
O'Costelloe h, Rich., pardon 6832.
O'Coufy, Oney, pardon, 180.
O'Coughlane, Philip, pardon, 4843.
O'Couigan, Derby and Hugh, pardon, 6884.
O'Coullaghane, Tho., pardon, 4824.
O'Coullane, Owen, pardon, 6714.
O'Coulaghan, Ea, pardon, 6418.

INDEX TO FIANTS—ELIZABETH.

O'Coultran, Felim and Neill, pardon, 6630.
O'Coungyn, Donogh, pardon, [illegible].
O'Counye, Shane, pardon, 4872.
O'Courinane, Shane, pardon, [illegible].
O'Cowan—Cowane—Kowan, persons of the name pardoned, [illegible], 4878, 5448, [illegible].
O'Cowgan, Wm., pardon, 6677.
O'Cowghane, Conor, pardon, 4478.
O'Cowhow, Shane, pardon, 5518.
O'Cowile, Wm., pardon, 5574.
O'Cowlane, Teig, pardon, [illegible].
O'Cowle, Edm., pardon, [illegible].
O'Cowltan, Tho. Balfe, pardon, [illegible].
O'Cowltayn, Gilladuff, English liberty, 177.
O'Cowne, James and Shane, pardon, 6761.
O'Cowman, James and William, pardon, 4080, [illegible].
O'Cownell, Donell, pardon, [illegible].
O'Cowny—Cowney—Cownie, persons of the name pardoned, [illegible], 5762.
O'Cowony, Donogh, pardon, [illegible].
O'Cowray, Morgan, English liberty, 177.
O'Coyll, pardon, [illegible].
" John, pardon, 6458.
O'Coylon, Mologhlin, pardon, [illegible].
O'Coyn, Padrickin, pardon, [illegible].
O'Coyne—Coyn—Koyne, persons of the name pardoned, 1608, 1589, 1879, 2041, 2771, [illegible], [illegible], 4115, [illegible], [illegible], 6487.
" Art m'Teig O'C. O'Byrne, pardon, [illegible].
O'Coynliske, Tomnliagh, pardon, 5815.
O'Coyune, Conor, pardon, 6622.
O'Coyske, persons of the name pardoned, 18.
O'Crahyn, Donald, pardon, 5774.
O'Cranyne, Donell, pardon, [illegible].
O'Craly, Dermot, pardon, 2284.
O'Crawie, Coole, pardon, [illegible].
O'Crean—Creane, Andrew, commission, 4732.
" James (of Sligo), pardon, [illegible].
" John, commission, 4732.
" others of the name pardoned, [illegible], 5498, 5761.
O'Crenyn, Rich., pardon, 6618.
O'Credane, Teig, pardon, 6487, [illegible].
" See O'Hredan.
O'Cremane, Morris, pardon, [illegible].
O'Creefe, Moriertagh, pardon, [illegible].
O'Creghan, Wm., pardon, [illegible].
" See O'Kreghan.
O'Crevan, Henry, pardon, 5424.
O'Creve, Teig and Moroghe, pardon, [illegible], [illegible].
" See O'Krew.
O'Crevy, Hugh, pardon, 1722.
O'Crey, Daniel, pardon, 4775.
O'Crieghan, Gillapatrick, pardon, 6714.
O'Crigan—Crigaine, Conor and Hugh, pardon, 6761.
O'Crinegan, Donell, pardon, [illegible].
O'Criohin, Shane, pardon, 6446.
O'Criane, persons of the name pardoned, 6761.
O'Crive, James, pardon, 5618.
O'Crivie, Meloghlin, pardon, 6367.
O'Crocrane, Cormac and Gillapatrick, pardon, [illegible].
O'Croghan, Conoghor, pardon, 6634.
O'Crokeran, Donogh, pardon, [illegible].
O'Croley, Conor, pardon, [illegible].
O'Croly, Edm., pardon, [illegible].
O'Crompe, Dermot, pardon, [illegible].
O'Cromane, Philip, pardon, 6742.
O'Cromine. See O'Cromyne.
O'Crompe, Dermot, pardon, 6612.
O'Cromy, Teig, pardon, [illegible].
O'Cromyne—Cromyn—Cromine—Kromyn, persons of the name pardoned, [illegible], 4742, [illegible], [illegible], 6467, 6469, [illegible], [illegible], 6784.
O'Cronan, Tho., robbery of, 142.
O'Crone, Shane, pardon, 6721.
O'Cronogill, Rory, pardon, [illegible].
O'Cronell, Neal, pardon, [illegible].
O'Cronoyll, Moriagh, pardon, 1442.
O'Cronigane, Dermod and Teig, pardon, [illegible].
O'Crunne. See O'Cronyne.
O'Cronogan, John, tailor, pardon, [illegible].
O'Cronowly, Wm., pardon, [illegible].
O'Cronully—Cronullie, Dermot and Hugh, pardon, [illegible], [illegible].
O'Cronyne—Cronine—Cronyn, persons of the name pardoned, [illegible], [illegible], 2048, [illegible], [illegible], [illegible], 4761, 4764, [illegible], [illegible], [illegible], [illegible], 6170, [illegible], 6477, [illegible], 6611, [illegible], [illegible], [illegible], [illegible], 6701, 6702, 6760.
O'Croson, Morris, pardon, [illegible].
O'Crottagh, Macurugh and Philip, pardon, 2234.
O'Crottie—Crotty—Krottie, persons of the name pardoned, [illegible], 4487, 6498, 6478, [illegible], [illegible], [illegible], 5534.
O'Crottine, Conor, pardon, [illegible].
O'Crotty. See O'Crottie.
O'Croweley, Awliff, pardon, 6770.
O'Crowine, Ellan Lasie, pardon, [illegible].
O'Crowle, Awliff, pardon, [illegible].
O'Crowly—Crowley—Crowlie—Crowlley—Crowllie—Crouly—Crwolie—I Crowly—Y Crowlie—I Crwoly:
" Dermod M'y Vallirty, pardon, 5518.
" Fynyn (of Dromgarriff), pardon, 2234.
" Florence: O'Crowly, pardon, [illegible].

INDEX TO FIANTS—ELIZABETH.

O'Crowly, Teig or Thady m'Dermot: O'Crowly, pardon, [illegible], [illegible], 6778.
" others of the name pardoned, 416, 1264, 2370, [illegible], [illegible], 4160, 4482, [illegible], [illegible], 6416-8, [illegible], [illegible], 6871, 6701, 6770.
O'Crowain—Crowaine—Crownyne, persons of the name pardoned, [illegible], [illegible].
O'Crownowe, Edm., pardon, 4267.
O'Crownyne. See O'Crowain.
O'Croyne, Shane, pardon, [illegible].
O'Croyne, Wm., pardon, 4491.
O'Crumveghane, Moris, pardon, [illegible].
O'Crunyne, Dermod, pardon, 6764.
O'Cruoegan, Donogh, and Fair., pardon, [illegible].
O'Cruoly—Crwolie—Crwoly. See O'Crowly.
O'Cryon, Teig, pardon, [illegible].
O'Cuayn, Rich., pardon, [illegible].
O'Cuacgrie, Rory, pardon, [illegible].
O'Cualane, John, pardon, [illegible].
O'Cuddie, Edm., pardon, 6704.
O'Cughlan, Wm., robbery from, 418.
O'Cughlane, Maurice, pardon, [illegible].
O'Cuirk—Cuircke—Cwirck, persons of the name pardoned, [illegible], [illegible].
O'Culan, David, pardon, 6034.
O'Culane, Shille, pardon, [illegible].
O'Culaine—Cullane—I Cullane, persons of the name pardoned, [illegible], 4416, 4484, [illegible], [illegible], [illegible], 6514, [illegible], [illegible], [illegible].
O'Cullan. See O'Cullen.
O'Cullanayne, Cowne, pardon, [illegible].
O'Cullane. See O'Cullaine.
O'Cullanie or O'Cullaine, Teig, pardon, [illegible].
O'Cullany, Tho. Crome, pardon, [illegible].
O'Cullayn, Fair., alias Groanye, pardon, 1161.
O'Cullayne, Dermod and Donell, pardon, 4416, 4493.
O'Culleman, John, pardon, 18.
O'Cullenane, Donell, pardon, 6837.
O'Cullen, Shane, pardon, [illegible]. See O'Cullen.
O'Culleman—Culliman—Cullyman—I Culliman —Y Cullinane:
" Conoghor, Daniel, Donogh, pipers, pardon, [illegible], 5971.
" others of the name pardoned, 4717, [illegible], [illegible], [illegible], [illegible], 6871, 6761, 6784.
O'Cullin. See O'Cullen.
O'Culliman. See O'Culleman.
O'Culline, Donill, pardon, [illegible].
O'Cullie, Farrell, pardon, 4158.
O'Cullen—Cullan—Cullen—Cullin—Cullens —Kullen—Hullen:
" Edm., surgeon, pardon, 6617.
" Shane, sheep stolen from, 3679.
O'Cullen, others of the name pardoned, 914, 2370, [illegible], [illegible], [illegible], [illegible], [illegible], [illegible], 4418, 4721, 4789, 4877, [illegible], 6170, 6190-8, [illegible], [illegible], [illegible], [illegible], [illegible], 6401, 6477, [illegible], [illegible], [illegible], [illegible], [illegible], [illegible], [illegible], [illegible], 6714, 6707, 6772.
O'Culloman, John, pardon, [illegible].
O'Cullogan. See O'Cullen.
O'Cullyman. See O'Culleman.
O'Cultacker, Donogh, pardon, [illegible].
O'Cumar, Onn, pardon, [illegible].
O'Cumna, Costor, pardon, 6741.
O'Cunnyn, Shane, pardon, [illegible].
O'Cunally, Shane, pardon, 4574.
O'Cunnie, Murtagh, pardon, [illegible].
O'Cunigan, Nich., pardon, [illegible].
O'Cunne, Neal, pardon, 6781.
O'Cunnaghan—Cunnoghane, persons of the name pardoned, 4761.
O'Cunnone, Tho., pardon, 4504.
O'Cunor, Falim, pardon, [illegible].
O'Curban, Conoghor, pardon, [illegible].
O'Curcke, Donogh, pardon, [illegible].
O'Curin—Curine, Donogh, pardon, [illegible], [illegible].
O'Curkye, Teig, pardon, 6714.
O'Curmok, John, English liberty, 144.
O'Curnyn, Manus, pardon, [illegible].
O'Curnyne, Tho., pardon, [illegible].
O'Curoly, Dermod, pardon, [illegible].
O'Curroane—Curran, persons of the name pardoned, [illegible], 5316, [illegible], [illegible], [illegible].
O'Curran — Currin — Curryn — Curryne — Curru — Cowren:
" Adam m'vicaria, pardon, [illegible], [illegible].
" others of the name pardoned, 146, 1744, 1748, [illegible], [illegible], [illegible], [illegible], [illegible], [illegible], [illegible], [illegible], 4115, [illegible], [illegible], [illegible], [illegible], [illegible], 5111, 5118, [illegible], [illegible], [illegible], 6114, [illegible], 6404, 6447, 6477, 6484, 6617, [illegible], 6742, 6774.
O'Currya—Curryne—Curye. See O'Curran.
O'Cuyll, Kennefuckly, pardon, [illegible].
O'Cuylly, Donogh, pardon, 6731.
O'Cwill, Donogh and Donell, pardon, [illegible], [illegible].
O'Cwirck. See O'Cuirck.
O'Cwonie, Edm., pardon, [illegible].
O'Cwnowe, Tho., pardon, [illegible].
O'Cwony, Mahon, pardon, [illegible].
O'Cynallie, Morish, pardon [illegible].
O'De, Tho. and Mahon, pardon, [illegible], [illegible].
O'Dea, persons of the name pardoned, [illegible], [illegible], [illegible].
O'Deally, Owen, pardon, 4781.
O'Dea, Dermot and Mahon (of Tulleghadee, co. Clare), indenture, 4781.

INDEX TO FIANTS—ELIZABETH.

O'Dae, others of the same pardoned, 5060, 5477, 6422, 6768.
O'Dacy, persons of the name pardoned, 5542.
O'Daffie, Teig, pardon, [illegible].
O'Daffine, Donogh, pardon, [illegible].
O'Dahe, John, pardon, 6121.
O'Dahill, John, pardon, 2547.
O'Dain, Owen, pardon, 6594.
O'Dalachain. See O'Dalaghan.
O'Dalee, Dermod, pardon, 4272.
O'Dalaghan—Dalachain—Daligan—Dallaghan, persons of the name pardoned, 4032, 4340, 4874, 6818.
O'Dalaghlan, Cormock, priest, pardon, 6818.
O'Dalany, Teig, pardon, [illegible].
O'Dale, persons of the name pardoned, 1272, 1734, 2134, [illegible], 5326, 6180, 6456.
O'Dales, Cowqnyngtiag and Donell, pardon, 4771.
„ See O'Daly.
O'Daley—Dali—Dalie. See O'Daly.
O'Daligan. See O'Dalaghan.
O'Dalle, Wm., pardon, 4672.
O'Dallagh, Dwyre, pardon, 6676.
O'Dallaghan. See O'Dalaghan.
O'Dallan, Geroit, alias Tyllan, pardon, 3461.
„ others of the same pardoned, 4777, 4732.
O'Dallarie, Donogh and Molaghlin, pardon, 6440.
O'Dalley—Dallie. See O'Dally.
O'Dallon, Hugh, pardon, 6727.
O'Dally—Dallie—Dalley—I Dally—Y Dally, persons of the name pardoned, 1677, 2244, 2262, [illegible], 3874, 4256, 4276, 4437, [illegible], 4673, 4741, 4782, 4741, [illegible], [illegible], 5425, 6017, [illegible], 6407, [illegible], 6430, [illegible], 6461, 6446, 6534, [illegible], 6535, [illegible], 6676, [illegible], 6713, 6724, 6751, 6762.
O'Dalvy, Cormick, pardon, [illegible].
O'Daly—Dalie—Dalye—Daley—Dali—Dales—Y Dalie—I Daly:
„ (in co. Westm.), chiefry from, 1418, 5471.
„ Brian or Barnaby (of Carrickylyon), English liberty, 2234; pardon, 2341.
„ Dermot (of Larry, co. Gal.), grant of land, [illegible]; pardon, [illegible].
„ Donogh (of Killimore), pardon, [illegible].
„ Owen or Eugene, English liberty, 2234.
„ Teig (of Lareyhe,) pardon, [illegible].
„ the rhymer, lands held by, 6618.
„ others of the same pardoned, 10, [illegible], 1422, 1566, 1601, 1645, 1684, 1771, 2044, 2138, 2234, 2341, 2344, 2378, 2423, 2494, 2498, 2518, 2774, 2815, 2941, [illegible], 3347, [illegible], [illegible], 3778, [illegible], 4078, 4142,
O'Daly:
„ [illegible]-7, 4414, 4410, 4444, [illegible], 4572, [illegible], [illegible], 4744, 4751, [illegible], [illegible], [illegible], 5100, 5238, 5487, 6148, [illegible], [illegible], 5514, [illegible], 5792, [illegible], 5113, [illegible], [illegible], 6319, [illegible], 6467, 6475-7, 6480, [illegible], 6487-8, [illegible], [illegible], 6500, 6511-2, 6515-7, [illegible]-8, [illegible]-41, 6550, 6646, [illegible]-8, [illegible]-4, 6571, 6616, 6651, [illegible], [illegible], [illegible], [illegible], 6701, 6743, 6770.
O'Dane, Teig, pardon, 4794, 6811.
O'Daniell, persons of the same pardoned, 5088, 6744.
O'Dagarty, Daniel, pardon, [illegible].
O'Dany, Brian, pardon, 4759.
O'Daran, Donald and Owen, pardon, 78, 1008.
O'Darguano, Philip, pardon, [illegible].
O'Darpano, Philip, pardon, 5347.
O'Darigan [ ] pardon, 4781.
O'Darmod, Donald and Shane, pardon, [illegible].
O'Darmodie, Teig, harpmaker, pardon, 6494.
O'Dassam, Donogh, pardon, 6812.
O'Dassanie, Donell and Donogh, pardon, 6808.
O'Dassen, Dermot, pardon, [illegible].
O'Dasshowne, Donogh, pardon, 4784.
O'Dassanie. See O'Dassany.
O'Dassanaghe, Awliff, pardon, 6640.
O'Dassany—Dassanie, Dermod and Donell, pardon, 6467, 6468, 6471.
O'Dauen, One, pardon, 182.
O'Daury, Wm., pardon, 6618.
O'Davan, Edm., pardon, 6618.
O'Daven, Donell, pardon, [illegible].
O'Daveony, Manus, pardon, 4761.
O'Daverin—Davorrin—Davoryn—Dawirne—Daworen, persons of the same pardoned, 5364, 4871, 4867, 6516, 6461.
O'Davourren—Davourran, persons of the name pardoned, 6642.
O'Davyne, James, pardon, 6817.
O'Dawe, Cormock, pardon, 182.
O'Daworen—Dawirne. See O'Daverin.
O'Dawry, Gilleduff, pardon, 6018.
O'Day, Thady, pardon, 5404.
O'Daye, Conor, pardon, 1641.
O'Dayle, Wm., pardon, [illegible].
O'Daylie, Enos, pardon, 6617.
Oddar, co. Meath, 5601.
„ abbey or nunnery, leased, 404, [illegible]; procurations of, 4747; possessions leased, 407, [illegible], 5611.
„ rectory, 5854, 5611.
O'Dea, Donell M'vic Gragh (of Disert, co. Clare), pardon, 0764.
„ others of the name pardoned, [illegible], [illegible], 4108, 4563, 4584-6, 4580, [illegible], [illegible], [illegible], [illegible], [illegible], [illegible], 6446, [illegible].

INDEX TO FIANTS—ELIZABETH.

O'Deadie, John and Hugh, pardon, 6477, [illegible].
O'Dean — Deane, persons of the name pardoned, [illegible], 6497, 6518.
O'Dearmin, Fear, pardon, [illegible].
O'Deasan, Donogh, pardon, 2341.
O'Deasy, persons of the name pardoned, 1034.
O'Dedy, Moriertagh, pardon, 6611.
O'Deelan, Tho., pardon, 4687.
O'Degoman, Teig, pardon, [illegible].
O'Degyll, Wm., pardon, [illegible].
O'Deid, Murtagh, pardon, 6604.
O'Deire, Gillipadrig, pardon, [illegible].
O'Deirmod, Conor, pardon, [illegible].
O'Delayne, Shane, pardon, 4306.
O'Dempsie—Dempsy—Demsy—Dempsey—Dampsey—Demsi—Demsy;
„ Dermot m'Hugh, remainder man, 694, 1523, 1606, 1654; his wife, [illegible]; his heir, 4397, [illegible].
„ Edm. carragh, pardon, [illegible], 4467, 6428.
„ Gilis, pardon at suit of, 2775.
„ Hugh m'Dermot, grant of land, 617.
„ Owen or Owny m'Hugh, captain of Clanmalier, grant of lands, [illegible], 1523, 1606, 1654-5; surrender, 1621; depredations committed on his lands, 2164; pardon, 430, 634, 810, 2411, 2694, 2849; commissions, 843, 1762, [illegible]; his heir, 4397, 4520.
„ Teig or Thady m'Owny (of Richardstown), pardon, 634, 1420.
„ Terence m'Hugh, remainder man, 694, 1523, 1606, 1654.
„ Terence (sir), wardship, 4397; livery, 4520; pardon, 4918, [illegible], 6471; sheriff of King's co., [illegible]; commission, 6171; licence to alien, [illegible]; pardon, 6491; wardship grant, [illegible]; conveyance by, [illegible].
„ others of the name pardoned, 18, 430, 614, 634, 810, 1163, 1168, 1874, [illegible], 1575, 1701, 2411, 2769, 2723, [illegible], 6467, [illegible], [illegible], 6775, 6780. See O'Dimpsie, O'Dymsie.
O Dempsies country, King's co., 649.
O'Demghis, Donogh, pardon, [illegible].
„ Donell, pardon, 6762.
O'Deniel, Feyne, pardon, [illegible].
O Denrathay, Moriagh, pardon, 4706.
O'Deolan, Laghlin, pardon, 4467.
O'Deoran—Deorane, persons of the name pardoned, 1617, 2348, [illegible], 4446, [illegible], 6422, [illegible], 6464, [illegible], [illegible].
„ Donell, priest, pardon, [illegible].
O'Deran, persons of the name pardoned, [illegible]-4.
O'Derane, Conoghor, pardon, [illegible].
O'Deveran, Shane, pardon, [illegible].
O'Dergane—Dergaan, persons of the name pardoned, 6480.
O'Dermod—Dermode, persons of the name pardoned, 10, [illegible], [illegible], [illegible].
O'Dermody—Dermodie, persons of the name pardoned, [illegible], [illegible]-6, [illegible].
O'Dermot, persons of the name pardoned, [illegible], [illegible].
O'Dermydie, Hugh, pardon, [illegible].
O'Derran, Wm., pardon, [illegible].
O'Derrelane, Teig, pardon, [illegible].
O'Deryleo, Wm., pardon, 1060.
O'Desmonde (see Desmond, John of), 4176.
O'Devlinge, Brian (of Muntir Devlinge, in Tyrone), chief of his name, pardon, 6718.
„ Gillpatrick, vicar, pardon, 6718.
„ others of the name pardoned, 6718-4.
O'Devrane, Cahir and Gerrall, pardon, [illegible].
O'Devy, Edm. and Donogh, pardon, [illegible], 4604.
O'Dewny, Dermod, pardon, 6464.
O'Dewryne, Donald, pardon, [illegible].
O'Dewy, Gerroll, pardon, 4775.
O'Deyiyn, Donald, pardon, [illegible].
Odhee, persons of the name pardoned, 4712.
O'Die, Wm., priest, pardon, [illegible].
„ others of the name pardoned, [illegible], 6762.
O'Dienore, Thady, pardon, 1882.
O'Diergan, Tho., pardon, [illegible].
O'Diermode, Moriagh, pardon, 4904.
O'Diermot, Shane and Wm., pardon, [illegible].
O'Diggan, Donogh and Teig, pardon, 4490, [illegible].
O'Digin, persons of the name pardoned, 4578.
O'Dihirde, Donald, pardon, [illegible].
O'Dimpsie, Wm., pardon, 4367.
O'Dinegane, Edm., pardon, 4574.
O'Dingine, Moroghe, pardon, [illegible].
O'Diomoe, Colliam, pardon, 1443.
O'Diomosie, Gillpatrick, pardon, [illegible].
O'Dirrellee, James, pardon, [illegible].
O'Dirrovane, Brian, pardon, 6480.

INDEX TO FIANTS—ELIZABETH.

O'Divi, Maurice, robbery from, [illegible].
O'Divie, Wm., pardon, [illegible].
O'Divyo, Hugh, pardon, [illegible].
O'Doagill, Mulledge, pardon, [illegible].
O'Doan, Donogh, pardon, [illegible].
O'Doane, Wm. and Derby, pardon, [illegible], [illegible].
O'Dochane, Teig, pardon, 6511.
O'Dochartie. See O'Dogharty.
Odode, Teig, pardon, [illegible].
O'Dody, Redmund, pardon, [illegible].
O'Doedy, Thady O'Connor, pardon, [illegible].
O'Doelaine, Terence, [illegible].
O'Doelan, persons of the name pardoned, [illegible], [illegible], [illegible], [illegible], [illegible].
O'Doelane, Edm. and Tho., pardon, [illegible].
O'Doelayn, Charles and John, pardon, [illegible].
O'Doell, Art and Donell, pardon, 6111.
O'Doffy, James and Patr., pardon, [illegible].
O'Dogan, persons of the name pardoned, [illegible], 6184, [illegible].
O'Dogharde. See O'Dogharty.
O'Doghog, John, pardon, 6404.
O'Doghon, persons of the name pardoned, [illegible].
O'Doghor, Donogh, pardon, [illegible].
O'Dogheran, Conoghor, pardon, [illegible].
O'Dogharty — Dogharde — Dogherde — Docharde—Dogharde:
 " Brian, persons of race of, pardoned, [illegible].
 " Cahir, pardon, [illegible].
 " Donell, persons of race of, pardoned, [illegible].
 " Felim, persons of race of, pardoned, [illegible].
 " Hugh, persons of race of, pardoned, [illegible].
 " sir John, [illegible]; surrender and regrant of his lands, [illegible], [illegible]; his title of O'Dogharty abolished, [illegible]; protection, [illegible].
 " Redmund, persons of race of, pardoned, [illegible].
 " Shane, persons of race of, pardoned, [illegible].
 " William, persons of race of, pardoned, [illegible].
 " Brennalie, persons of race called, pardoned, [illegible].
 " Clan Alin, persons of, pardoned, [illegible].
 " Clan David, persons of, pardoned, [illegible].
 " Clan Laughlin, persons of, pardoned, [illegible].
 " Mucler Banlaghan, persons of, pardoned, [illegible].
O'Dogharty, persons of the name in Inishowen, pardoned, [illegible], [illegible].
O'Dogharty—Docharde—Doherties country, granted to chief, [illegible]; commander of forces in, [illegible]; martial law in, [illegible].
O'Dogharty — Dogharde — Doghirtie — Doharrye—Dohirty:
 " Edm. roe, hanging of, [illegible].
 " others of the name (elsewhere than in co. Donegall), pardoned, 211, [illegible], [illegible], [illegible], [illegible], [illegible], [illegible], [illegible].
O'Dogharde—Doghirtie. See O'Dogharty.
O'Doghwyne, Shane, pardon, [illegible].
O'Doghy, Thady, pardon, [illegible].
O'Dogowyn, Wm., pardon, [illegible].
O'Doherian, Teig, pardon, [illegible].
O'Dohie, Dermot, pardon, [illegible].
O'Dohirty—Dohertie. See O'Dogharty.
O'Doier, Thady, pardon, [illegible].
O'Doigin, Molmore, pardon, [illegible].
O'Doigin, persons of the name pardoned, [illegible].
O'Doigne, Brian, pardon, [illegible].
O'Doile—Doill—Doille. See O'Doyle.
O'Doin—Doine. See O'Doyne.
O'Doingo, persons of the name pardoned, [illegible], [illegible].
O'Doire, Shane and Conogher, pardon, [illegible], [illegible].
O'Dolaghan, Hugh, pardon, [illegible].
O'Dolaine, Wm., pardon, [illegible].
O'Dolan, persons of the name pardoned, [illegible], [illegible], [illegible], [illegible], [illegible], [illegible], [illegible].
O'Doland, Donell, pardon, [illegible].
O'Dolane, persons of the name pardoned, [illegible], [illegible], [illegible], [illegible], [illegible], [illegible].
O'Dolany, Wm., pardon, [illegible].
O'Dolchyn, Wm., pardon, [illegible].
O'Dole, persons of the name pardoned, [illegible], [illegible].
O'Doleen, Philip, pardon, [illegible].
O'Doleane, Shane, pardon, [illegible].
O'Doleayn, Owen, pardon, [illegible].
O'Dolen. See O'Dolin.
O'Dolenne, Hugh, pardon, [illegible].
O'Dolere, Wm., pardon, [illegible].
O'Dolian, James, pardon, [illegible].
O'Dolin—Dolen, persons of the name pardoned, [illegible], [illegible], [illegible], [illegible], [illegible].
O'Doline, Phelim, pardon, [illegible].
O'Doling, Ellis, pardon, 2710.
O'Dollan, persons of the name pardoned, [illegible], [illegible], [illegible].
O'Dollane, persons of the name pardoned, [illegible], [illegible].
O'Dollany, Shane, pardon, [illegible].
O'Dolleam, Edm., pardon, [illegible].
O'Dolleanie, Edm. and Owen, pardon, [illegible].

INDEX TO FIANTS.—ELIZABETH.

O'Dulliams, Rory, pardon, [illegible].
O'Dolly, Donogo and John, pardon, [illegible].
O'Dollyan, Owen, pardon, [illegible].
O'Dologhanline, Donogh, pardon, 5101.
O'Dologhemie, Rory, pardon, 6734.
O'Dologher, persons of the name pardoned, [illegible].
O'Dologhintya, Mahony, pardon, [illegible].
O'Daly, persons of the name pardoned, [illegible], 6494, [illegible], [illegible].
O'Dolyn, Rich., pardon, [illegible].
" Thady, grant of land, [illegible].
O'Dolyne, Thady, pardon, [illegible].
O'Dom's (O'Dowde) country (see O'Dowde), 4407.
O'Domane, Donogh and Wm., pardon, 4807.
O'Domnagh, Garret, pardon, [illegible].
O'Domyn, Thaddeus, pardon, [illegible].
O'Don. See O'Doyne.
O'Donagan, Murcho, pardon, [illegible].
O'Donagh, Donell and John, pardon, 4444, [illegible].
O'Donaghie, Donogh and Morian, pardon, [illegible], [illegible].
O'Donaghow. See O'Donogho.
O'Donaile, Conell, pardon, [illegible].
O'Donall, persons of the name (in Queen's co.) pardoned, [illegible].
O'Donayne, Donell, pardon, 5440.
O'Doncho—Donchow—Donen, persons of the name (in co. Cavan) pardoned, [illegible], [illegible].
O'Donchowe, Teig, pardon, [illegible].
O'Donday, Mahon, pardon, [illegible].
O'Done. See O'Doyne.
O'Donegaine, Enn, pardon, [illegible].
O'Donegan, Morogh, priest, pardon, [illegible].
" others of the name pardoned, [illegible], [illegible], 5466, [illegible], [illegible].
O'Donegho, John, English liberty, [illegible].
O'Doneleghe, Tho., attainted, [illegible].
O'Donelan. See O'Donellan.
O'Donell — Donill — Donnell — Donnill — Donnyll — Donyll — I Donell — Y Donell—I Donill:
" Cafferie oge m'Cafferie, pardon, [illegible].
" Caffir (of Rathmelton), pardon, [illegible].
" Calvagh, named O'Donyll and captain of Tirconnell, [illegible]; late chief of Tyrconell, [illegible], [illegible].
" Costaine (of Rathmelton), pardon, [illegible].
" Conn oge, brother of Neill garve, pardon, [illegible].
" Donell, sheriff of co. Donegal, pardon, [illegible].
" Donell (of Rathmelton), pardon, [illegible].
O'Donell, Donell, brother of Neill garve, pardon, [illegible].
" Fynwall or Nyn duff, wife of O'Donell, pardon, 4914, [illegible].
" (sir) Hugh m'Manus, captain of Tyrconell, [illegible]; earl of Essex deals with, [illegible]; commission to, 4763; indenture, [illegible]; his wife pardoned, 4914.
" Hugh roe: O'Donell, commissions to treat with, [illegible], [illegible], [illegible]; war against, 6111, [illegible]; protection, 6127.
" Hugh, a pensioner, [illegible].
" Hugh, alias m'Edegan, pardon, 4906.
" Hugh (of Rathmelton), pardon, [illegible].
" Hugh boy m'Inaltie, lease, [illegible], [illegible].
" Hugh boy, brother of Neill garve, pardon, [illegible].
" Molaghlin, clerk, pardon, [illegible].
" Neill garrowe (or garve), chief of his name, grant of the custody of the country of Tyrconell, [illegible]; pardon, [illegible]; his son and brothers, [illegible].
" Rory, son of Hugh m'Manus, a hostage, [illegible]; pardon to him and his followers, [illegible].
" others of the name in co. Donegal and neighbouring districts, pardoned, [illegible], 3173, [illegible], [illegible], [illegible], [illegible], [illegible], [illegible], [illegible].
" country of, [illegible], [illegible], [illegible].
" Tirlogh, priest, pardon, 1158.
" persons of the name (elsewhere than in co. Donegal and neighbourhood), pardoned, [illegible].
O'Donellan—Donelan—Donellane:
" Gylernow, 1848, [illegible].
" Melaghlen reogh (of Ballydonelan), pardon, [illegible].
" Shane (of Ballydonelan), pardon, [illegible].

INDEX TO FIANTS.—ELIZABETH.

O'Donellan, Twohell, chapel of (Chapel Tully at Kilconnell, co. Gal.), 4878, 6811.
" others of the name pardoned, 3718, 4730, 5090, 4083, 4887, 4842, 4487, 5028, 5298, 5447, 5618, 5093, 6602, 3740, 6110, 6190, 6306, 6458, 6480.
O'Donelly—Donnelly, persons of the name pardoned, 5254, 5483, 5742.
O'Donest, Hugh, pardon, 6374.
O'Donevan — Donnevan — Donnevane — Donovane — Donovan — Donivane — Doniwane — Donovan — Dowaavane — I Donovan:
" Dermod (of Castledonevan), pardon, 6515, 6450.
" Donald Donovan called O'D., pardon, 5033.
" Donald juvenis, pardon, 5032.
" Donell or Daniel (of Castledonevan), pardon, 6515, 5550.
" Richard (of the Isle of Man), pardon, 6524.
" others of the name pardoned, 1648, 5063-4, 5066, 4738, 4450, 4595, 4604, 4488, 4460, 6509, 6314-6, 6455, 6465, 5571, 6575, 6638, 5490, 6701, 6702, 6764, 6770.
O'Donevaye, Conoghor, pardon, 4418.
O'Dongaine, Donogh, pardon, 6511.
O'Dongan, Dermod, pardon, 6783.
O'Donganne, Donald, pardon, 1854.
O'Dongus, Donell, pardon, 6190.
O'Dongho, Patr., pardon, 4980.
O'Donghnan, Perlaum, pardon, 5418.
O'Dongyn, Melaghlin, pardon, 867.
O'Donhie, James, pardon, 0422.
O'Donhowe, Shane, pardon, 4376.
O'Donichan, Murrogh, pardon, 4478.
O'Doniell, Wm., pardon, 4783.
O'Donigane, persons of the name pardoned, 4487, 4811.
O'Donigher, persons of the name pardoned, 4533.
O'Donill. See O'Donell.
O'Donillaine, Avoly, pardon, 4707.
O'Donivane—Doniwane. See O'Donovan.
O'Doniseth, Donell and Owen, pardon, 1854.
O'Donn. See O'Doyne.
O'Donnaghowe, Donell, pardon, 3478.
O'Donnall, Walter, pardon, 3323.
O'Donnane, Edm. Neale, pardon, 6393.
O'Donne. See O'Doyne.
O'Donnegan, Shane, pardon, 6511.
O'Donneghie, Conoghor, pardon, 4440.
O'Donnell. See O'Donell.
O'Donnellan, Donell, pardon, 5188, 4850.
" See O'Donellan.
O'Donnelly. See O'Donelly.
O'Donnertie, Donell, pardon, 4484.
O'Donnovan—Donnevane. See O'Donevan.
O'Donnill. See O'Donell.
O'Donnocartie, Shane and Wm., pardon, 4484.
O'Donnogh, Edm., pardon, 6409.
O'Donnogh Moore (or O'Donoghe), 5488.
O'Donnoghe. See O'Donoghe.
O'Donnoghor, Shane, pardon, 5486.
O'Donnoghow. See O'Donoghe.
O'Donnor, Tho., pardon, 4481.
O'Donnowan, Wm., pardon, 4483.
O'Donnowly, Donell, pardon, 4447.
O'Donnughoe, Jeffery, pardon, 6874.
O'Donnyll. See O'Donell.
O'Donnylle, Hugh, pardon, 4402.
O'Donnylly, James and Patr., pardon, 4423.
O'Donochie, Edm., pardon, 4453.
O'Donoche. See O'Donoghe.
O'Donochowe, Rich., pardon, 3917.
O'Donogan, Donogh and John, pardon, 4388, 6437.
O'Donogh—Donoghe, persons of the name pardoned, 2881, 6454, 4807, 5516, 5523.
O'Donoghohowe. See O'Donoghe.
O'Donoghe. See O'Donogh.
O'Donoghor, persons of the name pardoned, 6483.
O'Donoghie, Knocher, pardon, 1767.
O'Donogho—Donoghow—Donaghow—Donnoghe — Donnoghow — Donocho — Donoghohowe — Donoaho — I Donoghe — Y Donogho—I Donoghow:
" Rory (of Ross), alias O'Donogho More, pardon, 2783, 4070 ; his possessions granted, 4377, 4717 ; his son pardoned, 6468.
" Rory, son of O'Donogho More, pardon, 6469.
" Shearry or Geoffrey m'Teig, alias O'Donoghow in Glenn (of the Glen), pardon, 4467, 4716, 6488.
" Teig (of Killarney), pardon, 6070.
" others of the name in co. Kerry and Cork, pardoned, 4053, 6180, 4464, 4467, 4453, 4731, 6418, 6488, 6437, 5514-6, 5583, 5502, 6671, 5574, 6764, 6770.
" persons of the name in other districts, pardoned, 1308, 1651, 1684, 4484, 4480, 4594, 4782, 4844, 6794, 4808, 6180, 5928, 6451, 5598, 5513, 6517, 4588, 5585, 5577.

INDEX TO FIANTS—ELIZABETH.

O'Donocine, Marcus, pardon, 4577.
O'Donolan, persons of the name pardoned, [illegible], [illegible], 6618.
O'Donordy, Wm., pardon, 3175.
O'Donorty, Donald, pardon, 2964.
O'Donoshe. See O'Donoghue.
O'Donovan—Donovan. See O'Donevan
O'Donowan, Teig, pardon, 6082.
O'Donowey, Hugh, pardon, 6433.
O'Donowghowe, Hugh and Teig, pardon, 5796.
O'Donowly, Shane and Teig, pardon, 4453.
O'Donowre, Murcho and Petrus, pardon, 4073, [illegible].
O'Donwane, Donogh, pardon, 6176.
O'Dony, persons of the name pardoned, 6447, 6755, 6768.
O'Donyall, Gohyrie, pardon, 4063.
O'Donyen, Matthew or Mahon, pardon, [illegible].
O'Donyman, Maurice, pardon, 5462.
O'Donylan, Morough, pardon, 6654.
O'Donyll. See O'Donell.
O'Donyllan, Tho., pardon, 4231.
O'Donylle, Ennes, and Tirrelagh, pardon, 947, 1042.
O'Donylley, Tho., pardon, 5794.
O'Donyne, Cormock, pardon, 6614.
O'Doode—Doode. See O'Dowde.
O'Doodegan, Rory, pardon, 5802.
O'Doodregane, Donogh, pardon, 6615.
O'Doogaine, Cormock, pardon, 5965.
O'Doogenan, Farfeasy and Feafeasy, pardon, 6616. See O'Dowgenan.
O'Doohie, Donall, pardon, 4581.
O'Doolan, Gillernow, pardon, 6450.
O'Doole, Alexander, pardon, 4174.
O'Doolen, David, pardon, 5776.
O'Dooly, Dermot, pardon, [illegible].
O'Dooman, [ ], pardon, 6163.
O'Doomegaine—Doomegaine, persons of the name pardoned, 6806.
O'Dooryn, Wm., pardon, 5642.
O'Doonin, Cahir, pardon, 5836.
O'Doran—Dorane:
„ Cahir and Donell, indenture with, 6766.
„ persons of the name pardoned, 134, 140, 164, [illegible], [illegible], 494, 717, 754, 813, 867, 871, 876, 911, [illegible], 984, 1103, 1230, 1310, 1424, 1866, 2102, 2033-6, 2216, 2437, 2697, 3948, [illegible], 4438, 4461, 4464, 4702, [illegible], [illegible], 6062, 6110, 6151, [illegible], [illegible], 6432, 6438, 6417, 6432, 6577, 6614, 6664, 6771, 6772.
O'Doran, Moriagh, pardon, 6158.
O'Dorchane, Walter, pardon, 6477.
O'Dorchie, Donogh, pardon, 6457.
O'Doraky, persons of the name pardoned, 6617.
O'Dore, Melaghlin, pardon, [illegible].
O'Dorenne, Gillpatrick, pardon, 6477.
O'Doren, David, pardon, 5658.
O'Dorghy, Teig, pardon, 6423.
O'Dorichie, Hugh, pardon, 5712.
O'Doride, Shiddie, pardon, 6644.
O'Dorimle, David, pardon, 4115.
O'Dorme—Dormene, persons of the name pardoned, 6144, 6651, 6678.
O'Dornell, Ferdoragh, pardon, 4880.
Odorney, abbey of (Abbeydorney), co. Kerry, 4716.
„ abbey of Our Lady of Kirie eleison, leased, 2818, 3788, 6306; lands granted, 6128.
„ rectory, 2818, 4806.
O'Dorney, persons of the name pardoned, 4783, 6741.
O'Dornine, Nele, pardon, 6714.
O'Doroghie, Morogh and Donoghe, pardon, 4430, 4431.
O'Dorolinge, Conoghor, pardon, [illegible].
O'Dorrane—Dorran, persons of the name pardoned, 380, 445, 481, 5621.
O'Dorreahy, Conoghor, pardon, 6696.
O'Dorrery, persons of the name pardoned, 6465.
O'Dorrey, Shane, pardon, 4409.
O'Dorrine, Morish, pardon, 4411.
O'Dorroghie, Edm., pardon, 6460.
O'Dorryny, persons of the name pardoned, 1044, 2947.
O'Dosan, Conor, pardon, 6269.
O'Doud—Douda. See O'Dowda.
O'Douell, Owen, pardon, 4883.
O'Douffen, Brian, pardon, 6465.
O'Dougher, Wm. and Philip, pardon, 6433, 6628.
O'Dougher, Wm., pardon, 2087.
O'Dougherthe, Donell, pardon, 4781.
O'Dougyman. See O'Dowgenan.
O'Doule, persons of the name pardoned, 750, 2981, 4183, 4162.
O'Doulen, James, pardon, 4110.
O'Doulen—Doulin. See O'Dowlin.
O'Doullane, Ferdorogh, pardon, 697.
O'Doulye, Farrall, pardon, 4110.
O'Doulyn. See O'Dowlin.
O'Douthie, [ ], pardon, 6162.
O'Dovan, Conoghor and Mulmory, pardon, 4180, 6838.
O'Dovayne, Maurice, pardon, 6673.
O'Dovin, Owen, pardon, 2304.
O'Dovine, James, pardon, 5782.
O'Dovir, Tho. (O'Dwyre), pardon, 4688.
O'Dovire, Hugh and Shane, pardon, 6761.
O'Dovyeyn, John, pardon, 897.

INDEX TO FIANTS—ELIZABETH.

O'Dow, Murgh, pardon, [illegible].

O'Dowan—Dowane:
 " Derby, harper, pardon, 6784.
 " Melaghlin, harper, pardon, [illegible].
 " others of the name pardoned, 18, 1043, 4182, [illegible], [illegible], 6418, 6615, 6544, [illegible].

O'Dowarile, persons of the name pardoned, 6478.

O'Dowchy, Hugh, pardon, [illegible].

O'Dowde—Doude—Doudo—Doud—Douda—Dowda—Dowdae—Dowdie—Duda—Dwda:
 " Dahie (of Castleconnor), pardon, [illegible].
 " Teig or Thaddeus boy, pardon, 6480, 5848.
 " others of the name pardoned, [illegible], 4704, 4783, [illegible], 6430, 6456, 6478, 6438, 5748, 5788, [illegible], [illegible], [illegible].
 " country of (Tireragh, co. Sligo), 1288, 1488, 2186, 6461, 4407 (O'Doude).

O'Dowdy—Dowddy—Dowdye:
 " Owen, attainted (in co. Tip.), [illegible].
 " others of the name pardoned, [illegible], 4761, 4877, 6414, [illegible], [illegible].

O'Dowell—Dowll—Dowyll:
 " Edm. ro Kavanagh, pardon, [illegible].
 " others of the name pardoned, 811, 857, [illegible], 1044, 1141, [illegible], [illegible], [illegible], [illegible], [illegible], [illegible], [illegible], [illegible], [illegible], [illegible], 4712, [illegible], [illegible], [illegible], [illegible], [illegible], [illegible], 6462, 6488, 6484, [illegible], 6541, 6488, 6792.

O'Dowes, Davis, pardon, [illegible].

O'Doware, Adam, pardon, [illegible].

O'Dowgaine, Philip and John, pardon, [illegible], [illegible].

O'Dowgan—I Dowgan—Y Dowgan, persons of the name pardoned, [illegible], [illegible], [illegible], 5120, 6481, [illegible], 4467, 4728, 4761, 4761, 6412, 6178, 6443, 6457, 6475, [illegible], [illegible], 6571, 6702.

O'Dowgane, persons of the name pardoned, [illegible], [illegible], 5740, [illegible], [illegible], [illegible], [illegible], 6671.

O'Dowgayn, Donald, pardon, [illegible].

O'Dowgen, Donell, pardon, 6652.

O'Dowgenan — Doogenan — Dougynan — Dowgynane—Duganain—Dugenane—Duiganain—Dwganan:
 " Cogngria, pardon, [illegible].
 " Fariame—Fearinmy, pardon, 4706, [illegible], 6439, [illegible], [illegible].
 " Mulmorie, pardon, [illegible], [illegible].

O'Dowgenan, others of the name pardoned, 4708, 4717, 4767, 6430, [illegible], 5746, [illegible], [illegible], [illegible].

O'Dowggin, Donogh, pardon, 4726.

O'Dowghe, Edm., pardon, [illegible].

O'Dowghie, Edm., pardon, [illegible].

O'Dowgin, Edm., pardon, [illegible].

O'Dowgoe, Donoghe, pardon, 4457.

O'Dowgyn, Philip and Teig, pardon, [illegible], 4782.

O'Dowgynan. See O'Dowgenan.

O'Dowgyne, Tho., pardon, 1817.

O'Dowhirty, Conogher, pardon, [illegible].

O'Dowhye, Wm., pardon, [illegible].

O'Dowie, Philip, captain of his nation, English liberty, 818. See O'Dwyer.

O'Dowier, Shane, pardon, 2072.

O'Dowigine, Mahon, pardon, 6614.

O'Dowile, Teig, pardon, 4737.

O'Dowill. See O'Dowell.

O'Dowilly, Florence, pardon, [illegible].

O'Dowime, Donell, pardon, [illegible].

O'Dowinagham, David, pardon, [illegible].

O'Dowine, persons of the name pardoned, 6648, [illegible].

O'Dowinan, Donell, pardon, [illegible].

O'Dowire—Dowir. See O'Dwyer.

O'Dowlan, persons of the name pardoned, 4844, [illegible], [illegible].

O'Dowland, Edm., pardon, [illegible].

O'Dowlany—Dowlaney, persons of the name pardoned, [illegible], 6466, 4317, [illegible].

O'Dowle, Patrick, murder of, [illegible].
 " others of the name pardoned, [illegible], 1084, [illegible], [illegible], [illegible], [illegible], 4152, [illegible], 6722, [illegible], [illegible], [illegible], [illegible], 6416, 6216, [illegible], [illegible], [illegible], [illegible], [illegible], 6782.

O'Dowles, Tho., pardon, [illegible].

O'Dowlen. See O'Dowlin.

O'Dowley—Dowlie, persons of the name pardoned, [illegible], 1083, 2144, [illegible], 4110, [illegible], 6484, [illegible], 6541, 6652, [illegible].

O'Dowlin — Dowlen — Doulen — Doulin — Dowllen — Dowllin — Dowlyn, persons of the name pardoned, [illegible], 161, [illegible], [illegible], [illegible], 1583, 1601, 1684, [illegible], 1936, [illegible], [illegible], [illegible], 6544, 5848, 6776, [illegible], 4023, [illegible], [illegible], [illegible], [illegible], 6452, [illegible], [illegible], [illegible], 6181, 6183, [illegible], [illegible], 6450, 6482, 6496, [illegible], 6618, [illegible], [illegible], [illegible], [illegible], [illegible], 6574, 6772.

O'Dowlinge—Dowling—Dowlynge, persons of the name pardoned, [illegible], 4184, [illegible], [illegible], [illegible], 6571, 6575, 6577, [illegible], 6772.

O'Dowll, David and Wm., pardon, [illegible].

O'Dowllale, John, pardon, 4734.

O'Dowllen. See O'Dowlin.

O'Dowllie, persons of the name pardoned, [illegible], [illegible].

INDEX TO FIANTS—ELIZABETH.

O'Dowlin. *See* O'Dowlin.

O'Dowly, persons of the name pardoned, [illegible], [illegible], [illegible], [illegible], [illegible], 6374, 6777.

O'Dowlyn. *See* O'Dowlin.

O'Dowlynge. *See* O'Dowlinge.

O'Down. *See* O'Downe.

O'Downavane. *See* O'Donevan.

O'Downe—Down, persons of the name pardoned, 4114, 6274, [illegible], [illegible].

O'Downegane, persons of the name pardoned, [illegible], [illegible].

O'Downever, Cormack, pardon, [illegible].

O'Downghowe, Murtagh and Thos., pardon, [illegible].

O'Downie. *See* O'Downy.

O'Downilie, Patr., pardon, [illegible].

O'Downine, M'Igallagh duff, pardon, [illegible].

O'Downleigh, Dermot, pardon, [illegible].

O'Downy—Downie—Downye:

- „ Maurice m'Hugh, attainted, 6918, [illegible].
- „ Rory, attainted, [illegible], [illegible].
- „ Teig oge, attainted, 6912, [illegible].
- „ Wm. oge, harper, pardon, [illegible].
- „ others of the name pardoned, [illegible], 4107, 4118, 4492, 4534, [illegible], [illegible], 6477, 6479, 6814, 6571, 6576.

O'Downylye, Tirlagh, pardon, [illegible].

O'Downyne, persons of the name pardoned, 6497, [illegible], [illegible].

O'Dowran—Dowrane, persons of the name pardoned, [illegible], [illegible], 6714.

O'Dowrley, James, pardon, 6612.

O'Dowrye, Teig, pardon, [illegible].

O'Dowryn, Redmund, pardon, 1287.

O'Dowy, Derby, pardon, [illegible].

O'Dowyer, Fraghra, pardon, 2044.

O'Dowyle, John, pardon, [illegible].

O'Dowyll. *See* O'Dowell.

O'Dowyr, Derby and Nich., pardon, [illegible], [illegible].

O'Dowyre, Edm. (of Kilmery, co. Tip.), attainted, [illegible].

- „ Moroghoe, pardon, [illegible].
- „ *See* O'Dwyer.

O'Doygan, Wm., pardon, [illegible].

O'Doygin, James, pardon, 4110.

O'Doylain, John, pardon, 4072.

O'Doylan—Doylane, persons of the name pardoned, [illegible].

O'Doyle—Doile—Doyll—Doill:

- „ Bryan or Barnaby, murder of, [illegible].
- „ Teig m'Donogh, pardon, [illegible], [illegible].
- „ others of the name pardoned, [illegible], [illegible], 1443, 1477, 1716, [illegible], [illegible], [illegible], 4701, [illegible], [illegible], 6172, [illegible], [illegible], [illegible], [illegible], 6977, [illegible], 6742.

O'Doyllain, John, pardon, 4073.

O'Doylle, Gerrot, pardon, [illegible].

O'Doyne—Doin—Doine—Dun—Done—Doune—Doune—Doyn—Dun—Dune—Dunn—Dunne—Dwne:

- „ Fendle, English liberty, [illegible].
- „ Mahowry, house in Trim, 1714.
- „ Teig or Thady (of Tinnahinch), chief of his name, pardon, [illegible], 1878, [illegible], [illegible]; commission, [illegible]; English liberty for his sister, 1291; his sons, [illegible].
- „ Teig oge (of Castlebrack), pardon, [illegible], [illegible]; his sons, [illegible].
- „ Tirlagh or Terence (of Kilkevan), pardon, [illegible], [illegible].
- „ others of the name pardoned, [illegible], 432, [illegible], [illegible], [illegible], [illegible], [illegible], [illegible], 1304, 1178, 1297, [illegible], 1578, 1894, 2294, [illegible], [illegible], [illegible], [illegible], [illegible], [illegible], 2771, [illegible], [illegible], [illegible], [illegible], 4018, 4081, [illegible], [illegible], 4733, [illegible], [illegible], [illegible], 5798, [illegible], [illegible], [illegible], [illegible], [illegible], [illegible], [illegible], [illegible], [illegible], [illegible], [illegible], [illegible], [illegible], [illegible], [illegible], [illegible], [illegible], [illegible], [illegible], 6773, 6777.
- „ country of (now the barony of Tinnahinch, Queen's co.), 183, [illegible], [illegible]; made shire ground, [illegible]; martial law, [illegible]; rebels in, [illegible].

O'Doyran, persons of the name pardoned, 6743.

O'Doyrane, Edm., pardon, [illegible].

O'Doyre. *See* O'Dwyer.

O'Doyrin, John, parson, and others of the name pardoned, [illegible].

O'Dradie—Dradye, James and Wm., pardon, [illegible].

O'Dree, Dermot, pardon, [illegible].

O'Drendy, John, pardon, 4111.

O'Dreane, persons of the name pardoned, [illegible].

Odreanne, in Ulster, [illegible].

O'Dree, Dermot, pardon, 5742.

O'Drehiff, Maurice, pardon, 6002.

O'Dreman, Donell, pardon, [illegible].

O'Dreyn, Moriagh, pardon, 4767.

O'Drimane, Melaghlin, pardon, 1176.

O'Driscoll—Driscoll—Driscole—Driscolle—Driscoill—Driscole—Driscoyll—Eldriscoll—Hodriscoll:

- „ Cornell, economist of Ross cathedral, [illegible].
- „ sir Finin or Florence, knt. (of Downeshed), pardon, [illegible], [illegible].
- „ Finin (of Blackwilsky), pardon, 4418, 6719.
- „ Macon garvan (of Dunnegal), pardon, [illegible].

O'Driscoll, others of the name pardoned, 2046, 4618, 4489, 4894, 5406, 5632, 5580, 5610, 5601, 5619-6, 5618, 5630, 5671, 5815, 5701, 5703, 5770.
O'Drohy, persons of the name pardoned, 4761.
O'Dromen, Manus, pardon, 6433.
O'Dromay, Nich., pardon, 6518.
Odrone. See Idrone.
O'Droughane, Maurice, pardon, 744.
O'Droughie, Donogh, pardon, 3669.
O'Drowght, Wm., pardon, 377.
O'Droughye, Maurice, English liberty, 473.
O'Drughie, Teig, pardon, 4468.
O'Drumellan, Treara, pardon, 6445.
O'Drwoghane, Maurice, pardon, 4715.
O'Dryman, Patr. and John, pardon, 3946, 6146.
O'Drymane, Padine, pardon, 4332.
O'Dryscoll, Macqon, pardon, 4415.
O'Duan, persons of the name pardoned, 6636, 6732.
O'Duarty, Wm., pardon, 4584.
O'Duanane, Hugh, pardon, 4739.
O'Duahowny, Rob., pardon, 5139.
O'Duda. See O'Dowde.
O'Duegan — Duecen — Ducayn, persons of the name pardoned, 4681.
O'Dueygan, Wm., pardon, 4735.
O'Duff—Duf:
Wm., English liberty, 1137.
others of the name pardoned, 10, 2077, 5601, 5731, 6576.
O'Duffe, persons of the name pardoned, 10, 2661, 4056, 5237, 6003, 6306, 6587, 6734.
O'Duffedie, Patr., pardon, 6663.
O'Duffy—Duffe—Duffee—Duffey:
Owen, grant of land, 5036.
Patrick, grant of land, 5635.
others of the name pardoned, 3498, 4347, 4469, 5511, 5734, 5753, 5900, 5305, 6460, 6734.
O'Duffyn, Donell, pardon, 5815.
O'Dugane, persons of the name pardoned, 5457, 5439.
O'Dugenain—Dugenane. See O'Dowganan.
O'Duggan, Wm., pardon, 3412.
O'Dughierna, persons of the name pardoned, 2565.
O'Dughrune, Philip, pardon, 6463.
O'Duharhie, John, pardon, 6175.
O'Duhie, Patr., vicar; and others of the name pardoned, 5567.
O'Duhig, Dermod and Meloghlin, pardon, 4497, 6575.
O'Duigenain, Fiall, pardon, 5605. See O'Dowganan.
O'Duip, Rory alias Capell, pardon, 4078.
O'Duinighan, John, pardon, 4655.
O'Duire—Dair. See O'Dwyer.
O'Dulaghanty, Rory, pardon, 6407.
O'Dulany, Conor, pardon, 4561.
O'Dulchonty — Dulchontie — Dulchentie — Dulconie — Dulchente — Dulchonty:
„ Donogh (of Lounyvanna), pardon, 4083, 4120.
„ others of the name pardoned, 4046, 4766, 6963.
O'Dule, Dermot and Shane, pardon, 4123.
O'Duleciente—Duleycyente, Rory and Wm., pardon, 4884.
O'Dulisine, Edm. and Tho., pardon, 5712, 6478.
O'Dullane—Dullan, persons of the name pardoned, 367, 1517, 2235, 2467, 3542, 4079, 3749, 6180, 6477.
O'Dullany—Dullanie—Dullaney:
„ Matthew, chaplain, pardon, 4018,
„ others of the name pardoned, 1219, 1817, 2060, 2595, 4263, 6118, 6440, 6464, 6038, 6151, 6733, 6738, 6775.
O'Dullahenia. See O'Dulchonty.
O'Dullane, Donogh, pardon, 5017.
O'Dulleghonty — Dulleghonie, Gillpatrick and Wm., pardon, 5565.
O'Dullon, Wm. and Teig, pardon, 4044, 4341.
O'Dulline, Dermot, pardon, 4600.
O'Dulling, Meloghlin, pardon, 175.
O'Dullumaine, Teig, pardon, 6964.
O'Dulloughmotye, Shane, pardon, 4351.
O'Dulughontie, Donogh, pardon, 5456.
O'Duluie, Edm., pardon, 4694.
O'Dully, John and Any, pardon, 4538, 5744.
O'Dulye, persons of the name pardoned, 3486, 5654, 6116.
O'Duly, John, pardon, 6565.
O'Dulye, Dermot, pardon, 6463.
O'Dumiyee, persons of the name pardoned, 6761.
O'Dun—Dune. See O'Doyne.
O'Dunaghie, Morice, pardon, 5467.
O'Dunaghowe, Philip and Shane, pardon, 6497.
O'Dunaghan, **Conor and Edm., pardon,** 4934.
O'Duneghon, Owen, pardon, 5036.
O'Dunerae, Brien, pardon, 6370.
O'Dungane, Donoghe, pardon, 6158.
O'Dungie, John, pardon, 4763.
O'Dunim, Conor, pardon, 5609.
O'Dunivane, Teig, pardon, 5609.
O'Dunligh, John and Owen, pardon, 4456.
O'Dunn—Dunne. See O'Doyne.
O'Dunnogan, Philip, pardon, 4763.
O'Dunnedy, Wm., pardon, 4185.
O'Dunnflise, Donell, pardon, 6108.

INDEX TO FIANTS—ELIZABETH.

O'Dannye—Dunnyne, persons of the name pardoned, 2984, 6782.

O'Danert, Edw., pardon, 6484.

O'Duay, Dermod and Donell, pardon, 5811.

O'Duanyne, Donald, pardon, 6170.

O'Dnollan, John, pardon, 2904.

O'Duolly, Tho., pardon, 5722.

O'Duoygin, Donogh, pardon, 6[illegible].

O'Duryke, Conoghor and Morriogh, pardon, 6444.

O'Duran, Edm., pardon, 5800.

O'Durthie, Shane, pardon, 4514.

O'Durinn, Gilligrame, pardon, [illegible].

O'Duris, James, pardon, 4[illegible]1.

O'Durley—Durly, Brian and Melaghlin, pardon, 1[illegible], 5[illegible]8.

O'Durnye—Durnyne, persons of the name pardoned. 4[illegible]7, 4[illegible], 5[illegible]7, 6[illegible]7, 6761.

O'Durrogh, Donell, pardon, 6451.

O'Durry, Molaghlin, pardon, [illegible].

O'Durvin, Hugh, pardon, [illegible].

O'Dusgoole, Conoghor, pardon, 6[illegible].

O'Duvire, Hugh, pardon, 6742.

O'Duygan—Duygen. See O'Dwigin.

O'Duygennis, Diarmot, pardon, [illegible]. See O'Dowgenan.

O'Duygyne. See O'Dwigin.

O'Duyne. See O'Dwyne.

O'Duyr—Duyre. See O'Dwyer.

O'Dwaine—Dwayne, persons of the name pardoned, [illegible].

O'Dwane, Dermod and Molaghlin, pardon, 5304.

O'Dwartie, Wm., alias Donvarb, pardon, 6478.

O'Dwayne. See O'Dwaine.

O'Dwde. See O'Dowde.

O'Dwallany, Edm., pardon, [illegible].

O'Dware. See O'Dwyer.

O'Dwgenan. See O'Dowgenan.

O'Dwghie, Conoghor and Morogh, pardon, 6[illegible].

O'Dwghrane, Philip, pardon, [illegible].

O'Dwiall, Donogh, pardon, 6[illegible].

O'Dwier. See O'Dwyer.

O'Dwigan—Dwigen. See O'Dwigin.

O'Dwigher, Teig, pardon, 6444.

O'Dwigin—Daygan—Duygen—Duygyne—Dwigan—Dwigen—Dwygin—Dwygan—Dwygyn, persons of the name pardoned, 4[illegible], 4[illegible], 4[illegible], 5[illegible], 6[illegible], 6[illegible], 6[illegible], 6[illegible]-4, 6704.

O'Dwile, Edm., robbery by, [illegible].

O'Dwill, John, pardon, [illegible].

O'Dwine. See O'Dwyne.

O'Dwire—Dwir. See O'Dwyer.

O'Dwirky, Donell and Mahon, pardon, [illegible].

O'Dwiohan, Philip, pardon, 6[illegible].

O'Dwile, Wm., pardon, 3[illegible].

O'Dwlinge, Dermod and Teig, pardon, 6478.

O'Dwloghrigan, Conoghor, pardon, 6474.

O'Dwinogherie, Dermot, pardon, 6477.

O'Dwne's country (see O'Doyne), 6704.

O'Dwuyn, John, English liberty, 204.

O'Dwoill, Cahir, pardon, 6[illegible]7.

Odwoy, Edm., pardon, 4[illegible].

O'Dwoyle, persons of the name pardoned, 6[illegible].

O'Dwrigane, Donell, pardon, 6762.

O'Dwrrane, Edm., pardon, 6[illegible]7.

O'Dwull, John, pardon, 5[illegible].

O'Dwyer — Dowire — Dowyr — Dowyre — Doyre—Duir—Duire—Duyr—Duyre—Dware—Dwier—Dwir—Dwire—Dwyre—Dyer:

" Derby fitz Philip, pardon, [illegible].

" Dermot or Derby (of Clonyhorp), pardon, 4[illegible]7, 4[illegible], 6441, 6[illegible]1, 6704.

" Donell (of Crossmyle), attainted, [illegible].

" Donogh (of Crossmyle), attainted, 6[illegible]4.

" Edm., alias Evotty, attainted, 6[illegible].

" John (of Dundrum), pardon, [illegible]4, 6[illegible], 6707.

" John (of Cork), English liberty. 112.

" Philip, alias O'D., pardon, [illegible]4. See O'Dowie.

" Philip (of Ballymolyn), pardon, 2184.

" Philip (of Dondrum), pardon, 6[illegible]4.

" Shane, alias O'D. (in co. Donegal), pardon, 6721.

" Tho. (of Ballimanomy), pardon, [illegible], 6707.

" Tho. (of Waterford), English liberty, 1187.

" Wm., abbot of Holy Cross (in 1577), [illegible]14.

" others of the name pardoned, 1[illegible]4, [illegible], [illegible], 31[illegible], [illegible], [illegible]4, [illegible], [illegible], 4[illegible], 4[illegible], 4[illegible], 4[illegible], 4[illegible], 4767, 4[illegible], 4[illegible]07, [illegible], [illegible], [illegible], [illegible], [illegible], [illegible], [illegible], [illegible], [illegible], [illegible], [illegible], [illegible], [illegible]17, [illegible], [illegible], [illegible]-4, [illegible]-4, [illegible], [illegible], [illegible]704, [illegible], [illegible], [illegible].

O'Dwygin — Dwygan — Dwygyn. See O'Dwigin.

O'Dwyll, Wm., pardon, 4[illegible].

O'Dwynaghan. See O'Dwynighan.

O'Dwyne—Duyne—Dwine, persons of the name pardoned, 4[illegible], [illegible], 4[illegible], [illegible], 6[illegible]7, [illegible], [illegible], 67[illegible].

O'Dwyaighan—Dwyaughan—Dwyaaghan, persons of the same pardoned, 6188, 6477, [illegible].
O'Dwyre. See O'Dwyer.
O'Dwyrky, Donell, pardon, 6000.
O'Dwyry, Tho., pardon, [illegible].
O'Dye—Dy, persons of the name pardoned, 2378, 4714, 4767, [illegible], 6478-7, 6494, [illegible].
O'Dyonne, Derby, pardon, [illegible].
O'Dyer (see O'Dwyer), [illegible].
O'Dyllone, Donell and Wm., pardon, [illegible], [illegible].
O'Dymon, Dermot (O'Dempsy), pardon, 947.
O'Dymne, Maurice, pardon, 12.
O'Dyre, Donell, pardon, [illegible].
O'Dyrrollen, Morish, pardon, [illegible].
O'Dyrwy — Dyrwye — Dywwie — Dywy, persons of the same pardoned 170, 897, 2363, 4340.
Œconomus of S. Finbar's, Cork, [illegible].
O'Egir, Owen, pardon, [illegible].
O'Egharte, James, pardon, [illegible].
O'Egyn, Cale, pardon, [illegible].
Oelane, James macOwen, pardon, [illegible].
O'Emonnie, Wm., pardon, 6704.
O'Enaree, Rory, pardon, 2304.
O'Emone, Arthur, pardon, 2011.
O'Enen, Art, and others of the name pardoned, [illegible].
O'Eyfernane, Donogh, pardon, [illegible].
O'Eyne, Thady, pardon, 1341.
O'Fae, Gerald, pardon, [illegible].
O'Fagartie, Dermot and Donogh, pardon, 6817.
O'Fagh, Teig, pardon, [illegible].
O'Faghie, persons of the name pardoned, 6475, 6480, 6522, [illegible], 6708.
O'Faghnie, persons of the name pardoned, [illegible], [illegible].
O'Faghny, Gillerow, grant of land, [illegible].
O'Faghy, Wm., pardon, 6479.
O'Fagirtye, Shane, pardon, 1816.
O'Fahain — Fahan, persons of the name pardoned, [illegible].
O'Fahe, Gilledufe and Donogh, pardon, 2073, 7084.
O'Fahee, Eugene, pardon, [illegible].
O'Fahie — Fahhie — Fahi. See O'Fahy.
O'Faidin, Dermot, pardon, 6412.
O'Faie, Shane, pardon, 4857.
O'Faill, Rory, pardon, [illegible].
O'Fahy — Fahie — Fahi — Fahhie:
„ Cornelius, priest, pardon, 4140, 4794.
„ Edm. (of Lisnafill), pardon, 6470.
„ Shane (of Pobleowinfahy), pardon, [illegible].
„ Tho., clerk, pardon, [illegible].
„ others of the same pardoned, [illegible], [illegible], [illegible], 4079-81, 4140, [illegible], [illegible], 4707, 4734, 4738, 4795, [illegible], [illegible], 6100, [illegible], 6478, 6479, [illegible], 6611, [illegible], [illegible], 6697, 6471, [illegible], [illegible], 6704, 6704, 6768.
O'Faina, Conor, pardon, 6452.
O'Failan, Teig, pardon, 6178.
O'Faiove, Donell and Philip, pardon, [illegible].
Ofalie. See Offaly.
O'Faill, Auley, pardon, [illegible].
O'Fallan. See O'Fallon.
O'Fallenlocan, Finin, pardon, [illegible].
O'Fallowre, Amliff, pardon, 6878.
O'Fallie — Fallivie, Donogh, pardon, [illegible].
O'Fallo, Sowe, pardon, [illegible].
O'Fallon — Fallone — Fallan — Falon:
„ Conogh, grant of land, [illegible], pardon, [illegible]; livery to heir, [illegible].
„ Edm., leases, 1680, 3408, 3447, 6464.
„ Redmund, pardon, [illegible], [illegible]; livery, [illegible].
„ others of the name pardoned, [illegible], 3763, [illegible], 4766, 4780, 4874, [illegible], 5486, 5747, [illegible], 6106, 6110, [illegible], [illegible], 6440, 6874, [illegible].
„ country of, 1486, 3419.
„ grange of (co. Ross.), 1436, [illegible], 3418.
„ mills of, at Athlone, 4342, [illegible].
O'Fallow — Fallowe, Teig and Tho., pardon, 4768, [illegible].
O'Fallowan, Morogh, pardon, 1694.
O'Fallwe, Donogho, pardon, [illegible].
O'Fally — Fallye, persons of the name pardoned, 2070, 4378, [illegible].
O'Falon, Molaghlin, pardon, [illegible].
O'Falve, persons of the name pardoned, [illegible], [illegible].
O'Falvie, Conor, pardon, [illegible].
O'Falvy, Awly, pardon, 4877.
O'Faly, Moroghe, pardon, 4642.
O'Famee, Daniel, pardon, 4702.
O'Famlage, Conor, pardon, 6432.
O'Fany, Moriagh, pardon, [illegible].
O'Farall—Farall. See O'Ferrall.
O'Faremane, Ferdorgh and Patr., pardon, [illegible].
O'Faremie, James, pardon, 6484.
O'Fargonie, Shane, pardon, 4378.
O'Fargul, Hugh, pardon, 4028.
O'Farhy, Owny, pardon, 4812.
O'Fariell, Foy, pardon, [illegible].
O'Farilin, Teig, pardon, 4018.
O'Farill. See O'Ferrall.
O'Farle, Henry, pardon, [illegible].
O'Farmane, Edm., [illegible].
O'Faroll. See O'Ferrall.
O'Farrabwy, half hundred of (lying chiefly along north of Tralee Bay), co. Kerry, [illegible].

INDEX TO FIANTS,—ELIZABETH.

O'Farrell, David, pardon, 6534.
O'Farraghor, John, pardon, 6490.
O'Farrall, Shane, pardon, 6740.
O'Farrall. *See* O'Farrall.
O'Farran, Brian and Felim, pardon, 6482.
O'Farrall. *See* O'Farroll.
O'Farrely, Teig, 1069.
O'Farronane, Neal, pardon, 5484.
" *See* O'Faronane.
O'Farrill. *See* O'Farrall.
O'Farris, Owen and Con, pardon, 5462, 5848.
O'Farroll—Farrole. *See* O'Farrall.
O'Farrolld, James, pardon, 267.
O'Farry, Meleghlin, pardon, 5736.
O'Farylly, Philip, pardon, 4482.
O'Farye, James, pardon, 678.
O'Fasim, Owen, pardon, 4612.
O'Faughy, Teig, pardon, 2909.
O'Fay, Wm., pardon, 6080.
O'Faye, Owen, pardon, 4673.
O'Fayerty, Donogh, pardon, 5262.
O'Feagho, Wm., pardon, 6769.
O'Feaghie, John and Teig, pardon, 4498, 5621.
O'Feabine, Teig, pardon, 6456.
O'Fealan, Meleghlin, and Henry, pardon, 2848, 6534.
O'Feanighan, Wm., pardon, 6487.
O'Fearisle, Dermot, pardon, 6427.
O'Fearmey, Donchie, pardon, 5862.
O'Fearry, Meleghlin and Donnkive, pardon, 5897, 6306.
O'Fearrym, Conor, pardon, 4808.
O'Fearry, Morierragh, pardon, 2806.
O'Fearyne, Fearroghor, pardon, 5903.
O'Fegan, persons of the name pardoned, 2172, 5612.
O'Fegart—Fegarte, Donell and Donogh, pardon, 1124.
O'Fegurey, Donogh, pardon, 1124.
O'Feghy, Owin, pardon, 6543.
O'Fehin, Teig, pardon, 6122.
O'Feighrein, Conoghor, pardon, 5492.
O'Fein, Callo, pardon, 4811.
O'Felaloo, Pair., pardon, 6776.
O'Felano—Felane, persons of the name pardoned, 935, 1044-6, 1115, 1810, 2746, 3593, 4030, 4116, 4676, 5375, 5664, 6110, 6452, 6476, 6494, 6528, 6588.
O'Felime (or Felume), Donald, English liberty, 1127.
O'Felan, persons of the name pardoned, 1812, 2541, 2980.
O'Fellon, Tho., pardon, 5524.
O'Felome, John, pardon, 1633.
O'Felowe, Tho., pardon, 2744.
O'Felume, Donald, English liberty, 1127.
O'Fenaghe, Morogh and Shane, pardon, 4747.
O'Fenaght, Conor and Teig, pardon, 6456.
O'Fenaghtie, Donell, pardon, 4733.
O'Fenan—Fenane, persons of the name pardoned, 2317, 4793.
O'Fenaghty, Conohor, pardon, 4747.
O'Fenegane, Donell, pardon, 6377.
O'Fenelan—Fenelane, persons of the name pardoned, 4153, 6403.
O'Fenell, Dermot, pardon, 1617.
O'Fenellie, Wm., pardon, 6304.
O'Fenllane, Conoghor, pardon, 5873.
O'Fennaght, Conoghor, pardon, 5441.
O'Fenane, persons of the name pardoned, 5903, 5832, 6458.
O'Fenneclane, Donogh, pardon, 4733.
O'Fennell, Thady, pardon, 3374.
O'Fennen, Teig, pardon, 5423.
O'Feogherdie, Meleghlin, pardon, 1686.
O'Feolan, Donogh, pardon, 4714.
O'Feolane, Edm., pardon, 5477.
O'Feore, Wm., pardon, 5348.
O'Feovor, Conor, pardon, 5452.
O'Feralle—Forall — Farall — Feral. *See* O'Farrall.
O'Fergurti, Philip, pardon, 2049.
O'Ferane, persons of the name pardoned, 1101, 2562, 2584, 4379.
O'Ferall. *See* O'Farrall.
O'Ferowe, Gerrott, pardon, 5473.
O'Ferre, Wm., pardon, 4148.
O'Ferragh, Wm., pardon, 4292.
O'Ferrall, Kedagh, pardon, 6374.
O'Ferrall—Farall—Farell—Farill—Faroll—Farrall—Farrell—Farrill—Farrole—Farroll—Feralle—Ferall—Forall—Ferell—Ferral—Ferrell—Ferroll;
" Brian; O'Ferrall Boy, captain of his country of Moyvravin in Annaly, 1206; dead, 1871.
" Brian, son of Faghnoy O'F. Bane, pardon, 2801, 2881; vice seneschal of Clonlane, 2898.
" Brian roe (of Drumlane), attainted, 1949.
" Carbry m'Lysagh, attainted, 5404.
" Connell, seneschal of Slanght William, 3182.
" Conoke m'Kedagh, seneschal of Sleight William, 2221.
" Conwocke macHubert, captain of Clancobor, 1272, 1306.
" Cormac m'Geffry, murder of, 1177.
" Cormock, attainted, 2712.
" Cormuck m'Rory, late captain of Callagh, 308.
" Donagh, attainted, 5404.
" Donell avaughery—ovegharye or omaghery (son of Faghney), chief serjeant of O'F. Bane's

INDEX TO FIANTS—ELIZABETH.

O'Ferrall :
country, 1804 ; sheriff of Longford, comm., [illegible] ; seneschal of O'F. Bane's country, [illegible] ; pardon, 1447, [illegible], [illegible] ; his murder [illegible], [illegible] ; wardship and livery of his son and heir (James), [illegible], [illegible].

„ Edm., son of Tirlagh, wardship, [illegible].

„ Faghna (brother of Brian) : O'Ferrall Boy, chief of his name, captain of his country, 1871 ; surrender and regrant of his possessions, [illegible], [illegible] ; commission, 4157 ; his sons, [illegible].

„ Faghna m'Gillernew (of Rathcline), pardon, 5714, [illegible].

„ Faghnay m'Teig: O'F. Bane, made captain of his country of Clantane in the Annaly, 1110 ; pardon, [illegible], [illegible] ; his successor, [illegible].

„ Fergus or Ferris m'Brian (of Ballinamber and Tonaghick), sheriff of Longford, 17[illegible] ; pardon, 1447, [illegible], [illegible], [illegible] ; commissions, [illegible], [illegible], 5127.

„ Geoffrey oge, captain of the country of Callagh, 208.

„ Gerald or Garrald, pardon, [illegible], [illegible].

„ Gerald m'Hubert boy, pardon, [illegible] ; attainted, [illegible], [illegible], [illegible].

„ Gerald m'Rosse, attainted, [illegible].

„ Gerald m'Teig oge, wardship, [illegible].

„ Gerrot, killed, [illegible].

„ Gillernew m'Faghnay (of Rathcline), pardon, 5718 ; chief of Callee, grant of his lands, [illegible].

„ Hubert m'Liagh, pardon, [illegible], [illegible], [illegible].

„ Hugh, slain, [illegible].

„ Hugh duff, attainted, [illegible].

„ Iriel (of Mornin), son of Faghna O'F. Boy, sheriff of co. Longford, [illegible], [illegible], [illegible] ; pardon, [illegible], [illegible], [illegible] ; license of alienation, [illegible], [illegible] ; lease [illegible] ; commission, [illegible], [illegible] ; pardon to his followers, [illegible].

Iriel m'Gillernew, pardon, [illegible], [illegible].

„ Iriel m'Wm., seneschal of Clanconnor, [illegible].

„ James, son of Donell evaghery, wardship and livery, [illegible], [illegible].

„ John, captain of Sleightwilliam O'Ferrall, 1704.

O'Ferrall, Kedagh, his lands granted, [illegible].

„ Liagh mac Hubert, captain of Clanconnor, 1231.

„ Liagh mac Kedagh, seneschal of Sleightwilliam, [illegible] ; sheriff of Longford, comm., 5127.

„ Morogh or Morll, lands held by the heirs of, [illegible], 1401, [illegible], [illegible].

„ Morogh m'Conwick, pardon, [illegible] ; attainted, [illegible].

„ Morogh m'Teig, seneschal of Clanawile, [illegible].

„ Mortagh, attainted, [illegible].

„ Moylaghlin, attainted, [illegible].

„ Owen, attainted, [illegible], [illegible].

„ Rory, sheriff of Longford, [illegible] ; son of O'F. Boy, [illegible].

„ Rory (of Drumhoghily), pardon, [illegible].

„ Rory m'Donogh, pardon, [illegible] ; attainted, [illegible].

„ Shane m'Donogh, attainted, [illegible].

„ Shane m'Tirrelagh, wardship, [illegible].

„ Teig oge, son of Faghnay O'F. Bane, pardon, [illegible], [illegible] ; appointed tanist of Clantane, [illegible] ; wardship of his heir, [illegible].

„ Teig boy m'Hubert, chief sergeant and captain of Clanconnor, 1608 ; pardon, [illegible], 3771.

„ Teig m'James, attainted, [illegible]

„ Tho., vicar of Mayne, pardon, [illegible].

„ Tho., manslaughter of, [illegible].

„ Tirlagh m'Breyn, wardship of his heir, [illegible].

„ Tirlagh m'Kedagh, seneschal of Sleightwilliam, [illegible] ; pardon, [illegible].

„ Tirlagh m'Owen, attainted, [illegible] ; pardon, [illegible].

„ Tirlagh m'William reagh, pardon, [illegible] ; wardship of his heir, [illegible].

„ Tirrell, lands of, in co. Kild., [illegible].

„ William mac Donell : O'F. Bane, [illegible] ; surrender and regrant of his possessions, [illegible], [illegible] ; commission, 5127.

„ others of the name pardoned, 10, [illegible], [illegible], [illegible], [illegible], [illegible], [illegible], [illegible], [illegible], 1446–7, [illegible], 1770, [illegible]

O'Ferrall:
[illegible], 4163, [illegible], [illegible], 4418, [illegible], [illegible], [illegible], 4708, 4740, [illegible], [illegible], [illegible], [illegible], [illegible], 4874, [illegible], [illegible], 4913, [illegible], [illegible], 4980, 5000, 5122, 5162, [illegible], 5274, [illegible], 5440, 5462, [illegible], 6777, [illegible].

O'Ferrall Bane. See O'F., Faghnoy, William.
" country of, 614, 1465, 1604, [illegible], [illegible], [illegible], [illegible].

O'Ferrall Boy. See O'F., Brian, Faghna.
" title abolished, 4051.
" country of, 1083, 1737, [illegible], 4178, [illegible], [illegible], [illegible].

O'Ferralls — O'Ferrals, composition rent paid by, [illegible].

O'Ferralls, Redm., pardon, [illegible].

O'Ferran, Brian, pardon, 18.

O'Ferrayle, persons of the name (8 described as pipers) pardoned (co. Wex., ?) [illegible].

O'Ferrale, Rich., pardon, 4122.

O'Ferroy, Brian, pardon, 5740.

O'Ferris, Moriertagh, pardon, [illegible].

O'Ferroll. See O'Ferrall.

O'Ferrowle, James, pardon, 5477.

O'Fewre, Brian and Wm., pardon, 1673.

O'Fewre, Gillepatrick, pardon, [illegible].

O'Feye, persons of the name pardoned, [illegible].

O'Feylaghan, Shane, pardon, 836.

Offaley—Offalie. See Offaly.

Offallon in Uppercowney, [illegible].

Offaly—Ofalie—Offaley—Offalie—Offalley—Offayle — Ophalie — Ophalley — Ophallie — Ophaly, 62, 70, 123, 234, 345, 362, 674, [illegible], [illegible], [illegible], [illegible], [illegible], [illegible], [illegible], [illegible]; lordship, [illegible]; formed into King's co., [illegible]; martial law in, 52, 98, [illegible], [illegible].
" lieutenant of, [illegible], 4044, [illegible].
" seneschal of, [illegible].
" governor of forces in, [illegible].
" fort of, lieutenant of, 4, 12, [illegible], [illegible], [illegible].
" " victualler of, [illegible].
" O'Connors of, excepted from pardon, [illegible], [illegible], [illegible].
" barony of, in co. Kildare. See Aphaly [illegible].
" baron of (see Kildare, earl of), [illegible].

Offane (co. Leit. ?), [illegible].

Offayle. See Offaly.

Official, exempted from serving on juries, [illegible]; removed for insufficiency, [illegible]; neglects office for three years, [illegible]; deprived for misbehaviour, [illegible]; in rebellion, [illegible], [illegible].

Official hours—a fiant delivered about 6 a.m., [illegible].

Officials to take oath of supremacy, [illegible]; not to be deprived of office without sufficient cause proved, [illegible], [illegible], [illegible], [illegible].

Offlyny (Leyny ?), barony of, co. Sligo, [illegible].

O'Fiagh, Wm., pardon, [illegible].

O'Fiaghny, Dermot, pardon, [illegible].

O'Fiaghy, Tho., pardon, [illegible].

O'Fian, Dermot and Wm., pardon, [illegible], [illegible].

O'Fianaghta, Conchor, pardon, [illegible].

O'Fidnagh, Teig, pardon, [illegible].

O'Fiehe, persons of the name pardoned, [illegible].

O'Fiegles, Wm., pardon, [illegible].

O'Fieghidie, John, pardon, [illegible].

O'Fieghie, Teig, pardon, [illegible], [illegible].

O'Fieghny, Hugh, pardon, [illegible].

O'Fielagh, Cahill, pardon, [illegible].

O'Fielly or Fild, Dermot and Owen, pardon, [illegible].

O'Fierhie, Conghor, pardon, [illegible].

O'Fieris, persons of the name pardoned, [illegible], [illegible].

O'Figurty, Colagh, pardon, [illegible].

O'Fihel, Thomas. See Leighlin, bishop.

O'Fihilie, Rory, pardon, [illegible].

O'Fihilly, Dermot, pardon, [illegible].

O'Fihily or Filde, Owen, pardon, [illegible].

O'Fihylly, Wm., pardon, [illegible].

O'Fila, Fliagh, pardon, [illegible].

O'Filan, Ferrall, pardon, [illegible].

O'Filane, Evan, pardon, [illegible].

O'Finie, Ohanie, pardon, [illegible].

O'Fimilan, David, pardon, [illegible].

O'Fin, Dermod, pardon, [illegible].

O'Finane—Finan, persons of the name pardoned, 1048, 4794, [illegible], [illegible].

O'Finegan, Donogh, pardon, [illegible].

O'Finekane, Tho., pardon, [illegible].

O'Finen—Finin, Tho. and Owen, pardon, [illegible], [illegible].

O'Finley, Tho., pardon, [illegible].

O'Finn—Finne, Shane and Dermot, pardon, [illegible], [illegible].

O'Finy, Teig, pardon, [illegible].

O'Finygan, John, priest, pardon, [illegible].

O'Finyn, Thady, pardon, [illegible].

O'Fiorie, Conghor, pardon, [illegible].

O'Firrie, Tirlagh, pardon, [illegible].

O'Flaertie—Flaerty. See O'Flaherty.

O'Flaghavane. See O'Flahavan.

O'Flaghery, John, pardon, [illegible].
O'Flaghovan. *See* O'Flahavan.
O'Flaghie, Padin and Donell, pardon, [illegible], [illegible].
O'Flaghin, Wm., pardon, [illegible].
O'Flaghvane, Teig, pardon, 6477.
O'Flahane, Philip, [illegible].
O'Flahertie, Margaret, pardon, [illegible].
O'Flahavan — Flahovan — Flaghavane — Flaghevan—Flahevane—Flahewan, persons of the name pardoned, [illegible], [illegible], [illegible], [illegible], [illegible], [illegible], [illegible], [illegible], [illegible], 6494, [illegible], [illegible], [illegible], [illegible].
O'Flaherta, Rory, pardon, [illegible].
O'Flaherty—Flahertie—Fleartie—Flaarty—Flarety — Flarte — Flartie — Flarty:
„ Donald crone, captain of Iar Connaght, [illegible].
„ Donell crone, pardon, [illegible], [illegible], [illegible].
„ Donell in coggie, proposed surrender, [illegible]; daughter of, [illegible].
„ Donell m'Rory, pardon, 4474, [illegible], [illegible].
„ Morogh ne doe m'Teig (knight), captain of Iar Connaght, [illegible]; pardon, [illegible], [illegible], 6716, [illegible], [illegible], [illegible]; commission, [illegible], 4745; surrender and regrant of his possessions, [illegible]; his sons, [illegible], [illegible].
„ Morogh na moyre, son of Donell in coggie and Grany ny Maly, pardon, [illegible], [illegible], [illegible]; proposed surrender, [illegible].
„ Rory shaogh, son of Morogh ne doe, pardon, [illegible], [illegible], [illegible], [illegible]; Mr. Roger, pardon at suit of, [illegible].
„ Teig m'Morogh, pardon, [illegible], [illegible]; slain in rebellion, [illegible], [illegible].
„ Teig oge (of Ahinure), pardon, [illegible], [illegible]; slain in rebellion, [illegible].
„ Teig ne bully, pardon, [illegible], [illegible].
„ others of the name pardoned, [illegible], [illegible], [illegible], [illegible], [illegible], [illegible], [illegible], 4767, [illegible], [illegible], [illegible], [illegible], [illegible], 6415, [illegible], [illegible], [illegible], [illegible], [illegible], [illegible], [illegible].
„ country of, [illegible], [illegible], [illegible], [illegible], [illegible], [illegible].
„ Knight Rory roe, territories of, [illegible].
O'Flahevne — Flahovane — Flahewan. *See* O'Flahavan.
O'Flahie, Donogho, pardon, [illegible].
O'Flahiff, Shane, pardon, 6712.
O'Flaine, Teig, pardon, [illegible].
O'Flaingelye, Donell, pardon, [illegible].
O'Flamyle, John, pardon, 6731.
O'Flanagan — Flanagaine — Flanagane — Flanagyne — Flanegan — Flanegaine — Flanigan — Flanigane — Flannagan — Flannegan — Flannegaine — Flannigan—Flannogan—Flanygan:
„ Hugh, attainted, 6777.
„ Owen m'Dowallagh (of Bolhree), pardon, [illegible], [illegible], [illegible]; attainted, [illegible].
„ Owen gran, attainted, [illegible].
„ Redmund. *See* Flanegane.
„ others of the name (in co. Rosc.), pardoned, [illegible], [illegible], [illegible], [illegible], [illegible], [illegible], 4762, [illegible], [illegible], [illegible], [illegible], [illegible], [illegible], [illegible], [illegible], [illegible], [illegible], [illegible], [illegible], [illegible].
„ persons of the name in co. Clare pardoned, [illegible], [illegible], [illegible], [illegible], [illegible], [illegible], [illegible].
„ persons of the name in other districts, pardoned, [illegible], [illegible], [illegible], [illegible], [illegible], [illegible], [illegible], [illegible], [illegible], [illegible], [illegible], [illegible], [illegible], [illegible], [illegible], [illegible], [illegible], 6777.
„ country of (in co. Roscommon), [illegible], [illegible], [illegible].
O'Flanaghan — Flanaghan, persons of the name pardoned, 4447, [illegible], [illegible], [illegible].
O'Flanagyne. *See* O'Flanagan.
O'Flanawghan, Donogh, pardon, 4741.
O'Flanchy, Mohown, pardon, [illegible].
O'Flanechie, Teig, pardon, [illegible].
O'Flanegan — Flanegaine — Flanegane. *See* O'Flanagan.
O'Flaneghan. *See* O'Flanaghan.
O'Flangan, persons of the name pardoned, [illegible], [illegible], [illegible], [illegible].
O'Flanger, Wm., pardon, [illegible].
O'Flanhill, Dermod and Thady, pardon, [illegible].
O'Flanigagan [ ], pardon, [illegible].
O'Flanigan—Flanigane. *See* O'Flanagan.
O'Flanill, Marcus, priest, pardon, [illegible].
O'Flanmore, Dermot, attainted, [illegible].
O'Flannagagan, Hugh, pardon, [illegible].
O'Flannagaine, Molaghlin, pardon, [illegible].
O'Flannegan—Flannogan. *See* O'Flanagan.
O'Flannoghan, Cormock and Shane, pardon, [illegible].

INDEX TO FIANTS—ELIZABETH.

O'Flannelly—Flannellie, persons of the name pardoned, [illegible].
O'Flannerragh, Brian, pardon, [illegible].
O'Flannigan—Flannogan. *See* O'Flanagan.
O'Flannor, Dermod, attainted, [illegible].
O'Flannorne, Wm., pardon, [illegible].
O'Flannygan. *See* O'Flanagan.
O'Flannylie, Dermot crone, pardon, [illegible].
O'Flanor, Rory, pardon, 5401.
O'Flanory, Connor, pardon, [illegible].
O'Flanure, Wm., pardon, 4734.
O'Flanuragh, Mologhlin, pardon, [illegible].
O'Flanygan. *See* O'Flanagan.
O'Flanylie, persons of the name pardoned, [illegible].
O'Flarty—Flarte—Flartie—Flarety. *See* O'Flaherty.
O'Flatere, Ferall, pardon, [illegible].
O'Flaterie—Flatery—Flateye—Flatterie—Flattery, persons of the name pardoned, [illegible], [illegible], [illegible].
O'Flaterice country. *See* O'Flaherty.
O'Flatery, Morogh ne do (*see* O'Flaherty), [illegible].
O'Flathirte, Donoghe, pardon, [illegible].
O'Flateye. *See* O'Flaterie.
O'Flatteine, Murtagh, pardon, [illegible].
O'Flattery—Flatterie. *See* O'Flaterie.
O'Flaugh, Dermot and Donagh, pardon, [illegible].
O'Flavan—Flavane, persons of the name pardoned, [illegible], 4111, [illegible], [illegible], [illegible].
O'Flayne, persons of the name pardoned, [illegible], [illegible], [illegible], [illegible].
O'Flayne, Morish, pardon, [illegible].
O'Flayvane, John, pardon, [illegible].
O'Flaine, Daniel and Teig, pardon, [illegible].
O'Flee, Donke and Matthew, pardon, [illegible], [illegible].
O'Flemgan, Mologhlin, pardon, [illegible].
O'Flene, Owen and Knoghor, pardon, [illegible], [illegible].
O'Fleyne, Donell, [illegible].
O'Flin, Cahill and Donell, pardon, [illegible].
O'Flin. *See* O'Flyn.
O'Fline, persons of the name pardoned, [illegible], [illegible].
O'Flinge, persons of the name pardoned, [illegible].
O'Floime, Dermod, pardon, [illegible].
O'Floine. *See* O'Floyne.
O'Floinge, Tho., pardon, [illegible].
O'Floyne—Floine—Floyn—Floin:
   „ Conor, mesurage in Kells, [illegible].
   „ others of the name pardoned, [illegible], [illegible], 1048, [illegible], [illegible], [illegible], [illegible], [illegible], [illegible], [illegible], [illegible], [illegible], [illegible], [illegible], [illegible], [illegible].
O'Flun, Owen, pardon, [illegible].
O'Flyne, persons of the name pardoned, [illegible], [illegible], [illegible], [illegible], [illegible].
O'Flwin, David, pardon, [illegible].
O'Flwyn, persons of the name pardoned, [illegible], [illegible], [illegible].
O'Flyin, Daniel, pardon, [illegible].
O'Flyn—Flin—Flynn—Flynne:
   „ Thomas (of Myleagh), attainted, [illegible].
   „ others of the name pardoned, [illegible].
O'Flynn, persons of the name pardoned, [illegible], [illegible], [illegible], 4777, [illegible], [illegible], [illegible], [illegible].
O'Flynn—Flynne. *See* O'Flyn.
O'Foody, Wm., pardon, [illegible].
O'Foelan, Shane, pardon, [illegible].
O'Foelane, Donogh and Morris, pardon, [illegible], [illegible].
O'Foeliane, Morris, pardon, [illegible].
O'Forty, Shane, pardon, [illegible].
O'Fogartie. *See* O'Fogertie.
O'Fogard, Gorh, pardon, [illegible].
O'Fogertie, Wm., a rebel, [illegible].
O'Fogertie—Fogartie—Fogerty—Fogirtie—Fogortie—Fogurtie:
   „ Donell grany, attainted, [illegible].
   „ Mologhlin, slain in rebellion, [illegible].
   „ others of the name pardoned, [illegible], [illegible], [illegible], [illegible], [illegible], [illegible], [illegible], [illegible], [illegible], [illegible], [illegible], [illegible], [illegible], [illegible], [illegible], [illegible], [illegible].
O'Fogierte, Donell, pardon, [illegible].
O'Fogirtie. *See* O'Fogertie.
O'Fogortie, Shane, pardon, [illegible].
O'Fogurtie. *See* O'Fogertie.
O'Fogurtie, Edm., pardon, [illegible].
O'Fogurtie. *See* O'Fogertie.
O'Fohrane, John, pardon, [illegible].
O'Folan, persons of the name pardoned, [illegible], [illegible], [illegible], [illegible], [illegible].
   „ country of, co. Rosc., [illegible].
O'Folane, persons of the name pardoned, 10, [illegible].
O'Foleghe, Gillpatrick, pardon, [illegible].
O'Folian, persons of the name pardoned, [illegible].
O'Folleghe, Hugh, pardon, [illegible].
O'Follie, Hugh, pardon, [illegible].
O'Folligh, Wm., pardon, [illegible].
O'Follow—Follows—Folows, persons of the name pardoned, [illegible], [illegible], [illegible], [illegible], [illegible].
O'Folly, Wm., pardon, [illegible].

INDEX TO FIANTS—ELIZABETH.

O'Folowe. See O'Follow.
O'Foodie, Teig, pardon, 6708.
O'Fooelane, persons of the name pardoned, 4711.
O'Foran—Forane, persons of the name pardoned, 120, 4694, 6874.
O'Fordhane, Shane, pardon, 6696.
O'Foreban, Donell and Edm., pardon, 6[illegible].
O'Foreman, Bren and Donogho, pardon, 6459.
O'Forfinye, Gillpatrick, pardon, 6714.
O'Forgerthie, Conor, pardon, 6878.
O'Forhane — Forhane — Forhan, persons of the name pardoned, 2[illegible], 3941, 4[illegible].
O'Forman, Edm. and John, pardon, 6[illegible].
O'Fougherty, Rorie, pardon, 5[illegible].
O'Foullowe. See O'Fowle.
O'Foulve. See O'Fowlwe.
O'Foulohan, Edm., pardon, 6[illegible].
O'Foulue—Foulowe. See O'Fowle.
O'Foulwe. See O'Fowlwe.
O'Fowle, John, pardon, 1[illegible].
O'Fowlam, Rich., pardon, 1504.
O'Fowlan—Fowlane, persons of the name pardoned, 1[illegible], 4712, 6317.
O'Fowlant, Wm., pardon, 6711.
O'Fowle, Teig, pardon, 4749.
O'Fowle—Foullowe — Foulue — Foulowe — Fowlloe — Fowllow — Fowloe — Fowlow — Fowlue, persons of the name pardoned, 61, 2[illegible]-3, 2[illegible]-4, 3[illegible], 4115, 4[illegible], 4[illegible], 4[illegible], 4715-6, 4[illegible], 4[illegible], 5174, 5180, 5[illegible], 5[illegible], 6[illegible], 6[illegible], 6[illegible], 6[illegible], 6[illegible], 6[illegible], 6[illegible], 6[illegible], 6[illegible].
O'Fowlwe—Foulve—Foulwe, persons of the name pardoned, 6467, 6671.
O'Fowlwe, Edm., alias Farshinge, pardon, 6[illegible].
O'Fowly, John, pardon, 6[illegible].
O'Fowran—Fowrane, persons of the name pardoned, 2[illegible], 3[illegible], 4467, 6[illegible].
O'Fowre, Conor, pardon, 4[illegible].
O'Foylan—Foylane, persons of the name pardoned, 2[illegible], 6[illegible], 6[illegible], 1[illegible].
O'Frenslan, Geoffrey, pardon, 6[illegible].
O'Freney, David, pardon, 2[illegible].
O'Frinaghly, Conor, pardon, 4[illegible].
O'Fryertane, Donell, pardon, 6[illegible].
O'Fryle, Clement and Hugh, pardon, 6[illegible].
O'Fuareyne, Donogho, pardon, 2[illegible].
O'Fuathane, Teig, pardon, 6[illegible].
O'Fuer, Edm. and Tibbald, pardon, 6[illegible].
O'Fuery, Brian, pardon, 6[illegible].
O'Fullan—Fullane, persons of the name pardoned, 2[illegible], 6[illegible].
O'Fullve, Dermod, pardon, 6[illegible].
O'Furrhan, Teig, pardon, 6[illegible].
O'Fure, Wm. and Tho., pardon, 2[illegible], 6[illegible].
O'Furie. See O'Fury.
O'Furillie—Furielli, Donell and Teig, pardon, 6[illegible].
O'Furrie — Furry, Neal and Gillpatrick, pardon, 6[illegible], 6[illegible].
O'Fury—Furie—Fwry, persons of the name pardoned, 6[illegible], 4780, 6[illegible], 6450, 6[illegible], 6[illegible], 6[illegible].
O'Fwolce, Dermod, pardon, 6[illegible].
O'Fworan, Shane oge, pardon, 6[illegible].
O'Fworhan, Onoghor, pardon, 6[illegible].
O'Fworlahe, Cormock, pardon, 6[illegible].
O'Fwry. See O'Fury.
O'Fwylighane, Hugh, pardon, 4[illegible].
O'Fyan, Shane and Wm., pardon, 6[illegible], 6[illegible].
O'Fyegh, Moriertagh, priest, pardon, 5[illegible].
O'Fyeneghlle, Teig, pardon, 6[illegible].
O'Fyhie, Mahon, pardon, 6764.
O'Fyhye, Molmory, pardon, 6711.
O'Fylan—Fylane;
 „ Donogh, rimer, pardon, 6[illegible].
 „ Niall and Dowgin, pardon, 6[illegible], 6[illegible].
O'Fylloawghe, Fylliagh, pardon, 6741.
O'Fyn, persons of the name pardoned, 4[illegible], 4[illegible], 4[illegible], 5[illegible], 5[illegible], 6[illegible], 6[illegible].
O'Fynaghin, Morcho, pardon, 2[illegible].
O'Fynaghty, Conor, pardon, 2[illegible].
O'Fynan—Fynane—Fynen, persons of the name pardoned, 6709, 6[illegible], 6[illegible], 6[illegible].
O'Fynaught, Morgh, pardon, 1[illegible].
O'Fyne, Morgh, pardon, 4[illegible].
O'Fynen—Fynes, persons of the name pardoned, 4[illegible], 4761.
O'Fynegane, Shane, pardon, 6[illegible].
O'Fyneghan, Teig, pardon, 4[illegible].
O'Fyneigh, Moriertagh, pardon, 6[illegible].
O'Fynellan, Brien and Shane, pardon, 6[illegible], 6[illegible].
O'Fynen. See O'Fynan.
O'Fynise, Donogh, 1578.
O'Fynn. See O'Fynne.
O'Fynnan, Teig and Murtagh, pardon, 4797, 6[illegible].
O'Fynne—Fynn, persons of the name pardoned, 4641, 4703, 6[illegible], 6[illegible].
O'Fynnellan, Pair., pardon, 6[illegible].
O'Fynnlage, Edm., pardon, 6[illegible].
O'Fynnole, Conoghor, pardon, 6[illegible].
O'Fynnolan—Fynnolane, Dermot and Morish, pardon, 6[illegible].
O'Fynnoll, Edm., pardon, 6[illegible].
O'Fynnyly, Maurice, surgeon, pardon, 6[illegible].
O'Fynnysie, Dermod, pardon, 6[illegible].
O'Fynoely—Fynoele, Donoghow and Philip, 6[illegible], 6[illegible].
O'Fyny, persons of the name pardoned, 6[illegible], 4[illegible], 6[illegible], 6[illegible], 6[illegible], 6[illegible], 6[illegible].
O'Fyrasyn, Donald, pardon, 1[illegible].

INDEX TO FIANTS—ELIZABETH.

O'Fyrye, Owen, pardon, 4407.
O'Gahan, Shane, pardon, [illegible].
O'Galchow, Gillypatrick, pardon, [illegible].
O'Galcour, persons of the name pardoned, [illegible].
O'Galcowe, persons of the name pardoned, [illegible].
O'Galevaine, Teig, pardon, [illegible].
" See also Yalevain.
O'Galgan, Wm., pardon, [illegible].
O'Galla, Donogh, pardon, [illegible].
O'Gallacowe, Edm., pardon, [illegible].
O'Gallagan, Conoghor, alias Meyhin, pardon, [illegible].
O'Gallagher—Gallgr—Galgr:
" Art m'Ancoblg, pardon, [illegible].
" Owen m'Adegany, pardon, [illegible].
" Owen m'Shane, pardon, [illegible].
" See also O'Galcour, O'Galcowe, and O'Gallchair.
O'Gallavan, Teig, pardon, [illegible].
O'Gallchair, Eugenius Flavus, pardon, [illegible].
O'Gallchoe, Owen, pardon, [illegible].
O'Gallcowe, Rory, pardon, [illegible].
O'Gallegan, David, pardon, [illegible].
O'Galleghan, Shane, pardon, [illegible].
O'Galleghowe, Donogho, pardon, [illegible].
O'Galleghure, Brian and Donogh, pardon, [illegible].
O'Gallehow, Neal, pardon, [illegible].
O'Gallevane, Teig, pardon, [illegible].
O'Galligan, Donogh and David, pardon, [illegible], [illegible].
O'Gallikure, Donoghy, pardon, [illegible].
O'Gallivain, Thady, pardon, [illegible].
O'Gallochowe, Ro., pardon, [illegible].
O'Galloghan, Donogh, pardon, [illegible].
Ogallohore (Evegallahoo ?), co. Lim., [illegible].
O'Gallowkowe, Rory, pardon, [illegible].
O'Gallqr. See O'Gallagher.
O'Gallvaine—Gallvan—Gallvarn—Gallwaine. See O'Galvane.
O'Galpen, Shane, pardon, [illegible].
O'Galqr. See O'Gallagher.
O'Galvane—Gallvaine—Gallvan—Gallvane—Gallvarn—Gallwaine—Galvan—Galwan, persons of the name pardoned, [illegible].
Ogan, Ricard and Ogan m'Ricard I., pardon, [illegible].
" See O'Hogan.
Ogane, Shivane ny, pardon, [illegible], [illegible].
Ogangagha, Donogh, pardon, [illegible].
O'Ganie, Shane, pardon, [illegible].
O'Gara—Garoe—Garey—Garie—Garrie—Garry—Gary—Garye:
" Ercill (of Moy), chief of his name, pardon, [illegible], [illegible].
O'Gara, others of the name pardoned, [illegible].
" country of, in co. Sligo, [illegible].
O'Gargan, Murtagh, pardon, 4715.
O'Garie. See O'Gara.
O'Garran, persons of the name pardoned, [illegible], [illegible], [illegible], 4574.
O'Garrevey, Philip, pardon, [illegible].
O'Garrie—Garry. See O'Gara.
O'Garrywan, Teig, pardon, [illegible].
O'Garvan—Garvane, persons of the name pardoned, [illegible].
" See also Yarvane.
O'Garve, Conoghor, pardon, [illegible].
O'Garvey, Cahill, pardon, [illegible].
O'Garvie, Edm., pardon, [illegible].
O'Garvy, Conoghor, pardon, [illegible].
O'Garvyne, Eugene or Owen, pardon, [illegible].
O'Garwane, Conoghor and Donogho, pardon, [illegible].
O'Gary—Garye. See O'Gara.
O'Garyveigh, Tho., pardon, [illegible].
O'Garywan, Donald, pardon, [illegible].
O'Gasnan, Brian, pardon, [illegible].
O'Gavan, Loghlen and Wm., pardon, [illegible], [illegible].
O'Gawen. See O'Gawin.
O'Gawenan, Patrick or Ferdoragh, pardon, [illegible].
O'Gawin—Gawen—Gawne, persons of the name pardoned, [illegible].
O'Gawnan, Donagh, English liberty, [illegible].
O'Gawne, persons of the name pardoned, [illegible].
O'Gawney, Patrick, English liberty, 111.
" others of the name pardoned, [illegible].
O'Gawran, Tho., pardon, [illegible].
O'Gayn, Murchie, pardon, [illegible].
O'Gealane, Donogh and Melaghlin, pardon, [illegible].
O'Gealghona, Neil, murder of, [illegible].
O'Geallane, Patr., pardon, [illegible].
O'Gealvane, John, pardon, [illegible].
O'Gealwaine, Teig, pardon, [illegible].
O'Geane, Wm., pardon, [illegible].
O'Geanie, Dermod, pardon, [illegible].
O'Geary, Wm., attainted, [illegible].
O'Geatie, persons of the name pardoned, [illegible].
O'Gebhan, Brian, pardon, [illegible].
O'Gegin, persons of the name pardoned, [illegible].
O'Gehin, Donald, pardon, [illegible].
O'Geigin, John and Melaghlin, pardon, [illegible].
O'Geirie, Owen, pardon, [illegible].

INDEX TO FIANTS.—ELIZABETH.

O'Gelgan, Doughe, pardon, [illegible].
O'Gellain, Edm., pardon, 6818.
O'Gellchain, Donell, pardon, [illegible].
O'Geenyle, Rory and Shane, pardon, 6761.
O'Gemer, Shane, pardon, 6180.
O'Gerane—Geran, persons of the name pardoned, [illegible], 6498, [illegible].
O'Gereighan, Donell, pardon, [illegible].
O'Geria, persons of the name pardoned, 4478, 4688, [illegible].
O'Gerigh, Maurice, pardon, [illegible].
O'Geriles, Donogh, pardon, [illegible].
O'Gernan, John and Maurice, pardon, [illegible], [illegible].
O'Geryn, Shane, pardon, [illegible].
O'Gewregane, Shane, pardon, [illegible].
O'Geyne, John, pardon, 6494.
Oghelerra, co. Cav., 4891.
Ogheren, Gerald m'Wm. Y., pardon, [illegible].
Oghery, co. Gal. See Oheria.
Oghewalle — Oghewally (Noughaval, co. Westm. and Long.), chapel, &c., 6767.
Oghil Beg, co. Gal. See Oghylbegge.
Oghill (co. Gal.?), [illegible].
Oghill (Oghil), co. Kild., 1252.
Oghill, co. Mon. See Ballyoghill.
Oghe moore, pardon, 670.
Oghoherdon, Phelim, pardon, 634.
Oghterdiren (co. Ros. or Leit.), 4426. See Oughterhorey.
Oghie (co. Kerry?), 6878.
Oghered (or Ughtered), Henry, grant of land, 6782.
Oghvalle (Nohaval), co. Kerry, advowson, 6034.
Oghylbegge (Oghil Beg, co. Gal.), 1681.
Oghyll, co. Tip., 6700.
Ogieny, Wm., pardon, 6069.
O'Gibbelain, Hugh, pardon, 4078.
O'Gibbelen, Brian, pardon, 6487.
O'Gibbellayne, Morish, pardon, 4778.
O'Gibbenny, Edm., harper, pardon, 6737.
O'Gibbellan, Wm., pardon, 6808.
O'Gibleam, Murtagh, pardon, 6428.
O'Gibleny, Teig, pardon, 4883.
O'Gibne, persons of the name pardoned, 711, 5804, 6861.
O'Gigney, persons of the name pardoned, 87, 5804, 5618, 6421.
O'Gieran, Conor and Donogh, pardon, [illegible].
O'Gierey, Moriogh, pardon, 6812.
O'Gigen, Wm., pardon, 6434.
O'Gighine, Conor, pardon, 6477.
O'Gilbon—Gilbine, David and Wm., pardon, 6879.
O'Gilan, Donell, pardon, 6478.
O'Gilevoy, Neal and Tirlagh, pardon, 6704.
O'Gilgan, Dermod, pardon, 6435.
O'Gillahicain, Donell, pardon, 4484.
O'Gillain, Teig, pardon, 6874.
O'Gillegan—Gilligan—Gillygayne, persons of the name pardoned, 3780, 4684, 4887, 6848, 6867.
O'Gillhinan, Moriagh, pardon, 5184.
O'Gillikenan, Moriertagh, pardon, 4477.
O'Gillygayne. See O'Gillegan.
Ogirogh, Davie and John, pardon, 6878.
O'Glachane, Manus, pardon, 6761.
O'Glaeky, Owny, pardon, 5944.
O'Glasmine, persons of the name pardoned, 4476, 4744, 6461.
O'Glavan—Glasane—Glasson, persons of the name pardoned, 5041, 4460, 4478, 6457, 4462, 4678, 6682.
O'Glasphane, Dermod, pardon, 4489.
O'Glassnie, Conoghor, pardon, 6480.
O'Glasyn, Tho. and Hugh, pardon, 1204, 1807.
O'Glavine, John, pardon, 5068.
O'Glavyn, Maurice, pardon, 4107.
O'Glenane, Loghlen, pardon, 4752.
O'Glessane, Donogh, pardon, 6463.
O'Glessine, Shane, pardon, 6463.
O'Glissan—Glisane—Glishane. See O'Glissane.
O'Glishie, Donoghe, pardon, 6704.
O'Glissane—Glisan—Glisane—Glishane, persons of the name pardoned, 4482, 4678, 6512-6, 6516, 6522, 6541, 6549, 6542, 67-6, 6711.
O'Glishon—Glisshie, Hugh boy, pardon, 6550, 6551.
O'Glisten, Hugh, pardon, 4484.
O'Glissed, Edm. and Morierlagh, pardon, 6602.
Oglos, co. Ros., 4448.
O'Glussleine, David, pardon, 6528.
O'Glusson, John, pardon, 6166.
O'Glycean, Loghlen, pardon, 6817.
O'Glyeane, Dermot, pardon, 4484; alias (?), 4484.
O'Glyshane, David, pardon, 4484.
O'Glyssan, Donell, pardon, 4004.
Ognailf—Ognaile—Ognailde, persons of the name pardoned, 6603.
O'Gnyw, persons of the name pardoned, 6405.
O'Goan, persons of the name pardoned, 4478, 6867, 6882.
O'Goharye—Gogharie—Goharie—Goharighe persons of the name pardoned, 4486, 4488, 6604, 6608.
O'Goine, Philip, pardon, 4289.
O'Golgane, Donogh, pardon, 10.
O'Gomen, Fordorgh, pardon, 4478.
O'Gomely, Patr., pardon, 6782.
O'Gonaghtyn, Conoghor, pardon, 4478.
O'Gone, Kell, pardon, 6711.
O'Gonne, Edm. and Tirrelagh, pardon, 4469.
O'Gonne, Brian, robbery of, 142.
O'Gonyane, Wm., pardon, 2808.

INDEX TO FIANTS—ELIZABETH.

O'Gormann, Gerald, pardon, 6440.
O'Gormanan. *See* O'Gormogan.
O'Gormakan, Morish, pardon, 6437.
O'Gormaly, Cormock, pardon, 6468.
O'Gorman, persons of the name pardoned, 5078, 6344, 6478.
O'Gorman (in Inishowen), pardon, 6858.
O'Gormegan. *See* O'Gormogan.
O'Gormelan, Dermot, pardon, 6476.
O'Gormelo, Edm., pardon, 6783.
O'Gormeyle, Mortagh, 6182.
O'Gormle, Tho., pardon, 6407.
O'Gormley—Gormly, persons of the name pardoned, 5484, 6843, 6734.
O'Gormenan, Michael, pardon, 6443.
O'Gormochan, Conoghor and Gillduff, pardon, 6473, 6682.
O'Gormock, Donogh, pardon, 6481.
O'Gormogan, Owen, pardon, 776.
O'Gormogan — Gormagan — Gormegan, persons of the name pardoned, 1671, 4698, [illegible], [illegible], [illegible], [illegible], 6423, 6462, 6541, 6577, 6782.
O'Gormoge, persons of the name pardoned, 3981, 4682, 6703.
O'Gormoke, persons of the name pardoned, 1617, 6561.
O'Gormon, Conor and Donell, pardon, 4495, 6775.
O'Gormoly, Rich., pardon, 5468.
O'Gormoule — Gormowle, persons of the name pardoned, 6640.
O'Gormull, Philip, pardon, 6608.
O'Gormully, Don, pardon, 6628.
O'Gormuly, Philip, pardon, 6815.
O'Gormyle, Hugh, pardon, 5468.
Ogormaltelmas, barony, co. Cork, 5287.
O'Gorumley, Tirelagh, pardon, 5438.
O'Gowe, alias Smith, Moriertagh, pardon, 4867.
O'Gowen—Gowin, persons of the name pardoned, 1247, 1184, 4512, 4871, 4884, 5143, 5799, 6456, 6500, 6548, 6867.
O'Gowneght, Conoboneght, pardon, 5603.
O'Gownan—Gownane, persons of the name pardoned, 4614, 5223, 6442.
O'Gowne, Philip, English liberty, 944.
„ others of the name pardoned, 4398, 4808, 6784, 6791–2, 6199.
O'Gownee—Gownin, Donell or Daniel, pardon, 5813, 6818.
O'Gownowe, Edm. and Owen, pardon, 746.
O'Gowsero, Donogho, pardon, 4031.
O'Goyne, Patr. and Tho., pardon, 4498, 6379.
O'Goynen, Tho., pardon, 4828.
O'Grada. *See* O'Grady.
O'Gradda, Philip and Laghlin, pardon, 4716.
O'Grady — Grade — Graddey — Graddie — Graddy—Gradie:
„ Dionysius or Denis, knt., 5842; his son, 3794, 3842.
O'Grady, Donogh, livery, 2618.
„ Edmund, pardon, 1108; livery to his brother, 2619.
„ Henry (of Imbernan), indenture, 4761.
„ John or Shane (son of sir Denis), grant of land, 3842; pardon, 3794, 4682.
„ *See* Brady.
„ others of the name pardoned, 487, 1182, 1842, 1860, 2788, 1078, 1548, 4491, 4734, 4781, 4878, 5002, 5148, 5101, 5444, 6416, 5614, 6000, 6008, 6348, 6470, 6478, 6487, 6488, 6497, 6548, 6511, 6532, 6550, 6562, 6563, 6616, 6762.
„ country of, 4523.
O'Grady's island, co. Clare, 3542.
O'Grafty, Dermot, pardon, 6171.
O'Grahie, Thig, pardon, 4449.
O'Graine, John, pardon, 6488.
O'Grame, Conoghor, pardon, 6784.
O'Grane, Donogh, pardon, 2381.
O'Granie, John, pardon, 6487, 6571.
O'Grandie, Gillemorry, pardon, 6480.
O'Gredin, Donogh, pardon, 2904.
O'Grenie, Donell, pardon, 6469.
O'Greefin—Greefin. *See* O'Griffe.
O'Gresmane, Teig, pardon, 6577.
O'Greffe. *See* O'Griffe.
O'Greffane, Donell, pardon, 6782.
O'Greffee, Tho., pardon, 6849.
O'Greghan, Brian, pardon, 1492.
O'Greghane, Donell, pardon, 6768.
O'Greney, Donogh, pardon, 4881.
O'Greyenan, Thady, pardon, 6152.
O'Greynan, Cahill, pardon, 6269.
O'Gribie, Henry and Owen, pardon, 6464.
O'Griffe—Greeffe—Greaffe—Graffe—Griffe—Griffy—Gripha—Gryffe—Gryffie, persons of the name pardoned, 5077, 4780, 5712, 6208, 6304, 6463, 6616, 6617.
O'Griffe, persons of the name pardoned, 5434, 6490.
O'Griffen. *See* O'Griffin.
O'Griffie. *See* O'Griffe.
O'Griffin — Griffen — Griffine — Gryffine, persons of the name pardoned, 4497, 5418, 6494, 6314–5, 6436, 6469, 6576, 6634.
O'Griffy. *See* O'Griffe.
O'Grighie, persons of the name pardoned, 4465.
O'Griphe, Andrew and Mahowny, pardon, 6643.
O'Grouh, Edm., pardon, 2844.
O'Groe, Wm., pardon, 4780.
O'Grogan — Grogaine — Growgane — Grogan, persons of the name pardoned, 1694, 3542, 4782, 5089, 6128, 6280, 6477, 6487, 6485, 6768.

INDEX TO FIANTS—ELIZABETH.

O'Grohan, Hugh, pardon, 6805.
O'Gromagan, Rich., pardon, [illegible].
O'Grompanite, Wm., pardon, 6144.
O'Gromell, Donogh, pardon, [illegible].
O'Gronogan, Teig, pardon, 6464.
O'Growgane. See O'Grogan.
O'Growogane, John, pardon, 4867.
O'Groogan. See O'Grogan.
O'Gryffe—Gryffie. See O'Griffin.
O'Gryffine. See O'Griffin.
O'Grygyn, David and Philip, pardon, [illegible].
O'Gryhan, John, pardon, [illegible].
O'Gryhune, Teig, pardon, [illegible].
O'Guine, Fenale and Gorric, pardon, [illegible].
O'Gulligane, David, pardon, [illegible].
O'Guilin, Hugh, pardon, [illegible].
O'Gullyn, David, pardon, [illegible].
Oguly, Ph., chaplain, pardon, [illegible].
O'Gnoghane, Shane, pardon, [illegible].
O'Guyne, Brian, pardon, [illegible].
O'Gwlin, Rich., pardon, [illegible].
O'Gwule, David and Dermot, pardon, [illegible].
Ogwyn, Teig, pardon, [illegible].
Ogwynan, Owen, pardon, 10.
O'Gwyre, Owen, pardon, [illegible].
O'Gyenan, Morris, pardon, [illegible].
O'Gyrdvane, Wm., pardon, [illegible].
O'Gyhie, Teig, pardon, [illegible].
O'Gyllygayne, David, pardon, [illegible].
O'Gymnon, Onowlly, pardon, [illegible].
O'Gyreshane, Hugh, pardon, 4777.
O'Ha, Feaghy, pardon, [illegible].
O'Habran, Donald and Moriertagh, pardon, [illegible].
O'Hastry, Dermot, pardon, [illegible].
O'Hafferaghe, Rory, pardon, 6417.
O'Hagan—Hagans:
— Owen (of Tullaghoge), chief of his name, pardon, 6714.
— others of the same pardoned, [illegible], 6714, [illegible], 6772.
O'Hagasse, Ogha, pardon, [illegible].
O'Hageran, John, pardon, [illegible].
O'Hagane, Patr., pardon, [illegible].
O'Haggart, Mohmurry, pardon, [illegible].
O'Hagh, Morierlagh, pardon, [illegible].
O'Haghe, Dairmod, pardon, [illegible].
O'Haghairin. See O'Haghierin.
O'Haghan, Gilleduff and James, pardon, [illegible].
O'Hagher, Donoghe, pardon, [illegible].
O'Hagheran—Hagheren—Hagherin—Hagherne. See O'Haghierin.
O'Haghie, persons of the name pardoned, [illegible], [illegible].
O'Haghierin—Haghairin—Haghorne—Hagheren—Hagherin—Hagheron—Haghieray—Haghieryn—Haghiren—Haghy-
O'Haghierin:
eran—Haghyerin—Haherne—Haherty—Hahirny:
— persons of the name pardoned, [illegible]. See also Agheran, Iagherin, Yagherin, O'Agheherin.
O'Haghir, James and Patr., pardon, [illegible].
O'Haghiren—See O'Haghierin.
O'Haghir, Dermod and John, pardon, [illegible].
O'Haghy, Gillernow, pardon, [illegible].
O'Haghyeran—Haghyerin. See O'Haghierin.
O'Hagirtie, Dermot, pardon, [illegible].
O'Hahassie, Shane, pardon, [illegible].
O'Haherne—Haheray, Teig, alias Brooke, or Teig na Brocky, pardon, [illegible], [illegible], [illegible].
— See O'Haghierin.
O'Hahesse, Wm., pardon, [illegible].
O'Hahesy, Philip, pardon, [illegible].
O'Hahir, James and Tho., pardon, [illegible].
O'Hahirny. See O'Haghierin.
O'Hahisse, Dermot, pardon, 1016.
O'Hahrine, Dermod, pardon, 4738.
O'Haighie, [ ], pardon, 6146.
O'Hailie, Brian, pardon, [illegible].
O'Haify, Wm., pardon, 6180.
O'Hairt. See O'Hart.
O'Halanan. See O'Hallinan.
O'Halogan, Wm., pardon, [illegible].
O'Haleighie, John, pardon, [illegible].
O'Haleran, Owen, admiral, [illegible].
O'Halfpenny—Halfpeny, Rich. and Wm., pardon, [illegible].
— See also O'Halpen.
O'Halie. See O'Haly.
O'Halighan. See O'Halleghan.
O'Halinan. See O'Hallinan.
O'Halleghan—Halighan—Halloghane—Halleighane, persons of the name pardoned, [illegible], [illegible], [illegible], [illegible], [illegible], [illegible], [illegible], [illegible], [illegible].
O'Hallan, Morghe, pardon, [illegible].
O'Halleran. See O'Halloran.
O'Halloghane—O'Halleighaine. See O'Halleghan.
O'Hallonan. See O'Hallinan.
O'Halloran—Hallorane—Halloron. See O'Halloran.
O'Hallie, Teig and Tho., pardon, 6714, [illegible].
O'Hallihey, John, pardon, [illegible].
O'Hallihie, John, pardon, [illegible].
O'Hallin, Donogh, pardon, [illegible].

O'Halliman — Halaman — Haliman — Hallimane — Hallinan — Halluman — Hallynan — Hallynayne — Halynan :
- persons of the name pardoned, 1076, 2271, 2284, 3394, 3425, [illegible], 4686, 4735, 4741, [illegible], [illegible], [illegible], 5487, [illegible], [illegible], [illegible], [illegible], 6794.

O'Hallorane, Loghlin, pardon, [illegible].
O'Hallshy, Conoghor, pardon, 6914.
O'Halloran—Halloranе — Hallorayne—Hallowran — Halluran — Halleran —Halleraine — Halloren — Halloraine — Halaran — Halowrane :
- persons of the name pardoned, 2782, 2340, 2870, [illegible], [illegible], [illegible], 4618, [illegible], 4741, [illegible], [illegible], [illegible], [illegible], [illegible], 5417-8, [illegible], 5712, [illegible], [illegible], [illegible], [illegible], [illegible], [illegible], [illegible], [illegible], 6785.

O'Hally, persons of the name pardoned, [illegible], [illegible], [illegible], [illegible], [illegible], [illegible], [illegible], 6784.
O'Hallynan—Hallynayne. See O'Halliman.
O'Hallyne, Donogh, pardon, [illegible].
O'Hallyon, Donogh, pardon, [illegible].
O'Haloran—Halowrane. See O'Halloran.
O'Halpen — Halpin, persons of the name pardoned, [illegible], [illegible], [illegible], [illegible].
O'Halpeny, Teig. and Shane, pardon, [illegible].
O'Halran, Loghlen, pardon, [illegible].
O'Haly—Halie :
- Gillernow, pardon, [illegible]; made captain of his country of Towohally (co. Ross.), [illegible].
- others of the name pardoned, 19, 65, 1380, 2784, [illegible], [illegible], [illegible], [illegible].

O'Halynan. See O'Halliman.
O'Hamle, John, pardon, [illegible].
O'Hamim, Brian, pardon, [illegible].
O'Hamine, Gillerough, harper, pardon, [illegible].
O'Hammoyll, Donell, pardon, [illegible].
O'Hammea, Donogh, pardon, [illegible].
O'Hamoryrough, Thady, pardon, [illegible].
O'Hamye, Wm., pardon, [illegible].
O'Han, Shane, pardon, [illegible].
O'Hanagan, Donogh, pardon, [illegible].
O'Hanaghane. See O'Hannaghan.
O'Hanain. See O'Harmaine.
O'Hanaricke, Neal (of Tullyhog), pardon, 6714.
O'Handlon. See O'Hanlon.
O'Hanee, Donogh, pardon, [illegible].
O'Hanenme, persons of the name pardoned, [illegible].
O'Haneghan. See O'Hannaghan.
O'Hanely, Donell, pardon, [illegible].
O'Hanene, Teo., pardon, [illegible].
O'Hanerterughe, Shane, pardon, [illegible].
O'Hanfy, Manus and Wm., pardon, [illegible].
O'Hangan, Murtagh, pardon, [illegible].
O'Hangelen, Teig and Neavan, pardon, [illegible], [illegible].
O'Hanglen — Hanglin — Hanglyn, persons of the name pardoned, [illegible], [illegible], [illegible], [illegible].
O'Hanhie, Donogh, pardon, [illegible].
O'Hanhin, John, pardon, 3917.
O'Hanlhone, Teig, pardon, [illegible].
O'Hanim, Wm., pardon, [illegible].
O'Hanin—Hanine :
- John, priest, pardon, [illegible].
- others of the name pardoned, [illegible], [illegible], [illegible], [illegible], [illegible].

O'Hanlan. See O'Hanlon.
O'Hanle. See O'Hanly.
O'Hanlean, Teig, pardon, [illegible].
O Hanlee — Hanlele — Hanley. See O'Hanly.
O'Hanleyne, Hugh, pardon, [illegible].
O'Hanlie — Hanlly. See O'Hanly.
O Hanlon — Hanlan — Handlon — Honlone :
- Arthur (in O'Cahan's country), pardon, [illegible].
- John m'Cahyr, made captain of his country, [illegible].
- Oghie, knight, captain of his nation, surrender and regrant of his possessions, [illegible], [illegible]; names of his brothers, son, and reputed sons, [illegible]; protection, [illegible].
- others of the name pardoned, [illegible], [illegible], [illegible], [illegible], [illegible], [illegible], [illegible], [illegible], [illegible], [illegible], [illegible], [illegible], [illegible].
- title of, abolished, [illegible].
- country of (Orior, co. Armagh), [illegible], [illegible], [illegible], [illegible]; to be made shire ground, [illegible].

O'Hanlowne, Donogh, pardon, [illegible].
O'Hanly — Hanle — Hanlee — Hanlele — Hanley — Hanlie — Hanlly :
- Fergananym, appointed seneschal of Tomohanly, [illegible]; pardon, [illegible].
- Farall, house of, in Trim, [illegible].
- others of the name pardoned, [illegible].
- country of (in co. Ross.), [illegible].
- See also O Haly.

O'Hannaghan — Hanaghane — Haneghan — Hannighan, persons of the name pardoned, [illegible], [illegible], [illegible], [illegible].

INDEX TO FIANTS—ELIZABETH.

O'Hanraine — Hassin, Owen and Teig, pardon, 6487, 6294.

O'Hannane, Wm., pardon, 6428.

O'Hanneon, Dermod and Teig, pardon, [illegible].

O'Hanragan, John, pardon, 6460.

O'Hanraghe, Shane, pardon, 4087.

O'Hannighan. See O'Hannaghan.

O'Hanny, Brian, pardon, [illegible].

O'Hanayle, Teig, pardon, 6478.

O'Hanrn, John, pardon, [illegible].

O'Hanertye, Wm., pardon, 4079.

O'Hanraghane—Hanraghan—Hanrighane—Hanrahan, persons of the name pardoned, [illegible], 6548, 4713, 4867, 5878, 6182, 6814, 6818, 6470, 6787.

" See also Anraghan, Ianraghan.

O'Hanraghty — Hanraghtie, persons of the name pardoned, [illegible].

O'Hanrahan—Hanraghan. See O'Hanraghane.

O'Hanreighaine, Conoghor, pardon, [illegible].

O'Hanwick, Morish and Wm., pardon, [illegible].

O'Hanrigan, Donogh, pardon, 4467.

O'Hanrighane. See O'Hanraghane.

O'Hanys — Hanyne, persons of the name pardoned, 3830, 4618, 4827, 4790, 5123, [illegible], 6464, 4823, 6548, [illegible].

O'Hara — Harae — Haro — Haron — Hari — Harie — Harrae — Harre — Harren — Harroy — Harrie — Harry — Hary — Haryo:

" Arthur, attainted, [illegible].

" Brian, appointed tenant of O'Hara Boy's country, 3391.

" Brian m'Phelim, pardon, 4789; attainted, [illegible].

" Cormac, or O'H. Boy, appointed seneschal of O'Hara Boy's country, [illegible], pardon, 4873.

" Donogh, attainted, [illegible], [illegible].

" Donald, attainted, [illegible].

" Edmund (of Cashelcormick), attainted, [illegible].

" Rory ballagh (O'Harre), chief of his name, pardon, 4897, [illegible].

" Rory keagh, attainted, [illegible].

" Sleighte Shane boy mac Owen, territory of, [illegible].

" Teig, N. Dillon's man, 4782.

" Tumoltagh m'Wm., pardon, 4782; attainted, [illegible].

" others of the name pardoned, [illegible], [illegible], [illegible], 4717, 4781, 4782, 4784, 4873, 4897, [illegible], [illegible], 6420, 6434, 6478, 6473, [illegible], [illegible], 6411, 5740, 5790, [illegible], 6180, 6446, 6624.

O'Hara Boy. See O'H., Cormac.

" " country of, 3390-1.

O'Harege, Mahon, pardon, 5712.

O'Haraghian — Haraghiane — Haraghion, persons of the name pardoned, [illegible], [illegible], 6474.

O'Haran—Harane, persons of the name pardoned, 4867, 5464, [illegible].

O'Hardagane, Brian, pardon, [illegible].

O'Hare—Haren. See O'Hara.

O'Haregan, James, harper, pardon, [illegible].

O'Harety, Shane, pardon, [illegible].

O'Hargedaine—Hargedan—Hargidan, persons of the name pardoned, [illegible], [illegible], [illegible], 6687.

O'Harhen, Shane, pardon, 6604.

O'Hari—Harie. See O'Hara.

O'Harighane, Daniel, pardon, 6540.

O'Harighiane—Harighten. See O'Harrighian.

O'Haris, Enens, pardon, 6476.

O'Harlage, Teig na brocky, pardon, 4874.

O'Harkan, Donell, pardon, [illegible].

O'Harmady—Harmaly—Harmodie:

" Conoghor oge, pardon, 4814, 4867, 6818.

" Dermod, pardon, 6818.

O'Harne, Cormock, commission, 4782.

" others of the name pardoned, [illegible], 6482.

O'Harnel, Teig, pardon, 6878.

O'Harondie, Shane, pardon, 6487, 6371.

O'Harrogh, Donell Fursin and Teig, pardon, 6480.

O'Harnels, Conoghor and Shane, pardon, 6444.

O'Harpey, Meloghlin and Philip, pardon, [illegible], 4781.

O'Harnlady — Harnladie, persons of the name pardoned, 6814-5.

O'Haroy—Harnie, persons of the name pardoned, 1944, 4114, 6870, 6948, 6464.

O'Harrae. See O'Hara.

O'Harragan, Brian, pardon, [illegible].

O'Harraghan — Harroghan, Donogh and Wm., pardon, 3004, 6454.

O'Harrall, Gillepatrick, pardon, [illegible].

O'Harre, Rory ballagh, chief of his name, pardon, [illegible].

O'Harre—Harren. See O'Hara.

O'Harreghan. See O'Harraghan.

O'Harroghdane— Harroghiane. See O'Harrighian.

O'Harroryan, Morris, pardon, [illegible].

O'Harroy—Harrie. See O'Hara.

O'Harrighian — Harighten — Harighiane—Harroghdane — Harroghtane, persons of the name pardoned, 4444, 5457, 6477, 6487.

O'Harrough, Dermod, pardon, [illegible].

O'Harronghow, Teig, pardon, 4786.

Oharry, co. Gal., 4469.

INDEX TO FIANTS—ELIZABETH.

O'Harry. See O'Hara.
O'Hart—Harte—Hairt—Hartt:
„ Barnaby, official of diocese of Meath, commission, 5124.
„ Hugh, 5180; castle built by, 1444, 4487.
„ Owen, comm., 6782.
„ others of the name pardoned, 4561, 4570, 4598, 4704, 4800, 5236, 5431, 5478, 5804, 5827, 5898, 5740, 5808, 5815, 5843, 6261, 6516, 6767.
O'Harte, Teig, pardon, 6604.
O'Hartan, Art and Philip, pardon, 6173.
O'Harte. See O'Hart.
O'Hartegan. See O'Hartigan.
O'Harteron, Edm., pardon, 4282.
O'Hartie—Harty, persons of the name pardoned, 4578, 5173, 6485–6, 6487, 6197, 6511, 6518, 6532, 6694, 6764.
O'Hartigan—Hartogan:
„ Wm., death of, 498.
„ Laghlin and Wm., pardon, 3258, 6603.
O'Hartoedy, Conor and Shane, pardon, 6604.
O'Hartnallige, Conoghor and John, pardon, 6815.
O'Hartt. See O'Hart.
O'Harty. See O'Hartie.
O'Harughan, Rory, pardon, 6478.
O'Harvey, Teig, pardon, 4528.
O'Hary—Harye. See O'Hara.
O'Hasie, Wm., pardon, 6564.
O'Hassie, Donn, pardon, 5763.
O'Hassie—Hassey—Hasey, persons of the name pardoned, 698, 4821, 4935, 6173, 6230.
O'Haulwein, Edm., pardon, 4683.
O'Haveregan, Donogh, pardon, 6615.
O'Haveris, Wm., pardon, 4473.
O'Hawnraghan, Conoghor, pardon, 4854.
O'Hawram, Donell, pardon, 6477.
O'Hawroghane, Donell, pardon, 6615.
O'Haylan, Teig, pardon, 6533.
O'Haylie, Edm., pardon, 6123.
O'Hayne, Patt. and Tho., pardon, 1617, 6621.
O'Haynye, Melaghlin, pardon, 6608.
O'He, Gerald and Gillpatrick, pardon, 72, 6498, 6577.
O'Hea—I Ea—Y Ea, persons of the name pardoned, 2347, 3941, 3942, 4760, 4744, 5665, 6170, 6425, 6477, 6432, 6187, 6304–5, 6311, 6316, 6571, 6528, 6558, 6573, 6542, 6701.
„ John, alias Swynnade, pardon, 4807.
„ See also O'Hea.
O'Hean, Edm., pardon, 4712.
O'Headan—Headyne, persons of the name pardoned, 4283, 6494, 6727. See also O'Hedean.
O'Healagh, Darby, pardon, 6473.
O'Heagirtie—Heagertie, persons of the name pardoned, 6518, 6545.
O'Heabir—Heabire—Heaber, persons of the name pardoned, 3043, 4764, 6712. See also O'Hebir.
O'Healaee, Liseagh, pardon, 6577.
O'Healehy. See O'Hialihie.
O'Healie. See O'Healy.
O'Healiehie—Healihie. See O'Hialihie.
O'Healy—Healie—Heally, persons of the name pardoned, 4538, 5426, 5806, 6318, 5398, 6182, 6425, 6480, 6221, 6563.
O'Hean, James, pardon, 6420.
O'Heanegane, Philip and Shyhogh, pardon, 6452.
O'Heanessy—Heanissa, David and Teig, pardon, 6122, 6488.
O'Heany, persons of the name pardoned, 6582.
„ See also O'Heny.
O'Heanyne, Mahon and Wm., pardon, 4532.
O'Heare, Gildal, pardon, 6401.
O'Hearne, Moriah, pardon, 6494.
O'Heavane, alias O'Carine, Teig, pardon, 560.
O'Heawrine, Rory, pardon, 6169.
O'Hedayne, Tho., pardon, 6741.
O'Hedean, Hugh and Brian, pardon, 5417, 6411.
O'Hedegiane, Philip, pardon, 6427.
O'Hedeo—Hedie—Hedine, persons of the name pardoned, 1527, 3284, 3065, 4607, 5654, 6408, 6153.
O'Hedewan, Teig, pardon, 2274.
O'Hedian—Hedyan, persons of the name pardoned, 4622, 4346, 5403.
O'Hedin—Hedine. See O'Hedean.
O'Hedine, Walter, pardon, 6182.
O'Hedrean, Peter, pardon, 1582.
O'Hedrescoll. See O'Driscoll.
O'Hedyan. See O'Hedian.
O'Hedyne, Peter, pardon, 2282.
O'Hee, Donell, Iwras and Melaghlin skinnogh, slain in rebellion, 5483.
„ persons of the name pardoned, 534, 2789, 2317, 2778, 2780, 3079, 3281, 3143, 3564, 3822, 4410, 4420, 4438, 4436, 4763, 4857, 4615, 4973, 5608, 6461, 6120, 6571, 6313, 6453.
O'Heegan, Melaghlin, English liberty, 92.
O'Heer, Conor and Egh, pardon, 4283.
O'Heferman—Heffernan. See O'Hifferman.
O'Hefernan, Hugh, pardon, 4729.
O'Hegan—Hegane—Hogan, persons of the name pardoned, 1481, 2420, 3347, 5041, 4413, 6513, 6420, 6486, 6518, 6784.
O'Hegerdall, Donell, pardon, 6464.
O'Hegerte, James, pardon, 6577.
O'Hegertie, Donell and Murtagh, pardon, 6652.

INDEX TO FIANTS.—ELIZABETH.

O'Hegher, Muriagh, pardon, 6765.
O'Hegyn, Goghery, pardon, 5544.
O'Heheir, Owen, pardon, [illegible].
O'Heher. See O'Hehir.
O'Heidoe, Conor, pardon, [illegible].
O'Hehir—Heher, persons of the name pardoned, 1548, 2877, [illegible], 4677, [illegible], [illegible], 5712, 5748, [illegible], [illegible], 6114, [illegible], 6615, 6617.
O'Hein, Teig, pardon, [illegible].
O'Heigan, Donell, pardon, [illegible], [illegible].
O'Heighen, Gillemill, pardon, [illegible].
O'Heigher, Shane, pardon, [illegible].
O'Heiunia, Farriegh, pardon, [illegible].
O'Hein—Heine. See O'Heyne.
O'Hekie, John and Ferdorogh, pardon, 1623, [illegible].
O'Helan—Helane, persons of the name pardoned, [illegible], [illegible], 6116, 5175, [illegible].
O'Helegane, Moragh, pardon, [illegible].
O'Haleghane, Henry, 5442.
O'Heleman, Brian, pardon, [illegible].
O'Helie. See O'Hely.
O'Hellan, persons of the name pardoned, [illegible], [illegible].
O'Hellehan, Wm., pardon, [illegible].
O'Helley—Hellie. See O'Helly.
O'Hellier, Dermod, pardon, [illegible].
O'Helligan, Awlie, pardon, [illegible].
O'Helly—Helley—Hellie, persons of the name pardoned, [illegible], [illegible], [illegible], [illegible], [illegible], [illegible].
O'Hellyn[ ], Dermod, pardon, [illegible].
O'Helme, Tho., pardon, [illegible].
O'Hely—Helie, persons of the name pardoned, [illegible], 1574, [illegible], [illegible], [illegible], [illegible], [illegible], [illegible], [illegible], [illegible], 6740, [illegible], [illegible], [illegible], [illegible], [illegible], 6704, [illegible], [illegible].
O'Helyn, Connor and Donogh, pardon, [illegible], [illegible].
O'Hemergin, Hugh, pardon, [illegible].
O'Hempee, Wm., pardon, [illegible].
O'Henayne, Wm., pardon, 1761.
O'Henchirieyhe, Conoghor, pardon, [illegible].
O'Henessa, John, pardon, [illegible].
O'Henechan, Donald, pardon, [illegible].
O'Heneas, Tho., pardon, [illegible].
O'Henegan—Henegane, persons of the name pardoned, [illegible], [illegible], [illegible], 6877.
O'Henoh, Teig, pardon, [illegible].
O'Heneran, Marcus and Morhoe, pardon, [illegible].
O'Henes, persons of the name pardoned, 174, 1747, [illegible], [illegible], [illegible].
O'Henesa, Rory, pardon, [illegible].
O'Henessy, Peter, pardon, [illegible].
O'Henese, Rory and Dermit, pardon, [illegible], [illegible].
O'Henesey. See O'Henesy.
O'Henechie, Donogh, pardon, [illegible].
O'Henesie. See O'Henesy.
O'Henessa, Farr, pardon, [illegible].
O'Henesy—Henesie—Henessy—Lenisie—Lonyssie—Y Enesy—Y Enisie:
„ persons of the name pardoned, [illegible], [illegible], [illegible], [illegible].
O'Henesy, Cornelius, pardon, [illegible].
O'Heneyne, Philip, pardon, [illegible].
O'Hengerdell. See O'Hingerdell.
O'Hengerttye, John, alias Harrengton, pardon, [illegible].
O'Heni—Henie. See O'Heny.
O'Henlesy, John yileo, pardon, [illegible].
O'Henlaine, Donogh, pardon, [illegible].
O'Henigane, Shane, priest, pardon, [illegible].
O'Henle, Dermod and Shane, pardon, [illegible], 6314.
„ Mahon, pardon, [illegible].
O'Henly, Farrogh, pardon, [illegible].
O'Hennaine—Henane, Wm., pardon, [illegible], 6777.
O'Hennary, Tho., pardon, [illegible].
O'Hennes—Hennie, persons of the name pardoned, [illegible], 647, [illegible], [illegible].
O'Hennesy—Hennesie—Hennessye—Henysie, persons of the name pardoned, [illegible], [illegible], [illegible], [illegible]. See also O'Henesy.
O'Hennie. See O'Hennes.
O'Henniche, Walter, pardon, [illegible].
O'Hennos. See O'Henos.
O'Hennane, Rich., pardon, [illegible].
O'Henoe—Henoes—Henoge—Henes. See O'Henos.
O'Henny—Hennye, Conney and Owen, pardon, [illegible].
„ See also Henney.
O'Hennys—Hennyes, persons of the name pardoned, 19, 947, [illegible], [illegible], [illegible], 6777.
O'Hennyeh, Rory, pardon, [illegible].
O'Henos—Henoes—Henes—Henose—Henoge—Henonse—Henoys—Henois—Henos—Henoys—Henoe—Henne:
„ Dionysius, English liberty, 61.
„ persons of the name pardoned, 654, 461, 615, 796, 874, [illegible], [illegible], [illegible], [illegible], [illegible], [illegible], [illegible], [illegible], [illegible], [illegible], 5517.
O'Henrine, Dallagh, pardon, [illegible].
O'Henry, persons of the name pardoned, [illegible], [illegible], [illegible].
O'Hensey, Donogh, pardon, [illegible].
O'Hensie—Hensie. See O'Hensa.
O'Heny—Heni—Henie:
„ Gilduff, attainted, [illegible].
„ others of the name pardoned, [illegible], [illegible], [illegible], [illegible], [illegible].
O'Henyll, Shane, pardon, [illegible].
O'Henyne, Andrew, pardon, [illegible].

INDEX TO FIANTS.—ELIZABETH.

O'Henye—Henyen, persons of the name pardoned, 13, [illegible].
O'Henye [illegible], Brian, pardon, [illegible].
O'Henyssie. See O'Hennessy.
O'Hepharnan. See O'Hifernan.
Oher, Cormock m'Ricard, pardon, [illegible].
O'Heragh, John, pardon, 1178.
O'Heraght, Donogh, pardon, [illegible].
O'Heraghty, Fiers, pardon, 6784.
O'Heraey, Tho., pardon, 67[illegible].
O'Here, persons of the name pardoned, [illegible].
O'Herelagh, Awliff, pardon, 4876.
Oherie (Ogherry, co. Gal.), castle and land, [illegible]-1. See Oherry.
O'Heriell, Art, pardon, [illegible].
O'Herin. See O'Heryn.
O'Herke, Wm., pardon, 67[illegible].
O'Herlehey—Herlyhie—I Erlyhie—I Yerloghy—Y Erlyhy:
" persons of the name pardoned, [illegible], 3162, [illegible], [illegible], [illegible].
O'Herman, James and Wm., pardon, [illegible].
O'Hermody, Mahon, pardon, 4144.
O'Herane—Heraned—Herranc—Hiroan:
" Aharney, Faraghell, Mulmory, and MacCrah, yeomen, pardoned, 3162.
" persons of the name pardoned, [illegible], [illegible], [illegible], [illegible], [illegible], [illegible], [illegible], [illegible], [illegible], [illegible], [illegible], [illegible].
O'Herney, Donogh, pardon, 374[illegible].
Oherny, co. Gal., 4519.
O'Heron, Tho., pardon, [illegible].
O'Herraghton, Morris, pardon, [illegible].
O'Herroll, Patr., pardon, [illegible], [illegible].
O'Herrore, Knoghor, pardon, [illegible].
O'Herrick, Owen, pardon, [illegible].
O'Herrig—Herrigan—Herrigan, persons of the name pardoned, [illegible], [illegible].
O'Herrolahie Conor, pardon, [illegible].
Oherry—Ohiry, co. Gal., [illegible], [illegible].
O'Herrye, Rory, pardon, [illegible].
O'Hervan, Philip, pardon, [illegible].
O'Hery, Edm., pardon, 10.
O'Heryn—Herin—Heryne, persons of the name pardoned, 16, [illegible], [illegible].
O'Hessedy, Teig, pardon, 4867.
O'Heverin—Heveran—Heveron—Heverine—Heverye—Heveryne—Hevren—Hevryne, persons of the name pardoned, 448, [illegible], 717, 1781, [illegible], [illegible], [illegible], [illegible], [illegible], 4167, [illegible], [illegible], [illegible], [illegible], [illegible], [illegible], [illegible], [illegible], [illegible], [illegible], 6777.
O'Hevie, Dermot and Patr., pardon, [illegible].
O'Hevine—Hevyne, John and Donell, pardon, [illegible], [illegible].
O'Hevren—Hevryne. See O'Heverin.
O'Hevyne. See O'Hevine.
O'Hew—Hewe, Moriesh boy, pardon, [illegible], [illegible].
" Teig, pardon, [illegible].
O'Hewer, Conoghor, pardon, 4817.
O'Hewrie, Rory, pardon, [illegible].
O'Hewryn—Hewryne, persons of the name pardoned, [illegible], [illegible], [illegible].
O'Hey—Heye, persons of the name pardoned, 1781, [illegible], [illegible], 4734, [illegible], [illegible].
O'Heyden, Peter and Edm., pardon, [illegible], [illegible].
O'Heyin, Cowgeyllie, pardon, [illegible].
O'Heykey, John, pardon, 842.
O'Heylan, Teig, pardon, [illegible].
O'Heyle, Edm., pardon, 6877.
O'Heyley, John, pardon, [illegible].
O'Heymod—Heymode, persons of the name pardoned, [illegible], 4816, 67[illegible].
O'Heyn. See O'Heyne.
O'Heynan, Teig and Wm., pardon, [illegible], [illegible], [illegible].
O'Heyne—Hein—Heine—Heyn—I Eyne—Y Eyn:
" Donald and Thady, lands of, in co. Lim., [illegible].
" Ferrough and Cugollo, attainted, [illegible].
" Hugh boy, pardon, [illegible]; surrenders title of O'Heyne, [illegible]; surrender and regrant of his possessions, [illegible]-7.
" Owen mantagh, pardon, 464, [illegible], 4471, [illegible]; his son, [illegible]-7.
" Rory: O'Heyne, pardon, [illegible]; his son made tanist, [illegible].
" Torrelagh, made tanist of O'Heyne's country, [illegible].
" Uathgony, English liberty, 177.
" others of the name pardoned, [illegible], 1841, 1438, 1841, [illegible], [illegible], [illegible], [illegible]-8, [illegible], [illegible], [illegible]-8, [illegible], 4171, 4474, [illegible], [illegible], [illegible], [illegible], [illegible], [illegible], 4741, 4748, [illegible]-7, [illegible], [illegible], [illegible], [illegible], [illegible], [illegible], [illegible], [illegible], [illegible], [illegible], [illegible], [illegible], [illegible], [illegible].
O'Heyne. See Rory, Owen mantagh, and Hugh boy, O'H.
" title surrendered, [illegible].
" country of, in co. Gal., [illegible].
O'Heynee, Donell, pardon, [illegible].
O'Heynen, James, pardon, [illegible].
O'Heynie, Wm., pardon, [illegible].
O'Heysyene, Maurice, pardon, [illegible].
O'Heyren, persons of the name pardoned, 671, 1378.
O'Heyriell, Tirlagh, pardon, [illegible].
O'Heyrisy, David, pardon, [illegible].

O'Heyvrya, Dermot, pardon, 3122.
O'Hialall, Morris, pardon, [illegible].
O'Hialeghie—Hialehie. *See* O'Hialibie.
O'Hialeigh, Donell, pardon, [illegible].
O'Hialibie—Healahy—Healihie—Heallahie
—Heallihie—Hially—Hialeghie—Hialehie—Hiallighie—
Hiallhie—Hiallihy—Hially-
hie—Hyalahy—Hyalyhy:
„ Tho. oge: O'Hiallhie, pardon, 6457.
„ others of the name pardoned, 2041, 3021, [illegible], 4510, 4673, 4732, 4764, [illegible], 5416, [illegible], 6457, [illegible], [illegible], [illegible], [illegible], [illegible], 6471, 6764.
„ *See also* Hiallhie.
O'Hiallenhide, Morish, pardon, 4673.
O'Hialligirie — Hiallihy — Hiallyhie. *See* O'Hialibie.
O'Hiartighie, Wm., pardon, 6744.
O'Hicokien, David, land of, [illegible].
O'Hicken. *See* O'Hicky.
O'Hickon, Donell bane, pardon, [illegible].
O'Hickey—Hickie. *See* O'Hicky.
O Hickie, Shane m'Conoghor, pardon, [illegible].
O'Hicky — Hickee — Hickey — Hickie — Hickye—Hyckie—Hycky:
„ Daniel, surgeon, pardon, 6464.
„ Donogh, surgeon, pardon, [illegible].
„ Gillerully, physician, pardon, 4734, [illegible].
„ Wm., surgeon, pardon, 4742.
„ others of the name pardoned, 1148, [illegible], [illegible], [illegible], [illegible], [illegible], [illegible], [illegible], [illegible], [illegible], [illegible], [illegible], [illegible], [illegible], 6675, 6478, [illegible], [illegible], [illegible], [illegible], [illegible], 6571, [illegible], [illegible], 6708, 6769, [illegible], 6770, 6772.
„ *See also* Hickie, Iykye, O'Hiky.
O'Hiddon, Donogh, pardon, [illegible].
O'Hidie, Rory, pardon, [illegible].
O'Hidiane, James, pardon, [illegible].
O'Hidriscoll—Hedrescoll—Hidriscoll. *See* O'Driscoll.
O'Hieghoran, Derby, pardon, [illegible].
O Hiehie, Donogh roe, pardon, [illegible].
O Hielan, Teig, pardon, [illegible].
O'Hieron, Morris, pardon, 6701.
O'Hierihie—Hierighie—Hierlohy—Hierlyhy—Hyerlyhy, persons of the name pardoned, [illegible], [illegible], [illegible], 4467, [illegible], 6467, 6511, [illegible].
O'Hierman, Connor, pardon, [illegible].
O'Hiery, Derby, pardon, [illegible].
O'Hifernan—Hifernane. *See* O'Hifernan.
O'Hifferan, Mahowne, pardon, [illegible].
O'Hifernan — Hefernan — Heffrnan — Hophernan — Hifernan — Hifernane — Hifernain — Hifernane — Hifernaya — Hifernayne—Hyfernayn:
„ Rame roe (of Shronell, co. Tip.), alias O'Hifernane, pardon, 4644, [illegible].
„ Thady, clerk, pardon, [illegible].
„ William, bard, pardon, 1871.
„ others of the name pardoned, 1646, 3013, 3647, 4576, [illegible], 4457, 4643, 4732, 4718, [illegible], [illegible], [illegible], 6176, 6478, [illegible], [illegible], 6511, [illegible], [illegible], [illegible], 6764.
O'Higan—Higane—Higen. *See* O'Higgin.
O'Higeni, Dermot, pardon, [illegible].
O'Higgan—Higgon. *See* O'Higgin.
O'Higehie, Morris, pardon, [illegible].
O'Higgin—Higan—Higane—Higen—Higeni—Higgan—Higgon—Higgye—Higin — Higyn — Hygane — Hyggine — Hygin, persons of the name pardoned, 1082, [illegible], [illegible], 4637, 4074, 4240, [illegible], [illegible], [illegible], 4447, [illegible], [illegible], 4777, [illegible], [illegible], [illegible], 5078, 5113, 5434, 5467, [illegible], [illegible], [illegible], [illegible], [illegible], [illegible], [illegible], [illegible], [illegible], [illegible], 5740, [illegible], 5758, 5790, 5900, [illegible], [illegible], [illegible], 6171, 6480, [illegible], [illegible], [illegible], [illegible], 6312, [illegible], [illegible], 6551, 6457, [illegible], [illegible], 6786.
O'Higirdell, John, pardon, [illegible].
O'Higkin, John roe, pardon, [illegible].
O'Higyne, Gilderman, pardon, [illegible].
O'Higyn. *See* O'Higgin.
O'Hihorly, Conoghor and Shane, pardon, 64.
O'Hihir—Hihire, persons of the name pardoned, [illegible], [illegible].
O'Hiky — Hikie — Hikye — Hykie — Hyky, persons of the name pardoned, [illegible], [illegible], 1664, 1666, 1853, 1969, 2611, [illegible], [illegible], [illegible], [illegible], [illegible], 5447, [illegible], [illegible], [illegible], [illegible], [illegible], [illegible], 6749, [illegible], 6677.
O'Hilane, John, pardon, [illegible].
O'Hiley, Dionisa, pardon, 5178.
O'Hilleboyhiue, Teig, pardon, [illegible].
O'Hillichain, Tho., pardon, [illegible].
O'Himnes, Teige, pardon, 14.
O'Hinane, Dermot, pardon, [illegible].
O'Hinelane, Shane, pardon, [illegible].
O'Hingen, Brian, pardon, [illegible].
O'Hingerdell — Hengerdell — Hingerdle — Hingirdill—Hingurdill—Hingurdle:
„ Thady: O'Hingerdell, pardon, [illegible].

INDEX TO FIANTS.—ELIZABETH.

O'Hingerdell.

" others of the name pardoned, 2929, [illegible], [illegible], 4418, [illegible], [illegible], [illegible], [illegible], 6170, [illegible], [illegible], 6516, [illegible], [illegible].

" See also Ingerdell, Hingardell.

O'Hinowman, Wm., pardon, [illegible].

" See O'Hynowman.

O'Hinsele, Fisharie, pardon, [illegible].

O'Hire, persons of the name pardoned, [illegible].

O'Hirgy, Dourgh, pardon, 1654.

O'Hiriell, Teig, pardon, [illegible].

O'Hirick, Owen, pardon, [illegible].

O'Hirige, persons of the name pardoned, [illegible], [illegible].

O'Hirley—Hirly, Morgh and Conor, pardon, [illegible], [illegible].

O'Hirnan. See O'Hernan.

O'Hirraght, Edm. and Teig, pardon, [illegible].

O'Hirrell, Nich., pardon, [illegible].

O'Hirrely, Wm., pardon, [illegible].

O'Hirrille, John, pardon, [illegible].

O'Hirtaine, Philip, pardon, [illegible].

Ohiry. See Oherry.

O'Hision, Owen, pardon, [illegible].

O'Hisiemane, Tomultagh, pardon, [illegible].

O'Hiskeen, Donell, pardon, [illegible].

O'Hiskie, Gilladuff, pardon, [illegible].

O'Hiskennane, Laghlin, pardon, [illegible].

O'Hiskenane, persons of the name pardoned, [illegible].

O'Hissie, Teig, pardon, [illegible].

O'Hiur, Dourgh, pardon, [illegible].

Ohlasid, Morogh, pardon, [illegible].

O'Hoa, Patr., pardon, [illegible].

O'Hoaey, persons of the name pardoned, [illegible].

O'Hoan, Maurice, pardon, [illegible].

O'Hoarie, Nickoll, pardon, [illegible].

O'Hogan—Hogain—Hogaine—Hoganе:

" Malachy, deprived of rectory, [illegible].

" others of the name pardoned, [illegible], [illegible], 1948, [illegible], [illegible], [illegible], [illegible], [illegible], 3773, [illegible], [illegible], [illegible], [illegible], [illegible], 4284, [illegible], [illegible], [illegible], [illegible], [illegible], [illegible], [illegible], 4473, [illegible], [illegible], 4784, [illegible], 6477, [illegible], [illegible], [illegible], [illegible], [illegible], [illegible], [illegible], [illegible], [illegible], [illegible], [illegible], [illegible], [illegible], [illegible], [illegible], [illegible], [illegible], 6778.

O'Hogane, Miler, pardon, [illegible].

O'Hogane, Rorsard and Kithrin, pardon, [illegible].

O'Hogayne, Teige, pardon, [illegible].

O'Hogertie, Donell, pardon, [illegible].

O'Hoggan, Rich., pardon, [illegible].

" See also Loggayne.

O'Hoghagan, Wm., pardon, [illegible].

O'Hoghegane, Shane, pardon, [illegible].

O'Hoghery, Cherwoy, pardon, [illegible].

O'Hogirtie, Teige, pardon, [illegible].

O'Hokin, Connor, pardon, [illegible].

O'Hoky, Conor, pardon, [illegible], [illegible].

O'Holilehane, Maurice, pardon, [illegible].

O'Holane, Shane, pardon, [illegible].

O'Holahan, Conoghor, pardon, [illegible].

O'Holane, Edmund, pardon, [illegible].

O'Holeghan—Holeahan—Holeghane:

" persons of the name pardoned, [illegible], [illegible], [illegible].

" See also Ioleghan, Yehologhane.

O'Hollagan, Edm., [illegible].

O'Hollaghan—Hollahan. See O'Holloghan.

O'Hollan, Donill, pardon, [illegible].

O'Holleghan—Holleghan—Hollahan—Hollehan—Hollichan—Holligham—Holloghan:

" persons of the name pardoned, [illegible], [illegible], [illegible], [illegible], [illegible], [illegible], [illegible].

" See also Ionighane.

O'Hollighan, Wm., pardon, [illegible].

O'Hollichan—Holliganе. See O'Holleghan.

O'Hollogane, Peter, pardon, [illegible].

O'Holloghan. See O'Holleghan.

O'Hollohane, Teig, pardon, [illegible].

O'Holloe, Bren, pardon, [illegible].

O'Holowe, Morogh, pardon, [illegible].

O'Homnya, Melaghelin and Shane, pardon, 16.

O'Hopen, Mahown, pardon, [illegible].

O'Hone, persons of the name pardoned, [illegible], 4944, [illegible].

O'Honechan, persons of the name pardoned, [illegible].

O'Honegan, Mahowne, pardon, [illegible].

O'Honeghane, Donell, pardon, [illegible].

O'Honie, Teige, pardon, [illegible].

O'Honlane, Sir Oghie, [illegible]. See O'Hanlon.

O'Honnoghane, Donogh, pardon, [illegible].

O'Honnon, Owen, pardon, [illegible].

O'Honnoyan, Perce, pardon, [illegible].

O'Honnane, Mary, pardon, [illegible].

O'Honorane — Honnnine, persons of the name pardoned, [illegible].

O'Honyan, Donald, pardon, [illegible].

O'Honygane, John, pardon, [illegible].

O'Hoogan, Conohor, pardon, [illegible].

O'Hooligan, Philip, pardon, [illegible].

O'Hooregaine, Donogh, pardon, [illegible].

O'Horeghan, Shane, pardon, [illegible].

O'Horan—Horain:
" Donogh, dean of Clonfert, pardon, [illegible]; his successor, 4162.
" Donogh, dean of Killaloe, indenture, 4761.
" others of the name pardoned, [illegible], 1471, 1770, 1348, [illegible], [illegible], [illegible], [illegible], [illegible], [illegible], [illegible], [illegible], [illegible], [illegible], 6708.
O'Horaye, Teige, pardon, 6018.
O'Hordagan, Rob., clerk, [illegible].
O'Horegaine, Donogh, pardon, [illegible].
O Horeghan, Donell, pardon, [illegible].
O'Horgan—Horgaine—Horgane:
" persons of the name pardoned, 1944, [illegible], [illegible], [illegible], 5784.
O'Horghane, Melaughlen, pardon, [illegible].
O'Horichain, Sean, pardon, 2146.
O'Horiogane, Jowrus, pardon, [illegible].
O'Horigan, Shane, pardon, [illegible].
O'Horiske, Donogh, pardon, [illegible].
O'Horne, Brian, pardon, [illegible].
O'Horochain, Shane, pardon, 2343.
O'Horoshane, Gillepatrick, pardon, [illegible].
O'Horogh, Diermot, pardon, [illegible].
O'Horoghan — Horohan, persons of the name pardoned, [illegible], [illegible], 6778.
O'Hororan, Connoghor, pardon, 4312.
O'Horran, persons of the name pardoned, [illegible], [illegible], 6400.
O'Horregan, Shane, pardon, [illegible].
O'Horrogan, John and Teige, pardon, [illegible].
O'Hose, Melaghlen, pardon, [illegible].
O'Hosie, David, pardon, [illegible].
O'Hosse, Laghlen, killed, 6410.
O'Hossie, Donald, pardon, 6434.
O Hossye, Aghye, pardon, 6816.
O'Hosghine, Shane, pardon, [illegible].
O'Houlinghan, Magonius, student, pardon, [illegible].
O'Houne, Rob., pardon, [illegible].
O'Houre, Morris, pardon, 6479.
O'Hourigan, Ever, pardon, 6612.
O'Howlane, Shane, pardon, 5763.
O'Howen, persons of the name pardoned, [illegible], [illegible], 5411, 6144.
O'Howgan, Mahowne, pardon, 5041.
O'Howgin, Brian, pardon, 5110.
O'Howine, Rorie, pardon, [illegible].
O'Howlaughan, Richard, alias Murry, pardon, 82.
O'Howlegan, persons of the name pardoned, [illegible], [illegible].
O'Howleghan — Howleghan — Howleghane — Howlighan — Howloghan:
" Thady, carpenter, robbery from, [illegible].
O'Howloghan, others of the name pardoned, 1617, [illegible], 4743, [illegible], [illegible], [illegible], 4514, [illegible], [illegible], [illegible], 6701.
O'Howley, Hugh, pardon, 5794.
O'Howlig, John, pardon, 4731.
O'Howligane, John, pardon, 5501.
O'Howlighane—Howlighen—Howloghan. *See* O'Howloghan.
O'Howlycane, Gully Cudy, pardon, 4278.
O'Howneghan, Donill, pardon, [illegible].
O'Hownoghan, Rory and Melaghlin, pardon, 1024, 6424.
O'Howoyghan, Philip, pardon, 4697.
O'Hownyn, Gulliglas, pardon, [illegible].
O'Howraine, Moris, pardon, 5743.
O'Howran, persons of the name pardoned, 1453, [illegible].
O'Howrane, Dermod and Wm., pardon, 4444.
" *See also* Yowrane.
O'Howreohan, David and John, pardon, [illegible].
O'Howreo, Edm., pardon, 6447.
O'Howrogan, persons of the name pardoned, 6118, [illegible], [illegible], [illegible].
O'Howroghan, persons of the name pardoned, [illegible].
O'Howrigaine, Mahowne, pardon, [illegible].
O'Howrogan, Donnoghe, pardon, 6173.
O'Howyn, William, pardon, 1617.
O'Howyne, John, pardon, 1617.
O'Hoy, persons of the name pardoned, [illegible], [illegible], 6267.
O'Hoye, persons of the name pardoned, [illegible], [illegible], [illegible].
O'Hoylomy, Donald, pardon, [illegible].
O'Hoyn, Shan, pardon, 4644.
O'Hoyno rone, Owen, pardon, [illegible].
Ohrare. *See* Orier.
O'Huar, Shane, pardon, 4780.
O'Hubane, David, pardon, [illegible].
O'Hue. *See* O'Hugh.
O'Huelighan, Wm. Murry, pardon, [illegible].
O'Huenous, David, pardon, [illegible].
O'Hugen. *See* O'Hugin.
O'Huggen, Irriell, pardon, [illegible].
O'Huggyn, John, pardon, [illegible].
O'Hugh—Hue, persons of the name pardoned, [illegible], [illegible], [illegible], [illegible], [illegible], [illegible], [illegible], [illegible].
O'Hughen, Donald, pardon, [illegible].
O'Hughes, Feris, pardon, [illegible].
O'Hugin—Hugen, persons of the name pardoned, [illegible], 1040, [illegible], [illegible], 6161.
O'Huighen, James, pardon, 4144.
O'Huinan, Rorie, pardon, [illegible].
O'Huky, Shane, pardon, [illegible].
O'Hulahill, Donogh, land grant, [illegible].
O'Hullaghan, persons of the name pardoned, [illegible].
" *See also* Ulaghan

INDEX TO FIANTS—ELIZABETH.

O'Hullorane, Teige, pardon, 4512.

O'Hullig, persons of the name pardoned, [illegible].

O'Hultinan, persons of the name pardoned, 4674.

O'Hulloran, Moyler, pardon, 6519.

O'Humyn, Laghlin, pardon, 6808.

O'Hungerdell, persons of the name pardoned. 4414, 4[illegible], 4[illegible].

O'Hungrell[ ] pardon, [illegible].

O'Hunnye, Morogh, pardon, 6[illegible].

O'Hurgane, Donell, pardon, 44[illegible].

O'Hurvane, Rich., pardon, 4[illegible].

O'Hurwane, Mahown, pardon, 44[illegible].

O'Huoligan—Huoligaine—Huologhane—Huologhane;

" John, alias Merigh, pardon, 6170.

" others of the name pardoned, 6170, 6611.

O'Huraghiine, Donogho, pardon, [illegible].

O'Huran, Conner, pardon, 4[illegible].

O'Hurelly — Hureley — Hurilly, persons of the name pardoned, 2063, 2[illegible].

O'Hureny, Moleghlin, pardon, [illegible].

O'Hurgane—Hurgane:

" persons of the name pardoned, 4447, [illegible], [illegible], 4371, 4478.

O'Huricke, James, pardon, 6613.

O'Hurilly. See O'Hurelly.

O'Huring, Gilbert, pardon, [illegible].

O'Hurkahan, Donell, pardon, [illegible].

O'Hurkey, Manus, pardon, 6716.

O'Hurle, Donell and Tho.; pardon, 6616.

O'Hurley—Hurlie—Hurly:

" Knoghor, English liberty, 1167.

" others of the name pardoned. [illegible], [illegible], 4[illegible], 4[illegible], 4[illegible], [illegible], [illegible], [illegible], 6471, [illegible], 6[illegible].

O'Hurlihie, Connoghor, pardon, [illegible].

O'Hurly. See O'Hurley.

O'Hurnan, Gylledu[ ] and Wm., pardon, 3797, [illegible].

O'Hurowe, Shane, pardon, [illegible].

O'Hurrane, Conoghor, pardon, [illegible].

O'Hurre[ ], Randulph, pardon, [illegible].

O'Hurrelly — Hurroly — Hurrilie — Hurylr, persons of the name pardoned. 1804, 4418, 6447, [illegible].

O'Hurren, Teige, pardon, [illegible].

O'Hurrilie—Hurylr. See O'Hurrelly.

O'Hurye, Morogh, pardon, 1761.

O'Huryne, Edward, pardon, 17[illegible].

O'Huskie, Mahowne, pardon, [illegible].

O'Hussin, Conner, pardon, 6[illegible].

O'Hussine, Shane, pardon, [illegible].

O'Hustin, Ed., pardon, 4457.

O'Husyne, Teig or Tiedy, pardon, [illegible].

O'Huylan, Conor, pardon, 847.

O'Huyne or O'Henane, Rory, pardon, [illegible].

O'Hwoligan—Hwologhane — Hwolighane —Hwologhan:

" persons of the name pardoned, [illegible], [illegible], [illegible], [illegible].

O'Hwolohow, persons of the name pardoned [illegible].

O'Hwrye, persons of the name pardoned, [illegible].

O'Hyalahy—Hyalyhy. See O'Hialihie.

O'Hycky—Hyckie. See O'Hicky.

O'Hye, Patrick, pardon, [illegible].

O'Hyen, Donnogh, pardon, 37[illegible].

O'Hyerlyhy. See O'Hierlihie.

O'Hyffernyn. See O'Heffernan.

O'Hygane — Hyggins — Hygin. See O'Higgin.

O'Hykie—Hyky. See O'Hiky.

O'Hymmin, Donogh, pardon, 4[illegible].

O'Hynowran, alias Hynowran, Donagh, attainted. [illegible].

O'Hynownayn, Donell, pardon, 4478.

O'Hynnie, Mahowne, pardon, 6417.

O'Hyrrell, Morryghe, pardon, [illegible].

O'Hyver, Loghlen, pardon, [illegible].

O'Hywer, Teige, pardon, [illegible].

Oïlgles in Ossery, [illegible].

O'Ilehane, Richard, pardon, [illegible].

Oirghialla. See Oriall, Uriall.

Oirymagh (co. Mon. ?), 4[illegible].

O'Innasdan, Donogh, pardon, [illegible].

O'Hence, Hugh, pardon, [illegible].

O'Kadogane—Kadigan:

" Connor and Donogh, pardon, 4457, [illegible].

O'Kaell, Philip, attainted, [illegible].

O'Kagherne, Edm., pardon, [illegible].

O'Kahallane, Donell, pardon, [illegible].

O'Kahan—Kahane:

" persons of the name pardoned, [illegible], 4[illegible], 4[illegible], 4[illegible], 6467.

O'Kahasie—Kahassie. See O'Kahisy.

O'Kahill—Kahall—Kahille:

" persons of the name pardoned, [illegible], [illegible], 4[illegible], [illegible], 4[illegible], [illegible]. See O'Cahill.

O'Kahisse, Shane, pardon, [illegible].

O'Kahisy—Kahasie—Kahassie—Kahasy—Kahyssy:

" John, attainted, [illegible].

" others of the name pardoned, [illegible], 4[illegible], 4[illegible], 4[illegible]. See O'Cahissie.

O'Kaimban, Tho., pardon, [illegible].

O'Kallacan, Irelaghe, pardon, [illegible].

O'Kallegan, Cahir, pardon, [illegible].

O'Kallaghan. See O'Callaghan.

O'Kallaghe, Dermot, pardon, [illegible].
O'Kallahan, Conoghor, pardon, [illegible].
O'Kallan. See O'Callan.
O'Kalle, Dermot, pardon, [illegible].
O'Kallekhane. See O'Callaghan.
O'Kalley, Maurice, pardon, [illegible].
O'Kallign, Conoghor, pardon, [illegible].
O'Kalligie, Conoghor, pardon, [illegible].
O'Kalloran, Conchor, pardon, [illegible].
O'Kally, persons of the name pardoned, [illegible], [illegible], [illegible], [illegible].
O'Kanavan, Rowry, pardon, [illegible].
O'Kaneman Ladg, Hugh, pardon, [illegible].
O'Kanewane, Moriertagh, pardon, [illegible].
O'Kannenan, John, pardon, [illegible].
O'Kannife, persons of the name pardoned, 6614.
O'Kanvan, Shane, pardon, [illegible].
O'Kany, Gohere, pardon, [illegible].
O'Kanyen, Dermod, pardon, [illegible].
O'Kanylle, Donell, pardon, 6714.
O'Kaoyle, Teige, pardon, [illegible].
O'Kare, Donogh, pardon, [illegible].
O'Karell. See O'Carroll.
O'Karewhan, Patr., pardon, [illegible].
O'Karie, Ferrall, pardon, [illegible].
O'Karmody. See O'Carmodie.
O'Karne, Wm., pardon, 6767.
O'Karoll. See O'Carroll.
O'Karrelan — Karrelane, persons of the name pardoned, [illegible], [illegible]. See O'Karwellan.
O'Karrihall, Kahill, pardon, [illegible].
O'Karroll. See O'Carroll.
O'Karry, Donogh, pardon, [illegible].
O'Karymody, Donell, pardon, [illegible].
O'Kassrwe, Donoghe, pardon, [illegible].
O'Kaugney, Dermod, pardon, [illegible].
O'Kaylian, Donoghe, pardon, [illegible].
O'Kayliey, Rory, pardon, [illegible].
O'Kaylly, Manasses, pardon, [illegible].
O'Kea, Rich., pardon, [illegible].
O'Keadigan, Donogh, pardon, [illegible].
O'Keagalagh, John, pardon, [illegible].
O'Keagalagh, Dermott, pardon, [illegible].
O'Keaghan, Wm., pardon, [illegible].
O'Keagho, Mulmory and Rorie, pardon, [illegible].
O'Keahan, Cormock, pardon, [illegible].
O'Kealaghan, Diermod, pardon, [illegible].
O'Kealain, Patr., pardon, [illegible].
O'Keale, Dermod, pardon, [illegible].
O'Kealoghan, Dermod, pardon, [illegible].
O'Kealoghane, Dermod, pardon, [illegible].
O'Kealoghir, Conoghor, pardon, [illegible].
O'Kealie, Rorie, pardon, [illegible].
O'Kealigher, Shane, pardon, [illegible].
O'Kealle, Tho., pardon, [illegible].
O'Keallaghan—Keallaghane, persons of the name pardoned, [illegible], [illegible].
O'Keallaghir — Keallahir, Conoghor and Donogh, pardon, 6614.
O'Keallane, David and Mahowne, pardon, [illegible].
O'Kealle, Fernaghe, pardon, [illegible].
O'Keallone, Edm., pardon, [illegible].
O'Keally—Kealy, persons of the name pardoned, [illegible], [illegible], [illegible], [illegible], [illegible], [illegible], [illegible].
O'Kean—Keane, persons of the name pardoned, [illegible], [illegible], [illegible].
O'Keanally, Derby, pardon, [illegible].
O'Keannedy, Conoghor, pardon, [illegible].
O'Keanowan, Morice, pardon, [illegible].
O'Kear, Owen, pardon, [illegible].
O'Kearane, Dermod and Philip, pardon, [illegible].
O'Kearin, persons of the name pardoned, [illegible].
O'Kearnee, Moriertogh, pardon, [illegible].
O'Kearne, Nicoll, pardon, 4740.
O'Kearney — Kearnie — Kearny, persons of the name pardoned, [illegible], [illegible], [illegible], [illegible], [illegible], [illegible], [illegible], [illegible], [illegible], [illegible], [illegible], [illegible], [illegible].
O'Kearoll—Kearowell. See O'Carroll.
O'Kearyn—Kearyne, persons of the name pardoned, [illegible], [illegible], [illegible], [illegible].
O'Keaten, Shane, pardon, [illegible].
O'Keathan, Tho., pardon, [illegible].
O'Keatine, Donell, pardon, [illegible], [illegible].
O'Keatinge, persons of the name pardoned, [illegible].
O'Keatyne, Donogh, pardon, [illegible].
O'Keavane, Cormuck, pardon, [illegible].
" Ferrall, pardon, [illegible].
O'Keavicke, Wm., pardon, [illegible].
O'Keawan, John, pardon, [illegible].
O'Keddy, Edm., pardon, [illegible].
O'Keeffe — Keef — Keefe — Keif — Keife — Keiffe—Keyfe—Keyffe—Kief —Kiefe—Kieffe—Kif—Kife— Kiff — Kiffe — Kyefe — Kyf— Kyfe—Kyff—Kyffe:
" Art; O'Keeffe, pardon, [illegible], [illegible], [illegible].
" Finin m'Art (of Dunbulloge), pardon, [illegible], [illegible].
" others of the name pardoned, [illegible].
" country of, in co. Cork, [illegible].
O'Keelagh, Rorie, pardon, [illegible].
O'Keely, Conoghor, pardon, [illegible].
O'Keerroll, lordship of, [illegible].

INDEX TO FIANTS.—ELIZABETH.

O'Keeve, Owin, pardon, [illegible].
O'Kegan, persons of the name pardoned, [illegible], 1747, [illegible], [illegible], [illegible].
O'Kegelagh, Philip, pardon, [illegible].
O'Keggan, Shane, pardon, [illegible].
O'Keghnan, Maurice, pardon, 481.
O'Kegly, Brian, pardon, 5791.
O'Kehan—Kehana, Philip and Walter, pardon, [illegible], [illegible].
O'Keherne, Dermod, weaver, pardon, [illegible].
O'Keif—Keife—Keiffe. *See* O'Keeffe.
O'Keinde, Donill and Thady, pardon, [illegible].
O'Keinge, persons of the name pardoned, [illegible].
O'Kelaghan, Knoghor, pardon, [illegible].
O'Kelaghe, Shane and Teige, pardon, [illegible], [illegible].
O'Kelagher, persons of the name pardoned, [illegible], [illegible], [illegible].
O'Kelegan, Donell, pardon, [illegible].
O'Keleher, Tho., pardon, [illegible].
O'Kelie, Mellaghlin, pardon, 1304.
Ulrye, pardon, 1236.
O'Keligher, Teig, pardon, [illegible].
O'Kelle, David, pardon, [illegible].
O'Kelleghain, Laghlin, pardon, [illegible].
O'Kelleghan. *See* O'Callaghan.
O'Kellie, John, messuage in Cashel, [illegible].
others of the name pardoned, [illegible], [illegible], [illegible], [illegible], [illegible], [illegible], [illegible].
O'Kelleghain, Connor, pardon, [illegible].
O'Kellachan, Cormock, pardon, [illegible].
O'Kellecher, persons of the name pardoned, [illegible].
O'Kellegan, Connor, pardon, [illegible].
O'Kellegher, Donogh, pardon, [illegible].
" John, pardon, [illegible].
O'Kellen, Rich. and Thady, pardon, [illegible], [illegible].
O'Kellenan, Donnchoe and Gillegery, pardon, [illegible], [illegible].
O'Kelley. *See* O'Kelly.
O'Kelli, Edmund, pardon, [illegible]
tenement in Limerick, [illegible].
O'Kellichan, persons of the name pardoned, [illegible].
O'Kellie. *See* O'Kelly.
O'Kellios, Hugh, pardon, [illegible].
O'Kellogher, Dermod and Tho., pardon, [illegible].
O'Kelly—Kelley—Kellie—Kellys.
Abbot, [illegible].
Conor (of Lenckan), pardon, [illegible].
Conor og (of Cooliegeyer), pardon, [illegible].
Conor nagarrogh, son of Donogh reogh (of Callagh), grant of his lands, [illegible]; seneschal of Kilconnell, [illegible]; pardon, [illegible], [illegible], [illegible].
O'Kelly. Conor m'Teig og, attainted, [illegible].
" Conor m'Hugh m'Brien (of Turriak), pardon, [illegible], [illegible].
" Donell reogh (of Downe), his heir, [illegible].
" Donell, son of Donell reogh, wardship, [illegible].
" Donell m'Brian (of Rahagh), pardon, [illegible], [illegible].
" Donogh reogh, his son, seneschal of Kilconnell, [illegible].
" Dowdally, wardship of his heir, [illegible].
" Edm. row, rector of Reagh, [illegible].
" Egnahan (of Lackan), pardon, [illegible].
" Egneghan m'Edm. oge, attainted, [illegible].
" Ferdorche (of Aghrim), pardon, [illegible], [illegible].
" Ferragh (of Rathanlon), attainted, [illegible].
" Hugh (of Lisdalone), commission, [illegible]; pardon, [illegible].
" Hugh m'Wm., attainted, [illegible].
" Hugh (of Clogher), wardship, [illegible].
" John or Shane ne moy (of Oraagh), grant of his lands, [illegible]; pardon, [illegible], [illegible]; sons of, [illegible], [illegible], [illegible]; daughters of, [illegible].
" John oge or Shane ne moy, son of Shane ne moy, [illegible]; pardon, [illegible], [illegible], [illegible].
" John or Shane m'Egnaghan (of Lackan), attainted, [illegible].
" John (of Clogher), his heir, [illegible].
" John, curate, [illegible].
" Malaghlin m'en abb, pardon, [illegible]; seneschal of Kilconnell, [illegible], [illegible]; grant of lands, [illegible]; commission, [illegible]; his heir, [illegible].
" Morne ny moy, wife of O'Madden, [illegible].
" Onory ne moy, wife of O'Fallon, [illegible].
" Shane eniriagh, pardon, [illegible], [illegible].
" Teig or Thady m'William (of Mallaghmore), pardon, [illegible]; seneschal of bar. of Tiaquin, [illegible]; grant of land, [illegible]; commission, [illegible]; late tanist, [illegible]; pardon, [illegible].
" Teig m'abba, his son, [illegible].
" Teig oge, son of Teig m'abba (or m'enab), livery, [illegible]; castle to be delivered to, [illegible].
" William m'Melaghlin, pardon, [illegible]; made tanist, [illegible]; livery, [illegible].
" others of the name in cos. Galway and Roscommon pardoned, [illegible], [illegible], [illegible], [illegible], [illegible], [illegible], [illegible].

O'Kelly :
[illegible], 6771, 6780, 6783, [illegible], 4103, 4170, 4240, [illegible], 4661, 4711, 4731, 4741, 4779, 4780, 4805, [illegible], 4874, 4875, 4877, 4914, 5112, [illegible], 5421, 5423, 5428, 5428, 5432, 5447-8, 5474, 5486-7, [illegible], 5611, 5612, [illegible], 5712, 5740, [illegible], 6106, 6214, 6418, [illegible].
„ country of, 196, 949, 1846, [illegible], 4780, [illegible], 6740; burial of, 6761.
„ Cahill or Charles (of Ballhaspick), livery, 4180; attainted, 6678.
„ Donell (of Tullyhog, co. Tyrone), pardon, 6714.
„ Ever, livery to his son, 4158.
„ Fergananym, pardon, 171, 176; grant of land, 496.
„ Frynne, grant of land, 498.
„ Manus (a rebel), 2818.
„ Morgh and Rory (houses in Trim), 1714.
„ others of the name pardoned, 171, 227, 420, 438, 443, 614, 634, 717, 813, 871, 878, 906, 918, 954, 1080, 1104, 1378-80, 1398, 1443, 1467-8, 1488, 1559, 1583, 1617, 1751, 1858, 1849, 1867-4, 2044, 2086, 2149, [illegible], [illegible]-3, 2250, 2343, 2297, [illegible], 2310, 2348, 2397, [illegible], 2516, [illegible], [illegible], [illegible], [illegible], 3011, 3044, [illegible], 3247, [illegible], 3544, [illegible], 3871, [illegible], 4036, [illegible], 4232, [illegible], 4250, [illegible], 4589, [illegible], 4762, 4797, 4867, [illegible], 5445, [illegible], 5571, [illegible], 5576, 5788, [illegible]-30, [illegible], 4179-80, [illegible], 4322, [illegible], 5421, 5457-8, 5462, 5429, [illegible], 5477, 5479-80, [illegible], 5486-7, [illegible], 5613-15, 5617, [illegible], 5637, [illegible], 5662-3, [illegible], 5674-5, 5677, 5616, 5623-4, 5644-7, [illegible], 5670, 6714, 6720-7, 6735, 6742, [illegible], 6768.

O Kellyduan, Nele, pardon, 5482.

O'Kellye. *See* O'Kelly.

O'Kely—O'Kelye, persons of the name pardoned, 1063, 1306-7, 1391, 6189, 6724.

O'Kemai, Dowche, pardon, 4682.

O'Kempan, David and Tho., pardon, 4444.

O'Kemy, Philip, pardon, 6160.

O'Ken, Richard, pardon, 5012.

O'Kene, persons of the name pardoned, 6434, 6417, 6577.

O'Kenaghan, Patr. and Shane, pardon, 4073, 4580.

O'Kenaith, persons of the name pardoned, 4694.

O'Kenan—Kenane, persons of the name pardoned, 2224, 0162, 4577, 5516, 5659, 6683, 6714.

O'Kenay, Hugh, pardon, 4494.

O'Kenaly, persons of the name pardoned, 4410.

O'Kene, Conogher, pardon, 4732.

O'Kenelo, Edmund, pardon, 734.

O'Kenelay—Kenelie—Keneligh—Kenedy. *See* O'Kennedy.

O'Kenegan, persons of the name pardoned, 4088, 4307, 4431.

O'Kenelagh, Donogh, pardon, 4679.

O'Kenely—Kenelan—Kenelie—Kenelly:
„ persons of the name pardoned, 1463, 4348, 5484, 6579, 6689.

O'Kenevan, persons of the name pardoned, 4458, 5793, 5800.

O'Kenewane, Carberie, pardon, 4619.

O'Keney, persons of the name pardoned, 6328.

O'Kenga, Donyll and Rory, pardon, 58.

O'Kenga, Hugh, pardon, 4164.

O'Kengy—Kengie—Hengey:
„ persons of the name pardoned, 4310, 4338, 4450.

O'Kenidie, Teig, pardon, 5082.

O'Kenides, three races of, country, 4332.

O'Keniye, Donogh, pardon, 4084.

O'Kenig, persons of the name pardoned, 5949.

O'Kenighan — Kenighon, persons of the same pardoned, 1964.

O'Kenkevaine, Hugh, pardon, 5431.

O'Kenkenane, Donnogh, pardon, 4884.

O'Kenkevaine, Tho., pardon, 5451.

O'Kenlan, Donald, pardon, 2044.

O'Kenly, Thady, pardon, 6512.

O'Kennedy, Conor and Hugh, pardon, 5614, 6612.

O'Kenna, persons of the name pardoned, 4528, 6517, 4525, 6714.

O'Kenane, Dermod, pardon, 6511.

O'Kennevain, Conla, pardon, 4472.

O'Kennew, Conner, Donogh, and Murtagh, pardon, 6894.

O'Kennay, David, pardon, 6743.

INDEX TO FIANTS.—ELIZABETH.

O'Kennelly—Kennellie—Kentnoly, persons of the name pardoned, 6183, [illegible].

O'Kennedy—Kenedey—Kenelie—Kenedigh—Kenedy—Kennedie—Kenydy:

„ Conoghor, his son attainted, 6122.

„ Edm. (of Ballintot), pardon, 4902, 6513, 6708.

„ Gilliduffe (of Garranmore), pardon, 4646, 6708.

„ Gilleduffe (of Castletown), pardon, [illegible], 6764.

„ Gilleduffe (of Ballingarry), pardon, 6518.

„ Hugh (of Rapponlagh), pardon, 6542, 6704.

„ Iriell (of Garranmore), pardon, 6562, 6706, 6775.

„ John or Shane (of Lackin), pardon, 6514, 6708, 6734.

„ Wm. (of Ballichalill), pardon, 6543, 6703.

„ Wm. Hogh boye, attainted, 6122.

„ others of the name pardoned, 437, 677, 916, 1059, 1246, 1697, 1097, [illegible], [illegible], 2041, [illegible], 2087, 2083, 2046, 2247, [illegible], 2103, 3118, 3134, [illegible], 3964, 3002, 4033, 4316, 4370, 4376–8, 4449, 4506–8, 4528, 4532, 4553, 4555, 4670, 4694–6, 4713–14, 4767, 4705, 4896, 4933, 4937, 4975, [illegible], 5048, 5274, 5431, 5402, 5492, 5897, 6108, 6143, [illegible], [illegible], 6443, 6487, 6494–5, 6504, 6512, 6517, 6518, 6521, 6524, 6529, 6531–3, 6534, 6536, 6554, 6576, 6562, 6627, 6658, 6704, 6706–7, 6730, 6734, 6761, 6764, 6775.

„ country of, 125, 7822.

„ three races of, 6323.

„ *See* Kenedie, Kenedigh, &c.

O'Kennedy Doffee, pardon, 1066.

O'Kennuhane, Hugh carragh, pardon, 5294.

O'Kennell, Teig, pardon, 6523.

O'Kennelly, John roe cromme, pardon, 5746.

O'Kennerie, John, pardon, 6477.

O'Kennevan, Gillatuni, pardon, [illegible].

O'Kennevane, Owen, 5485.

O'Kenney, Brian and Dermot, pardon, 6496, 6494.

O'Kennovan, Nich., pardon, 5498.

O'Kennoy, Donnogh, pardon, 6216.

O'Kenny—Kennye, persons of the name pardoned, 4334, 4608, 4652, 4707, 4573, 5474, 5513, 5522, 5618, 5497, 6128, 6316, 6440, 6436, 6464, 6497, 6514, 6540, 6541, 6658, 6706.

O'Kennydy. *See* O'Kennedy.

O'Kennye. *See* O'Kenny.

O'Kenolan, Beaghan, wardship of his heir, 1157.

O'Kenolan, Edward, his wardship, 1157.

O'Kenty, persons of the name pardoned, 4079–80, 4213, 4050, 4547, 4864, 5712, 6108, 6218.

O'Kenydie, Hugh, pardon, 5702.

O'Kenye, Laghlin, pardon, 4972.

O'Kenye, Wm., pardon, 6532.

O'Keo, Conchor, pardon, 515.

O'Keogho, Thomas, pardon, 678.

O'Kerane—Keran—Keraine:

„ Shane, O'Kerane, pardon, 6761.

„ others of the same pardoned, 4767, 4782, 5214.

O'Kerby, Tho. pardon, 4611.

O'Kerogane, Gillpatrick, pardon, 5712.

O'Kerovan, Andrew and Rich., pardon, 4317, 6977.

O'Kergan, Shane, pardon, 5443.

O'Kerin—Kerine—Keryn—Keryne:

„ persons of the name pardoned, 1517, 2403, 2877, 4349, 5712, 5602, 6616, 6617, 6624, 6776.

O'Kermoly—Kermoddy:

„ persons of the name pardoned, 4378, 6401, 6570.

O'Kernan, Teige, pardon, 4767.

O'Kerne, persons of the name pardoned, 1767, 2353, 6454.

O'Kerny—Kerney—Kernie:

„ Donogh: O'Kerny, pardon, 5284.

„ others of the name pardoned, 1462, 2380, 5063, 5414, 6306, 6462, 6571, 6584.

O'Kerolan. *See* O'Kerrolan.

O'Keroll—Kerrall. *See* O'Carroll.

O'Kerrpaise, Wm., pardon, 6511.

O'Kerrin, Moriogh, pardon, 5065.

O'Kerrogan, Neile, pardon, 5488.

O'Kerrolle. *See* O'Carroll.

O'Kerrolan—Kerolan:

„ persons of the name pardoned, 2574, 4638, 4734.

O'Kerroll—Kerrole. *See* O'Carroll.

O'Kerry, Kermock, pardon, 5594.

O'Kerunlan, Brean, (of Nobber), pardon, 6544.

O'Kervan, Rich., pardon, 6127.

O'Kervellan, persons of the name pardoned, 6563, 6608. *See* O'Kerwellan.

O'Kervick, Conoghor and Philip, pardon, 5672, 5672.

O'Kervoll, Teige, pardon, 4586.

O'Kervy, David and Teige, pardon, 6634.

O'Kerwall, Kenny, pardon, 6561.

O'Kerwellan, persons of the name pardoned, 4402.

O'Kerwellans — Carrollans, certain excepted from pardon, 6694.

O'Kerwick—Kerwicke—Kerwyck:

„ persons of the name pardoned, 5507, 4474, 6406.

INDEX TO FIANTS—ELIZABETH.

O'Kerymakyn, John, pardon, [illegible].
O'Kerye—Keryne. See O'Herin.
O'Keredy, Gelygreme, pardon, [illegible].
O'Keran, Dermod, pardon, [illegible].
O'Keredye—Keridie—Kerydy:
" persons of the name pardoned, [illegible], [illegible].
Okerairie, country of, [illegible].
O'Kevan, persons of the name pardoned, [illegible], [illegible], [illegible], 1804, [illegible], 41[illegible], [illegible], [illegible], [illegible], [illegible].
O'Kewane, Robert, pardon, 1017.
O'Kewallane, Patr., pardon, 6734.
O'Kewlie, Laughlin, pardon, [illegible].
O'Kewyn, Arthur, pardon, 1318.
O'Key, Riccard, pardon, [illegible].
O'Keyfe—Keyffe. See O'Keaffe.
O'Keyghan, Dermod and Donogh, pardon, [illegible], [illegible].
O'Keyle, persons of the name pardoned, [illegible], [illegible].
O'Keyle, Kenghor, pardon, [illegible].
O'Keyley, Conoghor, pardon, [illegible].
O'Keylle, persons of the name pardoned, [illegible], [illegible], [illegible].
O'Keylly, Thomas, English liberty, [illegible].
O'Keyllye, Tho., pardon, [illegible].
O'Keyly, Kenghor and Teige, pardon, [illegible], [illegible].
O'Keyn, Emma, pardon, [illegible].
O'Keynaugher, Teig, pardon, [illegible].
O'Keyne, Farrall and James, pardon, [illegible].
O'Keynigan, Wm., pardon, [illegible].
O'Keynlewayn, Mahown, pardon, [illegible].
O'Keyrwick, Donogh and Morice, pardon, [illegible], [illegible].
O'Keyrvig, Taige, pardon, [illegible].
O'Keysey, Dermod, pardon, [illegible].
O'Keytra, Rich. and Teige, pardon, [illegible].
O'Keyve, Uligg, land of (co. Cork), [illegible].
O'Khyow, Edm., pardon, [illegible].
O'Kiadigaine, Teige, pardon, [illegible].
O'Kially, Conoghor and Donogh, pardon, [illegible].
O'Kie, Donogh, pardon, [illegible].
O'Kief—Kiefe—Kieffe. See O'Keaffe.
O'Kieghane, Donogho, pardon, [illegible].
O'Kieran, Diarmod, pardon, [illegible].
O'Kierny, Teige, pardon, [illegible].
O'Kierrogain, Wm., pardon, [illegible].
O'Kierrgaine, Torrnultagh, pardon, [illegible].
O'Kierviske, Diarmod, pardon, [illegible].
O'Kievane, Donogh, pardon, [illegible].
O'Kif—Kife—Kiff—Kiffe. See O'Keaffe.
O'Kigane, Mahowne, pardon, [illegible].
O'Kihan, John, pardon, [illegible].
O'Killane, Conoghor and Gillcisiff, pardon, [illegible].
O'Killen, Rowry, pardon, [illegible].
O'Killewaine, Edm., pardon, [illegible].
O'Killeynoy, John, pardon, [illegible].
O'Killie, Mahowne, pardon, [illegible].
O'Killigho, Mahowne, pardon, [illegible].
O'Killilly, Rorery, pardon, [illegible].
O'Killin—Killinc—Killyn—Killyne—Kylin—Kylinn—Kyllyn, persons of the name pardoned, [illegible], [illegible], [illegible], [illegible], [illegible], [illegible].
O'Killinane, Riccard, pardon, [illegible].
O'Killyn. See O'Killin.
O'Kilt, Edm. and John, pardon, [illegible].
" See also O'Kylt.
O'Kiltagh, Donald and Owin, pardon, [illegible].
O'Kilto, Brian and Brien, pardon, [illegible].
O'Kime, Gillebride, pardon, [illegible].
" See also O'Kyme.
O'Kimain, Mulrony, pardon, [illegible].
O'Kinan, Coconnaght, priest, pardon, [illegible].
" David, pardon, [illegible].
O'Kinane—Kynan, persons of the name pardoned, [illegible], [illegible].
O'Kindane, Conoghor, pardon, [illegible].
O'Kine, Mah, pardon, [illegible].
O'Kinedy, Teige, pardon, [illegible].
O'Kineghan, Teige, pardon, [illegible].
O'Kingolane, Brian and Teige, pardon, [illegible].
O'Kinely, Dermot arone, pardon, [illegible].
O'Kinet, Robert, pardon, [illegible].
O'King, Donogh and Rory, pardon, [illegible], [illegible].
O'Kinge, Thorrelagh and Tirlagh, pardon, [illegible], [illegible].
O'Kinge—Kynge, persons of the name pardoned, 1747, [illegible], [illegible], [illegible], [illegible], [illegible], [illegible], [illegible], [illegible], [illegible], [illegible], [illegible], [illegible], [illegible].
O'Kinkennice, Brian and Cahell, pardon, [illegible].
O'Kinregan—Kinrogane, persons of the name pardoned, [illegible], [illegible], [illegible].
O'Kircke, Dermod, pardon, [illegible].
O'Kirevin, James, pardon, [illegible].
O'Kirie, Hwonye, pardon, [illegible].
O'Kirran, M'Agus, pardon, [illegible].
O'Kirry, Wm., pardon, [illegible].
O'Kishane—Kishaine—Kishyn—Kishan—Kishan—Kyshane—Kyshan, persons of the name pardoned, [illegible], [illegible], 4107-8, [illegible], [illegible], [illegible], [illegible], [illegible].
O'Kivan—Kyvan, persons of the name pardoned, [illegible], [illegible], [illegible], [illegible].
O'Kive, Owin, pardon, [illegible].
O'Kivelaghan, Dyarmoit, pardon, [illegible].
O'Klaghny, Dermot, pardon, [illegible].
O'Klan, Wm., pardon, [illegible].
O'Klerkane, Hugh, pardon, [illegible].
O'Klery. See O'Clery.
O'Kloonay, Donogho, pardon, [illegible].
O'Knaffe—Knafe—Knayff, persons of the name pardoned, [illegible], [illegible], [illegible], 1846.
O'Knavin—Knavyn—Knavyne, persons of the name pardoned, [illegible], [illegible], [illegible], [illegible], [illegible].

INDEX TO FIANTS.—ELIZABETH.

O'Kenyll. *See* O'Kneile.
O'Keogher—Keogher. *See* O'Connor.
O'Keowe, Donell, pardon, 6515.
O'Keowane, John, pardon, 6434.
O'Keoyrk, Tho., pardon, 6179.
O'Keyghier, Calle, pardon, 2774.
O'Keyne, Cahill and Wm., pardon, [illegible].
O'Kobry, Donell, pardon, [illegible].
O'Koffe. *See* O'Coffe.
O'Koggie, Teig, pardon, 6457.
O'Koh, Rory, pardon, [illegible]
O'Kolenlan, Brian, pardon, 4468.
O'Kohee, Ennes, pardon, 2044.
O'Koigne. *See* O'Coigne.
O'Konan, Maurice, pardon, 2861.
O'Koneloure. *See* O'Connor.
O'Konell—Konill—Kounell. *See* O'Connell.
O'Konor. *See* O'Connor.
O'Konyll. *See* O'Connell.
O'Konnlayne—Konolleyne. *See* O'Conolan.
O'Konon, Donogh, pardon, 2204.
O'Konor. *See* O'Connor.
O'Konowe. *See* O'Connow.
O'Konyllan—Konylan. *See* O'Connellan.
O'Korcorane. *See* O'Corcheran.
O'Korkerie—Korkiree. *See* O'Corkery.
O'Korkrain—Korkran. *See* O'Corcran.
O'Korkyrye. *See* O'Corkory.
O'Kormick. *See* O'Cormick.
O'Korregan. *See* O'Corregan.
O'Kosse—Koss, Enys and Myllaghlyn, pardon, [illegible].
O'Kowan. *See* O'Cowan.
O'Kowne, Donald, pardon, [illegible].
O'Kowrke, Donoghe, pardon, [illegible].
O'Koyffe, John and Knogher, pardon, 6571.
O'Koyllegan, Daniel, pardon, 6574.
O'Koyne, Gylglasse, pardon, [illegible]. *See* O'Coyne.
O'Kredan, Donoghe, harper, pardon, 4626. *See* O'Credane.
O'Kregiane, Richard, pardon, 611. *See* O'Gregiane.
O'Krehan, Teige, pardon, 2544.
O'Krew, Donell, pardon, [illegible].
O'Krian—Kryane, persons of the name pardoned, 4153, 5408.
O'Krighan, Tho., pardon, 6008.
O'Kromyn. *See* O'Cromyne.
O'Kronane, Edm., pardon, [illegible].
O'Krottie. *See* O'Crottie.
O'Kryane. *See* O'Krian.
O'Kuddyhy. *See* O'Cuddihie.
O'Kuerke, Dermot and Wm., pardon, [illegible].
O'Kullane, Donogh, alienation to, [illegible].
O'Kullen—Kullen. *See* O'Cullen.
O'Kuondill, Conchor, pardon, [illegible].
O'Kurnane, Gyllynenaffe, pardon, 4574.
O'Kurnee, Murtagh, pardon, 1727.
O'Kusty, Dermot, pardon, 6480.
O'Kwllayn, John, pardon, [illegible].
O'Kwodghane, Donell, pardon, 5546.
O'Kwoine, Derbie, pardon, 4472.
O'Kwyn, Dermod, pardon, 6811.
O'Kyefe. *See* O'Keeffe.
O'Kyon Tho., pardon, [illegible].
O'Kyermeyck, Donoghe, piper, pardon, 4782.
O'Kyerwicke, Teig, pardon, 4474.
O'Kyf—Kyfe—Kyff—Kyffe. *See* O'Keaffe.
O'Kythy, persons of the name pardoned, 3774.
O'Kyll, Edmund and Wm., pardon, [illegible].
O'Kyllin—Kyllan—Kyllyn. *See* O'Killin.
O'Kylt, Moris, pardon, 4792.
O'Kymoe, Hugh, slain, [illegible].
O'Kyne, Awe, pardon, 6602.
O'Kyman. *See* O'Kinane.
O'Kymay, One, pardon, 811.
O'Kynealy, Donogh, pardon, 6427.
O'Kynge. *See* O'Kinge.
O'Kyngy, Rory, pardon, [illegible].
O'Kynilly, Tho., pardon, 4707.
O'Kynnighan, Dermot, pardon, [illegible].
O'Kynnaddy, Shane, pardon, 6074.
O'Kynnedy, John and Philip, English liberty, 900.
O'Kynny—Kynnye, Donogh and Patrick, pardon, 4680, 6472.
O'Kynnyne, Teige, pardon, 2827.
O'Kynsillaghe, Knogher, pardon, 778.
O'Kyrye, Hugh, pardon, 1848.
O'Kynylos, Teige, pardon, 4828.
O'Kyrine, Teige, pardon, 5448.
O'Kyshane—Kyshan. *See* O'Kissane.
O'Kyrye, John, pardon, [illegible].
O'Kyrny, Neale, pardon, 4234.
O'Kyvan. *See* O'Kivan.
O'Kyve, Cowne and Hugh, pardon, 6431.
O'Kywaine, persons of the name pardoned, [illegible].
O'Kywe, Arth oge, pardon, 1098.
O'Laane, Tho., pardon, 5740.
O'Lachnyn, Nich., pardon, [illegible].
O'Lachnin, Mahony, pardon, 6418.
O'Lackyne, Teige, harper, pardon, 4564.
O'Lacy—Lacye, persons of the name pardoned, 6028, 6428, 6827.
O'Laen, Tho., pardon, 4297.
O'Lafferty—Laffertie, persons of the name pardoned, 6644, 5761.
O'Laffie, persons of the name pardoned, 4440, [illegible].
O'Lagan—Lagane, persons of the name pardoned, [illegible], 4718.
O'Lagh, Teige, pardon, 5118.
O'Laghan, Shane and Tho., pardon, [illegible], 5794.
O'Laghen, Murtagh, pardon, 1178.

INDEX TO FIANTS—ELIZABETH:

O'Laghlen—Laghlane—Laghlin. See Loghlin.
O'Laghlor, Neale and Wm., pardon, 6494.
O'Laghlyn—Laghlyne. See Laghlin.
O'Laghnan—Laghnane, persons of the name pardoned, 1817, [illegible], 6718, [illegible], 6816.
O'Laghnan, Morirt, pardon, 431.
O'Lagtery, William, pardon, 658.
O'Lagine, Tho., pardon, 6477.
O'Lahan, Donogh, pardon, 6468.
O'Laherty, Shane, pardon, 6752.
O'Lahie. See O'Lahy.
O'Lahiff, Richard, English liberty, [illegible].
O'Lahy—Lahie, persons of the name pardoned, 1124, 4[illegible], 6[illegible], 6762.
O'Lalor—Lalar—Lallor—Lallore—Lallour—Lalour—Lalor—Lalure—Laulor—Lawlor:
„ persons of the name pardoned, 128, 6[illegible], 7[illegible], 871, 873, 967, 1118, 1874, 1913, [illegible], [illegible], 2144, [illegible], [illegible]–4, [illegible], [illegible], [illegible], [illegible], [illegible], [illegible], [illegible], [illegible], [illegible], 4[illegible], [illegible], [illegible], [illegible], [illegible], [illegible], [illegible], [illegible], [illegible], [illegible], [illegible], [illegible], [illegible], [illegible], [illegible], [illegible], [illegible], 6457, [illegible], [illegible], [illegible], [illegible], 6766, 6741, 6769, 6773.
O'Lanagan, John, pardon, 788.
O'Lanaghin, Donogh, pardon, 6791.
O'Laname, Donald, pardon, 6451.
O'Lane, Donogh and O'Ferrall, pardon, [illegible], 6378.
O'Lanan, Dermot, pardon, [illegible].
O'Lanegane, Cahir and Nicholas, pardon, 1[illegible], [illegible].
„ William, English liberty, 1[illegible].
O'Laneghan, Donoghe, pardon, 6758.
O'Langan, Dermott and Donogh, pardon, 6418, 6761.
O'Lanie, Redmond, pardon, 6152.
O'Lannan, Melaghlin and Robert, pardon, 931, 6554.
O'Lannegan, alias Lohane, Dermock, pardon, 1[illegible].
O'Lanneregane, Shane, murder of, [illegible].
O'Lapane—Lappan, persons of the name pardoned, [illegible], 6752.
O'Laran, Mahowne, pardon, 5009.
O'Larie, Morogh, pardon, 4[illegible].
O'Larryne, Connor, pardon, 4631.
Olase, Donill, pardon, [illegible].
O'Lasie, persons of the name pardoned, 6547.
O'Lasse, Gerald, pardon, [illegible].
O'Lassy, Morogh, pardon, 6741.
O'Laughlen. See O'Loghlin.
O'Laulor—Loulor. See O'Lalor.
O'Lavin—Lavon—Lavine—Lavyn:
„ persons of the name pardoned, 4[illegible], 4[illegible], 4[illegible], 4[illegible], 4777, [illegible], 6[illegible]–14, [illegible], 6724.
O'Lawan, Dermod and John, pardon, [illegible].
O'Lawlare, Wm., pardon, 4[illegible].
O'Lawlor. See O'Lalor.
O'Lawndoyr, Edm., pardon, 4[illegible].
O'Lawrie—Lawry, persons of the name pardoned, 6416, 6714, 6734.
O'Lay, persons of the name pardoned, 4[illegible].
O'Layflartie—Loyrellertie, persons of the name pardoned, [illegible].
Old Abbey—Abey—Abbaye—Abbie—Abby, co. Kilk., 1175, 1862, 1[illegible], [illegible], 4[illegible], [illegible].
Oldbawne, co. Dub., 4616.
Oldbridge, co. Meath, [illegible].
Old Cappaghe, co. Tip., 4[illegible].
Oldcasiell. See Oldcastle.
Oldcastelton. See Oldcastleton.
Old Castle, co. Cork, 3[illegible].
Oldcastle, co. Gal., 4[illegible].
Oldcastle, co. Meath, 4[illegible], 4[illegible], 4[illegible], 4[illegible].
„ manor, 1800.
„ rectory, 1[illegible], [illegible].
Old Castleton, co. Cork, [illegible], [illegible], 6[illegible], 4[illegible], [illegible].
„ manor, [illegible], [illegible], [illegible].
Oldcastleton, or Shanballecaryslelane (Castletown, co. Westm.), [illegible].
Oldcnoer, alias Tonore (Shanour, co. Meath), [illegible].
Oldcoolicall (Coolycull), co. Wex., 1[illegible].
Old Conoghie, alias Shanconoghie (Cona ?), co. Cork, [illegible].
Old Connell—Connell, co. Kild., 1[illegible], [illegible], [illegible], 6[illegible].
Oldconnaught, co. Dub. See Connaghe, Conoghor.
Oldconnell, co. Kild. See Connall, Old Connell.
Old Corck (co. Cork ?), 6[illegible].
Old Court, co. Kild. 2[illegible].
Old Court—Olde Courte, co. Cork, 4[illegible], [illegible], [illegible].
Oldcourt, co. Wick. See Ouldecourte, Butlerscourt.
Oldderrig, Queen's co. See Oldargo.
Olde Courte, Oldetoun, &c. See Old Court, Oldtown.
Oldefyne. See Elphin.
Olderfleete — Olderfleet (Olderfleet, co. Antrim), 6766; castle, 6766.
„ gauger of port, 1[illegible].
Oldargo (Oldderrig), Queen's co., 4[illegible].
Old Graig, (co. Tip. ?), 6[illegible].
Oldgrange of Moiaghmore, [illegible].
Old Grange—Grang, [illegible], [illegible], [illegible], 6713.
Old Grange—Grannage—Oulde Grange, co. Kild., 978, 1814, [illegible], [illegible], 6115.
Old Grannage, co. Kilk., [illegible].
Old head—Oldehedd, of Kinsale, co. Cork, [illegible], [illegible].

INDEX TO FIANTS—ELIZABETH.

Old Laughlin (Oldleighlin), co. Car., messuage and garden in, granted, [illegible].
Old mill, Queen's co. *See* Shanemullen.
Old Orchard, at Mellifont, co. Louth, 2971, 2972.
Old Parish, co. Meath, rectory, 1465, [illegible]-3, 5166, 6334.
Old Ross—Ros—Owlde Rosse, co. Wex., 1067, 4254, [illegible], 6787.
„ manor, [illegible], 2460.
„ vicar of, 464.
„ rector of, [illegible], 6080, [illegible].
Old Stone, alias Cloghloghortie, co. Antrim, [illegible].
Oldston, co. Meath, 2804.
Oldtown, 1032, [illegible].
Oldtown—Ouldtowne, co. Cork, 6310.
Oldtown—Oldeton, co. Kild., 1516, 2471, [illegible], 6409; rectory, 2471.
Oldtown of Donowre, co. Kild., [illegible].
Oldtown, co. Kilk., 4570, 6704.
(Oldtown)—Oldetowne (in par. Kilcarn, co. Meath.), 2804.
Oldtown, co. Tip., [illegible], [illegible].
Oldtown, co. Westm., [illegible].
Old Town—Oldetown, co. Wex., [illegible], [illegible].
Oldwood—Oldewood, co. Wat., [illegible].
O'Leaery, William, pardon, 1265.
O'Leaghea, persons of the name pardoned, 4464.
O'Leaghe, persons of the name pardoned, [illegible], 6467.
O'Leaghie, persons of the name pardoned, 6467, 6467, 6514-6, 6272, [illegible], [illegible].
O'Leaghre, Daniel, pardon, 6474.
O'Leaghy—Leahy, persons of the name pardoned, [illegible], 4216, [illegible], [illegible].
O'Lealor—Leallor—Leallour:
„ persons of the name pardoned, [illegible], 3646, [illegible].
O'Leamy, Morogh, pardon, 6477.
O'Leamygh, Wm., pardon, 3644.
O'Lean, Edm. and Morish, pardon, [illegible], 6511.
O'Leary—Learie:
„ persons of the name pardoned, [illegible], [illegible], 4444, [illegible], 6170, 6408, 6428, 6514-16, [illegible], [illegible], [illegible], 6701, [illegible].
O'Leaughy, Tho., pardon, 4611.
O'Leay, Patr., pardon, 6741.
Olehan, towns of, in Connello, co. Lim., [illegible].
O'Ledify, Rorie, pardon, [illegible].
O'Leery, Ellen, pardon, [illegible].
„ Wm., English liberty and pardon, [illegible].
O'Leghan, Owen, pardon, [illegible].
O'Leghie, John and Donell, pardon, [illegible].
O'Lehan, Donell, pardon, [illegible].
O'Leian, Laughlen and Redmund, pardon, 6617.
O'Leinsie, Donell, pardon, [illegible].
O'Leigh—Leighe:
„ persons of the name pardoned, [illegible], 6613, 4812, [illegible], [illegible].
O'Leighy—Leighie—Leighey:
„ persons of the name pardoned, [illegible], [illegible], [illegible], [illegible], 4764, [illegible], 6497, 6511.
O'Leigne, persons of the name pardoned, 6744.
O'Leine—Lein, persons of the name pardoned, [illegible], 3462, [illegible], [illegible], [illegible], [illegible], 6162, [illegible], 6516, [illegible], [illegible]-5, 6578.
O'Lempsey, Darby and Donogh, pardon, 4574.
O'Len, Molaghlyn, pardon, [illegible].
O'Lenagan, Edm., pardon, [illegible].
O'Lenaghan, Shane, pardon, 6443.
O'Lenan, persons of the name pardoned, 1714, 3169, [illegible], [illegible], 6711.
O'Lenargan, Rickard, pardon, 6701.
O'Lende—Lende, persons of the name pardoned, 6162.
O'Lenean, Moriertagh, pardon, [illegible].
O'Lenaghan—Lenaghaan, Patr. and Wm., pardon, 4187, [illegible].
O'Lenie, Connor, pardon, [illegible].
O'Lennan—Lennane, persons of the name pardoned, [illegible], 4193, 4403, 6517, [illegible], [illegible], [illegible], 6760.
O'Lenahie—Lenahye—Lenale:
„ persons of the name pardoned, 4923, 6451, 6467, [illegible], 6671.
O'Lenygtan, Philip and Teig, pardon, [illegible].
O'Leny, Morris, pardon, [illegible].
O'Lenyowean, Wm., pardon, [illegible].
O'Leochulle, Bete, pardon, 6517.
O'Leoghlie, Donell, pardon, [illegible].
Olera, co. Car., [illegible].
O'Lerie. *See* O'Lary.
O'Lerigane, Shane, pardon, [illegible].
O'Lerne, Art, alias O'Lery, pardon, 4764.
„ Conoghor, pardon, 4764.
O'Lery—Lerie—Lerye:
„ Art or Arther; O'Lery, pardon, 4416, 4764, 5069, 6467.
„ wife of, pardon, 6467, 4571.
„ Darmod oge, pardon, [illegible].
„ others of the name pardoned, 4416, 4418, 4764, [illegible], [illegible], [illegible], 5174, [illegible], [illegible], 6467, [illegible], 6511, [illegible], [illegible], [illegible], 6571, [illegible], [illegible].
O'Leskine, Walter, pardon, [illegible].
Olelon, co. Mayo, 6076.
O'Leeth, John, pardon, [illegible].
O'Ley, persons of the name pardoned, [illegible], 5069, [illegible].

INDEX TO FIANTS.—ELIZABETH.

O'Leyayn, Shervragh, pardon, [illegible].
O'Leyhan, Thomas, pardon, [illegible].
O'Leye, Rorye, pardon, 47[illegible].
O'Leyerie, alias O'Lerie, Donogh, pardon, [illegible].
O'Leygiemayne, Owen, pardon, [illegible].
O'Leyn. See O'Leyne.
O'Leyman, Hugh and John, pardon, [illegible].
O'Leyne—Leyn—Lyne:
" Edmund, commission, [illegible], [illegible]; pardon, [illegible].
" Awly, Donell, Eneas, John, and Patrick, surgeons, pardon, 1787, [illegible], [illegible], [illegible], [illegible], [illegible].
" John, physician, pardon, [illegible].
" others of the name pardoned, 1[illegible], 140, 912, 515, [illegible], 1[illegible], 1[illegible], 1417, 1[illegible], 1874, 2541, 2[illegible], [illegible], [illegible], 2[illegible], 2[illegible], [illegible], [illegible], [illegible], [illegible], [illegible], 4111, [illegible], [illegible], [illegible], 4613, [illegible], [illegible], [illegible], 4612, [illegible], 4675, [illegible], 4714, [illegible], [illegible], [illegible], [illegible], [illegible], [illegible], [illegible], [illegible], [illegible], [illegible], [illegible], [illegible], [illegible], [illegible], [illegible], [illegible], [illegible], [illegible]-7, [illegible], [illegible], [illegible], [illegible], [illegible], [illegible], [illegible], [illegible], [illegible], [illegible], [illegible], [illegible]-7, [illegible], [illegible].
O'Leyrie, Mahowne and Teig, pardon, [illegible], [illegible].
Olfine. See Elphin.
O'Liagha, Derby, pardon, [illegible].
Oliekuygesa, co. Gal., [illegible].
Olie, Brien, pardon, [illegible].
O'Lieghan, David, pardon, [illegible].
Oliehan barony, co. Cork (in bar. Barrymore), [illegible].
O'Lien, persons of the name pardoned, [illegible], [illegible].
O'Liengan, Hugh, pardon, [illegible].
O'Liffe, Dermond, pardon, [illegible].
O'Lighe, John and Philip, pardon, [illegible].
O'Limaffoyer, John, pardon, [illegible].
O'Linee. See O'Lynce.
O'Linch—Linche—Linshe:
" persons of the name pardoned, 10, [illegible], [illegible], [illegible], [illegible], [illegible], [illegible], [illegible], [illegible], [illegible], [illegible], [illegible]-7, [illegible].
O'Linchi, Donagh, priest, pardon, [illegible].
O'Lincy—Lincie—Lincey—Linsie—Linsy:
" persons of the name pardoned, [illegible], [illegible], [illegible], [illegible], [illegible], [illegible], [illegible].
O'Line, John, pardon, [illegible].
O'Linne, John, pardon, [illegible].
O'Linsey. See O'Linsy.
O'Linshe. See O'Linch.
O'Linshie, Dermod, pardon, [illegible].
O'Linsie. See O'Linsy.
O'Linsighan, persons of the name pardoned, [illegible].
O'Linsy. See O'Lincy.
Oliogo, Donell, pardon, [illegible].
O'Lishane, Donell, pardon, [illegible].
Olladoy, Donald, pardon, [illegible].
Ollane, Donoghe, pardon, [illegible].
Ollard, co. Kild., grant, [illegible].
Ollorde, co. Car., [illegible].
Ollordroch, [illegible].
O'Loaine, Dermod and Manus, pardon, [illegible].
O'Loane, Art, pardon, [illegible].
O'Loddie, Tho., pardon, [illegible].
O'Loghe, Manus, pardon, [illegible].
O'Loghan, Colman, pardon, 1874.
" Edmund, physician, pardon, [illegible].
O'Loghane, Wm., pardon, [illegible].
O'Loghden, Tirrelagh, pardon, [illegible].
O'Logher, Con and Owen, pardon, [illegible].
O'Loghin, Brien, pardon, [illegible].
O'Loghlein, Donogh, pardon, [illegible].
O'Loghlin—Loghlen—Loghlen—Loghlin—Loghlyn—Loughlen—Loghlyn:
" Brian m'Thirrely (of Glaseland), pardon, [illegible].
" Donogh m'Rossa (of Glancollumkille), pardon, [illegible], [illegible].
" Owly or Auliffe, clerk, pardon, [illegible].
" Owny m'Meloghlin, called O'Loghlin, pardon, [illegible]; indenture, [illegible]; his lands, [illegible].
" Rosse (of Glancolumkille), tanist to O'Loghlin, pardon, [illegible], [illegible], [illegible], [illegible]; indenture, [illegible].
" Tirrelagh m'orriggagh (of Cahirsloggan), pardon, [illegible], [illegible].
" Tirrelagh (of Glaseland), attainted, [illegible].
" others of the name pardoned, [illegible], 1641, [illegible], [illegible], [illegible], [illegible], [illegible], [illegible], [illegible], [illegible], [illegible], [illegible], [illegible]-7, [illegible], [illegible], [illegible], [illegible], [illegible], [illegible].
O'Loghnan—Loghnane, persons of the name pardoned, [illegible], [illegible], [illegible], [illegible]-2, [illegible], [illegible], [illegible], [illegible].
O'Loinshy, Dermond, pardon, [illegible].
O'Lonane, Morrogh, pardon, [illegible].
O'Lonasny, Donell, pardon, [illegible].
O'Lonan—Lonane, persons of the name pardoned, [illegible], [illegible], [illegible].
O'Lonaragayn, Maurice, English liberty, 177.
O'Londergan, Conor, pardon, [illegible].
O'Londen, Maurice, pardon, [illegible].
O'Lone, Wm., pardon, [illegible].

INDEX TO FIANTS—ELIZABETH.

O'Lonegan, Edm., pardon, 6108.

O'Lonergan—Lonergane—Lonnergane—Lonneryghan, persons of the same pardoned, 1044, 1310, [illegible], [illegible], 4296, 4422, [illegible].

O'Lonergan — Lonergane — Lonnergan, persons of the same pardoned, [illegible], [illegible], [illegible], [illegible], [illegible], [illegible], [illegible], [illegible], [illegible], [illegible], [illegible], 6457-8, 6764.

O'Longan, persons of the same pardoned, [illegible], [illegible], [illegible], [illegible], [illegible].

O'Longe, persons of the same pardoned, [illegible], [illegible], [illegible], [illegible], [illegible], [illegible].

O'Longy—Longie, persons of the same pardoned, 4518, 4576.

O'Lonie, James, pardon, [illegible].

O'Lonie, Wm., pardon, [illegible].

O'Lonine, Matthew, pardon, [illegible].

O'Lonnan, Donnell, pardon, [illegible].

O'Lonnaregane. See O'Lonergane.

O'Lonnergan. See O'Lonergan.

O'Lonneryghan. See O'Lonergane.

O'Lonney, Donnogh, pardon, [illegible].

O'Loogan—Loogan, persons of the same pardoned, [illegible], 6431.

O'Loonegan, Brian, pardon, [illegible].

O'Loonegan, Edm., pardon, [illegible].

O'Loayn—Loayne, persons of the same pardoned, 4734, [illegible].

O'Looba, Mellaghlen and Rory, pardon, [illegible], [illegible].

O'Looby, Cormak, pardon, [illegible].

O'Loran—Lorahan—Lorcane—Lorkan, persons of the same pardoned, 1770, [illegible], [illegible], [illegible], [illegible], 4676, [illegible], [illegible], [illegible], 6484, [illegible].

O'Lordane, Dermod and Donell, pardon, [illegible].

O'Loran, Moriart, pardon, 6091.

O'Lorkan. See O'Loran.

O'Lorrighan, Dermod, pardon, [illegible].

O'Lorrigane, David, pardon, [illegible].

O'Lorry, Conoghor, pardon, [illegible].

O'Loubby, John, pardon, [illegible].

O'Loughan, James, pardon, [illegible].

O'Loughlane, Melaughlin, pardon, [illegible].

O'Loughnan, Nicholas, pardon, 1154.

O'Loughnane, David, pardon, [illegible].

O'Loughorne, John, surgeon, pardon, 6464.

O'Lounargan, Brian, pardon, [illegible].

O'Lowan—Lowane, persons of the same pardoned, [illegible], 6794.

O'Lowargan, Tirelagh, pardon, [illegible].

O'Lowhan, persons of the same pardoned, [illegible].

O'Lowny—Lownie, persons of the same pardoned, [illegible], [illegible].

O'Lowony, Donell, pardon, [illegible].

O'Lowrone, Tho., pardon, [illegible].

O'Lowrowe, persons of the same pardoned, 1577, [illegible].

O'Lowre, Gillpatrick, pardon, 6764.

O'Lowrie, Gillpatrick and Teig, pardon, [illegible], 6764.

O'Loye, Donogh, pardon, 6714.

O'Loyneey, Teig, pardon, [illegible].

O'Loynsye, Wm., pardon, [illegible].

O'Luby, Donogho and Mellaghlyn, pardon, 4076, [illegible].

O'Lucry, Gillicome, pardon, [illegible].

O'Ludan, Donell, pardon, [illegible].

O'Luinye, James, priest, pardon, [illegible].

O'Lullane, Shane, pardon, [illegible].

O'Lunney, Donell and Shane, pardon, [illegible].

O'Lungane, persons of the same pardoned, [illegible].

O'Lunyghan, Theige, pardon, [illegible].

O'Lunym, Rory, pardon, [illegible].

O'Lurcan—Lurcayne—Lurkaine—Lurkan, persons of the same pardoned, [illegible], [illegible], [illegible], [illegible], 4491, [illegible], [illegible], [illegible], [illegible].

O'Lurgan, Conor, pardon, 6714.

O'Lurkan — Lurkaine — Lurkane. See O'Lurcan.

O'Lurreigh, Edm., pardon, [illegible].

O'Lwonshie — Lwonsie, Dermod, pardon, 6457, [illegible].

O'Lwoshie—Lwosie, persons of the same pardoned, 6457, [illegible].

O'Lwy, Dermot, pardon, [illegible].

O'Lyagh—Lyaghe, persons of the same pardoned, [illegible].

O'Lyan—Lyon, persons of the same pardoned, [illegible], 1720, [illegible], 4138, 6177, [illegible], [illegible], [illegible], [illegible].

O'Lydan, Thady, pardon, [illegible].

O'Lyddy, Diarmaid, pardon, [illegible].

O'Lye, persons of the same pardoned, [illegible], [illegible], [illegible].

O'Lyeghe, Teige, pardon, [illegible].

O'Lyensy, Donell, pardon, [illegible].

O'Lyffer, alias O'Morowe, Patrick, pardon, [illegible].

O'Lyhan, Teig, pardon, [illegible].

O'Lymon, Wm., pardon, [illegible].

O'Lynam, Ferdorogh, pardon, [illegible].

O'Lynan, Murtagh and Patrick, pardon, [illegible].

O'Lynce—Linne, persons of the same pardoned, [illegible], [illegible].

O'Lynche, Rory, pardon, [illegible].

O'Lynchy, persons of the same pardoned, [illegible], [illegible].

O'Lyncy—Lynsey—Linsie—Lynsy, persons of the same pardoned, [illegible], 6411, [illegible], [illegible], 6764.

O'Lyne. See O'Leyne.

O'Lynnan, persons of the same pardoned, [illegible], [illegible].

O'Lynne, Conoghor, pardon, [illegible].

O'Lynneghane, Ranell, pardon, [illegible].

INDEX TO FIANTS—ELIZABETH.

O'Lynaey. See O'Lyncy.
O'Lynahe, Donell, pardon, 6816.
O'Lynaie. See O'Lyncy.
O'Lynchy, persons of the name pardoned, 6811, 6[illegible], 6[illegible].
O'Lyney. See O'Lyncy.
O'Lyshane, Donell, pardon, 6371.
O'Macky, Hugh, pardon, 6[illegible].
O'M'akega, Hugh, pardon, 64[illegible].
O'Machaghane, Patr., 6140.
O'Machor—Machir, persons of the name, pardoned, 6[illegible], 6[illegible], 6[illegible], 67[illegible].
O'Mackan, Teig, pardon, 6764.
O'Mackane, Moragh, pardon, 6[illegible].
O'Mackessy, Gillepatrick, pardon, 671.
O'M'Hey, Deryll, pardon, 6[illegible].
O'Mackie, Farloroch, pardon, 61[illegible].
O'Mackine, Donell and Wm., pardon, 6[illegible].
O'Mackie, Donnell, pardon, 64[illegible].
O'Mackega, Teig, pardon, 6[illegible].
O'Macky, Ro, pardon, 4[illegible].
O'Macoghlan, Dermot, pardon, 6[illegible].
O'Madagane. See O'Maddegan.
O'Maddane, Donald, pardon, [illegible].
O'Maddegan — Maddigan — Madagane— Madegan — Madigan— Madigane:
" persons of the name pardoned, [illegible], 4[illegible], 4[illegible], 4712, 5746, 6[illegible], 6[illegible], 6[illegible], 6[illegible], 6[illegible], 6[illegible], 6[illegible].
" See also Vaddegane.
O'Madden—Maddin—Maddine—Maddyn— Maden — Madin — Madine— Madyn:
" Ambrose (of Clonfongh), pardon, 6100, 6[illegible].
" Awle oge (of Kilorna), attainted, 6[illegible].
" Coghe, a rebel, 1[illegible]; pardon, [illegible], 4[illegible], 4[illegible], 4[illegible], 6[illegible].
" Donell — Donald — Daniel: O'Madden, made captain of O'Madden's country, 10[illegible], 1715; pardon, [illegible]; grant of lands, 4716.
" Hugh mac Melaghlin ballagh, made captain of O'Madden's country, 617; his murder, 1[illegible].
" Melaghlin ballagh, late captain of his nation, 617.
" Melaghlin m'Awly oge, attainted, [illegible].
" Owe O'Melaghlyn, alias Melaghlin modder, captain of O'Maddan's country 41.
" Owen, a rebel, 1[illegible].
O'Madden, Owen m'Melaghlin ballagh (of Melock), pardon, [illegible], 4[illegible]; his title to O'Madden's country, 4716.
" others of the name pardoned, 423, 878, 1146, 1477, [illegible], [illegible], 3231-4, [illegible], [illegible], [illegible], [illegible], 4[illegible], 4874, 4[illegible], [illegible], 64[illegible], 64[illegible], 6476, 6[illegible], [illegible], [illegible], [illegible], [illegible], [illegible], [illegible], 6374, [illegible], 6400-12, 6477, 6[illegible], 6[illegible], [illegible], [illegible], 6[illegible], 6[illegible], 6[illegible].
" country of, 41, 1[illegible], [illegible], [illegible]; captain of, 41, 617, 1[illegible].
" Slough Callow, 47[illegible].
" Slough Donogh, 471[illegible].
O'Maddy, persons of the name pardoned, 41, [illegible], 3174, 4[illegible], 4744, [illegible].
O'Maddyn. See O'Madden.
O'Madegan—Madegane. See O'Maddegan.
O'Maden. See O'Madden.
O'Madigan—Madigane. See O'Maddegan.
O'Madin—Madine. See O'Madden.
O'Madmoghore, Cormock and Tirlagh, pardon, 6[illegible].
O'Madyn—Madyne. See O'Madden.
O'Maely, Melaghlin, pardon, 6[illegible].
O'Magnasie, James, pardon, 4[illegible].
O'Magh, Conghor, pardon, 1[illegible].
O'Maghair, Dermod, pardon, 4[illegible].
O'Maghan—Maghane:
" persons of the name pardoned, 6[illegible], 6[illegible], 6[illegible], 64[illegible].
" See also Ivaghain.
Omaghcorbe, co. Gal., 6[illegible].
O'Magher—Maghere—Maghir:
" Donell moyle m'Teig, pardon, [illegible], 1164, 1[illegible].
" Gillenenew: O'Magher, pardon, 6[illegible], [illegible].
" Gillenenew m'Teig, pardon, 11[illegible], 1910, [illegible], [illegible].
" Hugh macDonell moyle, pardon, [illegible], 1184, 1[illegible].
" Philip m'Donogh, pardon, 1[illegible], [illegible], 6164, 6[illegible].
" others of the name pardoned, 812, [illegible], 10[illegible], 1[illegible], 1184, 1[illegible], 1[illegible]-8, 1[illegible], 1[illegible]-0, 1918, [illegible], [illegible], [illegible], [illegible], [illegible], [illegible], [illegible], [illegible], [illegible], [illegible], [illegible], [illegible], [illegible], [illegible], [illegible], 4007, 4[illegible], 4[illegible], 4[illegible], 4[illegible], 4744, 4784, 4[illegible], 4[illegible], 4[illegible], [illegible], 6[illegible], 6144, 6[illegible], 6[illegible], 6[illegible], [illegible], 6[illegible], [illegible], 6[illegible], [illegible], [illegible], [illegible]-8, 6[illegible], 6[illegible], 67[illegible], 67[illegible].
O'Magher oo forosy, Tho., pardon, [illegible].
O'Magher roughe, Thomas, pardon, [illegible].
O'Magher row, Dermot, pardon, [illegible].

INDEX TO FIANTS—ELIZABETH.

O'Maghery — Maghery — Magherice — Magheryce country (the barony of Iberrin, co. Tip.), 162, 973, [illegible], [illegible].
O'Maghery, Edm. m'Laughlin doune, pardon, [illegible].
O'Maghonne, Darby and Teige pardon, [illegible].
O'Magh Ierny, Wm., pardon, [illegible].
O'Maghir. See O'Magher.
O'Maghlaghlin, Rory, pardon, [illegible].
O'Maghowne, Shane and Teige, pardon, [illegible], [illegible].
O'Maghyr, Dermot, pardon, [illegible].
O'Mahe( ), Donogh, pardon, [illegible].
O'Mahan—Mahand—Mahane:
„ persons of the name pardoned, [illegible], [illegible], [illegible], [illegible].
O'Mahany, Teige, pardon, [illegible].
O'Mahawne, Teig, pardon, [illegible].
O'Maher—Mahir—Mahire:
„ persons of the name pardoned, [illegible], [illegible], [illegible], [illegible].
O'Maholmihill, Avarogh, pardon, [illegible].
O'Mahon—Mahoney—Mahonie—Mahony—Mahoun. See O'Mahowny.
O'Mahonagh—Mahownagh, Dermod and Teig, pardon, [illegible].
O'Mahouney—Mahounie. See O'Mahowny.
O'Mahowney, Gerald, pardon, [illegible].
O'Mahown—Mahowne. See O'Mahowny.
O'Mahowney—Mahownie. See O'Mahowny.
O'Mahownigh, Donogh, pardon, [illegible].
O'Mahowny—Mahon—Mahoney—Mahonie — Mahony — Mahoun — Mahoune — Mahouney — Mahounie — Mahown — Mahowne — Mahowney — Mahownie:
„ Conoagher, alias Connor, lease, [illegible].
„ Conoghor (of Ardityman), wardship of son, [illegible].
„ Donel (son of Donogh), wardship, [illegible].
„ Donell m'Conoghor, attainted, [illegible], [illegible], [illegible], [illegible].
„ Donogh (son of Conoghor of Ardtynan), alias O'Mahowne Fin, wardship, [illegible]; wardship of his son, [illegible].
„ Florence, alias O'Mahony Carbery, pardon, [illegible], [illegible]; pardon of his men at his suit, [illegible].
„ Florence (son of Florence), pardon, [illegible], [illegible].
„ Shane m'Melmo (of Castlemahowny), pardon, [illegible], [illegible].
O'Mahowny, Moelmoe (of Castlemahowny), alias O'Mahony, pardon, [illegible].
„ Teig ne Reigr, pardon, [illegible], [illegible], [illegible], [illegible].
„ others of the name pardoned, [illegible], 5770.
„ —Carbery (Florence), pardon, [illegible].
„ Castle of, co. Cork, [illegible].
„ See also Ivahuny, Vahony.
O'Mahuny, Dermod, pardon, [illegible].
O'Maigher, Donell, pardon, [illegible].
O'Maile. See O'Mally.
Omalie. See Imeyle.
Omailie, Tho., pardon, [illegible].
O'Mairry, Teige, pardon, [illegible].
O'Maiveruddy, Teig, pardon, [illegible].
O'Makeny, Philip, pardon, [illegible].
O'Malaghlin—Malaghlyn. See O'Melaghlin.
O'Malalo, Teige, pardon, [illegible].
O'Malan—Malane:
„ Cormock, pardon, [illegible].
„ Shane, pardon, [illegible].
O'Malaughlin. See O'Melaghlin.
O'Malaunie, Edm., pardon, [illegible].
O'Malbogenagh, William, pardon, [illegible].
O'Malchly, Hugh, pardon, [illegible].
O'Malchonery, Brien, pardon, [illegible].
O'Male. See O'Mally.
O'Maledia, Morogh, pardon, [illegible].
O'Maledy, Thomas, lease, [illegible], [illegible].
O'Mallan—Mallane:
„ persons of the name pardoned, [illegible], [illegible], [illegible].
O'Mallaughlen. See O'Melaghlin.
O'Malleadie, Cormock and Hugh, pardon, [illegible].
Omallicy, Brien, pardon, [illegible].
O'Mallie. See O'Mally.
O'Mallmoghrie, Owen, pardon, [illegible].
O'Mallon—Mallone:
„ persons of the name pardoned, [illegible], [illegible], [illegible].
O'Malloy, Hene and Neill, pardon, [illegible].
O'Mally — Malle — Male — Mallie — Maly — Mayle—Maylly:
„ Dermod, pardon, [illegible]; surrender of his lands, [illegible].
„ Dodarogh or Dowdara, pardon, [illegible], [illegible], [illegible].

INDEX TO FIANTS.—ELIZABETH.

O'Mally, Donell, surrender of his lands [illegible].
" Melaghlin, chief of his name, appointed seneschal, [illegible].
" Mellaghlin (son of Teig roe), pardon, [illegible].
" Owen (of Cahirnamart), pardon, 4844, [illegible]; surrender of his lands, [illegible].
" Teige roe, pardon, [illegible]; traitor, [illegible].
" others of the name pardoned, [illegible], [illegible], [illegible]-3, [illegible], [illegible], [illegible], 4760, [illegible], [illegible], [illegible], [illegible], 5172, [illegible]-8, [illegible], [illegible], [illegible]-17, [illegible].
O'Malone, persons of the name pardoned, [illegible], [illegible], [illegible], [illegible], [illegible].
O'Malowny, Wm., pardon, [illegible].
O'Maloyn, Conor, pardon, [illegible].
O'Maly. See O'Mally.
O'Mameghan, Owen, pardon, [illegible].
O'Manehan, Brian, pardon, [illegible].
O'Manenan, Donogh, pardon, [illegible].
O'Mangan, Patrick and Shane, pardon, [illegible], [illegible].
O'Manikin, Tho., pardon, [illegible].
O'Manin. See O'Mannin.
O'Manine, Hugh and Shane, pardon, [illegible], [illegible].
O'Mann, Donoho, pardon, [illegible].
Omannane, Donogh, pardon, [illegible].
O'Mannarane, Dermod, pardon, [illegible].
O'Mannin—Manin—Mannyn—Manyn:
" Donell, chief of his nation, [illegible].
" Hugh (of Mynlogh), appointed tanist, [illegible].
" Wm., pardon, [illegible].
" others of the name pardoned, [illegible], [illegible], [illegible], [illegible], [illegible], [illegible], [illegible], 4711, [illegible], [illegible], [illegible], [illegible], [illegible], [illegible], [illegible], [illegible], [illegible], [illegible], [illegible], [illegible].
Omanny. See Imany.
O'Manoghow, Owen, pardon, 5411.
O'Mantane, David, pardon, [illegible].
Omany. See Imany.
O'Many, Mahown and Teig, pardon, [illegible].
O'Manyn. See O'Mannin.
O'Manynane, Loghlin, pardon, [illegible].
O'Manyne, Rory and Tho., pardon, [illegible], [illegible].
O'Manynge, Bryen, slaying of, [illegible].
O'Maoyltully, Murrogh, pardon, [illegible].
O'Marcahan, John, pardon, [illegible].
O'Marcus, Tho., pardon, [illegible].
O'Mare, William, pardon, [illegible].
O'Marey—Marie:
" persons of the name pardoned, [illegible], [illegible]-6, [illegible].
O'Marii, Conoghor, pardon, [illegible].
O'Markahane—Markaghaine—Markehan, persons of the name pardoned, [illegible], [illegible], [illegible].
O'Markellie, Teig, pardon, [illegible].
O'Marmane, Mawghon, pardon, [illegible].
O'Marnane, Donell, pardon, [illegible].
O'Marngan, Patrick, pardon, 124.
O'Marrho, Conner, pardon, [illegible].
O'Marrinan — Marrenan — Marynayn — Marynayne, persons of the name pardoned, [illegible], [illegible], [illegible], [illegible].
" See also Iwarrynane, Iverynane.
O'Marrogho—Marroghoe, Gillypatrick and Tho., pardon, [illegible], [illegible].
O'Marry—Marrye, persons of the name pardoned, [illegible], [illegible].
O'Marynayne. See O'Marrinan.
O'Martin—Martin, persons of the name pardoned, [illegible], [illegible], [illegible], [illegible], [illegible].
O'Martinan, Donell, pardon, [illegible].
O'Mary, persons of the name pardoned, [illegible], [illegible], [illegible], [illegible].
O'Mathuna, David, pardon, [illegible].
O'Maughan, Farrall, pardon, [illegible].
O'Maughery, Teig and Wm., pardon, [illegible], [illegible].
O'Mayghir, Teig, pardon, [illegible].
O'Mayle. See O'Mally.
Omayle. See Imayle.
O'Mayleghan, Owyne, pardon, [illegible].
Omaylle. See Imayle.
O'Maylly. See O'Mally.
O'Mayne, Patr., pardon, [illegible].
O'Maynane, Dermot, pardon, [illegible].
O'Maynloy, Wm., pardon, [illegible].
O'Meachair, Teig, pardon, [illegible].
O'Meehan, Meleaghlen, pardon, [illegible].
O'Meaghan—Meaghane, persons of the name pardoned, [illegible], [illegible], [illegible].
O'Meagharie, Philip, pardon, [illegible].
O'Meaghe, Philip, pardon, [illegible].
O'Meaghegan, Donogh, pardon, [illegible].
O'Meagher—Meaghere—Meaghir, persons of the name pardoned, [illegible], [illegible], [illegible]-8, [illegible], [illegible], [illegible], [illegible], [illegible]-8, [illegible], [illegible], [illegible], [illegible], [illegible], [illegible]-6, [illegible].
" See also Yeagher.
O'Meaghigan, Donogh and Shane, pardon, [illegible].
O'Meallane, persons of the name pardoned, [illegible].
O'Measine, John, pardon, [illegible].

INDEX TO FIANTS.—ELIZABETH.

O'Mearan, Donogho and John, pardon, 6707.
O'Meary—Meare:
" Donald (of Lisconsky), English liberty, 4097; pardon, [illegible], [illegible].
" Wm., pardon, 6443.
" others of the name pardoned, 2810, 4605, 4604, 6104, [illegible], [illegible], 6763.
O'Meawhan, Moriertagh, pardon, 613.
Omeaby, Grene, pardon, 4545.
O'Meale, Edm., pardon, 6504.
O'Meghan, Trige, pardon, 6161.
O'Meghir, Donell, pardon, 6612.
O'Mehogaine — Mehogane, Matthew and Teig, pardon, 5941, [illegible].
O'Mehaloran, Donell, pardon, 2816.
O'Meholloghan, Wm., pardon, 6761.
O'Meigher, Conchor, pardon, 5058.
Omeill. *See* Imayle.
O'Meintayne, Carnelius, pardon, 152.
O'Melaghlin — Molaghlyn — Malaghlin — Malanghlin—Mallaughlen —Melanghlin—Mellaughlen—Molaghlen—Molaghlin—Molaghlyn—Molaughlin — Molaughlyn — Molaghlen — Mollaughlen — Moylaghlin—Mulaghlin—Mullaghlen—Mullaglen — Mullaghlyn:
" chief of his name, comm., 4459.
" Arte, attainted, 5836.
" Arte m'Phelim, attainted, [illegible].
" Callagh, appointed captain of his country, 615; pardon, 1586, 1644, 3169; commission, 4161; pardon to his man, 1894.
" Colman, pardon, 4862; attainted, 4880; his lands, 5315.
" Con m'James, pardon, 1144, 1379, 1760, 2160, 2737, 5344, 5773.
" Irrell (of Cloonlonan), pardon, 6450.
" Kedagh oge, pardon, 1438, 1801, 2812, [illegible]; attainted, 5594.
" others of the name pardoned, 742, 875, 1596, 1664, 1771, 2168, 2911, 2978, 3408, 3458-4, 3200, 3170, 3344, 3484, 3718, 3761, 4014, 4622, 3160, [illegible], 3414, 4585, 4171, [illegible], 4484, 4450, 4420, 4412, 5530, 6457, 6377, [illegible], [illegible].
O'Melaghlin — country of (barony of Clonlonan, co. Westmeath), 165, 612, 1599, 1471, 1439, 1601, 3390, [illegible]; martial law and rebels in, 2182-4.
O'Melan—Melane, persons of the name pardoned, 3091, 5075, 5712, 6562, 6748.
O'Melanghan, Keadagh (of Moyally), attainted, 6777.
O'Melanghlin. *See* O'Melaghlin.
O'Melcrewe, Teig, pardon, 4146.
O'Melefy, Melaghlin, pardon, 6912.
O'Meleghlen, James (of Ballycor), pardon, 6819.
O'Mellan — Mellane, persons of the name pardoned, 4561, 5776, 6142, 6874, 6528, 6714.
O'Mellanghlen. *See* O'Melaghlin.
O'Mellawe, Shane, pardon, 1581.
O'Melleny — Melleny, persons of the name pardoned, 4407.
O'Mellon, Rowry, pardon, 6148.
O'Melloyne, Connor, pardon, 1843.
O'Mellisle, Edm., pardon, 6484.
O'Meloan, persons of the name pardoned, 14, 1463, 2852.
O'Meloy, Con, pardon, 6548.
O'Meloyes country, 1610. *See* O'Molloy.
O'Menine—Menane:
" Garbry and Gilleduff, pardon, 875, 3484.
O'Meoghan, Hugh, 3281.
O'Meolle, Edm., pardon, 6542.
O'Mergy, Shane, pardon, 6704.
O'Meran, Donell, pardon, 4793.
O'Merayne, Donogh, pardon, 6167.
O'Merehy, David, pardon, 4714.
O'Merga, Donell, pardon, 4681.
O'Mergey, Rich., pardon, 6333.
O'Mergin, Donald and William, pardon, 1113, 5409.
O'Mergyne, Tho., pardon, 5562.
O'Merick, Owen, pardon, 4948.
O'Merigan, Rae, pardon, 4681.
O'Meriss, Donnogh and Ennose, pardon, 3949, 3093.
O'Merran, Donogh, pardon, 6544.
O'Merry, Donnough, 5950.
Omescourte, alias Uppercourt, co. Kilk., 1144.
O'Meskill—Miskell—Mishill:
" persons of the name pardoned, 3068, 1838, 4210, 4434.
O'Mey—Mley:
" persons of the name pardoned, 3480, 3914, 6761.
O'Miagan, Pair., pardon, 6943.
O'Miagh, Donogh, pardon, 6762.
O'Miaghan—Mieghan:
" persons of the name pardoned, 6833-2, 6761, 6762.

INDEX TO FIANTS.—ELIZABETH.

O'Mieskell. *See* O'Meskill.
O'Miey. *See* O'May.
O'Mighan—Mighane:
„ persons of the name pardoned, [illegible], [illegible], [illegible], [illegible].
O'Mighcane, persons of the name pardoned, [illegible], [illegible].
O'Mihain, Charles, priest, pardon, [illegible].
O'Milcallon, Cormock, pardon, 6144.
O'Millen, Owin, pardon, [illegible].
Omine, Edmund, pardon, 1480.
O'Mire, Dermot and Teige, pardon, 6748.
O'Mirie, Donell, pardon, [illegible].
O'Miskill. *See* O'Meskill.
O'Miswney—Miswny—Miswnye:
„ John, attainder, 4115.
„ others of the name pardoned, [illegible], [illegible].
Omleny, Rowry, pardon, [illegible].
O'Mlawnye, Danyll, pardon, [illegible].
Omlinn, Rich., pardon, 4708.
O'Moare, Gilmoddir, pardon, [illegible].
O'Mochane, Wm., pardon, 4467.
O'Mocliegy, Tho., pardon, [illegible].
O'Moclan—Moclane, persons of the name pardoned, [illegible], [illegible], [illegible], [illegible].
O'Moclegane, Teig, pardon, [illegible].
O'Moclin, persons of the name pardoned, 4116, [illegible].
O'Moclinn, Darbey and Wm., pardon, 1784, [illegible].
O'Moclkny, Dermot, pardon, [illegible].
O'Mocltalye, Iriell, pardon, [illegible].
O'Mocny, Donell, pardon, [illegible].
„ Tho., pardon, [illegible].
O'Moghan—Moghane:
„ persons of the name pardoned, [illegible], [illegible], [illegible], [illegible], [illegible], [illegible], [illegible], [illegible].
O'Mogher—Moghir, Wm., pardon, [illegible], [illegible].
O'Moght, Gillpatrick and Hugh, pardon, [illegible].
O'Moghylaughlen, Dermot, pardon, [illegible].
O'Mohaire (or O'Maghir), Wm., pardon, [illegible].
O'Mohertie, Owen, pardon, [illegible].
O'Mohele, Rickard, pardon, [illegible].
O'Moheilachan, Philip, pardon, [illegible].
„ *See also* Voheighan.
O'Moholleyan, Gilleduffe, pardon, [illegible].
O'Moher, David and Dorond, pardon, [illegible].
O'Mohertie, Donsye, pardon, [illegible].
O'Mohery, David, pardon, 4714.
O'Mohilligham—Mohilleghane:
„ John and Morrie, pardon, [illegible], [illegible].
O'Moholeighan—Moholahane—Moholeghan—Moholeighan—Moholeghan—Mohelleghan—Moholochan:
O'Moholaghan, persons of the name pardoned, [illegible], [illegible], [illegible], [illegible], [illegible], [illegible].
O'Moholane, John, pardon, [illegible].
O'Moillallagh, Shane, pardon, [illegible].
O'Moilline, John, pardon, [illegible].
O'Moilryan, Connor, pardon, [illegible].
O'Moinielan, Teige, pardon, [illegible].
O'Mokan, Wm., pardon, [illegible].
O'Mokeran, Donell, pardon, [illegible].
Omoklaghe, co. Wex. [illegible].
O'Mokenney, Conoghor, pardon, [illegible].
O'Mole, Mortaghe, pardon, [illegible].
O'Moleghan, Donell, pardon, [illegible].
O'Molaghlin—Molaghlen—Molaghlyn. *See* O'Molaghlin.
O'Molallye, Laughlin, pardon, [illegible].
O'Molan—Molane:
„ Fardorogh, chief of his name (in O'Cahane's country), pardon, [illegible].
„ Moryce, house in Trim, 1714.
„ others of the name pardoned, [illegible], [illegible], [illegible], [illegible], [illegible], [illegible], [illegible], [illegible].
O'Molany, Conor, pardon, [illegible].
O'Molaughlin—Molaughlyn. *See* O'Molaghlin.
O'Molawne, Teige, pardon, [illegible], [illegible].
O'Molawnoghe, Moylmor, pardon, [illegible].
O'Molcahy. *See* O'Mulcahy.
O'Molchaha, Shane, pardon, 4473.
O'Molchaill, Pat. (or O'Mulcahel), pardon, [illegible].
O'Molchloy. *See* O'Mulcloy.
O'Molcherre, Donnogh, pardon, [illegible].
O'Molcloby, Brien, pardon, [illegible].
O'Molconre—Molconnere—Molconrie. *See* O'Mulconry.
O'Moldony. *See* O'Muldony.
O'Moldowney — Moldownie — Moldowny. *See* O'Muldowny.
O'Mole, Gilpatrycke, pardon, [illegible].
O'Molechan, John, pardon, [illegible].
O'Molidie—Molidy:
„ persons of the name pardoned, [illegible], [illegible], [illegible].
O'Molegan, persons of the name pardoned, [illegible], [illegible], [illegible].
O'Moleghan, Brene and Wm., pardon, [illegible], [illegible].
O'Molene, Wm., pardon, [illegible].
O'Molengo, Patr. boy, pardon, [illegible].
O'Moleran, John, pardon, [illegible].
O'Moley, Onin, pardon, [illegible].
O'Molgarre, Tho., pardon, [illegible].
O'Molgui, Edm., pardon, [illegible].
O'Molgurge, Cnnor, pardon, [illegible].
O'Molgoyhe, Donnogh, pardon, 4140
O'Molghan, Shane, pardon, [illegible].

INDEX TO FIANTS.—ELIZABETH.

O'Molinge, persons of the name pardoned, [illegible], [illegible], [illegible].
O'Molkery—Molkiery :
" persons of the same pardoned, 1946, 4553, 6495.
O'Molkiyby, John, pardon, [illegible].
O'Molkmery, Daniel, pardon, 1817.
O'Mollaggi, near Acrom, church of (Templemolaga, co. Cork), 6163.
O'Molaggie, lands of the abbey of the corb of, 6163.
O'Molleghehbye, Donagh, pardon, [illegible].
O'Molleghlen, Donald and Tirlagh, pardon, 676 See O'Meloghlin.
O'Mollalle, Morogh, pardon, 5700.
O'Mollan—Mollane :
" Teig, alias O'Molowne, pardon, 4915, 6373.
" others of the name pardoned, [illegible], [illegible], [illegible], [illegible], [illegible], [illegible], [illegible], 6714; 6761.
O'Mollany, Manrice, pardon, [illegible].
O'Mollaughlen. See O'Meloghlin.
O'Mollaye, Wm., pardon, [illegible].
O'Mollcahill. See O'Mulcahel.
O'Mollchony, Ollard, pardon, [illegible].
O'Molleghan, Dermot and Philip, pardon, [illegible].
O'Mollenanyne, Tomulagh, pardon, 4777.
O'Molline, Shane, pardon, [illegible].
O'Molling—Mollinge :
" persons of the name pardoned, [illegible], [illegible].
O'Mollmochory, Gillepatrowe, pardon, [illegible].
O'Mollory. See O'Molloy.
O'Mollgin. See O'Molloy.
O'Mollome, Edm., pardon, [illegible].
O'Mollone, Donall, pardon, [illegible].
O'Mollony, Riccard and Teig, pardon, [illegible], 4897.
O'Mollowne, Walter, pardon, [illegible].
O'Mollowne, John, pardon, [illegible].
O'Mollownywe, John, lands of, 6782.
O'Mollowny, Mac Crahe and Pair., pardon, [illegible], [illegible].
O'Molloy — Moloy — Molloye — Molmoy — Molloey — Mollolo — Mulmoy — Mulloy — Mulloye — Mulmoy — Muloy :
" Arthur, late captain of Fercall, 1806.
" Brian, pardon, [illegible], [illegible], [illegible].
" Brian (of Ballycowan), attainted, 1777.
" Callagh m'Conell, pardon, [illegible].
" Conatius or the prior, pardon, 8; his sons, [illegible], [illegible].
" Conatius or Con, pardon, 1767, [illegible].
O'Molloy—Conell, made captain, [illegible]; surrender and regrant of country, [illegible]-8.
" Donall or Donald, pardon, 3484; made captain, [illegible]; pardon to him and followers, [illegible].
" Donall or Donatus (of Ban Killtobert), wardship of his heir, [illegible].
" Edmond duff m'Connell, pardon, [illegible].
" Edward, wardship, [illegible].
" Edward (of Tullamore), his good service, [illegible]; pardon on his petition, [illegible].
" Hugh, pardon, [illegible].
" Phelim, made captain of Fercall, 4165.
" Teig m'Cahir, attainted, [illegible].
" Theobald or Tibbalt, made captain of Fercall, [illegible], 1227; his son pardoned, [illegible]; surrenders captaincy, [illegible].
" others of the name pardoned, 780, [illegible], 1767, [illegible]. See also Moloy.
" title of, abolished, [illegible].
O'Molloy, country of, [illegible], [illegible], [illegible], [illegible], [illegible], [illegible], [illegible], [illegible], [illegible].
" martial law in, [illegible].
" rebels in, [illegible].
" captain and seneschal of, [illegible]. See Fercall.
O'Molloye, Edm., pardon, [illegible].
O'Mollrane. See O'Mulrean.
O'Mollrenill, Gillacrist, pardon, [illegible].
O'Mollrona. See O'Mulrona.
O'Mollryan. See O'Mulryan.
O'Molltalle, Shane bane, pardon, [illegible].
O'Mollughayn, Derby and Donill, pardon, [illegible].
O'Mollvill. See O'Mulvihill.
O'Molly, Rorie, pardon, [illegible].
O'Molmochora. See O'Mulmochora.
O'Molmoy. See O'Molloy.
O'Molnolle, Tho., pardon, 4874.
O'Molocy. See O'Molloy.
O'Molona, Malachias, priest, pardon, 4618.
" Shane, pardon, 4877.
O'Molone, persons of the name pardoned, [illegible], [illegible], [illegible], [illegible].
O'Molowne—Molowne — Molowne, persons of the name pardoned, [illegible], [illegible] [illegible].

INDEX TO FIANTS.—ELIZABETH.

O'Molowne, Donogh and Owen, pardon, 6418.

O'Molowny—Molowmic—Molowney, persons of the name pardoned, 2797, [illegible].

O'Molowys, persons of the same pardoned, 5472.

O'Molpatrick. See O'Mulpatrick.

O'Molrany. See O'Mulrania.

O'Molrean. See O'Mulreun.

O'Molrian. See O'Mulryan.

O'Molrone, William, pardon, [illegible].

O'Molrone, Shane, pardon, 4478.

O'Molrowne, Thady, pardon, 1884.

O'Molryan. See O'Mulryan.

O'Molrydy, William, pardon, 16[illegible].

O'Moltolle—Moltole, persons of the name pardoned, 4346, 5436, 6874.

O'Moluhie—Molubye—Moluhie, persons of the name pardoned, 4784.

O'Molvey, William, pardon, 4[illegible].

O'Molvochohy, Gilledowe, pardon, 47[illegible].

O'Molvochory, persons of the name pardoned, 47[illegible].

O'Molvolly, Patr., pardon, 6348.

O'Molye, Hugh, pardon, [illegible].

O'Molyne—Molyn, persons of the name pardoned, 678, 4676.

O'Monaghan — Monechan — Monighan — Monnechan — Monnighan, persons of the name pardoned, 2711, 5450, 5467, 6487, 6071, 6478, 6764.

O'Monane, Dermod and John, pardon, [illegible].

Omonde, Philip, pardon, 4594.

O'Mone, persons of the name pardoned, 874, [illegible].

O'Monechan. See O'Monaghan.

O'Moneghar, Edm., pardon, 6486.

O'Money, persons of the name pardoned, 451, 614, 1472, [illegible], [illegible], 5[illegible], 6214.

O'Mongane—Mongane, persons of the name pardoned, [illegible], 1164, [illegible], 3723, 4518, 6[illegible], [illegible], [illegible].

O'Mongovalin, Donell, pardon, [illegible].

O'Monghan, persons of the name pardoned, 4[illegible], [illegible], 6487.

O'Monighan. See O'Monaghan.

O Monilloe, Cormock and Edm., pardon, 47[illegible].

O'Monnechan. See O'Monaghan.

O'Monnighan. See O'Monaghan.

O'Monoge, Don, pardon, 5478.

O'Mony—Monye, persons of the name pardoned, 1357-8, 1747, 2341, 3378, [illegible], 4[illegible], [illegible], 6[illegible].

O'Monylie—Monyllee, persons of the name pardoned, 67[illegible].

O Monyn, John, pardon, 2808.

O'Moone, John, pardon, [illegible].

O'Moony—Mooney, persons of the name pardoned, 1184, 6110, 6418, 6777.

O'Moonynce, Shane, pardon, 47[illegible].

O'Moore. See O'More.

O'Moores, Onye, pardon, 6846.

O'More, Conell and Wm., pardon, [illegible].

" Moriertagh m'Leenagh, pardon, 170.

O'Moraghan, Donagh, pardon, 5[illegible].

O'Moraghie, persons of the name pardoned, 6784.

O'Morane—Morain—Morane—Morann:

" Brian, priest, pardon, [illegible].

" others of the name pardoned, 677, 1178, 2469, 3434, [illegible], [illegible], [illegible], 4786, 4806, [illegible], [illegible], 4944, 6173, 5432, 5443, 5469, 5478, 5611, [illegible], 5740, [illegible], 6178, 6188, [illegible], [illegible], 6466, 6487, 6468, [illegible], [illegible], [illegible], 6577, 6663-4, 6784, 6777.

O'Morashy, Thady, pardon, 4[illegible].

O'Moraughe, Charles, priest, pardon, [illegible].

" Teig, pardon, 4918.

O'Morchallo, Patr., pardon, 6[illegible].

O'Morchan, persons of the name pardoned, 2785, 6468, 6777.

O'Morchghine, Donogh, pardon, 6784.

O'Morcho—Morchoe—Morchow—Morchowe:

" Arthur or Art's m'Donnell, pardon, 5878.

" Donald m'Donagh cnisckyne, pardon, 2978.

" Donogh m'Art ne hille, pardon, 6517.

" Moriertagh rowane m'Donnell, pardon, 2674, 6434.

" Teige m'Art ne hille, pardon, 4[illegible].

" others of the name pardoned, [illegible], 2236, 2346, 2335-6, [illegible], [illegible], 6133, 6188, [illegible], [illegible], 6468, 6517, 6[illegible], 6771.

O'More—Moore, Callough (son of Rory), grant of lands, 2468, [illegible], [illegible], 6467, 6748.

" Ferroe m'Rosse, sons of, in rebellion, 1511.

" Kedagh, a rebel, 1218.

" Lisagh m'Conell, pardon, 16[illegible], [illegible].

" Lisagh m'Mortagh oge, pardon, 47[illegible]; livery, 5[illegible].

" Mortagh, a rebel, 1216.

" Mortagh—Moreriagh or Murrice oge, grant of land, 418, 14[illegible]; pardon, [illegible]; livery to heir, [illegible].

" Owny m'Rory, a rebel, [illegible].

" Owny or Owen m'Shane, pardon, [illegible], 6484, 4[illegible], [illegible]; pension, [illegible]; his wife, 6[illegible].

" Patrick m'Lisagh m'Mortagh oge, attainted, 6578.

" Rory, his good service, grants to his son, 2468, 2686, [illegible].

O'More, Rory oge, pardon, 812, 2144, [illegible]; a rebel, 2997, [illegible]; his sons, [illegible], 6116, [illegible].
" Shane m'Kedagh, attainted, 6678.
" others of the name pardoned, 68, 186, 442, 715-16, 871, 876, 1043, 1118, 1557, 1564, 1597, 2014, 2116, [illegible], 2331, [illegible], [illegible], [illegible], [illegible], 2967, [illegible], 3397, [illegible], [illegible], [illegible], [illegible], [illegible], [illegible], 4729, [illegible], 4999, 5118, 5378, [illegible], 6110, 6182, [illegible], 6451, 6459, 6571, 6647, 6654.
" See also O'Mora.
O'Mores, 6077; pardon pursuant to promise to, [illegible]; rebels, war made upon, [illegible], [illegible], [illegible], [illegible], [illegible]; forfeited lands of, [illegible], [illegible], [illegible]; excepted from pardon, [illegible], [illegible], [illegible], [illegible].
O'Moregan, Donnine or Donald duf, pardon, 3172.
O'Moreghole, Conoghor, pardon, [illegible].
O'Moreghow. See O'Moroghoe.
O'Moreh, Dermod, pardon, [illegible].
O'Morehe, Maurice, pardon, [illegible].
O'Morehie—Morehy, persons of the name pardoned, [illegible], [illegible], [illegible], [illegible], [illegible].
O'Morehowe, Donell, pardon, [illegible].
O'Morehy. See O'Morehie.
O'Morely, Hugh, pardon, [illegible].
O'Moren, persons of the name pardoned, 514, 6467, 6971.
O'Mores, Avale, pardon, [illegible].
O'Moreun, Teig, pardon, [illegible].
O'Morewy, Donogho, pardon, [illegible].
O'Morey. See O'Mory.
O'Morfe, Rich., pardon, [illegible].
O'Morgan, persons of the name pardoned, [illegible], 6618.
O'Morghan — Morghane — Morghayn, persons of the name pardoned, 947, [illegible], [illegible].
O'Morgho, Barnaby, robbery from, [illegible].
" Edmund and Morghe, pardon, 461, 2148.
O'Morghon, Rossa, pardon, [illegible].
O'Morgho. See O'Moroghoe.
O'Morghow. See O'Moroghoe.
O'Morghy, William, pardon, [illegible].
O'Morgowne, Edm., pardon, [illegible].
O'Morhellie—Morhelly—Morherlly, persons of the name pardoned, [illegible].
O'Morhowe, Keannore, pardon, 1041.
O'Morice, persons of the name pardoned, [illegible].
O'Moriertie—Moriertie—Moriertagh—Moriarty;
" Donell (of Castledrumy), sons of, [illegible].
" Donall, grant, [illegible].
" Owen, grant, [illegible].
O'Moriertie, others of the name pardoned, [illegible], 4464, 6457-8.
O'Morighe, Teige m'Donell, pardon, [illegible].
O'Morihie, persons of the name pardoned, 6614, [illegible], [illegible].
O'Morine, Gillgroome and Tho., pardon, [illegible], [illegible].
O'Moris, persons of the name pardoned, 1787, [illegible], [illegible], [illegible].
O'Morise, persons of the name pardoned, [illegible], [illegible].
O'Morise, Donyll and Mahowne, pardon, [illegible], [illegible].
O'Morish—Morishe, persons of the name pardoned, [illegible], [illegible], [illegible], [illegible], [illegible], [illegible], [illegible], [illegible], [illegible], [illegible], [illegible], [illegible].
O'Morishee, Donogh and Loghlin, pardon, [illegible].
O'Morishey—Morishie—Morishie, persons of the name pardoned, [illegible], [illegible], [illegible], 5704.
O'Morisse, Thady, pardon, [illegible].
O'Morissy—Morisie, persons of the name pardoned, 4743, 4762, 6751.
O'Moriste or O'Morres, Donogh, pardon, 8170.
O'Moritagh, Teige, pardon, [illegible].
O'Morochoe. See O'Moroghoe.
O'Moroe. See O'Moroghoe.
O'Morogh — Moroghe — Morough — Moroughe—Morrogh — Morrough, persons of the name pardoned, [illegible], [illegible], [illegible], [illegible], 4732, [illegible], 5142, 5468, [illegible], [illegible], [illegible], [illegible], 8104, 6611, 6615-17, [illegible], 6471, 6577, 6762.
O'Moroghane, Thomas, pardon, [illegible].
O'Moroghie, Donell, pardon, [illegible].
O'Moroghoe — Moroghow — Morgho— Morghow—Morochoe—Moroe—Morogho ;— Muroghow — Morohowe—Moroue—Morougho — Morow — Morrohowe — Morroghow — Morro — Morrogho — Morroghoe—Morroghow—Morrone — Morroughoe — Morrow — Morrowe — Morrowghow—Murcho— Murchow —Murghow—Murghoe — Murghow — Murghne — Murgho — Murghowe — Murogho — Muroghowe — Murowghoe— Murroghowe —Murrogho — Murroghe — Murroghoe— Murroghow— Murroghu — Murroughoe— Murrowghoe—Murrogho — Murroghow—Murughow— Murrigho—I Moroghow:
" Arthur mikill, pardon, [illegible].

INDEX TO FIANTS.—ELIZABETH.

O'Moroghoe, Donell m'Art na killa, pardon, 4807, 5785.
Donell, attainted, 648, 5784.
Donell Evalley, pardon, 4617.
Donell m'Donnogh entrebin, pardon, 5447.
Donoghe ontoukyne mac Donell, pardon, 850.
Donogh m'Arte ne killy, pardon, 4807.
Gerald, m'Arte ne killy, pardon, 4807.
(or Murphie), James, English liberty, 2986.
(or Murphie), Richard, English liberty, 7804.
Teig m'Art no killa, pardon, 4817.
Tho. duffbirllagh, clerk, pardon, 6667.
others of the name pardoned in co. Wexford and adjoining districts, 63, 448, 856, 878, 897, 1001, 1518, 2021, 2882, 3146, 3992, 4032, 4132, 4168, 4174, 4307, 5488, 5108, 5100, 5193, 5592, 5494, 5517, 5542, 5577, 6647.
others of the name pardoned in co. Cork, 134, 2243, 2844, 2078, 2898, 4031, 4080, 4092-3, 4106, 4247, 5425, 4461, 4467, 4486, 4490, 4633, 4663-4, 4694, 4648, 4764, 4760, 4761, 4860, 4943, 4897, 4897-8, 5001, 6126, 6136, 6142, 6488, 6497, 5400, 6604-5, 6621, 6614-16, 6620, 6656, 6669, 6666, 6671, 6674, 6051, 6628, 6711, 6789, 6704.
others of the name pardoned, 24a, 1805, 2100, 2398, 2500, 2488, 2500, 3150, 3541, 4048, 4118, 4118, 4880, 4896, 4712, 4660, 4080, 5161, 5428, 5570, 5527, 5794, 6310, 6748, 6309, 6470, 6454, 6497, 6609, 6604, 6563, 6128, 6734, 6706, 6786, 6800.
See also Yoroghowo, Woroghe, Worrowhowe.
(O'Morroo — O'Morrowe — O'Morone — O'Morgho's) country in co. Wexf., 63, 853, 1192, 4062, 6306; customs payable from, 648, 5784. See Morroos.
O'Morohey, Wm., pardon, 5786.
O'Morohowe. See O'Moroghoe.
O'Morohnigh, Morogh, pardon, 5118.
O'Morono, Teig, pardon, 4104.
O'Moronie, Moighlin, pardon, 5466.
O'Morosie, Wm., pardon, 5058.
O'Morowe. See O'Moroghoe.
O'Morough — Murough. See O'Morogh.
O'Morowghe. See O'Moroghoe.
O'Morow. See O'Moroghoe.
O'Morowhowe, Donogho, pardon, 5012.
O'Morphy, Arte, pardon, 5468.
Omorri, Johanna, pardon, 4356.
O'Morran—Morrane:
" persons of the name pardoned, 4080, 4154, 4584, 6640.
O'Morro, Patrick, pardon, 403.
" Donell (or O'Moroghoe), 5784.
O'Morrehowo—Morroghow. See O'Moroghoe.
O'Morron, Murogh, pardon, 5508.
O'Morres or O'Moriahe, Donogh, pardon, 3370.
O'Morroy, Pardhdie, pardon, 4427.
" Nole, slain, 5748.
O'Morreyne, James, pardon, 5210.
O'Morreys, persons of the name pardoned, 5210.
O'Morrbie, Donell og, pardon, 5384.
O'Morrice. See O'Morris.
O'Morrice, Donogh, pardon, 4260.
O'Morrihie, Wm., pardon, 3503.
O'Morrin, James, pardon, 6512.
O'Morrioghe, Teige, pardon, 4487.
O'Morris — Morrice — Morrys — Morryse — Morys, persons of the name pardoned, 3504-5, 5617, 6402, 6679.
O'Morrisane, Solfe, pardon, 5781.
O'Morrishe—Moryshe:
" persons of the name pardoned, 3306, 4183, 6408, 6594-5.
O'Morrisie. See O'Morrissye.
O'Morrisse, Conoghor, pardon, 4681.
O'Morrissye — Morrisie — Morrisin — Morysy:
" persons of the name pardoned, 4218, 4281, 6617, 6704.
" See also Verrisey.
O'Morro—Morron. See O'Moroghoe.
O'Morrogh. See O'Morogh.
O'Morroghan, Gerald and Gerot, pardon, 448, 6466.
O'Morroghe. See O'Moroghoe.
O'Morroghe, Rich., pardon, 5476.
O'Morroghoe — Morroghow. See O'Moroghoe.
O'Morrohinigh, Maurice, pardon, 6576.
O'Morrohoy, Morris, pardon, 5784.
O'Morrone. See O'Moroghoe.
O'Morrough. See O'Morogh.
O'Morroughoe. See O'Moroghoe.
O'Morrow—Morrowe. See O'Moroghoe.
O'Morrowghow. See O'Moroghoe.

INDEX TO FIANTS.—ELIZABETH.

O'Morey, persons of the name pardoned, 18, [illegible], 2944, 6459, 6363.
O'Morryn—Morryne, persons of the name pardoned, 481, 2883, 4080, 6781.
O'Morrys—Morryse. See O'Morris.
O'Morthy, Richard, pardon, 2368.
O'Mortin, Donnogh, pardon, 6687.
O'Moreg, Edm., pardon, 4183.
O'Mory—Morey—Morye, persons of the name pardoned, 618, 1102, 2944, 6906, 4071, 4188, 6110, 6378.
O'Moryle, Thadeus, assaults and robberies on, 142.
O'Moryly, Rich., pardon, 6614.
O'Moryn—Moryne, persons of the name pardoned, 1060, 2120, 2883, 6124, 3467, 4049, 6411.
O'Morys. See O'Morris.
O'Moryssh. See O'Morrishe.
O'Moryssy. See O'Morrissye.
O'Moughan, Deirmot, pardon, 6761.
O'Mought, Rowrie, pardon, 6714.
O'Moukdowry, Teige, pardon, 6647.
O'Moulloure, Morierlagh, pardon, 6665.
O'Moune, Tuge, pardon, 781.
O'Moungwan—Moungwane, Donill and Donogho, pardon, 5091.
O'Mourane, Hugh, pardon, 4744.
" Lowreuce or Loghlen O'Moran, pardon, 677.
O'Mourowragh alias Oroonum, Wm., pardon, 6904.
O'Mowreghow, Donogh, pardon, 6616.
Omowr, co. Westm., 4779.
O'Mowgan, Teige, pardon, 5447.
O'Mowrkle, Edm. and Walter, pardon, 6963.
O'Mowfhill—Mowlicull, persons of the name pardoned, 6621.
O'Mowliane, Hugh and Manus, pardon, 6612.
O'Mowlonye, Dermot, pardon, 4481.
O'Mowlvonte, persons of the name pardoned, 6652.
O'Mowrpighan, John, pardon, 7637.
O'Moydan, Shane, pardon, 6371.
Omoye, Queen's co., 6434.
O'Moylaghlin. See O'Melaghlin.
O'Moylan—Moylane, Daniel and Donoghe, pardon, 4636, 6636.
O'Moylanrie, Downe, pardon, 6612.
O'Moylearky, Owne, pardon, 4761.
O'Moylegane, persons of the name pardoned, 6761.
O'Moylen, Rory, pardon, 4944.
" Thady, English liberty, 1187.
O'Moylary, Gillechrist, pardon, 6761.
O'Moylirragh, Teige, pardon, 6761.
O'Moylin—Moyline, Edm. and Wm., pardon, 4769, 6490.
O'Moylon, Shane, pardon, 6477.
O'Moyloy, Owny, pardon, 6687.
O'Moynaghan—Moynaghan—Mynaghane—Mynighan, persons of the name pardoned, 6173, 6469, 6674, 6637, 6764.
O'Moyse, persons of the name pardoned, 18.
O'Moynaghan. See O'Moynaghan.
O'Moyney—Moyne, Edm. and Cahill, pardon, 6403, 6514.
O'Moynig, Donell, pardon, 6516.
O'Moyssye, Owen, pardon, 6274.
Omulorghne, Conoghor, pardon, 4468.
O'Muckane, John or Shane oy Neganc, pardon, 4468.
O'Muckile, Conoghor, pardon, 6673.
O'Mucory, Ferlowe, pardon, 4679.
O'Mucelly, Tho., pardon, 5763.
O'Mugrohen, Philip, pardon, 4476.
O'Mughan, Diarmod and Wm., pardon, 6963, 6411.
O'Mughoule, Donogho, pardon, 4761.
O'Mulmighan, Donogh, pardon, 6611.
O'Mutrown, Donoho, pardon, 4584.
O'Mul[illegible]lshall, Shane, pardon, 4780.
O'Mulaghlin. See O'Melaghlin.
O'Mulane, Donill, pardon, 5638.
O'Mulanye, Tho., pardon, 6673.
O'Mulbridy, Dermot, pardon, 6794.
O'Mulcaell, Gilpatrick and James, pardon, 6974.
O'Mulcagh—Mulcaghe, persons of the name pardoned, 6468.
O'Mulcaghide, persons of the name pardoned, 4468. See O'Mulcahy.
O'Mulcahe, John, pardon, 6531.
O'Mulcahe, Donell, pardon, 6466, 6468.
O'Mulcahel—Mulcahill—Molchill, persons of the name pardoned, 671, 5766, 4316.
O'Mulcahy—Molcahy—Mulchahie—Mulchahy—Mulkahy—Mulloahy—Mulloahie, persons of the name pardoned, 1663, 2769, 2934, 4618, 4714, 6006, 6170, 6614–16, 6673, 6635, 6678.
" See also O'Molchahe, Ymulcahe.
O'Mulcallen—Mulcallan—Mulcallen—Mulchalen—Mulchallen—Mulchallen—Mulchallen—Mullchallane—Mullchallen, persons of the name pardoned, 4628, 6776, 6144, 6629, 6785.
O'Mulcashell—Mulchashell, John and Wm., pardon, 6188, 6761.
O'Mulcaphan, Patr., pardon, 6765.
O'Mulce, John, pardon 6763.
O'Mulchan, Ferrall, pardon, 4628.
O'Mulchan, John, pardon, 4765, 6767.
" See also Mulchan.
O'Mulchaha, Teige, pardon, 6764.
" See also Mulchaina.

INDEX TO FIANTS—ELIZABETH.

O'Mulchahy—Mulchahie. *See* O'Mulcahy.
O'Mulchallan—Mulchallon—Mulchalon. *See* O'Mulcallan.
O'Mulchamhell, *See* O'Mulcashell.
O'Mulcheary, Brian, pardon, 6108.
O'Mulchery, Donogh, pardon, 6917.
O'Mulchloran, Pollin, pardon, 6444.
O'Mulchone, Donnell, pardon, 4850.
O'Mulchirrill, Donell and Rorie, pardon, 6478.
O'Mulchiry, Cormock, pardon, 4667.
O'Mulchlohie. *See* O'Mulclohey.
O'Mulchloy. *See* O'Mulcloy.
O'Mulchonere, persons of the name pardoned, 6377.
O'Mulchonery. *See* O'Mulconry.
O'Mulchoralle, persons of the name pardoned, 6766.
O'Mulchonre, Donell, pardon, 6877.
O'Mulchonry. *See* O'Mulconry.
O'Mulchowry, Bergati, pardon, 4874.
O'Mulclare, Donogh, pardon, 6904.
O'Mulcleighe, Rory, pardon, 5799.
O'Mulcleighne, Shane, pardon, 4634.
O'Mulcleyhe, Hugh, pardon, 4508.
O'Mulclohey—Mulchlohie, persons of the name pardoned, 4101, 6618.
O'Mulcloigh, Teroghill, pardon, 6761.
O'Mulcloy—Mulchloy—Molchloy, persons of the name pardoned, 4680, 4683, 6467.
O'Mulconry—Mulconrie—Mulconery—Mulconnerie—Molconery—Mulconre—Molconere—Molconnere—Molconrie—Mulchonery—Mulchonry—Mulkonere—Mulkonery:
" Farfassa, pardon, 4483.
" Gales (of Coricaconyll), pardon, 4903.
" Moilen, chronicler, pardon, 6404.
" Tulligne, pardon, 3941, 4341, 4918.
" Uline, rimor, pardon, 4678.
" others of the name pardoned, 3941, 4373, 4077, 6348, 4740, 4818, 4880, 4887, 6451, 6488, 4400, 6617, 4888, 6171, 6188, 6241, 6464, 6677.
O'Mulconry, Padine oge, rimor, pardon, 4678.
O'Mulcreane, Gilleduff, pardon, 4838.
O'Mulcture, Connor, pardon, 6888.
O'Muldony—Muldoni—Moldony:
" persons of the name pardoned, 912, 6364, 4532, 6457.
O'Muldowne—Muldownie:
" persons of the name pardoned, 6367, 4643, 6724.
O'Muldownee, Shane, pardon, 4408
O'Muldowny—Muldowney—Muldownie—Moldownie—Moldowny, persons of the name pardoned, 1783, 6423, 6466, 6618, 6683, 6648, 6684, 6766.
O'Muldryn, Edmund, pardon, 6698.
O'Mulfadder, Wm., pardon, 6110
O'Mullodriske, Edm., pardon, 6910.
O'Mulgarane, Owen, pardon, 6781.
O'Mulgohy, Donell and Teig, pardon, 6148, 6616.
O'Mulgeran, John, pardon, 6748.
O'Mulgey, Oen, pardon, 4637.
O'Mulghahe, Eo., pardon, 2367.
O'Mulghorlek, persons of the name pardoned, 6486.
O'Mulgue, Owen, pardon, 4604.
O'Mulhane, Diermoid, pardon, 6718.
O'Mulish, Edmund and Philip, pardon, 6463.
O'Mulkahy. *See* O'Mulcahy.
O'Mulkeloy, Donell, pardon, 4068.
O'Mulkeran—Mulkerane—Mulkyran, persons of the name pardoned, 671, 4676, 6602, 6761.
O'Mulkerrie—Mulkirry—Mulkyrie, persons of the name pardoned, 2904, 6467, 6468.
O'Mulkie, Brian, pardon, 4673.
O'Mulkier, Ricard, pardon, 4698.
O'Mulkirry. *See* O'Mulkerrie.
O'Mulkrynye, Brien, pardon, 6718.
O'Mulkyran. *See* O'Mulkeran.
O'Mulkyle, Dermot, pardon, 6768.
O'Mulkyne, Gerhie, pardon, 4668.
O'Mulkyrie. *See* O'Mulkerrie.
O'Mulle—Mullae, persons of the name pardoned, 2083, 3618, 6868.
O'Mullaghlen—Mullaglen—Mullaghlyn. *See* O'Molaghlin.
O'Mullaghlyn, Owin, pardon, 6473.
O'Mullaly—Mullalie:
" alias Lealy, William, dean of Tuam, protection, 887.
" others of the name pardoned, 1848, 4673.
O'Mullan—Mullane:
" Donnys, lands of, 6687.
" William, messuage in Halls, co. Meath, 868.
" others of the name pardoned, 784, 4234, 4703, 4734, 4884, 6718, 6460, 6418, 6476, 6762.
O'Mullane, persons of the name pardoned, 4078.
O'Mullaner, Shane, pardon, 4677.
O'Mullaney, MacOmb, pardon, 6084.
O'Mullany—Mullanny:
" Donald, priest, pardon, 2288.
" others of the name pardoned, 3943, 3887, 4697, 4703, 4808, 5918-18, 6760, 6868, 6304, 6481.

INDEX TO FIANTS.—ELIZABETH.

O'Mallartey, Gillpatrick, pardon, 6450.
O'Mallowny — Mullowney — Mullowne, persons of the name pardoned, [illegible], [illegible], [illegible], 4237, 5786, 6480, 6490, 6502, 6712.
O'Mallayne, Donald and Tho., pardon, 5877, 6448.
" John, theft from, 184.
O'Mallcahy—Mullcahie. See O'Mulcahy.
O'Mallchallen—Mullchallane. See O'Mulcallen.
O'Mallconery—Mullconere. See O'Mulconry.
O'Mullconner, Shorney, pardon, 6078.
O'Mullealy, Cormock and Gildaf, pardon, 6437, 6624.
O'Mullegan, Thady, pardon, 6124.
O'Mulleghan, John, pardon, 6428.
O'Mullen, Murrogh, pardon, 4677.
O'Mulleven, Thady, pardon, 6458.
O'Mullgreem, Ene, pardon, 6464.
O'Mullgrinne, Edm., pardon, 6468.
O'Mullhallon, Hugh, pardon, 4673.
O'Mulline, Tirlagh, pardon, 6443.
O'Mullim, Shane, pardon, 6440.
O'Mullivine, Morogh, pardon, 6464.
O'Mullme. See O'Mulme.
O'Mullmihell. See O'Mulmichell.
O'Mullmochory—Mullmoghorie, Owen and Phelim, pardon, 5467, 6914.
O'Mullmorie. See O'Mulmorrie.
O'Mullmoy. See O'Molloy.
O'Mulloigny, Wm., pardon, 6173.
O'Mulloon, Dermod, pardon, 6763.
O'Mulloney—Mullonie, persons of the name pardoned, 2824, 2412, 6485, 6500, 6534, 6563.
O'Mulloroy, Shane, pardon, 4822.
O'Mullory—Mullorye, persons of the name pardoned, 4628, 5744, 6714, 6496, 6534.
O'Mullowane, Dyermod, pardon, 5768.
O'Mullowen, Owen, pardon, 6078.
O'Mullowne, Owen and Shane, pardon, 5434.
O'Mullownie, Rich., pardon, 6421.
O'Mullownowe, John, attainted, 6782.
O'Mulloway, persons of the name pardoned, 4237, 4782, 5512, 6522, 6765.
O'Mulloy—Mulloye. See O'Molloy.
O'Mullpatrick — Mullphedrick. See O'Mulpatrick.
O'Mullreane. See O'Mulrean.
O'Mullrohan, Dermod, pardon, 6808.
O'Mullrenan. See O'Mulrenan.
O'Mullrian. See O'Mulryan.
O'Mullronye. See O'Mulrony.
O'Mullryan. See O'Mulryan.
O'Mulltully. See O'Multully.
O'Mullvihile—Mullvichill. See O'Mulvihill.
O'Mully—Mullye, Conor and Loghlin, pardon, 5840, 6527.
O'Mullyn, Shane, pardon, 5867.
O'Mulme — Mullme, persons of the name pardoned, 6442.
O'Mulmee, Brian and John, pardon, 6443.
O'Mulmichell — Mullmihell, Morris and Rory, pardon, 6443, 6468.
O'Mulmochore — Molmoechore, persons of the name pardoned, 6488, 6441.
O'Mulmoy. See O'Molloy.
O'Mulmurrie—Mullmorie, Edm. and John, pardon, 6421, 6828.
O'Mulmany — Mulmaye, persons of the name pardoned, 6712-14.
O'Mulowne, Gullpatrick, pardon, 6477.
O'Muloway, Shane, pardon, 6214.
O'Muloy. See O'Molloy.
O'Muloyne, Rich., pardon, 6464.
O'Mulpatrick—Mulpatricke—Mulpadrick — Molpatrick—Mullpatrick — Mullphedrick:
" Conor, chief of his name, pardon, 6887.
" others of the name pardoned, 3082, 4602, 6403, 6416, 5762, 6271, 6460, 6416, 6438, 6461, 6364.
O'Mulranie—Molrany, John and Conogher, pardon, 4467, 6833.
O'Mulrean — Mullreane — Mulreayn—Mollrane—Molrean, persons of the name pardoned, 1652, 2049, 2624, 3149, 4226, 4117, 4314-6, 4561, 4712, 5029, 5688, 6179, 6458, 6508, 6704.
O'Mulrenan — Mullronan — Mulrenyn, persons of the name pardoned, 4921, 4777, 6484, 6494, 6761.
O'Mulreso, Rorie, pardon, 6464.
O'Mulriagan, Cornelius, pardon, 4628.
O'Mulriain, Dermod, pardon, 4894.
O'Mulrian. See O'Mulryan.
O'Mulriany, Rori, pardon, 5488.
O'Mulridie, Daniel and Molaghlyn, pardon, 4614, 6374.
O'Mulrigan, Thady, pardon, 4622.
O'Mulriah, Manus, pardon, 2685.
O'Mulrone—Molrona, Donogh and Rory, pardon, 3867, 5368.
O'Mulrony—Mulroni—Mullronye, persons of the name pardoned, 2078, 2234, 4868, 4608, 6383.
O'Mulrowne, Donogh, pardon, 4378.
O'Mulrowny, Donogho, pardon, 6143.
O'Mulryan—Mulrian—Mollryan—Molrian—Molryan—Mullrian—Mullryan—Mulryane. See also O'Mulrean.
" Conell m'Shane glas, pardon, 3323, 5448, 6628.
" Connor, son of William (of Annagh), 1086, 4975; chief of his name, 6483.

INDEX TO FIANTS.—ELIZABETH.

O'Mulryan, Daniel m'Keogher M'ollie, slain, 5554.
" Donell glas, slain in rebellion, 5584.
" Donell (of Killinlogh), pardon, [illegible], 6794.
" Henry fitz Donell, pardon, 2948, 2903.
" John glas, pardon, 1668.
" Moroghow no Kelly, pardon, 6406, 6411.
" Teig, slain in rebellion, 4983.
" William, chief of his name, pardon to him and his sons, 1664.
" others of the name pardoned. 1084, 1843, 1881, 2326, 2764, 2967, 3143, 3384, 3834, 4271, 4649, 4674, 4686, 4827, 4878, 5048, 5556, 5443, 5467, 5712, 6109, 6175, 6178, 6348, 6468, 6427, 6486, 6504–5, 6613, 6613, 6514, 6530–3, 6531, 6595, 6663, 6604–5, 6282, 6638, 6796, 6798–8.
" country of, 6323. See also O'wny O'Mulrian, 6322, 6834.
O'Mulshaghlen, Cowe, pardon, 6452.
O'Multellon, Thomas, mortgage in Kells, Meath, 848.
O'Multhomrie, Ferfecia, pardon, 6540.
O'Multilly, alias Fluid, Donnogh, pardon, 6030.
O'Multreo, Tho., garden in Youghal, 6168.
O'Multulbe, Connor, pardon, 4962.
O'Multolly—Multullee—Multtulle, persons of the name pardoned, 1627, 3800, 4813, 6618, 6674, 6719, 6487.
O'Mulule, Donell, pardon, 6477.
O'Mulveghell, Teige, pardon, 4630.
O'Mulvell, Manus ogo, pardon, 6633.
O'Mulverie, Thrrelagh, pardon, 6728.
O'Mulvihill — Mulvichill — Mulvyhill — Mollvill—Mullvibille, persons of the name pardoned, 2846, 2841, 5903, 5438, 6068.
O'Mulvoge, Dermot and James, pardon, 6781.
O'Mulvyhill. See O'Mulvihill.
O'Mulyrowe, Morris, pardon, 6714.
O'Mumeghane — Mineyghan, Connor and John, pardon, 2854, 5184.
O'Mungain, Tho., pardon, 4381.
O'Muggane, Murtagh, pardon, 4578.
O'Mungaria, Theag, pardon, 6661.
O'Muoyghan. See O'Mumeghane.
O'Muogmane, Edm., pardon, 6464.
O'Muragh—Muraghe, persons of the name pardoned, 6611.
O'Muraghton, Philip, pardon, 4313.
O'Murahan, Morierlagh, pardon, 4033.
O'Murcho—Murchow. See O'Moroghoe.
O'Murcarie, persons of the name pardoned, 5464.
O'Muroghow — Muroghoo — Muroghow — Muroghua. See O'Moroghoe.
O'Murley—Murlie, Donough and Garret, pardon, 6696, 6941.
O'Murgann, Conor and Owin, pardon, 6565.
O'Murghe, Morierlagh, pardon, 3932.
O'Murgheana, persons of the name pardoned, 6656.
O'Murgho—Murghowe. See O'Moroghoe.
O'Murholy—Murholie, persons of the name pardoned, 6614, 6671.
O'Murhie, Patr., pardon, 4532.
O'Murhilly—Murhillie, persons of the name pardoned, 3334, 6564, 6762.
O'Murhowe, Gerald, pardon, 3934.
O'Murico, Donell, pardon, 6578.
O'Murie, Molaghlin, pardon, 4768.
O'Murighe, Patr., pardon, 6621.
O'Murihy, David, pardon, 6173.
O'Murilly, John pardon, 6611.
O'Murien, Conchor, pardon, 934.
O'Murley, Mahony, pardon, 4630.
O'Murloy—Murlie, persons of the name pardoned, 6654, 6529.
O'Murogh, persons of the name pardoned, 4987, 6911.
O'Muroghe — Muroghowe — Murowghan. See O'Moroghoe.
O'Murphow, Donogh, pardon, 6618.
O'Murragh, Shan, pardon, 5648.
O'Murran, Shane, pardon, 6274.
O'Murre, John, pardon, 4467.
O'Murreghowe—Murreghe. See O'Moroghoe.
O'Murreley, Awley, pardon, 1068.
O'Murren, Dowlin and Tho., pardon, 2184, 6461.
O'Murretie, persons of the name pardoned, 6466, 6671.
O'Murrey—Murrie, Cahill and Donell, pardon, 6184, 6791.
O'Murrey, Owen, pardon, 6560.
O'Murrigane, Lainlaghe, pardon, 6617.
O'Murrighie, Donell, pardon, 6946.
O'Murrihey, John, pardon, 6784.
O'Murrilly, Donell, pardon, 6612.
O'Murrin, Eyrie, pardon, 6634.
O'Murris, Cormock, pardon, 6528.
O'Murrishe, Morish, pardon, 6168.
O'Murrishie, persons of the name pardoned, 6479, 6651.
O'Murrisee, Teige, pardon, 4668.
O'Murriske — Murrisye, John and Teig, pardon, 8134, 6168.
O'Murrogh—Murroghe, persons of the name pardoned, 6390, 6611, 6677.
O'Murroghan, Brian, pardon, 6404.
O'Murrogho — Murroghoo — Murroghow — Murroghn—Murronghoe. See O'Moroghoe

INDEX TO FIANTS.—ELIZABETH.

O'Marrow, Philip and Tho., pardon, 4478, 4487.
O'Murrowghoo. See O'Moroghoe.
O'Murragh, Owen, pardon, 6411.
O'Murrugho—Murraghow. See O'Moroghoe.
O'Murry—Murrye, persons of the name pardoned, 3796, 4577, 6702.
O'Murryes, Owaye, pardon 4378.
O'Murryes, Cnoghor and Dennys, pardon, 6150.
O'Murrygan, Donill, pardon, 4608.
O'Murryn, Murrogh and Philip, pardon, 4461, 4774.
O'Murthy. See Murfy.
O'Murughow. See O'Moroghoe.
O'Mury, Edm. and Shane, pardon, 4728, 4487.
O'Murymna, Pair., pardon, 6682.
O'Murynoe, Tho., pardon, 6411.
O'Mayraighan, Cormock, pardon, 6494.
Omvyne, Meagha, pardon, 10.
O'Mwrhillie, Donchl and Thady, pardon, 4538.
O'Mwrigho. See O'Moroghoe.
O'Myagher, Philip, pardon, 6708.
O'Myane, Shomino, pardon, 6009.
O'Myanie, Wm., pardon, 6421.
O'Myhan, Hugh, pardon, 5507.
O'Myhell, Diarmod, pardon, 6542.
O'Myhiden, Owen, pardon, 5600.
O'Mylime, Maurice, pardon, 4744.
O'Myllone, Breno and Owen, pardon, 914.
O'Mynan—Mynane, Donell and Shane, pardon, 4449, 4464.
O'Mynaghane. See O'Moynaghan.
O'Mynie, Cahill, pardon, 5475.
O'Mynighan. See O'Moynaghan.
O'Mynye, Gilleduff, pardon, 5475.
O'Myre, Donogh, pardon, 4401.
O'Nackline—Nackiyne, Edm. and Gillepatrick, pardon, 6464.
O'Naddene, Conor, pardon, 5049.
O'Naddy—Naddye, persons of the name pardoned, 6173, 6744.
O'Nade, Edm., pardon, 2408.
O'Nady, Edmund, pardon, 574.
O'Naghe (co. Rosc.?), 4728.
Onaghe O'Donochomore. See Onaght.
Onaght, co. Tip., grant of manor and lordship of, 3846; to be made shire ground, 3763.
Onaght—Onaught—Onaghe O'Donochomore, country of (in barony of Magunihy), co. Kerry, 5777, 6717.
O'Naghtan—Naghtan—Naghtin—Naghton—Naghtyne—Naighten—Naughten—Naughtin—Naughton:
" Conchor (of Moyneure), pardon, 5778, 5432.
O'Naghtan, Conchor, clerk, pardon, 6651.
" Conogher, land in tenure of, 5384.
" Conogher, attainted, 6284.
" Cornell, lease, 2687.
" Donald, attainted, 6117.
" Donogho, clerk, 5712.
" John or Shane (of Moyneure), livery to his heir, 5452.
" John m'Melaghlin, attainted 6372.
" Robert, grandson of John, livery, 6480.
" Rory boy, attainted, 6202, 6611.
" Shane, attainted, 6202, 6117.
" others of the name pardoned 572, 1607, 1820, 2778, 3844, 4613, 4574, 4782, 4779, 4809, 5082, 5724, 5725, 5422, 5438, 5414, 6848, 6480, 6480, 6804, 6611, 6516, 6540, 6284, 6777.
country of, (in barony of Athlone, co. Rosc.), 5128, 6478.
O'Naghtes, Marogh, pardon, 4482.
O'Nahane, Donell, pardon, 6514.
O'Naighten. See O'Naghtan.
O'Narde, John, pardon, 2081.
O'Narie. See O'Nary.
O'Narry, Hugh, pardon, 4741.
O'Nary—Narie—Narye:
" Philip, soldier, murder of, 75.
" others of the name pardoned, 2344, 2372, 2861, 3734, 3212, 4029, 4032, 4078, 4340, 4741, 4777, 4944, 5898, 5422, 5408, 5411, 6804, 6667, 6802.
O'Nashe, Maurice, pardon, 6548.
O'Nasye, Walter, pardon, 5373.
Onaught. See Onaght.
O'Naughtan—Naughtin. See O'Naghtan.
O'Nayllayne, Donell, pardon, 4481.
on dale, Marogh, pardon, 6298.
O'Ne. See O'Nea.
Onea, Moore mal, pardon, 4082.
O'Nea—Ne, persons of the name pardoned, 4824, 6461, 6598.
O'Neaghten, Donogh, priest, pardon, 4888.
O'Neaghtaine—Neaghtin—Neaghten, persons of the name pardoned, 5448, 5428, 5481, 6804.
O'Nealan. See O'Nolan.
O'Neal—Neale—Neall. See O'Neill.
Onedaly, Donell, pardon, 6487.
O'Nee, Donogh, pardon, 6398.
O'Neale. See O'Neill.
O'Neall. See O'Neill.
O'Nellane. See O'Nolan.

O'Neill — Neal — Neale — Neall — Neele — Neil — Neile — Neille — Nele — Nell — Neyle — Neyll — Neylle — Niall:

„ Arte m'Baron, pardon, 1881.

„ Arte or Arthur, knt., son of Tirlagh lenagh, pardon, 5713: his sons, 6488.

„ Art oge, race of, 5918.

„ Brian, livery to his brother Hugh, 1581.

„ Brian fertagho's country, 4782.

„ Brian m'Phelim, knt. (of Clandeboy), commission, 1480; pardon, 2144, 2158, 2419; earl of Essex deals with, 2463; son and heir of, 4901.

„ Brian puddoria, pardon, 6028, 5718.

„ Con m'Neile oge, knt., pardon, 1008, 2386, 2948; surrender and regrant of the lordship of Castlereagh, 4904-5.

„ Cormack (son of Tirlagh lenagh), pardon, 5918.

„ Cormack, pardon, 6480.

„ Donell (son of Phelim roe), pardon, 2172; his sons, 4682.

„ Donell oge (of the Fivagh, co. Antrim), pardon, 6718.

„ Henry oge m'Henry m'Shane, esq. (of Portnelligan, co. Armagh), pardon, 6734.

„ Hugh, livery, 1281; baron of Dungannon, pardon at suit of, 2884, 3844; commissions, 4064, 6791. *See* Tyrone, earl of.

„ Hugh macNeile more, pardon, 1683.

„ Hugh m'Phelim, late captain of Clandeboy, 4291.

„ Hugh (son of Con M'Neal oge), 4688; pardon, 4900.

„ John (Shane), pardon, 184; war with, 870, 542-3, 461, 1502, 2044.

„ Neile (father of Tirlagh lenagh), 6071.

„ Neile m'Brian fertagho, pardon, 2630; appointed captain of Clandeboy, 1142.

„ Neile, of the race of Art oge, pardon, 5918.

„ Neill m'Hugh, pardon, 5878, to him and his dependants, 6145. *See also* Neil m'H. M'Murthoe, 5710.

„ Phelim roe, pardon to son of, 2172.

„ Rose (wife of O'Cahan), pardon, 6062.

O'Neill, Shane m'Brian (son of Brian m'Phelim), captain of Clandeboy, 4901; pardon, 4966, 5472, 6145; pardon to dependants of, 6146.

„ Sophronia, matrimonial suit, 3847.

„ Tirlagh lenagh, chief of his name, treaty with, 2462, 2631; commission, 4763; contribution of Maguire to, 4900; grant of captaincy of Tyrone, 5913; pardon, 5918.

„ Tirlagh brisselagh, pardon, 1101.

„ Tirlagh m'Henry (chief of the Fues), pardon, 6062.

„ Tirlagh (son of sir Arthur), pardon, 6458.

„ Tirlagh oge (of Portnelligan, co. Armagh), pardon, 6734.

„ others of the name in Tyrone and neighbouring districts pardoned, 1616, 1181, 3172, 3790, 4058, [illegible], 5218, 5474, 5663, 5770, 5791, 6145, 6462, 6562, 6626, 6642, 6718, 6735.

„ others of the name in co. Carlow, and neighbouring districts, pardoned, 876, 916, 1840, 1867, 2618, 3184, 3894, 4818, 4163, 4844, 4448, 4018, 5028, 5118, 4896, 6160, 6161, 6168, 6200, [illegible], [illegible], 6454, 6517, 6641. *See* Ferren O'Neyle.

„ others of the name pardoned, 1584, 1636, 2043, 2086, 2488, 2708, 3978, 3974, 4280, 4677, 4769, 5646, 5948, 6280, 6454-6, 6468, 6512, 6572, 6629, 6586, 6576, 6682, 6764, 6782, 6745.

O'Nolan — Nolane — Neolan — Nolane — Noland:

„ Dormot oge, physician, pardon, 6462.

„ others of the name pardoned, 3042, 4877, 6401, 6712, 6404, 6642, 6652, 6618, 6617, 6745-6.

O'Nole. *See* O'Neill.

O'Nelogan, Thomas, pardon, 1089.

O'Noll. *See* O'Neill.

O'Nellan—Nollain—Nollaine—Nollane:

„ Donald, clerk, presentation to archdeaconry of Killfenora, 6782.

„ others of the name pardoned, 4478, 4462, 4788, 5068, 5465, 6168, 6478.

O'Nolle. *See* O'Neill.

O'Nellogane, Conoghor, pardon, 6478.

O'Nonane, Shane, pardon, 6762.

O'None, Conoghor, pardon, 4584.

O'Noyre, Nicholas, English liberty, 177.

O'Noshie, John, messuage at Boro Abbey, 7692.

O'Now, Hugh, pardon, 6628.

Onoy, Edm., pardon, 3941.

O'Noylan—Neylane, Connor and Edm., pardon, 4682, 6452.

INDEX TO FIANTS.—ELIZABETH.

O'Neyle—Neyll—Neylle. *See* O'Neill.
O'Neyman, Murtagh, pardon, 6487.
O'Niell, Tirrely, pardon, 5094. *See* O'Neill.
O'Nihill—Nihill—Nyhill, persons of the name pardoned, 4728, 5784, 6404.
O'Nilane, Donell roe, pardon, 6340.
O'Nilly, William, pardon, 5042.
O'Nimhane, Murrythirtagh, pardon, 5522.
Onilley, Donogh (*see* Cavanagh), pardon, [illegible].
O'Nirain, Dermot, attainted, 6042.
Onitayn, Shane, pardon, 3128.
Onivirin, persons of the name pardoned, 5923.
Onmoly. *See* Anmoly.
O'Nolane, Fardorogh, pardon, 6337.
O'Noallan, Tirrely, pardon, 5942.
O'Noble, Sydoy, pardon, 4328.
O'Noddagh, Edm., pardon, 4094.
O'Noglaghe, Gerrot, pardon, 6517.
O'Nolain, Donald, pardon, 5914.
O'Nolan—Noland—Nolane—Noulane—Nowlan—Nowlane:
 ,, persons of the name pardoned, 478, 697, 711, 914, 1161, 1615, 1617, 1628, 1640, 1666, 1771, 1851, 1887, 1890, 2057, 2060, 2108, 2202, 2224, 2409–10, 2738, 2848, 3166, 3904, 4371, 4370, 4441, 4501, 4691, 5115, 5615, 5788, 6118, 6187, 6218, 6221, 6348, 6382, 6428, 6346, 6447, 6304, 6517, 6540, 6525, 6417, 6604, 6622, 6704, 6783.
 ,, *See also* Nolan.
O'Nollan—Nollane, persons of the name pardoned, 614, 4182, 6394.
O'Nollegimlan, John, pardon, 6369.
O'Noonan, Shane, pardon, 4615.
O'Norane, Wm., pardon, 6091.
O'Noran, Teige M'Cartie, pardon, 4418.
O'Noulan. *See* O'Nolan.
O'Nourdan, Morrough, pardon, 4918.
O'Novan, Conor, pardon, 5402.
O'Nowan, Wm., pardon, 6978.
O'Nowlan—Nowlane. *See* O'Nolan.
O'Nowman, Donogho, attainted, 4761.
 ,, lands of, co. Cork, 5898.
O'Nowne, persons of the name pardoned, 4796, 6132.
O'Nownighan, Philip, pardon, 6681.
O'Nullaghe, Henry, pardon, 4282.
O'Nullan, Teige, pardon, 3844–5.
O'Nurgher, Teige, pardon, 4226.
O'Nuylan, Gillegrome, pardon, 3048.
Ony, Eleonora ny, pardon, 3972.
Ony Mulryan. *See* Owny Mulryan.
O'Nyallagan, Fyn and Thos., pardon, 4786.
O'Nyhill. *See* O'Nihill.
O'Nymane, Murtaghe, pardon, 4068.
O'Nywane, Dermod, pardon, 6409.
Oola, co. Lim. *See* Owlyn.
O'Polan, Wm., pardon, 3748.
O'Pottane, persons of the name pardoned, 6482.
O'Phalan, Donell, pardoned, 3428.
Ophalle—Ophalley—Ophallie—Ophally. *See* Offaly.
O'Phalvy, Dowell and Fa., pardon, 6315.
O'Phalwey, Donogh, pardon, 6248.
Ophaly. *See* Offaly.
O'Phealan. *See* O'Phelan.
O'Pheane, Edm., pardon, 4465.
O'Phelan—Phelane—Phelaine—Phealan, persons of the name pardoned, 1617, 1880, 2064, 2772, 2744, 3078, 3341, 3880, 4082, 4270, 4614, [illegible], [illegible], [illegible], [illegible], [illegible], 6471, [illegible], [illegible], [illegible], 6441, 6423–4.
O'Phelim, Donell, pardon, 6476.
O'Phellan—Phellane, persons of the name pardoned, 6196, 4322, 6851.
O'Phelme, Wm., pardon, 4083.
O'Phelume, Donough, pardon, 2884.
O'Phelan, John, Nicholas, and Richard, English liberty, 303.
 ,, others of the name pardoned, 1648, 1746.
O'Pherall, Cormac and Rory, pardon, 481.
O'Philan, Owen and Shane, pardon, 4848, 6309.
O'Philan, persons of the name pardoned, 6541, 6722.
O'Pholan—Phelane, persons of the name pardoned, 897.
O'Photane, Shane, pardon, 1160.
O'Phylan—Phyllan—Phyllane, persons of the name pardoned, 4461, 4762.
Opicyhane, Dermot, pardon, 1617.
O'Poxnie, Brene, pardon, 6784.
O'Pray—Praye, persons of the name pardoned, 2286.
O'Prist, Edm., pardon, 4728.
O'Prontye, Nale, pardon, 5408.
O'Pullie, Edm., pardon, 6374.
O'Quane, Shane, pardon, 3796.
O'Quanahan, Donill, pardon, 4848.
O'Quane, Ene, pardon, 6838.
O'Queinlan. *See* O'Quinlan.
O'Quigly—Quygley, Donogh and Gerrot, pardon, 4877, 6447.
O'Quillayne, Hugh, pardon, 4718.
O'Quillin, Donogh, pardon, 6392.
Oquin in the Annaly, country of, 2121. *See* Looynes country.
O'Quin—Quine. *See* O'Quyn.
O'Quinegane—Quynagan:
 ,, Donyll, homicide of, 6982.
 ,, others of the name pardoned, 6418, 6521.

INDEX TO FIANTS.—ELIZABETH.

O'Quingane — Quynegan — Owyngan — Quyngine, persons of the name pardoned, 4369, 5418, 6821, 6712.
O'Quinlan — Queulan — Quenlane — Quynlan — Quynland — Quynlane — Quynleane — Quyndane, persons of the name pardoned, 5686, 4177, 4186, 4439, 4573, 4691.
O'Quintreny, Murogh, pardon, 4318.
O'Quirk — Quirke — Quircke — Quyrcke — Quyrk — Quyrke:
" Mahowne ne Rowrye, pardon, 4627; attainted, 5144.
" others of the name pardoned, 3860, 5344, 4365, 4187, 4454, 4637, 4594, 4178-80, 5352, 6466, 6428, 6513, 6331-2, 4521-3, 6566, 6575, 6583.
O'Quenane, Gillecluffe and Teige, pardon, 6754.
O'Queddy, William, pardon, 415.
O'Queghane, Dermod, pardon, 6018.
O'Quelke, Edm., pardon, 5752.
O'Quelane, Thomas, English liberty, 336.
Oqueone, John, pardon, 4652.
O'Quenale, Morris, pardon, 6314.
O'Queyne — Queyn, persons of the name pardoned, 6146, 4371, 6287.
O'Quyan, Rich., pardon, 6791.
O'Quyggine — Quygine, persons of the name pardoned, 6718.
O'Quygley. See O'Quigly.
O'Quyn — Quynn — Quin — Quine — Quynn — Quynne:
" Hugh, priest, pardon, 4683.
" others of the name pardoned, 280, 648, 1574, 1696, 1948, 2918, 3011, 3304, 3597, 4367, 4885, 4677, 5065, 5288, 6418, 5398, 4578, 6103, 6143, 6333, 6309, 6214, 6473, 6489, 6496, 6533-4, 6574, 6576, 6681, 6638, 6644, 6662, 6713-14, 6761.
" See Cuynn, Inoyne, O'Qwyne.
O'Quynegan. See O'Quingane.
O'Quynggan — Quyngine. See O'Quingane.
O'Quynlan — Quyndane — Quynlane — Quynland — Quynleane. See O'Quinlan.
O'Quynnyne, Dermot, alias Stankerde, pardon, 482.
O'Quyrk — Quyrke — Quyrcke. See O'Quirk.
O'Quyrrice, James, pardon, 6706.
O'Qwyngan. See O'Quingane.
O'Qwyne, seneschal of Mointerguligan, co. Longford, 2582.
O'Rachaine, Shane, pardon, 129.
O'Raddygan, Hugh, pardon, 5740.
O'Raghell, Edm., pardon, 6172.
O'Raghtagan, Donell, pardon, 6102.
O'Raghter, Shane, pardon, 6421.
O'Raghtorane, Brian, pardon, 6616.
O'Raghtore, Shane, pardon, 6118.
O'Raghtoary, Manus, pardon, 6712.
O'Rah( ), Dermod, pardon, 6793.
O'Rahellie — Rahellie — Rahelie — Rahelly — Rahillo — Rahillie — Rahilly, persons of the name pardoned, 3931, 5284, 4467, 6479, 6516, 6548, 6571.
O'Rahill, Moriah and Morogh, pardon, 4764, 6695.
O'Raicke, Pharragh, pardon, 4488.
O'Raine, Redmund fitz Dey, pardon, 6133.
O'Raly — Ralye, persons of the name pardoned, 1898, 5791, 3962.
Oran Beg, co. Gal. See Cranbeg.
Orane (Oran, co. Ross.), 5118.
Oranmore — Owranmore, co. Gal., 1883; castle and lands, 6291.
O'Rannyve, John, pardon, 4678.
Oranstowne, co. Meath. See Overanston.
O'Rawghan, persons of the name pardoned, 3033, 6511.
O'Rawbane, John, pardon, 4672.
Orchard, co. Car., 1114.
Orchard, Queen's co. See Owllorte.
Orchardeston, King's co., 2768.
Ordmolivan, co. Gal., 4717.
Ordmond. See Ormond.
Ordnance, master of, 336, 3696, 5761, 5763-9.
" clerk of, 680, 673, 694, 714, 6362, 3910.
" clerk, controller, and surveyor of, 4380, 3843, 6361, 6738.
" smith of, 6097, 6188, 6366, 6567, 6568, chief smith to impress iron, workmen, &c., 4344.
" maker of horse collars to, 777.
" saddler to, 6062.
" general lieutenant of (in England), 5748.
Ore river, Queen's co. (Nore), 4738.
O'Readie, Moriah and Teig, pardon, 6469.
O'Reagan, Donell and Moleghlin, pardon, 6184, 6662.
O'Reale, Hugh, pardon, 6374.
O'Realy, Donell, pardon, 6114.
" See also Ireelaghe.
O'Reen — Reane, persons of the name pardoned, 140, 1882, 5790, 6434.
O'Redy, David and Shane, pardon, 1609, 6184.
O'Ree, Shane, pardon, 4488.
O'Reely, Dermod, 6753.
O'Reerdan, Ashowe, pardon, 6453.
O'Reeylie, Gerrott, pardon, 4683.
Oregan, Queen's co., rectory, 2698.
" See Irogan.

INDEX TO FIANTS—ELIZABETH.

Oregan in Connaught, 1471.
O'Regan—Regane—Regain—Regaine:
" Conogher oge m'ne Maddor, pardon, 6701.
" Dermot m'en Maddor, pardon, 6439.
" others of the name pardoned, 2237, 3938, [illegible], [illegible], [illegible], 1742, 4777, 5447, 5618, 6407, 6407, 6542, 6571, 6575, 6634, 6742, 6761.
Oregay, Donell, pardon, 5592.
O'Reggine, Shane, pardon, 6619.
O'Reyhelewin, Dermot, pardon, 4807.
O'Regin, James, pardon, 6618.
O'Regan, John, pardon, 4506.
O'Reignan—Reignane, persons of the name pardoned, 4747, 6454, 6515-16, [illegible].
O'Reigh, Donogh, pardon, 6378.
O'Reighlie—Reighly—Reiglie—Reigly. See O'Reilly.
O'Relle, Donogho and Molaughlin, pardon, 4477.
O'Reilly—Reighlie—Reighly—Reiglie—Reigly—Reiley—Reilie—Reilye—Reiel—Reley—Reli—Relie—Rellie—Relly—Rely—Relye—Reyle—Reyley—Reylie—Reylle—Reylley—Reyllie—Reylly—Reyly:
" Brian, attainted, 4562.
" Brian m'Cahir, attainted, 6840.
" Brian m'Mulmore, attainted, 6842.
" Cahir m'Prior, pardon, 4832; his lands custodiam, 5618.
" Cahir gare, surrender of his lands, 4541.
" Caher reoe, robbery by, 148.
" Edmund (of Kilmore), appointed tanist of Breny, 1017, 1286; pardon, 2714; surrenders barony of Castlerahan, 4543; commission, 5130; his son, 4231.
" Edm. m'Mulmore, attainted, 4562.
" Farrell m'Donell, attainted, 4562.
" Geoffrey, son of John (Reilli), pardon, 5446.
" Hugh (afterwards knt.), chief of his nation, commission to treat with, 783; recommends appointment of his brother Edmund as tanist, 1017, 1286; lease, 1601; his successor, 4197.
" Hugh, son of Prior Reilie, pardon, 4592.
" Hugh, son of the prior or m'Prior, pardon, 4592, 6657.
" Hugh reogh, surrender of his lands, 4541; pardon, 4592.
O'Reilly, Hugh, wife and sister of, 4239.
" John, knight, appointed captain of Breny, 4197; commission, 5130; pardon, 5612.
" Katherine (alias Adams), pardon, 5842.
" Maillmore moile, slain, 4562.
" Mulmore, attainted, 4562.
" Mulmurry, "the prior's son," surrender, 4541.
" Mulmory m'Shane, chief of his name, pardon, 6128.
" Mulmorrie (of the Cavan), pardon, 6445, 6481.
" Owen m'Hugh, pardon, 4592, 6793; chief of his name, 6457; his wife, 6457.
" Philip (of Ballinacargie), pardon, 4434, 4791; proposes to surrender his possessions, 4753, 4843.
" Philip m'Prior, pardon, 4592, 6628.
" the Prior, sons of, pardon, 4592.
" Shane m'Philip, attainted, 5618.
" others of the name pardoned, 149, 844, 780, 942, 1144, 1735, 1751, 1327, 2196-8, 2033, 2237, 2704, 3121, 3441, 3876, 3201, 3914, 3916, 3962, 3962, 3972, 4097, 4166, 4238, 4144, 4431, 4532, 4122, 4439, 4782, 4512-13, 4791-2, 4938, 4934, 4978, 5134, 5136, 5168, 5169, 5512, 5563, 5691, 5723, 5726, 5762, 5791-2, 6192, 6223, 6239, 6218, 6204, 6122, 6238, 6428, 6448, 6483, 6484, 6439, 6436, 6407, 6511, 6514, 6513, 6526, 6522-3, 6528, 6534, 6537, 6563-4, 6583, 6573-4, 6577, 6571, 6618, 6621, 6647, 6657, 6659-61, 6683, 6698, 6724, 6742, 6773, 6777.
" See also Iraghilliaghe, Irialli.
" country of (Breny), 823, 1651, 1736, 1949.
" country of, captain appointed, 4197.
" country of, clerk of crown and peace in, 6378, 6384.
O'Reilyde, Tho., pardon, 6779.
O'Reilye—Reiel—Reli—Relie—Rellie—Relly—Reley—Rely—Relye. See O'Reilly.
O'Reogh, James, pardon, 4168.
O'Reredan—Reredane, Rich. and William, pardon, 1617, 6634.
Orestone, co. Meath, 1770.
O'Revoey, Tho., pardon, 4698.
O'Rewe, Donogh, pardon, 2772.
O'Reyan, John, pardon, 4734.
O'Reygne, Ferrall and Tho., pardon, 4464.
O'Reygyne, Edm., pardon, 4661.

O'Reyle — Reyley — Reylie — Reylle—Reyllie—Reylly—Reyly. See O'Reilly.

O'Reyrye, Tho., pardon, [illegible].

Orghryer. See Orier.

Orgua, John m'Finlne, pardon, 2777.

O'Rhawly, Donall alias Daniel, pardon, [illegible].

Orhogile (Urrohogal), co. Kerry, [illegible].

O'Ria, Gilley and John, pardon, [illegible].

O'Riadiall, John or Shane, attainted, [illegible].

O'Rian—Riane. See O'Ryan.

O'Ridgan, John, pardon, [illegible].

O'Riede, Tho. oge, pardon, [illegible].

O'Riegan — Riegane — Riegain, persons of the name pardoned, [illegible], [illegible], [illegible], [illegible], [illegible]-16, [illegible], [illegible], [illegible], [illegible].

Oriell—Oryell—Ioriell (Oirghialla), M'Mahon's country (county Monaghan), surrendered, [illegible]; re-granted, [illegible].

" See Uriell.

O'Rien, persons of the name pardoned, [illegible], [illegible], [illegible], [illegible].

Orier—Ohrere—Orghryer—Orrier—Orrye—Orryer—Oryrry, alias O'Hanlon's country (Orier, co. Armagh), [illegible], [illegible]; captain appointed, [illegible]; commission to subdue the people of, [illegible]; surrender, [illegible]; grant of the country to O'Hanlon, [illegible].

O'Rierdan — Rierdane — Riorden. See O'Riurdan.

O'Riergan, Rich., pardon, [illegible].

O'Rigan, Patr., pardon, [illegible].

O'Rigay—Rigao—Rigney—Rignoye—Rignie—Rignye — Rygny, persons of the name pardoned, [illegible], [illegible], [illegible], [illegible], [illegible].

O'Rime, Wm., pardon, [illegible].

O'Rindane, Wm., pardon, [illegible].

O'Rine, persons of the name pardoned, [illegible].

O'Rinne, Cahell, pardon, [illegible].

O'Riode, John, pardon, 2776.

O'Rion, persons of the name pardoned, [illegible].

Orior, co. Arm. See Orier.

O'Riordan — Riordane — Riordaine. See O'Riurdan.

O'Riordawe, Owin, pardon, [illegible].

O'Riourdan. See O'Riurdan.

O'Rirke, Tirlagh, pardon, [illegible].

Oriry, co. Cork, pardon, [illegible].

Oris, co. Ross, [illegible].

O'Rithe, Farrell roe, pardon, [illegible].

O'Riune, Rob., pardon, [illegible].

O'Riurdan—Riordan—Rierdane—Riordon — Riordan — Riordane — Riordaine—Riourdan—Riourdane—Riurdane—Ryordan—Ryordane—Ryurdane:

" Donald m'Edm., slain in rebellion, [illegible].

" Maurice, attainted, [illegible].

O'Riurdan, Nich., [illegible].

" others of the name pardoned, [illegible], [illegible], [illegible], [illegible], [illegible], [illegible], [illegible], [illegible], [illegible], [illegible], [illegible], [illegible], [illegible], [illegible], [illegible], [illegible], [illegible]-4, [illegible], [illegible], [illegible], [illegible], [illegible], [illegible], [illegible], [illegible], [illegible], [illegible], [illegible], [illegible], [illegible], [illegible], [illegible].

" See also Iriordan, Yriordan.

Ormesby, Roger, searcher of Waterford, [illegible], [illegible].

Ormond—Ormonde — Ordmond—Ormound —Ormounde —Ormund:

" country of, co. Tip., [illegible], [illegible], [illegible], [illegible], [illegible], [illegible], [illegible], [illegible], [illegible], [illegible], [illegible], [illegible]; martial law in, [illegible], [illegible]; clerk of the crown, &c., in, [illegible].

" James alias, (fourth) earl of, [illegible].

" James, (ninth) earl of, [illegible], [illegible], [illegible].

" and Ossory, Thomas, earl of, made high treasurer, [illegible], [illegible]; chief leader of the army in Munster, [illegible], [illegible]; governor of Munster, [illegible], [illegible]; lieutenant general in Munster, [illegible]; general of the forces in Leinster, [illegible]-4, [illegible], [illegible]; lieutenant general of the queen's army, [illegible], [illegible]; authority conferred upon, [illegible], [illegible], [illegible], [illegible]; commission to make war on O'Mores and O'Connors, [illegible]; dispute with earl of Desmond, [illegible]-8, [illegible]; pardon, [illegible], [illegible], [illegible]; redemption from captivity among rebels, [illegible]; grant of lands, &c., [illegible], [illegible], [illegible], [illegible], [illegible], [illegible]-60, [illegible], [illegible], [illegible]-61, [illegible], [illegible]-2, [illegible], [illegible], [illegible], [illegible], [illegible], [illegible], [illegible], [illegible], [illegible], [illegible], [illegible], [illegible], [illegible], [illegible], [illegible], [illegible], [illegible]; commissions, [illegible], [illegible], [illegible], [illegible], [illegible]-7, [illegible], [illegible], 1417-18, [illegible], [illegible], [illegible], [illegible], [illegible], [illegible], [illegible], [illegible], [illegible], [illegible], [illegible], [illegible], [illegible]-8, [illegible]-4, [illegible], [illegible], [illegible], [illegible], [illegible]; release of debts to crown, [illegible]; export licence, [illegible]; grant of a wardship, [illegible]; leases, [illegible], [illegible], [illegible]-4, [illegible], [illegible], [illegible], [illegible]-60, [illegible]-8, [illegible], [illegible]-18, [illegible], [illegible], [illegible], [illegible], [illegible], [illegible], [illegible], [illegible]-8, [illegible], [illegible]; surrender, [illegible], [illegible]; houses and lands belonging to, [illegible], [illegible], [illegible],

Ormond:
 4150; pardons recommended by, 3793, 4189, 4251, 4707; his man, 3817; pardon to brother of, 4744, 4754.
Oremnde, Mount, seignory called, 5348.
Orney—Orny. See Urney, co. Cav.
Orney—Orrey. See Urey, King's co.
O'Roaghan, Donald bane, pardon, 4016.
O'Roan, persons of the name pardoned, 4726, 4711, 5489.
O'Rodan, alias Ussyon, Hugh, pardon, [illegible].
O'Rodane, Ony, pardon, [illegible].
O'Roddeehan — Rodeghan — Roedeghan, persons of the name pardoned, 4726, 5142.
O'Roddir, Shane, pardon, 5418.
O'Roddy — Roddie, persons of the name pardoned, 4616, 4807, 6761.
O'Rodeghan — Roedeghan. See O'Roddechan.
O'Roen, persons of the name pardoned, 5402, 6646, 6664.
O'Roerke. See O'Rourke.
O'Rogan, persons of the name pardoned, 6483.
O'Roghan, Dermot and Donogh, pardon, 6615, 6766.
Oroghor, co. Cav., 4254.
O'Roircke—Roirk—Roirke. See O'Rourke.
Orolle, co. Rosc., [illegible].
O'Rome, Daniel, pardon, [illegible].
O'Ronan, Wm., 6123.
 " others of the name pardoned, [illegible], 6171, [illegible], [illegible], 6434, 6627.
O'Ronayne, Wm., pardon, 4487.
Orone, Dermott, pardon, [illegible].
O'Roney, Hugh, pardon, [illegible].
O'Ronfile, Phelim, pardon, 3817.
Oronoone, Owen, pardon, [illegible].
O'Rone—Ronee—Ronow—Ronowe, persons of the name pardoned, [illegible], [illegible], 5151, 5156, [illegible], 4702, 4749, [illegible], [illegible], [illegible], [illegible], [illegible].
O'Rory, persons of the name pardoned, [illegible], 6615.
O'Rorke, Edm., pardon, [illegible].
O'Rorie, Laughlen oge, pardon, [illegible].
O'Rorke—O'Rorke. See O'Rourke.
O'Rotarke, John, pardon, 5462.
O'Rourcke. See O'Rourke.
O'Rourdane, Dermod and Donoghe, pardon, [illegible].
O'Rourke — Roerke — Roircke — Roirk — Roirke — Rorike — Rorke — Rourcke — Rourk — Roirck — Rowerk — Rowirk — Rowrcke — Rowrk — Rowrke — Royrke — Ruairc — Ruirk — Rwark — Rwarke — Rwirk — Rwrke — Rwirk — Rwarck — Rwarke — Rwrke — Owrarke — Owrourke:
 " Bernard or Brian, late captain of Breny O'Rourke, 1812.
 " Brian or Bernard (knight), chief of his name, appointed captain, 1812; pardon, 1816, 4786, 4789; surrender of his country, 4689; commissions, 3687, 4783, 4746; pardon to his followers, 4790–4822, 4827; protection to come to lord deputy, 4880; pardon to his daughters, 5448.
 " Brian or Bernard, appointed tanist of O'Rourke's country, [illegible]; pardon, [illegible].
 " Brian oge, excepted from general pardon, 6112.
 " Brian, attainted, [illegible].
 " Conarius, pardon, 1814.
 " Donell, pardon, 6764.
 " Hugh oge (of Drumahaire), pardon, 4797, 5448.
 " Phelim, priest, pardon, [illegible].
 " Teige (of Leitrim), excepted from general pardon, 5115.
 " Tiernan, pardon, 1816, 4784, 5749.
 " others of the name pardoned, [illegible], [illegible], [illegible], [illegible], [illegible], [illegible], 4702, 4687, 4252, [illegible], 4676, 4647, 4714, 4784, 4789–4, 4797, [illegible], [illegible], 4877, 5423, 5429–33, 5474, 5486, [illegible], [illegible], [illegible], [illegible], [illegible], 5468, 5477, 5480, [illegible], 6114, 6117, [illegible], [illegible], [illegible], [illegible], [illegible], [illegible], [illegible].
 " country of, [illegible], [illegible], [illegible].
O'Rowane, alias O'Morchoe, Murtogh, pardon, 6434.
O'Rowarty, Donell grana, pardon, 6761.
O'Rowe, Wm. (in Youghal), 5180.
O'Rowerk. See O'Rourke.
O'Rowghan—Rowhane:
 " Henry, death of, [illegible].
 " others of the name pardoned, 4784, 4869.
O'Rowhan, sir Dennys, priest, pardon, [illegible].
O'Rowirk. See O'Rourke.
O'Rowne, Shane, pardon, [illegible].
O'Rowneе, James, pardon, 6517.
Orowpon, Edm., vicar of Tharragh, Meath, [illegible].
O'Rowrcke — Rowrk — Rowrke. See O'Rourke.

INDEX TO FIANTS—ELIZABETH.

O'Rayn, Donald Eglamsy, pardon, [illegible].
O'Reynian, Dairoost, pardon, [illegible].
O'Reyrk—Royrk. *See* O'Rourke.
Orpe—Orphie, James, [illegible], [illegible].
Orrery, co. Cork. *See* Oryrry.
Orrior. *See* Orier.
Orrues, co. Mayo, barony of (Erris), [illegible].
Orrye—Orryer. *See* Orier.
O'Rruire. *See* O'Rourke.
O'Rsanan, Bryne, pardon, [illegible].
O'Ruayrke, Shane bruyo, pardon, [illegible].
O'Ruddan, persons of the name pardoned, [illegible], [illegible].
O'Ruddy—Ruddie:
„ William, house in Trim, 1714.
„ others of the name pardoned, [illegible], 6477, [illegible], [illegible].
O'Rugheis, David, pardon, [illegible].
Orughlin (co. Car. ?), [illegible].
O'Ruirdane, Teige ogo, pardon, [illegible].
O'Ruirk. *See* O'Rourke.
O'Rushe, persons of the name pardoned, [illegible], [illegible].
O'Rayne, Walter, pardon, [illegible].
O'Rwan, Shane, pardon, 1478.
O'Rwark. *See* O'Rourke.
O'Rwdan, Shane, pardon, [illegible].
O'Rwerke—Rwirk—Rwirke—Rwoirk. *See* O'Rourke.
O'Rwollen, Edm. oge, pardon, [illegible].
O'Rwrock—Rworke—Rwrke. *See* O'Rourke.
O'Ryede, Moroghe, pardon, [illegible].
O'Ryan—Rian—Riane—Ryane:
„ Art m'Art and twenty others of the name, attainted, [illegible].
„ Ferginanim, attainted, [illegible].
„ Onin m'Henry, slain in rebellion, [illegible].
„ Owen m'Moleshlin (of Gurtie), pardon, [illegible]; attainted, [illegible].
„ others of the name pardoned, [illegible], [illegible], [illegible], 1087, 1417, 1617, [illegible], [illegible], 1673, [illegible].
„ country of, [illegible]. *See* Farrin O'Ryan, [illegible].
O'Ryddy—Rydy, John and Wm., pardon, [illegible], [illegible].
O'Ryelle, Maloghlin duff, pardon, [illegible].
Oryell. *See* Oriell.
O'Ryelye, Cahier, English liberty, [illegible].
O'Ryerdane alias Dorive, Dermod, pardon, [illegible].
Oryers country, co. Down, [illegible], [illegible].
O'Rygny. *See* O'Rigny.
O'Rylan, John, pardon, [illegible].
O'Rylo, Tho., pardon, [illegible].
O'Ryne, Conoghor and Donogh, pardon, [illegible], [illegible].
O'Rynoy, Edmund, pardon, [illegible], [illegible].
O'Ryodde, Tho., pardon, [illegible].
O'Ryerdan—Ryerdane. *See* O'Riordan.
Oryrry. *See* Orier.
Oryrry, co. Cork, barony of (Orrery), [illegible].
O'Ryurdane. *See* O'Riordan.
O'Sallve—Saylve, Dermod and Morrogh, pardon, [illegible].
O'Sallo, Donoghe, pardon, [illegible].
O'Sanoghan—Sanoghane—Sannaghan, persons of the name pardoned, [illegible], [illegible], [illegible]. *See* O'Shanaghan.
O'Sawne—Sawane, persons of the name pardoned, [illegible], [illegible].
O'Sawrn—Sawrne, persons of the name pardoned, [illegible].
O'Saylve. *See* O'Sallve.
Osberistown—Osberston—Osberteston—Osbertiston—Osbertowne—Hosberston (Osberstown, co. Kild.), [illegible], [illegible], [illegible], [illegible], [illegible], [illegible], [illegible].
„ S. Bride's Church, near, [illegible].
Osborne, Robert, authority to impress hay, 4081.
O'Scalain—Scalyn, Dowagh and Malachy, pardon, [illegible].
O'Scandlon, Tho., pardon, [illegible].
O'Scanell. *See* O'Scannell.
O'Scanlan—Scanlane—Skanlaine—Skanlan—Skanlane—Skanlaine—Skanlon, persons of the name pardoned, [illegible], [illegible], 4714, [illegible], [illegible], [illegible], [illegible], [illegible], [illegible], [illegible], [illegible], [illegible], [illegible], [illegible], [illegible], [illegible], [illegible], [illegible], [illegible], [illegible], [illegible].
O'Scannell—Scanell—Scanill—Scannill—Skanill—Skannell, persons of the name pardoned, [illegible], [illegible], [illegible], [illegible], [illegible], [illegible].
O'Scopolane, Daniel, pardon, [illegible].
O'Schalain, Cormac, pardon, [illegible].
O'Schoe, Donogh, pardon, [illegible].
Oscolan, [illegible].
O'Scollo, Murrogh, pardon, [illegible].
O'Scollen, Donell, pardon, [illegible].
O'Scolly—Scollie:
„ persons of the name pardoned, [illegible], [illegible], [illegible], [illegible].
„ *See* O'Skully.
Osconell, Dermod, pardon, 4764.
O'Scott, Gillaglasse, pardon, [illegible].

O'Scully, Dermod and Morogh, pardon, 6489, 6632.
O'Seaghnase, Teige, pardon, 4654.
O'Seagusnasie, Donogh, pardon, 6407.
O'See, Rychard, pardon, 3087.
O'Senko, Brian, pardon, 5783.
O'Seoye, Conochwro, pardon, 2283.
O'Sele, James, surgeon, murder of, 1568.
" others of the name pardoned, 4222.
O'Selive — Soloiva, persons of the name pardoned, 6618.
O'Senaghan—Senechan—Sennaghan — Senighan, persons of the name pardoned, 4654, 5125, 6457, 6140, 6632. See O'Shanaghan.
O'Serie, Farrall, pardon, 6623.
O'Serkoil, Molaghlen, pardon, 6214.
O'Serrie, Neile, pardon, 5773.
O'Serrydane. See O'Sheredan.
O'Servan, Dermot, pardon, 5758.
O'Seyne, Donagh, pardon, 2280.
O'Seyry, John, pardon, 6257.
O'Shaghen, Donogh m'Wm., pardon, 6763.
O'Shaghnes—O'Shaghnesie—Shaghnishe—Shaghnisie—Shaghnese—Shaughnessy—Shaghnessy:
" Dermicius or Darby: O'Shaghnes, appointed seneschal of his country, 1778; pardon, 3763.
" Dermot (of Gort), pardon, 6645.
" John (of Gort), pardon, 3871, 4680.
" others of the name pardoned, 2488, 2809, 3089, 4280, 4280, 4471, 4717, 5009, 6447, 5818, 6408, 6477, 6478.
" country of, 1778.
O'Shaignes, John, priest, pardon, 4662.
O'Shallon, Gillaglasse, pardon, 4587.
O'Shallowe, Gilpatrick and Wm., pardon, 6483, 6702.
O'Shalon, Brian, pardon, 6098.
O'Shanacan, Derbye, pardon, 3484.
O'Shanaghan—Shanechane—Shanaghane—Shanahan — Shanechan — Shaneghan — Shanighan — Shanihan — Shannaghan—Shannechane — Shannaghane — Shannaghane — Shanohan, persons of the name pardoned, 1749, 3106, 3408, 3377, 3830, 3647-8, 4683, 4683, 4784, 4838, 5145, 6170, 6173, 6482, 6484, 6477, 6478, 6518, 6623, 6634, 6537, 6765, 6779. See also O'Senaghan, O'Shanaghan, O'Shanaghan.
O'Shanen, Connor and Wm., pardon, 6808.
O'Shanchan—Shanchane:
" Donogh, priest, pardon, 6827.
" others of the name pardoned, 4834, 6507.
O'Shanechan—Shonechane — Shaneghan — Shanighan—Shanihan. See O'Shanaghan.
O'Shannesan, Donill, pardon, 4634.
O'Shannaghan — Shannechane — Shanneghane — Shannaghane — Shannihan. See O'Shanaghan.
O'Sharvan, Dermot, pardon, 6477.
O'Shaughan, Owen, pardon, 6323.
O'Shaughnes. See O'Shaghnes.
O'Shavane, Tho., pardon, 6477.
O'Shavine, Wm., pardon, 6485.
O'Shea—Shee—She, persons of the name pardoned, 1863, 1880, 2883, 3828, 3866, 4370, 4334, 4458, 4618, 4617, 4780, 4744, 4781, 4833, 5102, 5144, 5294, 5488, 5553, 5683, 6108, 6123, 6172, 6173, 6309, 6452, 6468, 6467, 6519, 6521-2, 6524, 6528, 6534, 6553, 6564-6, 6569, 6571, 6576-7, 6583, 6621, 6646, 6706, 6764, 6772.
O'Sheane, Morris, pardon, 6170.
O'Sheaghane, Thady or Teig, pardon, 4444.
O'Sheaghnesse. See O'Shaghnes.
O'Sheahan, Moriagh, pardon, 6173.
O'Sheahe, Edm., pardon, 6149.
O'Sheall—Sheale, persons of the name pardoned, 6145, 6484, 6618.
O'Shean Oughan, Dermot, pardon, 2746.
O'Sheaughan — Sheaughaine — Sheanteghane, persons of the name pardoned, 854, 4477, 4851.
O'Shearane, Farrall, pardon, 4677.
O'Shearhie, Teig, pardon, 6871.
O'Sheathe, Thomas, pardon, 3078.
O'Sheghan—Sheghaine—Sheghane—Shehan—Shehane—Sheeghan, persons of the name pardoned, 3058, 4407, 6466, 6467, 6478, 6808, 6878, 6762.
O'Shehoghane, Donell and John, pardon, 4683, 6863.
O'Shehie—Sheiy, persons of the name pardoned, 4736, 6229, 6519.
O'Sheighan—Sheighane—Sheihane, persons of the name pardoned, 4281, 5847, 6488.
O'Sheile—Sheill—Sheile — Sheyle — Sheyll, persons of the name pardoned, 183, 683, 5770, 6183, 6488, 6863.
O'Sheilie—Sheillie—Sheiley, persons of the name pardoned, 6481, 6484, 6623.
O'Sheine — Shein, persons of the name pardoned, 4729, 4814, 4997, 6465, 6467, 6483.
O'Sheile. See O'Sheile.
O'Sheiley. See O'Sheilie.
O'Shelly—Shellie, persons of the name pardoned, 6178, 6761.
O'Shelon, Hugh, pardon, 6409.

INDEX TO FIANTS.—ELIZABETH.

O'Sheone, Tho., pardon, 6482.
O'Sheneloge, James, pardon, 1871.
O'Shenaghan. *See* O'Shenaghan.
O'Shenane, Shane, pardon, 6647.
O'Shenghan, Ferrall, pardon, 6567.
O'Shene, Tho., pardon, 4467.
O'Shenesane, Hugh, pardon, 1486.
O'Shenaghan — Shenaghan — Shenechan — Shenaghane — Shenchane, persons of the name pardoned, 985, 1831, 2681, 3082, 4168, 4386-7, 5303.
O'Shenan, Patr., pardon, 6360.
O'Sheoghan, Teig, pardon, 1894.
O'Sherin, Laghlin, pardon, 6636.
O'Sherdan — Sherdane, Coheneghi and Shane, pardon, 1898.
O'Sheredan — Sheredane — Sheridan — Sheridane — Sheriddane — Sheriden — Serydane — Shirdan — Shiridan — Shiridane — Shyredan — Shredane:
Hugh duff, chief of his nation, pardon, 4922.
Wm. (of the Haigh), called O'Sheredan, pardon, 5591.
others of the name pardoned, 1446, 4815, 4861-2, 5145, 5406, 5602, 5792, 5788, 6808, 6804, 6520, 6838, 4794.
O'Sheren. *See* O'Sherin.
O'Sheridan — Sheridane — Sheriddane — Sheridon. *See* O'Sheredan.
O'Sherin — Sheren, persons of the name pardoned, 5636, 1523.
O'Sheriell, Cahill, clerk, pardon, 4165.
O'Shernan, Dermod, pardon, 6823.
O'Sheman, Pate., pardon, 6839.
O'Sheil, Edmond and Walter, pardon, 579, 2295.
O'Shevan, Coneghor, pardon, 6718.
O'Shewan, Donell, pardon, 5229.
O'Shey, persons of the name pardoned, 3398, 4318, 5521, 6589, 6878.
O'Sheyle — Sheyll. *See* O'Sheile.
O'Sheyn — Sheyne, persons of the name pardoned, 4836, 5225, 3495, 6703.
O'Shaighane, Dermot, pardon, 4444.
O'Shigan, Dairmod, pardon, 6871.
O'Shieghan — Shieghane, persons of the name pardoned, 6496, 6871.
O'Shiell — Shiells — Shyell — Shyelle:
Cormock, surgeon, pardon, 6574, 6816.
Hugh, surgeon, pardon, 6574, 6816.
Rory, surgeon, pardon, 6574, 6818.
others of the name pardoned, 480, 4563, 4868, 6039, 6074, 6816, 6826.
O'Shielly, John, pardon, 2775.
O'Shighan — Shighane — Shihan — Shihane, persons of the name pardoned, 3678, 4744, 4781, 4784, 4888, 5456, 5487, 5186, 6018, 5656, 6871.
O'Shighrowe, Dermaghe, pardon, 6473.
O'Shihan — Shihane. *See* O'Shighan.
O'Shilie, Wm. and Wm. oge, pardon, 4719, 2764.
O'Shileagher, Tho., licence to make aqua vitæ, 5063.
O'Shilishan, Tho., pardon, 5043.
O'Shill, Nich., pardon, 4864.
O'Shillie, Edm., pardon, 6928.
O'Shineghan, Gilluse, pardon, 1858.
O'Shiridan — Shiredan — Shirodane — Shiridane. *See* O'Sheredan.
O'Shirin, persons of the name pardoned, 3406.
O'Shirikane, Maurus and Teige, pardon, 5761.
O'Shirine — Shirin, persons of the name pardoned, 2106, 3834, 4807.
O'Shishenan, Rich., attainder of, 3317.
O'Shissane, Connoghor and Donogh, pardon, 5694, 5838.
O'Sholovan — Sholovan. *See* O'Sullivan.
O'Shoughan, Neaflagh, pardon, 6483.
O'Shoulyvan. *See* O'Sullivan.
O'Shourt, Mohono, pardon, 4830.
O'Shovlovan. *See* O'Sullivan.
O'Shragane, Teige, pardon, 5615.
O'Shrahane, Teige, pardon, 5814.
O'Shrishane, Rorie, pardon, 6316.
O'Shrihane, Donell, pardon, 6818.
O'Shyaghane, Wm., pardon, 4462.
O'Shyell — Shyelle. *See* O'Shiell.
O'Shymon, Donogh, pardon, 6573.
O'Shymoghan, Henry and Teige, pardon, 5865.
O'Shyne, Wm., pardon, 6506.
O'Shyredan. *See* O'Sheredan.
O'Shyry, Henry, pardon, 6763.
O'Siall, persons of the name pardoned, 6632.
O'Siestie, Morice, pardon, 4925.
O'Sigall, Dairmod, pardon, 4816.
O'Siel, persons of the name pardoned, 6565.
O'Siredane. *See* O'Sheredan.
O'Sirin, Shane, pardon, 4674.
O'Sismane — Sysnane, persons of the name pardoned, 6152, 6686.
O'Skahain, Donogh, pardon, 4736.
O'Skelyn, John, pardon, 5902.
O'Skerikan, Dermod, pardon, 5063.
O'Skanell. *See* O'Scannell.
O'Skanlahe, Maurice, pardon, 5636.
O'Skanlan — Skanlaine — Skanlane — Skanlaine — Skanlon. *See* O'Scanlan.
O'Skannell. *See* O'Scannell.
O'Skeghan, Gillduff, alias Molaghlin, pardon, 5029.

INDEX TO FIANTS—ELIZABETH.

O'Skelly, John, pardon, 2943.
O'Skeveyn, Connoghor, pardon, 6871.
O'Skeyvine, Shane, pardon, 6478.
O'Skimmoghan, Dermod, pardon, 6814.
O'Skiterin, Fearrall and James, pardon, 6609.
O'Skuaby, Carbry, pardon, 6652.
O'Skolly—Skollie—Skolley, persons of the name pardoned, 3523, 4488, 4741, 6465, 6478, 6811, 6871, 6798, 6762.
Oskott, Hugh roo, pardon, 6481.
O'Skully—Skullie, persons of the name pardoned, 4684, 4745, 6814, 6811, 6633.
O'Skyain, John, clerk, pardon, 6448.
O'Sladdy, Patr., pardon, 4812.
O'Slattery, Dermod and Donogh, pardon, 3867, 6620.
O'Slaterie. See O'Slattery.
O'Slattery, Donoghe, pardon, 4871.
O'Slattery—Slatterye—Slatterie, persons of the name pardoned, 2739, 3041, 4763, 6372, 6814, 6425, 6444, 6482, 6798, 6714.
O'Slattery, Donell oge, pardon, 6482.
Osney—Oseney—Osney (near Oxford) abbey, possessions leased, 394, 3588, 4062.
O'Soghlaghahane, Cale and Rory, pardon, 4678.
O'Solochan, Brien, pardon, 6699.
O'Solevan—Solevan—Solivan—Solivane—Solivane. See O'Sullivan.
O'Sollaghan, Shane, pardon, 6142.
O'Solovan—Solyvan. See O'Sullivan.
O'Sonaghan, Odo, English liberty, 114.
O'Soolahan persons of the name pardoned, 4381.
O'Soroghan, Donell oge, pardon, 4714.
O'Sorcle, Donogh, pardon, 1747.
O'Soulyvan. See O'Sullivan.
O'Sovaine, Wm., pardon, 6834.
O'Sovan, Hugh and Rich., pardon, 6466.
O'Sowan, Hugh, pardon, 6428.
O'Sowlevaine — Sowlevan — Sowlevane — Sowlivan—Sowlivane. See O'Sullivan.
O'Sowlighan, Gillereewe, pardon, 6844.
O'Sowloo, Donogh, pardon, 314.
O'Sowlyvan. See O'Sullivan.
O'Spallan — Spalain — Spalan—Spallane — Spallon:
„ Moritagh, clerk, pardon, 4084.
„ others of the name pardoned, 1694, 3880, 4321, 4514, 4609, 4612, 4688, 6772.
O'Spallan —Spallane — Spalain — Spalan — Spalane—Spallayn, persons of the name pardoned, 1864, 1865, 2091, 2394, 3637, 3621, 4108, 4132, 6378, 5461, 6486, 4614, 6619, 6875, 6628, 6695.
O'Spallian, Molaughlin, pardon, 4489.
O'Spillan—Spillane, persons of the name pardoned, 2962, 3078, 5163, 4612.
O'Spollane, Donogh, pardon, 6494.
O'Sreighan, Teige, pardon, 6798.
Ossarie. See Ossory.
Osse, co. Gal., 6447.
Ossency. See Osney.
Ossorie—Ossory. See Ossory.
Osserye, Edm. m'Bryan, pardon, [illegible]
Ossney. See Osney.
Ossory—Ossarie—Ossery—Ossorie—Osserie:
„ country of, 169, 765, 1580, 2872, 3668, 5820, 6428, 6748, 6794.
„ (upper), 807, 945, 1714, 2279, 3074, 4012, 4788, 4828; martial law in, 1829, 4049; captain of, appointed, 1467; united to Queen's co., 4649.
„ earl of. See Ormond, earl of.
„ (upper), baron of. See Upper Ossory.
„ bishop of (John Thonery), commission, 164–7.
„ „ Christopher Gaffney, alienations by, 1844, 4682; pardon, 1617; commissions, 3117, 5454.
„ „ Nicholas Walsh, commission, 5942. See Walshe.
„ dean of, 4129.
„ archdeacon of, 1617.
„ chancellor of, 1617.
„ treasurer of S. Canice, 4872.
„ official of, 5491.
„ diocese, 1658, 5451; presentations in, 5495, 6144, 6123, 6498, 4614, 6605, 6715, 6780, 6771.
O'Streffan, Teig, pardon, 4698.
O'Suee, Nele, pardon, 1878.
O'Suleian. See O'Sullivan.
O'Sulaghan — Saleghane, persons of the name pardoned, 4649.
O'Sulovan—Sulivan. See O'Sullivan.
O'Sullaghan, Moriertagh, pardon, 6654.
O'Sullivan — Sheolevan—Sholevan—Shoulyvan—Showlevan—Solevan—Solevan—Solivan—Solivane—Sollivane—Solovan—Solyvan —Soolyvan —Sowlevaine—Sowlevan — Sowlevane — Sowlivan — Sowlivane — Sowlyvan—Suleian—Sulevan —Sulivan —Sullevan—Sullivain—Solyvaine—Swolevan —Swolivaine — Swolivan — Swollevan — Swollevane — Swilivaine — Swilivan — Swilivane — Swilivan — —Swillevane—Swillevant — Swillivan — Swillivane —

INDEX TO FIANTS—ELIZABETH.

O'Sullivan :
Swillivant — Swillovannt — Swillowan — Swillowane — Swillnan — Swilliwan — Swilliwant — Swillyvane — Swillywan—Swlovan—Swlivan—Swilivain—Swilivan — Swilivane—Swilyvan—Swllywane — Swlyvan — Swollivane—Swolovane—Swolivan —Swollovan — Swollyvan — Swollywan — Swylevan — Swylovant — Swylivan — Swyllovan — Swyllyvan — Swylwan — Swylyvan — Swylywan :
— Swoghe or Keogh, pardon, [illegible], [illegible], [illegible].
— Dermot (of Dunkeran), pardon, [illegible], 2911.
— Dermot calango, pardon, [illegible].
— Dermot m'Fynynalias M'Anahar, pardon, 1324.
— Donald : O'Sullivan More, pardon, [illegible].
— Donell : O'S. More, excepted from pardon, 6772.
— Donell : O'S. Bear, pardon, 6911 ; excepted from pardon, 6772.
— Donell (of Carrignessy), pardon, [illegible], 6761.
— Donell (of Bearhaven), esq., pardon, [illegible].
— Donell, alias Fuohe ny Carty, pardon, 6811.
— Owen (of Dunkerran), pardon, [illegible], 2941 ; O'S. More, 4812, [illegible].
— Owen, knt. : O'S. Bear, pardon, [illegible], [illegible], [illegible] ; pardons to his tenants, [illegible] ; grant of his rent charge due to earl of Desmond, [illegible].
— Owen (of Carrignessy), esq., pardon, [illegible].
— Philip (of Ardea), pardon, [illegible].
— others of the name pardoned, [illegible], [illegible], [illegible], [illegible], [illegible], [illegible], [illegible], 2750, [illegible], [illegible], [illegible], [illegible], 4518–19, [illegible], [illegible], [illegible], [illegible], [illegible], [illegible], [illegible], [illegible], [illegible], [illegible], 4764, [illegible], [illegible], [illegible], [illegible], [illegible], [illegible], [illegible], [illegible], [illegible], [illegible], [illegible], [illegible], 6179, 6447, [illegible], [illegible], [illegible], [illegible], [illegible], [illegible], [illegible], [illegible], [illegible], [illegible], [illegible], [illegible], [illegible], 6701, 6702, 6704, 6770.

O'Sullivan Bear. See Owen O'Sullivan, knt., and Donell O'Sullivan.
O'Sullivan More. See Donald, Donell, and Owen O'Sullivan.
O'Summy, Teig, pardon, 6471.
O'Sunny, persons of the name pardoned, 6467, 6471.
O'Susan, Donagh and Teige, pardon, [illegible].
O'Svy, Tho., pardon, 4752, 6434.
O'Swally, Donell, pardon, 6714.
O'Swolovan — Swolivaine — Swolivan — Swolloman—Swolovan. See O'Sullivan.
O'Swonie, Dorio, pardon, 6607.
O'Sworie, William, pardon, 14, 615.
O'Swoio, Donoughe, pardon, [illegible].
O'Swllovane—Swilivaine—Swilivan—Swillivane — Swillovan — Swillovane — Swillovant—Swillovannt—Swillowan — Swillowant—Swillivan—Swillivane—Swillivant — Swillyvane — Swlovan — Swilivane — Swllywane. See O'Sullivan.
O'Swivan, Donell, pardon, 6476.
O'Swolovane — Swolivan — Swollovan — Swollyvan—Swollywan. See O'Sullivan.
O'Sword, William, pardon, 461.
O'Sworth, Shane, pardon, [illegible].
O'Swylovan — Swylovant — Swylivan — Swylluvan—Swylwan. See O'Sullivan.
O'Swynie, persons of the name pardoned, 6467, [illegible], 6471.
O'Sydan, Hugh, pardon, [illegible].
O'Syoll, Conor, pardon, 4777.
O'Syridan—Syridon—Syrrydane, persons of the name pardoned, [illegible], [illegible], [illegible].
O'Sysnane. See O'Sianane.
O'Syvane, Morris, pardon, [illegible].
O'Syvaine, Donell and Manus, pardon, 6741.
O'Tagan, Nich., pardon, [illegible].
O'Taginy, Patr., pardon, [illegible].
O'Taipe, Dermot m'Cormocke O'Dowde, pardon, [illegible].
O'Tarpy, Shane and Tho. oge, pardon, [illegible].
O'Tarran, Wm., pardon, [illegible].
O'Tarrane, Wm. duff, pardon, [illegible].
O'Tarrolan, Donogh, pardon, 6114.
O'Taughan, Philip, pardon, [illegible].
O'Taulan, Teig, pardon, [illegible].
O'Tawragh, Conoghor m'Teig, pardon, [illegible].
O'Tearney, Riccard, pardon, 6077.
O'Teddie or O'Teddile, Donogh, pardon, 6781.
O'Teig—Teige, persons of the name pardoned, [illegible], [illegible], [illegible], [illegible], [illegible], [illegible], [illegible], 4647, [illegible], [illegible], 4777, [illegible], [illegible], [illegible], [illegible], [illegible], 6477, [illegible], [illegible], [illegible], [illegible], [illegible], [illegible], [illegible].
O'Teiggart, James, pardon, [illegible].
Oteland, instructions at, 1409.
O'Tait, Mac, pardon, [illegible].

INDEX TO FIANTS—ELIZABETH.

O'Termane, Tho., pardon, [illegible].
O'Te[illegible]mane, Wm., pardon, [illegible].
O'Terne, Brian, pardon, [illegible].
O'Terrey, Gillegluff Phillips, pardon, [illegible].
O'Tevan, Owen, pardon, [illegible].
O'Teyman—Teymane, persons of the name pardoned, [illegible], [illegible], [illegible].
O'Tharin, M'Loghlin, pardon, [illegible].
O'Tharne, Donial duffe, pardon, [illegible].
O'Theall, Shyhy, pardon, [illegible].
O'Thekin, Dermod, pardon, [illegible], [illegible].
O'Thole. See O'Toole.
O'Thoman, Wm., pardon, [illegible].
O'Thome, Dermot, pardon, [illegible].
O'Thomye, Thady and Tho., pardon, [illegible].
O'Thonher, Thady, pardon, [illegible].
O'Thorly, Conoghor, pardon, [illegible].
O'Thum, persons of the name pardoned, [illegible].
O'Tierne, persons of the name pardoned, [illegible], [illegible].
O'Tiernan, Donell, pardon, [illegible].
O'Tierne, Teig, pardon, [illegible].
O'Tierey, Dermod and Gillecoscave, pardon, [illegible].
O'Tinan, Rory, pardon, [illegible].
O'Tine, Donell oge, pardon, [illegible].
Otoaffe, Walter Ommlone, pardon, [illegible].
O'Toddile or Teddile, Donogh, pardon, [illegible].
O'Toell. See O'Toole.
O'Togher, persons of the name pardoned, [illegible], [illegible], [illegible].
O'Toghie, Shane, pardon, [illegible].
O'Tohile, Patr., pardon, [illegible].
O'Tohill. See O'Toole.
O'Tohmell, Edm., pardon, [illegible].
O'Tohy, Teige: O'Tohy, pardon, [illegible].
O'Toighell, Edm., pardon, [illegible].
O'Toill. See O'Toole.
O'Tolan, Owen grome O'Loghar m'Manus duffe, [illegible].
O'Tole. See O'Toole.
O'Toman—Tomane, persons of the name pardoned, [illegible], [illegible], [illegible].
O'Tomelty, Morghe, pardon, [illegible].
O'Tome, Melaghelan, pardon, [illegible].
O'Tomolle, Donagh, pardon, [illegible].
O'Tomane, Melaghlin, pardon, [illegible].
O'Toohicke, Shane, pardon, [illegible].
O'Toole—Thole—Toell—Tohill—Toill—Tole—Towell—Towhill—Towle—Towll—Toohill—Twle:
,, Art, pardon to son of, [illegible].
,, Alexander m'Feagh (of Corrickrose), pardon, [illegible], [illegible].
,, Barnaby (son and heir of Luke), wardship, [illegible]; livery, [illegible]; pardon, [illegible]; wardship of his heir, [illegible].
,, Dermick, messuage in Trim, [illegible].
,, Edm. (of Carone), pardon to him and his followers, [illegible].
,, Edm. (of co. Gal.), pardon, [illegible], [illegible], [illegible].
,, Feagh or Luke. See Luke.
,, Feagh (son of Barnaby), wardship, [illegible].
,, Ferall (of Powerscourt), pardon, [illegible], [illegible].
,, Hugh mac Edmond, pardon, [illegible], [illegible], [illegible].
,, John macFeagh (of Castlerudderry) pardon, [illegible], [illegible].
,, Luke or Feagh (of Castlekevin), pardon, 117, 170, [illegible]; sheriff of co. Dublin, [illegible]; pardon for him and his men, [illegible]; wardship of his heir, [illegible]; livery to heir, [illegible].
,, Owny nyn Feagh, wife of Phelim m'Feagh O'Byrne, pardon, [illegible], [illegible].
,, Phelim (of Powerscourt), pardon, [illegible], [illegible], [illegible], [illegible], [illegible], [illegible]; sheriff of co. Dublin, [illegible].
,, Phelim (of Fartry and Castlekevin), pardon, [illegible], [illegible], [illegible], [illegible].
,, Rose or Rois, wife of Feagh m'Hugh, pardon, [illegible], [illegible], [illegible].
,, Shane m'Feagh (of Omalle), pardon, [illegible], [illegible].
,, Terence, grant of manor of Powerscourt, [illegible].
,, Theobald (in co. Gal.), pardon, [illegible].
,, others of the name pardoned, [illegible], [illegible], [illegible], [illegible], [illegible], 641, [illegible].
,, See Toole, Tole.
O'Tooles, rebels, [illegible].
O'Torme, Shane, pardon, [illegible].
O'Torne, Cahell, pardon, [illegible].
O'Toughert, Donald, pardon, [illegible].
O'Tougher, Dermot and Mulreany, pardon, [illegible], [illegible].
O'Toughill, Morrish and Shane, pardon, [illegible].
O'Towell. See O'Toole.
O'Towere, Connor, pardon, [illegible].
O'Towghie, Owy, pardon, [illegible].
O'Towhill. See O'Toole.
O'Towkygg, John, pardon, [illegible].

INDEX TO FIANTS.—ELIZABETH.

O'Towle—Towll. See O'Toole.
O'Toyle, sir Owen, commission, 6704.
O'Traine, John, pardon, [illegible].
O'Trasey—Trasie—Trasy, persons of the name pardoned, [illegible], [illegible], [illegible], 6797.
O'Trasse, Thady and Teige, pardon, 970, [illegible].
O'Trasey—Trassye—Trasie, persons of the name pardoned, [illegible], [illegible], 4975, [illegible], [illegible], [illegible], [illegible].
O'Treasy. See O'Trasey.
O'Trauchisen, Maurice, pardon, [illegible].
O'Treughie, Rowland, pardon, [illegible].
O'Trensie, Wm., pardon, [illegible].
O'Trenane, Cahill, priest, pardon, [illegible].
O'Trenan, Morroughe, pardon, [illegible].
O'Trenvahaire, Diermot, pardon, [illegible].
O'Tredane, Teig, pardon, [illegible].
O'Trehi, Teige, pardon, [illegible].
O'Trehie, Donoghue, pardon, [illegible].
O'Treewire, Patr., pardon, [illegible].
O'Treasy, persons of the name pardoned, [illegible], [illegible], 6767.
O'Trewye, Teig m'Wm., pardon, [illegible].
O'Trevaire, persons of the name pardoned, [illegible].
O'Trighan groughe, Shane, pardon, [illegible].
O'Trighie, Daniel, pardon, [illegible].
O'Troddie, Maurice, pardon, [illegible].
O'Trohie, Donald, physician, pardon to daughters, [illegible].
O'Trone, Edm., pardon, [illegible].
O'Trye, Donnogh, pardon, [illegible].
Ottean—Otiyn, Teig and Thady, pardon, [illegible], [illegible].
Otteroske (Wotcreuk), co. Down, [illegible].
O'Tullinellaghe, Davye, pardon, 6517.
O'Tumage, Brian, pardon, [illegible].
O'Tumold, Edm. duff, pardon, [illegible].
O'Tungher, persons of the name pardoned, [illegible].
O'Tuohill. See O'Toole.
O'Twaite, Donnell, pardon, [illegible].
O'Twigher, Donell, pardon, [illegible].
O'Twirtie, Wm. reogh, pardon, 6418.
O'Twie. See O'Toole.
O'Twealan, persons of the name pardoned, [illegible].
O'Twogher, Donogh, pardon, [illegible].
O'Twohell, persons of the name pardoned, [illegible].
O'Twohill, persons of the name pardoned, [illegible], [illegible], [illegible], [illegible], [illegible], [illegible].
O'Twohillane, Conogher, pardon, [illegible].
O'Twohy, Moleyn, pardon, [illegible].
O'Twoill, Rowry, pardon, [illegible].
O'Twomagh, Dermod, pardon, [illegible].
O'Twomy, persons of the name pardoned, [illegible], [illegible], 6611, [illegible].
O'Twonie—Twoey, persons of the name pardoned, [illegible], [illegible], 6571.
O'Tworhan, Conogher and Teig, pardon, [illegible].
O'Twoyll, Gerrot, pardon, [illegible].
O'Tyarne, Molaughlen, pardon, [illegible].
O'Tyon, Tomultagh, pardon, [illegible].
O'Tyorne, Mahowne, pardon, [illegible].
O'Tyorny, persons of the name pardoned, [illegible], [illegible].
O'Tyman, Shane, pardon, [illegible].
O'Tyn, Brian and Moriertagh, pardon, [illegible], [illegible].
O'Tyne, Morriertagh and Shane, pardon, [illegible].
O'Tynine, Wm., pardon, [illegible].
O'Tyosan, Shane, pardon, [illegible].
O'Tyrry, Shane, pardon, [illegible].
O'Tyvnane, Owen, pardon, [illegible].
O'Tywnan, Shane oge, pardon, [illegible].
Oucanty, Mayllyn, pardon, [illegible].
Oughter Raih. See Oughterraih.
Ouman. See Owgan, Wogan.
Oughrestoune. See Owphrystoune.
Oughan, Rob. (of Rathcoffey), pardon, [illegible].
Oughaval, Queen's co. See Oroghavall, Noghavall.
Oughenalty, co. Mon., [illegible].
Oughfrestoun. See Owphryetoune.
Oughnaghtie, co. Mon., [illegible].
Oughteragh, co. Tip., [illegible].
Oughterany, co. Kild. See Oughterrany.
Oughterard, co. Gal., [illegible].
Oughterard—Oughterarde—Outerarde—Outrarde—Owghterard—Woghterard, co. Kild., [illegible], [illegible], 1600, [illegible], [illegible], [illegible], [illegible], [illegible], [illegible], [illegible]; rectory, [illegible], [illegible], [illegible]; presentation to vicarage, 767, [illegible].
Oughterherry, co. Ros. (Uachtar-thire, a district in barony of Boyle. See Annals of Loch Ce), [illegible]. See Oghterthire, Woghterhyre.
Oughterlaigan, co. Tip., [illegible].
Oughterrarde. See Oughterard.
Oughterraih—Oughter Raih—Oughterraih (co. Tip.?), [illegible], [illegible], [illegible].
Oughterrany (Oughterany), co. Kild., [illegible].
Oughtery, co. Clare, [illegible].
Ougterraih. See Oughterraih.
Ouldecorte (Oldcourt, co. Wick.), [illegible].
Oulde Grannge—Grange. See Old Grange.
Ould Rossack, co. Cork (Rossagh), [illegible].
Ouldtowne. See Oldtown.
Oulecordan (recte Oulcredan), co. Louth (Uncircredan), [illegible].
O'Ulmeye, Owye, pardon, [illegible].
Outreboulan, co. Car., [illegible].
Our Lady abbey, co. Tip., [illegible], [illegible], [illegible], [illegible], [illegible].

Oury, co. Car., 1877.
Ouskiagh, co. Tip., 6797.
Outeeardo—Outerardo. See Oughterard.
Ovally, Brian, pardon, 9861.
Ovare, co. Gal., 5826.
O'Vaughere, Philip duf, pardon, 1466.
O'Vayle, Robert, pardon, 5838.
Ovellin, Edm. m'Edmh., pardon, 5489.
Ovendon. See Ovingdon.
O'Venaghan, Connoghur, pardon, 6311.
Ovenstown, co. Kilk. See Owenestone.
Overstown (Ormastowne?), co. Meath, 1809.
Ovine, persons of the name pardoned, 6798.
Ovingdon — Ovendon — Ovington — Ovyngdon:
Giles. See Hovendon.
John, pardon, 3646, 4371.
" Peter, pardon, 3510, 3453.
Ovoghenye, Donell. See O'Ferrall.
Ovrtboyr, co. Gal., 6617.
Ovoman—Ovonne; persons of the name pardoned, 6811.
Ovyngdon. See Ovingdon.
Owl Igin, Tulmaloghe, pardon, 4465.
O'Walshe, Donell m'Donogh, pardon, 6147.
Owallis Inalle. See Owll O'Malle.
Owar, co. Gal., 4797.
Owed, alias Howed, Philip, pardon, 1676.
Owell Iage, pardon, 5151.
Owen, Lynch ennais, pardon, 6547.
Dermot, pardon, 6466.
Donnell, alias M'Keown, pardon, 6466.
Ellen, pardon, 6151, 6615, 6764.
Jone, pardon, 6788.
John, English liberty, 869, 1157; pardon, 4561.
Katherine nyne, pardon, 6431.
More euyn, pardon, 6433.
Nicholas, pardon, 6512, 6709.
Onor ny, pardon, 5167.
Owin m'Gill m'Rory, pardon, 5762.
Rich., pardon, 5517, 6768.
Shane, pardon, 5625.
Shillie ny, pardon, 6467.
Teig m'Donogh Vic, pardon, 5183.
Tirlagh, pardon, 6486.
" or Eugene, 1832.
Owenass, Queen's co. See Owenenasse.
Owenbeg, Queen's co. See Owenaberge.
Owenbeg, co. Tyr. See Avan-na-buyan buy.
Owenduff, co. Wex. See Owenduffe.
Owenestone (Ovenstowne), co. Kilk., rectory, 5962.
Ower, Dermott, pardon, 5244.
" James, pardon, 886.
" John, English liberty, vicar of Ritter, 3878.
" Wm. m'James, pardon, 6646.
Owesh, Rich., pardon, 4467.
Owett, Rich., pardon, 6878, 6898.
Owfrissenne. See Ovphersocine.
Owgan—Ougan:
" David, commission, 795. See Wogan.
" Nicholas (Rathcoffye), commission, 886. See Wogan.
" Nicholas, pardon, 4798.
" Oliver (of Downings), commission, 795, 6160, 4464. See Wogan.
" Rob., pardon, 4326.
Owghny. See Owney.
Owghtered. See Oughterard.
Owghteraght, co. Mon., 1657.
O'Whelans—Whealane, persons of the name pardoned, 6684, 5823.
O'Wheylane, Rory, pardon, 5695.
O'Whilaghan — Whileghan — Whilleghane, persons of the name pardoned, 4466, 5833.
O'Whillin, Donell, pardon, 6168.
O'Whoheran, Teig, pardon, 6163.
O'Whylaghn, Shane, pardon, 1674.
O'Whyleghane, Wm., pardon, 5316.
O'Wilkins, Terence, priest, pardon, 6401.
Owlaw, Donogha m'Shane Y, pardon, 4519.
Owlde Ross. See Old Ross.
Owlemane, Ferrall, pardon, 18.
Owles, co. Mayo, 4961-2.
" Lower (barony of Burrishoole), co. Mayo, 6346.
Owll O'Mallie—Owalle Inalle (barony of Murrisk), co. Mayo, 5346; seneschal of, appointed, 2694.
Owllerie (Orchard), Queen's co., 1278, 1529.
Owlly, co. Lim., 4726.
Owllyghan, Donogh and Philip, pardon, 2340.
Owlorribaykeh, co. Wex., 6647.
Owlorie, co. Wex., 4307, 5547.
Owlrian, Connell, pardon, 4690.
Owlster. See Ulster.
Owltagh, Derby, pardon, 5188.
Owltagh, James, death of, 460.
Owlloye, co. Gal., 5068.
Owlye, co. Cork, 6660.
Owlys (Oola, co. Lim.), rectory, 2669, 3547.
Owmore (Blackwater) river, weirs on, 1667, 2161.
Ownduffe, alias Donodowne (Owenduff, co. Wex.), 3406
Owne int Gal, pardon, 6161.
Ownebage, brook (Owenbeg, Queen's co.), 4793.
Ownenasse river (Owenass, Queen's co.), 6788.
Ownoy, Edm., pardon, 6606.
Owney — Owniby's — Ueny — Owghny — Oynagh, 2908, 3606, 4743, 5906, 5994; lands claimed by earl of Thomond, 5654.

INDEX TO FIANTS—ELIZABETH.

Owney, abbey of (Abington, co. Limerick), [illegible], [illegible]. *See* Woney.
Owny or Onhy O'Mulrian—Owny y Mollo-ran—Ony Mulryan — Owthainmulruan, [illegible], [illegible], [illegible]; to be made shire ground, [illegible].
Owenygallaiss (co. Cav. ?), [illegible].
Ownyn—Owenyne, co. Kilk., [illegible], [illegible].
O'Wolighan, alias Mary, John, pardon, [illegible].
Owphryetowne—Owghfreetowne—Owghfree-towne—Owfrirtowne (Humfrystown, co. Wick. ?), [illegible], [illegible].
Owraghe, Dermot m'Dermot, pardon, [illegible].
Owraght, Shane, pardon, [illegible].
Owranmore. *See* Oranmore.
Owrarke. *See* O'Rourke.
Owre, Gerald, pardon, [illegible].
" James, pardon, [illegible].
Owre, alias Renoghane, Tho., pardon, [illegible].
Owre in O'Flaherty's country, co. Gal., [illegible], [illegible].
Owrey, Edw., pardon, [illegible].
Owrian, co. Clare, [illegible].
Owrourke. *See* O'Rourke.
Owrange (co. Car. or Wex. ?), [illegible].
Owyll, Ross duff ny, pardon, [illegible].
Owynes, James, pardon, [illegible].
Owyr, Donnogh, pardon, [illegible].
Oxmantown—Oxmanton—Oxmonton, Dublin, [illegible], 1311, [illegible], [illegible], [illegible].
Oyewlla. *See* Oyolla.
Oygully, co. Rosc., [illegible].
Oylennorrevir, co. Gal., [illegible].
Oyn, Lighlin oge na, pardon, [illegible].
Oynagh. *See* Owney.
Oyne Cherry river, co. Down, [illegible].
Oyolla—Oyewlla—Oyolowe—Oyoloe, co. Rosc., [illegible], [illegible], [illegible], [illegible].
Oysters, tithe of, [illegible]; customary payment of, [illegible].

Paace. *See* Passe.
Paas. *See* Pace.
Paase. *See* Pace, co. Meath.
Paase. *See* Passe, co. Westm.
Pace—Pase by Clony (Littlepace), co. Dub., [illegible], [illegible], [illegible].
Pace—Passe (Pace), co. Meath, [illegible], [illegible].
Pace. *See* Passe, co. Westm.
Paddingstown, co. Westm. *See* Ballypaden.
Padenston—Padynston (Padinstown), co. Meath, [illegible], [illegible].
Padgett, Walter, grant of a wardship, [illegible].
Padmam, John, pardon, [illegible].
Padynston. *See* Padenston.
Page, Edw., chancellor of Limerick, [illegible].
Pagnam—Paignam, Edm., collector of wine duty in Dublin, [illegible]; grant of fines, [illegible].
Painestown, co. Kild., [illegible].
Painestown—Paynestown (Painestown in par. Colp), co. Meath, [illegible], [illegible].
Painestown—Paynston (Painestown in par. Macetown), co. Meath, 1460.
Painestown—Painston—Paynston, co. Meath, [illegible], [illegible], [illegible], [illegible].
Painestown—Painstowne, co. Westm., [illegible], [illegible], [illegible].
Painestown, co. Car. *See* Painston.
Painestown, co. Louth. *See* Paynestown.
Painestown, co. Meath. *See* Painestown.
Painston — Paynistown — Paynston (Painestown), co. Car., [illegible], [illegible], [illegible], [illegible], [illegible].
Painstown (Painestown), co. Kild., [illegible].
Painston. *See* Painestown, co. Meath.
Painston — Painstowne — Paynston—Paynestown (co. Tip.), [illegible], [illegible], [illegible], [illegible].
Painstowne. *See* Painestown, co. Westm.
Paintor—Paintorn. *See* Paynton.
Paittagon—Paltagoge (Pottigon, co. Donegal), [illegible], [illegible].
Palace. *See* Pallace.
Pale, English, natives of, may receive leases, [illegible], [illegible]; force allotted to repress malefactors in, [illegible]; cess on, [illegible]; main road from, [illegible]; borders of, [illegible].
Paleas (co. Wick. ?), [illegible].
Palen, co. Westm., [illegible].
Paleys. *See* Pallice, co. Lim.
Palgne, Francis (a Frenchman), pardon, [illegible].
Pallice—Palis. *See* Pallice.
Palisboye (King's co. ?), [illegible], [illegible].
Pallah, co. Tip. or Lim., [illegible].
Pallahalonfrey (co. Rosc. ?), [illegible].
Pallsha. *See* Pallice.
Pallace (Pallas). *See* Pallice, co. Cork.
Pallace. *See* Pallis, co. Kerry.
Pallace. *See* Pallice, co. Lim.
Pallace. *See* Pallice, co. Long.
Pallace. *See* Pallice, co. Tip.
Pallace. *See* Pallice, co. Westm.
Pallace more, co. Westm., [illegible].
Pallaicn. *See* Pallice.
Pallardstowne (Pallardstown), co. Cork, [illegible].
Pallas. *See* Pallice.
Pallas, Queen's co. *See* Palloyes.
Pallas Green, co. Lim. *See* Pallyshonreny.
Pallas More, co. Long. *See* Pallismore.
Pallays. *See* Pallice, co. Cork.
Pallcis. *See* Pallice, co. Westm.
Palles. *See* Pallice, co. Lim.
Palles. *See* Pallice, co. Long.
Pallice, Patr., pardon, [illegible].
Palloyes—Palloys (Pallas), Queen's co., [illegible], [illegible], [illegible].

INDEX TO FIANTS—ELIZABETH.

Pallis. *See* Palliece, co. Long.

Pallice — Pallice — Pallase — Palleys — Pallis (Pallas, co. Cork ?), [illegible], [illegible], [illegible], [illegible], [illegible], 6762.

Pallice. *See* Pallis, co. Kerry.

Pallice, co. Kerry, 6602.

Pallice—Pallice—Pallis, King's co., 6424, [illegible], [illegible], [illegible].

Pallice—Palleys—Pallice—Pallace — Pallaice —Pallas—Pallice — Pallis—Palliceb —Pallisco—Pallyce, co. Lim., [illegible], 3476, 3767, [illegible], [illegible], [illegible], [illegible], [illegible], [illegible], [illegible], [illegible], [illegible], [illegible], [illegible], 6178, [illegible], [illegible], 6457, [illegible].

„ grant of castle, &c., 5783.

Pallice (in Munster), 3477, [illegible].

Pallice— Palace — Pallice—Pallis — Pallace — Pallas — Pallic — Pallis (co. Long.), [illegible], [illegible], [illegible], [illegible], [illegible], [illegible], [illegible], [illegible]; escape of prisoner at, [illegible].

Pallice (Pallis), co. Mon., [illegible].

Pallice — Pallace — Pallis (co. Tip. ?), [illegible], [illegible], [illegible], [illegible], 6416, [illegible], [illegible].

Pallice—Pallice—Palisbe — Pallace—Pallris, co. Westm., 1423, 1771, 3776, [illegible], [illegible].

Pallice— Pallaice, co. Wex., 4184, [illegible], [illegible].

Pallice m'tough (co. Lim. ?), [illegible].

Pallis. *See* Pallice, co. Cork.

Pallis, co. Gal., [illegible].

Pallis—Pallice—Pallis — Pallace—Pallice, co. Kerry, [illegible], [illegible], [illegible], [illegible], [illegible], [illegible], [illegible], [illegible], [illegible].

Pallis. *See* Pallice, co. Lim., Long., and Tip.

Pallise—Pallyse, 1451, [illegible]. *See* Ellfuragh of Pallise.

Pallissmore (Pallas More, co. Long.), 4181.

Pallish, [illegible]. *See* Pallice, co. Lim.

Pallis m'Cartymore (Pallis, co. Kerry ?), [illegible].

Pallisse, [illegible]. *See* Pallice, co. Lim.

Pallyce. *See* Pallice, co. Lim.

Pallyshegreny (Pallas Green, co. Lim.), [illegible].

Pallyse. *See* Pallise.

Palmer, Elizabeth, grant, [illegible].

„ Francis, grant, 175.

„ Henry, pardon, 1072.

„ John, pardon, [illegible].

„ Michael (alias Scott), death, 344.

„ Peter, commission, [illegible], judge of Common Bench, [illegible], [illegible].

Palmerston, co. Dub., 1390, 1444, [illegible], [illegible], [illegible]; rectory, [illegible], 3747, [illegible].

Palmerston by Grenock, co. Dub., 847, [illegible], [illegible]; manor, [illegible].

Palmerston, co. Kild., [illegible].

Palmerston, co. Lim., [illegible].

Palmes, Elizabeth, grant of land, 1378, 1544, 1894.

Palrish (co. Lim. ?), 3476.

Palyce, co. Lim., [illegible].

Palyshane (co. Tip. or Lim.), [illegible].

Palyst (co. Long. ?), [illegible].

Pamnyn, Tho., pardon, [illegible].

Pannonia (Hungary ?), king of, [illegible].

Pantings, Rob., [illegible].

Papal provision, benefices obtained by, confirmed, 84, 237.

Papist priest to be punished, [illegible].

Paroke (King's co. ?), 4437.

Paroke (Park, co. Lim.), 6176.

Paroke (co. Wex.), 4418.

Pardon, conditions attached to, 4118, [illegible], [illegible], [illegible], [illegible], [illegible], 4976, [illegible], [illegible], [illegible], [illegible], [illegible], [illegible], 6042, [illegible], 6451, 6461, [illegible], [illegible], 4572, 6617, 6745; conditions of exceptional character, [illegible], [illegible], [illegible]; pardon enrolled and allowed before justices at sessions, 1031; report by law officers on the character of persons pardoned, 1430; pardon inoperative from failure to find sureties, 1016; usual provision omitted when persons known to be answerable, [illegible]; notes illustrating the practice connected with the granting of pardons, &c., [illegible], 1304, 1367, 1423, 1442, 1463, 1471, 1690, 1925-8, 1908, 1814, [illegible], [illegible], [illegible], [illegible], [illegible], [illegible], [illegible], 4211, [illegible], [illegible], 6778; pardon not to be sealed till security given for loyalty, 4204; delayed for fees, [illegible]; lapsed for non-payment of fine, 1737; fine to be paid by person who first pleads the pardon, [illegible], 4487, [illegible], [illegible], &c.; pardons may be granted by earl of Essex in Ulster, [illegible]; persons already pardoned not to benefit by a second pardon, [illegible], 4417, [illegible], [illegible], [illegible], [illegible]; pardon by Perrot not to include offences committed during his government, [illegible], [illegible], [illegible], [illegible], [illegible]; pardon postdated because no sessions had been held to take security, [illegible].

Pardon by Proclamation, 3767, &c. *See* Proclamation.

Pardon (General) to Queen's subjects in co. Mayo, [illegible]; to all dwelling in Tyrone, [illegible]; for the province of Connaught, [illegible]; to inhabitants of O'Cahan's country, [illegible]; to inhabitants of Munster and Thomond, [illegible].

Parish constables, [illegible].

Parish, Rich., pardon, [illegible].

Park—Parke, the (co. Gal.), [illegible], [illegible], [illegible].

Park (co. Kilk. ?) [illegible], [illegible].

Park—Parke, King's co., [illegible], [illegible].

Park, co. Lim. *See* Paroke, Parke.

Park, co. Meath. *See* Parke.

Parkbally — Parkeballye Envyne (Park and Ballinaveny, par. Aghnameadle, co. Tip.), [illegible], [illegible], [illegible], [illegible].

Parkcosscourt, 675.
Parke, (co. Gal. ?) 6467, [illegible].
Parke, Castle of (Castlepark ?), co. Cork. [illegible].
Parke. See Park, co. Gal.
Parke. See Park, King's co., 4153.
Parke, co. Lim., 4152.
Parke (co. Lim. ?), 4734, [illegible], [illegible], 6490.
Parke (Park), co. Meath, grant, 6527.
Parke (Queen's co.), 1357, [illegible], [illegible], 6661.
Parke, co. Tip., [illegible], [illegible], [illegible], [illegible].
Parke (co. Wat. ?) 6748.
Parke, co. Wat., 4713.
Parke, co. Westm., [illegible].
Parke, co. Wex., [illegible].
Parkeballye Eavyne. See Parkbally.
Parkeballye, co. Tip., 6151.
Parkefelde at Trim, co. Meath, 152.
Parke meadow, Duleek, co. Meath, [illegible].
Parkemountain (co. Cork ?), [illegible].
Parken, Henry. See Parkins.
Parkenydalle. See Parknealally.
Parker, John, master of the Rolls, appointed chief serjeant of Connaught, 118; pardon, 134; takes oath of supremacy, 127; commissions, 1[illegible], [illegible], [illegible], [illegible], [illegible], [illegible], [illegible], 375-[illegible], [illegible], [illegible]-1, [illegible], [illegible], [illegible]; license to export wool, 87; leases, [illegible], 5611; premises in his tenure, 1[illegible]1; assignee of, [illegible]; at his death his goods sold in satisfaction of his debts to the crown, 1[illegible].
„ John, a tailor in Dublin, [illegible].
„ John, commission, 4[illegible]7; pardon, [illegible], 4117, [illegible], [illegible]; land in tenure of, 6116.
Parkelogher, co. Wat., [illegible], 5[illegible].
Parkeston—Parkestown, co. Meath, [illegible], [illegible].
Parkestowne — Parkstone (Parkstown), co. Meath, [illegible], [illegible].
Parkfilde, Trim, 55.
Parkins — Parkens, Henry, controller of customs, Drogheda, [illegible], [illegible]; clerk of the ordnance, [illegible].
Parkiswood, co. Wat., 513, 587.
Parkloughter (co. Gal. ?), [illegible]1.
Parknealally—Parkenydalle, co. Cork, 5747, [illegible].
Parkegrove (co. Kilk.), [illegible].
Parkstown, co. Meath. See Parkestowne.
Parkstone. See Parkestowne, co. Meath.
Parle, James, pardon, 641.
„ Thomas, killed, 378.
Parliament, clerk of, appointed, 185, 1942.
„ of 2° Eliz., Roll of members, 185.
„ of 27° Eliz., Roll of members, 4834.
Parliament, lords of, petition for pardon of a poor, 1[illegible].
„ member of, named by charter, 1[illegible].
Parris, Wm., grant, 4[illegible].
Parrishagh (co. Cav. ?), [illegible].
Parrockes—Parrocks (Barronkstown ?), co. Meath, [illegible], 6182.
Parry, Morris, pardon, 6465.
Parrys, George, grant, 1[illegible].
Parselston—Parselistown, co. Westm., [illegible], 6052. See also Parselstowne.
Parsleston, co. Westm., [illegible].
Parson, privileged, 4120, [illegible], [illegible], [illegible].
Parsons, Edw., 6[illegible].
„ Tho., 6[illegible].
„ Wm., surveyor general, [illegible].
Parsonston, co. Kild., 1[illegible], [illegible].
Parsonstone —Parsonston (Parsonstown), co. Meath, 1[illegible], [illegible].
Parsonstown, co. Louth, rectory, 1[illegible], [illegible].
Partan (Portan), co. Meath, [illegible], [illegible].
Partefordeston (Proudfootstown), co. Meath, 1[illegible].
Partie, co. Cav., [illegible].
Partrye (co. Mayo ?), [illegible].
Partrynny (co. Rosc. ?), [illegible].
Party (co. Cav. ?), 4[illegible].
Paryerath, co. Meath, [illegible].
Pase (King's co. ?), [illegible].
Pase. See Passe.
Pase of Kilbride. See Passe.
Passadge (co. Kerry ?), [illegible].
Passage—Passadg, co. Wat., 41[illegible], [illegible].
Passe—Pace—Pass—Pace—Pase (Tyrrellspass, co. Westm.), [illegible], 1[illegible], 1[illegible], 1[illegible], [illegible], [illegible], [illegible], [illegible], [illegible], 4161, [illegible], [illegible], [illegible], [illegible], [illegible], [illegible].
Passe—Passe—Passe—Pace—Pase of Kilbride (Pass of Kilbride, co. Westm.), [illegible], 1[illegible], [illegible], [illegible], [illegible], [illegible].
Passport, license of absence called, [illegible].
Pattermith (Pottlerath ?), co. Kilk., 4[illegible].
Pattockerston, co. Westm., 1[illegible].
Pa[ ]tmoytyne, co. Cav., 4834.
Patrick, Rob., pardon, [illegible].
Patricke, Geoffry, pardon, [illegible].
Patrickeston—Patrickston, co. Meath, 1154, 3[illegible], 4[illegible].
Patrick, Stephen, pardon, [illegible].
Paulfreman — Paulfreman, Richard, surrender, 4[illegible]; lease, [illegible].
Pauliston, co. Kilk., 1[illegible]-7. See also Powleston.
Pawer, Nich., pardon, [illegible].
Pawlin, Wm., pardon, 1[illegible].
Payne, Hugh, serjeant at arms and marshal of four courts, [illegible], [illegible], [illegible], [illegible]; pardon, [illegible].

INDEX TO FIANTS—ELIZABETH.

Payne, John, lease, 159, 6257.
Paynestón—Paynestone (Painestown), co. Louth, 678, 752.
Paynestón. See Painestón, co. Meath.
Payneston—Paynston. See Painestón, co. Car.
Paynston. See Painestón, co. Tip.
Paynston—Paynstone. See Painestón, co. Meath.
Paynstown. See Painestón, co. Tip.
Paynter—Painter—Painture—Paynter—Poynter:
" John, premises in Maryborough, 1644, 6459, 6834.
" Robert, master gunner, 6548, 6902.
Payton. See Peyton.
Peace, clerk of. See under respective counties.
Peace, commissions of, justices, commissioners and keepers of, 878, &c. See Government, commissions during absence of chief governor.
Peace, justices of, to enquire of crimes and deliver gaols, 6782.
" justice of, sovereign of Dingle to be a, 4814.
Peackeston, co. Kilk., 6297.
Peacock, Rob., keeper of the seal, Common Pleas, 4142.
Peacockstown, co. Meath. See Pecokeston.
Peake, co. Cork, 4468, 6784.
Penllane, Donell, pardon, 4533.
Pearse, Nich., pardon, 5752.
Pears, confection of, 237.
Pearson, Rob., vicar of Carroughe, Kildare, 6634; vicar of Downings, 6678.
Peawterer (pewterer ?), 5873.
Peccott, John, 4383.
Peck, measure of Kilkenny = 26 gallons, 6628.
" of wheat, Kilkenny measure = 24 gallons, 6944.
" of wheat or malt, contents of (measure of Dublin), 4732.
Pecokeston (Peacockstown), co. Meath, 5573.
Peerde, John, tailor, 1631.
Pedler, pardon, 6630–1.
Peer, pardoned on petition of lords in Parliament, 1636.
Peeres, Wm. See Piers.
Peers, James fitz John, pardon, 6612.
" William. See Piers.
" Zachary. See Piers.
Peirce, Edm. m'Rob., pardon, 4403.
" Gerald leigh, pardon, 6566.
" Maurice, pardon, 6566.
" Moriah, pardon, 6569.
Peirsell, Robert fitz Jeffery, pardon, 6477.
Peires, Zachary. See Piers.
Peirs, Edm. m'Rob., pardon, 6497.
" Ellice fitz James, pardon, 6497.
" Henry. See Piers.
" James oge, pardon, 6477.
" Morris, pardon, 6497.
" Rich., pardon, 6497.
" Rob. m'Tho., pardon, 6467.
" Seån, pardon, 6497.
" Shane, pardon, 6477.
" William. See Piers.
Peirston, co. Meath, 6914.
Peirston. See Pierstown, co. Westm.
Peirstonlawndie—Peirston Lawndy. See Pierston Lawndy.
Peirstowne, co. Ross., 6673.
Peirstowne. See Pierstown, co. Westm.
Peke, Horiegho oe, pardon, 6659.
Pelham, Sir Edmund, chief baron of Exchequer, 6477; commission, 6594.
" Sir William, lord justice, 3537, 3713, 3732, 6354, 4225.
Peller, Shane oe, alias John M'Conor, pardon, 5458.
Pellick, co. Cork, 6426.
Pembroke, David, pardon, 6474.
Pennagle—Pennagell—Pennagle, Edmund, leases, 312, 1395, 2562.
Pembrockstowne (co. Cork ?), 6781.
Pennangle, Edmund. See Penangle.
Penubrok, Wm., pardon, 1505.
Pension for long-heued service, 4151.
Pensioner, gentleman, appointed, 3566.
Pensioners, queen's, 3604.
Penlotloye, Rich. See Penloye.
Penteny, Nich., estate of, 6171.
" Patr., 4814.
Penloye, Rich., attainted, 4688, 6171.
Pentney, Wm., vicar of Moreschurch, 4771.
Pepar—Pepard—Peper—Pepard. See Peppard.
Peperton, co. Meath, 1494.
Pepertowne. See Pepperton.
Peppard—Pepar—Pepard—Peper—Peperd—Pepparde—Pepper—Pippard:
" Andrew, lease, 6778.
" Anthony (of Glascarrick), commissions, 2668, 3612, 3458, 3653; indenture, 6786; leases, 1590, 3626, 4171, 4338; pardon, 6973, 4443; pardon at his suit, 4348-60.
" Elizabeth, pardon, 6973.
" Henry, pardon, 4328.
" Meave, pardon, 4328.
" Patrick, pardon, 6577.
" Richard, commissions, 1765, 2026, 2302, 3848, 6789; lease, 358; grant of land, 425; lands of, 1591, 3357, 4814; pardon, 2341.
" Thomas, pardon, 2132.

INDEX TO FIANTS.—ELIZABETH.

Peppard, Walter, commission, 860; lease to, recited, 1163, 1672, 2018; possessions, 1676, 4171; livery to heir, 1630.
" William, sheriff of Kildare, 1037, 1064; commissions, 1477, 2318; grant, 893; livery, 1636; pardon, 1004.
Peppardestowne, King's co., 1810.
Pepper, Rich. See Peppard.
Pepperstown, co. Louth. See Pippardestowne.
Pepperton—Peperstowne, co. Tip., 847, 1230, 1300, 6465; rectory, [illegible], 6408.
Peraghe, co. Meath, 1469.
Perce, Wm. See Piers.
Percell, Peter, pardon, [illegible].
Peregryne, Shane m'Donill I, pardon, 6617.
Peris, Edmund, pardon, 1561.
Perorel, alias Walsh, Rob., pardon, [illegible].
Perpoint—Perpoynte, Annys or Anne, messuage in Kilmainham, 1732, 3418.
Perpoynte — Perpointe, Agnes, lease to, recited, 3438, [illegible].
Perrot—Perrott:
" sir John, lord president of Munster, 1818, 2207; commissions, 2346, 3171, 3163; pardons, 2077, 2300; lord deputy, confines pardon to offences committed before his government, 4361, 4514, 4539, 4545; excludes from his pardons persons previously pardoned by him, 4613, 4663, 4729; indentures with chiefs, 4703, 4804, 4855; undated fiants, 3317-28.
" sir Thomas, master of the ordinance, 4836, 5731.
" Thomas, lease, [illegible].
Perrott, Janeck, pardon, [illegible].
Pers, William. See Piers.
Persiestowne—Persiestown—Perceiston, co. Westm., 3357, 4379, 4591.
Persston (see Pierston), [illegible].
Persevall, Hugh, rector of Holy Trinity, Cork, [illegible].
Persiyston. See Persiestowne.
Persus, Teig M'Caffrie alias, pardon, 5718.
Person, Thomas Moighan alias, pardon, 4, 1221.
Persinst, Nich., pardon, [illegible].
Persseston. See Persseston.
Perston. See Pierston, co. Dub.
Perston. See Pierston, co. Meath.
Perston—Persiston—Perstowne. See Pierstown, co. Westm.
Pessinkston (Pessinkstown, co. Meath?), 4494.
Peter boys (Gall?), pardon of his servant 3942.
Petor, Robin, alias Roe, pardon, [illegible].
Petor roe, pardon, 6348.
Petor or Ferros m'Teig ogo, pardon, [illegible].
Petit — Petite — Petitt — Pettit — Pettite — Pettitt—Pettyt—Pettytt — Petyte —Petytt:
" Andrew, pardon, 1128, 1582.
" Edmund, pardon, 776, 2818, 3327, 6574.
" Edward, commission, 2346.
" Edw., wardship, 401.
" Edw. (of Bordeston), pardon, 2507; wardship of his heir, 4371.
" Edw., pardon, 671, 5730, 6389.
" Gerald, knight (of Irishton), commissions, 100, 391, 842, 882, 2117, 2318, 2414, 2855, 3346; son of, pardoned, 776; his feoffees, 4222.
" Gerald or Gerrot (of Bordeston), wardship, 4371; pardon, 2858.
" Gerrot, pardon, 4263.
" Margaret, pardon, 6748.
" Meyler, grant of a wardship, 462.
" Nicholas, pardon, 6361.
" Peter, 401.
" Redmond, pardon, 1583, 3346, 4228.
" Robert, pardon, 5342.
" Simon (of Irishton), commission, 4241; his son and heir, 4873.
" Thomas, grandson and heir of sir Gerald, pardon, 6323, 6360.
" Thomas, pardon, 6448.
" William, pardon, 6[illegible], 4[illegible], [illegible], 6[illegible].
Petitions not received without signature of Clerk of Requests, 3746.
Pettit. See Petit.
Petit, Nicholas, provost marshal of Munster, commission, 1848.
Petitgue, co. Don. See Pallitogue.
Pettit. See Petit.
Pettingh, James roe, pardon, 4480.
Pettite—Pettitt—Pettyt—Pettytt—Petyte—Petytt. See Petit.
Peyton—Payton, Chas. (recte Christopher), 5718.
" Christopher, auditor general, 4373, 6710; commissions, 4814, 6457; absence licence, 4178, 6[illegible].
" Edward, 5692.
Phalane, Margaret ni, pardon, [illegible].
" Wm., pardon, 3[illegible].
Phawlie, Donogh m'ny Con my, pardon, 4[illegible].
Phaly, Edmund, pardon, 5946.
Phannyne, Rob., pardon, 4918.
Phasey, Randolph, pardon, 4[illegible].
Phelpte Barnaby, murder of, [illegible].

INDEX TO FIANTS—ELIZABETH.

Phelpes, Patrick, 283.
Phelan, Dermot, pardon to son, 1224.
" John, pardon, 6637.
" Nicholas, pardon, 1224.
" Peter, pardon, 1224.
" Thomas, pardon, 808, 7928.
" Wm., pardon, 4274.
Pheleane, John, pardon, 3434.
" Teige fitz John, pardon, 4170.
" Wm., pardon, 4448.
Phelim boy, Margaret duffe oyne, pardon, 6697.
Phelim boye, Shane oy, pardon, 4338.
Phellitale, Honora ny, pardon, 6618.
Phepo, Rob., pardon, 6838.
Pherkeall, martial law in, 68. *See* Forcall.
Pheypoo, ——, 284.
Philbine, Shile ny, pardon, 6602.
Philemynsland, at Trim, co. Meath, 631.
Philesyne, Redmund, pardon, 6177.
Philip and Mary, lease quoted, 2344.
Philipeston, co. Kild., 1540.
Philippeston. *See* Philipstown.
Philippe, Thomas, lease, 1411.
Philipston. *See* Philipstown.
Philipstoune (co. Tip. ?), 6764.
Philipstown (co. Cork ?), 4528.
Philipstown, co. Kild. *See* Philipston.
Philipstown — Philippeston — Philipston— Philipeston — Philipstown—Phillipiston — Phillippeston — Phillippistone — Phillipston — Phillipstoune — Phillipstowne, King's co., 481, 2326, 3423, 3381, 3364, 4307, 4406, 3618, 3725, 3971, 6138, 6467; sessions at, 4532.
" charter of incorporation 1640.
" boroughmaster and burgesses, grant of messuages, 1758.
" boroughmaster, commission, 6122.
" fort or castle, 188, 2843.
" fort or castle, lieutenant of, 4645, 5238, 5738.
" fort or castle, constable, 474, 2810, 4174, 3546; services to, 4834–6, 3573.
" fort or castle, usher, 4425, 5573, 5542, 6765.
" gaol, 4221.
" *See also* Doughnin.
Philipstown, co. Louth. *See* Phillippeston.
Philipstown, co. Meath. *See* Phillippeston.
Philliane, co. Limerick, 6188.
Phillimie, Shillie ny, pardon, 6618.
Phillip, James, pardon, 6484.
Phillipston — Phillipestown. *See* Philipstown.
Phillipstowne, alias Longhe, King's co., 481.
Phillipiane, Sawe ny, pardon, 4794.
Phillipiston. *See* Philipstown.
Phillippes, Geoffry. *See* Phillips.
Phillippeston. *See* Philipstown.
Phillippeston (Philipstown), co. Louth, 1612, 1468.
Phillippeston—Phillipston (Philipstown), co Meath, 1184, 4704.
Phillipple, Tho., lease, 1272.
Phillippistone. *See* Philipstown.
Phillipps. *See* Phillips.
Phillippston. *See* Phillipston.
Phillips—Phillipps—Phillippes—Phyllipps:
" Colley, customs comptroller, Dublin, 6346; licence of absence, 6762.
" Geoffrey, grant of land, 471; commission, 741, 2346.
" George, pardon, 6777.
" Henry, commission, 6246.
" Lewis, porter Carrickfergus castle, 5514.
" Thomas, 2238.
" Wm., clerk of the hamper, 3340; clerk of the crown, Chancery, 3341; licence of absence, 5640, 6754, 6878.
Phillipston—Phillippston (Philipstown), co. Kild., 1667, 6146.
Phillipston. *See* Philipstown.
Phillipston. *See* Phillippeston, co. Meath.
Phillipstoune—Phillipstown—Phillipstowne. *See* Philipstown.
Philopent—Phillipeston, co. Kild., 1549.
Philpott, Thomas, searcher and gauger of Cork, 3636; pardon, 3415, 6063.
Philpston, co. Meath, 1840.
Phisycianston (Physicianstown), co. Kild. 1491.
Phitton, Alexander, land grant, 6178.
" Richard, land grant, 5178.
Phitton's Fortune, 6179.
Phlinnstowne (co. Lim. ?), 6368.
Phoiry (co. Cork ?), 6618.
Pholegh (co. Clare ?), 3367.
Phoulkecorte — Phowlkecourt co. Kilk. *See* Foulkescourt.
Phreghane (Preghane), co. Cork, 4594.
Phreghane, 2331.
Phyllipps, Jeffery. *See* Phillips, Geoffrey.
Physic, doctor of, 3047.
Physicians, English liberty to, 177; aid for expenses of one at Universities, 214; protection for one travelling to his patients,

INDEX TO FIANTS.—ELIZABETH.

Physicians:
[illegible]; suit by one, [illegible]; physicians pardoned, 1012, 1847, [illegible], [illegible], [illegible], [illegible], 4734, [illegible], [illegible], [illegible], [illegible]; daughters of one pardoned, [illegible]. *See also* Leech, Surgeon.
Physiciamstown, co. Kild. *See* Phisycionston.
Piarre, Morighane, indenture, [illegible].
Picardeston — Picardston — Pycardiston (Pickardstown, co. Wat.), 1046, [illegible], [illegible].
Picket, John fitz Tho., pardon, [illegible].
Picket, Elyas, pardon, [illegible].
Picket, Rob., pardon, [illegible].
Pieres, James fitz Richard, bishop of Ardfert, appeal from, [illegible]; attainted, 6117.
" James m'Tho., pardon, [illegible].
" Richard m'Morrice, pardon, [illegible].
" William, knave. *See* Piers.
" Zachary. *See* Piers.
Pierce, Saundors, pardon, [illegible].
Piercetown. *See* Pierston, Pierstown.
Piers acre in Thurlaston, co. Dub., [illegible].
Piers, James m'Tho., pardon, [illegible].
" William. *See* Piers.
Piers, Capt. *See* Piers, William.
" Henry (of Tristernagh), seneschal of Dalton's country, [illegible]; pardon, [illegible], [illegible].
" James oge, pardon, 4718.
" Nicholas m'Shane, attainted, [illegible], [illegible].
" Thomas, pardon, [illegible].
Piers—Pers—Pearse—Peers—Peirs—Perse—Pierce—Pieres—Pyerse—Pyeres, captain William, constable of the castle of Carrickfergus, 830, 1740; seneschal of Clandeboy, 1439, 1478; collector of customs, Carrickfergus, [illegible]; commissions, 1196, [illegible], [illegible], [illegible], [illegible]; persons committed to gaol by, [illegible]; grant of land, 1678; land in tenure of, 3125; leases, 467, [illegible], 1285, 1670, 1784, [illegible], [illegible]; surrender, 1679; pardon, 1140, [illegible]; pardon at his suit, [illegible].
" William, junior, pardon, 1740.
" William, security, [illegible].
" William, pension, [illegible].
" Zachary, secretary to the deputy, chief chamberlain of the Exchequer, [illegible], [illegible]; clerk of crown and peace, co. Meath, [illegible], [illegible]; grant of a wardship, [illegible]; license of absence, [illegible].
Pierse, John oge, pardon, [illegible].
Pierson, Robert, pardon, [illegible].
" Tho., pardon, [illegible].
" Wm., grant of a wardship, [illegible].
Pierston—Perston—Pirston (Pierstown), co. Dub., [illegible] 1278, [illegible].
Pierston — Poirston — Porston—Pierstown — Pierstowne—Pirston—Pyerston (Pierstown), co. Meath, [illegible], [illegible], [illegible], 1548, 1683, [illegible], [illegible], [illegible], [illegible], [illegible].
" parish, [illegible].
Pierston, co. Tip., 6707.
Pierston. *See* Pierstown, co. Westm.
Pierston Lawndy — Poirston lawndie — Poirston Laundy — Pyerston Laudy, co. Meath, [illegible], [illegible]; rectory, [illegible], [illegible].
Pierstone. *See* Pierston, co. Meath.
Pierstown—Peirston—Poirstowne—Perston—Perston—Perstone—Perstowne—Pierston (Pierstown), co. Westm., [illegible], [illegible], 1618, 1577, 4012, [illegible], [illegible], [illegible], [illegible], [illegible], [illegible].
Pierstowne. *See* Pierston, co. Meath.
Pierstowne, co. Wexford, [illegible].
Pifolde, Robert. *See* Pypho.
Pigott, Rich., pardon, [illegible].
Piggot, Griffith, keeper of the queen's house, Kilmaynam, [illegible].
" Rich. fitz Gerrot, pardon, [illegible].
Pigott—Pigeott—Piggotte—Pigot—Pigotte—Pyggotte—Pygott;
" Andrew, pardon, [illegible].
" David roe, pardon, [illegible].
" Francis, pardon, [illegible].
" John (of Dysert, Queen's co.), grant of land, [illegible], [illegible]; commission, [illegible]; wardship and livery of his heir, [illegible], [illegible], 4271; grant to his son, [illegible].
" Nich., gunner, [illegible].
" Robert, wardship, [illegible]; livery [illegible]; grant of land, [illegible]; soldier, [illegible].
" Thomas, son of John, [illegible], [illegible].
" William, house in Dublin, [illegible].
Pigs rent paid in, 1240.
Pikethe, Donald, [illegible].
Pilkinton, Thomas, pardon, [illegible].
Pilkith, Donald, [illegible].
Pillemansland, Trim, [illegible].
Pillon, Geoffrey, pardon, [illegible].
Pilleston (Pilltown), co. Meath, [illegible], [illegible].
Pillotston, co. Dublin, [illegible], [illegible].
Pilline, Dominick, pardon, [illegible].
" Edm., pardon, [illegible].
" Shane, pardon, [illegible].
" Tho., pardon, [illegible].
Pillory, right to have, given by charter to Athenry, [illegible].
Pilltown, co. Meath. *See* Pilleston.
Pilltown, co. Wat. *See* Ballynafayle, [illegible], Pillown.
Pilots impressed, [illegible], [illegible], [illegible].
Pilston (co. Wat. ?), [illegible].

INDEX TO FIANTS—ELIZABETH.

Pilsworth, Wm., M.A., commission, [illegible].
Pilthowne, co. Wat., 1078.
Piltown—Piltowne (co. Wat. ?), 2971, 3273, [illegible], 3784.
Piltowne, co. Wex., 6402.
Pincerall, Fair., [illegible].
Pinkesion—Pynckesion, Gerald, pardon, [illegible], 6468.
Piper, Alexander, pardon, [illegible], [illegible], [illegible], 4389.
" Conor, pardon, [illegible].
" Dermot, pardon, 6110.
" Donell, pardon, 4377.
" Finin fitz John, pardon, 5802.
" Mornes, pardon, [illegible].
" Morgan, pardon, 4312.
" Owen, pardon, 444.
" Thomas, pardon, 1274.
" Tirlagh, pardon, [illegible], 6649.
" William, pardon, 871.
Pipers pardoned, 1482, 2078, 3146, 3141, [illegible], [illegible], 4644, 4782, 5478, 4687, [illegible], [illegible], [illegible], [illegible]-1, 6549, 5761, [illegible], 6572, 6477, 6618.
Pipho—Piphoo—Piphold, Robert. See Pypho.
Pippard, Anthony. See Peppard.
Pipparestowne (Pepperstown, co. Louth), [illegible].
Pipraith (Raithpiper ?), Queen's co., 6461.
Piracies, pardon for, 5015.
Piracy, by French subjects, 4175.
Pires, Maurice fitz Richard, pardon, [illegible].
Pirstion. See Pierstion.
Planks impressed for works, 3485.
Plantations, Essex in Clandeboy, [illegible]; Chatterton in Orior, [illegible]; Smith in Ards, 2148.
" King's and Queen's counties, conditions imposed on grantees, 474; grantee living in Connaught, and married to an Irishwoman, [illegible].
" of Munster, conditions imposed on Undertakers, 5034.
Plare, co. Westm., priory, [illegible].
Plarie, alias Loghsewdie, priory, [illegible].
Platten—Platen—Plattin—Platton—Platyn (Platin), co. Meath, 340, 687, 454, [illegible], 1490 1547, [illegible], [illegible], [illegible], 3430, [illegible]-4, 3781, 3774, 4149, 5046, [illegible], [illegible], [illegible].
Platterer, Rich., pardon, 4049.
Plattin—Platton—Platyn. See Platten.
Pleasington—Pleasenton, George, porter, Maryborough fortress, 4001; messuage in Maryborough, 4400.
Plebardstowne—Plebardiston—Pleberdston (Plebersdown), co. Kilk., [illegible], [illegible].
Plomen, Donogh ro, pardon, 6448.
" Richard duffe, pardon, 6448.
" Wm. duffe, pardon, 6448.
Plossington or Blossington, capt. Charles, pension, 4410.
Plockerry, Rich. O'Moroghow, pardon, [illegible].
Plohiriske (Ploresk), co. Kerry, 4128.
Plonckeston (Plunketstown, co. Kild. ?), 6402.
Plonkeston (co. Kild. ?), 6402.
Plonket, John, a horseman, 5169.
Plonkett. See Plunket.
Ploresk, co. Kerry. See Plohiriske.
Ploughland, co. Westmeath to be divided into, 1496, [illegible], [illegible]; Munster, 1842.
" contents of, equivalent in country acres, 4918, 4377, [illegible], [illegible]; in statute acres, [illegible], [illegible], [illegible], 4718, 4377, [illegible], [illegible], [illegible], [illegible], [illegible], 5782-3.
" equall, [illegible].
Plounkett—Plounket. See Plunket.
Plowsland, by Chapelized, co. Dub., 3159, 4378.
Plowland (co. Kild. ?), 6144.
Plucknes (Plunkness, co. Cork), [illegible].
Plucke, Owen, pardon, 4768.
" Rich. roe, pardon, 5160.
Plums, confection of, 137.
Plunket—Plunckett—Plunckett—Plunkett—Plonket—Plonkett—Plounckett—Plounket:
" Alexander (of Gibbeston), pardon, 6484, [illegible]; commission, 4149, 4461.
" Alexander (of Rathmore), protection, [illegible].
" Alexander, pardon, 711, 2418, 3204, [illegible], [illegible], [illegible], [illegible].
" Alson, pardon, 4087.
" Anne (or Bermingham), dower, [illegible].
" Anne, grant of a wardship, [illegible].
" Christopher. See Dunsany, baron of.
" Christopher. See Killeen, baron of.
" Christopher (of Carlanstown), commission, [illegible].
" Chr. (of Clonbroy), commission, 6148.
" Chr., sheriff of Meath, 5128.
" Chr. (of Dunsoghly, knt.), comm., 6448; pardon, [illegible].
" Chr., pardon, 1141, [illegible] *bis*, 3468, 4018, 4487, [illegible], [illegible], [illegible].
" Edward (of Balrath), comm., 6148.
" Edw. (of Castlecor), pardon, [illegible].
" Edw. (of Whiteraith), pardon, [illegible].
" Edw., pardon, [illegible], [illegible].

INDEX TO FIANTS—ELIZABETH.

Plunket, lady Elizabeth, widow, 616.
„ Elizabeth, pardon, 6547.
„ George (of Bewley), sheriff of Louth, 821; commissions, 821, 1822, 2117, 2848, 3444, 4147, 4465, 4166; a trustee, 5806.
„ George, pardon, 5417, 6621.
„ Gerald (of Grange), commissions, 4148, 4461.
„ Gerald (of Irishtown), pardon, 3877, 5854.
„ Gerald (of Loughcrew), party in a suit, 3160; pardon, 3469.
„ Gerald, pardon, 908, 3877, 5304.
„ Helen, widow of W. Marward, jointure, 622, 802.
„ Helena or Ellen, widow of N. Nugent, pardon, 5284.
„ Henry, pardon, 6408.
„ James. See Killeen, baron of.
„ James, son of sir John, 1284.
„ James (of Arranghbrage), pardon, 1141, 3418, 5804.
„ James (of Tatherath), pardon, 5788.
„ James (of Balrasand), pardon, 6884.
„ Jenet, 5715, 6804.
„ Joan, pardon, 6441.
„ John (of Dunsoghly, knt.), chief justice, 199, 448, 4182; takes oath of supremacy, 226; commissions, 188, 221, 418, 560, 579–81, 584, 642, 653–4, 666–7, 1082, 1417–8, 1491, 2117, 2543, 2349, 3444–6, 3576, 3704, 3963, 3984, 3047, 3183, 6401, 3657, 3467–8, 3708, 4006; pardon, 329; marriage, 838; his wife, 3488, 5804; leases, 1564, 1574, 4037; license of alienation to, 849; pardon of alienation, 3718; surrender, 2345; party to a suit, 3454.
„ John (of Bewley), commission, 843.
„ John (of Loughcrew), sheriff of Meath, 2349; commissions, 880, 1885, 2117, 2316, 3444, 4145, 4461; pardon, 3304, 3304.
„ John (of Tallonston), pardon, 4037.
„ John (of Longford), pardon, 6441.
„ John, pardon, 3304, 5844, 5621, 6681. See also Plunket.
„ Katherine (or Goldinge), matrimonial suit, 1156.
„ Katherine (or Nugent), pardon, 6451.
„ lady, pardon at her suit, 6480.
„ Laurence, pardon, 158.
„ dame Margaret (or Sarsfield), 5710.
Plunket, Mary (wife of Purcell of Loughmoe), pardon, 6544, 6623.
„ Nicholas, pardon, 3418, 4804, 6627.
„ Oliver (of Kilsaran, knt.), 1659.
„ Oliver (of Tallanston, knt.), 1656.
„ Oliver (of Tallanston). See Louth, baron of.
„ Oliver (of Rathmore, knt.), sheriff of Meath, 822, 3026; commissions, 318, 560, 581, 642, 682, 2117, 2848, 3444, 3630, 3182; pardon, 806, 1997, 3877; livery to son, 4376.
„ Oliver (of Clono), pardon, 3304.
„ Oliver (of Gibstown), pardon, 6271.
„ Oliver, pardon, 410, 3170, 6428, 6621, 6651.
„ Patrick. See Dunsany, lord of.
„ Patrick. See Louth, baron of.
„ Patrick (of Gibbstown), commission, 280; pardon, 789, 1114.
„ Patrick, pardon, 5788, 6223.
„ Richard (of Newhouse), pardon, 243; chief serjeant of co. Louth, 611.
„ Richard (of Rathmore), livery, 4376; commissions, 4148, 4461, 6227; protection, 5258.
„ Richard, pardon, 3138, 4508.
„ Robert, knt., lands of, 1482, 6444.
„ Robert (of Ushestown), pardon, 5871.
„ Robert (of Oldcastle), commission, 4149, 4461.
„ Robert (in co. Westm.), comn., 3248.
„ sir Thomas. See Louth, baron of.
„ Thomas (of Haristown), 3872.
„ Thomas (of Killallon), pardon, 3304, 3618; commission, 4148, 4461.
„ Thomas (of Rathmore), pardon, 256.
„ Thomas, leases, 840, 6528.
„ Thomas, controller of customs and searcher of Dublin and Drogheda, 3773, 4783, 4154, 4487, 4890, 4731.
„ Thomas, pardon, 3877, 3814, 6621.
„ Walter, deputy clerk of hanaper, 1280; to pass fiants, 1280, 1454, 1680; pardon, 3180; security, 4114.
„ Walter, pardon, 3304.
„ William, pardon, 6808.
Plunket's country, martial law in, 6212.
Plunket's lands, co. Meath, 3[illegible].

INDEX TO FIANTS—ELIZABETH.

Plunketstown, co. Kild. *See* Plunckeston.
Poare, David fitz Edm., pardon, 6473.
" John fitz Edm., pardon, 6473.
" Rich. fitz Edm., pardon, 6473.
" Rob., pardon, 6466.
Pobellbrien — Pobliobrien — Pobleleyen — Pobulbrien — Publebrene (Pubbliobrien barony), co. Lim., country, 4006, 4068, 5291, 6801, 6464.
" lord of, 4458, 4615.
Poblegrety (co. Lim. ?), 4066.
Poble I Callaghan (a district comprising parishes of Kilshannig, Clonmeen, and parts of Roskeen, Ballyclough, and Castlemagner), co. Cork, 6902.
Pobleoifogertie (probably Pobble Ui Fhogartaigh or Ellogarty), co. Tip., barony of, 6634.
Poblewinterfahy. *See* Pobulmunterfahy.
Pobulbrien. *See* Pobellbrien.
Pobullbane (co. Rosc. ?), 4806.
Pobulmunterfahy — Poblewinterfahy, co. Gal., 4767, 5232. *See also* Pople muinteraghfaye.
Pobwill M'Hubert, country of, co. Gal., 5111.
Poell, Rich., dean of Leighlin, 6102.
Poer, lord, 5466. *See* Power, John, lord Power.
Poer, Anastacia, pardon, 2469.
" Anthony, pardon, 1742.
" David, pardon, 1046.
" Donogh m'Shane, pardon, [illegible].
" Edm., pardon, 6416, 6373.
" Edmund fitz David, pardon, 1044.
" Edmund fitz John, pardon, 1046, 2546.
" Edm., fitz Nich., pardon, 6473.
" Edmund fitz Robert, pardon, 612, 926-7, 1046.
" Edmund fitz Thomas, pardon, 1046.
" Edmund fitz Walter, pardon, 867, 1046.
" Edm. fitz Wm., land in his tenure, 6373; pardon, 6473.
" Edm. oge, pardon, 6122.
" Edmund roe, pardon, 791.
" Ellin, pardon, 6522.
" Eustace, pardon, 4289.
" Geoffrey, pardon, 1749, 4146.
" Geoffrey fitz Robert, pardon, 926, 977, 1046.
" Geoffrey fitz Walter, pardon, 867, 1046.
" James fitz Nich., pardon, 4712.
" John (son of Peter of Ballelaghey), 6604.
" John, pardon, 4114.
" John fitz Edmond, pardon, 612, 837, 1046, 2546, 5222.
" John fitz Edmond, alias M'Eustace, pardon, 977.
Poer, John fitz Nicholas, alias Shane mallagh, pardon, 977.
" John fitz Peirs, pardon, 2541.
" John fitz Philip, pardon, 1046.
" John fitz Richard, pardon, 837, 1046, 6376.
" John fitz Walter, pardon, 977.
" John fitz William, pardon, 1046.
" Maurice backaghe, pardon, 1046.
" Maurice fitz Nicholas, pardon, 937, 1046.
" Maurice fitz Richard, pardon, 2546.
" Maurice fitz Robert, pardon, 2545.
" Maurice fitz Walter, pardon, 837, 1046.
" Maurice m'Edmond, pardon, [illegible].
" Morrish fitz Rich., pardon, 6922.
" Morrish fitz Tho., pardon, 6704.
" Nicholas, vicar of Kilmedan, 5321.
" Nicholas (son of John, son of Peter, of Ballelaghaye), wardship, 6604.
" Nicholas fitz Edmond, pardon, 912, 6783.
" Nicholas fitz Geffrey, pardon, [illegible], 1046.
" Nicholas fitz Pers, pardon, 1046.
" Nicholas fitz Thomas, pardon, 837, 1046.
" Nich. fitz Walter, 6058.
" Nicholas fitz William m'Shane dowlagh, pardon, 612.
" Nicholas leigh fitz Wm., pardon, 1298.
" Nicholas m'Thomas, pardon, 836.
" Peirs fitz Rich., alias Peirs leigh, pardon, 6373.
" Peter, pardon, 1046.
" Peter (of Ballelaghey), 6604.
" Peter fitz Rich., livery to brother, 6333.
" Peter fitz Robert, pardon, 1046.
" Peter fitz Walter, pardon, 867.
" Peter Eagle, pardon, 1046.
" Peter m'Thomas, pardon, 927.
" Philip fitz Nicholas, pardon, 977.
" Richard, pardon, 1046, 1748, 6338, 6707.
" Richard boy, pardon, 1673.
" Richard fitz Edmond, pardon, 837, 1046, 2542.
" Richard fitz James, pardon, [illegible].
" Richard fitz John, pardon, [illegible], 1046.
" Rich. fitz Peirs Enawelan, pardon, 6373.
" Richard fitz Robert, pardon, 977.
" Richard fitz Thomas, pardon, 837, 1046.
" Richard fitz Walter, pardon, 837, 1046, 2544.
" Richard fitz William, pardon, 912, 2546.
" Richard m'Edmond, pardon, 837.
" Robert fitz Edmond, pardon, 1046.
" Robert fitz John, pardon, 837.
" Rob. fitz Nich., pardon, 4734.

INDEX TO FIANTS—ELIZABETH.

Poer, Robert fitz Piers, pardon, 918.
" Rob. duffe m'Wm., pardon, 1044.
" Shane m'Ricard, pardon, 677.
" Shane m'Wm., pardon, 1044.
" Shane ballagh. See John fitz Nich.
" Tho., pardon, 4108, 4111.
" Tho. fitz Edm., pardon, 670a.
" Thomas fitz Edmond, wardship of son, 6779.
" Thomas fitz John m'Edmond, pardon, 677.
" Thomas fitz Nicholas, pardon, 677, 1046
" Thomas oge, wardship, 6778.
" Walter fitz David, pardon, 677, 1048.
" Walter fitz Geoffrey, pardon, 686, 1048.
" Walter fitz Piers, pardon, 918, 6896.
" Walter duf, pardon, 788.
" William, pardon, 1044.
" William duff, pardon, 1048.
" Wm. duff, livery, 6882.
" Wm. fitz Edm., pardon, 3342.
" William fitz John, pardon, 677.
" William fitz Nicholas, pardon, 677, 1046.
" William fitz Richard, pardon, 1048.
" William fitz Robert, pardon, 412, 636, 1048.
" William fitz Tho., pardon, 1078.
" William m'Shane, pardon, 1048.
Poere, John, baron of Curaghmore, 5397. See Curraghmore.
" Nicholas, 5397.
" Wm. m'Shane m'Morrish, pardon, 6412.
Poerstown (co. Wat. ?), 2868.
Poerstowne (Powerstown, co. Kilk. ?), 6708.
Pogheliestone, co. Louth, 1734.
Poile, Dermott duff m'Shane ne, pardon, 2202.
" Thady duff m'Shane ny, pardon, 2202.
Poisch, Rich. oge, pardon, 4188.
Poine, Katherine, pardon, 6514.
Poinestowne (Poynstown, co. Tip. ?), 4628.
Poinkherry. See Pollecurry.
Poishore, co. Wex. See Polhoare, Poole.
Poiskery. See Pollokary.
Poisseheane. See Poll na pianan.
Polamlong, co. Cork, 6894.
Polo villine (Poulawillan ?), co. Clare, 4806.
Polovcastle, co. Carlow, 782. See also Polmounty.
Polgile (Pollagnill, co. Donegal), 6682.
Polhoare (Poishore), co. Wex., 2477.
Polico: comm. to capt. Collyar to repress idle persons and malefactors, 2621.
Policurry or Polykirry, co. Cork, castle and lands granted, 3318.
Polkapall, 5336. See Pollecaple.
Polkirry. See Pollokary.
Poll of land, contents of, 1081. See also Pulls.
Poll or Cartron, 5548.
Pollagh, the, co. Cav., 6896.
Pollagh, co. Kilk. or Tip., 6437. See Pollogh.
Pollagh—Pollogh (co. Tip. ?), 6803, 6788.
Pollaghe, co. Lim., 6128.
Pollaghmoyne—Pollaghmeane (Queen's co. ?), 606, 1864.
Pollaghinogna (Poulnaiaggie ?), co. Clare, 5777.
Pollagnill, co. Don. See Polgile.
Pollakiay (co. Sligo ?), 6808.
Pollanally, co. Rosc. See Pollynallya.
Pollard, Edm., pardon, 2876.
" Nicholas (of Mayne, co. Westm.), pardon, 1611; wardship of his son Nicholas, 3482.
" Nich., wardship, 3482.
Pollardeston (Pollerton, co. Car. ?), 1808.
Pollardeston—Pollardestone—Pollardestowne (Pollardstown), co. Cork, 3873, 6882, 6517. See Pollardeston.
Pollardston—Pollardstone (Pollardstown), co. Kild., 2861, 6748.
Pollecaple—Polkapall—Poulecaple (Poulacapple), co. Tip., 600, 5336, 5344. See also Pollicapple, Powell Capell.
Pollecurry—Poinkherry—Pollycurry—Poulchurry (Poulacurry), co. Cork, 3363, 3973, 6841, 6974. See also Policurry, Poullinicurrie.
Polle Drumore (co. Cav.), 1881.
Polle in Ylinac and Dyrre (co. Cav.), 1881.
Pollegh, 6698. See Pollagh.
Pollokary—Poiskary—Polkirry—Pollekirry (Poulakerry), co. Tip., 1088, 3012, 4006, 6407. See also Poolcurry.
Pollemonie, 6836. See Polmounty.
Pollenchaine, co. Sligo, 4600.
Pollenton (Pullington), co. Wex., 1268.
Pollerton, co. Car. See Pollardeston.
Polleston, 2318. See Powleston.
Pollicapple, 6704.
Pollistowne, co. Kilk., 6879.
Pollitarre, co. Tip., 6664.
Poll na pianan—Pollnobyane—Poisseheane, co. Clare, 1517, 5080, 6820.
Pollnavengh, co. Gal. See Powlenaveighe.
Pollnchullie—Poulmacloilie, co. Kerry, 6572; grant, 6135.
Pollogh (Pollagh), co. Kilk., 6437.
Pollone (co. Car. ?), 6617.
Pollrathbegge, co. Car., 5836.
Pollrean—Polrean—Polrowan—Polruane—Poulruaine (Polroan), co. Kilk., 1084, 2941, 4256, 6610, 6664.
" rectory, 328, 1880.
" vicar, 6654.

Pollsallagho, co. Wex., 1810.
Pollwickgranstye, co. Gal., 6148.
Pollycurry. *See* Pollecurry.
Pollyzallyo (Pollazality), co. Rosc., 4777.
Polmoint, 1744. *See* Polmontey.
Polmolowhe, co. Wex., 1637.
Polmontsyne, 678. *See* Polmontey.
Polmontey—Pollemonte—Polmoint—Polmontayne—Polmoutie—Polmonty, co. Car., 678, 1677, 1744, [illegible], [illegible], [illegible], [illegible]. *See* also Polavantie.
Polmore, co. Rosc., 4542.
Polmoslagh (co. Lim. ?), [illegible].
Polroan—Polrowan—Polruane. *See* Pollrona.
Pollykobane (co. Clare or Tip. ?), 6782.
Polykirry, co. Cork, 6718.
Pomeston (co. Kilk. ?), [illegible].
Pouchersgrange—Punchersgrange (Punchersgrange), co. Kild., 3117, 6488.
Puncheston—Powncheston (Punchestown), co. Kild., 1687, 3144, 4159, [illegible].
Ponchyn, John, pardon, [illegible].
Pooinge—Poony:
„ Gilpatrick or Patrick m'Owen carragh, pardon, 5604; grant, 5684.
„ Patr. m'Gillegrome M'Kenna, pardon, 5604; grant, 5672.
„ Patr. m'Shane m'Patrick, pardon, 5604; grant, 5684.
Poorhill, co. Meath, 1148, [illegible].
Poore, Hellane, pardon, [illegible].
„ John fitz Edm., pardon, [illegible], 4762.
„ Maurice cantagh, pardon, [illegible].
„ Morris fitz John fitz Edm., pardon, 4794.
„ Peter fitz Geffrey, pardon, 4798.
„ Rich. fitz John fitz Edm., pardon, 4768.
„ Rich. fitz Wm., pardon, [illegible].
„ Tho. fitz John fitz Edm., pardon, [illegible].
„ Walter fitz Poore m'Rob., pardon, 6718.
„ William fitz Tho., pardon, [illegible].
Poolcurry (co. Tip. ?), 6785. *See* Pollokarry.
Poole (Polahore), co. Wex., [illegible].
Poole (co. Wex. ?), [illegible].
Poolempla. *See* Pollempla.
Poolearry, co. Rosc., 6188.
Poolemaloffie. *See* Pollmaloffie.
Poules of land, 5648. *See* Poll.
Poole, John, kut., grant of a wardship, [illegible].
Poor, Morris fitz Edm. ogo, pardon, [illegible].
„ Tho. fitz Rich., pardon, 4162.
Poore, Edm., pardon, [illegible].
„ Edm. fitz Philip, pardon, 4162.
„ Edm. fitz Rich., pardon, 6714, [illegible].
„ Edm. fitz Rob., pardon, 6314.
Poore, Edm. ogo, pardon, [illegible].
„ Geoffrey fitz Nich., pardon, [illegible].
„ John fitz Edm., pardon, 6676.
„ John fitz Rich., pardon, 6714.
„ Katherine, pardon, 4162.
„ Maurice, pardon, [illegible], 6612.
„ Maurice fitz Nich., pardon, 6718.
„ Maurice fitz Walter, pardon, 4162.
„ Michael, pardon, [illegible].
„ Nich. fitz John, pardon, 6614.
„ Nich. fitz Rich., pardon, 6714.
„ Nich. fitz Thos., pardon, [illegible].
„ Peirce fitz Rich., pardon, [illegible].
„ Rich. (of Poorestown, co. Tip.), lease, 5872.
„ Rich., pardon, 4162, 4773, [illegible].
„ Rich. fitz Edm., pardon, [illegible].
„ Rich. fitz John, pardon, [illegible].
„ Rich. fitz Nich., pardon, [illegible].
„ Rich. fitz Wm., pardon, [illegible].
„ Rob., pardon, 4162.
„ Rowland, pardon, 6444.
„ Shane, pardon, [illegible].
„ Tho. fitz John, pardon, 4162.
„ Tho. m'Shane, pardon, [illegible].
„ Wm., pardon, 5619, 6442.
„ Wm. fitz Edm., pardon, [illegible].
„ Wm. fitz Rob. m'Wm., pardon, 6714.
Poorestowne, co. Tip., 5872.
Pope, Roger, surrender, [illegible]; lease, [illegible].
Popham, sir John, ch. justice of England, [illegible].
Pople rointer faye, co. Gal., [illegible]. *See* Pobul muinter fahy.
Porchfield at Trim, 6118, [illegible].
Porchgate, Trim, alienation, [illegible].
Pore, Ellen fitz John, pardon, 4718.
„ Tho. fitz Morice, pardon, 4718.
Poreurry, co. Rosc., 4542.
Porkarin, co. Rosc., 4118.
Porks impressed for army, 1168; customably rendered to Irish chief, [illegible].
Portomothan, co. Kilk., [illegible].
Porpoynt's land in Kilmainham, 1849.
Porsell, Margaret, pardon, [illegible].
Porsykeston, co. Meath, [illegible].
Port of Carrickfergus to be repaired by crown, 1800. *See* Ports.
Portaferry, co. Down. *See* Ballyportaferrye.
Portagh, co. Mayo, 1804, 3418.
Portan, co. Lim., [illegible].
Portan, co. Meath. *See* Partan, Purtane.
Portane, co. Meath, [illegible].
Portanes (co. Lim. ?), 4794.
Portas—Portasse, captain William, commissions, 842, [illegible], [illegible], 3117, [illegible], [illegible], [illegible]; pardon, [illegible]; surrender of his lands, [illegible].
Portavrolan (Portavrolla), King's co., [illegible]. *See* also Portalnroghile.

INDEX TO FIANTS—ELIZABETH.

Porteromio (Porterushe, co. Lim. ?), 6490.
Portdobor, 1087.
Portdrawic (King's co. ?), 6981.
Portdrine, co. Clare. *See* Portroyne.
Porte (Port, co. Louth), 782.
Porte, co. Westm., 6286.
Portealiroghie (Portavrolle ?), King's co., 1888.
Porteclare, co. Mon., 6870.
Portedaf, Queen's co., 6768.
Porteglorians — Portegloria. *See* Portglorryan.
Porteleader. *See* Portleister.
Portell, Nich., pardon, [illegible].
Portemarnocke. *See* Portmarnocke.
Portemaghy (Portimaghy), co. Mon., 5877.
Portemacolley — Portemekylly (Portmacully), co. Kilk., rectory, 302, 1882.
Portemen (Portamore ?), co. Gal., castle and land, 6601.
Portenyn (co. Rosc. ?), 5458.
Porteninche. *See* Portnynche.
Porter, gentleman, 5768. *See* Connaught.
Porter, Richard, coroner, 5938.
„ Simon, 5834.
„ Walter, 5431.
Porters, pardoned, 6764.
Portesahen—Porteraven. *See* Portrahen.
Porterahin (Portrushen ?), co. Car., 4181.
Porterston, co. Meath, 6343.
Portersin—Portersin (co. Rosc. ?), 5432, 5468.
Porterngate, 712.
Porterstown—Porterstowne (Porterstown), co. Dub., 189, 208, 1832, 5802, 6811.
Porterston — Portereston — Porterstowne (Porterstown), co. Meath, 1460, 5564, 5808, 5343, 6121, 6468.
Porterston, 6352.
Porterston (co. Westm. ?), 6432.
Porterstowne. *See* Porterston, co. Dublin.
Porterstowne. *See* Porterston, co. Meath.
Portesshangan (Portmshangan, co. Westm.), rectory, 6268.
Portesse, William. *See* Portas.
Portfery, co. Down, 5782.
Portgloryan — Portegloriane — Portegloria (Portgloriam), co. Kild., 5852, 5817, 6380.
Portidielh, co. Cork, 6880.
Porticonligan (Portinolligan), co. Armagh, 6783.
Portimaghy, co. Mon. *See* Portemaghy.
Portingall, Arthur, pardon, 6312.
„ Brian, pardon, 1808.
„ John, pardon, 1082.
Portingall's lands, Youghal, 6294.
Portingall. *See* Portingesse.
Portinolligan (Portinolligan, co. Armagh), 6786.
Portinylan (co. Donegal), 6381.
Portirwo, co. Rosc., 4887.
Portlado (Portlaw, co. Wat. ?), 6878.
Portlaman. *See* Portloman.
Portlemer—Portlolester, co. Meath, 21, 1177, 2810, 3326, 4177, 5884; manor, 1840.
Portliko, co. Westm., 6084.
Portloman — Portlaman — Portlomman — Portlumman, co. Westm., 1340, 2848, 3342, 3656, 3877, 5948, 6874; rectory, 3880.
Portmarnocke — Portemarnocke — Portmarnocke — Portemarnocke (Portmarnock), co. Dub., 2818, 3880, 3717, 5411, 6863-78.
„ grange of, 3717.
Portmukke, alias Ilynderane (Portmuck, co. Antrim), rectory, 1888, 6767.
Portnahinch, Queen's co. *See* Portnynche.
Portnascully, co. Kilk. *See* Portemacolley.
Portnashangan, co. Westm. *See* Portesshangan.
Portnachully—Portnohoyle (near Ballycastle, co. Mayo), 5484, 5788.
Portnolligan, co. Arm. *See* Porticonligan.
Portnora (co. Rosc. ?), 6896.
Portnoskollie (Portnascully, co. Kilk. ?), 6464.
Portnygammocke, King's co., 618.
Portnynche — Portenynche (Portnahinch), Queen's co., 198, 1716.
Portollochane—Portlolichan—Portleighan, co. Tip., 4680, 5818, 6882.
Portowne (co. Wat. ?), 3366, 2838.
Portrahen — Portrahen — Porteraven — Portrane — Portram — Portraran — Portraven (Portrane), co. Dub., rectory, 528, 613, 1181-2, 2588; tithes of fish and lambs, 1780, 2321, 5082, 5403, 6878.
Portrashon, 2037.
Portraven. *See* Portrahen.
Portrowding, co. Car., 4181.
Portroyn, co. Rosc., 6682.
Portroyne (Portdrine), co. Clare, 1701.
Portrinard, co. Lim. *See* Portryaard.
Portromno (co. Kilk. ?), 3041.
Port Rusho (Portrush, co. Antrim), ganger of, 1304.
Portruston, co. Car. *See* Porterahin.
Portryaard (Portrinard, in par. Abbeyfeale, co. Lim.), 6486.
Ports of Connaught, except Galway and Sligo, unknown and unwarranted, 5748.
Portsollchan. *See* Portollochane.
Portugal, import of wine from, 5746.
Portugesse—Portingall—Portyngall, trade with, 1816, 1711; ships of, may be seized, 1161.
Portulghan. *See* Portollochane.
Portumna, co. Gal. *See* Portumny.
Portumny, co. Gal., 6661.

INDEX TO FIANTS—ELIZABETH.

Portymole, co. Down, 1602.
Portyngall. *See* Portagrane.
Portyrosty, co. Ross, [illegible].
Portyrryny (co. Ross ?), [illegible].
Posickston. *See* Possockstown, co. Meath.
Posickstowne. *See* Possockstown, co. Kild.
Possesion, alias Possikeston, co. Meath, 1340.
(Possockstown)—Podokstowne—Posickstowne — Possiston — Possiwickston — Poswickeston—Posswickstowne, co. Kild., 1[illegible], [illegible], [illegible], 6[illegible], 6[illegible].
(Possockstown)—Posickston — Possession — Possikeston — Possixton, co. Meath, 1[illegible], [illegible], [illegible], [illegible]. *See* also Possikeston.
Possickeston — Possixton (co. Westm. ?), [illegible], [illegible].
Possickstowne. *See* Possockstown, co. Kild.
Possikeston. *See* Possockstown, co. Meath.
Possiston—Possiwickston. *See* Possockstown, co. Kild.
Possixton. *See* Possickeston.
Possixton. *See* Possockstown, co. Meath.
Posswickeston — Poswickstowne. *See* Possockstown, co. Kild.
Posthorses, impressed for army, 1461.
Pottaghan—Pottoghane (Pullaghan), King's co., [illegible], [illegible].
Pottell, co. Cav., 4[illegible].
Pottelrath—Pottelrath. *See* Pottlerath.
Pottle of land, co. Cav., [illegible].
Pottlerath—Pottelrath—Pottlerath, co. Kilk. 1[illegible], [illegible], [illegible]. *See* also Pullerath.
Pottoghane. *See* Pottaghan.
Poudersough (Powdersough), co. Meath, 1340.
Poukston, [illegible]. *See* Powleston.
Pouer, Edmund, pardon, 11[illegible].
„ John carraghe, pardon, 1162.
„ Peirse m'Rich., pardon, [illegible].
„ Peirse m'Wm., pardon, [illegible].
„ Peter fitz Robert, pardon, 11[illegible].
„ Rich. m'Edmond, pardon, [illegible].
„ Tho. m'Edm., pardon, [illegible].
„ Walter duffe, pardon, [illegible].
„ Walter rowe, pardon, 4[illegible].
Pouer Inne. *See* Powers Inne.
Pouers mill. *See* Powers mill.
Pouerston. *See* Powerstown, co. Car.
Pouerstown. *See* Powerstown, co. Kilk.
Poulacapple, co. Tip. *See* Pollacapple.
Poulacurry, co. Cork. *See* Pollacurry.
Poulakerry, co. Tip. *See* Pollakerry.
Poulataggle, co. Clare. *See* Pollaghteggan.
Poulawillan, co. Clare. *See* Poulemullen. Polewillane.
Poulcherry. *See* Pollacurry.
Poule, Donell oy, pardon, 6764.
Poule mullen (Poulawillan), co. Clare, 4741.
Poulleston. *See* Powleston.
Poullnicorrie (co. Cork ?), [illegible].
Poulroulan. *See* Pollrone.
Poulroo, co. Clare. *See* Cearowenpolroe.
Pounne, Katilin, pardon, [illegible].
Pouncenall—Pounceall—Pinceall, Patrick, 1[illegible], [illegible].
Pounche, Rich. fitz Rich., pardon, [illegible].
Poullinghame (Pullinghan), King's co., [illegible].
Powcheston, [illegible]. *See* Pouncheston.
Powcheston (old) (Punchestown), co. Kild. [illegible].
Powdarhame, co. Devon, [illegible].
Powdersough, co. Meath. *See* Poudersough.
Powell, Rowland, attorney, [illegible].
„ Tho., chief serjeant, co. Kildare, [illegible]; pardon, [illegible].
„ Wm., pardon, [illegible].
Powell Capell, [illegible].
Powell mill (Poel mill), Dublin, [illegible].
Power, Anne, pardon, [illegible].
„ Anthony, sheriff of Waterford, [illegible], [illegible], [illegible]; commissions, [illegible], [illegible]; recital of grant to, [illegible]; leases, [illegible], [illegible], [illegible], [illegible], [illegible], [illegible]; pardon, [illegible], [illegible], [illegible], [illegible].
„ David, pardon, [illegible], [illegible], [illegible].
„ David bane, pardon, [illegible].
„ David brake m'Walter, pardon, [illegible].
„ David dal, pardon, [illegible].
„ David fitz John, pardon, [illegible].
„ David fitz Leonard, pardon, [illegible].
„ David fitz Maurice, pardon, [illegible], 1[illegible].
„ David fitz Richard, alias David Oskerye, pardon, 1[illegible].
„ David fitz Richard, pardon, 10[illegible], 1[illegible].
„ David fitz Robert, pardon, [illegible].
„ David fitz Walter, pardon, [illegible].
„ David fitz Wm., pardon, [illegible], [illegible], [illegible].
„ David Roche fitz Wm., pardon, [illegible].
„ David roe m'Wm., pardon, [illegible].
„ Donald, alias Denis, pardon, 10[illegible].
„ Edmund (of Ballen, co. Cork), attainted, [illegible].
„ Edm. (of Coulfyn), wardship, 1[illegible].
„ Edm. (of Mothell), sheriff of co. Waterford, 1[illegible], 1[illegible]; commissions, 1[illegible], 1[illegible]; pardon, 1[illegible], 1[illegible], [illegible].
„ Edm. (of Knocbako), livery to son, [illegible].
„ Edm. (of Shangarry), pardon, [illegible]; livery, [illegible].
„ Edmund, pardon, [illegible], [illegible], [illegible], [illegible], [illegible], [illegible], [illegible], [illegible].
„ Edm. beg, pardon, [illegible].
„ Edm. daff m'Wm., pardon, [illegible].

INDEX TO FIANTS.—ELIZABETH.

Power, Edm. duf fitz John, pardon, 1794.
,, Edm. duf fitz Philip, pardon, 5740.
,, Edm. duf m'Shane more, pardon, 3812.
,, Edm. duff m'Shane, pardon, 5748.
,, Edmund fitz Dave, pardon, [illegible].
,, Edmund fitz David, outlawed for murder, 12.
,, Edmund fitz David (of Kilbarry-meadan), pardon, [illegible], [illegible], [illegible].
,, Edmund fitz David, pardon, [illegible].
,, Edm. fitz Edm., pardon, 6477.
,, Edm. fitz John, pardon, 1044, [illegible], 5740, [illegible].
,, Edm. fitz Morris, pardon, 5748.
,, Edmund fitz Nicholas, pardon, 1848.
,, Edmund fitz Piers, pardon, [illegible], 4494, [illegible], 6477.
,, Edm. fitz Richard. *See* Edmund (of Moshell).
,, Edm. fitz Rich., pardon, 8108, 8477, [illegible].
,, Edmund fitz Thomas, pardon, [illegible].
,, Edm. fitz Walter, pardon, 1044, 2812, [illegible], 6470.
,, Edm. fitz Wm., pardon, 4494, [illegible], [illegible], [illegible].
,, Edm. m'Rich. more, pardon, [illegible].
,, Edm. mowall, pardon, 5748.
,, Edm. oge, pardon, [illegible], [illegible], 4415.
,, Edm. roe (of Killcurrarriggie), attainted, [illegible].
,, Edm. Roth fitz John, or Edm. Roth m'Shane, pardon, [illegible], [illegible], 6478.
,, Edmund roe m'Sean, pardon, [illegible].
,, Ellen, pardon, [illegible], [illegible].
,, Elenor fitz Tho., pardon, [illegible].
,, Ellie fitz Tho., pardon, [illegible].
,, Geoffrey, pardon, 207, [illegible], 718, 5748, [illegible].
,, Geoffrey fitz David, attainted, [illegible].
,, Geoffrey fitz Edm., pardon, [illegible].
,, Geoffrey fitz Maurice, pardon, 207.
,, Geoffrey fitz Walter, pardon, 2812, [illegible].
,, Geoffry mac Moriske, pardon, [illegible].
,, Hollsm, pardon, [illegible].
,, Henry, pardon, [illegible], 6477, [illegible].
,, Henry, knt., governor of the forces, Queen's co., [illegible].
,, Honora fitz Edm., pardon, 6477.
,, James (of Cooliffin), livery, [illegible].
,, James, pardon, [illegible], [illegible], [illegible].
,, Jeffery fitz Morris, pardon, [illegible]-4.
,, Jeffery fitz Walter, pardon, 6470.
,, Jeffrey, pardon, 6470-7.
,, Jeffrie boy, pardon, [illegible].
,, John, knt., lord Power and baron of Curraghmore, commissions, [illegible],

Power:
[illegible], [illegible]-7, [illegible], 1040, [illegible], [illegible], [illegible]; livery, [illegible]; pardon, [illegible], 2161, [illegible], [illegible]; grants to his son, [illegible], [illegible]-13, [illegible].
,, John (of Ballylanyn), pardon, [illegible]; inquisition on his death, [illegible].
,, John (of Carrigphilip), wardship and livery, [illegible], [illegible].
,, John (of Garrancrowally), livery to his heir, [illegible].
,, John, pardon, 207, [illegible], [illegible], [illegible], [illegible], 6477, [illegible].
,, John fitz Alseth, pardon, [illegible].
,, John fitz Edm., pardon, [illegible], [illegible], [illegible], 4494, [illegible], 6478.
,, John fitz Geffry, pardon, 1794.
,, John fitz Maurice, pardon, 5748.
,, John bane fitz Nich., pardon, [illegible].
,, John more fitz Padine, pardon, 1844.
,, John fitz Piers, pardon, [illegible], 4167, [illegible].
,, John fitz Rich., pardon, [illegible], 6476, [illegible].
,, John fitz Richard (of Fiddan), commissions, 1834, 1846.
,, John fitz Robert (Power ?), pardon, 1710.
,, John fitz Robert, pardon, [illegible], 3818, [illegible], [illegible].
,, John fitz Theobald, pardon, [illegible].
,, John fitz Tho., pardon, 5748.
,, John fitz Walter, pardon, 1044.
,, John fitz William, pardon, 207, 1044, 3512, [illegible].
,, John m'Rob. moyle, pardon, [illegible].
,, John moyle m'Walter, pardon, [illegible].
,, John m'Walter, pardon, [illegible].
,, John roe, pardon, [illegible].
,, John, alias Shane moyle, pardon, [illegible].
,, Katherine, pardon, 4744.
,, Katherine (daughter of Nicholas, of Kiltballykilly), wardship, [illegible].
,, Katherine nyo Nicholas, pardon, [illegible].
,, Laurence, pardon, 1818.
,, Margaret, pardon, [illegible], 6579.
,, Mary, pardon, 4494, 6477.
,, Maurice, murder of, 12.
,, Maurice, pardon, [illegible].
,, Maurice fitz David (of Ballykenlan), livery to son and heir, 1870.
,, Maurice fitz David, pardon, [illegible].
,, Maurice fitz Edmond, pardon, 1794, [illegible].
,, Maurice fitz John, pardon, 1044, [illegible].
,, Maurice fitz Nich., pardon, [illegible].
,, Maurice fitz Piers, pardon, [illegible].
,, Maurice roth fitz Nicholas, pardon, 207.

INDEX TO FIANTS—ELIZABETH.

Power, Maurice fitz Rich., pardon, [illegible].
„ Maurice fitz Robert, pardon, 64, [illegible].
„ Maurice fitz William, pardon, 1162, 1710, 3746.
„ Morice fitz Edm., pardon, 6494.
„ Moriah fitz Henry, pardon, 6477.
„ Morrice fitz Rich., pardon, [illegible].
„ Morrice fitz Rob., pardon, 6477.
„ Morris, pardon, 6478.
„ Morris fitz John, pardon, [illegible].
„ Nicholas (of Kilmeadan), sheriff of co. Waterford, commissions, 735, [illegible]; pardon, 1162, 1710; livery to heir, [illegible].
„ Nicholas (of Kilmeadan), livery, [illegible].
„ Nich. (of Cully), livery to heir, [illegible].
„ Nich. (of Killballykilly), pardon, [illegible]; wardship of heiress, [illegible].
„ Nich., pardon, 2746, 3473, 6408.
„ Nicholas fitz David, pardon, [illegible].
„ Nicholas fitz Edmond (of Rath-cormack), pardon, 734, 1162.
„ Nich. fitz Edm., pardon, [illegible], [illegible].
„ Nicholas fitz Gerone, pardon, 64.
„ Nicholas fitz John (of Garranoro-bally), pardon, 1163; livery, [illegible].
„ Nich. fitz John, pardon, [illegible].
„ Nich. fitz Morish, pardon, [illegible].
„ Nicholas fitz Peter, pardon, [illegible].
„ Nicholas fitz Piers, pardon, [illegible], [illegible], 1044.
„ Nich. fitz Rich., pardon, [illegible], [illegible].
„ Nich. fitz William, pardon, [illegible].
„ Nicholas roth, pardon, [illegible].
„ Peers fitz John, pardon, 6487.
„ Peirs or Peter (of Carrickphilip), pardon, 1162, 1710; wardship and livery to son, [illegible], [illegible].
„ Peirs or Peirse, pardon, [illegible], 6476-7.
„ Pers fitz Wm., pardon, [illegible].
„ Peter, knt., lord Curraghmore, livery to brother and heir, [illegible].
„ Peter, son of John lord Curragh-more, pardon, [illegible], 4094.
„ Peter (of Clondonill, probably same as the preceding), pardon, [illegible].
„ Peter (of Carrickphilip). See Power, Peirs.
„ Peter, pardon, 100, [illegible], [illegible], [illegible], [illegible].
„ Peter Evans, pardon, 1894.
„ Peter fitz Edmond (of Rathgormike), pardon, 1045, [illegible].
„ Peter fitz Edm. pardon, [illegible].
„ Peter fitz Moryah, pardon, 1162.
„ Peter fitz Robert meale, pardon, 404.
„ Peter fitz Robert, pardon, [illegible].
„ Peter fitz Robert moor, pardon, 1794.
„ Peter fitz Tho., pardon, [illegible].
Power, Peter m'Robert moell, pardon, 1726.
„ Piers fitz Rich., pardon, 62.
„ Richard, knt., lord Curraghmore, livery to his heir, [illegible], [illegible].
„ Richard, son of John lord Curragh-more, sheriff of county Waterford, [illegible]; grants of land, [illegible], [illegible]-18, [illegible]; matrimonial cause, [illegible]; pardon, [illegible], [illegible], (of Kilmanahen) [illegible].
„ Richard, pardon, 1044, 1517, [illegible], [illegible], [illegible], [illegible], [illegible].
„ Rich. carragh fitz John, pardon, [illegible].
„ Rich. fitz Abaik, pardon, [illegible].
„ Rich. fitz Edm., pardon, [illegible], 4418, [illegible], [illegible].
„ Rich. fitz John, pardon, [illegible], [illegible].
„ Richard fitz Moryah, pardon, 1162.
„ Richard fitz Nicholas, pardon, [illegible].
„ Richard fitz Robert, pardon, [illegible].
„ Rich. fitz Thomas, pardon, [illegible], 6704.
„ Richard fitz Walter, pardon, 1046.
„ Richard fitz William, pardon, [illegible], [illegible], 3746, [illegible], [illegible].
„ Rich. more, pardon, [illegible].
„ Richard more fitz Walter, [illegible].
„ Richard rothe, pardon, [illegible].
„ Robert (of Balleakanlane or Bally-kanlan), pardon, 1163; livery, [illegible].
„ Robert (of Dunhill), commission, [illegible]; pardon, 100, 1162.
„ Robert (of Kilmeadan), livery, [illegible]; inquisition on his death, [illegible]; livery to son and heir, [illegible].
„ Robert, pardon, 1637, 1710, [illegible], [illegible], [illegible], [illegible], 6477.
„ Rob. fitz David, pardon, [illegible].
„ Rob. fitz Edm., pardon, [illegible], [illegible], 4094, 6478.
„ Rob. fitz John, pardon, 1044, [illegible], 6704, [illegible].
„ Rob. fitz Morris, pardon, [illegible].
„ Rob. fitz Tho., pardon, 3746, [illegible].
„ Rob. fitz Walter, pardon, [illegible].
„ Rob. fitz William, pardon, 64, 1044.
„ Rob. m'Shane balmey, pardon, [illegible].
„ Rob. oge fitz Rob., pardon, [illegible].
„ Rowland, pardon, 6478.
„ Rowland, alias Gyllyduffe, pardon, 6714.
„ Shane, pardon, [illegible].
„ Shane m'Edm., pardon, 6494.
„ Shane m'Richarde, pardon, [illegible].
„ Shane m'Wm., pardon, [illegible].
„ Theobald, pardon, [illegible].
„ Thomas (of Coolfin), wardship and livery to son, [illegible], [illegible].
„ Thomas (of Karrebane), livery, [illegible].
„ Thomas, pension, [illegible].

INDEX TO FIANTS—ELIZABETH.

Power, Thomas, pardon, 1817, 2424, 6474.
" Tho. dul, pardon, 2746.
" Tho. fitz Dave, pardon, 2182.
" Tho. fitz Edm., pardon, 4414, [illegible], 6466.
" Tho. fitz Edm. (of Mothell), pardon, 6348, [illegible].
" Tho. fitz Edm. oge, pardon, 4194.
" Tho. fitz John, pardon, 4086, 6478.
" Tho. fitz Morish, pardon, 1163, 1718, 2512, 4684.
" Tho. fitz Nich., pardon, 724, [illegible].
" Tho. fitz Peirs, pardon, [illegible].
" Tho. fitz Walter, pardon, 6478.
" Tho. fitz Wm., pardon, [illegible].
" Thomas mac Morishe, pardon, 189.
" Thomas m'Shane, pardon, 2372.
" Thomas ne Carroges, 1041.
" Walter (of Kilmaidan), inquisition on his death, 2267.
" Walter, pardon, 1616, [illegible], 3434, 6780.
" Walter doul, pardon, 3492.
" Walter fitz Edmund, pardon, 237.
" Walter fitz Geoffrey or Jefferie, pardon, 1204, 6474.
" Walter fitz John, pardon, 6477.
" Walter fitz Nich., pardon, 4387.
" Walter fitz Peirse, pardon, 6824.
" Walter fitz Richard, pardon, 1944, 2408, 2746, 6478, 6493–4.
" Walter fitz Rob., pardon, 4068, 6478.
" Walter fitz Tho., pardon, 6824.
" Walter fitz Wm., pardon, 1184, 4718, [illegible], 6478, 6768.
" Walter fitz William de curraton, attainted, 3978.
" Walter roe fitz Rich., pardon, 4614.
" William (of Coolfin), livery to his heir, 4381.
" William (of Colly), livery to his heir, 4386.
" William (of Colly), livery, 4388.
" Wm. (of Shangarry, co. Cork), livery to his heir, 4604.
" Wm., pardon to his men, 4462, 4464.
" William, pardon, [illegible], 1446, 1784, [illegible], 3462, [illegible].
" Wm. boye, pardon, 3454, [illegible].
" Wm. duf, pardon, 2761.
" Wm. fitz David, pardon, 1944, 6424, 6478.
" Wm. fitz Edm., pardon, 837, 1457, [illegible], 6464.
" William oglasse fitz Geoffrey, pardon, 1944.
" Wm. fitz Nich., pardon, [illegible].
" William fitz Peter, grant of land, 6428.
" Wm. fitz Peirs, pardon, 6478.
Power, Wm. fitz Philip (Power?), pardon, 6746.
" Wm. fitz Philip, pardon, 6437.
" Wm. fitz Rich., pardon, 1044, 6783.
" Wm. duf fitz Rob., pardon, [illegible].
" Wm. fitz Tho., pardon, [illegible], 2341.
" *See also* Puer, Poare, Poor, Poor, Poore, Pouer, Powre.
Power and Curraghmore, lord baron of. *See* John Power.
Powere, Edm. fitz David, pardon, 4424.
Powerscort — Powerscourt — Powerscourte. *See* Powerscourt.
Powerston. *See* Powerstown, co. Car.
Powerstown (co. Tip.), 628.
Powerstown (co. Tip.?), 911.
Powerscourt — Powerscort — Powerscourt — Powerscourte — Powerscourte — Powerskourt — Powrscourte (co. Wick.), 181, [illegible], 894–5, 1182, 1789, 1898, 3492, 3718, 4836, [illegible]; grant of the manor, 6786.
Powers Inns — Power Innes, Dublin, 818, 2802.
Powerskourt. *See* Powerscourt.
Powersmyll — Powersmill, Ross, co. Wex., 1578, 3167.
Powerston — Pouerston, co. Car., 895, 1868.
Powerston, co. Dub., 844, 1222, 1872.
Powerston — Pouerston — Powerstone — Powerstowne, co. Kilk., 6843; rectory, 1231, 3883, 4708, 6774. *See also* Pourstoun.
Powerswood, 6534.
Powes, David, pardon, 4480.
Powher, James, pardon, 3461.
Powkeporvigise (Polkavaugh), co. Gal., 6784.
Powleston — Polleston — Pouleston — Poulestoe — Powlestowne — Powliston (Poulstown?), co. Kilk., 2117, 2348, 2444, 2461, 2780, 2841, 2840, 3843, 2341, 6441. *See also* Pauleston.
Powleycurry, co. Cork, 6780.
Powlinge, John, pardon, 6188.
Powliston. *See* Powleston.
Powlytwohill (co. Cork?), 2279.
Powr, Edm. fitz Wm. m'David, pardon, 4718.
Powre, Anthony, commission, 682.
" David fitz Rob., pardon, 4878.
" Edm. fitz Morish, pardon, 6864.
" John fitz John fitz Edm., pardon, 6018.
" lord, commission, 482.
" Peirse m'Rob., pardon, 6864.
" Rich., pardon, 6166.
" Rob. m'Morish, pardon, 6864.
" Rowland, pardon, 5171.
Powrescourte. *See* Powerscourt.
Powreston (co. Wat.?), 2324.
Poyn, David m'Shean, pardon, 6494.

INDEX TO FIANTS—ELIZABETH.

Poyning's law cited, 834, 1028.
Poynlstown, co. Tip. *See* Poinstowne.
Præmunire, offences against, pardoned, [illegible].
Pranky, Maurice me, pardon, 6464.
Pratleston (co. Meath ?), [illegible].
Pratt, Christopher, pardon, 4117; lease, 4431.
" Ellen, pardon, [illegible].
" William, lease, [illegible]; grant of right of presentation, [illegible]; commission, 6763.
Preacher, commission to, 6015, [illegible]; presentation of, [illegible], [illegible]; preacher of God's Word, [illegible].
Preachers, friars. *See* Dominicans.
Preban, co. Wick., [illegible].
Precentor, son of, 9[illegible].
Preceptories of Hospital of S. John of Jerusalem. *See* Aney, Ardee, Clonmell, co. Tip., Kilbarry, co. Wat., Kilbeg, co. Kild., Kilcloggan, Kilheele, Killerge, Killure, Kilmaynhambeg, Kilsaran, Morne, Tully.
Preeban, Donell m'Tirlagh me, pardon, [illegible].
Prendergase, Maurice, pardon, [illegible].
Preghane, co. Cork. *See* Phrogham.
Premelstone, co. Meath, 4477.
Prendergast — Prindergast — Prendegast — Prendercast — Prendercast — Prendergas — Prendergase — Prendergaste — Prendergost — Prendirgast — Prendrecast — Prindercasse — Prindergas - Prindergasse —Prindergaste —Prindircasse — Prindirgast — Prindirgaste — Prindregast:
" David, pardon, 6740.
" Donogh, pardon, [illegible].
" Edm., clerk, pardon, [illegible].
" Edm. fitz James, pardon, [illegible], [illegible], [illegible].
" Edm. duffe, pardon, 6462.
" Edmund, pardon, [illegible], [illegible], [illegible], [illegible], [illegible], [illegible].
" Edward, pardon, [illegible].
" Ellen, pardon, 6418, [illegible].
" Garrott, pardon, [illegible].
" Geoffrey (of Newcastle, co. Tip.), pardon, 978, [illegible], [illegible], [illegible].
" Geoffrey (of Ballymorroghow, co. Clare), pardon, 6562.
" Geoffrey, pardon, [illegible].
" Gerald, pardon, [illegible], [illegible], [illegible], [illegible].
" Gerrot, pardon, [illegible].
Prendergast, Gerrott, pardon, 6740.
" Henry, pardon, 6740.
" James (of Newcastle), pardon, [illegible], 1634.
" James (of Ballyfarnske), pardon, 4544, [illegible], [illegible].
" James, priest, pardon, [illegible].
" James, pardon, [illegible], [illegible], [illegible], 6411, [illegible], [illegible], [illegible], [illegible].
" Jeffrey — Jefferie, pardon, [illegible], [illegible], [illegible], [illegible], [illegible], [illegible].
" John, prebendary of Mora, [illegible]; claims treasurership of Waterford, [illegible].
" John roe m'James, pardon, [illegible], [illegible].
" John, pardon, [illegible], [illegible], [illegible], [illegible], 6477, [illegible], [illegible].
" Katherine, pardon, [illegible].
" Margaret, pardon, [illegible].
" Mary, pardon, 4714.
" Maurice, pardon, [illegible], [illegible], [illegible].
" Morghe, pardon, [illegible].
" Morish — Morris — Morice, pardon, [illegible], [illegible], [illegible], [illegible], [illegible], 6724.
" Moyler, pardon, 6740.
" Patrick, pardon, [illegible].
" Philip, pardon, [illegible].
" Redmund, pardon, [illegible], 6155.
" Richard, pardon, [illegible], [illegible], [illegible], [illegible], [illegible], [illegible], [illegible], [illegible].
" Robert, pardon, [illegible], [illegible], [illegible], [illegible], [illegible], 2778, [illegible], [illegible], [illegible], [illegible], [illegible].
" Thomas, pardon, [illegible], [illegible], [illegible], 1972, 2776, [illegible], [illegible], [illegible], [illegible], [illegible], [illegible], [illegible], [illegible], [illegible], [illegible].
" Walter, pardon, [illegible], [illegible], [illegible], [illegible], [illegible], [illegible], [illegible], [illegible].
" William, pardon, [illegible], [illegible], [illegible], [illegible]. *See also* Pryndergast.
Prendergast's lands or country to be made shire ground, 1564, [illegible].
Prerogative (royal) exerted to continue an expired statute, 4760; to grant protection against legal process, [illegible].
Prerogative Court, commissioners appointed with powers similar to the Prerogative Court of Canterbury, [illegible].

INDEX TO FIANTS—ELIZABETH.

Prerogative Court, master of (archbishop of Dublin), 4788, [illegible]; deputy, 4768.
" judges of, 6912, [illegible].
" general substitute or surrogate, 4[illegible], 44[illegible], 6[illegible].
" receiver of fines, 6646, [illegible].
Prescot, Thomas, marshal of courts, [illegible].
Prescott, Humfrey, pardon, [illegible].
" James, clerk of requests, 5746; grant of a wardship, 1640; lease, [illegible].
Presentations, note as to, 257. See XXI. Report, p. [illegible].
Presteston, co. Tip., 1[illegible].
Preston, Christopher. See Gormanston, viscount.
" Eleanor (or Talbot), [illegible].
" Elizabeth, widow of baron of Delvin, licence to marry, [illegible]; pardon of alienation, [illegible].
" James (of Balmadon), livery, [illegible]; commission, 4[illegible]; wardship of heir, [illegible].
" Jenico. See Gormanston, viscount.
" Robert (of Balmadon), [illegible]; livery to heir, [illegible].
" Robert (of Balmadon), wardship, 50[illegible].
" Thomas, pardon, [illegible].
" William. See Gormanston, viscount.
Preston (perhaps Pierstown), co. Meath, 1274.
Preston, co. Westm., [illegible].
Prestonghe, co. Kild., 4[illegible].
Prestown (co. Westm.?), 6778.
Preys, compensation for, 41[illegible].
Priaghane, Dermod m'Donogh I, pardon, 6467, [illegible].
Prices, enhanced by illegal exports, [illegible].
" of hay, oats, &c., 1[illegible], 1[illegible], [illegible]; of victual for soldiers, [illegible]; allowed for meals given to soldiers, [illegible].
" See Values; Victuals.
Prickmistowne, co. Meath, 6779.
Prickynshayes (co. Kilk.?), [illegible].
Priestestowne (co. Tip.?), 6[illegible].
Priest, pardoned, [illegible], [illegible], [illegible], [illegible], [illegible], 4472, 4[illegible], 4[illegible], 4[illegible], 4[illegible], 47[illegible], 4[illegible], 4[illegible], 4[illegible], 4[illegible], [illegible], [illegible], 5[illegible], 5[illegible], [illegible], 5[illegible], 6[illegible], [illegible], 6[illegible], 6[illegible], 6[illegible], 6[illegible], 6[illegible], [illegible], 67[illegible], 67[illegible].
" a Mass priest, 4[illegible].
Priests excluded from pardon, 6[illegible].
" mass, excluded from pardon, 6[illegible].
" seminary, excluded from pardon, 6[illegible], 6772.
Priesthaggard, co. Wex. See Prishaggard.
Priestlown, co. Westm. See Prisistown.
Priestestown, co. Meath. See Pryaston.
Prindergasse—Prindergas—Prindergrane—Prindergast—Prindergaste. See Prendergast.
Prinlergrasse, Rob., pardon, 47[illegible].
Prindirgasse—Prindirgast—Prindirgaste—Prindregast. See Prendergast.
Prior, Edm., pardon, 4[illegible], 6176, 6[illegible], [illegible].
" Patr., pardon, 67[illegible].
" Rich., pardon, [illegible], [illegible], 6[illegible], 6[illegible].
Priors farm, in Dunboyne, 11[illegible].
Priors park, Clonmel, [illegible].
Priorston—Prioriston—Priorstone—Priorstoune—Priorstowne—Pryoriston, co. Tip., 1[illegible], 1[illegible], [illegible], [illegible], [illegible], 67[illegible].
Priorstown. See Priorton.
Priors warren, co. Dub., [illegible].
Priors weir, co. Westm., [illegible], 67[illegible].
Priors wood, co. Dub., [illegible].
Priorton (Priorstown), co. Louth. [illegible], [illegible].
Priorton mede—Priortowne meade, co. Kild., 4[illegible], 1[illegible].
Priortone, co. Kild., 6744.
Priortoun, co. Tip., [illegible].
Priortowne meade. See Priorton mede.
Priorpratowne, co. Lim., 1[illegible].
Prishaggard—Prishogard (Priesthaggard), co. Wex., [illegible], 6743.
Prisons (co. Mayo?), [illegible].
Prisoners fees to marshal, 4[illegible]; payment for diet, [illegible]; profits from prisoners granted to serjeant at arms, [illegible].
Prisistone (Priestlown), co. Westm., [illegible].
Privy Council, clerk of, [illegible]. See Council.
" in England, letter from, [illegible]; Irish cause depending before, [illegible]. See Council.
Procession moor in Kilmainham, 15[illegible].
Proclamation, warrant for publication, [illegible].
" for surrender of prior of Kilmainham, 67[illegible].
" of persons indicted of treason, 1[illegible].
" of general pardon, [illegible], [illegible], 40[illegible], 67[illegible].
" for continuing wine duty after expiry of statute granting it, 40[illegible].
Proctor, [illegible].
Prodderghie or Bitherighe, William, licence of absence, 342.
Prohura, co. Cork. See Pruhes.
Promleston. See Prompelston.
Prompelston—Prompellan, co. Kild., 1[illegible], 67[illegible].
Prompelston—Promleston—Prompleastoune (Prompalstown), co. Kild., 1[illegible], [illegible], 67[illegible].
Proudeville, Edm., attainder, [illegible].

INDEX TO FIANTS—ELIZABETH.

Prendlivill, John, priest, pardon, 6122.
Prenewill, John, pardon, 6555.
„ Rich., pardon, 6565.
Protections may be granted by chief commissioner of Ulster, 5452.
Proudfootstown, co. Meath. See Proutlston, Prowtfordeston.
Proudstown, co. Meath. See Proutlston.
Prout, John, pardon, 2615. See Prowte.
Prowdfordston (Proudfootstown, co. Meath ?) 2573. See also Parlefordeston.
Proutlston—Prowtiston (Proudstown), co. Meath, 275, 283, 434.
Provealls, lands of, 5212.
Provisions. See Victuals.
Provost marshal general or vice marshal of the army (Ross ap Hugh), 2905, 4650, 6182.
„ (provincial). See Connaught, Leinster.
Prowte, David, pardon, 1914.
„ Philip, pardon, 2708.
„ Rich., pardon, 4765.
„ Tho., pardon, 6144.
Prowtfordeston (Proudfootstown), co. Meath, 6564.
Prowtlot, Rob., pardon, 4573.
Prowtiston. See Proutlston.
Prucklishtown, co. Long. See Pruhan.
Pruhes (Pruhus, co. Cork ?), 4542.
Pruhan (Prucklishtown ?), co. Long., 6329, 6107.
Prumpelstown, co. Kild. See Prumpelston.
Prussiatown, co. Kild. See Ballypercivall.
Fryndergus, William, clerk, pardon, 2360.
Pryndergast, Wm., pardon, 4162.
Prynes park, co. Meath, 1460.
Pryneston (Princetown), co. Meath, 1460.
Pryorleston. See Prioreston.
Pryorstowne (co. Lim. or Cork ?), 2317.
Pubbleshyton, co. Lim. See Pobelbrien.
Pubble Carraih, country of, co. Car., 4842.
Publebreen. See Pobelbrien.
Puble Dromo (Poble Drum, now the parish of Ardoyne), co. Car., 804.
Pubullmyntergwylane, co. Lim., 5782.
Puggvaly, Rob., escheator, commission, 2221.
Pulkane, co. Cork, 3941, 3163.
Pullagh, co. Tip., 2882.
Pullaghballenowe, Queen's co., 1323, 5948.
Pullen, Wm., pardon, 2157.
Pullford, Vrian, pardon, 6524.
Pullington, co. Wex. See Polleston.
Pullis, co. Mon. See Pallice.
Pulls of land—2 called ½ quarter, co. Cav.—6 known as "the town of," co. Cav., 5542. See Poll.
Puncheregrange. See Puncheregrange.
Punchestown, co. Kild. See Punchestown.
Puniaghan (Pultaghan), King's co., 522.
Purcell—Pursell—Persoll—Purshall—Pursill—Pursell:
„ Anastace fitz Patr., pardon, 4569.
„ David, pardon, 4302, 4877.
„ Edmund, pardon, 911, 1050, 1553, 2284, 2474, 2752, 3360, 4448, 5747, 6328, 6173, 6328, 6310, 6522, 6321, 6446, 6702.
„ Edm. (of Aghalay), pardon, 6708.
„ Edm. (of Crogh), pardon, 4473, 6446; pardon to his sons, 6446.
„ Edm. duffe, pardon, 6425.
„ Edmund fone, pardon, 3250.
„ Edm. fitz Geoffrey or Jefferie, pardon, 1665, 6565, 6524.
„ Edm. fitz James, pardon, 6744.
„ Edm. fitz Morish, pardon, 6442.
„ Edm. fitz Nich., pardon, 6447.
„ Edmund fitz Patrick, pardon, 911, 2284, 3462, 3782.
„ Edm. fitz Philip, pardon, 4464.
„ Edmund fitz Piers, pardon, 3443, 6622.
„ Edmund fitz Richard, pardon, 2086, 4142.
„ Edm. fitz Rob., pardon, 4437, 6527.
„ Edm. fitz William, pardon, 1184.
„ Edm. oge, pardon, 6442.
„ Edm. roe, pardon, 4464.
„ Edward, pardon, 4020.
„ Edw. fitz Jeffery, pardon, 6440.
„ Edw. fitz Tho., pardon, 6440.
„ Elleen, pardon, 4764.
„ Ellen, pardon, 6494, 4682.
„ Ellen leigh, pardon, 6342.
„ Ellinor, pardon, 6348.
„ Garret, pardon, 6479.
„ Geoffrey (of Ballyfoill, Ballyfowill, or Ballyfowill, co. Kilk.), pardon, 860, 1229; cows stolen from, 5152.
„ Geoffrey, pardon, 911, 1690, 2283, 2258, 3185, 6448, 6704.
„ Geoffrey fitz Redmund, pardon, 6464.
„ Geoffrey fitz Robert, pardon, 1287.
„ Geoffrey fitz Robert, pardon, 6152, 6268, 6494.
„ Geoffrey fitz Tho., pardon, 6262, 6582.
„ Geoffrey fitz Tibbot or Tibbalt, pardon, 2227, 6522.
„ Geoffrey fitz Wm., pardon, 1184.
„ Geoffrey reagh, pardon, 6440, 6478.
„ Gerald, pardon, 1686.
„ Helen, pardon, 6538.
„ Henry, pardon, 6356.
„ James, sub-sheriff co. Waterford, pardon, 3517, 4795.

INDEX TO FIANTS—ELIZABETH.

Purcell, James (of Ballycormick), pardon, 6443, 6616, 6702.
„ James, pardon, 611, 1784, 1864, 3746, [illegible], [illegible], [illegible], 6408, 6440, 6616.
„ James fitz Denis, pardon, 6467.
„ James fitz Geoffrey or Jeffery, pardon, 6448, [illegible], [illegible].
„ James fitz John, pardon, [illegible].
„ James fitz John glass, pardon, [illegible].
„ James fitz Patr., pardon, 6440, 6504, [illegible].
„ James fitz Philip, pardon, [illegible], [illegible], [illegible].
„ James fitz Richard, pardon, [illegible], [illegible], [illegible], 6511, 6764.
„ James fitz Robert, pardon, 6484, 6704.
„ James fitz Wm., pardon, 1445, [illegible], [illegible], [illegible], [illegible], 6745.
„ James fitz Wm. See James (of Ballycormick).
„ James m'Patrick, pardon, 6504.
„ James m'Philip, pardon, 1918.
„ James m'Shane glass, pardon, 6440.
„ James m'Wm., pardon, [illegible].
„ James boye, pardon, 6140.
„ James leigh fitz Rich., pardon, 6440.
„ James reagh, pardon, [illegible].
„ James roe fitz James m'Gilpatrick, pardon, [illegible].
„ Jeffery, pardon, 6443, 6702.
„ John, pardon, 2874, 6467, [illegible], [illegible].
„ John, alias Fordorogh, pardon, [illegible], [illegible], 1184, [illegible], 1667, [illegible], [illegible].
„ John fitz Edmond (of Barrianlokdu), pardon, [illegible], 1667, [illegible], [illegible]. See John, alias Fordorogh.
„ John fitz Edm. (of Portadrath), pardon, [illegible].
„ John fitz Jefferie, pardon, 6416, [illegible].
„ John fitz Patrick, pardon, 6161.
„ John fitz Philip, pardon, [illegible].
„ John fitz Piers, pardon, [illegible], [illegible].
„ John fitz Theobald, pardon, [illegible].
„ John fitz Tho., pardon, [illegible], 6440, [illegible].
„ John fitz Tibbot, pardon, [illegible], [illegible].
„ John fitz William, pardon, [illegible], [illegible], [illegible], 6440.
„ John glasse, pardon, [illegible].
„ John roe fitz Rich., pardon, [illegible], [illegible].
„ John m'Philip, pardon, [illegible].
„ Katherine, pardon, [illegible].
„ Leonard, pardon, [illegible].
„ Margaret, pardon, 6467.
„ Nicholas, pardon, [illegible].
„ Patrick, pardon, [illegible], [illegible], [illegible], [illegible], [illegible], [illegible], [illegible], [illegible], [illegible], [illegible], [illegible], [illegible], 6440, 6446.
Purcell, Patrick (of Bruff), pardon, [illegible].
„ Patrick (of Kilbeghera), pardon, [illegible], [illegible].
„ Patr. (of [illegible]), pardon, [illegible], [illegible].
„ Patr. duff fitz Rich., pardon, [illegible], 6464.
„ Patr. fitz Davy duf (or dowe), pardon, [illegible], [illegible].
„ Patr. fitz James, pardon, 6704.
„ Patr. fitz Jefferie, pardon, [illegible].
„ Patr. fitz Philip, pardon, [illegible].
„ Patrick fitz Piers or Peirce, pardon, 1184, [illegible], [illegible], [illegible], [illegible], [illegible].
„ Patr. fitz Rich., pardon, [illegible].
„ Patrick fitz Robert or m'Robert, pardon, [illegible], 6164.
„ Patrick fitz William, pardon, [illegible], 1184, [illegible].
„ Patrick m'James, pardon, [illegible].
„ Patrick oge, pardon, [illegible], [illegible].
„ Patr. oge, pardon, [illegible].
„ Patr. roe, pardon, [illegible].
„ Peter, robbery by, [illegible].
„ Peter. See Purcell, Piers.
„ Peter, pardon, 611, 1617, [illegible], [illegible], 6781.
„ Peter fitz Tho., pardon, 6702.
„ Philip, pardon, [illegible], [illegible], [illegible], [illegible].
„ Philip (of Ballyphull), pardon, [illegible].
„ Philip (of Loghmoe), pardon, [illegible].
„ Philip fitz Gerrot, pardon, 6184.
„ Philip fitz James, pardon, [illegible].
„ Philip fitz Piers, pardon, 1184, [illegible], [illegible].
„ Philip m'Philip, pardon, [illegible].
„ Philip m'Robert, pardon, [illegible].
„ Philip m'Theobald, Theobald or Tibbot, pardon, [illegible], 6311, [illegible], [illegible].
„ Philip m'William, pardon, [illegible].
„ Piers or Peter (of Crogh, co. Lim.), pardon, [illegible], [illegible], 6446; burgages of, [illegible].
„ Piers or Peirse, pardon, [illegible], [illegible], 6704.
„ Piers fitz James, pardon, [illegible].
„ Piers fitz Morish, pardon, 6440.
„ Piers fitz Patr., pardon, [illegible].
„ Piers fitz Rob., pardon, [illegible].
„ Piers fitz Tho., pardon, [illegible], [illegible], [illegible].
„ Redmond (of Craigorawe), pardon, [illegible].
„ Redmond fitz Edmund (of Craigorawe), pardon, 1184, [illegible].
„ Redmond fitz James, pardon, [illegible].
„ Redmond fitz Jefferie, pardon, 6440, [illegible], [illegible].
„ Redmond fitz Robert, pardon, [illegible].
„ Redmund reagh (of Craigorawe), pardon, [illegible], [illegible], [illegible], [illegible], 6464.

INDEX TO FIANTS—ELIZABETH.

Purcell, Richard, pardon, 911, 1617, 1784, [illegible], [illegible], [illegible], 4571, 4787, 6440, 6446, [illegible].
„ Rich. (of Browustown), pardon, 6440.
„ Rich. (of Gnaiguraws), pardon, 6702.
„ Rich. (of Kilmocar), pardon, [illegible].
„ Rich. (of Longhmoe), pardon, [illegible].
„ Rich., alias Baron, pardon, [illegible].
„ Rich. fitz Denis, pardon, 4487.
„ Rich. fitz Edm., pardon, [illegible].
„ Rich. fitz John, pardon, 6440.
„ Rich. fitz Patrick, pardon, [illegible], [illegible], [illegible], [illegible].
„ Rich. fitz Redmund, pardon, 6454.
„ Richard fitz Theobald, pardon, [illegible].
„ Rich. fitz Tibbot, pardon, 6440.
„ Rich. fitz William, pardon, 1184, [illegible].
„ Rich. m'Piers, pardon, [illegible].
„ Rich. m'William, pardon, 1576, [illegible].
„ Rich. moell, pardon, 6708.
„ Richard more, pardon, [illegible], 1844.
„ Richard more fitz Wm., pardon, [illegible], [illegible].
„ Richard more m'Shane, pardon, 6440.
„ Richard rwo fitz Piers, pardon, [illegible].
„ Robenet—Robinet—Robnet—Robenede, pardon, 1028, 1842, [illegible], [illegible], [illegible], [illegible], [illegible].
„ Robenet m'Jeffrey, pardon, 1184.
„ Robenet (Robonet), attainted, [illegible]. See Robnet, Romnet.
„ Robert, marshal of the four courts, [illegible].
„ Robert, pardon, 911, 1617, [illegible], [illegible], [illegible], [illegible], [illegible], 4787, 6071, [illegible], [illegible], [illegible], 6702.
„ Rob. (of Clone), pardon, [illegible], [illegible].
„ Robert fitz Edm., pardon, [illegible], [illegible], [illegible].
„ Robert fitz Geffri, pardon, 2067.
„ Robert fitz James, pardon, [illegible], 3041.
„ Robert fitz Patrick, pardon, 1184, [illegible].
„ Rob. m'Philip, pardon, [illegible].
„ Robnet, pardon, [illegible], [illegible]. See Robenet.
„ Robnet fitz Jeffery, pardon, [illegible].
„ Robnet fitz Philip, pardon, [illegible].
„ Robnet fitz Rich., pardon, [illegible].
„ Robnet fitz Tho., pardon, [illegible].
„ Robonet, attainted, 5404.
„ Romnet, pardon, 1884, [illegible].
„ Shaine fitz Theobald, pardon, [illegible].
„ Shane m'Gilpatrick, pardon, [illegible].
„ Shane m'Theobald, pardon, 6109.
„ Shane m'William, pardon, [illegible].
Purcell, Sivan, wife of Edm. Leo, pardon, 6487.
„ Srowe (of Bonadstle), pardon, 6440.
„ Syrowe (of Ballydnell), pardon, [illegible].
„ Theobald, pardon, [illegible].
„ Theobald fitz Patr., pardon, 6704.
„ Theobald fitz Redmund, pardon, [illegible].
„ Theobald fitz Tho., pardon, [illegible].
„ Thomas, baron of Longhmoe, pardon, [illegible], [illegible], 4417.
„ Thomas, pardon, 911, 1748, 1919, [illegible], [illegible], [illegible], [illegible], [illegible], [illegible], 6440, [illegible].
„ Tho. (of Barrisleigh), pardon, [illegible], 6704.
„ Tho. (of Foulkruib), pardon, [illegible], 4870.
„ Tho., pardon to son, [illegible].
„ Tho. fitz Edm., pardon, [illegible].
„ Thomas fitz James, pardon, 1617.
„ Thomas fitz Philip, pardon, 911, [illegible], [illegible], 6440.
„ Thomas fitz Piers, pardon, 1184, [illegible], [illegible], [illegible], [illegible], [illegible].
„ Tho. fitz Redmund (Purcell ?), pardon, [illegible].
„ Thomas fitz Robert, pardon, 1184, [illegible], [illegible], [illegible], 6464.
„ Tho. fitz Robnet or m'Robenet, pardon, [illegible], [illegible], [illegible].
„ Thomas fitz Theobald, pardon, 911, [illegible], 1184, [illegible], [illegible], [illegible], 6440.
„ Tho. fitz Thomas, pardon, [illegible], [illegible].
„ Thomas fitz Tibbot, pardon, 1867, [illegible].
„ Thomas fitz William, pardon, [illegible], 1184, [illegible].
„ Thomas m'Gilpatrick, pardon, 1578.
„ Tho. m'Wm. bey, pardon, [illegible].
„ Tho. oge, pardon, 6708.
„ Tho. roe, pardon, [illegible].
„ Tibbot fitz James, pardon, 6440.
„ Tibbot fitz Patrick, pardon, [illegible].
„ Walter, pardon, [illegible], [illegible].
„ Walter gar, pardon, [illegible].
„ Walter leigh, pardon, [illegible], [illegible].
„ William, house in Dublin, [illegible].
„ Wm., pardon, [illegible], [illegible], [illegible], [illegible].
„ Wm. (of Aghaboy), pardon, [illegible].
„ Wm. fitz Edm., pardon, 6704.
„ Wm. fitz John, pardon, [illegible], [illegible].
„ Wm. fitz Piers, pardon, 1184, [illegible].
„ Wm. fitz Redmund, pardon, [illegible], 1184, [illegible].
„ Wm. fitz Rich., pardon, 4487, [illegible], 6440, [illegible].
„ Wm. fitz Wm., pardon, [illegible], [illegible].

INDEX TO FIANTS.—ELIZABETH.

Purcell, Wm. m'Gilpatrick, pardon, [illegible].
" Wm. m'Tho., pardon, 6027.
Purcell bey, Edm., pardon, 1987.
Purcell glas, John, pardon, 1884.
Purcell more, Peter or Piers, pardon, 1007.
Purcell reogho, Redmund, 1906. See Redmund reogh Purcell.
Purcell rowe, Wm. m'James, pardon, 1816.
Purcelston, co. Westm. (see Porselstowne), [illegible].
Purchesstowne (Purcellstown ?), co. Louth, [illegible].
Purdeme, Simon, pension, 1606.
Purdon, Gilbert (of Tallagh), pardon, 6768.
" John, pardon, 6768.
" Simon, pensioner, 4002.
Purpoint, Agnes. See Perpoynte.
Perpoynte, Anne. See Perpoint.
Purscell—Pursell. See Purcell.
Pursellstowne—Purselstowne, co. Lim., 6171.
Purshell, John, 4239. See Purcell.
Pursill, Patr., 4078. See Purcell.
Purssell. See Purcell.
Pursuivants at arms appointed, [illegible]-8, [illegible], [illegible]-10, 6778.
Pursuivant, Athlone, [illegible], [illegible], 6798, 6018, [illegible].
Purtane (Portan), co. Meath, 672, [illegible].
Pursell, Rob. reogh, pardon, 4471.
Puttaghan, King's co. See Pottinghan, Puttoghan.
Puttnalestown, co. Westm., 1676.
Pyardiston. See Fiardeston.
Pyerce, Wm., capt. See Piers.
Pyerce or Piers, William. See Piers.
Pyers, Edm. fitz James, pardon 3712.
" Garret fitz James, pardon, 3762.
" James oge, pardon, 3762.
" John oge, pardon, 3762.
" Rich. fitz James, pardon, 3762.
Pyerse, William. See Piers.
Pyerston. See Pierston, co. Meath.
Pyerston Landy. See Pierston Lawndy.
Pyfold, Robert. See Pypho.
Pyggotte—Pygott. See Pigott.
Pyemerston, co. Meath, 1609.
Pynkeston, Gerald. See Pinkeston.
Pyne, John, pardon, [illegible].
Pyncocke, Michael, grant of a wardship, 6772.
Pyncocke—Pyncock, Thomas, house in Dublin, 1672, 5176.
Pypho, Janet, pardon, 5146.
Pypho—Fiefolde—Fipho—Fiphoo—Fiphold—Pyfold—Pyphold, Robert (of Hollywood), seneschal of district west of Wicklow mountains, 1414; sheriff of Kildare, 1834; commissions, 882, [illegible] (bis), [illegible], 1108, 1416, 1528, 1834, [illegible], [illegible], 5134, 6751; pardon, 427, 763, 5148, 5450; leases, 1608, 5446; surety, [illegible]; pardon at his suit, [illegible].

Quade, Maurice, English liberty, [illegible].
Quahirronagh, co. Cork, 1678.
Quallan, Maurice m'Teig I, pardon, 6511.
Quanne, Margaret or Marine, pardon, [illegible].
Quarleme, Jermaine, grant, [illegible].
Quarrykeale (see Carrowkeal, co. Rosc.) [illegible].
Quarrowomore (Carrowmore, co. Rosc. ?), [illegible].
Quarrowncheashill (Carrowcashel, co. Sligo ?), [illegible].
Quarter Jordane, 1468.
Quarter or carrow of land, 5377.
" or carucate, [illegible].
" or ploughland, 6761-2.
" fourth part of a town of land, [illegible].
" = 4 cartrons (see Cartron), [illegible], [illegible], &c.
" = 120 acres, 5377.
" = 60 acres (co. Kerry), 6717.
" = 60 acres (co. Antrim), 5702.
" = 40 acres (co. Kerry), 6717.
" equivalent in English acres, 6761-2.
" being fourth part of a ploughland (co. Tip.), 6640.
" small, [illegible].
Quatermas, Edm., pardon, [illegible].
" John, second remembrancer of the Exchequer, 6, 128, 872, 883, 153, 906, [illegible]; house in Dublin, 1311; lease, 1362.
" Thomas, pardon, [illegible]; marshal of ecclesiastical high court, 6162.
Quatermasse, Rosina, 2184.
Queen's attorney (see Attorney general), 1808. See also Connaught, Munster.
Queen's Bench. See Chief Place, court of.
Queen's county, commission and return setting out boundaries of the county (in 1562), 6780; Iregan to be surveyed and added to county, 1684, 5118; Upper Ossory united, [illegible].
" or Leix, [illegible].
" persons indicted of treason to be proclaimed, 1898.
" men of, pardoned, 857, 1115, 1176, 2140, 3467, 3768, [illegible], 4261, 4347, 6110, &c.
" war by O'Mores, 1319; O'Mores of, excepted from pardons, [illegible], [illegible].
" persons employed in, discharged from appearance in court, 3842.
" travelling unsafe in, 6077.
" commission to treat with Irish of, 188.

INDEX TO FIANTS.—ELIZABETH.

Queen's county, commissions for muster, 3117, [illegible], 3444, [illegible].
" commissions of peace, [illegible], [illegible], [illegible], [illegible], [illegible], [illegible], [illegible], [illegible], [illegible], [illegible], [illegible], [illegible], [illegible], [illegible], [illegible], [illegible], [illegible].
" martial law, [illegible], [illegible], [illegible], 1027, [illegible], [illegible], [illegible], [illegible], [illegible], [illegible], [illegible], [illegible], [illegible], [illegible], [illegible], [illegible], [illegible], [illegible], [illegible], [illegible], [illegible].
" commissions to enquire of lands of earl of Kildare, [illegible], [illegible].
" lieutenant of King's and Queen's counties, [illegible], [illegible], [illegible].
" seneschal, [illegible], [illegible], [illegible], [illegible], [illegible], [illegible]; persons pardoned to give security before, [illegible]; Liagh O'More to be answerable for his followers until renounced before, [illegible]; to proclaim persons indicted of treason, 1641.
" constable of castle of Maryborough, [illegible], [illegible]; his powers for government of the county, [illegible].
" sheriff, [illegible], 1027, [illegible], [illegible], [illegible], [illegible], [illegible], [illegible], [illegible], [illegible], [illegible], [illegible].
" clerk of the peace, &c., [illegible], [illegible].
" general of the forces in, [illegible], [illegible], [illegible], [illegible], [illegible].
" soldiers in, not to leave their places, [illegible].
" grants of land in, [illegible], [illegible], [illegible], [illegible], [illegible], [illegible], [illegible], [illegible], [illegible], [illegible], [illegible], [illegible], [illegible], [illegible], &c., conditions attached to grants, 474, [illegible], [illegible].
" licence to demise lands waste from rebellion, [illegible].
Questrot, James. *See* Questrod.
Quellenagh—Quellenaghe. *See* Oullenagh, Queen's co.
Quemerford—Quemberford—Quembirford—Quemerforde. *See* Comerford.
Questrod — Quaitrot — Queytrott, James, surrender and lease, [illegible], 1174; a trustee, [illegible].
Queyne. *See* Quinby, co. Clare.
Queyne, Tho., pardon, [illegible].
Queytrott. *See* Questrod.
Queytrott's land in Kilmainham, [illegible].
Quicke, Robert, pardon, 1572.
Quiddy (*See* Cuddihie), [illegible].
Quidengehe, Queen's co., 481.
Quidrathe, Irish custom called, [illegible].
Quile, Art m'Donogh I., pardon, [illegible].
Quillaghmedohrake, co. Gal., [illegible].
Quillan, Daniel, [illegible].
" John, [illegible].
Quillane (Quillan, co. Mayo), [illegible], [illegible].
Quilleen (Queen's co.), [illegible].
Quillenagh. *See* Oullenagh, Queen's co.
Quillenaghe (Oullenagh ?), co. Wat., [illegible].
Quillenmawan (King's or Queen's co. ?) [illegible].
Quillin—Quyllen (co. Wat.), 1053, [illegible].
Quillindroghe (Cullendragh), co. Meath, [illegible].
Quimerford—Quimarsford — Quimarforde. *See* Comerford.
Quin, co. Clare. *See* Quinby.
Quin. *See* Quyn.
Quinces, confection of, [illegible].
Quine. *See* Quyn.
Quinby—Queyne—Quyn (Quin), co. Clare, [illegible].
" house of Franciscan friars leased, [illegible], [illegible].
Quinlane, Wm., English liberty, [illegible].
Quirck—Quircke. *See* Quirke.
quirilcah. Dermod m'Philip I., pardon, [illegible].
Quirke—Quirck—Quircke—Quyrck :
" David, pardon, [illegible], [illegible].
" Dominick, pardon, [illegible].
" Edmund, pardon, [illegible].
" Edward, pardon, [illegible].
" Mahown m'Rich. Y., pardon, [illegible].
" Thady m'Shean Y., pardon, [illegible].
" Walter, pardon, [illegible].
" William, pardon, [illegible], [illegible], [illegible].
Quirkeston (co. Kilk. ?), [illegible].
Quommerforde, James, pardon, [illegible].
Quonan, John, vicar of Pollrean, [illegible].
Qualcaleig (Coollistoige), co. Clare, [illegible].
Quoyne, Henry, pardon, [illegible].
" Robert, pardon, [illegible].
" Wm., pardon, [illegible].
Qurin—Quryn (co. Clare ?), [illegible].
Quycke—Qwycke, Thomas, licensed to keep tennis courts, &c., [illegible], [illegible].
Quyigan. *See* Coyligan.
Quyll, co. Long., [illegible].
Quyllen. *See* Quillin, co. Wat.
Quyllenaghe (Cullenagh, in parish Killabban), Queen's co. [illegible].
Quyn. *See* Quinby, co. Clare, [illegible].

INDEX TO FIANTS.—ELIZABETH.

Quyn—Quin — Quine — Quyne — Quynn — Qwyn—Qwyne :
„ Barnaby, pardon, [illegible].
„ Connor, pardon, 4641.
„ Donogh, pardon, [illegible].
„ Ellen ny, pardon, 6163.
„ Garret, pardon, [illegible].
„ Gerald, pardon, 6497.
„ Gerrott, pardon, [illegible].
„ Hubert, pardon, [illegible].
„ Inyn duffe ne, pardon, 6166.
„ Ivanney, pardon, [illegible].
„ James, pardon, [illegible], 6377.
„ Jeffery, pardon, [illegible].
„ John, tenement in Trim, 1714.
„ John, tenement in Kilmainham, 1722, 6418.
„ John, pardon, 4624, 6704, 6773.
„ Laghlin, tenement in Kilmainham, 1722, 6418.
„ Moriah, pardon, [illegible].
„ Nicholas, pardon, 761, 4316.
„ Onora inie, pardon, [illegible].
„ Redmund, pardon, 6773.
„ Richard, appeal by, 3136.
„ Richard, pardon, 6773.
„ Robert, pardon, 6773.
„ Teig, pardon, [illegible].
„ Thomas, pardon, 6773.
„ William, pardon, [illegible], [illegible].
Quynie, Joan ny, pardon, [illegible].
Quynland—Qwinlane, David, pardon, 4660.
„ Darby, pardon, [illegible], 6494.
„ John, pardon, [illegible].
„ Thomas, pardon, 6734.
Quynn. See Quyn.
Quynnahe, co. Cork, [illegible].
Quyrck. See Quirke.
Quyshen—Qwyshen, Robert oge, attainted, 5721-2. See Cushin.
Qwade, Nicholas, English liberty, 784.
Qwomerford. See Comerford.
Qwille, co. Gal., 4654.
Qwilliasiack, co. Clare, 1540.
Qwinlaine—Qwinlane. See Quynland.
Qwycke. See Quycke.
Qwyn—Qwyne. See Quyn.
Qwyran Clynamoriaria, co. Clare, 4274.
Qwyshen. See Quyshen.

Raaocm, co. Tip., [illegible].
Raas, co. Lim., 6176.
Rabane, baron of. See Robane.
Rabie, S. Peter of, monastery, co. Long., 4176. See Monasterderge.
Rabody (Rathbody, co. Louth), 1728.
Rabran. See Rathbran, co. Wick.
Rabran by Athy, co. Kild., 1347.
Rabran rectory, co. Mayo, [illegible]. See also Rathbranna.
Rabronan (Rathbronan), co. Ros., [illegible].
Rabuck—Rabuik, rectory of S. Michael, co. Long., 2154, [illegible], [illegible].
Racammon (co. Lim. ?), 4387.
Racan, co. Lim. or Cork, [illegible].
Racashane, co. Louth, 1654.
Rachanye (co. Lim. or Cork ?), 2217.
Rachara (King's co. ?), [illegible].
Rachavra, co. Westm. See Killenahanekin, Rathvichy.
Rackett, Henry, pardon, 6496.
Rackwallace, co. Mon. See Ramakmallie.
Rackyully, co. Ros., [illegible].
Racoubraman (Ratholonbrackan), King's co. 462, [illegible].
Racunnall, co. Mon. See Ballymaconnyle.
Racowle (Rathcool ?, co. Dub. ?), 6488.
Racrohin—Racrohyn (Rathcrone ?), Queen's co., 463, [illegible], 6377.
Racreighan (Racreghan), co. Mon., [illegible].
Racronan, co. Long., [illegible].
Racrogna, co. Lim., 6674.
Racthooge (co. Long. ?), [illegible].
Ractoure, Tho., merchant, [illegible].
Radcliel — Radclif — Radcliff — Radcliffe — Radclyf—Radclyffe. See Radeclyff.
Raddlyowe (co. Sligo ?), [illegible]. See Rathlew.
Radeclyff — Radcliel — Radclif — Radcliff—Radcliffe—Radclyf— Radclyffe — Radcliff —Radecliff—Ratclif—Ratcliff—Ratclyf, sir Henry, lieutenant of Leix and Offaly, 4, 15, 679 ; license of absence, 13 ; takes oath of supremacy, 187 ; commissions, 165, [illegible], [illegible], 679-80, 684, 643, [illegible], [illegible], [illegible], 6794 ; pardon, 4, 487 ; leases, 363-4, [illegible], [illegible], 6115 ; earl of Sussex, 6411.
Radencro (see Rathmore, co. Kild.), 6146.
Radford, Roger, clerk of the peace, Wexford, 5479 ; lease, 4604.
Radin, 6447.
Radnorshire, 4894.
Radoywe (co. Kilk. ?), 5048.
Radonell. See Rathdonill, co. Car.
Radowgin, co. Car., 604.
Radronaghe (Rathdrinagh), co. Meath, [illegible].
Radrome. See Rathdrome, co. Wick.
Raduff—Raduffe. See Rathduff, co. Westm.
Racgrolgo, alias Rathcroughe, co. Lim., 463.
Raooyane (King's co. ?), 6726.
Rafe, John, grant, 1577.
Rafegh. See Rathleigh.
Raferilan, co. Down, 1633.
Rafernam, [illegible]. See Rathfarnam.
Raffeigh. See Rathfeigh.
Raffin—Raffyn—Raffyne — Rafyne — Rathfine—Rhafen, co. Meath, [illegible], 2437, [illegible], [illegible], 4461, 4465, [illegible].

INDEX TO FIANTS.—ELIZABETH.

Rafcada, co. Meath, 6510.
Rafter, Tho., 1106.
Rafyne. See Rafin.
Ragarf—Ragarie—Ragarfeit (Rathgarve), co. Westm. 4686; rectory, 1059, 5472.
Ragarrand (co. Meath ?), 6864.
Ragarroge (Rathgaroge, co. Wex. ?), 1377.
Raggad, Peter, pardon, 3424.
Raggad, Edw., clerk of the crown and peace, Wexford, 2598, 3573, 3534, 4234.
" Edw. (of Kilkenny), pardon, 3394.
" Rich., message in Kilkenny, 3394.
" Rob., pardon, 4661.
" Wm. fitz Rich., pardon, 4437.
Raggid, Edw., pardon, 4363.
" Nich. fitz Patr., pardon, 3174.
" Nich. fitz Piers, pardon, 3434.
" Patr., pardon, 3434.
" Peter fitz Edw., pardon, 3434.
" Rich. fitz Piers, pardon, 3491.
" Rich. fitz Tho., pardon, 3434.
" Tho., pardon, 3434.
" Walter, pardon, 3434.
Raggyd, Wm., pardon, 3434.
Ragh (co. Lim. ?), 4461.
Ragharrowe, co. Ross., 5842.
Raghbrennagh. See Rathbrennagh.
Raghelaghin (co. Clare ?), 5743.
Raghcolly, co. Cork, 4761.
Raghe (co. Clare ?), 6414.
Raghebegg, in Elie Ocarroll, King's co., 4561.
Raghechloghy, co. Cav., 4834.
Raghellone, 5234. See Raughlines.
Raghenan (King's co.), 438.
Raghenmagorren (Raheenagurren, co. Wex. ?) 6180.
Raghershellogs (Rathmoshillogs), co. Wat., 4834.
Raghhoney (co. Cork ?), 5284.
Raghill in Tirconnell, 6467.
Raghin, co. Westm., 5472.
Raghine (co. Tip. ?), 6381.
Raghincoser (co. Tip. ?), 6452.
Raghingherin (Raheenakeeran ?), King's co., 6439.
Raghinlea (Raheenleagh), co. Car., 1754.
Raghirynan (co. Tip. ?), 4562.
Raghisseshean — Raghlynnshean, alias Rathseshean Queen's co., 1562, 3780.
Raghmore (co. Wat. ?), 6477.
Raghogelly, co. Tip., 6112.
Raghonyne, 6477. See Rathonyne.
Raghre, King's co., 6612.
Raghrevagh, 4532. See Rathrievagh.
Raghrianmaie, co. Kerry, 5494.
Raghter, Murtogh, pardon, 6712.
Raghter, Tim., pardon, 5434.
Ragilbert (Rathgilbert), Queen's co., 5388.
Ragony (co. Westm. ?), 6432.
Ragorrine, co. Gal., 4534.
Ragowle, co. Tip. (see Rathcoole), 521.
Ragraleg, co. Lim., 6284.
Ragrowe (co. Cork ?), 6761.
Ragum. See Argum, 58.
Ragyharry (co. Clare ?), 6412.
Rah, the, co. Clare, 4563.
Rah, co. Cork, 6540. See Rahen.
Rahagall (co. Kilk. or Tip. ?), 4562.
Rahalle (co. Wex. ?), 6567.
Rahallean—Rahalhen, co. Gal., 5385, 5728.
Rahalle, 4160.
Rahalron. See Rathalron.
Rahan, co. Lim., 6271.
Rahane, King's co., 6241.
Rahanagh (co. Clare ?), 5497.
Rahanagh, co. Lim. See Rahenogh.
Rahanas, co. Kerry, 4672.
Rahanane (Ranahan), co. Lim., 5672.
Rahanasky (co. Cork ?), 6416.
Rahangan. See Rathangan, co. Kild.
Rahangan. See Rathangane, co. Wex.
Rahangan. See Rathangan.
Rahanlom, co. Gal., 1836.
Rahanlon (Rathanlon ?), co. Gal., 5256.
Rahanlonie, co. Gal., 4564.
Rahanne, co. Lim., 5189.
Rahanne, co. Louth. See Rathenagha.
Rahannan—Rahannane (co. Kerry ?), 6572.
Rahanagh (Rahanagh), co. Lim., 5682.
Rahara, co. Ross. See Rathharrowe.
Rahard, co. Mayo. See Rathards.
Rahardo (co. Lim.), 4826.
Raharragh (co. Mayo ?), 5782.
Raharowe, co. Ross. 5824.
Raharrownye, co. Mayo, 5782.
Raharrowe (co. Ross. ?), 4572, 4172.
Raharwoe (co. Mayo ?), 5784.
Rahaspick — Rahaspike — Rahaspuck—Rahaspoke. See Rathaspicke.
Rahassane, co. Gal., 4238.
Rahatemple, co. Cork, 5062.
Rahe, Morogh m'Shane m, pardon, 6477.
Raheden (co. Wex. or Car.), 6317.
Raheen, King's co. See Rahyne.
Raheen, co. Wick. See Rahin, Rathenne, Reyn.
Raheenagurren, co. Wex. See Raghenmagorren.
Raheenakeeran, King's co. See Raghingherin, Rahiraghirrin, Rathinachirrin.
Raheenanisky, Queen's co. See Rahynisky.
Raheendarragh, co. Car. See Rahinderigh, Raynsdeow.
Raheendonore, co. Kilk. See Rahendonore.
Raheenduff, King's co. See Rahinduffe.
Raheenduff, Queen's co. See Rahenduf, Rahindowne, Rahinduffe, Rayndef.

INDEX TO FIANTS.—ELIZABETH.

Rahcendi-vh, co. Car. See Raghinlen.
Rahcennahoen, co. Wex. See Rahinno-
 howen.
Rahcenroche, co. Kilk. See Rahinroch.
Rahcille (Rahelty), co. Tip., rectory, 462.
Raheile, co. Wex., 1577.
Raheloy, Thady m' Donill Y, pardon, [illegible].
Rahellie, Dermond m' Donagh I, pardon,
 [illegible].
Rahelly, Rich., pardon, [illegible].
Rahelly—Rahellie (co. Tip.), 6440, [illegible]. See
 also Rahellie, Rahelty.
Rahen—Rah — Rahin, co. Cork, [illegible], [illegible],
 [illegible], [illegible].
Rahen, King's co., [illegible].
Rahen, Queen's co., 1157.
Rahen, co. Westm., [illegible].
Rahenallo (co. Kilk. ?), 1674.
Rahendarrogh. See Rahindarigh.
Rahendower — Rahindowner (Rahende-
 owre), co. Kilk., 290, 1178.
Rahendnif (Rahendnff ?), Queen's co., 6163.
Rahenduffe, co. Wex., 4737.
Rahenesharon, Queen's co., 1578.
Rahene cowlie, co. Westm., [illegible].
Rahenekeraghfyna, co. Wex., [illegible].
Rahengura, co. Tip., [illegible].
Rahenisky (co. Cork ?), 4414.
Rahennemaganee (co. Wex. ?), [illegible].
Rahenlesnalan, Queen's co., 634, 3357.
Raheny, co. Dub. See Ralheny.
Rahe mullayne, co. Cork, [illegible].
Rahesker. See Rathesker.
Raheston, co. Meath, 6357.
Rahetanny (Rathanny ?), co. Kerry, [illegible].
Raheyn, co. Clare, [illegible].
Rahgabban (co. Cork), [illegible].
Rahiene—Rahyen, co. Wex., [illegible], 1577.
Rahill, co. Meath. See Rathyll.
Rahin. See Rahen, co. Cork.
Rahin (co. Gal. ?), 4707.
Rahin — Rahyne (now Rahin ; called
 Rahindorrie in Book of Survey and
 Distribution), Queen's co., castle and lands
 granted, [illegible], [illegible].
Rahin (co. Tip. ?), [illegible].
Rahin, co. Westm., [illegible].
Rahin (Raheen, co. Wick.), 1357.
Rahin (co. Wick. ?), [illegible].
Rahinaghbrrie—Rahynaghirrin (Rahenna-
 howen ?, King's co.), [illegible], 1554.
Rahin Conoghor (co. Wex. ?), [illegible].
Rahin Cormockmore — Rahine Cormick-
 more — Rahinecormockmore, co. Wex.,
 [illegible], 5731.
Rahindarigh — Rahendarrogh — Rahin-
 darighe — Rahindorogh — Rahindorough
 (Rahendarragh, co. Car. ?), [illegible], [illegible],
 [illegible].
Rahindorrie. See Rahin, Queen's co.
Rahindowne (Rahendnff ?), Queen's co.,
 1514.
Rahindowner. See Rahendower.
Rahinduffe (Rahendnff), King's co., [illegible].
Rahinduffe — Rahinedniffe — Rahyndnf
 (Rahendnff), Queen's co., 616, [illegible], [illegible],
 [illegible]. See also Raynduf.
Rahine, King's co., [illegible].
Rahine (Queen's co. ?), [illegible].
Rahine (co. Tip. ?), [illegible], [illegible].
Rahine Cormickmore — Rahinecormock-
 more. See Rahin Cormockmore.
Rahinedniffe. See Rahinduffe, Queen's co.
Rahinegore - Rahynagoer — Rahynegoer,
 co. Tip., 1162, 6464, [illegible]. See also Raghine-
 goer.
Rahinemanero, co. Car., [illegible].
Rahinemore—Rahynmore, co. Car., 1477, [illegible].
Rahinemore, co. Westm., [illegible].
Rahine necollyran — Rahynekhollenane,
 Queen's co., 1125, 6755.
Rahinnohowne (Rahennahoen, co. Wex. ?)
 [illegible].
Rahinnokrigy (co. Kilk. ?), [illegible].
Rahin ny gerr, co. Tip. or Lim., 6743.
Rahinynill (co. Westm. ?), [illegible].
Rahinro, co. Kilk., [illegible].
Rahinroch — Rahynroch (Rahenroche ?),
 co. Kilk., 5417, [illegible].
Rahinnake — Rahynnake, Queen's co., [illegible],
 [illegible].
Rahinygorroen, co. Tip., [illegible].
Rahiston, King's co., [illegible].
Rahkrane, [illegible].
Rahlackane—Rahlenkane (Rathlackan), co.
 Mayo, [illegible], [illegible].
Rahlye (co. Kerry ?), [illegible].
Rahmy, Moroghe ny, alias Moriarie m'Brien,
 pardon, 6170.
Rahodo—Rathode (co. Meath), 67, [illegible].
Rahorn, co. Clare, [illegible].
Rahon (co. Westm. ?), [illegible].
Rahowran (co. Cork ?), [illegible].
Rahowrn, co. Kerry. See Rathowyny,
 Rathonlyne.
Rahosker, co. Kild., [illegible].
Rahowsnaghe, co. Kerry, [illegible].
Rahugh, co. Westm. See Rathee, Rathhey.
Rahrilie—Rathulie, co. Dub., [illegible], [illegible], [illegible].
Rahvihyne, co. Clare, [illegible].
Rahy, co. Clare, 1640.
Rahynaoghor, [illegible].
Rahyne. See Rahiane, co. Wex.
Rahykely, co. Lim., 4831.
Rahyn, co. Clare, [illegible].
Rahyn, Queen's co., [illegible], [illegible].
Rahynaghirrin. See Rahinaghbrrie.
Rahynagoer, [illegible]. See Rahinegore.

INDEX TO FIANTS—ELIZABETH.

Rahyndaf. See Rahindaffe, Queen's co.
Rahyndaffe, co. Wex., 6617.
Rahyns, co. Cork, 4929.
Rahyne (Raheen), King's co., 896.
Rahyns, co. Lim., castle and lands, 6282.
Rahyns, Queen's co., 3947.
Rahyns. See Rahin.
Rahynesporcer, 1182. See Rahinesporc.
Rahyne Tyrrellsvalle, King's co. 1654.
Rahynske (Rahinnansky), Queen's co. 461.
Rahynkhollemane. See Rahinsrucallyman.
Rahynmore. See Rahinmore, co. Car.
Rahynemonoey (co. Car. or Wex.), 6617.
Rahynroch. See Rahinroch.
Rahynnske. See Rahinnaske.
Raieston, co. Meath, 1174.
Raieston (Raystown), co. Meath, 2578.
Raigine (co. Gal. ?), 6603.
Railiston — Rayleston — Rayliston — Reyleston (Raffstown), co. Tip., rectory, 922, 7985, 6160, 6408; vicarage, 922, 6423. See also Ballyreffe.
Raigonemarck, Queen's co., 428.
Rainestown, co. Car. See Ballinrahin.
Rainhollan, co. Mayo, 5777.
Rainsford — Raynesford — Raynsford — Raynsforde, Hercules, collector of customs, Kinsale, 1481; collector of customs, Limerick, 4767; constable of Limerick castle, 2303, 2649, 1467; lease, 3976, 5027; grant of wardships, 1763-4.
Raiordan—Raiordane. See Rathjordan.
Raispicke (Rathaspick ?), co. Westm., rectory, 5769.
Rajordan—Ra Jordane. See Rathjordan.
Rakeale. See Rathkeale.
Rakeragh, co. Mon. See Rathkeraght.
Rakeigh (co. Meath), 2344.
Rakeley—Rakelie—Rakelly—Rakely—Rakelye. See Rathkealie.
Rakelly, co. Mon. See Rathkelly.
Rakeryn (co. Gal.), 5012.
Rakeyle—Rakeylle. See Rathkeale.
Rakinvirran, co. Lim., 5686.
Rakivinane, co. Lim., 5690.
Rakynylie, co. Ross., 5164.
Ralaclan (Rathlaclan), co. Mayo, 5945, 6016.
Ralahyn, co. Clare, 5465.
Ralegh. See Rathlegh.
Ralegh — Raleghe — Rawley, sir Walter, Munster undertaker, 4963; pardon granted on letter from, 4998; grant of lands, 5043; enquiry as to lands granted to, 5297.
Ralehin, co. Clare, 1840.
Raleigh, alias Rowlie, Rich., pardon, 6423.
Raleighstown (Rawleystown ?), co. Lim., 6462.
Ralein, co. Westm., 5422.
Raleikine, co. Mayo, 4667.
Raleston, 962.
Ralian (Rathilihen ? King's co.), 1616.
Ralie—Rally—Raly (Rathlihen, King's co.), 4987-8, 6511.
Raligoornyne, co. Gal., 4684.
Raline, 910. See Rathlyne.
Ralitavreny (Ballytarsney ?), co. Kilk., 2840.
Rally, King's co., 6511. See Ralie.
Ralsannane (Rathsannon ?), co. Wex., 2882.
Ralowe (co. Antrim), 6428.
Ralphtown, co. Wex. See Rathmore.
Raly, King's co. See Ralie.
Ralye, John, pardon, 1634.
Ralyn — Ralyne (Rathlihen ? King's co.), 4498.
Ralyne, Queen's co., 497.
Ram—Rame—Ramme, Thomas, A.M., dean of Ferns, 4471; vicar of Balrothery, 4868; prebendary of Christ Church, 4575; dean of Cork, 4694.
Ramakwallis (perhaps Rackwallace), co. Mon., 5784.
Ramanny, co. Mon., 5442.
Ramaspok—Ramaspoke, alias Derry, Queen's co., 494, 5047.
Rame, Tho. See Ram.
Ramevegrage, 6617. See Ramyegrange.
Ramockine, co. Meath, 5654.
Ramowe. See Rathmowe.
Rameyloie, King's co., 1640, 1653.
Ramgholl (co. Dub. ?), 6512.
Ramme, Tho. See Ram.
Ramoan parish, co. Antrim. See Momeria.
Ramollan (Rathmollin, co. Meath), 862.
Ramolyane. See Rathmolian.
Ramor, co. Kilk., 2628.
Ramore (co. Gal ?), 4632.
Ramore (King's or Queen's co.), 5602.
Ramoveake (Rathmoveage), co. Tip., rectory, 462.
Ramoyle (Rathmoyle), Queen's co., 497.
Ramullan (Rathmullan), co. Donegal, 6661.
Ramyegrange—Ramevegrage (Ramsgrange), co. Wex., 1827, 6617.
Ramyakie (co. Cork ?), 6762.
Ranahan, co. Lim. See Rahanrane.
Ranelaghes (a district included in the barony of Ballinacor South, co. Wick.), martial law in, 6791. See also Gabhal Raghnaill.
Ranasier (Rathnasery, co. Lim.), 6457.
Randall, Francis. See Randell.
Randewylestown, co. Dub., 718.
Randell, Francis. See Randoll.
Randoll, Edward, esq., lieutenant of ordnance in England to be colonel of army in Ulster, 846.
Randoll—Randall—Randell, Francis, constable of Carlow, 850, 1156; commissions, 44, 881, 842, 885, 883.
Ranegh, 1682.

Ranegrumanaghe (co. Lim. ?), 6277.
Raneleigh. *See* Ranelaghe, Gabhal Raghnalli.
Ranelaghi, co. Sligo, 5468.
Ranell, Joan ny, pardon, 6316.
" Katherine ny, pardon, 5461.
" More ny, pardon, 5516.
Ranamnekan, co. Gal., 4734.
Ranewahey, co. Lim., 6464.
Ranforde, alias Ranforthe, George, pardon, 687.
Ranill, Ellyne ny, pardon, 5701.
Rankagh, Donogh, pardon, 4626.
Ranrowan, alias Rathrowgan, co. Westm., 5943.
Ranmore (Rathnamer, co. Lim.), 6171.
Ranvyle (co. Gal. ?), 4674.
Rany, Gilbert, pardon, 6143.
Rany (co. Rosc. ?), 6432.
Ranyskan, alias Moncktonowton (Monkneowton, co. Meath), 682.
Ranywro, 612. *See* Rathmore, co. Kilk.
Raogalle, co. Tip., 6784.
Rapaleigh. *See* Rapleigh.
Rapatricke. *See* Rathpatrik.
Rape, growth and export of, 4461.
Raphrilan—Raphrylan. *See* Rathphrilan.
Rapiers (Rathpieres), co. Wex., 3732.
Rapleigh—Rapaleigh—Rappaleagh—Rappallaghe (Raple), co. Tip., 4403-4, 4585, 6702.
Rarevagh, 6169. *See* Rathrievagh.
Rayodda (co. Gal.), 4634.
Raroo. *See* Rathroo.
Rarowan. *See* Rathrowan, co. Lim.
Rarownie (Rathrowanbin, Queen's co. ?), 614.
Raruske. *See* Rathrush.
Rarwiagh, co. Mon. *See* Rathrowtaght.
Rasallagh. *See* Rathsallagh, co. Wick.
Rasallagh (Rathsillagh), co. Wex., 6737.
Rashillagh, Queen's co., 6152.
Rashinagh, King's co. *See* Rossyny.
Rashordan, 2042. *See* Rathjordan.
Ratacline, 4071. *See* Rathclyne, co. Long.
Rataine, co. Meath. *See* Rathtaine.
Ratbrahaghe (Rathbreagh ?), co. Kilk., 1287.
Ratcliff—Ratcliff—Ratclyf, sir Henry. *See* Radeclyff.
Rate, co. Cork, 6678.
Ratekely. *See* Rathkeale, co. Lim.
Ratenen, co. Tip., 1642, 4616.
Rath, Henry, pardon, 5962.
Rath—Rathe, co. Cork, 2867, 2841, 5478, 5101.
Rath (co. Donegal), 6382.
Rath—Rath by the Naas—Rathe by the Naas, co. Dub. 1232, 1462, 5126; grant, 5771.
Rath of Killosmery—Rathe, co. Dub., 2466, 4616.
Rath, co. Long., 6784.
Rath, the—Rathe, co. Louth, 152, 5416, 4877.
Rath—Rathe, co. Meath, 653, 2280, 6254, 6411. *See also* Rathe by Crowcke.
Rath, co. Mon., 4643.
Rath—Rathe, Queen's co., 1174, 5484.
Rath (co. Rosc. ?), 6968.
Rath (co. Tip. ?), 6768.
Rathaagire, co. Long., 6461.
Rathafryne, co. Rosc., 5416.
Rathaghe, co. Long., 6362.
Rathagloe, co. Gal., 4871.
Rathallan—Rathallen, co. Meath, 1426, 2668, 5444.
Rathallan (co. Meath ?), 1424.
Rathally (co. Gal.), 6968.
Rathalron—Rahalroe—Rathalrone—Rathalron (Rathaldron), co. Meath, 102, 2344, 2398, 2444, 2638, 2548, 2877, 3664, 4784, 5422.
Rathan, co. Meath, 880.
Rathangan—Rahangan—Rahangan—Rathehangan—Rathhangan, co. Kild., 98, 230, 494, 2262, 2344, 3062, 3312, 5460, 6257; river, 6798.
" rector of, 4484.
Rathangane—Rahangan, co. Wex., 542, 2627.
Rathanloe, co. Gal. *See* Rahanlon.
Rathanagh (co. Tip. or Kilk. ?), 5984.
Rathanny, co. Kerry. *See* Rahotanny.
Rathard—Rathardo—Rathard (co. Tip. ?), 1818, 2846.
Rathards (Rahard), co. Mayo, 5777.
Rathardo. *See* Rathard.
Rathardmore, co. Kilk., 358, 1022.
Rathargot—Rathargitt—Rathargyt—Rathargott, co. Kild., 928, 2818, 3144, 4868.
Ratharne, co. Westm., 6458.
Ratharuman, co. Gal., 4717.
Rathashog (co. Westm.), 4288.
Rathaslege, co. Westm., 4642.
Rathaspicke—Rahaspick—Rahaspike—Rahaspeck—Rahaspoke—Rathaspick, Queen's co., 826, 2422, 5128, 6479.
Rathaspige, co. Car., 1268.
Rathaspike, co. Westm., 1940. *See also* Rahaspicke, Raysbucke.
Rathassell, Abbey of (Athassel), co. Tip., 6464.
Rathawle, co. Wex., 1323.
Rathbane, co. Lim., 2542.
Rathbarry—Rathbarrie—Rathebarry, co. Cork, 6287, 5458.
" rectory, 2380, 4261.
Rathbeagh, co. Kilk. *See* Rathbeaghe.
Rathbegan—Rathbeggan (Rathbeggan), co. Meath, 1462, 1546, 3181, 5412, 5844, 6211; manor, 1918; rectory, 1166; parish, 1862.
Rathbegge, co. Meath, 5891.
Rathbeggo (Rathbeggan), Queen's co., 4634. *See* Rathbegge.
Rathbeggan, co. Meath. *See* Rathbegan.

INDEX TO FIANTS.—ELIZABETH.

Rathbregghan, 1940. *See* Rathbregan.
Rathbody, co. Louth. *See* Rabody.
Rathbran, 4916. *See* Rathbranna.
Rathbran — Rahran — Rathbrand — Rathbrane (Rathbran, co. Wick.), 1367, 5748, [illegible]; rectory, 1367.
Rathbranna — Rathbran (Rathbran?), co. Mayo, house of friars preachers leased, [illegible], 4916. *See also* Rabran.
Rathbrannoghe — Rathbrenagh — Raghbrenagh, co. Lim., 4173, 4461; grant, [illegible].
Rathbreany, co. Lim., 3647.
Rathbrenan — Rathebrenan — Rathebrenan (Rathbrennan, Queen's co.), 1158, 1947, 1424, [illegible], [illegible].
Rathbrenn, 5748. *See* Rathbran, co. Wick.
Rathbrenagh — Raghbrenagh (Rathbranagh, co. Lim.?). *See* Rathbrannoghe.
Rathbrennan, Queen's co. *See* Rathbrenan.
Rathbrennan, co. Rosc. *See* Rahrenan.
Rathbride — Rathbryd — Rathbryde — Rathebride, co. Kildare, 1940, 1407, [illegible], 3187, [illegible], [illegible], [illegible], 3484, 5789, 5748, [illegible], [illegible], [illegible], [illegible].
Rathbride (King's co.?), 4627.
Rathbrieda, co. Louth, 1512.
Rathbrim (co. Tip.), [illegible].
Rathbroge, co. Car., 404.
Rathbryd — Rathbryde. *See* Rathbride.
Rathbyn, co. Kilk., [illegible].
Rathcahill, co. Lim. *See* Rathkeale.
Rathcall, co. Kilk., 2173.
Rathcally, co. Kilk., grant, 4654.
Rathcam, co. Westm. *See* Rathkam.
Rathcan, co. Meath, [illegible].
Rathcane (co. Lim.?), 3467.
Rathcanaghe, co. Tip., 3378.
Rathcannon (co. Lim.), 4479.
Rathcaroge — Rathcaroge, co. Car., [illegible].
Rathcarragh, co. Westm., [illegible].
Rathcarren — Rathcarrin — Rathcarryn, co. Mayo, [illegible], 3911, 4324.
Rathcash (co. Kilk.), [illegible].
Rathcassan, co. Louth. *See* Rathkassan.
Rathcath. *See* Rathkerhait, Rathkinalle.
Rathcelaryne, co. Cork, [illegible], 4514.
Rathclein. *See* Rathclyne.
Rathcline, co. Long. *See* Rathclyne, Rathklen.
Rathcline barony, co. Long. *See* Clanconnoghor.
Rathclonbrackan, King's co. *See* Racorbracane.
Rathclowen, co. Lim., 3647.
Rathclyne — Rateclinge — Rathclein — Rathclyn — Rathecclyne (Rathcline), co. Long., 3718, 4159, 3974, 4942; rectory, 1170.
Rathcobican, King's co. *See* Rathcolbikan.
Rathcoffey — Rathcoffe — Rathcoffe — Rathcoffy — Rathcoffye, co. Kild., 294, [illegible], [illegible], 3137, 3345, 3444, [illegible], 4027, [illegible], 4779, 4778.
Rathcolbikan — Rathcolbykyn (Rathcobican), King's co., 477, 4352.
Rathcollomkill — Rathcollumkilley, alias Rathecollomkill, King's co., 182, 877.
Rathcommane, co. Cork, [illegible].
Rathconre (co. Tip.?), 4722, [illegible].
Rathcone alias Rathlean, co. Wex., 218, [illegible].
Rathconnan, co. Kerry, 6496.
Rathconnell, co. Westm., rectory, 3384.
 „ water of, [illegible]. *See also* Rosconnell, Rathconell.
Rathconrath — Rathconrethd barony, co. Westm., 1823; martial law in, [illegible].
Rathcool, co. Meath. *See* Rathcoole land.
Rathcoole, co. Dub. *See* Rathcowlle, Racowle.
Rathcorbally — Rathcorballie, co. Westm., 447, 5769.
Rathcorbe (co. Kilk.?), 3484.
Rathcore, co. Meath. *See* Rathcowre.
Rathcormick. *See* Rathgormock.
Rathcormick. *See* Rathcormock, [illegible].
Rathcormicke. *See* Rathgormock.
Rathcormock — Rathcormick — Rathcormok — Rathcorgyck, co. Cork, 1636, 2261, 3426, 4814, 4478, 4496, [illegible].
Rathcormycke. *See* Rathgormock.
Rathcowle, alias Rathcowlibe, co. Tip., 4462.
Rathcowle — Ragowle, co. Tip., rectory, 822, 4462. *See also* Rathgowle.
Rathcowre — Rathcowre (Rathcore), co. Meath, 815, 3387.
Rathcowrsy — Rathcourcy, co. Cork, 5920, 4123.
Rathcowle, co. Tip., 4271.
Rathcowlle (Rathcoole, co. Dub.), 848.
Rathcowre. *See* Rathcowre.
Rathcowlbe — Rathecowlbe, co. Tip., 1468, 3494, [illegible].
Rathcreva, Queen's co. *See* Racrevan.
Rathcredan, co. Dub., 845, [illegible].
Rathcroman, co. Tip., parsonage, [illegible].
Rathculliheen, co. Wat. *See* Rathculhen.
Rathdahiffe (co. Cork?), 4488.
Rathdaniel, co. Car. *See* Rathdonill.
Rathdenwny (Rathdowney, Queen's co.?), 4916.
Rathdonill — Radonell (Rathdaniel?), co. Car., 618, 3797, 4168.
Rathdonne (co. Wex.?), 1289.
Rathdowe, co. Louth, 3627.
Rathdown, co. Louth, 4163.
Rathdown (co. Wick.), 4494.
Rathdowne — Rathedowne, barony, co. Dub., [illegible], [illegible].
Rathdowne (co. Kild.?), [illegible].

INDEX TO FIANTS—ELIZABETH.

Rathdowny (Rathdowney), Queen's co., 5551. *See also* Rathdownay.

Rathdowny te (co. Lim. ?), 6480.

Rathdrangh—Rathdreagh (Rathdrishoge), co. Westm., 1733, 4378.

Rathdrinagh, co. Meath. *See* Radronaghe.

Rathdroma, co. Tip., 5817.

Rathdrome — Radrome (Rathdrum, co. Wick.), 4357.

Rathdrummogh, co. Meath, 5938.

Rathdromy (co. Tip. ?), 6784.

Rathdromyn (Rathdrum), co. Cork, 4695.

Rathdrum, King's co. *See* Ratromen.

Rathdrum, co. Wick. *See* Rathdrome.

Rathduf (Rathduff), Queen's co., 5858.

Rathduff—Rathduffe, co. Cork, 5280, 5822.

Rathduff—Radoff—Rathduffe, co. Westm., 1888, 2384, 2347, 5485, 6312.

Rathduffe, co. Lim., 4460.

Rathduffe. *See* Rathduff.

Rathe, Christopher, chantor of Christchurch, refuses oath of Supremacy, 236.

„ John, pardon, 6512.

Rathe, co. Carlow, 5151.

Rathe (co. Clare), 4783.

Rathe. *See* Rath, co. Cork.

Rathe, co. Cork or Kerry, 6874.

Rathe, co. Dub. 1696.

Rathe. *See* Rath of Killossery, co. Dub.

Rathe by the Naul. *See* Rath, co. Dub.

Rathe, co. Gal., 5978.

Rathe, Little, co. Kild., 5940.

Rathe. *See* Rath, co. Louth.

Rathe by Grenoke (co. Meath), 648, 854.

Rathe. *See* Rath, co. Meath.

Rathe. *See* Rath, Queen's co.

Rathe, co. Westm., 5778.

Rathealy, co. Kilk. *See* Rathhele.

Ratheard. *See* Rathard.

Rathebarry. *See* Rathbarry.

Rathebeg, co. Cork, 5969.

Rathebrahhragh (co. Kilk. ?), 5631.

Rathebreane (co. Mayo ?), 4758.

Rathebreanan — Rathebrenan. *See* Rathbrenan.

Rathebride. *See* Rathbride.

Rathebride by Whiteon, co. Kild. (*see* Rathbride), 1240.

Rathecasan (Rathcassan, co. Louth), 1211.

Rathecleyne. *See* Rathclyne.

Rathecolbykyn. *See* Rathcoulibeen.

Rathecolleskill. *See* Rathcolleskill.

Rathecomire land (Rathcool), co. Meath, 5878.

Rathecowche. *See* Rathcowthe.

Rathecoulbin, co. Kilk., 5318.

Rathedmond — Rathedmonde (Rathredmond), co. Mayo, 5385, 6016.

Rathedowne. *See* Rathdowne.

Rathee (Rahugh ?), co. Westm., 6370.

Rathefornan. *See* Rathfarnan.

Rathegerroke, co. Car. (Rathgarogue, co. Wex. ?), 3165.

Rathegelasse. *See* Rathglas, co. Gal.

Rathegowre, co. Wex., chapel, 668.

Rathegriffen, 784. *See* Griffinrath, co. Kild.

Rathehangan. *See* Rathangan.

Ratheharron, in Munster, 6314.

Ratheholler. *See* Rathoder.

Rathekealy. *See* Rathkealie, co. Lim.

Rathekenbatt in M'Cartan's country (Rathcalb, now Clough, in par. Loughinisland, co. Down—Reeves' Ant. Down and Connor), 5787.

Rathekillon, co. Kilk. (Rathculliheen, co. Wat.), 1709.

Rathekilly. *See* Rathkille.

Rathelan (co. Ross. ?), 6618.

Rathelogo (Rathlook), co. Meath, 478.

Ratheloge. *See* Rathlogo, Queen's co.

Ratheley, co. Kilk., 4188.

Ratheleyco. *See* Rathleyne.

Rathelle. *See* Rathlie.

Rathelin, King's co., 6680.

Rathelly, co. Kilk., 651.

Rathemakneo. *See* Rathmackneo.

Rathemane (co. Kerry ?), 6488.

Rathemallen. *See* Rathmullen, co. Down.

Rathemore. *See* Rathmore, co. Car.

Rathemore. *See* Rathmore, co. Kild.

Rathemore. *See* Rathmore, co. Meath.

Rathenaghe (Rahanna, co. Louth), 1728.

Rathenally—Rathenallye. *See* Rathnallie.

Rathenebaron, Queen's co., 1622.

Ratheneganagh. *See* Rathnegananghe.

Rathenegerry (co. Car. or Wex. ?), 6817.

Rathenekenenaghe, co. Tip., 5472.

Rathenekincr—Rathenekyner, co. Tip., 5373, 5472.

Rathenemoddagh (Rathtamuddagh, co. Westm.), 1346.

Rathenenarran, Queen's co., 1347.

Rathenenyell. *See* Rathnenell.

Rathenower. *See* Rathnure, co. Kilk.

Rathenowhittaghe, co. Lim., 5987.

Rathenowr. *See* Rathnure, co. Kilk.

Rathenpille (co. Tip. ?), 4038.

Rathenne, co. Carlow (Rahema, co. Wick.), rectory, 1867.

Rathennie — Rathenny. *See* Rathnoy, co. Dub.

Rathenny (co. Kilk. ?), 5042.

Rathenny. *See* Rathny, co. Westm.

Rathenur. *See* Rathnure, co. Kilk.

Rathenwskoy (co. Cork), 5874.

Rathony—Rathonnie—Rathenny (Rahenny, co. Dub.), 848, 887, 2814; rectory, 4485-70.

Rathony—Rathenny, co. Westm., 1898, 5878.

INDEX TO FIANTS—ELIZABETH.

Rathcokelly. *See* Rathkokelly.
Rathcopadenboy. *See* Rathpadisboy.
Rathcopatricke. *See* Rathpatrik.
Rathcreaghe, alias Racreigh, co. Lim., 462. *See* Rathriaghe.
Rathcorgell. *See* Rathangot.
Rathcrum, co. Kild., 1914.
Rathcronan—Rathcronane. *See* Rathronan, co. Tip.
Rathcrown, co. Gal., 4897.
Rathcrowe, co. Wex., 1577.
Rathcualaghe. *See* Rathsallagh, co. Wick.
Rathcusar, co. Louth. *See* Rathesker.
Rathcallagh (Rathsillagh, co. Wex. ?), 4626.
Rathcallaghe. *See* Rathsillagh, co. Kild.
Rathesker—Rahesker—Rathchesker—Rathesker (Rathescar), co. Louth, 675, 1230, 1673, 2346, 2877, 4147, 4166, 6183.
Rathespike, co. Kild., rectory, 322.
Rathesleary, co. Wex., 3015.
Rathcton. *See* Rathton, co. Wex.
Rathetowe. *See* Ratowe, co. Kerry.
Rathetowne, co. Meath, 1292.
Rathetran—Rathetrwone. *See* Rathirone, co. Kild.
Rathevan, Queen's co. *See* Rativine, Ratyvin.
Rathewogan—Rathewogane. *See* Rathwogan.
Rathfa. *See* Rathfaill.
Rathfadinvoye, 4494. *See* Rathpadinboy.
Rathfarnam, 6021. *See* Rathfarnan.
Rathfarnan, co. Westm., 6158.
Rathfarnan—Rafernan—Rathefarnan—Rathfernan—Rathfarnam, co. Dub., 4129, 4177, 4898, 6208, 6080–1.
Rathfarre, co. Lim. *See* Ravarye.
Rathfaill—Rathfa, King's co., 436, 1654.
Rathfeigh—Rafeagh—Rafeigh, co. Meath, 1686, 2117, 5779.
Rathfeild—Rathfilde, at Trim, co. Meath, 80, 972.
Rathfornan. *See* Rathfarnan.
Rathferne, co. Westm., 6152.
Rathfanstone—Rathfyanston (Rathfeston ?), King's co., 394, 1554.
Rathfilde. *See* Rathfeild.
Rathflen. *See* Raffin.
Rathflemynge, co. Tip., 6142.
Rathfolan, co. Clare. *See* Rathmolan.
Rathforyd, 1467.
Rathfoyle, co. Lim., 6782.
Rathfran, co. Mayo. *See* Rathbranagh.
Rathfready, co. Lim. *See* Rathphyrie.
Rathfryland, co. Down. *See* Rathphrilan.
Rathfyanston. *See* Rathfanstone.
Rathgallyr (co. Tip. ?), 1878.
Rathganny, co. Westm., 2968.
Rathgarret, 6766.
Rathgaroge, co. Wex. *See* Ragarroge, Rathgarroke.
Rathgarvan, co. Kilk., 6118, 6438.
Rathgarve, co. Westm. *See* Ragarf.
Rathgorin—Rathgorine (Rathgoran, co. Car. ?), 6641.
Rathgorinlogilgreige, Newton of (perhaps Newtownrathganley, Kilgraigue), co. Meath, 6304.
Rathgorone, co. Louth, 1612.
Rathgilbert, Queen's co. *See* Ragilbart.
Rathglas—Rathglass—Rathoglasse, co. Gal., 1682, 4618, 6713.
Rathgobban, co. Cork, 1698, 2387.
Rathgoggan—Rathgogan, co. Cork, 6068, 6828.
Rathgormeley (see Newton of Rathgormeley), 6342.
Rathgormock—Rathcormick—Rathcormicke—Rathcormock—Rathcormycke—Rathgormick—Rathgurmicke—Rathgurmog—Rathgurmike (Rathgormuck), co. Wat., 734, 1046, 1686, 1152, 4294, 6474, 6614, 6798; rectory, 5828.
Rathgormuck, 6838.
Rathgurmog. *See* Rathgormock.
Rathgowell, co. Tip., 4621, 6949.
Rathgowle (co. Tip.), 6611, 6254.
Rathgowles, co. Tip., 6072.
Rathgurgine, co. Gal., castle and land, 6942.
Rathgurrygin, co. Gal., 6818. *See also* Ragorgine.
Rathhalron. *See* Rathalron.
Rathhangan, 4458. *See* Rathangan.
Rathharrowe (Raharo), co. Ross., rectory, 6348.
Rathhele (Rathealy, co. Kilk. ?), 1076.
Rathhey (Rahugh, co. Westm.), 1760.
Rathhialmen, co. Long., 5063. *See also* Rathyhalmen.
Rathile (co. Kilk. ?), 6062.
Rathill (co. Kilk. ?), 6238.
Rathimacbairkin (Rahenmaheerran ?), King's co., 4202.
Rathimally. *See* Rathmollie.
Rathinclare, co. Cork, 4486.
Rathine, co. Tip. or Lim., 2942.
Rathinebarrowe, Queen's co., 1114.
Rathinecarthye (co. Tip. ?), 1868.
Rathinkilletane, Queen's co., 4284.
Rathinmore, co. Westm., 1622.
Rathinroth (co. Kilk. ?), 6038.
Rathinure, co. Kilk. *See* Rathnure.
Rathinusky—Rathinuskie, co. Cork, 5974, 6574
Rathinusky (co. Wat. ?), 6634.
Rathistone (co. Kilk. ?), 1918.
Rathjordan—Rajordan—Rajordane—Rajordan—Ra Jurdane—Reshordan—Rath Jordan, co. Lim., 3043, 3448, 4482, 6753, 4878; grant, 5747; rectory, 462, 5768, 6604.
Rathkam (Rathcam, co. Westm.), 1874.

Rathkenan, co. Lim., [illegible].
Rathkeale (Rathcahill), co. Lim., grant, [illegible].
Rathkealle—Rakeale—Rakeley—Rakelle—Rakelly—Rakely—Rakelye—Rakeyle—Rakeylle—Ratekely—Rathcheally—Rathkellie—Rathkeale—Rathkelly—Rathkeylle (Rathkeale, co. Lim.), [illegible], [illegible], [illegible], [illegible], [illegible], 6464, [illegible]; lands in, granted, 6171; tenement in, [illegible]; customs and profits of fairs granted, [illegible].
" merchant of, [illegible].
" abbey granted, 6171; priory, lands of granted, [illegible].
" house of friars leased, [illegible].
" parish, [illegible], [illegible].
" See also Rathkille.
Rathkelly (Rakelly), co. Mon., [illegible].
Rathkena, co. Tip., [illegible].
Rathkennie. See Rathkenny.
Rathkenny, co. Cav., [illegible].
Rathkenny—Rathkennie—Rathkenny, co. Kerry, [illegible], [illegible], [illegible], [illegible].
Rathkenny, co. Meath, rectory, [illegible], [illegible].
Rathkeraght—Rathkyraght (Rakeraugh), co. Mon., [illegible], [illegible].
Rathkerane (Rathkieran co. Kilk. ?), [illegible].
Rathkevan (co. Tip. ?), [illegible], [illegible]. See also Rathkyvane.
Rathkeylle. See Rathkealle, co. Lim.
Rathkhelte (Rathcath, now Clough, co. Down) rectory, [illegible].
Rathkiegine, co. Westm., [illegible].
Rathkien, [illegible].
Rathkieran, co. Kilk. See Rathkerane, Rathkirin.
Rathkilkedy, Queen's co., [illegible].
Rathkille—Rathekilly (Rathkeale ?), co. Lim., [illegible], [illegible].
Rathkirin (co. Kilk. ?), [illegible].
Rathkine (Rathcline), co. Long., [illegible].
Rathkravin, co. Cav., [illegible].
Rathkuddery, co. Kerry, [illegible].
Rathkwen, co. Meath, [illegible].
Rathkyraght. See Rathkeraght.
Rathkyvane (co. Tip ?), [illegible], [illegible].
Rathlacken, co. Mayo. See Carrowkeele Ralacken, Rathlackane, Ralacken.
Rathlarnee, co. Wex. See Ralarnane.
Rathleague, Queen's co. See Rathlege.
Rathleash, Queen's co. See Rathleyne.
Rathlee, co. Sligo. See Rathlie, Rathliew.
Rathlesk, co. Meath. See Rathalege.
Rathlag (Rathlillig ?), Queen's co., [illegible].
Rathlege—Ralege—Rathlage—Rathlegg—Rathleige (Rathleague), Queen's co., 494, [illegible], [illegible], [illegible], [illegible].
Rathlege—Rathelege—Rathleg (Rathlillig ?), Queen's co., [illegible], [illegible], [illegible].
Rathlegg—Rathleige. See Rathlege, Queen's co.
Rathleaky (co. Tip ?), [illegible].
Rathleem, co. Tip., [illegible].
Rathlevagh, Queen's co., [illegible].
Rathlewe. See Rathliew.
Rathleyne—Ralien—Rathaleyne (Rathleash, Queen's co.), [illegible], [illegible], [illegible].
Rathlie—Rathlolle (Rathlee ? co. Sligo), [illegible], [illegible], [illegible].
Rathliew—Rathlewe—Rathliewe (Rathlee ?) co. Sligo, [illegible], [illegible], [illegible].
Rathlihen, King's co. See Ralien, Ralie, Ralyn, Rhalyen.
Rathlin island. See Raughlin, Raughlines.
Rathlin, co. Kilk., [illegible].
Rathlinane—Rathlinaane, co. Wat., [illegible], [illegible].
Rathlinn, co. Mon., [illegible].
Rathlyn, alias Molbowne, co. Kilk., [illegible].
Rathlyne (King's co. ?), [illegible].
Rathlyworth, co. Lim., [illegible].
Rathmacandice, co. Lim., [illegible].
Rathm'artie—Rathm'cartie—Rathmackarty, co. Tip., [illegible], [illegible], [illegible].
Rathmacowen. See Rathmacknee.
Rathmackarty. See Rathm'artie.
Rathmacknee—Rathemaknee—Rathmacnee—Rathmackne—Rathmaknee—Ramakenee, co. Wex., [illegible], [illegible], [illegible], [illegible].
" vicar of, [illegible].
Rathmadocke, Queen's co. (alias Blackford) [illegible].
Rathmagrumagh, co. Kerry, [illegible].
Rathmaknee. See Rathmacknee.
Rathmallan—Rathmallias—Rathmallisye—Rathmollis—Rathmaullisyn (Rathmelton, co. Donegal ?), [illegible].
Rathmashackenire, Queen's co., [illegible].
Rathmaullisyn. See Rathmallan.
Rathmelton, co. Don. See Rathmallan.
Rathmewe—Ramewe (Rathnew), co. Wick., [illegible], [illegible].
Rathmickforlie, co. Cav., [illegible].
Rathmilice, Queen's co. See Rathmoyle.
Rathmolan (Rathfolan ?), co. Clare, [illegible].
Rathmolan, co. Wat., rectory, [illegible].
Rathmolane, co. Wat., [illegible].
Rathmoleme—Rathmolenan. See Rathmollan.
Rathmoles, co. Tip., [illegible].
Rathmolian—Ramolyane—Rathmolian—Rathmolenan (Rathmolyon), co. Meath, [illegible]; parish, [illegible]; rectory, [illegible], [illegible].
" vicar, [illegible].

Rathmoor. *See* Rathmore, co. Kild.
Rathmoore, co. Cork. 4803.
Rathmore—Rathemore, co. Car., 911, 918, 2341, 6642.
„ rectory, 826, 1160, 1385, 3488, 4224.
„ vicar, 1381.
Rathmore, in manor of Carlow, 1863.
Rathmore, co. Cork, 5224.
Rathmore (co. Kerry ?), 6679.
Rathmore — Rathemore — Rathmoor, co. Kild., 1097, 4223, 5164.
„ manor, 5143.
„ rectory, 2041, 4361, 6028.
„ advowson of church, 6146.
„ vicar, 1284.
Rathmore King's co. *See* Renathmore.
Rathmore, co. Lim., 2310, 4813.
Rathmore, co. Long., 6797.
Rathmore — Rathemore — Rhamore, co. Meath, 148, 808, 213, 881, 1967, 1842, 2877, 4373, 4461, 6227, 6344.
Rathmore, Queen's co., 6763.
Rathmore (co. Rosc. ?), 5608.
Rathmore (co. Tip. ?), 3046, 4484.
Rathmore, co. Wex., 417.
Rathmore (co. Wick. ?), 6477.
Rathmorrel, co. Kerry. *See* Rathwirigill.
Rathmowe, co. Long., 5062, 4397.
Rathmoylan, co. Wat., 4143. *See also* Rathmolan.
Rathmoyle, Queen's co. *See* Ramoyle.
Rathmoyle, co. Westm., 2180.
Rathmoyles (Rathmiles, Queen's co.), 498, 1454.
Rathmullan, co. Meath. *See* Ramollan.
Rathmullen, co. Donegal, monastery of friars preachers of the B. V. M., lease of site, 6653.
Rathmullen—Rathemollen, co. Down, 4639; rectory, 1589, 4767.
Rathmullen (Carrickrathmullen ?), co. Sligo, 4363, 5478.
Rathmyn, co. Cork, 1697.
Rathnacally, co. Cork. *See* Rathnekally.
Rathnacrosse—Rathnacrosse (co. Donegal), 4892, 6687.
Rathnagearagh, co. Car. *See* Rathnakeraghe, Rathnagaragh.
Rathnagearagh, co. Wex. *See* Rathnageraughe.
Rathnaggadan (co. Kilk. ?), 6704.
Rathnaghane, co. Lim., 5462.
Rathnagire, co. Rosc. *See* Carrow Raghew.
Rathnagore, co. Lim. *See* Rathnegor.
Rathnakeyle (co. Clare ?), 3708.
Rathnakeraghe—Rathnakeragh (Rathnageragh, co. Car. ?), 1808, 3648.
Rathnalle — Rathenally — Rathenallye — Rathkenally, co. Meath, 1171, 1228, 6978, 6542.
Rathnaltaye (co. Ferm. ?), 5483.
Rathnamanagh, Queen's co. *See* Rathnemanaghe.
Rathnamanshan, co. Gal., 4082.
Rathnamnddagh, co. Westm. *See* Rathenemoddagh, Rathnemoddagh.
Rathnarygyt (co. Kild. ?), 5143.
Rathnaseer, co. Lim. *See* Ranasler, Rannaers.
Rathnaskilloge, co. Wat. *See* Raghnaskelloge.
Rathnaveoge, co. Tip. *See* Ramoveoke.
Rathne( ) (co. Tip. ?), 6112.
Rathnecrosse. *See* Rathnacrosse.
Rathnedorturaghe (co. Cav. ?), 6697.
Rathnegarragh (co. Wex.), 1388.
Rathnegeragh (Rathnageeragh, co. Car.), 6778.
Rathnegeraghe, Queen's co., 5687.
Rathnegeraughe—Rathnegeraugh (Rathnegeeragh), co. Wex., 60, 1890.
Rathnegor (Rathnagore), co. Lim., 5947.
Rathnegrome, co. Kilk., 4325.
Rathnekally (Rathnacally co. Cork), 5928.
Rathnekill (co. Kild ?), 3146.
Rathnemanaghe (Rathnamanagh), Queen's co., 5838.
Rathnemoddagh, co. Westm., 3460.
Rathnemoddagh — Rathnemodagh, co. Westm., 3468, 4308.
Rathnerviall—Rathenerryall, co. Cork, 6161.
Rathneshane — Rathneshian, alias Raghnasheane, Queen's co., 160, 1348, 1780.
Rathnesker, 6497.
Rathnoge, co. Kerry, 5657.
Rathnoge, (co. Lim. ?), 4497.
Rathnolane, co. Cork, 4117.
Rathnure — Ranywre — Rathenerwer — Rathenerwy — Rathnur (Rathinure, co. Kilk.), 179, 813, 1826, 2038, 2438, 2488.
Rathnure (co. Westm.), 6622.
Rathnure (co. Wex.), 4541.
Rathnuskie (co. Cork ?), 6718.
Rathnysky (co. Cork), 5063. *See also* Rathynisky, Rathynuskie.
Rathode. *See* Rahode.
Rathogallagh (co. Tip. ?), 4708. *See also* Rategally.
Rathogormuke, 1586. *See* Rathgormuck.
Rathogowtyn, co. Mon., 5969.
Rathokelly—Rathecokelly, co. Tip., 2778, 6591.
Rathoenan, co. Kerry, 6117.
Rathoue, co. Tip., 5648.
Rathonell (Rathconnell), co. Westm., rectory, 1440.
Rathonell, water of, at Mullingar, co. Westm., 4261, 5423.
Rathonyne — Raghonyne — Rathonyn, co. Kerry, 5238, 6477, 6637, 6642.

INDEX TO FIANTS—ELIZABETH.

Rathowe (Rathery, co. Louth), 1773.
Rathowran—Rathowrane, co. Car., 611.
Rathowkor, 678, 1328. See Rathocker.
Rathowth. See Ratouth.
Rathowe, co. Kerry, [illegible].
Rathowney (King's or Queen's co. ?), [illegible].
Rathowyny (Rahoon), co. Kerry, [illegible].
Rathpadan (Rathphaddin), co. Wex., [illegible].
Rathpadinhoy — Rathepadenhoy — Rathfadinwoye — Rathpadinehoye, co. Car., [illegible], 6454, 5561.
Rathpatrik —Rapatricke—Rathepatricke, co. Kilk., rectory, [illegible], 1269.
" vicar, [illegible].
Rathphaddin, co. Wex. See Rathpadan.
Rathphillipp, co. Lim., [illegible].
Rathphrilan — Raphrilan — Raphrylan (Rathfryland), co. Down, 4713, 4677. See also Rafrilan.
Rathphyrie (Rathfrendy ?), co. Lim., [illegible].
Rathpierce, co. Wex. See Rapierce.
Rathpiper, Queen's co. See Pipraith.
Rathraghe, co. Car., 464.
Rathraynell (Rathreynolds), co. Meath, [illegible].
Rathreagh, co. Long. See Rathreoughe.
Rathredmond, co. Mayo. See Rathedmond.
Rathregan, co. Meath, rectory, 810, 1546, [illegible], [illegible].
Rathregane, co. Meath, [illegible].
Rathreogh (co. Kilk.), [illegible].
Rathreoughe (Rathreagh), co. Long., rectory, [illegible].
Rathreynolds, co. Meath. See Rathraynell.
Rathrieghe — Rathereaghe, co. Lim., 463, [illegible].
Rathrievagh—Raghravagh—Rarovagh, co. Long., [illegible], [illegible], [illegible].
Rathrinnon, King's co., 672.
Rathroan (Rathronan ?), co. Lim., [illegible].
Rathroe—Rarne, co. Ros., [illegible]; grant, [illegible].
Rathrollo, co. Louth, 1514.
Rathrum, King's co., [illegible].
Rathronan — Raronan, co. Lim., grant, [illegible].
" parish, [illegible]; patronage, [illegible]. See also Rathroan.
Rathronane — Rathoronan — Rathoronane — Rathronane — Rothronan, co. Tip., [illegible], 1663, [illegible], [illegible], [illegible], [illegible], [illegible].
" rectory, [illegible], [illegible], [illegible].
Rathrone, co. Meath, [illegible].
Rathroushie — Rathrouchie (Rathronshin, Queen's co.), [illegible], 1654. See also Raronshe.
Rathrowgh, co. Lim., [illegible].
Rathrowiaght (Rarningh), co. Mon., [illegible].
Rathrush—Rarushe—Rathrushe, co. Car., [illegible], 1571, [illegible].
Rathry, co. Meath.
Rathsallagh — Rasallagh — Rathesallaghe — Rathsalloghe, co. Dub. (now Wick.), [illegible], 1416, [illegible], [illegible], 6417, [illegible].
Rathsenlagh, co. Long., [illegible].
Rathsalloghe. See Rathsallagh, co. Wick.
Rathsallagh—Rathesillaghe, co. Kild., [illegible], 6182.
Rathsallagh, co. Wex. See Rasallagh, Rathesillagh.
Rathskeaghe — Rathskeaghe, co. Westm., 1940, [illegible].
Rathsnagg (co. Tip. ?), [illegible].
Rathsonnagee (co. Kilk. ?), [illegible].
Rathspike, co. Kild., rectory, [illegible].
Rathspike (Rathspick), co. Westm., [illegible].
Rathstowne, in Munster, [illegible].
Rathtaine—Rathtayn—Rathtayne (Rataine), co. Meath, [illegible].
" rectory, 818, 1468, 1814, [illegible], [illegible].
" parish, [illegible].
Rathtellig, Queen's co., 4181.
Rathtenny, co. Wex., 4034.
Rathtilling, Queen's co. See Rathtegan.
Rathtiom—Rathtoian, co. Wex., [illegible], [illegible].
Rathton (Ralphtown ?), co. Wex., [illegible].
Rathtough, co. Kerry, [illegible].
Rathtoole, co. Wick. See Ratoole.
Rathtouth. See Ratouth.
Rathtowe, See Ratowe, co. Kerry.
Rathtowe, alias Rathoon, co. Wex., [illegible].
Rathtoweth, co. Car., 1946. See also Rauthtowth.
Rathtowghe — Rathtowth, co. Car., [illegible], [illegible], [illegible], 6411.
Rathtowth, 2576. See Ratouth.
Rathtowth, co. Tip., 1560.
Rathtowth. See Rathtowghe, co. Car.
Rathtowthe, [illegible]. See Ratouth.
Rathtowthe, 847. See also Rathowthe, co. Tip.
Rathtrone — Rathotrone — Rathotrwne, co. Kild., 1577, [illegible], [illegible].
Rathturkyll (co. Kild. ?), [illegible].
Rathtyron, Queen's co., [illegible].
Rathumdle, co. Car., 1824.
Rathurgo, co. Meath, 1184, [illegible].
Rathunlk—Rathunlke. See Rahulk.
Rathumoy (co. Tip. ?), [illegible].
Rathurd (co. Lim.), castle and land, [illegible].
Rathvenan, co. Car., [illegible].
Rathvewghe, co. Long., rectory, [illegible]. See also Rathreoughe.
Rathvickie' (Rackavan ?, co. Westm.), [illegible].
Rathvickdulaffe, King's co., [illegible].
Rathville—Rathvillen. See Rathvilly.
Rathvillek (co. Cork ?), [illegible].
Rathvilly—Rathville—Rathvillen—Raville—Ravillie, co. Car., 614, 1647, [illegible], [illegible], [illegible], [illegible], 5194, [illegible].

INDEX TO FIANTS—ELIZABETH.

Rathvoge (co. Kerry ?), [illegible].
Rathwarigy (co. Cork ?), [illegible].
Rathwearo, [illegible]. *See* Rathwier.
Rathweate (co. Car. ?), [illegible].
Rathwier—Rathweare—Rathwyer—Rathwyre (Rathwire), co. Westm., [illegible], [illegible].
" manor and lands granted, [illegible].
" martial law, [illegible].
Rathwiriell (Rathmorrel ?), co. Kerry, [illegible], [illegible].
Rathwoe, co. Kerry, [illegible].
Rathwogan—Rathewogan—Rathewegane, in Farbillagha, co. Westm., [illegible], [illegible], [illegible].
Rathwyer. *See* Rathwier.
Rathwyll, in manor of Carlow, [illegible].
Rathwyre. *See* Rathwier.
Rathybalmon, co. Long., [illegible].
Rathyll (Rahill), co. Meath, [illegible].
Rathyly, Mwroghe m'Conoghor Y, pardon, [illegible].
Rathysisky (co. Cork ?), [illegible].
Rathynne, Queen's co., [illegible].
Rathynnre (co. Kilk. ?), [illegible].
Rathynuskie, co. Cork, [illegible].
Rathyuy, co. Clare, [illegible].
Rathyuyttg, co. Cork, [illegible].
Rathyonge, co. Westm., [illegible].
Rathywer, co. Lim., [illegible].
Ratin, co. Westm., [illegible].
Ratirine (Rathovean ?), Queen's co., [illegible].
Ratouth, co. Meath. *See* Ratouth.
Ratogally (co. Tip.), [illegible].
Ratole (Rathtoole), co. Wick., [illegible].
Raton. *See* Ratowe.
Ratouth—Ratouthe—Rathouth—Rathtouth—Rathtowth—Rathtowthe—Ratowthe (Ratoath), co. Meath, [illegible]; manor, [illegible], [illegible].
" rectory, [illegible], [illegible], [illegible], [illegible], [illegible].
" vicar, [illegible].
Ratowe—Rathetowe—Rathtowe—Raton—Ratow (Ratton), co. Kerry, [illegible]; messuages and gardens granted, [illegible], [illegible], [illegible]; land in, granted, [illegible], [illegible].
" rectory, [illegible].
" abbey, alias Arraghtownle or Arraguunle, leased, [illegible], [illegible], [illegible]; possessions granted, [illegible], [illegible].
Ratowthe. *See* Ratouth.
Ratrumon (Rathdrum), King's co., [illegible].
Rattin—Rattyn, co. Westm., [illegible], [illegible], [illegible].
Rattoo, co. Kerry. *See* Ratowe.
Rattyn. *See* Rattin.
Ratugh (co. Car. ?), [illegible].
Ratwogh (co. Kerry ?), [illegible].
Ratyfrynge (co. Rosc. ?), [illegible].
Ratyvin—Ratyvyne (Rathevan ?), Queen's co., [illegible], [illegible], [illegible].
Raucester—Rocester—Rocetter—Rawcester, John (of Rathmacknee), indenture, [illegible].
" Richard (of Tomhagard), livery, [illegible].
" Thomas (of Rathmacknee), commission, [illegible], [illegible]; his heir, [illegible].
" Walter (of Tomhagard), livery to son, [illegible].
" William (of Bargy), lands of, [illegible], [illegible].
" of Taccumshane, lands of, [illegible].
" *See* Rawcester.
Raughan, co. Dub. (Wick. ?), [illegible].
Raughlin, fiants dated at, [illegible], [illegible].
Raughlines—Ragheliens (Rathlin island, co. Antrim), to be made shire ground, [illegible]; martial law in, [illegible].
Raughter, Philip, pardon, [illegible].
Rauleghan, Moster, in Inishowen, men of pardoned, [illegible].
Raulestoe (co. Cork or Wat. ?), [illegible].
Rauly, Rich. fitz David, pardon, [illegible].
Raurenny (co. Mayo ?), [illegible].
Raurie, co. Meath, [illegible].
Rauthtowth, co. Car., [illegible].
Ravarye (Rathlarre ?), co. Lim., [illegible].
Ravage, brook, Queen's co., [illegible].
Ravarnet, co. Down. *See* Ballyravarnan.
Ravarnet river. *See* Garvologhy.
Raville—Ravillie. *See* Rathvilly, co. Car.
Ravo pavois, King's co. [illegible].
Ravrane (co. Mayo ?), [illegible].
Rawcester, David, pardon, [illegible].
" James, pardon, [illegible].
" John fitz Rob., pardon, [illegible].
" Matthew, pardon, [illegible].
" Thomas, [illegible]. *See* Raucester.
Rawcestor, Wm. [illegible]. *See* Raucester.
Rawe, capt. George, comn. for martial law, [illegible].
" Nich, [illegible].
Rawelenmeahan, alias Rathmeahlan, Queen's co., [illegible].
Rawghter, Tho., pardon, [illegible].
Rawlaghe, co. Dub. (Wick. ?), castle and land, [illegible].
Rawley, Daniel, alias Donell O'Rhawly, pardon, [illegible].
" Gerrott roe, pardon, [illegible].
" Morris fitz Garrott, pardon, [illegible].
" Nich. roe, pardon, [illegible].
" Walter. *See* Ralegh.
Rawleystown, co. Lim. *See* Ballyrowley, Raleighston, Rollestown, Rolleston.
Rawlie, Daniel, pardon, [illegible].

INDEX TO FIANTS—ELIZABETH.

Rawle, Edm. fitz James, pardon, 6470.
„ James fitz Edm., pardon, 6470.
„ James oge, pardon, 6470.
Rawlins, Johanna, testamentary appeal, 4744.
Rawlistowe, co. Lim., 6554.
Rawlistown, co. Lim., 6570.
Rawty, Ellice, pardon, 6497.
„ Rich., pardon, 6497.
„ of Rawlistown, wife of, pardoned, 6606.
Rawore, co. Gal., 4897.
Rawson, John, prior of S. John of Jerusalem, lease from, recited, 1067, 1438, 1781, 6360, 3639, 3341, 6411.
„ John, soldier, leases, 4040-1, 6323.
„ Rich., 1781.
Rayn, co. Gal., 5348.
Rayeston, co. Meath, 318, 5332.
Rayeston, alias Brayston, co. Meath, 1494.
Rayhan, co. Kild., 6296.
Rayhymymagh in Upper Ossory, 807.
Rayiad, 5534.
Rayiagbe, 534.
Rayleston — Rayliston. See Ralleston, co. Tip.
Raymore, Queen's co., 6441.
Rayndu[illegible]—Rayndu[illegible] (Rahen[illegible]), Queen's co., 323, 571, 647, 5594.
Raynedorow (Rahenndarragh, co. Car. ?), 4034.
Raynsforde, Rich., pardon, 6454.
Raynekame (Rianagan, co. Ros.), 5941.
Raynekenagh, co. Wex., 1380.
Raynesford, Hercules. See Rainsford.
Raynewilaghe—Raynewilawghe, co. Lim., 5578, 4517.
Raynsford — Raynsforde, Hercules. See Rainsford.
Rayschacke (Raihaspick ?), co. Westm., rectory, 447.
Raytown, co. Meath. See Ralston.
Read mountain. See Reid mounteyne.
Reade, David, pardon, 2283.
„ Rob., pardon, 2283.
Readestowne, co. Dub. (Wick.), 5391.
Reagh, Donell, pardon, 6487, 6578.
„ John, pardon, 1471.
„ Thomas, pardon, 5684.
Reaghe, Rory, pardon, 4897.
Reaghestown, co. Louth. See Riaghestown.
Realtirragh (co. Clare or Ros. ?), 4808.
Realy, John, pardon, 6263.
Rean, Derby, pardon, 6384.
„ James, pardon, 6363.
„ Wm. m'Donell, pardon, 6363.
Reane, Anle oy, pardon, 4787.
Reanes, co. Cork, 6916.
Rearybeg, Queen's co. See Rorybeg.
Rearymore, Queen's co. See Rierymore.
Reaskavalla, co. Tip. See Rioag in valy.
Reban, co. Kild., 6468. See Castletown of Rebane, 5823; and Rebane.
Reban, co. Mayo, rectory, 4902.
Reban, Rory, 1723, 6418.
Rebane—Rabane, baron of, commission, 320; freedom from subsidy, 489.
„ Walter, baron of, livery (as St. Michaell), 6383.
Rebellion, persons having been in, to find security, 5084.
Rebellion of W. Nugent, 6817.
Rebels, commission to make war on, 1463, 3164, 3402, 3987.
„ instructions for defence against, 1411.
„ Irish services against, 539, 594.
„ in Tyrone, their goods to be seized to queen's use, 1097.
„ treating with, 4392.
„ wine not to be sold to, 4154.
Recardstowne (Rickardstown, co. Kild. ?), 6467.
Rechill (co. Tip. ?), 5734.
Rechounisck (co. Cork ?), 6804.
Records in Brymyngham's tower, keeper appointed, 6614, 4680, 4871.
Records of Chancery, inventories to be made of, 3890.
Records of court of Com. Pleas lost; placed in Bermingham's Tower; inventory to be made of, 4450.
Records, keeper of, of counties, 6418. See clerks of peace, &c., under several counties.
Records, pardon for fabrications, 723.
Rector, son of, pardoned, 834, 2372.
Rectorial tithes leased to a butcher, 1718.
Red Barries country (Barryroe), co. Cork, 5676, 6255, 5084.
Redcitie, the (Redcity, co. Tip.), 6863.
Red logh — Reid logh (Lough Derg, co. Donegal), 4894, 4897.
Red Mountains, co. Dub. (the range of Wicklow and Dublin mountains, called in Irish Annals Sliabh Ruadh or Slieve Roe), seneschal of country adjoining, 1415; commission for martial law, 1416.
Red river called Dearge (Derg river, co. Donegal and Tyrone), 6896, 5397.
Redd logh. See Red logh.
Redd mounteyne — Read mountain in Tipperkevan, co. Dub. (Slievroe in par. Tipperkevin, co. Kild.), 1925, 4430.
Rede, Margery, pardon, 272.
„ Thomas, pardon, 798.
Redemedow, co. Tip., 3466.
Redemore, co. Louth, 1723.

INDEX TO FIANTS—ELIZABETH.

Redemption of Captives, friars of the Trinity for (see Adare), 1162, 6787.
Rederston, co. Meath, 4677.
Redmayne, Marmaduke, [illegible].
Redmon, Andrew, pardon, [illegible].
" Rob., pardon, [illegible].
" Wm., pardon, [illegible].
Redmond—Redmund—Remon, Alexander (of Redmond's Hall), theft from, [illegible]; wardship and livery of heir, [illegible], 6787.
" Alexander, son of Alexander (of Redmond's Hall), wardship, [illegible], 6787.
" of the Hoke (or Hook), lands of, 918, 4[illegible].
" Ellinor ny, pardon, 6477.
" Ellis ny, pardon, [illegible].
" James m' Wm., pardon, [illegible].
" Rich. fitz Patr., pardon, [illegible].
" Shilie ny, pardon, 470[illegible].
" William, pardon, [illegible].
Redmondes Hall, co. Wexford, 6787.
Redmondston—Redmondeston, co. Westm., 4181, 44[illegible], [illegible].
Redmore, co. Kilk., 2012, 4[illegible], [illegible].
Redmunsryde by Ardee, co. Louth, 17[illegible].
Redmund, Alexander. See Redmond.
Redmund of Hoke, 918, 4[illegible]. See Redmond.
Redmund oge, [illegible], [illegible]. See Fitzgerald.
Redmund oge, pardon, [illegible].
Redmund oge (of Lisenode or Lisnoyd, co. Westm.), [illegible], [illegible].
Redmund reagh, pardon, [illegible].
Redmunde, James m'Shane, pardon, [illegible].
Redwarde, alias Allmanaghe, Dermot, pardon, [illegible].
Redwardes, alias Allmanaghe, Rich., pardon, [illegible].
Ree, Thomas, lease, [illegible].
Ree, Lough. See Rye.
Reeburge, Chr., pardon, [illegible].
" Nich., pardon, [illegible].
Reenbeg, co. Kerry. See Rinbegge.
Reenmaharagh, co. Kerry. See Rincaharragh.
Reens, co. Lim. See Reyne.
Reenydonagan, co. Cork. See Rendogan.
Reesale, Wm., pardon, [illegible].
Reerdan, John m'Moleghlen Y, pardon, [illegible].
Regaine lands, Queen's co., 67[illegible].
Regaine, Donell m'Dermody I, pardon, [illegible].
Regan, Connor m'Donoghe, pardon, [illegible].
" Ellyn m'Murrogh I, pardon, [illegible].
" Morogh, [illegible].
" Onora, pardon, [illegible].
Regane, John, English liberty, [illegible].
" Teige m'Donogh I, pardon, [illegible].
" Thomas, English liberty, [illegible].
Regimon, Owen m'Shane duff, pardon, [illegible].
Reghill, co. Tip., 6774, 6784. See Reighill.
Regles, co. Dub., [illegible].
Regles, co. Dub. See Reighles.
Rehadin (co. Car.?), [illegible].
Rehill, co. Tip. See Reighill.
Reiaston, co. Meath, [illegible].
Reighe, James, pardon, 6787.
Reighely, Owin, pardon, [illegible].
Reighill (Rehill, co. Tip.?), [illegible], [illegible].
Reighlie, Evlin ny, pardon, 67[illegible].
Reighles—Reyghes—Reygles—Ryegles—Rygles (Regles?), co. Dub., [illegible], 1780, [illegible], [illegible], [illegible].
Reillane (co. Wex.?), 3804.
Reile, Dermot m'Donoghe I, pardon, 3[illegible].
Reile, John m'Donell I, alias Boingadany, pardon, [illegible].
Reilie, Anably, pardon, [illegible].
" Margaret, pardon, [illegible].
" Reise, jointure of, 4116.
Reille, Moleghlin, pardon, [illegible].
Reilton, Christopher, soldier, robbery of, [illegible].
Reilly, Katherine ny, pardon, [illegible].
Rein castle, co. Clare, [illegible].
Reinaghmore, co. Kild., [illegible].
Reirdan, Morierlagh m'Donogh I, pardon, 47[illegible].
Reiry, Jonan oyne, pardon, [illegible].
Reiston, co. Westm., [illegible].
Rekall, co. Ros. or Gal., [illegible].
Rekrafecke (co. Cork?), [illegible].
Rekill, co. Gal. or Ros., [illegible].
Relangrove, co. Wex., [illegible].
Reley, Connor, pardon, [illegible].
" Philip, pardon, [illegible].
Relickestown, co. Kild., 4[illegible].
Relickmore (Relickmurry), co. Tip., mill, [illegible].
" rectory, 1[illegible], [illegible], [illegible].
" See Religvory.
Relie, John, burgess, Athlone, [illegible].
" John, pardon, [illegible].
" Mary fitz John, pardon, [illegible].
Religion (see Ecclesiastical Causes), [illegible].
Religvory (Relickmurry, co. Tip.), [illegible].
Relligy, Teig boy (O'Mahon), pardon, [illegible].
Relly, Connor m'Shane, pardon, [illegible].
" Feolly, pardon, [illegible].
" Reiz, pardon, [illegible].
Rely, Cahall m'Molmor, pardon, [illegible].
" Cahir m'Tirlagh, pardon, [illegible].
" Edmund, pardon, [illegible].
" Farrall, pardon, [illegible].
" Gerald, pardon, [illegible].
" Garret m'Connor, pardon, [illegible].
" Hugh m'Phelim oge, pardon, [illegible].
" James, pardon, [illegible], [illegible], [illegible].
" Philip, pardon, [illegible].

INDEX TO FIANTS—ELIZABETH.

Roly, Tirrelagh, pardon, [illegible].
Rolye, Amory, pardon, [illegible].
" Margaret, pardon, 6186.
" Phelim A., pardon, [illegible].
" Tho., pardon, [illegible].
" Tirelagh, pardon, 6454.
Remembrancer's Office (Chief), Lessee to give security in, 4312, [illegible].
Romane, Alexander. See Redmond.
Renagan—Renaganne (Rinnagan), co. Rosc., [illegible], [illegible].
Renagh, Uny, pardon, [illegible].
Renaghan, John, [illegible].
Renaghane, co. Westm., [illegible].
Renagha, Carbery, pardon, [illegible].
Renaghe—Renanghe—Renagh (Roynagh, King's co.), rectory, 1461, [illegible], [illegible], [illegible].
Renan, Rich., pardon, [illegible].
Renany, [illegible].
Renanghe. See Renaghe.
Renecrane, co. Cork, 6764.
Rendogan (Reaurydonagan), co. Cork, [illegible].
Renenyn, [illegible].
Rengeraion—Rengeraione (Rangeralown?), co. Meath, [illegible], [illegible].
Ringowenaghe (Ringagowagh), co. Wat., [illegible], [illegible].
Renagh. See Renaghe.
Rennobylly, co. Cork, 6616.
Renogh, Wm., pardon, [illegible].
Renoghan (Rinaghan), co. Kild., [illegible].
Renaghan Hals, co. Kild., [illegible].
Rent, commissions to determine amount of rent and services in Munster, 2771, [illegible]; certain rents to replace uncertain services to crown and lords in Connaught and Thomond, 4746; in Thomond, 4741; under M'William, [illegible]; rents payable to earl of Desmond, [illegible]; fixed rents reserved to crown and chief in Monaghan, [illegible], [illegible], &c., [illegible] n [illegible], [illegible].
" of beeves or cows, [illegible], [illegible], [illegible], [illegible]; gloves, [illegible], [illegible]; goshawks, [illegible], [illegible], [illegible]; a red rose, [illegible], [illegible].
" of pension being too high, a new survey allowed, [illegible].
" of 1600 marks payable by earl of Tyrone to Turlogh leinagh, [illegible].
Renticolan, co. Rosc., [illegible].
Renwick, Thomas, lease, [illegible].
Renygrowre, co. Cork, [illegible].
Reoloff (or Realiff), co. Westm., [illegible].
Reogh, Connor, pardon, [illegible].
" Donell, pardon, [illegible].
" Donoghow, pardon, [illegible].
" Gerald, pardon, [illegible].
" Murrogh, pardon, [illegible].
Reogh, Owyne, pardon, [illegible].
" Shane, pardon, [illegible], [illegible].
" Teige m'Donill ogo, pardon, [illegible].
" Tho., pardon, [illegible], [illegible].
" Wm., pardon, [illegible].
Reoghe, Donogh, pardon, 6517.
" Donogh, pardon, [illegible].
" Edm., pardon, 6517.
" Moloughlin, pardon, [illegible].
" Tho., pardon, 6742.
Reough, James, pardon [illegible].
" Wm., pardon, [illegible].
Repcoste, clerk of, [illegible].
Rerego Ruddery, co. Lim., [illegible].
Reriske—Rerike—Reryck (Abbeydorey), co Long., rectory, [illegible], 1737, 4178.
Rerie, Katelyne ny, pardon, [illegible].
Rerike. See Reriske.
Rery, James, 1723, [illegible].
Reryck. See Reriske.
Reson, co. Kilk., [illegible].
Resillogh, co. Wex., [illegible].
Reslinary (co. Cork?), [illegible].
Resmonough (co. Kilk.?), [illegible].
Reughe, Teig, pardon, [illegible].
Reulville, co. Gal., [illegible].
Reurlane, John m'Conohor I., pardon, [illegible].
Reveghe, Reamyn, pardon, [illegible].
Revell, Tho., pardon, [illegible].
Revenue abuses, commission to enquire of, [illegible].
Revoston, co. Meath, [illegible], [illegible].
Revy, Hubbert m'Edm., pardon, [illegible].
" Moregh m'Edm., pardon, [illegible].
Rewdull, Andrew, pardon, 6178.
Rewe (Roe), co. Gal., [illegible].
Reyce, Christian, pardon, 1617.
Reyghne. See Reighne.
Reylan (co. Wex. or Car.?), 6617.
Reyland (co. Wex.?), [illegible].
Reylandmore, co. Wex., [illegible].
Reylanemore (co. Wex. or Car.?), [illegible].
Reylanmore (co. Car.), 6617.
Reyle, Gerald, pardon, [illegible].
Reyleston. See Raileston.
Reyley, Richard, pardon, [illegible].
Reylie, Rowe, pardon, 778.
" Tho., authorised to impress hay, [illegible].
" Tirrelagh, pardon, [illegible].
Reylly, Anabla, pardon, [illegible].
" John, pardon, 1744.
" Katherin ny, pardon, [illegible].
" Thomas, pardon, 1744.
Reyly, Edmund, pardon, [illegible].
" Katherine, pardon, [illegible].
" James, pardon, [illegible].
" John, pardon, 1136.
" Onor ny, pardon, [illegible].
" Pheylim, pardon, [illegible].

INDEX TO FIANTS—ELIZABETH.

Reyly, Tho., pardon, [illegible].
Reylye, Garret A., pardon, [illegible].
" John, pardon, [illegible].
Reyn, co. Car. (Raheen, co. Wick. ?), [illegible].
Reynagh, King's co. *See* Renagha.
Reynaghan, Wm., pardon, 3434.
Reynaghmor common, co. Kild., 1444.
Reynaldstown. *See* Reynoldeston.
Reyne (Reens), co. Lim., 5781.
Reynell, wife of Tirlagh m'Brian duff, [illegible].
Reynolds, Humfrey, grant of land, [illegible].
Reynoldes, Henry, manslaughter of, [illegible].
" John, pardon, [illegible].
Reynoldeston — Reynaldstown (Reynoldstown) co. Dub., 1440; manor, 4131.
Reynoldeston, [illegible].
Reynolds, James, lease, [illegible].
" Tho., [illegible].
" Thomasin, pardon, [illegible].
Reynoldstown, co. Dub. *See* Reynoldeston.
Reynold, James buoy, pardon, 6478.
Rhafen, [illegible]. *See* Raffin.
Rhalyon (Raithlihen ?), King's co., [illegible].
Rhamore, 4451. *See* Rathmore, co. Meath.
Rhise, alias Springe, Elizabeth, pardon, [illegible].
" Redmund, pardon, [illegible].
Rhymer. *See* Rimer.
Riagh (co. Gal. ?), [illegible].
Riagh, Patr., pardon, [illegible].
Riaghston — Riaghstowne — Ryaghston (Reaghstown), co. Louth, [illegible], 3414, [illegible].
Riallie, Donell m'Dermod I., pardon, 6764.
" Donell m'Moroghow I., pardon, 6764.
" Donell m'Teige I., pardon, 6764.
Rian, David, pardon, [illegible].
" Dermot, pardon, [illegible].
" Dermot, recognizance by, [illegible].
" Dionysius, alias Donogh duff O'Rian, pardon, 4413.
" Edm. fitz Derby, pardon, 6742.
" Edm. m'Donell I., pardon, [illegible].
" Hugh ny bowly, pardon, [illegible].
" James. *See* Ryan.
" James m'Redmond, pardon, 7230.
" John, late archdeacon of Cashel, [illegible].
" John m'Tho. I., pardon, [illegible].
" Matthew, pardon, [illegible].
" Matthew fitz Owen, pardon, [illegible].
" Morgan, pardon, 7434.
" Philip, [illegible].
" Roger Juhos, pardon, [illegible].
" Rorie boy, pardon, [illegible].
" Rowe ny, pardon, [illegible].
" Teige m'Donell m'Melaghlin, pardon, [illegible].
" Wm., pardon, [illegible], 6467, [illegible], 6534, 6707.
See Ryan.
Rian, co. Wexford, [illegible].
Riane, Daniel fitz Henry, pardon, 6179.
Riane, David, pardon, [illegible].
" Derby, [illegible].
" Maibe, pardon, [illegible].
" Walter more, pardon, [illegible].
Riane of Downe, Donald m'Melaghlin rough of the, pardon, 5314.
Rianston, co. Wex., [illegible].
Riare, Thomas, [illegible].
Riasg in vally (Reaskavalla, co. Tip ?), [illegible].
Ribbeston — Ribbestowne (Ribstown), co. Meath, [illegible], [illegible].
Ricardmor, country of (Clanrickard), [illegible].
Ricardmor of Glanwilliam, country of, (Clanwilliam), [illegible].
Rice, Edw., pardon, [illegible].
" Edw. fitz George, pardon [illegible].
" George, merchant, holdings in Ardfert, 6117; pardon, [illegible].
" James, pardon (*see* Ryce), [illegible].
" John, [illegible].
" John, pardon (*see* Ryse), [illegible].
" John fitz Piers, pardon, [illegible].
" Marc, pardon, [illegible].
" (alias Maxwell), Marian, [illegible].
" Nich., attainder of, 6117.
" Rich. fitz Dominick, pardon, [illegible].
" Rich. fitz Tho., pardon, [illegible].
" Rob., pardon, [illegible].
" Rowland, pardon, [illegible].
" Stephen (-Ryse), of Dingle, pardon, [illegible]; lands of, [illegible].
" Tho., pardon, [illegible], [illegible].
" Walter, pardon, [illegible], [illegible].
" *See* Ryan.
Rich, Rob., lord, commission, [illegible].
Richard, Shane, pardon, [illegible].
Richard, Shylly ny, pardon, [illegible].
Richards, Evan Ap. *See* Ap Richard.
Richardes park, in the burgage of Clonmel, [illegible].
Richardeston. *See* Richardiston, co. Kild.
Richardestowne, co. Louth, 1782.
Richardiston. *See* Richardston, co. Car.
Richardiston—Richardeston (Richardstown) co. Kild., 1514, [illegible].
Richardistowne, co. Cork, 1673.
Richardson, Rich., pardon, [illegible].
" Robert, precentor of Christ Church, Dublin, commission, [illegible]; license of absence, [illegible].
Richardston — Richardiston (Rickardstown, co. Car. ?), [illegible], [illegible].
Richardston. *See* Richardistowne.
Richardston—Richardeston, co. Kild., [illegible], [illegible], [illegible].
Richardston, co. Kild., [illegible].
Richardston, co. Meath, [illegible], [illegible], [illegible].
Richardstowne (Richardstown), co. Meath, 1460.

INDEX TO FIANTS—ELIZABETH.

Richardstown—Richardston, 434, 6447.
Richardstowne — Richardestowne, co. Louth, 1712.
Richarmston. See Richardston, co. Kild.
Richie, Barnaby, pension, [illegible].
„ Nich., pardon, 6647.
„ Patr. fitz Tibbot, pardon, [illegible].
„ Stephen, pardon, 6494.
Richeford, Gerald fitz James fitz Garrett, pardon, 6418.
Richeforde, Garrett, pardon, 4676.
Richefordestowne. See Richkerdestowne, co. Cork.
Richmeley, in manor of Leixlip, 1444, [illegible].
Richardston (co. Westm. ?) [illegible].
Richewardstowne (Rochfordstown ?), co. Cork, [illegible].
Richford, James, pardon, 6784.
Richford, Patr. fitz Michell, pardon, [illegible]
„ Walter, pardon, [illegible], [illegible].
„ Wm., [illegible].
„ Wm. fitz Edm., pardon, 6374.
„ See Richeforde.
Richfords, co. Meath, 2678.
Richkerdestowne—Richerderdestowne (Rochfordstown ?), co. Cork, 4575, 4528.
Richford, Walter roe, pardon, [illegible].
Richmond, Queen's letter dated at, 6430.
Richward, John, pardon, [illegible].
Rickardstown, co. Kild. See Ballyrichard, Bourdstown, Richardiston.
Rickenhede—Rikenheade (co. Dub.), 1223, [illegible].
Rickenboro—Riggenboro, 790, 4672.
Richard, Katherine nyne, pardon, 6431.
Ricketstown, co. Car. See Richardston.
Ricolfakin, co. Cork, 6448.
Riddry, Feilim, pardon, 6471.
Rider—Ryder, John, dean of S. Patrick's, Dublin, licence of absence, [illegible]; promoted to prebend of Geashill, [illegible]; commission, [illegible].
Ridye, John m'Rory oe, pardon, 4080.
Riegan, Daniel m'Murrigh I, pardon, 6540.
„ Dermod m'Rickard, pardon, 6571.
„ Dermod m'Teig I, pardon, 6540.
„ John m'Morough I, pardon, 6540.
„ Murrohie and Teig m'Dermody I, pardon, 6540.
Rieffie, Gilbert, pardon, 6108.
Rien, Tirlagh I, pardon, 6176.
Rierdan, Donell m'Shane I, pardon, 4753.
„ Donell m'Teig I, pardon, 4912.
„ John m'Donogh I, pardon, 6751.
Rierdane, Donell m'Teig I, pardon, [illegible].
„ John m'Donoghy I, pardon, 6846.
Riesymore (Reerymore) rectory, Queen's co., [illegible].
Rieske, co. Cork, [illegible].
Rievagh, Morghe m'Edm., pardon, [illegible]
Riffe, John, pardon, [illegible].
Riggenboro, 4672. See Rickenboro.
Riggos, Gregory, pardon, 6106.
Rigney, Brian, Edm., Hugh, Owen and Wm. A., pardon, [illegible].
Rilhir, co. Clare, 1641.
Rikenheade, [illegible]. See Rickenhede.
Rilandes—Rilands, Wm., porter of Dublin castle, 5614, 5944.
Rimer—Rhymer—Rimor—Rymer—Rymore pardoned, 1478, 2049, [illegible], 2272, 3102, [illegible], 4378, 4912, 4944, 4678, 5782, [illegible], [illegible]; punishment of, 1844, 6612; to be banished, 6168; lands held by O'Daly the rymer, 3518. See Harpers, &c.
Rimolline (co. Gal. ?), [illegible].
Rimor. See Rimer.
Rinaghan, co. Kild. See Renoghan.
Rinanool, co. Mayo. See Runyniell.
Rinardie, co. Kerry, 6152.
Rinbegan (Ronabeg, co. Kerry ?), 4678.
Rinconhurraghe — Rincahirragh — Rynnaharragh (Reenconlorragh), co. Kerry, 4125; rectory, [illegible], 6173.
Rinche (co. Clare ?), [illegible].
Rinchoun—Rynnahone (now Island Magee, co. Antrim), rectory, 1650, 5767.
Rinckell, Nich., pardon, 3494.
Rincolevan, co. Donegal. See Ryncolevan.
Rincolle—Ryncoll (co. Long. ?), [illegible], 1491, 4416.
Rincrew, co. Wat. See Rinckro, [illegible]; Rinkroe.
Rincurrane (co. Cork ?), 4871.
Rine, co. Cork (Kerry ?), 6152.
Rine, co. Leit., 5441.
Rine—Ryne, co. Long., 4416, 4422.
Rinekrowe (co. Lim. ?), 6453.
Rinervile—Rynorvile, co. Gal., [illegible], 4612.
Ring, gold, stolen, 447.
Ringawnaghe — Ringewonagh — Ryngawonaghe (Ringagonagh), co. Wat., [illegible], 6152.
Ringcurran — Ringcurran, co. Cork, [illegible], 6742.
Ringe of Carne, co. Wex., [illegible].
Ringe Lirolancy (co. Cork ?), 4464.
Ringewonagh — Ringowonaghe. See Ringawnaghe.
Ringhestown, co. Meath. See Ryngleston.
Ringmayne (Rinmeen), co. Cork, [illegible]. See also Ryncmyne.
Ringroone (Ringrone), co. Cork, [illegible]. See Rynrone.
Riniskiddy (co. Cork ?), 4630.
Rinkell, Chr., pardon, 4462.
„ Theobald, pardon, [illegible].
„ Tho., pardon, 6397.
Rinknockin, co. Cork, 4870.
Rinkroe (Rincrew, co. Wat.), 6167.

INDEX TO FIANTS—ELIZABETH.

Rinnagh, co. Ross. See Raynekame, Renagan, Raynekane.
Rinnarogue, co. Sligo. See Ronyroge.
Rinvallakeyne — Rynvallakeyne, co. Wat., 836, 5163.
Riordan, Donald m'Donoghe I, pardon, 6911.
„ Donald m'Teig I, pardon, 5091.
„ Donogh m'Donill I, pardon, 3538.
Riordane, Conoghor m'Owen I, pardon, 6761.
„ Donogh m'Dermody I, pardon, 6764.
„ Donell m'Dermod I, pardon, 6764.
„ Mahowne m'Donell Y, pardon, [illegible].
„ Owen m'Rairie Y, pardon, 6516.
„ Shane m'Teige I, pardon, 4463.
Riough, Wm. oge, pardon, 6416.
Rioughe, Donogh, indenture, [illegible].
Riourdan, Gillynenewe m'Teige Itolane I, pardon, [illegible].
Riourdane, Conoghor m'Moriertagh I, pardon, 6761.
„ Dermod m'Conoghor I, pardon, 6761.
„ Donell m'Owen I, pardon, 6764.
„ Donell m'Teige I, pardon, 6761.
„ Edm. m'Donell I, pardon, 6761.
„ Melaghlin m'Teige I, pardon, 6764.
„ Rich. m'Donell I, pardon, 6761.
„ Riordane m'Donogh I, pardon, 6764.
„ Teig m'Shane oge I, pardon, [illegible].
Riowoghvna, Queen's co., 1314.
Rise, Peter, pardon, 2476.
Rissdon, co. Meath, 3438.
Risford, Edm. m'Shane, pardon, [illegible].
Rism, Tho., pardon, 4617.
Risligey, Ricard, pardon, [illegible].
Rithericke, alias Proderaghie, William, license of absence, 342.
Riuordane, Shillie ny, pardon, 6107.
Riurdain, Conoghor m'Wm. Y, pardon, 4014.
„ Donollag m'Owen Y, pardon, 4414.
Riurdan, Conoghor m'Donogh E, pardon, 6634.
„ Conoghor m'Shane Igulla I, pardon, 6538.
„ Dermod m'Conoghor E, pardon, [illegible].
„ Dermot m'Donell I, pardon, 5531.
„ Donell m'Shane I, pardon, 4623, [illegible].
„ Donoghe m'Dermode Y, pardon, 4163.
Riurdan, Mahowne m'Donogh I, pardon, [illegible].
„ Mahowne m'Teige I, pardon, [illegible].
„ Shane m'Donogh I, pardon, [illegible].
„ Teig m'Melaghlin I, pardon, [illegible].
Riurdane, Conoghor m'Donill Y, pardon, 3187, 5163.
„ Conoghor m'Donogh I Loughlin I, pardon, 4571.
„ Conoghor m'Morierty I, pardon, 4571.
„ Conoghor m'Shane I, pardon, [illegible].
„ Dermond m'Donogh, pardon, 4167, 4571.
„ Donald m'Teige Y, pardon, 5100.
„ Donell m'Donogh I, pardon, [illegible], 6764.
„ Donogh m'Donell I, pardon, 6761.
„ Donogh m'Owen I, pardon, [illegible], 6764.
„ Donoghe m'Teige I, alias Donoghe ny Dary, pardon, 6764.
„ Edm. m'Donell I, pardon, 4157, 4571.
„ John m'Mahowny I, pardon, 6744.
„ John m'Teig I, pardon, [illegible].
„ Owen m'Dermod Y, pardon, 4167, 4571.
„ Owen m'Shane I, pardon, 6137.
„ Teige m'Melaghlin I, pardon, 6761.
Rivane, Katherine, pardon, [illegible].
Riverdan, Donell m'Shane I, pardon, 5412.
Riverston—Ryverstowne, co. Meath, 2115, 2444, [illegible], 3160, [illegible], 5913, [illegible].
Riverston (great, much or mich), co. Meath (Riverstowne), 180, 784, 1360, 1466, 3647, 4737.
Riverston, Little, co. Meath, 180, 1366, 1400, 2347, 4737.
Riverston (mich, moch, or mache). See Riverston, great.
Ro, Conilegh, pardon, [illegible].
„ Conoghor, pardon, [illegible].
Roa, Teig, pardon, [illegible].
Road through his country to be maintained by M'Rory, [illegible].
Roadston, co. Tip., [illegible].
Roaghan, King's co., [illegible].
Roan, Brian m'Ferganenim m'Muriagh, pardon, [illegible].
„ Rich., pardon, 4107.
Roane, Nich., pardon, [illegible].
Roane (co. Tip.), [illegible].
Robartston. See Robertstown, co. Meath.
Robartstown, co. Gal., [illegible].
Robartstowne, co. Kilk. (Ballyrobin, co. Wat. ?), [illegible].
Robartstowne. See Robertstown, co. Meath.
Robbery of cows from Santry by O'Byrnes, &c., 1148. See Preys, [illegible].

INDEX TO FIANTS—ELIZABETH.

Robinakes walls (Robswalls), co. Dub., [illegible].
Robbyneston. See Robinstown, co. Westm.
Robon—Robin—Robyn (Robeen), co. Mayo, [illegible], [illegible]; rectory, 1424, [illegible].
Roberston. See Robinstowne, co. Long.
Roberston (Robinstown ?), co. Meath, 3137.
Robenston. See Robinstown, co. Westm.
Robenstowne (Robinstown ?), co. Wex., [illegible].
Roberston (co. Clare ?), [illegible].
Roberston. See Robertstown, co. Meath.
Roberstown. See Robertstown, co. Lim.
Robert, Edm., pardon, [illegible].
Roberteston. See Robertston, co. Kild.
Robertesten. See Robertstown, co. Meath.
Robertestown. See Robertstown, co. Cork.
Robertiston. See Robertston, co. Kild.
Robertiston. See Robertstown, co. Lim.
Robertiston. See Robertstown, co. Meath.
Robertiston (co. Tip. ?), [illegible].
Robertston—Robertstowne, co. Kerry, [illegible], [illegible], [illegible].
Robertston — Robertston — Robertiston (Robertstown), co. Kild., 1316, [illegible]; grant, [illegible].
Robertston. See Robertstown, co. Lim.
Robertston. See Robertstown, co. Meath.
Robertstone. See Robertstown, co. Meath.
Robertstown — Robertstown — Robertstowne (co. Cork ?), [illegible], [illegible].
Robertstown, co. Kild. See Robertston.
Robertstown—Robertstown—Robertstone—Robertston—Robertstowne, co. Lim., [illegible], [illegible], [illegible], [illegible], [illegible]. See also Ballyrobert.
Robertstown—Robertston—Robertstowne—Roberston—Robertestown—Robertstown — Robertston — Robertstone — Robertstowne — Robertyston, co. Meath, [illegible], [illegible], [illegible], 1010, 1328, 1728, [illegible], [illegible], [illegible], [illegible], [illegible], [illegible], [illegible], 4422, [illegible], [illegible], [illegible], [illegible], [illegible]; rectory, [illegible], 4714, [illegible].
" Hills, and much, 791, [illegible], [illegible].
Robertstowne. See Robertstown, co. Cork.
Robertstowne. See Robertston, co. Kerry.
Robertstowne. See Robertstown, co. Lim. and co. Meath.
Robertstowne (co. Wat. ?), [illegible].
Robertyston. See Robertstown, co. Meath.
Robeston (co. Cork), [illegible].
Robeston, co. Meath, [illegible].
Robie, Teig e, lands of (co. Kerry), [illegible].
Robin. See Robon.
Robins, Arthur, grant of land, [illegible]; commissions, [illegible], [illegible].
Robins Rock, seignory called, [illegible].
Robinson, George, prothonotary, Common Bench, [illegible], [illegible]; temporary justice, [illegible]; commission, [illegible]; licence of absence, [illegible].
" William, attorney general of Munster, [illegible], [illegible]; prothonotary, Common Bench, [illegible].
Robinston (co. Cork ?), [illegible].
Robinstown, co. Meath. See Balrobin, Robeston.
Robinstown — Robbyneston — Robineston — Robinston— Robynston, co. Westm., 1448, [illegible], [illegible], [illegible], [illegible], [illegible], [illegible], [illegible]; rebellion of, [illegible]. See also Balrobbyn, [illegible].
Robinstown, co. Wex. See Robenstowne.
Robinstowne—Roberston— Robynston, co. Long., 1447, [illegible], [illegible], 4163.
Robswalls, co. Dub. See Robinockes walls.
Robyn. See Robon.
Robyns, James, [illegible].
Robynston. See Robinstowne, co. Long.
Robynston. See Robinstown, co. Westm.
Rocester, (of Rathmalnoo), commission, [illegible]. See Rancotor.
" (of Tacumshane), lands of, 818.
Rocetter, Tho., [illegible]. See Rancotor.
" William, 910. See Rancotor.
Rochan, John, pardon, [illegible].
Roche, co. Louth. See Roich.
Roche—Roch—Rooche:
" Adam fitz John, pardon, [illegible].
" Alexander (of Ardcavan, co. Wex.), pardon, 180; pardon to son of, [illegible]; wardship of heir, [illegible].
" Amy, pardon, [illegible].
" Andrew, English liberty, 44.
" Anthony, English liberty, 44.
" Brian, pardon, [illegible], [illegible].
" Conoghor buoy, pardon, [illegible].
" David, lord Roche, viscount Fermoy or Ardmoyn, livery, [illegible]; commissions, [illegible], 1019, [illegible], [illegible], 1849; authorised to lead his people against rebels, [illegible]; pardon, [illegible], [illegible]; lands of, [illegible]; lease, [illegible]; his wife, [illegible]; his sons, [illegible], [illegible], [illegible], [illegible], [illegible], [illegible], [illegible]; livery to his heir, [illegible].
" David, gauger of Limerick, [illegible].
" David, pardon, [illegible], [illegible], [illegible], [illegible].
" David (alias O'Hogan), pardon, 1481.
" David dowgh, pardon, [illegible].
" David fitz Edw., attainted, [illegible].
" David fitz James, pardon, [illegible], [illegible], 4418, [illegible].
" David fitz John or m'Shane (of Killahaly), pardon, [illegible], 1073, 2344, [illegible], [illegible], [illegible], [illegible].

INDEX TO FIANTS—ELIZABETH.

Roche, David fitz John, pardon, [illegible], [illegible], [illegible], 4386-7, 4484.
„ David fitz John fitz Gerot (Roche?) pardon, [illegible].
„ David fitz Morish, pardon, [illegible].
„ David fitz Philip, pardon, [illegible], [illegible].
„ David fitz Tibbot or Theobald, pardon, [illegible], [illegible], [illegible].
„ David fitz Wm., pardon, [illegible], [illegible].
„ David m'Edm., pardon, [illegible].
„ David m'Garrett, pardon, [illegible].
„ David m'Philip, pardon, [illegible].
„ David m'Rich., pardon, [illegible].
„ David m'Shane. See David fitz John.
„ David m'Shane, pardon, [illegible], [illegible].
„ David m'Shane bane, pardon, [illegible].
„ David m'Shane wanne, pardon, [illegible].
„ David m'Shane, lands of, granted, [illegible]. See David fitz John.
„ David row, pardon, [illegible].
„ Dominic, pardon, 1083.
„ Edmund, pardon, [illegible], [illegible], [illegible].
„ Edmund fitz David, pardon, [illegible], [illegible], [illegible], [illegible].
„ Edm. fitz James, pardon, [illegible].
„ Edm. fitz John, pardon, [illegible], [illegible], [illegible], [illegible].
„ Edmund fitz Moriskie, pardon, [illegible].
„ Edm. fitz Redmond, pardon, [illegible].
„ Edm. fitz Robert, pardon, [illegible], [illegible].
„ Edm. m'Philip, pardon, [illegible].
„ Edmund og fitz Edmond, pardon, [illegible], [illegible], [illegible].
„ Edm. rough, pardon, [illegible].
„ Edm. yvillaine, pardon, [illegible].
„ Edw., pardon, [illegible].
„ Edw. fitz Wm., pardon, [illegible].
„ Ellen, pardon, [illegible].
„ Ellen ny ne David, pardon, [illegible].
„ Ellen oge, pardon, [illegible].
„ Eustace, pardon, [illegible], [illegible], [illegible].
„ Eustace fitz Thomas, pardon, [illegible], [illegible] (bis).
„ Garrett, pardon, [illegible].
„ Geoffrey fitz Theobald (Roche?), pardon, [illegible].
„ George, English liberty, 64.
„ George, pardon, 1947.
„ George fitz John, pardon, [illegible].
„ George fitz Jordan, pardon, 79.
„ George fitz Philip, pardon, [illegible].
„ Gerald, pardon, [illegible].
„ Gerald fitz Edmond, pardon, [illegible].
„ Gerrot, pardon, [illegible], [illegible].
„ Gerrott fitz Edm., pardon, [illegible].
„ Gerrott m'Wm. rough, pardon, [illegible].
„ Henry, pardon, 41, [illegible], 1742, [illegible].
„ Henry ne Boyre, pardon, 191.
Roche, James, son of viscount Roche, lease, [illegible], [illegible], [illegible].
„ James, pardon, [illegible], [illegible], [illegible], [illegible], [illegible], [illegible], [illegible], [illegible].
„ James (alias Macbenry), pardon, [illegible].
„ James (alias m'Maurice), pardon, [illegible].
„ James boy, [illegible]. See James, son of viscount Roche.
„ James carrough, pardon, [illegible].
„ James fitz ( ), pardon, [illegible].
„ James fitz James, pardon, [illegible].
„ James fitz John, pardon, [illegible], [illegible], [illegible], [illegible].
„ James fitz Maurice, or Morish, or Morris, pardon, [illegible], [illegible], [illegible], [illegible], [illegible], [illegible].
„ James fitz Morish fitz John (Roche?), pardon, [illegible].
„ James fitz Patr., pardon, [illegible], [illegible].
„ James fitz Philip, pardon, [illegible], [illegible], [illegible], [illegible].
„ James fitz Theobald, pardon, [illegible].
„ James fitz Thomas, pardon, [illegible], [illegible], [illegible], [illegible].
„ James fitz Tibot, pardon, [illegible].
„ James fitz Ulick, pardon, [illegible].
„ James fitz Wm., pardon, [illegible], [illegible], [illegible].
„ James m'Morrish, pardon, [illegible].
„ James galde or galte, pardon, [illegible], [illegible].
„ James m'Tho., pardon, [illegible].
„ James ny goylagh, ny gillagh or [illegible], pardon, [illegible], [illegible]; death of, [illegible].
„ James oig, pardon, [illegible].
„ Johan, pardon, [illegible].
„ John, son of viscount Roche, grant of a wardship, [illegible]. See John boy.
„ John (of Kinsale), wardship and livery to his son, [illegible], [illegible].
„ John (son of Maurice, of Cork), wardship and livery, [illegible], [illegible].
„ John (of Rochland, co. Wex.), wardship of his heir, [illegible].
„ John, pardon, 1310, [illegible], [illegible], [illegible], [illegible], [illegible], [illegible], [illegible].
„ John, alias M'Sarine, pardon (of Wexford), [illegible].
„ John balli fitz Edmond riough, pardon, [illegible].
„ John ballyf, pardon, [illegible].
„ John bag, pardon, [illegible], [illegible], [illegible].
„ alias de Rupe, John boy, son of viscount Fermoy, pardon, [illegible].
„ John boy, gent., cessor, co. Limerick, [illegible].

INDEX TO FIANTS—ELIZABETH.

Roche, John boy, wife of, [illegible].
„ John duff, pardon, [illegible].
„ John fitz David, pardon, [illegible], [illegible].
„ John fitz Edmond, pardon, [illegible], [illegible], [illegible], [illegible].
„ John fitz Gerrold, pardon, [illegible].
„ John fitz James, pardon, [illegible], [illegible], [illegible].
„ John fitz James gankagh, pardon, [illegible].
„ John fitz Morice or Morish, pardon, [illegible], [illegible], [illegible].
„ John fitz Morris dowlegh, pardon, [illegible].
„ John fitz Richard, pardon, [illegible].
„ John fitz Robert, pardon, [illegible].
„ John fitz Thomas, pardon, [illegible], [illegible], [illegible], [illegible].
„ John fitz Tibot, pardon, [illegible].
„ John fitz Ulick or Uliake, pardon, [illegible], [illegible].
„ John fitz William, pardon, [illegible], [illegible], [illegible], [illegible].
„ John m'Philip, pardon, [illegible].
„ John m'Tho. m'Eustace, pardon, [illegible].
„ John m'Tibott, pardon, [illegible].
„ John m'William boy, pardon, [illegible].
„ John m'Wm. m'Edm., pardon, [illegible].
„ John moyle fitz Edmond, pardon, [illegible].
„ Jordan, knap, [illegible].
„ Jordan, pardon, [illegible].
„ lord. See Fermoy, viscount, and Roche, David and Maurice.
„ Margaret, pardon, [illegible], [illegible], [illegible].
„ Mary, house in the care of, at Limerick, [illegible].
„ Mary fitz John, pardon, [illegible].
„ Mathew, pardon, [illegible].
„ Maurice, viscount Fermoy, livery to his son David, [illegible].
„ Maurice, son and heir of David viscount Fermoy, pardon, [illegible], [illegible], [illegible], [illegible]; lord Roche and viscount Fermoy livery, [illegible]; commission, [illegible]; pardon, [illegible], [illegible]; lease, [illegible]; grant of land, [illegible]; lands of, [illegible], [illegible]; pardon to his men, [illegible]; release of recognizance, [illegible].
„ Maurice (son of Alexander of Ardcrowman), wardship, [illegible].
„ Maurice (of Cork), wardship and livery of son, [illegible], [illegible].
„ Maurice, pardon, [illegible], [illegible].
„ Maurice fitz David og, pardon, [illegible].
„ Maurice fitz Gerot, pardon, [illegible], [illegible].
Roche, Maurice fitz James, pardon, [illegible], [illegible].
„ Maurice fitz John, pardon, [illegible], [illegible], [illegible].
„ Maurice fitz Philip, pardon, [illegible].
„ Maurice Imaylet, pardon, [illegible].
„ Michael, pardon, [illegible].
„ Milo, pardon, [illegible].
„ Morice fitz John fitz Redmond, pardon, [illegible].
„ Morish. See Maurice.
„ Morish, pardon, [illegible].
„ Morish fitz Alexander, pardon, [illegible].
„ Morish fitz James, pardon, [illegible], [illegible].
„ Morish fitz John, pardon, [illegible].
„ Morish fitz Rich., pardon, [illegible].
„ Morris fitz Gerald, pardon, [illegible].
„ Morris m'Rich., pardon, [illegible].
„ Morris m'Wm. m'Thos., pardon, [illegible].
„ Morrish, pardon, [illegible].
„ Nicholas, security, [illegible].
„ Nich., commission, [illegible].
„ Nich., pardon, [illegible].
„ Nich. fitz Wm., pardon, [illegible].
„ Oliver, pardon, [illegible].
„ Patrick, pardon, [illegible], [illegible], [illegible].
„ Patrick fitz Philip, pardon, [illegible].
„ Pate fitz Robert, pardon, [illegible], [illegible].
„ Peirs fitz Garret leacy, pardon, [illegible].
„ Peirs m'Wm., pardon, [illegible].
„ Peirse fitz Gerrot, pardon, [illegible].
„ Peirse fitz James, pardon, [illegible].
„ Peter fitz William, pardon, [illegible], [illegible].
„ Philip (son of John, of Kinsale), wardship and livery, [illegible], [illegible].
„ Philip, pardon, [illegible], [illegible], [illegible], [illegible].
„ Philip, rector of Kenmagh, [illegible].
„ Philip carragh, pardon, [illegible], [illegible].
„ Philip fitz Alexander, pardon, [illegible].
„ Philip fitz John (Roche?), pardon, [illegible].
„ Philip fitz John, land claimed by, [illegible].
„ Philip fitz Patrick, pardon, [illegible].
„ Philip fitz Philip, pardon, [illegible], [illegible].
„ Philip fitz Redmond, pardon, [illegible].
„ Philip fitz Rob., pardon, [illegible].
„ Philip fitz Walter, pardon, [illegible].
„ Philip fitz Wm., pardon, [illegible].
„ Philip roe, pardon, [illegible].
„ Redmond (of Castletown), son of lord Roche, pardon, [illegible], [illegible].
„ Redmond (in co. Wex.), pardon, [illegible], [illegible].
„ Redmond boy or bwy, pardon, [illegible], [illegible], [illegible], [illegible], [illegible].

INDEX TO FIANTS—ELIZABETH.

Roche, Redmund fitz James, pardon, [illegible].
" Redmund fitz Theobald or Tibbott, pardon, 4186, [illegible], 6742.
" Redmund m'Wm., pardon, 6707.
" Risard fitz James, pardon, 6170.
" Richard, house in Clonmines, 816.
" Richard, English liberty, 44.
" Richard, merchant, house at Kinsale, 861.
" Rich., alderman of Cork, pardon, 1098.
" Rich., pardon, 4946, [illegible], 6737.
" Rich. fitz David, pardon, [illegible].
" Rich. fitz James, pardon, 4186, [illegible], [illegible].
" Rich. fitz John, pardon, 4078.
" Rich. fitz Petre, pardon, 2310.
" Rich. fitz Philip, pardon, [illegible], [illegible].
" Rich. fitz Philip, allocation to, [illegible].
" Rich. fitz Richard, pardon, [illegible].
" Richard fitz Walter, pardon, [illegible], [illegible].
" Robert, English liberty, 44.
" Robert, commission, [illegible].
" Rob., pardon, 6432.
" Rob. carragh, pardon, [illegible].
" Rob. fitz Alexdrin, pardon, 4045.
" Rob. fitz James, pardon, 6132.
" Rob. fitz Philip, pardon, 4807.
" Rob. garuffe fitz John, pardon, [illegible].
" Shane boy, pardon, 4617.
" Shane boye, his lands in co. Limerick, 2973, 4817.
" Shane boye fitz Robert, pardon, [illegible].
" Shane lyeh, pardon, [illegible].
" Shane m'Wm., pardon, [illegible].
" Sharrie m'Wm., pardon, [illegible].
" Sheane m'Dale m'Cale I, pardon, [illegible].
" Stephen, attorney general, temp. Hen. VI., [illegible].
" Thady, pardon, [illegible].
" Theobald (of Castletown), pardon, [illegible].
" Theobald or Tybbott (of Crag, Cregg or Crag, co. Cork), son of lord Roche, sheriff of co. Cork, [illegible]; lease, [illegible], 3179; grant of land, 3133; pardon, [illegible], 3140.
" Theobald, son of Maurice lord Roche, pardon, [illegible]; (of Crogh) pardon, 4374.
" Theobald (in co. Wex.), pardon, [illegible], 784, 1748, [illegible], 6433.
" Theobald fitz David, pardon, [illegible], [illegible], [illegible].
" Theobald fitz Morish Doulagh, or Morrice dowlagh, pardon, [illegible], 6511.
Roche, Theobald fitz Philip, pardon, [illegible].
" Theobald fitz Robert, pardon, [illegible].
" Theobald fitz Walter, pardon, 432.
" Theobald m'David, pardon, 6762.
" Tho., messuage at Hore, Cashel, [illegible].
" Thomas (of Dowpe, co. Wex.), lease, 7416; pardon, [illegible]; pardon to son of, [illegible].
" Tho. (of Ballimadden), pardon, 3782.
" Tho. bery, pardon, [illegible].
" Tho. fitz David, pardon, 4467.
" Tho. fitz James, pardon, [illegible].
" Tho. fitz Philip, pardon, [illegible].
" Tho. fitz Tho., pardon, [illegible].
" Tho. fitz Walter, pardon, [illegible].
" Tho. owre, pardon, [illegible].
" Tho. owre fitz Alexander, pardon, [illegible].
" Tibbot, pardon, [illegible].
" Tibbot fitz Water or m'Walter, pardon, 4181, 4617.
" Tybbott, [illegible]. See Theobald.
" Tybbott m'Philip, pardon, [illegible].
" Ulick fitz James Nygilcigh, pardon, [illegible].
" Ulick, son of James, lease, [illegible].
" Ulick, pardon, 646, 6432.
" Ulick fitz Philip, pardon, 4807.
" Ulick fitz Wm., pardon, [illegible], 6762.
" Ulcocke fitz Walter, pardon, 432.
" Ulück fitz James, pardon, [illegible].
" Ulisses, pardon, 1045.
" viscount. See Roche, David.
" Walter, lawyer, commission, 2314.
" Walter, pardon, [illegible].
" Walter (son of John of Rochland, co. Wex.), wardship, [illegible].
" Walter boye, pardon, [illegible], 6742.
" Walter fitz William, pardon, [illegible], [illegible].
" Walter moore, pardon, [illegible].
" Walter oge fitz William, pardon, [illegible], [illegible].
" William, pardon, [illegible].
" William (of Cork), commission, 1946; alderman of Cork, pardon, [illegible].
" Wm., house in Dublin, 4314.
" Wm., pardon, [illegible].
" Wm., pardon to son of, [illegible].
" Wm. tuke ruagh, pardon, [illegible].
" William oties, pardon, [illegible].
" Wm. duf fitz James, attainted, [illegible].
" Wm. fitz Edm., pardon, [illegible], [illegible].
" Wm. fitz Garrott, pardon, [illegible].
" Wm. fitz Gerrot, pardon, [illegible], [illegible].
" William fitz James, pardon, [illegible], [illegible].

INDEX TO FIANTS—ELIZABETH.

Roche, Wm. fitz John, pardon, 4714, [illegible], [illegible].
,, William fitz Morish, pardon, 2741.
,, Wm. fitz Rich., pardon, 6874.
,, William fitz Tibbot, pardon, 2343.
,, Wm. m'Alexander, pardon, 6418.
,, Wm. m'Philip, pardon, 2078, 2874.
,, Wm. m'Shane, pardon, 6762.
,, Wm. m'Theobald, pardon, 6766.
,, William oge fitz William, pardon, [illegible].
,, Wm. riogh, pardon, 2344, 7531.
,, (of Ballinrossy, co. Lim.), heir of, 6874.
Roche's tomb (co. Wat.?), 2810.
Roche's country — lord Roche's country, co. Cork, 1107, [illegible], [illegible], 2030, 2116, 2182, [illegible].
Roche's country, co. Ross (recte O'Conor Roe's country), 3102.
Roche's (lord) lands, co. Cork, 0792.
Rocheford, John, pardon, 6581.
Rocheford—Rochefords. See Rochfort.
Rochefordston (Rochfordstown, co. Cork), 4418.
Rochefort. See Rochfort.
Rocheiston. See Rochestown, co. Tip.
Rocheland (co. Wex.), 61.
Rocheston—Rochestowne (co. Cork), [illegible], 6814, 6770.
Rocheston — Rocheston, co. Kild., [illegible]; grant, 6378.
Rocheston — Rochiston — Rochston (co. Kilk.), 618, [illegible], 3428, [illegible].
Rocheston—Rocheston, co. Lim., 1528.
Rocheston. See Rochestown, co. Tip.
Rocheston, co. Wat., 6478.
Rocheston, co. Westm., [illegible].
Rocheston — Rochiston, co. Wex., 3449, [illegible], [illegible], [illegible], 6341.
Rochestone. See Rocheston, co. Kild.
Rochestown—Rochiston (co. Lim. ?), rectory, [illegible], 6347. See Rocheston.
Rochestown — Rocheiston — Rocheston — Rochestowne—Rochstowne, co. Tip., [illegible], [illegible], [illegible], [illegible], [illegible], [illegible]-4.
Rochestown. See Rocheston.
Rochestowne. See Rocheston, co. Cork.
Rochestowne. See Rochestown, co. Tip.
Rocheton. See Rocheston, co. Lim.
Rochetown (co. Tip. ?), [illegible].
Rochey, co. Lim., 8874.
Rochford, Katheline ny Redmond, pardon, 6762.
Rochfordestown, co. Cork. See Richardes-towne, Richardstowne, Rochefordston.
Rochfort—Rochefort—Rochforde—Roche-fort—Rochford—Rochforde—Rochforte:
Rochfort, Arthur, pardon, [illegible].
,, Christopher (in co. Meath), commission, 880; heir and widow of, [illegible].
,, Chr., pardon, 4817, 4934.
,, David, pardon, 1562, 3426.
,, Edward, pardon, 6158.
,, Gerald, pardon, 4934.
,, James, pardon, 4934.
,, Jenet, pardon, 6178, 6778.
,, John (in co. Kilk.), pardon, 1323, 6137, 6708.
,, John, premises in Dublin, 2747.
,, John, lands in co. Meath, [illegible].
,, Katherine, widow of N. Dillon, 3401.
,, Luke, pardon, 4530, 6158.
,, Nicholas, parson of S. Mary's, Wexford, 3015.
,, Oliver, pardon, [illegible].
,, Patrick, pardon, [illegible], 6462.
,, Piers, pardon, 4817.
,, Richard, pardon, 4817.
,, Robert (of Killbride, co. Meath), commission, 880; livery to heir, 2830.
,, Rob. (of Killbride), livery, [illegible]; commission, 4491.
,, Rob., chaplain, conspiracy, 4182.
,, Rob., lease, 6310.
,, Rob., pardon, [illegible], 6418.
,, Thomas, pardon, 4817, 6400, [illegible].
,, Walter, pardon, 4817, [illegible], 6764.
,, Wm., pardon, 6794.
,, See also Richeford, Richford, Richfort, Rishward, Rotchford.
Rochforth, Tho., pardon, [illegible].
Rochilordane, co. Lim., [illegible].
Rochiston. See Rocheston, co. Kilk.
Rochiston. See Rochestown, co. Lim.
Rochiston. See Rocheston, co. Wex.
Rochland, co. Wex., 1718, 6602, 6763.
Rochston. See Rocheston, co. Kilk.
Rochstowne. See Rochestown, co. Tip.
Rock Barkley, seignory called, 5162.
Rock of the Shannon, Limerick, 6183.
Rockell, Edw., pardon, 3698.
,, James, pardon, 836, 1046.
,, Nichol, pardon, 4850.
,, Nich., pardon, 4712.
,, Redmund (or R. de la Rockell, of Rockellscourt), pardon, 837, 1046.
,, Richard, pardon, [illegible], 1046.
Rockelles Court. See Rockellscourte.
Rockellie, Nich., pardon, 4852.
Rockellscourte—Rockelles Court — Rockelscourte, co. Wat., 837, 1046, 4712.
Rocker, Patr., pardon 4185.

INDEX TO FIANTS—ELIZABETH.

Rocke, Nicholas (son of Redmond of Athassy-part), livery, 6742.
Rockeslie, James, pardon, 531.
„ Redmund, pardon, 531.
Rockett, James leymaghe fitz Piers, pardon, 1894.
Rockettscourte or Knockmowllin, co. Wat., 931. See Rockellscorte, Roconticourte.
Rockett, James, pardon, 1502.
„ Richard, pardon, 1502.
Rockettestowne, alias Roconticourte, co. Wat., 1202.
Rockmorage, Cheshire, 6394.
Rocowill—Roconyll—Rokowill—Rokocyll, co. Westm., 1795, 6918, 6731.
Roconticourte, alias Rockottstowne, co. Wat., 1202.
Roda, Brian a., pardon, 6866.
Rodanstown, co. Meath. See Balrodan.
Rodder, alias Rydder, co. Meath, 163.
Roddery, William fitz William, pardon, 6702.
Rode, the (co. Wick.), 814, 7863.
Rodenams bushe, co. Wex., 1517.
Rodestowne, co. Meath, 4122.
Rodstone — Rodstowne — Roodstown (co. Wick.), 6748, 6041; rectory, 1867.
Rodin (co. Tip. or King's), 4861.
Rodine, co. Tip., 6818, 5782.
Rodmagh, co. Wick., 6877.
Roe, Edm., pardon, 6517.
„ John, pardon, 6522.
„ Laghlin, pardon, 6517.
„ Margaret, 4418.
„ Owin, pardon, 4874.
„ Patr., pardon, 4408.
„ Roben (alias Peter), pardon, 3400.
„ Rory, pardon, 6576.
„ Torge, pardon, 6487.
Roemile (co. Lim. ?), 4042.
Roedstown. See Rodstone.
Roefin, co. Cork, 6761.
Roetsward, Gerald fitz James fitz Gerrot, pardon, 4418. See Richaford.
Roer. See Rower, co. Lim.
Roestown, co. Meath. See Rowestown.
Roestowne, co. Kild., 5771.
Roeth, Helen, pardon, 2989.
Roethe, Peter, commission, 6744.
Rogan, Chr., 6048.
„ Patr., 6048.
Roge, Edm., pardon, 5408.
Rogers, Anthony, lease, 1168, 1646; messuage in his tenure, 2894.
„ Edw., pardon, 6367.
„ James, pardon, 2873.
„ sir Owen, clk., 2510.
„ Thomas, lease, 803; pardon, 5184.
Rogerston—Rogerstowne (Rogerstown), co. Meath, 1480, 3898, 6462.
Rogerston, co. Westm., 2297, 6378, 6484, 6525, 6464.
Rogerstowne (co. Kilk.), 6464.
Roghain (King's co. ?), 6574.
Roghan, William, chancellor of Cashel, 698.
Roghbee (co. Car. ?), 6817.
Roghgrancy, 802.
Roghoyn (co. Clare ?), 6741.
Roharroe (Roharroe), co. Kerry, 6786.
Rohonell, co. Westm., 6708.
Roich—Roiche (Roche), co. Louth, 3894-11, 4798.
Roirk, James, 2862.
Roirke, Farrall, pardon, 6471.
„ Uonny, pardon, 5692.
„ Wm., pardon, 4261.
Rokeby, Ralph (chief justice of Connaught), commissions, 1617-18, 1674, 1528.
Roket, Redmond, livery to son, 6748.
Rokowill—Rokocyll. See Rocowill.
Rolande, alias Smythe, Robert, 1878.
Rolandston, co. Meath, 1294.
Roll of lords spiritual and temporal, and commoners, &c., 183, 6434.
Rolle, Rich. fitz David, pardon, 4935.
Rolleston. See Rollestown.
Rolleston. See Rowleston, co. Dub.
Rollesloo (co. Meath), 2117.
Rollestown—Rolleston (Rawleystown ?), co. Lim., 2961, 6473, 4914.
Rolley, Garret gannagh, pardon, 2362.
„ James, pardon, 2478, 4132.
„ Richd, pardon, 4432.
„ Rich. bay, pardon, 2362, 3082.
Rolleyston, co. Meath, 1602.
Rollickestone, co. Kild., 6713, 5822.
Rollin, Garret roe fitz William, pardon, 4712.
Rollies lands, Youghal, 6694.
Rollisson (Rawleystown ?), co. Lim., 6262.
Rolls, Master of. See Parker, John; Draycott, Henry; White, Nicholas; Saintleger, Anthony.
„ a justice of assize, 1002.
„ E. Fitzsymons, appointed temporarily pending a sequestration, 6067.
„ powers of, 6856.
Rolonghirton, co. Meath, 745.
Romalmee. See Rathgonachme.
Rome, court of, benefices held under provision, 367. See Papal provision.
Rome runners to be punished, 4301.
Romish clerk, deprivation of, reversed, 4880.
Ronan, James, pardon, 1084.
„ John, pardon, 4497.
„ Patrick, pardon, 854.
„ Philip, pardon, 1008.
„ Rich., pardon, 6810.
„ Rich., house in Youghal, 6694.

INDEX TO FIANTS.—ELIZABETH.

Romane, James, vicar of Ardfonan and Noddanen, 4125.
" John, kern, 4158.
" John, pardon, 3894.
" Mallads, pardon, 2424.
" Margaret, 3152.
Romdon, Edm. fitz Rich., pardon, 6176.
Romelaght (co. Sligo ?), 5478.
Romo, Shane, pardon, 4161.
Romper (co. Westm. ?), [illegible].
Romugh, James, pardon, 4180.
Ronceane, David, pardon, 6485.
Ronno, James, pardon, 891.
Ronow, James, pardon, 4638.
Ronowe, Patrick, pardon, 6158.
Ronyroge (Rinnarogue), co. Sligo, 5151.
Roo, co. Gal., 1466, 3152. See also Rowe.
Roo, Gerald, pardon, 3285.
" Henry, 4158.
" John, commission, 2146.
" Tair, pardon, 3471.
" Simon, 4158.
Roode land (co. Gal. ?), 3467, [illegible].
Roolagh, alias Acre ne Croghnow, co. Long. 6181.
Roon, Hugh, pardon, 6182.
" John, sheriff of Carlow, comn. for martial law, 1855, 3168. See Rowe.
Rooghaun, co. Mayo. See Leigh Garowe Rowghane.
Rooen, Bartholomew, ganger of Limerick, 181.
Roomer, Laurence, English liberty, 462.
Roose (co. Leit. ?), 6442.
Rooskagh (Rossky, co. Donegal), 6381.
Rossky, co. Leit. See Rossky.
Rooth—Roothe, Robert. See Rothe.
Roowen, co. Cork. See Rwo.
Ropagh (co. Mayo ?), 6788.
Ropes impressed for army, 1461, 2121.
Rorestown (co. Tip.), 6488.
Rorsh, Rich., pardon, 4488.
Rorie, Mary oyne, pardon, 4802.
Roriston — Roryeston, alias Ballyrory (Roristown), co. Meath, 44, 871.
Rorin, Cornelius oy, pardon, 6487.
Rorwan, James, pardon, 6461.
Rory duffe, pardon, 6417.
Rory, Johanna ny, pardon, 4872.
Roryeston, alias Ballyorry. See Roriston.
Ros. See Rosse, co. Wex.
Rosan (Rossan), co. Meath, 4128.
Rosard, co. Car., 4665.
Rosbarrie, co. Kild., 6587.
Rosbahy (Rossbehy, co. Kerry ?), 6678.
Rosberean, 6484.
Rosbercon—Rosbrekon—Rossbarron, co. Kilk., 6464.
Rosberean, house of friars preachers, possessions granted, 4688.
" rectory, 1588.
Rosberie, 6511.
Rosborie—Rosbery (Rosberry), co. Kild., 1316, 3716, 6158, 6788. See also Rossbery, Rossebery.
Rosbirne, Tryone, co. Sligo, 6677.
Rosbranagh (co. Kild. ?), 6231.
Rosbrekan, 4880. See Rosbercon.
Rosbrenagh (co. Kild. ?), 2682.
Rosbrin—Rosbryn. See Rossbryn.
Roscagho (co. Cav. ?), 6687.
Rosshill, co. Don., 6382.
Roscam—Rosscam, co. Gal., 1438, 4888, 6568.
Roscanoo (co. Gal. ?), 4707.
Rossarbarie—Rosarborie — Rossarbery—Rossarbrie — Rossarbry — Rossarbrye — Rossarebre. See Rossarbrie.
Rosarike (Rosserk), co. Mayo, friary leased, 2368. See Rosserike.
Roselure (co. Wex. ?), 6728.
Roselavra, co. Mayo. See Rosselavra.
Roscolaine, or Rosscollaine, Queen's co., 2846.
Roscolaine — Roscollayne — Rosscollayne (Rosskelton), Queen's co., 818, 2830, 3862.
Roscommon — Roscoman — Roscomon — Roscomyn — Roscomen — Rosscommon, 2778, 3852, 3828, 4078, 4188, 4763, 4778, 5143, 5607, 5808, 6106.
" royal castle and manor, surrendered by O'Conor Don, 458; excepted from his rule, 1911; given to Malby, 3134, 3849; ward in, 3356, 4780; possession of, 4638.
" constable of castle, 3384.
" priory of canons, leased, 2364, 3134, granted, 3540.
" house of friars, leased, 2356, 3134; granted, 3848.
" barony, 4684, 6886, 6777.
" county, commission to form county, 1626; place now in co. Gal. described as in Roscommon, 1861; crimes committed outside excepted from pardon, 3787, 4888; grant of his country to O'Conor Don, 4886; men of, pardoned, 3838, 3894, 4078-7, 4178, &c.
" county, commission for government, 1285.
" county, martial law commissions, 2848, 3432, 4826.

INDEX TO FIANTS—ELIZABETH.

Roscommon — county, sheriff, [illegible], [illegible], [illegible], [illegible].
Roscouran, King's co. See Roscouragh, Roscorown.
Rosecon—Rosseton, co. Kilk., 550, 1063, 1184, 1843, 5678.
Roseoalan, or Rossolloyne, Queen's co. [illegible].
Roscomell — Roscomyll, Queen's co., 1112, 6861, 6796.
Roscourragh—Roscourtibe — Roscouroghe (Roscomroe, King's co.), 978, 5298, 4622.
Roscomyll. See Roscomell.
Roscualayne or Roscolloyne, Queen's co., 819.
Roscrea — Roscro — Roscrae — Roscrey— Roskero—Roskre—Roskrea— Roskrey, co. Tip., 1058, 1188, 1230, 4057, 4871, 4058, [illegible], [illegible], 6612, 6262, 6706.
" rectory, 348.
" house of friars, leased, 978, 1818, 5793, 6522.
Rosenfib — Rosoribbe — Rosorribe (Rosorib), co. Sligo, 6814, 5954, 6916.
Roslavagh (co. Wex. ?), 6901.
Roslogheen (Rosseloban, co. Kerry ?), 6476.
Rose, reserved as rent, 1493, 5161.
Roseinane (co. Wick.), 1843.
Rosebery (Rosberry, co. Kild. ?), 6182.
Rosebrine —Rossbryne, co. Cork, 1983, 4673. See Rosebryn.
Rosecarbrie — Rosecarbrye, co. Cork, 5098, 6672. See Rosscarbrie.
Rosecomman. See Roscommon.
Rosecrena, co. Kilk., 1184.
Rosegarlande—Rosegarlon — Rosegarlone— Rosgarlan — Rosgarlande (Rosegarland), co. Wex., 916, 1570, 1769; manor, 4091, 6316.
Roseilliarie, 5088. See Rosscarbrie.
Roseleyne (Rosselline, co. Cork ?), 2262.
Rosellisiou (co. Wick. ?), 2282.
Rosellarie, [illegible]. See Rosscarbrie.
Roselnoghe, co. Sligo, 4898.
Rosemeakan, co. Louth, 1312.
Rosemeelan, co. Gal., 6447.
Rosemenog—Rosemynog (Rossminoge), co. Wex., 6734.
Rosemore, co. Gal., 4615.
Rosemyd, co. Westm., 1469.
Rosemyn (co. Long ?), [illegible].
Rosemynog. See Rosemenog.
Rosenallis, Queen's co. See Rossenoles.
Rosenecarrie (co. Lim. ?), 6342.
Rosenemoltiny (Rossmultieny), co. Tip., 6612.
Rosenbarley (co. Tip. ?), 1858, 2012.
Roseweylie — Rosswilie (Ross, in par. Killeran, co. Gal.), 1087, 6418.
Rosery, co. Lim., 3426.
Rossinn, co. Meath, 3242.
Rosetown, co. Wex. See Rowsetoon.
Rosfarnhan (Rosfarnaghan, King's co. ?), 6166.
Rosgarbery, co. Cork, 6761.
Rosgarlan — Rosgarlande. See Rosegarlande.
Rosgrelle—Rosgrelly—Rossgrell — Rossgrellan (Rosegrilla, co. Wat. ?), 1044, 2798, 3810, 4173, 6763.
Rosgulll, co. Donegal. See Rosgolle.
Rosharline, co. Tip., 2943.
Roshillarie, 6840. See Rosscarbrie.
Roskinealan, co. Rosc., 4678.
Rosier, Rob., queen's attorney in Munster, 4342.
Roskgyne, co. Cork, 2231.
Roske (co. Leit. ?), 6794.
Roske (co. Wick.), 6477.
Roskeragh, co. Tip., 6446.
Roskinan, co. Cork. See Roskyen, Roswkin.
Roskelion — Rossakelion or Rosquillan (Rosskellton), Queen's co., 1878, 5734.
Roskere. See Roscrea.
Roskcabell, Queen's co., 1528, 5678.
Roskene (co. Ros. ?), 6497.
Roskro—Roskrea—Roskrey. See Roscrea.
Roskryny (Rossnacreena ?), Queen's co., 6311.
Roskyne (Roskeen), co. Cork, 3978, 5012. See also Rossakeyne.
Roskyne (co. Tip. ?), 5639.
Rosle (co. Cork ?), 6456.
Roslure, co. Wex., 6743.
Roslevan. See Rosslavan.
Roslie (co. Sligo ?), 6806.
Rosley (co. Car. ?), 1263.
Rosley (Rosslee, co. Mayo), rectory, 1494.
Rosly (co. Sligo ?), 6806.
Rosmanaher (Rossmanagher, co. Clare), 6816.
Rosmaure. See Rosmayre.
Rosmeen, co. Rosc. See Rosmyn.
Rosmolan, co. Gal., 6591.
Rosmayre—Rosmier. See Rosmayre.
Rosmore (Rossmore), Queen's co., 6543.
Rosmorow, co. Tip. (Rossmurrow, King's co. ?), rectory, 348.
Rosmoylan, co. Gal. See Karowe Rosmoylan.
Rosmyde, co. Westm., 6562.
Rosmyn (Rossmeen), co. Rosc., 6586.
Rosmynoge (Rossminoge ?), co. Wex., 6718.
Rosmyre. See Rosmayre.
Rosnacartan, co. Kerry. See Rossnaycartan.
Rosnalvan (Graigurosnalvan), co. Kild., 4401, 6297.
Rosnamultieny, co. Tip. See Rosenemultiny.
Rosnasleagh (Rossnagleagh), co. Mon., 6626.

INDEX TO FIANTS.—ELIZABETH.

Rosgovell (co. Kilk.?), [illegible].

Rosogianl — Rossuyany (Rossanowy, co. Kilk.?), [illegible], [illegible].

Rosguile — Rosgoyle (Rosspile?), co. Wex., 616, 4791.

Rosqnile (Rosgull, co. Donegal), [illegible].

Rosquillan—Rossequillan, alias Roshcilton, Queen's co., 1278, [illegible].

Rosrun — Rosroco — Rosro — Rosse Ro — Rose roo — Rosse roo, co. Clare, 1004, [illegible], [illegible], [illegible], [illegible], [illegible]. See also Rosrea.

Ross, co. Gal. See Rosseryle, Rossevelle.

Ross, co. Meath, [illegible].

Ross (co. Tip.?), [illegible], [illegible].

Ross, (co. Westm.?), [illegible].

Ross. See Rosse, Old Rosse.

Ross castle. See Rosse I Donoghe, Ross I Donoghue, Rosydonoghowe.

Rossana — Rossanne (co. Wick.), 1038, 1048.

Rossack, Ould (Rossagh), co. Cork, [illegible].

Rossan, co. Meath. See Rosse.

Rossane. See Rossan.

Rossanany, co. Kilk. See Rossenlanl, Rossenegane.

Rossard — Rossarde, co. Wex., [illegible], [illegible]; grant, [illegible].

Rossary, co. Tip., [illegible].

Rossaugh (co. Cork), rectory, [illegible].

Rossbehy, co. Kerry. See Rosbehy.

Rossbroy (Queen's co.?), [illegible].

Rossbryn—Rosbrin—Rosbrye—Rossbrine—Rossbryne—Rossebren—Rossebryn (Rossbrin), co. Cork, [illegible], [illegible], [illegible], [illegible]; manor and castle, [illegible], [illegible], [illegible], [illegible].

Rosscahan, co. Clare, [illegible].

Rosscam. See Rossan.

Rosscarberie — Rosscarborie — Rosscarborie — Rosscarbery — Roscarbrie — Rosscarbry — Rosscarbrye — Rosscarebre — Rosscarbrye — Rosscarebroy — Rosse Carbery, co. Cork, [illegible], [illegible], [illegible]; lands leased, [illegible], [illegible], [illegible].

" priory leased, [illegible], [illegible], [illegible], [illegible].

" rectory, [illegible], [illegible], [illegible], [illegible].

" bishop Dermot, [illegible].

" bishop William (Lyon), commissions, [illegible], [illegible].

" dean, commission, [illegible].

" cathedral, treasury, [illegible].

" diocese, ecclesiastical commissions, [illegible], [illegible], [illegible].

Rosschgram — Rosschrane — Rosshchonse or Rosshowe, Queen's co., [illegible], [illegible], [illegible].

Rossclavo (Rosslavo?), co. Mayo, [illegible].

Rossdohan, co. Kerry. See Rosdoghan.

Rossdroyle (Rossdroill), co. Wex., church, [illegible].

Rosse (co. Cav.), [illegible].

Rosse (co. Clare?), [illegible], [illegible].

Rosse, co. Cork, [illegible], [illegible], [illegible], [illegible], [illegible], [illegible].

Rosse or Rosscarebre. See Rosscarberie, co. Cork.

Rosse (Ross, co. Gal.), [illegible]; barony, [illegible], [illegible].

Rosse (Ross, near Killarney), co. Kerry, [illegible], [illegible].

Rosse (co. Lim.?), [illegible], [illegible].

Rosse (co. Mayo?), [illegible], [illegible].

Rosse, co. Mayo (now Galway), barony. See Rosse, co. Gal.

Rosse rectory (see Maghercross, co. Mon.), [illegible].

Rosse, the, (Queen's co.?), [illegible].

Rosse (co. Sligo?), [illegible].

Rosse, co. Westm., [illegible], [illegible], [illegible].

Rosse—Ros—New Ross—New Rosse, co. Wex., [illegible], [illegible], [illegible], [illegible], [illegible]; fiant dated at, [illegible]; fort built to protect its trade from the Irish, [illegible]; men mustered against invasion, [illegible]; messuage in, granted, [illegible], leased, [illegible]. See also Rosspont.

" sovereign, commissions, [illegible], [illegible], [illegible], [illegible]; like powers granted to sovereign of Kilkenny, [illegible].

" sovereign and council, [illegible].

" Earlsmeadow, [illegible].

" ferry, [illegible], [illegible].

" hospital of Holy Trinity, [illegible], [illegible].

" house of friars granted, [illegible].

" Powersmill, [illegible].

" S. Michael cemetery, [illegible]; chapel, [illegible].

" S. Saviour chapel, [illegible], [illegible], [illegible].

" haven, [illegible], [illegible].

" supervisor of port, [illegible].

" searcher, [illegible].

" collector of impost on wines, [illegible], [illegible], [illegible], [illegible], [illegible], [illegible], [illegible].

" controller of same, 1464, [illegible], [illegible], [illegible], [illegible], [illegible], [illegible].

" wine impost, leased, [illegible].

" vicar, [illegible].

Rosse (co. Wex.?), [illegible], [illegible], [illegible], [illegible].

Rosse, Old. See Old Rosse, co. Wex.

Rossebarran, alias Rossebarre, [illegible]. See Rosbarran.

Rossebert, co. Kild., [illegible].

Rossebren—Rossebryn. See Rossbryn.

Rosse Carbery. See Rosscarberie.

Rossechonce. See Rosschrane.

Rossecomman. See Roscommon.

INDEX TO FIANTS—ELIZABETH.

Rosecon. *See* Roscon.
Rosecowe (Roscon, co. Kilk.?), 680.
Rosecreyne in Upperossory, 637.
Rosedirelan, co. Meath, 6371.
Rosegarlan, co. Wex., 612.
Rosegrell—Rosegrellan. *See* Rosgrelle, co. Wat.
Rosegreenagh (co. Ferm.?), 4910.
Roseguyne (co. Cork ?), 2291.
Rosehalen (co. Wick.?), 5902.
Rosehillarie, co. Cork, priory, 4473. *See* Rosecartaria.
Rose I Doroghe in Desmonde (Ross castle, Killarney), manor and castle, and lands, 6777, 6717. *See also* Rowydoneghowe.
Rosekelton. *See* Roskelton.
Rosekeyne (co. Cork ?), 5326.
Rosekin (Roskeen, co. Cork ?), 5257.
Roseleaghanbegg (Rosleaghan), Queen's co., 2328.
Roseleaghanmore, Queen's co., 2328.
Roseled, co. Sligo, 4586.
Roselekyne (Rosleaghan), Queen's co., 499.
Roseloy (Rosslee ?), co. Carlow, 544.
Rosely (co. Sligo ?), 5808.
Roselynn (co. Sligo ?), 4578.
Roselye (co. Sligo ?), 4525.
Rosemoment, Queen's co., 534. *See* Rosemonele.
Rosemenoge (Rossminoge), co. Wex., 5760. *See also* Rosemenoyncy.
Rosemeran, 4900.
Rosemonyncy, co. Wex. (*see* Rosemenoge), 1344.
Rosemore (Rossmore), Queen's co., 2328.
Rosen (King's co. ?), 4128.
Roseneaghe (Rossmore), Queen's co., 534, 5357.
Rosemalgan, Queen's co., 532, 2328.
Rosenebeggie (co. Tip. ?), 6704.
Rosemonele—Rosemement—Rosemonene, Queen's co., 438, 6746, 6652.
Rosenahone (Rosmanony, co. Kilk. ?), 6186.
Rosenerayn, co. Kilk., 5564.
Rosenmolee (Rosemallin), Queen's co., rectory, 2328.
Rosenne, co. Clare, 5821.
Roseneraghar in Thomond manor, 238.
Rosennaky, co. Cork ?, 5614.
Roseny carten (Rosmarten), co. Kerry, 5472.
Rosepoula. *See* Rosepoul.
Rosequillan (*see* Rosquillan, Queen's co.), 5694.
Roserrane, co. Clare, 5517.
Rosewelle (Ross Reilly—Ross, bar. Clare, co. Gal.), monastery granted, 1581.
Rosericke—Rosirike—Rosdirk—Rosirike, co. Mayo, 5798.
" friary leased, 4283, 5280; possessions granted, 5882.
Rosse Ro—Rosse roo—Rosse roo. *See* Rosvue.
Rossereddery—Rosseraderie, co. Wat., 2828, 6478.
Rosseshinnan. *See* Roshinnan.
Rossehynsyan, co. Kilk., 1217.
Rossewbinnan. *See* Rosebignan.
Rossetemple (*see* Rostylemple), 5178.
Rosseyn (King's co. ?), 4361.
Rossyrilla, co. Wat. *See* Rosgrelle.
Rossbehagan. *See* Rossbanan.
Rossheghyman. *See* Rosshinnan.
Rossetillarie (*see* Rosecartarie), co. Cork, 6877.
Rossbinnan—Rossrahigan—Rossowbinnan—Rosshestyman (Rossinan, co. Kilk.), rectory, 2872, 5066, 6153. *See also* Rossebynyan.
Ross I Donnoghe, manor 6737. *See* Rosse I Doroghe.
Rosdirk—Rosirike. *See* Rosericke.
Rossiter, John, sheriff of Wexford, 1892.
Roskdole, co. Lim., 4850.
Roskelton, Queen's co. *See* Rosecoknine, Roskniton.
Rosleaghan, Queen's co. *See* Roseleaghanbegg, Roselekyne.
Roslee, co. Car. *See* Roseloy.
Roslee, co. Mayo. *See* Rosiny, Rowyre.
Roslevan—Roslevan, co. Clare, 6108, 6914.
Roslina, co. Cork. *See* Roseleyne.
Rossiny, co. Car., 1116.
Rosely, co. Sligo, 5142. *See also* Roseled, Rosely.
Rossm'owen (Rossmickowen, co. Cork), 6511.
Rosmanagher, co. Clare. *See* Rosemanagher.
Rosmeyre—Rosmeare—Rossmeyre—Rosmier—Rosmyre (Rossmire), co. Wat., 654, 844, 1072, 2117; chapel, 844, 5123.
Rosminoge, co. Wex. *See* Rosemenoncy, Rosemyneoge, Rosemenoge.
Rosmore, co. Gal., 4570.
Rosmore, Queen's co. *See* Rosemore, Rosemore.
Rosmacreena, Queen's co. *See* Roskryny.
Rossnagadon, 878.
Rosnagleagh, co. Mon. *See* Rosemaleagh.
Rosmuree, co. Meath. *See* Rosyury.
Rosnaballagy, co. Tip., 6708.
Rosnemoeke, co. Wex., 5780.
Rosnecerwe (co. Kilk. ?), 2044.
Rosnemane, co. Kilk., 6704.
Rospile, co. Wex. *See* Rospole.
Rospont—Rossponte (New Ross), co. Wex., 1058, 2451, 2183, 2408, 5743, 2834, 6294. *See* Rosse, co. Wex.
Rosree (Rossroe ?), co. Clare, 5577. *See also* Roserrane.
Ross Reilly, co. Gal. *See* Rosewelle.

INDEX TO FIANTS—ELIZABETH.

Rosstympple—Rossimple, co. Lim., 3943.
Rossyn (co. Westm. ?), 6900.
Rosvyary (Rossmare ?), co. Meath, 682.
Rostard, Walter, pardon, 4182.
Rostaville, Michell, pardon, 4408.
Rostalan in Imokall, co. Cork, rectory, 3131.
Rostalcome (co. Cork ?), 6511.
Rostellan — Rostellayne — Rostillan, co. Cork, 3783, 4107, 6452.
Rostowse (co. Wex. or Kilk.), 1087.
Rosvrellayn, co. Cork, 4166.
Rosmerka, co. Kilk., rectory, 282.
Roswye (Rossiee), co. Mayo, rectory, 6712.
Rosydonaghowe (Ross, co. Kerry), 6282.
Rotalan, John fitz Tho., pardon, 3472.
″ Tho., pardon, 3432.
″ Wm. fitz John fitz Wm., pardon, 3472.
Rotchaford, Rob. See Rochford.
Rotchford, John, pardon, 4478.
″ Roland, pardon, 4478.
Roth (co. Westm. ?), 6874.
Rothe—Roth, Edm. Power fitz John, pardon, 6616.
″ Ellen, lease, 4628.
″ Geoffrey, pardon, 3164.
″ Geoffrey fitz David, pardon, 1417, 3434.
″ Geoffrey fitz John, pardon, 3434.
″ Geoffrey fitz Tho., pardon, 3434.
″ Geoffrey fitz Rich., pardon, 1044.
″ Geoffrey fitz Wm., pardon, 3434.
″ George, pardon, 1617, 3434.
″ Isabella, pardon, 2361.
″ James fitz Edw., pardon, 1431.
″ James fitz Rob., pardon, 3434.
″ John, pardon, 3488.
″ John or Jenkon, pardon, 968, 1817.
″ John Oheragh fitz Tho., pardon, 6618.
″ John Eplache, pardon, 1042.
″ John fitz David, pardon, 3434.
″ John fitz Rob., pardon, 3434.
″ John fitz Piers, pardon, 4794.
″ Margaret, pardon, 1462, 1617.
″ Marion, pardon, 1462.
″ Nicholas fitz William, pardon, 1044.
″ Oliver fitz Robert, pardon, 1617.
″ Pair., pardon, 3434.
″ Peter fitz Robert, pardon, 1617.
″ Peter fitz Rob., official of Ossory, 3134.
″ Piers, bachelor of law, commission, 3697.
″ Richard, archdeacon of Ossory, pardon, 1617, 3434.
″ Richard, pardon, 4441.
″ Richard fitz Edw., pardon, 4877.
″ Richard fitz Walter, pardon, 3434.
Rothe, Robert (—Rooth—Roothe), commissions, 2884, 3426, 4456; treats with rebels in Munster, 4882; pardon, 1617, 4298; pardon at his suit, 4693; custodiam grant, 4316; land in Kilkenny, 5384; surrender and lease, 6697.
″ Rosina or Rose, pardon, 1042, 1462.
″ Simon, pardon, 3424.
″ Tho. fitz John, pardon, 3434.
″ Thomas fitz Richard, pardon, 1617, 3431.
″ Tho. fitz Rob., pardon, 3434.
″ Walter, wife of, pardon, 3465.
″ Walter fitz Oliver, pardon, 1617.
″ Walter fitz Richard, pardon, 3434.
″ Walter fitz Rob., pardon, 3434.
″ Walter m'William na corrane, pardon, 108.
″ William, pardon, 4443.
″ Wm. (alias Tobon), pardon, 2888.
″ Wm. fitz Joffery, pardon, 6702.
″ Wm. m'Mevrery, pardon, 6657.
Rothevion (co. Kilk. ?), 3467.
Rothkewlon, co. Louth, 2806.
Rothesdown, John, (co. Kilk. ?), 6587.
Rothiston, 6672.
Rothrowan. See Rathronan.
Rotomay, co. Wex., 4884.
Rouse, Barnabas, pardon, 3466.
″ Enens, pardon, 108.
Rough (King's co. ?), 3778.
Roughgrange, co. Meath. See Rughegrange.
Roulyghellis (co. Cork ?), 3434.
Rourke, Kahill m'Teig I., pardon, 6663.
Rous, Edm., constable, Athlone castle, 4325.
Rousk, co. Mon., 5480.
Rouske (co. Kild. ?), 6408.
Rouske, co. Meath or Cav., 5536.
Rouske, co. Mon., 5462.
Rouskie, co. Meath or Cav., 5462.
Rouskoughlie, King's co., 3778.
Rousky (Rousky, co. Leit.), 6797.
Rousselwood. See Russellswood.
Rout—Route. See Rowte.
Routh, Walter, pardon, 2880.
Routhe, John fitz Peirs, 6634.
Routlandiston, co. Kild., 5957.
Rouseell, Richard, house in Dublin, 1811.
Rovale, Diarmot m'Brien, pardon, 2817.
Rove, co. Cork, 3941.
Row, Rich., clerk of the pleas Exchequer, 6442.
″ Thady, pardon, 4354.
Row (co. Rosc. ?), 5452.
Row, co. Westm., 1682.
Rowan, Kirrien m'Moriegh, pardon, 6161.
Rowan, co. Meath, 282.
Rowcansell (co. Westm. ?), 6621.

INDEX TO FIANTS—ELIZABETH.

Rowe, Barnabe, pardon, [illegible].
„ Donoughe, pardon, [illegible].
„ Gilbert, pardon, 777.
„ Henry, pardon, [illegible].
„ John, pardon, [illegible], 1[illegible]; sheriff of Carlow, commission, [illegible]. See Rose.
„ Patr., pardon, [illegible].
„ Thomas, 17[illegible].
Rowe, co. Gal., [illegible], [illegible].
Rowe, co. Kild., 6777.
Rowe, co. Westm., 1[illegible], [illegible], [illegible].
Rower—Roer—Rowre, co. Lim., 1143, [illegible], 4787, [illegible], 5115; grant, [illegible], [illegible]. See Rowre
Rower More, co. Lim. See Rowremore.
Rowesion—Rowestowne, co. Kilk., 847, [illegible], [illegible], 4287, [illegible].
Rowestion — Rowyston (Rocstown), co. Meath, 1[illegible], 2[illegible], [illegible].
Rowestion, co. Meath, [illegible].
Rowestion (Rosstown), co. Wex., 1[illegible].
Rowestown, co. Wex., 710.
Rowestowne. See Rowesion.
Rowgarran—Rwogarrane (co. Cork), [illegible], [illegible].
Rowghan, King's co., [illegible].
Rowhan, Honor ffitz Hugh, pardon, [illegible].
Rowhie (co. Ross. ?), [illegible].
Rowilfeane, co. Westm., 17[illegible].
Rowir. See Rowre.
Rowles, Wm., receiver of fines, [illegible].
Rowleston—Rolleston, co. Dub., [illegible], [illegible].
Rowleston, alias Ballendrolan, co. Westm., 1[illegible].
Rowley, Davy, pardon, [illegible].
„ Garett, pardon, [illegible].
„ James, [illegible].
Rowlie, Garrott gankagh, pardon, [illegible].
„ alias Raleigh, Rich., pardon, [illegible].
Rowlle, William, pension, [illegible].
Rowne, Donell A., pardon, [illegible].
Rowne, Nich., pardon, [illegible].
„ alias Tobin, James, pardon, [illegible]. See also Rownie.
Rowniston, co. Meath, 1[illegible].
Rownoe, Donill, pardon, [illegible].
Rowrdan, Donoghowe intergymon Y, pardon, 4781.
Rowre, Gerald m'Brene oe, pardon, [illegible].
Rowre—Rowir—Rowrye (Rower, co. Kilk.), 812, 1[illegible], [illegible].
„ Cavanaghs of, [illegible].
„ rectory, [illegible], [illegible].
Rowre, co. Lim., [illegible].
Rowremore (Rower More, co. Lim.), [illegible].
Rowrie, Owney nyne, pardon, [illegible].
Rowrk, Mary ne, pardon, [illegible].
„ Owne ne, pardon, [illegible].
„ Sawe ne, pardon, [illegible].
Rowrke, Ellen ny, pardon, [illegible].
„ Shilie ny, pardon, [illegible].
Rowry, Donyne nyne, pardon, [illegible].
Rowrye, [illegible]. See Rowre, co. Kilk.
Rowske (co. Leit. ?), [illegible].
Rowske (co. Tip. ?), [illegible].
Rowston, co. Meath, [illegible].
Rowston, co. Wex., [illegible].
Rowte—Rout—Route—Rowt (north western part of co. Antrim), to be made shire ground, 1[illegible]; M'Quillen appointed seneschal and captain, [illegible]; rebellious intrusion of Sorley M'Donnell, [illegible]; under rule of governor of Clandeboy, [illegible], [illegible], [illegible].
„ commission to punish rebels, [illegible], [illegible].
„ „ for martial law, 11[illegible], 1[illegible], [illegible], [illegible], [illegible], [illegible], [illegible].
Rowte M'William (i.e. M'Quillen), 1[illegible]. See Rowte.
Rowth, Rob., pardon, [illegible].
„ Wm., pardon, [illegible].
Rowthe, Walter fitz Robert, pardon, [illegible].
Rowyston. See Roweston, co. Meath.
Roydon, Thomas, slaying of, [illegible].
Roygles or Reigles, co. Dub., 17[illegible], [illegible].
Royke, Tho., pardon, [illegible].
Roymaile (co. Gal. ?), [illegible].
Roymmoly (co. Gal. ?), [illegible].
Roymoyle (co. Gal.), [illegible].
Roynough, Teige m'Wm., pardon, [illegible].
Royrke, co. Kerry, [illegible].
Royrke, Thomas, pardon, 1[illegible].
Ruan, Robert, pardon, [illegible].
Rubbe, Dermod m'Teig y, pardon, [illegible]. See also Robie.
Rubestown, co. Cork, [illegible].
Ruddermagh, co. Wex., [illegible].
Ruddy, Wm., [illegible].
Ruderie, Edm. fitz Thomas, pardon, [illegible].
Rudmore, John, land of, 815.
Rue (co. Ross. ?), [illegible].
Ruerdane, Thady m'Mortertagh Y, pardon, [illegible].
Rughegrange, alias Grange (Roughgrange), co. Meath, 1[illegible].
Rulagh, Shane m'Teige I, pardon, [illegible].
Rumnahpakan, co. Ross. See Garrowrinbakan.
Runtagh, Connor, pardon, [illegible].
Rusyaleil—Rusynell (Rinnseel), co. Mayo, [illegible], [illegible].
Ruodrek, Gilecrin ny, pardon, [illegible].
Ruoirk, Gormaly ny Quyn ny, pardon, [illegible].
Ruonowe, Garret, pardon [illegible].

INDEX TO FIANTS.—ELIZABETH.

Rupe, abbey of the B.V.M. de, at Cashel, co. Tip., [illegible], [illegible], 6114, [illegible], 6482. See Hore abbey.
" rectory, co. Tip., [illegible], 6483.
Rupe, co. Tip., 6162.
Rupe, John de. See Roche.
Ruaylbag (Rearybag, Queen's co.), 1826.
Rush, co. Dub. See Rusho.
Rushane, co. Clare, 6317.
Rushern, co. Kerry. See Russin.
Rushall, Edm., pardon, [illegible].
" Edm. m'Philip, pardon, 6744.
Rushinel, co. Wat., [illegible], [illegible].
Rushock, in Munster, [illegible].
Rusk (co. Mon. ?), 1403.
Ruskagh — Ruskaghe (co. Car. ?), 3018. 5411.
Rusko, co. Mon., [illegible].
Rusko, little, co. Westm., 1940.
Ruskeighbegg, co. Lim., [illegible].
Ruskeighe (co. Tip. ?), 3304.
Ruskeighmore, co. Lim., [illegible].
Ruskogh (co. Westm. or King's ?), 5463.
Rusile (co. Sligo ?), 4723.
Rusragh—Russaghe, co. Westm., 3046; rectory [illegible].
Russaghe, co. Cork, rectory, [illegible].
Russe, sir Francis, pardon at his suit, 5729.
Russell, Bartholomew, clerk of the crown, Chief Place, [illegible]; takes oath of supremacy, 234, 317; licence to go to England to gain experience in his duties, 1157, [illegible], third justice of Chief Place, 364, 4154, 4467, [illegible]; clerk of crown and peace, Carlow, &c., 163, Munster, 1163; commissions, [illegible], 4430, 4463; lease, [illegible]; pardon, 63, 730, 1574.
" Charles, lease, [illegible].
" Christopher (of Castlebright, co. Down), pardon, [illegible], [illegible].
" Chr. (in co. Lim.), pardon, [illegible].
" David (son of Tho. of Cookstown, co. Meath), wardship, 6341; livery, 6760.
" David, pardon, [illegible], [illegible], [illegible], [illegible], 6417.
" Edmund, pardon, [illegible], [illegible].
" George, grant of a wardship, 3448.
" George, pardon, 1761, 5731.
" Gerald or Gerrot (of Russellstown, co. Westm.), wardship, 5181; pardon, [illegible].
" James, garden in Youghal, 5180.
" James, house in Dingle, [illegible].
" James, pardon, [illegible], [illegible], 5470, [illegible], [illegible], [illegible], [illegible].
" Janet, pardon, [illegible].
" John, comptroller of wine duty, [illegible].
Russell, John, pardon, [illegible], 4760, 6470, [illegible], 6704.
" Katherine, pardon, [illegible].
" Maurice, late ganger of Limerick, 131, [illegible], 2310.
" Maurice (in co. Cork), pardon, [illegible], 4462.
" Michael, grant of a wardship, [illegible]; lease, [illegible].
" Morrice or Morris, pardon, [illegible], [illegible], [illegible].
" Nicholas (of Russellstown, co. Westm.), pardon, [illegible]; wardship of his heir, [illegible].
" Nich., pardon, [illegible].
" Owen, pardon, 1784; commission, [illegible].
" Patrick, commission, 6341.
" Patr., pardon, [illegible].
" Philip, pardon, 6474, 1834.
" Richard, original member of guild of barbers, Dublin, [illegible].
" Rich., house in Dublin, 1311.
" Rich. (of Maponstown), lease, [illegible]; pardon of intrusion, [illegible].
" Rich., pardon, [illegible], [illegible], [illegible].
" Robert, pardon, [illegible], [illegible].
" Thomas (of Cookstown), wardship and livery of heir, [illegible], 6760.
" Thomas, pardon, 1884, [illegible], 4764, [illegible], 5465, 6460, [illegible], 6634, [illegible].
" sir William, son of the earl of Bedford, lease, 5745; lord deputy, [illegible] note; repairs to Ulster, [illegible], [illegible]; in O'Byrnes country, [illegible]; undated fiants, 6103-4; pension to a knight who came to Ireland in his train, 6602.
" William, pardon, 4712.
Russell's burgages, co. Lim., 5047.
Russell's lands, Youghal, 6094.
Russelleston (Russellstown), co. Kild., [illegible].
Russelleston. See Russellstown, co. Westm.
Russellestowne. See Russellstown, co. Wat.
Russellleston. See Russellstown, co. Wick.
Russelleton. See Russellstown, co. Car.
Russellstown (Ballyrussel, co. Wat.), 1687.
Russellstown—Russelleston—Russelston, co. Car., 6144, [illegible].
Russellstown, co. Kild. See Russelleston.
(Russellstown)—Russellestowne—Russelston, co. Wat., [illegible], [illegible]. See Ballinarussell.
Russellstown — Russelleston — Russelston, co. Westm., 5343, 5181, [illegible].
(Russellstown) — Russellleston — Russelston (co. Wick.), 1418, [illegible], [illegible], 4184.
Russellswood — Rousselswood — Russelswood — Russelwoode, co. Kild., [illegible], [illegible], [illegible], [illegible], [illegible], [illegible].

INDEX TO FIANTS—ELIZABETH.

Russelstown. See Russellstown, co. Car.
Russelston, co. Gal., [illegible].
Russelston. See Russellstown, cos. Wat., Westm., and Wick.
Russelstowne (co. Tip.?), [illegible].
Russelswood — Russelwoode. See Russells-wood.
Russeny (co. Ross.?), 6447.
Russhaghe. See Rossagh, co. Westm.
Russhe (Rush), co. Dub., [illegible], 1792.
Russhe, Thomas, commission, [illegible]; pardon, [illegible].
Russhin, co. Tip., [illegible].
Russin (Rusheen), co. Kerry, 6131.
Russyne, co. Wat., [illegible], [illegible].
Russyny (Rashinagh, King's co.), 1[illegible].
Rustum, Donell, pardon, [illegible].
Rutland, earl of, Thomas Manors, brother of, [illegible].
Rutledge, Andrew, pardon, 1737.
Rutledg, Edw., pardon, [illegible].
Rutledge, Allan, pardon, [illegible], [illegible].
Rutriche, Roland, pardon, [illegible].
Ruttelege, John, pardon, [illegible].
Ruttlege, Andrew, pardon, [illegible].
Ruyenkane (Rinnagan, co. Rosc.), [illegible].
Ruyrkyane (co. Wat.), [illegible].
Ruyshagh (co. Lim.?), [illegible].
Rwe — Rw (Roowes?), co. Cork, [illegible], [illegible], [illegible].
Rwoboke, Walter, killed, [illegible].
Rwogarrane. See Rowgarran.
Rwoule, alias Tobin, James, pardon, [illegible].
Ryaghe, co. Down, [illegible].
Ryaghston. See Riaghston.
Ryamoyn, Elleoner ny, pardon, [illegible].
Ryan, Anstace, pardon, [illegible].
,, Conoghor m'Shane, pardon, [illegible].
,, Darby oge, alias Mulrean, clerk, pardon, [illegible].
,, Dermod m'Shane, pardon, [illegible].
,, Dermot m'Melaghlin, pardon, [illegible].
,, Dermot m'Shane, pardon, [illegible].
,, Donagh m'Melaghlen, pardon, [illegible].
,, Donald (of Sollaghod), livery to son of, [illegible].
,, Donell fitz Matthew, pardon, [illegible].
,, Donell m'Conoghor, pardon, [illegible].
,, Donogho, pardon, [illegible].
,, —Rian — Ryane, James, clerk in Chancery, appointed engrosser to the seal, [illegible]; master in Chancery, [illegible], [illegible]; leases, [illegible], 17[illegible], [illegible]; surety, [illegible]; exemption from serving as juror, mayor, sheriff, &c., [illegible].
,, John m'Rorie, pardon, [illegible].
,, Moore ny Conoghor, pardon, [illegible].
,, Teig m'Wm., pardon, [illegible], [illegible], [illegible].
Ryan, Terence or Tirlagh m'Donill m'Edm., attainted, [illegible].
,, Tho., pardon, [illegible].
,, William (son of Donald of Sollaghod), livery, [illegible]; alienation licence, [illegible].
,, Wm. fitz Donell, pardon, [illegible].
Ryan (co. Long.?), [illegible].
Ryane, James. See Ryan.
Rybinkestowne (co. Wat.?), [illegible].
Ryce, James, pardon (see Rice), [illegible].
Rycott, privy signet dated at, 19[illegible], 1[illegible].
Rydall, Richard, attainted, [illegible].
Rydder, alias Rudder, co. Meath, [illegible].
Ryddyn, McEdig, pardon, [illegible].
Ryde, John, pardon, [illegible].
Ryder, John. See Rider.
Rye impressed for army, [illegible].
Rye, lough (Lough Ree on Shannon), 1[illegible].
Ryegane, Katherine ny, pardon, [illegible].
Ryegles. See Reigles, co. Dub.
Ryerdane, Conoghor m'Teig I, pardon, [illegible].
Ryglas. See Reiglas.
Rykesltowne, Queen's co., [illegible].
Rymer, the, O'Daley, lands held by, [illegible].
Rymore. See Rimor.
Rynaany (co. Clare?), [illegible].
Rynabarragh. See Rinnabarraghe, co. Kerry.
Rynchtone, alias Forunukka. See Rinchtun.
Rynceill. See Rinceile.
Rynco wlisky—Rynkollesky—Rynkule l-sky, co. Cork, [illegible], [illegible], [illegible].
Ryne (co. Cork?), [illegible].
Ryne. See Rine, co. Long.
Ryne, Donogh m'Dermody I, pardon, [illegible].
,, John m'Dermod, pardon, [illegible].
,, Wm. m'Teige I, pardon, [illegible].
Ryneclevan (Rinclevan, co. Donegal), [illegible].
Rynegawnaghe. See Ringawnaghe.
Ryneenyne (Ringmeen, co. Cork?), [illegible].
Rynane, co. Clare, [illegible].
Rynerone (Ringrone, co. Cork?), [illegible].
Rynervile. See Rinervile.
Rynglestone (Ringlestown), co. Meath, 1[illegible].
Ryngrahne, co. Kerry, [illegible].
Rynkenyicke—Rynne Kynnelmeke, co. Cork, 410[illegible].
Rynkollesky—Rynkole lsky. See Rynerowlisky.
Rynnobily (co. Cork?), 41[illegible].
Rynnyle, co. Gal., [illegible].
Rynne Kynnelmeke, [illegible]. See Rynkenyicke.
RynvaDeleyge. See Rinvalleleyge.
Ryaye (co. Clare?), [illegible].
Ryordan, Conoghor m'Dermod I, pardon, [illegible].
,, Dermod m'Donill I, pardon, [illegible].
,, Owen m'Donoghe I, pardon, [illegible].

Ryordan, Thady m'Dermod I, pardon, 5941.
Ryordane, Owen m'Rory I, pardon, [illegible].
Ryse, Dominick, pardon, [illegible].
" John, pardon (see Rice), 4894.
" Patr., pardon, 4854.
" Peter, pardon, 1781.
" Stephen, pardon (see Rice), 4894.
" Tho., pardon, 4854.
" Tho. fitz James, pardon, 4960.
Ryses place, by bridge of Galway, 1469.
Ryurdayne, Edm. m'Donald I, pardon, 3150.
Ryvers, Margaret, house in Dublin, 1711.
Ryverstown. See Riverston, co. Meath.
Rywardan, Thady m'Moriertagh I, pardon, [illegible].
Rywes crosse, co. Meath, [illegible].

Sacheverell, Christopher, deputy constable of castle of Dungarvan, [illegible]; constable, [illegible], [illegible], [illegible].
Sack wine, trade in, [illegible]; impressed for army, 1402, 1402, [illegible].
Sackford—Sackforde—Sackforde, Thomas, general surveyor of victuals, 1481, [illegible], [illegible]; seneschal of Clandeboy, [illegible]; commission, [illegible]; certificate by, [illegible].
Sacro Bosco, church of, co. Wex., [illegible].
Saddeiston—Sadliston (Saddlestown), co. Meath, [illegible], 1460.
Saddler of the ordnance, [illegible].
Sadgrave, Walter, sheriff, Dublin, [illegible].
Sadliston. See Saddeiston.
Sadler, Crosby, 1311.
Sadler, John, pardon, [illegible].
Safe conduct for O'Rorke country to lord deputy, [illegible].
Sagard (Saggart), co. Dub., burned by rebels, 4184. See Tassagard.
Sabe, Donel and Hugh m'Enaus, pardon, [illegible].
Sale O'Gromnyn (Rosgroman, co. Tyrone), [illegible].
Salghaes, Wm. m'Morris, pardon, 6487.
S. Anne's chapel, Cork, [illegible].
S. Anne's lands in Kilmainham, 1549.
S. Augustin's abbey, co. Kerry, See Ballowe abbey.
S. Augustin friars. See Augustinian friaries.
S. Augustin monastery. See Annaghdowne, Galway.
S. Barries, co. Cork, [illegible].
S. Bartholomew, Kilcoole fair on feast of, [illegible].
S. Beynan's church, Gyltons, co. Kild., 3148.
S. Brandan, co. Wex., [illegible], [illegible].
S. Brandan, college of, in Annaghdowne, [illegible].
S. Bride chapel, Castleknock, co. Dub., [illegible].
S. Bride church, near Osberston, co. Kild., 4178, 4434.
S. Brides hospital, Carrickfergus, [illegible], [illegible].
S. Brides, Waterford, [illegible].
S. Brigid of Grangefort, church of, co. Car., 3148.
S. Brigid of Oddar, [illegible].
S. Brigid, street of (see Dublin), [illegible].
S. Brigid in Tamon, co. Wex., [illegible].
S. Burioke, chapel of, co. Wex., [illegible].
S. Catherine. See S. Katherine.
S. Columba's church, Rathmore, co. Kild., [illegible].
S. Columbe of Kells, rectory of, [illegible]. See Kells, co. Meath.
S. Columba, Inistioke, [illegible], [illegible].
S. Crosses island—S. Crucis island (Skellig, co. Kerry), [illegible], 1762.
S. Dominic's monastery—S. Dominick friars. See Dominicans.
S. Edan cathedral, Ferns, 612.
S. Edan of Kynnegha, Dublin diocese, 740.
S. Evod, co. Down, rectory, [illegible], [illegible].
S. Fekins—S. Fekyn, in Fower, rectory of (S. Feighins, co. Westm.), [illegible], [illegible]. See also Foghines church.
S. Fenton of Clownenagh, parish church of, 470, [illegible], [illegible].
S. Finbar, astro de. See Gillabbey.
S. Francis abbey, friars, monastery. See Franciscans.
S. Funbar (Finbar), cathedral (see Cork), [illegible].
S. Funien of Clonogh, Queen's co., rectory, 694.
S. Gianocdius, [illegible].
S. Hillary juxta Ierdlam, parish of, co. Wexford (the places named as in this parish appear to be in par. S. Iberius, the next parish to which is Ladysisland), 417.
S. Imocby, co. Wex., 1258.
S. Ivorie—S. Ivories—S. Ivoryes—S. Ivorys (S. Iberius, co. Wex.), rectory, [illegible], [illegible], [illegible], [illegible], [illegible].
S. James chapel, Palmerston, co. Dublin, [illegible], [illegible].
S. James of Ueke, Dublin diocese, rector, [illegible].
S. James, co. Meath, 1440, [illegible].
S. James (nr. Westminster), letters dated at, [illegible], [illegible].
S. Jhon, Edm. fitz Rich., pardon, [illegible].
" Johanna nyn Richard, pardon, [illegible].
" Pierce, pardon to his wife, [illegible].
" Wm. fitz Rich., pardon, [illegible].
S. John Baptist church, Cork, [illegible], [illegible].
S. John Baptist, house of "crowched" friars (or Cross Bearers), by Longford (S. Johns, co. Rosc.), leased, [illegible], [illegible], [illegible], [illegible], [illegible].
S. John Baptist alias Taghoe (S. Johns), co. Rosc., rectory, [illegible].
S. John the Baptist, hospitals. See Ardee, Dublin, Trim.

INDEX TO FIANTS—ELIZABETH.

S. John, hospital of. *See* Athy, Castledermot, Drogheda, Kilkenny, co. Westm., Wexford.
S. John of Jerusalem, in Ireland, hospital, possessions leased, [illegible], 1323, 1486, 1560, 1591, 1620, 1722, [illegible], 2337–8, 2316, 2408, 2436, 2606, [illegible], 3161, 3176, 3142, 3187, [illegible], 3227–8, [illegible], 4159, 4174, 4158, 4401, 4492, [illegible], 6424, 6121, 6721, 6704; granted, [illegible], 4974, 6317, [illegible]
" prior, proclamation for his surrender, 6704; recitals of leases by, 1027, [illegible], 1484, 1571, [illegible], 6411, 6428.
St. John, Edmund duf, pardon, [illegible]
" Edm. fitz James, pardon, [illegible]
" Edm. fitz Rich., pardon, [illegible]
" Ellice, pardon, [illegible]
" James, pardon, [illegible]
" John, pardon, [illegible], 2015.
" John, pardon, [illegible]
" John fitz Edm., pardon, 6177.
" John fitz Wm., pardon, [illegible]
" Nicholas, pardon, [illegible]
" Peirce, pardon, [illegible]
" Peirs fitz Wm., pardon, [illegible]
" Peter oyre, pardon, [illegible]
" Piers fitz David, pardon, [illegible]
" Rich., pardon, [illegible]
" Richard, pardon to son of, [illegible]
" Rich. fitz Edm., pardon, [illegible]
" Robert (of Scadanston), pardon, [illegible], 9014.
" Tho., pardon, [illegible]
" Walter fitz Peirs, pardon, 6477.
" Wm., pardon, [illegible], 3911, [illegible]
S. John, vicarage of (S. John's, co. Rosc.), [illegible]
S. John's in Castledermot, co. Kild., [illegible]
S. John's by Athie, co. Kild., [illegible]
S. John's, hospital of, Athie, co. Kild., possessions of, [illegible]
S. John's, co. Rosc., [illegible]; town of, [illegible]. *See* S. John Baptist.
" vicarage of, [illegible]
S. John's (co. Tip. or Kilk.?), [illegible]
S. John's—Johnes, co. Wex., 798, 797, 4171.
S. John's of Enniscorthie, co. Wex., [illegible]
S. John's Grange—Orainge, co. Tip., [illegible]
S. John's lands—S. Johnes land, in Inchmacnidder, co. Kild., [illegible]
S. John's lands, Ballygawran, co. Kilk., [illegible]
S. John's land in Dunboyne, co. Meath, [illegible]
S. John's lees, leyes, or leas, at Teranure, co. Dub., [illegible], 4120, [illegible]
S. Johnes Rathe (Saintjohnsfort), co. Meath, [illegible]
S. John's Rathe by Slane, co. Meath, [illegible]
S. John's town (S. John's, co. Rosc.), [illegible]
St. Johnstown, co. Tip., [illegible]
S. Johnstowne, co. Meath, [illegible]
S. Kateryn's—S. Katheryne's, Waterford. *See* S. Katherine's.
S. Katherin's—S. Katheryn's, co. Kild., [illegible]
S. Katherine by Cork, rectory, [illegible]
St. Katherine's — Katherine — Katheryns (S. Catherines Park), co. Dub., [illegible]
S. Katherine's — Kateryn — Katheryne's, Waterford, [illegible]
S. Katherine, abbey of. *See* Waterford.
S. Katherine's grange — S. Katheryns grange, Waterford, [illegible]
S. Katherine's monastery, co. Lim., or Mynasher ne Kayllaghe, nunnery, [illegible], 4787, 5116, [illegible]
S. Katherine the virgin, Killdemoke, co. Louth, vicarage, [illegible]
S. Katheryns. *See* S. Katherine's.
S. Kelly of Beoghe, co. Gal., [illegible]
S. Keran—Keryan—Kerean (Saintkierans), co. Wex., [illegible]; rectory, [illegible]
S. Kevine, co. Kild., prebendal church of (Tipper), [illegible]
St. Leger, James, pardon, [illegible]
" Rob., pardon, [illegible]
S. Laurence. *See* S. Lawrence.
S. Lawrence, chapel of, near Ballyfermot, co. Dub., [illegible]; land of, [illegible]
S. Lawrence — Lawrance — Laurance — Lawranse:
" Alice (alias Howth, alias Howson), leases, [illegible]
" Almera, [illegible]
" sir Christopher, commander of garrison at Cavan, [illegible]; of garrison at Naas, [illegible]; commissions, [illegible]; pardon, [illegible]
" George, pardon, [illegible]
" Mary, divorce suit, [illegible]
" Nicholas, commissions, [illegible]
" Nicholas (of Clowston) grant of a wardship, [illegible]

INDEX TO FIANTS—ELIZABETH.

S. Laurence, Nicholas, pardon, [illegible]. *See* Howth, earl of, 6044, [illegible].
„ Thomas de, justice chief place, 772.
S. Lazarinus, cathedral at Leighlin, [illegible].
St. Leger, Anthony, knt. *See* Sentleger.
„ Edm. (of Graigueskill), pardon, 6792.
„ Edm. (of Tullaghanbrog), pardon, 6792.
„ James (of Tullaghbrogh), pardon, [illegible].
„ James (of Ballesow), pardon, 6794.
„ John, pardon, [illegible].
„ Margaret, pardon, [illegible], [illegible].
„ Meg, pardon, [illegible].
„ Oliver, pardon, [illegible].
„ Patrick, sub-sheriff of co. Kilkenny, [illegible]; clerk of crown, Kilkenny, [illegible].
„ Patr. (alias Lister), pardon, [illegible].
„ Rob., pardon, [illegible].
„ Rob. (alias Lister), pardon, [illegible].
„ Rob. fitz James, pardon, [illegible].
„ Rob. fitz Oliver, pardon, 6794.
„ Tho., 2841.
„ Tho. *See* Sevntlever.
„ Tho., fitz Oliver, pardon, [illegible].
„ Warham. *See* Sentleger.
„ Wm., pardon, 6794, 6792.
St. Legers—Sentlegers castle, Ardee, co. Louth, constable of, 1452, 2016, [illegible], 4312, 4168.
St. Leiger, Anthony. *See* Sentleger.
St. Leoger, Warham. *See* Sentleger.
S. Leonard. *See* S. Leonard, co. Wex.
S. Leonard, hospital of (*see* Dundalk), 142.
S. Leonard—Lenard—Leonard of the Nashe—Leonards (Saintleonards), co. Wex., 165, [illegible], [illegible], [illegible], [illegible].
St. Lowe, sir Edw., lease, [illegible]. *See* Sentlo.
S. Machona's church, Carrickbrennan, co. Dub., 6164.
S. Macnis of Diserigallen, rectory, 671.
S. Malinge, new fort, 4042. *See* S. Moling.
Saint Mallowes in France, [illegible].
S. Macvidagha, chapel of, 618.
S. Margaret's—Margarettes—Margaretts, co. Wex., rectory, 417, [illegible], [illegible], [illegible], 5114, [illegible].
S. Margaret's, co. Wex., 4434.
S. Martins—Martyns, co. Kilk., [illegible], [illegible].
S. Mary abbey. *See* Dublin, abbey of the B. V. M.
S. Mary of Borugus, rectory, [illegible].
S. Mary of Doungarvane, vicar of, 786.
S. Mary in Fower, rectory of (S. Mary's, co. Wexf.), 1562.
S. Mary of Laracor, co. Meath, vicarage of, [illegible].
S. Mary Iland, co. Wex., [illegible], 1577, 4944.
S. Mary Magdalene, Dublin, charter of guild, 5164.
Saint Molloe, co. Meath, 4141.
S. Michael's rectory, Athlo, 1362.
S. Michael (Templemichael), co. Lim., church of, [illegible], [illegible].
S. Michael's—Michaells—Mighels, co. Long., [illegible], [illegible], 4162.
S. Michaels—Michael of Rabuck—Michaels Rabuil — Michaels Rabuils — Michaels Rabuils (Templemichael, co. Long.?), rectory, [illegible], [illegible], [illegible], [illegible], 4131.
S. Michael (co. Rosc. or Gal.), [illegible].
S. Michaels—Michaelles—Michellen (Templemichael), co. Tip., [illegible], [illegible], [illegible].
St. Michaell's. *See* S. Michael's.
St. Michaell, Walter, baron of Rehan, livery, [illegible].
S. Michaelles. *See* S. Michaels, co. Tip.
St. Michell, Christopher (of Rehan), livery to son, [illegible].
„ Elizabeth, pardon, [illegible].
„ Nich., pardon, [illegible].
„ Walter, pardon, [illegible].
S. Michellen. *See* S. Michaels, co. Tip.
S. Mighels. *See* S. Michael's, co. Long.
S. Mocho of Tymocho, Queen's co., 876.
S. Mochud of Lismore cathedral, [illegible].
S. Moling — Molinge — Malinge — Molinge—Mollinge—Molyne (S. Mullins, co. Car.), 4024, [illegible], 4871, [illegible].
„ barony, enquiry as to title, [illegible].
„ new fort on Barrow, 4042.
„ *See* also Symolinge, Symolins, and Tymolin.
S. Molingbeg (Timolin), co. Kild., priory, possessions granted, 6162.
St. Molinge—Mollinge. *See* S. Moling.
S. Mollins alias Tamollin, co. Kild., monastery, [illegible].
S. Molman of Clonecurry, vicarage in Kildare diocese, 794.
S. Molyne, barony of, [illegible]. *See* S. Moling.
S. Mullins, co. Car. *See* S. Moling, Symolinge, Thamolinge, Tymolin.
S. Nicholas (Kill St. Nicholas), co. Wat., rectory, [illegible].
S. Nicholas, co. Wex., 417; rectory, [illegible], [illegible], [illegible], 5114, [illegible].
S. Nogan, church of, co. Mon., [illegible].
S. Nymock—Nymoke, co. Wex., 714, [illegible].
S. Owen, parish of. *See* Dublin, S. Andoen.
S. Patrick's day, [illegible].
S. Patrick's. *See* Dublin, cathedral of S. Patrick and S. Patrick's church.
S. Patrick, Cashell, metropolitan church of, [illegible].

INDEX TO FIANTS,—ELIZABETH.

S. Patrick's (co. Tip.?), [illegible].
S. Patrick's of Moymore or Moyvore, co. Westm., rectory, [illegible], [illegible], [illegible], [illegible].
S. Patrick's Ryke (Croagh Patrick), Connaught, 1279.
S. Peter's park, Staffordstown, co. Meath, 1794.
S. Peter's priory. See Trim.
S. Peter de Rabio, monastery, 1777. See Monasterdargan.
S. Peter de Rabio, [illegible]. See Monasterdargan.
S. Peter and S. Tulloks rectory, Wexford, [illegible].
SS. Cuoan and Brogan, vicarage of, Mothell, 787.
Saint saviours, New Ross, chapel, [illegible].
S. Selskar, Wexford. See Selsker.
S. Senanus. See Synnan.
S. Skrean (or S. Keran), co. Wex., [illegible].
S. Turga's church, Killenge, co. Car., [illegible].
S. Thomas the Martyr. See Dublin, abbey of S. Thomas.
S. Thomas (rectè Thome), co. Tip., priory, [illegible].
S. Thomas court, monastery. See Dublin, abbey of S. Thomas.
S. Trinity's island (Trinity island in Lough Oughter, co. Cavan), monastery of Holy Trinity, leased, [illegible].
S. Tullocks—Tulloks rectory, Wexford, [illegible], [illegible], [illegible], [illegible], [illegible].
S. Tulloks and S. Peter's rectory, co. Wex., [illegible].
S. Ubban of Killabban, rectory, [illegible], [illegible], [illegible].
S. Werburga. See Dublin, S. Warburg.
S. Wolstanes—Wolstowne—Wolstons—Woolstons—Wulstans, co. Kild., 1172, [illegible], [illegible], [illegible], [illegible].
Saire, co. Westm., [illegible].
Salconough (Sallaghan? co. Cav.), [illegible].
Saladin, Shane, pardon, [illegible].
Sale, John, messuage in Cashel, [illegible]; pardon, [illegible].
Sale—Salle, Richard, pardon, [illegible], [illegible]; rent from his land, [illegible], [illegible].
Salestou—Salleston (Salestown), co. Meath, [illegible], [illegible], [illegible].
Salighoda. See Sollogbod.
Sall, Benet, pardon, [illegible].
" Edm., pardon, [illegible].
" Edw., pardon, [illegible], [illegible].
" Geoffrey, pardon, [illegible].
" John, burgess of Casshell, [illegible].
" John, pardon, [illegible].
" John fitz Simon, pardon, [illegible].
" John fitz Wm., pardon, [illegible].
" Nicholas, pardon, [illegible].
" Patrick, pardon, [illegible]; lands at Cashel, [illegible].
Sall, Rob., [illegible].
" Rob., pardon, [illegible]; messuage at Cashel, [illegible].
" Simon, pardon, [illegible].
" Walter, pardon, [illegible].
" William, pardon, [illegible].
Sallaghan, co. Cav. See Salconough.
Salleghoda. See Sollogbod.
Salle, Richard. See Sale.
Sallechodda. See Sollogbod.
Sallerumy, co. Gal., [illegible].
Salleston. See Salestou.
Sallie park, Trym, [illegible].
Sallins, co. Kild. See Sollons.
Salloghe, Mortagh, attainted, [illegible].
Salloghodbeg. See Sollogbod beg.
Sallye park, Trym, 1714.
Salmon fishing, leased, [illegible].
Salmon leap on the Liffey, [illegible], [illegible], [illegible].
Salmoye, Rob., [illegible].
Salop, earl of, his possessions granted, [illegible], [illegible]. See Shrewsbury.
Salsbury alias Stanley, Agnes, livery, [illegible].
Salt, impressed for army, [illegible], [illegible], [illegible], [illegible], [illegible], [illegible], [illegible]; trade in, [illegible], [illegible], [illegible], [illegible].
Saltaherett, co. Wat., [illegible].
Saltashe, co. Cornwall, [illegible].
Salte—Sawte, barony, co. Kild., [illegible], [illegible].
Saltee islands, co. Wex. See Saltes, Shalte.
Saltes, Great, co. Wex., island, [illegible].
Saltes, Little, co. Wex., island, [illegible].
Saltfish impressed for army, [illegible], [illegible].
Salthowse, co. Louth, [illegible].
Salneche [illegible], co. Car., [illegible].
Samoraghe alias Samkonaghe, co. Tip., rectory, [illegible].
Samford, Tho., pardon, [illegible].
Samforde, John, pardon, [illegible].
Samkonaghe alias Samoraghe, co. Tip., rectory, [illegible].
Sampson, [ ] leases, [illegible].
Sampson, Anne, pardon, [illegible].
Samson, Thomas, pardon, [illegible].
Sanckie, John. See Sankye.
Sanckill. See Shankill.
Sanky, John. See Sankye.
Sandeford. See Sandford.
Sanders, James, pardon, [illegible].
Sandford—Sandeford, Foulk, controller of Drogheda port, [illegible]; collector of wine duty, [illegible], [illegible].
Sands, Novell, clerk, controller and surveyor of the ordnance, &c., [illegible], 714.
Sane, co. Cork, [illegible].
Saneganagh, Queen's co. (see Shanganagh), [illegible].
Sanekill (Shankill, co. Kilk.?), [illegible].
Sanevaeherron (co. Gal.), [illegible].
Snagarry (Shangarry, co. Car.) [illegible].

INDEX TO FIANTS—ELIZABETH.

Sanggannagh (co. Kilk. ?), [illegible].

Sanitary laws at Kilmallock—cnockheap. 4574.

Sankeiston. See Sankystone.

Sankeston. See Sankystone.

Sankey—Sankis, John. See Sankys.

Sankhill (Shankill, co. Kilk.), 4824.

Sankill—Sanckill (Shankill ?), co. Kilk., 1087; rectory, [illegible], [illegible].

Sankright (co. Wat. ?), rectory, 6162.

Sanky (tailor), house of, in Dublin, 1311.

Sankys—Sanckis—Sancky—Sankey—Sankis—Sanky, John, under marshal, 463; sheriff of King's co., [illegible]; pardon, 67, 811; commissions, 453 (septies), 1362, 1738, [illegible]; grant of land, 462, [illegible]; lease, 1408; livery to heir, 5431.

" Nicholas, son of John, livery, 5431.

Sankystone—Sankeston—Sankeiston alias Ballylakin, King's co., 462, 1294.

Santire (Santry), co. Dub., 1777.

" See also Sauntre.

Sanvallyamm (Shantallyanne, co. Wat. ?), 3753.

Sanyvallymore (Shanbally ?), co. Lim., 6277.

Saran alias Tsesaran, which see.

Saransfeld. See Sarsfield.

Sarenick (Shercock, co. Cav. ?), 5762.

Sardellestone (Swordlestown), co. Kild., 6411.

Sarde (co. Tip. ?), 4[illegible].

Sare (co. Lone. ?), 6161.

Sare, co. Westm., [illegible].

Sarfeld, Stephen, pardon, 6118.

Sarisfelde, Patr. See Sarsfield.

Sarrawe, Shane, pardon, 6317.

Sarreley, Hugh, pardon, 6741.

Sarsalagh, Maurice m'Edm., pardon, 4[illegible].

Sarsfield—Saresfeld—Sarisfelde—Sarsfelde—Sarsfeild—Sarsfellde—Sarsfold—Sarsfelde—Sarsfelde—Sarsffld—Sarsfyld—Sarsfylde—Sarswell:

" David, pardon, 6176, 6437.

" Dominick, queen's attorney in Munster, 6138, 6786, 6772.

" Edmund, pardon, 1[illegible].

" lady Jonet or Janet, widow of lord Dunsany, 749; wife of sir Tho. Cusake, 1401, 1900; surrender, 2341; premises in her hands, 4[illegible].

" John, commission, 6517; pardon, 6786.

" dame Margaret, 6310.

" Nicholas, pardon, 4762.

Sarsfield, Patrick, justice of peace, co. Kild., takes oath of supremacy, 234; commissions, [illegible], 542, [illegible], 662, 704.

" Patrick (of Baggotrath), license to import merchandise, 81; license to alien, 481-2; his servant pardoned, 4[illegible].

" Patrick (of Tully), lease, 6748; pardon, 6754.

" Richard, pardon, 6478.

" Stephen, pardon, 6[illegible].

" sir William, mayor of Dublin, 1083; sheriff of co. Dublin, 1049; seneschal of manors of Newcastle Lyons &c., 6718; commissions, [illegible], 6117, [illegible], 2348, 3444, [illegible], 6118, 3162, 4[illegible], [illegible], 4156, 4464, 6128; lease, 1467, 3458; rectory in his tenure, 6160; allocation, [illegible].

" William, pardon, 1024.

Sarsfieldcarte — Sarsfeildscorte, co. Cork, 6[illegible]4, 6701.

(Sarsfieldstown)—Sarsfeldeston, co. Meath, 6[illegible]4.

Sart—Sarte, co. Kilk., 1078, 4[illegible], 6442, 6704.

Sartell, James, pardon, 5348, 6[illegible].

" John, pardon, 5341.

" Nicholas, pardon, 5342.

" Oliver, pardon, 5341.

" Patrick, pardon, 5341.

" Thomas, pardon, 6348.

" William, pardon, 6447.

" See Shortall.

Sarte. See Sart.

Sary fyn (co. Gal. ?), 4707.

Sason, Andrew, license, 3159.

Saul, co. Down. See Sawle.

Saunders, Henry, pardon, 6[illegible].

" John, pardon, 6[illegible].

" Margaret, pardon, [illegible].

Saundros, Thomas, pardon, 48.

Saunton, Wm., [illegible].

Sauntre — Saunlryf (Santry), co. Dub., 1169; tithes of parish, 2916.

Savage—Savaile—Savaige—Savag—Savaig—Savaige:

" lord. See Patrick.

" Anthony, clerk, 1[illegible].

" Arthur, knt., pardon, 6416.

" Christopher, pardon, 4634.

" Edmund, pardon, [illegible], 6786.

" Edm., slain, 6762.

" Edmund alias Fardoragh, pardon, [illegible], [illegible].

" George, pardon, [illegible], 6711.

" Henry, pardon, 5364, [illegible], 6711, 6728.

" James, pardon, [illegible], [illegible], 6734.

INDEX TO FIANTS—ELIZABETH.

Savage, Jenkin, pardon, 6711, 6728.
" Jonyonk, pardon, 5401.
" sir John (of Rocksavage, Cheshire), 5534.
" sir John, constable of Castlemaine, 5169, 6159, 6461.
" Owen—Owynn, pardon, 6712, 6725.
" Owney, pardon, 6711.
" Patrick, lord Savage of Little Ards, appointed seneschal, 2080; livery, 5394; pardon, 6711.
" Patr. boy, pardon, 2348, 2048.
" Patrick, pardon, 5401, 6711-2, 6728.
" Redmond, disputes the captainship of Ards, 2080.
" Redmond, pardon, 6712.
" Revelyn, pardon, 2368.
" Richard, lease, 3428.
" Richard, pardon, 1617, 2368, 6711, 6728.
" Robert, pardon, 2368, 2348, 5401.
" Rowland, late captain of Ards, 2080, 5394.
" Rowland, pardon, 4530, 6711-2.
" William, pardon, 6145, 6028.
Savadg, Rich., pardon, 3434.
Sawle (Saul), co. Down, monastery, possessions leased, 1539.
Sawle, Edward, pardon, 6271.
Sawlyshe, Meath diocese, 6787.
Sawney, Conoghor O Derry m'Conner, pardon, 4723.
Sawnie, Donogh boye m'Connor oy, pardon, 6164.
" Fynine m'Conoghor oy, pardon, 6164.
" John m'Connor oy, pardon, 6465.
Sawny, More ny, pardon, 6814.
" Teige ny, O'Mahowny, pardon, 6614.
Sawnye, Dermod m'Conoghor ne, pardon, 6568.
Sawrebyne, co. Cork, rectory, 2933.
Sawte. See Salle, co. Kildare.
Saxey—Saxei, Wm., chief justice of Munster 5880; second justice chief place, 6298; commissions, 6144, 6285, 6773.
Saxons house (see Taghsaxon), 3278.
Say, Dionysius, keeper of Dublin gaol, 543.
" Tho., registrar in chancery, 6161.
Saye or Haye, Rich. fitz Shane, pardon, 6711.
Saye, Thomas, grant of land, 4322.
Sayfyn, co. Gal., 4678.
Sayhelmon, co. Long., 5091.
Sayn, Tho., 6041.
Sayntleger, Warham. See Sentleger.
Say Ogroman (Sergrottan, co. Tyrone), 4697.
Sayre, co. Westmeath, 683.
Scablerman (co. Kild.?), 5864.
Scadamiston—Scadaxton (co. Tip.?), 883, 6711.
Scadamston, co. Tip., 4878.
Scadeston, co. Tip., 1250.
Scainlaine, John m'Edm. I, pardon, 6468.
Scalestone (Scalestown), co. Meath, 4477.
Scally, Patrick, pardon, 6289.
Scally, Tho., pardon, 6873.
Scannell, Dermod, pardon, 4471.
Scanlane, Margaret ny Conoghor ny, pardon, 6698.
Scarcity caused by illegal exports, 638.
Scardan—Scarden—Scardon, co. Sligo, 4364, 4570, 4698, 5649, 6527.
Scarid (co. Cork?), 5364.
Scarke, co. Kilk., 1049.
Scarletiston—Scarleston (Scarletstown), co. Kild., 1514, 5716.
Scarriff, co. Clare. See Skariffe.
Scarrough—Scarrowe (Skarragh), co. Cork, 6903.
Scart, co. Cork. See Skart.
Scart, co. Kerry. See Skart, Skarth.
Scart, co. Kilk., 1788, 4254.
Scart, co. Wat. See Scartcriston, Scartriston, Skaart.
Scarlogh (co. Tip.?), 5452.
Scarnaghbeg (co. Tip.?), 5575, 6480.
Scartbeg, co. Tip. See Skartaghbeg.
Scartcriston (Scart?), co. Wat., 664.
Scarte, co. Cork, 3878, 5034, 5432, 5517.
Scarte, co. Wex., 1230, 2530.
Scarte, alias m'Morris, Thomas m'Shane, [illegible], 5424.
Scartie, 1012.
Scartine Kilcoleman, co. Cork or Limerick, 5567.
Scartriston (Scart?), co. Wat., 5152.
Scarvey, Rob., pardon, 6447.
Scartywarrigg (co. Cork?), 2540, 2582.
Scarvaghoyadoo (Scarvagh), co. Down, 4257.
Scatternaghe (Scatternagh), co. Meath, 163, 1480.
Scattery island. See Iniskattie.
Scaughan (co. Lim.?), 6594.
Scaheriewna, co. Cork, 5065.
Schanhoe (Shancough?), co. Sligo, 4704.
Scholar, pardoned, 4784, 6858.
Scholarstown, co. Dub. See Skallardston.
Scian (co. Westm.?), 4023.
Sclan Dorre, co. Cav., 5455.
Sclavonia, 80.
Scleraghe—Sclerathe. See Slerathe.
Sclobyston, co. Wex., 712.
Scolboka (co. Wex.?), 4234.
Scoll, co. Cork, 6868.
Scollagh, co. Wex. See Skallocke.
Scolly alias O'Daly, Conoghor ny, pardon, 4585.

INDEX TO FIANTS—ELIZABETH.

Scoruisse, co. Cav., [illegible].

Scotriske, Walter, pardon, [illegible]47.

Scotrasure, co. Ross., 6417, [illegible].

Scotboras, co. Cav., [illegible].

Scotland, service in wars in, consideration for grant of land, 2978, [illegible], [illegible], [illegible], [illegible], [illegible], 6414, 6514, [illegible].

" trade with, [illegible], [illegible].

Scots—Scottishmen, licence to trade, [illegible], 1519, 1711; denization, [illegible], [illegible]; pardon, [illegible]; one robbed upon the sea, [illegible].

" captain of fighting men pardoned, [illegible].

" rebels, [illegible]; earl of Essex to punish, [illegible]; to be retained in Ulster, [illegible]; to be prosecuted in co. Antrim, 4787; indenture with, [illegible]; slay the constable in Dunluce castle, [illegible]; to be prosecuted, [illegible], [illegible]; bonaght answered to, [illegible].

Scott, Edm., pardon, [illegible].

Scott alias Palmer, Michael, death of, 844.

Scottis, Matthew, pardon, [illegible].

Scottish or Galloglasses, [illegible].

Scottishmen—Scottish nation. See Scots.

Scottiston, [illegible].

Scotton, Edmund, homicide of, [illegible].

Scrabby, co. Cav. See Ballyvickinleny.

Scrarden, co. Sligo, [illegible].

Scrowtemarte, co. Sligo, [illegible].

Scrihan alias O'Flannegan, Morgan, pardon, [illegible].

Scriling—Scrybolge (co. Tip.), [illegible], [illegible], [illegible]. See also Shribogo.

Scrumakallye. See Strongcally.

Scrwell (Shrowell, co. Tip. ?), 4722.

Scrybolge. See Scriling.

Scryne. See Skryne, co. Meath.

Scryne, co. Ross., [illegible], 4467.

Scullye, Donell, [illegible].

Scuring, Barnaby. See Scurlock.

Scuriageston. See Scurlockston.

Scurlock—Scuring—Scurlocke—Scurlok—Scurloke—Skurlock—Skurlok—Skurloke:

" Barnaby, attorney general, [illegible]; commissions, [illegible], [illegible], [illegible]-4, [illegible], [illegible], [illegible], [illegible], [illegible], [illegible], [illegible], [illegible], [illegible], [illegible]; surrender, [illegible]; lease, [illegible], [illegible]; pardon, of alienation, [illegible], [illegible], [illegible].

" Barnaby, pardon, [illegible], [illegible].

" John, commission, [illegible].

" Martin, wardship of his heir [illegible].

" Nicholas, his lands, [illegible], [illegible].

" Oliver, pardon, [illegible].

Scurlock, Patrick, pardon, [illegible].

" Patrick, wardship, [illegible].

" Philip, pardon, [illegible].

" Richard, alienation, [illegible].

" Robert, pardon [illegible].

" Walter, pardon [illegible].

" Walter, queen's attorney for Connaught, [illegible].

" William, pardon, [illegible].

Scurlockeston. See Scurlockston, co. Meath.

Scurlockeston, co. Westm., [illegible].

Scurlockston—Scuriageston—Scurlockeston—Scurlokeston—Scurlokestowne—Skurlokeston, co. Meath, [illegible], [illegible], [illegible]; rectory or church, [illegible], [illegible], [illegible], [illegible].

Scurlok—Scurloke, William. See Scurlock.

Scurlokeston—Scurlokestone—Scurlokestowne. See Scurlockston.

Scwrlockstowne, co. Tip., [illegible].

Scygoe (Seagoe, co. Armagh), church of, [illegible].

Sealgrawe, Walter, mayor of Dublin, [illegible]. See Sedgrave.

Seagoe, co. Arm. See Scygoe.

Seal, Great, Keeper of, appointed, [illegible], [illegible], [illegible].

" officer appointed to engross writs passing, [illegible].

Seamer, Wm., pardon, [illegible].

Sean. See Shean.

Seanabaliduff (Shanballyduff, co. Tip. ?), [illegible].

Seanabolho (co. Tip. ?), [illegible].

Seanbolge (co. Ross. ?), [illegible].

Seanboythcrossys, co. Clare, [illegible].

Seanickeghimnanig (co. Lim. ?), [illegible].

Seantullagho, [illegible]. See Shanavullagho.

Searcher. See under names of ports.

Searchers, negligence of, [illegible].

Seaskand Tullabalaind (Tullylilan, co. Don. ?), [illegible], [illegible].

Seassoclyncgranell—Seassie Clyneranell, co. Clare, [illegible], [illegible].

Seat, Dionysius, pardon, [illegible].

Seatown, co. Dub. See Coton, [illegible]. Shaston.

Seavough, co. Mon. See Syvncho.

Secretary of Ireland (John Challoner), [illegible], [illegible], [illegible]; secretary of estate, [illegible]; principal secretary [illegible].

" one of the secretaries of state (Fenton), [illegible]; principal secretary of the council, secretary of estate, or secretary of Ireland (Fenton), [illegible], [illegible], [illegible], [illegible], [illegible], [illegible], [illegible], [illegible], [illegible].

Secretary to the lord deputy (Molyneux), [illegible]; (Spenser), [illegible]; (Trare), [illegible]-4.

Sedanistone, co. Tip., [illegible].
Seddinycorre, co. Gal., 6451.
Sedgrave—Sedgrawe :
" Christopher, mayor of Dublin, [illegible] ; alderman, [illegible] ; trade licences, 41, 1743 ; land of, [illegible], 6010.
" Katherine, pardon, 1944.
" Nicholas, pardon, [illegible].
" Patr., second baron of the exchequer, [illegible] ; commissions, [illegible].
" Rich., commissions, [illegible]17, [illegible], [illegible].
" Rich., second baron, exchequer, [illegible], [illegible] ; commissions, [illegible], [illegible].
" Rich., slain, [illegible].
" Stephen, pardon, [illegible].
" Walter, mayor of Dublin, [illegible] ; alderman, [illegible] ; lease, [illegible] ; grant of a wardship, [illegible]. See also Sedgrave.
" See also Sedgre.
Sedgrawe. See Sedgrave.
Sedgre, Christopher, livery, 23.
" Richard (of Balliboghill), livery to heir, [illegible].
Sedgreo, Patrick, [illegible].
" Stephen, constable, Dublin castle, [illegible].
Sedinycorre, co. Gal., [illegible].
Seegrona, co. Tyr. See Sele O'Gromya, Say Ogromain.
Segar—Segare—Seger, Stephen, constable of Dublin castle, [illegible], [illegible], [illegible], [illegible] ; lease, [illegible] ; builds the king's mills, [illegible].
Segarston—Segerston, Edmund, pardon, [illegible], [illegible].
Seger, Stephen. See Segar.
Segerston, Edmund. See Segarston.
Seice, Walter, pardon, [illegible].
Seignory of Munster undertakers, size of, [illegible].
Seintleger, Warham. See Sentleger.
Seirkieran, King's co. See Syrekeran, Seyre.
Seis, Wm., pardon, [illegible].
Seise, Edm., pardon, [illegible].
" William m'Fores, pardon, [illegible].
Seisgrume (co. Tip. ?), [illegible].
Seisse, Edm. m'Gerot, pardon, [illegible].
Seithfine—Seithfine, lake called, (co. Donegal or Tyrone), [illegible], [illegible].
Seix, Adam fitz John, pardon, [illegible].
" Edmund, pardon, [illegible], [illegible].
" Edmund fitz John, pardon, [illegible].
" James, pardon, [illegible], [illegible], [illegible].
" John, pardon, [illegible].
" Roland, robbed, [illegible].
Seix, Rowland, pardon, [illegible], [illegible], [illegible].
" Tho., pardon, [illegible].
" Walter, pardon, [illegible].
" Wm., pardon, [illegible], [illegible].
Seixe, Edm., pardon, [illegible].
" Henry, pardon, [illegible].
Sekrenore (co. Ross. ?), [illegible].
Selalagh—Selalaghe. See Shillelaghe.
Selenger, Robert boye, pardon, [illegible].
Selhirny, co. Gal., [illegible].
Sellenger, John m'Eneris, pardon, [illegible].
Sellerna, co. Gal., [illegible].
Sellinger, alias Liston, John, pardon, [illegible].
Selloe, co. Mon. See Sillowe.
Selsker—Selskere (St. Selskar), co. Wex., abbey of, commission to survey possessions, [illegible] ; possessions leased, [illegible], [illegible], [illegible], [illegible], [illegible].
" rectory, [illegible], [illegible], [illegible], [illegible], [illegible].
Semer, John, pardon, [illegible], [illegible].
Seminaries excluded from pardon, [illegible], [illegible].
Semyvyn, Edm. begg, pardon, [illegible].
Senbeo (Shanboe, Queen's co.), [illegible].
Senbohy, Queen's co., [illegible].
Sendell, Patr., pardon, [illegible].
Seneschal of Irish country appointed, [illegible].
Seneschal, vice, or tanist of Irish country, appointed, [illegible].
Seneschal (English), of Irish country, appointed, [illegible], [illegible], [illegible].
Seneschal of country, authority and emolument of, [illegible], [illegible], [illegible], [illegible], [illegible] ; powers of, [illegible].
Seneschalstown, co. Meath. See Senshialeston.
Sengarry—Sengary, Queen's co., [illegible].
Sengles, Michael, pardon, [illegible].
Senkill. See Shankill, co. Dub.
Senleger, Thomas. See Sentleger.
Senlisse (co. Cork ?), [illegible].
Sennaghan, Melaughlin m'Donoghe, pardon, [illegible].
Senshialeston (Seneschalstown), co. Meath, [illegible].
Sentagh, Dermot, pardon, [illegible].
Sentleger—St. Leger, sir Anthony, late lord deputy, fiant signed by, [illegible] ; lease recited, [illegible].
" sir Anthony, master of the rolls, [illegible] ; commissions, [illegible], [illegible], [illegible], [illegible], [illegible], [illegible], [illegible], [illegible], [illegible], [illegible], [illegible], [illegible], [illegible], [illegible], [illegible], [illegible] ; lease, [illegible], [illegible] ; pardon recommended by, [illegible].

INDEX TO FIANTS.—ELIZABETH.

Sentleger, Edmund, clerk, presentation, [illegible].
„ Edm., pardon, 1459, 2042, [illegible].
„ dame Elizabeth, lease, [illegible].
„ John, pardon, [illegible].
„ Oliver, pardon, 4[illegible].
„ Patrick, pardon, 1434.
„ Robert, pardon, [illegible], 1614, [illegible].
„ Thomas (or Senleger), pardon, [illegible], 077, [illegible]. See also Seyntleger.
Sentleger—St. Leger—Seyntleger—Sele[illegible]leger, sir Warham, commissions, [illegible], [illegible], 1[illegible], 3417-8, 1434, 3741, 4[illegible], 41[illegible], 44[illegible], [illegible], [illegible], [illegible]; general of levies in the field in Munster, [illegible]; chief colonel and commander of the forces in Munster, 3740; lease, 1143; disputes about Munster lands, [illegible]; to receive grant of land under great seal of England, [illegible]; grant of land as an undertaker, [illegible].
„ captain Warham, provost marshal of Munster, [illegible], 4037, [illegible]; commissions, [illegible], 4[illegible], [illegible], [illegible].
„ Warham, esquire (afterwards knight), constable of the castle of Castlemaigne, [illegible], [illegible]; governor of forces in Queen's co., [illegible]; commissions, [illegible], [illegible], [illegible]-4, [illegible]; soldier serving under, [illegible]; leases recited, [illegible]-7; lease to his widow, [illegible]. (This sir Warham was probably the same as captain Warham, but he has usually been identified with sir Warham above.)
Sentleger's castle in Arden. See S. Leger's castle.
Sentle—Sentlowe—St. Lowe—Seyntlowe, Edward, colonel of footmen, [illegible]; leases, 1517, [illegible], [illegible], [illegible].
Seore, Henry, pardon, [illegible].
Serebose, co. Kilk., [illegible].
Seregan, King's co., [illegible].
Seriantstown, co. Wex., 7[illegible].
Serim alias M'Cowck, pardon, 4071.
Serjeant at arms, appointments, 3436, [illegible], [illegible], [illegible], [illegible], [illegible]. See Connaught and Munster.
Serjeant at laws, [illegible]; appointments, 2161, [illegible], [illegible], [illegible]; ex-officio commissioner, [illegible].
Serjeant, chief, of Irish countries appointed, 1[illegible]-5, [illegible], 1[illegible], [illegible].
Serjeantown (Charlestown, co. Louth), 17[illegible].
Serrill, Nich. m'James, pardon, [illegible].
„ Rich. m'James, pardon, [illegible].
"Servant of the queen," 1434.
Service of precepts of eccl. comn. by affixing to doors, and proclamation, [illegible].
Seseweyrnmayn (Sesseoconnon, co. Sligo ?), 47[illegible].
Sesknaman (co. Sligo ?), [illegible].
Seskoman (co. Kerry ?), 4[illegible]7.
Seskin, Maurice m'Hugh, pardon, [illegible].
Seskin (co. Car. or Kilk.), 6434.
Seskin (co. Kilk. ?), [illegible].
Seskin (co. Tip. ?), [illegible].
Seskine, co. Car., [illegible].
Seskinryan, co. Car. See Siskinrian.
Seskyn, co. Kilk., [illegible].
Sessnagh (co. Donegal), [illegible].
Sessnaghe (co. Donegal), [illegible].
Sessorighkell, co. Tip. or Lim., 4[illegible].
Sessinaghe, [illegible].
Sessions in co. Carlow, [illegible].
Sessions in Connaught, persons availing themselves of pardon to appear before, 6112.
Sessions in counties, [illegible].
Sessrighell, co. Tip. or Lim., 4[illegible].
Sesseoconnon, co. Sligo. See Seseweyrnmayn.
Sever, William, clk., deprived, [illegible]; rector of Kilclonfert, [illegible].
Sewell, Anthony, chief serjeant of Kinnalegh, 1[illegible].
„ Anthony, pardon, [illegible], [illegible].
„ Rich., pardon, 4341.
Sex, ( ), 61[illegible].
Sex, Edmund, pardon, [illegible], [illegible], [illegible], [illegible], [illegible].
„ Edmund fitz Richard, pardon, 1[illegible].
„ James, pardon, [illegible], 3[illegible]7.
„ Michael, pardon, 61[illegible].
„ William, pardon, [illegible], 1578, [illegible], [illegible].
Sexe, Rob., pardon, [illegible].
Sexton, Maurice, [illegible].
„ Nich., pardon, [illegible].
„ —Sexten, Stephen, livery, [illegible]; lease, [illegible].
Sexton, Edmund, livery to heir, [illegible].
Seyn, Cornelius, pardon, 2974.
Seyn, Desmond m'Tho. L, pardon, [illegible].
Seynonny (co. Tip. ?), [illegible].
Seyntleger, Thomas, gent., grant of land, [illegible].
Seyntlowe, Edward. See Sentle.
Seymon (co. Waterf. ?), 6130.
Seyre (Seirkieran, King's co.), [illegible].
Seyse, John, merchant, [illegible].
„ Wm., pardon, [illegible].
Shadagyn, co. Cork [illegible].

INDEX TO FIANTS—ELIZABETH.

Shean—Shane—Shean, Francis (afterwards knight), sheriff of co. Galway, 4454; sheriff of Westmeath, [illegible]; commissions, 4176, 5948, 6080, 6308, [illegible], 6313; pardon, 3479, 4364, 6813; pardon at his suit, 4497; leases, [illegible], 6181; surrender, 6180; livery, [illegible].
" Mary, pardon, 4396.
" See Shane.
Shean, Queen's co. See Sheean.
Sheaghesse, Grany ny, pardon, 4627.
" Rose ny, pardon, 4627.
Sheaghneshara (co. Wat.?), 6544.
Sheghiam, alias O'Conill, Godfrey, pardon, 4098.
Shehanaghs (Shehanagh), co. Lim., 5761.
Shainakill (Shanakill), co. Wat., 614, 6169.
Shainagarry, co. Cork, 6765.
Shalaghe, Moelloorde m'Edm., pardon, 6444.
Shall, Pair, pardon, 6641.
Shellam Rathe — Shallamraithe. See Shellam Rosh, co. Kilk.
Shallon. See Shally.
Shallie (see Shally), co. Clare, 4780.
Shallie, John, 2948.
Shallon—Shallone, co. Meath, 897, 1460, 2328, 4811. See also Shallon.
Shallon, Richard, English livery, 14.
Shallone. See Shallon.
Shally—Shallie (Shallee?), co. Clare, 1286, 1848, 4780, 6617; castle and lands, 5777.
Shally (Shallon), co. Tip., 4978, 4704.
Shalton (Shalton), co. Meath, 4811.
Shaltie (Saltee islands), co. Wex., 1369.
Shalve (Shelvins), co. Mon., 5451.
Shamyd (co. Cork?), 6548.
Shamydangen, co. Cork, 5761.
Shanaghan, Wm., pardon, 6513.
Shanaclogh, co. Lim. See Shaneclogh.
Shanacloine (Shanacloon), co. Cork, 6591.
Shanacloon. See Shane Cloane.
Shanaloyle, co. Cork, 6584.
Shanagarrie (co. Cork), 6608.
Shanaghillie (co. Cork?), 6572.
Shanaghkilly, Donell m'Felamy oy, pardon, 6497.
Shanagolden, co. Lim. See Shanagowlly.
Shanakill, co. Wat. See Shainakill, Shenkill.
Shanakyll, co. Cork, 6472.
Shanamrock—Shamarocke (co. Mon.?), 6647.
Shanballe by Aghmacart, Queen's co., 897.
Shanballeard—Shanaballiard, co. Tip., 6516, 6581.
Shanballecayshalane alias Oldcastletown (Castletown, co. Westm.), 1401.
Shanballeduffe — Shanaballeduffe — Shanaballyduffe (co. Tip.), 6515-6, 6583, 6763.
Shanbally—Shanbaylle, King's co., 474, 1847, 6978.
Shanbally, co. Lim. See Sanyvallymore, Shanavallymore, Shanyvalymore.
Shanbally, co. Westm., 1624.
Shanballyanne, co. Wat. See Sanvallyanne.
Shanballyduff, co. Tip. See Sanaballiduff, Shanaballeduffe, Shanwalleduff.
Shanballymore, co. Cork. See Shanyvally-more.
Shanbaylle. See Shanbally, King's co.
Shanbeigh (co. Kilk.?), 6042.
Shanboe, Queen's co. See Senboe.
Shanbogh, county Kilk., rectory, 202. See Shanavough.
Shanbohe, co. Lim. See Templeshanabuy.
Shanboy (co. Car.?), 3320.
Shanclogh bane, co. Lim., 6647.
Shancloone (co. Long.?), 4152.
Shancoo (Shanoon), co. Wex., 1232.
Shancogh, co. Mon., 6644.
Shancor, co. Meath. See Tancre.
Shancough, co. Sligo. See Schanboe, Shancho.
Shandagen (co. Clare), 5800.
Shandangen (co. Clare), 5808. See also Shanedingan.
Shandangin (co. Cork), 6419.
Shandanyn (co. Cork), 6499.
Shandon manor, Cork, 6904.
Shandonecastell — Shandone castle, co. Cork, 1874, 6583.
Shandrum, co. Cork. See Shanedrome.
Shane, Ellis ny, pardon, 6511.
" Francis. See Shean.
" John, pardon, 6859.
" Margaret ny ne, pardon, 6434.
" Nicholas, livery to son, 6339; his wife, 6830.
Shane a Kyll, pardon, 1151.
Shaneballeduffe (see Shanballeduffe), 6583.
Shaneballeghbaine (co. Gal.?), 6662.
Shaneballiard. See Shanballeard.
Shanebally (co. Cork?), 6486.
Shaneballyduffe. See Shanballeduffe.
Shanebally Mortaghe (Queen's co.), 482.
Shaneboy, Queen's co., 2868.
Shanebroe, co. Meath, 4761.
Shanecullagh. See Shanecullaghe.
Shanechan, John, pardon, 4188.
Shanecoharte (co. Wick.?), 6877.
Shane cloane (Shanacloon?), 6612.
Shaneclogh (Shanaclogh?), co. Lim., 4616.
Shanecloghecoonoghorchowny (Shanaclogh?), co. Lim., 4484.
Shanecooneoghie alias Old Conoghie (Connagh?) co. Cork, 6663.
Shanedingan (Shandangan, co. Clare?), 6618.
Shanedrome (Shandrum), co. Cork, 6364.
Shane enallayne. See Enellan.

INDEX TO FIANTS.—ELIZABETH.

Shane glarum. See Sherwyn.
Shanegarie (co. Cork), [illegible].
Shanegarrie, in Munster, 6477.
Shanegarrye. See Shangarry.
Shanogh, Loyshagh, pardon, [illegible].
Shanogowlly (Shanagolden), co. Lim., 6472.
Shanokell (co. Kilk. or Tip.), 5761.
Shanskill—Shanickell, co. Kilk., 6342, 6476.
Shanskill (co. Wat.?), 6476.
Shanslaraghe (Shanlaragh), co. Cork, [illegible].
Shanslimo (co. Cork ?), [illegible].
Shanemollen — Shanemollen (Oldmill ?), Queen's co., 462, 501, [illegible], [illegible].
Shaneraghe (Shannora), co. Kerry, [illegible].
Shanetallaghe — Seantallaghe — Shanetallaghe—Shanecallaghe — Shean Callagh (Shanecallig), co. Cork, [illegible], 4452, 4514, [illegible], [illegible].
Shaneinlloghe (co. Mon.), 5043.
Shanevallymore (Shanbally ?), co. Lim., 6444.
Shanevough (Shanbogh), co. Kilk., rectory, [illegible].
Shangenagh—Shangenaghe—Shanganagh—Shanganaghe—Shangenaugh, co. Dub., [illegible], 3444, 3434, [illegible], [illegible], [illegible], 4453, 4530. See also Shanganaghe.
Shangenagh (co. Gal. ?), 4787.
Shanganagh — Shanganaghe, Queen's co., 871, 1340, 1573, 1687, 5762.
Shanganaghbegg—Shanganaghbeggo (Shanganagh Beg), Queen's co., [illegible], 5472.
Shanganaghe. See Shanganagh.
Shanganas (Shanganagh ?, co. Dub.), 5604.
Shanganaugh. See Shanganagh, co. Dublin.
Shangarrie, co. Car., [illegible], [illegible]. See Sangarry.
Shangarry — Shanegarrye — Shangary — Shanygarry (in Imokilly), co. Cork, [illegible], [illegible], [illegible]; rectory, [illegible].
Shangarry, Queen's co., [illegible].
Shangary. See Shangarry, co. Cork.
Shanghill (co. Wat. ?), [illegible], 1348.
Shanihaggard, co. Tip., 6448.
Shanid, co. Lim. See Shanyd.
Shanickell, [illegible]. See Shanekill, co. Kilk.
Shanidaly alias Cartie, John m'Dermodie, pardon, [illegible].
Shankayne, co. Lim., [illegible].
Shankill, Belfast. See Shankyll.
Shankill church (Shankill-Lurgan, co. Armagh), 4277.
Shankill (co. Car. ?), 6457, [illegible].
Shankill—Sankill—Shankyll—Shanekill, co. Dub., [illegible], 1782, [illegible], [illegible].
Shankill—Shankyll, co. Gal., [illegible], 1891, [illegible].
Shankill, co. Kilk. See Sankhill, Sanckill, Sankill.
Shankill, co. Rosc., 5777.
Shankill, co. Wat., 1944-6, 1731, [illegible].
Shankyll. See Shankill, co. Dub.
Shankyll. See Shankill, co. Gal.
Shanlaragh, co. Cork. See Shanslaraghe.
Shanlice country (O'Hanly's ?), co. Rosc., [illegible].
Shanlie—Shanlye, co. Louth, 1786, [illegible].
Shanlie grenage, co. Louth, 1722.
Shanlongurte—Shanlungart, Queen's co., 1167, 1336, [illegible].
Shanlye. See Shanlie.
Shannollagh, co. Mon., [illegible].
Shannagh, Phelim, pardon, [illegible].
Shannagh alias Rory m'Shane, pardon, [illegible].
Shannaghan, Donogh oge, pardon, [illegible].
" John, pardon, 5762.
" John m'Conoghor, pardon, [illegible].
Shannaghe, Brasell, pardon, [illegible].
Shannavallymore (co. Lim. ?), [illegible].
Shannekill (co. Kild. ?), [illegible].
Shannore, co. Kerry. See Shaneraghe.
Shannot, co. Lim., 6457.
Shannigarry (co. Cork ?), [illegible].
Shannon. See Shenan.
Shannrath (co. Lim. ?), 6478.
Shannygarry. See Shangarry, co. Cork.
Shannyn river. See Shenan.
Shanocloon, co. Lim., [illegible].
Shanon. See Shenan.
Shanoo, co. Wex. See Shanon.
Shanowyne (co. Cork ?), 5764.
Shanraghan — Shanraughan (Shanrahan), co. Tip., [illegible], [illegible].
Shanraghe, co. Meath, [illegible], [illegible].
Shanrath (co. Lim. ?), [illegible].
Shanraughan. See Shanraghan.
Shanrenagh (co. Kilk. ?), 5458.
Shanrighe, Teig m'Dermod, pardon, [illegible].
Shantemore (co. Cav. ?), [illegible].
Shantallig, co. Cork. See Shanetallaghe.
Shantway, King's co., [illegible].
Shantwinghe, co. Clare, [illegible].
Shanvanister alias Old Abbaye, co. Kilk., 1175.
Shanwalladuff (Shanballyduff, co. Tip. 4784.
Shanyarrie, 6477.
Shanycashill (co. Cork ?), 5418.
Shanyd, higher, (Shanid), co. Lim., [illegible].
Shanyd, lower, co. Lim., 6476.
Shanygcollin, co. Lim., [illegible].
Shanyvalymore (Shanbally ?), co. Lim., 5717.
Shanyvyaloid, co. Cork, [illegible].
Shanywallymore (Shanballymore, co. Cork ?), [illegible].
Sharagh, Queen's co., [illegible].
Sharles, Mary or Marion, pardon, [illegible].
Sharlocke, James fitz Thomas, comm. for martial law, 1814.

Sharloe, Patrick, commission, 64.
Sharo, John, pardon, 4618.
Sharpe, Simon, house in Dublin, 1811.
Sharre, co. Sligo, [illegible], [illegible].
Shart (co. Kilk. ?), [illegible].
Shartall, Edm. fitz Wm., pardon, [illegible].
„ James, pardon, 1061.
„ Leonard, pardon, 1801.
„ Oliver, pardon, 5182.
„ Wm. fitz Oliver, pardon, 6468.
Sharve, Mortertagh, pardon, 4494.
Sharywe, Shane, indenture, 6780.
Shashanes, James, pardon, 6873.
She, Rich., pardon, 6763.
She, Teige m'Dermody Y, pardon, [illegible].
Shea, Henry. See Shee.
„ Mary, pardon, 4744.
„ Rich. See Shee.
„ Shane m'Conogher I, pardon, 6467.
„ Tho., pardon, 6466.
„ Walter fitz John, pardon, 6477.
„ Wm. m'Shane, pardon, 6477.
Sheale, Christopher, clk., 1643.
„ Patr., pardon, [illegible].
Shealealy, [illegible].
Shealiahe (co. Cork ?), [illegible].
Shean (co. Clare ?), [illegible].
Shean, co. Cork or Wat., 1049.
Shean, King's co., 474, 1567, [illegible].
Shean—Sean—Sheane — Shyan —Sine — Syan (Shaen, Queen's co.), [illegible], 1347, [illegible], 1[illegible], 1[illegible], [illegible], [illegible].
Shean (co. Wick. ?), [illegible].
Shean, Francis. See Sheane.
„ Shillie oyne, pardon, 6594.
Sheanagh, Daniel, dean of Kilfenora, indenture, 4761.
Sheanaghill, co. Wat., 1076.
Sheanbega, Queen's co., 413.
Sheane Callagh. See Shanecallagha.
Sheane. See Shean, Queen's co.
Sheane (Sheanemore), co. Wat., castle and lands, 5046.
Sheanekill in Clonehoy (Shankill, Belfast), rectory, 6767.
Sheanganaghe—Sheangaunagh. See Shanganagh, co. Dub.
Sheankill. See Shankill, co. Dub.
Sheanemore, co. Wat. See Sheane.
Shearlocke, George, grant of land, 4444.
„ Peter, [illegible].
Shearman—Shearmen—Sherman—Sherman, pardoned, 3184, [illegible], 6614.
Shearmer, co. Cav., [illegible].
Sheath, Donnogh, fitz Walter, pardon, [illegible].
„ Donough Oduff, pardon, [illegible].
„ Nicholas fitz Donnell, pardon, [illegible].
„ Rich. See Shee.
Sheathe, Christopher, lease, [illegible], 4703.
Sheathe, Richard fitz Walter, pardon, [illegible].
Shebtown (Sextown, co. Dub. ?), 186.
Shee, Balthazar, pardon (see Sheethe), [illegible].
„ Donell oge m'Donell duffe Y, pardon, 4761.
„ Donell m'Shane Y, pardon, 4761.
„ Donell m'Teige Y, pardon, 4761.
„ Edm. m'Wm. boey, pardon, [illegible].
„ Elias, or Helias (—Sheethe) (of Kilkenny), pardon, 3434, [illegible].
„ Henry (or Shea—Sheethe—Sherthe) (of Kilkenny), commission, [illegible], [illegible]; grant of custodiam, [illegible]; lease, 6844; pardon, 3434, [illegible], 6441.
„ Jasper, pardon, 6394.
„ Jovan ny Teige Y, pardon, 4761.
„ Luke (son of sir Richard), pardon, 6441.
„ Michael, pardon, 6763.
„ Michael fitz Adam, pardon, [illegible].
„ (—Shea—Sheath—Sheeth—Sheethe—Sheth—Shethe), Richard (of Kilkenny, afterwards knight), [illegible]; treasurer of liberty of Tipperary, 3149; treats with rebels in Munster, [illegible]; sheriff of co. Kilkenny, [illegible], [illegible]; commissions, [illegible], [illegible], [illegible], [illegible], 3444, [illegible], [illegible], [illegible], 4761; alienation to, 1566; custodiam of lands of the earl of Desmond and other rebels, [illegible], [illegible]; leases, [illegible], [illegible], [illegible]; land of, in Kilkenny, [illegible]; pardon, [illegible], 3434, [illegible], 4[illegible], [illegible], 6441; pardon at his suit, [illegible], [illegible].
„ Rich., pardon, 4870.
„ Rob., pardon, 6441.
„ See Sheeth, Sheethe, Sheth, Shethe.
Sheele, James, pardon, 4763, 4763.
Sheep, value of, 444, 987; robbery of, [illegible], [illegible], [illegible], [illegible]; rent paid in, [illegible].
Sheep fell, illegal export, [illegible].
Sheep skins stolen, [illegible]; monopoly of export from Dublin and Drogheda, [illegible].
Sheep, summer, custom, in Irish countries, [illegible], [illegible], [illegible].
Sheepgrange, co. Louth. See Shepe grange.
Sheephouse, co. Meath. See Shepetown.
Sheepsbottom, co. Cork, [illegible].
Sheerman. See Shearman.
Sheeth, Peter, pardon, 3434.
„ Richard, [illegible]. See Shee.
„ Wm., commission to son of, 3117; pardon, 3434.
Sheethe, Arthur, pardon, 3434.
„ Balthasar, pardon (see Shee), 3434.
„ Edm., pardon, 3434.
„ Edw., pardon, 3434.
„ Helias, 3434. See Shee, Elias.
„ Henry, 3434, [illegible]. See Shee.

INDEX TO FIANTS—ELIZABETH.

Sheethe, Nich., pardon, 5434.
" Rich., 2946, 5434. *See* Shee.
" William, pardon, 1942.
Sheffeilde — Sheffeild — Sheffyelde, Henry, customs collector, 5749; grant of a wardship, 5947; leases, 4462, 6480.
Sheghan (co. Cork ?), [illegible].
Sheghan, Maurice, pardon, 5100.
" Morgan, pardon, [illegible].
Sheghanagh (co. Lim. ?), 4470.
Sheghane, Morish, pardon, 4512.
Sheheghan, Philip oge m'Shane, pardon, [illegible].
Shehy, Katherin ny, pardon, 4498.
Sheill, Edm., pardon, 5314.
" James, pardon, [illegible].
Sheigan, Maurice, pardon to son, [illegible].
" Wm., pardon, [illegible].
Shein, Dermot oge I., pardon, [illegible].
Sheinstroyne — Siorowne — Syaroyn — Syonrone (Shinrone, King's co.), [illegible], 4474, 5191, 6677.
Sheiloe — Sheislow, co. Wex. (Shillelagh, co. Wick. ?), 1882.
Sheilanwhye. *See* Shillanghyn.
Sheikuroe, co. Wex. *See* Shilbrin.
Sheisle (co. Wick.), 6677.
Sheisleymstowne, co. Dub., alias Ballyhelion (Hoddlerstown, co. Wick ?), [illegible].
Shelsyke, co. Down, 4227.
Shelle, Moylin oy, pardon, 4546.
Shelloe — Shelyne (Shilchorne ?), co. Wat., 856, 5152.
Shellem Rath — Shellam rathe (Shelinmerath), co. Kilk., 2916, 4967, 4908.
Shellyane, co. Long., [illegible].
Shelston (King's co. ?), [illegible].
Shellon, Henry, pardon, 4085.
Sheltonsmeads, co. Kild., 4960.
Sheltonsmore, co. Kild., [illegible].
Shelvin, co. Mon. *See* Shelve.
Shelyne. *See* Shelloe.
Shamykyn, Donyll oge moele, pardon, 2774.
" Gilleboy m'Donyll oge, pardon, 2774.
Shemagh, Phelym, pardon, [illegible].
" Tirrelagh, pardon, [illegible].
Shenagh, co. Westm., 1[illegible].
Shenaghe, Bryen, pardon, 3311.
" Owen, pardon, 3311, [illegible].
Shenagro, Queen's co., 6768.
Shenon — Shennyn — Shenon — Shenon — Shenin — Shennan — Shennon — Shenyn — Shenon — Shenyn — Shenyne — Shianon — Shinon — Shynon — Shynin — Shynnon — Shynnelngo — Shynnyn (river Shannon), [illegible], 917, 1611, 1938, 2434-6, 2971, 2827, 3198, 3729, 3488, 3977, 4[illegible]-6, 4078, [illegible], 5131, 5160, 5757; countries south of, 1848, [illegible], [illegible], 4489; islands leased or granted, 3872, 4428, 4494; mills, 3402, 5164; boats to be registered, 1996, 3118, 3841, 4299; rock of, 5188.
" weirs and fishing, 1434, 1994, 1689-1, 2872, 3160, 3402, 4290, 4318, 4428, 5177, 5496, 5915; weirs to be removed, 3641, 5[illegible].
" chief serjeant and water bailiff, 1649, 3118.
" overseer and keeper, 3841, [illegible].
" overseer, water bailiff and keeper, 4[illegible].
Shenan, Pairse, pardon, 5444.
Shenahe alias Gowagh (Shanecough), co. Sligo, rectory, 5077.
Shenclone, co. Kild., 5268, 5359, 6740.
Shene, King's co., 813.
Shenen — Shenin. *See* Shenon.
Shenkill (Shanakill), co. Wat., [illegible], [illegible].
Shenkyll — Sheanekill (Shankill, Belfast), rectory, 1650, 5767.
Shenleshe, co. Louth, 4561.
Shenle, John, pardon, [illegible].
Shenler, co. Westm., 1256.
Shenlis (co. Cork ?), 5412.
Shennagh, Owin, alias Fox, pardon, [illegible].
" Phelim, pardon, 4015.
" Rory O'Toig, pardon, 1[illegible].
Shennoghe, Brassell, alias Foxe, pardon, 58.
" Bryen, sons of, pardon, 58.
" Carbry, pardon, 58.
" Coughogory, pardon, 58.
" Kedaugh m'Tybbote, pardon, 58.
" Tybbote m'Tybbote, pardon, 58.
" *See* Fox.
Shenon — Shenon — Shennyn — Shenon. *See* Shenon river.
Sheey, John, pardon, 4072.
Shenygeyne, Yomhar, pardon, 6758.
Shevyn — Shevyne. *See* Shenon river.
Shee, Edm., pardon, 6411.
" Garrett, pardon, 4494.
" Gerott, pardon, 4[illegible].
" Maurice, pardon, 3472.
" Morris, pardon, 6470.
" Redmund, pardon, 6470.
" Theobald, pardon, 6516.
" Tho., pardon, [illegible].
" Wm., pardon, 5494.
Sheenan, co. Westm., 2[illegible].
Sheee, Richard, pardon, 4676.
Sheey, Edm. m'Wm., pardon, 6457.
" Gerrott, pardon, 6457.
" John m'Wm., pardon, 6457.
" Wm. fitz Gerrott, pardon, 6457.

INDEX TO FIANTS—ELIZABETH.

Sheoy, Wm. m'Edm., pardon, 4487.
Sheoye, Shane, pardon, [illegible].
Shepardo, Richard. *See* Sheppard.
Shepe grange—Shepegrange (Sheepgrange, co. Louth), 183, [illegible].
Shepehouse, co. Louth, 1751.
Shepehowse (Sheephouse, co. Meath), [illegible].
Shepeston, co. Cork, [illegible].
Shepeston (co. Tip.?), [illegible].
Shepestown (co. Kilk.?), 6704.
Sheppard—Shepardo—Shephearde, Rich., clerk of the ordnance, [illegible], 2910, [illegible].
Shercock, co. Cav. *See* Barcoick.
Shergold—Shergoll, William, commissions, 703-4, 752, [illegible].
Sheridan. *See* Siridanne, Siridan, Siridane.
Sheriff appointed for MacWilliam Eughter's country, 1239; *for* Breny O'Rorke, 1515; difficulty of introducing in new Shires, 1[illegible].
" exemption from serving as, 5371.
" manner of executing writ in co. Galway, [illegible].
" *See* under respective counties.
Sheriff, under, statute forbidding continuance for more than a year, [illegible].
Sheriffield—Sheriefeilde, alias Churchfield, at Trim, co. Meath, [illegible], 1[illegible].
Sherkin island, co. Cork. *See* Inisherkan.
Sherleestowne (Charlestown), co. Louth, 1752.
Sherley, Thomas, knight, commissions, [illegible], [illegible].
Sherlock—Sherlocke—Sherlok—Sherloke—Shurlock—Shurlocke—Shurlog—Shyrloke:
" Edward, pardon in Waterford, [illegible].
" Ellyce, lease, [illegible].
" George (of Dublin), pardon, [illegible].
" George, grants of lands and tithes, [illegible], [illegible], [illegible], [illegible], [illegible]; grant recited, [illegible].
" James, mayor of Waterford, [illegible].
" James (of Butlerstown, co. Wat.), sheriff of co. Waterford, freedom from subsidy, 794; commission, 1811; pardon, [illegible].
" James, executor of Patrick, [illegible].
" James, land in his tenure in Waterford, [illegible], [illegible].
" James (of Naas), sub-sheriff of Kildare, [illegible]; pardon, [illegible]; land of, [illegible].
" James, treasurer of co. Wexford, [illegible].
" James fitz John, commission, [illegible].
" James fitz Patrick, commission, [illegible].
Sherlock, James fitz Tho., pardon, 1784.
" James fitz Tho. (of [illegible]), mortgage to him, [illegible]; livery to his heir, [illegible].
" John, commission, [illegible].
" John (of Waterford), his widow, [illegible].
" John (of Naas), pardon of, [illegible].
" Patrick (of Burnchurch) sheriff of Kilkenny, [illegible]; sheriff of Tipperary, [illegible], [illegible]; commissions, [illegible], [illegible], [illegible], [illegible], 1016, 1196; pardon, 1[illegible], [illegible].
" Patr. (of Priorstown), co. Tip., commission, 1844.
" Patr., commissions, 2808, [illegible], [illegible].
" Patr. (of S. Katherines, Waterford), sheriff of co. Waterford, [illegible], [illegible]; commission, [illegible]; pardon, [illegible]; lease, [illegible], [illegible]; widow of his son, [illegible].
" Patr. (of Killure, co. Wat.), pardon, [illegible].
" Patr., sheriff of Kilkenny, [illegible].
" Patr., pardon at his suit, [illegible].
" Patr. (of Gologhmore, co. Kilk.), pardon, [illegible].
" Paul, pardon in Waterford, [illegible].
" Paul, son of James, livery, [illegible].
" Peter or Pearse (of Waterford), sheriff of cross of Tipperary, commission, [illegible]; pardon, [illegible], [illegible]; lease, [illegible]; grant of land, [illegible], [illegible]; grant to son, [illegible].
" William, pardon, [illegible], [illegible].
" *See* suit to attorney-general by, 1[illegible].
Sherlockestowne—Sherlockeston—Sherlokiston—Shirlockston, co. Kild., [illegible], 1067, [illegible], [illegible], [illegible].
Sherloge, James, pardon, [illegible].
Sherlok—Sherloke. *See* Sherlock.
Sherlokeston—Sherlokiston. *See* Sherlockestowne.
Sherlyestoun, co. Louth, [illegible].
Sherman. *See* Shearman.
Sherpstowne, co. Tip., [illegible].
Shertall, John, pardon, [illegible], 1078.
" Oliver, pardon, [illegible].
" Peter, pardon, 1078.
" Robert, pardon, [illegible].
" William, pardon, 1078.
Shertoll, Rob. fitz Nich., pardon, [illegible].
Sheshireagle (Shesheraghkeale, co. Tip.), [illegible].
Shesken, co. Kilk., [illegible].
Sheskeneste, co. Kerry, [illegible].
Sheskenvine, [illegible].

3 F

Sheasy, co. Gal. *See* Shanlakigan.
Sheath, Adam, pardon, 3434.
" Edmund, pardon, 167.
" John, pardon, 1648.
" Richard. *See* Shee.
" Robert fitz Nicholas, pardon, 1081.
Shethe, Donagh fitz Walter, pardon, 610.
" Donagh m'Teig, pardon, 800.
" Donald m'Teig, pardon, 800.
" Edmund, pardon, 611.
" Henry. *See* Shee.
" Nicholas, pardon, 930.
" Nicholas oig, pardon, 620.
" Richard. *See* Shee.
" Rich. fitz Rob., pardon, 2840.
" Richard fitz Walter, pardon, 800.
" Robert, pardon, 167; member of parliament for Kilkenny, 152.
" Robert fitz Nicholas, pardon, 800.
" Walter, pardon, 611.
" William, lease, 1581.
" William m'Teig, pardon, 800.
Sherven, Nich., pardon, 6452.
Shevers, John, 4145. *See* Chevers.
Shewrstone—Sherwiston, co. Wex., 614, 4261.
Shey, Conochor oge, pardon, 5538.
Shey, George, pardon, 6782.
Sheyne, Wm., pardon, 5487.
Shieghane, Ellen ny, pardon, 6481.
Shielere (Shewer), co. Tip., 4978.
Shian, co. Clare, 4668.
Shian (King's co.?), 6468.
Shian, co. Wat., 1845, 3471, 3054, 4290.
Shian, co. Wick., 6577.
Shichalan, Maurice, pardon, 2512.
Shichan, Donogh m'Awliff I, pardon, 6546.
Shien, Shane m'Cnogher I, pardon, 6371.
Shieghan, Ellen, pardon, 5528.
" John, pardon, 5528.
Shiolanlaghe, co. Dub., 2707. *See* Shillelaghe.
Shiell, Connor, pardon, 6160.
" Moriagh, pardon, 6362.
" Patr., pardon, 6160, 6280.
" Rich., pardon, 6159.
" Wm., pardon, 6162, 6280.
Shighan, Donogh m'Donell Y, pardon, 6702.
Shighane, Conoghor m'Shal[ ] Y, pardon, 6702.
" Joan ny, pardon, 6407.
" Morish oge, pardon, 4818.
Shigin, Thomas, surrender of pension, 6403.
Shihie, Brien m'Rich., pardon, 6478.
" Dermod m'Donogh, pardon, 6478.
" Donogh m'Cahill, pardon, 6478.
" Donogh m'Wm., pardon, 6782.
" Edm. oge, his son, attainted, 6122.
" Ellinor ny, pardon, 6467.
" Ellinor, pardon, 6487.
Shihie, Honor ny, pardon, 6467.
" John m'Tirlagh, pardon, 6470.
" Katherine ny, pardon, 6477.
" Manus, indicted and pardon, 6371.
" Manus m'Cahill, pardon, 6478.
" Margaret nyne, pardon, 6484.
" Margaret nyne Edm., pardon, 6478.
" Mary ny, pardon, 6467.
" Moriertagh m'Edm., pardon, 6478.
" Morrogh m'Cahill, pardon, 6478.
" Owen m'Edmund, attainted, 6122.
" Owen m'Cahill, pardon, 6478.
Shiby alias Brulagh, Thorlagh m'Owen, pardon, 6510.
Shilaghe. *See* Shillanghye.
Shilbegan, co. Wex., 5445-7.
Shilboken, co. Wex., 1837.
Shilbrin—Shilvirye (Shelburne), co. Wex., martial law in, 1807, 1884.
Shilelaghe—Selelagh—Selelaghe—Sheleloe—Shelelow—Shielealaghe—Shilealogh—Shilealoghe—Shilealye—Shilelalie—Silelaghe—Sylelaghe (Shillelagh, co. Wick.), 1862, 1408, 5111; country leased, 6973; granted, 6767; martial law in, 486, 1125, 1520, 1618, 2180, 2284.
Shill, Wm., pardon, 6778.
Shillagh—Shillanghe (Sillagh), co. Kild., 1667, 3984, 4411.
Shillinghan, Tho., pardon, 4881.
Shillanghye — Shelanwhye — Shileghe — Sylleanghy — Silleanchi — Sylanaghey (Siol Anmchadha, O'Madden's country in Galway and King's co.), 1681, 1770; captain appointed, 617, 1050, 1718; granted to O'Madden, 6718.
Shillanghe. *See* Shillagh.
Shillelagh, co. Wick. *See* Shelelaloe, Shilelaghe.
Shillihane (co. Gal.?), 5428.
Shillingeford, Rob., 6364.
Shillingesford's garden in Mary's abbey, Dublin, 6772.
Shillingfordes land, in Dublin, 6364, 6663.
Shillock (Sillogue), co. Dub., 3612.
Shillton's lands, co. Kild., 1164.
Shilumyn, co. Wex., 6267.
Shilmoston, co. Kild., 1164.
Shilvirye. *See* Shilbrin.
Shiman, Wm., 2344. *See* Shyman.
Shinane, Shane, pardon, 6477.
Shindale, co. Kild. *See* Stratyll.
Shinon river. *See* Shannon.
Shinnagho, Cahir m'Thybalde, pardon, 1418, 1420.
Shinnon river. *See* Shannon.
Shinoke alias Foxes country, 152.
Shinrone, King's co. *See* Ginron, 5101, Sheineroyne, Sibourone, Toyareyne.

INDEX TO FIANTS—ELIZABETH.

Ships impressed for army victualling service, 875, 1041, 3421, 5028; vice-treasurer authorised to impress ship for a journey to England, 9521.

Ship of Brittany robbed in Shannon by men of Limerick, 1518.

Ships, queen's, authority to press men for, 5023, 3867, 3451.

Ship, queen's, Handmaid, captain of, 5858.

Ship, the queen's, master gunner of, 5018.

Shipspoole (co. Cork ?), 6185.

Shirlockstown. See Sherlockestowne.

Shirpeston (co. Tip. ?) (See Sharpestowne), 4673.

Shirrelane, Thirelagh, pardon, 6452.

Shirwin, William, lease, 464.

Shoe, David, pardon, 6477.

„ David bog, pardon, 6477.

„ David fitz Morris, pardon, 6477.

„ David Iniatane—Inioiaine, pardon, 8183, 6477.

„ John, pardon, 6477.

„ Rob., pardon, 4542, 6477.

„ Tho. m'Rob., pardon, 6477.

„ Tho. m'Tho., pardon, 6477.

„ Tho. reogh m'Rob. more, pardon 6477.

Shoemakers of Cork license to tan, &c., 5068.

„ in Kilkenny, privilege to, 3451.

„ guild in Waterford, 5788.

„ pardoned, 3857, 4608, &c.

Shoemakers towne, co. Cork, 5713.

Shoes stolen, value of, 5858.

Sholanne, co. Mayo or Rosc., 4600.

Shollyvan, Owen m'Awlly Y, pardon, 4781.

Sholohoda. See Solloghod.

Sholis, Simon ne, O'Maly, pardon, 4844.

Sholyvan, Connor m'Fynyn Y, pardon, 4781.

Shorough begg, co. Wat., 6034.

Shorsallagh, Moriah m'Shane, pardon, 5234.

Shoranboye (co. Kilk. ?), 1250.

Shortall, Edmund, pardon, 847, 3494, 5494.

„ Edm. fitz Leonard, pardon, 5454.

„ Edward fitz Piers, pardon, 5800.

„ James, pardon, 1067.

„ James (of Ballylorcan), commissions, 2117, 2345, 3444; pardon, 1822, 4297, 4833.

„ James (of Prickysheyne), pardon, 5494.

„ alias Ferdorgh, James, pardon, 1868.

„ James, pardon, 911, 1867, 1868, 2888, 3048, 4503, 4683.

„ James roe, pardon, 2701.

„ John, pardon, 90, 2821, 5288, 3546.

„ John fitz Ehm, pardon, 4473.

„ John fitz Robert, pardon, 2824, 2870.

„ John gare, pardon, 6447.

Shortall, Katherine, conveyance of lands to, 4162.

„ Katherine fitz Edm., pardon, 5494.

„ Leonard, pardon, 1880, 1883; conveyance of lands to, 6162.

„ Nich., a surety, 4128.

„ Nich., pardon, 2541, 6441.

„ Nich. fitz Patr., pardon, 5841.

„ Oliver, pardon, 1912, 1794, 1261, 6363, 6793.

„ Oliver, pardon to widow of, 1048.

„ Oliver fitz Robert, pardon, 629.

„ Oliver ro, pardon, 6447, 6484, 6704.

„ Patrick, clerk, pardon, 4831.

„ Patr. (of Ballyvonle), sub-sheriff of Kilk., pardon, 5902, 4234.

„ Patrick (of Dunmore), pardon, 1833.

„ Patr. (of Fowlkesath), pardon, 5864.

„ Patr., pardon, 788, 4870.

„ Peirs fitz Leonard, pardon, 5704.

„ Peirs fitz John, pardon, 6348.

„ Peter, pardon, 1888, 5144.

„ Peter fitz Edmond, pardon, 157.

„ Peter fitz Leonard, pardon, 5798.

„ Peter fitz Oliver, pardon, 2082.

„ Peter fitz Richard, pardon, 611.

„ Peter fitz Robert, pardon, 682.

„ Peter m'Shane, pardon, 6602.

„ Philip, pardon, 5868.

„ Piers, pardon, 4698.

„ Richard, pardon, 158, 627, 1264, 2041.

„ Rich. fitz John, pardon, 1638, 2349, 5960.

„ Rich. fitz Patr., pardon, 6168.

„ Richard fitz Robert, pardon, 1920, 2088, 2860.

„ Richard m'Shane, pardon, 1087, 1957.

„ Robert, pardon, 2047, 6211, 6370, 5447, 4425, 5465.

„ Rob. fitz Edm., pardon, 6452.

„ Rob. fitz James, pardon, 6364.

„ Rob. fitz Oliver, pardon, 5182.

„ Rob. fitz Patr., pardon, 6360, 6484.

„ Shane, pardon, 6728.

„ Thomas, pardon, 2048, 4397, 6704, 6793.

„ Tho. fitz Oliver, pardon, 4628.

„ Walter m'Shane, pardon, 1087.

„ Wm., pardon, 880, 2048, 4328.

„ Wm. fitz Leonard, pardon, 5704.

„ Wm. m'Edw., pardon, 6447.

„ William roe, pardon, 1888.

„ See Shortall.

Shortallstown, co. Kilk. See Shotaleston.

Shortale, Nich., 4383.

Shortcastle, co. Cork, 4812.

Shortcourse, Waterford, 448.

Shortelops, co. Meath, 6477.

INDEX TO FIANTS—ELIZABETH.

Shortquarter, co. Lim., 5783.
Sholmleston, Great (Shortsallestown), co. Kild., 2862.
Showre, Gerolt fitz Thomas, pardon, 5611.
,, John fitz Tho., pardon, 5487.
,, Rob. fitz Tho., pardon, 5487.
,, Wm., pardon, 5487.
Shower, co. Tip. See Shinlore.
Shower river, co. Tip. See Shuer.
Showher, 3364. See Showre.
Showre river. See Shuer.
Shracullin (Sracullen, Queen's co.), 5532.
Shraduffe (Sradure, King's co.), 1834, 3871.
Shragadile, co. Wex., 5547.
Shragh. See Strahenmarte.
Shragh (Srah ?), Queen's co., 6683.
Shraghanmore (Stramordan), co. Mon., 5854.
Shraghede, Wm. m'Molaghlin m'Donill, pardon, 6683.
Shraghmyle, Queen's co., 5696.
Shranashymeagha, 4334.
Shrewsbury—Shrewsbury—Shrewisburie, earl of, possessions of, leased or granted, 153, 1294, 3632. See also Salop.
Shronakeogh (co. Gal ?), 5617.
Shroher — Sroher — Srower (Shrule ? co. Long.), 1651, 6366, 6622, 6574, 6669. See also Srure.
Shrohill. See Shrowle, Queen's co.
Shromcarton, co. Cork. See Shromy-charton.
Shrone, co. Kerry, 6117.
Shronecally—Shronkhall. See Shrongnally.
Shronell, co. Tip. See Scronell—Sronell.
Shromycharton—Shronyoharton (Shrone-carton, co. Cork), 6618.
Shroull (Shrule, Queen's co. ?), 6775.
Shroure (co. Gal. ?), 6718.
Shrowe, co. Sligo, 1682.
Shrowell—Shrowill—Shrowle — Shrowlie— Shroyll — Shrowell — Shrowill (Abbeyshrule, co. Long.), 1054.
,, abbey of the B. V. M., 2685, 6794; leased, 1023; granted, 1513; possessions leased, 4160, 6811, 6183; granted, 5404.
,, rectory, 1523, 5163.
Shrowina (co. Lim. ?), 1461.
Shrowle, Abbey of. See Shrowell.
Shrowle—Shroill—Shrowll (Shrule, Queen's co.), 1654, 2611, 2823, 5175.
Shrowlie. See Shrowell.
Shrowre — Shrowher — Shrowyr— Shroher— Sroghar — Srowher — Srowir (Shrule co. Mayo), 1278, 1288, 3364, 3153, 2626, 4690.
,, rectory, 1728.
Shroylerunka, brook, Queen's co. 5789.
Shroyll, abbey. See Shrowell.
Shruer, co. Mayo, 4663. See Shrowre.
Shrubane (co. Lim. ?), 1404.
Shrule, co. Gal. See Srowroboy.
Shrule, co. Long. See Shroher, Srure.
Shrule barony, co. Long. See Clanconnog-hor, Moyharowe.
Shrule, co. Mayo. See Shrowre.
Shrule, Queen's co. See Shroull, Shrowle.
Shrynninge river. See Shenan.
Shnogolde, Tho., 5411.
Shuer — Showor — Showre — Shure (Suir) river, 1566, 6317, 2854, 5850; weirs, &c., on, 2846.
Shully (Shallee ?), co. Tip., 4678.
Shure river. See Shuer.
Shureton, co. Westm. See Sweryme.
Shurlock—Shurlocke. See Sherlock.
Shute, John, captain, pardon, 1438.
Shyne, co. Car., 504.
Shyon. See Shane.
Shyanmocke — Shyanmolck (King's or Queen's co.), 542, 1854.
Shyan moyglas, Queen's co., 1588.
Shyffe, John, pardon, 5517.
Shyggins land, co. Lim., 4152.
Shyghan, Maurice, pardon, 2516.
Shyhye, Ellen, pardon, 4538.
Shylicke, co. Down, 4327.
Shylicke, alias Ballaghbogs, co. Down, 6718.
Shylloghy. See Shillanghye.
Shyllyngford, Robert, 1709.
Shyman, Gilleduff, pardon, 836, 2944.
,, James riough, pardon, 2944.
,, Philip, pardon, 2944.
,, William, pardon, 2944, 4111.
,, William crone, pardon, 2944.
,, William fitz John, pardon, 2944.
Shymane, Edm., pardon, 6782.
,, Rob. fitz John, pardon, 6794.
Shynan river. See Shenan.
Shynagh, Brasell, followers of, pardoned, 46.
Shyraghe, Brean m'Oyn, pardon, 1168.
,, Cahir m'Tybbote, pardon, 88.
,, Keddagh, pardon, 1184.
Shynnon—Shynnye river. See Shenan.
Shyragh, Donell, pardon, 440.
Shyricke, Peerce. See Sherlock.
Shyvry, Rowney, pardon, 2780.
Sian, 1760. See Shean, Queen's co.
Sicurin, Dermod m'Conoghor I, pardon, 6696.
Siddan —Siddane—Suddan—Syddan—Syd-dane — Syddan, co. Meath, 151, 260, 637, 738, 1540, 1587, 1236, 1412, 1725, 2344, 2450, 2467, 2605, 3787, 4098, 4146, 4461.
,, rectory, 637, 2942.
Sidney, Dorcas. See Sydney.
,, Sir Henry. See Sydney.

INDEX TO FIANTS—ELIZABETH.

Sidney, William, licence to export wool, [illegible].
Sifline—Syffyn, co. Westm., [illegible], 6762.
Siffinton by Marlbrogh, 1642.
Signet, fees of, [illegible].
Sibes, Richard, commission, 4454.
Sihemrone (Shinrone, King's co. ?), [illegible].
Sikewe, co. Kerry, [illegible].
Silelaghe. *See* Shilelaghe.
Silk stolen, 407.
Sillagh, co. Kild. *See* Shillagh.
Sillelurons, co. Wat. *See* Shelune, Sylyam.
Silleroghl. *See* Shillaughyn.
Sillie, Donell oy, pardon, [illegible].
Silliot, co. Kild., [illegible], [illegible], 6740.
Silliotshill (Silliotshill), co. Kild., 6761.
Silloge, co. Dub. *See* Shillock.
Sillowe (Salloo), co. Mon., [illegible].
Silmarvyn, in O'Conor Don's country, co. Ros., 4486.
Silmerere meadow. *See* Silvererre.
Silver, illegal export of, [illegible], [illegible]; prevention of export, [illegible].
Silvererre—Silverce—Silmerere meadow at Mellifont, co. Louth, [illegible], 3771, 3872.
Silver hand river, co. Westm. *See* Low-argill.
Simcot, John. *See* Symcott.
Simon, Redmond, pardon, 6401.
Simkin, Maurice m'Philip, pardon, [illegible].
" Rich. m'Philip, pardon, 2040.
" Tho. m'Morish, pardon, [illegible].
Simondeston—Symondiston (Simmonstown, co. Kild.), 1688, 2690. *See* also Simmeston.
Simondeston—Simondstone—Simoneston—Symondeston—Symneston, co. Meath, [illegible], 2271, 2348, 2842, 3878, 4727.
Simmeston. *See* Simonston, co. Kild.
Simoneston. *See* Simondeston, co. Meath.
Simonston—Simoneston (Simmonstown ?), co. Kild., 1444, 2690.
Simonstown, co. Westm. *See* Symneston.
Simson, alias Drum, George, pardon, [illegible].
Sindyll—Syndyll, King's co. (Shindale, co. Kild. ?), 1808, 1444.
Synod, James roragho, pardon, [illegible].
" John (of Dublin), [illegible].
" Nich. reoughe, pardon, [illegible].
" Patr. *See* Synnot.
" Philip, pardon, 2844.
" Rich., lease (see Symnot), [illegible].
Sinod, Jasper, pardon, [illegible].
" Matthew, pardon, [illegible].
" —Sinott, Oliver, pardon, [illegible], [illegible].
Sinottanagh (Srunttanagh, co. Mayo ?), 5767.
Sinrowne, [illegible]. *See* Sheinarroyne.
Siol Ammchada. *See* Shillanghyn.
Sion (co. Wat. ?), 2162.
Sippell, Morris, pardon, [illegible].
Siridanus, Eugenius albus, pardon, 5444.
" Thady, pardon to son, 5462.
Siridanus an leithbaill, Cornelio son of Padin, pardon, [illegible].
Siridan, Terence son of Fergal albus I., pardon, [illegible].
Sirideus, Bernard, son of Terence, pardon, [illegible].
" Bernard, son of Tho., pardon, 5464.
" Caroll, son of Tho., pardon, [illegible].
" Cognatus, son of Tho., pardon, 5464.
" Cognatus, son of Wm., pardon, [illegible].
" Corvell, pardon to son, [illegible].
" Domnius, pardon to son, [illegible].
" Edmund, son of Unerus, pardon, [illegible].
" Edm., son of Edm., pardon, [illegible].
" Felem, pardon to son, [illegible].
" Gotredus, pardon to son, 5464.
" Hugh, son of Unerus, pardon, 5464.
" Hugh, son of Gotredus, pardon, 5464.
" John, pardon, 5464.
" Malachias, pardon, [illegible].
" Nich., son of Wm., pardon, 5464.
" Nicholas, pardon to son, 5464.
" Patrick, pardon to son, [illegible].
" Terence, pardon to son, [illegible].
" Tho., pardon to son, 5464.
" Tho., son of Felem, pardon, 5462.
" Unerus, son of Patrick, pardon, 5464.
" Unerus, son of Terence, pardon, 5462.
" Unerus, pardon to sons, 5464.
" Wm., son of Domnius, pardon, 5464.
" Wm., pardon to sons, 5464.
Siskiarian (Seskinryan, co. Car.), [illegible].
Sirewicidgan (Shessy ?), co. Gal., [illegible].
Sitesor, pardoned, 4110; Sessor, 4112.
Sitell—Sitell ground near Athlone, co. Westm., 1894, [illegible].
Sivine, Honorny, pardon, [illegible].
" James, pardon, [illegible].
Skadarton—Skaddanston, co. Tip., 847; rectory, [illegible], 5408, [illegible].
Skagh, co. Clare, [illegible].
Skaghanagh (co. Lim. ?), [illegible].
Skaghanagh (Skehana ?), co. Kilk., 1184.
Skaghe, co. Clare, [illegible].
Skahanagh (co. Lim. ?), [illegible].
Skahannaghe. *See* Skeghanagh, co. Lim.
Skalle, John, pardon, [illegible].
Skallan, Conoghor m'Diermody I., pardon, 4764.
" Donill m'Hugh, pardon, [illegible].
Skallardston (co. Wick. ?, perhaps Scholarstown, co. Dub.), 4018.

INDEX TO FIANTS—ELIZABETH.

Skenaghe, Queen's co., 834.
Skanlan, Edm. m'Shane ogo I, pardon, [illegible].
Skanill, Wm. m'Dermody I, pardon, 4761.
Skanlane, Conoghor m'Teig I, pardon, [illegible].
" Donogh m'Teig I, pardon, [illegible].
Skanlan, Dermod m'Edm. I, pardon, [illegible].
" Donald m'Dermodie I, pardon, [illegible].
" Shane m'Hugh, pardon, [illegible].
Skanlane, Donald m'Diermody I, pardon, [illegible].
" Donoghy m'Conoghor I, pardon, [illegible].
Skanlon, Dermod m'Ea I, pardon, 6477.
" Edm. m'Tho. Y, pardon, 6487.
" Sayve ny, pardon, 6487.
Skannell, Dermod m'Donoghe Y, pardon, [illegible].
Skannell, Wm. m'Dermody Y, pardon, [illegible].
Skannill, Teige m'Diermody I, pardon, 4761.
Skanteschristone, co. Waterford, [illegible].
Skardane—Skardan, co. Sligo, [illegible], [illegible].
Skariffe (Scarriff), co. Clare, [illegible].
Skariff—Skaryffe isle (co. Wat. ?), 1687, 3151.
Skarke (co. Wex.), [illegible].
Skarragh, co. Cork. See Scarrough.
Skarrough (co. Cork ?), [illegible].
Skart (Scart, co. Cork), [illegible].
Skart (Scart, co. Kerry ?), 6477.
Skartagh (co. Tip. ?), [illegible].
Skarte (co. Cork), [illegible].
Skarte, co. Wat., [illegible].
Skarteghbeg (Scartbeg, co. Tip. ?), [illegible].
Skart Ebole, co. Cork, [illegible].
Skarte ny gearigh, co. Cork, [illegible].
Skarth (Scart ?), co. Kerry, [illegible], [illegible].
Skart Idonyne (co. Cork ?), [illegible].
Skartie, Thomas ny, heir to, [illegible].
Skarton, co. Lim., [illegible].
Skart Valle Vohogan, co. Cork, [illegible].
Skaryffe isle. See Skariff.
Skassbrick, James, overseer of tanning, [illegible].
Skaurt (Scart ?), co. Wat., 4718.
Skavage (co. Rosc. ?), [illegible].
Skeagh, co. Don. See Skeagh.
Skeagh, co. Down. See Skieghbleidane.
Skeagh—Skeaghe, co. Mon., [illegible], [illegible].
Skeaghe, co. Westm., [illegible].
Skeahanagh, co. Westm. See Skeanagh, Skenaghe.
Skeahanagh (co. Lim. ?), [illegible].
Skealie, Dermodie, Donell, and Donoghe m'Teig ny, pardon, [illegible].
Skeanagh—Skeanrathe, in manor of Carlow, [illegible], [illegible].
Skeanagh — Skeanaghe (Skeahanagh), co. Westm., [illegible], [illegible], [illegible].
Skeanaghe (Skehanagh), Queen's co., [illegible] [illegible].
Skeanagrue, Queen's co., [illegible].
Skeanaghe. See Skeanagh, co. Westm.
Skear, co. Wex., 1743.
Skeave (co. Cork ?), [illegible].
Skeenoor, co. Gal. See Skowgh Coore.
Skeenyle, co. Mon., [illegible].
Skeen, co. Cav., [illegible].
Skeffyn, co. Westm., [illegible].
Skeffyngton, Sir Wm. See Skevington.
Skeghanagh—Skeghanaghe — Skehanaghe (Skehanagh), co. Lim., [illegible], [illegible]; grant, [illegible]. See also Skeghanagh, Skeharagh.
Skeghanaghe (co. Cork or Lim.), [illegible].
Skeghbegge, Half, co. Cork, [illegible].
Skeghen (co. Rosc.), [illegible], [illegible].
Skeqin, co. Rosc., [illegible].
Skeharne, co. Kilk. See Skeghanagh.
Skehanagh, co. Lim. See Shahanaghe, Skeghanagh.
Skeharagh, Queen's co. See Skenaghe.
Skehanye, co. Lim., 1541.
Skeirke (Skirk), Queen's co., [illegible].
Skelligge Michaell—Skelligg michell island, co. Kerry, [illegible], [illegible].
Skelloghe, co. Mayo, [illegible].
Skelocan, co. Mayo, [illegible].
Skelton, Martin, livery, [illegible].
Skelton alias Lynd, Matthew, grant of land, [illegible], [illegible]; pardon, [illegible]; livery to his heir, [illegible].
Skelton rathe—Skeltons rathe, Queen's co., [illegible], [illegible].
Skenaghe (Skeahanagh), co. Westmeath (see Skeanagh), [illegible].
Skene (co. Cork ?), [illegible].
Skeoge, [illegible].
Skerish, co. Dub., [illegible].
Skermore (co. Rosc. ?), [illegible].
Skerne—Skerney (Skerries ?), co. Kild., [illegible], [illegible].
Skerres. See Skerries.
Skerret, Chr., pardon, [illegible].
" Henry fitz Rowland, pardon, [illegible].
Skerries, co. Antrim. See Skirryes.
Skerries—Skerres—Skeryes—Skires—Skiryes—Skyrries, co. Dub., [illegible].
" haven and pier, [illegible].
" See also Skerish, Skerrye.
Skerries, co. Kild. See Skerne.
Skerrye (co. Dub. ?), [illegible].
Skeryes. See Skerries.
Skevenaghe, co. Westmeath, [illegible].
Skevington, sir William, formerly lord deputy, [illegible].
Skowgh Coore (Skecoor), co. Gal., 4718.

INDEX TO FIANTS—ELIZABETH.

Skey, co. Cav., 4594.
Skeyokes (co. Kild. ?), 5148.
Skiagh (Skeagh), co. Donegal, [illegible].
Skieghan (co. Long.), [illegible].
Skieghbaddans (Skeagh ?), co. Down, 4680.
Skiemaughdan, co. Tip., 4617.
Skiddie. See Skiddy.
Skiddmore, Oliver, grant of a wardship, 4180.
Skiddy — Skiddie — Skiddye — Skyddie— Skyddy—Skydy :
„ Andrew. See Skyddy.
„ Clement, pardon, 4858, 6764.
„ Edward, pardon, 5157.
„ Nicholas, license to import wine, 4155; pardon, 6511, 6578, 6762.
„ Richard, bailiff of Cork, pardon, 1885.
„ Roger, chaplain, warden of Youghal, pardon, 1080.
„ Thomas, pardon, 6468.
„ William, pardon, 6085.
Skiffen, co. Westm., 6494.
Skihin, co. Westm., 4857.
Skillenglas — Skillinglas — Skyllenglas, co. Dub., 138, 1891, 4815.
Skimyne. See Lskimyne.
Skinnaherngne, co. Mon. See Skynnaherne.
Skinners-street, Dublin, 1340.
Skirk, Queen's co. See Skeirke.
Skirres. See Skerries.
Skirret, Clement, priest, 5097.
Skirryne port (Skerries, co. Antrim), ganger, &c., of, 1889.
Skn—Skne, co. Sligo, 4346, [illegible].
Skolard, Maurice, pardon, 4643.
Skolbake, co. Wex., 5737.
Skoll, co. Cork, 4469.
Skollie, Dermot, 6414.
„ Katherine, pardon, 6458.
Skollocke (Scollagh, co. Wex. ?), 5581.
Skool, co. Lim. See Skulls.
Skootaghe, Donald m'Owen, attainted, [illegible].
Skormoder, co. Ross., 5712.
Skoll, James, pardon, 6864.
Skowle, Edm., pardon, 1518.
Skraghly (Srahleagh), Queen's co., 1861.
Skreen, co. Meath. See Skryne.
Skreen, co. Sligo. See Skroine.
Skreen, co. Wex. See Skryne.
Skregan, King's co., [illegible], 5611.
Skregge amenaige — Skrege armenarye (co. Donegal or Tyrone), [illegible], 5907.
Skroine, co. Ross. (Skreen, co. Sligo), 4894.
Skrevock (co. Ross. or Leit.), 4828.
Skrevoge, co. Ross., 6567.
Skrihoge (Scrihoge, co. Tip.), [illegible].
Skrin—Skrine. See Skryne.
Skrine, co. Ross. See Skryne.
Skrine. See Skryne, co. Wex.
Skroon alias Ekkarone (Iskaroon, co. Meath), 5940.
Skrubly (co. Cork ?), 7584.
Skryne — Scryne—Skrin—Skrine (Skreen), co. Meath, 185, 898, 870, 885, 434, 1498, 1898, 2878, 2872, 4424, 4461, 5325, 6511, 6671.
„ church, 6767.
„ frankhouse in, 5594.
„ barony, 1894.
„ vicar of, 6384.
„ baron of, Walter Marward, 116, 588, 672, 3008.
Skryne (Skrine ?), co. Ross. 4237, 4941, 5616, 6878.
„ See also Scryne.
Skryne—Skrine (Skreen), co. Wex., rectory, 658, 2682, 4808, 5118, 6081.
Skule, co. Cork, 5618.
Skull, co. Cork, 6518.
Skulls, the two (Skool), co. Lim., 5774.
Skurlock, Barnaby. See Scurlock.
Skurlocke, Walter, queen's attorney, Connaught, 5446. See Scurlock.
Skurlogstown (co. Tip. or Lim.), 6722.
Skurlok—Skurloke, Barnaby. See Scurlock.
Skurloke, Richard, alienation to, 6607. See Scurlock.
Skurlokeston. See Scurlockstown, co. Meath.
Skurr, the, (co. Wex. ?), 6647.
Skyddy — Skiddie — Skiddy — Skiddye — Skyddie, Andrew, recorder of Cork, 1646, 5777; commissions, 887, 2748, 2771, 2843, 2846, 3188, 5489; lease, 895, 1388; grant of land, 884.
Skydy. See Skiddy.
Skyllenglas. See Skillenglas.
Skynnaherne (Skinnaherngne), co. Mon., 4088.
Skyrovan—Skyrowan (Iskaroon, co. Meath), 857, 948. See Eskaroan.
Skyrries. See Skerries.
Skyrvog, co. Ross., 4428.
Slabagh—Slabaghe, David, pardon, 6784, 6142.
„ Edm., pardon, 4408.
„ James, pardon, 6412.
„ Maurice or Murris, pardon, 4142, 6467.
„ Richard, pardon, 2384, 3488.
„ Rich. fitz David, pardon, 6511.
„ Robert, pardon, 6512.
„ William, pardon, 2384, 4467, 6871.
Slabbagh, Ellis, pardon, 6518.
Slabogh, Edm. fitz Tho., pardon, 6478.
„ James fitz Wm., pardon, 6742.
„ Morris m'fits Wm., pardon, 6440.
Slade, John, chirographer, Common Bench, 5870; license of absence, 5948.

INDEX TO FIANTS—ELIZABETH.

Slade—Slaide (co. Wex.), 65.
Slaffnylaston, co. Dub., 1654.
Slafformoly (co. Ros. ?), [illegible].
Slaghtwilliam. *See* Sleightwilliam, co. Long.
Slaide, 65. *See* Slade.
Slaighte M'Oneilan country (the greater part of the present bar. of Upper Castlereagh, co. Down. *See* Reeves, Ecc. Ant., Down, &c., p. 647), 1738.
Slale, co. Wex., [illegible].
Slandaf, [illegible].
Slane, co. Meath, [illegible].
„ barony, martial law, 1415, [illegible].
„ James Fleming, baron of, commissions, 218, 290, 679-81, 834, 643, [illegible], 965, 1120, [illegible]; to give evidence, [illegible]; livery to his heir, [illegible].
Thomas baron of, livery, [illegible]; commissions, [illegible], [illegible], [illegible], [illegible], [illegible], [illegible], [illegible], [illegible], [illegible], [illegible], [illegible]. *See* Fleming, Thomas.
„ baron of, commission, [illegible]; pardon at his suit, [illegible].
Slane, Edmund (of Slanestown, co. Westm.), pardon, [illegible], [illegible].
Slane river (the Slaney), 1178, 2541, [illegible].
Slane, co. Wex., 417.
Slaneston—Slanedown—Slanestown, co. Westm., 1448, [illegible], [illegible], [illegible].
Slaney. *See* Slane.
Slatter, Thomas, English liberty, [illegible].
Slatteragh, Lawrence, pardon, [illegible].
Slatteri, Wm. *See* Slattery, [illegible].
Slattery, Derby, pardon, [illegible].
„ Tho. fitz David, pardon, [illegible].
Slattery—Slatteri, Wm., land in Kilmainham [illegible], [illegible].
Slaught William. *See* Sleightwilliam.
Slavoy, co. Wex., [illegible].
Slawein (co. Westm. ?), [illegible].
Slawinghe — Slawnagh, co. Ross., [illegible], [illegible].
Sleanarbragh. *See* Slowcartry.
Sleaty, Queen's co. *See* Sloyty.
Sleawo (co. Ros. ?), [illegible].
Sleaville (co. Ros. ?), [illegible].
Sleawemanoughe. *See* Slowmanough.
Slehoine—Slehoyn (co. Tip.), [illegible], [illegible].
Slemaine, co. Wex., barony of, [illegible].
Sledge throwing, [illegible].
Sledoff, co. Car., [illegible].
Slengeith (co. Wat. ?), [illegible].
Sleovoharbre. *See* Slewcartry.
Slevowe, co. Mon., [illegible].
Sleyhinly, co. Wat., [illegible].
Sleyre, in O'Many, co. Ros., [illegible].
Sleighicmarybown, in O'Kelly's country, [illegible].
Sleight Coyne, co. Car., 604.
Sleight Donell Clery, in O'Kelly's country, [illegible].
Sleight Donogh O'Loghlyne, co. Clare, [illegible].
Sleight Irryell, co. Clare, 4761.
Sleightllewhinan, in O'Kelly's country, [illegible].
Sleight M'Brien, in O'Kelly's country, [illegible].
Sleight M'Donell, in O'Kelly's country, [illegible].
Sleight Mahon, in O'Kelly's country, [illegible].
Sleight Morish—Slyght Morish, sept of, in Dalton's country, co. Westm., 1618, [illegible].
Sleight O'Morhoe, co. Car., 861.
Sleightowen, in O'Kelly's country, [illegible].
Sleight Shane, in O'Kelly's country, [illegible].
Sleight Shean, co. Car., 604.
Sleightwilliam — Slaghtwilliam — Slaught William—Sleghtwilliam, co. Long.
„ captain, 1708.
„ chief serjeant, 1694.
„ seneschal of, [illegible], [illegible], 4183, [illegible].
Sleivgtaine (co. Cav. ?), [illegible].
Slelogher, co. Lim., mountain, [illegible].
Slelogher, co. Lim., [illegible]. *See* Slevelogher.
Slemarg—Slemargo—Slemargey. *See* Slewmargo
Slemison, co. Tip., 4431.
Sleoughle, Abis ne, co. Tip., [illegible].
Sleowynnery, co. Mayo, [illegible].
Slerolbie — Sclerogho — Sclorabo (Slevoragh. co. Wick. ?), 1387, [illegible], [illegible].
Slevogroth, co. Tip., [illegible].
Slevelogher—Slevloghirye—Slevlogher, co. Kerry (Slieve Loachra or Loughar hills, N.W. of Castleisland), [illegible], [illegible]. *See also* Slelogher.
Slevumish—Slevemisho (Slieve Mish), co. Kerry, [illegible].
Slevloghar. *See* Slevelogher.
Slevmarg. *See* Slewmargo.
Slevye (co. Wex. or Car. ?), [illegible].
Slew (co. Ros. ?), 4779.
Slewartry, co. Gal., [illegible].
Slewban. *See* Slewbran.
Slewcartry. *See* Slowcartry.
Slewnoil. *See* Slewnoid.
Slewdonarde (Slieve Donard, co. Down), [illegible].
Slewelmane—Slewban, co. Ros., [illegible], [illegible].
Slewnoid — Slewnoil (perhaps Slieve Gadoe mountain, co. Wick.), [illegible], [illegible].
Slewemargo. *See* Slewmargo.
Slewin, [illegible].
Slew Invroy, co. Mayo, [illegible].
Slewmargo—Slemarg — Slemargo—Slemargey—Slevmarg—Slewemargo—Slowmargo (Slievemargy barony), Queen's co., [illegible], [illegible], [illegible]; bounds of, [illegible]; sometime in possession of Walter Peppard, [illegible]; grant

INDEX TO FIANTS—ELIZABETH.

Slewmarge:
of land in, 505, 508, 511, 518, 572, 590, 533-4, 540, 1946, [illegible], 6157, [illegible]; surrender of lands, 6748; indenture as to lands in, 6749.
Slewnymanwyne in Mourne mountains, 4237.
Slewsancough—Slewseancoghe—Slyowshanneknogh, co. Gal., [illegible].
" house of friars of S. Francis Issued, 5467, [illegible].
Slewshan Uowo (co. Gal. ?), 5758.
Slewys, co. Westm., 283.
Sleycarbery. See Sliewcarbry.
Sleyty—Sleytye (Slenty), Queen's co., 539, [illegible].
" vector of, 603.
Sliddery river, co. Down. See Brunshe.
Slievardagh, co. Tip. See Slivardagh.
Slievcarbragh, co. Long. See Mount Carbre.
Slieve Donard, co. Down. See Slewdonorthe.
Slieve Gadon, co. Wick. See Slewcoul.
Slievelairnugh mountain, co. Kerry, 5042.
Slieve Luachra. See Slevaloghry.
Slievemargy, Queen's co. See Slewmarge.
Slieve mish, co. Kerry, 5042.
Sliev en torm (co. Leit. ?), 8112.
Slieve gwearriene (co. Cork ?), 1868.
Slievrough, co. Wick. See Slerothie.
Slieve roe, co. Kild. See Redd mountain.
Slievglahe (co. Cav. ?), 5567.
Sliewcarbry—Sleevcharbre—Slewcarbry—Sleycarbery—Sincarbrey (a district in barony of Granard. The Slewcarbragh mountains are marked on Petty's map in this barony near the boundary of the barony of Longford), co. Long., [illegible], [illegible], 5107, 5112, 6857. See also Mount Carbre.
Sligagh—Sligaghe—Sligaughe. See Sligo.
Slight ny Ivelles country, co. Down, 4237.
Slight vic Tibbot, lands of, in barony of Kilmaine, co. Mayo, 4773.
Sligo—Sligagh—Sligaghe—Sligaughe—Sligon—Sligoo, 4460-1-2, 4704, 4783, [illegible], 5434, 5504, [illegible], 5315, 5848.
" castle, betrayal and treasonable taking of, 4846, 4771.
" supervisor of port, [illegible].
" collector of wine duty, 5745, 5414, 5446, [illegible], 5461, 8042.
" controller of wine duty, [illegible], [illegible], 6617.
" county, commission to form county, 1873; men of, pardoned, 4638, &c.; crimes outside excepted from pardon, 5797.
" county, commission to prosecute rebel, 6378.
" county, sheriff, 4447.
Slivardagh (Slievardagh), co. Tip., 5087.
Slive Brennagh, co. Kilk. (see Walshe mountain), 2038.
Slivglaghe (co. Cav. ?), 5567.
Slobiston—Slobleiston, co. Wex., 4081, 6194.
Slought, abbey of, co. Tip., 6704.
Slough Cahell I Madden, co. Gal., 4718.
Slough Cahell Leye, co. Gal., 4718.
Slough Dermode Kowgh, co. Gal., 4718.
Slough Donell I Madden, co. Gal., 4718.
Slough Donell ogo, in O'Maddens country, co. Gal., 4718.
Sloughe Cahell, co. Gal., 4718.
Sloughe Callow O'Madden, co. Gal., 4718.
Sloughe M'e Cowlye, co. Gal., 4718.
Sloughe M'Shane, co. Gal., 4718.
Sloughe Molaghlin, co. Gal., 4718.
Slough M'e Cara, co. Gal., 4718.
Slough M'Coghla, co. Gal., 4718.
Slough M'e Colaghan, co. Gal., 4718.
Slough M'e Keoghe, co. Gal., 4718.
Slough Mollrona, co. Gal., 4718.
Slough Morogh I Madden, co. Gal., 4718.
Slough Morough duff I Madden, co. Gal., 4718.
Slough Owen I Madden, co. Gal., 4718.
Slough Shane I Madden, co. Gal., 4718.
Slncarbrey (see Sliewcarbry), [illegible].
Slneghtvicteigh (co. Lim. ?), 6504.
Slue (co. Gal. ?) (see Slywe), 4783.
Slught Rowry roe O'Flartie, territories of, co. Gal., [illegible].
Slughtwilliam O'Ferrall. See Sleightwilliam
Slullis (co. Ross. ?), 4340.
Slyeveloghnie (Slieve Logher), co. Kerry, 8042.
Slyeveamishe (Slieve Mish mountains), co. Kerry, 5045.
Slyeve O'Lone—Slyeveolone, co. Mayo, [illegible], 4902.
Slyewshanneknogh. See Slewsancough.
Slyght Morish. See Sleight Morish.
Slywe (co. Gal. ?), 1894.
Slywe leranile, 5497.
Smale more—Smalmore, co. Kild., common of, 463, 1858, 2080.
Smart, Patrick, messuage in Trim, 1714.
Smarte, Patrick, messuage in Trim, 1714.
Smerewicke. See Smerewicke.
Smeremore. See Smermore.
Smerewicke—Smeerewicke (Smerwick), co. Kerry, grant, [illegible]; port, 4858.
Smermore—Smeremore—Swermore alias Smermoth, co. Louth, 1394, 6159; manor, 6899.
" rectory, 9452.
Smerwick, co. Kerry. See Smerewicke.
Smith, Art, pardon, 5711.
" David fitz Davy, pardon, 5711.
" Dowaltagh fitz Gillduff, pardon, 5711.

INDEX TO FIANTS—ELIZABETH.

Smith, Fardorogh, pardon, [illegible].
,, Henry, pardon, [illegible], 6711.
,, Hugh, pardon, 6711.
,, alias Gowe, James, pardon, [illegible].
,, Jenkin, pardon, 6711.
,, John (—Smythe), premises in Trim, 1714, [illegible].
,, John, rector of Kilmaboy, [illegible].
,, John, pardon, [illegible].
,, John, saddler of the ordnance, [illegible].
,, Martin, pardon, [illegible]; son of, [illegible].
,, Matthew (—Smyth), commissioner in Ulster, [illegible]; pardon, [illegible]; land valued by, [illegible].
,, capt. Nathaniel (—Smithe—Smyth—Smythe), provost marshal of Connaught, [illegible], [illegible], [illegible]; commissions, [illegible], [illegible], 6180, [illegible], [illegible], [illegible], [illegible]; pardon, [illegible], [illegible]; horse lately under his command, [illegible]; his lieutenant, [illegible].
,, Nicholas, vicar of Balrath, [illegible].
,, Owyne (in co. Down), pardon, 6711.
,, Patrick, pardon, 6711.
,, Rowry, pardon, 6711.
,, Shane, pardon, [illegible].
,, sir Thomas (Smyth — Smythe), principal secretary in England, colonel of soldiers in the Ards, 2140; commissions, 2140, 2487.
,, Thomas (son of preceding), colonel of soldiers in the Ards, 2140; commission, 2140; deceased, 2487.
,, Thomas, pardon, [illegible].
,, William, pardon, [illegible], [illegible], [illegible], [illegible], [illegible].
Smithe, Dermote, land in Kilkenny, [illegible].
,, alias M'Iguyne, John, license, [illegible].
,, Nathaniel. See Smith.
,, Thomas, alderman of Dublin, [illegible].
Smithes, Jasan. See Smythes.
Smithe's — Smyth — Smythe's meadow, at Duleek, co. Meath, [illegible], [illegible], [illegible], [illegible].
Smithestone. See Smithestowne, co. Wex.
Smithestowne, co. Kilk., [illegible].
Smithestowne—Smithestone—Smythestowne, co. Wex., 417, 1060, [illegible].
Smithston, King's co., [illegible].
Smithstown, co. Meath. See Smythestowne.
Smithstowne—Smythestown, co. Clare, [illegible], [illegible].
Smorte, co. Wat., [illegible].
Smoutrone, [illegible].
Smutinagh, co. Mayo. See Shrutinagh.
Smythe, Katherine nyn Robert, pardon, [illegible].
,, Robert, pardon, [illegible].
Smytche, Tho., pardon, [illegible].
Smyth, Edm., pardon, [illegible].
Smyth, Henry (—Smythe), chief serjeant, co. Kildare, 1078, 3110, [illegible].
,, Henry, pardon, [illegible].
,, John, pardon, [illegible].
,, Matthew. See Smith.
,, Morgan, pardon, [illegible].
,, Nathaniel. See Smith.
,, Robert, pardon, 1184, [illegible].
,, Stephen, [illegible].
,, Thomas. See Smith.
Smythe, Edward, pension, [illegible].
,, Henry. See Smyth.
,, John. See Smith.
,, (alias O'Gowe), Moriertagh, pardon, [illegible].
,, Nathaniel. See Smith.
,, (alias Rolande), Robert, [illegible].
,, Thomas. See Smith.
,, (alias Davenport), William, controller of customs, Dublin, [illegible].
Smythes—Smithes, Jasan, solicitor general, [illegible], [illegible], [illegible]; chief justice of Munster, [illegible], [illegible]; commissions, [illegible], [illegible], [illegible], [illegible], [illegible], [illegible], [illegible], [illegible], [illegible].
Smythe's — Smyth's meadow. See Smithe's meadow.
Smythestom. See Smythestowne.
Smythestowne, alias Ballinegowne (co. Wat.), [illegible].
Smythestown. See Smithstowne.
Smythestowne—Smythestone (Smithstown), co. Meath, [illegible], [illegible].
Smythestowne. See Smithestowne.
Smythson, Edward fitz Hugh M'Egowne, pardon, [illegible].
,, Maurice, pardon, [illegible].
Snagg—Snagge, Thomas, attorney general, [illegible], [illegible]; commissions, [illegible], [illegible], [illegible].
Snakeel, co. Cav. See Snavekill.
Snaighten, Donogh O'Graddey, pardon, [illegible].
Snavekill—Snawekele (Snakeel?), co. Cav., [illegible], [illegible].
Snaveloghor (co. Cav.), [illegible].
Snawekele. See Snavekill.
Snawewille weir on Shannon, [illegible].
Soggan (co. Gal.?), rectory, [illegible].
Sogrwe, Conoghor m'Donogh I, pardon, [illegible].
Solobolibeg. See Sologhod beg.
Soloboyed—Soloone—Solooyd. See Sologhod.
Soldiers, not to leave their appointed places on pain of death, [illegible]; marshals court for punishment of, [illegible]; extortion and outrage by, to be punished by martial law, [illegible]; pay and allowances, 1211, [illegible], [illegible], [illegible], [illegible]; great defects in bands of, [illegible]; impressed for queen's ships, [illegible], [illegible]; to be maintained by Irish chiefs, [illegible], [illegible], [illegible]; to be cessed on co. Tipperary, [illegible]. See Army.

INDEX TO FIANTS—ELIZABETH.

Soleghed. *See* Solloghod.
Solovan, Tho., pardon, 4114.
Solovane, Donell, pardon, [illegible].
" John m'Dermod I., pardon, [illegible].
Solovant, Shane m'Dermod I., pardon, [illegible].
Solgbod—Solgose. *See* Solloghod.
Solicitor, principal or chief, James Dowdall, [illegible]; Lucas Dillon, 789; Nich. Nugent, [illegible]; John Bathe, [illegible]; Richard Beling, [illegible].
" general, John Bathe, [illegible]; Richard Finglas, [illegible]; Richard Beling, [illegible].
" chief or principal solicitor-general James Smythes, [illegible], 4477; Roger Wilbraham, [illegible].
Solicitor general, ex-officio commissioner of Ulster, [illegible].
Solivan, Conor and Donell m'Donogho Y., pardon, [illegible].
Solloidbegg. *See* Sollogbodbeg.
Solloyd. *See* Solloghod.
Solloydbegg. *See* Sollogbodbeg.
Solloyde — Sollichede — Sollihold. *See* Solloghod.
Sollivane, Beale ny, pardon, 6477.
Sollochad, John, pardon, [illegible].
Solloghod—Salighede — Balleghede — Salleoheide—Shaloihede—Solohoyd—Solocte—Solcoyd—Soleghed — Solghot — Solgote — Solloyd — Sollnyde — Sollichede — Sollihold — Solohed — Solohed — Sallucoyd, co. Tip., [illegible], [illegible], [illegible], [illegible], [illegible], [illegible], 4743, [illegible], [illegible], [illegible], [illegible], [illegible], [illegible], [illegible], [illegible]; rectory, 1042, [illegible].
Solloghod beg—Salloghed beg—Solchold beg—Solloid begg—Solloyd begg—Sollochold beg, co. Tip., 4732, [illegible], [illegible], [illegible], [illegible], [illegible].
Solloms (Sollims ?), co. Kild., 6787.
Sollowe, Wm., pardon, 6417.
Sololand. *See* Solloghod.
Somerston, co. Meath, [illegible].
Somersetshire, undertakers for Munster lands from, [illegible], [illegible].
Somerton, Edw., serjeant at laws, [illegible].
Somerton, in Somersetshire, [illegible].
Somaghe. *See* Sonnagh.
Sonnelon (co. Cork ?), [illegible].
Sonnagh (co. Cork ?), [illegible].
Sonnagh—Sonnaghe—Sonnaghe—Sonnagh I.—Sonnaugh—Sonnoghe, co. Westm., [illegible], [illegible], [illegible], [illegible], [illegible], [illegible], [illegible], [illegible], [illegible]; rectory, [illegible], [illegible].
Sonnaghe (co. Long. ?), [illegible].
Sonugan, Peter, pardon, [illegible].
Soore—Sore, Edward, constable of Longford castle, 3148, [illegible]; commissions, 3148, [illegible]; pardon, [illegible]; grant of land, [illegible]; wardship of his heir, [illegible].
Soure, Margery, [illegible].
" William, wardship, [illegible].
Sore, city in Germany, [illegible].
Sorhin—Sorren, illegal Irish exaction, 2771, [illegible], [illegible].
Sorley boy. *See* M'Connell.
Sorren. *See* Sorhin.
Sotche, John. *See* Zouche.
Soughaginneylaghe (co. Rosc. ?), [illegible].
Sourdowliston, [illegible]. *See* Surdalston.
Sowche, John. *See* Zouche.
Sowder (Ballynamuddery, co. Westm. ?), [illegible].
Sowlerwood, co. Kild., [illegible].
Sowlina, co. Cav., [illegible].
Sowlyvane, Shane m'Donell I., and others of the same, pardoned, [illegible].
Sowny, Donogho m'Dermody ny, pardon, [illegible].
Spackman, Nicholas, wardship &c., grant, [illegible].
Spain, wine trade, [illegible], [illegible], [illegible], [illegible], [illegible], [illegible], [illegible].
" wheat not to be exported to, [illegible].
" king of, designation of subject of, [illegible]; ship belonging to subjects seized, [illegible]; Daventry delivered to, [illegible].
Spainagh—Spaynagh, Donell (Cavanagh), pardon, [illegible], [illegible], [illegible]. *See* Cavanagh.
Spaniard, designation of a, [illegible].
" trade with, [illegible], 1711.
Spanish ship seized, [illegible], [illegible].
Spart Ardoblmire, co. Cav., [illegible].
Spaynagh, Donell. *See* Spainagh.
Spayniard. *See* Spaniard.
Spear, borne by county levies, [illegible].
Spearman or scolors, [illegible].
Spedell (Spiddle), co. Gal., [illegible], [illegible].
Spelane, Tho. (alias Spensfeld), [illegible].
Spencer, Edm. *See* Spenser.
" William, [illegible], [illegible], [illegible].
Spencerscroke, co. Louth, [illegible].
Spensfeld—Spensfelde, Thomas. *See* Spensfeld.
Spending and cutting of the lords to be compounded for rent, [illegible].
Spenser, James, constable, Limerick castle, [illegible].
Spenser, Edmund, secretary to the lord deputy, registrar in Chancery for faculties, [illegible]; leases, [illegible], [illegible], [illegible]; grant of lands, [illegible]; commissions, [illegible], [illegible].
Spensfeld—Spensfeld—Spensfelde — Spensfelde—Spyrsfeld, Thomas, learned in the law, official of Meath, [illegible]; commissions, [illegible], [illegible], [illegible], [illegible], [illegible], [illegible], [illegible].
Spicery, trade in, [illegible].
Spices stolen, [illegible].
Spiddle, co. Gal. *See* Spedell, Serpdell.
Spidell (co. Gal. ?), [illegible].

INDEX TO FIANTS.—ELIZABETH.

Spike island, co. Cork. *See* Inyspicke.
Spinan in Emale (Spinans, co. Wick.), 5111.
Spincer, Giles ny Flyn, pardon, [illegible].
Spinner, John fitz Rich., pardon, [illegible].
Spinster, description of a wife, 1818.
Spittal, co. Lim., [illegible].
Spittle house. *See* Spittell.
Spittell (co. Cork), 4157-8.
Spittell—Spittle—Spittle houses (Spital or Hospital).
„ at Ardfert, [illegible].
„ Carrickfergus, [illegible], [illegible].
„ Kinsale, [illegible].
„ Mullingar, [illegible], [illegible], [illegible].
„ *See* Athlone.
Spittle houses (Leper Hospitals), [illegible], [illegible].
Sprakstown, co. Kild. *See* Balliesparte.
Springe, Cheshire, [illegible].
Springe, Elizabeth (alias Ithiel), pardon, 6314.
„ Susan, pardon, 6314.
„ —Spryngs, Thomas, controller of customs, [illegible]; constable of Castlemaigne, [illegible], [illegible], [illegible], [illegible]; commissions, [illegible], [illegible]; pardon, [illegible]; leases, [illegible], 6314.
Springer, Wm., pardon, [illegible].
Spryngs, Edw., pardon, [illegible].
„ Tho. *See* Springe.
Spydell (co. Gal. ?), [illegible].
Spyrefeild, Thomas. *See* Sparefeild.
Spynery, Dermot, alias O'Calliglann, pardon, [illegible].
Sracurra, King's co., 1767.
Srachtaleare (co. Ferm. ?), [illegible].
Sracullen, Queen's co. *See* Shracullin.
Sracnewre (Sracnure), King's co., [illegible], [illegible].
Sragh (co. Tip. ?), [illegible].
Sraghicktll—Sraghickyll, King's co., [illegible], [illegible].
Sraghfinor, co. Long., [illegible].
Sraghmahon, King's co., [illegible], [illegible].
Sraghmulleghroe, King's co., [illegible], [illegible].
Srah, [illegible].
Srah, Queen's co. *See* Shragh.
Srahe, illegal custom, [illegible].
Srahe (co. Westm. ?), [illegible].
Srahleagh, Queen's co. *See* Shraghly.
Srahleagh, Queen's co., [illegible].
Srahy (co. Westm. ?), [illegible].
Srahe in the Morroe, co. Wex., [illegible].
Sranagh, Queen's co., [illegible].
Sranelaghan, co. Kild., [illegible], [illegible].
Sranure, King's co. *See* Shranenover, Sranewre.
Srathuar (co. Tyrone ?), [illegible].
Sraughandonl, co. Car., [illegible].
Sraun, Patr., pardon, [illegible].
Srembury, Queen's co., [illegible].
Sroha. *See* Strahee, 1347.
Srohow, co. Car. (see Struhee), [illegible].
Sroll (co. Tip. ?), [illegible].
Sromhmaollaghe — Srothamollaghe (co. Wick. ?), [illegible], [illegible].
Srowlar. *See* Shrowre, co. Mayo.
Srohar. *See* Shrohar, co. Long.
Sroine (co. Kild. ?), [illegible].
Sromkelly. *See* Strongally.
Sronkelly—Sronkally. *See* Strongally.
Sronell—Sronill—Sronyll (Shronell, co. Tip.), [illegible], [illegible], [illegible], [illegible], [illegible], [illegible], [illegible], [illegible], [illegible], [illegible], [illegible], [illegible]; rectory, [illegible]. *See* Stranis.
Sroncoman, co. Lim., [illegible].
Sronemonlagh, Queen's co., brook, [illegible].
Sronill—Sronyll. *See* Sronell.
Srothamollaghe, [illegible]. *See* Sroghmaollaghe.
Sroner. *See* Sroure.
Sroughboe, co. Car., [illegible].
Srower, co. Long., [illegible].
Srowher—Srowir. *See* Shrowre.
Srowle (co. Car. ?), [illegible].
Srowrobeg (Shrule ?), co. Gal., [illegible].
Sruffane (co. Cork), [illegible].
Srughan Rovagh—Srughan Rlavagh brook (co. Donegal), [illegible], [illegible].
Sruhill, co. Long., [illegible].
Sruhir, co. Long., land and vicarage, [illegible].
Sruro—Sruuer (Shrule, co. Long.), rectory, [illegible], [illegible], [illegible], [illegible], [illegible].
Stabally (Stradbally), Queen's co., [illegible].
Stabannan—Stabanon (Stabannan), co. Louth, [illegible], [illegible], [illegible].
Stable, the Deputy's, surveyor of, [illegible].
Stablerstown (co. Car. ?), [illegible].
Stablerstown, co. Kild., [illegible], [illegible].
Stablerstown (Stapolstown), co. Kild., [illegible], [illegible], [illegible].
Stacule (co. Kilk. ?), [illegible].
Stacallan — Stacallon — Stacallne (Stackallan), co. Meath, [illegible], [illegible], [illegible].
Stacbold. *See* Stackbold.
Stacboldton, Redm. fitz Edm., pardon, [illegible].
Stacboll, Redmund, pardon, [illegible]. *See* Stackbold.
Staccallen. *See* Stacallan.
Stacock, Morris, pardon, [illegible].
Stacooll. *See* Stacoll.
Stacre, John, summonister of the Exchequer, [illegible], [illegible].
Stack—Stacke:
„ Anslace, pardon, [illegible].
„ Edm. gancagh fitz Gerrald oge, pardon, [illegible].
„ Edm. fitz Morice, pardon, [illegible], [illegible].
„ Edm. fitz Morice fitz Redmond, pardon, [illegible].

INDEX TO FIANTS—ELIZABETH.

Stack, Edm. fitz Robert, pardon, [illegible].
„ Edm. fitz Wm., pardon, [illegible].
„ Edm. m'Rob, pardon, [illegible], 6497.
„ Garred fitz Redmond, pardon, 6457.
„ Garrett duff, pardon, 6494.
„ Garrett fitz James, pardon, 6494.
„ Garrot og, pardon, 6158.
„ Gerald gancaghe, pardon, [illegible].
„ Gerald fitz Philip, pardon, [illegible].
„ Gerald fitz Robert, pardon, 6182.
„ Gerald m'Morris, pardon, 6183.
„ Gerrad roe fitz Rekard fitz James oge, pardon, 6457.
„ Gerrot oge roe (of Listowel), pardon, [illegible].
„ Gerrot m'Moriah, pardon, [illegible].
„ Gerrot m'Tho., pardon, 6497.
„ James, pardon, [illegible].
„ James duffe, pardon, 6578, 6177.
„ James m'Morris or fitz Morice, pardon, 6182, [illegible].
„ James fitz Rickard or m'Rykard, pardon, [illegible], [illegible].
„ James m'Shane, pardon, [illegible].
„ John, priest, pardon, 6182.
„ John, pardon, [illegible].
„ John fitz James, pardon, 6457.
„ John m'Garrot, pardon, [illegible], 6497.
„ John m'Morris, pardon, [illegible], 6457.
„ John m'Richard duffe, pardon, 6457.
„ John m'Robert, pardon, [illegible].
„ John m'Tho., pardon, [illegible], 6497.
„ John ne brcicke, pardon, 6457.
„ Maurice, pardon, 6457.
„ Maurice, pardon, 6183.
„ Maurice fitz Gerald oge, attainted, [illegible], [illegible].
„ Maurice fitz Moris fitz Gerrote oge Stake, pardon, [illegible].
„ Maurice gancaghe, pardon, [illegible], 6457, 6110.
„ Moriah m'Ricard, pardon, [illegible].
„ Morrice fitz Redmund, pardon, 6457.
„ Morris oge, pardon, [illegible], [illegible].
„ Philip, pardon, [illegible].
„ Philip negallagh, pardon, [illegible].
„ Philip fitz Rich. fitz John, pardon, 6457.
„ Philip m'Rich., pardon, [illegible], 6497.
„ Richard, pardon, [illegible].
„ alias Totan, Richard, pardon, 6457.
„ Rob. fitz Garret duff, pardon, 6494.
„ Rob. m'Edm., pardon, 6497.
„ Rob. m'Garrett oge, pardon, 6457.
„ Rob. m'James, pardon, [illegible].
„ Rob. m'Rickard duf, pardon, [illegible].
„ Rob. oge, pardon, [illegible], 6497.
„ Thomas, pardon, [illegible], [illegible], [illegible], [illegible], 6497.
Stack, Thomas schoolis, pardon, 6457.
„ Tho. garve, pardon, 6457.
„ Tho. fitz Gerott, pardon, [illegible].
„ Tho. fitz John, pardon, [illegible].
„ Tho. fitz Wm., pardon, [illegible].
„ Tho. m'James m'Rich., pardon, 6477.
„ Tho. m'Morice, pardon, [illegible].
„ Tho. m'Wm., pardon, 6477.
„ Tho. m'Wm. m'Rich., pardon, 6477.
„ Tho. oge fitz Tho. fitz Ricard duffe, pardon, 6457.
„ Tho. oge fitz Tho. fitz Ricard oge, pardon, 6457.
„ Tho. fitz Morice fitz Ricard duffe, pardon, 6457.
„ Tho. fitz Morice ne manesiragh, pardon, 6457.
„ Tho. fitz Wm., pardon, 6457.
„ Wm. bag, pardon, [illegible].
„ Wm. fitz Nicholas, pardon, [illegible].
„ Wm. fitz Rich. fitz John, pardon, 6457.
„ Wm. kinghe, attainted, [illegible], [illegible].
„ Wm. tegan, pardon, 6457.
„ *See* Stak.
Stackaboll, Redmond, pardon, 1818.
Stackmaleighe (co. Car.?), [illegible].
Stackallen, co. Meath. *See* Stacallan.
Stackbold—Stacbold—Stacboll—Stackbolle—Stackbole—Stackbould—Stackebold:
„ Edmund, archdeacon of Cashel, [illegible].
„ Edm., pardon, [illegible].
„ Edm. fitz Hibberd, pardon, [illegible].
„ Edm. fitz Richard, pardon, [illegible].
„ James, pardon, [illegible], [illegible], [illegible].
„ John, pardon, [illegible], [illegible], 1297, [illegible].
„ Patr. fitz Redmond, pardon, [illegible].
„ Peirs, pardon, [illegible].
„ Peirs fitz Theobald, pardon, [illegible].
„ Philip fitz Rich., pardon, [illegible], [illegible].
„ Redmond, pardon, [illegible], [illegible].
„ Richard, chaplain, [illegible].
„ Rich., pardon, [illegible], [illegible].
„ Rich. fitz John, pardon, [illegible], [illegible].
„ Theobald, pardon, 1297, [illegible], [illegible].
„ Theobald fitz Pers, pardon, [illegible].
„ Theobald fitz Richard, pardon, [illegible], [illegible].
„ Thomas fitz Richard, pardon, [illegible].
„ Thomas fitz Robert, pardon, [illegible], [illegible].
„ Walter, pardon, [illegible], [illegible].

INDEX TO FIANTS.—ELIZABETH.

Stackbold, William, dean of Cashel, [illegible].
" Wm., pardon, 4463.
" See Stackpole, Stacpoll.
Stackbole. See Stackbold.
Stackbould, James fitz Redmund. See Stackbold.
Stackbowe, Hobbert, [illegible].
Stacke. See Stack.
Stackebold. See Stackbold.
Stackally (co. Kilk. or Tip.), 6778.
Stackepole, Walter, pardon, 4627.
Stackpoll, Wm., pardon, 4671.
Stackpooll, Patrick, pardon, 1034.
Stackmilighe (co. Car. ?), [illegible].
Stacoll—Stacolt (Stotkhole ?), co. Dub., 1238, [illegible], [illegible], 4614.
Stacom—Stacon, co. Westmeath, 944, 1954.
Stacomney—Stacoony—Stacony—Stacumny (Stacumny), co. Kild., 443, 1528, [illegible], 4386.
Stacon. See Stacom.
Stacoony—Stacony alias Stacoony. See Stacumney.
Stacpoll, James ryoghe, pardon, 1094.
Stacumny, co. Kild. See Stacomney.
Stacy, Rich., pardon, 5744.
Stadall, co. Meath. See Saydall.
Staferton (Tyfarnham), co. Westm., rectory, 427, 5762.
Staffordston. See Staffordeston.
Stafford—Staforde:
" Constance, 6754.
" Francis (afterwards knight), governor of Clandeboy, &c., 4767, [illegible]; to deliver up the constableship of Dunlare, 4884; commissions, 5135, [illegible], 6428, 6877, [illegible].
" Henry, constable of Dungarvan, 89; sheriff of Waterford, 144, 718; member of parliament for Dungarvan, 129; commissions, 58, [illegible], [illegible]-7, 1013; pardon, 284, [illegible], 714; lease, 672.
" John, clerk, pardon, [illegible].
" Nich., chancellor of Ferns, made bishop of Ferns and Leighlin, 4479-4.
" Philip, pardon, [illegible].
" Richard, pardon, 1748, 6787.
" Rob., pardon, [illegible].
" Tho., pardon, 4[illegible], 6787.
" Wm., [illegible].
Staffordeston—Staffardston—Staffordistone, co. Meath, 1784, [illegible], 4709; rectory, 5716.
Staffordshire, undertaker from, [illegible].
Staford, Tho., pardon, 4447.
Stagobb—Stagobbe (Astagob), co. Dublin, 1238, [illegible].
Stagony—Stagonny, co. Dub., 1468, 5134, [illegible]. See Tigony.
Stagroman (Stagroonan), co. Meath, 1465, [illegible].
Stahonny or Harlestowne, co. Dub., 1273, [illegible].
Stahalmock—Stahalmok—Stahalmoke—Stahalmock (Staholmog), co. Meath, [illegible], [illegible], 6374; rectory, 5718.
Staine, at Dublin, 1462.
Staines, Richard. See Stayne.
Stak, James, pardon, 6184.
" Tho., pardon, 6484.
Stakillene—Stakyllen (Stickillen, co. Louth), 1723.
Stakillin, co. Wex., 417.
Stakin alias Tobin, John, pardon, 4173.
Stakyllen. See Stakillene.
Stalcban (Nowtowntalaban), co. Louth, [illegible].
Stalingo (Staffoon), co. Meath, [illegible].
Stalorgan (Stallorgan), co. Dub., 4[illegible], [illegible], 1123, 1786, 5406.
Stamacartie rectory, co. Kilk., 872.
Stamaine—Stamyn, Great, (Stamen), co. Meath, 1499, 5942.
Stamaine—Stamyn, Little, (Stamen), co. Meath, 1440, 5443.
Stamcartie—Stamcarty—Stammacartie—Stamcartie—Stomcartie (Stamcartby) co. Kilk., 4[illegible], 5434; rectory, 5334, 5[illegible].
Stamenes (Stamen, co. Meath), [illegible]. See Stamaine.
Stamkarie, co. Kilk., 4848.
Stammacartie (see Stamcartie), 4544.
Stamollen — Stamollen (Stamullin), co. Meath, 5475; rectory, 1448, 5504.
" vicar of, 5471.
Stamyn, great. See Stamaine.
Stamyn, little. See Stamaine.
Stancartie. See Stamcartie.
Standard, Henry, pardon, 5574.
Standeforde, Henry, pardon, 4874.
Standard (queen's) in general hosting borne by O'Molloy, 1877, 5463-40.
Stanelon, Anthony, knt., pension, [illegible].
Stanelsho, John, archdeacon of Glendalough, pardon, 158; license of absence, 158, 445.
Stanelley. See Stanley.
Standon, Patr., pardon, 5534.
Stanehurst, James. See Stanyhurst.
Staneley, George, knt. See Stanley.
Stang of land, 4787, 5572.
Stangaraghe (Stangaragh, co. Dub.), 4148.
Stangarde (co. Mayo ?), 5486;
Stangford, Tho., pardon, 5414.
Stanihurst—Staniburste. See Stanyhurst.

INDEX TO FIANTS—ELIZABETH.

Stanbords, Dermot, alias O'Quynnyne, pardon, 482.

Stanley — Standley — Stanely — Stanlaye — Stanly:

Agnes (alias **Salsbury**), livery, 5090.

sir George, knight, marshal of the army, 306, 561; takes oath of supremacy, 217; commissions, 189, 198, 224, 225, 260, 283-4, 395, 462, 586, 694, 722, 1780; pardon, 67, 211, 5461; leases, 168, 314, 488.

Giles or Egidius, pursuivant at arms, 5909-10.

Henry, leases, 3447, 5396; livery to his sister, 5090.

John, pardon, 243.

John, messuage in Trim, 1714.

John, pardon of intrusion, 6006.

Walter, homicide of, 743.

sir William, knight, master of the ordnance, 5871; commissions, 4454, 4429, 4715; lease, 4715, 6814; outlawed, 5879; his treason, 5846.

Stanyhurstc, Henry. See Stanyhurst.

Stanry, Tho., pardon, 6875.

Stanton, Kvine, pardon, 6675.

" John, pardon, 5624.

" m'Ivylly, pardon (see Stanton, William), 2528.

" Miles fitzMiles, 5945.

" Moriagh, pardon, 5536.

" Nich., pardon, 4107, 5882.

" Patr., pardon, 6480.

" Ricard m'Wm. m'Walter, pardon, 6675.

" Rich., pardon for murder of, 2298, 5523.

" Rich. m'Shane boye, pardon, 5736.

" Tho., pardon, 5675.

" Walter roogh m'Wm., pardon, 6675.

" William (alias M'Ivylly—M'Ivilo—M'Iuylly), pardon, 2528, 3674, 5701.

" Wm. oge m'Wm. m'Walter, pardon, 6675.

Stanton alias Stanton, Wm., 6030.

Stanyerstowne, co. Kilk., 806.

Stanyhurst — Stanihurst — Stanihurste — Stanyhurstc:

Henry, lease, 2454; deputy valour for first fruits, 4817.

James, clerk of the parliament, 164, 1349; clerk of the crown in chancery, 237, 2982; seneschal of Kilcon, &c., 175, 217; recorder of Dublin, 842; master in chancery, 680, 3157, 3619, 3749, 4080; late customer of Dublin, 2805; late general escheator, 2763; takes oath of supremacy, 227; commissions, 542, 2325; leases, 806-7, 935, 2833-40, 5836.

Nicholas, late clerk of crown and hanaper, 2353, 5346; lease recited, 307, 5738, 5679.

" Walter, pardon, 2831.

Staple, granted to Carlingford, 1781, **Carrickfergus**, 1802.

Staplestown (co. Car. ?), 6275.

Staplestown, co. Kild. or Car., 6715.

Staplestown, co. Kild. See Stablerstown.

Stapleton (Steeplestown), co. Meath, 85.

Stapleton, Edm., pardon, 6455, 6619.

" Edm. fitz Redmund, pardon, 6449.

" Edm. more, pardon, 5698.

" Edm. oge, pardon, 5561.

" James, pardon, 6708.

" James fitz Redmund, pardon, 6495.

" James fitz Rich., pardon, 5562.

" John, pardon, 6558.

" John fitz Redmund, pardon, 6449.

" Patrick, pardon, 6443, 5708.

" Patr. fitz Redmond, pardon, 6475.

" Patr. fitz Walter, pardon, 6598.

" Patr. roe, pardon, 6521.

" Peirs, pardon, 6442, 6519.

" Peter, pardon, 6706.

" Redmund, pardon, 4435.

" Richard, pardon, 6534, 6545.

" Rich. fitz Hubert, pardon, 4585.

" Rich. fitz John, pardon, 6706.

" Rich. roe, pardon, 5706.

" Robert, pardon, 6442.

" Sawe, pardon, 4548.

" Thomas, pardon, 5584.

" Tho. fitz Rob. gankagh, pardon, 6488.

" Walter, pardon, 6443, 5708.

" Walter m'Edm. (or Stappelton), pardon, 4507, 6594.

" Walter roe, pardon, 4706.

" William, pardon, 6442, 5565, 6706.

" Wm. fitz Patr., pardon, 5708.

" Wm. fitz Tho., pardon, 6490.

" Wm. m'Redmond, alias M'Ygrill, pardon, 4507.

Stappelton, Walter fitz Edm., pardon, 4504.

Stappolliston, co. Wat., 4625.

Stapulton, Elinor, pardon, 4623.

Starbould, Patr., pardon, 5654.

Star Chamber, Dublin. See Castle Chamber.

Star Chamber, court of, casualties from, 5903.

INDEX TO FIANTS—ELIZABETH.

Star Chamber, England, court of, fine imposed on Irish bishop, [illegible].
Starelinge, John. *See* Sterling.
Starrenaghe, co. Meath, [illegible].
Starky, John, pardon, [illegible].
Starkye, Arthur, lease, [illegible].
Starling—Starelinge—Starlinge or Sterlinge, John, grant of a wardship, 4794; several messuages in Maryborough in his tenure, [illegible].
Statutes recited:
40 & 41 Edw. III., relating to under sheriffs, [illegible].
5 Edw. IV., tax on foreign fishing vessels, [illegible], [illegible].
28 Hen. VIII., Faculties, [illegible], 3010, [illegible], [illegible].
" English habit and language, [illegible].
" Spiritual appeals, [illegible].
3 & 4 Ph. and Mary, Aqua vitæ, [illegible], [illegible], [illegible].
" Forming counties, [illegible].
" Exemptions from subsidy, [illegible].
5 Eliz., Attainder of prior of Kilmainham, [illegible].
5 Eliz., Supremacy, [illegible], [illegible], &c. *See* Supremacy, Act and Oath of.
11 Eliz., ch. 1, Subsidy, [illegible], [illegible].
" ch. 2, Tanning, [illegible], [illegible], [illegible], [illegible], [illegible], [illegible], [illegible], [illegible], [illegible].
" sess. 3, ch. 6, Forming counties, [illegible], [illegible], [illegible], [illegible], [illegible].
" sess. 4, ch. 1, Wine impost, [illegible], [illegible], [illegible], [illegible].
12 Eliz., ch. [illegible], Attainders, [illegible].
Statute expired, continued by proclamation, [illegible].
Staunton, co. Louth, manor of, [illegible].
Staunton alias Stanton, Wm., pardon, [illegible].
Stawton, Gerrot, pardon, [illegible].
Stayne—Staines—Steynes, Richard, constable of Longford, [illegible], [illegible]; lease, [illegible]; commission, [illegible], [illegible].
Staynes, William, house in Dublin, [illegible].
Staynings, George, gent., [illegible].
Steale, Donogh roe mac Teige na, pardon, [illegible].
" William m'Donogh m'Teige na, pardon, [illegible].
Steeplestown, co. Meath. *See* Stapleton.
Steilbocke (co. Wex.?), [illegible].
Stephenstone, co. Lim., [illegible].
Stephens, John, livery to brother, [illegible].
Stephens, Robert, livery, [illegible].
" Thomas, mayor of Knocktopher, [illegible].
" Tho., houses in Dublin in his tenure, [illegible], [illegible], [illegible].
" *See also* Stephins.
Stephenson, John, pardon, [illegible], [illegible].
" Oliver (Stevenson—Stevensonn), lease, [illegible]; grant of land, [illegible]; pardon, [illegible], [illegible], [illegible]; pardon at his suit, [illegible].
" Thomas, [illegible].
" *See* Stephinston.
Stephenston, [illegible].
Stephenston, co. Kild., [illegible], [illegible].
Stephenston, co. Lim., [illegible].
Stephenston—Stephenstone, co. Louth, [illegible], [illegible].
Stephenstown, co. Lim. *See* Ballystephen.
Stephins, Thomas, late constable of Wicklow castle, [illegible]; lease recited, [illegible].
Stephinston—Stephenson—Stevenston—Stevinston, co. Meath, [illegible], [illegible], [illegible], [illegible], [illegible].
Steplestown, co. Meath, [illegible].
Sterlinge or Starlinge, John, [illegible].
Stermont, David, pardon, [illegible].
Sterminston, co. Louth, [illegible].
Steuart (co. Kilk.?), [illegible].
Stevens, Edw., pardon, [illegible].
" Nich., chaplain, lease, [illegible].
" Oliver, lease, [illegible].
Stevenson—Stevensonn, Oliver. *See* Stephenson.
Stevenston, co. Dub., [illegible].
Stevenston—Stevinston. *See* Stephinston co. Meath.
Steward—Stoward—Stewarde:
" Alexander, pardon, [illegible].
" Alexander roy, pardon, [illegible].
" John, pardon, [illegible], [illegible].
" John oge, pardon, [illegible].
" Wm., pardon, [illegible].
Stewkly, Elizabeth, lease, [illegible].
Stewsley, Thomas. *See* Stucley.
Steynes, Richard, [illegible]. *See* Stayne.
Stickerry (co. Leit.?), [illegible].
Stickillen, co. Louth. *See* Stakillen.
Stickeroymanor (co. Cork?), [illegible].
Stikil, Tuly ne, (M'Donell), pardon, [illegible].
Stillorgan, co. Meath, [illegible].
Stile, Tho., pardon, [illegible].
Stillorgan, co. Dub. *See* Stalorgan.
Stiles, Alexander, vicar of Aghamarta, &c., [illegible].
Stokes, Wm., shoemaker, [illegible].
Stonagh, Donald, pardon, [illegible].
Stoakane (co. Tip.), [illegible].
Stocke (co. Leit.?), [illegible].

Stockeston. See Stokeston, co. Westm.
Stockhole, co. Dub. See Stocoll.
Stocke—Stocke, John, sub-sheriff of Kildare, pardon, 2760; commission, 3801.
Stockston, co. Westm., 6460.
Stock keepers pardoned, 4636.
Stokagh, Donell m'Teig, pardon, 6754.
" Donogh oge, pardon, 6818.
Stoke, John, pardon, 2004.
" Patrick, pardon, 512.
Stokberry (co. Lett. ?), 6412.
Stokes, George, sub-sheriff, co. Dublin, 366.
George, pardon, 1574, 6034.
Henry, pardon, 6426.
" Patrick, pardon, 2064.
" Tho., lease, 4350, 4401-2.
" Wm., pardon, 3323.
Stokeston (co. Meath), 6058.
Stokeston — Stockeston (Stokestown), co. Westm., 405, 1490, 1529, 2068, 2544. See also Stockeston.
Stokiston, co. Wex., 5045.
Stoke, Nicholas, freedom from subsidy, 349.
Stolkyn, co. Dub., 349.
Stomcartie, alias Stamcartie, co. Kilk., 3708.
Stondon, Gerald m'Shane, pardon, 5154.
Rich., homicide of, 3796.
Shane m'Edmond, 4117.
Stondon, Murtogh, pardon, 6150.
Stone, George, grant of land, 5806.
Stone, impressed for works, 5466.
Stone, co. Cav., 4592.
Stone (the) (co. Wat. ?), 685.
Stonecarthy, co. Kilk. See Stonecartie.
Stonehilde—Stonehille, at Trim., 94, 125.
Stonehall, 5175.
Stonehall, co. Westm., rectory, 866, 6797.
Stonestown (co. Lim., or Cork ?), 6606.
Stonetowne, co. Louth, 1741.
Stonetowne—Stonetonne (Stonestown, co. Meath), 846, 6601.
Stonton, co. Louth, 1781.
Stonton, co. Westm., 845.
Stouton, alias Stonishton, co. Westm., 1366.
Stontown (King's co. ?), 6613.
Stontowne, co. Louth, 1761.
Stonyfurlongs, co. Meath, 4577.
Stooke, David fitz Edward, pardon, 2061.
" Patrick, pardon, 3063.
Stooke, John, pardon, 2760. See Stocke.
Stort, William, pardon, 2027.
Storie, James, pardon, 5445.
" Leonard, pardon, 6469.
Storkay (co. Leit. ?), 5440.
Stormanstown, co. Dub. See Stromanstone.
Storton, Gregory, pardon, 5714.
Story, Tho., pardon, 4557.
Stoughton—Stoughton, Anthony, clerk of Castle Chamber, 4977, 5187; grant of a wardship, 5187.
Gilbert, protection, 16.
John, grant of a wardship, 5247.
Stoughton alias Stupton, co. Westmeath, 1596.
Stounding, James fitz Wm., pardon, 6561.
Stowell, sir John, Munster undertaker, 4901.
Stoughton, Anthony. See Stoughton.
Stoykagh, John, pardon, 6128.
Strabeo—Strabeo—Strabon, co. Car., rectory, 534, 1156, 1366, 3438, 4794.
Strabon — Strabo — Strabee, alias Strobo (Strabee, Queen's co.), 659, 1454, 1720; rectory, 1847.
Strad, 626. See Strade, co. Westm.
Stradballis, co. Kerry, 6574.
Stradballis — Stradballye — Stradebally, co. Lim., 6170; rectory, 1846, 4633.
Stradballie. See Stradbally, Queen's co.
Stradballie. See Stradbally, co. Wat.
Stradbally, co. Gal., 4901.
Stradbally — Stradballie — Stradballye, Queen's co., 463, 1798, 2365, 4613, 5454, 5918, 6017, 6773.
" house of friars leased, 2396; granted, 2497.
" rectory, 1214.
" See Stabally.
Stradbally — Stradballie, co. Wat., rectory, 2372, 2901. See also Stradvally.
Stradbally Bag, co. Wat. See Stradvalbeggs.
Stradballye. See Stradballis, co. Lim.
Stradballye. See Stradbally, Queen's co.
Strade, co. Mayo, castle, 4478.
" friary leased, 3846, 4390; possessions granted, 2864.
Strade—Stread (Strad, co. Westm.), 1658, 2790, 6499; rectory, 626, 1461, 5685.
Stradebally. See Stradballis.
Stradlocheanbeibe (co. Car. ?), 2270.
Stradowe, co. Kild., 1547.
Stradvalbegge (Stradbally Bag), co. Wat., 5554.
Stradvally (Stradbally), co. Wat., 5550.
Straffan — Straffane, co. Kild., 537, 6604; rectory, 328, 3778, 3780, 5408-9.
Stragrettan, co. Louth, 1612.
Straid, co. Westm., 6834.
Strakegare, King's co., 4504.
Strahemmarte (Bluragh and courts in Desmond survey), custom, 4165.
Strahikerin. See Strahykerin.
Straby (co. Westm. ?), 6832.
Strahykeran — Strahikerin, King's co., 445, 3038.

INDEX TO FIANTS—ELIZABETH.

Strangally, co. Wat. See Strongally.
Strand. See Strond.
Strande at Passage, co. Wat., granted, 4462.
Strandelaugh, Queen's co., 481.
Strang, Mr., [illegible]. See Le Strange, Tho.
" Richard fitz Peter, pardon, 1764.
Strange, Absolom, [illegible].
" Mrs. (probably wife of Tho. Le Strange), pardon at her suit, 2911.
" Patr., possessions of, granted, 4493.
" Patre m'Rich., pardon, [illegible].
" Rich., lease, [illegible]; garden in Waterford, 4462.
" Tho. See Le Strange.
Strangford Lough. See Coine.
Strangford—Strangforde, port, collector of customs, 1772.
" gauger and searcher of, 1760.
" supervisor of, [illegible].
" water, 1539.
Strancodan, co. Mon. See Slanaghnacodon.
Stranis, co. Tip., rectory (represented by Grazill in 1441), 4818.
Strantedrumboke, Queen's co., 468.
Stranbore (co. Tyrone ?), 4467.
Straughnough, Queen's co., 418.
Straunge, Rob., pardon, 4[illegible].
" Thomas. See Le Strange.
Straw impressed for army, 1402, 1441, 2303; for use of lord deputy, price of, 1600.
Strawbridge, Hugh. See Strowbridge.
Streate—Streete, Robert, marshal of Courts and gaols in Munster, 5147, 6445.
Stredamlon, co. Westm., 2872.
Strenaston (King's co. ?), 4818.
Streicke, John, 5274.
Strete, Rob., killed, 2[illegible].
Stricke—Strich, Bartholomew, alderman, Limerick, 4186.
" James (—Stritche), commission, 5[illegible].
" Richard, surrender, 5101; lease, 5[illegible].
" Richard, divorce suit, 4[illegible].
Stridemore, co. Dub., 4459.
Strich, Nicholas, wardship, 4830.
Stritche, James. See Stricke.
Strobe—Strobes. See Straboe.
Stroboo. See Straboe, co. Car.
Strobridge, Hugh. See Strowbridge.
Stroghboe, co. Car., 5732.
Strolle, Queen's co., 5497.
Strolleon, co. Kild., 5[illegible].
Stromanstone (Stormanstown), co. Dub., 5[illegible].
Stromane (co. Kilk. ?), 1[illegible].
Strond, (Strand), co. Dub. Newton by the, 1[illegible].
Stroncally—Strenckallye—Strone Cally—Stronkhall—Stroncally — Stroncbally—Stronckally (Stratcally), co. Wat., 1646, 1657, 3374, 3171, 5946; castle and lands, [illegible], [illegible].
Strongle, queen's letter dated at, 584, 582.
Stronde, Robert, land grant, 4761.
Strowan, co. Meath, 5082.
Strowbridge — Strawbridge — Strobridge—Strowbrige, Hugh, deputy valuer for first fruits 4517; clerk of the first fruits, &c., [illegible]; searcher of Youghal, [illegible], [illegible]; commissions, 5763, [illegible]; grant of a wardship, [illegible]; lease, [illegible]; grant of land, 5739.
" Rob., pardon, [illegible].
Strowde, John, customs controller, Drogheda, grant of office, 4791.
Strowell—Strowill, abbey of. See Shrowell.
Stubbes, William, pardon, 214.
Stuckery (co. Leit.), 5448.
Stuckins, co. Kildare, 5777.
Stucley — Stewcley — Stukely — Stewcley, Thomas, seneschal of co. Wexford, 1162, 1444, 1513; commissions, 1116; pardon, 1464; surrenders, 1177-8; leases, 1178, 1188, 1185-6.
Students pardoned, 5728, 4726, 5425, 6441, 6351.
Studkeepers pardoned, 4[illegible]. See Stud-keepers.
Stukely, Thomas. See Stucley.
Stukle (co. Leit. ?), 5463.
Stuogaghoh, Conoghor m'Teig, pardon, 6511.
Sturghonellagh, co. Dub. (Wick.), 1414.
Sturmon, Patr., pardon, 4817.
Sturmys, Tho., owner of co. Cork, [illegible].
Sturkry (co. Leit. ?), 5462.
Stwcley, Thomas. See Stucley.
Stydall (Stedalt), co. Meath, 1460.
Stydolt, co. Cav., 4631.
Suard, co. Westm., 2[illegible].
Subjects to be raised against rebels, 578.
Subjects, rights not barred by grant to chief, 4556, 4560.
Subsidy collected by ploughlands, [illegible], [illegible].
Subsidy, freedoms from, 96, 173-5, 242, 243, 253, 325, 341, 356, 362, 364, 416, 473, 725, 763-6, 791, 745-6, 774, 790, 875, 945, 968, 1384, 1397, 1467, 1514, 1519, 1528-9, 1541, 2023, 4787.
Suck river, congiries on, 5791, 5[illegible].
Suddan. See Siddan.
Sudlowe, John, rector of Mosey, Killaloe, 6139.
Sugar stolen, 537.
Sulfys, co. Gal., 4082.
Suir river. See Shure.
Sulivaine, Dermod m'Conoghor, pardon, [illegible].

INDEX TO FIANTS.—ELIZABETH.

Sullwane, Dermod m'Teige, pardon, 6491.
Sullevan, Anne m'Donogh I, and many others of the name pardoned, 6544.
Sullevane, Murtagh m'Donell I, pardon, 6544.
„ Shane m'Donogh I, pardon, 6544.
Sullivan, Owin m'Fynine I, pardon, 6434.
Sullivane, Ane m'Conoghor I, pardon, 6521.
„ Donoghe, pardon, 6594.
Sulloocyd. See Sellogbed.
Sullyvane, Thady m'Owen ny Ivory I, pardon, 4383.
Sullywayne, Donald roe, pardon, 4487.
Sulvaine, Wm. m'Donnell I, pardon, 6612.
Sulywane, alias M'Gullachad, Donogh m'Dermod Y, pardon, 4471.
Summer sheep, custom charged on Irish countries, 643, 1025, 1215, 3784.
Sumpter, David, grant of land, 518; livery to son, 3420; without heirs male, 6347.
„ Henry, livery, 3420.
Sunaghs (co. Cork ?), 5036.
Supdell (perhaps Spiddle), co. Gal., 4493.
Supell, John. See Suppell.
Superstitious uses, grant made for, confirmed freed from uses, 5776.
Suple, John. See Suppell.
Suppel (of Kilmalow), pardon, 3474.
Suppell—Supple—Supell—Suple—Suppel:
„ Edmond fitz John, pardon, 3335.
„ Edmund, pardon, 4537, 4874.
„ Egidia, pardon, 4471.
„ Ellis, pardon, 6496.
„ Garrott, pardon, 6464.
„ Gerott fitz Gibbon, pardon, 4482.
„ Gerald, pardon, 6173.
„ Gerrott, pardon, 4893.
„ Joan, pardon, 6465.
„ John, attainted, his lands granted, 5171, 4392, 4647, 5152.
„ John, pardon, 1594, 4471, 6511.
„ John fitz Gibbon, pardon, 6492.
„ John fitz James, 4820.
„ Margaret, pardon, 6319.
„ Maurice, Morishe or Morris, pardon, 4394, 4467, 4879, 6130.
„ Philip, pardon, 3317, 4471, 4811; his land, 5023, 5535.
„ Philip, pardon, 6464.
„ Rich., pardon, 6464, 6470.
„ Rowland, pardon, 6470.
„ Shane oge, pardon, 6470.
„ William, pardon, 3317.
Supple. See Suppell.
Supremacy, Act of, 2 Eliz., commissions to execute, 2366, 5067, 5534, 5363.
Supremacy oath, special commissions for taking, and returns, 185-6, 231-7, 235, 647, 5321, 5830; several commissions empowered to administer the oath, 715-6.
Surell, Edmond, m'Morrys, attainted (Purcell ?), co. Lim., lands granted, 5171.
Surdalston—Sourdowliston—Surdalstone—Surdalstowne—Surdewalleston—Surdewallestowne — Surdwalleston — Surdwalston—Surwalstowne—Swordewalliston — Swordwalston (Swordlestown, co. Kild.), 634, 1867, 2394, 2870, 2876, 2973, 3762, 5741, 4970, 5756. See also Sardallmange.
Surgent, pardoned, 4315.
Surgeon, lease to, 576.
„ murdered, 1523.
Surgeons, pardoned, 587, 2349, 2543, 2543, 3883, 4225, 4564, 4730, 4627, 4738, 4748, 4734, 4781, 4835, 4751, 5377, 6464, 6479, 6517.
Surgeons of Dublin incorporated, 3125.
Surgeon of the army, 618.
Surnings, co. Kild. (Surnings alias Turning: Inquisitions), 4784.
Surrenders of lands by Irish chiefs. See Chief.
Surrem, Gillepatrick oge, pardon, 4914.
Surreman, Henry, pardon, 4453.
Survey, in Munster, commissioners of, 4833; comm. to survey lands of the Knight of Glin, 5615.
Surveyor General of the queen's manors and lands (Fitzwilliams), 371, 1919; (Alford), 3184, 3894; (Fenton), 5720; (Parsons), 5729.
„ deputy, 5920, 5745.
Surveyor general of Victuals, 1682.
Surwaldestown. See Surdalston.
Suspected persons found at night to be punished by martial law, 1126.
Sussex, Thomas, earl of, lord lieutenant, 475, 543; undated fiants of, 567.
„ sir Henry Radcliff, earl of, lease, 6411; surrender of premises, 6297.
Sutor, Nich., shoemaker, pardon, 4517.
Sutherton, G., registrar, eccl. comm., 6362.
Suthistone (co. Westm. ?), 694.
Suton, Gerald, 4254. See Sutton.
Sutter-lane, Dublin, 6570.
Sutton (of Richardson), commissions, 4186, 4464.
„ Christopher, castle and messuage in tenure of, 1480, 5105, 4878.
„ David (of Rathbride), lease to, recited, 1407, 3197, 4174, 5220, 5428, 5341, 5516.
„ David (of Castleton Kildrought), livery, 3127; attainted, his possessions leased, 3971, 4137, 4180-1, 4314, 4317, 4373-4, 4622, 4911, 4942,

Sutton [illegible]
5152, [illegible], [illegible], [illegible], 5745, [illegible], 6011, [illegible], [illegible], 4740; granted, 4214, [illegible], [illegible], [illegible], [illegible], [illegible], [illegible], [illegible], [illegible], 5777, 5778, [illegible], [illegible]; pension to his widow, [illegible].
" David, land in his tenure, 5414.
" David, house in Naas, 5192.
" David (alias De burgo), pardon, [illegible].
" David, pardon, [illegible], 5756.
" David fitz John, pardon, [illegible].
" Edmond, pardon, 842, [illegible], 5742.
" Edward, lease, [illegible]; wardship of his son, [illegible].
" Gerald or Garret (of Tully, Connell, and Castleton Kildrought), commissions, [illegible], [illegible], [illegible], 2117, [illegible]; freedom from subsidy, [illegible]; lease, [illegible], [illegible]; grant of a wardship, [illegible]; pardon, [illegible]; livery to son, [illegible].
" Garrott fitz David, pardon, [illegible].
" Gerald (of Rahmadroght), commission, [illegible].
" Gerald (of Richardston), [illegible].
" Gerald or Garrott (of Ballykerock, co. Wex.), pardon, 87, 710, [illegible], [illegible]; wardship of heir, [illegible].
" Garrot fitz David, pardon, [illegible].
" Garrott, pardon, [illegible].
" James fitz Rob., pardon, [illegible].
" John (of Castletown), attainted, his goods granted, [illegible].
" John (of Tipper), justice of peace, co. Kild., takes oath of supremacy, [illegible]; commissions, [illegible], [illegible], 2117, [illegible], [illegible]; license to alien, [illegible]; pardon, [illegible].
" John, pardon, [illegible].
" John (of Great Connell), pardon, [illegible].
" John fitz Rich., pardon, [illegible].
" Katherine, pension, [illegible].
" Laurence, pardon, 1129, [illegible], [illegible], [illegible], [illegible], [illegible].
" Margaret fitz Patrick, pardon, [illegible].
" Nicholas fitz David, pardon, [illegible].
" Oliver, commission, [illegible].
" Patrick, pardon, [illegible], [illegible], [illegible], [illegible].
" Patrick fitz Thomas, pardon, [illegible].
" Patrick roe m'Thomas or fitz Tho., pardon, 1744, [illegible].
" Robert, archdeacon of Dublin, [illegible].
" Rob., pardon, [illegible].
" Robert fitz William, pardon, [illegible].
" Robiston, pardon, [illegible].
" Shane, pardon, [illegible].
" Simon, pardon, [illegible].
" Tho., pardon, [illegible].
Sutton, Wm. (of Tipper), commissions, [illegible], [illegible], [illegible]; pardon, [illegible]; a trustee, [illegible]; land held of, [illegible].
" William (of Ballykerock, co. Wex.), pardon, 87, 772a.
" William (of Ballykerock), wardship, [illegible].
Suttonrath (Suttonsrath, co. Kilk.?), [illegible], [illegible].
Sutton Rath, co. Tip., [illegible].
Swytfeild, co. Meath, [illegible].
Swaine, Edm., pardon, [illegible].
Swans on Shannon placed in charge of overseer, [illegible].
Swe, Tho., [illegible].
Swerds. See Swords, co. Dub.
Swetiman — Swetioman — Swetiman. See Swetman.
Swallovan, Dermot m'Connoghor Y, pardon, [illegible].
" Donell m'Teige Y, pardon, [illegible].
" Gullyeaddy m'Dermodie Y, pardon, [illegible].
" Moriaghe m'Rory Y, pardon, [illegible].
Swerdes—Swords. See Swords.
Swerin. See Sweryne.
Swermore, co. Louth (See [illegible]), 1124, [illegible].
Sweryne — Swerin — Swirine — Swyren (Shureen), co. Westm., [illegible], [illegible], [illegible], [illegible], grant, [illegible].
Swetoman. See Swetman.
Swetman—Swetiman—Swetioman—Swetiman—Swetoman:
" Anstas, pardon, [illegible].
" Edmund, pardon, 1961, 1812, [illegible], [illegible], 5708.
" Edward, pardon, 1664, [illegible], [illegible].
" George, pardon, [illegible], [illegible], [illegible].
" John, pardon, 1617, [illegible], [illegible], 5144.
" John, land in Killenny, [illegible].
" Nicholas, sub-sheriff of Kilkenny, pardon, [illegible].
" Oliver, pardon, [illegible], [illegible].
" Petroe fitz Edm., pardon, [illegible].
" Pulm, pardon, [illegible].
" Peter or Piers (of Athsnell), pardon, [illegible], [illegible].
" Peter, pardon, [illegible].
" Richard, pardon, [illegible], [illegible].
" Robert, pardon, [illegible].
" Walter, pardon, 1041.
" William, sheriff of Kilkenny, [illegible].
" William, pardon, 1941, [illegible], [illegible].
Swiffin — Swifin — Swyffin — Swyfine — Swyfyn, co. Tip., [illegible], [illegible], [illegible], [illegible], [illegible]; grant of castle and land, [illegible].

INDEX TO FIANTS.—ELIZABETH.

Swilewan, Conchor, priest, pardon, 3774.
Swillivane, Katherine ny, pardon, 6614.
Swilewan, Teige m'Moriertagh I, pardon, 5764.
Swillivane, Ellis nyne Tane I, pardon, [illegible].
" Teig m'Dermody I, pardon, [illegible].
" Teig m'Shane I, pardon, [illegible].
Swillivane, Awliff oge m'Awliff I, pardon, [illegible].
" Donogho roe m'Awliff I, [illegible].
Swillywan, Conoghor m'Teige Y, pardon, [illegible].
Swine, winter, custom rendered to O'Byrne, [illegible].
Swinesyn (co. Tip. ?), [illegible].
Swirim. See Sweryne.
Swivan, Donell m'Teige Y, pardon, [illegible].
Swlivane, Dowell m'Donogh Y, pardon, [illegible].
Swillivane, Donell m'Dermod I, pardon, 6784.
" Owen m'Cragh I, pardon, 6784.
" Shane m'Dermod I, pardon, 6784.
Swllyvane, Morierragh m'Teige I, pardon, 5764.
Swivan, Owen m'Donell I, pardon, [illegible].
Swlywan, Dermot m'Conoghor I, pardon, 6100.
Swlywane, Teige m'Shane Y, pardon, [illegible].
Swulivane, Margaret ny, pardon, [illegible].
Sworagh, Gillepatrick, pardon, [illegible].
Swordes. See Swords.
Swordewalliston, co. Kild. (see Surdalston), [illegible].
Swordlestown, co. Kild. See Surdalston.
Swords — Swordis — Swardis — Swerdes — Swordes, co. Dub., [illegible], 1187, 1287, 1378, [illegible]; charter, [illegible]; commission to measure and mark the bounds of liberties, [illegible]; tenements in, leased, [illegible].
" burgesses, [illegible].
" Broad meadow, [illegible].
" Franceman land, [illegible].
" parish, [illegible].
" See Glogirna Swords.
Swordwalston (see Surdalston), [illegible].
Swyffin—Swyfine—Swylyn. See Swiffin.
Swylewan, Thady m'Boirs, pardon, [illegible].
Swyllivane, Donaghy and Shane m'Dermody, pardon, [illegible].
Swylyvan, Owin m'Auliffe, pardon, [illegible].
Swyne, Honora oge ne, pardon, [illegible].
" Honory ny, pardon, [illegible].
" Margaret ny, pardon, [illegible].
" Mary ny, pardon, [illegible].
Swyne's galloglasses, pardon, 4447. See M'Swyne.
Swynie, Honora ny (wife of M'Awliffe), pardon, [illegible].
Swynie, Jone ny, pardon, [illegible].
" Owen m'Donell, pardon, [illegible].
" Philip, pardon, [illegible].
Swynnowe, William, pardon, [illegible].
Swynoume, co. Tip., [illegible].
Swynston, co. Louth, [illegible].
Swyny, Donell fitz Edm., pardon, [illegible].
" Katherine ny, pardon, [illegible].
Swyran. See Sweryne, co. Westm.
Swyvonde, alias O'Hea, John, pardon, [illegible].
Swy[illegible], co. Lim., [illegible].
Syan (co. Cork ?), [illegible].
Syan, alias Sean. See Shean, Queen's co.
Syan, co. Westm., [illegible].
Syan near Patrestowne, co. Westm., [illegible].
Sycomnyll, co. Westm., [illegible].
Sydian—Syddane—Syddon. See Siddan, co. Meath.
Sydney—Sidney, Dorcas, grants of land, [illegible], [illegible]; grant of a wardship, [illegible].
" Sir Henry, lord justice, 149; lord deputy, [illegible], [illegible]; constable of castle of Athlone, [illegible]; fiants signed by, 142, [illegible], 1183-84, [illegible], [illegible]; notes made by, on pardons, 871, 874, 1101, [illegible], [illegible]; composition made with Irish countries, [illegible], [illegible], [illegible], [illegible].
" William. See Sidney.
Sydney Island (in L. Neagh, near mouth of Blackwater), surrendered for pardon of Tyrlagh brasselagh O'Neill, 1161.
Syerrone, [illegible]. See Sheineroyne.
Syeve, the, (co. Gal. or Mayo), [illegible].
Syffyn. See Siffin, co. Westm.
Syfin, co. Gal., [illegible].
Sygenston, co. Kild., [illegible], [illegible].
Sykeran, 874. See Syrcksran.
Sylamohy, co. Gal. (see Shillanghye), [illegible].
Sylelaghe. See Shilelaughe.
Sylyanmaage, co. Long., [illegible].
Sylyarde, Nich., commissions, [illegible], [illegible].
Sylmarwyne (see Silmarvyn), [illegible].
Sylmanhhey, [illegible]. See Shillanghye.
Sylye, alias Gyles, pardon, [illegible].
Sylyhin (Shileburne), co. Wat., [illegible].
Symackin, James m'Rich., pardon, [illegible].
Syman, Richard, pardon, [illegible].
Symckine, Edm. oge mac Edm., pardon, [illegible].
Symons — Symcotts — Simcot, John, second remembrancer, [illegible], 2707; commission, [illegible] (in No. [illegible] the name has been incorrectly printed Symonis).
Symekine, Philip oge, pardon, [illegible].
Symickone, Ellishe ny Morish, pardon, [illegible].
Symickyne, Gerald m'Davi, pardon, [illegible].
Symkyn, Nich., slaying of, [illegible].
Symoliage (St. Mullins, co. Car. and Wex.) rectory, [illegible].

INDEX TO FIANTS.—ELIZABETH.

Symolins—Symolyn (St. Mullins barony), co. Car., 4918, 6944, 6411; martial law, 6082. See St. Moling.
Symondes parke. See Symons park.
Symondeston. See Simondeston, co. Meath.
Symondston. See Simondeston.
Symonderwood (co. Cork?), 6468.
Symonspark—Symondes parke, Cork, 1384, 6425.
Symonston. See Simondeston, co. Meath.
Symonston—Symonstown—Symonstowne (Simonstown), co. Westm., 4868, 4812, 6487.
Symonswold, co. Dub., 1782.
Symons, Edm., slaying of, 4578.
„ Jony, pardon, 1804.
Symyckins, James m'Philip, pardon, 4658.
Synane, Nich., pardon, 6471.
Syman, Gilleduff, pardon, 4284.
„ James, pardon, 4287.
„ John, pardon, 4287.
„ Rich., pardon, 5940.
„ Wm., alias Syvan, pardon, 4268.
„ Wm. Crowne, pardon, 4367.
„ Wm. oge, pardon, 5940.
Symme, James, pardon, 4302.
„ John fitz Wm., pardon, 4302.
„ Patr., pardon, 6462.
„ Philip, pardon, 5940.
„ Wm., pardon, 5940.
„ Wm. fitz Nich., pardon, 5451.
Syndyll. See Sindyll.
Synenny (co. Tip.?), 6768.
Syngnagh (co. Tip.?), 6678.
Synnemonte, tongh of, co. Antrim, 6214.
Synnen, co. Lim. (S. Seanan), 6284.
Synneganagh (co. Clare?), 4752.
Synnodestowne (co. Tip.?), 6632.
Synnot—Synnott—Synot—Synote—Synotte:
„ Anstace, dower, 6784.
„ David, pardon, 4397, 6517, 6647.
„ Edmund, sons of, 2863.
„ Edmund, pardon, 4307, 6647, 6737.
„ Egidia or Gilles, 6662.
„ Gaspar, death of, 72.
„ Gerald, pardon, 6682.
„ Gerrot, pardon, 6647.
„ Henry, pardon, 6647.
„ James fitz Piers, pardon, 4628, 4607.
„ James, pardon, 4297, 6647.
„ James fitz Rich., commission, 6601.
„ Jasper, pardon, 6617, 6646.
„ John, justice of liberty of Wexford, 144; commissions, 443, 684, 708, 3117, 3345, 3277, 3763, 3771, 3867, 4176, 4486; lease, 884.
„ John fitz Piers, pardon, 4297, 6647.
„ John, grant of a wardship, 6014.
„ John, pardon, 4617, 6647.
„ Martyn, pardon, 6617.
Synnot, Nicholas, pardon, 6647.
„ Patrick (—Simnot), clerk of the peace, Wexford, 2778, 6408, 2824.
„ Pers, pardon, 6651.
„ Peter, pardon, 1447, 4867.
„ Philip, pardon, 6647.
„ Piers fitz Davie, 4517.
„ Richard (or Simnot) (of Ballybrennan) vice seneschal of Wexford, 2117, 2179; sheriff of Wexford, 2346; commissions, 810, 2062, 3117, 3172, 3346, 3444, 3894, 4637, 5168; pardon, 1618, 2749, 3880, 3973, 3808, 4434; leases, 1653-4, 4784, 4022, 4880-6; licence to alien, 1386; conveyance to, 6963.
„ Richard (of Balmagyr), commission, 621.
„ Richard fitz Poiren, pardon, 5737.
„ Rich. fitz Rowland, pardon, 6647.
„ Robert, pardon, 4617.
„ Stephen, pardon, 6652.
„ Walter, pardon, 6617.
„ William (of Waterford), pardon, 4136.
„ William, justice of Wexford, 3800; commission, 3390, 3343, 5415.
„ (of Cloyhand), 414.
Synodestowne (co. Tip.), 6462.
Synorin, co. Tip., 6768.
Synon. See Synone.
Synonan, co. Westm., 1549.
Synone—Synon, co. Tip., 2221, 4465, 4962, 6317, 5709, 6764.
Synot—Synote—Synott. See Synnot.
Synroye in Ely (see Sheimeroyne), 4674.
Synur, John, pardon, 4944.
Syotan, co. Westm., 1622, 6751.
Syrekoran — Sykoran — Syrakaran (Seirkieran, King's co.), religious house, leased, 974, 6686, 4632.
„ rectory, 474.
Syullagh, Edm., pardon, 6691.
Syvacke (Seavaugh), co. Mon., 4622.
Syvan, alias Syman, Wm., pardon, 4284.

Taaffe—Taaf—Taafe—Taaff—Tafe—Taff—Taffe:
„ Christopher (of Gilbertstown), 5972.
„ Edw. fitz Rob., pardon, 6662.
„ James, pardon, 4364, 6180.
„ Johanne, 6678.
„ Katherine, pardon, 4208.
„ Laurence, pardon, 5784.
„ Laurence, matrimonial suit, 4022.
„ Laurence, pension, 4832.
„ Nicholas (of Ballybraghan or Bolbrogan), commissions, 3117, 3345, 3444 (Taih), 4148, 4404.

INDEX TO FIANTS—ELIZABETH.

Taaffe, Nicholas (of Rathcaker), chief serjeant of co. Louth, 1930; freedom from subsidy, 678; commissions, [illegible] (Taths), [illegible]; lease, [illegible], [illegible] (Taths).
" Nich. (of Athclare), commission, 4147, 4465, [illegible]; grant of land and rents, 4777, [illegible], [illegible].
" Peter, commissions, 4147, 4465.
" Richard, [illegible].
" Robert, sheriff of Louth, [illegible].
" Rob. (of Mollaghary), coroner of Louth, 763; commission, [illegible].
" Rob. (of Cookstown), commissions, [illegible] (Taths), 2117, 2444 (Taths), 4147, 4465, [illegible].
" Rob. (of Clonmorath), 1672.
" William (of Bonnoundane, co. Sligo), pardon, [illegible] (Taith), 6749; lease, 6014.
" Wm., keeper of gaol, Ardee, [illegible].
" Wm. (of Harryestown), pardon, [illegible].
Tabh na minisagh. See Tachhnamynisgh.
Tabnimg creir (Tongmore?), co. Cav., [illegible].
Tahnnighbeg, co. Cav., [illegible].
Tackillen. See Takillen.
Tacollat, co. Mon., [illegible].
Tacummshane—Tacoumshane—Tacumshane—Tacgmshean—Tacomshane—Ticomshane, co. Wex., 30, [illegible], 916, 1749, [illegible].
" rector of, 712.
Tachhnamyniagh—Tabh na minisagh (Tievenamanta, co. Tyrone), [illegible], [illegible].
Taena, co. Leit., [illegible].
Taeve narodda (co. Tyrone?), [illegible].
Taeva twaye (Tievetooey, co. Donegal?), [illegible].
Taffe—Taff—Taffe. See Taaffe.
Taffe lands, co. Meath, [illegible].
Tagan, Edm., pardon, [illegible], [illegible].
" Moriagh, pardon, [illegible], [illegible], [illegible].
" Rich., pardon, [illegible].
" Thomas, pardon, 1152.
Tagham church, co. Kilk., rectory, [illegible].
Tagharagh, co. Mon., [illegible].
Taghboy, co. Clare or Rosc., [illegible].
Taghelone or Clonoghe, alias Tanclone, Queen's co., 1448.
Taghelowe, [illegible].
Taghduffe (co. Kild.?), [illegible].
Taghenowran, co. Car. (Thowran, co. Wick.), [illegible].
Taghar or Togher, Queen's co., [illegible].
Taghessen. See Taghessen.
Taghestemple. See Taghtemple.
Taghlanre, King's co., [illegible].
Taghleslan (Taleydan), co. Mon., [illegible].
Taghmacconell (Taghmaconnell, co. Rosc.), rectory, [illegible].
Taghmon, co. Westm., 2117. See also Thamon.
Taghmon, co. Wex. See Tamon.
Taghmone, co. Dub. (Wick. or Wex.?), [illegible].
Taghmone (co. Wick.?), [illegible].
Taghmonis (co. Wick.?), [illegible].
Taghmory, co. Westm., 2444.
Taghoe, alias S. John Baptist, co. Rosc., [illegible].
Taghrough (co. Mon.?), [illegible].
Taghsany—Tisinye, co. Long., [illegible], [illegible].
Taghessen—Taghessen, alias the house of the Saxons (Tisaxon, co. Gal.), house of friars leased, 2878; granted, [illegible].
Taghshinai — Taghsinale — Tessenort — Tessynort—Tesynort (Taghshinod), co. Long., [illegible], 6121; rectory, [illegible], [illegible], [illegible], 6121.
Taghshinny, co. Long. See Taghsynewe, Tenghsyny.
Taghsinall, alias Taghsynye, co. Long., [illegible].
Taghsynewe—Tassenny—Tessenny—Tesyny (Taghshinny, co. Long.), rectory, [illegible], [illegible], [illegible], [illegible], 6121.
Taghsynnye, alias Taghsinall, co. Long., 6122.
Taghtaby, Connor, pardon, [illegible].
Taghtemple, co. Sligo, 5341, [illegible].
Taghtemple—Taghstemple—Tonghtemple, rectory, in O'Conor Sligo's country, co. Sligo, [illegible], 5341, 5343, [illegible]; land, [illegible], [illegible].
Taghtogher, Queen's co., [illegible].
Taghtullie, King's co., [illegible].
Taghtully, co. Westm., [illegible].
Taillior, Tho., lease, [illegible].
Taillior, Gerrott, pardon, [illegible].
Tailler, a, pardoned, [illegible], [illegible], [illegible], [illegible].
Tailor, George, recorder, Dublin, pardon, [illegible].
" Maurice, house in Dublin, [illegible].
" Philip, pardon, [illegible].
" Rich., pardon, [illegible].
" Sanky, 1811.
" Thomas, footman, Dublin Castle, [illegible].
Tailor's hall, Dublin, [illegible], [illegible], [illegible].
Taithe—Taythe (Tait), [illegible].
Takillen—Tackillen—Takyllen (Tikillin), co. Wex., [illegible]; rectory, [illegible], [illegible], [illegible], [illegible], [illegible].
Talaght. See Tallaght.
Talbot—Talbott:
" Appolinaris — Appolinarus, or Pollinar, pardon, [illegible], [illegible].
" Bartholomew, prothonotary Common Bench, [illegible], [illegible]; license of absence, [illegible].
" Christopher, pardon, [illegible], [illegible].

INDEX TO FIANTS.—ELIZABETH.

Talbot, Edward, pardon, 1404.
,, Eleanor, [illegible].
,, Elizabeth, widow, [illegible].
,, Gilbert (of Belgard), wardship, [illegible]; livery, [illegible]; commissions, [illegible], 4462.
,, James, pardon, [illegible].
,, Jane, pardon, [illegible].
,, John, justice of liberty of Tipperary, [illegible].
,, John, clerk of the Crown, &c., in several counties, [illegible].
,, John, esq., leases, [illegible], [illegible], [illegible].
,, John (of Cammerstown, co. Westm.), pardon, [illegible].
,, John (of Crumlin), [illegible].
,, John (of Feasaghroe), wardship, [illegible]; livery, [illegible]; livery to his heir, [illegible].
,, John (of Malahide), commission, [illegible].
,, John (of Rolleston), commission, [illegible].
,, John (of Robertstown), lease, [illegible]; commission, [illegible]; wardship of his heir, [illegible].
,, John, rector of Karragh, Ferns, [illegible].
,, Katherine, [illegible].
,, Matthew, commission, [illegible].
,, Nicholas, rector of Moymaile, [illegible], 1448.
,, Nich. (of Robertstown), [illegible].
,, Patrick, [illegible].
,, Peter (of Feasaghroe), wardship and livery of son, 1779, 1[illegible].
,, Peter, son of John (of Feasaghroe), livery, [illegible].
,, Pollinar. See Appolinaris.
,, Reginald, widow of, 644.
,, Richard, messuages in Dublin, [illegible], [illegible].
,, Richard, second justice, Common Bench, 18, 144, [illegible]; oath of supremacy, [illegible]; commissions, [illegible], [illegible], [illegible], 2117, 2444; lease, [illegible].
,, Rich., grandson of Wm. of Malahide, [illegible]; wardship, [illegible].
,, Richard (of Dublin), pardon, 776.
,, Rich. pardon, [illegible], [illegible], [illegible].
,, Robert (of Belgard), commission, [illegible]; wardship and livery of heir, 644, [illegible].
,, Rob., a horseman, [illegible].
,, Thomas (of Dardistown), commissions, 4149, 4461; house and land of, [illegible], [illegible].
,, Tho., prior of Kylmaynham, temp. Hen. VI., 2104.
,, William, house in Dublin, 1948.
Talbot, William (of Malahide), commissions, [illegible], [illegible], [illegible], [illegible], [illegible], 4068, 4148, [illegible]; pardon, [illegible], [illegible]; surrender, [illegible]; a feoffee, [illegible]; wardship of heir, [illegible], [illegible].
,, William (of Dublin), pardon, 344.
,, Wm. (of Robertstown), wardship, [illegible].
Talbotston, co. Dub., 437.
Talbott. See Talbot.
Talbott's lands in Kilmainham, [illegible].
Talemohoo, Upper (Tullyhunco), co. Cav. [illegible].
Talight, co. Kerry, [illegible].
Talleagh, co. Leix., [illegible].
Tallagh (Queen's co.?), [illegible].
Tallaght — Talaght — Taloughl, co. Dub., [illegible], [illegible].
Tallan, Hubert m'Richard, pardon, [illegible].
,, James rough m'William, pardon, 1376.
,, Pierse m'Richard, pardon, [illegible].
,, Roger, pardon, [illegible].
,, Shane m'William, pardon, [illegible].
Tallanston, co. Louth, [illegible].
Tallant, Edm., pardon, [illegible].
,, Hubert, pardon, [illegible].
,, Morish, pardon, [illegible].
,, Peirse, pardon, [illegible].
Tallaughan, Nich., [illegible].
Tallaughanbrooke, co. Kilk., rectory, [illegible].
Tallen, Edw., pardon, [illegible].
Talleraght, co. Wex., [illegible].
Tallon, Anne, pardon, [illegible].
,, Carroll, pardon, [illegible].
,, Charles (of Rathmallagh), pardon, [illegible], 4447.
,, Charles, pardon, [illegible].
,, Edmund, pardon, [illegible].
,, Edm. fitz Rich., pardon, [illegible].
,, Edm. m'Hobbert, pardon, [illegible].
,, Edward, pardon, [illegible].
,, Eleanora, pardon, [illegible].
,, Ismay or Isme, pardon, [illegible], [illegible].
,, James, pardon, [illegible].
,, John, pardon, [illegible], [illegible], [illegible], [illegible].
,, Maurice, pardon, [illegible].
,, Maurice fitz Redmond, pardon, [illegible].
,, Maurice fitz Rich., pardon, [illegible].
,, Maurice fitz Rob., pardon, [illegible].
,, Morish, pardon, [illegible], [illegible].
,, Nicholas, [illegible].
,, Oliver, pardon, [illegible].
,, Patr. fitz Perse, pardon, [illegible].
,, Patrick m'Rich., pardon, [illegible].
,, Perse, pardon, [illegible].
,, Philip, or Phelim, pardon, [illegible].
,, Redmund, pardon, [illegible], 4577.
,, Richard, pardon, [illegible].

INDEX TO FIANTS—ELIZABETH.

Tallon, Shane fitz Pairs, pardon, [illegible].
" Shane rough, pardon, [illegible], [illegible], 6762.
" Thomas, pardon, [illegible].
" Tahbot m'Redmond, pardon, [illegible].
" Walter, pardon, [illegible].
" Walter fitz Charles, pardon, [illegible].
Tallone, James, pardon, 6447.
Tallonsion—Tallonstown, co. Louth, 841, [illegible], [illegible], [illegible], [illegible].
Tallow, export of, [illegible]; export prevented, [illegible], [illegible], [illegible]; grant of monopoly of export from Dublin and Drogheda, [illegible].
Tallow, co. Wat. See Tallowe, Tullaghrusha.
Tallowe, Tibbot, pardon, [illegible].
Tally Lough, [illegible].
Talonght (see Tullaght), [illegible].
Talvin, James, pardon, [illegible].
Tamasion (Thomastown, co. Kild. ?), 848.
Tamblesanvaghe (Templeshanbo, co. Wex.), [illegible].
Tame, lady Margaret Wilkins of (wife of James Crofts), [illegible].
Tameraiston, co. Meath (Tankardstown), 1[illegible].
Tamhagarde (Tombaggard), co. Wex., [illegible].
Tamlat, co. Mon. See Towlaght.
Tamsaghe (co. Sligo ?), [illegible].
Tamshaharry, co. Down. See Towinghoury.
Tamnyvane, co. Antrim. See Domnyvynge.
Tamolliage (co. Wex. ?), [illegible].
Tamon (Taghmon, co. Wex.), [illegible], [illegible], [illegible], 6787.
" rector of, 918.
" S. Brigit's in, tithes of parish, [illegible], [illegible].
Tamoon, co. Wex., [illegible].
Tampolpatricke (see Tempelpatricke), 1182.
Tamplavenyn, co. Sligo, 6434.
Tamplebege, co. Tip., rectory, [illegible].
Templebrandd, co. Cork, 6315.
Templebreickan, co. Cork, rectory, [illegible].
Templebriand, co. Cork, 6518.
Temple Cloe, co. Lim., parish, [illegible].
Templeconnelly (Templeconnell, co. Cork ?), 2748.
Templedelgin, co. Dub. (in Byrne's country, perhaps Delgany), [illegible].
Temple shee (co. Tip. ?), [illegible].
Temple sheane (co. Tip. ?), [illegible].
Templefeighane, co. Kilk., rectory, 3548.
Templegall—Templegall (Whitechurch), co. Wat., [illegible], [illegible]; chapel, [illegible], [illegible].
Templehodegan (Templeludigan, co. Wex. ?), [illegible].
Temple Ihyraghe, co. Cork, [illegible].
Temple Irhirhaghe (co. Cork ?), [illegible].
Templekargan, co. Dub., [illegible].
Templekenwy—Templekenny in Ardes, (now Witter parish), co. Down, rectory, [illegible], 5787.
Templeletun, co. Gal., [illegible].
Templelodan (co. Wex. or Car. ?), [illegible].
Templeloran. See Templeorane.
Templeloran rectory (co. Gal. ?), [illegible].
Templemaghell alias Kinckre. See Temple Mighell.
Templemighell. See Temple Mighell.
Templemoel Kiltullagne (Kilfullagh), co. Gal., church of third order of Franciscan Friars, granted, [illegible].
Templemore (co. Cork ?), [illegible].
Templemore, co. Tip., 4784.
Templemore (co. Tip. ?), [illegible].
Templemyyhell. See Temple Mighell.
Templenahorney (Templenahurney), co. Tip., [illegible].
Templenamenagh—Templenamannaghe, co. Sligo, 1488, [illegible], 4[illegible].
Templenerie (Templenoiry), co. Tip., rectory 1[illegible].
Templendogan. See Templeowdygan.
Templeorane — Templeloran alias Ballyshane (Templeoran), co. Westm., [illegible], [illegible], [illegible].
Templeowdygan—Templeodogan (Templeludigan, co. Wex.), 878, [illegible].
Templereny (Templerainy, co. Wick.), [illegible].
Temple Robin — Temple Robyn (Templerobin), co. Cork, rectory, 1167, [illegible].
Templerowne (co. Cork ?), [illegible].
Templesallagh—Templeshallogh (co. Wex. or Car. ?), [illegible].
Templesambogha. See Templeshanboyh.
Templesnobe (Templescoby), co. Wex., [illegible].
Templeshanbogh—Templeshanboghe (Templeshanbo, co. Wex.), [illegible], [illegible].
Templeshanwoe (co. Wex.), [illegible].
Templeshanet—Templeshaffort, King's co., [illegible], [illegible].
Templevihille (Templemichael, co. Tip. ?), [illegible].
Templevrik (Templeyvrick ?), co. Wat., 877.
Templewy—Templeowy (Fews ?), chapel, co. Wat., [illegible], [illegible].
Templism. See Templeton.
Tempollosswygh (co. Wat. ?), rectory, [illegible].
Tempullorum (Templeorum, co. Kilk.), [illegible].
Tempulnomrahir, co. Cork, [illegible].
Tancarde, James, pardon, [illegible].
Tancardeston — Tancardiston (Tankardstown), co. Meath, 1[illegible], [illegible].
Tancardiston — Tanckardiston (Tankardstown), co. Car., 911, [illegible].
Tancardiston. See Tancardeston, co. Meath.
Tanckardeston. See Tankardstown.
Tan kardiston. See Tancardiston.

Tamorrick, co. Leit., 4443.
Tancre alias O'donnor (Shancor), co. Meath, [illegible].
Tanderagee, co. Kild. See Toragigh.
Tane, Ellen ny, pardon, 6814.
„ Ellinor nyn, pardon, [illegible].
„ Honora ny, pardon, 4515.
„ Shillie ny, pardon, 6816.
Tane y [ ] ghalone, Joan nyn, pardon, [illegible].
Taneheney in Iregan (Tinnahinch, Queen's co.), 1879.
Tang (co. Westm. ?), [illegible].
Tangatey, co. Wex., [illegible].
Tan house, license to erect, 4467, 5794.
Tanist appointed by crown, 1047, 1308, 2291-2, 2234, [illegible], 2780-1, 2818, [illegible]; right of succession to chieftaincy recognised, 4780, [illegible]; promotion to captaincy, 184; title abolished, 4761, 4871, [illegible], 5841, 6060-1, 6397; replaced by under-serjeant, 1698; called vice seneschal, 1972, [illegible]; rights merged in seneschalship, 1768.
Tankard, James, pardon, 6858, 5257.
Tankardeston. See Tankardstown, co. Kild.
Tankardeston (Tankardstown, par. Gernonstown), co. Meath, 1481.
Tankardstone—Tankardstown—Tankardiston—Tankardyston, Queen's co., 1496, 2222, 3497, [illegible]. See also Ballintankards.
Tankardstown. See Tancardiston.
Tankardstown—Tankardeston—Tankardeston—Tankardeston—Tankardstown, co. Kild., 4779; rectory, [illegible], 1138, 1965, 5628, 4594, 5878.
Tankardstown, co. Meath. See Tancardstown, Tancardeston, Tankardeston.
Tankardyston. See Tankardstone, Queen's co.
Tankardeston. See Tankardstown.
Tankardston, co. Kilk. or Tip., 4452.
Tankillye (co. Mon. ?), 5043.
Tanmacnally, co. Mon. See Tonrvickennally.
Tanmacurt, co. Lim., 4139.
Tanner, William, pardon, 634.
Tanner, pardoned, [illegible].
Tanners privileges to Kilkenny, 6451; none in Cork, [illegible].
Tanning, shoemakers at Waterford licensed to tan, 2769; shoemakers at Cork, [illegible]; glovers at Cork licensed to dress skins, 5311.
Tanning, overseers or surveyors, 1757, 2613, 2724, 2218, 2838, 4218, 4146, 6744.
Tanny, Dermot, 834.
Tanrego, co. Sligo. See Toorego.
Tantoure in Upper Ossory, 877.
Tany, Donell, pardon, 4411.
„ Philip m'Tho., pardon, 4412.
Tanycorragh, co. Sligo, 5918.
Tapystry making in Ireland, 61.
Tara, co. Meath. See Taraghe, Tharragh.
Tarbart, co. Kerry, 4714.
Tarbeston, co. Westm., 4181.
Tardaron (Ardcrone ?), co. Kerry, 6312.
Taremodo, 6067.
Taragh, co. Clare, 4723.
Tarman, Dermot oy, pardon, 6457.
Tarman, Moroghe ie, 7136.
Tarmon, co. Mayo, 6457.
Tarmon I Gradille. See Tormon O'Grady, 4683.
Tarmonmackrowyn, co. Clare, 4573.
Tarmon tenants, 4684.
Tarmon tennants, co. Kerry, 6153.
Tarmore, the, (co. Mayo ?), 6484.
Tarryman (co. Lim. ?), 6846.
Tartaine—Tartain—Tartayne (Artaine), co. Dub., 770, 4603; manor, 1777.
Tartanople, co. Car., 804.
Tarlandland, co. Car., 1452.
Tartayne. See Tartaine.
Tarvies, Edm., pardon, 4577.
Tassinone, co. Gal., 6412. See Taghrennen.
Tassagard (Saggart), co. Dub., manor, 178, 877, 2328, 6718.
„ prebend, 6081.
Tassaran—Tassarane alias Seran (Tisaran, King's co.), rectory, 1461, 3306, 4362.
Taiogaro (Taltygaro), co. Mon., 6324.
Taltercacks (Tatlincake), co. Mon., 6492.
Tate, equivalent to acres, 5013, 6474.
Tates, 4 equal a carow, 6631; 16 equal a bally bodagh, 6474.
Taafe, Edw., pardon, 2800.
„ Nicholas, 3444. See Taafe.
„ Wm., 6430. See Taaffe.
„ Wm., pardon, 6740.
Taaffe, Nicholas, 1852, 6166. See Taaffe.
„ Robert, 1823, 3444. See Taaffe.
Tatheraith, co. Meath, 2760.
Tathraith, co. Meath, 4094.
Tattigarran (Gaeran, co. Mon. ?), 5012.
Tattinranke, co. Mon. See Tatcrewicks.
Tattygare, co. Mon. See Taiogare.
Tauchkine, Wm., pardon, 4362.
Tauelone alias Taghelone or Clonoyne, Queen's co., 1848.
Taulaght—Taulaght—Taullaght—Tawlaghe (Tawlaght), co. Kerry, 4680, 4687; grant, 6048.
Tauraghe, co. Meath, 5867.
Taunaghe (Tara), co. Meath, 4459.
„ Castleton of, 5867.
„ parish of S. Patrick, 3781.
„ rectory, 6652.
Tavern not to be kept by stranger, 4571.
Tawe, the, (co. Donegal), 5007.

INDEX TO FIANTS—ELIZABETH.

Tawenagh (Tawnies, co. Cork ?), 6770.
Tawir, co. Cork, [illegible], [illegible].
Tawiagh, co. Dub., 5718.
Tawleit, co. Cav., 4834.
Tawloughe, [illegible]. See Tanlaght.
Tawnagh—Tawnaghe—Tawnaghe—Tawnaghe, co. Gal., [illegible], [illegible], [illegible], [illegible], [illegible].
Tawnagh (co. Sligo ?), [illegible], [illegible].
Tawnagh, 5740.
Tawnagh duluk, co. Mon., [illegible].
Tawnaghe. See Tawnagh.
Tawnaghe, co. Lim., toghe of, [illegible].
Tawnaghmarry (Thannaharry), co. Down, [illegible].
Tawnies, co. Cork. See Tawny.
Tawnaghe. See Tawnagh.
Tawnaghe, co. Rosc., [illegible].
Tawny (Tawnies ?), co. Cork, [illegible], [illegible]. See also Tawenagh.
Tawnyagh (co. Cork ?), [illegible].
Tawnytragh (co. Sligo ?), [illegible].
Tawre, Queen's co., [illegible].
Tawterstown, co. Cork, [illegible].
Tax to be assessed by Parliament or by order of deputy or president, [illegible].
Taxes, cessor of, appointed, [illegible].
Taxing of spiritual benefices, commission for, [illegible].
Taylafurdeston. See Tayllordston.
Tayler, Thomas, surrender by, 1181.
Taylor Finn, Dermod O'Cameonan, [illegible].
Tayllordston—Taylafurdeston—Tayllorston, co. Meath, [illegible], [illegible], [illegible].
Tayllor, Bryan. See Taylor.
" Thomas, lease, [illegible]; garden in his tenure, [illegible].
Tayllorston. See Taylorston.
Taylor, Bryan (or Tayllor), [illegible], [illegible].
" David fitz Thomas, pardon, [illegible].
" George, recorder of Dublin, [illegible], [illegible]; commissions, [illegible], [illegible], [illegible].
" John, overseer of tanning, Meath, &c., [illegible].
" John, pardon, [illegible], [illegible].
" (alias O'Deveiany), John, pardon, [illegible].
" Maurys, pardon, [illegible].
" Peter, pardon, [illegible].
" Rich., pardon, [illegible].
" Thomas, footman, Dublin Castle, [illegible], [illegible]. See Tayllor.
" Walter, pardon, [illegible].
Taylorston—Tayllorston, co. Westm., [illegible], [illegible].
Tayne, Hilline ny, pardon, [illegible].
Taynle, Margaret ny, pardon, [illegible].
Tayre, co. Louth, [illegible].
Teacroghan—Teacrohan. See Tecroghan.
Teaghane Dymrie (Dysart), co. Rosc., rectory, [illegible].
Teaghboyes (co. Mayo ?), 5740.
Teaghcloige (co. Cork ?), [illegible].
Teaghcoyne. See Tisquin, co. Gal.
Teaghcroime alias Kyllarde, co. Kild., [illegible]. See Tecroghan, co. Meath.
Teaghar, co. Mayo, [illegible].
Teaghfinnarone, co. Rosc., rectory, [illegible].
Teaghsin, co. Long., [illegible].
Teaghsyny (Teghshinny, co. Long. ?), [illegible].
Teaghtample. See Teghtample.
Teampleguill. See Teampleguill.
Teampleguill, co. Cork (alias Whitechurch; which see), [illegible].
Teampleheine, co. Tip., rectory, [illegible].
Teamplekenny in Arden. See Tamplekewy.
Teamplemolehie (Molahy ?, co. Cork), [illegible].
Teamplemolaghe alias Teample molehie, co. Cork, [illegible].
Teamplepeter (Templepeter), co. Car., [illegible].
Teamplebroye, co. Cork, rectory, [illegible].
Teamplewry chapel. See Templewry.
Tean, Ellis ny, pardon, [illegible].
Teane m'Robert, Savina nyne, pardon, [illegible].
Teane, Shely ny [illegible], pardon, [illegible].
Teaqenne—Teaquene—Teaquin—Teaquine—Teaquyn. See Tisquin.
Tearmoid—Thermond (co. Donegal and Tyrone), [illegible], [illegible].
Tearmond Magrath—Tearmondo Magrath—Thearmond Magrath, Ulster, lands of, [illegible], [illegible].
" chieftain of, [illegible], [illegible].
Teason, Egidius, pardon for homicide of, [illegible].
Teawir, co. Cork, [illegible].
Teayn nye, Una nyn, pardon, [illegible].
Tobehin, co. Westm., [illegible].
Tebrogh (co. Tip. or Kilk. ?), [illegible].
Tecalme, Queen's co. See Tecolme.
Techbuy, co. Rosc., [illegible].
Teckagin—Teckagin—Teckagyn, co. Lim., rectory, vicarage, and patronage, [illegible].
Tecloy (co. Westm. ?), [illegible].
Tecolme, co. Car., [illegible].
Tecolme—Tecolme (Tecolm), Queen's co., [illegible], 1347, [illegible], [illegible]. See also Colme.
Tecommalmon. See Tacommalman.
Tecroghan — Tecroghan — Tecrohan — Teaghcrohan — Tecroghane — Tecroughan — Teigcroghane — Tycroghan (Ticroghan), co. Meath, 184, [illegible], [illegible], [illegible], [illegible], [illegible], [illegible], [illegible], [illegible]; manor, [illegible], [illegible].
Tecmoroghan, [illegible]. See Tecroghan.
Tecroughan, co. Meath, manor, [illegible].
Tedivnet—Tydevned (Tedavnet), co. Mon., [illegible]; tenures, [illegible].
Tedusse (Tideff), co. Kerry, [illegible].
Teelin, John, sheriff of Knockfergus, 1808.

INDEX TO FIANTS—ELIZABETH.

Tearanne, co. Gal. See Carrowtirine.
Tearbrin, co. Kerry. See Tierbruyn.
Tearlehan, co. Clare. See Tirlehan.
Tearvane, co. Lim. See Tyrwanaghe.
Tervenny, co. Cork. See Tyvynye.
Teghbany (co. Gal. ?), [illegible].
Teghbodlam, co. Car., 1768.
Teghdaiaghe—Tegh Dahigh (co. Don.), [illegible], 5507.
Teghemrylane, co. Car., 5102.
Teghkerievan—Teghkyrievan (Tikerlevan, co. Kilk.), [illegible], 1174.
Teghnaskoll, co. Kilk., 1117.
Teghmeloey (co. Wex. or Car., perhaps Timaclash, co. Car.), 4848.
Teghanran (Tearan, King's co.), [illegible].
Teghmeany (King's co.), [illegible].
Tehallan, co. Mon. See Tihallan, Tihallen.
Teig, Ellin ny, pardon, 6468.
„ Fynollie nyne Edmund ynyne, pardon, [illegible].
„ Grany ny, pardon, 4534.
„ Katherine ny, pardon, 4457.
„ Meave ni, pardon, 4380.
Teigeroghane. See Terroghane.
Teige Roy, pardon, [illegible], 1467.
Teige, Donell m'Donoghe, pardon, 4777.
„ Ellen, pardon, 6616-6.
„ Ellinor nyne, pardon, 6468.
„ Giles nyne, pardon, 4378.
„ Grany duff nyne, pardon, 6837.
„ John, pardon, 6467, 5871.
„ Katherine ny, pardon, 6511, 4651.
„ Margaret ny, pardon, 4573, 6451, 6511.
„ Mawe nyne, pardon, 4293.
„ Morre ne, pardon, 4168.
„ Onora nyne, pardon, 6661.
„ Selve ny, pardon, 5614.
„ Selve ny Donogh ny, pardon, 6764.
„ Shiele inine William inine, pardon, [illegible].
„ Shilly ny, pardon, 6616.
„ Sorryhine William, pardon, 6452.
„ William, 6517.
„ Wonne nyne, pardon, 6834.
Teige enellane, indenture, 6790.
Teige kittagh, Shilie ny, pardon, 6514.
Teige roughe, indenture, 6788.
Teigeane, Donald, pardon, 4582.
Teighfeighbeighrie (probably Tifeaghna, co. Kilk.), 4454.
Teighmurane (Tinoran, co. Wick.), 6561.
Teimamoike (King's co. ?), 6776.
Teinydan, co. Mon. See Teghlerdan.
Teimeran, co. Long., 6162.
Temlreane, co. Car., 4058.
Temockoe, Queen's co., 1112.
Temoka, alias Tymoko, alias Ferrymakalla, Queen's co., 636.
Temolin. See Timolin, co. Kild.
Tempoe, co. Meath, 6861.
Temoran, co. Wex., 1289.
Tempellmychild (Templemichael ?), co. Wat., 4496.
Tempellpatrick. See Templepatricke.
Tempelmorye. See Templemory.
Templasaion, co. Westm., 94.
Templeathea, co. Lim. See Templella.
Templeahanne, co. Sligo, 4494.
Templebeanne, co. Wex., 6517.
Templebrohir (co. Cork ?), 6526.
Templebrianid (co. Cork ?), 6414. See also Templebranid.
Templebridan—Templebrydan, co. Lim., 1288, 6597. See also Templibrydan.
Templecloey, co. Lim., 6528.
Templeconnell, co. Cork. See Templeconnylly.
Templecrowne, Queen's co., 6661.
Templedire (Templederry), co. Tip., rectory, 681.
Templedirr — Templedirre — Templedirrie (Templederry), co. Wex., 1080, 5925, 4171.
Temple Dowgan, 1680. See Templedowdigan.
Templedrinig, co. Kerry, 4477.
Templeforan—Tempelloran (Templeoran ?), co. Westm., 467, 6788.
Templegalo, alias Whitechurch, vic., Ossory, 6851.
Templegall (Whitechurch), co. Wat., 6848. See also Templegall.
Templeglentan—Templeglantan (Templeglentan), co. Lim., 6461; grant, 6628.
Templeharry, King's co. See Templeeharry.
Temple Logan, alias Carig in edye (Castlehyde), co. Cork, 1281, 6782.
„ parish (now Litter), 6782.
Temple Iurick (Templeyvrick, co. Wat. ?), 4284.
Templekeran (Templekeeran, co. Meath), rectory, 5662.
Templeleenan, co. Gal., 4808.
Templeloran rectory, 1528.
Templeowdigan—Temple Dowgan, co. Car. (Templeindigna, co. Wex.), rectory, 1680, 2838. See also Templehodegan, Templeowdygan.
Temple m'tyer—Temple m'tyre (Templemacateer), co. Westm., 1684, 3347.
Temple Macoy (co. Sligo ?), 4676.
Templemchail (Templemichael, co. Wick. ?), 5541.
Templemary (Templemoley), co. Tip., rectory, 4618.
Templemichael, co. Tip. See Templevillie.
Templemichael, co. Wat. See Temple Mighell.

INDEX TO FIANTS—ELIZABETH.

Templemichael, co. Wick. See Templemichall.
Templemichael. See S. Michael, S. Michaels.
Templemichall (co. Cork ?), [illegible].
Templemichell (co. Wat. ?), [illegible].
Templemighell (co. Wat. ?), [illegible].
Templemighell (co. Wex. ?), [illegible].
Temple Mighell—Templemighell—Templemyghell (Templemichael), co. Wat., 1687, 5161, 6763; castle and lands, 5015; rectory, 1687, 5161. See also Templemychell.
Templemolbie (co. Leit. ?), 5448.
Templemolaga, co. Cork. See O'Mollaggi, Corbe O'Mollaggie.
Templemore, co. Tip., 5018, [illegible], 6144, 6173, 6704.
Templemory — Templemorye, co. Car., rectory, [illegible], 3418, 6411.
Templenacarriga, co. Cork. See Templenycarrigh.
Templenaburney, co. Tip. See Templeneburney.
Templenaharry, co. Tip. (Templeharry, King's co.), rectory, [illegible].
Templeneiry, co. Tip. See Templeneirie, Templenery.
Templenemanaghe, 1464.
Templenequillan, co. Cork, 5667.
Templeno (co. Tip.), [illegible].
Templenoe—Templenoae, alias Newchurche, co. Kerry, rectory, [illegible], 6172.
Templenovagge, co. Cork, 5667.
Templenooe. See Templenoe, co. Kerry.
Templenycarrigh (Templenacarriga, co. Cork), [illegible].
Templenyre (co. Tip.), [illegible].
Templeogan, co. Cork, vicarage, 5667.
Templeoge, co. Dub., 18, 164. See also Timologe.
Temple Ogryne, co. Down, 1777.
Templeoharry, co. Tip., 5776.
Templeoran, co. Westm. See Templeorane, Templeforan.
Templeoram, co. Kilk. See Tampuliorum.
Templepatricke—Tampolpatricke—Tempellpatrick, co. Westm., 1147, 1182, [illegible].
Templepeter, co. Car. See Teampleped.
Templeporte rectory, co. Cav., 4964.
Templeraincy, co. Wick. See Templereny.
Templerevaghe, co. Ross., [illegible].
Templeriston (co. Westm. ?), [illegible].
Templerobin, co. Cork. See Temple Robin.
Templescoby, co. Wex. See Templescobin.
Templeshanaboy (Shanbohe Church in towneland of Granagh, co. Lim.), 6171.
Templeshanbo, co. Wex. See Tamblesanvaghe, Templeshanbogh.
Templeshenane (Templeshannon, co. Wex.), 6047.
Templetain, co. Mon. See Intemple, 6942.
Templetie—Templetiy (Templenibee ?), co. Lim., grant, [illegible].
Templeton (Templetown, co. Louth), 1466.
Templeton, co. Cork, 1818, [illegible], 6427.
Templeton, co. Westm., 1291.
Templeton—Templtun (Templetown), co. Wex., 1987, [illegible].
Templetown—Templetowne (co. Cork ?), [illegible], [illegible]. See Templeton.
Templetown (co. Lim. ?), [illegible].
Templetown, co. Louth. See Templeton.
Templetown, co. Wex. See Templeton.
Templetowndage, co. Tip., rectory, [illegible].
Templeyvrick, co. Wat. See Templevrik, Temple Irrick.
Tempilbrydan, alias Karrygyrolavis, vicarage of, 84.
Tempimore, alias Ballymadare, co. Sligo, [illegible].
Tempulloran. See Templeforan.
Tempuliolvredain (co. Tip. ?), 5267.
Tenaghe, co. Gal., 1774.
Tenaght, co. Mon., [illegible].
Tenaghte, Conghor or Connor O'Swievan, pardon, 4463.
Tenants, customs payable by, [illegible], [illegible]; rents and services of tenants in Munster to be determined by commission, 5771; tenants of Maguire to hold by knight service, and to be permitted to enjoy their lands, [illegible].
Tenawran, co. Car. (Tinoranhill, co. Wick.), rectory, 1287.
Tenecurragh, co. Car., 5045.
Tenecorre, co. Wex. or Car., 5154.
Tenehenole—Tenehenne—Tenehynne (Tinnahinch), co. Car., 4812, [illegible], 5411.
Tenehinch—Tenehinche—Tenhenshie—Tenhensie—Tenybynch (Tinnahinch), Queen's co., 1337-8, [illegible], 4422.
Tenebynne. See Tenehenole, co. Car.
Tenekill—Tenekille—Tenekyll—Tenekylle (Tinnakill), Queen's co., [illegible], [illegible], 1718, [illegible], [illegible], 6452.
Tenekille (co. Wick. ?), 6577.
Tenekyll—Tenekylle. See Tenekill, Queen's co.
Tenelick—Tenelick—Tynelick (Tenealick), co. Long., [illegible], 6128, 6433, 6467, 6474.
Tenemoyck, King's co., 1344.
Teneran, co. Car., 6344.
Teneroogh (Tenrengh), co. Kerry, 6158.
Teneran (Tireran ?), Queen's co., 5267.
Tenesearle, co. Kerry, [illegible].
Tenesnolle, co. Kilk. See Tinnescolly.
Tenescolly, co. Wat., [illegible].
Teneslragh — Teneshraghe (Tinnasragh), Queen's co., 478, 4748, 6163.
Tenganeghe, co. Tip. 5344.

INDEX TO FIANTS.—ELIZABETH.

Tenbeamhie.—Tenbonnie, 1897-8. *See* Tonebinch.
Tumaliok, co. Long. *See* Tonaliok.
Temaghanna, co. Car., [illegible].
Temploart (co. Car. or Wex. ?), [illegible].
Temple court erected in Dublin, [illegible].
Tennis, game of, [illegible].
Tencran, co. Dub. (Tinotenhill, co. Wick. ?), [illegible].
Tenrent, co. Wex., [illegible].
Tenrenry, co. Car., [illegible], [illegible].
Tenrilland (Thurland, co. Car. ?), [illegible].
Tentorpaugha, co. Lim., [illegible].
Tenlaghar (Queen's co. ?), [illegible].
Tentore (Tintore), Queen's co., [illegible].
Tenures of land, uncertainty of, [illegible]; W., earl of Essex, to compound with Ulster chief for rents in cattle or money, [illegible]; English tenures to be introduced by O'Molloy, [illegible]; Irish freeholders to hold of the crown, [illegible], [illegible], [illegible].
Tenyeboria, co. Wat., [illegible].
Tenyeyle—Tenyle (Tinneel), Queen's co., [illegible], [illegible].
Tenybynch. *See* Tonehinch, Queen's co.
Tenyle, [illegible]. *See* Tenyeyle.
Teoghlinybin, co. Ross., [illegible].
Teotample (co. Sligo ?), [illegible].
Teowor (King's co. ?), [illegible].
Tepe, Wm. fitz John, pardon, [illegible].
Tequin, [illegible]. *See* Tinquin, co. Gal.
Terbert, co. Lim., [illegible].
Terell, Wm., [illegible]. *See* Tyrrell.
Terenane (co. Gal. ?), [illegible].
Teresure, co. Dub. *See* Tiriuntre, Tyuoure, Tyryoure.
Terevna. *See* Tyrone.
Terrroan. *See* Tirevnan.
Terloghan, 1812. *See* Termonfeighan.
Terglashe (Terryglasse ?), co. Tip., [illegible].
Termaine, co. Sligo, [illegible].
Terman, co. Gal., [illegible], [illegible].
Termane, co. Ross., [illegible], [illegible].
Termanfecan. *See* Termonfeighan.
Terman M'Crayn (co. Gal. ?), [illegible].
Termon of the Nobber, co. Meath, [illegible].
Termone (co. Ross. ?), [illegible].
Termon lands in co. Longford, granted, [illegible].
Termon lands in co. Mon., granted, [illegible], [illegible], [illegible], [illegible].
Termon or church lands, granted, co. Lim., [illegible].
Termon or corb, in Kerry, lands granted, [illegible].
Termon or hospital lands granted, [illegible], [illegible].
Termon, river, co. Donegal. *See* Ava an Tearmoind.
Termonammongan, co. Tyrone. *See* Termond Imongha*n*.
Termonbarye (Termonbarry), co. Ross., parson, [illegible].
Termond Imonghan—Thermond Imonghain, (Termonammongan, co. Tyrone), [illegible], [illegible].
Termone, Edm. m'Shane, pardon, [illegible].
Termone, the lands of, co. Mayo, [illegible].
Termone (co. Meath ?), [illegible].
Termonocmonagho, co. Kerry, [illegible].
Termonfeighan—Terloghan—Termanfecan —Termonfeghan—Termonfeighan—Termonfeighin—Tyrmonfeighan, co. Louth, [illegible], [illegible], [illegible], [illegible], [illegible], [illegible], [illegible], [illegible], [illegible], [illegible]; tithes of parish, [illegible].
—— priory of nuns leased, [illegible], [illegible].
Termonkelna, co. Ross., 1881.
Termon O'Grady—Termon I Graddie—Termonygrady, co. Clare, [illegible], 4761, [illegible].
Teronyn, John o, attainted, [illegible].
Termygriddy, co. Car., [illegible].
Ternamacroughe (co. Mon. ?), [illegible].
Terone. *See* Tyrone.
Terenagh, Teige m'Shane, pardon, [illegible].
Terraghiye (co. Sligo ?), [illegible].
Terreconnel. *See* Tirconnell.
Terre, co. Gal., [illegible].
Terrolagh, Mary ny Kenygan ny, pardon, [illegible].
Terrolaigh, Margaret ny, pardon, [illegible].
Terrell. *See* Tyrrell.
Terrelspace (Tyrrellspass, co. Westm.), [illegible].
Terreragho. *See* Tiraragh.
Terrowoghter, co. Ross., country of, [illegible].
Terryglass, co. Tip. *See* Terglashe.
Tervoe, co. Lim. *See* Tirovowe, Tirovowe.
Terwen, co. Kild., 1487.
Terwrye (co. Kerry ?), [illegible].
Tesernort, [illegible]. *See* Taghshinel.
Tesrony—Tesrony. *See* Taghshynvery.
Teshanfochan in Kylloghan, Queen's co., [illegible].
Tesrynort, [illegible]. *See* Taghshinel.
Testamentary causes commission, [illegible].
Testamentary praemunire, [illegible].
Tethilkeran, co. Meath, 1040.
Tester, silver, stolen, [illegible], [illegible].
Tesynort. *See* Taghshinel.
Tesynidby, co. Long., [illegible].
Tesryhy, [illegible]. *See* Taghsynowe.
Tetemple, co. Sligo, [illegible].
Tova na Boldie (co. Tyrone ?), [illegible].
Tovaiwaye (Tievelowny, co. Donegal ?), [illegible].
Towe, Wm., pardon, [illegible].
Tower (see Togher, Queen's co.), [illegible].
Towenlie (Tievenbilly, co. Down), [illegible].
Towry, co. Gal., [illegible].

INDEX TO FIANTS—ELIZABETH.

Taylor, Connor m'Morris, pardon, 6478.
" Donogh m'Shane, pardon, 6478.
Teyman, Elizabeth, pardon, 6146.
Teyman alias Tyman (Inan ?), co. Meath, rectory, 5708.
Thamolinge (St. Mullins, co. Car. ?), 4418.
Thamon (Taghmon, co. Westm. ?), parson of, 1872.
Thamondstown, co. Meath (Hammondstown), 1480.
Tharaght, in Connaught, 1504.
Tharragh (Tara), co. Meath, vicar of, 4800.
Thatch roof on castle, 1588, 6792.
Thawyten, Henry, first portgreave, Athboy, 6213.
Thaylor, Donald moyle m'Thomas, pardon, 5842.
Thayrne Nabanive—Thayrr na banive (co. Donegal), 5993, 5997.
Theard, co. Kilk., 5938.
Thearmond Magrath — Thearmond Magrathe. See Tearmond Magrath.
Thekraghi, 893.
Theglam, in O'Maloye's country (King's co.), 1418, 1480.
Thenmoylo (co. Tip. ?), 4822.
Thomand (co. Wick. or Dub.), 5560.
Thermond, 6797. See Tearmoind.
Thermond Imonghain. See Termond Imonghan.
Thesker co. Gal., 1894.
Theynner (co. Tip. ?), 2824.
Thevenon (co. Wex. ?), 6488.
Thewe, [ ], house occupied by, 4402.
Thickpenny—Thickepenny—Thickepennye —Thickpennye—Thickpeny —Thyckepenny—Tickepenny
" Anne, widow, land in her occupation, 5046 ; grants of land, 5281, 5572.
" John, victualler of garrisons in Munster, 1519 ; collector of duty on wine, 1546, 2777 ; commission to contract for import of corn, &c., 5789 ; leases, 1687, 5161, 5148.
" Wm., pardon, 5619.
Thieves, measures taken to prevent their crossing Shannon, 6112.
Thihallan (Tehallan), co. Mon., 6744. See Tihallan.
Thilligh, Shane m'Donogh, pardon, 6432.
Thirasy, Matthew, 2868.
Thobbin, Philip fitz Water, pardon, 6155.
Thoben, James roe, pardon, 2794.
" Wm., pardon, 2794.
Tholsell, Dublin, commissioners sit in the, 6287.
Thomas, Edward, 1844.
Thomas, Ellice nyn, pardon, 6821.
" Honor ny, pardon, 6444.
" Joan nyn, pardon, 4824.
" John (alias Bowene of Ballyadams, Queen's co.), commission, 913 ; livery to son, 1490.
" John, chief remembrancer, Exchequer, 1030, 1363 ; surrender, 1130 ; leases, 1129, 1313 ; grant of a wardship, 1235 ; pardon, 1770.
" Joan, grant of a wardship, 4591.
" Katherine ny, pardon, 6634.
" Kallin ny, pardon, 6812.
" Margaret nyne, pardon, 4487.
" Martin, commission, 3492.
" Owen ny, pardon, 4823.
" Rice, commission, 1726 ; grant of a wardship, 4898.
" Robert (alias Bowene), livery, 1490. See Bowen.
" Rose nyne, pardon, 6288.
" Wm., pardon, 4484.
Thomas more, indenture, 6788.
Thomascourt, Dublin, 1708, 6627. See Dublin, abbey of S. Thomas.
Thomas is land, co. Wex., 5630.
Thomaston (Thomastown, par. Cadamstown), co. Kild., 1344, 2148, 3422, 5978.
Thomaston. See Thomastown, co. Kilk.
Thomaston. See Thomastown, co. Lim.
Thomaston, 1178.
Thomaston, co. Meath, 1184, 1428, 5136, 3474, 4506.
Thomastone, 948.
Thomastone, co. Louth, 5418.
Thomastoune. See Thomastowne, co. Kild.
Thomastown—Thomaston—Thomastowne, co. Kilk., 285, 872, 904, 1945, 3012, 3018, 3837, 4387, 4458, 4808, 6864 ; rectory, 3811, 4182.
" sovereign, commissions, 3117, 3444.
" sovereign and burgesses, pardon, 3974.
Thomastown, King's co. See Ballythomas, 488, Tomaston.
Thomastown — Thomaston — Tomaston, co. Lim., 41, 887, 2088, 6464, 6474, 6505.
Thomastown (co. Tip. ?), 6564.
Thomas Towne, co. Kerry, 5048.
Thomastowne — Thomastowne (co. Kild.), 6228, 6882. See Tamaston, Thomaston.
Thomastowne. See Thomastown, co. Kilk.
Thomastowne (co. Wick.), 6461.
Thomdaly (Tomdeely, co. Lim.), 6468.
Thome, co. Tip., 4886, 6151.
Thome, co. Tip. (stated by Archdall to be Toem, but apparently Toomyvara in par,

Aghamanagh), priory leased, 2375, [illegible], [illegible], [illegible], 6151; lease surrendered, [illegible], [illegible].

Thomas, co. Wex., [illegible].

Thomas, William, archbishop of. See Tuam.

Thomaskin, Thomas fitz Morish, pardon, [illegible].

Thomlynson, Tho., fletcher, 3474.

Thomond — Thomon — Thomonde — Thomound—Thomounde—Thowmonde—Toman—Tomond — Towmonde, country (the county of Clare), 1034, 1108, 1443, 1775, 2782, 3448, 3443, 4383, 4374, 4781, [illegible]; to be made shire ground, 1528, 2788; united to the Government of Connaught, 1434; transferred to government of Munster, [illegible]; restored to Connaught, [illegible]-8; persons pardoned to appear before commissioners, 1886; wasted by rebellion and war, 1819; unable to support garrison, 2780; indenture of composition, 4780; revenues of, 4384; general pardon to inhabitants, 6112, 6773; commission of concealments, 6712.

" commissions of peace, [illegible], [illegible]. See Connaught.

" ecclesiastical commission, [illegible].

" commission of musters, 3172.

" commission for martial law, 344, [illegible], [illegible], 4072, 4086, [illegible], 4730, 4807, [illegible], [illegible], [illegible], [illegible].

" president, chief commissioner, or governor. See Connaught.

" lieutenant governor. See Connaught.

" justice. See Connaught.

" clerk of the council (see Connaught), 4144.

" provost marshal. See Connaught.

" clerk of the crown and peace, [illegible]. See also under Connaught, 1427, &c.

" chief serjeant and receiver, [illegible],

" serjeant at arms, 2742.

" Maurice, earl of, his daughter, 3177.

" Conor, Conoghor, Cornelius, or Conacius, earl of, grants of land, [illegible], 3444-6; commissions, [illegible], [illegible], 1418, 1434, 2142, [illegible], 2742, 3447; pardons, 1428, [illegible]; queen's letter in favour of, [illegible]; livery to heir, [illegible].

Thomond, Donogh or Donatus, earl of, livery, [illegible]; commissions, 4484, 4743, 5031, 6138, [illegible], [illegible], [illegible], [illegible], 4334-6, [illegible]; pardon, 4534; indenture of composition, 4781; claims barony of Ibrickan, 4781; pension, 6384; grants of land, [illegible], 6436; lease, [illegible].

Thomondo towne (Tuam, co. Gal.), monastery of Holy Trinity, leased, 2573. See Tuam.

Thomound—Thomounde. See Thomond.

Thompson—Thomson—Tompson—Tomson, Richard, precentor of Christ Church, Dublin, licence of absence, 2438; treasurer of S. Patrick's, 2438, 3647; commissions, 1433, 3938, 3717, 4135, 4158, 4179, 4438, 4473, 4744, 4830, 4373, 4447, 4783; vicar of Balrothery, [illegible].

Thomye, Sylly ny, pardon, [illegible].

Thomyn, James, pardon, 857.

Thoneagrony (perhaps Tomgraney, co. Clare), 4795.

Thoronton, Geo. See Thornton.

Thornburgh, John. See Limerick, bishop of.

Thornton, Egidius, treasurer of Ireland (temp. Hen. VI.), 3166.

Thorne, Nicholas, pardon, 1817.

Thornton, in Yorkshire, [illegible].

Thornton—Thoroston—Thoronton, George, captain of ship Handmaid, [illegible]; empowered to press men for queen's service on the seas, 3636, 3857, 5071; provost marshal of Munster, 4448, 5378; vice marshal, [illegible]; commissions, 4153, 4448, 4436, 5418, [illegible], [illegible], 5416, [illegible], 6144, [illegible]; pardon, [illegible], [illegible], 4327, [illegible]; pension, [illegible], [illegible]; grant of land, [illegible].

Thowmonde. See Thomond.

Thoyore, co. Westm., [illegible].

Thread stolen, value of, 407, [illegible].

Thre Castelles of Footesland, co. Kild., [illegible].

Three Castles—Three Castells—Threecastels—Threecastelle (co. Wick.), 850, 1887, 1418, 3148, 4010, 4441, [illegible], 4417, [illegible].

Thuby, Darby m'Teig yny, pardon, [illegible].

Thuohy, Donogho m'Dermodie ny, pardon, [illegible].

Thurin (co. Westm. ?), 6773.

Thurkell, co. Kild., 1848.

Thurles — Thurlos — Thurlis — Thurls, co. Tip., 443, 867, 812, [illegible], [illegible], 5047, [illegible], 4784, 4787, 6814, [illegible].

" house of friars, granted, 864.

" rectory, 443.

" viscount, title of earl of Ormond, 7194, [illegible].

Thurlesbeg—Thurles bege—Thurles begg—Thurles beig, co. Tip., 873, 1887, 2812, 2814, [illegible], 4630, [illegible]. See also Durlesbeg.

INDEX TO FIANTS—ELIZABETH.

Thurleston alias Tyrrelleston, co. Dub., [illegible], [illegible].
Thurley (perhaps Thurles), 1868.
Thurles—Thurlis—Thurls. See Thurles.
Thurlonstowne, co. Lim., 1494.
Thurlogston (Thurlingstown), co. Meath, 1494.
Thuyre—Thwire, co. Westm., 7142, 6824, [illegible].
Thwayts, Thomas, grant, 6016.
Thwire. See Thuyre.
Thyckepenny, John. See Thickpenny.
Tiaghegrinan, co. Gal. or Mayo, 4880.
Tiaquin—Teagheoyne—Teaquane—Tea-
quene—Teaquin—Teaquine—
Teaquyn—Tequin—Tyaquyn,
co. Gal., 1346, 4822, 5319; lord-
ship and manor, 2942,
" barony, 4916, 5470, 5536, 6979; sene-
schal appointed, 2916.
Tibberaghny, co. Kilk. See Tibraghney.
Tibberaght (co. Kilk. ?), 1647. See also Tip-
peraght.
Tibberbards, co. Wex., 578.
Tibberbir. See Tubberber.
Tibberclare (Toberclare, co. Westm.), 6798.
Tibberdalaghe—Tibberdaloghe. See Tub-
berdanlaghe.
Tibberkeveo. See Tipperkevin.
Tibberlanughte, in Birne's country (co.
Wick.), 1823.
Tibberaght (co. Kilk. ?) (see also Tibberaght),
6118.
Tibbred—Tibbred (co. Tip. ?), 6482.
Tibburyhe, co. Gal., 6625.
Tibraghne, alias Tubbernaghny (Tibber-
aghny, co. Kilk.), 6771.
Tibronghne, 2801.
Tibruit (co. Kerry ?), 6497.
Tibruraghne, alias Tibraghne, co. Kilk.,
6771.
Tiband, Fynine m'Donell, pardon, 6363.
Tickepenny, John. See Thickpenny.
Tickinhorne, co. Wat., 4772.
Ticonaghane. See Tacumshan.
Ticosker, co. Cav. See Tigh Cosgner.
Ticroghan, co. Meath. See Tacroghan.
Tiduff, co. Kerry. See Teduffe.
Tiemalin alias Ballintample (co. Wick. ?)
2824.
Tier[ ], Fynoly ny, pardon, 6411.
Tieracloa, co. Kerry. See Tirighly.
Tierbrayn (Tearbrin, co. Kerry), 6164.
Tierichien—Tyerichyun (Tearichean), co.
Clare, 4882, 4774.
Tiermore, co. Lim. See Tirmoire.
Tieraskelly, co. Gal., 2813.
Tiernay, Gilliduffe, pardon, 4421.
Tierchanaghan, co. Kerry. See Tircheanig-
han.
Tierwhirrye, co. Cork, 4896.
Tievenamuckala, co. Tyrone. See Teebb-
namynleagh.
Tievesbilly, co. Down. See Ballyntedbye,
8281, Towerville.
Tievenmoey, co. Donegal. See Thevalwaye.
Tevalwaye.
Tifeaghine, co. Kilk. See Toighfeighrighrie.
Tighmane, Teige o, pardon, 4828.
Tigh Cosgner (Ticosker), co. Cav., 5186.
Tiguny (co. Dub.), 8901. See Stagony.
Tihallan (Tehallan), co. Mon., termon gran-
ted, 6744.
Tikerievan, co. Kilk. See Teghkerievan.
Tikillin, co. Wex. See Tukillen.
Tiknock, co. Car. See Tynekenocke.
Tiler, pardoned, 6763.
Tilers impressed for army, 5168, 7121.
Till, John, grant of land, 120; escheat on his
death without heirs, 2614. See Tyll.
Tillegarie (co. Leit. ?), 4120.
Tilligarie (Tallygarran ?), co. Kerry, 4122.
Timacled, alias Tomocloyge, Queen's co., 313.
Timber impressed for army, 376, 1185; cus-
toms of, 3782.
Timinaghoe. See Tunoghoe.
Timmore, co. Wick. See Twomore.
Timoghoe—Timinaghoe—Timoghe—Ty-
mochoe—Tymoco—Tymocoe—Tymoghe
—Tymoghoe—Tymohow, co. Kild., 123,
434, 2187, 2288, 5443, 2974, 6737, 6044, 6772,
6776; rectory, 3266; parish, 5463.
Timogue, Queen's co. See Tymoge.
Timoleage—Timoleage—Tymolage—Tymo-
lage—Tymolagge—Tymolagge
—Tymolagey—Tymoleage—
Tymoleig—Tymoleige, co.
Cork, 2341, 2841, 2874, 4886, 6158,
6371, 6834, 6781, 6761.
" house of friars leased, 2275, 2942,
4887.
Timolin—Teamolin—Timolingbegge—
Tymolenbegg—Tymolin—
Tymolinbegg—Tymolinbegg
—Tymollingbeg—Tymolin-
begge—Tymolinge—Tymo-
lingebegge—Tymolinbeg—
Tymolyn, co. Kild., 2481, 2971,
4277, 3387, 5440.
" rectory, 4394.
" house of nuns, leased, 1314, 2804;
granted, 3700; possessions
leased, 1613, 3377, 4294; granted,
3414, 4436, 6281. See also B.
Mollingbeg.
" house of monks (probably a
mistake for preceding), 3377
Timologe (Templeoge ?), co. Dub., 4117.
Timon—Tymon, co. Westm., 6687, 6772.

INDEX TO FIANTS—ELIZABETH.

Timcole, co. Meath. *See* Tyrcole.
Timealiegh, co. Gal. *See* Towtamellah.
Timltyo, Wm. M'Kennedy, attainted, 5777.
Timknoyhn (co. Wex. ?), 6541.
Timnerigh, [illegible].
Timnarigo, 6541.
Tinckick. *See* Tenalick.
Tinecolly—Tennecolle—Tinickolly (Tinnecolly, co. Kilk. ?), 5798, 6494.
Tinecolly, [illegible].
Tinlenarie (Timmanart, co. Cork), [illegible].
Tinickolly, 6494. *See* Tennecolly.
Tinker, pardoned, 6212.
Tinnaclash, co. Car. *See* Toghmoclasy.
Tinnahinch, co. Car. *See* Tenahenche.
Tinnahinch, Queen's co. *See* Tenehinch, Tenehencey.
Tinnahinch barony, Queen's co. *See* Irogan.
Tinnakill, Queen's co. *See* Tenakill, Tinnykill.
Tinnaranny, co. Kilk. *See* Tyonranna.
Tinnemart, co. Cork. *See* Tinlenarie.
Tinnescart, co. Wat. *See* Trenescart, Tynnekairty.
Tinnescolly, co. Kilk. *See* Tinecolly.
Tinnesragh, Queen's co. *See* Trenesragh.
Tinnoel, Queen's co. *See* Tenycyle, Tynyll.
Tinnykill—Tynekilly—Tynekylly — Tynnekill (Tinnakill), Queen's co., [illegible], 1804, [illegible]. *See also* Tenekill.
Tinoran, co. Wick. *See* Teghonowran, Teighonran, Tenowren, Tenoran.
Tinrland, co. Car. *See* Tourlleam.
Tintern—Tinterne—Tinteyrne—Tynterne, co. Wex., 1259, 2186, [illegible], 4043, 4314, 5162, 6452, 6647.
abbey leased, 1259; granted, [illegible]; possessions leased, 2278, 6541.
„ barony, 117.
„ rectory, [illegible].
Tintobber—Tyntobber, co. Wat., [illegible], 4097, 6511.
Tintore, Queen's co. *See* Tentore.
Tiparkevin. *See* Tipparkevin.
Tipheragha, 4697. *See* Theragh.
Tippar. *See* Tipper.
Tippeman—Typpemane, co. Kild., [illegible], 6188, 5762, 6146.
Tipper—Tippar—Typpar—Typper, co. Kild., 224, 293, 344, [illegible], 2117, [illegible], 3444, 8146, 4150, 4159, 4464, 5128, 5281, [illegible], 6348, 6734.
„ prebendary of, [illegible], [illegible].
Tipper (co. Tip. ?), 6464.
Tipper—Typper, of Tipperstown, commissions, 4150, 4164.
Tipperaght (co. Kilk. ?), 5641.
Tipperary — Tipperare — Tipperarie — Tipperarye — Typperare — Typperary, 1648, 4693, [illegible], [illegible], [illegible]; rectory, 4918.
„ county, commission to set out county and divide into baronies and ploughlands, [illegible]; doubtful lands to be surveyed and made shire ground, 1464, 2758, [illegible]; injuries done by men of, 436; persons pardoned, to give security before commissioners in county, 960, 1670; persons indicted of treason proclaimed, 1828, 1848; lands of White Knight in, [illegible]; of earl of Desmond, 4739; escheated, lands allotted to undertakers, 4901, granted, [illegible], [illegible].
„ „ commission of peace, 612-3, [illegible].
„ „ commission to lead inhabitants against rebels, 891.
„ „ ecclesiastical comm., 666-7.
„ „ commissions for martial law, 469, [illegible], 728, 839, [illegible], 1126, 3430, [illegible], [illegible], 3910, 4061, 4776, [illegible], [illegible].
„ „ sheriff, 728, [illegible], 1049, 4461, [illegible], [illegible].
„ „ justice of peace, 6521.
„ „ clerk of crown and peace, 142.
„ „ collector of cess, 6272.
„ liberty, lord of the liberties and royalties of the county, the earl of Ormond, 3134, [illegible], 6734.
„ „ seneschal, [illegible], 1870, 2148, 6521.
„ „ justice, 2140, 4697.
„ „ treasurer, 2148.
„ „ attorney, 2148.
„ „ sheriff, 2148.
„ „ martial law in, 1614, 1194, 2148, [illegible].

INDEX TO FIANTS—ELIZABETH.

Tipperary cross, or county of the cross (church lands exempted from the earl's liberty), 5348, 4460, 5578, 5461.
" " sheriff, 1538, 2324, 5828, 3867, 4364.
" " sub-sheriff, 5258, 5867.
" " clerk of the crown, 4457.
" " marshal of courts, 4153.
" " collector of cess, 5175.
" " martial law in, 1014, 1164, 2537, [illegible], [illegible].

Tipperhesy (Toberaheena), co. Tip., 5361.
Tipperkeagh, co. Gal., 5587.
Tipperkevin—Tibberkeven—Tipperkevin—Tipperkeavin—Tipperkenvyn—Tipperkevan—Tipperkevan—Tobberkeven—Tobberkevin, co. Dub. (now Kild.), 1415, 3874, 3973, 4083, 4928, 5468, 6116, [illegible].
" prebendary of, 581, 712.
Tipperstowle—Typpersowle (Tobersool?), co. Dub., 4168, 4465, [illegible].
Tipperston — Typperston, co. Kild., 4152, 4484.
Tiptyman — Typtyman (Tobertynan), co. Meath, [illegible], [illegible].
Tiraglasse, co. Tip., 6706.
Tirardan, co. Mon. See Tyreardan.
Tiraun, co. Mayo. See Turan.
Tiravera, co. Mon. See Tyrerawra.
Tirawlie—Tirauly—Tirawly—Tirrawle—Tirrawly—Tirowly—Tyrawly—Tyrawlye—Tyreawle—Tyrrawley (barony of Tirawley, co. Mayo), 1238, 5443, 4873, 4876, 5817, [illegible], [illegible], [illegible], [illegible].
Tirbieg, Harman, English liberty, 1578.
Tir Briuin na Sinna. See Tirerowyn.
Tircagar (Tirhogar), Queen's co., 6458.
Tircollin—Tirecollin, King's co., 1824, 2871.
Tirconnell — Tyrconnel — Tireconnell — Tirreconnell — Tyrconell — Tyrconnell — Tyrconnell — Tyrconnell (co. Donegal), captaincy and chief rule of, [illegible]; indenture fixing annual payment of beeves, 4908; grant, [illegible]; surrender and grant of lands of chiefs in, [illegible], [illegible]; martial law, 4376; pardon to men of, [illegible], 6741. See also Connalia.
" captain, [illegible], 1871.
" general of forces, 6113, [illegible], [illegible].

Tircullen, co. Wat. See Tyrecullen.
Tirawle—Tirrawly. See Tirawlie.
Tireberon, co. Ross., 4878.
Tirecollin. See Tircollin.
Tireconnell. See Tirconnell.
Tiredaghe, co. Clare, 4869.
Tiredigan, co. Mon. See Treredegan.
Tireeraghe Moy, co. Sligo (see Tireragh), 4460.
Tirehane, co. Gal., 4897.
Tirehanighan (Tirehannaghan), co. Kerry, 6634.
Tirehill (Tirerrill, co. Sligo?), 1794.
Tire Hugh—Tyre Enodha (Tirhugh, co. Donegal), 5565; commander of the forces at, 6573.
Tireihane, co. Gal., 4728.
Tireirell—Tirrerell—Tirreryll—Tyrerell—Tyrrerell (Tirerrill), co. Sligo, [illegible], 4469, 4623, [illegible], [illegible].
Tirekennedy (Tirkennedy, co. Fermanagh), [illegible].
Tirelagh, Elizabeth ny, pardon, [illegible].
" Ionna ny, pardon, 6312.
Tirell, John, 4452. See Tyrell.
" sir John. See Tyrrell.
Tiremagraper, co. Gal., 4857.
Tiremalkaraghe (co. Gal.?), 1572.
Tirendarrill, co. Ross. or Gal., 5437.
Tirenane, co. Mayo, territory of, [illegible].
Tirenegher, co. Gal., 1771.
Tirerowne. See Tirerowyn.
Tireragh — Turreraghe — Tipheraghe — Tireeraghe Moy—Tireraghe—Tirreragh—Tirreragh—Tireraghe—Tyreraghe—Tyreheraghe—Tyrreraighe—Tyrheragh, or O'Dowd's country (Tireragh barony), co. Sligo, 1228, 1464, 2160, 3462, 3387, 3407, 4360, 4752, 5341, 5266, 4539, 5577.
Tireran, co. Mon. See Tyreran.
Tirernan—Tereruan, Queen's co., 644, 6405. See also Tececruan.
Tirerowne (co. Ross.?), 4549.
Tireron woughter, co. Ross., [illegible].
Tirerowyn—Tirerowne—Tirrowyn—Tirrowyne—Tirrerowne—Tyreowyne—Tyrrowyn (Tir ui Bhriuin or Tir Briuin na Sinna), co. Ross., country of, 4484, 5577; chief of, 1428, 3123; seneschal appointed, 3352. See also Tireron woughter, Tyrerowne, Tyrrerwyn.
Tirerragh. See Tireragh.
Tirerrill, co. Sligo. See Tireirell, Tirehill.
Tirevichbrayn, co. Clare, 1854. See Tir m'brien.
Tirevowe (Tervoe), co. Lim., 6465.
Tirewan (co. Lim.?), 5804.
Tirhogar, Queen's co. See Tircagar, Tyrrogher.

Tirhugh, co. Donegal. *See* Tiro Hugh, Tyre Raodha, Tyrone.
Tirighly (Tieracles ?), co. Kerry, [illegible].
Tirin—Tirine—Tyrane—Tyrine—Tyrran—Tyrrye—Tyryne (Tourone ?), King's co., [illegible], 1894, 1844, 2871, 4831.
Tirinaire (Turanure), co. Dub., 4573.
Tiriwoy (co. Lim. ?), 6467.
Tirkennedy, co. Ferm. *See* Tirokenada.
Tirkill in Killocan, co. Westm., 6297.
Tirkullen, 6312.
Tirlagh, alias M'Gillerwiss, Garill, pardon, 6541.
Tirlagh, Joan ny, pardon, [illegible].
„ Katheryne ny, pardon, 6478.
„ Margaret ny, pardon, 6515.
„ Owny nyne, pardon, [illegible].
Tirlaughe, Amy nyn, pardon, [illegible].
Tirlickan, co. Long., 5771.
Tirmfeelan—Tinvickraye, co. Clare, 1298, [illegible].
Tironemone, co. Mon. *See* Tyrem'nowe.
Tiromdown, co. Mon. *See* Tyrem'divan.
Tirommervin (co. Leit. ?), 4489.
Tironoire (Tieromore), co. Lim., 5874.
Tironkille (co. Gal. ?), [illegible].
Tironleaghan (co. Kerry ?), 6167.
Tiroky (co. Gal. ?), [illegible].
Tirokbaye, co. Gal., [illegible].
Tirone. *See* Tyrone.
Tirowly. *See* Tirawlie.
Tirraghe, co. Sligo, [illegible].
Tirreconnell. *See* Tirconnell.
Tirrel, Patr. fitz Francis, pardon, [illegible].
Tirrelagh, Ellen ny, pardon, 6467.
„ Joan ny, pardon, 6467.
„ Margaret nine, pardon, [illegible].
„ Onor ny, pardon, 6467.
Tirrelagh oge (of Ballygoyne, co. Kerry), pardon, 6151.
Tirrelockyn, co. Long., 5719.
Tirreleigh—Tirrelleghe, co. Tip., 4576.
Tirrell. *See* Tyrrell.
Tirrelston (Tyrrelstown, co. Westm.), 6329.
Tirrenoghilin, co. Mayo, territory, [illegible].
Tirreragh—Tirreraghe. *See* Tireragh.
Tirrerell. *See* Tirerell.
Tirrenowre. *See* Tirerowyn.
Tirreryll. *See* Tirerell.
Tirretowre, co. Lim. (Tervoe), 4415.
Tirrie. *See* Tirry.
Tirrinkowne, co. Cork, [illegible].
Tirrilaughaghie—Tirrilaughaghaye—Tyrrylaughaughaye (Tullaghan ?), co. Kerry, [illegible], [illegible], [illegible].
Tirroe, Rob., pardon, 6125.
Tirrough, King's co., [illegible].
Tirry, Henry m'Shane, pardon, 6114.
Tirry—Tirrie—Tirrye, Clement, 1836, 6122.
Tirry, Michael, 1836, 6122.
„ *See* Tyrry.
Tir ui Bhriain. *See* Tirowteryn, Tyrowryn.
Tirvighclane—Tirvicklane (co. Clare ?), [illegible], 6763.
Tirvicklane, 6763.
Tirvickuran, co. Clare, [illegible].
Tirvoe, co. Lim., 3090.
Tirvowe, co. Lim., [illegible].
Tirwoe, co. Lim., 3090.
Tiryo, William, 1651.
Tisaran, King's co. *See* Tasseran, Teghsaran.
Tisaxon, co. Gal. *See* Taghsaxon.
Tisieye, co. Long. (see Tagheseny), 2914.
Tithes assigned to curate, 815; measured by copies of corn, 5186, 5860; by pooks, 6153; tithes of lambs, calves, and fish, 1153; impropriate tithes used for victualling fort, 1187.
Tituell, King's co., [illegible].
Tivo, Nicholas, pardon, 1680. *See also* Tyvo.
Tivmore, co. Long., [illegible].
Tiony, Redmund fa. pardon, [illegible].
Tionin (co. Lim. ?), 2363.
Toe, Diermod m'Teig ny, pardon, 6514.
Toe, M'Swyne of, in Tirconnell, [illegible], [illegible].
Toe anoghe, co. Clare, 4761.
Toecalle, co. Clare, 4761.
Toeclean, co. Clare, 4761.
Toe Clonecollan Woghiraghe, co. Clare, 4761.
Toeneghtraghe Trudry, co. Clare, 4761.
Toefiarmott, co. Clare, 4761.
Toegh of Clangorbery (Glin), co. Lim., 6156.
Toeglasye, co. Clare, 4761.
Toeggennyll, co. Clare, 4761.
Toehaghdene, co. Clare, 4761.
Toeholanly (O'Hanly's country in bar. Ballintober, co. Rosc.), 4844. *See* Twoyhanly.
Toe (Inchecuyne), co. Clare, 4761.
Toe Kynalwye, co. Clare, 4761.
Toellych, co. Lim., 4874.
Toem, Wm., archbishop of. *See* Tuam.
Toemmagh—Toemlaugh, co. Clare, 4[illegible], 4874.
Toemolke, co. Clare, 4761.
Toemore, co. Clare, 4761.
Toemadwale, [illegible].
Toeno (co. Cork ?), 6467.
Toenelgorny, co. Clare, 4761.
Toenehowne, co. Clare, 4761.
Toe nekeave, co. Clare, 4761.
Toe ne Kylly, co. Clare, 4761.
Toenemarrod, co. Clare, 4761.
Toe ne verchone, co. Clare, 4761.
Toenreugh, co. Kerry. *See* Tonereoughe.
Toe Ronye, co. Clare, 4761.
Toero, co. Clare, 5942.
Toe Resparde, co. Clare, 4761.
Toe Ronye, co. Clare, 4761.
Toe Rushbarte, co. Clare, 4761.

INDEX TO FIANTS.—ELIZABETH.

Toaughe of Synnamont (co. Antrim), [illegible].
Toavenmughe Truslery, co. Clare, 4761.
Toavolaryuo, co. Clare, 4761.
Toawaghtragh Tradry, co. Clare, 4761.
Toawoynter Fishiriye, co. Clare, 4761.
Toawoynter Thom, co. Clare, 4761.
Tobye, Hugh, pardon, 10.
Tobber, 694.
Tobber, co. Dub. (Tober, co. Wick.), 4183.
Tobber (co. Kild. ?), [illegible], 4373.
Tobber (King's co. ?) 6778.
Tobber (Tober, co. Wick.), 4678.
Tobber (co. Wick. ?), 4377.
Tobber, Wards of (Wards of Tober, co. Wick.), 4189 4673.
Tobberaghay, alias Tibraghne, co. Kilk., 6771.
Tobber asighoy, co. Rosc., 4678.
Tobberboy ae, co. Dub., 5941.
Tobbercormock—Tobbercormucke (Tobercormick), co. Westm., 4138, 5484.
" monastery leased, 4830.
Tobberdower (co. Car. or Wex.), 4548.
Tobberelley (Toberelva), co. Rosc., chapel or cell, 5544.
Tobbergall (Tubergal), co. Wex., 6517.
Tobbergragan. See Tobergragan.
Tobberkeigh—Tubberkeagh (Blindwell ?, co. Gal.), 4860, 6224.
Tobberkeven—Tobberkevin. See Tipperkevin.
Tobbermachie. See Tobermakye.
Tobbermally, co. Clare, 4761.
Tobbermanan, co. Wex., 1259.
Tobberogan—Tobberrogan—Tobberrogane (Toberogan), co. Kild., 2859, 4128, 5424; castle and lands, 6010.
Tobberroe (Toberroe, co. Gal.), 4628.
Tobberrogan—Tobberrogane. See Tobberogan.
Tobberton (Tobertown ?), co. Dub., 6013.
Tobbin, David, pardon, 4611.
" David mode fitz James, pardon, 5834.
" James, pardon, 5701. See Tobin.
" John fitz Richard, pardon, 2094.
" John fitz Walter, pardon, 2961.
" Rich., pardon, 4611.
" Richard fitz Thomas, pardon, 2084.
" Richard, pardon, 1322.
" Rob., clk., rector of Glascro, 4633.
" Tho. ballagh, pardon, 2821.
" Tho. fitz James, pardon, 1328.
" Thomas bogh fitz James, pardon, 2084. See Tobin.
" Tho. fitz Philip, pardon, 4623.
" Thomas fitz Richard, pardon, 2084.
" William fitz Walter, pardon, 2084.
Tobbine, James bog fitz Edmond, pardon, 5078.
Tobbine, James fitz Moriche, pardon, 2843.
" Richard fitz Walter, pardon, 2271.
Tobbyn, Tho., pardon, 2778.
Tobbyne, Jowen fitz Tho., pardon, 4620.
Tobeen—Tobeene. See Tobin.
Tobenston (Tobinstown), co. Car., 5424.
Tober, King's co., 4428.
Tober, co. Tip. See Tubbir.
Tober, co. Wick. See Tobber, Tober, Tubber.
Toberadora, co. Tip. See Tuberydary, Tybberdora.
Toberabeane, co. Tip. See Tipperheny, Typperbeaye.
Toberbury, co. Dub. See Tubberber.
Toberclare, co. Westm. See Tibberclare.
Tobercormoke—Tybbercormyke, co. Westm., 923, 3422. See Tobbercormock.
Toberdaly, King's co. See Tubberdaslughe.
Toberelva, co. Rosc. See Tobberelley.
Tobergal, co. Wex. See Tobbergall.
Tobergragan—Tobbergragan (Tobergragan), co. Dub., 1363, 4772.
Tober in ersig (co. Wex. ?), 2733.
Toberkeogh (co. Rosc.), 4968.
Toberkewgh, 4877.
Toberkewghe, co. Gal., 4067.
Tobermakye—Tobbermachie (Tobermakee co. Rosc. ?), 4416, 4777.
Tobermoenghan (King's co. ?), 6448.
Tobernamole, co. Kerry. See Tyboranamolte.
Toberneasen, co. Wex., 2894.
Toberogan, co. Kild. See Tobberogan.
Toberroe, co. Gal. See Tobberroe.
Tobersool, co. Dub. See Tippersowle, Tubbersoule.
Toberthoule, 4238.
Tobertown, co. Dub. See Tobberton.
Tobertyane, co. Meath. See Tipertyne.
Tobin—Toben—Tobene—Tobine—Tobyn—Tobyne:
" Adam, attainted, 1084, 2647.
" Adam, pardon, 1887, 2840, 4234, 4732, 6246, 6484, 6471, 6363-4, 6382, 6704.
" Conoghor, pardon, 6414.
" David, pardon, 800, 1769, 2840, 3963, 3669, 4523, 4133, 4831, 5412, 6214, 6436, 6508, 6579, 6678, 6534.
" Edmund, pardon, 400, 830, 1861, 2078, 3408, 2918, 2440, 3394, 3467, 4430, 4741, 6235, 6461, 6514, 6518, 6522, 6534, 6511, 6463, 6784.
" Ellen, pardon, 4828, 6222, 6346, 6763, 6768.
" Garrett, pardon, 4688.
" Gerald, pardon, 3473.
" Gerrot, pardon, 4477, 6763.
" Gibbon, pardon, 3869, 6344, 4823.
" Henry, pardon, 2844, 4114, 6223,

INDEX TO FIANTS.—ELIZABETH.

Tobin, James (of Killaby, co. Tip.), sheriff of liberty of Tipperary, [illegible]; commissions, [illegible], [illegible]; pardon, [illegible], 1678, [illegible], [illegible] (Tobbin).
„ James (of Kilbancrie), livery to heir, [illegible].
„ James (of Kilkenny), pardon, [illegible].
„ James, pardon, [illegible], [illegible], 1184, [illegible], 1816, [illegible], [illegible], [illegible], [illegible], [illegible], [illegible], 4714, [illegible], [illegible], [illegible], 6122, [illegible], [illegible], [illegible], [illegible].
„ James (alias Rowno or Rwonio), pardon, [illegible], [illegible].
„ Joan, pardon, 2167.
„ Johanna, widow, [illegible].
„ John (of Garrangibbon), pardon, 874, [illegible]; attainted, [illegible].
„ John (of Killaby), livery, [illegible]; pardon, [illegible], [illegible].
„ John (of Ballaghtobin), pardon, 6411.
„ John (of Conny), pardon, [illegible].
„ John, pardon, [illegible], [illegible], 1481, 1884, [illegible], [illegible], 2971, [illegible], [illegible], [illegible], [illegible], [illegible], [illegible], 4714, [illegible], [illegible], [illegible], 6443, 6477, [illegible], [illegible], [illegible], [illegible], [illegible], 6788.
„ John, alias gowname, pardon, [illegible].
„ John, alias Slakin, pardon, [illegible].
„ Margaret, matrimonial cause, [illegible]; pardon, 4712, [illegible], [illegible], [illegible].
„ Maurice, pardon, [illegible]–4, [illegible], [illegible], [illegible], [illegible].
„ Moris—Morish—Morrice—Morris—Morrish, pardon, [illegible], [illegible], [illegible], [illegible], 6477, [illegible], [illegible].
„ Nicholas, pardon, [illegible], [illegible], [illegible], [illegible], [illegible], [illegible].
„ Philip, pardon, [illegible], [illegible], [illegible], [illegible], [illegible], [illegible], [illegible], [illegible].
„ Philip, alias Llowine, pardon, 6477.
„ Ricard—Riccard, pardon, [illegible], [illegible], [illegible], [illegible], [illegible], [illegible].
„ Richard (of Ballagh), pardon, [illegible], [illegible].
„ Rich. (of Garrangibbon), pardon, [illegible].
„ Rich., serjeant of lordship of Innislawnagh, [illegible].
„ Richard, pardon, [illegible], 1481, [illegible], [illegible], [illegible], [illegible], [illegible], [illegible], [illegible], [illegible], [illegible], [illegible], [illegible], [illegible], [illegible], [illegible], [illegible], [illegible], [illegible].
„ Richard, pardon, [illegible], 6701, [illegible].
„ Robert, pardon, [illegible].
„ Rob., mortgagee of premises in Youghal, [illegible].
„ Robin, pardon, [illegible].
„ Rycard, pardon, [illegible].
„ Theobald, pardon, [illegible], [illegible].
„ Thomas, lease recited, [illegible].
Tobin, Tho. (of Ballaghtobin), pardon, [illegible], [illegible].
„ Tho. (of Killaby), pardon, 6701, [illegible].
„ Tho. fitz James (of Conny), pardon, [illegible].
„ Thomas, pardon, [illegible], [illegible], [illegible], 1678, [illegible], [illegible], 1873, [illegible], [illegible], [illegible], [illegible], [illegible], [illegible], [illegible], [illegible], [illegible], [illegible], 6712, [illegible], [illegible], [illegible], [illegible], [illegible], [illegible], [illegible], [illegible].
„ Tho. Hogh fitz James, pardon, [illegible] (Tobbin), [illegible], [illegible], [illegible].
„ Tho., alias ne Fabio, pardon, [illegible].
„ Walter, pardon, [illegible], [illegible], [illegible]–6, [illegible], [illegible], [illegible], [illegible], [illegible], [illegible], [illegible], [illegible], [illegible], [illegible], [illegible], [illegible], [illegible], [illegible], [illegible].
„ William, pardon, [illegible], [illegible], [illegible], [illegible], [illegible], [illegible], [illegible], [illegible], [illegible], 4714, [illegible], [illegible], [illegible], 6706.
„ William, alias Roth, pardon, [illegible].
„ William dorrough, pardon, [illegible], [illegible].
„ William na moghyn, pardon, [illegible].
„ *See also* Tobbin.
Tobinstown, co. Car. *See* Ballytobyn, Tobenstown.
Tobor (Tober, co. Wick.), 1416.
Toborkegh — Toborkeagh (Blandwell, co. Gal. ?), [illegible], [illegible].
Tobrestiky, co. Ross., [illegible].
Toby, Wm., pardon, [illegible].
Tobyn—Tobyne. *See* Tobin.
Tochar, [illegible]. *See* Togher, co. Cav.
Tocher, [illegible]. *See* Togher, co. Cork.
Tooker—Toker, Denis, [illegible], [illegible].
Toddo, John, gent., constable of Wicklow castle, [illegible].
Toe, co. Lim., [illegible].
Toeaghmoneagh, co. Clare, [illegible].
Toedromy (co. Cork ?), [illegible].
Toegan (Togan), co. Mon., [illegible].
Toeghwyne, co. Clare, [illegible].
Toem (co. Cork ?), [illegible].
Toem, co. Tip. *See* Thome.
Toemonie (Toomone), co. Ross., house of Franciscan friars leased, [illegible], [illegible].
Togan, co. Mon. *See* Toegan.
Toghe of Glancorbarie, co. Lim., [illegible].
Toghe of Kilcummin, co. Kerry, [illegible], [illegible].
Togher—Tochar, co. Cav., [illegible], [illegible], [illegible].
Togher—Tocher, co. Cork, [illegible].
Togher, King's co. *See* Tougher.
Togher, co. Mayo, [illegible], [illegible]–9.
Togher, alias Tower or Tower (Togher), Queen's co., [illegible], [illegible].
Togher, co. Westm., [illegible].
Toghes in Connello, [illegible].
Toghir (co. Cork ?), [illegible].
Toghiro (co. Cork ?), [illegible].
Toghmacdironick (co. Car. ?), [illegible].
Togharoyn, co. Lim., [illegible].

INDEX TO FIANTS.—ELIZABETH.

Tolahobanly, co. Ross., [illegible]7. *See* Twoy-banly.
Tolan, co. Westm., [illegible].
Tohell, Alson, pardon, [illegible].
" Edm. m'Donell I, pardon, [illegible].
Tohill, John, pardon, [illegible].
Toker, Denis, [illegible]. *See* Tocker.
Tolabane (co. Gal. ?), chapel of, [illegible]. *See* Tollabane.
Tolcane. *See* Tolghan.
Tolcunnon, King's co., [illegible].
Tolchan. *See* Tolghan.
Tolchane in Tolharne. *See* Tolhan.
Tolchmanion (King's co. ?), [illegible].
Tolchobradam (Tallybradan, co. Leit. ?), [illegible].
Tole, Dorithe, pardon, [illegible].
" Elizabeth, pardon, [illegible].
" Grany, pardon, [illegible].
" Margaret, pardon, [illegible].
" More, pardon, [illegible].
" Oney, pardon, [illegible].
Tole's country. *See* Toole.
Tolcagh (co. Cork ?), [illegible].
Tolev( ), co. Ross., [illegible].
Tolghan — Tolchan — Tolcane — Tolkane (Tullaghan), co. Westm., [illegible], [illegible], [illegible], [illegible], [illegible], [illegible], [illegible].
Tolghan ne Brenhye, King's co., [illegible].
Tolgbrung (Tullaghanog ?), co. Meath, [illegible].
Tolhan—Tolchane—Tolhane in Tolharne, co. Westm., [illegible], [illegible], [illegible].
Tolharne, co. Westm., [illegible].
Tolkane. *See* Tolghan.
Toll, freedom from, to inhabitants of Dingle, [illegible].
Tolls payable at Kilmallock, [illegible].
Tollabane—Tolabane (co. Gal. ?), chapel, [illegible], [illegible].
Tollaghcrassane, [illegible]. *See* Tullycassan.
Tollaghe, co. Cork, [illegible].
Tollaghe (co. Ross. ?), [illegible].
Tollaghbelarrels. *See* Tullaghfarren.
Tollagher. *See* Tullaghen.
Tollaghgorie. *See* Tullaghgowere.
Tollaghmenan. *See* Tullaghmenan.
Tollaghmelane. *See* Tullaghmelan.
Tollakyhain. *See* Tullakehan.
Tollalcane (Tullykane, co. Cork ?), [illegible].
Tollalonge (King's co. ?), [illegible].
Tollaughbanghe (Tullalough ? ?), co. Kilk., [illegible].
Tollaughe Coole, King's co., [illegible].
Tollaughmaine. *See* Tullamayne.
Tollcheryn, co. Kilk., [illegible].
Tolle (co. Tip. ?), [illegible].
Tollebrick. *See* Tollebricke.
Tollechambroge (co. Tip. ?), [illegible].
Tolleighe rectory, [illegible].
Tollekeele (Tullykeel), co. Kild., [illegible].
Tollemogane (Tullymongan ?), co. Cav., [illegible].
Tollemoylin (Tullamoylin, co. Tip.), [illegible].
Tollengebrane, co. Car., [illegible].
Tollemanarny (Tullymarny), co. Mon., [illegible].
Tollemlaughlen—Tollemaclaughlen, co. Kild., [illegible], [illegible].
Tolley, co. Leit., [illegible].
Tolliard (Tullyard), co. Mon., [illegible], [illegible].
Tolligillan (Tullygillan), co. Mon., [illegible].
Tollimacrewe (Tullymacrew, co. Down), [illegible].
Tollnogor, in Ards, co. Down, [illegible].
Tollocke, in Connaught, [illegible], [illegible].
Tollocne, co. Cav., [illegible].
Tollocrosan, co. Tip., [illegible].
Tollogballon. *See* Tullaghballon.
Tolloghecoole—Tolloughe Coole, King's co. [illegible], [illegible].
Tolloghborde, co. Louth, [illegible].
Tollohanny, co. Westm., [illegible].
Tolloughe Coole. *See* Tolloghecoole.
Tolloughkill (co. Donegal), [illegible].
Tollowe, town of (Tallow), co. Wat., [illegible].
Tollyomy, co. Down, [illegible].
Tolnevanely, in Ards, co. Down, [illegible].
Tologhan, Queen's co., [illegible], [illegible].
Tolokyman, co. Gal., [illegible].
Tolowan, Derbie, pardon, [illegible].
Tolphelam in Clan Colman, co. Westm., [illegible].
Tolrone (co. Gal. ?), [illegible].
Tolsell, Drogheda, [illegible].
Tolsell. *See* Dublin.
Toltharne, co. Westm., [illegible].
Tolzhorne alias Tolhane, co. Westm., [illegible].
Tolwyraine (Tullygarran ?), co. Kerry, [illegible].
Tomagaddy, co. Wex. *See* Tomgaddy, Tomogaddye.
Tomagbard rectory, co. Wex., [illegible].
Tomaghareyne, co. Gal., [illegible].
Tomagbrim—Tomaghryne, co. Gal., [illegible], [illegible].
Tomalyn, co. Kild., [illegible].
Tomaston — Tomastone (Thomastown, King's co.), [illegible], [illegible].
Tomaston. *See* Thomastown, co. Lim.
Tomastone. *See* Tomaston.
Tombegh, [illegible].
Tombreackne—Tombreanne — Tombreenan —Tombreckane (Tombrickane, co. Tip.), [illegible], [illegible], [illegible].
Tombrick, co. Wex. *See* Tomrricke.
Tomcoyle. *See* Tomkoyle.
Tomdarragh—Tomdarroghe—Tomdoragh—Tomdorogh—Tomdarroghe, co. Car., [illegible], [illegible], [illegible], [illegible].
Tomdilly—Thomdely — Tomdellye (Tomdaely), co. Lim., [illegible], [illegible], [illegible]. *See also* Thomdely, Tomegwelly.

INDEX TO FIANTS—ELIZABETH.

Tomdoragh — Tundoragh — Tomdarroghe. See Tumdarragh.
Tome. See Team.
Tome, Peter, pardon, [illegible].
Tome (Toomyvara, co. Tip. ?), 4275, [illegible].
Tomeclarin, co. Gal., 6108.
Tomecorro (co. Car. ?), 4621.
Tomecreniac, 6318. See Tomgreny.
Tomegerily, co. Cork, 6616.
Tomegroghe, co. Car., 2278.
Tomegwelly (Tomdeely ?), co. Lim., castle and land, 5406.
Tomelyn, Thomas fitz Morish, pardon, 2362.
Tome m'Moriske, co. Car. or Wex., 5795.
Tomen, Arthur, grant of land, [illegible].
„ Dermot, pardon, [illegible].
„ Donill, pardon, [illegible].
„ Edm., pardon, 4782.
„ Edm. m'Arte, pardon, [illegible].
„ Edm. m'Edm., pardon, 6108.
„ James, pardon, [illegible].
„ John, pardon, [illegible].
„ Morierlagh, pardon, 1528.
„ Morrogh, pardon, [illegible].
„ Walter, pardon, [illegible].
„ Wm., pardon, [illegible].
„ See Tomyn.
Tomenaloo, co. Kild., 673, 2351, 5708.
Tomevegranyll—Tomour'ranyll — Towmacgranell—Toyme M'Granell—Toomackgranill, co. Rosc., [illegible], 6777, 4844, 6421, [illegible]. See also Two M'Granell.
Tomgaddy (Tomagaddy), co. Wex., [illegible], 6617.
Tomgarrow, co. Wex. See Tomgarrow.
Tomgill, co. Lim., 5374, 5941.
Tomgreny — Tomecreniac — Tomygrouyre (Tomgrenoy), co. Clare, 3618, 5943, 6761. See also Thomegreny.
Tomgroghe, co. Car., [illegible].
Tomhaggard, co. Wex. See Tomhagarde, Tomaghard.
Tomhallogh, co. Gal., 4654.
Tomillin, [illegible].
Tomineerly, co. Wex. See Townerly.
Tomineka, 6441.
Tomiker—Tomkere (co. Kilk. ?), 3941.
Tomkoyle (Tomcoyle, co. Wex. or Wick.) 6942.
Tomkyns, John, 1644, 4881.
Tomlane, co. Wex., 6712.
Tomline (co. Wex. ?), 6917.
Tomloyle (co. Lim. ?), [illegible].
Tomly, in Munster, 6477.
Tom-mighelar (co. Wex. ?), 667.
Tommogaddye (Tomagaddy), co. Wex., 6160.
Tommore, in O'Byrne's country, 1618.
Tomna (Tumna), co. Rosc., rectory, 6163.
Tomnoclare, co. Wex., 128.
Tomnohao, co. Kilk., 691.
Tomnonaghtire (co. Car. ?), [illegible].
Tomnyndan, co. Gal., 6617.
Tomoclavin, Queen's co. See Towinlevan.
Tomoclogo alias Thimoukhal, Queen's co., 616.
Tomolyne (co. Clare ?), 4878.
Tomon, Connilius, earl of. See Thomond.
Tomongh, co. Rosc., 6646.
Tomond. See Thomond.
Tomond, archbishop of, [illegible]. See Tuam.
Tomonglagh, co. Lim., 6916.
Tomore (co. Gal. ?), 6155.
Tompkins, John, general examiner in Connaught, 4680.
Tompson, Richard. See Thompson.
Tompson, Wm., pardon, 7728.
Tomrullagh, co. Wex., 1068.
Tomsfile, co. Wex., 4[illegible].
Tomsnavy, [illegible].
Tomson, Peter, pardon, 4117.
„ Richard. See Thompson.
Tomuhlagh more (of Ballikillin, co. Rosc.), pardon, 6712.
Tomultoly, co. Clare, [illegible].
Tomvricko (Tumbrick, co. Wex. ?), [illegible].
Tomygale, in Munster, 6477.
Tomyn, Arthur, pardon, 1118, 1142.
„ Edmond, pardon, 637.
„ Edm. m'Art, pardon, 6752.
„ Edm. m'Edm., pardon, 6752.
„ James, pardon, 1118.
„ Wm., pardon, 4782.
„ See Tomen.
Tomyne, James, pardon, 6183.
„ Patr. m'Rhame, pardon, [illegible].
Tonaclamor, co. Cav., 6657.
Tonagh, co. Mon., 6667. See also Tonnagh.
Tonaghan, co. Mon., [illegible].
Tonaghmor, co. Cav., 6657.
Tonaghmore (Tonymore, co. Long.), 276, 1681, 6616.
Tonagilhan, co. Mon., 6669.
Tonaght, co. Mayo, 5574.
Tonboe (co. Car. ?), 4182.
Tonerlagha, co. Mon., [illegible].
Tonerowe, co. Wex., 1673.
Tonchillin (Tonyrallivan ?), co. Mon., 6612.
Tondanmpill (Tullynample ?), co. Mon., [illegible].
Tonalogin — Tonelogy (Toologan, co. Cav.), 4981.
Tonelogy (co. Rosc. ?), 6606.
Tonem'magyll, co. Rosc., 4844. See Tomovegranyll.
Tonemore, co. Cav., 6659.
Tonemmony (co. Gal.), 6756.
Tonerragyo, co. Kild., 6168.
Tonerae—Tonomaoe, co. Car., 4916, 6314.
Tonesgrolla, co. Kild., 817.
Tonerogilly (co. Westm. ?), 5657.

INDEX TO FIANTS—ELIZABETH.

Tamerooagho (Tonnurragh), co. Kerry, [illegible].
Tonaskeary, co. Mon., [illegible].
Toneerickenally (Tanmacnully), co. Mon., [illegible].
Toneygan, co. Mon., [illegible].
Tongarrow (Tongurrow, co. Wex ?), 6181.
Tonge, co. Antrim, [illegible].
Tonie, co. Mon., 4610.
Tonilie, in Munster, 6477.
Toniomeaka, co. Mon., [illegible].
Tonlagee, co. Cav. See Tonlagie.
Tonlegeiho, co. Westm., [illegible].
Tonlegyge (co. Meath ?), [illegible].
Tonneyll, co. Gal., [illegible].
Tonnagh (Tonagh), co. Mon., [illegible].
Tonnaghmore (co. Leit. ?), 5740.
Tonnanesna, co. Westm., [illegible].
Tonne, Donagh, pardon, [illegible].
Tonnesye, co. Lim., [illegible].
Tonnemackdirye (co. Wex. ?), [illegible].
Tonne m'Tyre (co. Wex. ?), [illegible].
Tonnemore, co. Cav., [illegible].
Tonnoghe (co. Mayo ?), [illegible].
Tonogh, co. Westm., 4779.
Tonragigh—Tonragighe (Tandoragee), co. Kild., 1947, [illegible], [illegible].
Tonreagh, co. Kerry. See Tonerough.
Tonrege (co. Sligo ?), [illegible].
Tonregoe (Tanrego), co. Sligo, [illegible], [illegible], [illegible], [illegible].
Tonrin (co. Tip. ?), [illegible].
Tonyancake (co. Cav. ?), [illegible].
Tonymore, co. Cav. See Tabuinag oreir.
Tonymore, co. Long. See Tonnyghmore.
Tonyuenle (co. Wex. or Car. ?), [illegible].
Tonyacallan, co. Mon. See Tonackillen.
Tongheasgroy (co. Lim. ?), [illegible].
Toole, Anne, pardon, [illegible].
" Barnaby, [illegible]. See O'Toole.
" Darbie fitz Edm., pardon, [illegible].
" Dermod fitz Edmonde, [illegible], [illegible].
" Derby, pardon, [illegible].
" Dorithy, pardon, [illegible].
" Ellen, pardon, [illegible].
" Honor, pardon, [illegible].
" Katherine, pardon, [illegible].
" Rose, pardon, [illegible]. See O'Toole.
" Rich. m'Edm., pardon, [illegible].
" See Tole, O'Toole.
Tooles—Toles—Towles—Towll's country (in co. Wick.), martial law in, [illegible], [illegible], [illegible], [illegible], [illegible], [illegible].
" seneschal of, 741, 1948-9, 1414.
" serjeant of, 2178.
Toollacobbin (co. Lim. ?), [illegible].
Toome, Christopher, archbishop of. See Tuam.
Toome (co. Cork), [illegible].
Toome, co. Wex. See Twome.
Toomna, co. Ross. See Toymna.
Toomona, co. Ross. See Toomonie.
Toomyvara, co. Tip. See Thome, Tome.
Toomoroghe, co. Cork, [illegible].
Toor, co. Tip. See Tore.
Tooreen, co. Gal. See Twoorynedrinaghe.
Tooreen, King's co. See Tirin.
Toorora, co. Tip. See Toorin, Towrin.
Toorfelim, co. Westm. See Turfelim.
Toora (Tirana ?), co. Mayo, [illegible].
Torlay, co. Long. See Etworthey, [illegible].
Torough alias the Woodehouse, co. Wat., [illegible].
Tore (Toor ?) co. Tip., [illegible].
Torefelem (Toorfelim), co. Westm., [illegible].
Toregoin (co. Long. ?), [illegible].
Torbe (co. Tip. or Wat.), [illegible].
Torbin, co. Tip., [illegible].
Torighe (co. Car. or Wex. ?), [illegible].
Torlavaghar, co. Gal., [illegible].
Torloghvumin, co. Gal., [illegible].
Torman, co. Ros., [illegible].
Tormond, co. Gal., [illegible].
Tormanie, co. Dub. (Tormant, co. Wick.), 1414.
Tornaghmore (co. Leit. ?), 4794.
Turner, Paul, 417.
Torny (co. Tip. ?), [illegible].
Torpan, co. Mon., [illegible].
Torragh, co. Car., [illegible].
Torrens, Feur m'Rory, pardon, [illegible].
Torrey island (Tory), co. Donegal, [illegible].
Tortanelan (Forth O'Nolan ?), [illegible].
Tory, co. Donegal. See Torrey.
Torye, co. Tip., [illegible].
Toryn (co. Mayo ?), [illegible].
Toryn, co. Tip., [illegible].
Toryne, co. Gal. or Mayo, [illegible].
Tosey—Toswee, co. Gal., [illegible], [illegible].
Tosey, co. Mon. See Carowe losais.
Toswee. See Tosey.
Totan, alias Stack, Ricard, pardon, [illegible].
Totbe (co. Lim. ?), [illegible].
Totbie, James, pardon, [illegible].
Touaghty, co. Mayo. See Toughty.
Tough, co. Lim. or Tip., [illegible].
Toughe (Tuogh, co. Lim.), [illegible].
Tougharye, co. Fermanagh, [illegible].
Tougher—Towgher (Togher), King's co., castle, 479, [illegible], [illegible].
Toughercdirvall, Queen's co., [illegible].
Toughes, in Carbrie, [illegible].
Toughir (co. Cork ?), [illegible].
Tougher, co. Kerry, [illegible].
Toughraby (co. Ferm. ?), [illegible].
Toulleme, co. Clare, [illegible].
Tourin (Toureen ?), co. Tip., [illegible]. See also Towrin.
Toumany. See Turnye.

Towacushin (co. Cork ?), [illegible].
Towagh Bellamoyra (Ballymoney, co. Antrim), [illegible].
Towe, Elizabeth ny, pardon, [illegible].
Towem (co. Wex. ?), 17[illegible].
Tower alias Togher, Queen's co., [illegible].
Towercowlie, co. Wex., 6047.
Towerre, co. Gal., 1061.
Togher castle. See Towerhar.
Towhoboly, [illegible]. See Twoyhoaly.
Towhy, Dermod m'Teige ny, pardon, 6446.
Towinlevan — Towinlevan — Towniloven (Tomaslavin), Queen's co., 1178, 1634, [illegible].
Towkenna (co. Tip. ?), [illegible].
Towleght (Tamlat ?), co. Mon., 5641.
Towlan, co. Wex., [illegible].
Towlaugh, co. Wex., [illegible].
Towles country. See Toolea.
Towlevolly, co. Kilk., [illegible].
Towley, Rich., pardon, [illegible].
Towlloonalagh, co. Cav., [illegible].
Towllowbralch (co. Lim. ?), [illegible].
Towlls country. See Toolea.
Towlaglasse (Tullyglass), co. Lim., [illegible].
Towlaknocke (co. Westm.), [illegible].
Towloughe, Queen's co., [illegible].
Towlought, Queen's co., 572.
Towlaky—Towlakye, [illegible], 6407. See Tulakir.
Towlyne, co. Cav., [illegible].
Towlyvyrry (co. Rosc. ?), [illegible].
Towmackranell, [illegible]. See Tomorogranyll.
Towmewater (Tuath M'Walter in bar. Ballymoe), co. Gal., [illegible].
Towmonde. See Thomond.
Townafearna, co. Clare, [illegible].
Townagh, co. Clare, [illegible].
Townaghe, [illegible]. See Townagh, co. Gal.
Townaghmore, co. Cav., [illegible].
Townarath of Lemadon (Townarath), co. Louth, [illegible].
Towneris (Tominearly), co. Wex., [illegible].
Towntallagh (Timmalagh ?), co. Gal., 4718.
Towneyne (co. Cork ?), [illegible].
Townilevan, 1634. See Towinlevan.
Townley, Rich., pardon, [illegible].
Townoughe (co. Cork ?), [illegible].
Towns in Munster, tenants of, excluded from pardons, [illegible].
Town of Lorrha containing 12 cottages, built after Irish manner, with great ditches, [illegible].
Towns, 2—3 quarters, [illegible].
Towrath, co. Louth. See Townarath.
Township, [illegible].
Towrye (Doony ? co. Cork), [illegible].
Towrin, co. Cork, [illegible].
Towrin—Towryn (Toorean or Tourean), co. Tip., [illegible]; grant, [illegible].
Towskart, co. Mayo, [illegible].
Towwyanmoo in Forhaill (King's co.), [illegible].
Towyn (co. Rosc. ?), [illegible].
Toy (co. Westm. ?), 6574.
Toynloigo, co. Rosc., 4825.
Toyhor, Wm., pardon, 4876.
Toymo M'Granell, 4777. See Tomorogranyll.
Toymholly, 5767.
Toym Ivor (co. Rosc. ?), 4940.
Toymme (Tuman or Toorane), co. Rosc., 2941.
Toynrayne, co. Tip. (Shinrone, King's co.), rectory, [illegible].
Tra, Wm. ny, pardon, 4116.
Traholleena, co. Cork, [illegible].
Tracie, John. See Tracye.
Tracton—Tracton — Traciane — Tracten — Trachton—Traughton, co. Cork, 1408, 3120, 4038, 5514, [illegible], [illegible].
 „ abbey, 4446, 4[illegible], [illegible].
 „ abbey de Albo Tractu, leased, [illegible], 6411; lands granted, 5512.
Tracye—Tracie, John, vicar of Dallinax, 6611-12.
Trade, licences to export wheat, 1719, 1737, 1742, 1788, 2247; to export corn in time of plenty, in return for scarcer commodities, [illegible], 6176, 6204, 6219; to export wool, [illegible], 203; to export meat and butter, [illegible]; overseers appointed to prevent illegal exports, [illegible], [illegible], [illegible]; restrictions evaded, [illegible]; licences to import wine, salt, iron, &c., from foreign countries, 50, 51, 58, 3746, 4153; commissions to contract with foreigners for import of corn, wine, salt, &c., for garrison, 1610, 1711, 6750; prohibition of trade with Spain, 2171; trade with France, 6176, [illegible]; citizens of Cork empowered to trade with foreigners in time of war, [illegible]; licence to trade with Scotland, [illegible]; trading licence, 1468; licence to grow and export woad, 4801; fort to protect inland trade, 4912.
 „ See Monopoly.
Tradesmen using deception to be punished by clerk of market, 6418.
Tradry, co. Clare. See Towraghtragh Tradry, Towronamaghe Tradery, and Toanaghtraghe Tradry, 4761.
Tradvallye, co. Kerry, 6480.
Trafford alias Branle, Mary, lease, [illegible], [illegible].
Traghton. See Tracton.
Trale, John fitz Rob. ny, pardon, [illegible].
Tralee—Traley—Tralie — Traly — Traile, co. Kerry, 4877, [illegible], [illegible], 6407-8, [illegible], [illegible].

INDEX TO FIANTS—ELIZABETH.

Tralee, merchants of, 6414, 6383.
" abbey, granted, 6043.
" burgage lands, 6043.
" lordship, 6043.
Traly bisagesse (Tralee, burgess ?), 4462.
Tramon, 6572.
Tramore, co. Wat., 1046, 4872.
Trandar, John, pardon, 4830.
Tranerraghe, co. Gal., 4813.
Trancston, co. Lim., 4452.
Transport, authority to press vessels, men, &c., for, 1442, 3471, 3887, 5642.
Trant, Christian, pardon, 6376.
" Gerald, pardon, 3472.
" James, commission, 5879.
" James fitz Morice (of the Dingnal), commission, 6913, 5991.
" Jonas oy Richard, pardon, 4781.
" Nicholas, pardon, 3491.
" Nicholas fitz Gerrot, pardon, 1721.
" Nich. oge, pardon, 6378.
" Philip, pardon, 3462.
" Richard, pardon, 5678.
" William, pardon, 3472.
" *See* Antrawntaghe, Traunt.
Trapiare, Rich., pardon, 5323.
Traute, James, pardon, 3472.
Trassie, Tadge, pardon, 5772.
Tracy, John, pardon, 5308.
" Shane fyn, pardon, 4478.
Trasye, Katherine, pardon, 6378.
" Wm., pardon, 6808.
Trasteraghe, co. Gal., 4836.
Traverragh, 5923.
Tra:erragh, co. Gal. *See* Drafferraghe.
Traughton. *See* Tracton.
Traunt—Traunte, Dominick, pardon, 6376.
" Garret fitz Nich., pardon, 4864, 6494.
" Garrett fitz Dominick, pardon, 6491.
" Garrett fitz James, pardon, 6494.
" Gerrot, pardon, 4284.
" James, pardon, 4884, 6120, 6876.
" James (of Caherconnell), pardon, 6494.
" James fitz Morris, pardon, 6494.
" James fitz Rich., pardon, 6152, 6378.
" John, pardon, 6494.
" John m'Philip, pardon, 6494.
" Nich., pardon, 4884, 6494.
" Patrick, pardon, 6194.
" Richard, provost of Dingle, 4818.
" Richard, pardon, 4884, 6494, 6811, 6878.
" Thomas, pardon, 4864, 6494.
" Wm., pardon, 4884.
" *See* Antrawntaghe, 3462.
Travellers, tenant of manor of Carlow to keep accommodation for, 1628.
Traver, Randall, doctor of physic, 2047.
Traverse, Philip. *See* Travers.
Travers, vicar of Castleknock, 6816.
Travers, Edm., pardon, 6823.
" Gilbert, summonister of the Exchequer, 4329, 6776; clerk of the crown for Wicklow, 6821.
" Henry (of Cavorstown), pardon, 4694, 6344.
" James, pardon, 2440, 6528.
" John, knight, commissions, 760, 874-81, 394; his lands held by his heiresses, 3149; lease and grant to, recited, 6423, 6765.
" Mary, called viscountess Baltinglas, intrusion in lands of sir John, 3144; grant of land, 4184, 5268.
" Mora, pardon, 2294.
" Peirs, pardon, 6318.
" Philip (of Moriniston), pardon, 6327.
" Philip (of Kedragh), pardon, 6344 (Traverse), 4463.
" Philip fitz Rob., pardon, 6282.
" Rich., pardon, 6318.
" Richard fitz Patr., pardon, 2940, 4738.
" Rob., pardon, 2910, 4838.
" Thomas, pardon, 1962.
" Walter, pardon, 2440.
Traverston — Traverstown (co. Tip.), 6761, 6783.
Travet, Edm., pardon, 3774.
" James, pardon, 3328.
Travel. *See* Trevet.
Travet, Walter, preacher, commission, 3114.
Tray lavellis or the Mill shore, Limerick, 6042.
Treaford alias Nugent, Mary, pardon, 6423.
Trean, co. Leit. *See* Treen.
Trean, co. Lim., 6558.
Treanacreeve, co. Ross. *See* Treengrewe, Triancrevy.
Trean Caltaghe, co. Lim., 6762.
Treanmeane, co. Lim., 5762.
Trean merane (Mayne ?), co. Lim., 6761.
Trean Tawnaghe, co. Lim., 6762.
Treason, persons indicted and not surrendering to be attainted, 1828.
Treasury of Ireland, 7134, 8168.
Treasurer (vice), and Treasurer at Wars. *See* FitzWilliam, Fitton, Wallop, Cary.
Treasurer, deputy vice, 6452.
Tredagh — Tredaghe — Tredaihe. *See* Drogheda.
Treddynes, co. Cork, 4318.
Treffan, Philip, pardon, 6814.
" Rich., pardon, 6814.
Trelyne, Ellen, pardon, 6814.
" James, pardon, 6814.

INDEX TO FIANTS.—ELIZABETH.

Tredyne, Philip, pardon, 5314.
Treen (Trean, co. Leit.?), 5481.
Trees (ash) reserved in leases, [illegible], 5911.
Tregrane, co. Mayo, 4578.
Treer, John, soldier, pardon, [illegible].
Treiden, David, pardon, 4594.
Trelair Tyrytough, co. Cork, [illegible].
Trelick (Trellick), co. Gal., [illegible].
Trelis, [illegible]. See Tralee.
Trembler, Pier, English liberty, [illegible].
Trenchard, Wm., land grant, [illegible].
Trenegrewe (Trenecreeve?), co. Rosc., 4944.
Trennescart—Trenescarte (Tinnescart), co. Wat., [illegible], [illegible].
Trenvolegan—Trevolegan, co. Rosc., [illegible], 4944. See also Tryen volegaine.
Trenlawnaghe, co. Lim., country of, [illegible].
Trenvolgan. See Trenvolegan, [illegible].
Tren, Philip m'Thomas, pardon, 6714.
Trevelegan (Thaligan), co. Mon., [illegible].
Tresham, George, comptroller of the ordnance and clerk of works, [illegible], [illegible].
Tressle, James, pardon, [illegible].
Tresteraghe. See Tristeragh.
Treuse, Patr., pardon, [illegible].
Treugh—Treughe. See Trough.
Treven, co. Kild., [illegible].
Treverock or Tralock, Wm., pardon, [illegible].
Travers, Patr., pardon, [illegible].
Treves, David, pardon, [illegible].
Trevet—Travet—Trevett—Trivet, co. Meath, 1674; manor, 4477.
" grange beside, [illegible].
" rectory, [illegible], [illegible], 6797.
Trewe, Sawsly, lease, 1794, [illegible].
Trewman, Robert, pardon, [illegible].
Treydyn, James fitz Wm., pardon, [illegible].
" Rich. fitz Wm., pardon, [illegible].
Treyly, co. Rosc., 1280.
Tridine, Dee ogo, pardon, [illegible].
" James m'Philip, pardon, [illegible].
" James m'Rob., pardon, [illegible].
" Wm. m'Dao, pardon, [illegible].
Triell (co. Rosc.?), [illegible].
Triemmoeany, co. Galway, [illegible].
Triene or Tryon of land, co. Sligo, [illegible], [illegible].
Triencrevy—Tryongecreven (Trenacreeve), co. Rosc., [illegible], [illegible].
Trienieragh—Trienieraghe—Trienyeraghe (Triemeragh), co. Kerry, [illegible], [illegible], [illegible].
Trien reade (co. Rosc.?), [illegible].
Trienyeraghe. See Trienieragh.
Trille, co. Rosc. See Trylle.
Trim—Trym—Trime—Tryme, (mention), [illegible], [illegible], [illegible], [illegible], [illegible], [illegible], [illegible], [illegible], [illegible], [illegible], [illegible], [illegible], [illegible], [illegible], 6077, [illegible], [illegible], [illegible], [illegible]; the liberties extended to other

Trim:
towns, [illegible], [illegible]; premises in, leased, [illegible], 1714, [illegible]; granted, [illegible], [illegible].
" portreeve and burgesses, lease of market and tolls, [illegible]; surrender, [illegible]; leased anew, [illegible].
" portreeve or provost, commissions, [illegible], [illegible], [illegible], [illegible].
" castle, reserved to crown, [illegible], [illegible]; customs due to, [illegible], [illegible].
" castle, constable and keeper of castle and gaol, [illegible], [illegible], [illegible], [illegible], [illegible]; his fees, 4547.
" gaol, delivery, [illegible], [illegible].
" abbey of the B. V. M., proprietor, [illegible]; alienation, [illegible]; possessions leased, [illegible], [illegible], 1714, [illegible], [illegible], [illegible], [illegible], [illegible], [illegible], [illegible]; granted, [illegible], [illegible], [illegible]; pension, [illegible].
" house of friars minor observant, [illegible].
" house of friars preachers, [illegible].
" priory of S. Peter of the Newtown, possessions leased, [illegible], [illegible], [illegible], [illegible], [illegible], [illegible], [illegible], [illegible], 1614, [illegible], 1714, [illegible], [illegible], [illegible], [illegible], [illegible], [illegible], [illegible], [illegible], [illegible], [illegible], [illegible], [illegible], [illegible]; pension, 6787.
" hospital of S. John of the Newtown, surrender of lease, [illegible]; leased, [illegible], [illegible], [illegible]; pension, 6787.
" Black hall, 1714, [illegible].
" Castle moss, 1714.
" Ferre street, 1714, [illegible].
" Frank house, [illegible], [illegible].
" Gates, north and south, 1714.
" Grange of, [illegible].
" Haggard street, 1714.
" High street, 1714, [illegible].
" Market, [illegible], [illegible], [illegible].
" Mandolin land, [illegible].
" Mandleysfield, [illegible].
" Mendlin chapel, [illegible].
" Park, [illegible].
" Pillory street, 1714.
" Porch street, 1714.
" Rathfield, [illegible].
" Saille park, [illegible].
" Scarlet street, 1714, [illegible].
" Skinner's street, [illegible].
" Turk mill, [illegible].
" Wyne street—Wynetavern street, 1714, [illegible].
" manor, [illegible], [illegible], [illegible], [illegible], [illegible].
" rectory of the B. V. M., [illegible], [illegible], [illegible], [illegible].
" parson of, [illegible].
" See Newtown of Trim.

INDEX TO FIANTS—ELIZABETH.

Trimletston — Trimleston — Trimletiston — Trimletestone — Trimleiston—Trimlettiston— Trimlettiston— Trymeletiston — Trymleiston — Trymleston —Trymletteston—Trymletestowne — Trymlettiston — Trymletston — Trymletstown — Trymlettiston, co. Meath, 4[illegible].

" John (Barnewall), baron of, lease to recited. [illegible], 6751.

" Patrick, baron of, commissions, 201, 279-81, 294; lease, 619; livery to heir, 861.

" Robert, baron of, livery, 871; commissions, 682, 698, 782, 952, 2117; licence of absence, 2162; livery, [illegible].

" Peter, baron of, livery, [illegible]; commissions, 3144-6, [illegible], 3[illegible], 3401, [illegible], 4085, 40[illegible], 4149, 4461, 4618, 4[illegible], 43[illegible], 53[illegible], 5[illegible], 6716, 6781.

Trinagh (co. Mayo ?), 67[illegible].

Trinitie land, Fethard, co. Tip., 4[illegible].

Trinity College, Dublin, charter, 5718; first provost, fellows and scholars, 5719; annuity granted to, 6414; the provost an ecclesiastical commissioner, [illegible]; crown wards to be educated in, 6[illegible], 6[illegible], 6311, 6[illegible], 6[illegible], 6[illegible], 6[illegible], 6[illegible], 6406, 6416, 6[illegible], 6[illegible], 6[illegible], 6[illegible], 6[illegible], 6[illegible], 6[illegible], 6676, 6[illegible], 67[illegible], 6778.

Trinity, friars of (Trinitarians or Order for the Redemption of Captives), at Adare, 1148, 3174, 4186, 4767, 5118, 5[illegible].

Trinity island. *See* Holy Trinity.

Trippetts (triped) stolen, value of, 3[illegible].

Trishill, Gilpatrick keaghe, pardon, 4[illegible].

Tristan, co. Gal., 5918.

Tristan, Moris, pardon, 47[illegible].

Tristeldermot — Tristeldermote — Tristeldermott—Tristledermot (Castledermot), co. Kild., 1854, 5[illegible], 67[illegible]; rectory, 432.

" hospital of S. John, leased, 678, 5[illegible]; granted, 5[illegible]; possessions granted, 5[illegible].

" house of friars leased, [illegible], 4[illegible], 44[illegible].

" vicar of, [illegible].

" *See also* Castledermot.

Tristell—Tristle, co. Kild., 1[illegible], 7[illegible].

Tristernagh — Tresternaghe — Trysternagh, co. Westm., 467, 6[illegible], 6[illegible].

Tristernagh, priory of the B. V. M., leased, 467, 1[illegible], [illegible], 6[illegible]; possessions granted, [illegible], 6[illegible]; proxies, 67[illegible].

" rectory, 467, 37[illegible].

Tristerman (King's co. ?), 6[illegible].

Tristle. *See* Tristell.

Tristledermot. *See* Tristeldermot.

Tristram, Rob., pardon, 4[illegible].

Trivel. *See* Trovel.

Troddon, Cahir, pardon, [illegible].

Troddy, Wm., pardon, 4712.

Troe, Philip fitzThos., pardon, 6178.

Troghe, 6[illegible]. *See* Trough.

Troghe, Rob., pardon, 6[illegible].

Trohanackesy (Troghanmeny ?), co. Kerry, 6[illegible].

Trohie, Gramy, pardon, [illegible].

" Katherine, pardon, [illegible].

" Margaret, pardon, [illegible].

Trolley, William, clerk, death of, [illegible].

Troman (Tromman), co. Meath, [illegible], [illegible].

Tromhender, Donald, pardon, [illegible].

Tromro (Trumra), Queen's co., 1876, [illegible].

Tromroe—Trumroe, co. Westm., [illegible], 6[illegible].

Tromry, co. Clare, 4[illegible].

Tromry (co. Long.), [illegible].

Tronell, co. Dub. (co. Wick.), [illegible].

Trostan—Trostane, Nich., pardon, [illegible], [illegible].

Trott, Richard, pardon, 772.

Trough —Trogh — Troughe — Troghe, co. Mon., barony, 6753; surrender and regrant to M'Mahon, 4[illegible], 4[illegible]; grants of land in, [illegible]-72, [illegible], [illegible].

Trowegh Kyllolowe, co. Clare, 4781.

Troye, David, pardon, [illegible].

" James, pardon, 1617, [illegible], [illegible].

" Philip, pardon, 1044.

Troyvoyanna (King's co. ?), 6[illegible].

Trubley, co. Meath 2[illegible].

Trughanmeny, co. Kerry. *See* Trohanackesy, Trughmeny.

Trughland or hufedred, 6042.

Trughmeny (Trughanmeny), co. Kerry, [illegible]. *See also* Trohanackesy.

Trulock or Treverock, Wm., pardon, 4[illegible].

Trumamacroughe (Trumra), Queen's co., 4[illegible].

Trumpeter, pay of, [illegible].

Trumra, Queen's co. *See* Tromro, Trummacroghe.

Trumroe. *See* Tromroe, co. Westm.

Trunaballie, [illegible].

Truston—Trustane, co. Gal., 4[illegible], 4[illegible].

Trustane, Wm., pardon, [illegible].

Truit, John fitz Nich., pardon, [illegible].

Tryen of land, [illegible]. *See* Triena.

Tryen Roshirna, co. Sligo, [illegible].

Tryenagh (co. Mayo ?), 67[illegible].

Tryenescreven, [illegible]. *See* Triencrevy.

INDEX TO FIANTS—ELIZABETH.

Trynsvalgan, [illegible].
Tryan volagalan, [illegible]. See Trunsvolagan.
TryBe (Trille ?), co. Ross, [illegible].
Tryllye, [illegible].
Tryme—Tryme. See Trim.
Trymelstston — Trymladston — Trymles-ton — Trymlestown — Trymlestowne — Trymlesteston — Trymletston — Trymlestown—Trymlettston. See Trimlestown.
Trynytie monastery. See Holy Trinity.
Trysteldelan (Castledillon ?), co. Kild., rectory, [illegible].
Trystelkeran (Castlekeeran, co. Meath ?), church, [illegible].
Trysteragh. See Tristernagh.
Trytrane (co. Donegal), [illegible].
Tryver, grange of, co. Meath, [illegible].
Tuaghs, surrendered by M'Donell, co. Antrim, [illegible].
Tuaim. See Tuam.
Tually, co. Ross., [illegible].
Tuam—Tome—Tuame—Tweme, co. Gal., [illegible], [illegible], [illegible].
" monastery of the Holy Trinity, leased, [illegible] (under form of Thomonde); granted, [illegible].
" monastery of S. John Baptist, granted, [illegible].
Tuam—Thome—Tuam — Tome — Tome — Tuaim:
" archbishop Christopher (Bodkyn), takes oath of supremacy, 196; commissions, [illegible] (Tomond), 1417-8, 1454, [illegible].
" " William (Mallaly), commissions, [illegible], [illegible], [illegible], [illegible], [illegible], [illegible], [illegible], [illegible], [illegible], [illegible], [illegible]; appeal from, [illegible].
" " (Nehemiah Donellan), commissions, [illegible], [illegible], [illegible]-4.
" " tithes belonging to, [illegible].
" dean, [illegible].
" diocese, [illegible].
Tuame. See Tuam.
Tuam Ighter—Twayne Ightare — Twayne Ighter, co. Gal., [illegible], [illegible].
Tuam Iwyre, co. Leit., [illegible].
Tuamcelasan, co. Gal., [illegible].
Tuan mack granill. See Tunnevegranyll.
Tuathclogin (Taughcloggin, co. Lim.), vicarage of, 84.
Tuath M'Walter, co. Gal. See Towneswater.
Tuath. See Toe, Toagh, Tuaghe, Too, Toghe, Toghe, Towagh, Tow—, Toy—, Tuagh, Tuogh, Twho—, Two—, Twugh.
Tubber, co. Kild. (Tober, co. Wick.), rectory, [illegible], 1720, [illegible], 2708.
Tubber, King's co., [illegible].
Tubberbor—Tibberbir (Toberburr), co. Dub., 1777, [illegible].
Tubbercowell, co. Westm., [illegible].
Tubberdanlaghe—Tibberdalaghe — Tibberdaloghe (Tobertoly, King's co.), [illegible], [illegible], [illegible], [illegible].
Tubberkeagh. See Tobberkeigh.
Tubbersoule (Toberseol, co. Dub.), [illegible].
Tubbervilly (co. Wick. ?), [illegible].
Tubbir (Tober ?), co. Tip., [illegible].
Tubbred, Robert, death of, [illegible].
Tuberidd, Donald my, pardon, [illegible].
Taberydary (Toberadera ?), co. Tip., [illegible].
Tuckemill (see Tuckmill), [illegible].
Tucker, Robert, constable, Dublin castle, [illegible] marshal of four courts, [illegible], [illegible].
" Rob., gunner, Dublin castle, [illegible].
" Wm., pardon, [illegible].
tuckers, pardoned, [illegible], [illegible].
Tucking mill at Galway, [illegible].
Tuckmill—Tuckemill, co. Dub. (Wick.), [illegible], [illegible].
Tuck mill at Trim, [illegible].
Tuo, Nicholas, pardon, [illegible], [illegible].
" See Two.
Tuabe (co. Lim. ?), [illegible].
Tuallery (co. Gal. ?), [illegible].
Tuamore alias Clontykho, Queen's co., [illegible].
Tueaadrosine, co. Cork or Lim., [illegible].
Tuel, William, comm. for martial law, [illegible].
Tugh Cloggyne (Tuaghcloggin), co. Lim., [illegible].
Tuhanedromyn (co. Cork ?), [illegible].
Tuite—Tuit—Tute—Tuyt—Tuyte:
" Andrew (of Moneloy), pardon, [illegible]; alienation by, [illegible]; wardship of his heir, [illegible].
" Andrew (of Moneloy), pardon, [illegible].
" Edmund (of Mollenly), wardship of his son, [illegible].
" Edm. (of Tuitestown), wardship, [illegible].
" Edm., pardon, [illegible].
" Edward (of Bakemill), pardon, [illegible], 4708, 4731.
" Edward (of Tuitestown), wardship of his son, [illegible].
" Edw., pardon, [illegible], [illegible], [illegible].
" Farrall (alias M'Illroy), pardon, [illegible].
" Garrett, pardon, [illegible], [illegible].
" Gerald, son of, commission, [illegible].
" Gerald, pardon, [illegible].
" Gerrott, pardon, [illegible].
" James, murder of, [illegible].
" James, pardon, 18, [illegible], [illegible].
" Janett, pardon, [illegible].
" Jenne, pardon, [illegible].

INDEX TO FIANTS—ELIZABETH.

Tuite, John (of Sonnagh), wardship, 5152; livery, 5151.
„ John (of Brackagh), commissions, 4181, 4463; alienation by, 5348.
„ John (of Cloghran), his heir, 5170, 5152.
„ John (of Cloghran), wardship, 5170; livery, 5152.
„ John (of Balnegall), alienation by, 5348.
John, pardon, 498 (Twyt), 4018, 4978, [illegible].
John fitz Rich., pardon, 4872.
m'Rickard, son of, commission, 262.
„ Nicholas, pardon, 5053, 6457.
„ Oliver (of Balirusane), commissions, 4168, 4463; pardon, 6471.
„ Oliver (of Moylin), commissions, 4181, 4463.
„ Patrick, pardon, 6424.
„ Redmund, pardon, 4783.
„ Richard (of Tuitestown, knight), commissions, 262, 891, 843; grant of land, 289; pardon of alienation, 403.
„ Richard, son of sir Richard, 289.
„ Rich. (of Tuitestown), pardon, 2710.
„ Rich., pardon, 2771, 4847.
„ Robert (of Cloghran), livery to his son, 5152.
„ Rob., pardon, 6450.
„ Simon, pardon, 6154.
„ Thomas or Tho. m'Riccard (of Sonnagh), sheriff of Westm., 2274, 2841; commissions, 982, 2215, 2274, 2484, 2881; pardon, 906; freedom from subsidy, 1459; wardship and livery to son, 5152, 5151.
„ Thomas, pardon, 82, 498, 674, 6348, 4173, 6621.
„ Tibbott, pardon, 4521.
„ Walter (of Tuitestown, son of sir Richard), 289; pardon, 2710.
„ Walter (of Johnston), commission, 4181, 4463.
„ Walter (son of Andrew, of Molyaley), wardship, 1510.
„ Walter (son of Edm., of Mollenly), wardship, 5223.
„ Walter, house of, in Mullingar, 1441, 2296.
„ Walter (of Rosmyll), pardon, 1224.
„ William (of Tuiteston), sheriff of Westmeath, 2221, 2710, 2818; commissions, 1863, 2117, 2444, 2484, 2884, 4181, 4463, 5181; grant in remainder, 289; freedom from subsidy, 1459; pardon, 2710, 2818, 2845; pardon to his tenants, 4818.
Tuite, William (of Killenan), commission, 2444.
„ Wm. fitz Rob. (of Sonnagh), pardon, 2671.
„ Wm. (alias M'Gilleroy), pardon, 4294.
„ Wm., pardon, 6273.
„ (of Balirusane), commission, 891.
Tuiterath, co. Meath. See Tuteratho.
Tuiteston, co. Meath, 6499.
Tuiteston—Tuitestowne—Tuiston—Tuiteston—Tuitestone—Tuiestoun—Tuitestowne—Tuiteton—Tuitstone—Tuyteston—Twytiston, co. Westm., 82, 498, 1575, 1863, 2117, 2444, 2888, 2710, 2767, 2818, 2845, 2884, 4183, 4463, 4104, 4632. See also Tuiteston.
Tuitt, Edw., pardon, 6150.
Tulagh (see Tullagh, King's co.), 5664.
Tulahody (Tullahedy, co. Tip.), 4974.
Tulanydala, co. Gal. or Mayo, 4708.
Tulchanston, King's co., 6404.
Tulerin, co. Gal., 4614.
Tulfarnis, co. Wick. See Tullaghfarnes.
Tulghan, co. Tip., 4658.
Tulghane (co. Sligo?), 6601.
Tulghanemilke (Tullaghanmiok), co. Westm., 2428.
Tulhighe, co. Cork, 6820.
Tulla, co. Clare. See Tullaa, Tullaughe.
Tulla, co. Clare, barony. See Tullaghconnyll, Tullaghyneagill.
Tulla Beg, co. Kerry. See Tullybeg.
Tullabracky, co. Lim. See Tulloghbracky.
Tullacoman, co. Clare, 1834.
Tullae (Tulla), co. Clare, 4761.
„ abbey, 4761.
Tullagchmaun (co. Tip.?), 6708.
Tullagh, co. Car., 4440.
Tullagh, co. Clare, 4563, 6178.
Tullagh (co. Gal.), 4878, 6543.
Tullagh—Twlagh (co. Kerry?), 6468, 6477.
Tullagh (co. Kilk. or Car.), 2098.
Tullagh — Tulagh — Tullaghe — Tullaugh (King's co.?), 1767, 2784, 6101, 6657.
Tullagh, co. Lim., 4463.
Tullagh (Tully), co. Mon., 5477.
Tullagh (co. Ros.?), 6777.
Tullagh, co. Sligo, 5493, 5780.
Tullagh (co. Tip.), 5113, 4364.
Tullagh, Twig na, pardon, 6161.
Tullaghadae, co. Clare, 4761.
Tullaghadae (the barony of Inchiquin), co. Clare, 4761.
Tullaghallon—Tolloghallon (Tullyallen), co. Louth, 649, 2574.
Tullaghan, co. Westm. See Tulghan, Tullen, Tullham.
Tullaghanbroge—Tullaghan broge, co. Kilk., 4587, 6704. See Tullaghanbrooke, Tullighane broge.

INDEX TO FIANTS—ELIZABETH.

Tullaghanecrudere, co. Gal., 5718.
Tullaghan Idovane, 4394.
Tullaghanog, co. Meath. See Tolghynoge.
Tullaghamy, grange, co. Kilk., 1178.
Tullaghanalesk, co. Westm. See Tulghanes-
  kea.
Tullagharay, co. Clare, 3912.
Tullagharde (Tullyard), co. Louth, 5867.
Tullagharman (Tullycarman?, co. Down),
  [illegible].
Tullaghbane (Tullybane), co. Westm., 5528.
Tullaghbrogo (co. Kilk.?), 1960.
Tullagh Carne—Tullagh Carne (Tullycorn,
  co. Donegal), 5862, 5887.
Tullagh Comme (co. Clare?), 4732.
Tullagh cammon (Tullycammon), co. Clare,
  6731.
Tullaghcomyskie (Tullycommasky), co. Mon.,
  [illegible].
Tullaghcrokhorrigh ter alias Kyllehuorn
  (Killadandra in bar. Tullyhonco, co.
  Cav.), 1691.
Tullaghcrevane, co. Kilk. or Tip., 4152.
Tul'aghe, 6423.
Tullaghe (co. Ferm.?), 4510.
Tullaghe. See Tullagh, King's co.
Tullaghe (co. Rosc.), rectory, 1311.
Tullaghe, co. Wat., 3294.
Tullaghea (co. Tip.?), 6768.
Tullaghecrome (co. Car.?), 911.
Tullagheclarris. See Tullaghfcrees.
Tullaghegallegan. See Tullagh Gallegan.
Tullaghegowrye, co. Kild., 932.
Tullaghekeltie, co. Louth, 5187.
Tullaghenaspyll (the barony of Tullo), co.
  Clare, 4761.
Tullaghene (co. Wat.?), 6674.
Tullaghenemrace, co. Car., 1652.
Tullaghenske, church of, 6787.
Tullagh e—Tullaghes, co. Louth, 5116, 5367.
Tullaghew, co. Tip., 2612.
Tullaghfelim—Tullaghfelym—Tullaghophe-
      lem (Tullow), co. Car., 1560,
      1577, 3145; rectory, 482.
      house of friars, 894.
Tullaghferres — Tullagheclarris—Tullagho-
  ferris — Tullaghferyes — Tullaghferrise—
  Tullaghfeerys (Tullorris, co. Wick.), 1414,
  1615, 2572, 3145, 3996, 4134.
Tullagh Gallegan — Tullaghegallegan, co.
  Mon., manor and land, 4663, 4661.
Tullaghgeegan, co. Mayo, 6314.
Tullaghgorey (co. Wick.?), 6577.
Tullaghgowere — Tullaghgorie—Tullaghg-
  wery (Tullygorey), co. Kild., 6323, 6664,
  6783. See also Tullaghegowrye.
Tullaghhaghe — Tullaghugh — Tullehugh
  (Tullyhugh), co. Sligo, 4540, 5478.
Tullaghhogan, co. Mayo, 6611.
Tullaghisto, co. Mon., 5444.
Tullaghkyle, co. Louth, 6563.
Tullaghlarge—Tullaghlarge—Tullaghlarge
  (Tullytark, co. Donegal), 5852, 5887; hill
  and river of, 5863, 5887.
Tullaghleighe (Tullyleague?), co. Lim., 6158.
Tullaghlifferoghe (Lisronagh), co. Tip.,
  rectory, 4018.
Tullaghlinnan, co. Clare, 4263, 4374.
Tullaghmain—Tullaghmayne. See Tulla-
  mayne, co. Kilk.
Tullaghmcan — Tullaghmeane—Tullereane
  (Tullamain, co. Tip.?), 1016, 1928, 2288-9.
Tullaghmeddan — Tullamethan — Tullo-
  methane — Tullemethan, co. Meath,
  tithes of the grange, 1462, 2822-4, 6146,
  6334.
Tullaghmolan — Tullaghmolane, co. Tip.,
  2778, 3394.
Tullaghmore, co. Clare, 4860.
Tullaghmore, co. Gal., 5402.
Tullaghmore (Tullamore, King's co.), 2828,
  6130.
Tullagh more, co. Westm., 718, 1364.
Tullaghmoyn (co. Kilk.?), 3631.
Tullaghna, co. Kerry. See Tirrillaughlaghie.
Tullaghnogloge — Tullenagloge (Tullanag-
  loge), co. Sligo, 4544, 5696, 6316.
Tullaghnemrace — Tullaghnemrake, co.
  Car., 778, 1787.
Tullaghophelem. See Tullaghfelim.
Tullaghoressae (co. Tip.?), 6794.
Tullaghphall (Tullow?), co. Car., 5363.
Tullaghrathe, co. Cork (Tallow, co. Wat.?),
  1007.
Tullaghter, 3732.
Tullaghviane—Tullaghwian (Tullamain?),
  co. Tip., rectory, 1614, 4618, 5621.
Tullaghydae (barony of Inchiquin), co.
  Clare, 4761.
Tullaghynaspill — Tullaghynaspyll — Tul-
  laghynaspyll (barony of Tullo), co. Clare,
  4761.
Tullagiogan, co. Mayo, 6605.
Tullaluan, 6764.
Tullahealy, co. Tip. See Tulahedy, Tullaha-
  den.
Tullahuneill (Tullahennel), co. Kerry, 6152.
  See also Tullobyneill, Tullihineill.
Tullahaughe, co. Kilk. See Tollaughanglie.
Tullakeshna—Tullakyhain (co. Gal.?), 6025,
  6711.
Tullalane (co. Cork), 6566.
Tullamain, co. Tip. See Tullaghmcan, Tull-
  aghviane.
Tullamayne—Tullaughmaine—Tullaghmain
  —Tullaghmayne, co. Kilk., 348, 3012, 4267,
  6606.
Tullamethan. See Tullaghmeddan.

INDEX TO FIANTS—ELIZABETH.

Tullamore, co. Kerry. *See* Tullamore, Tully-more.
Tullamore, King's co., 4750. *See* Tullagh-more.
Tullamoylin, co. Tip. *See* Tollemoylin.
Tullan (Tullaghan), co. Westm., 1884.
Tullanaghug, co. Sligo. *See* Tullaghnegiog.
Tullan e mecill, co. Sligo, 4888.
Tullanamoyle, co. Sligo, 4561.
Tullanoge, co. Meath, rectory, 825.
Tullaugh. *See* Tullagh, King's co.
Tullaughe (Tulla ?), co. Clare, 5777.
Tullaugha (co. Rosc.), rectory, 5782.
Tullaughokillie, co. Louth, 6414.
Tullchalaind (Tullylinn, co. Donegal ?), 5948, 6807.
Tulle. *See* Tully, co. Car.
Tulle. *See* Tully, co. Long.
Tulle. *See* Tully, co. Tip.
Tullebraske, co. Cav., 4891.
Tullebricke — Tollebrick (Tullybrick), co. Cav., 4918, 6457.
Tullecarbet—Tullecarbidd (Tullycorbet), co. Mon., rectory, 2042; termon granted, 5728.
Tulleenalon, co. Cav., 4891.
Tullegalkhork — Tullegalkhorke, co. Cav., 4908.
Tulleghugh. *See* Tullaghhaghe.
Tullegolanorke, co. Cav., 4908.
Tullehady. *See* Tullyhady.
Tullehugh, 6474. *See* Tullaghhaghe.
Tullehynell (Tullahonnel, co. Kerry ?), 6916.
Tullekrwly (co. Clare ?), 6414.
Tullemacke, co. Mon., 4631.
Tullemenahane—Tullemeihan. *See* Tullagh-meidan.
Tullemore (Tullamore), co. Kerry, 6493.
Tullenalle—Tullenalley. *See* Tulleenally, co. Westmeath.
Tullenally, King's co., 4464.
Tullenally — Tulleenalle — Tullenalley (Tullynally), co. Westm., 2878, 4151, 4463, 5274.
Tullenan, co. Long., 4404.
Tullenecrosse (co. Mon. ?), 5041.
Tullenegloggs. *See* Tullaghnegiog.
Tulleneyane, co. Rosc., 4567.
Tullenor (Tullyanmore ?), co. Mon., 4682.
Tullery—Tullerye, co. Gal., 4078, 4894, 5414.
Tullevenna, 1936. *See* Tullaghmenna, co. Tip.
Tullevin. *See* Tullyvyn, co. Cav.
Tullevine. *See* Tullyvyn, co. Lim.
Tullevohalle (co. Cork ?), 4754.
Tullewine. *See* Tullyvyn, co. Lim.
Tulley. *See* Tully, co. Kild.
Tulley (Tully, co. Leit. ?), 5440.
Tulleyman, co. Long., 1799.
Tulleyre (co. Gal. or Rosc.), 4928.
Tullham (Tullaghan), co. Westm., 648.
Tullibeg (Tulla Beg ?), co. Kerry, 6183.
Tullie. *See* Tully, co. Kild.
Tullie. *See* Tully, King's co.
Tullie (Tully, co. Leit. ?), 5453.
Tullie. *See* Tully, co. Rosc.
Tullighan (co. Kilk. ?), 1018.
Tullighanebroge (Tullaghanbrogue, co. Kilk.), 2267;
" vicar, 749.
Tulligenie, Grany 8ix, pardon, 6704.
Tullihinell (Tullahennel, co. Kerry ?), 6477.
Tullindoney, co. Down. *See* Ballytollydony, 1488.
Tullinemoyle (co. Sligo ?), 4514.
Tullivine. *See* Tullyvyn.
Tullo (King's co. ?), 4483.
Tullo. *See* Tulloe, co. Long.
Tullocke (Tulloy), co. Meath, 1460, 2706, 3472, 3888, 3943.
Tulloe, co. Car., 4319.
Tulloe—Tullo, co. Long., 2973, 4143, 5028.
Tulloy, co. Meath. *See* Tullocke.
Tullogh (perhaps Tully, co. Dub.), 1144.
Tullogh, in Ely (King's co.), 1298.
Tullogh, co. Long., 2291.
Tullogh, 2768.
Tullogh (co. Wat. ?), 5782.
Tulloghmane, 4834.
Tulloghbracky (Tullabracky, co. Lim.), prebend, 6415.
Tulloghegles (Tullyglass), co. Lim., 2377.
Tulloghirin (co. Lim. ?), 4466.
Tulloghoge (Tullyhoge), co. Tyrone, 6714.
Tulloghwere, co. Kild., 6793.
Tullokheine, co. Gal., 6944.
Tullomer (co. Clare ?), 4978.
Tullore, Queen's co. *See* Tulloyer.
Tullough, co. Dub. (Wick. ?), 1544.
Tulloughdonnell, co. Louth, 1038.
Tulloughotyn, co. Lim., 1694.
Tullovin, co. Lim., 6930. *See also* Tullyvyn.
Tullow, co. Car. *See* Tullaghfellim, Tullagh-phelim.
Tullowe (co. Tip. ?), 4671.
Tulloyer — Tulloyre (Tullore), Queen's co., 1167, 1898, 3348.
Tullske, co. Rosc., 4624.
Tullw (co. Lim. ?), 6479.
Tully—Tulle, co. Car., 148, 911, 4161.
Tully, co. Dub. *See* Tullogh.
Tully—Tulley—Tullie—Tullye, co. Kild., 764, 1708, 2344, 5710, 5943, 6489, 6749, 6754,
" rectory 1407.
" preceptory leased, 1407; granted, 5710; possessions granted, 5738.
Tully—Tullie, King's co. 6488, 6637.
Tully, co. Leit. *See* Tulley, Tullie.
Tully — Tulle — Tullye, co. Long., 2381, 2880, 2888, 3243, 4294, 4298, 5344, 6598.

INDEX TO FIANTS—ELIZABETH.

Tully, co. Mon. *See* Tullagh.
Tully—Tullie, co. Rosc., [illegible], [illegible], [illegible].
Tully, co. Sligo. *See* Tullye.
Tully—Tulle, co. Tip., [illegible], [illegible].
Tully—Tullye, co. Westm., [illegible], [illegible].
Tully (co. Wex. ?), [illegible].
Tully, Owen m'Teige ny, pardon, [illegible].
Tullyaghe, co. Kilk., rectory, [illegible].
Tullyallon, co. Louth. *See* Tullaghallon.
Tullyard, co. Louth. *See* Tullagharde.
Tullyard, co. Mon. *See* Tolliard.
Tullybane, co. Westm. *See* Tullaghbane.
Tullybeard, co. Down. *See* Ballytolloborde, [illegible].
Tullybradan, co. Leit. *See* Tuichobradan.
Tullybrick, co. Cav. *See* Tullebricke.
Tullycam, co. Donegal. *See* Tullagh Camm.
Tullycarran, co. Down. *See* Ballytollyecarton, Tulloghcarran.
Tullycassan — Tolloghcassane (co. Tip. ?), [illegible], [illegible]. *See also* Tollocossan, Tullaghcassan.
Tullychim (co. Clare ?), [illegible].
Tullycommon, co. Clare. *See* Tullaghcommone.
Tullycorbet, co. Mon. *See* Tullecorbet.
Tullycumasky, co. Mon. *See* Tullaghcomyskie.
Tullye. *See* Tully, co. Kild.
Tullye. *See* Tully, co. Long.
Tullye, Queen's co., [illegible].
Tullye (Tully), co. Sligo, [illegible].
Tullye. *See* Tully, co. Westm.
Tullygarran, co. Kerry. *See* Tillgarte, Tolerrraine.
Tullygillan, co. Mon. *See* Tulligillan.
Tullyglass, co. Lim. *See* Towloglasse, Tulloghglas.
Tullygorey, co. Kild. *See* Tulloghgorore.
Tullyhedy—Tullehedy (co. Tip. ?), [illegible], [illegible].
Tullyherron, co. Down. *See* Ballytolloherran, [illegible].
Tullyhog, co. Tyr. *See* Tullaghoge.
Tullyhugh, co. Sligo. *See* Tullaghhughe.
Tullyhunco, co. Cav. *See* Collis Duncha, Taloonchna, Tullaghoneheerightier.
Tullylane, co. Kilk., 1112.
Tullylark, co. Donegal. *See* Tullaghlairge.
Tullyleague, co. Lim. *See* Tullaghleigtre.
Tullylease, co. Cork. *See* Tollaleishe.
Tullyleyce rectory, co. Lim., [illegible].
Tullylinn, co. Donegal. *See* Seaskand Tullchalaid.
Tullylost, co. Kild. *See* Tolleloste.
Tullymongan, co. Cav. *See* Tullamongane.
Tullymonrath, King's co., [illegible].
Tullymore castle, co. Clare, 4742.
Tullymore (Tullemore), co. Kerry, [illegible], [illegible], [illegible].
Tullymoyrath, King's co., [illegible].
Tullymacrow, co. Down. *See* Ballytolloscrowe, [illegible]; Tullmocrowe.
Tullynally, co. Westm. *See* Tullenally.
Tullynample, co. Mon. *See* Tumclampill.
Tullymaruro, co. Mon. *See* Tullenor.
Tullynarny, co. Mon. *See* Tulloneumarny.
Tullynore, co. Down. *See* Ballytolloknoir, [illegible].
Tullyvyn—Tullevin, co. Cav., [illegible], [illegible].
Tullyvyn — Tullevine — Tullewine — Tullivine (Tullovin ?), co. Lim., [illegible], [illegible], [illegible], [illegible].
Tulmore, Queen's co., [illegible].
Tulrean (Tulrohann), co. Mayo, [illegible], [illegible].
Tulrohain, co. Mayo, [illegible].
Tulske — Tulskie — Tulskye — Twylskye, co. Rosc., house of friars leased, 1454, [illegible], [illegible]; possessions leased, [illegible], granted, [illegible]. *See also* Tullske, Twilsk.
Tulskir—Towisky—Towiskye—Tulskyrre—Turskye, belonging to abbey of Boyle, co. Rosc., 1455, [illegible], [illegible].
Tulskirvis, Grange of, in O'Conor Sligo's country, [illegible].
Tulskye. *See* Tulske.
Tulskye, co. Gal. (Rosc. ?), [illegible].
Tulskyrre (see Tulskir), 1455.
Tulyveran, co. Long., [illegible].
Tumagh (King's or Queen's co. ?), [illegible].
Tumbermoren. Murrogho M'Ememy, pardon, [illegible].
Tumna, co. Rosc. *See* Tomme, Toymaa, Twomma.
Tumulta, Brian and Donill m'Cormick vic, pardon, [illegible].
Tunagh (co. Cork ?), [illegible].
Tuncho (co. Westm. ?), [illegible].
Tuncke, Thomas, controller of customs in Carrickfergus, 2111.
Tunnagh, co. Mon., [illegible].
Tuocunham, co. Cork. *See* Twogh I Cunnig.
Tuogh — Twogh — Twoth (co. Lim.), [illegible], [illegible], [illegible], [illegible]. *See also* Tongin, Two, Twoghosquroney, Twothe Currogh.
Tuogh of Blarney, co. Cork. *See* Twoheblarny.
Tuoghcluggin, co. Lim. *See* Tualhclugin, Tugh Clogyne.
Tuoghgrony, co. Lim., [illegible].
Tuolgh (co. Lim. ?), [illegible].
Turbotston — Turbotstown, co. Westm., [illegible], [illegible].
Turcke, John. *See* Turk.
Turcnagh (co. Kilk. ?), [illegible].
Turf, as fuel, [illegible]; liberty to cut, [illegible].
Turgheleg—Turbalan, co. Gal., [illegible], [illegible].
Turgher, co. Mon., [illegible].

INDEX TO FIANTS—ELIZABETH.

Turhelan. *See* Turghelan.
Turlen, Dermod, pardon, 6467.
Turk — Turcke — Turke alias Linche, John, pursuivant at arms, [illegible], 4413, [illegible].
Turlagh—Twrlagh, co. Clare, 4785, 5801, [illegible].
Turlagh voggane, co. Gal., [illegible].
Turlagmoghanne, co. Gal., 5451.
Turlaughe. *See* Turlonghe.
Turlegh voghan, co. Gal. or Mayo, [illegible].
Turliskyn, co. Long., 5711.
Turlogh. *See* Turlonghe.
Turloghnighane, co. Gal., 5451.
Turlogh vaghan, co. Gal., [illegible].
Turlonghe — Turlaghe — Turlogh, co. Mayo, 5777, [illegible]; castle and land granted, 5777.
Turmoin (co. Clare ?), 4763.
Turneglogh, co. Sligo, [illegible].
Turnegrawen, ford of, co. Antrim, [illegible].
Turner, Martin, collector of fines, Munster, [illegible].
„ Walter, dean of Ferns, 6471.
Turners pardoned, 6467, [illegible].
Turnings, co. Kild., [illegible]. *See* Sutelings.
Turnor, Ellinor, pardon, [illegible].
„ Nicholas, clerk of peace, Wexford, 2771; commission, 2345; alienations by him and value of his lands, [illegible].
„ *See* Turnir.
Turuye (Tourney), a native of, [illegible].
Turraghie (co. Wex. ?), [illegible].
Turran, co. Mayo, [illegible].
Turran, in Desmond, co. Kerry, 6117.
Turrock—Turrick—Turracke, co. Rosc., [illegible], 3748, 4877, 6108.
Turrogh, co. Rosc., [illegible].
Turrarke (co. Rosc. ?), 4794.
Turrucke. *See* Turrock.
Turry, Donogh m'Teig I, pardon, [illegible].
Turryck, co. Gal., [illegible].
Turryck, co. Rosc., [illegible].
Turskyr, co. Rosc., 5150. *See* Tulskie.
Turvey, co. Dub., [illegible], [illegible].
Turwey, [illegible].
Tuskine, Edm. m'Donnogh, pardon, 6467.
Tuie. *See* Tuile.
Tuisraihe — Twithraihe (Tuiespaith), co. Meath, 1800, [illegible].
Tuiston, co. Meath (Tuilestown, co. Westm.), 1450.
Tuisston—Tuistone — Tuistown — Tuisstowne—Tuiston—Tuistone. *See* Tuileston, co. Westm.
Tuyloghgory, co. Clare, [illegible].
Tuyt—Tuyte. *See* Tuile.
Tuyteston. *See* Tuiteston.
Twayne Ighlare—Twayne Ightor, 4897. *See* Tuam Ightor.
Twe, John, pardon, [illegible].
„ Wm., pardon, [illegible], [illegible].
Twellegan, co. Gal., [illegible].
Twema, 1821. *See* Tuam, co. Gal.
Twerlee begge, co. Tip., [illegible]. *See* Thurles beg.
Twerynbringhe — Twerynbryngh (Thorton, co. Gal.), 1464, [illegible].
Twithraihe, co. Meath, 1800. *See* Tuisraih.
Twhoosbiarey, co. Cork, [illegible].
Twhoundroman, a territory in Muskerry, co. Cork, [illegible].
Twhoncromkragh, a territory in Muskerry, co. Cork, [illegible].
Twigheri, Shelee, pardon, 5448.
Twileig, co. Wat., [illegible].
Twilak (Tulsk), co. Rosc., [illegible], 6074.
Twiscart, co. Mayo, 5817.
Twile, James m'Robbad, pardon, [illegible].
Twith, co. Tip. or Lim., [illegible].
Twisvallogh, [illegible].
Twilagh, [illegible]. *See* Tullagh.
Twlagh Comman, 4784. *See* Tullagh Comman.
Twllaght (co. Lim. ?), 6479.
Twllehelan (perhaps Tullahedy, co. Tip.), 6755.
Twllymobilly (co. Cork ?), [illegible].
Twllymadalle, co. Gal., [illegible].
Twummary, co. Gal., 5519.
Two (Twogh), co. Lim., 1143.
Twomleige, co. Rosc. or Gal., [illegible].
Twohallnagey — Twoghinallcnegey, co. Westm., 1846, 1471.
Twohallyestya, co. Tip., rectory, 453.
Twohrohill, co. Lim., 5948.
Twocrymary — Twoskeamore (Kenmare, co. Kerry ?), [illegible], [illegible].
Twoe, Dermod m'Teig oy, pardon, [illegible].
Twoe, co. Mayo, [illegible].
Twooe, co. Mayo, [illegible].
Twooghyaro (co. Lim. ?), [illegible].
Twoskeamore, [illegible]. *See* Twocrymary.
Twogh. *See* Twogh, co. Lim.
Twoghinallenegey. *See* Twohallnagey.
Twogher (co. Cork ?), 5912.
Twoghenegrealy (Twogh, co. Lim. ?), 6479.
Twogh I Cusinig—Two I Cusing (Tuocusheen, co. Cork ?), [illegible].
Twoght (co. Mayo ?), [illegible].
Twoght (Toughty), co. Mayo, castle and land, [illegible].
Twohaeghinyne (co. Lim. or Kerry), [illegible].
Twohinymmaylehyn, co. Gal., [illegible].
Twohmehiarey (Twogh of Blarney), co. Cork, [illegible].
Two I Cusing. *See* Twogh I Cusinig.
Twolle (co. Lim. ?), 6478.
Twollovin (co. Lim. ?), 6478.
Twollrine, co. Gal., 4897.

INDEX TO FIANTS.—ELIZABETH.

Twdotane, co. Gal., castle and land, [illegible].
Twoly, Donogh m'Shane ny, pardon, [illegible].
Two m'Grenall (co. Ross. ?), 5748. See Twomvegranyll.
Two M'Walter (in bar. of Ballymoe), co. Gal. [illegible].
Twomalen, 848.
Twomanlogh (co. Clare ?), 6615.
Twome (Toome), co. Wex., 5782.
Twomally (co. Cork ?), 6611.
Twomen rectory (Tumme, co. Ross.), 1484, 1487.
Twomomane, co. Westm., country of, rent to earl of Kildare (in the Kildare Rental 9th Report Hist. MSS. Comm., p. 276, it is called Moyamm, apparently in O'Molloy's country), 1246.
Twomoor—Twomore (Timmore, co. Wick.), 214, [illegible].
Twomdromen—Twonedromyn—Twonydromyn, a territory in Muskerry, co. Cork, [illegible], [illegible], [illegible].
Twomervodinghe, co. Cork, territory, [illegible], [illegible].
Twonydromye. See Twomdromen.
Twonykyly (co. Cork ?), [illegible].
Tworisdera (co. Gal. ?), [illegible].
Twoth (Tough), co. Lim., 4787, 5116.
Twothe Ovragh (Tough), co. Lim., [illegible].
Twoy, co. Westm., [illegible].
Twoyhealy—Towhohaly — Tohahohaly — Towhohally (Duthy Hanly, O'Hanly's country along the Shannon, in bar. Ballintober, co. Ross.), [illegible].
" captain of, 1220.
" seneschal of, 2217.
Twoyne, co. Gal., [illegible].
Twoynegallice, co. Gal., 3464.
Twrlagh (or Turlagh), 4782.
Twtymcon, co. Westm., [illegible].
Twumrewe (co. Ross. ?), [illegible].
Twykkyo. See Tuleke, co. Ross.
Twyny, alias Caytie, Dermod m'Donogh ney, pardon, 1784.
Twyughter, co. Gal., 4697.
Twyt, John, pardon, 423. See Tuite.
Twyttiston. See Tuiteston.
Tyaickmooke (Tikmock, co. Car. ?), 5543.
Tyaquyn, [illegible]. See Tiaquin.
Tyaing ny Gerogaine, Katherine nyne, pardon, [illegible].
Tybberenemy'ne, co. Westm., [illegible]. See Tobercormicke.
Tybbore (co. Meath ?), [illegible].
Tybburdore (Tobaradora ?), co. Tip., [illegible].
Tybernamolie (Tobernamoll in townland of Tubridmore), co. Kerry, [illegible].
Tycroghan. See Tecroghan.
Tydswned, [illegible]. See Todimnet.
Tyerichyon. See Theriohien.
Tyermon, co. Meath, 8478.
Tyovenlabe, co. Mayo or Gal., [illegible].
Tyfarnham, co. Westm. See Stalerman.
Tyhyngyarph, co. Cork, [illegible].
Tyll, Hugh, wardship, 8348.
" John (of Kilsiemicrt), wardship of his heir, [illegible]. See Till.
Tyllan, alias O'Dallan, Gerott, pardon, [illegible].
Tymarelanden, co. Meath, [illegible].
Tymachoo — Tymochoo — Tymacow — Tymogho—Tymoho, Queen's co., 1162, 1214, 1876, 1029; rectory, 878, 1816; advowson, [illegible].
Tymalen, alias Ballystample, co. Dub., rectory, 1846.
Tymolino (co. Car. ?), 6782.
Tymall (King's co. ?), 4004.
Tym Ihor, co. Ross., [illegible].
Tymooho. See Timoghoe, co. Kild.
Tymochoo. See Tymachoo, Queen's co.
Tymook, Queen's co., 8467. See Tymog.
Tymoco, 404. See Timoghoe, co. Kild.
Tymocono, 129. See Timoghoe, co. Kild.
Tymocow, 1162. See Tymachoo.
Tymog — Tymock — Tymoke — Tymooke (Timogue), Queen's co., 1946, [illegible]; manor, 1248.
" rector of, 6782.
" advowson, 424.
Tymogho. See Timoghoe, co. Kild.
Tymogho. See Tymachoo, Queen's co.
Tymoghoe, co. Dub., 6706.
Tymoghoo. See Timoghoe, co. Kild.
Tymoho. See Tymachoo.
Tymohow, 6567. See Timoghoe, co. Kild.
Tymoke. See Tymog, Queen's co.
Tymolag — Tymolago — Tymolagy— Tymolaggo — Tymolaggy. See Timolage, co. Cork.
Tymole (Timole), co. Meath, rectory, 1468, [illegible].
Tymolegge — Tymoleig — Tymoleige. See Timolage.
Tymolenbegg. See Timolin, co. Kild.
Tymolin (co. Car. ?), 5541.
Tymolin—Tymolyn, (R. Mullins, co. Car. and Wex.) barony, 1886, [illegible]; rectory, [illegible].
Tymolin — Tymolinbego — Tymolinbegg— Tymolingbeg — Tymolingbogge — Tymolinge — Tymolingebege — Tymolinbegg. See Timolin, co. Kild.
Tymolyn. See Tymolin.
Tymolyn. See Timolin, co. Kild.
Tymon, 6778. See Timon, co. Westm.
Tymooke, 1946. See Tymog, Queen's co.
Tynagh, co. Gal., 4461.
Tynaighe, co. Gal., 8718.

INDEX TO FIANTS—ELIZABETH.

Tyman—Teynan (Inan ?), co. Meath, rectory, 6708.

Tymakairly (Timmeart ?), co. Wat., 1678, 8071.

Tynbeghe in Dublin, [illegible].

Tyne( ) (Queen's co. ?), 1172.

Tynakerragh, co. Cork, [illegible].

Tynakilly — Tynekylly. See Tinnykill, Queen's co.

Tynelick, 4467. See Tanelick, co. Long.

Tyneranne (Tinneranny), co. Kilk., [illegible].

Tyneranny (co. Car. ?), 4071.

Tynerane, co. Car., [illegible].

Tynickmocke (co. Car. ?), [illegible].

Tynicore (co. Wex. or Car. ?), [illegible].

Tynikick (co. Long. ?), [illegible].

Tynnekill, [illegible]. See Tinnykill.

Tynnure—Tynure (Terenure, co. Dub.), 847, 1[illegible].

Tynny, co. Kerry, 4136.

Tynoyll (Tinneel ? Queen's co.), [illegible].

Tynstorne. See Tintern, co. Wex.

Tyntobber. See Tintobber.

Tyntobberne (co. Car. ?), 4617.

Tynure, 1236. See Tynnure.

Tyone, co. Tip., [illegible].

Typper. See Tipper, co. Kild.

Typperane. See Tipperan, [illegible].

Typper. See Tipper, co. Kild.

Typper, of Tipperstown. See Tipper.

Typperary—Typperary. See Tipperary.

Typperhouye mill (Toberaheena ? co. Tip.), [illegible].

Typpertowle. See Tippertowle.

Typperston. See Tipperston.

Typtynne. See Tiptynne.

Tyrawly—Tyrawlye. See Tirawlie.

Tyrbruyn (co. Kerry ?), [illegible].

Tyrbuny, [illegible].

Tyreconell—Tyreconnell. See Tirconnell.

Tyre, alias Eyre, Queen's co., 1018.

Tyreardan (Tirardan), co. Mon., [illegible].

Tyreawle—Tyreawley. See Tirawlie.

Tyrechoweghlin—Tyrechoweghlyn, King's co., [illegible], 1464.

Tyreckihle (co. Kerry ?), [illegible].

Tyreconnell—Tyre Connyll. See Tirconnell.

Tyrecullen, little, co. Cork (Tireullen, co. Wat.), 1[illegible].

Tyrecullene, great, co. Cork (Tireullen, co. Wat.), 1[illegible].

Tyre Enedha (Tirhugh, co. Donegal), [illegible].

Tyregownyn, co. Clare, [illegible].

Tyrehoyle (co. Rosc. ?), [illegible].

Tyrekewle, co. Gal., [illegible].

Tyrekelkine, co. Clare, [illegible].

Tyrell, James, pardon, [illegible]. See Tyrrell.

Tyrelake, co. Mon., [illegible].

Tyremadivan (Tirmadown), co. Mon., [illegible].

Tyremmore (Tirmacmoe), co. Mon., [illegible].

Tyremasey, in Munster, [illegible].

Tyrene, 1[illegible]. See Tirin.

Tyreoghar (Tirhogar, Queen's co.), [illegible], 1[illegible].

Tyreowyne. See Tirerowyn.

Tyreragh, co. Mon., [illegible].

Tyreraghe. See Tireragh.

Tyreran (Tireran), co. Mon., [illegible].

Tyrerawre (Tiravera), co. Mon., [illegible].

Tyrerell. See Tirerell.

Tyrerle, co. Mon., 6671.

Tyreramore, co. Mon., 6477.

Tyrerowne, co. Rosc. (see Tirerowyn), 1[illegible].

Tyreue (Tirhugh, co. Don.), [illegible].

Tyrhenuie, co. Gal. or Mayo, [illegible].

Tyrhoyle (co. Rosc. ?), [illegible].

Tyrine, King's co., [illegible].

Tyringh oge, Margaret ny, pardon, [illegible].

Tyrmonaleighan, 1[illegible]. See Termonfeighen.

Tyroberaghe, [illegible]. See Tireragh.

Tyrohme, co. Car., 804.

Tyrone—Tarone—Terone—Tirone—Tyron, [illegible], [illegible]; commission to enquire of possessions of abbeys, 1077; commission to enquire of offences committed in, 1[illegible], 1[illegible]; queen's forces in, [illegible], [illegible]; part of country demised to earl Hugh, [illegible]; commission to set out manors and lands and amount of rents, &c., [illegible]; called a county, [illegible]-14.
" martial law in, [illegible]; general pardon, [illegible]; pardon to inhabitants, [illegible]-14.
" commander of forces in, [illegible]-1.
" captain of; Turlogh lenagh (O'Neill) appointed, [illegible].
" earl, Con (O'Neill), his son pardoned (Shane O'Neill), 1[illegible]; death, 1[illegible]; services rendered to, [illegible].
" earl, Hugh, commission, 47[illegible]; part of country demised to, [illegible], [illegible]; indenture, [illegible]; rights of, [illegible]; commission to treat with, [illegible], [illegible], [illegible]; pardon, [illegible]; protection, [illegible]; bonaghts, [illegible].

Tyromytkry, co. Clare, [illegible].

Tyrovain, co. Clare, [illegible].

Tyrovane (co. Gal. or Mayo ?), [illegible].

Tyrovanny (co. Clare ?), [illegible].

Tyrow, co. Louth, 4017.

Tyrre, co. Gal., [illegible].

Tyrre, Queen's co., [illegible].

Tyrremanne, co. Mon., [illegible].

Tyrrebarnasky, co. Mon., [illegible].

Tyrrole, co. Gal., [illegible].

Tyrrelaghe, Onora ny, pardon, [illegible].

Tyrrell—Terrell—Tirrell:

INDEX TO FIANTS—ELIZABETH.

Tyrrell, Alison, Alicona, or Alson, wardship, 3374; livery, 5941; wardship of her son, 4378.
Christopher, pardon, 4888, 5349.
Edmund, pardon, [illegible], 1874, 2009, 4298, 4499, [illegible], 4528, 4807, 6064.
Edward, pardon, 2087, 4858.
Elizabeth, pardon, 6587.
Ellinor, pardon, 2550.
Evelin, pardon, 6653.
Falduck or Fedlog, pardon, 3827, 6503.
Garrett fitz Redmond, pardon, 6513.
Garrett m'Hubert, pardon, 3647, 6651.
George, pardon, 3887.
Gerald (of Pass), pardon, 3648, 3842.
Gerald, pardon, 1670, 4638, 6840.
Gerrot, pardon, 2897, 6374.
Hubert, pardon, 1185, 4966, 6800.
James (of Castlelost), pardon, 4827, 6146.
James (of Clonmoyle), commission, 3562.
James (of Pass), pardon, 1674, 3649, 3842.
James, pardon, [illegible] (Tyrrell), 3827, [illegible], [illegible], 4298, [illegible], [illegible], 5538.
James boy, bwoy or bwy, pardon, [illegible], 3943, 6180, 6265.
John (of Pass or of Fertullagh, afterwards knight), livery, [illegible]; captain of Fertullagh, 571; sheriff of Westmeath, 1458; commissions, 309, 1306, 1466, 1621, 3117, 3346, 3144, 3494, 4141, [illegible] (Tyrryll), 4142, 6393, 6494, 6289; pardon, 471, 1674, 3048, 3648, 3807, 5148, 6355; lease, 1676; his wife, 3843.
John, constable of Dunganvan, commission, 2287.
John, grant of house in Dublin, 3171.
John, pardon, 1043, [illegible], 3027, 3427, 3299, 5146, 6313, 6485, 6580.
John (Tirell), house in Naas, 6453.
Lucas or Luke, wardship, 3557; wardship and livery, 3374, 5941.
Margaret, lease, 3121.
Margaret, wardship, 3374; livery, 5941.
Margaret, pardon, 3164.
Margery, pardon, 4831.
Mary, pardon, 6902, 6550.
Maurice, pardon, 3448, 5365, 6139.
Morish, pardon, 6338.
Nicholas, wardship and livery, 2357, 3814, 5941.
Nich., pardon, 3559.
Owney, pardon, 6651.
Owen, pardon, 3837.
Tyrrell, Patrick, 6314.
" Philbock, pardon, 6388.
" Redmond, attainted, 2312, 4274.
" Redmond (of Pass), pardon, 5144, 6580.
" Redmond, pardon, [illegible], [illegible], [illegible], 6592.
" Howard, pardon, 3897, 3997.
" Richard, lands of, 1931.
" Richard, commission, 2344.
" Richard, pardon, 1184, 1674, 3480, 3897, 4998, 5146, 6513, 6582.
" Richard, pardon, 1672.
" Robert, pardon, 1674, 3168.
" Rose, pardon, 5513.
" Shane, pardon, 731, 3646.
" Thomas, knight, captain of the barony of Fertullagh, commissions, 300, 381, 543; grant of land, 482; livery to heir, 694.
" Thomas (of Molliniry), commission, 2314.
" Thomas, pardon, 621, 1668, 3341, 3827, 6588, 6806.
" Walter (of Clonmoyle), sheriff of Westmeath, 3897, 4262, 4182; commissions, 3501, 4151, 4163 (Tyrrill), pardon, 871, 2642, 3827, 3997, 4327.
" Walter, lease recited, 2181; widow of, 3834.
" Walter, executors of, 4814.
" Walter, land in his occupation, 5519.
" Walter (of Porteloon), pardon, [illegible], 1857.
" Walter fitz Edm. (of Pass of Kilbride), pardon, 885, 1275, 3548.
" Walter, pardon, 1393, 1674, 3897, 6412.
" William (of Portlomon), pardon, 2646, 3346, 3686 (Tirrell), 3827, 4874.
" William, pardon, 3827, 3342, 3484, 3861, 3775, 3897, 3997, 5146, 4518, 6581.
" William, allocation to, 1658.
Tyrrells, aid against rebels, 3154.
Tyrrellon country, co. Westm., 6798.
Tyrrellowton, alias Thurloghton, co. Dub., 3608.
Tyrrellsvallis, King's co., 396, 1034.
Tyrrellspass, co. Westm. See Passe, Terrelspass.
Tyrrellstown, co. Westm. See Tirrellston.
Tyrrolston, alias Broklestown, King's co., 483.
Tyrron, King's co. (see Tirin), 4384.
Tyrrnaighe, co. Sligo, 4580. See Tirenagh.
Tyrrerell, co. Sligo, 4580. See Tirerell.
Tyrrie (co. Gal.?), 4713.
Tyrrill, Walter, 4163. See Tyrrell.
Tyrry, David, collector of customs, Cork, 1456.

INDEX TO FIANTS.—ELIZABETH.

Tyrry, David (of Cork), livery to son, 4863.
″ Edmund, livery, 4888.
″ Edm., pardon, 4411.
Nich., pardon, 2068.
Richard, pardon, 1068.
Robert fitz Oliver, pardon, 183.
″ See Tirry.
Tyrrylanghaghtys. See Tirrilaughaghts.
Tyrryll, John, 4463. See Tyrrell.
Tyrue, Henry m'Shane, pardon, 2303.
Tyrurwyn—Tyrurwyne (Tir ui Bhriuin), co. Rosc., 4838. See Tirerrwyn.
Tyrvyran (co. Clare ?), 4780.
Tyrwatinghe (Toorreena ?), co. Lim., 5781.
Tytyn—Tyryne, King's co. See Thein.
Tyrryrg, co. Meath, 5885.
Tyrynure (Tenenure), co. Dub., 4330.
Tyssnakehs, in Osongish, 1471.
Tyvaton, co. Kilk., 1361.
Tyvyrine (Taeveany), co. Cork, 5088.
Tyxre, Nicholas, pardon, 911, 1658. See Tive.
Tywhanagh, 1458. See Tireragh, co. Sligo.

Uachtar-tiire. See Oughterhurey.
Uandy tennghorie (co. Cork ?), 2970.
Udall, Wm., grant, 6484.
Ughtred, Henry, grant, 6783.
Uhamey, Tho., pardon, 5085.
Ui Briuin na Sinna. See Tyirue.
Ui Laeghaire. See Iveleary.
Ui Muireadhaigh. See Murify.
Uirsebeg (co. Gal. ?), 4888.
Uirgure, 3414. See Uregare.
Ukerrell, Moyle, pardon, 6741.
Ulaghan, Awly m'Philip I, pardon, 4803.
″ Conor, pardon, 6586.
″ Donell, pardon, 4804.
″ Donogh, pardon, 4898.
Gillecoidh, pardon, 5088.
″ Shane, pardon, 4868.
Ulin, Peirse, pardon, 5684.
Uliyne. See Elphin.
Ullan m'Gillevally, co. Mayo, 4808, 4808.
Ullard—Ollarde—Illard, co. Car., 904, 6617, 6351.
Ullenagha, co. Mayo, 1804, 3419.
Ullendame, co. Cork, 4781.
Ullick, Jone ayne, pardon, 6481.
″ Oneile ayne, pardon, 4886.
Ullickstan, co. Meath, 1506.
Ullid, co. Kilk. See Illed.
Ulster, province of, 1080, 3749, 3326, 3414, 3808, 3930, 3932, 3858-60, 3781, 3977, 4221, 4327, 4450, 4483, 4676, 4848, 5210, 5708, 5763, 4508, 5985, 6022, 4565, 5390-1, 6418, 6482, 6062, 4467, 6910-2; lord deputy absent in, 328, 1417-8, 4418, 4780, 4926, 5001, 6658, 6115, 6249.
Ulster, to be divided into counties, 4781, 5575, 6763.
″ committed to government of Sentle, 641.
″ captain general of, 2946, 2951, 3462. See Essex, Walter, earl of.
″ resident provincial government established, 3071.
″ commissions for government, 3543, 3871, 3837, 4040, 4044, 4882.
″ chief commissioner. See Bagenall, 3922, 5462.
″ martial law in, 1333, 1412, 2278 (Cowley ?), 3361, 3808 (Wallister), 3935, 3824, 4063.
″ commn. to treat with Tyrone, &c., 5851, 5972, 5960.
″ protection to chief persons of, 6197.
″ commander of forces in, 640, 4330, 5545, 6366.
″ soldiers in, 1402, 4982, 4238; victualling of, 2421.
″ war in, 2218, 5084.
″ governor of Clandeboy in, 4267, 4787, 4443, &c.
″ seneschal of co. Monaghan, 4693.
″ constable of Carrickfergus, 3343, &c.
″ clerk of crown and peace, 3845, 3274, 3386.
″ Queen's earldom of, 2854.
Ulster—Ulvester, King of arms, 3816, 6324; to hold visitation of arms, 5168.
Ultagh, Cormock, pardon, 4487, 4781.
″ Dermot, pardon, 5697, 6761.
″ Donell, pardon, 4427.
″ Donogh, pardon, 6781.
″ Eugene, lease, 453; license to 781.
″ Francis, pardon, 6484, 6761,
″ Gilleduff, pardon, 6761.
″ James, pardon, 5808, 6761.
″ Morish, pardon, 4227, 4882, &c.
″ Owen, pardon, 5497, 6761.
″ Patrick, pardon, 4387.
″ Shane, pardon, 4227, 5532, &c.
Ulwellie, Murtagh, pardon, 6830.
Ulvester. See Ulster.
Ulynighan, Donoghe m'Teig, pard
Umfrey, James, vicar, 1378.
Unaga, co. Westm. See Uainoge.
Umrie, King's co. (Unmerka, co. 1606, 1685.
Undertakers in Munster. See under several counties.
″ plot for planting by, 4901.
″ schedule of lands passed to, cited, 4036.
″ commission to examine disputes between, 5351, 5561.

INDEX TO FIANTS—ELIZABETH.

Undoun, Donell m'Horie, pardon, 6608.
Uniacke. See Unyack.
Uniegan (co. Lim. ?), 6487.
Uniformity, Act of, pardon for offences against, [illegible].
" comm. to execute, [illegible], [illegible].
Unimoe (Umma ?), co. Westm., [illegible].
Universities, English, Dublin dignitary studying at, [illegible].
University of Dublin. See Dublin, Trinity College.
Unkill, co. Car., [illegible].
Unnyo, co. Gal., [illegible].
Unredon, Maurice, pardon, [illegible].
Unsboke (perhaps Funshog), co. Louth, [illegible].
Untenkem, Donogh, pardon, [illegible].
Unyack—Unyake—Uniacke:
" James, his heir, [illegible], [illegible].
" John, [illegible].
" John, wardship, [illegible]; livery, [illegible].
Unyake's land, in Youghal, [illegible].
Uolgrainge (Woollengrange ?), co. Kilk., [illegible].
Upper Bean, co. Kild., [illegible].
Upper Caragh, co. Kilk., 1884, [illegible].
Upper Court, co. Kilk., [illegible]; manor, [illegible].
Upper Grange, [illegible].
Upperhill by Kilkenny, 1068.
Uppermost Owle O'Malle (Murrisk barony), co. Mayo, [illegible].
Upperossory—Upperosserie, Queen's co., [illegible], [illegible], 4117, [illegible], [illegible]; martial law in, [illegible], [illegible]; formed into a barony and included in Queen's co., [illegible]. See Ossory.
Upperossory, Barnaby Fitz Patrick, first baron of, pardon, [illegible], [illegible]; being incapacitated by age his son Barnaby appointed captain of his country, 1437.
" Barnaby Fitz Patrick, knt., baron of, pardon, [illegible]; lieutenant of King's and Queen's cos., [illegible]; commissions, [illegible], [illegible], [illegible], [illegible], [illegible], 4043; pardons at his suit, [illegible], [illegible]; surrender, [illegible]; grant of lands, [illegible], 3415; licence to alien, [illegible]; lease, [illegible]; livery to heir, [illegible]. See Fitz Patrick, Barnaby, knt.
" Florence, lord of, livery, [illegible]; comm., [illegible], [illegible]; pardon, [illegible], [illegible], [illegible]; pardon at his suit, [illegible]; grant, [illegible]; suit to have his country united to Queen's co., [illegible].
" Joan, lady of, [illegible].
Upraith (co. Tip. ?), [illegible].
Uranbog—Uranbegg (Oran Bog ?), co. Gal., [illegible], [illegible], 4916, [illegible].
Urbb (co. Clare ?), [illegible].
Urohlin (Urglin), co. Car., [illegible].
Urdalue, Ellin ny, pardon, [illegible].
Urdan, co. Rosc., [illegible].
Uregare—Nuregare—Urgarre—Uirgare, co. Lim., [illegible], [illegible]; rectory, 4114, [illegible].
Urghly, alias Urly, co. Gal., 1681.
Urglin, co. Car. See Urohlin.
Uriell—Uryell (Oirghialla, a district in Ulster including co. Louth, to which in later times the name is frequently confined), 1487, [illegible]; martial law, [illegible]. See also Oriell.
Uriell, Rob., pardon, [illegible], [illegible].
Urlan, co. Clare. See Urlin.
Urlie (Urlan, co. Kerry), [illegible].
Urlin—Urlyane—Urlen (Urlan, co. Clare), [illegible], [illegible], [illegible], [illegible].
Urly, co. Gal., 1681.
Urney—Urnoy—Ornoy—Orny, co. Cav., [illegible], [illegible], [illegible].
Urnoy—Urny, co. Kild., 1848, 3107.
Urny—Ornoy—Orny (Urney), King's co., 1834, [illegible], [illegible]. See also Nowrny.
Urra—Urrogh, co. Tip., [illegible], [illegible].
Urre, co. Long., [illegible], [illegible], [illegible]; alias Shrule, rectory, [illegible].
Urrogh. See Urra.
Urrney (or Urney, co. Cav.), [illegible].
Urrobogal, co. Kerry. See Orbogle.
Uryell. See Uriell.
Ushere—Ussher—Ushiere—Ussher—Usher
" Arland, [illegible], [illegible]; lease, [illegible], [illegible]; registrar of appeals spiritual, [illegible], [illegible]; registrar of faculties, [illegible]; surrender, [illegible].
" Arlandon or Arlonton, [illegible], [illegible].
Usher—Ussher—Ussher:
" Christopher, merchant, [illegible], [illegible].
" Christopher, Ulster King of Arms, [illegible], 4134; bachelor of laws, comm., [illegible].
" Garrett, pardon, [illegible].
" Henry, treasurer of Christ Church, [illegible], [illegible]; archdeacon of Dublin, [illegible], [illegible]; fellow of Trinity College, Dublin [illegible]; archbishop of Armagh, [illegible]; commissions, [illegible], [illegible], [illegible], [illegible], [illegible], [illegible], [illegible], [illegible], 4163, 4163, 4176, [illegible], 4461, [illegible], [illegible], [illegible], [illegible], [illegible], [illegible], [illegible], [illegible]; charter of Trinity College granted at his request, [illegible].
" John, pardon, 1777; lease, [illegible]; alderman, [illegible], [illegible]; his heir, [illegible].
" Thomas, 1777.
" Walter, wardship, [illegible].

INDEX TO FIANTS.—ELIZABETH.

Usher, William, clerk of the council, [illegible]; constable of Wicklow castle, [illegible]; lease, [illegible], [illegible]; pardon, [illegible].
Ushestowne, co. Meath, [illegible].
Usk, co. Kild. See Uske.
Uskane—Uskane Tipperarye, co. Tip., 4787, 6181.
Uske (Usk), co. Kild., [illegible], [illegible], [illegible].
" Portor of, 748.
Uskentagh (co. Kilk. ?), [illegible].
Uskyfyrrin, King's co., 4784.
Ussher. See Usshers, Usher.
Usshiers. See Usshers.
Ussyan, Hugh O'Rorian, pardon, [illegible].
Ustace. See Eustace.
Usury, cognizance of by ecclesiastical comm., [illegible].

Vaskey, Morogh, pardon, [illegible].
" Murtertagh, pardon, [illegible].
Vaddegane—Vadegaine (see O'Maddegan), Donell m'Owen I, [illegible].
" Donogh m'Kenedy Y, [illegible].
Vadden, Amable ny, pardon, [illegible].
Vagabonds to be punished, [illegible], [illegible], [illegible].
Vagaige, Edm. m'Tirlagh, pardon, [illegible].
Vaghan. See Vaughan.
Vagher, Margaret ny, pardon, [illegible].
Vaghon, Alson ny, pardon, [illegible].
Vagrants to be searched out by ecclesiastical comm., [illegible].
Vahony—Vahowny, Finin and Owen m'Teig I (see O'Mahowny), [illegible].
Vakin, Wm., pardon, [illegible].
Vale, Gerald, pardon, [illegible].
" James, attainted, 5777.
" John, [illegible].
" Rich., [illegible].
" Walter, pardon, [illegible], [illegible].
" Wm., pardon, [illegible].
Valencie, co. Kerry, [illegible].
Valiee, Gerald m'Shane, pardon, [illegible].
Valle, John m'Teige, pardon, [illegible].
Valleghe, Morys fitz Edm., pardon, [illegible].
Valley, [illegible].
Valley, Knight of, attainted, 5777. See Fitzgerald, Tho.
Valley Fraghe, co. Mayo, 5777.
Vallive, Conogher m'Donell, pardon, [illegible].
Vallye, James Butler, pardon, [illegible].
Value of clothing, [illegible], [illegible], [illegible].
" cattle, &c., [illegible], [illegible], [illegible].
Vanchymore (Banaby ?), co. Cork, [illegible].
Vanee, Hastings, [illegible].
Varentagh, Philip m'Shane, pardon, [illegible].
Varhie, Owen m'Donoghe, pardon, [illegible].
Varniell, Shane m'Tho. I, [illegible].
Varnone, John, pardon, [illegible].
Vartry. See Farter.
Varvagh (Maragh, co. Donegal), [illegible].
Varymane, Dermod m'Dermod I, pardon, [illegible].
Vasnoie, John, pardon, [illegible].
Vasline (now Castletownkindalen), co. Westm., rectory, [illegible].
Vandraye, Rich., comm., [illegible], [illegible].
Vaughan—Vaghan:
" George, pardon, [illegible].
" James, lease, [illegible], [illegible]; soldier, [illegible].
" John, [illegible]; lease, [illegible].
" Katherine, lease, [illegible].
" Sevranus, pardon, [illegible].
" Thomas, comm., [illegible], [illegible], [illegible].
Vause or Vawse, John, lease, [illegible].
Vayngr, Edm. m'James, pardon, [illegible].
Veagher (O'Meagher), Fynola ny, pardon, [illegible].
" Hugh m'Conogher Y, pardon, [illegible].
Veanwly, Ellen ny, pardon, [illegible].
Veoon, Ellen ny, pardon, [illegible].
Veartin, John, pardon, [illegible].
Vegily—Vegille, Donogh m'Morys I, [illegible].
" Donogh m'Ee Y, [illegible].
" Tho. m'Ee Y, [illegible].
" See O'Regelly.
Velden, Chr., pardon, [illegible].
" Henry, pension, [illegible].
" Katherine, pardon, [illegible].
" Rich., pardon, [illegible].
" Tho., pardon, [illegible].
" William, vicar of Clonenrry, 702, 798.
" William (of Rathfine), pardon, [illegible], [illegible], [illegible]; comm., [illegible], [illegible].
" ( ) (of Rafyne), comm., [illegible].
Veldonston (Veldonstowne), co. Meath, [illegible].
Velle, Moriah m'Donell, pardon, [illegible].
Venadas, co. Mayo (Banada, co. Sligo ?), friary leased, [illegible].
Ventrye—Ventree—Vhintry (Ventry), co. Kerry, [illegible], [illegible].
Very, Rich., pardon, [illegible].
Verdon, Chr., [illegible].
" David, pardon, [illegible], [illegible], [illegible], [illegible].
" Edward, [illegible], [illegible].
" Geo., pardon, [illegible].
" John, pardon, [illegible], [illegible]; comm., [illegible].
" Patrick, [illegible]; livery, [illegible].
" Patrick, pardon, [illegible].
" Tho., 4214.
Verdonston (Verdonstown, co. Louth), [illegible].
Veremygh, John m'Tho., pardon, [illegible].
Vernochstowne, co. Meath, [illegible].
Vernon, Wm., lease, [illegible], [illegible], [illegible].
Verveldston, co. Westm., [illegible].
Vervoraugh, Grany, pardon, [illegible].

INDEX TO FIANTS—ELIZABETH.

Vessey, Fair., pardon, [illegible].
Vestiarius pardoned, [illegible], [illegible], 4783.
Vestments, &c., may be seized, 6934.
Viall (co. Cork ?), 5571.
Vierlighan, co. Cork, 5850.
Vibillion (co. Kerry ?), 6477.
Vicar disqualified being a minor and layman, 6240.
" pardoned, 4471, 4237, 6649, 6661, 6667, 6712.
Vicars, Wm. m'Owen, pardon, [illegible].
Vicars, Tho., pardon, 6654.
" Wm., 1466, 4824; lease, 464.
Vicarstown, King's co. See Vickerstonne.
Vicarstown, Queen's co. See Ballymvicar.
Vicman, John, usher of Philipstown fort, 4371, 6682.
Vice Treasurer of Ireland. See Treasurer.
Vic Gillisowrchin, Donoghe, pardon, 6817.
Vickerman, George, pardon, 2164.
Vickevarid, Evelin ny, pardon, 3178.
Vickenchariggo, Mahon m'Morierlagh (O'mccorrigge), pardon, 6817.
Vickerstonne — Ballyvicaryo (Vicarstown, King's co.), 1461, 6815.
Vick Iongo, Donell m'Teige, pardon, 6817.
Vic Kynwroith alias Mackyncroith, Donald and Mathew, 2187.
Vicmon, Loghlin m'Shanb, pardon, 6817.
Vicormick, Teig m'Donell (M'Gorman), pardon, 2087.
Vic Tibbot, Slight, lands of, in bar. Kilmaine, co. Mayo, 4978.
Victorious mountain (Knockmoy), co. Gal., monastery, 6230.
Victualler, pardoned, 4768; grant of land in discharge of debt to, 6844; of garrison in Munster, 1819.
Victuals or provisions for army, supply of, 641, 1168, 1457, 2862, 3441, 2784, 2878, 4858; carriage of, 3615; prices to be paid and mode of assessment, 3411, 2861, 4861; not to be taken in town against will of burgesses, 1729; to be imported, the harvest having been destroyed, 1818.
" for Lord deputy's household, 3789.
" surveyor general of, 828, 1108, 1462, 2621, 4288, 5314, 6718.
Vic Tummin, Brian and Donell m'Cormick, pardon, 6817.
Vige, Wm. m'Dermot oge, pardon, 4867.
Vilanstown, co. Westm. See Villanston.
Villa Gonill, co. Tip., 2814.
Villanston—Villeaston—Vyllanston—Villastion—Vilanston (Vilanstown), co. Westm., 308, 1524, 1637, 3643, 4947, 4824.
Villa Tempil (Ballintemple, co. Cav.), 5448.
Villars, Elizabeth, 6314.
Vin, Redmund, &c. See Vyn.
Vintros—Vintray. See Vestryn.
Viron, Fennollay ny, pardon, 4462.
Virling, John (see also Varlinge), pardon, 4162.
" Tho., pardon, 3740, 4118.
Voncroitaine, Conoghor m'Shane, pardon, 4611.
Vody, Donoghy ny, pardon, 4442.
Voelane, More ny, pardon, 4763.
Vogh (co. Rosc. ?), 4545.
Vohaleghan, John fitz Donald I, pardon, 4688.
Voiade, Edm., pardon, 6252.
Voiade—Void or Woyde, Walter, pardon, 123, 1224.
Volane, Reynat ny Keyne I, pardon, 6062.
Volcororan, co. Wat., 6622.
Volguirime, [ ] I, pardon, 6610.
" See Moiguirran.
Voroghowo—Voroghe—Voroghowo—Voroghue (O'Moroghoo), Conoghor m'Shane I, pardon, 4469.
" Dermod m'Donell Y, pardon, 6093.
" Dermod m'Shane I, pardon, 4468.
" Donell m'Tho. I, pardon, 6468.
" Ellice ny, pardon, 4985.
" Honora ny Donoghe I, pardon, 5162.
Vorierlagh, Onor ny, pardon, 5541.
" Owne ny, pardon, 6641.
" See Morierlagh.
Vorin, Katherine ny, pardon, 6811.
Vorlinge, John (see Virling), pardon, 4778.
Vorrisey (O'Morrisey), John and Wm. m'Teig, pardon, 4782.
Voulfe, Shane m'Patrick, pardon, 6418. See Woulf.
Vowell or Hoker, John, comm., 1362.
Voy, Owen m'Donogh, pardon, 1621.
Vreddine, More ny, pardon, 4671. See O'Breddan.
Vroynan — Vroman — Vronain, Conoghor m'Donogh, &c. (see O'Brennan), 4418-9, 4617, 4782.
Vrice, John fitz David, pardon, 4478.
Vrion, Slany ny, pardon, 4428.
" Teig m'Donoghy I (see O'Brien), pardon, 6868.
Vrohio, Granee ny, pardon, 4578.
Vroiskagh—Vroyskaghe (Briska), co. Lim., 4486, 4612.
Vromaghan, Dermod m'Teig I (see O'Bromoghan), 4477.
Vryen, Tirlagh m'Donoghy I (see O'Brien), 6854.
Vryn, Tho., a pursuivant, 4409.

INDEX TO FIANTS.—ELIZABETH.

Vyllanston. *See* Villanston.
Vyn—Vin, John, pardon, 6765.
" Redmund, pardon, 4621.
" Shane, pardon, [illegible].
Vyn or Vyner, Tho., pardon, [illegible].
Vyusy, Rich., overseer of tanning, [illegible]; pardon, 3798.
Vyrn—Vyrne, Dineyn, pardon, 5063.
" Katherine, pardon, 5069.
" Meaw, pardon, 5064.

Waale, James, attainted, 5960. *See* Wale.
" Patrick, pardon, [illegible].
" Stephen, attainted, 5950.
Waall, Peter, pardon, [illegible].
Wackmley, Tho. *See* Wakley.
Wackelly, Shane, pardon, 6547.
Wackleston, King's co., 1851.
Wackley—Wacklie—Wackly—Wacley. *See* Wakley.
Wacoume, Donnogho Dymalliagh, pardon, [illegible].
Wadding—Waddinge—Wading—Wadinge, Richard, commission, [illegible].
" Thomas, pardon, 1794, [illegible], 4591; commissions, 1836, [illegible], [illegible], [illegible] (Wadinge), 4456, [illegible]; licence of alienation, [illegible].
" Walter, pardon, 1781.
" Wm., pardon, 4478.
Waddy, Onorye ny Taig I., pardon, 4639.
Wadgore, murder of the, 4781. *See* Wager.
Wadhouse (Woodhouse, co. Wat. ?), 6764.
Wading—Wadinge, Tho. *See* Wadding.
Wadinger, Rich., 4183.
Wafer, Lucas or Luke, [illegible]; pardon, [illegible].
Waffer, Francis, pardon, 6317.
" James, pardon, 2517.
Waffer—Waffre—Wafre, Roger, clerk of the crown and peace of Connaught, 1457, 4791, 5471; commission, [illegible].
Wager, Jasper, murder of, 4478, [illegible], 4914.
" John, murder of, 4478, [illegible].
Waghary, Edmund, pardon, 1478.
Waghyre, Ansy ny, pardon, 4683.
Wald, Wm., pardon, 5464.
Walish, Adam fitz Rob., [illegible]. *See* Walshe.
" Henry fitz Rob., pardon, 6031.
" Maurice, pardon, [illegible].
" Walter (of Moyglare), pardon, [illegible], 5434.
Walishe, Edmund, pardon, 1043.
" James, pardon to son, 1043.
" James oge (of Moyvally), pardon, 5433.
" Matthew, pardon to son, 1043.
" Oliver more m'Edmond, pardon, 1043.
Walishe, Peter (Clonmore, co. Kilk.), pardon, 1043.
" Peter, pardon, 1043.
" Richard, pardon, 1043.
" Robert fitz Philip, pardon, 1043.
" Shane fitz James, pardon, 1043.
" Thomas, pardon to sons, 1043.
" Walter, pardon, 1043.
" William (alias Brenagho), pardon, 1041, 1043.
Walnaxxin, Francis, comm., [illegible].
Wake, Rich., customs controller, Dublin, [illegible].
Wakeleston, alias Ballebursley, King's co., [illegible].
Wakley—Wackmley—Wackley—Wacklie—Wackly—Wacley—Wakeley—Wakeleye:
" Christopher, grant of a wardship, 6406.
" George, wardship, 1764.
" John (of Navan and Ballybursley), M.P. for Navan, 129; sheriff of King's co., 1810; commissions, [illegible], [illegible], [illegible], 1810, 6776; leases, 1184, 1712; wardship, livery and license of alienation of his sons, 1764, 1867, [illegible].
" John, jointure for his wife, [illegible].
" Mary, jointure, [illegible].
" Thomas, livery, 1851; commissions, 5117, 5444, [illegible], 6123; lease, 5169; farmer of rectory of Navan, 4152, [illegible]; license to alien, [illegible].
Walche, James, pardon, [illegible]. *See* Walshe.
" Rosmetus, pardon, 138. *See* Walshe.
" Tho., pardon, [illegible].
" Wm., pardon, [illegible].
Walchestion. *See* Walshestown, co. Kild.
Walchestown (co. Lim. ?), 4638.
Wale, Austace, pardon, [illegible].
" Charles, pardon, [illegible].
" David (of Fethard), license to make aqua vitae, 7158.
" David (of Kilmallock), pardon, 567, 1470.
" David, pardon, 3441.
" Eady, pardon, 4571.
" Edm. (of Johnstown, co. Car.), livery to son, 4874.
" Edm. (of Urchlin, co. Car.), pardon, 3497, 5737.
" Edm. (of Walltown, co. Cork), pardon, [illegible], 4632.
" Edm., pardon, 1894, [illegible], [illegible], [illegible], 6477, [illegible], [illegible].
" Edm. fitzTho., pardon, [illegible].
" Edm. m'Ullick, pardon, [illegible].
" Ellena, pardon, 1043.
" Ellis (alias Tho.), pardon, 5063.

INDEX TO FIANTS—ELIZABETH.

Wale, Garett, pardon, [illegible].
„ Garret, pardon, [illegible], [illegible], 6703.
„ Gerald, premises in Dublin, [illegible].
„ Gerald, pardon, [illegible], [illegible], [illegible].
„ Gilbert, pardon, 4073.
„ Hugh boye, pardon, [illegible].
„ Isabella, attainted, [illegible].
„ James (—Waale—Walle, of Clonecrane, co. Lim.), attainted, [illegible] (Walle), [illegible], [illegible] (Waale).
„ James, pardon, [illegible], [illegible], [illegible], [illegible], [illegible].
„ James fitzWalter, pardon, [illegible], [illegible].
„ James m'Shane, pardon, [illegible].
„ John, pardon, 1057, [illegible], [illegible], [illegible], [illegible], [illegible], [illegible], [illegible], [illegible], [illegible], [illegible].
„ John fitzMorice or Morris, pardon, [illegible], [illegible].
„ John fitzPhilip, pardon, [illegible].
„ John fitzTho., pardon, [illegible].
„ John fitzUlick, pardon, [illegible].
„ John fitzWalter, pardon, 6123, 6484.
„ John keoghe, pardon, [illegible].
„ John Hacy or Lacy, pardon, [illegible].
„ Jonyne, pardon, [illegible].
„ Maurice, pardon, [illegible].
„ Moreny, pardon, [illegible].
„ Morrice fitzJohn, pardon, [illegible].
„ Nich. fitzWalter, pardon, [illegible], [illegible], [illegible].
„ Oner fitzRichard, pardon, [illegible].
„ Patrick, pardon, [illegible], [illegible], [illegible], [illegible].
„ Patr. fitz James, pardon, [illegible].
„ Patrick fitz Richard, pardon, [illegible].
„ Patrick fitzWilliam, [illegible].
„ Peirce fitz Patrick, pardon, [illegible].
„ Peirse, pardon, [illegible], [illegible].
„ Peirse fitz John, pardon, [illegible].
„ Peres roe, pardon, [illegible].
„ Peter, attainted, [illegible].
„ Peter, pardon, [illegible].
„ Peter fitz Richard, pardon, [illegible].
„ Peter fitz Walter, pardon, [illegible].
„ Philip, pardon, [illegible].
„ Philip, merchant of Cashel, [illegible], [illegible].
„ Philip, son of Richard, premises held by, [illegible].
„ Philip fitz Richard, pardon, [illegible].
„ Philip fitz Wm., pardon, [illegible].
„ Redmund, attainted, [illegible].
„ Redmund, pardon, [illegible], [illegible].
„ Redmund oge fitz Redmund, pardon, [illegible].
„ Richard (of Cloghscotired), attainted, lands granted, [illegible]; pardon, [illegible] (Wall).
„ Rich., burgess of Cashel, [illegible].
„ Richard, commission (co. Kild.), [illegible].

Wale, Richard, pardon, [illegible], [illegible], [illegible], [illegible], [illegible], [illegible], [illegible], [illegible].
„ Robert, pardon, [illegible], [illegible], [illegible].
„ Rob fitz John, pardon, [illegible].
„ Shane m'Gillebert, pardon, [illegible].
„ Thomas, pardon, 877, [illegible], [illegible], [illegible].
„ Thomas, treasurer of Ossory, allocation by, [illegible].
„ Tho. fitz Edm., pardon, [illegible].
„ Thomas fitz Philip, pardon, [illegible].
„ Tho. fitz Redmund, pardon, [illegible].
„ Thomas fitz Richard, pardon, [illegible], [illegible].
„ Thomas m'Redmond, attainted, [illegible].
„ Ulick, pardon, [illegible].
„ Ulick oge, pardon, [illegible].
„ Ulick (or de Wale) called the Faltagh (of Dunmoylan), attainted, his lands leased and granted, [illegible], [illegible], [illegible].
„ Ulick (of Dunmoylan), pardon, [illegible], [illegible].
„ Ulick fitz John, pardon, 4744.
„ Ulick oge (of Droght, co. Gal.), pardon, [illegible], [illegible].
„ Walter, land in Clonmel, [illegible]. *See* Walle.
„ Walter (of Drought, co. Gal.), chief of his name, [illegible]; pardon, [illegible], [illegible]; grant of lands, [illegible].
„ Walter, pardon, [illegible], [illegible], [illegible], [illegible], [illegible].
„ Walter fitz Peirs, pardon, [illegible], [illegible].
„ Walter m'Shane, pardon, [illegible].
„ William, robbery from, 842.
„ William (son of Edm. of Johnstown, co. Car.), livery, [illegible].
„ William, pardon, [illegible], [illegible].
„ Wm. fitz Richard, pardon, [illegible].
„ Wm. fitz Walter, pardon, [illegible], [illegible].
Wales, [illegible]; exports to, [illegible].
Wales lands, co. Lim., [illegible].
Wales loughe—Waleslogh (Wallslough, co. Kilk.?), [illegible], [illegible].
Waleston (Wallstown, co. Cork?), [illegible], [illegible].
Waleston (co. Kild.?), [illegible].
Walestowne, alias Ballynwale, co. Kilk., [illegible].
Waleslogh, [illegible]. *See* Walesloughe.
Walleston (co. Cork?), [illegible].
Walker, Anneis, pardon, [illegible].
„ Farmna, pardon, 748.
„ Henry, [illegible].
„ John, pardon, [illegible].
„ Margery, pardon, [illegible].
„ Nich., pardon, [illegible].
„ Nich., land in his tenure, [illegible].
Wall of Dungarvan to be erected as condition of pardon of inhabitants, [illegible].
Wall, Charles, pardon, [illegible].

INDEX TO FIANTS.—ELIZABETH.

Wall, Edmund, pardon, 4394.
„ Edm. fitz John, pardon, 6744.
„ Gerald, pardon, 6748.
„ Gerrott fitz Rich., pardon, [illegible].
„ James, pardon, 3972, 4080, 6462.
„ James, [illegible].
„ James fitz Nich., pardon, 6461.
„ John, pardon, [illegible], 6764.
„ John fitz Edy, pardon, 6461.
„ John m'Teige, pardon, 6461.
„ Patr., pardon, [illegible].
„ Patrickie, pardon, 3011.
„ Petrie, pardon, 6189, 6704.
„ Peter, pardon, 6242.
„ Ricard, pardon, [illegible].
„ Rich., pardon, [illegible], 6461, 6748. See Wale.
„ Shane keagh, pardon, 6458.
„ Tho., pardon, 6764.
„ Ullick, pardon, 6461.
„ Walter, pardon, 1828, [illegible].
„ Wm., pardon, 3774.
Wallace, Michael, protection, 63.
Wallane, John, alias M'Donnogho, pardon, [illegible].
Walle, James, land of, 6494.
„ James, pardon, 4463, [illegible], [illegible].
„ James fitz John, pardon, 6768.
„ John, attainted, lands leased (co. Gal.), 6940.
„ Morryes m'Shane, the lands of, granted (co. Lim.), 6494.
„ Oliver, pardon, 6348.
„ Rich., pardon, [illegible], [illegible].
„ Rob., pardon, [illegible].
„ Thomas, attainted, 6781.
„ Tho. fitz Morishe, pardon, 6748.
„ Tho. m'Rickard, pardon, [illegible].
„ Ulighe, attainted, 6781.
„ Walter, land in Clonmel, [illegible]. See also Wale.
„ Walter, pardon, 6308, 6774.
„ Wm., pardon, [illegible].
Waller, Apollo, treasurer of Ferns, 6460.
Wallestowne (Wallstown), co. Cork, [illegible].
Walley, John, registrar ecclesiastical commission, [illegible].
Walleys, Edward, clerk of works, [illegible].
Wallibeg (co. Kilk. ?), 6462.
Wallington, Alis, 3438.
Wallop — Wallope — Wallopp — Walloppe, sir Henry, vicetreasurer and treasurer at war, 3601, 6439; constable of Athlone castle, [illegible]; appointed lord justice of Ireland, 3978, 4494; authorised to treat with Tyrone, [illegible]; footmen under his command, [illegible]; commissions, [illegible], [illegible], 3947, [illegible], 3720, 4042, 4044, [illegible],

Wallop:—
[illegible], [illegible], [illegible], 4740, [illegible], [illegible], [illegible], 5108, [illegible], [illegible], [illegible], [illegible], [illegible], [illegible], [illegible], [illegible], [illegible], [illegible], [illegible], [illegible], [illegible], [illegible]; grant of the lordship of Athlone, [illegible]; grants of land, [illegible]; leases, 4787-8, [illegible], [illegible], 6081; surrender, [illegible]; licences of alienation, [illegible], [illegible].
„ Oliver, second son of sir Henry, license of alienation, 6318.
„ Richard and William, principal registrars of the high commission, [illegible].
Wallslough, co. Kilk. See Wales loughe.
Wallstown, co. Cork. See Walestowe, Wallestowne.
Walshe—Walsh—Walsche:
„ Adam (of Abbey of Owny), pardon, 6788.
„ Adam fitz Rob., pardon, 6081 (Walshe), 4463, 6704.
„ Alexander, pardon, 6864.
„ Alson, 5804.
„ Agne, pardon, 847.
„ Anstace, 3150.
„ Charles, pardon, [illegible].
„ Christopher (of Lexale), pardon, 6794.
„ Chr. (of Kilgoban), pardon, 6773.
„ Chr., pardon, 6189, 6494, 6496.
„ Clement, pardon, 6434.
„ David, parson of Tamon, 1676.
„ David (of Rathronan), pardon, [illegible], 5001.
„ David, pardon, 3434, 4434, [illegible].
„ Edmund, vicar of Oughterard, 787.
„ Edm. (of Ballyvan, co. Dub.), pardon, 3791.
„ Edm. (of Carrickmale), pardon, [illegible].
„ Edm. (of Corke), pardon, 634.
„ Edm. (of Frompston), pardon, 1728.
„ Edm. (of Owny, co. Lim.), pardon, 3148, 4129; livery, [illegible].
„ Edm. m'Charles, pardon, [illegible], [illegible], 6394.
„ Edm. fitz Rob., pardon, [illegible], 6454, 6791.
„ Edmund, pardon, 1788, 1972, [illegible], [illegible], 3417, [illegible], [illegible], [illegible], [illegible], 4878, 6398, 4188, [illegible], 6468, 6486, 6364, 6704.
„ Edward, leases, 881, 1431; license to alien, [illegible]; pardons granted at his suit, 1648.
„ Edw., pardon, 4016, 6712, 5360, 6183, [illegible].

INDEX TO FIANTS.—ELIZABETH.

Walshe, George, grant of a wardship, 4371.
" Gerald, pardon, 3141, [illegible].
" Gerrott, pardon, [illegible].
" Henry (of Arklow), pardon, 2851.
" Henry (of Dalkey), pardon, [illegible].
" Henry (of Killenurrig), pardon, [illegible].
" Henry (of Monkton, co. Meath), pardon, [illegible], [illegible].
" Henry (of Newton), pardon, [illegible].
" Henry (of Three Castles), pardon, [illegible], [illegible].
" Henry, pardon in Waterford, [illegible].
" Henry, pardon, [illegible], [illegible], [illegible], [illegible].
" Heill, pardon, 971.
" Howell, pardon, [illegible].
" James, alderman of Waterford, commission, [illegible]; pardon, [illegible], [illegible]; wardship and livery of heir, [illegible], [illegible].
" James (of Clonard), pardon, [illegible].
" James (of Molragh), pardon, 3727.
" James (of Rathronan), pardon, [illegible], [illegible] (Walshe), [illegible].
" James (of Three Castles), pardon, [illegible].
" James, pardon in his tenure in Waterford, [illegible].
" James fitz Oliver (of Lisronagh), pardon, [illegible], [illegible].
" James fitz Rob. (of Waterford), pardon, [illegible], 1234.
" James fitz Rob. (alias Brenagh), pardon, 1768, [illegible].
" James, pardon, [illegible], 1725, [illegible], 1671, [illegible], [illegible], 2700, [illegible], [illegible], 4441, [illegible], [illegible], [illegible], [illegible], [illegible], [illegible], [illegible], [illegible], [illegible], [illegible].
" Jasper, pardon, 3124.
" Jeffery, pardon, [illegible].
" Joan, pardon, [illegible], [illegible].
" Joan, party in matrimonial cause, 4372.
" Johanna, grant of a wardship, [illegible].
" John (of Ardery), pardon, [illegible].
" John (of Balawly), livery, [illegible]; pardon, 1782.
" John (of Castleboole), pardon, [illegible].
" John (of Kilgobbin), commission, [illegible]; wardship of heir, [illegible].
" John, late gauger of Limerick, [illegible], [illegible].
" John (of Shanganagh), commissions, 3444, [illegible], [illegible]; pardon, [illegible], [illegible], [illegible], [illegible], [illegible]; party to a suit, [illegible] (Walsh).

Walshe, John, sheriff of co. Dublin, comm., [illegible].
" John (of Wony), pardon, [illegible].
" John (alias Brenagh), murder of, [illegible], [illegible].
" John, pardon to his wife, [illegible].
" John fitz Rob., pardon, [illegible], [illegible], [illegible].
" John, pardon, [illegible], [illegible], 1788, [illegible], [illegible], [illegible], [illegible], [illegible], [illegible], [illegible], [illegible], [illegible], [illegible], [illegible], [illegible], [illegible], [illegible], [illegible], [illegible], [illegible], [illegible].
" Katherine, pardon, [illegible], [illegible].
" Laurence (of Kilkenny), pardon, 1617, [illegible].
" Laurence (of Moyvaly), pardon, [illegible], [illegible].
" Laurence, pardon, [illegible], [illegible], [illegible].
" Lewis, pardon, [illegible].
" Marcus, pardon, [illegible].
" Margaret, pardon, [illegible], [illegible].
" Margaret, pardon in Waterford, [illegible].
" Martin, grant of duty on French imposts, [illegible], [illegible].
" Maurice—Morice (of Thorngham), attainted, [illegible], [illegible].
" Maurice — Moris — Morish, pardon, [illegible], [illegible], [illegible], [illegible], [illegible], [illegible].
" Morgan, pardon, [illegible].
" Murragh, pardon, [illegible].
" Nicholas (alias Walsh and Welshe), second justice of Munster, [illegible], [illegible], [illegible]; chief justice of Munster, [illegible], [illegible]; second justice of the Chief Place, [illegible], [illegible]; chief justice Common Bench, [illegible], [illegible]; a commissioner in Munster, [illegible], [illegible], [illegible]; commissions, [illegible]; at musters, [illegible]; grant of a wardship, [illegible]; trustee of Cormac m'Teig M'Carty, [illegible]; pardon at his suit, [illegible]; grants of land, [illegible], [illegible]; leases, [illegible], [illegible], [illegible]; pardon of alienation, [illegible]; export licence, [illegible].
" Nicholas, chancellor of St. Patrick's, commission, [illegible], [illegible] (Walshe), [illegible], [illegible]; bishop of Ossory, [illegible].
" Nicholas fitz James (of Waterford), pardon, 1784.
" Nicholas, pardon, [illegible], [illegible], [illegible], [illegible], [illegible], [illegible], [illegible], [illegible].

INDEX TO FIANTS—ELIZABETH.

Walshe, Nicholas, house in Naas, 6108.
„ Nicholas, garden in Waterford, 6183.
„ Oliver (of Kilmore bremagh), pardon, [illegible].
„ Oliver (of Slieve Breamagh), pardon, [illegible].
„ Oliver (of Merrion), pardon, [illegible].
„ Oliver, pardon, 1812, [illegible], 3347, [illegible], [illegible], 4484, [illegible], 6437, [illegible], 6704.
„ Owen, lease, 446 (Walshe), grant of a wardship, [illegible]; pardon, 1732, [illegible], [illegible].
„ Patrick, pardon, [illegible].
„ Patr., widow of, [illegible].
„ Patr., knt., grant at request of, [illegible].
„ Patr., lands in Youghal, [illegible].
„ Petrus, pardon, [illegible], [illegible].
„ Peter, mayor of Waterford, commission, 1658.
„ Peter, alderman of Waterford, pardon, 1784.
„ Peter (of Clonongh or Clonniffe, co. Kild.), pardon, 2727; attainted, [illegible] pardon, [illegible].
„ Peter, garden in Waterford, 6183.
„ Peter, pardon, 1746, [illegible], 2434, 2801, [illegible].
„ Peter. *See* Piers.
„ Philip, chaplain, [illegible].
„ Sir Philip, land at Cashel, [illegible].
„ Philip Artur, pardon, [illegible].
„ Philip, pardon, [illegible], [illegible], [illegible], [illegible], [illegible], 6740, [illegible], [illegible], 6466, [illegible], 6704.
„ Piers—Pers—Peter (of Grange, co. Kilk., and Owney, co. Lim.), grant of lands, 483; sheriff of Limerick, [illegible], 1744, 3401; commissions, [illegible], 1644, [illegible]; pardon, 1769; livery to son, 6704.
„ Piers (of Kilgobban), wardship, [illegible]; pardon, 6774 (Walshe).
„ Redmond, pardon, [illegible].
„ Reimlotus, pardon, [illegible].
„ Ricard, pardon, [illegible].
„ Richard m'Robert (of Carrickmines), pardon, 604.
„ Richard (son of William of Carrickmines), livery, [illegible]; commission, 2344; pardon, [illegible], [illegible].
„ Richard (son of Theobald of Carrickmines), wardship, [illegible].
„ Richard, gauger of Cork, [illegible], [illegible].
„ Richard (of Curraghmore, co. Kild.), pardon, [illegible].

Walshe, Richard fitz James (of Knockmaillan), pardon, [illegible], 6704.
„ Richard, parson of Loughmerdie, attainted, 1172, [illegible].
„ Richard (of Tveroghan ?), attainted, [illegible], 3488, [illegible].
„ Richard (of Temple m'tyer), pardon, 1684, 3347.
„ Richard, tenement in Waterford, [illegible].
„ Richard, marshal of the gaol of Waterford, [illegible].
„ Richard, pardon, 1768, [illegible], [illegible], [illegible], [illegible], 4384, 4660, [illegible], [illegible], 6443, [illegible], 6704.
„ Robert (of Ballenclowre), pardon, 1769, 2434.
„ Rob. (of Ballincase), pardon, 6704.
„ Rob. (of Castlehowell), pardon, 6443, [illegible].
„ Rob. (of Grange), pardon, 6704.
„ Rob. (of Hilltown), pardon, 6704.
„ Rob. (of Tveroghan), attaint [illegible]
„ Rob. (of Waterford), war[illegible] livery, 3194, [illegible].
„ Rob. (alias Cushie), par[illegible]
„ Rob. (alias Perman[illegible] [illegible].
„ Rob., land in Waterfo[illegible]
„ Robert, pardon, 140, 31[illegible] [illegible], [illegible], 4441, [illegible], [illegible]
„ Romnoius, pardon, 1[illegible] 737.
„ Shane, pardon, 1877, 6[illegible]
„ Simon, pardon, [illegible].
„ Theobald (of Carrick[illegible] mission, 4443; ward[illegible] [illegible].
„ Theobald (of Killenan[illegible] [illegible]; livery, [illegible].
„ Theobald (of Three C[illegible] don, [illegible].
„ Theobald, pardon, [illegible]
„ Thomas (of Ballanlr), heir, 857.
„ Thomas (of Dublin), the Chamber, 448, (Walshe); grant a[illegible]
„ Tho. (of Kilkenny), [illegible] [illegible].
„ Tho. (of Carrickfer[illegible] 6712.
„ Tho., land of, [illegible].
„ Thomas, pardon, 670, [illegible], [illegible], [illegible], [illegible] [illegible], 6484, [illegible], [illegible].
„ Tibbott (of Kilgob[illegible] [illegible].

Walshe, Tirlagh, pardon, 6462.
„ Walter (of Castlehoale—Castlekelam—Castlehowell, co. Kilk.), sheriff of Kilkenny, [illegible], 4463; commission, [illegible]; pardon, [illegible], [illegible], 4398, [illegible], 6704.
„ Walter oge (of Garrangood), wife of, [illegible].
„ Walter, pardon, [illegible], 842, 1788, [illegible], [illegible], 3948, 4267, 6442, 6418, [illegible]-6.
„ William. See Meath, bishop of.
„ William (of Carrickmaines), commission, [illegible]; lease, [illegible], 6794; livery to heir, 2100; his son, [illegible].
„ Wm. (of Corke, co. Dub.), pardon, [illegible].
„ Wm. (of Kildare), clerk, pardon, 1908.
„ Wm. (of Tacroghan), his son attainted, [illegible].
„ Wm., murdered, 1683, 1980.
„ Wm., house in Naas, 5166.
„ Wm., pardon, 1681, 1788, 2824, [illegible], 3043, [illegible], [illegible], [illegible], [illegible], [illegible], [illegible], [illegible], [illegible], [illegible], [illegible], [illegible], [illegible], 6446, 6463, 6517, 6764, [illegible], 6772.
„ See Walsh, Walshe, Walche, Walshe, Welche, Welsh, Welshe.
Walsheman's land, co. Dub., 4626.
Walshemontayne—Walsh mountay, co. Kilk., [illegible], 1628.
Walshe sallon, co. Dublin, [illegible].
Walsheston, 846.
Walsheston (co. Cork ?), 6761.
Walsheston — Walcheston— Walsheton, co. Kild., 1427, 1716, 1963, [illegible], 3073; rectory, 3671.
Walshestowne (Walshestown), co. Wex., 6724.
Walshestown (co. Cork ?), 4463, 6464.
Walshestowne, co. Cork or Lim., [illegible].
Walsheton. See Walsheston, co. Kild.
Walshton—Walshtowne in diocese of Dublin, 3615, 6411.
Walshtown (co. Westm. ?), [illegible].
Walshtown (co. Cork ?), [illegible].
Walshtowne. See Walshton.
Walsh, commissioner, temp. Henry VIII., 6722.
Walshe, Owen, lease, 466. See Walshe.
„ Peter fitz Nicholas, pardon, 7132.
„ William, lease, 466. See Walshe.
Walstone, co. Westm., [illegible].
Walter, Gaber, pardon, 4377.
„ Dorothy ny, pardon, [illegible].
„ Ellena fitz Rob., pardon, [illegible].
„ George, pardon, 6977.
„ James oge, pardon, 6484.
Walter, John, pardon, 1889.
„ Wm., pardon, 6423.
„ Wm. boyye, pardon, [illegible].
Walter duffe, pardon, 6464.
Walterestou. See Walterston, co. Meath.
Walteriston. See Walterston, co. Kild.
Walteriston, co. Tip., 960.
Walteriston — Walteristoune. See Walterstown, co. Westm.
Walterston—Walterstone (Waterstown, co. Car.), 2727, 4334.
Walterston—Walteriston—Walterstown, co. Kild., 1484, [illegible], 6778, 6712.
Walterston, co. Louth, 4677.
Walterston — Walterestou (Walterstown), co. Meath, 674, 1683, [illegible], [illegible], 4236, 5878.
Waltersion (co. Wex. ?), 6417.
Walterstoun. See Walterston, co. Car.
Walterstoun. See Walterston, co. Kild.
Walterstoune, co. Westm., 6462.
Walterstown (co. Cork ?), 6462.
Walterstown, co. Meath. See Walterston.
Walterstowne—Walteriston—Walteristoune—Walterstowne (Walterstown), co. Westm., 846, 1946, 1256, [illegible].
Walterstown, co. Westm. See Waltertowne
Walterstowne, near Lucan, co. Dub., [illegible].
Walterstowne. See Walterstown, co. Westm.
Waltertowne—Walterrston (Walterstown), co. Westm., 1622, 2861.
Walton, Tho., pardon, 5616.
Wapell, Tho., burgess, Athlone, 6312.
War: rebels make war, 3134, 1216; commission to make war on rebels, 5184, 5828; grants of land given in consideration of service in the wars in Ireland, [illegible], 5130, 5166, [illegible], [illegible], 5317, 6414, 5874, 5816; treasurer at wars. See Treasurer (vice).
Ward, Tho., pardon, [illegible].
„ Wm., pardon, [illegible].
Warde, Bernard, pardon, 782, 4471.
„ John, captain, pardon, 1114, [illegible].
„ John, pardon to son of, 782.
„ Nicholas, surveyor general of ordnance, 5381-6, 6728.
Wards, co. Dub., 6834.
Wards of Tobber (Wards of Tober, co. Wick.), 4189, 5878.
Wardston—Wardstowne, co. Meath, 4471, [illegible].
Wardships, commission to enquire of concealed, 6761.
Wardslough (co. Kilk. ?), 4377.
Wardton, co. Meath, 1828.
Ware, James, clerk of pleas of Exchequer, [illegible]; auditor of the accounts, 6716; grant, [illegible]; pension, 6441, [illegible]; authority to take hay, 5416.

Ware, James, footman, Dublin Castle, 5148, 6161.
Waren, Elinora, [illegible].
" Henry. *See* Warren.
" Humfrey. *See* Warren.
Waring, Henry. *See* Warren.
" James, pardon, 2943.
" Nicholas, 6717.
" Peter, freedom of subsidy, [illegible].
" William, pardon, 6294.
Waringe, Andrew, son of John, of Navan, wardship, 6918.
" Patrick, livery to, [illegible].
" Rob., pardon, 6469.
" Tho., pardon, [illegible].
" Thomas, son and heir of, [illegible].
Waringeston (Warrenstown, in par. of Dunboyne), co. Meath, 874, 1881.
Waringestone. *See* Warrenston, King's co.
Waringiston, co. Meath, 894.
Warn—Warne, Henry. *See* Warren.
Warne, Humfrey. *See* Warren.
Warneston — Warmston (alias Warmaston), King's co., 477, [illegible].
Warr, Nich., [illegible].
" Rich., [illegible].
Warren, Anne, pardon, 6768.
" Ellinor, pardon, 6454.
" Henry (also Waren — Waring — Warn, afterwards knight), [illegible]; sheriff of King's co., 4040, 5136; commissions, 4046, 4574, 5186, [illegible], 6049, [illegible], [illegible]-4; grants of land, 477, 4184, [illegible]; leases, 4181, 4411; surrender, 4301; license for alienation, [illegible]; farmer of rectory, [illegible]: pardon, 4117, 4136, [illegible]-6.
" Humfrey (also Waren — Warne), captain, and member of privy council, commissions, 47, 188, 218, 735, 4788; takes oath of supremacy, [illegible]; grant of land to his heirs, 477; his services, 4181.
" Tho. (of the Navan), pardon, [illegible], 6394, 6410.
" Tho. fitz John, pardon, 6494.
" William, brother of sir Henry, [illegible].
" Wm., pardon, 6782.
Warrenston, 6945.
Warrenston—Waringestone, King's co., 477, 5846, 6385.
Warrenston, or Great Warrenston (Warrenstown, in parish of Rathbeggan), co. Meath, 1480, 2864.
Warrenston (Warrenstowne in parish of Knockmark), co. Meath, 162.
Warrenston, little (Warrenstown), co. Meath, 1940, 1468, 2864.
Warrenstown, co. Meath. *See* Waringeston, Warrenston, Warringston.
Warringe, John (of Navan), 6919. *See* Waringe.
Warringstown (Warrenstown, in barony of Deece), co. Meath, 6280.
Warrinstone (co. Wat. ?), 5474.
Waslye, Robert. *See* Wesley.
Waspallston — Waspailston. *See* Waspailiston.
Waspailston. *See* Waspailston.
Waspalngton (in manor of Newcastle), co. Dub., [illegible].
Waspaylston. *See* Waspailston.
Waspaylliston — Waspeliston — Waspelston. *See* Waspailiston.
Wasse, Rob., pardon, 6519.
Wasterton, co. Kild., 6081.
Waston, John fitz Rich., pardon, 6447.
" Oliver (or Weston, of Rathcloy, co. Kilk.), pardon, 1076; attainder of his son, 6163.
" Patrick, attainder of, 6163.
" Richard, pardon, 1076, [illegible].
Watch and ward, to be kept in co. Meath, [illegible]; in bar. Newcastle, co. Dub., 4118.
Watchmen at night to be employed by sheriff of Meath, 1111; slay a man who would not submit to them, 6708.
Water, the, co. Louth, 2348, 4147, 4466.
Water bailiff of Shannon appointed, 1908, 6118.
Water, James, son and heir of, wardship, 5778.
" James, alias M'Twaterig, pardon, [illegible].
" Michael, wardship, [illegible].
" Richard, pardon, 6701.
" Richard, pardon, 6782.
" Stephen, lease, 6377, 6962.
Watercastle—Watercastell—Waster Castell Queen's co., 697, 6861, 6762. *See also* Castle Uany.
Watereska, co. Down. *See* Ottereska.
Waterfield, co. Tip., [illegible].
Waterfoot river, co Donegal. *See* Ava Iniurragh.
Waterford — Waterforde — Waterfourd (mentioned), 13, 14, 40, 294, 411, 416, 428, 457, 488, 613, 676, 731, 754, 781, 862, 954, 980, 1032, 1044, 1162, 1180, 1208, 1234, 1302, 1482, 1848, 2378, 2507, 2218-4, 2848, 2712, 2528, 3034-5, 3087, 3018, 3026, 3182, 3174, 3191, 3191, 3280, [illegible], [illegible], 3311, [illegible], 4118, 4188, 4163, 4282, 4224, 4728, 4818, 4819, 5013, [illegible], [illegible], [illegible], [illegible],

INDEX TO FIANTS.—ELIZABETH.

Waterford:
[illegible], 4416, [illegible], [illegible]; English liberty to men of, 1187, 1234; export of wheat, 1758, [illegible], 4210; illegal exports, [illegible]; shoemakers licensed to tan, [illegible]; goldsmith, [illegible]; men to be mustered against foreign invasion, [illegible]; premises leased, [illegible], 1421, 1878, [illegible], 4253, [illegible], granted, [illegible], [illegible], [illegible], [illegible]; gardens and ground leased, [illegible], 6123-3; license to erect tan house, [illegible].
" mayor, bayllyes, and commons, lease, [illegible].
" mayor, bailiffs, and citizens, lease, [illegible].
" mayor, sheriffs, and citizens confirmation of grant to, [illegible].
" mayor and bailiffs, to proclaim persons indicted of treason, [illegible].
" mayor, commissions to, [illegible], [illegible], [illegible], [illegible], 1012, 1844, [illegible], [illegible], [illegible], [illegible], [illegible], [illegible], 4157, [illegible]; copy of articles between queen and earl of Desmond sent to, [illegible]; accuses the bishop of plundering the cathedral, 3743.
" sheriff, 3743.
" recorder, [illegible].
" aldermen, 1794, 1799, [illegible], [illegible].
" merchants, [illegible], 1234, 1334, 1876, 1794, 1799, [illegible], 3344, [illegible], 6114, [illegible].
" physician, [illegible].
" Archery butt, [illegible].
" Barron strand, [illegible], [illegible].
" Christ church, or church of Holy Trinity, plundered, 3743; land of, [illegible]. See cathedral below.
" Colbeck street, [illegible].
" Colbecks island, [illegible].
" Colbecks mill, [illegible].
" Courthouse, [illegible].
" ferry, [illegible], [illegible], 4121.
" Flesh shambles, [illegible], [illegible].
" Guild hall, [illegible].
" Magdalen, [illegible].
Milk-street, [illegible].

Waterford, Monastery of Friars Preachers, [illegible], [illegible], [illegible].
" S. Bride's hermitage, [illegible].
" S. John the Evangelist, hospital, possessions granted, [illegible]; rectory, [illegible]; backgate, [illegible].
" S. Katherine abbey, leased, [illegible], 4318, [illegible]; possessions leased, [illegible], [illegible], [illegible], [illegible]; granted, [illegible], [illegible].
" S. Michael parish, [illegible], [illegible].
" S. Patrick parish, [illegible], [illegible], 4163, [illegible]; gate, [illegible]; church, [illegible].
" S. Peter parish, [illegible].
" S. Peter street, [illegible], [illegible], [illegible].
" S. Stephen's parish, [illegible].
" Shortcourse, [illegible].
" Suburbs, [illegible], [illegible].
" bishop of Waterford and Lismore, Patrick (Walshe), commissions, [illegible], [illegible], [illegible], 1062, [illegible], 1446; suit against archbishop of Cashel, [illegible]; appeal from his court, [illegible].
" bishop, Marmaduke (Middleton), commission, [illegible]; made provost of college of Youghal, [illegible]; accused of plundering his cathedral, 3743.
" bishop commendatory, Meiler Magrath, commission, 4139; appeals from, 4169, [illegible].
" dean, [illegible], [illegible], [illegible], [illegible], [illegible].
" president of cathedral, [illegible].
" chancellor, [illegible], [illegible], [illegible].
" treasurer, 705, 1626, [illegible], [illegible], [illegible].
" chaplains pardoned for offences against Act of Uniformity, [illegible].
" diocese, benefices in, [illegible], [illegible].
" port or haven, trade of, [illegible], [illegible], [illegible], [illegible]; great fleet of fishermen at, [illegible].
" " supervisor of, [illegible].
" " searcher and gauger, [illegible], [illegible], [illegible], [illegible].
" wine impost leased, [illegible].
" collector of impost on wine, 1494, [illegible], [illegible], [illegible], 4009, [illegible], [illegible].

INDEX TO FIANTS.—ELIZABETH.

Waterford, controller, 1466, 2152, 2777, [illegible], [illegible], [illegible], [illegible], [illegible].
" county, to be surveyed and made shire ground, 1333, 1344, [illegible], [illegible]; to be divided into baronies and ploughlands, [illegible], 1348; injuries done by men of, [illegible]; commission to hear disputes between inhabitants and earl of Desmond, 464; general session for county, [illegible]; persons indicted of treason, [illegible]; plenty of corn, [illegible]; lands in, exchanged by N. White, [illegible]; custodiam of lands of earl of Desmond, [illegible]; escheated lands measured, [illegible]; allotted to undertakers, [illegible]; grants to undertakers, [illegible], [illegible], [illegible], [illegible]; other grants of land, [illegible], [illegible], &c.
" county, commission of peace, [illegible], [illegible].
" county, command of soldiers in, [illegible], [illegible].
" county, ecclesiastical commission, [illegible].
" county, martial law, [illegible].
" county, sheriff, [illegible], 144, [illegible], [illegible], [illegible], [illegible], [illegible], 1346, [illegible], [illegible], [illegible], [illegible], [illegible], [illegible], [illegible], [illegible], [illegible], [illegible], [illegible], [illegible], [illegible], [illegible], [illegible], [illegible], [illegible], [illegible], [illegible].
" county, sub-sheriff, [illegible], [illegible], [illegible], [illegible], [illegible].
" county, clerk of crown and peace, 142.
" county, chief serjeant, [illegible].
" county, marshal of courts and keeper of gaol, [illegible], [illegible].
" county, overseer of tanning, [illegible].
Waterhous — Waterhouse — Waterhowse — Watirhous — Watirhouse — Watirhowse, Edward (afterwards knight), clerk of the Castle Chamber, [illegible], [illegible]; secretary to the lord deputy, [illegible]; to be member of parliament for Carrickfergus, [illegible]; collector of
Waterhous:
custom on wines, [illegible], [illegible], [illegible]; commissioner for check of the army, [illegible]; receiver general of the Exchequer, [illegible]; receiver of casual profits, [illegible]; overseer of river Shannon, [illegible], [illegible]; chancellor of the Exchequer, [illegible], [illegible]; party to indentures with chiefs, [illegible], [illegible]; commissions, [illegible]; pension, [illegible], [illegible]; licence of absence, [illegible], [illegible], [illegible], [illegible], [illegible]; pardon, [illegible]; pardon at his suit, [illegible]; divorce cause, [illegible]; grant of land, [illegible]; lands confirmed by indenture, [illegible]; grant of a wardship, [illegible]; leases, [illegible], [illegible], [illegible]; surrenders, [illegible], [illegible]; license to alien, [illegible], [illegible].
Watermen impressed, [illegible].
Waters, James (of Rathjordan), heir of, [illegible].
" Michael, livery, [illegible].
" Stephen, commissions, [illegible], [illegible].
Waters land, Lu[illegible], co. Dub., [illegible].
Waterston (co. Westm.?), [illegible].
Waterstown, co. Car. See Walterston.
Waterstown, co. Westm. See Walterstown.
Watervion, John, pensioner, [illegible].
Watirhous—Watirhouse—Watirhowse. S Waterhous.
Watkyngs, Wm., pardon, [illegible].
Watson, Edm., pardon, [illegible].
" Oliver, pardon, [illegible], [illegible].
Watonsgrow (co. Kilk.,) [illegible].
Watson, Thomas, rector of Old [illegible].
Watter, Ellis, pardon, [illegible].
Watton, Oliver, pardon, [illegible].
" Philip, pardon, [illegible].
Waulker, Ferman, pardon, [illegible].
Wauter Castell. See Watercastl[illegible]
Wax, chief rent paid in, [illegible]; [illegible] of, [illegible], [illegible], [illegible].
Wayes, James, pardon, [illegible].
Wayle, Redmund fitz John, par[illegible]
Waynman—Wayneman, Edmo[illegible] [illegible], [illegible]; capt. and provost [illegible] Connaught, [illegible].
Wayre, James, lease, [illegible].
Wealsh, James, pardon, [illegible].
Weavers pardoned, [illegible], [illegible], [illegible], [illegible], [illegible], [illegible], [illegible], [illegible], [illegible], [illegible], [illegible], [illegible].
Webb, Wm., pardon, [illegible].
Webbe, John, pardon, [illegible].
Webbister, Henry, killed, [illegible].
Wegwood, Roger, pardon, [illegible].
Weights and measures (false), to be corrected, [illegible], [illegible].
Weingfield, Jacques, [illegible]. See Wingfield[illegible]

INDEX TO FIANTS—ELIZABETH.

Weirs on Shannon to be destroyed, [illegible], [illegible].
Weisley, Gerrott, commission, [illegible].
Weisly, Rob., [illegible]. *See* Wesley.
Welche, John fitz Edm., pardon, [illegible].
" Oliver fitz James, pardon, [illegible].
" Walter fitz Edw., pardon, [illegible].
" Wm., pardon, [illegible].
Welches garden, co. Wat., [illegible].
Weldon, Nich., [illegible].
" Rob., pardon, [illegible].
Welestye, John, servant of, pardon, [illegible].
Welford, John, grant of wardship, [illegible].
Wellesley—Welisley—Wellesleye—Wellesle—Wellesly—Wellesleye—Wellisley:
" Chr. (of Dengin), alienation by, [illegible].
" Edw., pardon, [illegible].
" Gerald (of Blackhall), commission, [illegible]. *See* Wesley.
" Gerald (of Dengin), livery, 46; commissions, [illegible], [illegible]. *See* Wesley.
Nicholas, son of baron of Norragh, [illegible]. *See* Wesley.
" Peter or Piers (of Blackhall), freedom from subsidy, [illegible]; commission, [illegible]; alienation by, [illegible].
" Robert, archdeacon of Dublin. *See* Wesley.
" William, 44.
Wells, co. Car., [illegible].
Wellshestowne, co. Lim., [illegible].
Welsh, Edm., pardon, [illegible].
" Edm. (or Brenagh), pardon, [illegible].
" Edm. fitz Rob., pardon, [illegible].
" Elizabeth, pardon, [illegible].
" Henry, pardon, [illegible].
" James fitz Nich., pardon, [illegible].
" Joan, pardon, [illegible].
" John, [illegible]. *See* Walshe.
" John m'Davy, pardon, [illegible].
" Katherine, pardon, [illegible].
" Moriah, pardon, [illegible].
" Nicholas, commission, [illegible].
" Nich., knt. *See* Walshe.
" Oliver duff (or Brenagh), pardon, [illegible].
" Peirs fitz Edm., pardon, [illegible].
" Wm., pardon, [illegible].
Welsh nation, men of, permitted to receive alienation of lands, 4804; soldiers may be of, [illegible].
Welshe, Charles, pardon, [illegible].
" Chief justice. *See* Walshe, Nicholas.
" Edm. m'Wm., pardon, [illegible].
" Henry, pardon, [illegible].
Welshe, James, pardon, [illegible], [illegible], [illegible].
" John, pardon, [illegible].
" John fitz David, pardon, [illegible].
" John fitz Oliver (or Brenagh), pardon, 812.
" John fitz Phillipp, pardon, [illegible].
" John fitz Rich., pardon, [illegible].
" Laurence, pardon, [illegible].
" Nicholas. *See* Walshe.
" Nich., pardon, [illegible].
" Nich. m'Tobbott, pardon, [illegible].
" Peirs (or Brenagh), pardon, [illegible].
" Peirs, pardon, [illegible].
" Peirse, of Kilgobau. *See* Walshe.
" Peirse, pardon, [illegible].
" Rich., pardon, [illegible], [illegible].
" Rich. fitz Rob., pardon, [illegible].
" Rob., pardon, [illegible], [illegible].
" Rob. (or Brennagh), pardon, [illegible].
" Rob. fitz James, pardon, [illegible].
" Shane m'Charles, pardon, [illegible].
" Thomas, 1452. *See* Walshe.
" Tho., pardon, [illegible].
" Tibbot m'Edm., pardon, [illegible].
" Tirlagh, pardon, [illegible].
" Wm. (or Brenagh), pardon, [illegible].
Welshes lands, Youghal, [illegible].
Wenaghan, John m'Donell I., pardon, [illegible].
Weny, Katherine ny, pardon, [illegible].
Werre, Nicholas, [illegible].
Wesbie—Wesby—Wesbhy—Wesbye—Wespey, Richard, pardon, 1707, [illegible]; serjeant of the Birnes and Tooles countries, commissions, [illegible], [illegible]; pardon, [illegible], [illegible].
Wesby, James, pardon, [illegible].
Wesle, Maurice, pardon, [illegible].
Weslele, Chr. fitz Walter, pardon, [illegible].
Wesley—Wesleye—Weslie—Wesly—Weslye—Wessesley—Weysley:
" David, pardon, [illegible].
" Edmund, pardon, [illegible], [illegible], [illegible], [illegible].
" Garret (of Blackhall), commission, [illegible]. *See* Wellesley.
" Gerald—Gerrott—Gerard (of Dangan), sheriff of Meath, [illegible]; commissions, [illegible], [illegible], [illegible], [illegible], [illegible], [illegible], [illegible]; grant of a wardship, [illegible]; pardon at his suit, [illegible]; lands of, [illegible]. *See* Weisley, Wellesley, Wesly.
" Gerald, commission, [illegible]; pardon, of intrusion, [illegible].
" Gerald, pardon, [illegible].
" James, vicar of Manlaug, [illegible].
" James, pardon, [illegible].
" Jane, pardon, [illegible].
" John, pardon, [illegible], [illegible], [illegible].

INDEX TO FIANTS—ELIZABETH.

Wesley, Nicholas (of Norragh), pardon, [illegible]. *See* Wellesley.
„ Oliver, pardon, [illegible].
„ Piers (of Blackhall), [illegible]. *See* Wellesley.
„ Redmund, pardon, [illegible].
„ Richard, pardon, [illegible], [illegible].
„ Robert, archdeacon of Dublin, takes oath of supremacy, [illegible]; commission, [illegible] (Wellesley), [illegible] (Weslye), [illegible], [illegible], [illegible], [illegible], [illegible] (Wellesly), [illegible], [illegible] (Wesly), [illegible].
„ Robert, pardon, [illegible].
„ Walter, baron of Norragh, commissions, [illegible], [illegible]; pardon, [illegible].
Wesminster. *See* Westminster.
Wespaileston—Wespilliston—Wespayleston—Wespaylston, co. Dub., tithes, 1150, [illegible], [illegible], [illegible].
Wespanstone, co. Meath, [illegible].
Wespayleston. *See* Wespaileston.
Wespilliston—Wespaileston—Wespaleston—Waspayleston—Waspelliston—Waspalston (Westpalstown), co. Dub., [illegible], [illegible], [illegible], [illegible], [illegible]; rectory, [illegible].
Wespey, Rich. *See* Wesbie.
Wessley. *See* Wesley.
Westby—Westbye, Rich. *See* Wesbie.
Westcrewe (Westcrave), co. Dub., 1777.
Westerkernes—Westkurnes, co. Meath, [illegible], [illegible], [illegible].
Wester park, Duleek, co. Meath, [illegible], [illegible], [illegible].
Westerton, co. Kild., [illegible].
Westkernes. *See* Westerkernes.
Westley, Wm., pardon, [illegible].
Westmeath — West Meithe — Westmeithe county, commission to survey and extend as shire ground part of county, [illegible]; part transferred to King's co., [illegible], [illegible]; excluded from government of Ulster, [illegible]; to be divided into plough lands, [illegible], [illegible], [illegible]; wages of soldiers employed against O'Mores owned on, 1911; O'Madden's tribute to be paid in, [illegible]; taxing, [illegible]; survey of forfeited lands, [illegible]; hay impressed in, [illegible], [illegible], [illegible], [illegible], [illegible]; appointments of seneschals and other officers of countries in, [illegible], [illegible], [illegible], 1760, [illegible], [illegible], [illegible], [illegible], [illegible].
commissions of peace, [illegible].
Westmeath:
„ commissions of musters, [illegible], [illegible], [illegible], [illegible], [illegible], [illegible], [illegible].
„ ecclesiastical commission, [illegible].
„ commission of concealments, [illegible].
„ commissions for martial law, [illegible].
„ general of army in, [illegible].
„ provost marshal, [illegible], [illegible].
„ sheriff, [illegible]; security to be given before, [illegible].
„ sub-sheriff, [illegible], [illegible], [illegible].
„ coroner, [illegible].
„ clerk of the crown, [illegible]; of crown and peace, [illegible], [illegible], [illegible].
„ general cessor and collector of cesses, [illegible], [illegible].
Westminster—Wesminster, commissions, &c. dated at, [illegible].
Weston, John, pardon, [illegible], [illegible].
„ Nicholas, alderman of Dublin, [illegible].
„ Oliver, lands of, [illegible]. *See* Waston.
„ Rich., pardon, [illegible].
„ sir Robert, lord chancellor, made lord justice, [illegible]; commissions, [illegible], [illegible], [illegible], [illegible]; pardon, [illegible]; death, [illegible].
„ sir William, chief justice of the Common Bench, [illegible], [illegible]; commissions, [illegible], [illegible], [illegible], [illegible], [illegible], [illegible]; deceased, [illegible], [illegible].
„ *See* Waston.
Weston of the Nall (Westown), co. Dub., [illegible], 1777.
Westpalstown, co. Dub. *See* Wespilliston.
Westparke, at Duleek, co. Meath, [illegible].

Weiston, 6110.
Wexford—Wexforde—Wexfourd (mentioned) 381, 849, 453, [illegible], [illegible], [illegible], 5763, 4434, 5418; tenement in, leased, [illegible]; burgage granted, [illegible]; land by, leased, 610; illegal exports, 5040; assizes at, 6080; measure of malt, [illegible].
„ sovereign to proclaim persons indicted of treason, 1841; commissions, 3117, 3444, [illegible], [illegible], 5788.
„ merchants, 5545, 5844.
„ constable of castle, 648, 1188, 1850, 1444, 2211, 4779, 6160.
„ Crow street, 417.
„ Ferry, 915, 4167.
„ High ball, 417.
„ hospital of S. John, leased, [illegible]; granted, 5750.
„ house of friars minor, 417.
„ Kenny's mill, 6312.
„ S. John street in suburbs, [illegible].
„ S. Mary, parish, 417; rectory, 4473.
„ „ parson, [illegible].
„ S. Michael, parish, 4613; rectory, [illegible].
„ S. Patrick, vicar of, 417, 5518, [illegible].
„ S. Peter's rectory, 665, [illegible], 4003, 5115, [illegible].
„ S. Tullock, rectory, 168, 4005, 5118, [illegible].
„ Selskar abbey. See Selskar.
„ Selskar, rectory, [illegible], 2549, 4012, 5118, [illegible].
„ port or haven, 51, 58, 62, [illegible].
„ „ supervisor, [illegible].
„ collector of wine duty, 1584, 2087, 2788, 2818, 4219, 5241, 6041.
„ comptroller of wine duty, 2788, [illegible], 3884, 4524, [illegible].
„ searcher and gauger, 576, 2030, 6347.
„ liberty, seneschal (Philip Isam), 57, 69; (Nich. Horan), 646, 465, 465, 653, 1116, 1164; (Thomas Stanley), 1139, 1442, 1444, 1618; (Nich. White), 1520, 1686, 1742, 1748, 2127, 2144; (Tho. Masterson), 3421, 4912, 4944-6, 6771; (Rich. Masterson), 6440; security to be given before seneschal, 1806; seneschal may direct chief to raise his forces, 5736; commission to enquire of lands, [illegible].
„ „ vice or sub-seneschal, 1448, 3117, 5574.
Wexford, liberty, justice, 131, 542, 646, 1029, 1166, 1674, 2504, 2766, [illegible], 5844, [illegible].
„ „ treasurer, receiver, and bailiff, 1297, [illegible].
„ county, enquiry as to lands of earl of Kildare in, 702, 712; lands excepted from grant to the earl, 1340; survey of forfeited lands, 4043; enquiry as to lands of Cavanagh, 4690; persons pardoned to find security in, 1067; proclamation of persons indicted of treason, 1828, 1843; cess in lieu of broughs, 5090, 5763.
„ „ commissions of peace, 542-3, 2601, 3057, 4086-7, 4168, 4615, 4760, [illegible], 5543, [illegible], 5297, [illegible], 6204, [illegible], [illegible], 6428, 6827, [illegible].
„ „ commissions of musters, 3117, 3348, 3444, 5103.
„ „ commissions of martial law, 97, [illegible], 810, 848, 1116, 1770, 1838, 1624, 2092, 2174, 2184, 2722-3, 3144, 3182, 3464, 3627-8, 3431, 4944, [illegible], 5108, 5317, [illegible], [illegible], 5943, 6416.
„ „ ecclesiastical commission, 947.
„ „ warrants to impress hay, [illegible], 4172, 4429, 4280.
„ „ general of army in, [illegible], [illegible], 5110, [illegible].
„ „ sheriff, 24, 57, [illegible], [illegible], [illegible], 1892, 1448, 2174, 2544, 2671, 3170, 3364, 4679, 4844, 5781, [illegible].
„ „ general cashier, [illegible].
„ „ clerk of crown and peace, 3772, 3436, 3478, 5534, 6294.
„ „ chief serjeant, [illegible]; chief serjeant of Kinshelagh, 1082, 2944.
„ „ overseer of tanning, 3418.
Weyry, John, pardon, 3494.
„ Morgan, pardon, 3494.
Weysley, Garret. See Wesley.
Whalington, co. Wat., rectory, 4158.
Whalicaine (co. Cork ?), 2944.
Whealan, Dorby, pardon, 787.
Wheat, illegal export forbidden, [illegible], 3060, 3690; licences to export, 1719, 1727, 1749, 1753,

INDEX TO FIANTS—ELIZABETH.

Wheat:
[illegible], (in time of plenty), [illegible], [illegible], [illegible]; impressed for army, [illegible], 1198, [illegible], [illegible], [illegible]; price, [illegible].
Wheeler, James, dean of Christchurch, [illegible], 6704.
Whoery, King's co. See Fwyre.
Whelan, Katherine, pardon, [illegible].
" William, pardon, [illegible].
Whelocke, Hugh, slain, [illegible].
Wheylan (co. Kild. ?), [illegible].
Whiddy, co. Cork. See Whiddy.
Whilam, co. Kild., 1942.
Whiloman, co. Kild., [illegible].
Whit, Edm., pardon, [illegible].
" Gilleduff, pardon, [illegible].
" Joanna, pardon, [illegible].
" John, pardon, 1404.
" Margery, pardon, 1058.
" Nicholas. See White.
" Nich., pardon, [illegible].
" Owen, serjeant at arms, [illegible].
" Patrick. See White.
" Richard, pardon, [illegible].
" Thomas, pardon, [illegible].
" Walter, pardon, [illegible].
" William, alienation, [illegible].
" William. See White.
Whit Knight. See White Knight.
Whitchurch — Whitchurche. See Whitechurch.
White, Andrew, chaplain, pardon, [illegible].
" Andrew, son of sir Nicholas, [illegible]; surrender, [illegible]; wardship of his heir, [illegible].
" Bartholomew, house in Naas, [illegible].
" Bennet, pardon, [illegible].
" Christopher, pardon, [illegible].
" —Whyte, David or Davy (of Grenan, co. Wat.), commissions, [illegible], [illegible]; pardon, [illegible].
" David, pardon, [illegible], [illegible].
" Davy, pardon, [illegible].
" Dominick, pardon, [illegible].
" Edmund, land in Waterford, [illegible], [illegible].
" Edm., pardon, [illegible], [illegible], [illegible], [illegible], [illegible].
" Edward. See Whyte.
" Ellis or Ellen, pardon, [illegible], [illegible], [illegible].
" Henry (of Clonmel), land of, [illegible]; wardship of his heir, [illegible].
" Honor, pardon, 6704.
" Isolde, [illegible].
" Isaac, wardship and livery, [illegible], [illegible]; garden of, in Maryborough, [illegible].
" James, land in Waterford, [illegible], [illegible].
" James, clerk, land in Kilmainham, [illegible].
White—James, pardon, [illegible], [illegible], [illegible], [illegible].
" Joan, pardon, [illegible].
" Johanna, land in Fethard, [illegible].
" John (of Waterford), chaplain, pardon, [illegible].
" John (of Dublin), chaplain, pardon, 1777.
" John, house in Dublin, 1511, [illegible].
" John (of Clonmel), wardship, [illegible]; sheriff of Waterford, [illegible].
" John (of Balrogan, co. Louth), wardship, [illegible].
" John, pardon, 1417, [illegible], [illegible], [illegible], [illegible], [illegible], [illegible].
" —Whyte, John (of Dangan, co. Rosc.), pardon, [illegible], [illegible]. See Whyte.
" Katherine, pardon, [illegible].
" Margaret, pardon, [illegible].
" Mary, widow of Chr. Darcie, [illegible]; wife of Nich., lord Howth, [illegible].
" Michael, pardon, [illegible].
" Nicholas (—Whit—Whitt — Whyte), recorder of Waterford, [illegible]; seneschal of the liberty and constable of the castle of Wexford, [illegible], [illegible]; master of the Rolls, [illegible]; his office sequestered, [illegible], [illegible]; restored, [illegible]; his successor, [illegible]; commissions, [illegible]; grants of land, [illegible], [illegible], [illegible], [illegible]; exchange of lands, [illegible]; grants of custodiam, [illegible]; leases, [illegible], [illegible], [illegible], [illegible], [illegible], [illegible], [illegible]; surrenders, [illegible], [illegible], [illegible]; suit as to Dunbrody, [illegible], [illegible]; licence of absence, [illegible], [illegible], [illegible]; pardon, [illegible], [illegible]; pardon of alienation, [illegible]; pardon at his suit, [illegible]; surrender by his son, [illegible]. See Whitte.
" Nicholas (of Leixlip, grandson of preceding), wardship, [illegible].
" Nicholas, grants of land in Queen's co., [illegible], [illegible]; wardship and livery of his heir, [illegible], [illegible].
" Nich. (of Kilmaynan), matrimonial suit, [illegible].
" Nich., land in tenure of (co. Kild.), [illegible].
" Nich., pardon, [illegible], [illegible], [illegible].
" —Whyte, sir Patrick, second baron of Exchequer, 17, [illegible], [illegible]; oath of supremacy, [illegible]; commission, [illegible].

INDEX TO FIANTS—ELIZABETH.

White, Patr. (of Clongell), commissions, [illegible], 4461; chief serjeant of co. Cavan, [illegible].
— Patr. (of Flemington), freedom from subsidy, [illegible].
— Patr., premises in Cashel, [illegible].
— Patr., house in Drogheda, [illegible].
— Patr., clerk, pardon, 4114.
— Patr., pardon, 4714, [illegible].
— Peirs, pardon, [illegible], [illegible].
— Peter, rector of Mayne, pardon, [illegible].
— Peter, pardon, [illegible], 4115.
— Reimund, pardon, [illegible].
— Richard (of Rush), robbery from, [illegible].
— Rich., land in Clonmel, [illegible].
— Rich., pardon, 4115, [illegible], [illegible], 6113, [illegible], [illegible], [illegible].
— Rowland, commissions, 874, 1198.
— Salomon, pardon, [illegible]. See also Whyte.
— Shane de, pardon, [illegible].
— Stephen, alderman of Limerick, commissions, [illegible], 4168.
— Stephen fitz Dominick, merchant of Limerick, lease, [illegible].
— Stephen, scholar T.C.D., [illegible].
— Thomas, commission, [illegible].
— Tho., vicar of Skrine, [illegible].
— Tho., pardon, 4115, [illegible], [illegible], [illegible], [illegible].
— —Whitt, Victor, pardon, [illegible]; land in Clonmel, [illegible].
— Vincent, pardon, [illegible].
— Walter (of Navan), wardship, [illegible].
— Walter (of Dalrugna, co. Louth), wardship of heir of, [illegible].
— Walter, pardon, 4114.
— —Whit, William, marshal of four courts, 837, [illegible].
— Wm. (of Navan), wardship of heir of, [illegible].
— Wm., house in Dublin, 1311.
— Wm., land in Waterford, [illegible], [illegible].
— Wm. (of Anguilleston), livery to heir, [illegible].
— Wm., pardon, [illegible].
— [ ] (of Clongell, co. Meath), commission, [illegible].
White bay, Kinsale, co. Cork, [illegible].
Whitehaven, Kinsale, co. Cork, [illegible].
Whitecastle—White castell, Queen's co., [illegible], [illegible].
Whitechurch, co. Cork, rectory, [illegible].
Whitechurch — Whitchurche, co. Kild., manor, [illegible]; rectory, [illegible], [illegible].
Whitechurch — Whitechurche — Whitechurche, co. Kilk., rectory, [illegible], [illegible], [illegible]; vicar, [illegible].
Whitechurch — Whitechurche — Whyte Church (co. Tip.?), [illegible], [illegible], [illegible].
Whitechurch, co. Tip., rectory, [illegible].
Whitechurch (co. Wat.?), [illegible]. See also Templegall.
Whitechurch—Whitchurch — Whitechurche —Whytchurch, co. Wex., [illegible], [illegible], [illegible], [illegible].
— prebendary, [illegible].
Whitechurch — Whitchurche, in Faraghbearie (Whitechurchglynn?), co. Wex., rectory, [illegible].
Whitefriars, Kildare, [illegible], [illegible].
White friars. See Carmelite friars.
White Knight (John oge FitzGibbon), pardon, [illegible], [illegible]; his sons, [illegible], [illegible]; attainted, and lands given to his son, [illegible], [illegible], [illegible], [illegible].
— (Edmund FitzGibbon), pardon, [illegible], [illegible], [illegible]; leases and grants to him of lands forfeited by his father, [illegible], [illegible], [illegible], [illegible]; pardon of his men, [illegible].
— sons of, [illegible], [illegible].
White—Whyte Knight's country to be made shire ground, [illegible], [illegible].
White leis, co. Kild., [illegible].
White Leys — Whiteleise (Whiteleas), co. Meath, [illegible], [illegible].
Whitemore, co. Kild., [illegible].
Whitepark, co. Louth, [illegible].
Whitesmithe—Whitsmithe, co. Louth, [illegible], [illegible].
Whiteshall — Whitshall — Whiteshall, co. Kilk., [illegible], [illegible], [illegible], [illegible], [illegible], [illegible].
Whites—Whitte Island, [illegible]; enclosed lands adjoining, co. Cork, [illegible].
Whiteisland (co. Cork?), [illegible].
Whites lands, co. Kild., [illegible].
Whiteston (co. Kild.?), [illegible].
Whiteston. See Whitestown, co. Lim.
Whiteston — Whitteston, co. Meath, [illegible], [illegible].
Whiteston. See Whitestown, co. Wat.
Whiteston — Whiteston (co. Wick.?), [illegible], [illegible], [illegible].
Whitestown—Whiteston, co. Lim., [illegible], [illegible]; [illegible], [illegible].
Whitestown—Whiteston (co. Wat.?), [illegible], [illegible].
Whitewall — Whitewall — Whitwall — Whytewall, co. Kilk., [illegible], [illegible], [illegible], [illegible], [illegible].
Whitewood (co. Kilk.?), [illegible].
Whitewall. See Whitewall, co. Kilk.
Whitishall. See Whiteshall.
Whitiston. See Whiteston, co. Wick.
Whitleston, co. Wat., [illegible].

INDEX TO FIANTS.—ELIZABETH.

Whitney, James, chief serjeant of Connaught, 782.
" —Whytney, John (of Shean), grant of land, 1648, 1780; commissions, 1486, 2118, 2117, 3846; house in Dublin, 1894; house in Maryborough, 4020; livery to heir, 6934.
" Robert, livery, 6828.
Whitraithe. See Whitewraithe.
Whitroodo, Wm., vicar of Skrine, 6353.
Whitshall. See Whiteshall.
Whitstown, co. Lim. or Cork, 1887-8.
Whitt, Beale or Ballina, land in Clongal, 4444.
" sir Nich. See White.
" Victor. See White.
" Walter, livery, 5788.
Whittchurche, co. Kilk., rectory, 308.
Whitte, Edw. See White.
" Nicholas, grant of a wardship, 612.
Whittleston. See Whiteston, co. Meath.
Whittleston (co. Wat.?), 5748.
Whittley, Nicholas, prebendary of Clone, 6314; vicar of Carne, 1811.
" Patrick, son of Patrick, livery, 5948.
" Richard, livery, 4788.
" Walter, livery to his heir, 6798.
Whittle, Adam, vicar of Killagh, 714.
Whittleston (co. Wat.?), 2815.
Whitton, Thomas, commission, 3947.
Whitts Island. See Whites Island.
Whitwall. See Whitewall.
Whitworth—Whitworthe, Michael, pardon, 6488, 6877.
Whody, Katherine ny, pardon, 6414.
Whoheran, Margery ny, pardon, 4888.
Whohill, Una ny, pardon, 6488.
Whuiddy island (Whiddy), co. Cork, 4611.
Whylom, co. Kild., 4987.
Whyt, James, lease of wine duties, 4328.
" sir Patrick. See White.
Whytchurch. See Whitechurch, co. Wex.
Whyte, David. See White.
" Donal, house in Maryborough, 4422.
" Edmund, pardon, 6740.
" Edward (—White—Whitte), clerk of the council in Connaught, 4127, 4144, 4783, 4741; commissions, 4117, 4783, 6848; party to indenture of composition, 4761; his lands in co. Clare confirmed, 4761; pardon, 5443.
" James (of Kells, co. Kilk.), commission, 5544.
" James, pardon, 6479.
" John (of co. Mayo), pardon, 4580.
" John. See White.
Whyte, Maurice, pardon, 3478.
" Nicholas, pardon, 3478.
" Nicholas. See White.
" Patrick, pardon, 3478.
" Richard, pardon, 4878.
" Salamon or Salomon, pardon, 4498, 6742. See also White.
" Thomas, pardon, 167.
" Walter, pardon, 4090.
Whyte Church. See Whitechurch,
Whyte Knight. See White Knight.
Whytewall. See Whitewall.
Whytney, John. See Whitney.
Wickcombe, Marc. See Wycombe.
Wicklow—Wickelow—Wicklos—W Wicklowe—Wicklows lowe—Wycklo—Wy Wyclow—Wyclowe:
" constable of castle, [illegible] 6984, 6962.
" church of S. Patrick, [illegible]
" prebendary, 7, 192.
" Frank house, 5414, 6463.
" gaol to be built, 3958.
" haven, 92.
" hospital or Maudlens, [illegible]
" house of Franciscans [illegible] 3898; granted, 5708.
" Churchtown by, 517, 129[illegible]
" Inchboyne near, 3454.
" mountain land near, [illegible]
" county, commission [illegible] county, 28[illegible] by persons to be give[n] commission 5994, sale: [illegible] in the more 6947.
" " commission [illegible] 6887.
" " clerk of the [illegible] peace, 4682.
" " chief serjeant [illegible]
Wickman, Wm., pardon, 4817.
Widdimeston (co. Tip.?), 5877. Almgaston.
Wicaton, co. Meath, 1940.
Wight, Isle of, in England, 128.
Wikelowe. See Wicklow.
Willenham, Richard, commiss[ion] 6964.
" —Wyllenme, Roge[r] and general sol[dier] commissions, 42[illegible] 4220, 5351, 6578, 64[illegible] 6948, 6452, 6286-8, custodiam grant[ed] covery, 6964.

Wilcocks—Wilcockes, Anthony, clerk of the Castle Chamber, 5148, 5782.
Wilford, Thomas, commission, 2348.
Wilkes, John. See Wilkes.
Wilkenston. See Wilkenston.
Wilkenson, John. See Wilkinson.
Wilkeston. See Wilkinston.
Wilkins—Wilkes, John, pardon in Dublin, [illegible], 4514.
Wilkinson—Wilkynson, John, 4962; pardon, [illegible].
Wilkinston — Wilkenston — Wilkeston — Wylkenston, co. Meath, 1480, [illegible], [illegible], [illegible].
Wilkynson, Richard, pardon, [illegible].
Willen, Donyll m'Donagh in, pardon, [illegible].
Willes, Leonard, death of, 104.
Willeys, captain, list of pardons made by, [illegible].
Willestowne (co. Armagh ?), 5726.
William, Edward, grant, [illegible].
" Gylee or Gyllee ny, pardon, 4164, 4513.
" Katherine nyne, pardon, [illegible].
" Mary ny, pardon, [illegible], [illegible].
" Shile nyn, pardon, [illegible].
William Carrighe — William Carraghe's Grange, [illegible], 1172.
William leighe, Donogh, pardon, [illegible].
Williams, dame Clare, pardon, 5162.
" Edmund, pardon, [illegible], [illegible].
" Henry, grant of a wardship, [illegible].
" James, burgess of Athlone, [illegible].
" John (of Punchestown), commissions, [illegible], [illegible].
" John (of London), license to plant and export wood, madder, &c., [illegible].
" John, keeper of gaol of Galway, [illegible].
" John, marshal of Ecclesiastical High Court, [illegible].
" John, pardon, [illegible].
" Meredith, searcher of Waterford, [illegible].
" Nich., pardon, [illegible].
" Philip, granted of fines, [illegible], [illegible], [illegible]-80; clerk of the market, 5414, [illegible].
" Stephen, commission, [illegible].
" Thomas, soldier, pardon, [illegible].
" sir Thomas, clerk of the check, [illegible]; muster master and clerk of the check, 5118, 5178, [illegible], [illegible]; commissions, 5117, [illegible]; license of absence, [illegible], 5119; pardon, [illegible]; deceased, [illegible].
" Walter, clerk of the market, [illegible], [illegible].
Williamston (co. Car. ?), [illegible], [illegible], 1477, [illegible], [illegible]. See also Ballywilliam, 4814.
Williamston, co. Gal., [illegible].
Williamston, King's co., [illegible].
Williamston—Williamstowne, co. Lim., [illegible], [illegible].
Williamston—Wylliamston, co. Meath, 1194, [illegible].
Willingston (co. Tip. ?), [illegible].
Williamston, co. Westm., [illegible]. See also Ballyvickwilliam, [illegible].
Williamstowne or Ballyichone, co. Wat., [illegible].
Willies, captain Humfrey, grant of land, [illegible], 5718.
Willins, lady Margaret or Margery, [illegible].
Willinstowne. See Williamston, co. Lim.
Willing, John, pardon, [illegible].
Willmore, Anne, pardon, [illegible].
Willowhill, co. Cork. See Knockeawilla.
Wilmott, sir Charles, constable of Castlemaine, [illegible].
Wilso or Wilsonne, Adam, pardon, [illegible].
Wilton, Arthur, lord Grey of, [illegible].
Wiltshire, native of, [illegible].
Windmilland — Wyndemill land, co. Dub., 1661, [illegible], [illegible].
Windsor, letters dated at, [illegible], 1188, [illegible], [illegible].
Wine, trade, [illegible], [illegible], 1721, [illegible], 5748; discharged without paying duty, [illegible]; imported into unwarranted ports in Connaught, [illegible]; license to import free of duty, [illegible]; impressed for army, [illegible], [illegible], 1198, [illegible], 1441, [illegible], [illegible]; license to take up, [illegible]; purveyed for deputy's household, [illegible]; customs on, [illegible], [illegible], [illegible], &c. See Customs.
" custom, collector, 3316, [illegible].
" " general controller, [illegible], [illegible], [illegible]. See also under several ports.
Wingfelde — Weingfield — Wingefelde — Wingefeilde — Winkfeld — Wingfeld — Wingfield — Wingfelde — Wingfilde — Wynchefelde — Wyndfeld — Wynfeld — Wyngefelde — Wyngfeld — Wyngfelde — Wyngfild — Wyngfylde:
" Jacques, master of the ordnance, 198, [illegible], [illegible]; constable of Dublin castle, [illegible], 4514; takes oath of supremacy, [illegible]; commissions, 198, [illegible], [illegible], [illegible], [illegible], [illegible], [illegible]; his charge in the Byrne's and Toole's coun-

INDEX TO FIANTS—ELIZABETH.

Wingfields :
ary, 741 ; pardon, [illegible], [illegible] ; pardon at his suit, [illegible] ; ground in Dublin in his tenure, 2816, [illegible] ; grant of a wardship, [illegible] ; his son and executor, [illegible], [illegible].
" sir Richard, marshal of the army, [illegible] ; commissions, [illegible], [illegible], [illegible], [illegible] ; pardon at his suit, [illegible].
" Thomas Maria (captain), pardon, [illegible], [illegible].
" Thomas (Wingfeilde), son and executor of Jaques, [illegible] ; surrender, [illegible] ; lease, [illegible].
Winstodan alias Nugent, Edward, pardon, [illegible].
" Margaret, pardon, [illegible].
" William, pardon, [illegible].
Winston, Roger, collector of customs, [illegible].
Winter, Hugh, pardon, [illegible].
Winterford, Patr., pardon, [illegible].
Wintervarie (co. Cork ?), [illegible].
Winton, Statute of, [illegible].
Wise, Anastacia, [illegible].
" Andrew. See Wyse.
" Christopher. See Wyse.
" George. See Wyse.
" Henry. See Wyse.
" James. See Wyse.
" Johanna, widow, 701.
" John, chancellor of Waterford, [illegible], [illegible].
" Matthew, commission, [illegible] ; pardon, 1784, [illegible].
" Maurice, commission, 302.
" Thomas. See Wyse.
" ( ), garden in Waterford in tenure of, [illegible].
Wiseman—Wyseman, Rob., pardon, [illegible].
" Thomas, commission, [illegible] ; grant of a wardship, [illegible].
Wisse. See Wyse.
Witter, co. Down. See Templetawy.
Withocks, grange of, co. Kild., [illegible].
Wood, growth and export of, [illegible].
Woade, Ricard, pardon, [illegible].
Wonyde, Walter, pardon, [illegible].
Wodd, John, commission, [illegible].
" Richard, pensioner, [illegible].
Wodde, Richard, [illegible]. See Wood.
" Tho., pardon, [illegible].
Weddingstown — Weddingeston — Weddingstowne — Wodingston (Woodinstown, co. Tip. ?), [illegible], [illegible], [illegible], [illegible].
Woddyngton, Nycolas, [illegible].
Wode, Morris, pardon, [illegible].
Wodgralk (Woodgraigue, co. Wex. ?), [illegible].
Wodgrange, [illegible]. See Woodgrange.
Wodhous, Tho., pardon, [illegible].
Wodhouse, Mary, [illegible].
Wodhouse (Woodhouse, co. Wat. ?), [illegible], [illegible], [illegible].
Woding, Nicholas, pardon, [illegible].
Wodinge, Thomas, commission, [illegible]. See Wadding.
Wodingston, [illegible]. See Weddingstown.
Wodlan, [illegible].
Wodlock, David, pardon, [illegible].
Wodlocke—Wodloke. See Woodlok.
Wodman, Katheline ny Donell, pardon, [illegible].
Wodton, Matilda, pardon, [illegible].
Woltowne, co. Wex., [illegible].
Wodwale in Newton, co. Meath, [illegible]
Wogan, Alson, pardon, [illegible].
" Caher duff mac Donogho m, [illegible].
" Christopher, pardon, [illegible].
" David (—Owgan) (of Lat... freedom from subsidy, re... missions, [illegible], [illegible].
" Edward, (of Rathcoffey), [illegible].
" Edw., pardon, [illegible].
" Gerald (of Downings), pard... wardship of his heir, [illegible].
" James, pardon, [illegible].
" John, alias Brian duff, pardo...
" Laurence, pardon, [illegible].
" Mary, pardon, [illegible].
" Nicholas (—Owgan) (of Rat... justice of peace, co. Kilda... oath of supremacy, [illegible] ; ... sions, [illegible], [illegible], [illegible].
" Nicholas, grant, [illegible].
" Nich. (—Owgan), pardon, [illegible]
" Oliver (— Ougan — Owg... Downings), commissions, [illegible] ; pardon, [illegible].
" Robert, pardon, [illegible], [illegible].
" Robert (Owgan), pardon, ... Ougan.
" William (of Rathcoffey), ... sions, [illegible], [illegible] ; attainted
" William (of Downings), ... gan.
Woganne, Edw., pardon, [illegible].
Woghterard, co. Kild., [illegible]. See ... ard.
Woghterhyre — Woghtirhyre (co. ... [illegible]. See Oughterhery.
Woghtyre, co. Rosc., [illegible].
Wohillane, Donogh m'Dermod I., pardon, [illegible].
Wohnle, Edm., pardon, [illegible].
Wolcote, Anthony, pardon, [illegible].
Wolf, Edmond, pardon, [illegible].
" John, pardon, [illegible].

INDEX TO FIANTS—ELIZABETH.

Wolf, Nicholas, pardon, 1701, 2797. See Wolfe.
Patragin, pardon, 3374.
Patrick (or Woulfe), admitted, 3121, 5751, 5847.
Robert, pardon, 2481.
Thomas (or Woulfe), sheriff of Down, commission, 1716, 2524.
Tho. (or Woulfe), lands of, 2771, 5836.
" Walter, pardon, 2494. See Wulff.
Wolfe, John oge, pardon, 5468.
Morris m'Shane, pardon, 6052.
" See Woulf, Woulfe.
Wolfeston (Wolfestown), co. Kild., 1467.
Wolff, Edm. m'John, pardon, 4485.
Wolgrange (Woollengrange), co. Kilk., 104.
Wolle, John, pardon, 4164.
" Rob., pardon, 4164.
Wollies, Thomas, robberies by, 4584.
Wolls, 1602.
Wollster (Ulster), 2465.
Wolrene, Annora ny, pardon, 6156.
Wolverston—Wulverston, George, commission, 822; pardon, 886, 1154, 1768.
Thomas, pardon, 1162.
" See Wulverston, Woolverstone.
Women's gowns, &c., stolen, value of, 851.
Wone (co. Cork ?), 5121.
Wonekstowne (co. Kilk. ?), 1973.
Woney, Cahir m'James, pardon, 4914.
Woney, James, pardon, 473.
Woney. See Woney.
Wonie, Donnell m'Donell, pardon, 5654.
Wonsallwrady (co. Down or Antrim), 4967.
Wonnestowne, co. Kilk., 6318.
Wony—Woney—Wonye (Owney, now Abington), abbey, co. Lim., 463, 5664,
" monastery, 4132.
" rectory, 463, 6324.
" See Owney.
Wony, Diarmod m'Conner m'Dermod, pardon, 4804.
" James, pardon, 6610.
" Rich. m'Edmond, pardon, 4855.
Wonye. See Wony.
Wony Ikyrryn, co. Tip., rectory, 463.
Wonyn, Philip, English liberty, 142.
Wood, Bernard, pardon, 4726.
Hubert, house in Dublin, 1821.
Rich. (— Wodde — Woodde), sheriff of Carlow, 1506, 2361, 2640; commissions, 1672, 2161; pardon, 2616, 2666.
Thomas, assignment, 2806. See Woodde.
William (or Wodde), pardon, 3564, 3565.
" See Wodde.
Wood taken for army, 1128, 1408, 1461, 3862.
" for deputy, price of, 1309.
" as fuel, impressed for victualling, 3651.
Wood, sale of, 4264.
Woods in Chancelery, &c., 5125.
Woodborn. See Goodborne.
Woodcockstowne, co. Meath, 2280.
Woodd, Rich., pardon, 6616.
Wooddde, Thomas, 1169.
Woddice, Tho., pardon, 2453.
Wooddington, 2754.
Woode, Richard. See Wood.
" Wm. See Wood.
Woodehouse or Tarerich (Woodhouse), co. Wat., 6626. See Wodhouse, Wadhouse.
Woodewarde, Rob., lease, 4898.
Woodfall, John, commission, 1193; pardon, 1262, 1268.
Woodford — Woodfford, Robert, to impress victual, 2735; lease, 2827.
Woodgraigue, co. Wex. See Wodgrafe, Woodgranga.
Wood grange — Woodesgrange — Wodgrange, co. Kilk., 130, 831, 1178.
Woodgrange (Woodgraigue, co. Wex. ?), 6431.
Woodgreenage. See Woodgrange.
Woodhame—Woodhavyn, captain Thomas, 4406; monopoly of making glass, 5671. See Woodhaven.
Woodhouse, co. Wat. See Wadhouse, Wodhouse, Woodehouse.
Woodington, co. Tip., 6441.
Woodinstown, co. Tip. See Woddingstown.
Woodland, co. Meath, [illegible], [illegible].
Woodlocke, James, pardon, [illegible].
Woodlok — Wodlocke — Wodlokn, Thomas, sub sheriff of Waterford, commissions, 722, 872; pardon, 1161.
Woodlocke, James, 6126.
" James roe, pardon, 6665.
Woodlocke, David fitz Philip, pardon, 4726.
Wood meadow, co. Louth, 2071, 3273.
Woodstock — Woodstocke, co. Kild., 1247, 3412, 6228.
Woodton (Wotton, co. Meath), [illegible].
Woodtowne. See Woodtowne, co. Meath.
Woodtowne, co. Dub., 6158.
Woodtowne, co. Meath, 1328.
Woodtowne — Woodtonne, co. Meath, 1102, 2580.
Woodtowne (co. Wex. ?), 6146. See Wodtonne.
Woodward, Katherine, 6460. See Woodewarde.
Woolway — Wodwaie — Woodwye, co. Meath, 1460, [illegible], [illegible].
Wooulloun, Wm. m'Shane Y, pardon, [illegible].
Wool, licence to export, [illegible], 245, 2131; illegal carriage of, 863, 5606; grant of monopoly of export from Dublin and Drogheda, 4973; export prevented, 6360; stolen, value of, [illegible].

INDEX TO FIANTS—ELIZABETH.

Woulfe, John, pardon, 6461.
„ Rob., pardon, [illegible].
Woollen cloth (Irish), 4574.
Woollengrange, co. Kilk. See Wolgrainge, Wolgrange, Woulgrannge.
Woolverstone, James, pardon, 4798.
Woory, co. Lim., 4431.
Worroghoe, Donogh m'Donell I, pardon, 5406.
Worcestershire, Irish landowner living in, 2594.
Worohan, Margaret ny, pardon, 4[illegible].
Worough, Shane more, pardon, 3172.
Worghow, Conoghor m'Edm. I, pardon, 4421.
Worghowe, Owen m'Wm. I, pardon, 3920.
Works, clerk of, of queen's castles, &c., 660, 672, 694, 714.
„ clerk general of, appointed, 4236, [illegible], 5914, 6326, 6482.
Works (her majesty's), power to impress workmen and materials for, 2462.
Works in county, men to be supplied by chief for, 4549.
Worlome, Edm., pardon, [illegible].
Worroghe, Donoghe m'Donell I, pardon, 4481.
„ Donoghe m'Shane I, pardon, 4482.
Woroghe, Conoghor m'Donoghe Y, pardon, 3062.
„ John m'Dermod I, pardon, 4136.
„ Morthirroghe m'Donell I, pardon, 4642.
„ Philip m'Donell I, pardon, 4513.
Woroghowe, Donogh m'Teig Y, pardon, 4491.
Worren, Johanna ny, pardon, 6676.
Worroaghowe, Donoghe and Teig m'Conoghor I, pardon, 5181.
Worrowhowe, Dermot m'Donnell I, pardon, 6974.
Worsh, Hugh, grant of land, 6944.
Worrampstown, co. Dub., theft at, 547.
Wosly, David, pardon, 3342.
„ Gerald, pardon, 3342.
„ Gerald (of Dowcill), pardon, 3342. See Wesley.
Wossman, Rob., pardon, 6772.
Wotrillagh, co. Meath, 2280.
Wotton, co. Meath, 886, 2144, 6873. See also Wootton.
Wottone, Walter, pardon, 1758.
Wottone, John, pardon, 3768.
Woulf, Oliver, pardon, 1102.
„ Thomas, 1732. See Wolf.
„ Tho., 3772. See Wolf.
Woulfe, James, pardon, 6677.
Woulfe, Patrick, lands of, granted, 5171. See Wolf.
Woulfe. See also Voulfe.
Woulgrannge (Woollengrange), co. Kilk., rectory, 3948.
Wouncton (co. Westm.?), 1138.
Woyde, John, pardon, 2208.
Woyo, Any ny vic, pardon, 2297.
Woyrioe, Teige m'Donell ny, pardon, 6496.
Wren—Wrenne, Christopher, commission, 2863; grant of a wardship, 6266; pardon, 1458, 1461.
Wrenan, Dermod m'Shane Y, pardon, 4791.
Wrenne, Christopher (see Wren), 2863.
Wrestling, death from injuries received in, 6361.
Wright, Anthony, pardon, 5819.
Writ, extension of, in co. Galway, 4786.
Writs, return of, by chief magistrate of town, 2726.
Wroskernagh (Brisearnagh), co. Mon., 5696.
Wryan, Teige m'Donoghe I, pardon, 4782.
„ Tirrelagh m'Diermodie I, pardon, 4782.
Wryt, Tho., pardon, 4281.
Wuddingtone, Nich., pardon, 5887.
Wulfe, Nicholas, pardon, 1488.
Walff, Walter, pardon, 5744.
Wulverston, George. See Wolverston.
„ James, pardon, 3408.
„ William, pardon, 880.
Wyat, Nich., pardon, 6764.
„ Tho. fitz Walter, pardon, 5466.
Wyckam, Mark. See Wycombe.
Wyckham, Thomas. See Wycombe.
Wycklo—Wycklowe—Wyclow—Wyclowe, See Wicklow.
Wycombe—Wickcombe—Wyckam—Wyckham:
„ John, 118.
„ Marc or Mark, livery, 1799; sheriff of co. Dublin, 1838; commissions, 1830, 2142, [illegible]; pardon, 3429; inquisition on, 6006.
„ Thomas, sheriff of co. Dublin, commissions, 1189, 1190; livery to son, 1799.
Wyddingeston—Wyddingistoun—Wydingestown—Wydingiston, co. Tip., 1388–89, 2677. See Waddingstown.
Wye, Tho., lease, 2949, 6302.
Wyese, James, lease, 1672.
Wygon, Isabel ny Philip I, pardon, 4567.
Wykes, John, pardon, 54.
Wylbrame, Roger. See Willbraham.
Wylkeston. See Wilkinston.
Wyles, Nicholas, sheriff of Carrickfergus, 1689.
Wyllyamston. See Williamston, co. Meath.
Wylson, William, pardon, 1032.

INDEX TO FIANTS.—ELIZABETH.

Wynagh, Donell, pardon, 4611.
Wynaghe. *See* Wynnaghe.
Wyndesfelde, Jaques. *See* Wingfielde.
Wyndemill land—Wynde myll lande. *See* Windmillland, co. Dub.
Wyndfeld—Wynfeld—Wyngefelde—Wyngfeld—Wyngfeilde—Wyngfild—Wyngfylde. *See* Wingfielde.
Wynickaine, Donogh m'Donell I, pardon, [illegible].
Wynn, George, marshal of courts and gaols of Munster, 6444.
Wynnaghe—Wynaghe, isle (co. Wat. ?), 1687, [illegible].
Wynall, John, lease, 6810.
" Thomas, pardon, [illegible].
Wyrey, Laughlin m'Philip I, pardon, 4867.
Wyrryhirtighe, Morris m'Owen I, pardon, [illegible].
Wyse—Wise—Wisse, Andrew, late constable of Limerick, 1588, 2946, 2467; wardship of heir, 1532.
" Christopher, sub-sheriff of Waterford, 2428; sheriff, 4085; pardon, 2408, 3341, 4685.
" George, lease, 527; lease recited, 2568, 4152, 4153; deceased, 2[illegible]; lands in Waterford in occupation of his relict, 2978; his executors, 5304.
" Henry, commission, 619; wardship and livery of his heir, 619, 1809; license to his widow to marry, [illegible].
" James (of Waterford), wardship and livery, 619, 1809; sheriff of Waterford co., 2379, 2545; commissions, 2373, 2392, 2897; pardon, 1698, 2544.
" James, lease recited, 2441.
" James, leave in Waterford, 4573.
" John, livery to his son, 1809.
" John or Jenkin, pardon, 2548.
" Mary, wardship, 1839.
" Robert, pardon, 2541.
" Thomas, lease, 1681, 4389; grant of duties on imports, 5178, 5191.
" sir Wm., widow of, 619.
" Wm., pardon, 2548.
" *See* Wise.
Wyseland, co. Kild., 464.
Wyseman, Thomas. *See* Wiseman.
Wyskam, John, constable of gaol of Longford, 3850.

Yadevor (co. Lim. ?), 6048.
Yagheria, Shane m'Gerald, pardon, 4808.
Yagogonston. *See* Jagogeston.
Yalevain, Conochor and Teig m'Donoghe, and Donell m'Teig Y, pardon, 4519.
Yallowe Island. *See* Yellow island.
Yamrighian, Tho. m'Sean, pardon, 6487.
Yarhin, Dermod m'Owen, pardon, 6487.
Yarthody, Morris m'Teig, pardon, 6468.
Yarvane, Conoghor m'Dermody I, pardon 6948.
Yarwardston, co. Meath, 4477.
Yalserie, Teig o, attainted, 5138.
Yaughall. *See* Youghal.
Ybawne. *See* Bawne.
Ybohir, Donell m'Teig, pardon, 4618.
Ycayle, Teig m'Hugh, pardon, 4469.
Ychessell, Dermod m'Brian, pardon, 4675.
Ychinan, Wm. m'Rory, pardon, 6458.
Ydoganig, Edm. fitz Edm., pardon, 6418.
Ydoloe, Owen m'Dermodie, pardon, 6514.
Ydolough, Jone ny Donell, pardon, 6518.
Yea, Donell m'Donell, pardon, 4766.
Yeardun, Tuoly m'Murtoriagh, pardon, 5780. *See* Haghan.
Yeaghirawrith, co. Lim., 5947.
Yeagogiston. *See* Jagogeston.
Yeally, John m'Teig, pardon, 4367.
Yearnane, Teig m'Conoghor I, pardon, 4462.
Yegeston. *See* Iagogeston.
Yelleagane, Soyve ny, pardon, 6561.
Yellow island—Yellowe Island (at Menlich), co. Gal., 1841, 2975, 4125, 4656.
Yellow river, co. Don., 4698, 5037.
Yengestowne. *See* Yongeston.
Yeniaska (co. Mayo ?), 4562.
Yeriaghy, John m'Dogell I, pardon, 4458.
Yerndheny (King's co. ?), 4162.
Yerowly, Teig m'Dermodie, pardon, 6414.
Yerrigan (co. Car. ?), 6467.
Yfahill, Honora ny Dermodie, pardon, 6618.
Yfe, John fitz John, pardon, 2424.
Yfallaghowe (co. Lim. ?), 5784.
Yghoshkiy, Owen m'Brian, and Bowen and Owen m'Owen, pardon, 2168.
Yghieonrowe, Donogh m'Awley, 4617.
Yghilaghane, Donoghe m'Denis, pardon, 5867.
Yhinwe, Edm. oge, pardon, 6962.
Yhagthane, Conoghor m'Conoghor, pardon, 4601.
Yhowne—Yhwone, Teig m'Conoghor, and Dermod and John m'Teig, pardon, 5777.
Yhbellon, James Nogle, 2864.
Yiandes, the, co. Gal., 4339.
Yiancy, Dermot m'Donell, pardon, 6818.
Yllhan, Donogh m'Teig, pardon, 4418.
Ylhane, co. Cav., 1881.
Ylian m'Kegan, co. Gal., 4081.
Yllstrie, co. Kerry, 4868.
Ylogh'o, Thriagh m'Owen, pardon, 4784.
Ylonan, Donogh m'Conoghor, and Owen m'Teig, pardon, 4468.
Ymbolan, Edm. m'Tho., pardon, 4617.

INDEX TO FIANTS—ELIZABETH.

Ymalaghehegge. See Ymalaghbegg.
Ymalaghnagry. See Ymalaghnygry.
Ymanmagha, Teig O'Callaghan, pardon, [illegible].
Ymalaghbegg — Ymalaghehegge (Emlagh Beg), co. Ross, [illegible], [illegible].
Ymalaghnygry — Ymalaghnagry (Emlagh nagrea), co. Ross, [illegible], [illegible].
Ymlaghfiaddie (Emlaghfiad), co. Sligo, [illegible].
Ymlotta, Ricard m'Ricard, pardon, [illegible].
Ymorill, Conoghor m'Shane, pardon, [illegible].
Ympar. See Emper.
Ymulample, Wm. m'David, pardon, [illegible].
Ymulcaho—Ymulcaghe, John m'Owen, John m'Tho., and Rich. m'Mahoe, pardon, [illegible].
Ymullory (Ivolcary, co. Cork ?), [illegible].
Ymunga, Queen's co., [illegible].
Ynche. See Inche.
Yncheadrumeniller (Drumeanlire, co. Ross ?), [illegible].
Ynchiqoyne—Ynchyqoyne. See Inchequin, co. Cork.
Yngalla, Brian m'Donell, pardon, [illegible].
Ynnessag. See Eniscnaga.
Ynskill, Callogh m'Owen, pardon, [illegible].
Ynishemore (co. Long. ?), [illegible].
Ynishkine. See Inishkean, co. Cork.
Ynnaghty, Donell m'Teig I, pardon, [illegible].
Ynoan, Daniel macDonyll, pardon, [illegible].
Ynsterdrisly. See Inshtaddrisly.
Ypsham (co. Cork ?), [illegible].
Yndoarcy, Donogho, pardon, [illegible].
Ywly (co. Cork ?), [illegible].
Ymeshy, co. Cork, [illegible].
Yerrowghie, Tirlagh m'Teig, pardon, [illegible].
Ynylemry, Johanna, pardon, [illegible].
Ynyshenmore (co. Long. ?), [illegible].
Yoghall—Yoghell—Yoghill—Yoghull. See Youghal.
Yole, Rob., pardon, [illegible].
Yolle, Anastasia ne, pardon, [illegible].
Yong—Yonge. See Younge.
Yonge Castletowne, alias Yonge Collestowne, King's co., [illegible], [illegible], [illegible].
Yongeston—Yongestowne (Youngstown), co. Wex., [illegible], [illegible], [illegible], [illegible].
Yonnasam, David m'Edm., pardon, [illegible].
Yorcke, Tho., lease, [illegible].
Yordaston, co. Meath, [illegible]. See Jordanston.
Yorkshire, undertaker of lands from, [illegible].
Youghall in Ara (Youghalarra, co. Tip.), [illegible].
Youghal—Yonghall—Youghall—Youghill—Youghull—Yoghall—Yoghell—Yoghill—Yoghull—Yaughall—Yowghill, co. Cork, [illegible], [illegible], [illegible], [illegible], [illegible], [illegible], [illegible], [illegible], [illegible], [illegible], [illegible], [illegible], [illegible], [illegible], [illegible], [illegible].
Youghal, mayor of, commissions to, [illegible], [illegible], [illegible], [illegible], [illegible].
" alderman of, [illegible].
" merchants of, [illegible].
" goldsmith of, [illegible].
" premises in, [illegible], [illegible]; granted, [illegible], [illegible], [illegible].
" escheated lands near, [illegible], [illegible].
" Abbey lane, [illegible].
" Blind lane, [illegible].
" Bow street, [illegible].
" castle of Holy Trinity, [illegible].
" chantry, [illegible].
" chapel of S. Anne near, [illegible].
" Church lane, [illegible].
" College lands, [illegible], [illegible].
" Key lane, [illegible], [illegible].
" North gate, [illegible].
" College, possessions of, [illegible], [illegible].
" " warden of, [illegible], [illegible], [illegible], [illegible], [illegible], [illegible].
" house of Black friars, lease, [illegible]; grant, [illegible].
" " of Franciscans, grant, [illegible]; lease, [illegible].
" " of sick or lepers, [illegible].
" port, [illegible].
" Spanish ship seized at, [illegible], [illegible].
" prize wines, suit as to, [illegible].
" customer of, [illegible].
" searcher of, [illegible], [illegible].
" supervisor of, [illegible].
" collector of wine impost, [illegible], [illegible], [illegible], [illegible], [illegible].
" comptroller of wine impost, [illegible], [illegible], [illegible], [illegible].
Youghalarra, co. Tip. See Youghall in Ara.
Youghell, co. Kild., [illegible].
Young—Younge—Yong—Yonge:
" John, [illegible], [illegible], [illegible], [illegible].
" Robert, [illegible].
" Thomas, pardon, [illegible].
" William, merchant of Cashel, [illegible]; pardon, [illegible], [illegible]; provost of Cashel, [illegible].
" William, pardon, [illegible], [illegible].
Youngestown, co. Kild. See Ballyounge, [illegible].
Youngstowne, co. Wex. See Yongeston.
Yowghill, co. Cork. See Youghal.
Yowrane, Conoghor m'Wm., pardon, [illegible].
Yoyner, Peter, pardon, [illegible].
Ypbadyn, Conoghor m'Shane, pardon, [illegible].
Ygniffe, Cowe m'Conogho, pardon, [illegible].
Yrean, Moriertagh m'Conor, pardon, [illegible].
Yreagho, Dermod, attainted, [illegible].
Yrell, Garret, pardon, [illegible].
Yriadle, Donogho m'Dae, pardon, [illegible].
Yriardon, Conoghor m'Dermod, pardon, [illegible].
Yrishtowne. See Irishtowne, co. Westm.

INDEX TO FIANTS—ELIZABETH.

Yroghlagh, co. Kild., 1176.
Yrwan, David O'Hancy, [illegible].
Ysbertkierane. *See* [illegible].
Ysharcastell (King's co. ?), [illegible].
Yskarowen. *See* [illegible].
Ytorney, Philip m'Taig vicke, pardon, [illegible].
Ytleyn, John O'Hancy, [illegible].
Yvoughill, Owen oy Teag, pardon, [illegible].
Yvogily, Donogho m'Ea, pardon, [illegible].
Yvolerie. *See* Ivolcary.
Yvryne, Owen m'Donogho, pardon, [illegible].
Ywobir, Philip Magnor, [illegible].

Zouche—Zowch, John, colonel, [illegible]; lieutenant of the forts of Leix and Offaly, [illegible]; lease, [illegible]; pardon at his suit, [illegible].

ADDITIONAL REFERENCES.

Abbeydorg, co. Long. *See* Monasterdergs, Begicke.
Abbeydorney, co. Kerry. *See* Manistero-dorny, Odorney.
Abbeygormacan, co. Gal. *See* Monaster Macgormacan.
Abbeylara, co. Long. *See* Larragh.
Abbeyleix, Queen's co. *See also* Leix, abbey of.
Allen, George, pardon, [illegible], [illegible].
Ardcrone, co. Kerry. *See* Tardoron.
Ariem, Queen's co. *See* Narlen.
Balliegarry, co. Lim. *See also* Garry.
Ballygowny, co. Wex. *See* Gayneston.
Ballymacodane, co. Cork. *See* Monaster valle m'Idane.
Ballymagauran, co. Cork. *See* Magawran-towne.
Ballymaglin, co. Meath. *See* O'Blaranton.
Ballymore, co. Westm. *See also* Loughsewdy.
Ballymanne, co. Kild. *See* Moreton.
Ballyneanane, co. Lim. *See also* Morenon.
Ballyrobin, co. Wat. *See* Robertstowne.
Ballytarsney, co. Kilk. *See also* Ballitarsney.
Barrockstown, co. Meath. *See* Parrocken.
Blindwell, co. Gal. *See* Toberloagh.
Bourke, Ullick roe, pardon, [illegible].
Brackloonagh, co. Mayo. *See* Leighcarrow-brackloon.
Brisnaragh, co. Mon. *See* Wreskernagh.
Callow, co. Long. *See also* Callagh.
Cappagh, co. Car. *See also* Keppaghe.
Cappagh, co. Leix. *See* Keapaghe.
Carranmanna, co. Kilk. *See also* Garranmanan.
Carrickrodinagallen, co. Sligo. *See* Rath-mallen.
Carrigdownbary. *See also* Loymbary
Carrowcloghagh, co. Mayo. *See* Leigh-carrow ne Cloghe.
Carrowcrin, co. Sligo. *See also* Karro-creyn.
Casey, Wm. *See* Limerick, bishop of.
Cashel, Queen's co. *See also* Galshell.
Cashel, co. Tip., burgesses, [illegible].
" merchants, [illegible].
Castledermot, co. Kild. *See also* Tristel-dermot.
Castlekillion, co. Kild. *See* Trystelkilean.
Castlekeeran, co. Meath. *See* Trystelkeran.
Cavanagh, Edm. m'Morgh (of Rathgeddin-boy). *See also* M'Mortigh.
Clanbrassalagh, co. Armagh. *See* Klin-brislaghes.
Clare island, co. Mayo. *See* Innisbooleire.
Clogher, co. Louth. *See* Kilclogher.
Clonagath, co. Kild. *See also* Glangas.
Cloonlyhillow, co. Mayo. *See also* Leigh Carrow Cloudehillie Bealick.
Cloydagh, co. Car. *See* Dallougho.
Conwal, co. Mayo. *See* Leigh Carrow Cownalle.
Cork, gauger of port, [illegible].
Carrowvaggan, co. Mayo. *See* Leigh Carrow Carrovagan.
Curroge, co. Tip. *See* Garroghe
Curry, co. Long. *See* Monaster o kory.
Fitz Edmund, Maurice (of Garranjames), wardship, [illegible].
Fitz Gerald, Redmond (of Broghill). *See also* M'Gerald.
Ivolcary, co. Cork. *See also* Yvoullery.
Jordanstown, co. Meath. *See also* Yordans-ton.

DUBLIN: Printed for Her Majesty's Stationery Office,
By ALEX. THOM & CO. (Limited), 87, 88, & 89 Abbey-street,
The Queen's Printing Office.

www.ingramcontent.com/pod-product-compliance
Lightning Source LLC
Chambersburg PA
CBHW021932110726
47901CB00003B/813
* 9 7 8 3 7 4 2 8 1 0 5 9 5 *